Dedalus European Classics

The Wandering Jew-Eugene Sue

The legend of Ahaserus condemned to wander the world until the second coming of Christ has exercised a strong fascination on European Literature since the Middle Ages. This Autumn Dedalus will bring together the best of the existing stories in its anthology *Tales of the Wandering Jew*, alongside specially commissioned contributions from Brian Stableford, Robert Irwin, Geoffrey Farrington and other leading fantasy writers.

Also available from Dedalus is Jan Potocki's *Tales from the Zaragossa Manuscript*, in which the Wandering Jew appears as a character

Dedalus / Hippocrene

EUGENE SUE

THE
WANDERING
JEW

with an introduction by
Brian Stableford

Dedalus / Hippocrene

Published in the UK by Dedalus Ltd,
Langford Lodge, St Judith's Lane, Sawtry, Cambs, PE17 5XE
Published in the USA by Hippocrene Books Inc.,
171 Madison Avenue, New York, NY10016

ISBN 0 946626 33 2

First published in France in 1844–45
Dedalus edition 1990

Introduction copyright © Dedalus 1990

Printed in Great Britain by
Richard Clay Ltd, Bungay, Suffolk

A CIP listing for this title is available on request

INTRODUCTION TO THE WANDERING JEW
by Brian Stableford

Eugene Sue's father and grandfather were distinguished doctors, and he was intended to follow in their footsteps. After completing his education he did indeed embark upon such a career, serving for a while as a ship's doctor, but in 1829 - when he was 25 years old - he elected to "retire" from that employment in order to become a man of letters. His early works drew upon such experience of the world as he had, but contrived only to be hollow adventures in sensationalism, and they brought him no great celebrity; such small success as he enjoyed, however, established him sufficiently to allow him to play a crucial role in the development of popular fiction in France, when the opportunity to play such a role came along.

In the 1830s France was recovering economically from the devastation of the Napoleonic wars of 1795-1815, but the humiliation of military defeat - redoubled for those who still clung to the ideals of the Revolution which seemed to have been betrayed by the restoration of Louis XVIII to the throne - was by no means so easily forgotten. All Europe was in political turmoil thanks to the advancing cause of democratic reform and the evolving spectre of revolutionary socialism, but history had amply demonstrated that the head which wore the crown of France had better reason to be uneasy than any other, and the French political élite were particularly ambivalent in the matter of maintaining a precarious balance between repression and concession. Prominent among those legacies of the Revolution which were carried forward, however, were the movement towards universal literacy and the notion that a healthy press was a vital cornerstone of a free and just society. In these respects France had much more in common with post-revolutionary America than with her neighbours in Europe. The situation in France as regards the development of popular literacy contrasted very strongly with the situation in Britain.

In Britain the spread of literacy in the 1830s was

gradual, encouraged far more by religious groups and trade unions than by the government, and the freedom of the press was subtly but effectively restricted by taxation. British newspapers were subject to stamp duty, which made them artificially expensive and forced them to forge unbreakable and intimate links with the interests of a bourgeois audience. At the same time, the advertising which they carried was also taxed, compounding the disincentive to would-be advertisers of ordinary consumer goods. Price-fixing also exerted a powerful influence upon the British literary scene because the circulating libraries which took a large percentage of the print runs of novels did not want their business threatened by falling prices, and thus blackmailed publishers into maintaining a three-volume format and an economically unnecessary high retail price; the development of popular fiction which could appeal to working people was thus drastically inhibited.

In France, by contrast, the spread of literacy in the 1830s was relatively rapid, and the demand for reading material which was thus created offered a golden opportunity for the proprietors of newspapers - aided by advertisers - to provide a product of universal appeal. The inevitable result of such competition was a circulation war, and it quickly transpired that one of the key weapons in that circulation war was to be the *feuilletonist*.

A *feuilleton* was a line ruled across the page of a newspaper, which marked the foot of the news section; the space below the line was used for serial fiction. This innovation was first introduced in 1836 in *Le Siècle*, and was quickly imitated. Because French newspapers were aiming for the largest possible audience, natural selection demanded that successful editors must discover the kind of fiction which would appeal to the largest possible audience, and exploit it for all it was worth. As things turned out, it was worth quite a lot; the newspaper editors of Paris soon discovered the remarkable truth which is responsible for the seemingly paradoxical face of modern journalism: the vast majority of potential newspaper readers are not really interested in the news which is of real political and economical significance; they prefer "human interest stories", and what they like best of all is to read of matters sensational and scandalous, especially when they have a royal connection of some kind.

The market space beneath the *feuilleton* was colonised by a number of writers, of whom two in particular stood out. These two stood out because they were the two who came through the rigorous testing most spectacularly, commanding the vastest audiences because they wrote about the most popular subjects in the most popular manner; the writers in question were Alexandre Dumas and Eugene Sue. When the hectic decade of the 1840s began - building, though its protagonists could not know it as yet, towards a second revolution and the establishment of a new Napoleon - Dumas was known only as a playwright and Sue was hardly known at all. Within five years, though, they had become the two most popular fiction-writers in history - and probably the highest paid, though neither showed any conspicuous ability to handle money sensibly.

The two writers were great rivals in commercial terms, but their works were in some ways very different. They appealed to two great sections of the audience, using broadly similar literary methods but tending to opposite extremes ideologically. They were both shameless melodramatists, but Dumas made his name with extravagant adventures set in a gorgeous and grandiouse past when the *Ancien Régime* had allegedly not yet fallen prey to the wholesale corruptions which brought about the Revolution. In Dumas, particular kings might be weak and particular cardinals villainous, but the system was fine and beautiful and entirely worthy of the loyalty of valiant men, because the ideals of chivalry were not dead and still had power to generate optimism. Sue, on the other hand, adopted modern Paris as his literary ground, and directed his invective against systems rather than individuals. In Sue, the occasional aristocrat might be virtuous and generous, and even the occasional priest, but on the broader stage of history the aristocratic system of government and the hierarchical organization of the Catholic Church were infallible destroyers of idealism which enabled the worst of villians to find a niche and thrive. Sue refused to prettify the past, and looked forward instead to an imaginary future when social justice would triumph and new social institutions would facilitate virtue in all men.

It was only to be expected that Dumas the nostalgic conservative would achieve a far greater measure of respectability than Sue the fervent radical - though those historians of literature who have blinkered themselves against the possibility of glimpsing historical contexts and sociological factors in the shaping of literature continue to argue even today that Sue had a less-sophisticated audience because he was the less-sophisticated writer, and not *vice versa*.

****

The Wandering Jew (1844-45), which ran beneath the *feuilleton* in competition with Dumas' two most famous works, *The Three Musketeers* and *The Count of Monte Cristo*, was the second of Sue's major newspaper serials. The first of them, *The Mysteries of Paris* (1842-43), is somewhat better-known, but the ones which he wrote subsequently are now virtually forgotten. The reason for this neglect has more to do with the evolving political consciousness of the stories than their literary craftsmanship. *Les Sept péchés capitaux* (1847-49), whose pun on the word "capital" is unreproduced in the English title *The Seven Deadly Sins*, is now entirely forgotten, while *The Mysteries of the People* (1849-56) - which is Sue's *magnum opus* - might also have been relegated to total obscurity had it not been for a handful of champions who worked to preserve it - one such was the noted American socialist Daniel de Leon, who translated it for a 19-volume edition issued by the New York Labor News

Company in the 1900s.

Within the sequence of Sue's major works *The Wandering Jew* is crucial, because it represents the calculated importation into his world-view of a broader historical perspective, which attempts to move beyond the pseudo-journalistic railing against injustice and misery which is the hallmark of some of his work. The perspective is here represented in an allegorical fashion, whereby the predicament of working men and (all) women throughout history is linked to the legendary curses placed upon the Wandering Jew by Jesus and upon Herodias, mother of Salome, by John the Baptist.

Fans of supernatural fantasy may be disappointed to find that these two immortal characters hardly impinge upon the action at all, though the linch-pin of the plot is the spectacularly valuable legacy which the former wishes to divided among the descendants of a man who once gave him succour at a time of dire need. Their true purpose within the text is to focus the sense of outrage which the narrative attempts to convey in arguing that women - who have the social status of property even in the upper classes - and those who labour to produce the world's goods have been omitted from that measure of salvation from misery which mankind has managed to acquire. (A more radical writer might have taken the argument so far as to suggest that some fault might be found here with Jesus, whose alleged condemnation of Ahasuerus must surely seem at odds with his general character, but in spite of his rabid anti-Clericalism - which led him to make the Society of Jesus the chief villain of the story - Sue remained a devout Christian.)

In his later works - particularly *The Mysteries of the People*, which chronicles the travails of a "proletarian family" from prehistoric to modern times - Sue attempted to develop this historical perspective further, but he failed to bring any real theoretical sophistication to his theme when he abandoned the allegorical frame. For Sue, the sufferings of the poor at the hands of the rich were simply the result of an evil conspiracy of Church and State, which might be solved if only the world could embrace the essential message of Christ ("Love One Another") and the spirit of justice enshrined in the ideals of the Revolution (Liberty, Equality, Fraternity). The weakness of this perspective is amply demonstrated by the peculiar ending of *The Wandering Jew*, which shows how ill-fitting the formulae of popular literature are with the ideals of social justice. Sue - who died in 1857 - probably never had the chance to read Karl Marx; he drew his main political inspiration from Proudhon, whom Marx dismissed as a starry-eyed Utopian. It would have been interesting to see how Sue's career might have developed had it not been terminated by premature death (and it is interesting to note that Marx was living in Paris between October 1843 and February 1845, and was there while *The Wandering Jew* was being serialised).

****

In its full version *The Wandering Jew* is well over half a million words long; almost all the English editions are abridged. In a way, this is a shame, because the novel's main feature of interest is the amazing intricacy of its plot - but it has to be admitted that there are passages which seem to have been written in a desperate hurry (as might be expected from a man who had a daily deadline to meet for months on end), and a retrospective view of the plot reveals a vast profusion of loose ends and unfulfilled promises, some of which can be tidied up by careful abridgement.

The most striking feature of the text is that it is really two texts run together, the second of which only exists because the first proved so popular that as it approached its planned climax either Sue or his editor must have decided that it could not be allowed to end. Because of this, we find in the middle of the text what is perhaps the most spectacular example of an aborted climax to be found in the entire history of popular fiction.

The subsequent narrative never manages to achieve the same clarity of focus and sureness of direction as the former; from the moment of lost climax onwards the plot is lame, and its limp gets steadily worse - until the second ending, which is not so much a climax as a collapse, finally puts it out of its misery. Those readers who can bear in mind the circumstances of the story's composition, however, may still find much to fascinate them in this second part, whose eventual winding-up callously violates all the conventional expectations of the reader, to the extent that it becomes astonishing in its temerity.

A recent dramatization of *The Wandering Jew* which was staged at the National Theatre - in which a relatively small cast of actors demonstrated unparalleled heroism is playing half a dozen parts each (including a horse and a panther) - has served to demonstrate both the merits and the faults of the storyline, as well as brining the existence of the work to the attention of a modern British audience. In the book, as in the play, the quasi-Gothic moments of high drama and the shameless sentimentality are shaken and stirred with wild abandon, and the movement from subplot to subplot is marvellously relentless. The fanatical Rodin emerges by degrees to become a truly charismatic villain, in a story whose villains are far more important than its heroes. The play makes it all too clear, though, that the most abysmal of Sue's failures was his attempt to import into the plot something of the Oriental exoticism of which the French literary men of the day were so very fond. The incredibly naive and noble Indian prince is too silly an invention by half, and it is absurd to require him to play Romeo to Adrienne's Juliet - an absurdity recognised by audiences at the National, who could not help but dissolve into embarrassed laughter when that affair nightly reached its tragic end.

In a book such as this, though, a measure of absurdity might be considered simply one more element of an extraordinary and remarkably complex tapestry.

****

The Wandering Jew did appear in English, like *The Mysteries of Paris* before it, in the form of a three-decker novel, but it made little or no appeal in that form to the select *bourgeois* audience which patronised Mr. Mudie's guinea-a-year libraries. This was, however, by no means the only form in which it was published - and its greatest success was in another and very different stratum of the English literary marketplace.

Throughout the 1830s attempts had been made in Britain to export *bourgeois* culture to the lower orders, in the form of such charitably funded publications as the *Penny Magazine*. Charles Dickens - first as a writer and subsequently also as a publisher - became a key figure in the attempt to extend literary culture in such a way as to take in such an emergent audience. While *The Pickwick Papers* (1836-37) did enjoy some success in that vein when it first appeared as a serial, though, it was not Dickens himself but his plagiarisers who began to explore and exploit the true nature of working-class demand.

Despite the best of intentions Dickens was never more than half successful in his mission to capture the hearts and minds of the poor (his most radical attempt to strike and ideological blow on their behalf - in the second of his Christmas stories, *The Chimes* - largely passed them by; the story was far outstripped in popularity by its cosy and sickly sentimental successor, *The Cricket on the Hearth*). Those hack writers who specialised in producing coarser and more downmarket imitations of his work, however - who produced, among others, *The Penny Pickwick*, *Pickwick Abroad*, *Oliver Twiss* and *Nicholas Nicklebery* - provided the first economic base for a new kind of publishing aimed specifically at working-class readers. A vast gulf separated the *demi-monde* in which publishers of working-class fiction came to operate during the 1840s from the genteel world of the three-decker novel. This "middlebrow gap" remained agape at least until the 1890s, despite the attempts made by Dickens and a handful of others to build bridges across it. The fiction produced to meet the demand of the working-class audience was stigmatised in the world above as "penny dreadful" fiction, and deplored for the crudity of its prose and its sensationalism. The rigorous natural selection which had produced Dumas and Sue in France could not produce an identical result in England, because it was working within a much narrower range, but it worked according to the same logic, fostering a similar penchant for sensationalism and melodrama.

Dumas, when he was translated, could be promoted upwards into *bourgeois* culture without too much difficulty because of his ideological affilations, but Sue inevitably found a more appreciative audience in the nether regions of the market. *The Mysteries of Paris* proved to be popular in penny partwork reissues, and by the time *The Wandering Jew* started serialization in Paris the English penny dreadful market had begun to boom. No less than nine English publications set out to offer their own versions of it, if one condescends to include plagiarisms and parodies. Sue's next serial after *The Wandering Jew, The Seven Deadly Sins*, began serialization in two London weeklies within weeks of its commencement in *Le Constitutionnel*, and was subsequently picked up by a third. The popularity of these three works with this particular audience seems to have been immense - and so, if only within this curious literary underworld, was their influence.

Sue was the major inspiration for the most prolific and most successful of all the penny dreadful writers, G. W.M. Reynolds. Reynolds had the same political sympathies as Sue, and shared the same naive political philosophy. All his most popular and most famous works owe a heavy debt to Sue - a debt clearly acknowledged in the titles of *The Mysteries of London* (1846-48) and *The Mysteries of the Court of London* (1849-56). The specific influence of *The Wandering Jew* can be seen in three works which share the same method, establishing supernatural figures which display in some allegorical fashion the sufferings of the poor beneath the aristocratic yoke: *Faust* (1846); *Wagner the Wehr-Wolf* (1846-47); and

The Necromancer (1851-52). Of the three the second-named was by far the most popular, partly because it gives a central and much more extravagant role to supernatural horror - but in its insistence that the aristocratic monster's predations upon the poor and innocent provide a model for the everyday exploitations of the poor by the rich it remains true to Sue's passion and Sue's principle. (And if Sue seems to the modern reader to be a more sophisticated writer than Reynolds, that is probably because his audience made him so, rather than *vice versa*.) What direct influence Sue may have had on other penny dreadful writers it is very difficult to say, because literary history has passed over the entire genre so lightly and so contemptuously that we know little or nothing about its other prolific contributors, but if James Malcolm Rymer's *Varney the Vampyre* (1847) does not take any inspiration directly from *The Wandering Jew*, it certainly takes a full measure indirectly, via *Wagner the Wehr-Wolf*.

Penny dreadful fiction has been all but obliterated from the official record of English literary history, and Eugene Sue's English reputation, such as it ever was, has been erased along with it. This is to be regretted, not so much because Sue was a better writer than G.W.M. Reynolds, but because the erasure hides - for reasons of pure snobbery - a significant episode in the history of popular fiction and the history of the press. If it is true that we can understand the present only by first understanding the past, this obliteration should and must be made good. For this reason, if for no other, there-issue of one of Sue's major works is a publishing event of some significance.

Eugene Sue was one of the men who discovered - and subsequently taught that discovery to a generation of early English journalists - what sort of thing people who have a free choice really like to read. He was, in consequence, one of the men who laid the foundation stones for modern soap opera and modern tabloid journal-

-ism, and is worthy of interest on that account. *The Wandering Jew* is one of the most curiously-wrought of those foundation stones, and it too is worthy of our interest.

****

THE WANDERING JEW.

PROLOGUE.

THE LAND'S END OF TWO WORLDS.

THE Arctic Ocean encircles with a belt of eternal ice the desert confines of Siberia and North America—the uttermost limits of the Old and New worlds, separated by the narrow channel, known as Behring's Straits.

The last days of September have arrived.

The equinox has brought with it darkness and Northern storms, and night will quickly close the short and dismal polar day. The sky of a dull and leaden blue is faintly lighted by a sun without warmth, whose white disc, scarcely seen above the horizon, pales before the dazzling brilliancy of the snow that covers, as far as the eyes can reach, the boundless *steppes*.

To the North, this desert is bounded by a ragged coast, bristling with huge black rocks.

At the base of this Titanic mass lies enchained the petrified ocean, whose spell-bound waves appear fixed as vast ranges of ice mountains, their blue peaks fading away in the far-off frost smoke, or snow vapour.

Between the twin-peaks of Cape East, the termination of Siberia, the sullen sea is seen to drive tall icebergs across a streak of dead green. There lies Behring's Straits.

Opposite, and towering over the channel, rise the granite masses of Cape Prince of Wales, the headland of North America.

These lonely latitudes do not belong to the habitable world ; for the piercing cold shivers the stones, splits the trees, and causes the earth to burst asunder, which, throwing forth showers of icy spangles, seems capable of enduring this solitude of frost and tempest, of famine and death.

And yet, strange to say, foot-prints may be traced on the snow, covering these headlands on either side of Behring's Straits.

On the American shore, the footprints are small and light, thus betraying the passage of a woman.

She has been hastening up the rocky peak, whence the drifts of Siberia are visible.

On the latter ground, footprints larger and deeper betoken the passing of a man. He also was on his way to the Straits.

It would seem that this man and woman had arrived here from opposite directions, in hope of catching a glimpse of one another across the arm of the sea dividing the two worlds—the Old and the New.

More strange still ! the man and the woman have crossed the solitudes during a terrific storm ! Black pines, the growth of centuries, pointing their bent heads in different parts of the solitude like crosses in a churchyard, have been uprooted, rent, and hurled aside by the blasts !

Yet the two travellers face this furious tempest, which has plucked up trees, and pounded the frozen masses into splinters, with the roar of thunder.

They face it, without for one single instant deviating from the straight line hitherto followed by them.

Who then are these two beings who advance thus calmly amidst the storms and convulsions of nature ?

Is it by chance, or design, or destiny, that the seven nails in the sole of the man's shoe form a cross—thus:

```
          ✿
       ✿ ✿ ✿
          ✿
          ✿
          ✿
```

Everywhere he leaves this impress behind him.

On the smooth and polished snow, these footmarks seem imprinted by a foot of brass on a marble floor.

Night without twilight has soon succeeded day—a night of foreboding gloom.

The brilliant reflection of the snow renders the white steppes still visible beneath the azure darkness of the sky ; and the pale stars glimmer on the obscure and frozen dome.

Solemn silence reigns.

But, towards the Straits, a faint light appears.

At first, a gentle, bluish light, such as precedes moonrise ; it increases in brightness, and assumes a ruddy hue.

Darkness thickens in every other direction ; the white wilds of the desert are now scarcely visible under the black vault of the firmament.

Strange and confused noises are heard amidst this obscurity.

They sound like the flight of large night-birds—now flapping—now heavily skimming over the steppes—now descending.

But no cry is heard.

This silent terror heralds the approach of one of those imposing phenomena that awe alike the most ferocious and the most harmless of animated beings. An Aurora Borealis (magnificent sight !) common in the polar regions, suddenly beams forth.

A half circle of dazzling whiteness becomes visible in the horizon. Immense columns of light stream forth from this dazzling centre, rising to a great height, illuminating earth, sea, and sky. Then a brilliant reflection, like the blaze of a conflagration, steals over the snow of the desert, purples the summits of the mountains of ice, and imparts a dark red hue to the black rocks of both continents.

After attaining this magnificent brilliancy, the Northern Lights faded away gradually, and their vivid glow was lost in a luminous fog.

Just then, by a wondrous mirage, an effect very common in high latitudes, the American Coast, though separated from Siberia by a broad arm of the sea, loomed so close, that a bridge might seemingly be thrown from one world to the other.

Then human forms appeared in the transparent azure haze overspreading both forelands.

On the Siberian Cape, a man, on his knees, stretched his arms towards America, with an expression of inconceivable despair.

On the American promontory, a young and handsome woman replied to the man's despairing gesture by pointing to heaven.

For some seconds, these two tall figures stood out, pale and shadowy, in the farewell gleams of the Aurora.

But the fog thickens, and all is lost in darkness.

Whence came the two beings, who met thus amidst polar glaciers, at the extremities of the old and new worlds?

Who were the two creatures, brought near for a moment by a deceitful mirage, but who seemed eternally separated?

CHAPTER I.

MOROK.

THE month of October, 1831, draws to its close.

Though it is still day, a brass lamp, with four burners, illumines the cracked walls of a large loft, whose solitary window is closed against outer light. A ladder, with its top rungs coming up through an open trap, leads to it.

Here and there at random on the floor lie iron chains, spiked collars, saw-toothed snaffles, muzzles bristling with nails, and long iron rods set in wooden handles. In one corner stands a portable furnace, such as tinkers use to melt their spelter; charcoal and dry chips fill it, so that a spark would suffice to kindle this furnace in a minute.

Not far from this collection of ugly instruments, putting one in mind of a torturer's kit of tools, there are some articles of defence and offence of a bygone age. A coat of mail, with links so flexible, close, and light, that it resembled steel tissue, hangs from a box, beside iron cuishes and arm-pieces, in good condition, even to being properly fitted with straps. A mace, and two long three-corner-headed pikes, with ash handles, strong, and light at the same time, spotted with lately-shed blood, complete the armoury, modernized somewhat by the presence of two Tyrolese rifles, loaded and primed.

Along with this arsenal of murderous weapons and out of-date instruments, is strangely mingled a collection of very different objects, being small glass-lidded boxes, full of rosaries, chaplets, medals, AGNUS DEI, holy-water bottles, framed pictures of saints, etc., not to forget a goodly number of those chap-books, struck off in Friburg on coarse bluish paper, in which you can hear about miracles of our own time, or 'Jesus Christ's Letter to a true believer,' containing awful predictions, as for the years 1831 and '32, about impious revolutionary France.

One of those canvas daubs, with which strolling showmen adorn their booths, hangs from a rafter, no doubt to prevent its being spoilt by too long rolling up. It bore the following legend:

'THE DOWNRIGHT TRUE AND MOST MEMORABLE CONVERSION OF IGNATIUS MOROK, KNOWN AS THE PROPHET, HAPPENING IN FRIBURG, 1828TH YEAR OF GRACE.'

This picture, of a size larger than natural, of gaudy colour, and in bad taste, is divided into three parts, each presenting an important phase in the life of the convert, surnamed 'The Prophet.' In the first, behold a long-bearded man, the hair almost white, with uncouth face, and clad in reindeer skin, like the Siberian savage. His black foreskin cap is topped with a raven's head; his features express terror. Bent forward in his sledge, which half-a-dozen huge tawny dogs draw over the snow, he is fleeing from the pursuit of a pack of foxes, wolves, and big bears, whose gaping jaws, and formidable teeth, seem quite capable of devouring man, sledge, and dogs, a hundred times over. Beneath this section, read:

'IN 1810, MOROK, THE IDOLATER, FLED FROM WILD BEASTS.'

In the second picture, Morok, decently clad in a catechumen's white gown·

kneels, with clasped hands, to a man who wears a white neckcloth, an flowing black robe. In a corner, a tall angel, of repulsive aspect holds a trumpet in one hand, and flourishes a flaming sword with the other, while the words which follow flow out of his mouth, in red letters on a black ground :

'MOROK, THE IDOLATER. FLED FROM WILD BEASTS ; BUT WILD BEASTS WILL FLEE FROM IGNATIUS MOROK, CONVERTED AND BAPTIZED IN FRIBURG.'

Thus, in the last compartment, the new convert proudly, boastfully, and triumphantly parades himself in a flowing robe of blue ; head up, left arm akimbo, right hand outstretched, he seems to scare the wits out of a multitude of lions, tigers, hyænas, and bears, who, with sheathed claws, and masked teeth, couch at his feet, awestricken, and submissive.

Under this, is the concluding moral :

'IGNATIUS MOROK BEING CONVERTED, WILD BEASTS CROUCH BEFORE HIM.'

Not far from this canvas are several parcels of halfpenny books, likewise from the Friburg press, which relate by what an astounding miracle Morok, the Idolater, acquired a supernatural power almost divine, the moment he was converted—a power which the wildest animal could not resist, and which was testified to every day by the lion-tamer's performances, ' given less to display his courage than to show his praise unto the Lord.'

Through the trap-door which opens into the loft, reek up puffs of a rank, sour, penetrating odour. From time to time are heard sonorous growls and deep breathings, followed by a dull sound, as of great bodies stretching themselves heavily along the floor.

A man is alone in this loft. It is Morok, the tamer of wild beasts, surnamed the Prophet.

He is forty years old, of middle height, with lank limbs, and an exceedingly spare frame ; he is wrapped in a long, blood-red pelisse, lined with black fur ; his complexion, fair by nature, is bronzed by the wandering life he has led from childhood ; his hair, of that dead yellow peculiar to certain races of the Polar countries, falls straight and stiff down his shoulders ; and his thin, sharp, hooked nose, and prominent cheek-bones, surmount a long beard, bleached almost to whiteness. Peculiarly marking the physiognomy of this man is the wide-open eye, with its tawny pupil ever encircled by a rim of white. This fixed, extraordinary look, exercises a real fascination over animals—which, however, does not prevent the Prophet from also employing, to tame them, the terrible arsenal around him.

Seated at a table, he has just opened the false bottom of a box, filled with chaplets and other toys, for the use of the devout. Beneath this false bottom, secured by a secret lock, are several sealed envelopes, with no other address than a number, combined with a letter of the alphabet. The Prophet takes one of these packets, conceals it in the pocket of his pelisse, and, closing the secret fastening of the false bottom, replaces the box upon a shelf.

This scene occurs about four o'clock in the afternoon, in the White Falcon, the only hostelry in the little village of Mockern, situated near Leipsic, as you come from the north towards France.

After a few moments, the loft is shaken by a hoarse roaring from below.

'*Judas !* be quiet !' exclaims the Prophet, in a menacing tone, as he turns his head towards the trap-door.

Another deep growl is heard, formidable as distant thunder.

' Lie down, *Cain !*' cries Morok, starting from his seat.

A third roar, of inexpressible ferocity, bursts suddenly on the ear.

' *Death !* will you have done ?' cries the Prophet, rushing towards the trap-door, and addressing a third invisible animal, which bears this ghastly name.

Notwithstanding the habitual authority of his voice—notwithstanding his reiterated threats—the brute-tamer cannot obtain silence; on the contrary, the barking of several dogs is soon added to the roaring of the wild beasts. Morok seizes a pike, and approaches the ladder; he is about to descend, when he sees some one issuing from the aperture.

The new comer has a brown, sun-burnt face; he wears a grey hat, bell-crowned and broad-brimmed, with a short jacket, and wide trousers of green cloth; his dusty leathern gaiters show that he has walked some distance; a game-bag is fastened by straps to his back.

'The devil take the brutes!' cried he, as he set foot on the floor; 'one would think they'd forgotten me in three days. Judas thrust his paw through the bars of his cage, and Death danced like a fury. They don't know me any more, it seems?'

This was said in German. Morok answered in the same language, but with a slightly foreign accent.

'Good or bad news, Karl?' he inquired, with some uneasiness.

'Good news.'

'You've met them?'

'Yesterday; two leagues from Wittenberg.'

'Heaven be praised!' cried Morok, clasping his hands with intense satisfaction.

'Oh, of course, 'tis the direct road from Russia to France, 'twas a thousand to one that we should find them somewhere between Wittenberg and Leipsic.'

'And the description?'

'Very close: two young girls in mourning; horse, white; the old man has long moustache, blue forage-cap, grey top-coat, and a Siberian dog at his heels.'

'And where did you leave them?'

'A league hence. They will be here within the hour.'

'And in this inn—since it is the only one in the village,' said Morok, with a pensive air.

'And night drawing on,' added Karl.

'Did you get the old man to talk?'

'Him!—you don't suppose it!'

'Why not?'

'Go, and try yourself.'

'And for what reason?'

'Impossible.'

'Impossible—why?'

'You shall know all about it. Yesterday, as if I had fallen in with them by chance, I followed them to the place where they stopped for the night. I spoke in German to the tall old man, accosting him, as is usual with wayfarers, "*Good day, and a pleasant journey, comrade!*" But, for an answer, he looked askant at me, and pointed with the end of his stick to the other side of the road.'

'He is a Frenchman, and, perhaps, does not understand German.'

'He speaks it, at least, as well as you; for at the inn I heard him ask the host for whatever he and the young girls wanted.'

'And did you not again attempt to engage him in conversation?'

'Once only; but I met with such a rough reception, that, for fear of making mischief, I did not try again. Besides, between ourselves, I can tell you this man has a devilish ugly look; believe me, in spite of his grey moustache, he looks so vigorous and resolute, though with no more flesh on him than a carcass, that I don't know whether he or my mate Giant Goliath, would have the best of it in a struggle. I know not your plans: only take care, master—take care!'

'My black panther of Java was also very vigorous and very vicious,' said Morok, with a grim, disdainful smile.

What, Death? Yes, in truth; and she is vigorous and vicious as ever. Only to you she is almost mild.'

'And thus I will break in this tall old man, notwithstanding his strength and surliness.'

'Humph! humph! be on your guard, master. You are clever: you are as brave as any one; but, believe me, you will never make a lamb out of the old wolf that will be here presently.'

'Does not my lion, Cain—does not my tiger, Judas, crouch in terror before me?'

'Yes, I believe you there—because you have means——'

'Because I have *faith:* that is all—and it *is* all,' said Morok, imperiously interrupting Karl, and accompanying these words with such a look, that the other hung his head and was silent.

'Why should not he whom the Lord upholds in his struggle with wild beasts, be also upheld in his struggle with men, when those men are perverse and impious?' added the Prophet, with a triumphant, inspired air.

Whether from belief in his master's conviction, or from inability to engage in a controversy with him on so delicate a subject, Karl answered the Prophet, humbly: 'You are wiser than I am, master; what you do must be well done.'

'Did you follow this old man and these two young girls all day long?' resumed the Prophet, after a moment's silence.

'Yes; but at a distance. As I know the country well, I sometimes cut across a valley, sometimes over a hill, keeping my eye upon the road, where they were always to be seen. The last time I saw them, I was hid behind the water-mill by the potteries. As they were on the highway for this place, and night was drawing on, I quickened my pace to get here before them, and be the bearer of what you call good news.'

'Very good—yes—very good: and you shall be rewarded; for if these people had escaped me——'

The Prophet started, and did not conclude the sentence. The expression of his face, and the tones of his voice, indicated the importance of the intelligence which had just been brought him.

'In truth,' rejoined Karl, 'it may be worth attending to; for that Russian courier, all plastered with lace, who came, without slacking bridle, from St. Petersburg to Leipsic, only to see you, rode so fast, perhaps, for the purpose——'

Morok abruptly interrupted Karl, and said:

'Who told you that the arrival of the courier had anything to do with these travellers? You are mistaken; you should only know what I choose to tell you.'

'Well, master, forgive me, and let's say no more about it. So! I will get rid of my game-bag, and go help Goliath to feed the brutes, for their supper time draws near, if it is not already past. Does our big giant grow lazy, master?'

'Goliath is gone out; he must not know that you are returned; above all, the tall old man and the maidens must not see you here—it would make them suspect something.'

'Where do you wish me to go, then?'

'Into the loft, at the end of the stable, and wait my orders; you may this night have to set out for Leipsic.'

'As you please; I have some provisions left in my pouch, and can sup in the loft whilst I rest myself.'

'Go.'

'Master, remember what I told you. Beware of that old fellow with the grey moustache; I think he's devilish tough; I'm up to these things—he's an ugly customer—be on your guard!'

'Be quite easy! I am always on my guard,' said Morok.

'Then good luck to you, master?'—and Karl, having reached the ladder, suddenly disappeared.

After making a friendly farewell gesture to his servant, the Prophet walked up and down for some time, with an air of deep meditation; then, approaching the box which contained the papers, he took out a pretty long letter, and read it over and over with profound attention. From time to time, he rose and went to the closed window, which looked upon the inner court of the inn, and appeared to listen anxiously; for he waited with impatience the arrival of the three persons whose approach had just been announced to him.

CHAPTER II.

THE TRAVELLERS.

WHILE the above scene was passing in the White Falcon at Mockern, the three persons whose arrival Morok was so anxiously expecting, travelled on leisurely in the midst of smiling meadows, bounded on one side by a river, the current of which turned a mill; and on the other by the highway leading to the village, which was situated on an eminence, at about a league's distance.

The sky was beautifully serene; the bubbling of the river, beaten by the mill-wheel and sparkling with foam, alone broke upon the silence of an evening profoundly calm. Thick willows, bending over the river, covered it with their green transparent shadow; whilst, further on, the stream reflected so splendidly the blue heavens and the glowing tints of the west, that, but for the hills which rose between it and the sky, the gold and azure of the water would have mingled in one dazzling sheet with the gold and azure of the firmament. The tall reeds on the bank bent their black velvet heads beneath the light breath of the breeze that rises at the close of day—for the sun was gradually sinking behind a broad streak of purple clouds, fringed with fire. The tinkling bells of a flock of sheep sounded from afar in the clear and sonorous air.

Along a path trodden in the grass of the meadow, two girls, almost children —for they had but just completed their fifteenth year—were riding on a white horse of medium size, seated upon a large saddle with a back to it, which easily took them both in, for their figures were slight and delicate.

A man of tall stature, with a sun-burnt face, and long grey moustache, was leading the horse by the bridle, and ever and anon turned towards the girls, with an air of solicitude at once respectful and paternal. He leaned upon a long staff; his still robust shoulders carried a soldier's knapsack; his dusty shoes, and step that began to drag a little, showed that he had walked a long way.

One of those dogs which the tribes of Northern Siberia harness to their sledges—a sturdy animal, nearly of the size, form, and hairy coat of the wolf —followed closely in the steps of the leader of this little caravan, never quitting, as it is commonly said, the heels of his master.

Nothing could be more charming than the group formed by the girls. One held with her left hand the flowing reins, and with her right encircled the waist of her sleeping sister, whose head reposed on her shoulder. Each step of the horse gave a graceful swaying to these pliant forms, and swung their little feet, which rested on a wooden ledge in lieu of a stirrup.

These twin sisters, by a sweet maternal caprice, had been called Rose and Blanche; they were now orphans, as might be seen by their sad mourning vestments, already much worn. Extremely like in feature, and of the same size, it was necessary to be in the constant habit of seeing them, to distinguish one from the other. The portrait of her who slept not, might serve then for both of them; the only difference at the moment being, that Rose was awake, and discharging for that day the duties of elder sister—duties thus divided between them, according to the fancy of their guide, who, being an old soldier of the empire, and a martinet, had judged fit thus to alternate obedience and command between the orphans.

Greuze would have been inspired by the sight of those sweet faces, coifed in close caps of black velvet, from beneath which strayed a profusion of thick ringlets of a light chestnut colour, floating down their necks and shoulders, and setting, as in a frame, their round, firm, rosy, satin-like cheeks. A carnation, bathed in dew, is of no richer softness than their blooming lips ; the wood violet's tender blue would appear dark beside the limpid azure of their large eyes, in which are depicted the sweetness of their characters, and the innocence of their age ; a pure and white forehead, small nose, dimpled chin, complete these graceful countenances, which present a delightful blending of candour and gentleness.

You should have seen them too, when, on the threatening of rain or storm, the old soldier carefully wrapped them both in a large pelisse of rein-deer fur, and pulled over their heads the ample hood of this impervious garment ; then nothing could be more lovely than those fresh and smiling little faces, sheltered beneath the dark-coloured cowl.

But now the evening was fine and calm ; the heavy cloak hung in folds about the knees of the sisters, and the hood rested on the back of their saddle.

Rose, still encircling with her right arm the waist of her sleeping sister, contemplated her with an expression of ineffable tenderness, akin to maternal ; for Rose was the eldest for the day, and an elder sister is almost a mother.

Not only did the orphans idolize each other ; but, by a psychological phenomenon, frequent with twins, they were almost always simultaneously affected ; the emotion of one was reflected instantly in the countenance of the other ; the same cause would make both of them start or blush, so closely did their young hearts beat in unison ; all ingenuous joys, all bitter griefs, were mutually felt, and shared in a moment between them.

In their infancy, simultaneously attacked by a severe illness, like two flowers on the same stem, they had drooped, grown pale, and languished together ; but together also had they again found the pure, fresh hues of health.

Need it be said, that those mysterious, indissoluble links which united the twins, could not have been broken without striking a mortal blow at the existence of the poor children ?

Thus the sweet birds called love-birds, only living in pairs, as if endowed with a common life, pine, despond, and die, when parted by a barbarous hand.

The guide of the orphans, a man of about fifty-five, distinguished by his military air and gait, preserved the immortal type of the warriors of the republic and the empire—some heroic of the people, who became, in one campaign, the first soldiers in the world—to prove what the people can do, have done, and will renew, when the rulers of their choice place in them confidence, strength, and their hope.

This soldier, guide of the sisters, and formerly a horse-grenadier of the Imperial Guard, had been nicknamed Dagobert. His grave, stern countenance was strongly marked ; his long, grey, and thick moustache completely concealed his upper lip, and united with a large imperial, which almost covered his chin ; his meagre cheeks, brick coloured, and tanned as parchment, were carefully shaven ; thick eye-brows, still black, overhung and shaded his light blue eyes ; gold ear-rings reached down to his white-edged military stock ; his top-coat, of coarse grey cloth, was confined at the waist by a leathern belt ; and a blue foraging cap, with a red tuft falling on his left shoulder, covered his bald head.

Once endowed with the strength of Hercules, and having still the heart of a lion—kind and patient, because he was courageous and strong—Dagobert, not-withstanding his rough exterior, evinced for his orphan charges an exquisite solicitude, a watchful kindness, and a tenderness almost maternal. Yes, motherly ; for the heroism of affection dwells alike in the mother's heart and the soldier's.

Stoically calm, and repressing all emotion, the unchangeable coolness of Dagobert never failed him ; and, though few were less given to drollery, he was now and then highly comic, by reason of the imperturbable gravity with which he did everything.

From time to time, as they journeyed on, Dagobert would turn to bestow a caress or friendly word on the good white horse upon which the orphans were mounted. Its furrowed sides and long teeth betrayed a venerable age. Two deep scars, one on the flank and the other on the chest, proved that his horse had been present in hot battles ; nor was it without an act of pride that he sometimes shook his old military bridle, the brass stud of which was still adorned with an embossed eagle. His pace was regular, careful, and steady ; his coat sleek, and his bulk moderate ; the abundant foam, which covered his bit, bore witness to that health which horses acquire by the constant, but not excessive, labour of a long journey, performed by short stages. Although he had been more than six months on the road, this excellent animal carried the orphans, with a tolerably heavy portmanteau fastened to the saddle, as freely as on the day they started.

If we have spoken of the excessive length of the horse's teeth—the un-questionable evidence of great age—it is chiefly because he often displayed them, for the sole purpose of acting up to his name (he was called *Jovial*), by playing a mischievous trick, of which the dog was the victim.

This latter, who, doubtless for the sake of contrast, was called Spoil-sport (*Rabat-joie*), being always at his master's heels, found himself within the reach of Jovial, who from time to time nipped him delicately by the nape of the neck, lifted him from the ground, and carried him thus for a moment. The dog, protected by his thick coat, and no doubt long accustomed to the practical jokes of his companion, submitted to all this with stoical complacency ; save that, when he thought the jest had lasted long enough, he would turn his head and growl. Jovial understood him at the first hint, and hastened to set him down again. At other times, just to avoid monotony, Jovial would gently bite the knapsack of the soldier, who seemed, as well as the dog, to be perfectly accustomed to his pleasantries.

These details will give a notion of the excellent understanding that existed between the twin sisters, the old soldier, the horse, and the dog.

The little caravan proceeded on its way, anxious to reach, before night, the village of Mockern, which was now visible on the summit of a hill. Ever and anon, Dagobert looked around him, and seemed to be gathering up old re-collections ; by degrees, his countenance became clouded, and when he was at a little distance from the mill, the noise of which had arrested his attention, he stopped, and drew his long moustache several times between his finger and thumb, the only sign which revealed in him any strong and concentrated feeling.

Jovial, having stopped short behind his master, Blanche, awaked suddenly by the shock, raised her head ; her first look sought her sister, on whom she smiled sweetly ; then both exchanged glances of surprise, on seeing Dagobert motionless, with his hands clasped and resting on his long staff, apparently affected by some painful and deep emotion.

The orphans just chanced to be at the foot of a little mound, the summit of which was buried in the thick foliage of a huge oak, planted half way down the slope. Perceiving that Dagobert continued motionless and absorbed in thought,

Rose leaned over her saddle, and, placing her little white hand on the shoulder of their guide, whose back was turned towards her, said to him, in a soft voice: 'Whatever is the matter with you, Dagobert?'

The veteran turned; to the great astonishment of the sisters, they perceived a large tear, which traced its humid furrow down his tanned cheek, and lost itself in his thick moustache.

'You weeping—*you!*' cried Rose and Blanche together, deeply moved. 'Tell us, we beseech, what is the matter?'

After a moment's hesitation, the soldier brushed his horny hand across his eyes, and said to the orphans in a faltering voice, whilst he pointed to the old oak beside them: 'I shall make you sad, my poor children: and yet what I'm going to tell you has something sacred in it. Well, eighteen years ago, on the eve of the great battle of Leipsic, I carried your father to this very tree. He had two sabre-cuts on the head, a musket-ball in his shoulder; and it was here that he and I—who had got two thrusts of a lance for my share —were taken prisoners; and by whom, worse luck?—why, a renegado! By a Frenchman—an *emigrant* marquis, then colonel in the service of Russia— and who afterwards—but one day you shall know all."

The veteran paused; then, pointing with his staff to the village of Mockern, he added: 'Yes, yes, I can recognise the spot. Yonder are the heights where your brave father—who commanded us and the Poles of the Guard—over- threw the Russian Cuirassiers, after having carried the battery. Ah, my children!' continued the soldier, with the utmost simplicity, 'I wish you had seen your brave father, at the head of our brigade of horse, rushing on in a desperate charge in the thick of a shower of shells!—there was nothing like it—not a soul so grand as he!'

Whilst Dagobert thus expressed, in his own way, his regrets and recollec- tions, the two orphans—by a spontaneous movement, glided gently from the horse, and holding each other by the hand, went together to kneel at the foot of the old oak. And there, closely pressed in each other's arms, they began to weep; whilst the soldier, standing behind them, with his hands crossed on his long staff, rested his bald front upon it.

'Come, come, you must not fret,' said he softly, when, after a pause of a few minutes, he saw tears run down the blooming cheeks of Rose and Blanche, still on their knees. 'Perhaps we may find General Simon in Paris,' added he; 'I will explain all that to you this evening at the inn. I pur- posely waited for this day, to tell you many things about your father; it was an idea of mine, because this day is a sort of anniversary.'

'We weep because we think also of our mother,' said Rose.

'Of our mother, whom we shall only see again in heaven,' added Blanche.

The soldier raised the orphans, took each by the hand, and gazing from one to the other with ineffable affection, rendered still the more touching by the contrast of his rude features, 'You must not give way thus, my children,' said he; 'it is true your mother was the best of women. When she lived in Poland, they called her the *Pearl of Warsaw*—it ought to have been the Pearl of the Whole World—for in the whole world you could not have found her match. No—no!'

The voice of Dagobert faltered; he paused, and drew his long grey moustache between finger and thumb, as was his habit. 'Listen, my girls,' he resumed, when he had mastered his emotion; 'your mother could give you none but the best advice, eh?'

'Yes, Dagobert.'

'Well, what instructions did she give you before she died? To think often of her, but without grieving?'

'It is true; she told us that our Father in heaven, always good to poor mothers whose children are left on earth, would permit her to hear us from above,' said Blanche.

'And that her eyes would be ever fixed upon us,' added Rose.

And the two, by a spontaneous impulse, replete with the most touching grace, joined hands, raised their innocent looks to heaven, and exclaimed, with that beautiful faith natural to their age : 'Is it not so, mother ?—thou seest us ?—thou hearest us ?'

'Since your mother sees and hears you,' said Dagobert, much moved, 'do not grieve her by fretting. She forbade you to do so.'

'You are right, Dagobert. We will not cry any more.'—And the orphans dried their eyes.

Dagobert, in the opinion of the devout, would have passed for a very heathen. In Spain, he had found pleasure in cutting down those monks of all orders and colours, who, bearing crucifix in one hand, and poniard in the other, fought *not* for liberty—the Inquisition had strangled *her* centuries ago—but for their monstrous privileges. Yet, in forty years, Dagobert had witnessed so many sublime and awful scenes—he had been so many times face to face with death—that the instinct of *natural religion*, common to every simple, honest heart, had always remained uppermost in his soul. Therefore, though he did not share in the consoling faith of the two sisters, he would have held as criminal any attempt to weaken its influence.

Seeing them less downcast, he thus resumed : 'That's right, my pretty ones : I prefer to hear you chat as you did this morning and yesterday—laughing at times, and answering me when I speak, instead of being so much engrossed with your own talk. Yes, yes, my little ladies ! you seem to have had famous secrets together these last two days—so much the better, if it amuses you.'

The sisters coloured, and exchanged a subdued smile, which contrasted with the tears that yet filled their eyes, and Rose said to the soldier, with a little embarrassment. 'No, I assure you, Dagobert, we talk of nothing in particular.'

'Well, well, I don't wish to know it. Come, rest yourselves, a few moments more, and then we must start again ; for it grows late, and we have to reach Mockern before night, so that we may be early on the road to-morrow.'

'Have we still a long, long way to go ?' asked Rose.

'What, to reach Paris? Yes, my children ; some hundred days' march. We don't travel quick, but we get on ; and we travel cheap, because we have a light purse. A closet for you, a straw mattress and a blanket at your door for me, with Spoil-sport on my feet, and a clean litter for old Jovial, these are our whole travelling expenses. I say nothing about food, because you two together don't eat more than a mouse, and I have learnt in Egypt and Spain to be hungry only when it suits.'

'Not forgetting that, to save still more, you do all the cooking for us, and will not even let us assist.'

'And to think, good Dagobert, that you wash almost every evening at our resting-place. As if it were not for us to——'

'You !' said the soldier, interrupting Blanche, 'I allow you to chap your pretty little hands in soap suds ! Pooh ! don't a soldier on a campaign always wash his own linen ? Clumsy as you see me, I was the best washerwoman in my squadron—and what a hand at ironing ! Not to make a brag of it.'

'Yes, yes—you can iron well—very well.'

'Only sometimes, there will be a little singe,' said Rose, smiling.

'Hah ! when the iron is too hot. Zounds ! I may bring it as near my cheek as I please ; my skin is so tough that I don't feel the heat,' said Dagobert, with imperturbable gravity.

'We are only jesting, good Dagobert.'

'Then, children, if you think that I know my trade as a washerwoman, let me continue to have your custom : it is cheaper ; and, on a journey, poor people like us should save where we can, for we must, at all events, keep enough to reach Paris. Once there, our papers and the medal you wear will do the rest—I hope so, at least.'

'This medal is sacred to us ; mother gave it to us on her death-bed.'

'Therefore, take great care that you do not lose it : see, from time to time, that you have it safe.'

'Here it is,' said Blanche, as she drew from her bosom a small bronze medal, which she wore suspended from her neck by a chain of the same material. The medal bore on its faces the following inscriptions :

VICTIM of L. C. D. J. Pray for me ! —— PARIS, February the 13th, 1682.	AT PARIS, No. 3, Rue Saint François. In a century and a half you will be. February the 13th, 1832. —— PRAY FOR ME !

'What does it mean, Dagobert?' resumed Blanche, as she examined the mournful inscriptions. 'Mother was not able to tell us.'

'We will discuss all that this evening, at the place where we sleep,' answered Dagobert. 'It grows late : let us be moving. Put up the medal carefully, and away !—We have yet nearly an hour's march to arrive at quarters. Come, my poor pets, once more look at the mound where your brave father fell—and then—to horse ! to horse!'

The orphans gave a last pious glance at the spot which had recalled to their guide such painful recollections, and, with his aid, remounted Jovial.

This venerable animal had not for one moment dreamed of moving ; but, with the consummate forethought of a veteran, he had made the best use of his time, by taking from that foreign soil a large contribution of green and tender grass, before the somewhat envious eyes of Spoil-sport, who had comfortably established himself in the meadow, with his snout protruding between his fore-paws. On the signal of departure, the dog resumed his post behind his master, and Dagobert, trying the ground with the end of his long staff, led the horse carefully along by the bridle, for the meadow was growing more and more marshy ; indeed, after advancing a few steps, he was obliged to turn off to the left, in order to regain the high road.

On reaching Mockern, Dagobert asked for the least expensive inn, and was told there was only one in the village—the White Falcon.

'Let us go then to the White Falcon,' observed the soldier.

———

CHAPTER III.

THE ARRIVAL.

ALREADY had Morok several times opened with impatience the window-shutter of the loft, to look out upon the inn-yard, watching for the arrival of the orphans and the soldier. Not seeing them, he began once more to walk slowly up and down, with his head bent forward, and his arms folded on his bosom, meditating on the best means to carry out the plan he had conceived. The ideas which possessed his mind, were, doubtless, of a painful character, for his countenance grew even more gloomy than usual.

Notwithstanding his ferocious appearance, he was by no means deficient in intelligence. The courage displayed in his taming exercises (which he gravely attributed to his recent conversion), a solemn and mystical style of speech, and a hypocritical affectation of austerity, had given him a species of influence over the people he visited in his travels. Long before his conversion, as may well be supposed, Morok had been familiar with the habits of wild beasts. In fact, born in the north of Siberia, he had been, from his boyhood, one of the boldest hunters of bears and reindeer ; later, in 1810, he had abandoned this profession, to serve as guide to a Russian engineer, who was charged with an exploring expedition to the Polar regions. He afterwards followed him to St. Petersburg, and there, after some vicissitudes of fortune, Morok became one of the imperial couriers—those iron *automata*, that the least caprice of the despot hurls in a frail sledge through the immensity of the empire, from Persia to the Frozen Sea. For these men, who travel night and day, with the rapidity of lightning, there are neither seasons nor, obstacles, fatigues nor dangers ; living projectiles, they must either be broken to pieces, or reach the intended mark. One may conceive the boldness, the vigour, and the resignation, of men accustomed to such a life.

It is useless to relate here, by what series of singular circumstances Morok was induced to exchange this rough pursuit for another profession, and at last to enter, as catechumen, a religious house at Friburg ; after which, being duly and properly converted, he began his nomadic excursions, with his menagerie of unknown origin.

    ✿   ✿   ✿   ✿   ✿   ✿   ✿

Morok continued to walk up and down the loft. Night had come. The three persons whose arrival he so impatiently expected had not yet made their appearance. His walk became more and more nervous and irregular.

On a sudden he stopped abruptly, leaned his head towards the window, and listened. His ear was quick as a savage's.

' They are here !' he exclaimed, and his fox-like eye shone with diabolic joy. He had caught the sound of footsteps—a man's and a horse's. Hastening to the window-shutter of the loft, he opened it cautiously, and saw the two young girls on horseback, and the old soldier who served them as a guide, enter the inn-yard together.

The night had set in, dark and cloudy ; a high wind made the lights flicker in the lanterns which were used to receive the new guests. But the description given to Morok had been so exact, that it was impossible to mistake them. Sure of his prey, he closed the window.

Having remained in meditation for another quarter of an hour—for the purpose, no doubt, of thoroughly digesting his projects—he leaned over the aperture from which projected the ladder, and called, ' Goliath !'

' Master !' replied a hoarse voice.

' Come up to me.'

' Here I am—just come from the slaughter-house with the meat.'

The steps of the ladder creaked as an enormous head appeared on a level with the floor. The new comer, who was more than six feet high, and gifted with herculean proportions, had been well named Goliath. He was hideous. His squinting eyes were deep set beneath a low and projecting forehead ; his reddish hair and beard, thick and coarse as horse-hair, gave his features a stamp of bestial ferocity ; between his broad jaws, armed with teeth which resembled fangs, he held by one corner a piece of raw beef weighing ten or twelve pounds, finding it, no doubt, easier to carry in that fashion, whilst he used his hands to ascend the ladder, which bent beneath his weight.

At length the whole of this tall and huge body issued from the aperture. Judging by his bull-neck, the astonishing breadth of his chest and shoulders, and the vast bulk of his arms and legs, this giant need not have feared to wrestle single-handed with a bear He wore an old pair of blue trousers with red stripes, faced with tanned sheep's-skin, and a vest, or rather cuirass, of thick leather, which was here and there slashed by the sharp claws of the animals.

When he was fairly on the floor, Goliath unclasped his fangs, opened his mouth, and let fall the great piece of beef, licking his blood-stained lips with greediness. Like many other mountebanks, this species of monster had begun by eating raw meat at fairs for the amusement of the public. Thence having gradually acquired a taste for this barbarous food, and uniting pleasure with profit, he engaged himself to perform the prelude to the exercises of Morok, by devouring, in the presence of the crowd, several pounds of raw flesh.

' My share and Death's are below stairs, and here are those of Cain and Judas,' said Goliath, pointing to the chunk of beef. ' Where is the cleaver, that I may cut it in two ?—No preference here—beast or man—every gullet must have its own.'

Then, rolling up one of the sleeves of his vest, he exhibited a fore-arm hairy as the skin of a wolf, and knotted with veins as large as one's thumb.

' I say, master, where's the cleaver ?' he again began, as he cast round his eyes in search of that instrument. But instead of replying to this inquiry, the Prophet put many questions to his disciple.

' Were you below when just now some new travellers arrived at the inn ?'

' Yes, master ; I was coming from the slaughter-house.'

' Who are these travellers ?'

' Two young lasses mounted on a white horse, and an old fellow with a big moustache. But the cleaver ?—my beasts are hungry and so am I—the cleaver !'

' Do you know where they have lodged these travellers ?'

' The host took them to the far end of the court-yard.'

' The building which overlooks the fields ?'

' Yes, master –but the cleaver——' A burst of frightful roaring shook the loft, and interrupted Goliath.

' Hark to them !' he exclaimed ; ' hunger has driven the beasts wild. If I could roar, I should do as they do. I have never seen Judas and Cain as they are to-night ; they leap in their cages as if they'd knock all to pieces. As for Death, her eyes shine more than usual like candles— Poor Death !'

' So these girls are lodged in the building at the end of the court-yard,' resumed Morok, without attending to the observations of Goliath.

' Yes, yes—but, in the devil's name, where is the cleaver ? Since Karl went away I have to do all the work, and that makes our meals very late.'

' Did the old man remain with the young girls ?' asked Morok.

Goliath amazed that, notwithstanding his importunities, his master should still appear to neglect the animals' supper, regarded the Prophet with an increase of stupid astonishment.

' Answer, you brute !'

' If I am a brute, I have a brute's strength,' said Goliath, in a surly tone : ' and brute against brute, I have not always come the worst off.'

' I ask if the old man remained with the girls,' repeated Morok.

' Well, then—no !' returned the giant. ' The old man, after leading his horse to the stable, asked for a tub and some water, took his stand under the porch— and there—by the light of a lantern—he is washing out clothes. A man with a grey moustache !--paddling in soap-suds like a washerwoman—it's as if I were to feed canaries !' added Goliath, shrugging his shoulders with disdain. ' But now I've answered you, master, let me attend to the beasts' supper—and,' looking round for something, he added, ' where is the cleaver ?'

After a moment of thoughtful silence, the Prophet said to Goliath, ' You will give no food to the beasts this evening.'

At first the giant could not understand these words, the idea was so incomprehensible to him.

'What is your pleasure, master?' said he.

'I forbid you to give any food to the beasts this evening.'

Goliath did not answer, but he opened wide his squinting eyes, folded his hands, and drew back a couple of steps.

'Well, dost hear me?' said Morok, with impatience. 'Is it plain enough?'

'Not feed? when our meat is there, and supper is already three hours after time!' cried Goliath, with ever-increasing amazement.

'Obey, and hold your tongue.'

'You must wish something bad to happen this evening. Hunger makes the beasts furious—and me also.'

'So much the better!'

'It'll drive 'em mad.'

'So much the better!'

'How, so much the better?—But——'

'It is enough!'

'But, devil take me, I am as hungry as the beasts!'

'Eat then—who prevents it? Your supper is ready, as you devour it raw.'

'I never eat without my beasts, nor they without me.'

'I tell you again, that, if you dare give any food to the beasts—I will turn you away.'

Goliath uttered a low growl as hoarse as a bear's, and looked at the Prophet with a mixture of anger and stupefaction.

Morok, having given his orders, walked up and down the loft, appearing to reflect. Then, addressing himself to Goliath, who was still plunged in deep perplexity, he said to him :

'Do you remember the burgomaster's, where I went to get my passport signed?—to-day his wife bought some books and a chaplet.'

'Yes,' answered the giant shortly.

'Go and ask his servant if I may be sure to find the burgomaster early to-morrow morning.'

'What for?'

'I may, perhaps, have something important to communicate ; at all events, say that I beg him not to leave home without seeing me.'

'Good! but may I not feed the beasts before I go to the burgomaster's?— only the panther, who is most hungry? Come, master ; only poor Death? just a little morsel to satisfy her ; Cain and I and Judas can wait.'

'It is the panther, above all, that I forbid you to feed. Yes, her, above all the rest.'

'By the horns of the devil!' cried Goliath, 'what is the matter with you to-day? I can make nothing of it. It is a pity that Karl's not here ; he, being cunning, would help me to understand why you prevent the beasts from eating when they are hungry.'

'You have no need to understand it.'

'Will not Karl soon come back?'

'He has already come back.'

'Where is he, then?'

'Off again.'

'What can be going on here? There is something in the wind. Karl goes, and returns, and goes again, and——'

'We are not talking of Karl, but of you ; though hungry as a wolf you are cunning as a fox, and, when it suits you, as cunning as Karl.' And, changing on the sudden his tone and manner, Morok slapped the giant cordially on the shoulder.

'What! am I cunning?'

'The proof is, that there are ten florins to earn to-night—and you will be keen enough to earn them, I am sure.'

'Why, on those terms, yes—I am awake,' said the giant, smiling with a stupid, self-satisfied air. 'What must I do for ten florins?'

'You shall see.'

'Is it hard work?'

'You shall see. Begin by going to the burgomaster's—but first light the fire in that stove.' He pointed to it with his finger.

'Yes, master,' said Goliath, somewhat consoled for the delay of his supper by the hope of gaining ten florins.

'Put that iron bar in the stove,' added the Prophet, 'to make it red-hot.'

'Yes, master.'

'You will leave it there ; go to the burgomaster's, and return here to wait for me.'

'Yes, master.'

'You will keep the fire up in the stove.'

'Yes, master.'

Morok took a step away, but, recollecting himself, he resumed : 'You say the old man is busy washing under the porch?'

'Yes, master.'

'Forget nothing : the iron bar in the fire—the burgomaster—and return here to wait my orders.' So saying, Morok descended by the trap-door and disappeared.

CHAPTER IV.

MOROK AND DAGOBERT.

GOLIATH had not been mistaken, for Dagobert was washing with that imperturbable gravity with which he did everything else.

When we remember the habits of a soldier a-field, we need not be astonished at this apparent eccentricity. Dagobert only thought of sparing the scanty purse of the orphans, and of saving them all care and trouble ; so every evening when they came to a halt he devoted himself to all sorts of feminine occupations. But he was not now serving his apprenticeship in these matters ; many times, during his campaigns, he had industriously repaired the damage and disorder which a day of battle always brings to the garments of the soldier; for it is not enough to receive a sabre-cut—the soldier has also to mend his uniform ; for the stroke which grazes the skin makes likewise a corresponding fissure in the cloth.

Therefore, in the evening or on the morrow of a hard-fought engagement, you will see the best soldiers (always distinguished by their fine military appearance) take from their cartridge-box or knapsack a huswife, furnished with needles, thread, scissors, buttons, and other such gear, and apply themselves to all kinds of mending and darning, with a zeal that the most industrious workwoman might envy.

We could not find a better opportunity to explain the name of Dagobert, given to Francis Baudoin (the guide of the orphans) at a time when he was considered one of the handsomest and bravest horse-grenadiers of the Imperial Guard.

They had been fighting hard all day, without any decisive advantage. In the evening, the company to which our hero belonged was sent as outliers to occupy the ruins of a deserted village. Videttes being posted, half the troopers remained in saddle, whilst the others, having picketed their horses, were able to take a little rest. Our hero had charged valiantly that day without receiving any wound—for he counted as a mere memento the deep scratch on his thigh, which a kaiserlitz had inflicted in awkwardly attempting an upward thrust with the bayonet.

'You donkey! my new breeches!' the grenadier had exclaimed, when he saw the wide yawning rent, which he instantly avenged by running the Austrian through with a thrust scientifically administered. For if he showed a stoical indifference on the subject of injury to his skin, it was not so with regard to the ripping up of his best parade uniform.

He undertook, therefore, the same evening, at the bivouac, to repair this accident. Selecting his best needle and thread from the stores of his huswife, and arming his finger with a thimble, he began to play the tailor by the light of the watch-fire, having first drawn off his cavalry-boots, and also (if it must be confessed) the injured garment itself, which he turned the wrong side out the better to conceal the stitches.

This partial undress was certainly a breach of discipline : but the captain, as he went his round, could not forbear laughing at the sight of the veteran soldier, who, gravely seated, in a squatting position, with his grenadier cap on, his regimental coat on his back, his boots by his side, and his galligaskins in his lap, was sewing with all the coolness of a tailor upon his own shop-board.

Suddenly, a musket-shot is heard, and the videttes fall back upon the detachment, calling to arms. 'To horse !' cries the captain, in a voice of thunder.

In a moment, the troopers are in their saddles, the unfortunate clothesmender having to lead the first rank : there is no time to turn the unlucky garment, so he slips it on, as well as he can, wrong side out, and leaps upon his horse, without even stopping to put on his boots.

A party of Cossacks, profiting by the cover of a neighbouring wood, had attempted to surprise the detachment : the fight was bloody, and our hero foamed with rage, for he set much value on his equipments, and the day had been fatal to him. Thinking of his torn clothes and lost boots, he hacked away with more fury than ever ; a bright moon illumined the scene of action, and his comrades were able to appreciate the brilliant valour of our grenadier, who killed two Cossacks, and took an officer prisoner, with his own hand.

After this skirmish, in which the detachment had maintained its position, the captain drew up his men to compliment them on their success, and ordered the clothes-mender to advance from the ranks, that he might thank him publicly for his gallant behaviour. Our hero could have dispensed with this ovation, but he was not the less obliged to obey. Judge of the surprise of both captain and troopers, when they saw this tall and stern-looking figure ride forward at a slow pace, with his naked feet in the stirrups, and naked legs pressing the sides of his charger.

The captain drew near in astonishment ; but recalling the occupation of the soldier at the moment when the alarm was given, he understood the whole mystery. 'Ha, my old comrade !' he exclaimed, 'thou art like King Dagobert —wearing thy breeches inside out.'

In spite of discipline, this joke of the captain's was received with peals of illrepressed laughter. But our friend, sitting upright in his saddle, with his left thumb pressing the well-adjusted reins, and his sword-hilt carried close to his right thigh, made a half-wheel, and returned to his place in the ranks without changing countenance, after he had duly received the congratulations of his captain. From that day, Francis Baudoin received and kept the nickname of Dagobert.

Now Dagobert was under the porch of the inn, occupied in washing, to the great amazement of sundry beer-drinkers, who observed him with curious eyes from the large common room in which they were assembled.

In truth, it was a curious spectacle. Dagobert had laid aside his grey topcoat, and rolled up the sleeves of his shirt ; with a vigorous hand, and good supply of soap, he was rubbing away at a wet handkerchief, spread out on the board, the end of which rested in a tub full of water. Upon his right arm, tattooed with warlike emblems in red and blue colours, two scars, deep enough to admit the finger, were distinctly visible. No wonder then, that, while smoking their pipes, and emptying their pots of beer, the Germans should display some surprise at the singular occupation of this tall, moustached, bald-headed old man, with the forbidding countenance—for the features of Dagobert assumed a harsh and grim expression, when he was no longer in presence of the two girls.

The sustained attention, of which he saw himself the object, began to put him out of patience, for his employment appeared to him quite natural. At this moment, the Prophet entered the porch, and, perceiving the soldier, eyed him attentively for several seconds ; then approaching, he said to him in French, in a rather sly tone : ' It would seem, comrade, that you have not much confidence in the washerwomen of Mockern ?'

Dagobert, without discontinuing his work, half turned his head with a frown, looked askant at the Prophet, and made him no answer.

Astonished at this silence, Morok resumed : ' If I do not deceive myself, you are French, my fine fellow. The words on your arm prove it, and your military air stamps you as an old soldier of the empire. Therefore I find, that, for a hero, you have taken rather late to wear petticoats.'

Dagobert remained mute, but he gnawed his moustache, and plied the soap, with which he was rubbing the linen, in a most hurried, not to say angry style ; for the face and words of the beast-tamer displeased him more than he cared to show. Far from being discouraged, the Prophet continued : ' I am sure, my fine fellow, that you are neither deaf nor dumb ; why, then, will you not answer me ?'

Losing all patience, Dagobert turned abruptly round, looked Morok full in the face, and said to him in a rough voice : ' I don't know you : I don't wish to know you ! Chain up your curb !' And he betook himself again to his washing.

' But we may make acquaintance. We can drink a glass of Rhine-wine together, and talk of our campaigns. I also have seen some service, I assure you ; and that, perhaps, will induce you to be more civil.'

The veins on the bald forehead of Dagobert swelled perceptibly ; he saw in the look and accent of the man, who thus obstinately addressed him, something designedly provoking ; still he contained himself.

' I ask you, why should you not drink a glass of wine with me—we could talk about France. I lived there a long time ; it is a fine country ; and when I meet Frenchmen abroad, I feel sociable—particularly when they know how to use the soap as well as you do. If I had a house-wife I'd send her to your school.'

The sarcastic meaning was no longer disguised ; impudence and bravado were legible in the Prophet's looks. Thinking that, with such an adversary, the dispute might become serious, Dagobert, who wished to avoid a quarrel at any price, carried off his tub to the other end of the porch, hoping thus to put an end to the scene which was a sore trial of his temper. A flash of joy lighted up the tawny eyes of the brute-tamer. The white circle which surrounded the pupil seemed to dilate. He ran his crooked fingers two or three times through his yellow beard, in token of satisfaction ; then he advanced slowly towards the soldier, accompanied by several idlers from the common-room.

Notwithstanding his coolness, Dagobert, amazed and incensed at the impudent pertinacity of the Prophet, was at first disposed to break the washing-board on his head ; but, remembering the orphans, he thought better of it.

Folding his arms upon his breast, Morok said to him, in a dry and insolent tone : ' It is very certain you are not civil, my man of suds !' Then, turning to the spectators, he continued in German : ' I tell this Frenchman, with his long moustache, that he is not civil. We shall see what answer he'll make. Perhaps it will be necessary to give him a lesson. Heaven preserve me from quarrels !'

he added, with mock compunction ; ' but the Lord has enlightened me—I am his creature, and I ought to make his work respected.'

The mystical effrontery of this peroration was quite to the taste of the idlers ; the fame of the Prophet had reached Mockern, and, as a performance was expected on the morrow, this prelude much amused the company. On hearing the insults of his adversary, Dagobert could not help saying in the German language : ' I know German. Speak in German—the rest will understand you.'

New spectators now arrived, and joined the first comers ; the adventure had become exciting, and a ring was formed around the two persons most concerned.

The Prophet resumed in German : ' I said that you were not civil, and I now say you are grossly rude. What do you answer to that ?"

' Nothing !' said Dagobert, coldly, as he proceeded to rinse out another piece of linen.

' Nothing !' returned Morok ; 'that is very little. I will be less brief, and tell you, that, when an honest man offers a glass of wine civilly to a stranger, that stranger has no right to answer with insolence, and deserves to be taught manners if he does so.'

Great drops of sweat ran down Dagobert's forehead and cheeks ; his large imperial was incessantly agitated by nervous trembling—but he restrained himself. Taking, by two of the corners, the handkerchief which he had just dipped in the water, he shook it, wrung it, and began to hum to himself the burden of the old camp ditty :

> ' Out of Tirlemont's flea-haunted den,
> We ride forth next day of the sen,
> With sabre in hand, ah !
> Good-bye to Amanda,' etc.

The silence to which Dagobert had condemned himself, almost choked him ; this song afforded him some relief.

Morok, turning towards the spectators, said to them, with an air of hypocritical restraint : ' We knew that the soldiers of Napoleon were pagans, who stabled their horses in churches, and offended the Lord a hundred times a day, and who, for their sins, were justly drowned in the Beresino, like so many Pharaohs ; but we did not know that the Lord, to punish these miscreants, had deprived them of courage—their single gift. Here is a man, who has insulted, in me, a creature favoured by divine grace, and who affects not to understand that I require an apology ; or else——"

' What ?' said Dagobert, without looking at the Prophet.

' Or you must give me satisfaction !— I have already told you that I have seen service. We shall easily find somewhere a couple of swords, and to-morrow morning, at peep of day, we can meet behind a wall, and show the colour of our blood—that is, if you have any in your veins !'

This challenge began to frighten the spectators, who were not prepared for so tragical a conclusion.

' What, fight ?—a very fine idea !' said one. 'To get yourselves both locked up in prison : the laws against duelling are strict.'

' Particularly with relation to strangers or nondescripts,' added another. ' If they were to find you with arms in your hands, the burgomaster would shut you up in gaol, and keep you there two or three months before trial.'

' Would you be so mean as to denounce us ?' asked Morok.

' No, certainly not,' cried several ; 'do as you like. We are only giving you a friendly piece of advice, by which you may profit, if you think fit.'

' What care I for prison ?' exclaimed the Prophet. 'Only give me a couple of swords, and you shall see to-morrow morning if I heed what the burgomaster can do or say.'

' What would you do with two swords ?' asked Dagobert. quietly.

'When you have one in your grasp, and I one in mine, you'd see. The Lord commands us to have a care of his honour!'

Dagobert shrugged his shoulders, made a bundle of his linen in his handkerchief, dried his soap, and put it carefully into a little oil-silk bag—then, whistling his favourite air of Tirlemont, moved to depart.

The Prophet frowned; he began to fear that his challenge would not be accepted. He advanced a step or so to encounter Dagobert, placed himself before him, as if to intercept his passage, and, folding his arms, and scanning him from head to foot with bitter insolence, said to him: 'So! an old soldier of that arch-robber, Napoleon, is only fit for a washerwoman, and refuses to fight!'

'Yes, he refuses to fight,' answered Dagobert, in a firm voice, but becoming fearfully pale. Never, perhaps, had the soldier given to his orphan charge such a proof of tenderness and devotion. For a man of his character to let himself be insulted with impunity, and refuse to fight—the sacrifice was immense!

'So you are a coward—you are afraid of me—and you confess it?'

At these words Dagobert made, as it were, a pull upon himself—as if a sudden thought had restrained him the moment he was about to rush on the Prophet. Indeed, he had remembered the two maidens, and the fatal hindrance which a duel, whatever might be the result, would occasion to their journey. But the impulse of anger, though rapid, had been so significant—the expression of the stern, pale face, bathed in sweat, was so daunting, that the Prophet and the spectators drew back a step.

Profound silence reigned for some seconds, and then, by a sudden reaction, Dagobert seemed to have gained the general interest. One of the company said to those near him: 'This man is clearly not a coward.'

'Oh, no! certainly not.'

'It sometimes requires more courage to refuse a challenge than to accept one.'

'After all, the Prophet was wrong to pick a quarrel about nothing—and with a stranger, too.'

'Yes, for a stranger, if he fought and was taken up, would have a good long imprisonment.'

'And then, you see,' added another, 'he travels with two young girls. In such a position, ought a man to fight about trifles? If he should be killed or put in prison, what would become of them, poor children?'

Dagobert turned towards the person who had pronounced these last words. He saw a stout fellow, with a frank and simple countenance; the soldier offered him his hand, and said with emotion:

'Thank you, sir.'

The German shook cordially the hand which Dagobert had proffered, and, holding it still in his own, he added: 'Do one thing, sir—share a bowl of punch with us. We will make that mischief-making Prophet acknowledge that he has been too touchy, and he shall drink to your health.'

Up to this moment the brute-tamer, enraged at the issue of this scene, for he had hoped that the soldier would accept his challenge, looked on with savage contempt at those who had thus sided against him. But now his features gradually relaxed; and, believing it useful to his projects to hide his disappointment, he walked up to the soldier, and said to him, with a tolerably good grace: 'Well, I give way to these gentlemen. I own I was wrong. Your frigid air had wounded me, and I was not master of myself. I repeat, that I was wrong,' he added, with suppressed vexation; 'the Lord commands humility—and—I beg your pardon.'

This proof of moderation and regret was highly appreciated and loudly applauded by the spectators. 'He asks your pardon; you cannot expect more, my brave fellow!' said one of them, addressing Dagobert. 'Come, let us all drink together; we make you this offer frankly—accept it in the same spirit.'

'Yes, yes; accept it, we beg you, in the name of your pretty little girls,' said the stout man, hoping to decide Dagobert by this argument.

'Many thanks, gentlemen,' replied he, touched by the hearty advances of the Germans; 'you are very worthy people. But, when one is treated, he must offer drink in return.'

'Well, we will accept it—that's understood. Each his turn, and all fair. We will pay for the first bowl, you for the second.'

'Poverty is no crime,' answered Dagobert; 'and I must tell you honestly that I cannot afford to pay for drink. We have still a long journey to go, and I must not incur any useless expenses.'

The soldier spoke these words with such firm, but simple dignity, that the Germans did not venture to renew their offer, feeling that a man of Dagobert's character could not accept it without humiliation.

'Well, so much the worse,' said the stout man. 'I should have liked to clink glasses with you. Good night, my brave trooper!—good night—for it grows late, and mine host of the Falcon will soon turn us out of doors.'

'Good night, gentlemen,' replied Dagobert, as he directed his steps towards the stable, to give his horse a second allowance of provender.

Morok approached him, and said in a voice even more humble than before: 'I have acknowledged my error, and asked your pardon. You have not answered me; do you still bear malice?'

'If ever I meet you,' said the veteran, in a suppressed and hollow tone, 'when my children have no longer need of me, I will just say two words to you, and they will not be long ones.'

Then he turned his back abruptly on the Prophet, who walked slowly out of the yard.

The inn of the White Falcon formed a parallelogram. At one end rose the principal dwelling; at the other was a range of buildings which contained sundry chambers, let at a low price to the poorer sort of travellers; a vaulted passage opened a way through this latter into the country; finally, on either side of the court-yard were sheds and stables, with lofts and garrets erected over them.

Dagobert, entering one of these stables, took from off a chest the portion of oats destined for his horse, and, pouring it into a winnowing-basket, shook it as he approached Jovial.

To his great astonishment, his old travelling companion did not respond with a joyous neigh to the rustle of the oats rattling on the wicker-work. Alarmed, he called Jovial with a friendly voice; but the animal, instead of turning towards his master a look of intelligence, and impatiently striking the ground with his fore-feet, remained perfectly motionless.

More and more surprised, the soldier went up to him. By the dubious light of a stable-lantern, he saw the poor animal in an attitude which implied terror —his legs half bent, his head stretched forward, his ears down, his nostrils quivering; he had drawn tight his halter, as if he wished to break it, in order to get away from the partition that supported his rack and manger; abundant cold-sweat had speckled his hide with bluish stains, and his coat altogether looked dull and bristling, instead of standing out sleek and glossy from the dark background of the stable; lastly, from time to time, his body shook with convulsive starts.

'Why, old Jovial!' said the soldier, as he put down the basket, in order to soothe his horse with more freedom, 'you are like thy master—afraid!—Yes,' he added with bitterness, as he thought of the offence he had himself endured, 'you are afraid—though no coward in general.'

Notwithstanding the caresses and the voice of his master, the horse continued to give signs of terror; he pulled somewhat less violently at his halter, and approaching his nostrils to the hand of Dagobert, sniffed audibly, as if he doubted it were he.

'You don't know me!' cried Dagobert. 'Something extraordinary must be passing here.'

The soldier looked around him with uneasiness. It was a large stable, faintly lighted by the lantern suspended from the roof, which was covered with innumerable cobwebs; at the further end, separated from Jovial by some stalls with bars between, were the three strong, black horses of the brute-tamer—as tranquil as Jovial was frightened.

Dagobert, struck with this singular contrast, of which he was soon to have the explanation, again caressed his horse; and the animal, gradually reassured by his master's presence, licked his hands, rubbed his head against him, uttered a low neigh, and gave him his usual tokens of affection.

'Come, come, this is how I like to see my old Jovial!' said Dagobert, as he took up the winnowing-basket, and poured its contents into the manger. 'Now eat with a good appetite, for we have a long day's march to-morrow; and, above all, no more of these foolish fears about nothing! If thy comrade, Spoil-sport, was here, he would keep you in heart; but he is along with the children, and takes care of them in my absence. Come, eat! instead of staring at me in that way.'

But the horse, having just touched the oats with his mouth, as if in obedience to his master, returned to them no more, and began to nibble at the sleeve of Dagobert's coat.

'Come, come, my poor Jovial! there is something the matter with you. You have generally such a good appetite, and now you leave your corn. 'Tis the first time this has happened since our departure,' said the soldier, who was now growing seriously uneasy, for the issue of his journey greatly depended on the health and vigour of his horse.

Just then a frightful roaring, so near that it seemed to come from the stable in which they were, gave so violent a shock to Jovial, that with one effort he broke his halter, leaped over the bar that marked his place, and, rushing at the open door, escaped into the court-yard.

Dagobert had himself started at the suddenness of this wild and fearful sound, which at once explained to him the cause of his horse's terror. The adjoining stable was occupied by the itinerant menagerie of the brute-tamer, and was only separated by the partition which supported the mangers. The three horses of the Prophet, accustomed to these howlings, had remained perfectly quiet.

'Good!' said the soldier, recovering himself; 'I understand it now. Jovial has heard another such roar before, and he can scent the animals of that insolent scoundrel. It is enough to frighten him,' added he, as he carefully collected the oats from the manger; 'once in another stable, and there must be others in this place, he will no longer leave his peck, and we shall be able to start early to-morrow morning.'

The terrified horse, after running and galloping about the yard, returned at the voice of the soldier, who easily caught him by the broken halter; and a hostler, whom Dagobert asked if there was another vacant stable, having pointed out one that was only intended for a single animal, Jovial was comfortably installed there.

When delivered from his ferocious neighbours, the horse became tranquil as before, and even amused himself much at the expense of Dagobert's top-coat, which, thanks to his tricks, might have afforded immediate occupation for his master's needle, if the latter had not been fully engaged in admiring the eagerness with which Jovial despatched his provender. Completely reassured on his account, the soldier shut the door of the stable, and proceeded to get his supper as quickly as possible, in order to rejoin the orphans, whom he reproached himself with having left so long.

CHAPTER V.

ROSE AND BLANCHE.

THE orphans occupied a dilapidated chamber in one of the most remote wings of the inn, with a single window opening upon the country. A bed without curtains, a table, and two chairs, composed the more than modest furniture of this retreat, which was now lighted by a lamp. On the table, which stood near the window, was deposited the knapsack of the soldier.

The great Siberian dog, who was lying close to the door, had already twice uttered a deep growl, and turned his head towards the window—but without giving any further effect to this hostile manifestation.

The two sisters, half recumbent in their bed, were clad in long white wrappers, buttoned at the neck and wrists. They wore no caps, but their beautiful chestnut hair was confined at the temples by a broad piece of tape, so that it might not get tangled during the night. These white garments, and the white fillet that like a halo encircled their brows, gave to their fresh and blooming faces a still more candid expression.

The orphans laughed and chatted, for, in spite of some early sorrows, they still retained the ingenuous gaiety of their age. The remembrance of their mother would sometimes make them sad, but this sorrow had in it nothing bitter ; it was rather a sweet melancholy, to be sought instead of shunned. For them, this adored mother was not dead—she was only absent.

Almost as ignorant as Dagobert, with regard to devotional exercises, for in the desert where they had lived there was neither church nor priest, their faith, as was already said, consisted in this—that God, just and good, had so much pity for the poor mothers whose children were left on earth, that he allowed them to look down upon them from highest heaven—to see them always, to hear them always, and sometimes to send fair guardian angels to protect them. Thanks to this guileless illusion, the orphans, persuaded that their mother incessantly watched over them, felt, that to do wrong would be to afflict her, and to forfeit the protection of the good angels.——This was the entire theology of Rose and Blanche—a creed sufficient for such pure and loving souls.

Now, on the evening in question, the two sisters chatted together whilst waiting for Dagobert. Their theme interested them much, for, since some days, they had a secret, a great secret, which often quickened the beatings of their innocent hearts, often agitated their budding bosoms, changed to bright scarlet the roses on their cheeks, and infused a restless and dreamy languor into the soft blue of their large eyes.

Rose, this evening, occupied the edge of the couch, with her rounded arms crossed behind her head, which was half turned towards her sister ; Blanche, with her elbow resting on the bolster, looked at her smilingly, and said : ' Do you think he will come again to-night ?'

' Oh, yes ! certainly. He promised us yesterday.'

' He is so good, he would not break his promise.'

' And so handsome, with his long fair curls.'

' And his name—what a charming name !—how well it suits his face.'

' And what a sweet smile and soft voice, when he says to us, taking us by the hand : " My children, bless God that He has given you one soul. What others seek elsewhere, you will find in yourselves." '

' " Since your two hearts," he added, " only make one." '

' What pleasure to remember his words, sister !'

' We are so attentive ! When I see you listening to him, it is as if I saw myself, my dear little mirror !' said Rose, laughing, and kissing her sister's forehead. ' Well—when he speaks, your—or rather *our* eyes—are wide, wide open, our lips moving as if we repeated every word after him. It is no wonder we forget nothing that he says.'

' And what he says is so grand, so noble, and generous.'

' Then, my sister, as he goes on talking, what good thoughts rise within us ! If we could but always keep them in mind.'

' Do not be afraid ! they will remain in our heart, like little birds in their mother's nests.'

' And how lucky it is, Rose, that he loves us both at the same time !'

' He could not do otherwise, since we have but one heart between us.'

' How could he love Rose, without loving Blanche ?'

' What would have become of the poor neglected one ?'

' And then again he would have found it so difficult to choose.'

' We are so much like one another.'

' So, to save himself that trouble,' said Rose, laughing, ' he has chosen us both.'

' And is it not the best way ? He is alone to love us ; we are two together to think of him.'——' Only he must not leave us till we reach Paris.'

' And in Paris, too—we must see him there also.'

' Oh, above all at Paris ; it will be good to have him with us—and Dagobert, too—in that great city. Only think, Blanche, how beautiful it must be.'

' Paris !—it must be like a city all of gold.'

' A city, where every one must be happy, since it is so beautiful.'

' But ought we, poor orphans, dare so much as to enter it ? How people will look at us !'

' Yes—but every one there is happy, every one must be good also.'

' They will love us.'

' And, besides, we shall be with our friend with the fair hair and blue eyes.'

' He has yet told us nothing of Paris.'

' He has not thought of it ; we must speak to him about it this very night.'

' If he is in the mood for talking. Often, you know, he likes best to gaze on us in silence—his eyes on our eyes.'

' Yes. In those moments, his look recalls to me the gaze of our dear mother.'

' And, as she sees it all, how pleased she must be at what has happened to us !'

' Because, when we are so much beloved, we must, I hope, deserve it.'

' See what a vain thing it is !' said Blanche, smoothing with her slender fingers the parting of the hair on her sister's forehead.

After a moment's reflection, Rose said to her : ' Don't you think we should relate all this to Dagobert ?'

' If you think so, let us do it.'

' We tell him everything, as we told everything to mother. Why should we conceal this from him ?'

' Especially as it is something which gives us so much pleasure.'

' Do you not find that, since we have known our friend, our hearts beat quicker and stronger ?'

' Yes, they seem to be more full.'

' The reason why is plain enough ; our friend fills up a good space in them.'

' Well, we will do best to tell Dagobert what a lucky star ours is.'

' You are right——' At this moment the dog gave another deep growl.

' Sister,' said Rose, as she pressed closer to Blanche, ' there is the dog growling again. What can be the matter with him ?'

' Spoilsport, do not growl ! Come hither,' said Blanche, striking with her little hand on the side of the bed.

The dog rose, again growled deeply, and came to lay his great, intelligent-looking head on the counterpane, still obstinately casting a side-long glance at the window ; the sisters bent over him to pat his broad forehead, in the centre of which was a remarkable bump, the certain sign of extreme purity of race.

' What makes you growl so, Spoilsport ?' said Blanche, pulling him gently by the ears—' eh, my good dog ?'

' Poor beast ! he is always so uneasy when Dagobert is away.'

' It is true ; one would think he knows that he then has a double charge over us.'

' Sister, it seems to me, Dagobert is late in coming to say good-night.'

' No doubt he is attending to Jovial.'

' That makes me think that we did not bid good-night to dear old Jovial.'

' I am sorry for it.'

' Poor beast ! he seems so glad when he licks our hands. One would think that he thanked us for our visit.'

' Luckily, Dagobert will have wished him good-night for us.'

' Good Dagobert ! he is always thinking of us. How he spoils us ! We remain idle, and he has all the trouble.'

' How can we prevent it ?'

' What a pity that we are not rich, to give him a little rest.'

' We rich ! Alas, my sister ! we shall never be anything but poor orphans.'

' Oh, there's the medal !'

' Doubtless, there is some hope attached to it, else we should not have made this long journey.'

' Dagobert has promised to tell us all, this evening.'

She was prevented from continuing, for two of the window-panes flew to pieces with a loud crash.

The orphans, with a cry of terror, threw themselves into each other's arms, whilst the dog rushed towards the window, barking furiously.

Pale, trembling, motionless with affright, clasping each other in a close embrace, the two sisters held their breath ; in their extreme fear, they durst not even cast their eyes in the direction of the window. The dog, with his fore-paws resting on the sill, continued to bark with violence.

' Alas ! what can it be ?' murmured the orphans. ' And Dagobert not here !'

' Hark !' cried Rose, suddenly seizing Blanche by the arm ; ' hark !—some one coming up the stairs !'

' Good heaven ! it does not sound like the tread of Dagobert. Do you not hear what heavy footsteps ?'

' Quick ! come, Spoilsport, and defend us !' cried the two sisters at once, in an agony of alarm.

The boards of the wooden staircase really creaked beneath the weight of unusually heavy footsteps, and a singular kind of rustling was heard along the thin partition that divided the chamber from the landing-place. Then a ponderous mass, falling against the door of the room, shook it violently ; and the girls, at the very height of terror, looked at each other without the power to speak.

The door opened. It was Dagobert.

At the sight of him Rose and Blanche joyfully exchanged a kiss, as if they had just escaped from a great danger.

' What is the matter ? why are you afraid ?' asked the soldier in surprise.

' Oh, if you only knew !' said Rose, panting as she spoke, for both her own heart and her sister's beat with violence.

' If you knew what has just happened ! We did not recognise your footsteps —they seemed so heavy—and then that noise behind the partition !'

'Little frightened doves that you are ! I could not run up the stairs like a boy of fifteen, seeing that I carried my bed upon my back—a straw mattress that I have just flung down before your door, to sleep there as usual.'

'Bless me ! how foolish we must be, sister, not to have thought of that !' said Rose, looking at Blanche. And their pretty faces, which had together grown pale, together resumed their natural colour.

During this scene the dog, still resting against the window, did not cease barking a moment.

'What makes Spoilsport bark in that direction, my children ?' said the soldier

'We do not know. Two of our window-panes have just been broken. That is what first frightened us so much.'

Without answering a word Dagobert flew to the window, opened it quickly pushed back the shutter, and leaned out.

He saw nothing ; it was dark night. He listened ; but heard only the moaning of the wind.

'Spoilsport,' said he to his dog, pointing to the open window, 'leap out, old fellow, and search !' The faithful animal took one mighty spring and disappeared by the window, raised only about eight feet above the ground.

Dagobert, still leaning over, encouraged his dog with voice and gesture 'Search, old fellow, search ! If there is any one there, pin him—your fangs are strong—and hold him fast till I come.'

But Spoilsport found no one. They heard him go backwards and forwards snuffing on every side, and now and then uttering a low cry like a hound at fault

'There is no one, my good dog, that's clear, or you would have had him by the throat ere this.' Then, turning to the maidens, who listened to his words and watched his movements with uneasiness : 'My girls,' said he, 'how were these panes broken ? Did you not remark ?'

'No, Dagobert ; we were talking together when we heard a great crash, and then the glass fell into the room.'

'It seemed to me,' added Rose, 'as if a shutter had struck suddenly against the window.'

Dagobert examined the shutter, and observed a long movable hook, designed to fasten it on the inside.

'It blows hard,' said he ; 'the wind must have swung round the shutter, and this hook broke the window. Yes, yes ; that is it. What interest could anybody have to play such a sorry trick ?' Then, speaking to Spoilsport, he asked 'Well, my good fellow, is there no one ?'

The dog answered by a bark, which the soldier no doubt understood as a negative, for he continued : 'Well, then, come back !—Make the round—you will find some door open—you are never at a loss.'

The animal followed this advice. After growling for a few seconds beneath the window, he set off at a gallop to make the circuit of the buildings, and come back by the court-yard.

'Be quite easy, my children !' said the soldier, as he again drew near the orphans ; 'it was only the wind.'

'We were a good deal frightened,' said Rose.

'I believe you. But now I think of it, this draught is likely to give you cold. And seeking to remedy this inconvenience, he took from a chair the reindeer pelisse, and suspended it from the spring-catch of the curtainless window, using the skirts to stop up as closely as possible the two openings made by the breaking of the panes.

'Thanks, Dagobert, how good you are ! We were very uneasy at not seeing you.'

'Yes, you were absent longer than usual. But what is the matter with you ?' added Rose, only just then perceiving that his countenance was disturbed and pallid, for he was still under the painful influence of the brawl with Morok ; 'how pale you are !'

'Me, my pets ?—Oh, nothing.'

'Yes, I assure you, your countenance is quite changed. Rose is right.'

'I tell you there is nothing the matter,' answered the soldier, not without some embarrassment, for he was little used to deceive ; till, finding an excellent excuse for his emotion, he added : 'If I do look at all uncomfortable, it is your fright that has made me so, for indeed it was my fault.'

'Your fault !'

'Yes ; for if I had not lost so much time at supper, I should have been here when the window was broken, and have spared you the fright.'

'Anyhow, you are here now, and we think no more of it.'

'Why don't you sit down ?'

'I will, my children, for we have to talk together,' said Dagobert, as he drew a chair close to the head of the bed. 'Now tell me, are you quite awake ?' he added, trying to smile in order to re-assure them. 'Are those large eyes properly open ?'

'Look, Dagobert !' cried the two girls, smiling in their turn, and opening their blue eyes to the utmost extent.

'Well, well,' said the soldier ; 'they are yet far enough from shutting; besides, it is only nine o'clock.'

'We also have something to tell, Dagobert,' resumed Rose, after exchanging glances with her sister.

'Indeed !'

'A secret to tell you.'

'A secret ?'

'Yes, to be sure.'——'Ah, and a very great secret !' added Rose, quite seriously.

'A secret which concerns us both,' resumed Blanche.

'Faith ! I should think so. What concerns the one always concerns the other. Are you not always, as the saying goes, " two faces under one hood ?" '

'Truly, how can it be otherwise, when you put our heads under the great hood of your pelisse ?' said Rose, laughing.

'There they are again, mocking-birds ! One never has the last word with them. Come, ladies, your secret, since a secret there is.'

'Speak, sister,' said Rose.

'No, miss, it is for you to speak. You are to-day on duty, as eldest, and such an important thing as telling a secret like that you talk of belongs of right to the elder sister. Come, I am listening to you,' added the soldier, as he forced a smile, the better to conceal from the maidens how much he still felt the unpunished affronts of the brute-tamer.

It was Rose (who, as Dagobert said, was doing duty as eldest) that spoke for herself and for her sister.

CHAPTER VI.

THE SECRET.

'FIRST of all, good Dagobert,' said Rose, in a gracefully caressing manner, 'as we are going to tell our secret—you must promise not to scold us.'

'You will not scold your darlings, will you ?' added Blanche, in a no less coaxing voice.

'Granted !' replied Dagobert gravely; 'particularly as I should not well know how to set about it—but why should I scold you ?'

'Because we ought perhaps to have told you sooner what we are going to tell you.'

'Listen, my children,' said Dagobert sententiously, after reflecting a moment on this case of conscience; 'one of two things must be. Either you were right, or else you were wrong, to hide this from me. If you were right, very well; if you were wrong, it is done: so let's say no more about it. Go on—I am all attention.'

Completely reassured by this luminous decision, Rose resumed, while she exchanged a smile with her sister: 'Only think, Dagobert; for two successive nights we have had a visitor.'

'A visitor!' cried the soldier, drawing himself up suddenly in his chair.

'Yes, a charming visitor—he is so very fair.'

'Fair!—the devil!' cried Dagobert, with a start.

'Yes, fair—and with blue eyes,' added Blanche.

'Blue eyes—blue devils!' and Dagobert again bounded on his seat.

'Yes, blue eyes—as long as that,' resumed Rose, placing the tip of one forefinger about the middle of the other.

'Zounds! they might be as long as that,' said the veteran, indicating the whole length of his arm from the elbow—'they might be as long as that, and it would have nothing to do with it. Fair, and with blue eyes   Pray what may this mean, young ladies?' and Dagobert rose from his seat with a severe and painfully unquiet look.

'There now, Dagobert, you have begun to scold us already!'

'Just at the very commencement,' added Blanche.

'Commencement !——what, is there to be a sequel? a finish?'

'A finish? we hope not,' said Rose, laughing like mad.

'All we ask is, that it should last for ever,' added Blanche, sharing in the hilarity of her sister.

Dagobert looked gravely from one to the other of the two maidens, as if trying to guess this enigma; but when he saw their sweet, innocent faces gracefully animated by a frank, ingenuous laugh, he reflected that they would not be so gay if they had any serious matter for self-reproach, and he felt pleased at seeing them so merry in the midst of their precarious position.

'Laugh on, my children!' he said.   'I like so much to see you laugh.'

Then, thinking that was not precisely the way in which he ought to treat the singular confession of the young girls, he added in a gruff voice: 'Yes, I like to see you laugh—but not when you receive fair visitors with blue eyes, young ladies!—Come, acknowledge that I'm an old fool to listen to such nonsense— you are only making game of me.'

'Nay, what we tell you is quite true.'

'You know we never tell stories,' added Rose.

'They are right—they never fib,' said the soldier, in renewed perplexity. 'But how the devil is such a visit possible? I sleep before your door—Spoilsport sleeps under your window—and all the blue eyes and fair locks in the world must come in by one of those two ways—and, if they had tried it, the dog and I, who have both of us quick ears, would have received their visits after our fashion. But come, children! pray, speak to the purpose. Explain yourselves!'

The two sisters, who saw, by the expression of Dagobert's countenance, that he felt really uneasy, determined no longer to trifle with his kindness.   They exchanged a glance, and Rose, taking in her little hand the coarse, broad palm of the veteran, said to him: 'Come, do not plague yourself!   We will tell you all about the visits of our friend, Gabriel.'

'There you are again!—He has a name, then?'

'Certainly, he has a name.   It is Gabriel.'

'Is it not a pretty name, Dagobert?   Oh, you will see and love, as we do, our beautiful Gabriel!'

'I'll love your beautiful Gabriel, will I?' said the veteran, shaking his head—

Love your beautiful Gabriel?—that's as it may be. I must first know——'
Then, interrupting himself, he added : ' It is queer. That reminds me of something.'

' Of what, Dagobert ?'

' Fifteen years ago, in the last letter that your father, on his return from
France, brought me from my wife. she told me that, poor as she was, and with
our little growing Agricola on her hands, she had taken in a poor deserted child,
with the face of a cherub, and the name of Gabriel—and only a short time since
I heard of him again.'

' And from whom, then ?'

' You shall know that by-and-by.'

' Well, then—since you have a Gabriel of your own—there is the more reason
that you should love ours.'

' Yours ! but who is yours ? I am on thorns till you tell me.'

' You know, Dagobert,' resumed Rose, ' that Blanche and I are accustomed
to fall asleep, holding each other by the hand.'

' Yes, yes, I have often seen you in your cradle. I was never tired of looking
at you : it was so pretty.'

' Well, then—two nights ago, we had just fallen asleep, when we beheld——'

' Oh, it was in a dream !' cried Dagobert. ' Since you were asleep, it was in
a dream !'

' Certainly, in a dream—how else would you have it ?'

' Pray let my sister go on with her tale !'

' Ah, well and good !' said the soldier with a sigh of satisfaction ; ' well and
good ! To be sure, I was tranquil enough in any case—because—but still—I
like it better to be a dream. Continue, my little Rose.'

' Once asleep, we both dreamt the same thing.'

' What ! both the same ?'

' Yes, Dagobert ; for the next morning when we awoke we related our two
dreams to each other.'

' And they were exactly alike.'

' That's odd enough, my children ; and what was this dream all about ?'

' In our dream, Blanche and I were seated together, when we saw enter a
beautiful angel, with a long white robe, fair locks, blue eyes, and so handsome
and benign a countenance, that we clasped our hands as if to pray to him.
Then he told us, in a soft voice, that he was called Gabriel ; that our mother
had sent him to be our guardian angel, and that he would never abandon us.'

' And, then,' added Blanche, ' he took us each by the hand, and, bending his
fair face over us, looked at us for a long time in silence, with so much goodness
—with so much goodness, that we could not withdraw our eyes from his.'

' Yes,' resumed Rose, ' and his look seemed, by turns, to attract us, or to go
to our hearts. At length, to our great sorrow, Gabriel quitted us, having told
us that we should see him again the following night.'

' And did he make his appearance ?'

' Certainly. Judge with what impatience we waited the moment of sleep, to
see if our friend would return, and visit us in our slumbers.'

' Humph !' said Dagobert, scratching his forehead ; ' this reminds me, young
ladies, that you kept on rubbing your eyes last evening, and pretending to be
half asleep. I wager, it was all to send me away the sooner, and to get to your
dream as fast as possible.'

' Yes, Dagobert.'

' The reason being, you could not say to me, as you would to Spoilsport : " Lie
down, Dagobert !" Well—so your friend Gabriel came back ?'

' Yes, and this time he talked to us a great deal, and gave us, in the name of
our mother, such touching, such noble counsels, that the next day, Rose and

I spent our whole time in recalling every word of our guardian angel—and h
face, and his look——'

'This reminds me again, young ladies, that you were whispering all alo
the road this morning ; and that when I spoke of white, you answered black.

'Yes, Dagobert, we were thinking of Gabriel.'

'And, ever since, we love him as well as he loves us.'

'But he is only one between both of you !'

'Was not our mother one between us ?'

'And you, Dagobert—are you not also one for us both ?'

'True, true ! And yet, do you know, I shall finish by being jealous of th
Gabriel ?'

'You are our friend by day—he is our friend by night.'

'Let's understand it clearly. If you talk of him all day, and dream of hi
all night, what will there remain for me ?'

'There will remain for you your two orphans, whom you love so much,' sa
Rose.

'A nd who have only you left upon earth,' added Blanche, in a caressing ton

'H umph ! humph ! that's right, coax the old man over ! Nay, believe m
my children,' added the soldier, tenderly, 'I am quite satisfied with my lot.
can afford to let you have your Gabriel. I felt sure that Spoilsport and myse
could take our rest in quiet. After all, there is nothing so astonishing in wh
you tell me ; your first dream struck your fancy, and you talked so much abo
it that you had a second ; nor should I be surprised if you were to see this fi
fellow a third time.'

'Oh, Dagobert ! do not make a jest of it ! They are only dreams, but w
think our mother sends them to us. Did she not tell us that orphan childre
were watched over by guardian angels ? Well, Gabriel is our guardian angel
he will protect us, and he will protect you also.'

'Very kind of him to think of me ; but you see, my dear children, for th
matter of defence, I prefer the dog ; he is less fair than your angel, but he ha
better teeth, and that is more to be depended on.'

'How provoking you are, Dagobert—always jesting !'

'It is true ; you can laugh at everything.'

'Yes, I am astonishingly gay ; I laugh with my teeth shut, in the style of o
Jovial. Come, children, don't scold me : I know I am wrong. The remem
brance of your dear mother is mixed with this dream, and you do well to spea
of it seriously. Besides,' added he, with a grave air, 'dreams will sometime
come true. In Spain, two of the Empress's dragoons, comrades of min
dreamt, the night before their death, that they would be poisoned by the monk
—and so it happened. If you continue to dream of this fair angel Gabriel,
is—it is—why, it is, because you are amused by it ; and, as you have none to
many pleasures in the daytime, you may as well get an agreeable sleep at nigh
But, now, my children, I have also much to tell you ; it will concern you
mother ; promise me not to be sad.'

'Be satisfied ! when we think of her we are not sad, though serious.'

'That is well. For fear of grieving you, I have always delayed the moment c
telling what your poor mother would have confided to you as soon as you wer
no longer children. But she died before she had time to do so, and that whic
I have to tell broke her heart—as it nearly did mine. I put off this communi
cation as long as I could, taking for pretext that I would say nothing till w
came to the field of battle where your father was made prisoner. That gav
me time ; but the moment is now come ; I can shuffle it off no longer.'

'We listen, Dagobert,' responded the two maidens, with an attentive an
melancholy air.

After a moment's silence, during which he appeared to reflect, the vetera
thus addressed the young girls :

'Your father, General Simon, was the son of a workman, who remained a workman; for, notwithstanding all that the general could say or do, the old man was obstinate in not quitting his trade. He had a heart of gold and a head of iron, just like his son. You may suppose, my children, that when your father, who had enlisted as a private soldier, became a general and a count of the empire, it was not without toil or without glory.'

'A count of the empire? what is that, Dagobert?'

'Flummery—a title, which the emperor gave over and above the promotion, just for the sake of saying to the people, whom he loved because he was one of them: "Here, children! you wish to play at nobility! you shall be nobles. You wish to play at royalty! you shall be kings. Take what you like—nothing is too good for you—enjoy yourselves!"'

'Kings!' said the two girls, joining their hands in admiration.

'Kings of the first water. Oh, he was no niggard of his crowns, our Emperor! I had a bed-fellow of mine, a brave soldier, who was afterwards promoted to be king. This flattered us; for, if it was not one, it was the other. And so, at this game, your father became count; but, count or not, he was one of the best and bravest generals of the army.'

'He was handsome, was he not, Dagobert!—mother always said so.'

'Oh, yes! indeed he was—but quite another thing from your fair guardian angel. Picture to yourself a fine, dark man, who looked splendid in his full uniform, and could put fire into the soldiers' hearts. With him to lead, we would have charged up into Heaven itself—that is, if Heaven had permitted it,' added Dagobert, not wishing to wound in any way the religious beliefs of the orphans.

'And father was as good as he was brave, Dagobert.'

'Good, my children? Yes, I should say so!—He could bend a horse-shoe in his hand as you would bend a card, and the day he was taken prisoner he had cut down the Prussian artillerymen on their very cannon. With strength and courage like that, how could he be otherwise than good? It is then about nineteen years ago, not far from this place—on the spot I showed you before we arrived at the village—that the general, dangerously wounded, fell from his horse. I was following him at the time, and ran to his assistance. Five minutes after, we were made prisoners—and by whom, think you?—by a Frenchman.'

'A Frenchman?'

'Yes, an emigrant marquis, a colonel in the service of Russia,' answered Dagobert, with bitterness. 'And so, when this marquis advanced towards us, and said to the general: "Surrender, sir, to a countryman!"—"A Frenchman, who fights against France," replied the general, "is no longer my countryman; he is a traitor, and I'd never surrender to a traitor!" And, wounded though he was, he dragged himself up to a Russian grenadier, and delivered him his sabre, saying: "I surrender to you, my brave fellow!" The marquis became pale with rage at it.'

The orphans looked at each other with pride, and a rich crimson mantled their cheeks, as they exclaimed: 'Oh, our brave father!'

'Ah, those children,' said Dagobert, as he proudly twirled his moustache. 'One sees they have soldier's blood in their veins! Well,' he continued, 'we were now prisoners. The general's last horse had been killed under him; and, to perform the journey, he mounted Jovial, who had not been wounded that day. We arrived at Warsaw, and there it was that the general first saw your mother. She was called the *Pearl of Warsaw;* that is saying everything. Now he, who admired all that is good and beautiful, fell in love with her almost immediately; and she loved him in return; but her parents had promised her to another—and that other was the same——'

Dagobert was unable to proceed. Rose uttered a piercing cry, and pointed in terror to the window.

CHAPTER VII.

THE TRAVELLER.

Upon the cry of the young girl, Dagobert rose abruptly.

' What is the matter, Rose ?'

' There—there !' she said, pointing to the window. ' I thought I saw a hand move the pelisse.'

She had not concluded these words before Dagobert rushed to the window and opened it, tearing down the mantle which had been suspended from the fastening.

It was still dark night, and the wind was blowing hard. The soldier listened but could hear nothing.

Returning to fetch the lamp from the table, he shaded the flame with his hand, and strove to throw the light outside. Still he saw nothing. Persuaded that a gust of wind had disturbed and shaken the pelisse, and that Rose had been deceived by her own fears, he again shut the window.

' Be satisfied, children ! The wind is very high ; it is that which lifted the corner of the pelisse.'

' Yet methought I saw plainly the fingers which had hold of it,' said Rose still trembling.

' I was looking at Dagobert,' said Blanche, ' and I saw nothing.'

' There was nothing to see, my children ; the thing is clear enough. The window is at least eight feet above the ground ; none but a giant could reach it without a ladder. Now, had any one used a ladder, there would not have been time to remove it ; for, as soon as Rose cried out, I ran to the window, and when I held out the light, I could see nothing.'

' I must have been deceived,' said Rose.

' You may be sure, sister, it was only the wind,' added Blanche.

' Then I beg pardon for having disturbed you, my good Dagobert.'

' Never mind !' replied the soldier musingly ; ' I am only sorry that Spoilsport is not come back. He would have watched the window, and that would have quite tranquillised you. But he no doubt scented the stable of his comrade, Jovial, and will have called in to bid him good night on the road. I have half a mind to go and fetch him.'

' Oh, no, Dagobert ! do not leave us alone,' cried the maidens ; ' we are too much afraid.'

' Well, the dog is not likely to remain away much longer, and I am sure we shall soon hear him scratching at the door, so we will continue our story,' said Dagobert, as he again seated himself near the head of the bed, but this time with his face towards the window.

' Now the general was prisoner at Warsaw,' continued he, ' and in love with your mother, whom they wished to marry to another. In 1814, we learned the finish of the war, the banishment of the Emperor to the Isle of Elba, and the return of the Bourbons. In concert with the Prussians and Russians, who had brought them back, they had exiled the Emperor. Learning all this, your mother said to the general : "The war is finished ; you are free, but your Emperor is in trouble. You owe everything to him ; go and join him in his misfortunes. I know not when we shall meet again, but I will never marry any one but you, I am yours till death !"—Before he set out the general called me to him, and said : ' Dagobert, remain here ; Mademoiselle Eva may have need of you to fly from her family, if they should press too hard upon her ; our correspondence will have to pass through your hands ; at Paris, I shall see your wife and son ; I will comfort them, and tell them you are my friend."'

' Always the same,' said Rose, with emotion, as she looked affectionately at Dagobert.

'As faithful to the father and mother as to their children,' added Blanche.

'To love one was to love them all,' replied the soldier. 'Well, the general joined the Emperor at Elba; I remained at Warsaw, concealed in the neighbourhood of your mother's house; I received the letters, and conveyed them to her clandestinely. In one of those letters—I feel proud to tell you of it, my children—the general informed me that the Emperor himself had remembered me.'

'What, did he know you?'

'A little, I flatter myself—" Oh! Dagobert!" said he to your father, who was talking to him about me; " a horse-grenadier of my old guard—a soldier of Egypt and Italy, battered with wounds—an old dare-devil, whom I decorated with my own hand at Wagram—I have not forgotten him !"—I vow, children, when your mother read that to me, I cried like a fool.'

'The Emperor—what a fine golden face he has on the silver cross with the red riband that you would sometimes show us when we behaved well!'

'That cross—given by him—is my relic. It is there in my knapsack, with whatever we have of value—our little purse and papers. But, to return to your mother; it was a great consolation to her, when I took her letters from the general, or talked with her about him—for she suffered much—oh, so much! In vain her parents tormented and persecuted her; she always answered: " I will never marry any one but General Simon." A spirited woman, I can tell you—resigned, but wonderfully courageous. One day she received a letter from the general; he had left the Isle of Elba with the Emperor; the war had again broken out, a short campaign, but as fierce as ever, and heightened by soldiers' devotion. In that campaign of France, my children, especially at Montmirail, your father fought like a lion, and his division followed his example. It was no longer valour—it was frenzy. He told me that, in Champagne, the peasants killed so many of those Prussians, that their fields were manured with them for years. Men, women, children, all rushed upon them. Pitchforks, stones, mattocks, all served for the slaughter. It was a true wolf-hunt !'

The veins swelled on the soldier's forehead, and his cheeks flushed as he spoke, for this popular heroism recalled to his memory the sublime enthusiasm of the wars of the republic—those armed risings of a whole people, from which dated the first steps of his military career, as the triumphs of the Empire were the last days of his service.

The orphans, too, daughters of a soldier and a brave woman, did not shrink from the rough energy of these words, but felt their cheeks glow, and their hearts beat tumultuously.

'How happy we are to be the children of so brave a father !' cried Blanche.

'It is a happiness and an honour too, my children—for the evening of the battle of Montmirail, the Emperor, to the joy of the whole army, made your father Duke of Ligny and Marshal of France.'

'Marshal of France !' said Rose in astonishment, without understanding the exact meaning of the words.

'Duke of Ligny !' added Blanche, with equal surprise.

'Yes; Peter Simon, the son of a workman, became duke and marshal—there is nothing higher except a king !' resumed Dagobert, proudly. 'That's how the Emperor treated the sons of the people, and, therefore, the people were devoted to him. It was all very fine to tell them : " Your Emperor makes you food for cannon." " Stuff !" replied the people, who are no fools, "another would make us food for misery. We prefer the cannon, with the chance of becoming captain or colonel, marshal, king—or invalid ; that's better than to perish with hunger, cold, and age, on straw in a garret, after toiling forty years for others."'

'Even in France—even in Paris, that beautiful city—do you mean to say there are poor people who die of hunger and misery, Dagobert ?'

'Even in Paris? Yes, my children; therefore, I come back to the point—the cannon is better. With it, one has the chance of becoming, like your father, duke and marshal: when I say duke and marshal, I am partly right and partly wrong, for the title and the rank were not recognised in the end; because, after Montmirail, came a day of gloom, a day of great mourning, when, as the general has told me, old soldiers like myself wept—yes, wept!—on the evening of a battle. That day, my children, was Waterloo!'

There was in these simple words of Dagobert an expression of such deep sorrow, that it thrilled the hearts of the orphans.

'Alas!' resumed the soldier, with a sigh, 'there are days which seem to have a curse on them. That same day, at Waterloo, the general fell, covered with wounds, at the head of a division of the Guards. When he was nearly cured, which was not for a long time, he solicited permission to go to St. Helena—another island at the far end of the world, to which the English had carried the Emperor, to torture him at their leisure; for if he was very fortunate in the first instance, he had to go through a deal of hard rubs at last, my poor children.'

'If you talk in that way, you will make us cry, Dagobert.'

'There is cause enough for it—the Emperor suffered so much! He bled cruelly at the heart, believe me. Unfortunately, the general was not with him at St. Helena; he would have been one more to console him; but they would not allow him to go. Then, exasperated, like so many others, against the Bourbons, the general engaged in a conspiracy to recall the son of the Emperor. He relied especially on one regiment, nearly all composed of his old soldiers, and he went down to a place in Picardy, where they were then in garrison; but the conspiracy had already been divulged. Arrested the moment of his arrival, the general was taken before the colonel of the regiment. And this colonel,' said the soldier, after a brief pause, 'who do you think it was again? Bah! it would be too long to tell you all, and would only make you more sad; but it was a man whom your father had many reasons to hate. When he found himself face to face with him, he said: " If you are not a coward, you will give me one hour's liberty, and we will fight to the death; I hate you for this, I despise you for that "—and so on. The colonel accepted the challenge, and gave your father his liberty till the morrow. The duel was a desperate one; the colonel was left for dead on the spot.'

'Merciful heaven!'

'The general was yet wiping his sword, when a faithful friend came to him, and told him he had only just time to save himself. In fact, he happily succeeded in leaving France—yes, happily—for, a fortnight after, he was condemned to death as a conspirator.'

'What misfortunes, good heaven!'

'There was some luck, however, in the midst of his troubles. Your mother had kept her promise bravely, and was still waiting for him. She had written to him : " The Emperor first, and me next!" Not able to do anything more for the Emperor, nor even for his son, the general, banished from France, set out for Warsaw. Your mother had lost her parents, and was now free; they were married—and I am one of the witnesses to the marriage.'

'You are right, Dagobert; that was great happiness in the midst of great misfortunes!'

'Yes, they were very happy; but, as it happened with all good hearts, the happier they were themselves, the more they felt for the sorrows of others—and there was quite enough to grieve them at Warsaw. The Russians had again begun to treat the Poles as their slaves; your brave mother, though of French origin, was a Pole in heart and soul; she spoke out boldly what others did not dare speak in a whisper, and all the unfortunate called her their protecting angel. That was enough to excite the suspicions of the Russian governor. One day, a friend of the general's, formerly a colonel in the lancers, a brave and worthy man, was condemned to be exiled to Siberia, for a military plot against the Russians. He took refuge in your father's house, and lay hid there; but his retreat was discovered. During the next night, a party of Cossacks, commanded by an officer and followed by a travelling-carriage, arrive at our door; they rouse the general from his sleep, and take him away with them.'

'Oh, heaven! what did they mean to do with him?'

'Conduct him out of the Russian dominions, with a charge never to return, on pain of perpetual imprisonment. His last words were: 'Dagobert, I entrust to thee my wife and child!'—for it wanted yet some months of the time when you were to be born. Well, notwithstanding that, they exiled your mother to Siberia; it was an opportunity to get rid of her; she did too much good at Warsaw, and they feared her accordingly. Not content with banishing her, they confiscated all her property; the only favour she could obtain was, that I should accompany her, and, had it not been for Jovial, whom the general had given to me, she would have had to make the journey on foot. It was thus, with her on horseback, and I leading her as I lead you, my children, that we arrived at the poverty-stricken village, where, three months after, you poor little things were born!'

'And our father?'

'It was impossible for him to return to Russia; impossible for your mother to think of flight, with two children; impossible for the general to write to her, as he knew not where she was.'

'So, since that time, you have had no news of him?'

'Yes, my children—once we had news.'

'And by whom?'

After a moment's silence, Dagobert resumed with a singular expression of countenance: 'By whom?—by one who is not like other men. Yes—that you may understand me better, I will relate to you an extraordinary adventure, which happened to your father during his last French campaign. He had been ordered by the emperor to carry a battery, which was playing heavily on our army; after several unsuccessful efforts, the general put himself at the head of a regiment of cuirassiers, and charged the battery, intending, as was his custom, to cut down the men at their guns. He was on horseback, just before the mouth of a cannon, where all the artillerymen had been either killed or wounded, when one of them still found strength to raise himself upon one knee, and to apply the lighted match to the touch-hole—and that when your father was about ten paces in front of the loaded piece.'

'Oh! what a peril for our father!'

'Never, he told me, had he run such imminent danger—for he saw the artilleryman apply the match, and the gun go off—but, at the very nick, a man of tall stature, dressed as a peasant, and whom he had not before remarked, threw himself in front of the cannon.'

'Unfortunate creature! what a horrible death!'

'Yes,' said Dagobert, thoughtfully; 'it should have been so. He ought by rights to have been blown into a thousand pieces. But no—nothing of the kind!'

'What do you tell us?'

'What the general told me. "At the moment when the gun went off," as he often repeated to me, "I shut my eyes by an involuntary movement, that I might not see the mutilated body of the poor wretch who had sacrificed himself in my place. When I again opened them, the first thing I saw in the midst of the smoke, was the tall figure of this man, standing erect and calm on the same spot, and casting a sad, mild look on the artilleryman, who, with one knee on the ground, and his body thrown backward, gazed on him with as much terror as if he had been the devil in person. Afterwards, in the tumult of the battle, I lost sight of this man," added your father.'

'Bless me, Dagobert! how can this be possible?'

'That is just what I said to the general. He answered me, that he had never been able to explain to himself this event, which seemed as incredible as it was true. Moreover, your father must have been greatly struck with the countenance of this man, who appeared, he said, about thirty years of age—for he remarked, that his extremely black eyebrows were joined together, and formed, as it were, one line from temple to temple, so that he seemed to have a black streak across his forehead. Remember this, my children; you will soon see why.'

'Oh, Dagobert! we shall not forget it,' said the orphans, becoming more and more astonished as he proceeded.

'Is it not strange—this man with a black seam on his forehead?'

'Well, you shall hear. The general had, as I told you, been left for dead at Waterloo. During the night, which he passed on the field of battle, in a sort of delirium brought on by the fever of his wounds, he saw, or fancied he saw, this same man bending over him, with a look of great mildness and deep melancholy, stanching his wounds, and using every effort to revive him. But as your father, whose senses were still wandering, repulsed his kindness—saying, that after such a defeat, it only remained to die—it appeared as if this man replied to him: "You must live for Eva!"—meaning your mother, whom the general had left at Warsaw, to join the Emperor, and make this campaign of France.'

'How strange, Dagobert!—And since then, did our father never see this man?'

'Yes, he saw him—for it is he who brought news of the general to your poor mother.'

'When was that? We never heard of it.'

'You remember that, on the day your mother died, you went to the pine-forest with old Fedora?'

'Yes,' answered Rose, mournfully; 'to fetch some heath, of which our mother was so fond.'

'Poor mother!' added Blanche; 'she appeared so well that morning, that we could not dream of the calamity which awaited us before night.'

'True, my children; I sang and worked that morning in the garden, expecting, no more than you did, what was to happen. Well, as I was singing at my work, on a sudden I heard a voice ask me in French: "Is this the village of Milosk?"—I turned round, and saw before me a stranger; I looked at him attentively, and, instead of replying, fell back two steps, quite stupefied.'

'Ah, why?'

'He was of tall stature, very pale, with a high and open forehead; but his eyebrows met, and seemed to form one black streak across it.'

'Then it was the same man who had twice been with our father in battle?'

'Yes—it was he.'

'But, Dagobert,' said Rose, thoughtfully, 'is it not a long time since these battles?'

'About sixteen years.'

'And of what age was this stranger?'

'Hardly more than thirty.'

'Then how can it be the same man, who sixteen years before, had been with our father in the wars?'

'You are right,' said Dagobert, after a moment's silence, and shrugging his shoulders: 'I may have been deceived by a chance likeness—and yet——'

'Or, if it were the same, he could not have got older all that while.'

'But did you ask him, if he had not formerly relieved our father?'

'At first I was so surprised that I did not think of it ; and afterwards, he remained so short a time, that I had no opportunity. Well, he asked me for the village of Milosk. "You are there, sir," said I, "but how do you know that I am a Frenchman ?" "I heard you singing as I passed," replied he ; "could you tell me the house of Madame Simon, the general's wife ?" "She lives here, sir." Then, looking at me for some seconds in silence, he took me by the hand and said : "You are the friend of General Simon—his best friend ?" Judge of my astonishment, as I answered : "But, sir, how do you know ?" "He has often spoken of you with gratitude." "You have seen the general then ?" "Yes, some time ago, in India. I am also his friend : I bring news of him to his wife, whom I knew to be exiled in Siberia. At Tobolsk, whence I come, I learned that she inhabits this village. Conduct me to her !"

'The good traveller—I love him already,' said Rose.

'Yes, being father's friend.'

'I begged him to wait an instant whilst I went to inform your mother, so that the surprise might not do her harm : five minutes after, he was beside her.'

'And what kind of man was this traveller, Dagobert ?'

'He was very tall ; he wore a dark pelisse, and a fur cap, and had long black hair.'

'Was he handsome ?'

'Yes, my children—very handsome ; but with so mild and melancholy an air, that it pained my heart to see him.'

'Poor man ! he had doubtless known some great sorrow.'

'Your mother had been closeted with him for some minutes, when she called me to her and said that she had just received good news of the general. She was in tears, and had before her a large packet of papers ; it was a kind of journal, which your father had written every evening to console himself ; not being able to speak to her, he told the paper all that he would have told her.'

'Oh ! where are these papers, Dagobert ?'

'There, in the knapsack, with my cross and our purse. One day I will give them to you : but I have picked out a few leaves here and there for you to read presently. You will see why.'

'Had our father been long in India ?'

'I gathered from the few words which your mother said, that the general had gone to that country, after fighting for the Greeks against the Turks—for he always liked to side with the weak against the strong. In India he made fierce war against the English : they had murdered our prisoners in pontoons, and tortured the Emperor at St. Helena, and the war was a doubly good one, for in harming them he served a just cause.'

'What cause did he serve then ?'

'That of one of the poor native princes, whose territories the English lay waste, till the day when they can take possession of them against law and right. You see, my children, it was once more the weak against the strong, and your father did not miss this opportunity. In a few months he had so well-trained and disciplined the twelve or fifteen thousand men of the prince, that, in two encounters, they cut to pieces the English sent against them, and who, no doubt, had in their reckoning left out your brave father, my children. But come, you shall read some pages of his journal, which will tell you more and better than I can. Moreover, you will find in them a name which you ought always to remember : that's why I chose this passage.'

'Oh, what happiness ! To read the pages written by our father, is almost to hear him speak,' said Rose.

'It is as if he were close beside us,' added Blanche.

And the girls stretched out their hands with eagerness, to catch hold of the leaves that Dagobert had taken from his pocket. Then, by a simultaneous movement, full of touching grace, they pressed the writing of their father in silence to their lips.

' You will see also, my children, at the end of this letter, why I was surprised that your guardian angel, as you say, should be called Gabriel. Read, read,' added the soldier, observing the puzzled air of the orphans. ' Only I ought to tell you, that, when he wrote this, the general had not yet fallen in with the traveller who brought the papers.'

Rose, sitting up in her bed, took the leaves, and began to read in a soft and trembling voice, Blanche, with her head resting on her sister's shoulder, followed attentively every word. One could even see, by the slight motion of her lips, that she too was reading, but only to herself.

CHAPTER VIII.

EXTRACTS FROM GENERAL SIMON'S DIARY.

Bivouac on the Mountains of Ava, February the 20th, 1830.

' EACH time I add some pages to this journal, written now in the heart of India, where the fortune of my wandering and proscribed existence has thrown me—a journal which, alas ! my beloved Eva, you may never read—I experience a sweet, yet painful emotion ; for, although to converse thus with you is a consolation, it brings back the bitter thought that I am unable to see or speak to you.

' Still, if these pages should ever meet your eyes, your generous heart will throb at the name of the intrepid being, to whom I am this day indebted for my life, and to whom I may thus perhaps owe the happiness of seeing you again—you and my child—for of course our child lives. Yes, it must be—for else, poor wife, what an existence would be yours amid the horrors of exile ! Dear soul ! he must now be fourteen. Whom does he resemble ? Is he like you ? Has he your large and beautiful blue eyes ?—Madman that I am ! how many times, in this long day-book, have I already asked the same idle question, to which you can return no answer !—How many times shall I continue to ask it ?—But you will teach our child to speak and love the somewhat savage name of *Djalma.*'

' Djalma !' said Rose, as with moist eyes she left off reading.

' Djalma !' repeated Blanche, who shared the emotion of her sister. ' Oh, we shall never forget that name.'

' And you will do well, my children : for it seems to be the name of a famous soldier, though a very young one. But go on, my little Rose !'

' I have told you in the preceding pages, my dear Eva, of the two glorious days we had this month. The troops of my old friend the prince, which daily make fresh advances in European discipline, have performed wonders. We have beaten the English, and obliged them to abandon a portion of this unhappy country, which they had invaded in contempt of all the rights of justice, and which they continue to ravage without mercy ; for, in these parts, warfare is another name for treachery, pillage, and massacre. This morning, after a toilsome march through a rocky and mountainous district, we received information from our scouts, that the enemy had been reinforced, and was preparing to act on the offensive ; and, as we were separated from them by a distance of a few leagues only, an engagement became inevitable. My old friend the prince, the father of my deliverer, was impatient to march to the attack. The action began about three o'clock ; it was very bloody and furious. Seeing that our men wavered for a moment, for they were inferior in number, and the English reinforcements consisted of fresh troops, I charged at the head of our weak reserve of cavalry. The old prince was in the centre, fighting, as he always fights, intrepidly ; his son, Djalma, scarcely eighteen, as brave as his father, did not leave my side. In the hottest part of the engagement, my horse was killed under me, and rolling over into a ravine, along the edge of which I was riding, I found myself so awkwardly entangled beneath him, that for an instant I thought my thigh was broken.'

'Poor father!' said Blanche.

'This time, happily, nothing more dangerous ensued—thanks to Djalma! You see, Dagobert,' added Rose, ' that I remember the name.' And she continued to read :

'The English thought—and a very flattering opinion it was—that, if they could kill me, they would make short work of the prince's army. So a Sepoy officer, with five or six irregulars—cowardly, ferocious plunderers—seeing me roll down the ravine, threw themselves into it to despatch me. Surrounded by fire and smoke, and carried away by their ardour, our mountaineers had not seen me fall ; but Djalma never left me. He leaped into the ravine to my assistance, and his cool intrepidity saved my life. He had held the fire of his double-barrelled carbine ; with one load, he killed the officer on the spot ; with the other he broke the arm of an irregular, who had already pierced my left hand with his bayonet. But do not be alarmed, dear Eva ; it is nothing—only a scratch.'

'Wounded—again wounded—alas !' cried Blanche, clasping her hands together, and interrupting her sister.

'Take courage!' said Dagobert : 'I dare say it was only a scratch, as the general calls it. Formerly, he used to call wounds, which did not disable a man from fighting, blank wounds. There was no one like him for such sayings.'

'Djalma, seeing me wounded,' resumed Rose, wiping her eyes, 'made use of his heavy carbine as a club, and drove back the soldiers. At that instant, I perceived a new assailant, who, sheltered behind a clump of bamboos which commanded the ravine, slowly lowered his long gun, placed the barrel between two branches, and took deliberate aim at Djalma. Before my shouts could apprise him of his danger, the brave youth had received a ball in his breast. Feeling himself hit, he fell back involuntarily two paces, and dropped upon one knee ; but he still remained firm, endeavouring to cover me with his body. You may conceive my rage and despair, whilst all my efforts to disengage myself were paralysed by the excruciating pain in my thigh. Powerless and disarmed, I witnessed for some moments this unequal struggle.

'Djalma was loosing blood rapidly ; his strength of arm began to fail him ; already one of the irregulars, inciting his comrades with his voice, drew from his belt a huge, heavy kind of bill-hook, when a dozen of our mountaineers made their appearance, borne towards the spot by the irresistible current of the battle. Djalma was rescued in his turn, I was released, and, in a quarter of an hour, I was able to mount a horse. The fortune of the day is ours, though with severe loss ; but the fires of the English camp are still visible, and tomorrow the conflict will be decisive. Thus, my beloved Eva, I owe my life to this youth. Happily, his wound occasions us no uneasiness ; the ball only glanced along the ribs in a slanting direction.'

'The brave boy might have said : "A blank wound," like the general,' observed Dagobert.

'Now, my dear Eva,' continued Rose, 'you must become acquainted, by means of this narrative at least, with the intrepid Djalma. He is but just eighteen. With one word, I will paint for you his noble and valiant nature ; it is a custom of this country to give surnames, and, when only fifteen, he was called "The Generous"—by which was, of course, meant generous in heart and mind. By another custom, no less touching than whimsical, this name has reverted to his parent, who is called "The Father of the Generous," and who might, with equal propriety, be called "The Just," for this old Indian is a rare example of chivalrous honour and proud independence. He might, like so many other poor princes of this country, have humbled himself before the execrable despotism of the English, bargained for the relinquishment of sovereign power, and submitted to brute force—but it was not in his nature. "My whole rights, or a grave in my native mountains !"—such is his motto. And this is no empty boast : it springs from the conviction of what is right and just. "But you will be crushed in the struggle," I have said to him.—" My friend," he answered, " what if, to force you to a disgraceful act, you were told to yield or die ?"—From that day I understood him, and have devoted myself, mind and body, to the ever sacred cause of the weak against the strong. You see, my Eva, that Djalma shows himself worthy of such a father. This young Indian is so proud, so heroic in his bravery, that, like a young Greek of Leonida's age, he fights with his breast bare ; while other warriors of his country (who, indeed, usually have arms, breast, and shoulders uncovered) wear, in time of battle, a thick, impenetrable vest. The rash daring of this youth reminds me of Murat, King of Naples, who, I have so often told you, I have seen a hundred times leading the most desperate charges with nothing but a riding-whip in his hand.'

'That's another of those kings I was telling you of, whom the Emperor set up for his amusement,' said Dagobert. 'I once saw a Prussian officer prisoner, whose face had been cut across by that mad-cap King of Naples' riding-whip ; the mark was there, a black and blue stripe. The Prussian swore he was dishonoured, and that a sabre-cut would have been preferable. I should rather think so ! That devil of a king ; he only had one idea : " Forward, on to the cannon !" As soon as they began to cannonade, one would have thought the guns were calling him with all their might, for he was soon up to them with his " Here I am !" If I speak to you about him, my children, it's because he was fond of repeating ; "No one can break through a square of infantry, if General Simon or I can't do it." '

Rose continued :

' I have observed with pain, that, notwithstanding his youth, Djalma is often subject to fits of deep melancholy. At times, I have seen him exchange with his father looks of singular import. In spite of our mutual attachment, I believe that both conceal from me some sad family secret, in so far as I can judge from expressions which have dropped from them by chance.

' It relates to some strange event, which their vivid imaginations have invested with a supernatural character.

' And yet, my love, you and I have no longer the right to smile at the credulity of others. I, since the French campaign, when I met with that extraordinary adventure, which, to this day, I am quite unable to understand——'

' This refers to the man who threw himself before the mouth of the cannon,' said Dagobert.

' And you,' continued the maiden, still reading, 'you, my dear Eva, since the visits of that young and beautiful woman, whom, as your mother asserted, she had seen at her mother's house forty years before.'

The orphans, in amazement. looked at the soldier.

' Your mother never spoke to me of that, nor the general either, my children ; this is as strange to me as it is to you.'

With increasing excitement and curiosity, Rose continued :

' After all, my dear Eva, things which appear very extraordinary, may often be explained by a chance resemblance or a freak of nature. Marvels being always the result of optical illusion or heated fancy, a time must come, when that which appeared to be superhuman or supernatural, will prove to be the most simple and natural event in the world. I doubt not, therefore, that the things, which we denominate our prodigies, will one day receive this commonplace solution.'

You see, my children—things appear marvellous, which at bottom are quite simple—though for a long time we understand nothing about them.'

'As our father relates this, we must believe it, and not be astonished—eh, sister?'

'Yes, truly—since it will all be explained one day.'

'For example,' said Dagobert, after a moment's reflection, 'you two are so much alike, that any one, who was not in the habit of seeing you daily, might easily take one for the other. Well! if they did not know that you are, so to speak, "doubles," they might think an imp was at work instead of such good little angels as you are.'

'You are right, Dagobert; in this way many things may be explained, even as our father says.' And Rose continued to read:

'Not without pride, my gentle Eva, have I learned that Djalma has French blood in his veins. His father married, some years ago, a young girl, whose family, of French origin, had long been settled at Batavia in the island of Java. This similarity of circumstances between my old friend and myself—for your family also, my Eva, is of French origin, and long settled in a foreign land—has only served to augment my sympathy for him. Unfortunately, he has long had to mourn the loss of the wife whom he adored.

'See, my beloved Eva! my hand trembles as I write these words. I am weak—I am foolish—but, alas! my heart sinks within me. If such a misfortune were to happen to me—Oh, my God!—what would become of our child without thee—without his father—in that barbarous country? But no! the very fear is madness; and yet what a horrible torture is uncertainty! Where may you now be? What are you doing? What has become of you? Pardon these black thoughts, which are sometimes too much for me. They are the cause of my worst moments—for, when free from them, I can at least say to myself: I am proscribed, I am every way unfortunate—but, at the other end of the world, two hearts still beat for me with affection—yours, my Eva, and our child's!'

Rose could hardly finish this passage; for some seconds her voice was broken by sobs. There was indeed a fatal coincidence between the fears of General Simon and the sad reality; and what could be more touching than these outpourings of the heart, written by the light of a watch-fire, on the eve of battle, by a soldier who thus sought to soothe the pangs of a separation, which he felt bitterly, but knew not would be eternal?

'Poor general! he is unaware of our misfortune,' said Dagobert, after a moment's silence; 'but neither has he heard that he has two children, instead of one. That will be at least some consolation. But come, Blanche; do go on reading: I fear that this dwelling on grief fatigues your sister, and she is too much affected by it. Besides, after all, it is only just, that you should take your share of its pleasure and its sorrow.'

Blanche took the letter, and Rose, having dried her eyes, laid in her turn her sweet head on the shoulder of her sister, who thus continued:

'I am calmer now, my dear Eva; I left off writing for a moment, and strove to banish those black presentiments. Let us resume our conversation! After discoursing so long about India, I will talk to you a little of Europe. Yesterday evening, one of our people (a trusty fellow) rejoined our outposts. He brought me a letter, which had arrived from France at Calcutta; at length, I have news of my father, and am no longer anxious on his account. This letter is dated in August of last year. I see by its contents, that several other letters, to which he alludes, have either been delayed or lost; for I had not received any for two years before, and was extremely uneasy about him. But my excellent father is the same as ever! Age has not weakened him; his character is as energetic, his health as robust, as in times past—still a workman, still proud of his order, still faithful to his austere republican ideas, still hoping much.

'For he says to me, "the time is at hand," and he underlines those words. He gives me also, as you will see, good news of the family of old Dagobert, our friend—for in truth, my dear Eva, it soothes my grief to think, that this excellent man is with you, that he will have accompanied you in your exile—for I know him—a kernel of gold beneath the rude rind of a soldier! How he must love our child !'

Here Dagobert coughed two or three times, stooped down, and appeared to be seeking on the ground the little red and blue check-handkerchief spread over his knees. He remained thus bent for some seconds, and, when he raised himself, he drew his hand across his moustache.

'How well father knows you !'

'How rightly has he guessed that you would love us !'

'Well, well, children ; pass over that !—Let's come to the part where the general speaks of my little Agricola, and of Gabriel, my wife's adopted child. Poor woman ! when I think that in three months perhaps——But come, child ; read, read,' added the old soldier, wishing to conceal his emotion.

'I still hope against hope, my dear Eva, that these pages will one day reach you, and therefore I wish to insert in them all that can be interesting to Dagobert. It will be a consolation to him, to have some news of his family. My father, who is still foreman at Mr. Hardy's, tells me that worthy man has also taken into his house the son of old Dagobert. Agricola works under my father, who is enchanted with him. He is, he tells me, a tall and vigorous lad, who wields the heavy forge-hammer as if it were a feather, and is light spirited as he is intelligent and laborious. He is the best workman on the establishment ; and this does not prevent him in the evening, after his hard day's work, when he returns home to his mother, whom he truly loves, from making songs and writing excellent patriotic verses. His poetry is full of fire and energy ; his fellow-workmen sing nothing else, and his lays have the power to warm the coldest and the most timid hearts.'

'How proud you must be of your son, Dagobert,' said Rose, in admiration ; 'he writes songs.'

'Certainly, it is all very fine—but what pleases me best is, that he is good to his mother, and that he handles the hammer with a will. As for the songs, before he makes a "Rising of the People," or a "Marseillaise," he will have had to beat a good deal of iron ; but where can this rascally sweet Agricola have learned to make songs at all ?—No doubt, it was at school, where he went, as you will see, with his adopted brother Gabriel.'

At this name of Gabriel, which reminded them of the imaginary being whom they called their guardian angel, the curiosity of the young girls was greatly excited. With redoubled attention, Blanche continued in these words :

'The adopted brother of Agricola, the poor deserted child whom the wife of our good Dagobert so generously took in, forms, my father tells me, a great contrast with Agricola ; not in heart, for they have both excellent hearts ; but Gabriel is as thoughtful and melancholy as Agricola is lively, joyous, and active. Moreover, adds my father, each of them, so to speak, has the aspect which belongs to his character. Agricola is dark, tall, and strong, with a gay and bold air ; Gabriel, on the contrary, is weak, fair, timid as a girl, and his face wears an expression of angelic mildness.'

The orphans looked at each other in surprise ; then, as they turned towards the soldier their ingenuous countenances, Rose said to him : 'Have you heard, Dagobert? Father says, that your Gabriel is fair, and has the face of an angel. Why, 'tis exactly like ours !'

'Yes, yes, I heard very well ; it is that which surprised me, in your dream.'

'I should like to know, if he has also blue eyes,' said Rose.

'As for that, my children, though the general says nothing about it, I will answer for it : your fair boys have always blue eyes. But, blue or black, he will not use them to stare at young ladies ; go on, and you will see why.'

Blanche resumed :

' His face wears an expression of angelic mildness. One of the Brothers of the Christian Schools, where he went with Agricola and other children of his quarter, struck with his intelligence and good disposition, spoke of him to a person of consequence, who, becoming interested in the lad, placed him in a seminary for the clergy, and, since the last two years, Gabriel is a priest. He intends devoting himself to foreign missions, and will soon set out for America.'

' Your Gabriel is a priest, it appears?' said Rose, looking at Dagobert.

' While ours is an angel,' added Blanche.

' Which only proves that yours is a step higher than mine. Well, every one to his taste ; there are good people in all trades ; but I prefer that it should be Gabriel who has chosen the black gown. I'd rather see my boy with arms bare, hammer in hand, and a leathern apron round him, neither more nor less than your old grandfather, my children—the father of Marshal Simon, Duke of Ligny—for, after all, marshal and duke he is by the grace of the Emperor. Now finish your letter.'

' Soon, alas, yes !' said Blanche ; ' there are only a few lines left.' And she proceeded :

' Thus, my dear, loving Eva, if this journal should ever reach its destination, you will be able to satisfy Dagobert as to the position of his wife and son, whom he left for our sakes. How can we ever repay such a sacrifice? But I feel sure, that your good and generous heart will have found some means of compensation.

' Adieu !—Again adieu, for to-day, my beloved Eva ; I left off writing for a moment, to visit the tent of Djalma. He slept peacefully, and his father watched beside him ; with a smile, he banished my fears. This intrepid young man is no longer in any danger. May he still be spared in the combat of to-morrow ! Adieu, my gentle Eva ! the night is silent and calm ; the fires of the bivouac are slowly dying out, and our poor mountaineers repose after this bloody day ; I can hear, from hour to hour, the distant all's-well of our sentinels. Those foreign words bring back my grief ; they remind me of what I sometimes forget in writing—that I am far away, separated from you and from my child ! Poor, beloved beings ! what will be your destiny? Ah ! if I could only send you, in time, that medal, which, by a fatal accident, I carried away with me from Warsaw, you might, perhaps, obtain leave to visit France, or at least to send our child there with Dagobert ; for you know of what importance——But why add this sorrow to all the rest? Unfortunately, the years are passing away, the fatal day will arrive, and this last hope, in which I live for you, will also be taken from me : but I will not close the evening by so sad a thought. Adieu, my beloved Eva ! Clasp our child to your bosom, and cover it with all the kisses which I send to both of you from the depths of exile !

' Till to-morrow—after the battle !'

The reading of this touching letter was followed by a long silence. The tears of Rose and Blanche flowed together. Dagobert, with his head resting on his hand, was absorbed in painful reflections.

Without doors, the wind had now augmented in violence ; a heavy rain began to beat on the sounding panes ; the most profound silence reigned in the interior of the inn. But, whilst the daughters of General Simon were reading with such deep emotion these fragments of their father's journal, a strange and mysterious scene transpired in the menagerie of the brute-tamer.

CHAPTER IX.

THE CAGES.

MOROK had prepared himself. Over his deer-skin vest he had drawn the coat of mail—-that steel tissue, as pliable as cloth, as hard as diamonds; next, clothing his arms and legs in their proper armour, and his feet in iron-bound buskins, and concealing all this defensive equipment under loose trousers and an ample pelisse carefully buttoned, he took in his hand a long bar of iron, white hot, set in a wooden handle.

Though long ago daunted by the skill and energy of the Prophet, his tiger Cain, his lion Judas, and his black panther Death, had sometimes attempted, in a moment of rebellion, to try their fangs and claws on his person; but, thanks to the armour concealed beneath his pelisse, they blunted their claws upon a skin of steel, and notched their fangs upon arms or legs of iron, whilst a slight touch of their master's metallic wand left a deep furrow in their smoking, shrivelled flesh.

Finding the inutility of their efforts, and endowed with strong memory, the beasts soon learned that their teeth and claws were powerless when directed against this invulnerable being. Hence, their terrified submission reached to such a point that, in his public representations, their master could make them crouch and cower at his feet by the least movement of a little wand covered with flame-coloured paper.

The Prophet, thus armed with care, and holding in his hand the iron made hot by Goliath, descended by the trap-door of the loft into the large shed beneath, in which were deposited the cages of his animals. A mere wooden partition separated this shed from the stable that contained his horses.

A lantern, with a reflector, threw a vivid light on the cages. They were four in number. A wide iron grating formed their sides, turning at one end upon hinges like a door, so as to give ingress to the animal; the bottom of each den rested on two axle-trees and four small iron castors, so that they could easily be removed to the large covered wagon in which they were placed during a journey. One of them was empty; the other three contained, as already intimated, a panther, a tiger, and a lion.

The panther, originally from Java, seemed to merit the gloomy name of Death, by her grim, ferocious aspect. Completely black, she lay crouching and rolled up in the bottom of her cage, and her dark hues mingling with the obscurity which surrounded her, nothing was distinctly visible but fixed and glaring eyes—yellow balls of phosphoric light, which only kindled, as it were, in the night-time; for it is the nature of all the animals of the feline species to enjoy entire clearness of vision but in darkness.

The Prophet entered the stable in silence : the dark red of his long pelisse contrasted with the pale yellow of his straight hair and beard; the lantern, placed at some height above the ground, threw its rays full upon this man, and the strong light, opposed to the deep shadows around it, gave effect to the sharp proportions of his bony and savage-looking figure.

He approached the cage slowly. The white rim, which encircled his eye-ball, appeared to dilate, and his look rivalled in motionless brilliancy the steadily sparkling gaze of the panther. Still crouching in the shade, she felt already the fascination of that glance; two or three times she dropped her eyelids with a low, angry howl; then, reopening her eyes, as if in spite of herself, she kept them fastened immovably on those of the Prophet. And now her rounded ears clung to her skull, which was flattened like a viper's; the skin of her forehead became convulsively wrinkled; she drew in her bristling, but silky muzzle, and twice silently opened her jaws, garnished with formidable fangs. From that moment a kind of magnetic connection seemed to be established between the man and the beast.

The Prophet extended his glowing bar towards the cage, and said, in a sharp, imperious tone: ' Death ! come here !'

The panther rose, but so dragged herself along that her belly and the bend of her legs touched the ground. She was three feet high, and nearly five in length ; her elastic and fleshy spine, the sinews of her thighs as well developed as those of a race-horse, her deep chest, her enormous jutting shoulders, the nerve and muscle in her short, thick paws—all announced that this terrible animal united vigour with suppleness, and strength with agility.

Morok, with his iron wand still extended in the direction of the cage, made a step towards the panther. The panther made a stride towards the Prophet. Morok stopped ; Death stopped also.

At this moment the tiger, Judas, to whom Morok's back was turned, bounded violently in his cage, as if jealous of the attention which his master paid to the panther. He growled hoarsely, and, raising his head, showed the under-part of his redoubtable triangular jaw, and his broad chest of a dirty white, with which blended the copper colour, streaked with black, of his sides ; his tail, like a huge red serpent, with rings of ebony, now clung to his flanks, now lashed them with a slow and continuous movement ; his eyes, of a transparent, brilliant green, were fixed upon the Prophet.

Such was the influence of this man over his animals, that Judas almost immediately ceased growling, as if frightened at his own temerity ; but his respiration continued loud and deep. Morok turned his face towards him, and examined him very attentively during some seconds. The panther, no longer subject to the influence of her master's look, slunk back to crouch in the shade.

A sharp cracking, in sudden breaks, like that which great animals make in gnawing hard substances, was now heard from the cage of the lion. It drew the attention of the Prophet, who, leaving the tiger, advanced towards the other den.

Nothing could be seen of the lion but his monstrous croup of a reddish yellow. His thighs were gathered under him, and his thick mane served entirely to conceal his head. But by the tension and movement of the muscles of his loins, and the curving of his backbone, it was easy to perceive that he was making violent efforts with his throat and his forepaws. The Prophet approached the cage with some uneasiness, fearing that, notwithstanding his orders, Goliath had given the lion some bones to gnaw. To assure himself of it, he said in a quick and firm voice : ' Cain !'

The lion did not change his position.

' Cain ! come here !' repeated Morok in a louder tone. The appeal was useless ; the lion did not move, and the noise continued.

' Cain ! come here !' said the Prophet a third time ; but, as he pronounced these words, he applied the end of the glowing bar to the haunch of the lion.

Scarcely did the light track of smoke appear on the reddish hide of Cain, when, with a spring of incredible agility, he turned and threw himself against the grating, not crouching, but at a single bound—upright, superb, terrifying. The Prophet being at the angle of the cage, Cain, in his fury, had raised himself sideways to face his master, and, leaning his huge flank against the bars, thrust between them his enormous fore-leg, which, with his swollen muscles, was as large as Goliath's thigh.

' Cain ! down !' said the Prophet, approaching briskly.

The lion did not obey immediately. His lips, curling with rage, displayed fangs as long, as large, and as pointed as the tusks of a wild boar. But Morok touched those lips with the end of the burning metal ; and, as he felt the smart, followed by an unexpected summons of his master, the lion, not daring to roar, uttered a hollow growl, and his great body sank down at once in an attitude of submission and fear.

The Prophet took down the lantern to see what Cain had been gnawing. It was one of the planks from the floor of his den, which he had succeeded in tearing up, and was crunching between his teeth in the extremity of his hunger For a few moments the most profound silence reigned in the menagerie. The Prophet, with his hands behind his back, went from one cage to the other observing the animals with a restless, contemplative look, as if he hesitated to make between them an important and difficult choice.

From time to time he listened at the great door of the shed, which opened on the courtyard of the inn. At length this door turned on its hinges, and Goliath appeared, his clothes dripping with water.

"Well! is it done?' said the Prophet.

'Not without trouble. Luckily, the night is dark, it blows hard, and it pours with rain.'

'Then there is no suspicion?'

'None, master. Your information was good. The door of the cellar opens on the fields, just under the window of the lasses. When you whistled to let me know it was time, I crept out with a stool I had provided; I put it up against the wall, and mounted upon it; with my six feet, that made nine, and I could lean my elbows on the window-ledge; I took the shutter in one hand, and the haft of my knife in the other, and, whilst I broke two of the panes, I pushed the shutter with all my might.'

'And they thought it was the wind?'

'Yes, they thought it was the wind. You see, the "brute" is not such a brute, after all. That done, I crept back into my cellar, carrying my stool with me. In a little time, I heard the voice of the old man; it was well I had made haste.'

' Yes; when I whistled to you, he had just entered the supper-room. I thought he would have been longer.'

'That man's not built to remain long at supper,' said the giant, contemptuously. 'Some moments after the panes had been broken, the old man opened the window, and called his dog, saying: "Jump out !"—I went and hid myself at the further end of the cellar, or that infernal dog would have scented me through the door.'

'The dog is now shut up in the stable with the old man's horse. Go on!'

'When I heard them close shutter and window, I came out of my cellar, replaced my stool, and again mounted upon it. Unfastening the shutter, I opened it without noise, but the two broken panes were stopped up with the skirts of a pelisse. I heard talking, but I could see nothing; so I moved the pelisse a little, and then I could see the two lasses in bed opposite to me, and the old man sitting down with his back to where I stood.'

' But the knapsack—the knapsack?—That is the most important.'

'The knapsack was near the window, on a table, by the side of a lamp; I could have reached it by stretching out my arm.'

' What did you hear said?'

'As you told me to think only of the knapsack, I can only remember what concerns the knapsack. The old man said he had some papers in it—the letters of a general—his money—his cross.'

' Good—what next?'

'As it was difficult for me to keep the pelisse away from the hole, it slipped through my fingers. In trying to get hold of it again, I put my hand too much forward. One of the lasses saw it, and screamed out, pointing to the window.'

'Dolt !' exclaimed the Prophet, becoming pale with rage, 'you have ruined all.'

'Stop a bit! there is nothing broken yet. When I heard the scream, I jumped down from my stool, and got back into the cellar; as the dog was no longer about, I left the door ajar, so that I could hear them open the window, and see, by the light, that the old man was looking out with the lamp; but he could find no ladder, and the window was too high for any man of common size to reach it !'

'He will have thought, like the first time, that it was the wind. You are less awkward than I imagined.'

'The wolf has become a fox, as you said. Knowing where the knapsack was to be found with the money and the papers, and not being able to do more for the moment, I came away—and here I am.'

'Go upstairs and fetch me the longest pike.'

'Yes, master.'

'And the red blanket.'

'Yes, master.'

'Go!'

Goliath began to mount the ladder; half-way up he stopped. 'Master,' said he, 'may I not bring down a bit of meat for Death?—you will see that she'll bear me malice; she puts it all down to my account; she never forgets, and on the first occasion——'

'The pike and the cloth!' repeated the Prophet, in an imperious tone. And whilst Goliath, swearing to himself, proceeded to execute his instructions, Morok opened the great door of the shed, looked out into the yard, and listened.

'Here's the pike and the cloth,' said the giant, as he descended the ladder with the articles. 'Now what must I do next?'

'Return to the cellar, mount once more by the window, and when the old man leaves the room——'

'Who will make him leave the room?'

'Never mind! he will leave it.'

'What next?'

'You say the lamp is near the window?'

'Quite near—on the table next to the knapsack.'

'Well, then, as soon as the old man leaves the room, push open the window, throw down the lamp, and if you accomplish cleverly what remains to do—the ten florins are yours—you remember it all?'

'Yes, yes.'

'The girls will be so frightened by the noise and darkness, that they will remain dumb with terror.'

'Make yourself easy! The wolf turned into a fox; why not a serpent?'

'There is yet something.'

'Well, what now?'

'The roof of this shed is not very high, the window of the loft is easy of access, the night is dark—instead of returning by the door——'

'I will come in at the window.'

'Ay, and without noise.'

'Like a regular snake!' and the giant departed.

'Yes!' said the Prophet to himself, after a long silence, 'these means are sure. It was not for me to hesitate. A blind and obscure instrument, I know not the motives of the orders I have received: but from the recommendations which accompany them—but from the position of him who sends them—immense interests must be involved—interests connected with all that is highest and greatest upon earth!—And yet how can these two girls, almost beggars, how can this wretched soldier represent such interests?—No matter,' added he, with humility; 'I am the arm which acts—it is for the head, which thinks and orders, to answer for its work.'

Soon after the Prophet left the shed, carrying with him the red cloth, and directed his steps towards the little stable that contained Jovial. The crazy door, imperfectly secured by a latch, was easily opened. At sight of a stranger Spoilsport threw himself upon him; but his teeth encountered the iron leggings of the Prophet, who, in spite of the efforts of the dog, took Jovial by his halter, threw the blanket over his head to prevent his either seeing or smelling, and led him from the stable into the interior of the menagerie, of which he closed the door,

CHAPTER X.

THE SURPRISE.

THE orphans, after reading the journal of their father, remained for some moments silent, sad and pensive, contemplating the leaves yellowed by time. Dagobert, also plunged in a reverie, thought of his wife and son, from whom he had been so long separated, and hoped soon to see again.

The soldier was the first to break the silence, which had lasted for several minutes. Taking the leaves from the hand of Blanche, he folded them carefully, put them into his pocket, and thus addressed the orphans :

'Courage, my children ! you see what a brave father you have. Think only of the pleasure of greeting him, and remember always the name of the gallant youth, to whom you will owe that pleasure—for without him your father would have been killed in India.'

'Djalma ! we shall never forget him,' said Rose.

'And if our guardian angel Gabriel should return,' added Blanche, 'we will ask him to watch over Djalma as over ourselves.'

'Very well, my children ; I am sure that you will forget nothing that concerns good feeling. But to return to the traveller, who came to visit your poor mother in Siberia, he had seen the general a month after the events of which you have read, and at a moment when he was about to enter on a new campaign against the English. It was then that your father entrusted him with the papers and medal.'

'But of what use will this medal be to us, Dagobert ?'

'And what is the meaning of these words engraved upon it ?' added Rose, as she drew it from her bosom.

'Why it means, my children, that on the 13th of February, 1832, we must be at No. 3, Rue Saint François, Paris.'

'But what are we to do there ?'

'Your poor mother was seized so quickly with her last illness, that she was unable to tell me. All I know is, that this medal came to her from her parents, and that it had been a relic preserved in her family for more than a century.'

'And how did our father get it ?'

'Among the articles which had been hastily thrown into the coach, when he was removed by force from Warsaw, was a dressing case of your mother's, in which was contained this medal. Since that time the general had been unable to send it back, having no means of communicating with us, and not even knowing where we were.'

'This medal is, then, of great importance to us ?'

'Unquestionably ; for never, during fifteen years, had I seen your mother so happy, as on the day the traveller brought it back to her. " Now," said she to me, in the presence of the stranger, and with tears of joy in her eyes, " now may my children's future be brilliant as their life has hitherto been miserable. I will entreat of the governor of Siberia permission to go to France with my daughters ; it will perhaps be thought I have been sufficiently punished, by fifteen years of exile, and the confiscation of my property. Should they refuse, I will remain here ; but they will at least allow me to send my children to France, and you must accompany them, Dagobert. You shall set out immediately, for much time has been already lost ; and, if you were not to arrive before the 13th of next February, this cruel separation and toilsome journey would have been all in vain '

'Suppose we were one day after ?'

'Your mother told me that if we arrived the 14th instead of the 13th, it would be too late. She also gave me a thick letter, to put into the post for France, in the first town we should pass through—which I have done.'

'And do you think we shall be at Paris in time?'

'I hope so ; still, if you are strong enough, we must sometimes make forced marches—for, if we only travel our five leagues a day, and that without accident, we shall scarcely reach Paris until the beginning of February, and it is better to be a little beforehand.'

'But as father is in India, and condemned to death if he return to France, then shall we see him?'

'And where shall we see him?'

'Poor children ! there are so many things you have yet to learn. When the traveller quitted him, the general could not return to France, but now he can do so.'

'And why is that?'

'Because the Bourbons, who had banished him, were themselves turned out last year. The news must reach India, and your father will certainly come to meet you at Paris, because he expects that you and your mother will be there on the 13th of next February.'

'Ah! now I understand how we may hope to see him,' said Rose with a sigh.

'Do you know the name of this traveller, Dagobert?'

'No, my children ; but whether called Jack or John, he is a good sort. When he left your mother, she thanked him with tears for all his kindness and devotion to the general, herself, and her children ; but he pressed her hands in his, and said to her, in so gentle a voice that I could not help being touched by it : "Why do you thank me ? Did He not say—LOVE YE ONE ANOTHER !"'

'Who is that, Dagobert?'

'Yes, of whom did the traveller speak?'

'I know nothing about it ; only the manner in which he pronounced those words struck me, and they were the last he spoke.'

'Love one another !' repeated Rose, thoughtfully.

'How beautiful are those words !' added Blanche.

'And whither was the traveller going?'

'Far, very far into the North, as he told your mother. When she saw him depart, she said to me : "His mild, sad talk has affected me even to tears ; whilst I listened to him, I seemed to be growing better—I seemed to love my husband and my children more—and yet, to judge by the expression of his countenance, one would think that this stranger had never either smiled or wept !" She and I watched him from the door as long as we could follow him with our eyes ; he carried his head down, and his walk was slow, calm, and firm ; one might fancy that he counted his steps. And, talking of steps, I remarked yet another thing.'

'What was it, Dagobert?'

'You know that the road which led to our house was always damp, because of the overflowing of the little spring.'

'Yes.'

'Well, then, the mark of the traveller's footsteps remained in the clay, and I saw that he had nails under his shoe in the form of a cross.'

'How in the form of a cross?'

'Look !' said Dagobert, placing the tip of his finger seven times on the coverlet of the bed ; 'they were arranged thus beneath his heel :

You see it forms a cross.'

'What could it mean, Dagobert?'

' Chance, perhaps—yes, chance—and yet, in spite of myself, this confounded cross left behind him struck me as a bad omen, for hardly was he gone when misfortune after misfortune fell upon us.'

' Alas ! the death of our mother !'

' Yes—but, before that, another piece of ill-luck. You had not yet returned, and she was writing her petition to ask leave to go to France or to send you there, when I heard the gallop of a horse. It was a courier from the governor-general of Siberia. He brought us orders to change our residence; within three days we were to join other condemned persons, and be removed with them four hundred leagues further north. Thus, after fifteen years of exile, they redoubled in cruelty towards your mother.'

' Why did they thus torment her ?'

' One would think that some evil genius was at work against her. A few days later, the traveller would no longer have found us at Milosk ; and if he had joined us further on, it would have been too far for the medal and papers to be of use—since, having set out almost immediately, we shall hardly arrive in time at Paris. " If they had some interest to prevent me and my children from going to France," said your mother, " they would act just as they have done. To banish us four hundred leagues further, is to render impossible this journey, of which the term is fixed." And the idea overwhelmed her with grief.'

' Perhaps it was this unexpected sorrow that was the cause of her sudden illness.'

' Alas ! no, my children ; it was that infernal cholera, who arrives without giving you notice —for he too is a great traveller—and strikes you down like a thunderbolt. Three hours after the traveller had left us, when you returned quite pleased and gay from the forest, with your large bunches of wild-flowers for your mother, she was already in the last agony, and hardly to be recognised. The cholera had broken out in the village, and that evening five persons died of it. Your mother had only time to hang the medal about your neck, my dear little Rose, to recommend you both to my care, and to beg that we should set out immediately. When she was gone, the new order of exile could not apply to you ; and I obtained permission from the governor to take my departure with you for France, according to the last wishes——'

The soldier could not finish the sentence ; he covered his eyes with his hand, whilst the orphans embraced him sobbing.

' Oh ! but,' resumed Dagobert, with pride, after a moment of painful silence, ' it was then that you showed yourselves the brave daughters of the general. Notwithstanding the danger, it was impossible to tear you from your mother's bedside ; you remained with her to the last, you closed her eyes, you watched there all night, and you would not leave the village till you had seen me plant the little wooden cross over the grave I had dug for her.'

Dagobert paused abruptly. A strange, wild neighing, mingled with ferocious roarings, made the soldier start from his seat. He grew pale, and cried : ' It is Jovial ! my horse ! What are they doing to my horse ?' With that, opening the door, he rushed down the stairs precipitately.

The two sisters clung together, so terrified at the sudden departure of the soldier, that they saw not an enormous hand pass through the broken panes, unfasten the catch of the window, push it violently open, and throw down the lamp placed on the little table, on which was the soldier's knapsack. The orphans thus found themselves plunged into complete darkness.

CHAPTER XI.

JOVIAL AND DEATH.

MOROK had led Jovial into the middle of the menagerie, and then removed the cloth which prevented him from seeing and smelling. Scarcely had the tiger, lion, and panther caught a glimpse of him, than they threw themselves, half-famished, against the bars of their dens.

The horse, struck with stupor, his neck stretched out, his eye fixed, and trembling through all his limbs, appeared as if nailed to the ground; an abundant icy sweat rolled suddenly down his flanks. The lion and the tiger uttered fearful roarings, and struggled violently in their dens. The panther did not roar, but her mute rage was terrific.

With a tremendous bound, at the risk of breaking her skull, she sprang from the back of the cage against the bars : then, still mute, still furious, she crawled back to the extreme corner of the den, and with a new spring, as impetuous as it was blind, she again strove to force out the iron grating. Three times had she thus bounded—silent, appalling—when the horse, passing from the immobility of stupor to the wild agony of fear, neighed long and loud, and rushed in desperation at the door by which he had entered. Finding it closed he hung his head, bent his knees a little, and rubbed his nostrils against the opening left between the ground and the bottom of the door, as if he wished to inhale the air from the outside ; then, more and more affrighted, he began to neigh with redoubled force, and struck out violently with his fore-feet.

At the moment when Death was about once more to make her spring, the Prophet approached her cage. The heavy bolt which secured the grating was pushed from its staple by the pike of the brute-tamer, and, in another second, Morok was half way up the ladder that communicated with the loft.

The roaring of the lion and tiger, mingled with the neighing of Jovial, now resounded through all parts of the inn. The panther had again thrown herself furiously on the grating, and this time yielding with one spring, she was in the middle of the shed.

The light of the lantern was reflected from the glossy ebon of her hide, spotted with stains of a duller black. For an instant she remained motionless, crouching upon her thick-set limbs, with her head close to the floor, as if calculating the distance of the leap by which she was to reach the horse ; then suddenly she darted upon him.

On seeing her break from her cage Jovial had thrown himself violently against the door, which was made to open inwards, and leaned against it with all his might, as though he would force it down. Then, at the moment when Death took her leap, he reared up in almost an erect position ; but she, rapid as lightning, had fastened upon his throat and hung there, whilst at the same time she buried the sharp claws of her fore-feet in his chest. The jugular vein of the horse opened ; a torrent of bright red blood spouted forth beneath the tooth of the panther, who, now supporting herself on her hind-legs, squeezed her victim up against the door, whilst she dug into his flank with her claws, and laid bare the palpitating flesh. Then his half-strangled neighing became awful.

Suddenly these words resounded : 'Courage, Jovial !—I am at hand ! Courage !'

It was the voice of Dagobert, who was exhausting himself in desperate exertions to force open the door that concealed this sanguinary struggle. 'Jovial !' cried the soldier, ' I am here. Help! help !'

At the sound of that friendly and well-known voice, the poor animal, almost at its last gasp, strove to turn its head in the direction whence came the accents of his master, answered him with a plaintive neigh, and, sinking beneath the efforts of the panther, fell prostrate, first on its knees, then upon its flank, so that its backbone lay right across the door, and still prevented its being opened. And now all was finished. The panther, squatting down upon the horse, crushed him with all her paws, and, in spite of some last faint kicks, buried her bloody snout in his body.

'Help ! help ! my horse !' cried Dagobert, as he vainly shook the door. 'And no arms !' he added with rage ; 'no arms !'

'Take care !' exclaimed the brute-tamer, who appeared at the window of the loft ; 'do not attempt to enter—it might cost you your life. My panther is furious.'

·'But my horse ! my horse !' cried Dagobert, in a voice of agony.

'He must have strayed from his stable during the night, and pushed open the door of the shed. At sight of him the panther must have broken out of her cage and seized him. You are answerable for all the mischief that may ensue,' added the brute-tamer, with a menacing air ; 'for I shall have to run the greatest danger, to make Death return to her den.'

'But my horse ! only save my horse !' cried Dagobert, in a tone of hopeless supplication.

The Prophet disappeared from the window.

The roaring of the animals and the shouts of Dagobert, had roused from sleep every one in the White Falcon. Here and there lights were seen moving and windows were thrown open hurriedly. The servants of the inn soon appeared in the yard with lanterns, and surrounding Dagobert, inquired of him what had happened.

'My horse is there,' cried the soldier, continuing to shake the door, 'and one of that scoundrel's animals has escaped from its cage.'

At these words the people of the inn, already terrified by the frightful roaring, fled from the spot and ran to inform the host. The soldier's anguish may be conceived, as pale, breathless, with his ear close to the chink of the door, he stood listening. By degrees the roaring had ceased, and nothing was heard but low growls, accompanied by the stern voice of the Prophet, repeating in harsh, abrupt accents : 'Death ! come here ! Death !'

The night was profoundly dark, and Dagobert did not perceive Goliath, who, crawling carefully along the tiled roof, entered the loft by the attic window.

And now the gate of the court-yard was again opened, and the landlord of the inn appeared, followed by a number of men. Armed with a carbine, he advanced with precaution ; his people carried staves and pitchforks.

'What is the row here?' said he, as he approached Dagobert. 'What a hubbub in my house ! The devil take wild-beast showmen, and negligent fellows who don't know how to tie a horse to the manger ! If your beast is hurt, so much the worse for you ; you should have taken more care of it.'

Instead of replying to these reproaches, the soldier, who still listened atten-tively to what was going on in the shed, made a sign to entreat silence. Suddenly a ferocious roar was heard, followed by a loud scream from the Prophet ; and, almost immediately after, the panther howled piteously.

'You are no doubt the cause of some great accident,' said the frightened host to the soldier ; 'did you not hear that cry ? Morok is, perhaps, dangerously wounded.'

Dagobert was about to answer, when the door opened, and Goliath appeared on the threshold.

'You may enter now,' said he ; 'the danger is over.'

The interior of the menagerie presented a singular spectacle. The Prophet, pale, and scarcely able to conceal his agitation beneath an apparent air of calmness, was kneeling some paces from the cage of the panther, in the attitude of one absorbed in himself ; the motion of his lips indicating that he was praying. At sight of the host and the people of the inn, he rose, and said in a solemn voice : ' I thank thee, my Preserver, that I have been able to conquer, by the strength which Thou hast given me.'

Then, folding his arms, with haughty brow and imperious glance, he seemed to enjoy the triumph he had achieved over Death, who, stretched on the bottom of her den, continued to utter plaintive howlings. The spectators of this scene, ignorant that the pelisse of the brute-tamer covered a complete suit of armour, and attributing the cries of the panther solely to fear, were struck with astonishment and admiration at the intrepidity and almost supernatural power of this man. A few steps behind him stood Goliath, leaning upon the ashen pikestaff. Finally, not far from the cage, in the midst of a pool of blood, lay the dead body of Jovial.

At sight of the blood-stained and torn remains, Dagobert stood motionless, and his rough countenance assumed an expression of the deepest grief : then, throwing himself on his knees, he lifted the head of Jovial ; and when he saw those dull, glassy, and half-closed eyes, once so bright and intelligent, as they turned towards a much-loved master, the soldier could not suppress an exclamation of bitter anguish. Forgetting his anger, forgetting the deplorable consequences of this accident, so fatal to the interests of the two maidens, who would thus be prevented from continuing their journey—he thought only of the horrible death of his poor old horse, the ancient companion of his fatigues and wars, the faithful animal, twice wounded like himself, and from whom for so many years he had never been separated. This poignant emotion was so cruelly, so affectingly visible in the soldier's countenance, that the landlord and his people felt themselves for a moment touched with pity, as they gazed on the tall veteran kneeling beside his dead horse.

But, when following the course of his regrets, he thought how Jovial had also been the companion of his exile, how the mother of the orphans had formerly (like her daughters) undertaken a toilsome journey with the aid of this unfortunate animal, the fatal consequences of his loss presented themselves on a sudden to his mind. Then, fury succeeding to grief, he rose, with anger flashing from his eyes, and threw himself on the Prophet with one hand he seized him by the throat, and with the other administered five or six heavy blows, which fell harmlessly on the coat of mail.

' Rascal ! you shall answer to me for my horse's death !' said the soldier, as he continued his correction. Morok, light and sinewy could not struggle with advantage against Dagobert, who, aided by his tall stature, still displayed extraordinary vigour. It needed the intervention of Goliath and the landlord to rescue the Prophet from the hands of the old grenadier. After some moments, they succeeded in separating the two champions Morok was white with rage. It needed new efforts to prevent his seizing the pike to attack Dagobert.

' It is abominable !' cried the host, addressing the soldier, who pressed his clenched fists in despair against his bald forehead. 'You expose this good man to be devoured by his beasts, and then you wish to beat him into the bargain. Is this fitting conduct for a greybeard ? Shall we have to fetch the police ? You showed yourself more reasonable in the early part of the evening.'

These words recalled the soldier to himself. He regretted his impetuosity the more, as the fact of his being a stranger might augment the difficulty of his position. It was necessary above all to obtain the price of his horse, so as to be enabled to continue his journey, the success of which might be compromised by a single day's delay. With a violent effort, therefore, he succeeded in restraining his wrath.

' You are right—I was too hasty,' said he to the host, in an agitated voice, which he tried to make as calm as possible. " I had not the same patience as before. But ought not this man to be responsible for the loss of my horse ? I make you judge in the matter.'

'Well then, as judge, I am not of your opinion. All this has been your own fault. You tied up your horse badly, and he strayed by chance into this shed, of which no doubt the door was half-open,' said the host, evidently taking part with the brute-tamer.

'It was just as you say,' answered Goliath. 'I can remember it. I left the door ajar, that the beasts might have some air in the night. The cages were well shut, and there was no danger.'

'Very true,' said one of the standers-by.

'It was only the sight of the horse,' added another, 'that made the panther furious, so as to break out of its cage.'

'It is the Prophet who has the most right to complain,' observed a third.

'No matter what this or that person says,' returned Dagobert, whose patience was beginning to fail him, 'I say, that I must have either money or a horse on the instant—yes, on the instant—for I wish to quit this unlucky house.'

'And I say, it is you that must indemnify me,' cried Morok, who had kept this stage trick for the last, and who now exhibited his left hand all bloody, having hitherto concealed it beneath the sleeve of his pelisse. 'I shall perhaps be disabled for life,' he added ; 'see what a wound the panther has made here !'

Without having the serious character that the Prophet ascribed to it, the wound was a pretty deep one. This last argument gained for him the general sympathy. Reckoning no doubt upon this incident, to secure the winning of a cause that he now regarded as his own, the host said to the hostler : 'There is only one way to make a finish. It is to call up the burgomaster, and beg him to step here. He will decide who is right or wrong.'

'I was just going to propose it to you,' said the soldier; 'for, after all, I cannot take the law into my own hands.'

'Fritz, run to the burgomaster's !'—and the hostler started in all haste. His master, fearing to be compromised by the examination of the soldier, whose papers he had neglected to ask for on his arrival, said to him : 'The burgomaster will be in a very bad humour, to be disturbed so late. I have no wish to suffer by it, and I must therefore beg you to go and fetch me your papers, to see if they are in rule. I ought to have made you show them, when you arrived here in the evening.'

'They are upstairs in my knapsack ; you shall have them,' answered the soldier—and turning away his head, and putting his hand before his eyes, as he passed the dead body of Jovial, he went out to rejoin the sisters.

The Prophet followed him with a glance of triumph, and said to himself : 'There he goes !—without horse, without money, without papers. I could not do more—for I was forbidden to do more—I was to act with as much cunning as possible, and preserve appearances. Now every one will think this soldier in the wrong. I can at least answer for it, that he will not continue his journey for some days—since such great interests appear to depend on his arrest, and that of the young girls.'

A quarter of an hour after this reflection of the brute-tamer, Karl, Goliath's comrade, left the hiding-place where his master had concealed him during the evening, and set out for Leipsic, with a letter which Morok had written in haste, and which Karl, on his arrival, was to put immediately into the post.

The address of this letter was as follows :

'A MONSIEUR RODIN, Rue du Milieu-des-Ursins, No. 11, A Paris, France.'

CHAPTER XII.

THE BURGOMASTER.

DAGOBERT'S anxiety increased every moment. Certain that his horse had not entered the shed of its own accord, he attributed the event which had taken place to the spite of the brute-tamer ; but he sought in vain for the motive of this wretch's animosity, and he reflected with dismay, that his cause, however just, would depend on the good or bad humour of a judge dragged from his slumbers, and who might be ready to condemn upon fallacious appearances.

Fully determined to conceal, as long as possible, from the orphans the fresh misfortune which had befallen them, he was proceeding to open the door of their chamber, when he stumbled over Spoilsport—for the dog had run back to his post, after vainly trying to prevent the Prophet from leading away Jovial. ' Luckily the dog has returned ; the poor little things have been well guarded,' said the soldier, as he opened the door. To his great surprise, the room was in utter darkness.

' My children,' cried he, 'why are you without a light?' There was no answer. In terror, he groped his way to the bed, and took the hand of one of the sisters : the hand was cold as ice.

' Rose, my children !' cried he. ' Blanche ! Give me some answer ! you frighten me.' Still the same silence continued ; the hand which he held remained cold and powerless, and yielded passively to his touch.

Just then, the moon emerged from the black clouds that surrounded her, and threw sufficient light into the little room, and upon the bed, which faced the window, for the soldier to see that the two sisters had fainted. The bluish light of the moon added to the paleness of the orphans ; they held each other in a half embrace, and Rose had buried her head on Blanche's bosom.

' They must have fainted through fear,' exclaimed Dagobert, running to fetch his gourd. ' Poor things ! after a day of so much excitement, it is not surprising.' And, moistening the corner of a handkerchief with a few drops of brandy, the soldier knelt beside the bed, gently chafed the temples of the two sisters, and held the linen, wet with the spirituous liquor, to their little pink nostrils.

Still on his knees, and bending his dark, anxious face over the orphans, he waited some moments before again resorting to the only restorative in his power. A slight shiver of Rose gave him renewed hope ; the young girl turned her head on the pillow with a sigh ; then she started, and opened her eyes with an expression of astonishment and alarm ; but, not immediately recognising Dagobert, she exclaimed : ' Oh, sister !' and threw herself into the arms of Blanche.

The latter also was beginning to experience the effect of the soldier's care. The exclamation of Rose completely roused her from her lethargy, and she clung to her sister, again sharing the fright without knowing its cause.

' They've come to—that's the chief point,' said Dagobert, 'now we shall soon get rid of these foolish fears.' Then, softening his voice, he added : 'Well, my children, courage ! you are better. It is I who am here—me, Dagobert !'

The orphans made a hasty movement, and, turning towards the soldier their sweet faces, which were still full of dismay and agitation, they both, by a graceful impulse, extended their arms to him and cried : 'It is you, Dagobert—then we are safe !'

' Yes, my children, it is I,' said the veteran, taking their hands in his, and pressing them joyfully. ' So you have been much frightened during my absence?'

' Oh, frightened to death !'

' If you knew—oh, goodness ! if you knew——'

' But the lamp is extinguished—why is that ?'

' We did not do it.'

' Come—recover yourselves, poor children, and tell me all about it. I have no good opinion of this inn ; but, luckily, we shall soon leave it. It was an ill wind that blew me hither—though, to be sure, there was no other in the village. But what has happened ?'

' You were hardly gone, when the window flew open violently, and the lamp and table fell together with a loud crash.'

'Then our courage failed—we screamed and clasped each other, for we thought we could hear some one moving in the room.'

'And we were so frightened, that we fainted away.'

Unfortunately, persuaded that it was the violence of the wind which had already broken the glass and shaken the window, Dagobert attributed this second accident to the same cause as the first, thinking that he had not properly secured the fastening and that the orphans had been deceived by a false alarm. 'Well, well—it is over now,' said he to them : 'calm yourselves, and don't think of it any more.'

'But why did you leave us so hastily, Dagobert?'

'Yes, now I remember—did we not hear a great noise, sister, and see Dagobert run to the staircase, crying: "My horse! what are they doing to my horse?"'

'It was then Jovial who neighed?'

These questions renewed the anguish of the soldier ; he feared to answer them, and said, with a confused air: 'Yes—Jovial neighed—but it was nothing. By the by, we must have a light here. Do you know where I put my flint and steel last evening? Well, 1 have lost my senses ; it is here in my pocket. Luckily, too, we have a candle, which I am going to light ; I want to look in my knapsack for some papers I require.'

Dagobert struck a few sparks, obtained a light, and saw that the window was indeed open, the table thrown down, and the lamp lying by the side of the knapsack. He shut the window, set the little table on its feet again, placed the knapsack upon it, and began to unbuckle this last in order to take out his portfolio, which had been deposited along with his cross and purse, in a kind of pocket between the outside and the lining. The straps had been readjusted with so much care, that there was no appearance of the knapsack having been disturbed ; but when the soldier plunged his hand into the pocket above-mentioned, he found it empty. Struck with consternation, he grew pale, and retreated a step, crying: 'How is this?—Nothing!'

'What is the matter?' said Blanche. He made her no answer. Motionless, he leaned against the table, with his hand still buried in the pocket, Then, yielding to a vague hope—for so cruel a reality did not appear possible —he hastily emptied the contents of the knapsack on the table—his poor half-worn clothes—his old uniform-coat of the horse-grenadiers of the Imperial Guard, a sacred relic for the soldier—but, turn and return them as he would, he found neither his purse, nor the portfolio that contained his papers, the letters of General Simon, and his cross.

In vain, with that serious childishness which always accompanies a hopeless search, he took the knapsack by the two ends, and shook it vigorously: nothing came out. The orphans looked on with uneasiness, not understanding his silence or his movements, for his back was turned to them. Blanche ventured to say to him in a timid voice : 'What ails you—you don't answer us—What is it you are looking for in your knapsack?'

Still mute, Dagobert searched his own person, turned out all his pockets —nothing!—For the first time in his life, perhaps, his two children, as he called them, had spoken to him without receiving a reply. Blanche and Rose felt the big tears start into their eyes ; thinking that the soldier was angry, they durst not again address him.

'No, no! it is impossible—no!' said the veteran, pressing his hand to his forehead, and seeking in his memory where he might have put those precious objects, the loss of which he could not yet bring himself to believe. A sudden beam of joy flashed from his eyes. He ran to a chair, and took from it the portmanteau of the orphans ; it contained a little linen, two black dresses, and a small box of white wood, in which were a silk handkerchief that had belonged to their mother, two locks of her hair, and a black ribbon she had worn round her neck. The little she possessed had been seized by the Russian government, in pursuance of the confiscation. Dagobert searched and researched every article—peeped into all the corners of the portmanteau —still nothing !

This time, completely worn out, leaning against the table, the strong, energetic man felt himself giving way. His face was burning, yet bathed in a cold sweat ; his knees trembled under him. It is a common saying, that drowning men will catch at straws ; and so it is with the despair that still clings to some shred of hope. Catching at a last chance—absurd, insane, impossible—he turned abruptly towards the orphans, and said to them, without considering the alteration in his voice and features : 'I did not give them to you—to keep for me ?—speak ?'

Instead of answering, Rose and Blanche, terrified at his paleness, and the expression of his countenance, uttered a cry. 'Good heavens ! what is the matter with you ?' murmured Rose.

'Have you got them—yes or no ?' cried in a voice of thunder the unfortunate, distracted man. 'If you have not—I'll take the first knife I meet with, and stick it into my body !'

'Alas ! you are so good : pardon us if we have done anything to afflict you ! You love us so much, you would not do us any harm.' The orphans began to weep, as they stretched forth their hands in supplication towards the soldier.

He looked at them with haggard eye, without even seeing them ; till, as the delusion passed away, the reality presented itself to his mind with all its terrible consequences. Then he clasped his hands together, fell on his knees before the bed of the orphans, leaned his forehead upon it, and amid his convulsive sobs—for the man of iron sobbed like a child—these broken words were audible : 'Forgive me—forgive !—I do not know how it can be ! —Oh ! what a misfortune—what a misfortune !— Forgive me !'

At this outbreak of grief, the cause of which they understood not, but which in such a man was heart-rending, the two sisters wound their arms about his old grey head, and exclaimed amid their tears : 'Look at us ! Only tell us what is the matter with you ?—Is it our fault ?'

At this instant, the noise of footsteps resounded from the stairs, mingled with the barking of Spoilsport, who had remained outside the door. The nearer the steps approached, the more furious became the barking ; it was no doubt accompanied with hostile demonstrations, for the host was heard to cry out in an angry tone : 'Hollo ! you there ! Call off your dog, or speak to him. It is Mr. Burgomaster who is coming up.'

'Dagobert—do you hear ?—it is the burgomaster,' said Rose.

'They are coming upstairs—a number of people,' resumed Blanche.

The word *burgomaster* recalled whatever had happened to the mind of Dagobert, and completed, so to express it, the picture of his terrible position. His horse was dead, he had neither papers nor money, and a day, a single day's detention, might defeat the last hope of the sisters, and render useless this long and toilsome journey.

Men of strong minds, and the veteran was of the number, prefer great perils, positions of danger accurately defined, to the vague anxieties which precede a settled misfortune. Guided by his good sense and admirable devotion, Dagobert understood at once, that his only resource was now in the justice of the burgomaster, and that all his efforts should tend to conciliate the favour of that magistrate. He therefore dried his eyes with the sheet, rose from the ground, erect, calm, and resolute, and said to the orphans : 'Fear nothing, my children ; it is our deliverer who is at hand.'

'Will you call off your dog or no?' cried the host, still detained on the stairs by Spoilsport, who, as a vigilant sentinel, continued to dispute the passage. 'Is the animal mad, I say? Why don't you tie him up? Have you not caused trouble enough in my house? I tell you, that Mr. Burgomaster is waiting to examine you in your turn, for he has finished with Morok.'

Dagobert drew his fingers through his grey locks and across his moustache, clasped the collar of his top-coat, and brushed the sleeves with his hand, in order to give himself the best appearance possible ; for he felt that the fate of the orphans must depend on his interview with the magistrate. It was not without a violent beating of the heart, that he laid his hand upon the door-knob, saying to the young girls, who were growing more and more frightened by such a succession of events : 'Hide yourselves in your bed, my children ; if any one must enter, it shall be the burgomaster alone.'

Thereupon, opening the door, the soldier stepped out on the landing-place, and said : 'Down, Spoilsport !— Here !'

The dog obeyed, but with manifest repugnance. His master had to speak twice, before he would abstain from all hostile movements towards the host. This latter, with a lantern in one hand and his cap in the other, respectfully preceded the burgomaster, whose magisterial proportions were lost in the half shadows of the staircase. Behind the judge, and a few steps lower, the inquisitive faces of the people belonging to the inn, were dimly visible by the light of another lantern.

Dagobert, having turned the dog into the room, shut the door after him, and advanced two steps on the landing-place, which was sufficiently spacious to hold several persons, and had in one corner a wooden bench with a back to it. The burgomaster, as he ascended the last stair, was surprised to see Dagobert close the door of the chamber, as though he wished to forbid his entrance. 'Why do you shut that door?' asked he in an abrupt tone.

'First, because two girls, whom I have the charge of, are in bed in that room ; secondly, because your examination would alarm them,' replied Dagobert. 'Sit down upon this bench, Mr. Burgomaster, and examine me here ; it will not make any difference, I should think.'

'And by what right,' asked the judge, with a displeased air, 'do you pretend to dictate to me the place of your examination?'

'Oh, I have no such pretension, Mr. Burgomaster !' said the soldier hastily, fearing above all things to prejudice the judge against him : 'only, as the girls are in bed, and already much frightened, it would be a proof of your good heart to examine me where I am.'

'Humph !' said the magistrate, with ill-humour : 'a pretty state of things, truly !—It was much worth while to disturb me in the middle of the night. But, come, so be it ; I will examine you here.' Then, turning to the landlord, he added : 'Put your lantern upon this bench, and leave us.'

The innkeeper obeyed, and went down, followed by his people, as dissatisfied as they were at being excluded from the examination. The veteran was left alone with the magistrate.

CHAPTER XIII.

THE JUDGMENT.

THE worthy burgomaster of Mockern wore a cloth cap, and was enveloped in a cloak. He sat down heavily on the bench. He was a corpulent man, about sixty, with an arrogant, morose countenance ; and he frequently rubbed, with his red, fat fist, eyes that were still swollen and blood-shot, from his having been suddenly roused from sleep.

Dagobert stood bare-headed before him, with a submissive, respectful air, holding his old foraging-cap in his hands, and trying to read in the sullen physiognomy of his judge what chance there might be to interest him in his favour—that is, in favour of the orphans.

In this critical juncture, the poor soldier summoned to his aid all his presence of mind, reason, eloquence and resolution. He, who had twenty times braved death with the utmost coolness—who, calm and serene, because sincere and tried, had never quailed before the eagle-glance of the Emperor, his hero and idol—now felt himself disconcerted and trembling before the ill-humoured face of a village burgomaster. Even so, a few hours before, he had submitted, impassive and resigned, to the insults of the Prophet—that he might not compromise the sacred mission with which a dying mother had entrusted him—thus showing to what a height of heroic abnegation it is possible for a simple and honest heart to attain.

' What have you to say in your justification ? Come, be quick !' said the judge roughly, with a yawn of impatience.

' I have not got to justify myself—I have to make a complaint, Mr. Burgomaster,' replied Dagobert in a firm voice.

' Do you think you are to teach me in what terms I am to put my questions ?' exclaimed the magistrate, in so sharp a tone that the soldier reproached himself with having begun the interview so badly. Wishing to pacify his judge, he made haste to answer with submission : 'Pardon me, Mr. Burgomaster, I have ill-explained my meaning. I only wished to say that I was not wrong in this affair.'

' The Prophet says the contrary.'

' The *Prophet ?*' repeated the soldier, with an air of doubt.

' The Prophet is a pious and honest man,' resumed the judge, 'incapable of falsehood.'

' I cannot say anything upon that subject ; but you are too just, and have too good a heart, Mr. Burgomaster, to condemn without hearing me. It is not a man like you that would do an injustice ; oh, one can see that at a glance !'

In resigning himself thus to play the part of a courtier, Dagobert softened as much as possible his gruff voice, and strove to give to his austere countenance a smiling, agreeable, and flattering expression. 'A man like you,' he added, with redoubled suavity of manner, 'a respectable judge like you, never shuts his ear to one side or the other.'

' Ears are not in question, but eyes ; and, though mine smart as if I had rubbed them with nettles, I have *seen* the hand of the brute-tamer with a frightful wound on it.'

' Yes, Mr. Burgomaster, it is very true ; but consider, if he had shut his cages and his door, all this would not have happened '

" Not so : it is your fault. You should have fastened your horse securely to the manger.'

' You are right, Mr. Burgomaster, certainly, you are right,' said the soldier, in a still more affable and conciliating voice. ' It is not for a poor devil like me to contradict you. But supposing my horse was let loose out of pure malice, in order that he might stray into the menagerie—you will then acknowledge that it was *not* my fault. That is, you will acknowledge it if you think fit,' hastily added the soldier ; ' I have no right to dictate to you in anything.'

' And why the devil should any one do you this ill turn ?'

' I do not know, Mr. Burgomaster—but——'

' You do not know—well, nor I either,' said the Burgomaster impatiently. ' Zounds ! what a many words about the carcass of an old horse !'

The countenance of the soldier, losing on a sudden its expression of forced suavity, became once more severe ; he answered in a grave voice, full of emotion : 'My horse is dead—he is no more than a carcass—that is true ; but an hour ago, though very old, he was full of life and intelligence. He neighed joyously at my voice—and, every evening, he licked the hands of the two poor children, whom he had carried all the day—as formerly he had carried their mother. Now he will never carry any one again ; they will throw him to the dogs, and all will be finished. You need not have reminded me harshly of it, Mr. Burgomaster—for I loved my horse !'

By these words, pronounced with noble and touching simplicity, the burgomaster was moved in spite of himself, and regretted his hasty speech. ' It is natural that you should be sorry for your horse,' said he, in a less impatient tone ; ' but what is to be done ?—It is a misfortune.'

' A misfortune ?—Yes, Mr. Burgomaster, a very great misfortune. The girls, who accompany me, were too weak to undertake a long journey on foot, too poor to travel in a carriage—and yet we have to arrive in Paris before the month of February. When their mother died, I promised her to take them to France, for these children have only me to take care of them.'

' You are then their——'

' I am their faithful servant, Mr. Burgomaster ; and now that my horse has been killed, what can I do for them ? Come, you are good, you have perhaps children of your own : if, one day, they should find themselves in the position of my two little orphans—with no wealth, no resources in the world, but an old soldier who loves them, and an old horse to carry them along—if, after being very unfortunate from their birth—yes, very unfortunate, for my orphans are the daughters of exiles—they should see happiness before them at the end of a journey, and then, by the death of their horse, that journey become impossible—tell me, Mr. Burgomaster, if this would not touch your heart ? Would you not find, as I do, that the loss of my horse is irreparable ?'

' Certainly,' answered the burgomaster, who was not ill-natured at bottom, and who could not help taking part in Dagobert's emotion ; ' I now understand the importance of the loss you have suffered. And then your orphans interest me : how old are they ?'

' Fifteen years and two months. They are twins.'

' Fifteen years and two months—that is about the age of my Frederica.'

' You have a young lady of that age,' cried Dagobert, once more awaking to hope ; ' ah, Mr. Burgomaster ! I am really no longer uneasy about my poor children. You will do us justice.'

' To do justice is my duty. After all, in this affair, the faults are about equal on both sides. You tied up your horse badly, and the brute-tamer left his door often. He says : " I am wounded in the hand." You answer : " My horse has been killed—and, for a thousand reasons, the loss of my horse is irreparable." '

' You make me speak better than I could ever speak on my own account, Mr. Burgomaster,' said the soldier, with a humble, insinuating smile ; ' but 'tis what I meant to express—and, as you say yourself, Mr. Burgomaster, my horse being my whole fortune, it is only fair——'

' Exactly so,' resumed the magistrate, interrupting the soldier ; ' your reasons are excellent. The Prophet—who is a good and pious man withal—has related the facts to me in his own way ; and then, you see, he is an old acquaintance. We are nearly all zealous Catholics here, and he sells to our wives such cheap and edifying little books, with chaplets and amulets of the best manufacture, at less than the prime cost. All this, you will say, has nothing to do with the affair ; and you will be right in saying so : still I must needs confess that I came here with the intention——'

'Of deciding against me, eh, Mr. Burgomaster?' said Dagobert, gaining more and more confidence. 'You see, you were not quite awake, and your justice had only one eye open.'

'Really, master soldier,' answered the judge, with good humour, 'it is not unlikely; for I did not conceal from Morok that I gave it in his favour. Then he said to me (very generously, by the way): "Since you condemn my adversary, I will not aggravate his position by telling you certain things"——'

'What! against me?'

'Apparently so; but, like a generous enemy, when I told him that I should most likely condemn you to pay him damages, he said no more about it. For I will not hide from you that, before I heard your reasons, I fully intended that you should make compensation for the Prophet's wound.'

'See, Mr. Burgomaster, how the most just and able persons are subject to be deceived,' said Dagobert, becoming once more the courtier; then, trying to assume a prodigiously knowing look, he added: 'But such persons find out the truth at last, and are not to be made dupes of, whatever *prophets* may say.'

This poor attempt at a jest—the first and only one, perhaps, that Dagobert had ever been guilty of—will show the extremity to which he was reduced, and the desperate efforts of all kinds he was making to conciliate the good graces of his judge. The burgomaster did not at first see the pleasantry; he was only led to perceive it by the self-satisfied mien of Dagobert, and by his inquiring glance, which seemed to say: 'Is it not good, eh?—I am astonished at it myself.'

The magistrate began, therefore, to smile with a patronising air, and, nodding his head, replied in the same jocular spirit: 'Ha! ha! ha! you are right; the Prophet is out in his prophesy. You shall not pay him any damages. The faults on both sides are equal, and the injuries balance one another. He has been wounded, your horse has been killed; so you may cry quits, and have done with it.'

'But how much, then, do you think he owes me?' asked the soldier, with singular simplicity.

'How much?'

'Yes, Mr. Burgomaster, what sum will he have to pay me? Yes—but, before you decide, I must tell you one thing, Mr. Burgomaster. I think I shall be entitled to spend only part of the money in buying a horse. I am sure, that, in the environs of Leipsic, I could get a beast very cheap from some of the peasants; and, between ourselves, I will own to you, that, if I could meet with only a nice little donkey—I should not be over particular—I should even like it just as well: for, after my poor Jovial, the company of another horse would be painful to me. I must also tell you——'

'Hey-day!' cried the Burgomaster, interrupting Dagobert, 'of what money, what donkey, and what other horse are you talking? I tell you, that you owe nothing to the Prophet, and that he owes you nothing!'

'He owes me nothing?'

'You are very dull of comprehension, my good man. I repeat, that, if the Prophet's animals have killed your horse, the Prophet himself has been badly wounded; so you may cry quits. In other words, you owe him nothing, and he owes you nothing. Now do you understand?'

Dagobert, confounded, remained for some moments without answering, whilst he looked at the burgomaster with an expression of deep anguish. He saw that his judgment would again destroy all his hopes.

'But, Mr. Burgomaster,' resumed he, in an agitated voice, 'you are too just not to pay attention to one thing: the wound of the brute-tamer does not prevent him from continuing his trade; the death of my horse prevents me from continuing my journey; therefore, he ought to indemnify me.'

The judge considered he had already done a good deal for Dagobert, in not making him responsible for the wound of the Prophet, who, as we have already said, exercised a certain influence over the Catholics of the country by the sale of his devotional treasures, and also from its being known that he was supported by some persons of eminence. The soldier's pertinacity, therefore, offended the magistrate, who, reassuming his lofty air, replied, in a chilling tone : ' You will make me repent my impartiality. How is this? instead of thanking me, you ask for more.'

' But, Mr. Burgomaster, I ask only for what is just. I wish I were wounded in the hand, like the Prophet, so that I could but continue my journey.'

' We are not talking of what you wish. I have pronounced sentence—there is no more to say.'

' But, Mr. Burgomaster——'

' Enough, enough. Let us go to the next subject. Your papers?'

' Yes, we will speak about my papers ; but I beg of you, Mr. Burgomaster, to have pity on those two children. Let us have the means to continue our journey, and——'

' I have done all I could for you—perhaps, more than I ought. Once again, your papers !'

' I must first explain to you——'

' No explanation—your papers !—Or would you like me to have you arrested as a vagabond?'

' Me—arrested !'

' I tell you that, if you refuse to show me your papers, it will be as if you had none. Now, those people who have no papers we take into custody till the authorities can dispose of them. Let me see your papers, and make haste !—I am in a hurry to get home.'

Dagobert's position was the more distressing, as for a moment he had indulged in sanguine hope. The last blow was now added to all the veteran had suffered since the commencement of this scene, which was a cruel as well as dangerous trial, for a man of his character—upright, but obstinate—faithful, but rough and absolute—a man who, for a long time a soldier, and a victorious one, had acquired a certain despotic manner of treating with civilians.

At these words—' your papers,' Dagobert became very pale ; but he tried to conceal his anguish beneath an air of assurance, which he thought best calculated to gain the magistrate's good opinion. ' I will tell you all about it, Mr. Burgomaster,' said he. ' Nothing can be clearer. Such a thing might happen to any one. I do not look like a beggar and a vagabond, do I ? And yet—you will understand, that an honest man who travels with two young girls——'

' No more words ! Your papers !'

At this juncture two powerful auxiliaries arrived to the soldier's aid. The orphans, growing more and more uneasy, and hearing Dagobert still talking upon the landing-place, had risen and dressed themselves ; so that just at the instant, when the magistrate said in a rough voice—' No more words ! Your papers !'—Rose and Blanche, holding each other by the hand, came forth from the chamber.

At sight of those charming faces, which their poor mourning vestments only rendered more interesting, the burgomaster rose from his seat, struck with surprise and admiration. By a spontaneous movement, each sister took a hand of Dagobert, and pressed close to him, whilst they regarded the magistrate with looks of mingled anxiety and candour.

It was so touching a picture, this of the old soldier presenting as it were to his judge the graceful children, with countenances full of innocence and beauty, that the burgomaster, by a sudden reaction, found himself once more disposed to sentiments of pity. Dagobert perceived it; and, still holding the orphans by the hand, he advanced towards him, and said in a feeling voice: 'Look at these poor children, Mr. Burgomaster! Could I show you a better passport?' And, overcome by so many painful sensations—restrained, yet following each other in quick succession—Dagobert felt, in spite of himself, that the tears were starting to his eyes.

Though naturally rough, and rendered still more testy by the interruption of his sleep, the burgomaster was not quite deficient in sense or feeling. He perceived at once, that a man thus accompanied, ought not to inspire any great distrust. 'Poor dear children!' said he, as he examined them with growing interest; 'orphans so young, and they come from far——.'

'From the heart of Siberia, Mr. Burgomaster, where their mother was an exile before their birth. It is now more than five months that we have been travelling on by short stages—hard enough, you will say, for children of their age. It is for them that I ask your favour and support—for them, against whom everything seems to combine to-day—for, only just now, when I went to look for my papers, I could not find in my knapsack the portfolio in which they were, along with my purse and cross—for you must know, Mr. Burgomaster—pardon me, if I say it—'tis not from vain glory—but I was decorated by the hand of the Emperor; and a man whom he decorated with his own hand, you see, could not be so bad a fellow, though he may have had the misfortune to lose his papers—and his purse. That's what has happened to me, and made me so pressing about the damages.'

'How and where did you suffer this loss?'

'I do not know, Mr. Burgomaster; I am sure that the evening before last, at bed-time, I took a little money out of the purse, and saw the portfolio in its place; yesterday I had small change sufficient, and did not undo the knapsack.'

'And where then has the knapsack been kept?'

'In the room occupied by the children: but this night——'

Dagobert was here interrupted by the tread of some one mounting the stairs: it was the Prophet. Concealed in the shadow of the staircase, he had listened to this conversation, and he dreaded lest the weakness of the burgomaster should mar the complete success of his projects.

CHAPTER XIV.

THE DECISION.

MOROK, who wore his left arm in a sling, having slowly ascended the staircase, saluted the burgomaster respectfully. At sight of the repulsive countenance of the lion-tamer, Rose and Blanche, affrighted, drew back a step nearer to the soldier. The brow of the latter grew dark, for he felt his blood boil against Morok, the cause of all his difficulties—though he was yet ignorant that Goliah, at the instigation of the Prophet, had stolen his portfolio and papers.

'What did you want, Morok?' said the burgomaster, with an air half friendly and half displeased. 'I told the landlord that I did not wish to be interrupted.'

'I have come to render you a service, Mr. Burgomaster.'

'A service?'

'Yes, a great service; or I should not have ventured to disturb you. My conscience reproaches me.'

'Your conscience?'

'Yes, Mr. Burgomaster, it reproaches me for not having told you all that I had to tell about this man ; a false pity led me astray.'

'Well, but what have you to tell ?'

Morok approached the judge, and spoke to him for some time in a low voice. At first apparently much astonished, the burgomaster became by degrees deeply attentive and anxious ; every now and then he allowed some exclamation of surprise or doubt to escape him, whilst he glanced covertly at the group formed by Dagobert and the two young girls. By the expression of his countenance, which grew every moment more unquiet, severe, and searching, it was easy to perceive that the interest which the magistrate had felt for the orphans and for the soldier, was gradually changed, by the secret communications of the Prophet, into a sentiment of distrust and hostility.

Dagobert saw this sudden revolution, and his fears, which had been appeased for an instant, returned with redoubled force; Rose and Blanche, confused, and not understanding the object of this mute scene, looked at the soldier with increased perplexity.

'The devil !' said the burgomaster, rising abruptly ; 'all this never occurred to me. What could I have been thinking of ?—But you see, Morok, when one is roused up in the middle of the night, one has not always presence of mind. You said well : it is a great service you came to render me.'

'I assert nothing positively, but——'

'No matter ; 'tis a thousand to one that you are right.'

'It is only a suspicion founded upon divers circumstances ; but even a suspicion——'

'May give you scent of the truth. And here was I, going like a gull into the snare !—Once more, what could I have been thinking of ?'

'It is so difficult to be on guard against certain appearances.'

'You need not tell me so, my dear Morok, you need not tell me so.'

During this mysterious conversation, Dagobert was on thorns ; he saw vaguely that a violent storm was about to burst. He thought only of how he should still keep his anger within bounds.

Morok again approached the judge, and glancing at the orphans, recommenced speaking in a low voice. 'Oh !' cried the burgomaster, with indignation, 'you go too far now.'

'I affirm nothing,' said Morok, hastily ; 'it is a mere supposition founded on——' and he again brought his lips close to the ear of the judge.

'After all, why not ?' resumed the magistrate, lifting up his hands ; 'such people are capable of anything. He says that he brings them from the heart of Siberia : why may not all this prove to be a tissue of impudent falsehoods ?—But I am not to be made a dupe twice,' cried the burgomaster, in an angry tone, for, like all persons of a weak and shifting character, he was without pity for those whom he thought capable of having beguiled his compassion.

'Do not be in a hurry to decide—don't give to my words more weight than they deserve,' resumed Morok with a hypocritical affectation of humility. 'I am unhappily placed in so false a position with regard to this man'— pointing to Dagobert—'that I might be thought to have acted from private resentment for the injury he has done me ; perhaps I may so act without knowing it, while I fancy that I am only influenced by love of justice, horror of falsehood, and respect for our holy religion. Well—who lives long enough will know—and may heaven forgive me if I am deceived !—In any case, the law will pronounce upon it ; and if they should prove innocent, they will be released in a month or two.'

'And, for that reason, I need not hesitate. It is a mere measure of precaution ; they will not die of it. Besides, the more I think of it, the more it seems probable. Yes, this man is doubtless a French spy or agitator, especially when I compare these suspicions with the late demonstration of the students at Frankfort.'

'And, upon that theory, nothing is better fitted to excite and stir up those hot-headed youths than——' He glanced significantly at the two sisters ; then, after a pause, he added with a sigh, 'Satan does not care by what means he works out his ends !'

'Certainly, it would be odious, but well-devised.'

'And then, Mr. Burgomaster, look at him attentively : you will see that this man has a dangerous face. You will see——'

In continuing thus to speak in a low tone, Morok had evidently pointed to Dagobert. The latter, notwithstanding his self-command, felt that the restraint he had imposed upon himself, since his arrival at this unlucky inn, and above all since the commencement of the conversation between Morok and the burgomaster, was becoming no longer bearable ; besides, he saw clearly that all his efforts to conciliate the favour of the judge were rendered completely null by the fatal influence of the brute-tamer ; so, losing patience, he advanced towards him with his arms folded on his breast, and said to him in a subdued voice : 'Was it of me that you were whispering to Mr. Burgomaster ?'

'Yes,' said Morok, looking fixedly at him.

'Why did you not speak out loud ?' Having said this, the almost convulsive movement of his thick moustache, as he stood looking Morok full in the face, gave evidence of a severe internal conflict. Seeing that his adversary preserved a contemptuous silence, he repeated in a sterner voice : 'I ask you, why you did not speak out loud to Mr. Burgomaster, when you were talking of me ?'

'Because there are some things so shameful, that one would blush to utter them aloud,' answered Morok, insolently.

Till then Dagobert had kept his arms folded ; he now extended them violently, clenching his fists. This sudden movement was so expressive that the two sisters uttered a cry of terror, and drew closer to him.

'Harkye, Mr. Burgomaster !' said the soldier, grinding his teeth with rage ; 'bid that man go down, or I will not answer for myself !'

'What !' said the burgomaster, haughtily ; 'do you dare to give orders to me ?'

'I tell you to make that man go down,' resumed Dagobert, quite beside himself, 'or there will be mischief !'

'Dagobert !—good heaven !—be calm,' cried the children, grasping his hands.

'It becomes you, certainly—miserable vagabond that you are—not to say worse,' returned the burgomaster, in a rage : 'it becomes you to give orders to me !—Oh ! you think to impose upon me, by telling me you have lost your papers !—It will not serve your turn, for which you carry about with you these two girls, who, in spite of their innocent looks, are perhaps after all——'

'Wretch !' cried Dagobert, with so terrible a voice and gesture that the official did not dare to finish. Taking the children by the arm before they could speak a word, the soldier pushed them back into the chamber ; then, locking the door, and putting the key into his pocket, he returned precipitately towards the burgomaster, who, frightened at the menacing air and attitude of the veteran, retreated a couple of steps, and held by one hand to the rail of the staircase.

'Listen to me!' said the soldier, seizing the judge by the arm. 'Just now, that scoundrel insulted me—I bore with it—for it only concerned myself. I have heard patiently all your idle talk, because you seemed for a moment to interest yourself in those poor children. But since you have neither soul, nor pity, nor justice—I tell you that, burgomaster though you are—I will spurn you as I would spurn that dog,' pointing again to the Prophet, 'if you have the misfortune to mention those two young girls, in any other way than you would speak of your own child!—Now, do you mark me?'

'What!—you dare to say,' cried the burgomaster, stammering with rage, that if I happen to mention two adventuresses——'

'Hats off!—when you speak of the daughters of the Duke of Ligny,' cried the soldier, snatching the cap of the burgomaster and flinging it on the ground. On this act of aggression, Morok could not restrain his joy. Exasperated and losing all hope, Dagobert had at length yielded to the violence of his anger, after struggling so painfully against it for some hours.

When the burgomaster saw his cap at his feet, he looked at the brute-tamer with an air of stupefaction, as if he hesitated to believe so great an enormity. Dagobert, regretting his violence, and feeling that no means of conciliation now remained, threw a rapid glance around him, and, retreating several paces, gained the topmost steps of the staircase. The burgomaster stood near the bench, in a corner of the landing-place, whilst Morok, with his arm in the sling, to give the more serious appearance to his wound, was close beside him. 'So!' cried the magistrate, deceived by the backward movement of Dagobert, 'you think to escape, after daring to lift hand against me!—Old villain!'

'Forgive me, Mr. Burgomaster! It was a burst of rashness that I was not able to control. I am sorry for it,' said Dagobert, in a repentant voice, and hanging his head humbly.

'No pity for thee, rascal! You would begin again to smooth me over with your coaxing ways, but I have penetrated your secret designs. You are not what you appear to be, and there is perhaps an affair of state at the bottom of all this,' added the magistrate, in a very diplomatic tone. 'All means are alike to those who wish to set Europe in flames.'

'I am only a poor devil, Mr. Burgomaster; you, that have a good heart, will show me some mercy.'

'What! when you have pulled off my cap?'

'And you,' added the soldier, turning towards Morok, 'you, that have been the cause of all this—have some pity upon me—do not bear malice!—You, a holy man, speak a word in my favour to Mr. Burgomaster.'

'I have spoken to him what I was bound to speak,' answered the Prophet ironically.

'Oho! you can look foolish enough now, you old vagabond! Did you think to impose on me with lamentations?' resumed the burgomaster, advancing towards Dagobert. 'Thanks be, I am no longer your dupe!—You shall see that we have good dungeons at Leipsic for French agitators and female vagrants, for your damsels are no better than you are. Come,' added he, puffing out his cheeks with an important air, 'go down before me—and as for you, Morok——'

The burgomaster was unable to finish. For some minutes Dagobert had only sought to gain time, and had cast many a side-glance at a half-open door on the landing-place, just opposite to the chamber occupied by the orphans : finding the moment favourable, he now rushed quick as lightning on the burgomaster, seized him by the throat, and dashed him with such violence against the door in question, that the magistrate, stupefied by this sudden attack, and unable to speak a word or utter a cry, rolled over to the further end of the room, which was completely dark. Then, turning towards Morok, who, with his arm encumbered by the sling, made a rush for the staircase, the soldier caught him by his long, streaming hair, pulled him back, clasped him with hands of iron, clapped his hand over his mouth to stifle his outcries, and notwithstanding his desperate resistance, dragged him into the chamber, on the floor of which the burgomaster lay bruised and stunned.

Having double-locked the door, and put the key in his pocket, Dagobert descended the stairs at two bounds, and found himself in a passage that opened on the court-yard. The gate of the inn was shut, and there was no possibility of escape on that side. The rain fell in torrents. He could see through the window of a parlour, in which a fire was burning, the host and his people waiting for the decision of the burgomaster. To bolt the door of the passage, and thus intercept all communication with the yard, was for the soldier the affair of an instant, and he hastened upstairs again to rejoin the orphans.

Morok, recovering from his surprise, was calling for help with all his might ; but, even if the distance had permitted him to be heard, the noise of the wind and rain would have drowned his outcries. Dagobert had about an hour before him, for it would require some time to elapse before the length of his interview with the magistrate would excite astonishment; and, suspicion or fear once awakened, it would be necessary to break open two doors—that which separated the passage from the court-yard, and that of the room in which the burgomaster and the Prophet were confined.

'My children, it is now time to prove that you have a soldier's blood in your veins,' said Dagobert, as he entered abruptly the chamber of the young girls, who were terrified at the racket they had heard for some minutes.

'Good heaven, Dagobert ! what has happened?' cried Blanche.

'What do you wish us to do ?' added Rose.

Without answering, the soldier ran to the bed, tore off the sheets, tied them strongly together, made a knot at one end, passed it over the top of the left half of the casement, and so shut it in. Thus made fast by the size of the knot, which could not slip through, the sheets, floating on the outside, touched the ground. The second half of the window was left open, to afford a passage to the fugitives.

The veteran next took his knapsack, the children's portmanteau, and the reindeer pelisse, and threw them all out of the window, making a sign to Spoilsport to follow, to watch over them. The dog did not hesitate, but disappeared at a single bound. Rose and Blanche looked at Dagobert in amazement, without uttering a word.

'Now, children,' said he to them, ' the doors of the inn are shut, and it is by this way,' pointing to the window, 'that we must pass—if we would not be arrested, put in prison—you in one place, and I in the other—and have our journey altogether knocked on the head.'

'Arrested ! put in prison !' cried Rose.

'Separated from you !' exclaimed Blanche.

'Yes, my poor children !—They have killed Jovial—we must make our escape on foot, and try to reach Leipsic—when you are tired, I will carry you, and, though I have to beg my way, we will go through with it. But a quarter of an hour later, and all will be lost. Come, children, have trust in me—show that the daughters of General Simon are no cowards—and there is yet hope.'

By a sympathetic movement, the sisters joined hands, as though they would meet the danger united. Their sweet faces, pale from the effect of so many painful emotions, were now expressive of simple resolve, founded on the blind faith they reposed in the devotion of the soldier.

'Be satisfied, Dagobert! we'll not be frightened,' said Rose, in a firm voice.

'We will do what must be done,' added Blanche, in a no less resolute tone.

'I was sure of it,' cried Dagobert ; 'good blood is ever thicker than water. Come ! you are light as feathers, the sheet is strong, it is hardly eight feet to the ground, and the pup is waiting for you.'

'It is for me to go first—I am the eldest for to-day,' cried Rose, when she had tenderly embraced Blanche ; and she ran to the window, in order, if there were any danger, to expose herself to it before her sister.

Dagobert easily guessed the cause of this eagerness. 'Dear children !' said he, 'I understand you. But fear nothing for one another—there is no danger. I have myself fastened the sheet. Quick, my little Rose !'

As light as a bird, the young girl mounted the ledge of the window, and, assisted by Dagobert, took hold of the sheet, and slid gently down according to the recommendation of the soldier, who, leaning out his whole body, encouraged her with his voice.

'Don't be afraid, sister !' said she, as soon as she touched the ground ; 'it is very easy to come down this way. And Spoilsport is here, licking my hands.' Blanche did not long keep her waiting ; as courageous as her sister, she descended with the same success.

'Dear little creatures ! what have they done to be so unfortunate ?—Thousand thunders ! there must be a curse upon the family,' cried Dagobert, as, with heavy heart, he saw the pale, sweet face of the young girl disappear amid the gloom of the dark night, which violent squalls of wind and torrents of rain rendered still more dismal.

'Dagobert, we are waiting for you; come quickly !' said the orphans in a low voice, from beneath the window. Thanks to his tall stature, the soldier rather leaped than glided to the ground.

Dagobert and the two young girls had not fled from the inn of the White Falcon more than a quarter of an hour, when a long crash resounded through the house. The door had yielded to the efforts of the burgomaster and Morok, who had made use of a heavy table as a battering-ram. Guided by the light, they ran to the chamber of the orphans, now deserted. Morok saw the sheets floating from the casement, and cried : 'Mr. Burgomaster, they have escaped by the window—they are on foot—in this dark and stormy night, they cannot be far.'

'No doubt, we shall catch them, the miserable tramps !— Oh, I will be revenged ! Quick, Morok ; your honour is concerned as well as mine.'

'My honour ?—Much more is concerned than that, Mr. Burgomaster,' answered the Prophet, in a tone of great irritation. Then, rapidly descending the stairs, he opened the door of the court-yard, and shouted in a voice of thunder : 'Goliath ! unchain the dogs !—and, landlord ! bring us lanterns, torches—arm your people—open the doors !—We must pursue the fugitives; they cannot escape us ; we must have them—*alive or dead !*"

CHAPTER XV.

THE DESPATCHES.

When we read, in the rules of the order of the Jesuits, under the title *De formulâ scribendi* (Institut. 2, 11, p. 125 129), the development of the 8th part of the constitutions, we are appalled by the number of letters, narratives, registers, and writings of all kinds, preserved in the archives of the society.

It is a police infinitely more exact and better informed than has ever been that of any state. Even the government of Venice found itself surpassed by the Jesuits : when it drove them out in 1606, it seized all their papers, and reproached them for *their great and laborious curiosity.* This police, this secret inquisition, carried to such a degree of perfection, may give some idea of the strength of a government, so well-informed, so persevering in its projects, so powerful by its unity, and, as the constitutions have it, by the *union of its members.* It is not hard to understand, what immense force must belong to the heads of this society, and how the general of the Jesuits could say to the Duke de Brissac : ' *From this room, your grace, I govern not only Paris, but China—not only China, but the whole world—and all without any one knowing how it is done.*'

(CONSTITUTION OF THE JESUITS, edited by PAULIN, Paris, 1843.)

MOROK, the lion-tamer, seeing Dagobert deprived of his horse, and stripped of his money and papers, and thinking it was thus out of his power to continue his journey, had, previous to the arrival of the burgomaster, despatched Karl to Leipsic, as the bearer of a letter which he was to put immediately into the post. The address of this letter was as follows : ' A Monsieur Rodin, Rue du Milieu des Ursins, Paris.'

About the middle of this obscure and solitary street, situate below the level of the Quai Napoleon, which it joins not far from the Rue Saint Landry, there stood a house of unpretentious appearance, at the bottom of a dark and narrow court-yard, separated from the street by a low building in front, with arched doorway, and two windows protected by thick iron bars. Nothing could be more simple than the interior of this quiet dwelling, as was sufficiently shown by the furniture of a pretty large room on the ground floor. The walls of this apartment were lined with old grey wainscot ; the tiled floor was painted red, and carefully polished ; curtains of white calico shaded the windows.

A sphere of about four feet in diameter, raised on a pedestal of massive oak, stood at one end of the room, opposite to the fire-place. Upon this globe, which was painted on a large scale, a host of little red crosses appeared scattered over all parts of the world—from the North to the South, from the rising to the setting sun, from the most barbarous countries, from the most distant isles, to the centres of civilisation, to France itself. There was not a single country which did not present some spots marked with these red crosses, evidently indicative of stations, or serving as points of reference.

Before a table of black wood, loaded with papers, and resting against the wall near the chimney, a chair stood empty. Further on, between the two windows, was a large walnut-wood desk, surmounted by shelves full of pasteboard boxes.

At the end of the month of October, 1831, about eight o'clock in the morning, a man sat writing at this desk. This was M. Rodin, the correspondent of Morok, the brute-tamer.

About fifty years of age, he wore an old, shabby, olive greatcoat, with a greasy collar, a snuff-powdered cotton handkerchief for a cravat, and waistcoat and trousers of threadbare black cloth. His feet, buried in loose varnished shoes, rested on a petty piece of green baize upon the red, polished floor. His grey hair lay flat on his temples, and encircled his bald forehead ; his eyebrows were scarcely marked ; his upper eyelid, flabby and overhanging, like the membrane which shades the eyes of reptiles, half concealed his small, sharp, black eye. His thin lips, absolutely colourless, were hardly distinguishable from the wan hue of his lean visage, with its pointed nose and chin ; and this livid mask (deprived as it were of lips) appeared only the more singular, from its maintaining a death-like immobility. Had it not been for the rapid movement of his fingers, as, bending over the desk, he scratched along with his pen, M. Rodin might have been mistaken for a corpse.

By the aid of a *cipher* (or secret alphabet) placed before him, he was copying certain passages from a long sheet full of writing, in a manner quite unintelligible to those who did not possess the key to the system. Whilst the darkness of the day increased the gloom of the large, cold, naked-looking apartment, there was something awful in the chilling aspect of this man, tracing his mysterious characters in the midst of profound silence.

The clock struck eight. The dull sound of the knocker at the outer door was heard, then a bell tinkled twice, several doors opened and shut, and a new personage entered the chamber. On seeing him, M. Rodin rose from the desk, stuck his pen between his teeth, bowed with a deeply submissive air, and sat down again to his work without uttering a word.

The two formed a striking contrast to one another. The new comer, though really older than he seemed, would have passed for thirty-six or thirty-eight years of age at most. His figure was tall and shapely, and few could have encountered the brightness of his large grey eye, brilliant as polished steel. His nose, broad at the commencement, formed a well-cut square at its termination ; his chin was prominent, and the bluish tints of his close-shaved beard were contrasted with the bright carnation of his lips, and the whiteness of his fine teeth. When he took off his hat, to change it for a black velvet cap which he found on the small table, he displayed a quantity of light chestnut hair, not yet silvered by time. He was dressed in a long frock-coat, buttoned up to the neck in military fashion.

The piercing glance and broad forehead of this man revealed a powerful intellect, even as the development of his chest and shoulders announced a vigorous physical organization ; whilst his gentlemanly appearance, the perfection of his gloves and boots, the light perfume which hung about his hair and person, the grace and ease of his least movements, betrayed what is called the man of the world, and left the impression that he had sought or might still seek every kind of success, from the most frivolous to the most serious. This rare combination of strength of mind, strength of body, and extreme elegance of manners, was in this instance rendered still more striking by the circumstance, that whatever there might be of haughtiness or command in the upper part of that energetic countenance, was softened down and tempered by a constant but not uniform smile—for, as occasion served, this smile became either kind or sly, cordial or gay, discreet or prepossessing, and thus augmented the insinuating charm of this man, who, once seen, was never again forgotten. But, in yielding to this involuntary sympathy, the doubt occurred if the influence was for good—or for evil.

M. Rodin, the secretary of the new comer, continued to write.

'Are there any letters from Dunkirk, Rodin ?' inquired his master.

'Post not yet in.'

'Without being positively uneasy as to my mother's health, since she was already convalescent,' resumed the other, ' I shall only be quite reassured by a letter from my excellent friend, the Princess de Saint-Dizier. I shall have good news this morning, I hope.'

'It is to be desired,' said the secretary, as humble and submissive as he was laconic and impassible.

'Certainly it is to be desired,' resumed his master ; 'for one of the brightest days of my life was when the Princess de Saint-Dizier announced to me that this sudden and dangerous illness had yielded to the care and attention with which she surrounds my mother. Had it not been for that, I must have gone down to her instantly, though my presence here is very necessary.'

Then, approaching the desk, he added : ' Is the summary of the foreign correspondence complete ?'

' Here is the analysis.'

' The letters are still sent under envelope to the places named. and are then brought here as I directed?'

' Always.'

' Read to me the notes of this correspondence ; if there are any letters for me to answer, I will tell you.' And Rodin's master began to walk up and down the room, with his hands crossed behind his back, dictating observations of which Rodin took careful note.

The secretary turned to a pretty large pile of papers, and thus began :

' Don Raymond Olivarez acknowledges from Cadiz receipt of letter No. 19 ; he will conform to it, and deny all share in the abduction.'

' Very well ; file it.'

' Count Romanoff, of Riga, finds himself in a position of pecuniary embarrassment.'

' Let Duplessis send him fifty louis ; I formerly served as captain in his regiment, and he has since given us good information.'

' They have received at Philadelphia the last cargo of Histories of France, expurgated for the use of the faithful : they require some more of the same sort.'

' Take note of it, and write to Duplessis. Go on.'

' M. Spindler sends from Namur the secret report on M. Ardouin.'

' To be examined.'

' M. Ardouin sends from the same town the secret report on M. Spindler.'

' To be examined.'

' Doctor Van Ostadt, of the same town, sends a confidential note on the subject of Messrs. Spindler and Ardouin.'

' To be compared. Go on !'

' Count Malipierri, of Turin, announces that the donation of 300,000 francs is signed.'

' Inform Duplessis. What next?'

' Don Stanislaus has just quitted the waters of Baden with Queen Marie Ernestine. He informs us that her majesty will receive with gratitude the promised advices, and will answer them with her own hand.'

' Make a note of it. I will myself write to the queen.'

Whilst Rodin was inscribing a few remarks on the margin of the paper, his master, continuing to walk up and down the room, found himself opposite to the globe marked with little red crosses, and stood contemplating it for a moment with a pensive air.

Rodin continued : ' In consequence of the state of the public mind in certain parts of Italy, where sundry agitators have turned their eyes in the direction of France, Father Orsini writes from Milan, that it would be of importance to distribute profusely in that country, some little book, in which the French would be represented as impious and debauched, rapacious and bloody.'

' The idea is excellent. We might turn to good account the excesses committed by our troops in Italy during the wars of the Republic. You must employ Jacques Dumoulin to write it. He is full of gall, spite, and venom : the pamphlet will be scorching. Besides, I may furnish a few notes ; but you must not pay Dumoulin till after the delivery of the manuscript.'

' That is well understood ; for, if we were to pay him beforehand, he would be drunk for a week in some low den. It was thus we had to pay him twice over for his virulent attack on the pantheistic tendencies of Professor Martin's philosophy.'

' Take note of it—and go on !'

'The merchant announces that the clerk is about to send the banker to give in his accounts. You understand?' added Rodin, after pronouncing these words with a marked emphasis.

'Perfectly,' said the other, with a start; 'they are but the expressions agreed on. What next?'

'But the clerk,' continued the secretary, 'is restrained by a last scruple.'

After a moment's silence, during which the features of Rodin's master worked strongly, he thus resumed: 'They must continue to act on the clerk's mind by silence and solitude; then, let him read once more the list of cases in which regicide is authorised and absolved. Go on!'

'The woman Sydney writes from Dresden, that she waits for instructions. Violent scenes of jealousy on her account have again taken place between the father and son; but neither from these new bursts of mutual hatred, nor from the confidential communications which each has made to her against his rival, has she yet been able to glean the information required. Hitherto, she has avoided giving the preference to one or the other; but, should this situation be prolonged, she fears it may rouse their suspicions. Which ought she then to choose—the father or the son?'

'The son—for jealous resentment will be much more violent and cruel in the old man, and, to revenge himself for the preference bestowed upon his son, he will perhaps tell what they have both such an interest to conceal. The next?'

'Within the last three years, two maid-servants of Ambrosius, whom we placed in that little parish in the mountains of the Valais, have disappeared, without any one knowing what has become of them. A third has just met with the same fate. The Protestants of the country are roused—talk of murder with frightful attendant circumstances——'

'Until there is proof positive and complete of the fact, Ambrosius must be defended against these infamous calumnies, the work of a party that never shrinks from monstrous inventions. Go on!'

'Thompson, of Liverpool, has at length succeeded in procuring for Justin the place of agent or manager to Lord Stewart, a rich Irish Catholic, whose head grows daily weaker.'

'Let the fact be once verified, and Thompson shall have a premium of fifty louis. Make a note of it for Duplessis. Proceed.'

'Frantz Dichstein, of Vienna,' resumed Rodin, 'announces that his father has just died of the cholera, in a little village at some leagues from that city; for the epidemic continues to advance slowly, coming from the north of Russia by way of Poland.'

'It is true,' said Rodin's master, interrupting him; 'may its terrible march be stayed, and France be spared.'

'Frantz Dichstein,' resumed Rodin, 'says that his two brothers are de-termined to contest the donation made by his father, but that he is of an opposite opinion.'

'Consult the two persons that are charged with all matters of litigation. What next?'

'The Cardinal Prince d'Amalfi will conform to the three first points of the proposal: he demands to make a reservation upon the fourth point.'

'No reserve!—Either full and absolute acceptance—or else war—and (mark me well!) war without mercy—on him and his creatures. Go on!'

'Fra Paolo announces that the Prince Boccari, chief of a redoubtable secret society, in despair at seeing his friends accuse him of treachery, in consequence of suspicions excited in their minds by Fra Paolo himself, has committed suicide.'

'Boccari! is it possible?' cried Rodin's master. 'Boccari! the patriot Boccari! so dangerous a person!'

'The patriot Boccari,' repeated the impassible secretary.

'Tell Duplessis to send an order for five-and-twenty louis to Fra Paolo. Make a note of it.'

'Hausman informs us that the French dancer, Albertine Ducornet, is the mistress of the reigning prince : she has the most complete influence over him, and it would be easy through her means to arrive at the end proposed, but that she is herself governed by her lover (condemned in France as a forger), and that she does nothing without consulting him.'

'Let Hausman get hold of this man—if his claims are reasonable, accede to them—and learn if the girl has any relations in Paris.'

'The Duke d'Orbano announces, that the king his master will authorise the new establishment, but on the conditions previously stated.'

'No conditions !—either a frank adhesion or a positive refusal. Let us know our friends from our enemies. The more unfavourable the circumstances, the more we must show firmness, and overbear opposition by confidence in ourselves.'

'The same also announces, that the whole of the corps diplomatique continues to support the claims of the father of that young Protestant girl, who refuses to quit the convent where she has taken refuge, unless it be to marry her lover against her father's will.'

'Ah! the corps diplomatique continues to remonstrate in the father's name?'

'Yes.'

'Then, continue to answer, that the spiritual power has nothing to do with the temporal.'

At this moment, the bell of the outer door again sounded twice. 'See who it is,' said Rodin's master ; and the secretary rose and left the room. The other continued to walk thoughtfully up and down, till, coming near to the huge globe, he stopped short before it.

For some time he contemplated, in profound silence, the innumerable little red crosses, which appeared to cover, as with an immense net, all the countries of the earth. Reflecting doubtless on the invisible action of his power, which seemed to extend over the whole world, the features of this man became animated, his large grey eye sparkled, his nostrils swelled, and his manly countenance assumed an indescribable expression of pride, energy, and daring. With haughty brow and scornful lip, he drew still nearer to the globe, and leaned his strong hand upon the pole.

This powerful pressure, an imperious movement, as of one taking possession, seemed to indicate, that he felt sure of governing this globe, on which he looked down from the height of his tall figure, and on which he rested his hand with so lofty and audacious an air of sovereignty.

But now he no longer smiled. His eye threatened, and his large forehead was clad with a formidable scowl. The artist, who had wished to paint the demon of craft and pride, the infernal genius of insatiable domination, could not have chosen a more suitable model.

When Rodin returned, the face of his master had recovered its ordinary expression. 'It is the postman,' said Rodin, showing the letters which he held in his hand ; 'there is nothing from Dunkirk.'

'Nothing?' cried his master—and his painful emotion formed a strange contrast to his late haughty and implacable expression of countenance—'nothing? no news of my mother?—Thirty-six hours more, then, of anxiety.'

'It seems to me, that, if the princess had bad news to give, she would have written. Probably, the improvement goes on.'

'You are doubtless right, Rodin—but no matter—I am far from easy. If, to-morrow, the news should not be completely satisfactory, I set out for the estate of the princess. Why would my mother pass the autumn in that part of the country? The environs of Dunkirk, do not, I fear, agree with her.'

After a few moment's silence, he added, as he continued to walk : 'Well —these letters—whence are they ?'

Rodin looked at the post-marks, and replied : ' Out of the four, there are three relative to the great and important affair of the medals.'

' Thank heaven !—provided the news be favourable,' cried his master, with an expression of uneasiness, which showed how much importance he attached to this affair.

' One is from Charlestown, and no doubt relative to Gabriel the missionary,' answered Rodin ; 'this other from Batavia, and no doubt concerns the Indian, Djalma. The third is from Leipsic, and will probably confirm that received yesterday, in which the lion-tamer, Morok, informed us, that, in accordance with his orders, and without his being compromised in any way, the daughters of General Simon would not be able to continue their journey.'

At the name of General Simon, a cloud passed over the features of Rodin's master.

CHAPTER XVI.

THE ORDERS.

The principal houses correspond with that in Paris ; they are also in direct communication with the General, who resides at Rome. The correspondence of the Jesuits, so active, various, and organised in so wonderful a manner, has for its object to supply the heads with all the information they can require. Every day, the General receives a host of reports, which serve to check one another. In the central house, at Rome, are immense registers, in which are inscribed the names of all the Jesuits, of their adherents, and of all the considerable persons, whether friends or enemies, with whom they have any connexion. In these registers are reported, without alteration, hatred or passion, the facts relating to the life of each individual. It is the most gigantic biographical collection that has ever been formed. The frailties of a woman, the secret errors of a statesman, are chronicled in this book with the same cold impartiality. Drawn up for the purpose of being useful, these biographies are necessarily exact. When the Jesuits wish to influence an individual, they have but to turn to this book, and they know immediately his life, his character, his parts, his faults, his projects, his family, his friends, his most secret ties. Conceive, what a superior facility of action this immense police-register, which includes the whole world, must give to any one society ! It is not lightly that I speak of these registers ; I have my facts from a person who has *seen* this collection, and who is perfectly well acquainted with the Jesuits. Here then is matter to reflect on for all those families, who admit freely into their houses the members of a community that carries its biographical researches to such a point.

(LIBRI, Member of the Institute. *Letters on the Clergy.*)

WHEN he had conquered the involuntary emotion which the name or remembrance of General Simon had occasioned, Rodin's master said to the secretary : ' Do not yet open the letters from Leipsic, Charlestown, and Batavia; the information they contain will doubtless find its place presently. It will save our going over the same ground twice.'

The secretary looked inquiringly at his master.

The latter continued—' Have you finished the note relating to the medals ?'

' Here it is,' replied the secretary ; ' I was just finishing my interpretation of the cipher.'

' Read it to me, in the order of the facts. You can append to it the news contained in those three letters.'

' True,' said Rodin ; ' in that way the letters will find their right place.'

' I wish to see,' rejoined the other, ' whether this note is clear and fully explanatory ; you did not forget that the person it is intended for ought not to know all ?'

' I bore it in mind, and drew up the paper accordingly.'

' Read,' said the master.

M. Rodin read as follows, slowly and deliberately :

' " A hundred-and-fifty years ago, a French protestant family, foreseeing the speedy revocation of the edict of Nantes, went into voluntary exile, in order to avoid the just and rigorous decrees already issued against the members of the reformed church—those indomitable foes of our holy religion.

' " Some members of this family sought refuge in Holland, and afterwards in the Dutch colonies ; others in Poland, others in Germany ; some in England, and some in America.

' " It is supposed that only seven descendants remain of this family, which underwent strange vicissitudes since ; its present representatives are found in all ranks of society, from the sovereign to the mechanic.

' " These descendants, direct or indirect, are :

' " On the mother's side—

' " Rose and Blanche Simon—minors.

' " General Simon married, at Warsaw, a descendant of the said family.

' " Françoise Hardy, manufacturer at Plessis, near Paris.

' " Prince Djalma, son of Kadja-sing, King of Mondi.

' " Kadja-sing married, in 1802, a descendant of the said family, then settled at Batavia, in the island of Java, a Dutch colony.

' " On the father's side—

' " Jacques Rennepont, surnamed Sleepinbuff, mechanic.

' " Adrienne de Cardoville, daughter of the Count of Rennepont, Duke of Cardoville.

' " Gabriel Rennepont, priest of the foreign missions.

' " All the members of this family possess, or should possess, a bronze medal bearing the following inscriptions :

Victim of L. C. D. J. Pray for me ! —— Paris, February the 13th, 1682.	At Paris, Rue Saint François, No. 3, In a century and a half you will be. February the 13th, 1832. —— Pray for me !

' " These words and dates show that all of them have a great interest to be at Paris on the 13th February, 1832 ; and that, not by proxy, but in person, whether they are minors, married or single.

' " But other persons have an immense interest that none of the descendants of this family be at Paris on the 13th February, except Gabriel Rennepont, priest of the foreign missions.

' " At all hazards, therefore, Gabriel *must* be *the only person* present at the appointment made with the descendants of this family, a century and a half ago.

' " To prevent the other six persons from reaching Paris on the said day, or to render their presence of no effect, much has been already done ; but much remains to be done to ensure the success of this affair, which is considered as the most vital and most important of the age, on account of its probable results." '

' 'Tis but too true,' observed Rodin's master, interrupting him, and shaking his head pensively. 'And, moreover, that the consequences of success are incalculable, and there is no foreseeing what may follow failure. In a word, it almost involves a question of existence or non-existence during several years. To succeed, therefore, "all possible means must be employed. Nothing must be shunned," except, however, that appearances must be skilfully maintained.'

'I have written it,' said Rodin, having added the words his master had just dictated, who then said,

'Continue.'

Rodin read on :

' " To forward or secure the affair in question, it is necessary to give some private and secret particulars respecting the seven persons who represent this family.

' " The truth of these particulars may be relied on. In case of need they might be completed in the most minute degree ; for contradictory information having been given, very lengthened evidence has been obtained. The order in which the names of the persons stand will be observed, and events that have happened up to the present time will only be mentioned.

' " Note, No. 1.

' " Rose and Blanche Simon, twin sisters, about fifteen years of age ; very pretty, so much alike, one might be taken for the other ; mild and timid disposition, but capable of enthusiasm. Brought up in Siberia by their mother, a woman of strong mind and deistical sentiments, they are wholly ignorant of our holy religion.

' " General Simon, separated from his wife before they were born, is not aware, even now, that he has two daughters.

' " It was hoped that their presence in Paris, on the 13th of February, would be prevented, by sending their mother to a place of exile, much more distant than the one first allotted her ; but their mother dying, the Governor of Siberia, who is wholly ours, supposing, by a deplorable mistake, that the measure only affected the wife of General Simon personally, unfortunately allowed the girls to return to France, under the guidance of an old soldier.

' " This man is enterprising, faithful, and determined. He is noted down as *dangerous*.

' " The Simon girls are inoffensive. It is hoped on fair grounds, that they are now detained in the neighbourhood of Leipsic." '

Rodin's master interrupted him, saying :

' Now, read the letter just received from Leipsic ; it may complete the information.'

Rodin read it, and exclaimed :

' Excellent news ! The maidens and their guide had succeeded in escaping during the night from the White Falcon Tavern, but all three were overtaken and seized about a league from Mockern. They have been transferred to Leipsic, where they are imprisoned as vagabonds ; their guide, the soldier, is accused and condemned of resisting the authorities, and using violence to a magistrate.'

' It is almost certain, then, considering the tedious mode of proceeding in Germany (otherwise we would see to it), that the girls will not be able to be here on the 13th February,' added Rodin's master. ' Append this to the note on the back.'

The secretary obeyed, and endorsed ' An abstract of Morok's letter.'

' It is written,' he then added.

' Go on,' resumed his master.

Rodin continued reading.

'"NOTE, NO. II.

'"François Hardy, manufacturer at Plessis, near Paris, forty years old ; a steady, rich, intelligent, active, honest, well-informed man, idolised by his workmen—thanks to numberless innovations to promote their welfare. Never attending to the duties of our holy religion. Noted down as a very dangerous man : but the hatred and envy he excites among other manufacturers, especially in M. le Baron Tripeaud, his competitor, may easily be turned against him. If other means of action on his account, and against him, are necessary, the evidence may be consulted ; it is very voluminous. This man has been marked and watched for a long time.

'" He has been so effectually misguided with respect to the medal, that he is completely deceived as to the interests it represents. He is, however, constantly watched, surrounded, and governed, without suspecting it; one of his dearest friends deceives him, and through his means we know his secret thoughts.

'"NOTE, No. III.

'" Prince Djalma; eighteen ; energetic and generous, haughty, independent, and wild ; favourite of General Simon, who commanded the troops of his father, Radja-sing, in the struggle maintained by the latter against the English in India. Djalma is mentioned only by way of reminder, for his mother died young, while her parents were living. They resided at Batavia. On the death of the latter, neither Djalma nor the king, his father, claimed their little property. It is, therefore, certain that they are ignorant of the grave interests connected with the possession of the medal in question, which formed part of the property of Djalma's mother. "'

Rodin's master interrupted him.

'Now read the letter from Batavia, and complete the information respecting Djalma.'

Rodin read, and then observed :

'Good news again. Joshua Van Dael, merchant at Batavia (he was educated in our Pondicherry establishment), learns from his correspondent at Calcutta that the old Indian king was killed in the last battle with the English. His son, Djalma, deprived of the paternal throne, is provisionally detained as a prisoner of state in an Indian fortress.'

'We are at the end of October,' said Rodin's master. ' If Prince Djalma were to leave India now, he could scarcely reach Paris by the month of February.'

'Van Dael,' continued Rodin, 'regrets that he has not been able to prove his zeal in this case. Supposing Prince Djalma set at liberty, or having effected his escape, it is certain he would come to Batavia to claim his inheritance from his mother, since he has nothing else left him in the world. In that case, you may rely on Van Dael's devotedness. In return, he solicits very precise information, by the next post, respecting the fortune of M. le Baron Tripeaud, banker and manufacturer, with whom he has business transactions.'

'Answer that point evasively. Van Dael as yet has only shown zeal ; complete the information respecting Djalma from these new tidings.'

Rodin wrote.

But in a few minutes his master said to him with a singular expression :

'Does not Van Dael mention General Simon in connection with Djalma's imprisonment and his father's death ?'

'He does not allude to him,' said the secretary, continuing his task.

Rodin's master was silent, and paced the room.

In a few moments Rodin said to him : ' I have done it.'

'Go on, then.'

"Note, No. IV.

' " Jacques Rennepont, surnamed ' Sleepinbuff,' *i. e.* Lie-naked, workman in Baron Tripeaud's factory. This artisan is drunken, idle, noisy, and prodigal ; he is not without sense, but idleness and debauch have ruined him. A clever agent, on whom we rely, has become acquainted with his mistress, Cephyse Soliveau, nicknamed the Bacchanal Queen. Through her means the agent has formed such ties with him that he may even now be considered beyond the reach of the interests that ought to insure his presence in Paris on the 13th of February.

"Note, No. V.

' " Gabriel Rennepont, priest of foreign missions, distant relation of the above, but he is alike ignorant of the existence of his relative and the relationship. An orphan foundling, he was adopted by Frances Baudoin, the wife of a soldier, going by the name Dagobert.

' " Should this soldier, contrary to expectation, reach Paris, his wife would be a powerful means of influencing him. She is an excellent creature, ignorant and credulous, of exemplary piety, over whom we have long had unlimited control. She prevailed on Gabriel to take orders, notwithstanding his repugnance.

' " Gabriel is five-and-twenty ; disposition as angelic as his countenance ; rare and solid virtues : unfortunately he was brought up with his adopted brother, Agricola, Dagobert's son. This Agricola is a poet and workman— but an excellent workman ; he is employed by M. Hardy ; has imbibed the most detestable doctrines ; fond of his mother ; honest, laborious, but without religious feeling. Marked as very dangerous. This causes his intimacy with Gabriel to be feared.

' " The latter, notwithstanding his excellent qualities, sometimes causes uneasiness. We have even delayed confiding in him fully. A false step might make him, too, one of the most dangerous. Much precaution must be used then, especially till the 13th of February ; since, we repeat it, on him, on his presence in Paris at that time, depend immense hopes, and equally important interests.

' " Among other precautions, we have consented to his taking part in the American mission, for he unites with angelic sweetness of character a calm intrepidity and adventurous spirit which could only be satisfied by allowing him to engage in the perilous existence of the missionaries. Luckily, his superiors at Charlestown have received the strictest orders not to endanger, on any account, so precious a life. They are to send him to Paris, at least a month or two before February the 13th." '

Rodin's master again interrupted him, and said : ' Read the letter from Charleston, and see what it tells you, in order to complete the information upon this point also.'

When he had read the letter, Rodin went on : ' Gabriel is expected every day from the Rocky Mountains, whither he had absolutely insisted on going alone upon a mission.'

' What imprudence !'

' He has no doubt escaped all danger, as he himself announces his speedy return to Charlestown. As soon as he arrives, which cannot (they write) be later than the middle of this month, he will be shipped off for France.'

' Add this to the note which concerns him,' said Rodin's master.

' It is written,' replied the secretary, a few moments later.

' Proceed, then,' said his master. Rodin continued :

' "Note, No. VI.

' " Adrienne Rennepont de Cardoville.

' " Distantly related (without knowing it) to Jacques Rennepont, *alias* Sleepinbuff, and Gabriel Rennepont, missionary priest. She will soon be twenty-one years of age, the most attractive person in the world—extraordinary beauty, though red-haired—a mind remarkable for its originality—immense fortune—all the animal instincts. The incredible independence of her character makes one tremble for the future fate of this young person. Happily, her appointed guardian, Baron Tripeaud (a baron of 1829 creation, formerly agent to the late Count of Rennepont, Duke of Cardoville), is quite in the interest, and almost in the dependence, of the young lady's aunt. We count, with reason, upon this worthy and respectable relative, and on the Baron Tripeaud, to oppose and repress the singular, unheard-of designs which this young person, as resolute as independent, does not fear to avow—and which, unfortunately, cannot be turned to account in the interest of the affair in question—for——' "

Rodin was here interrupted by two discreet taps at the door. The secretary rose, went to see who knocked, remained a moment without, and then returned with two letters in his hand, saying : ' The princess has profited by the departure of a courier to——'

' Give me the letter !' cried his master, without leaving him time to finish. ' At length,' he added, ' I shall have news of my mother !'

He had scarcely read the first few lines of the letter, when he grew deadly pale, and his features took an expression of painful astonishment and poignant grief. ' My mother !' he cried, ' oh, heavens ! my mother !'

' What misfortune has happened !' asked Rodin, with a look of alarm, as he rose at the exclamation of his master.

' The symptoms of improvement were fallacious,' replied the other, dejectedly ; ' she has now relapsed into a nearly hopeless state. And yet the doctor thinks my presence might save her, for she calls for me without ceasing. She wishes to see me for the last time, that she may die in peace. Oh, that wish is sacred ! Not to grant it would be matricide. If I can but arrive in time ! Travelling day and night, it will take nearly two days.'

' Alas! what a misfortune !' said Rodin, wringing his hands, and raising his eyes to heaven.

His master rang the bell violently, and said to the old servant that opened the door : ' Just put what is indispensable into the portmanteau of my travelling-carriage. Let the porter take a cab, and go for post-horses instantly. Within an hour, I must be on the road. Mother ! mother !' cried he, as the servant departed in haste. ' Not to see her again—oh, it would be frightful !' And sinking upon a chair, overwhelmed with sorrow, he covered his face with his hands.

This great grief was sincere—he loved tenderly his mother : that divine sentiment had accompanied him, unalterable and pure, through all the phases of a too often guilty life.

After a few minutes, Rodin ventured to say to his master, as he showed him the second letter : ' This, also, has just been brought from M. Duplessis. It is very important—very pressing——'

' See what it is, and answer it. I have no head for business.'

' The letter is confidential,' said Rodin, presenting it to his master. ' I dare not open it, as you may see by the mark on the cover.'

At sight of this mark, the countenance of Rodin's master assumed an indefinable expression of respect and fear. With a trembling hand he broke the seal. The note contained only the following words : ' Leave all business.

and, without losing a minute, set out and come. M. Duplessis will replace you. He has orders.'

'Great God!' cried this man in despair. 'Set out before I have seen my mother! It is frightful, impossible—it would perhaps kill her—yes, it would be matricide!'

Whilst he uttered these words, his eyes rested on the huge globe, marked with red crosses. A sudden revolution seemed to take place within him; he appeared to repent of the violence of his regrets; his face, though still sad, became once more calm and grave. He handed the fatal letter to his secretary, and said to him, whilst he stifled a sigh : 'To be classed under its proper number.'

Rodin took the letter, wrote a number upon it, and placed it in a particular box. After a moment's silence, his master resumed : ' You will take orders from M. Duplessis, and work with him. You will deliver to him the note on the affair of the medals ; he knows to whom to address it. You will write to Batavia, Leipsic, and Charlestown, in the sense agreed. Prevent, at any price, the daughters of General Simon from quitting Leipsic ; hasten the arrival of Gabriel in Paris ; and should Prince Djalma come to Batavia, tell M. Joshua Van Dael, that we count on his zeal and obedience to keep him there.'

And this man, who, while his dying mother called to him in vain, could thus preserve his presence of mind, entered his own apartments ; whilst Rodin busied himself with the answers he had been ordered to write, and transcribed them in cipher.

In about three quarters of an hour, the bells of the post-horses were heard jingling without. The old servant again entered, after discreetly knocking at the door, and said : ' The carriage is ready.'

Rodin nodded, and the servant withdrew. The secretary, in his turn, went to knock at the door of the inner room. His master appeared, still grave and cold, but fearfully pale, and holding a letter in his hand.

'This for my mother,' said he to Rodin ; 'you will send a courier on the instant.'

'On the instant,' replied the secretary.

'Let the three letters for Leipsic, Batavia, and Charlestown, leave to-day by the ordinary channel. They are of the last importance. You know it.'

Those were his last words. Executing merciless orders with a merciless obedience, he departed without even attempting to see his mother. His secretary accompanied him respectfully in his carriage.

'What road, sir?' asked the postilion, turning round on his saddle.

'The road to ITALY!' answered Rodin's master, with so deep a sigh that it almost resembled a sob.

   ✧   ✧   ✧   ✧   ✧   ✧

As the horses started at full gallop, Rodin made a low bow ; then he returned to the large, cold, bare apartment. The attitude, countenance, and gait of this personage seemed to have undergone a sudden change. He appeared to have increased in dimensions. He was no longer an automaton, moved by the mechanism of humble obedience. His features, till now impassible, his glance, hitherto subdued, became suddenly animated with an expression of diabolical craft ; a sardonic smile curled his thin, pale lips, and a look of grim satisfaction relaxed his cadaverous face.

In turn, he stopped before the huge globe. In turn, he contemplated it in silence, even as his master had done. Then, bending over it, and embracing it, as it were, in his arms, he gloated with his reptile-eye on it for some moments, drew his coarse finger along its polished surface, and tapped his flat, dirty nail on three of the places dotted with red crosses. And, whilst he thus pointed to three towns, in very different parts of the world, he named them aloud, with a sneer. ' Leipsic—Charlestown—Batavia.'

' In each of these three places,' he added, ' distant as they are from one another, there exist persons who little think that here, in this obscure street, from the recesses of this chamber, wakeful eyes are upon them—that all their movements are followed, all their actions known—and that hence will issue new instructions, which deeply concern them, and which will be inexorably executed ; for an interest is at stake, which may have a powerful influence on Europe—-on the world. Luckily, we have friends at Leipsic, Charlestown, and Batavia.'

This funny, old, sordid, ill-dressed man, with his livid and death-like countenance, thus crawling over the sphere before him, appeared still more awful than his master, when the latter, erect and haughty, had imperiously laid his hand upon that globe, which he seemed desirous of subjecting by the strength of his pride and courage. The one resembled the eagle, that hovers above his prey—the other the reptile, that envelops its victim in its inextricable folds.

After some minutes, Rodin approached his desk, rubbing his hands briskly together, and wrote the following epistle in a cipher unknown even to his master :

' PARIS, ¾ past 9 A.M.

' He is gone—but he hesitated !

' When he received the order, his dying mother had just summoned him to her. He might, they told him, save her by his presence, and he exclaimed : " Not to go to my mother would be matricide !"

' Still, he is gone—but he hesitated. I keep my eye upon him continually. These lines will reach Rome at the same time as himself.

' P.S.—Tell the Cardinal-Prince that he may rely on me, but I hope for his active aid in return.'

When he had folded and sealed this letter, Rodin put it into his pocket. The clock struck ten, M. Rodin's hour for breakfast. He arranged and locked up his papers in a drawer, of which he carried away the key, brushed his old greasy hat with his sleeve, took a patched umbrella in his hand, and went out.*

✧   ✧   ✧   ✧   ✧   ✧

Whilst these two men, in the depths of their obscure retreat, were thus framing a plot, which was to involve the seven descendants of a race formerly proscribed—a strange, mysterious defender was planning how to protect this family, which was also his own.

INTERVAL.

THE WANDERING JEW'S SENTENCE.

THE site is wild and rugged. It is a lofty eminence covered with huge boulders of sandstone, between which rise birch trees and oaks, their foliage

---

* Having cited the excellent, courageous letters of M. Libri, and the curious work edited by M. Paulin, it is our duty likewise to mention many bold and conscientious writings on the subject of the ' Society of Jesus,' recently published by the Elder Dupin, Michelet, Quinet, Génin, and the Count de Saint Priest—works of high and impartial intellects, in which the fatal theories of the order are admirably exposed and condemned. We esteem ourselves happy, if we can bring one stone towards the erection of the strong, and, we hope, durable embankment which these generous hearts and noble minds are raising against the encroachments of an impure and always menacing flood.—E. S.

already yellowed by autumn. These tall trees stand out from the back-ground of red light, which the sun has left in the west, resembling the reflection of a great fire.

From this eminence the eye looks down into a deep valley, shady, fertile, and half-veiled in light vapour by the evening mist. The rich meadows, the tufts of bushy trees, the fields from which the ripe corn has been gathered in, all blend together in one dark, uniform tint, which contrasts with the limpid azure of the heavens. Steeples of grey stone or slate lift their pointed spires, at intervals, from the midst of this valley ; for many villages are spread about it, bordering a high road which leads from the north to the west.

It is the hour of repose—the hour when, for the most part, every cottage window brightens to the joyous crackling of the rustic hearth, and shines afar through shade and foliage, whilst clouds of smoke issue from the chimneys, and curl up slowly towards the sky. But now, strange to say, every hearth in the country seems cold and deserted. Stranger and more fatal still, every steeple rings out a funeral knell. Whatever there is of activity, movement, or life, appears concentrated in that lugubrious and far-sounding vibration.

Lights begin to show themselves in the dark villages, but they rise not from the cheerful and pleasant rustic hearth. They are as red as the fires of the herdsmen, seen at night through the midst of the fog. And then these lights do not remain motionless. They creep slowly towards the churchyard of every village. Louder sounds the death-knell, the air trembles beneath the strokes of so many bells, and, at rare intervals, the funeral chant rises faintly to the summit of the hill.

Why so many interments ? What valley of desolation is this, where the peaceful songs which follow the hard labours of the day are replaced by the death-dirge ? where the repose of evening is exchanged for the repose of eternity ? What is this valley of the shadow, where every village mourns for its many dead, and buries them at the same hour of the same night ?

Alas ! the deaths are so sudden and numerous and frightful that there is hardly time to bury the dead. During day the survivors are chained to the earth by hard but necessary toil ; and only in the evening, when they return from the fields, are they able, though sinking with fatigue, to dig those other furrows, in which their brethren are to lie heaped like grains of corn.

And this valley is not the only one that has seen the desolation. During a series of fatal years, many villages, many towns, many cities, many great countries, have seen, like this valley, their hearths deserted and cold—have seen, like this valley, mourning take the place of joy, and the death-knell substituted for the noise of festival—have wept in the same day for their many dead, and buried them at night by the lurid glare of torches.

For, during those fatal years, an awful wayfarer had slowly journeyed over the earth, from one pole to the other—from the depths of India and Asia to the ice of Siberia—from the ice of Siberia to the borders of the seas of France.

This traveller, mysterious as death, slow as eternity, implacable as fate, terrible as the hand of heaven, was the CHOLERA !

      ◇   ◇   ◇   ◇   ◇   ◇

The tolling of bells and the funeral chants still rose from the depths of the valley to the summit of the hill, like the complaining of a mighty voice ; the glare of the funeral torches was still seen afar through the mist of evening ; it was the hour of twilight—that strange hour, which gives to the most solid forms a vague, indefinite, fantastic appearance—when the sound of firm and regular footsteps was heard on the stony soil of the rising ground, and, between the black trunks of the trees, a man passed slowly onward.

His figure was tall, his head was bowed upon his breast ; his countenance was noble, gentle, and sad ; his eye-brows, uniting in the midst, extended from one temple to the other, like a fatal mark on his forehead.

This man did not seem to hear the distant tolling of so many funeral bells—and yet, a few days before, repose and happiness, health and joy, had reigned in those villages through which he had slowly passed, and which he now left behind him mourning and desolate. But the traveller continued on his way, absorbed in his own reflections.

' The 13th of February approaches,' thought he ; ' the day approaches, in which the descendants of my beloved sister, the last scions of our race, should meet in Paris. Alas ! it is now a hundred and fifty years since, for the third time, persecution scattered this family over all the earth—this family, that I have watched over with tenderness for eighteen centuries, through all its migrations and exiles, its changes of religion, fortune, and name !

' Oh ! for this family, descended from the sister of the poor shoemaker,* what grandeur and what abasement, what obscurity and what splendour, what misery and what glory ! By how many crimes has it been sullied, by how many virtues honoured ! The history of this single family is the history of the human race !

' Passing, in the course of so many generations, through the veins of the poor and the rich, of the sovereign and the bandit, of the wise man and the fool, of the coward and the brave, of the saint and the atheist, the blood of my sister has transmitted itself to this hour.

' What scions of this family are now remaining ? Seven only.

' Two orphans, the daughters of proscribed parents—a dethroned prince —a poor missionary priest—a man of the middle class—a young girl of a great name and large fortune—a mechanic.

' Together, they comprise in themselves the virtues, the courage, the degradation, the splendour, the miseries of our species !

' Siberia—India—America—France—behold the divers places where fate has thrown them !

' My instinct teaches me when one of them is in peril. Then, from the North to the South, from the East to the West, I go to seek them. Yesterday amid the Polar frosts—to-day in the temperate zone—to-morrow beneath the fires of the tropics—but often, alas ! at the moment when my presence might save them, the invisible hand impels me, the whirlwind carries me away, and the voice speaks in my ear : " GO ON ! GO ON !"

' Oh, that I might only finish my task !—" GO ON !"—A single hour—only a single hour of repose !—" GO ON !"—Alas ! I leave those I love on the brink of the abyss !—" GO ON ! GO ON !"

' Such is my punishment. If it is great, my crime was greater still ! An artisan, devoted to privations and misery, my misfortunes had made me cruel.

' Oh, cursed, cursed be the day, when, as I bent over my work, sullen with hate and despair, because, in spite of my incessant labour, I and mine wanted for everything, the Saviour passed before my door.

' Reviled, insulted, covered with blows, hardly able to sustain the weight

---

* It is known that, according to the legend, the Wandering Jew was a shoemaker at Jerusalem. The Saviour, carrying his cross, passed before the house of the artisan, and asked him to be allowed to rest an instant on the stone bench at his door. ' Go on ! go on !' said the Jew harshly, pushing him away. ' Thou shalt go on till the end of time,' answered the Saviour, in a stern though sorrowful tone. For further details, see the eloquent and learned notice by Charles Magnin, appended to the magnificent poem of ' Ahasuerus,' by Ed. Quinet.—E. S.

of his heavy cross, He asked me to let Him rest a moment on my stone bench. The sweat poured from His forehead, His feet were bleeding, He was well-nigh sinking with fatigue, and He said to me, in a mild, heart-piercing voice : " I suffer !" "And I too suffer," I replied, as with harsh anger I pushed Him from the place : " I suffer, and no one comes to help me ! I find no pity, and will give none. Go on ! go on !" Then, with a deep sigh of pain, He answered, and spake this sentence : " Verily, thou shalt go on till the day of thy redemption, for so wills the Father which art in heaven !"

'And so my punishment began. Too late I opened these eyes to the light, too late I learned repentance and charity, too late I understood those divine words of Him I had outraged, words which should be the law of the whole human race, "LOVE YE ONE ANOTHER."

'In vain through successive ages, gathering strength and eloquence from those celestial words, have I laboured to earn my pardon, by filling with commiseration and love hearts that were overflowing with envy and bitter-ness, by inspiring many a soul with a sacred horror of oppression and in-justice. For me, the day of mercy has not yet dawned !

'And even as the first man, by his fall, devoted his posterity to misfortune, it would seem as if I, the workman, had consigned the whole race of artisans to endless sorrows, and as if they were expiating my crime : for they alone, during these eighteen centuries, have not yet been delivered.

'For eighteen centuries, the powerful and the happy of this world have said to the toiling people what I said to the imploring and suffering Saviour : "Go on ! go on !" And the people, sinking with fatigue, bearing their heavy cross, have answered in the bitterness of their grief : " Oh, for pity's sake ! a few moments of repose ; we are worn out with toil."—" Go on !"—" And if we perish in our pain, what will become of our little children and our aged mothers ?"—" Go on ! go on !" And, for eighteen centuries, they and I have continued to struggle forward and to suffer, and no chari-table voice has yet pronounced the word, " Enough !"

'Alas ! such is my punishment. It is immense, it is twofold. I suffer in the name of humanity, when I see these wretched multitudes consigned without respite to profitless and oppressive toil. I suffer in the name of my family, when, poor and wandering, I am unable to bring aid to the descendants of my dear sister. But, when the sorrow is above my strength, when I foresee some danger from which I cannot preserve my own, then my thoughts, travelling over the world, go in search of that woman like me accursed, that daughter of a queen, who like me, the son of a labourer, wanders, and will wander on, till the day of her redemption.*

'Once in a century, as two planets draw nigh to each other in their revolu-tions, I am permitted to meet this woman during the dread week of the Passion. And after this interview, filled with terrible remembrances and boundless griefs, wandering stars of eternity, we pursue our infinite course.

'And this woman, the only one upon earth who, like me, sees the end of every century, and exclaims : " What ! another?" this woman responds to my thought, from the furthest extremity of the world. She, who alone shares my terrible destiny, has chosen to share also the only interest that has con-soled me for so many ages. Those descendants of my dear sister, she too loves, she too protects them. For them she journeys likewise from East to West and from North to South.

* According to a legend very little known, for which we are indebted to the kind-ness of M. Maury, the learned sub-librarian of the Institute, Herodias was condemned to wander till the day of judgment, for having asked for the death of St. John the Baptist.—E. S.

' But alas ! the invisible hand impels her, the whirlwind carries her away, and the voice speaks in her ear : " Go on !"—" Oh that I might finish my sentence !" repeats she also.—" Go on !"—" A single hour—only a single hour of repose !"—" Go on !"—" I leave those I love on the brink of the abyss."—" Go on ! Go on !"——'

Whilst this man thus went over the hill absorbed in his thoughts, the light evening breeze increased almost to a gale, a vivid flash streamed across the sky, and long, deep whistlings announced the coming of a tempest.

On a sudden this doomed man, who could no longer weep or smile, started with a shudder. No physical pain could reach him, and yet he pressed his hand hastily to his heart, as though he had experienced a cruel pang. ' Oh !' cried he ; ' I feel it. This hour, many of those whom I love—the descendants of my dear sister—suffer, and are in great peril. Some in the centre of India —some in America—some here in Germany. The struggle recommences, the detestable passions are again awake. Oh, thou that hearest me—thou, like myself wandering and accursed—Herodias ! help me to protect them ! May my invocation reach thee, in those American solitudes where thou now lingerest—and may we arrive in time !'

Thereon an extraordinary event happened. Night was come. The man made a movement, precipitately, to retrace his steps—but an invisible force prevented him, and carried him forward in the opposite direction.

At this moment, the storm burst forth in its murky majesty. One of those whirlwinds, which tear up trees by the roots, and shake the foundations of the rocks, rushed over the hill rapid and loud as thunder.

In the midst of the roaring of the hurricane, by the glare of the fiery flashes, the man with the black mark on his brow was seen descending the hill, stalking with huge strides among the rocks, and between trees bent beneath the efforts of the storm.

The tread of this man was no longer slow, firm, and steady—but painfully irregular, like that of one impelled by an irresistible power, or carried along by the whirl of a frightful wind. In vain he extended his supplicating hands to heaven. Soon he disappeared in the shades of night, and amid the roar of the tempest.

CHAPTER XVII.

THE AJOUPA.

WHILE Rodin despatched his cosmopolite correspondence, from his retreat in the Rue du Milieu des Ursins, in Paris—while the daughters of General Simon, after quitting as fugitives the White Falcon, were detained prisoners at Leipsic along with Dagobert—other scenes, deeply interesting to these different personages, were passing, almost as it were at the same moment, at the other extremity of the world, in the furthermost parts of Asia—that is to say, in the island of Java, not far from the city of Batavia, the residence of M. Joshua Van Dael, one of the correspondents of Rodin.

Java ! magnificent and fatal country, where the most admirable flowers conceal hideous reptiles, where the brightest fruits contain subtle poisons, where grow splendid trees, whose very shadow is death—where the gigantic vampire bat sucks the blood of its victims whilst it prolongs their sleep, by surrounding them with a fresh and balmy air, no fan moving so rapidly as the great perfumed wings of this monster !

The month of October, 1831, draws near its close. It is noon—an hour well nigh mortal to him who encounters the fiery heat of the sun, which spreads a sheet of dazzling light over the deep blue enamel of the sky,

An ajoupa, or hut, made of cane mats, suspended ..om long bamboos, which are driven far into the ground, rises in the midst of the bluish shadows cast by a tuft of trees whose glittering verdure resembles green porcelain. These quaintly formed trees, rounded into arches, pointing like spires, over-spreading like parasols, are so thick in foliage, so entangled one with the other, that their dome is impenetrable to the rain.

The soil, ever marshy, notwithstanding the insupportable heat, disappears beneath an inextricable mass of creepers, ferns, and tufted reeds, of a fresh-ness and vigour of vegetation almost incredible, reaching nearly to the top of the ajoupa, which lies hid like a nest among the grass.

Nothing can be more suffocating than the atmosphere, heavily laden with moist exhalations like the steam of hot water, and impregnated with the strongest and sharpest scents ; for the cinnamon-tree, ginger plant, stepha-notis and Cape jasmin, mixed with these trees and creepers, spread around in puffs their penetrating odours. A roof, formed of large Indian fig-leaves, covers the cabin ; at one end is a square opening, which serves for a window, shut in with a fine lattice-work of vegetable fibres, so as to prevent the rep-tiles and venomous insects from creeping into the ajoupa. The huge trunk of a dead tree, still standing, but much bent, and with its summit reaching to the roof of the ajoupa, rises from the midst of the brushwood. From every crevice in its black, rugged, mossy bark, springs a strange, almost fantastic flower ; the wing of the butterfly is not of a finer tissue, of a more brilliant purple, of a more glossy black : those unknown birds we see in our dreams, have no more grotesque forms than these specimens of the orchis—winged flowers, that seem always ready to fly from their frail and leafless stalks. The long, flexible stems of the cactus, which might be taken for reptiles, encircle also this trunk, and clothe it with their bunches of silvery white, shaded inside with bright orange. These flowers emit a strong scent of vanilla.

A serpent, of a brick-red, about the thickness of a large quill, and five or six inches long, half protrudes its flat head from one of those enormous, per-fumed calyces, in which it lies closely curled up.

Within the ajoupa, a young man is extended on a mat in a profound sleep. His complexion of a clear golden yellow, gives him the appearance of a statue of pale bronze, on which a ray of the sun is playing. His attitude is simple and graceful ; his right arm sustains his head, a little raised and turned on one side ; his ample robe of white muslin, with hanging sleeves, leaves uncovered his chest and arms worthy of the Antinoüs. Marble is not more firm, more polished than his skin, the golden hue of which contrasts strongly with the whiteness of his garments. Upon his broad manly chest a deep scar is visible—the mark of the musket-ball he received in defending the life of General Simon, the father of Rose and Blanche.

Suspended from his neck, he wears a medal similar to that in the possession of the two sisters. This Indian is Djalma.

His features are at once very noble and very beautiful. His hair of a blue black, parted upon his forehead, falls waving, but not curled, over his shoulders ; whilst his eyebrows, boldly and yet delicately defined, are of as deep a jet as the long eyelashes, that cast their shadow upon his beardless cheek. His bright, red lips are slightly apart, and he breathes uneasily ; his sleep is heavy and troubled, for the heat becomes every moment more and more suffocating.

Without, the silence is profound. Not a breath of air is stirring. Yet now the tall ferns, which cover the soil, begin to move almost imperceptibly, as though their stems were shaken by the slow progress of some crawling body. From time to time, this trifling oscillation suddenly ceases, and all is again motionless. But, after several of these alternations of rustling and deep silence, a human head appears in the midst of the jungle, a little distance from the trunk of the dead tree.

The man to whom it belonged was possessed of a grim countenance, with a complexion the colour of greenish bronze, long black hair bound about his temples, eyes brilliant with savage fire, and an expression remarkable for its intelligence and ferocity. Holding his breath, he remained quite still for a moment; then, advancing upon his hands and knees, pushing aside the leaves so gently, that not the slightest noise could be heard, he arrived cautiously and slowly at the trunk of the dead tree, the summit of which nearly touched the roof of the ajoupa.

This man, of Malay origin, belonging to the sect of the Lughardars (Stranglers), after having again listened, rose almost entirely from amongst the brushwood. With the exception of white cotton drawers, fastened around his middle by a parti-coloured sash, he was completely naked. His bronzed, supple, and nervous limbs were overlaid with a thick coat of oil. Stretching himself along the huge trunk on the side furthest from the cabin, and thus sheltered by the whole breadth of the tree with its surrounding creepers, he began to climb silently, with as much patience as caution. In the undulations of his form, in the flexibility of his movements, in the restrained vigour, which fully put forth would have been alarming, there was some resemblance to the stealthy and treacherous advance of the tiger upon his prey.

Having reached, completely unperceived, the inclined portion of the tree, which almost touched the roof of the cabin, he was only separated from the window by a distance of about a foot. Cautiously advancing his head, he looked down into the interior, to see how he might best find an entrance.

At sight of Djalma in his deep sleep, the Thug's bright eyes glittered with increased brilliancy; a nervous contraction, or rather a mute, ferocious laugh, curling the corners of his mouth, drew them up towards the cheek-bones, and exposed rows of teeth, filed sharp like the points of a saw, and dyed of a shining black.

Djalma was lying in such a manner and so near the door of the ajoupa, which opened inwards, that, were it moved in the least, he must be instantly awakened. The Strangler, with his body still sheltered by the tree, wishing to examine more attentively the interior of the cabin, leaned very forward, and in order to maintain his balance, lightly rested his hand on the ledge of the opening that served for a window. This movement shook the large cactus-flower, within which the little serpent lay curled, and, darting forth, it twisted itself rapidly round the wrist of the Strangler. Whether from pain or surprise, the man uttered a low cry; and as he drew back swiftly, still holding by the trunk of the tree, he perceived that Djalma had moved.

The young Indian, though retaining his supine posture, had half opened his eyes, and turned his head towards the window, whilst his breast heaved with a deep-drawn sigh, for, beneath that thick dome of moist verdure, the concentrated heat was intolerable.

Hardly had he moved, when, from behind the tree, was heard the shrill, brief, sonorous note, which the bird of paradise utters when it takes its flight —a cry which resembles that of the pheasant. This note was soon repeated, but more faintly, as though the brilliant bird were already at a distance. Djalma, thinking he had discovered the cause of the noise which had aroused him for an instant, stretched out the arm upon which his head had rested, and went to sleep again, with scarcely any change of position.

For some minutes, the most profound silence once more reigned in this solitude, and everything remained motionless.

The Strangler, by his skilful imitation of the bird, had repaired the imprudence of that exclamation of surprise and pain, which the reptile bite had forced from him. When he thought all was safe, he again advanced his head, and saw the young Indian once more plunged in sleep. Then he descended the tree with the same precautions, though his left hand was somewhat swollen from the sting of the serpent, and disappeared in the jungle.

At that instant a song of monotonous and melancholy cadence was heard in the distance. The Strangler raised himself, and listened attentively, and his face took an expression of surprise and deadly anger. The song came nearer and nearer to the cabin, and, in a few seconds, an Indian, passing through an open space in the jungle, approached the spot where the Thug lay concealed.

The latter unwound from his waist a long thin cord, to one of the ends of which was attached a leaden ball, of the form and size of an egg ; having fastened the other end of this cord to his right wrist, the Strangler again listened, and then disappeared, crawling through the tall grass in the direction of the Indian, who still advanced slowly, without interrupting his soft and plaintive song.

He was a young fellow scarcely twenty, with a bronzed complexion, the slave of Djalma, his vest of blue cotton was confined at the waist by a particoloured sash ; he wore a red turban, and silver rings in his ears and about his wrists. He was bringing a message to his master, who, during the great heat of the day was reposing in the ajoupa, which stood at some distance from the house he inhabited.

Arriving at a place where two paths separate, the slave, without hesitation took that which led to the cabin, from which he was now scarce forty paces distant.

One of those enormous Java butterflies, whose wings extend six or eight inches in length, and offer to the eye two streaks of gold on a ground of ultramarine, fluttering from leaf to leaf, alighted on a bush of Cape jasmin, within the reach of the young Indian. The slave stopped in his song, stood still, advanced first a foot, then a hand, and seized the butterfly.

Suddenly, he sees a dark figure rise before him ; he hears a whizzing noise like that of a sling ; he feels a cord, thrown with as much rapidity as force, encircle his neck with a triple band ; and, almost in the same instant, the leaden ball strikes violently against the back of his head.

This attack was so abrupt and unforeseen, that Djalma's servant could not even utter a single cry, a single groan. He tottered—the Strangler gave a vigorous pull at the cord—the bronzed countenance of the slave became purple, and he fell upon his knees, convulsively moving his arms. Then the Strangler threw him quite down, and pulled the cord so violently, that the blood spirted from the skin. The victim struggled for a moment— and all was over.

During his short but intense agony, the murderer, kneeling before his victim, and watching with ardent eye his least convulsions, seemed plunged in an ecstasy of ferocious joy. His nostrils dilated, the veins of his neck and temples were swollen, and the same savage laugh, which had curled his lips at the aspect of the sleeping Djalma, again displayed his pointed black teeth, which a nervous trembling of the jaws made to chatter. But soon he crossed his arms upon his heaving breast, bowed his forehead, and murmured some mysterious words, which sounded like an invocation or a prayer. Immediately after, he returned to the contemplation of the dead body. The hyena and the tiger-cat, who, before devouring, crouch beside the prey that they have surprised or hunted down, have not a wilder or more sanguinary look than this man.

But, remembering that his task was not yet accomplished, tearing himself unwillingly from the hideous spectacle, he unbound the cord from the neck of his victim, fastened it round his own body, dragged the corpse out of the path, and, without attempting to rob it of its silver rings, concealed it in a thick part of the jungle.

Then the Strangler again began to creep on his knees and belly, till he arrived at the cabin of Djalma—that cabin constructed of mats suspended from bamboos. After listening attentively, he drew from his girdle a knife, the sharp-pointed blade of which was wrapped in a fig-leaf, and made in the matting an incision of three feet in length. This was done with such quickness, and with so fine a blade, that the light touch of the diamond cutting glass would have made more noise. Seeing, by means of this opening, which was to serve him for a passage, that Djalma was still fast asleep, the Thug, with incredible temerity, glided into the cabin.

CHAPTER XVIII.

THE TATTOOING.

THE heavens, which had been till now of transparent blue, became gradually of a greenish tint, and the sun was veiled in red, lurid vapour. This strange light gave to every object a weird appearance, of which one might form an idea, by looking at a landscape through a piece of copper-coloured glass. In those climates, this phenomenon, when united with an increase of burning heat, always announces the approach of a storm.

From time to time there was a passing odour of sulphur ; then the leaves, slightly shaken by electric currents, would tremble upon their stalks ; till again all would return to the former motionless silence. The weight of the burning atmosphere, saturated with sharp perfumes, became almost intolerable   Large drops of sweat stood in pearls on the forehead of Djalma, still plunged in enervating sleep—for it no longer resembled rest, but a painful stupor.

The Strangler glided like a reptile along the sides of the ajoupa, and, crawling on his belly, arrived at the sleeping-mat of Djalma, beside which he squatted himself, so as to occupy as little space as possible. Then began a fearful scene, by reason of the mystery and silence which surrounded it.

Djalma's life was at the mercy of the Strangler. The latter, resting upon his hands and knees, with his neck stretched forward, his eye fixed and dilated, continued motionless as a wild beast about to spring. Only a slight, nervous trembling of the jaws agitated that mask of bronze.

But soon his hideous features revealed a violent struggle that was passing within him—a struggle between the thirst, the craving for the enjoyment of murder, which the recent assassination of the slave had made still more active, and the orders he had received not to attempt the life of Djalma, though the design, which brought him to the ajoupa, might perhaps be as fatal to the young Indian as death itself. Twice did the Strangler, with look of flame, resting only on his left hand, seize with his right the rope's end ; and twice his hand fell—the instinct of murder yielding to a powerful will, of which the Malay acknowledged the irresistible empire.

In him, the homicidal craving must have amounted to madness, for, in these hesitations, he lost much precious time : at any moment, Djalma, whose vigour, skill, and courage were known and feared, might awake from his sleep, and, though unarmed, he would prove a terrible adversary. At length the Thug made up his mind ; with a suppressed sigh of regret, he set about accomplishing his task.

This task would have appeared impossible to any one else. The reader may judge.

Djalma, with his face turned towards the left, leaned his head upon his curved arm. It was first necessary, without waking him, to oblige him to turn his face towards the right (that is, towards the door), so that, in case of his being half-roused, his first glance might not fall upon the Strangler. The latter, to accomplish his projects, would have to remain many minutes in the cabin.

The heavens became darker ; the heat arrived at its last degree of intensity ; everything combined to increase the torpor of the sleeper, and so favour the Strangler's designs. Kneeling down close to Djalma, he began, with the tips of his supple, well-oiled fingers, to stroke the brow, temples, and eyelids of the young Indian, but with such extreme lightness, that the contact of the two skins was hardly sensible. When this kind of magnetic incantation had lasted for some seconds, the sweat, which bathed the forehead of Djalma, became more abundant : he heaved a smothered sigh, and the muscles of his face gave several twitches, for the strokings, although too light to rouse him, yet caused in him a feeling of indefinable uneasiness.

Watching him with his restless and burning eye, the Strangler continued his manœuvres with so much patience, that Djalma, still sleeping, but no longer able to bear this vague, annoying sensation, raised his right hand mechanically to his face, as if he would have brushed away an importunate insect. But he had not strength to do it ; almost immediately after, his hand, inert and heavy, fell back upon his chest. The Strangler saw, by this symptom, that he was attaining his object, and continued to stroke, with the same address, the eyelids, brow, and temples.

Whereupon Djalma, more and more oppressed by heavy sleep, and having neither strength nor will to raise his hand to his face, mechanically turned round his head, which fell languidly upon his right shoulder, seeking, by this change of attitude, to escape from the disagreeable sensation which pursued him. The first point gained, the Strangler could act more freely.

To render as profound as possible the sleep he had half interrupted, he now strove to imitate the vampire, and, feigning the action of a fan, he rapidly moved his extended hands about the burning face of the young Indian. Alive to a feeling of such sudden and delicious coolness, in the height of suffocating heat, the countenance of Djalma brightened, his bosom heaved, his half-opened lips drank in the grateful air, and he fell into a sleep only the more invincible, because it had been at first disturbed, and was now yielded to under the influence of a pleasing sensation.

A sudden flash of lightning illumined the shady dome that sheltered the ajoupa : fearing that the first clap of thunder might rouse the young Indian, the Strangler hastened to complete his task. Djalma lay on his back, with his head resting on his right shoulder, and his left arm extended ; the Thug, crouching at his left side, ceased by degrees the process of fanning ; then, with incredible dexterity, he succeeded in rolling up, above the elbow, the long wide sleeve of white muslin that covered the left arm of the sleeper.

He next drew from the pocket of his drawers a copper box, from which he took a very fine, sharp-pointed needle, and a piece of a black looking root. He pricked this root several times with the needle, and on each occasion there issued from it a white, glutinous liquid.

When the Strangler thought the needle sufficiently impregnated with this juice, he bent down, and began to blow gently over the inner surface of Djalma's arm, so as to cause a fresh sensation of coolness ; then, with the point of his needle, he traced almost imperceptibly on the skin of the sleeping youth some mysterious and symbolical signs. And this was performed so cleverly, and the point of the needle was so fine and keen, that Djalma did not feel the action of the acid upon his skin.

The signs, which the Strangler had traced, soon appeared on the surface, at first in characters of a pale rose-colour, as fine as a hair ; but such was the slowly corrosive power of the juice, that, as it worked and spread beneath the skin, they would become in a few hours of a violet red, and as apparent as they were now almost invisible.

The Strangler, having so perfectly succeeded in his project, threw a last look of ferocious longing on the slumbering Indian, and creeping away from the mat, regained the opening by which he had entered the cabin ; next, closely uniting the edges of the incision, so as to obviate all suspicion, he disappeared just as the thunder began to rumble hoarsely in the distance.*

CHAPTER XIX.

THE SMUGGLER.

THE tempest of the morning has long been over. The sun is verging towards the horizon. Some hours have elapsed, since the Strangler introduced himself into Djalma's cabin, and tattooed him with a mysterous sign during his sleep.

A horseman advances rapidly down a long avenue of spreading trees. Sheltered by the thick and verdant arch, a thousand birds salute the splendid evening with songs and circlings ; red and green parrots climb, by help of their hooked beaks, to the top of pink-blossomed acacias ; large Morea birds of the finest and richest blue, whose throats and long tails change in the light to a golden brown, are chasing the *prince-oriels*, clothed in their glossy feathers of black and orange ; Kolo doves, of a changeable

---

* We read in the letters of the late Victor Jacquemont upon India, with regard to the incredible dexterity of these men : 'they crawl on the ground, ditches, in the furrows of fields, imitate a hundred different voices, and dissipate the effect of any accidental noise by raising the yelp of the jackal or note of some bird—then are silent, and another imitates the call of the same animal in the distance. They can molest a sleeper by all sorts of noises and slight touches, and make his body and limbs take any position which suits their purpose.' Count Edward de Warren, in his excellent work on English India, which we shall have again occasion to quote, expresses himself in the same manner as to the inconceivable address of the Indians : 'They have the art,' says he, 'to rob you, without interrupting your sleep, of the very sheet in which you are enveloped. This is not "a traveller's tale," but a fact. The movements of the *bheel* are those of a serpent. If you sleep in your tent, with a servant lying across each entrance, the *bheel* will come and crouch on the outside, in some shady corner, where he can hear the breathing of those within. As soon as the European sleeps, he feels sure of success, for the Asiatic will not long resist the attraction of repose. At the proper moment, he makes a vertical incision in the cloth of the tent, on the spot where he happens to be, and just large enough to admit him. He glides through like a phantom, without making the least grain of sand creak beneath his tread.. He is perfectly naked, and all his body is rubbed over with oil ; a two-edged knife is suspended from his neck. He will squat down close to your couch, and, with incredible coolness and dexterity, will gather up the sheet in very little folds, so as to occupy the least surface possible ; then, passing to the other side, he will lightly tickle the sleeper, whom he seems to magnetise, till the latter shrinks back involuntarily, and ends by turning round, and leaving the sheet folded behind him. Should he awake, and strive to seize the robber, he catches at a slippery form, which slides through his hands like an eel ; should he even succeed in seizing him, it would be fatal—the dagger strikes him to the heart, he falls bathed in his blood, and the assassin disappears.'—E. S.

violet hue, are gently cooing by the side of the birds of paradise, in whose brilliant plumage are mingled the prismatic colours of the emerald and ruby, the topaz and sapphire.

This avenue, a little raised, commanded the view of a small pond, which reflected at intervals the green shade of tamarind trees. In the calm, limpid waters, many fish were visible, some with silver scales and purple fins, others gleaming with azure and vermilion : so still were they that they looked as if set in a mass of bluish crystal, and, as they dwelt motionless near the surface of the pool, on which played a dazzling ray of the sun, they revelled in the enjoyment of the light and heat. A thousand insects—living gems, with wings of flame—glided, fluttered and buzzed over the transparent wave, in which, at an extraordinary depth, were mirrored the variegated tints of the aquatic plants on the bank.

It is impossible to give an adequate idea of the exuberant nature of this scene, luxuriant in sun-light, colours, and perfumes, which served, so to speak, as a frame to the young and brilliant rider, who was advancing along the avenue. It was Djalma. He had not yet perceived the indelible marks, which the Strangler had traced upon his left arm.

His Japanese mare, of slender make, full of fire and vigour, is black as night. A narrow red cloth serves instead of saddle. To moderate the impetuous bounds of the animal, Djalma uses a small steel bit, with headstall and reins of twisted scarlet silk, fine as a thread.

Not one of those admirable riders, sculptured so masterly on the frieze of the Parthenon, sits his horse more gracefully and proudly than this young Indian, whose fine face, illumined by the setting sun, is radiant with serene happiness ; his eyes sparkle with joy, and his dilated nostrils and unclosed lips inhale with delight the balmy breeze, that brings to him the perfume of flowers and the scent of fresh leaves, for the trees are still moist from the abundant rain that fell after the storm.

A red cap, similar to that worn by the Greeks, surmounting the black locks of Djalma, sets off to advantage the golden tint of his complexion ; his throat is bare ; he is clad in his robe of white muslin with large sleeves, confined at the waist by a scarlet sash ; very full drawers, in white cotton stuff, leave half uncovered his tawny and polished legs ; their classic curve stands out from the dark sides of the horse, which he presses tightly between his muscular calves. He has no stirrups ; his foot, small and narrow, is shod with a sandal of morocco leather.

The rush of his thoughts, by turns impetuous and restrained, was expressed in some degree by the pace he imparted to his horse—now bold and precipitate, like the flight of unbridled imagination—now calm and measured, like the reflection which succeeds an idle dream. But, in all this fantastic course, his least movements were distinguished by a proud, independent, and somewhat savage grace.

Dispossessed of his paternal territory by the English, and at first detained by them as a state-prisoner after the death of his father—who (as M. Joshua Van Dael had written to M. Rodin) had fallen sword in hand—Djalma had at length been restored to liberty Abandoning the continent of India, and still accompanied by General Simon, who had lingered hard by the prison of his old friend's son, the young Indian came next to Batavia, the birth-place of his mother, to collect the modest inheritance of his maternal ancestors. And amongst this property, so long despised or forgotten by his father, he found some important papers, and a medal exactly similar to that worn by Rose and Blanche.

General Simon was not more surprised than pleased at this discovery, which not only established a tie of kindred between his wife and Djalma's

mother, but which also seemed to promise great advantages for the future.
Leaving Djalma at Batavia, to terminate some business there, he had gone
to the neighbouring island of Sumatra, in the hope of finding a vessel that
would make the passage to Europe directly and rapidly; for it was now
necessary that, cost what it might, the young Indian also should be at Paris
on the 13th February, 1832. Should General Simon find a vessel ready to
sail for Europe, he was to return immediately, to fetch Djalma : and the
latter, expecting him daily, was now going to the pier of Batavia, hoping to
see the father of Rose and Blanche arrive by the mail-boat from Sumatra.

A few words are here necessary on the early life of the son of Kadja-sing.

Having lost his mother very young, and brought up with rude simplicity,
he had accompanied his father, whilst yet a child, to the great tiger hunts,
as dangerous as battles ; and, in the first dawn of youth, he had followed
him to the stern and bloody war, which he waged in defence of his country.
Thus living, from the time of his mother's death, in the midst of forests and
mountains and continual combats, his vigorous and ingenuous nature had
preserved itself pure, and he well merited the name of "The Generous"
bestowed on him. Born a prince, he was—which by no means follows—a
prince indeed. During the period of his captivity, the silent dignity of his
bearing had overawed his gaolers. Never a reproach, never a complaint—
a proud and melancholy calm was all that he opposed to a treatment as unjust as it was barbarous, until he was restored to freedom.

Having thus been always accustomed to a patriarchal life, or to a war of
mountaineers, which he had only quitted to pass a few months in prison,
Djalma knew nothing, so to speak, of civilised society. Without its exactly
amounting to a defect, he certainly carried his good qualities to their extreme
limits. Obstinately faithful to his pledged word, devoted to the death, confiding to blindness, good almost to a complete forgetfulness of himself, he
was inflexible towards ingratitude, falsehood, or perfidy. He would have
felt no compunction to sacrifice a traitor, because, could he himself have
committed a treason, he would have thought it only just to expiate it with
his life.

He was, in a word, the man of natural feelings, absolute and entire. Such
a man, brought into contact with the temperaments, calculations, falsehoods,
deceptions, tricks, restrictions, and hollowness of a refined society, such as
Paris, for example, would without doubt form a very curious subject for
speculation. We raise this hypothesis, because, since his journey to France
had been determined on, Djalma had one fixed, ardent desire—to be in Paris.

In Paris—that enchanted city—of which, even in Asia, the land of enchantment, so many marvellous tales were told.

What chiefly inflamed the fresh, vivid imagination of the young Indian,
was the thought of French women—those attractive Parisian beauties,
miracles of elegance and grace, who eclipse, he was informed, even the
magnificence of the capitals of the civilised world. And at this very moment,
in the brightness of that warm and splendid evening, surrounded by the intoxication of flowers and perfumes, which accelerated the pulses of his
young fiery heart, Djalma was dreaming of those exquisite creatures, whom
his fancy loved to clothe in the most ideal garbs.

It seemed to him as if, at the end of the avenue, in the midst of that sheet
of golden light, which the trees encompassed with their full, green arch, he
could see pass and repass, white and sylph-like, a host of adorable and
voluptuous phantoms, that threw him kisses from the tips of their rosy
fingers. Unable to restrain his burning emotions, carried away by a strange
enthusiasm, Djalma uttered exclamations of joy, deep, manly, and sonorous,
and made his vigorous courser bound under him in the excitement of a mad

delight. Just then a sunbeam, piercing the dark vault of the avenue, shone full upon him.

For several minutes, a man had been advancing rapidly along a path, which, at its termination, intersected the avenue diagonally. He stopped a moment in the shade, looking at Djalma with astonishment. It was indeed a charming sight, to behold, in the midst of a blaze of dazzling lustre, this youth, so handsome, joyous, and ardent, clad in his white and flowing vestments, gaily and lightly seated on his proud black mare, who covered her red bridle with her foam, and whose long tail and thick mane floated on the evening breeze.

But, with that reaction which takes place in all human desires, Djalma soon felt stealing over him a sentiment of soft, undefinable melancholy. He raised his hand to his eyes, now dimmed with moisture, and allowed the reins to fall on the mane of his docile steed, which, instantly stopping, stretched out its long neck, and turned its head in the direction of the personage, whom it could see approaching through the coppice.

This man, Mahal the Smuggler, was dressed nearly like European sailors. He wore jacket and trousers of white duck, a broad red sash, and a very low-crowned straw-hat. His face was brown, with strongly marked features, and, though forty years of age, he was quite beardless.

In another moment, Mahal was close to the young Indian. 'You are Prince Djalma?' said he, in not very good French, raising his hand respectfully to his hat.

'What would you?' said the Indian.

'You are the son of Kadja-sing?'

'Once again, what would you?'

'The friend of General Simon?'

'General Simon?' cried Djalma.

'You are going to meet him, as you have gone every evening, since you expect his return from Sumatra?'

'Yes, but how do you know all this?' said the Indian, looking at the Smuggler with as much surprise as curiosity.

'Is he not to land at Batavia, to-day or to-morrow?'

'Are you sent by him?'

'Perhaps,' said Mahal, with a distrustful air. 'But are you really the son of Kadja-sing?'

'Yes, I tell you—but where have you seen General Simon?'

'If you are the son of Kadja-sing,' resumed Mahal, continuing to regard Djalma with a suspicious eye, 'what is your surname?'

'My sire was called the "Father of the Generous,"' answered the young Indian, as a shade of sorrow passed over his fine countenance.

These words appeared in part to convince Mahal of the identity of Djalma; but, wishing doubtless to be still more certain, he resumed : 'You must have received, two days ago, a letter from General Simon, written from Sumatra?'

'Yes ; but why so many questions?'

'To assure myself that you are really the son of Kadja-sing, and to execute the orders I have received.'

'From whom?'

'From General Simon.'

'But where is he?'

'When I have proof that you are Prince Djalma, I will tell you. I was informed that you would be mounted on a black mare, with a red bridle. But——'

"By the soul of my mother ! speak what you have to say ?"

'I will tell you all—if you can tell me what was the printed paper, con-tained in the last letter that General Simon wrote you from Sumatra.'

'It was a cutting from a French newspaper.'

'Did it announce good or bad news for the general?'

'Good news—for it related, that, during his absence, they had acknow-ledged the last rank and title bestowed on him by the Emperor, as they had done for others of his brothers in arms, exiled like him.'

'You are indeed Prince Djalma,' said the Smuggler, after a moment's re-flection. 'I may speak. General Simon landed last night in Java, but on a desert part of the coast.'

'On a desert part?'

'Because he has to hide himself.'

'Hide himself!' exclaimed Djalma, in amazement; 'why?'

'That I don't know.'

'But where is he?' asked Djalma, growing pale with alarm.

'He is three leagues hence—near the sea-shore—in the ruins of Tchandi.'

'Obliged to hide himself!' repeated Djalma, and his countenance ex-pressed increasing surprise and anxiety.

'Without being certain, I think, it is because of a duel he fought in Sumatra,' said the Smuggler, mysteriously.

'A duel—with whom?'

'I don't know—I am not at all certain on the subject. But do you know the ruins of Tchandi?'

'Yes.'

'The general expects you there; that is what he ordered me to tell you.'

'So you come with him from Sumatra?'

'I was pilot of the little smuggling coaster, that landed him in the night on a lonely beach. He knew that you went every day to the mole, to wait for him; I was almost sure that I should meet you. He gave me details about the letter you received from him, as a proof that he had sent me. If he could have found the means of writing, he would have written.'

'But he did not tell you *why* he was obliged to hide himself?'

'He told me nothing. Certain words made me suspect what I told you—a duel.'

Knowing the mettle of General Simon, Djalma thought the suspicions of the Smuggler not unfounded. After a moment's silence, he said to him: 'Can you undertake to lead home my horse? My dwelling is without the town—there, in the midst of those trees—by the side of the new mosque. In ascending the mountain of Tchandi, my horse would be in my way; I shall go much faster on foot.'

'I know where you live; General Simon told me. I should have gone there, if I had not met you. Give me your horse.'

Djalma sprang lightly to the ground, threw the bridle to Mahal, unrolled one end of his sash, took out a silk purse, and gave it to the Smuggler, saying: 'You have been faithful and obedient. Here!—it is a trifle—but I have no more.'

'Kadja-sing was rightly called the "Father of the Generous,"' said the Smuggler, bowing with respect and gratitude. He took the road to Batavia, leading Djalma's horse. The young Indian, on the contrary, plunged into the coppice, and, walking with great strides, he directed his course towards the mountain, on which were the ruins of Tchandi, where he could not arrive before night.

CHAPTER XX.

M. JOSHUA VAN DAEL.

M. JOSHUA VAN DAEL, a Dutch merchant, and correspondent of M. Rodin, was born at Batavia, the capital of the island of Java ; his parents had sent him to be educated at Pondicherry, in a celebrated religious house, long established in that place, and belonging to the 'Society of Jesus.' It was there that he was initiated into the order, as 'professor of the three vows,' or lay member, commonly called 'temporal coadjutor.'

Joshua was a man of a probity that passed for stainless ; of strict accuracy in business, cold, careful, reserved, and remarkably skilful and sagacious ; his financial operations were almost always successful, for a protecting power gave him ever in time knowledge of events which might advantageously influence his commercial transactions. The religious house of Pondicherry was interested in his affairs, having charged him with the exportation and exchange of the produce of its large possessions in this colony.

Speaking little, hearing much, never disputing, polite in the extreme—giving seldom, but with choice and purpose—Joshua, without inspiring sympathy, commanded generally that cold respect, which is always paid to the rigid moralist ; for, instead of yielding to the influence of lax and dissolute colonial manners, he appeared to live with great regularity, and his exterior had something of austerity about it, which tended to overawe.

The following scene took place at Batavia, while Djalma was on his way to the ruins of Tchandi in the hope of meeting General Simon.

M Joshua had just retired into his cabinet, in which were many shelves filled with paper boxes, and huge ledgers and cash-boxes lying open upon desks. The only window of this apartment, which was on the ground-floor, looked out upon a narrow empty court, and was protected externally by strong iron bars ; instead of glass, it was fitted with a Venetian blind, because of the extreme heat of the climate.

M. Joshua, having placed upon his desk a taper in a glass globe, looked at the clock. 'Half-past nine,' said he. 'Mahal ought soon to be here.'

Saying this, he went out, passed through an antechamber, opened a second thick door, studded with nail-heads, in the Dutch fashion, cautiously entered the court (so as not to be heard by the people in the house), and drew back the secret bolt of a gate six feet high, formidably garnished with iron spikes. Leaving this gate unfastened, he regained his cabinet, after he had successively and carefully closed the two other doors behind him.

M. Joshua next seated himself at his desk, and took from a drawer a long letter, or rather statement, commenced some time before, and continued day by day. It is superfluous to observe, that the letter already mentioned, as addressed to M. Rodin, was anterior to the liberation of Djalma and his arrival at Batavia.

The present statement was also addressed to M. Rodin, and Van Dael thus went on with it :

'Fearing the return of General Simon, of which I had been informed by intercepting his letters—I have already told you, that I had succeeded in being employed by him as his agent here ; having then read his letters, and sent them on as if untouched to Djalma, I felt myself obliged, from the pressure of the circumstances, to have recourse to extreme measures—taking care always to preserve appearances, and rendering at the same time a signal service to humanity, which last reason chiefly decided me.

'A new danger imperiously commanded these measures. The steam-ship "Ruyter" came in yesterday, and sails to-morrow in the course of the day. She is to make the voyage to Europe *viâ* the Arabian Gulf : her passengers will disembark at Suez, cross the Isthmus, and go on board another vessel at Alexandria, which will bring them to France. This voyage, as rapid as it is direct, will not take more than seven or eight weeks. We are now at the end of October ; Prince Djalma might then be in France by the commencement of the month of January ; and according to your instructions, of which I know not the motive, but which I execute with zeal and submission, his departure must be prevented at all hazards, because, you tell me, some of the gravest interests of the Society would be compromised, by the arrival of this young Indian in Paris before the 13th of February. Now, if I succeed, as I hope, in making him miss this opportunity of the " Ruyter" it will be materially impossible for him to arrive in France before the month of April ; for the " Ruyter" is the only vessel which makes the direct passage, the others taking at least four or five months to reach Europe.

" Before telling you the means which I have thought right to employ, to detain Prince Djalma—of the success of which means I am yet uncertain—it is well that you should be acquainted with the following facts.

' They have just discovered, in British India, a community whose members call themselves " Brothers of the Good Work," or " Phansegars," which signifies simply " Thugs" or " Stranglers ;" these murderers do not shed blood, but strangle their victims, less for the purpose of robbing them, than in obedience to a homicidal vocation, and to the laws of an infernal divinity named by them " Bowanee."

' I cannot better give you an idea of this horrible sect, than by transcribing here some lines from the introduction of a report by Colonel Sleeman, who has hunted out this dark association with indefatigable zeal. The report in question was published about two months ago. Here is the extract ; it is the colonel who speaks :

' " From 1822 to 1824, when I was charged with the magistracy and civil administration of the district of Nersingpore, not a murder, not the least robbery was committed by an ordinary criminal, without my being immediately informed of it ; but if any one had come and told me at this period, that a band of hereditary assassins by profession lived in the village of Kundelie, within about four hundred yards of my court of justice—that the beautiful groves of the village of Mundesoor, within a day's march of my residence, formed one of the most frightful marts of assassination in all India—that numerous bands of ' Brothers of the Good Work,' coming from Hindostan and the Deccan, met annually beneath these shades, as at a solemn festival, to exercise their dreadful vocation upon all the roads which cross each other in this locality—I should have taken such a person for a madman, or one who had been imposed upon by idle tales. And yet nothing could be truer ; hundreds of travellers had been buried every year in the groves of Mundesoor ; a whole tribe of assassins lived close to my door, at the very time I was supreme magistrate of the province, and extended their devastations to the cities of Poonah and Hyderabad. I shall never forget, when, to convince me of the fact, one of the chiefs of the Stranglers, who had turned informer against them, caused thirteen bodies to be dug up from the ground beneath my tent, and offered to produce any number from the soil in the immediate vicinity."[*]

' These few words of Colonel Sleeman will give some idea of this dread society, which has its laws, duties, customs, opposed to all other laws human and divine. Devoted to each other, even to heroism, blindly obedient to their chiefs, who profess themselves the immediate representatives of their dark divinity, regarding as enemies all who do not belong to them,

---

[*] This report is extracted from Count Edward de Warren's excellent work, ' British India in 1831.'—E. S.

gaining recruits everywhere by a frightful system of proselytism—these apostles of a religion of murder go preaching their abominable doctrines in the shade, and spreading their immense net over the whole of India.

'Three of their principal chiefs, and one of their adepts, flying from the determined pursuit of the English governor-general, having succeeded in making their escape, had arrived at the Straits of Malacca, at no great dis-tance from our island; a smuggler, who is also something of a pirate, attached to their association, and by name Mahal, took them on board his coasting vessel, and brought them hither, where they think themselves for some time in safety—as, following the advice of the smuggler, they lie con-cealed in a thick forest, in which are many ruined temples, and numerous subterranean retreats.

'Amongst these chiefs, all three remarkably intelligent, there is one in particular, named Faringhea, whose extraordinary energy and eminent qualities make him every way redoubtable. He is of the mixed race, half-white and Hindoo, has long inhabited towns in which are European fac-tories, and speaks English and French very well. The other two chiefs are a Negro and a Hindoo; the adept is a Malay.

'The smuggler, Mahal, considering that he could obtain a large reward by giving up these three chiefs and their adept, came to me, knowing, as all the world knows, my intimate relations with a person who has great influ-ence with our governor. Two days ago, he offered me, on certain conditions, to deliver up the Negro, the half-caste, the Hindoo, and the Malay. These conditions are—a considerable sum of money, and a free passage on board a vessel sailing for Europe or America, in order to escape the implacable vengeance of the Thugs.

'I joyfully seized the occasion to hand over three such murderers to human justice, and I promised Mahal to arrange matters for him with the governor, but also on certain conditions, innocent in themselves, and which concerned Djalma. Should my project succeed, I will explain myself more at length; I shall soon know the result, for I expect Mahal every minute.

'But before I close these despatches, which are to go to-morrow by the "Ruyter"—in which vessel I have also engaged a passage for Mahal the Smuggler, in the event of the success of my plans—I must include in paren-theses a subject of some importance.

'In my last letter, in which I announced to you the death of Djalma's father, and his own imprisonment by the English, I asked for some informa-tion as to the solvency of Baron Tripeaud, banker and manufacturer at Paris, who has also an agency at Calcutta. This information will now be useless, if what I have just learned should, unfortunately, turn out to be correct, and it will be for you to act according to circumstances.

'His house at Calcutta owes considerable sums both to me and our col-league at Pondicherry, and it is said that M. Tripeaud has involved himself to a dangerous extent in attempting to ruin, by opposition, a very flourishing establishment, founded some time ago by M. François Hardy, an eminent manufacturer. I am assured that M. Tripeaud has already sunk and lost a large capital in this enterprise: he has no doubt done a great deal of harm to M. Fraçonis Hardy; but he has also, they say, seriously compromised his own fortune—and, were he to fail, the effects of his disaster would be very fatal to us, seeing that he owes a large sum of money to me and to us.

'In this state of things it would be very desirable if, by the employment of the powerful means of every kind at our disposal, we could completely discredit and break down the house of M. François Hardy, already shaken by M. Tripeaud's violent opposition. In that case, the latter would soon regain all he has lost; the ruin of his rival would insure his prosperity, and our demands would be securely covered.

'Doubtless, it is painful, it is sad, to be obliged to have recourse to these extreme measures, only to get back our own ; but, in these days, are we not surely justified in sometimes using the arms that are incessantly turned against us ? If we are reduced to such steps by the injustice and wickedness of men, we may console ourselves with the reflection that we only seek to preserve our worldly possessions, in order to devote them to the greater glory of God ; whilst, in the hands of our enemies, those very goods are the dangerous instruments of perdition and scandal.

After all, it is merely a humble proposition that I submit to you. Were it in my power to take an active part in the matter, I should do nothing of myself. My will is not my own. It belongs, with all I possess, to those to whom I have sworn absolute obedience.'

Here a slight noise interrupted M. Joshua, and drew his attention from his work. He rose abruptly, and went straight to the window. Three gentle taps were given on the outside of one of the slats of the blind.

'Is it you, Mahal ?' asked M. Joshua, in a low voice.

'It is I,' was answered from without, also in a low tone.

'And the Malay ?'

'He has succeeded.'

'Really !' cried M. Joshua, with an expression of great satisfaction ; 'are you sure of it ?'

'Quite sure : there is no devil more clever and intrepid.'

'And Djalma ?'

'The parts of the letter, which I quoted, convinced him that I came from General Simon, and that he would find him at the ruins of Tchandi.'

'Therefore, at this moment——'

'Djalma goes to the ruins, where he will encounter the black, the half-blood, and the Indian. It is there they have appointed to meet the Malay, who tattooed the prince during his sleep.'

'Have you been to examine the subterraneous passage ?'

'I went there yesterday. One of the stones of the pedestal of the statue turns upon itself ; the stairs are large ; it will do.

'And the three chiefs have no suspicion ?'

'None—I saw them in the morning—and this evening the Malay came to tell me all, before he went to join them at the ruins of Tchandi—for he had remained hidden amongst the bushes, not daring to go there in the day-time.'

'Mahal—if you have told the truth, and if all succeed—your pardon and ample reward are assured to you. Your berth has been taken on board the " Ruyter ;" you will sail to-morrow ; you will thus be safe from the malice of the Stranglers, who would follow you hither to revenge the death of their chiefs, Providence having chosen you to deliver those three great criminals to justice. Heaven will bless you !— Go and wait for me at the door of the governor's house ; I will introduce you. The matter is so important that I do not hesitate to disturb him thus late in the night. Go quickly !—I will follow on my side.'

The steps of Mahal were distinctly audible, as he withdrew precipitately, and then silence reigned once more in the house. Joshua returned to his desk, and hastily added these words to the despatch, which he had before commenced :

'Whatever may now happen, it will be impossible for Djalma to leave Batavia at present. You may rest quite satisfied ; he will not be at Paris by the 13th of next February. As I foresaw, I shall have to be up all night.— I am just going to the governor's. To-morrow I will add a few lines to this long statement, which the steam-ship " Ruyter" will convey to Europe.'

Having locked up his papers, Joshua rang the bell loudly, and, to the great astonishment of his servants, not accustomed to see him leave home in the middle of the night, went in all haste to the residence of the governor of the island.

We now conduct the reader to the ruins of Tchandi.

CHAPTER XXI.

THE RUINS OF TCHANDI.

To the storm in the middle of the day, the approach of which so well served the Strangler's designs upon Djalma, has succeeded a calm and serene night. The disc of the moon rises slowly behind a mass of lofty ruins, situate on a hill, in the midst of a thick wood, about three leagues from Batavia.

Long ranges of stone, high walls of brick, fretted away by time, porticoes covered with parasitical vegetation, stand out boldly from the sheet of silver light which blends the horizon with the limpid blue of the heavens. Some rays of the moon, gliding through the opening on one of these porticoes, fall upon two colossal statues at the foot of an immense staircase, the loose stones of which are almost entirely concealed by grass, moss, and brambles.

The fragments of one of these statues, broken in the middle, lie strewed upon the ground ; the other, which remains whole and standing, is frightful to behold. It represents a man of gigantic proportions, with a head three feet high ; the expression of the countenance is ferocious, eyes of brilliant slaty black are set beneath grey brows, the large, deep mouth gapes immoderately, and reptiles have made their nest between the lips of stone ; by the light of the moon, a hideous swarm is there dimly visible. A broad girdle, adorned with symbolic ornaments, encircles the body of this statue, and fastens a long sword to its right side. The giant has four extended arms, and, in his great hands, he bears an elephant's head, a twisted serpent, a human skull, and a bird resembling a heron. The moon, shedding her light on the profile of this statue, serves to augment the weirdness of its aspect.

Here and there, enclosed in the half-crumbling walls of brick, are fragments of stone bas-reliefs, very boldly cut ; one of those in the best preservation represents a man with the head of an elephant, and the wings of a bat, devouring a child. Nothing can be more gloomy than these ruins, buried among thick trees of a dark green, covered with frightful emblems, and seen by the moonlight, in the midst of the deep silence of night.

Against one of the walls of this ancient temple, dedicated to some mysterious and bloody Javanese divinity, leans a kind of hut, rudely constructed of fragments of brick and stone ; the door, made of woven rushes, is open, and a red light streams from it, which throws its rays on the tall grass that covers the ground. Three men are assembled in this hovel, around a claylamp, with a wick of cocoa-nut fibre steeped in palm-oil.

The first of these three, about forty years of age, is poorly clad in the European fashion ; his pale, almost white, complexion, announces that he belongs to the mixed race, being offspring of a white father and Indian mother.

The second is a robust African negro, with thick lips, vigorous shoulders, and lank legs ; his woolly hair is beginning to turn grey ; he is covered with rags, and stands close beside the Indian. The third personage is asleep, and stretched on a mat in the corner of the hovel.

These three men are the three Thuggee chiefs, who, obliged to fly from the continent of India, have taken refuge in Java, under the guidance of Mahal the Smuggler.

'The Malay does not return,' said the half-blood, named Faringhea, the most redoubtable chief of this homicidal sect : 'in executing our orders, he has perhaps been killed by Djalma.'

'The storm of this morning brought every reptile out of the earth,' said the negro ; 'the Malay must have been bitten, and his body ere now a nest of serpents.'

'To serve the good work,' proceeded Faringhea, with a gloomy air, 'one must know how to brave death.'

'And to inflict it,' added the negro.

A stifled cry, followed by some inarticulate words, here drew the attention of these two men, who hastily turned their heads in the direction of the sleeper. This latter was thirty years old at most. His beardless face, of a bright copper colour, his robe of coarse stuff, his turban striped brown and yellow, showed that he belonged to the pure Hindoo race. His sleep appeared agitated by some painful vision ; an abundant sweat streamed over his countenance, contracted by terror ; he spoke in his dream, but his words were brief and broken, and accompanied with convulsive starts.

'Again that dream !' said Faringhea to the negro. 'Always the remembrance of that man.'

'What man ?'

'Do you not remember, how, five years ago, that savage Colonel Kennedy, butcher of the Indians, came to the banks of the Ganges, to hunt the tiger, with twenty horses, four elephants, and fifty servants ?'

'Yes, yes,' said the negro ; 'and we three, hunters of men, made a better day's sport than he did. Kennedy, his horses, his elephants, and his numerous servants, did not get their tiger—but we got ours,' he added, with grim irony. 'Yes ; Kennedy, that tiger with a human face, fell into our ambush, and the brothers of the good work offered up their fine prey to our goddess Bowance.'

'If you remember, it was just at the moment when we gave the last tug to the cord round Kennedy's neck, that we perceived on a sudden a traveller close at hand. He had seen us, and it was necessary to make away with him. Now, since that time,' added Faringhea, 'the remembrance of the murder of that man pursues our brother in his dreams,' and he pointed to the sleeping Indian.

'And even when he is awake,' said the negro, looking at Faringhea with a significant air.

'Listen !' said the other, again pointing to the Indian, who, in the agitation of his dream, recommenced talking in abrupt sentences ; 'listen ! he is repeating the answers of the traveller, when we told him he must die, or serve with us on Thuggee. His mind is still impressed—deeply impressed —with those words.'

And, in fact, the Indian repeated aloud in his sleep, a sort of mysterious dialogue, of which he himself supplied both questions and answers.

' "Traveller,"' said he, in a voice broken by sudden pauses, ' "why that black mark on your forehead, stretching from one temple to the other ? It is a mark of doom, and your look is sad as death. Have you been a victim ? come with us ; Kallee will avenge you. You have suffered ?"—" Yes, I have greatly suffered."—" For a long time ?"—" Yes, for a very long time."— " You suffer even now ?"—" Yes, even now."—" What do you reserve for those who injure you ?"—" My pity."—" Will you not render blow for blow ?" —" I will return love for hate."—" Who are you, then, that render good for evil ?"—" I am one who loves, and suffers, and forgives."'

'Brother, do you hear ?' said the negro to Faringhea ; 'he has not forgotten the words of the traveller before his death,'

'The vision follows him. Listen! he will speak again. How pale he is!' Still under the influence of his dream, the Indian continued :

"'Traveller, we are three ; we are brave; we have your life in our hands— you have seen us sacrifice to the good work. Be one of us, or die—die— die ! Oh, that look ! Not thus—do not look at me thus !' As he uttered these last words, the Indian made a sudden movement, as if to keep off some approaching object, and awoke with a start. Then, passing his hand over his moist forehead, he looked round him with a bewildered eye.

'What ! again this dream, brother ?' said Faringhea. 'For a bold hunter of men, you have a weak head. Luckily, you have a strong heart and arm.'

The other remained a moment silent, his face buried in his hands ; then he replied . ' It is long since I last dreamed of that traveller.'

' Is he not dead ?' said Faringhea, shrugging his shoulders. ' Did you not yourself throw the cord around his neck ?'

' Yes,' replied the Indian, shuddering.

' Did we not dig his grave by the side of Colonel Kennedy's ? Did we not bury him with the English butcher, under the sand and the rushes ?' said the negro.

' Yes, we dug his grave,' said the Indian, trembling ; 'and yet, only a year ago, I was seated one evening at the gate of Bombay, waiting for one of our brothers—the sun was setting behind the pagoda, to the right of the little hill—the scene is all before me now—I was seated under a fig-tree— when I heard a slow, firm, even step, and, as I turned round my head—I saw him—coming out of the town.'

' A vision,' said the negro ; ' always the same vision !'

' A vision,' added Faringhea, ' or a vague resemblance.'

' I knew him by the black mark on his forehead ; it was none but he. remained motionless with fear, gazing at him with eyes aghast. He stopped, bending upon me his calm, sad look. In spite of myself, I could not help exclaiming : " It is he !"—" Yes," he replied, in his gentle voice, " it is I. Since all whom thou killest must needs live again," and he pointed to heaven as he spoke, " why shouldst thou kill ?—Hear me ! I have just come from Java : I am going to the other end of the world, to a country of never-melt- ing snow ; but, here or there, on plains of fire or plains of ice, I shall still be the same. Even so is it with the souls of those who fall beneath thy *kalleepra;* in this world or up above, in this garb or in another, the soul must still be a soul ; thou canst not smite it. Why then kill ?"—and shaking his head sorrowfully, he went on his way, walking slowly, with downcast eyes ; he ascended the hill of the pagoda ; I watched him as he went, without being able to move : at the moment the sun set, he was standing on the summit of the hill, his tall figure thrown out against the sky—and so he disappeared. Oh ! it was he !' added the Indian with a shudder, after a long pause : ' it was none but he.'

In this story the Indian had never varied, though he had often entertained his companions with the same mysterious adventure. This persistency on his part had the effect of shaking their incredulity, or at least of inducing them to seek some natural cause for this apparently superhuman event.

' Perhaps,' said Faringhea, after a moment's reflection, ' the knot round the traveller's neck got jammed, and some breath was left him, the air may have penetrated the rushes, with which we covered his grave, and so life have returned to him.'

'No, no,' said the Indian, shaking his head ; 'this man is not of our race.'

' Explain.'

' Now I know it !'

' What do you know ?'

'Listen !' said the Indian, in a solemn voice ; 'the number of victims that the children of Bowanee have sacrificed since the commencement of ages, is nothing compared to the immense heap of dead and dying, whom this terrible traveller leaves behind him in his murderous march.'

'He ?' cried the negro and Faringhea.

'Yes, *he !*' repeated the Hindoo, with a convinced accent, that made its impression upon his companions. 'Hear me and tremble !— When I met this traveller at the gates of Bombay, he came from Java, and was going towards the north, he said. The very next day, the town was a prey to the cholera, and we learned some time after, that this plague had first broken out here, in Java.'

'That is true,' said the negro.

'Hear me still further !' resumed the other. ' " I am going towards the north, to a country of eternal snow," said the traveller to me. The cholera also went towards the north, passing through Muscat—Ispahan—Tauris—Tiflis—till it overwhelmed Siberia.'

'True,' said Faringhea, becoming thoughtful.

'And the cholera,' resumed the Indian, 'only travelled its five or six leagues a day—a man's tramp—never appeared in two places at once—but swept on slowly, steadily,—even as a man proceeds.'

At the mention of this strange coincidence, the Hindoo's companions looked at each other in amazement. After a silence of some minutes, the awe-struck negro said to the last speaker : 'So you think that this man——'

'I think that this man, whom we killed, restored to life by some infernal divinity, has been commissioned to bear this terrible scourge over the earth, and to scatter round his steps that death, from which he is himself secure. Remember !' added the Indian, with gloomy enthusiasm, 'this awful wayfarer passed through Java—the cholera wasted Java. He passed through Bombay—the cholera wasted Bombay. He went towards the north—the cholera wasted the north.'

So saying, the Indian fell into a profound reverie. The negro and Faringhea were seized with gloomy astonishment.

The Indian spoke the truth as to the mysterious march (still unexplained) of that fearful malady, which has never been known to travel more than five or six leagues a day, or to appear simultaneously in two spots. Nothing can be more curious, than to trace out, on the maps prepared at the period in question, the slow, progressive course of this travelling pestilence, which offers to the astonished eye all the capricious incidents of a tourist's journey. Passing this way rather than that—selecting provinces in a country—towns in a province—one quarter in a town—one street in a quarter—one house in a street—having its place of residence and repose, and then continuing its slow, mysterious, fear-inspiring march.

The words of the Hindoo, by drawing attention to these dreadful eccentricities, made a strong impression upon the minds of the negro and Faringhea—wild natures, brought by horrible doctrines to the monomania of murder.

Yes—for this also is an established fact—there have been in India members of an abominable community, who killed without motive, without passion—killed for the sake of killing—for the pleasure of murder—to substitute death for life—to make of a living man a corpse, as they have themselves declared in one of their examinations.

The mind loses itself in the attempt to penetrate the causes of these monstrous phenomena. By what incredible series of events, have men been induced to devote themselves to this priesthood of destruction ? Without doubt, such a religion could only flourish in countries given up, like India, to the most atrocious slavery, and to the most merciless iniquity of man to man.

Such a creed !—is it not the hate of exasperated humanity, wound up to its highest pitch by oppression ?—May not this homicidal sect, whose origin is lost in the night of ages, have been perpetuated in these regions, as the only possible protest of slavery against despotism ? May not an inscrutable wisdom have here made Phansegars, even as are made tigers and serpents?

What is most remarkable in this awful sect, is the mysterious bond, which, uniting its members amongst themselves, separates them from all other men. They have laws and customs of their own, they support and help each other, but for them there is neither country nor family ; they owe no allegiance save to a dark, invisible power, whose decrees they obey with blind submission, and in whose name they spread themselves abroad, to make corpses, according to their own savage expression.*

* The following are some passages from the Count de Warren's very curious book, ' British India in 1831 ':—' Besides the robbers, who kill for the sake of the booty they hope to find upon travellers, there is a class of assassins, forming an organised society, with chiefs of their own, a slang-language, a science, a free-masonry, and even a religion, which has its fanaticism and its devotion, its agents, emissaries, allies, its militant forces, and its passive adherents, who contribute their money to the *good work*. This is the community of the Thugs or Phansegars (deceivers or stranglers, from *thugna*, to deceive, and *phansna*, to strangle), a religious and economical society, which speculates with the human race by exterminating men ; its origin is lost in the night of ages.

' Until 1810 their existence was unknown, not only to the European conquerors, but even to the native governments. Between the years 1816 and 1830, several of their bands were taken in the fact, and punished ; but until this last epoch, all the revelations made on the subject by officers of great experience, had appeared too monstrous to obtain the attention or belief of the public; they had been rejected and despised as the dreams of a heated imagination. And yet for many years, at the very least for half a century, this social wound had been frightfully on the increase, devouring the population from the Himalayas to Cape Comorin, and from Cutch to Assam.

' It was in the year 1830 that the revelations of a celebrated chief, whose life was spared on condition of his denouncing his accomplices, laid bare the whole system. The basis of the Thuggee Society is a religious belief—the worship of Bowanee, a gloomy divinity, who is only pleased with carnage, and detests above all things the human race. Her most agreeable sacrifices are human victims, and the more of these her disciple may have offered up in this world, the more he will be recompensed in the next by all the delights of soul and sense, by women always beautiful, and joys eternally renewed. If the assassin meets the scaffold in his career, he dies with the enthusiasm of a martyr, because he expects his reward. To obey his divine mistress, he murders, without anger and without remorse, the old man, woman and child ; whilst, to his fellow-religionists, he may be charitable, humane, generous, devoted, and may share all in common with them, because, like himself, they are the ministers and adopted children of Bowanee. The destruction of his fellow-creatures, not belonging to his community—the diminution of the human race—that is the primary object of his pursuit ; it is not as a means of gain, for though plunder may be a frequent, and doubtless an agreeable accessory, it is only secondary in his estimation. Destruction is his end, his celestial mission, his calling ; it is also a delicious passion, the most captivating of all sports—this hunting of men !—" You find great pleasure," said one of those that were condemned, " in tracking the wild beast to his den, in attacking the boar, the tiger, because there is danger to brave, energy and courage to display. Think how this attraction must be redoubled, when the contest is with man, when it is man that is to be destroyed. Instead of the single faculty of courage, all must be called into action—courage, cunning, foresight, eloquence, intrigue. What springs to put in motion ! what plans to develop ! To

For some moments the three Stranglers had maintained a profound silence.

Outside the hut, the moon continued to throw great masses of white radiance, and tall bluish shadows, over the imposing fabric of the ruins ; the stars sparkled in the heavens ; from time to time, a faint breeze rustled through the thick and varnished leaves of the bananas and the palms.

The pedestal of the gigantic statue, which, still entire, stood on the left side of the portico, rested upon large flag-stones, half hidden with brambles. Suddenly, one of these stones appeared to fall in ; and from the aperture, which thus formed itself without noise, a man, dressed in uniform, half pro-truded his body, looked carefully around him, and listened.

Seeing the rays of the lamp, which lighted the interior of the hovel, tremble upon the tall grass, he turned round to make a signal, and soon, accompanied by two other soldiers, he ascended, with the greatest silence and precaution, the last steps of the subterranean staircase, and went gliding amongst the ruins. For a few moments, their moving shadows were thrown upon the moon-lit ground ; then they disappeared behind some fragments of broken wall.

At the instant when the large stone resumed its place and level, the heads of many other soldiers might have been seen lying close in the excavation. The half-caste, the Indian, and the negro, still seated thoughtfully in the hut, did not perceive what was passing.

CHAPTER XXII.

THE AMBUSCADE.

THE half-blooded Faringhea, wishing doubtless to escape from the dark thoughts which the words of the Indian on the mysterious course of the Cholera had raised within him, abruptly changed the subject of conversa-tion. His eye shone with lurid fire, and his countenance took an expression of savage enthusiasm, as he cried : ' Bowanee will always watch over us, intrepid hunters of men ! Courage, brothers, courage ! The world is large ; our prey is everywhere. The English may force us to quit India, three chiefs of the good work—but what matter? We leave there our brethren, secret, numerous, and terrible, as black scorpions, whose presence is only known by their mortal sting. Exile will widen our domains. Brother, you shall have America !' said he to the Hindoo, with an inspired air. ' Brother, you shall have Africa !" said he to the negro. ' Brothers, I will take Europe ! Wherever men are to be found, there must be oppressors and victims— wherever there are victims, there must be hearts swollen with hate—it is for us to inflame that hate with all the ardour of vengeance ! It is for us, ser-vants of Bowanee, to draw towards us, by seducing wiles, all whose zeal, courage, and audacity may be useful to the cause. Let us rival each other

---

sport with all the passions, to touch the chords of love and friendship, and so draw the prey into one's net—that is a glorious chase—it is a delight, a rapture, I tell you!"

' Whoever was in India in the years 1831 and 1832, must remember the stupor and affright, which the discovery of this vast infernal machine spread through all classes of society. A great number of magistrates and administrators of provinces refused to believe in it, and could not be brought to comprehend that such a system had so long preyed on the body politic, under their eyes as it were, silently, and without betraying itself.'—See ' British India in 1831,' by Count Edward de Warren, 2 vols, in 8vo, Paris, 1844.—E. S,

in devotion and sacrifices ; let us lend each other strength, help, support ! That all who are not with us may be our prey, let us stand alone in the midst of all, against all, and in spite of all. For us, there must be neither country nor family. Our family is composed of our brethren ; our country is the world.'

This kind of savage eloquence made a deep impression on the negro and the Indian, over whom Faringhea generally exercised considerable influence, his intellectual powers being very superior to theirs, though they were themselves two of the most eminent chiefs of this bloody association. 'Yes, you are right, brother !' cried the Indian, sharing the enthusiasm of Faringhea ; 'the world is ours. Even here, in Java, let us leave some trace of our passage. Before we depart, let us establish the good work in this island ; it will increase quickly, for here also is great misery, and the Dutch are rapacious as the English. Brother, I have seen in the marshy rice-fields of this island, always fatal to those who cultivate them, men whom absolute want forced to the deadly task--they were livid as corpses—some of them, worn out with sickness, fatigue, and hunger, fell—never to rise again. Brothers, the good work will prosper in this country !'

'The other evening,' said the half-caste, 'I was on the banks of the lake, behind a rock ; a young woman came there—a few rags hardly covered her lean and sun-scorched body--in her arms she held a little child, which she pressed weeping to her milkless breast. She kissed it three times, and said to it : "You, at least, shall not be so unhappy as your father"—and she threw it into the lake. It uttered one wail, and disappeared. On this cry, the alligators, hidden amongst the reeds, leaped joyfully into the water. There are mothers here who kill their children out of pity.—Brothers, the good work will prosper in this country !'

'This morning,' said the negro, 'whilst they tore the flesh of one of his black slaves with whips, a withered old merchant of Batavia left his country-house to come to the town. Lolling in his palanquin, he received, with languid indolence, the sad caresses of two of those girls, whom he had bought, to people his harem, from parents too poor to give them food. The palanquin, which held this little old man, and the girls, was carried by twelve young and robust men. There are here, you see, mothers who in their misery sell their own daughters—slaves that are scourged—men that carry other men, like beasts of burden.—Brothers, the good work will prosper in this country !'

'Yes, in this country—and in every land of oppression, distress, corruption, and slavery.'

'Could we but induce Djalma to join us, as Mahal the Smuggler advised,' said the Indian, 'our voyage to Java would doubly profit us ; for we should then number among our band this brave and enterprising youth, who has so many motives to hate mankind.'

'He will soon be here ; let us envenom his resentments.'

'Remind him of his father's death !'

'Of the massacre of his people !'

'His own captivity !'

'Only let hatred inflame his heart, and he will be ours.'

The negro, who had remained for some time lost in thought, said suddenly: 'Brothers, suppose Mahal the Smuggler were to betray us ?'

'He ?' cried the Hindoo, almost with indignation ; 'he gave us an asylum on board his bark ; he secured our flight from the Continent ; he is again to take us with him to Bombay, where we shall find vessels for America, Europe, Africa.'

'What interest would Mahal have to betray us ?' said Faringhea.

Nothing could save him from the vengeance of the sons of Bowanee, and that he knows.'

'Well,' said the black, 'he promised to get Djalma to come hither this evening, and, once amongst us, he must needs be our own.'

'Was it not the Smuggler who told us to order the Malay to enter the ajoupa of Djalma, to surprise him during his sleep, and, instead of killing him as he might have done, to trace the name of Bowanee upon his arm? Djalma will thus learn to judge of the resolution, the cunning and obedience of our brethren, and he will understand what he has to hope or fear from such men. Be it through admiration or through terror, he must become one of us.'

'But if he refuse to join us, notwithstanding the reasons he has to hate mankind?'

'Then—Bowanee will decide his fate,' said Faringhea, with a gloomy look; 'I have my plan.'

'But will the Malay succeed in surprising Djalma during his sleep?' said the negro.

'There is none bolder, more agile, more dexterous, than the Malay,' said Faringhea. 'He once had the daring to surprise in her den a black panther, as she suckled her cub. He killed the dam, and took away the young one, which he afterwards sold to some European ship's captain.'

'The Malay has succeeded!' exclaimed the Indian, listening to a singular kind of hoot, which sounded through the profound silence of the night and of the woods.

'Yes, it is the scream of the vulture seizing its prey,' said the negro, listening in his turn: 'it is also the signal of our brethren, after they have seized their prey.'

In a few minutes, the Malay appeared at the door of the hut. He had wound around him a broad length of cotton, adorned with bright coloured stripes.

'Well,' said the negro, anxiously; 'have you succeeded?'

'Djalma must bear all his life the mark of the good work,' said the Malay, proudly. 'To reach him, I was forced to offer up to Bowanee a man who crossed my path—I have left his body under the brambles, near the ajoupa. But Djalma is marked with the sign. Mahal the Smuggler was the first to know it.'

'And Djalma did not awake?' said the Indian, confounded by the Malay's adroitness.

'Had he awoke,' replied the other, calmly, 'I should have been a dead man—as I was charged to spare his life.'

'Because his life may be more useful to us than his death,' said the half-caste. Then, addressing the Malay, he added: 'Brother, in risking life for the good work, you have done to-day what we did yesterday, what we may do again to-morrow. This time, you obey; another, you will command.'

'We all belong to Bowanee,' answered the Malay. 'What is there yet to do?—I am ready.' Whilst he thus spoke, his face was turned towards the door of the hut; on a sudden, he said in a low voice: 'Here is Djalma. He approaches the cabin. Mahal has not deceived us.'

'He must not see me yet,' said Faringhea, retiring to an obscure corner of the cabin, and hiding himself under a mat; 'try to persuade him. If he resists—I have my project.'

Hardly had Faringhea disappeared, saying these words, when Djalma arrived at the door of the hovel. At sight of those three personages with their forbidding aspect, Djalma started in surprise. But ignorant that these men belonged to the Phansegars, and knowing that, in a country where there are no inns, travellers often pass the night under a tent, or beneath the shelter of some ruins, he continued to advance towards them. After the first moment, he perceived by the complexion and the dress of one of these men, that he was an Indian, and he accosted him in the Hindoo language : ' I thought to have found here a European—a Frenchman——'

' The Frenchman is not yet come,' replied the Indian ; ' but he will not be long.'

Guessing by Djalma's question the means which Mahal had employed to draw him into the snare, the Indian hoped to gain time by prolonging his error.

' You knew this Frenchman ?' asked Djalma of the Phansegar.

' He appointed us to meet him here, as he did you,' answered the Indian.

' For what ?' inquired Djalma, more and more astonished.

' You will know when he arrives.'

' General Simon told you to be at this place ?'

' Yes, General Simon,' replied the Indian.

There was a moment's pause, during which Djalma sought in vain to explain to himself this mysterious adventure. ' And who are you ?' asked he, with a look of suspicion ; for the gloomy silence of the Phansegar's two companions, who stared fixedly at each other, began to give him some uneasiness.

' We are yours, if you will be ours,' answered the Indian.

' I have no need of you—nor you of me.'

' Who knows ?'

' I know it.'

' You are deceived. The English killed your father, a king ; made you a captive ; proscribed you, you have lost all your possessions.'

At this cruel reminder, the countenance of Djalma darkened. He started, and a bitter smile curled his lip. The Phansegar continued :

' Your father was just and brave—beloved by his subjects—they called him " Father of the Generous," and he was well named. Will you leave his death unavenged ? Will the hate, which gnaws your heart, be without fruit ?'

' My father died with arms in his hand. I revenged his death on the English whom I killed in war. He, who has since been a father to me, and who fought also in the same cause, told me, that it would now be madness to attempt to recover my territory from the English. When they gave me my liberty, I swore never again to set foot in India—and I keep the oaths I make.'

' Those who despoiled you, who took you captive, who killed your father —were men. Are there not other men, on whom you can avenge yourself ! Let your hate fall upon them !'

' You, who speak thus of men, are not a man !'

' I, and those who resemble me, are more than men. We are, to the rest of the human race, what the bold hunter is to the wild beasts, which they run down in the forest. Will you be, like us, more than a man ? Will you glut surely, largely, safely—the hate which devours your heart, for all the evil done you ?'

' Your words become more and more obscure : I have no hatred in my heart,' said Djalma. ' When an enemy is worthy of me, I fight with him ; when he is unworthy, I despise him. So that I have no hate—either for brave men or cowards.'

' Treachery !' cried the negro on a sudden, pointing with rapid gesture to the door, for Djalma and the Indian had now withdrawn a little from it, and were standing in one corner of the hovel,

At the shout of the negro, Faringhea, who had not been perceived by Djalma, threw off abruptly the mat which covered him, drew his crease, started up like a tiger, and with one bound was out of the cabin. Then, seeing a body of soldiers advancing cautiously in a circle, he dealt one of them a mortal stroke, threw down two others, and disappeared in the midst of the ruins. All this passed so instantaneously, that, when Djalma turned round, to ascertain the cause of the negro's cry of alarm, Faringhea had already disappeared.

The muskets of several soldiers, crowding to the door, were immediately pointed at Djalma and the three Stranglers, whilst others went in pursuit of Faringhea. The negro, the Malay, and the Indian, seeing the impossibility of resistance, exchanged a few rapid words, and offered their hands to the cords, with which some of the soldiers had provided themselves.

The Dutch captain, who commanded the squad, entered the cabin at this moment. 'And this other one?' said he, pointing out Djalma to the soldiers, who were occupied in binding the three Phansegars.

'Each in his turn, captain!' said an old sergeant. 'We come to him next.'

Djalma had remained petrified with surprise, not understanding what was passing round him ; but, when he saw the sergeant and two soldiers approach with ropes to bind him, he repulsed them with violent indignation, and rushed towards the door where stood the officer. The soldiers, who had supposed that Djalma would submit to his fate with the same impassibility as his companions, were astounded by this resistance, and recoiled some paces, being struck, in spite of themselves, with the noble and dignified air of the son of Kadja-sing.

'Why would you bind me like these men?' cried Djalma, addressing himself in Hindostanee to the officer, who understood that language from his long service in the Dutch colonies.

'Why would we bind you, wretch?—because you form part of this band of assassins. What?' added the officer in Dutch, speaking to the soldiers, 'are you afraid of him?—Tie the cord tight about his wrists ; there will soon be another about his neck.'

'You are mistaken,' said Djalma, with a dignity and calmness which astonished the officer ; 'I have hardly been in this place a quarter of an hour—I do not know these men. I came here to meet a Frenchman.'

'Not a Phansegar like them?—Who will believe the falsehood?'

'Them!' cried Djalma, with so natural a movement and expression of horror, that with a sign the officer stopped the soldiers, who were again advancing to bind the son of Kadja-sing ; 'these men form part of that horrible band of murderers! and you accuse me of being their accomplice! —Oh, in this case, sir! I am perfectly at ease,' said the young man, with a smile of disdain.

'It will not be sufficient to say that you are tranquil,' replied the officer ; 'thanks to their confessions, we now know by what mysterious signs to recognise the Thugs.'

'I repeat, sir, that I hold these murderers in the greatest horror, and that I came here——'

The negro, interrupting Djalma, said to the officer with a ferocious joy : 'You have hit it ; the sons of the good work do know each other by marks tattooed on their skin. For us, the hour is come—we give our necks to the cord. Often enough have we twined it round the necks of those who served not with us the good work. Now, look at our arms, and look at the arm of this youth!'

The officer, misinterpreting the words of the negro, said to Djalma : 'It is quite clear, that if, as this negro tells us, you do not bear on your arm the mysterious symbol—(we are going to assure ourselves of the fact)—and if you can explain your presence here in a satisfactory manner, you may be at liberty within two hours.'

'You do not understand me,' said the negro to the officer ; 'Prince Djalma is one of us, for he bears on his left arm the name of Bowanee.'

'Yes ! he is like us, a son of Kaile !' added the Malay.

'He is, like us, a Phansegar,' said the Indian.

The three men, irritated at the horror which Djalma had manifested on learning that they were Phansegars, took a savage pride in making it believed that the son of Kadja-sing belonged to their frightful association.

'What have you to answer?' said the officer to Djalma. The latter again gave a look of disdainful pity, raised with his right hand his long, wide left sleeve, and displayed his naked arm.

'What audacity !' cried the officer, for on the inner part of the fore-arm, a little below the bend, the name of the Bowanee, in bright red Hindoo characters, was distinctly visible. The officer ran to the Malay, and uncovered his arm ; he saw the same word, the same signs. Not yet satisfied, he assured himself that the negro and the Indian were likewise so marked.

'Wretch !' cried he, turning furiously towards Djalma ; 'you inspire even more horror than your accomplices. Bind him like a cowardly assassin,' added he to the soldiers ; 'like a cowardly assassin, who lies upon the brink of the grave, for his execution will not be long delayed.'

Struck with stupor, Djalma, who for some moments had kept his eye rivetted on the fatal mark, was unable to pronounce a word, or make the least movement : his powers of thought seemed to fail him, in presence of this incomprehensible fact.

'Would you dare deny this sign?' said the officer to him, with indignation.

'I cannot deny what I see—what is,' said Djalma, quite overcome.

'It is lucky, that you confess at last,' replied the officer. 'Soldiers, keep watch over him and his accomplices—you answer for them.'

Almost believing himself the sport of some wild dream, Djalma offered no resistance, but allowed himself to be bound and removed with mechanical passiveness. The officer, with part of his soldiers, hoped still to discover Faringhea amongst the ruins ; but his search was vain, and, after spending an hour in fruitless endeavours, he set out for Batavia, where the escort of the prisoners had arrived before him.

   ⁕   ⁕   ⁕   ⁕   ⁕   ⁕

Some hours after these events, M. Joshua van Dael thus finished his long despatch, addressed to M. Rodin of Paris :

'Circumstances were such, that I could not act otherwise ; and, taking all into consideration, it is a very small evil for a great good. Three murderers are delivered over to justice, and the temporary arrest of Djalma will only serve to make his innocence shine forth with redoubled lustre.

'Already this morning, I went to the governor, to protest in favour of our young prince. "As it was through me," I said, "that those three great criminals fell into the hands of the authorities, let them at least show me some gratitude, by doing everything to render clear as day the innocence of Prince Djalma, so interesting by reason of his misfortunes and noble qualities. Most certainly," I added, "when I came yesterday to inform the governor, that the Phansegars would be found assembled in the ruins of Tchandi, I was far from anticipating, that any one would confound with those wretches the adopted son of General Simon, an excellent man, with whom I have had for some time the most honourable relations. We must then, at any cost, discover the inconceivable mystery that has placed Djalma in this dangerous position ; and," I continued, "so convinced am I of his innocence, that, for his own sake, I would not ask for any favour on his behalf. He will have sufficient courage and dignity to wait patiently in prison for the day of justice." In all this, you see, I spoke nothing but the truth, and had not to reproach myself with the least deception, for nobody in the world is more convinced than I am of Djalma's innocence.

'The governor answered me as I expected, that morally he felt as certain as I did of the innocence of the young prince, and would treat him with all possible consideration ; but that it was necessary for justice to have its course, because it would be the only way of demonstrating the falsehood of the accusation, and discovering by what unaccountable fatality that mysterious sign was tattooed upon Djalma's arm.

'Mahal the Smuggler, who alone could enlighten justice on this subject, will in another hour have quitted Batavia, to go on board the "Ruyter," which will take him to Egypt ; for he has a note from me to the captain, to certify that he is the person for whom I engaged and paid the passage. At the same time, he will be the bearer of this long despatch, for the "Ruyter" is to sail in an hour, and the last letter-bag for Europe was made up yesterday evening. But I wished to see the governor this morning, before closing the present.

'Thus then is Prince Djalma enforcedly detained for a month, and, this opportunity of the "Ruyter" once lost, it is materially impossible that the young Indian can be in France by the 13th of next February. You see, therefore, that, even as you ordered, so have I acted according to the means at my disposal—considering only the end which justifies them—for you tell me a great interest of the society is concerned.

'In your hands, I have been what we all ought to be in the hands of our superiors—a mere instrument : since, for the greater glory of God, we become corpses with regard to the will.* Men may deny our unity and power, and the times appear opposed to us ; but circumstances only change ; we are ever the same.

'Obedience and courage, secrecy and patience, craft and audacity, union and devotion—these become us, who have the world for our country, our brethren for family, Rome for our queen !

'J. V.'

* * * * * *

About ten o'clock in the morning, Mahal the Smuggler set out with this despatch (sealed) in his possession, to board the 'Ruyter.' An hour later, the dead body of this same Mahal, strangled by Thuggee, lay concealed beneath some reeds on the edge of a desert strand, whither he had gone to take boat to join the vessel.

When at a subsequent period, after the departure of the steam-ship, they found the corpse of the smuggler, M. Joshua sought in vain for the voluminous packet, which he had entrusted to his care. Neither was there any trace of the note which Mahal was to have delivered to the captain of the 'Ruyter,' in order to be received as passenger.

Finally, the searches and bush-whacking ordered throughout the country for the purpose of discovering Faringhea, were of no avail. The dangerous chief of the Stranglers was never seen again in Java.

---

* It is known that the doctrine of passive and absolute obedience, the main-spring of the Society of Jesus, is summed up in those terrible words of the dying Loyola : 'Every member of the Order shall be, in the hands of his superiors, even as a corpse (*Perinde ac Cadaver*).'—E. S.

CHAPTER XXIII.

M. RODIN.

THREE months have elapsed since Djalma was thrown into Batavia Prison accused of belonging to the murderous gang of Megpunnas. The following scene takes place in France, at the commencement of the month of February, 1832, in Cardoville Manor House, an old feudal habitation standing upon the tall cliffs of Picardy, not far from Saint Valery, a dangerous coast on which almost every year many ships are totally wrecked, being driven on shore by the north-westers, which render the navigation of the Channel so perilous.

From the interior of the Castle is heard the howling of a violent tempest, which has arisen during the night; a frequent formidable noise, like the discharge of artillery, thunders in the distance, and is repeated by the echoes of the shore; it is the sea breaking with fury against the high rocks which are overlooked by the ancient Manor House.

It is about seven o'clock in the morning. Daylight is not yet visible through the windows of a large room situate on the ground-floor. In this apartment, in which a lamp is burning, a woman of about sixty years of age, with a simple and honest countenance, dressed as a rich farmer's wife of Picardy, is already occupied with her needle-work, notwithstanding the early hour. Close by, the husband of this woman, about the same age as herself, is seated at a large table, sorting and putting up in bags divers samples of wheat and oats. The face of this white-haired man is intelligent and open, announcing good sense and honesty, enlivened by a touch of rustic humour; he wears a shooting-jacket of green cloth, and long gaiters of tan-coloured leather, which half conceal his black velveteen breeches.

The terrible storm which rages without renders still more agreeable the picture of this peaceful interior. A rousing fire burns in a broad chimney-place faced with white marble, and throws its joyous light on the carefully polished floor; nothing can be more cheerful than the old-fashioned chintz hangings and curtains with red Chinese figures upon a white ground, and the panels over the door painted with pastoral scenes in the style of Watteau. A clock of Sèvres china, and rosewood furniture inlaid with green—quaint and portly furniture, twisted into all sorts of grotesque shapes—complete the decorations of this apartment.

Out-doors, the gale continued to howl furiously, and sometimes a gust of wind would rush down the chimney, or shake the fastenings of the windows. The man who was occupied in sorting the samples of grain was M. Dupont, bailiff of Cardoville manor.

'Holy Virgin!' said his wife; 'what dreadful weather, my dear! This M. Rodin, who is to come here this morning, as the Princess de Saint-Dizier's steward announced to us, picked out a very bad day for it.'

'Why, in truth, I have rarely heard such a hurricane. If M. Rodin has never seen the sea in its fury, he may feast his eyes to-day with the sight.'

'What can it be that brings this M. Rodin, my dear?'

'Faith! I know nothing about it. The steward tells me in his letter to show M. Rodin the greatest attention, and to obey him as if he were my master. It will be for him to explain himself, and for me to execute his orders, since he comes on the part of the princess.'

'By rights he should come from Mademoiselle Adrienne, as the land belongs to her since the death of the duke her father.'

'Yes; but the princess being aunt to the young lady, her steward manages

Mademoiselle Adrienne's affairs—so whether one or the other, it amounts to the same thing.'

' May be M. Rodin means to buy the estate. Though, to be sure, that stout lady who came from Paris last week on purpose to see the château appeared to have a great wish for it.'

At these words the bailiff began to laugh with a sly look.

' What is there to laugh at, Dupont ?' asked his wife, a very good creature, but not famous for intelligence or penetration.

' I laugh,' answered Dupont, ' to think of the face and figure of that enormous woman : with such a look, who the devil would call themselves Madame de la Sainte Colombe—Mrs. Holy Dove ? A pretty saint, and a pretty dove, truly ! She is round as a hogshead, with the voice of a town-crier, has grey moustachios like an old grenadier, and, without her knowing it, I heard her say to her servant : " Stir your stumps, *my hearty !*"—and yet she calls herself Sainte Colombe !'

' How hard on her you are, Dupont ; a body don't choose one's name. And, if she has a beard, it is not the lady's fault.'

' No—but it is her fault to call herself Sainte Colombe. Do you imagine it her true name ? Ah, my poor Catherine, you are yet very green in some things.'

'While you, my poor Dupont, are well read in slander ! This lady seems very respectable. The first thing she asked for on arriving was the chapel of the Castle, of which she had heard speak. She even said that she would make some embellishments in it ; and, when I told her we had no church in this little place, she appeared quite vexed not to have a curate in the village.'

' Oh, to be sure ! that's the first thought of your upstarts—to play the great lady of the parish, like your titled people.'

' Madame de la Sainte Colombe need not play the great lady, because she is one.'

' She ! a great lady ? Oh, lor' !'

' Yes—only see how she was dressed, in scarlet gown, and violet gloves like a bishop's ; and, when she took off her bonnet, she had a diamond band round her head-dress of false, light hair, and diamond ear-drops as large as my thumb, and diamond rings on every finger ! None of your tuppenny beauties would wear so many diamonds in the middle of the day.'

' You are a pretty judge !'

' That is not all.'

' Do you mean to say there's more ?'

' She talked of nothing but dukes, and marquises, and counts, and very rich gentlemen, who visit at her house, and are her most intimate friends ; and then, when she saw the summer house in the park, half-burnt by the Prussians, which our late master never rebuilt, she asked : " What are those ruins there ?" and I answered : " Madame, it was in the time of the Allies that the pavilion was burnt."—" Oh, my dear," cried she ; " our allies, good, dear allies ! they and the Restoration began my fortune !" So you see, Dupont, I said to myself directly : " She was no doubt one of the noble-women who fled abroad——" '

' Madame de la Sainte Colombe !' cried the bailiff, laughing heartily ; ' Oh, my poor, poor wife !'

' Oh, it is all very well ; but because you have been three years at Paris, don't think yourself a conjuror !'

' Catherine, let's drop it : you will make me say some folly, and there are certain things which dear, good creatures like you need never know.'

' I cannot tell what you are driving at ; only try to be less slanderous—for after all, should Madame de la Sainte Colombe buy the estate, will you be sorry to remain as her bailiff, eh ?'

'Not I—for we are getting old, my good Catherine ; we have lived here twenty years, and we have been too honest to provide for our old days by pilfering—and truly, at our age, it would be hard to seek another place, which perhaps we should not find. What I regret is, that Mademoiselle Adrienne should not keep the land ; it seems that she wished to sell it, against the will of the princess.'

'Good gracious, Dupont ! is it not very extraordinary that Mademoiselle Adrienne should have the disposal of her large fortune so early in life ?'

'Faith ! simple enough. Our young lady, having no father or mother, is mistress of her property, besides having a famous little will of her own. Dost remember, ten years ago, when the count brought her down here one summer ?—what an imp of mischief ! and then what eyes ! eh ?—how they sparkled, even then !'

'It is true that Mademoiselle Adrienne had in her look—an expression—a very uncommon expression for her age.'

'If she has kept what her witching, luring face promised, she must be very pretty by this time, notwithstanding the peculiar colour of her hair—for, between ourselves, if she had been a tradesman's daughter, instead of a young lady of high birth, they would have called it red.'

'There again ! more slander.'

'What? against Mademoiselle Adrienne? Heaven forbid !—I always thought that she would be as good as pretty, and it is not speaking ill of her, to say she has red hair. On the contrary, it always appears to me so fine, so bright, so sunny, and to suit so well her snowy complexion and black eyes, that in truth I would not have had it other than it was ; and I am sure, that now this very colour of her hair, which would be a blemish in any one else, must only add to the charm of Mademoiselle Adrienne's face. She must have such a sweet vixen look !'

'Oh ! to be candid, she really was a vixen—always running about the park, aggravating her governess, climbing the trees—in fact, playing all manner of naughty tricks.'

'I grant you, Mademoiselle Adrienne was a chip of the old block ; but then what wit, what engaging ways, and above all, what a good heart !'

'Yes—that she certainly had. Once I remember she gave her shawl and her new merino frock to a poor little beggar girl, and came back to the house in her petticoat, and bare arms.'

'Oh, an excellent heart—but headstrong—terribly headstrong !'

'Yes—that she was ; and 'tis likely to finish badly, for it seems that she does things at Paris—oh ! such things——'

'What things ?'

'Oh, my dear ! I can hardly venture——'

'Well, but what are they ?'

'Why,' said the worthy dame, with a sort of embarrassment and confusion, which showed how much she was shocked by such enormities, 'they say, that Mademoiselle Adrienne never sets foot in a church, but lives in a kind of heathen temple in her aunt's garden, where she has masked women to dress her up like a goddess, and scratches them very often, because she gets tipsy—without mentioning, that every night she plays on a hunting horn of massive gold—all which causes the utmost grief and despair to her poor aunt the princess.'

Here the bailiff burst into a fit of laughter, which interrupted his wife. 'Now tell me,' said he, when this first access of hilarity was over, 'where did you get these fine stories about Mademoiselle Adrienne ?'

' From René's wife, who went to Paris to look for a child to nurse ; she called at Saint-Dizier House, to see Madame Grivois, her godmother,— Now Madame Grivois is first bedchamber-woman to the princess—and she it was who told her all this—and surely she ought to know, being in the house.'

' Yes, a fine piece of goods that Grivois ! once she was a regular bad 'un, but now she professes to be as over-nice as her mistress ; like master like man, they say. The princess herself, who is now so stiff and starched, knew how to carry on a lively game in her time. Fifteen years ago, she was no such prude : do you remember that handsome colonel of hussars, who was in garrison at Abbeville ? an exiled noble who had served in Russia, whom the Bourbons gave a regiment on the Restoration ?'

' Yes, yes —I remember him ; but you are really too backbiting.'

' Not a bit—I only speak the truth. The colonel spent his whole time here, and every one said he was very warm with this same princess, who is now such a saint. Oh ! those were the jolly times. Every evening, some new entertainment at the château. What a fellow that colonel was, to set things going ; how well he could act a play !—I remember——'

The bailiff was unable to proceed. A stout maid-servant, wearing the costume and cap of Picardy, entered in haste, and thus addressed her mistress : ' Madame, there is a person here that wants to speak to master ; he has come in the post-master's calash from Saint-Valery, and he says that he is M. Rodin.'

' M. Rodin ?' said the bailiff rising. ' Show him in directly !'

A moment after, M. Rodin made his appearance. According to his custom, he was dressed even more than plainly. With an air of great humility, he saluted the bailiff and his wife, and at a sign from her husband, the latter withdrew.

The cadaverous countenance of M. Rodin, his almost invisible lips, his little reptile eyes, half concealed by their flabby lids, and the sordid style of his dress, rendered his general aspect far from prepossessing ; yet this man knew how, when it was necessary, to affect, with diabolical art, so much sincerity and good-nature--his words were so affectionate and subtly penetrating—that the disagreeable feeling of repugnance, which the first sight of him generally inspired, wore off little by little, and he almost always finished by involving his dupe or victim in the tortuous windings of an eloquence as pliant as it was honied and perfidious ; for ugliness and evil have their fascination, as well as what is good and fair.

The honest bailiff looked at this man with surprise, when he thought of the pressing recommendation of the steward of the Princess de Saint-Dizier ; he had expected to see quite another sort of personage, and, hardly able to dissemble his astonishment, he said to him : ' Is it to M. Rodin that I have the honour to speak ?'

' Yes, sir ;—and here is another letter from the steward of the Princess de Saint-Dizier.'

' Pray, sir, draw near the fire, whilst I just see what is in this letter. The weather is so bad,' continued the bailiff, obligingly, ' may I not offer you some refreshment ?'

' A thousand thanks, my dear sir ; I am off again in an hour.'

Whilst M. Dupont read, M. Rodin threw inquisitive glances round the chamber ; like a man of skill and experience, he had frequently drawn just and useful inductions from those little appearances, which, revealing a taste or habit, give at the same time some notion of a character ; on this occasion, however, his curiosity was at fault

'Very good, sir,' said the bailiff, when he had finished reading ; 'the steward renews his recommendation, and tells me to attend implicitly to your commands.'

'Well, sir, they will amount to very little, and I shall not trouble you long.'

'It will be no trouble, but an honour.'

'Nay, I know how much your time must be occupied, for, as soon as one enters this château, one is struck with the good order and perfect keeping of everything in it—which proves, my dear sir, what excellent care you take of it.'

'Oh, sir, you flatter me.'

'Flatter you?—a poor old man like myself has something else to think of. But to come to business : there is a room here which is called the Green Chamber?'

'Yes, sir ; the room which the late Count-Duke de Cardoville used for a study.'

'You will have the goodness to take me there.'

'Unfortunately, it is not in my power to do so.   After the death of the Count-Duke, and when the seals were removed, a number of papers were shut up in a cabinet in that room, and the lawyers took the keys with them to Paris.'

'Here are those keys,' said M. Rodin, showing to the bailiff a large and a small key tied together.

'Oh, sir ! that is different. You come to look for papers?'

'Yes—for certain papers—and also for a small mahogany casket, with silver clasps—do you happen to know it?'

'Yes, sir ; I have often seen it on the count's writing-table.   It must be in the large, lacquered cabinet, of which you have the key.'

'You will conduct me to this chamber, as authorised by the Princess de Saint-Dizier?'

'Yes, sir ; the princess continues in good health?'

'Perfectly so.   She lives altogether above worldly things.'

'And Mademoiselle Adrienne?'

'Alas, my dear sir !' said M. Rodin, with a sigh of deep contrition and grief.

'Good heaven, sir ! has any calamity happened to Mademoiselle Adrienne?'

'In what sense do you mean it?'

'Is she ill?'

'No, no—she is, unfortunately, as well as she is beautiful.'

'Unfortunately !' cried the bailiff, in surprise.

'Alas, yes ! for when beauty, youth, and health are joined to an evil spirit of revolt and perversity—to a character which certainly has not its equal upon earth—it would be far better to be deprived of those dangerous advantages, which only become so many causes of perdition.   But I conjure you, my dear sir, let us talk of something else : this subject is too painful,' said M. Rodin, with a voice of deep emotion, lifting the tip of his little finger to the corner of his right eye, as if to stop a rising tear.

The bailiff did not see the tear, but he saw the gesture, and he was struck with the change in M. Rodin's voice.   He answered him, therefore, with much sympathy : 'Pardon my indiscretion, sir ; I really did not know——'

'It is I who should ask pardon for this involuntary display of feeling—tears are so rare with old men—but if you had seen, as I have, the despair of that excellent princess, whose only fault has been too much kindness, too much weakness, with regard to her niece—by which she has encouraged her—but, once more, let us talk of something else, my dear sir !'

After a moment's pause, during which M. Rodin seemed to recover from his emotion, he said to Dupont : 'One part of my mission, my dear sir—

that which relates to the Green Chamber—I have now told you ; but there is yet another. Before coming to it, however, I must remind you of a circumstance you have perhaps forgotten—namely, that some fifteen or sixteen years ago, the Marquis d' Aigrigny, then colonel of the hussars in garrison at Abbeville, spent some time in this house.'

'Oh, sir ! what a dashing officer was there ! It was only just now, that I was talking about him to my wife. He was the life of the house !—how well he could perform plays—particularly the character of a scapegrace.   In the *Two Edmonds*, for instance, he would make you die with laughing, in that part of a drunken soldier—and then, with what a charming voice he sang *Joconde*, sir—better than they could sing it at Paris !'

Rodin, having listened complacently to the bailiff, said to him : ' You doubtless know, that, after a fierce duel he had with a furious Bonapartist, one General Simon, the Marquis d'Aigrigny (whose private secretary I have now the honour to be) left the world for the church.'

' No, sir ! is it possible ?   That fine officer !'

' That fine officer—brave, noble, rich, esteemed, and flattered—abandoned all those advantages for the sorry black gown ; and, notwithstanding his name, position, high connections, his reputation as a great preacher, he is still what he was fourteen years ago—a plain *abbé*—whilst so many, who have neither his merit nor his virtues, are archbishops and cardinals.'

M. Rodin expressed himself with so much goodness, with such an air of conviction, and the facts he cited appeared to be so incontestable, that M. Dupont could not help exclaiming : ' Well, sir, that is splendid conduct !'

' Splendid ?   Oh, no !' said M. Rodin, with an inimitable expression of simplicity ; ' it is quite a matter of course—when one has a heart like M. d'Aigrigny's.   But amongst all his good qualities, he has particularly that of never forgetting worthy people—people of integrity, honour, conscience— and therefore, my dear M. Dupont, he has not forgotten you.'

" What, the most noble marquis deigns to remember——'

' Three days ago, I received a letter from him, in which he mentions your name.'

' Is he then at Paris ?'

' He will be there soon, if not there now.   He went to Italy about three months ago, and, during his absence, he received a very sad piece of news —the death of his mother, who was passing the autumn on one of the estates of the Princess de Saint-Dizier.'

' Oh, indeed ! I was not aware of it.'

' Yes, it was a cruel grief to him ; but we must all resign ourselves to the will of Providence !'

'And with regard to what subject did the marquis do me the honour to mention my name ?'

' I am going to tell you.   First of all, you must know that this house is sold.   The bill of sale was signed the day before my departure from Paris.'

' Oh, sir ! that renews all my uneasiness.'

' Pray, why ?'

' I am afraid that the new proprietors may not choose to keep me as their bailiff.'

' Now see what a lucky chance :   It is just on that subject that I am going to speak to you.'

' Is it possible ?'

' Certainly.   Knowing the interest which the marquis feels for you, I am particularly desirous that you should keep this place, and I will do all in my power to serve you, if——'

' Ah, sir !' cried Dupont, interrupting Rodin ; ' what gratitude do I not owe you ! It is Heaven that sends you to me !'

' Now, my dear sir, you flatter me in your turn ; but I ought to tell you, that I am obliged to annex a small condition to my support.'

' Oh, by all means ! Only name it, sir—name it !'

' The person who is about to inhabit this mansion, is an old lady in every way worthy of veneration ; Madame de la Sainte-Colombe is the name of this respectable——'

' What, sir ?' said the bailiff, interrupting Rodin ; ' Madame de la Sainte-Colombe the lady who has bought us out ?'

' Do you know her ?'

' Yes, sir, she came last week to see the estate. My wife persists that she is a great lady ; but—between ourselves—judging by certain words that I heard her speak——'

' You are full of penetration, my dear M. Dupont. Madame de la Sainte-Colombe is far from being a great lady. I believe she was neither more nor less than a milliner, under or e of the wooden porticoes of the Palais Royal. You see, that I deal openly with you.'

' And she boasted of all the noblemen, French and foreign, who used to visit her !'

' No doubt, they came to buy bonnets for their wives ! However, the fact is, that, having gained a large fortune—and, after being in youth and middle age—indifferent—alas ! more than indifferent to the salvation of her soul—Madame de la Sainte-Colombe is now in a likely way to experience grace—which renders her, as I told you, worthy of veneration, because nothing is so respectable as a sincere repentance—always providing it be lasting. Now to make the good work sure and effectual, we shall need your assistance, my dear M. Dupont.'

' Mine, sir ! what can I do in it ?'

' A great deal ; and I will explain to you how. There is no church in this village, which stands at an equal distance from either of two parishes. Madame de la Sainte-Colombe, wishing to make choice of one of the two clergymen, will naturally apply to you and Madame Dupont, who have long lived in these parts, for information respecting them.'

' Oh ! in that case the choice will soon be made. The incumbent of Danicourt is one of the best of men.'

' Now that is precisely what you must not say to Madame de la Sainte-Colombe.'

' How so ?'

' You must, on the contrary, much praise, without ceasing, the curate of Roiville, the other parish, so as to decide this good lady to trust herself to his care.'

' And why, sir, to him rather than to the other ?'

' Why?—because, if you and Madame Dupont succeed in persuading Madame de la Sainte-Colombe to make the choice I wish, you will be certain to keep your place as bailiff. I give you my word of it, and what I promise I perform.'

' I do not doubt, sir, that you have this power,' said Dupont, convinced by Rodin's manner, and the authority of his words ; ' but I should like to know——'

' One word more,' said Rodin, interrupting him ; ' I will deal openly with you, and tell you why I insist on the preference which I beg you to support. I should be grieved if you saw in all this the shadow of an intrigue. It is only for the purpose of doing a good action. The curate of Roiville, for whom I ask your influence, is a man for whom M. d'Aigrigny feels a deep interest. Though very poor, he has to support an aged mother. Now, if he had the spiritual care of Madame de Sainte-Colombe, he would do more good than any one else, because he is full of zeal and patience ; and then it is clear he would reap some little advantages, by which his old mother might profit—there you see is the secret of this mighty scheme. When I knew that this lady was disposed to buy an estate in the neighbourhood of our friend's parish, I wrote about it to the marquis ; and he, remembering you, desired me to ask you to render him this small service, which, as you see, will not remain without a recompense. For I tell you once more, and I will prove it, that I have the power to keep you in your place as bailiff.'

' Well, sir,' replied Dupont, after a moment's reflection, ' you are so frank and obliging, that I will imitate your sincerity. In the same degree that the curate of Danicourt is respected and loved in this country, the curate of Roiville, whom you wish me to prefer to him, is dreaded for his intolerance —and, moreover——'

' Well, and what more ?'

'Why, then, they say——'

' Come, what do they say ?'

'They say—he is a Jesuit.'

Upon these words, M. Rodin burst into so hearty a laugh, that the bailiff was quite struck dumb with amazement—for the countenance of M. Rodin took a singular expression when he laughed. ' A Jesuit !' he repeated, with redoubled hilarity ; ' a Jesuit !—Now really, my dear M. Dupont, for a man of sense, experience, and intelligence, how can you believe such idle stories ? — A Jesuit—are there such people as Jesuits ?—in our time, above all, can you believe such romance of the Jacobins, hobgoblins of the old freedom lovers ?—Come, come ; I wager, you have read about them in the *Constitu-tionnel !'*

' And yet, sir, they say——'

' Good heavens ! what will they not say ?—But wise men, prudent men like you, do not meddle with what is said—they manage their own little matters, without doing injury to any one, and they never sacrifice, for the sake of nonsense, a good place, which secures them a comfortable provision for the rest of their days. I tell you frankly, however much I may regret it, that should you not succeed in getting the preference for my man, you will not remain bailiff here.'

'But, sir,' said poor Dupont, ' it will not be my fault, if this lady, hearing a great deal in praise of the other curate, should prefer him to your friend.'

' Ah ! but if, on the other hand, persons who have long lived in the neigh-bourhood—persons worthy of confidence, whom she will see every day—tell Madame de la Sainte-Colombe a great deal of good of my friend, and a great deal of harm of the other curate, she will prefer the former, and you will continue bailiff.'

' But, sir—that would be calumny !' cried Dupont.

' Pshaw, my dear M. Dupont !' said Rodin, with an air of sorrowful and affectionate reproach, 'how can you think me capable of giving you evil counsel ?—I was only making a supposition. You wish to remain bailiff on this estate. I offer you the certainty of doing so—it is for you to consider and decide.'

' But, sir——'

'One word more—or rather one more condition—as important as the other. Unfortunately, we have seen clergymen take advantage of the age and weakness of their penitents, unfairly to benefit either themselves or others : I believe our protégée incapable of any such baseness—but, in order to discharge my responsibility—and yours also, as you will have contributed to his appointment—I must request that you will write to me twice a week, giving the most exact detail of all that you have remarked in the character, habits, connections, pursuits, of Madame de la Sainte-Colombe—for the influence of a confessor, you see, reveals itself in the whole conduct of life, and I should wish to be fully edified by the proceedings of my friend, without his being aware of it—or, if anything blameable were to strike you, I should be immediately informed of it by this weekly correspondence.'

' But, sir—that would be to act as a spy?' exclaimed the unfortunate bailiff.

' Now, my dear M. Dupont ! how can you thus brand the sweetest, most wholesome of human desires—mutual confidence ?—I ask of you nothing else—I ask of you to write to me confidentially the details of all that goes on here.   On these two conditions, inseparable one from the other, you remain bailiff ; otherwise, I shall be forced, with grief and regret, to recommend some one else to Madame de la Sainte-Colombe.'

' I beg you, sir,' said Dupont, with emotion, ' be generous without any conditions !—I and my wife have only this place to give us bread, and we are too old to find another.   Do not expose our probity of forty years' standing to be tempted by the fear of want, which is so bad a counsellor !'

' My dear M. Dupont, you are really a great child : you must reflect upon this, and give me your answer in the course of a week.'

' Oh, sir ! I implore you——'   The conversation was here interrupted by a loud report, which was almost instantaneously repeated by the echoes of the cliffs.   ' What is that ?' said M. Rodin.   Hardly had he spoken, when the same noise was again heard more distinctly than before.

' It is the sound of cannon,' cried Dupont, rising ; ' no doubt a ship in distress, or signalling for a pilot.'

' My dear,' said the bailiff's wife, entering abruptly, ' from the terrace, we can see a steamer and a large ship nearly dismasted—they are drifting right upon the shore—the ship is firing minute guns—it will be lost.'

' Oh, it is terrible !' cried the bailiff, taking his hat and preparing to go out, ' to look on at a shipwreck, and be able to do nothing !'

' Can no help be given to these vessels ?' asked M. Rodin.

' If they are driven upon the reefs, no human power can save them ; since the last equinox two ships have been lost on this coast.'

' Lost with all on board ?—Oh, very frightful,' said M. Rodin.

' In such a storm, there is but little chance for the crew ; no matter,' said the bailiff, addressing his wife, ' I run down to the rocks with the people of the farm, and try to save some of them, poor creatures !—Light large fires in several rooms—get ready linen, clothes, cordials—I scarcely dare hope to save any, but we must do our best.   Will you come with me, M. Rodin ?'

' I should think it a duty, if I could be at all useful, but I am too old and feeble to be of any service,' said M. Rodin, who was by no means anxious to encounter the storm.   ' Your good lady will be kind enough to show me the Green Chamber, and when I have found the articles I require, I will set out immediately for Paris, for I am in great haste.'

' Very well, sir.   Catherine will show you.   Ring the big bell,' said the bailiff to his servant ; ' let all the people of the farm meet me at the foot of the cliff, with ropes and levers.'

' Yes, my dear,' replied Catherine ; ' but do not expose yourself.'

' Kiss me—it will bring me luck,' said the bailiff ; and he started at a full run, crying : ' Quick ! quick ; by this time, not a plank may remain of the vessels.'

' My dear madam,' said Rodin, always impassible, ' will you be obliging enough to show me the Green Chamber ?'

' Please to follow me, sir,' answered Catherine, drying her tears—for she trembled on account of her husband, whose courage she well knew.

CHAPTER XXIV.

THE TEMPEST.

THE sea is raging. Mountainous waves of dark green, marbled with white foam, stand out, in high, deep undulations, from the broad streak of red light, which extends along the horizon. Above are piled heavy masses of black and sulphurous vapour, whilst a few lighter clouds of a reddish grey, driven by the violence of the wind, rush across the murky sky.

The pale winter sun, before he quite disappears in the great clouds, behind which he is slowly mounting, casts here and there some oblique rays upon the troubled sea, and gilds the transparent crest of some of the tallest waves. A band of snow-white foam boils and rages as far as the eye can reach, along the line of the reefs that bristle on this dangerous coast.

Half-way up a rugged promontory, which juts pretty far into the sea, rises Cardoville Castle ; a ray of the sun glitters upon its windows ; its brick walls and pointed roofs of slate are visible in the midst of this sky loaded with vapours.

A large, disabled ship, with mere shreds of sail still fluttering from the stumps of broken masts, drives dead upon the coast. Now she rolls her monstrous hull upon the waves—now plunges into their trough. A flash is seen, followed by a dull sound, scarcely perceptible in the midst of the roar of the tempest. That gun is the last signal of distress from this lost vessel, which is fast forging on the breakers.

At the same moment, a steamer, with its long plume of black smoke, is working her way from east to west, making every effort to keep at a distance from the shore, leaving the breakers on her left. The dismasted ship, drifting towards the rocks, at the mercy of the wind and tide, must some time pass right ahead of the steamer.

Suddenly, the rush of a heavy sea laid the steamer upon her side ; the enormous wave broke furiously on her deck ; in a second, the chimney was carried away, the paddle-box stove in, one of the wheels rendered useless. A second white-cap, following the first, again struck the vessel amidships, and so increased the damage that, no longer answering to the helm, she also drifted towards the shore, in the same direction as the ship. But the latter, though further from the breakers, presented a greater surface to the wind and sea, and so gained upon the steamer in swiftness that a collision between the two vessels became imminent—a new danger added to all the horrors of the now certain wreck.

The ship was an English vessel, the ' Black Eagle,' homeward bound from Alexandria, with passengers, who, arriving from India and Java, *viâ* the Red Sea, had disembarked at the Isthmus of Suez, from on board the steamship ' Ruyter.' The ' Black Eagle,' quitting the Straits of Gibraltar, had gone to touch at the Azores. She headed thence for Portsmouth, when she was overtaken in the Channel by the north-wester. The steamer was the ' William Tell,' coming from Germany, by way of the Elbe, and bound, in the last place, from Hamburg to Havre.

These two vessels, the sport of enormous rollers, driven along by tide and tempest, were now rushing upon the breakers with frightful speed. The deck of each offered a terrible spectacle ; the loss of crew and passengers appeared almost certain, for before them a tremendous sea broke on jagged rocks, at the foot of a perpendicular cliff.

The captain of the ' Black Eagle,' standing on the poop, holding by the remnant of a spar, issued his last orders in this fearful extremity with courageous coolness. The smaller boats had been carried away by the waves ; it was in vain to think of launching the long-boat ; the only chance of escape, in case the ship should not be immediately dashed to pieces on touching the rocks, was to establish a communication with the land by means of a life-line—almost the last resort for passing between the shore and a stranded vessel.

The deck was covered with passengers, whose cries and terror augmented the general confusion. Some, struck with a kind of stupor, and clinging convulsively to the shrouds, awaited their doom in a state of stupid insensibility. Others wrung their hands in despair, or rolled upon the deck uttering horrible imprecations. Here, women knelt down to pray ; there, others hid their faces in their hands, that they might not see the awful approach of death. A young mother, pale as a spectre, holding her child clasped tightly to her bosom, went supplicating from sailor to sailor, and offering a purse full of gold and jewels to any one that would take charge of her son.

These cries, and tears, and terror contrasted with the stern and silent resignation of the sailors. Knowing the imminence of the inevitable danger, some of them stripped themselves of part of their clothes, waiting for the moment to make a last effort, to dispute their lives with the fury of the waves ; others, renouncing all hope, prepared to meet death with stoical indifference.

Here and there, touching or awful episodes rose in relief, if one may so express it, from this dark and gloomy background of despair.

A young man of about eighteen or twenty, with shiny black hair, copper-coloured complexion, and perfectly regular and handsome features, contemplated this scene of dismay and horror with that sad calmness peculiar to those who have often braved great perils ; wrapped in a cloak, he leaned his back against the bulwarks, with his feet resting against one of the bulkheads. Suddenly, the unhappy mother, who, with her child in her arms, and gold in her hand, had in vain addressed herself to several of the mariners, to beg them to save her boy, perceiving the young man with the copper-coloured complexion, threw herself on her knees before him, and lifted her child towards him with a burst of inexpressible agony. The young man took it, mournfully shook his head, and pointed to the furious waves—but, with a meaning gesture, he appeared to promise that he would at least try to save it. Then the young mother, in a mad transport of hope, seized the hand of the youth, and bathed it with her tears.

Further on, another passenger of the ' Black Eagle' seemed animated by sentiments of the most active pity. One would hardly have given him five-and-twenty years of age. His long, fair locks fells in curls on either side of his angelic countenance. He wore a black cassock and white neck-band. Applying himself to comfort the most desponding, he went from one to the other, and spoke to them pious words of hope and resignation ; to hear him console some, and encourage others, in language full of unction, tenderness, and ineffable charity, one would have supposed him unaware or indifferent to the perils that he shared.

On his fine, mild features, was impressed a calm and sacred intrepidity, a religious abstraction from every terrestrial thought ; from time to time, he raised to heaven his large blue eyes, beaming with gratitude, love, and serenity, as if to thank God for having called him to one of those formidable trials in which the man of humanity and courage may devote himself for his brethren, and, if not able to rescue them all, at least die with them, pointing to the sky. One might almost have taken him for an angel, sent down to render less cruel the strokes of inexorable fate.

Strange contrast ! not far from this young man's angelic beauty, there was another being, who resembled an evil spirit !

Boldly mounted on what was left of the bowsprit, to which he held on by means of some remaining cordage, this man looked down upon the terrible scene that was passing on the deck. A grim, wild joy lighted up his countenance of a dead yellow, that tint peculiar to those who spring from the union of the white race with the East. He wore only a shirt and linen drawers ; from his neck was suspended, by a cord, a cylindrical tin box, similar to that in which soldiers carry their leave of absence.

The more the danger augmented, the nearer the ship came to the breakers, or to a collision with the steamer, which she was now rapidly approaching— a terrible collision, which would probably cause the two vessels to founder before even they touched the rocks—the more did the infernal joy of this passenger reveal itself in frightful transports. He seemed to long, with ferocious impatience, for the moment when the work of destruction should be accomplished. To see him thus feasting with avidity on all the agony, the terror, and the despair of those around him, one might have taken him for the apostle of one of those sanguinary deities, who, in barbarous countries, preside over murder and carnage.

By this time the ' Black Eagle,' driven by the wind and waves, came so near the 'William Tell' that the passengers on the deck of the nearly dismantled steamer were visible from the first-named vessel.

These passengers were no longer numerous. The heavy sea, which stove in the paddle-box and broke one of the paddles, had also carried away nearly the whole of the bulwarks on that side ; the waves, entering every instant by this large opening, swept the decks with irresistible violence, and every time bore away with them some fresh victims.

Amongst the passengers, who seemed only to have escaped this danger to be hurled against the rocks, or crushed in the encounter of the two vessels, one group was especially worthy of the most tender and painful interest. Taking refuge abaft, a tall old man, with bald forehead and grey moustache, had lashed himself to a stanchion, by winding a piece of rope round his body, whilst he clasped in his arms, and held fast to his breast, two girls of fifteen or sixteen, half-enveloped in a pelisse of reindeer-skin. A large, fallow Siberian dog, dripping with water, and barking furiously at the waves, stood close to their feet.

These girls, clasped in the arms of the old man, also pressed close to each other ; but, far from being lost in terror, they raised their eyes to heaven, full of confidence and ingenuous hope, as though they expected to be saved by the intervention of some supernatural power.

A frightful shriek of horror and despair, raised by the passengers of both the vessels, was heard suddenly above the roar of the tempest. At the moment when, plunging deeply between two waves, the broadside of the steamer was turned towards the bows of the ship, the latter, lifted to a prodigious height on a mountain of water, remained, as it were, suspended over the ' William Tell,' during the second which preceded the shock of the two vessels.

There are sights of so sublime a horror, that it is impossible to describe them. Yet, in the midst of these catastrophes, swift as thought, one catches sometimes a momentary glimpse of a picture, rapid and fleeting, as if illumined by a flash of lightning.

Thus, when the ' Black Eagle,' poised aloft by the flood, was about to crash down upon the ' William Tell,' the young man with the angelic countenance and fair, waving locks bent over the prow of the ship, ready to cast himself into the sea to save some victim. Suddenly, he perceived on board the steamer, on which he looked down from the summit of the immense wave, the two girls extending their arms towards him in supplication. They appeared to recognise him, and gazed on him with a sort of ecstacy and religious homage '

For a second, in spite of the horrors of the tempest, in spite of the approaching shipwreck, the looks of those three beings met. The features of the young man were expressive of sudden and profound pity; for the maidens with their hands clasped in prayer, seemed to invoke him as their expected Saviour. The old man, struck down by the fall of a plank, lay helpless on the deck. Soon all disappeared together.

A fearful mass of water dashed the 'Black Eagle' down upon the 'William Tell,' in the midst of a cloud of boiling foam. To the dreadful crash of the two great bodies of wood and iron, which, splintering against one another, instantly foundered, one loud cry was added—a cry of agony and death—the cry of a hundred human creatures swallowed up at once by the waves!

And then- -nothing more was visible!

A few moments after, the fragments of the two vessels appeared in the trough of the sea, and on the caps of the waves—with here and there the contracted arms, the livid and despairing faces of some unhappy wretches, striving to make their way to the reefs along the shore, at the risk of being crushed to death by the shock of the furious breakers.

CHAPTER XXV.

THE SHIPWRECKED.

WHILE the bailiff was gone to the sea-shore, to render help to those of the passengers who might escape from the inevitable shipwreck, M. Rodin, conducted by Catherine to the Green Chamber, had there found the articles that he was to take with him to Paris.

After passing two hours in this apartment, very indifferent to the fate of the shipwrecked persons, which alone absorbed the attention of the inhabitants of the Castle, Rodin returned to the chamber commonly occupied by the bailiff, a room which opened upon a long gallery. When he entered it he found nobody there. Under his arm he held a casket, with silver fastenings, almost black from age, whilst one end of a large red morocco portfolio projected from the breast-pocket of his half-buttoned great coat.

Had the cold and livid countenance of the Abbé d'Aigrigny's secretary been able to express joy otherwise than by a sarcastic smile, his features would have been radiant with delight; for, just then, he was under the influence of the most agreeable thoughts. Having placed the casket upon a table, it was with marked satisfaction that he thus communed with himself:

'All goes well. It was prudent to keep these papers here till this moment, for one must always be on guard against the diabolical spirit of that Adrienne de Cardoville, who appears to guess instinctively what it is impossible she should know. Fortunately, the time approaches when we shall have no more need to fear her. Her fate will be a cruel one; it must be so. Those proud, independent characters are at all times our natural enemies—they are so by their very essence—how much more when they show themselves peculiarly hurtful and dangerous! As for La Sainte Colombe, the bailiff is sure to act for us; between what the fool calls his conscience, and the dread of being at his age deprived of a livelihood, he will not hesitate. I wish to have him because he will serve us better than a stranger; his having been here twenty years will prevent all suspicion on the part of that dull and narrow-minded woman. Once in the hands of our man at Roiville, I will answer for the result. The course of all such gross and stupid women is traced beforehand: in their youth, they serve the devil; in riper years, they make others serve him; in their old age, they are horribly afraid of him; and this fear must continue till she has left us the Château de Cardoville, which, from its isolated position, will make us an excellent college. All then goes well. As for the affair of the medals, the 13th of February approaches, without news from Joshua—evidently, Prince Djalma is still kept prisoner by the English in the heart of India, or I must have received letters from Batavia. The daughters of General Simon will be detained at Leipsic for at least a month longer. All our foreign relations are in the best condition. As for our internal affairs——'

Here M. Rodin was interrupted in the current of his reflections by the entrance of Madame Dupont, who was zealously engaged in preparations to give assistance in case of need.

' Now,' said she to a servant, ' light a fire in the next room ; put this warm wine there : your master may be in every minute.'

' Well, my dear madam,' said Rodin to her, ' do they hope to save any of these poor creatures ?'

' Alas ! I do not know, sir. My husband has been gone nearly two hours. I am terribly uneasy on his account. He is so courageous, so imprudent, if once he thinks he can be of any service.'

' Courageous even to imprudence,' said Rodin to himself, impatiently ; ' I do not like that.'

' Well,' resumed Catherine, ' I have here at hand my hot linen, my cordials — heaven grant it may all be of use !'

' We may at least hope so, my dear madam. I very much regretted that my age and weakness did not permit me to assist your excellent husband. I also regret not being able to wait for the issue of his exertions, and to wish him joy if successful—for I am unfortunately compelled to depart—my moments are precious. I shall be much obliged if you will have the carriage got ready.'

' Yes, sir ; I will see about it directly.'

' One word, my dear, good Madame Dupont. You are a woman of sense, and excellent judgment. Now I have put your husband in the way to keep, if he will, his situation as bailiff of the estate——'

' Is it possible ? What gratitude do we not owe you ! Without this place what would become of us at our time of life ?'

' I have only saddled my promise with two conditions—mere trifles—he will explain all that to you.'

' Ah, sir ! we shall regard you as our deliverer.'

' You are too good. Only, on two little conditions——'

' If there were a hundred, sir, we should gladly accept them. Think what we should be without this place—penniless—absolutely penniless !'

' I reckon upon you then ; for the interest of your husband, you will try to persuade him.'

' Missus ! I say, missus ! here's master come back,' cried a servant, rushing into the chamber.

' Has he many with him ?'

' No, missus ; he is alone.'

' Alone ! alone ?'

' Quite alone, missus.'

A few moments after, M. Dupont entered the room ; his clothes were streaming with water ; to keep his hat on in the midst of the storm, he had tied it down to his head by means of his cravat, which was knotted under his chin ; his gaiters were covered with chalky stains.

' There I have thee, my dear love !' cried his wife, tenderly embracing him. ' I have been so uneasy !'

' Up to the present moment—THREE SAVED.'

' God be praised, my dear M. Dupont !' said Rodin ; ' at least your efforts will not have been all in vain.'

'Three ! only three ?' said Catherine. 'Gracious heaven !'

'I only speak of those I saw myself, near the little creek of Goëlands. Let us hope there may be more saved on other parts of the coast.'

'Yes, indeed ; happily, the shore is not equally steep in all parts.'

'And where are these interesting sufferers, my dear sir ?' asked Rodin, who could not avoid remaining a few instants longer.

'They are mounting the cliffs, supported by our people. As they cannot walk very fast, I ran on before to console my wife, and to take the necessary measures for their reception. First of all, my dear, you must get ready some women's clothes.'

'There is then a woman amongst the persons saved ?'

'There are two girls—fifteen or sixteen years of age at the most—mere children—and so pretty !'

'Poor little things !' said Rodin, with an affectation of interest.

'The person to whom they owe their lives is with them. He is a real hero !'

'A hero ?'

'Yes ; only fancy——'

'You can tell me all this by-and-by. Just slip on this dry, warm dressing-gown, and take some of this hot wine. You are wet through.'

'I'll not refuse, for I am almost frozen to death. I was telling you that the person who saved these young girls was a hero ; and certainly his courage was beyond anything one could have imagined. When I left here with the men of the farm, we descended the little winding path, and arrived at the foot of the cliff—near the little creek of Goëlands, fortunately somewhat sheltered from the waves by five or six enormous masses of rock stretching out into the sea. Well, what should we find there ? Why, the two young girls I spoke of, in a swoon, with their feet still in the water, and their bodies resting against a rock, as though they had been placed there by some one, after being withdrawn from the sea.'

'Dear children ! it is quite touching !' said M. Rodin, raising, as usual, the tip of his little finger to the corner of his right eye, as though to dry a tear, which was very seldom visible.

'What struck me was their great resemblance to each other,' resumed the bailiff ; 'only one in the habit of seeing them could tell the difference.'

'Twin-sisters, no doubt,' said Madame Dupont.

'One of the poor things,' continued the bailiff, 'held between her clasped hands a little bronze medal, which was suspended from her neck by a chain of the same material.'

Rodin generally maintained a very stooping posture ; but, at these last words of the bailiff, he drew himself up suddenly, whilst a faint colour spread itself over his livid cheeks. In any other person, these symptoms would have appeared of little consequence ; but in Rodin, accustomed for long years to control and dissimulate his emotions, they announced no ordinary excitement. Approaching the bailiff, he said to him in a slightly agitated voice, but still with an air of indifference : 'It was doubtless a pious relic. Did you see what was inscribed on this medal ?'

'No, sir ; I did not think of it.'

'And the two young girls were like one another—very much like, you say ?'

'So like, that one would hardly know which was which. Probably they are orphans, for they are dressed in mourning.'

'Oh ! dressed in mourning ?' said M. Rodin, with another start.

'Alas ! orphans so young !' said Madame Dupont, wiping her eyes.

'As they had fainted away, we carried them further on, to a place where the sand was quite dry. While we were busy about this, we saw the head of a man appear from behind one of the rocks, which he was trying to climb, clinging to it by one hand ; we ran to him, and luckily in the nick of time, for he was clean worn out, and fell exhausted into the arms of our men. It was of him I spoke, when I talked of a hero ; for, not content with having saved the two young girls by his admirable courage, he had attempted to rescue a third person, and had actually gone back amongst the rocks and breakers—but his strength failed him, and, without the aid of our men, he would certainly have been washed away from the ridge to which he clung.'

' He must indeed be a fine fellow !' said Catherine.

Rodin, with his head bowed upon his breast, seemed quite indifferent to this conversation. The dismay and stupor, in which he had been plunged, only increased upon reflection. The two girls, who had just been saved, were fifteen years of age ; were dressed in mourning ; were so like, that one might be taken for the other ; one of them wore round her neck a chain with a bronze medal ; he could scarcely doubt that they were the daughters of General Simon. But how could those sisters be amongst the number of shipwrecked passengers ? How could they have escaped from the prison at Leipsic ? How did it happen, that he had not been informed of it ? Could they have fled, or had they been set at liberty ? How was it possible that he should not be apprised of such an event ? But these secondary thoughts, which offered themselves in crowds to the mind of M. Rodin, were swallowed up in the one fact : ' The daughters of General Simon are here !' —His plan, so laboriously laid, was thus entirely destroyed.

' When I speak of the deliverer of these young girls,' resumed the bailiff, addressing his wife, and without remarking M. Rodin's absence of mind, ' you are expecting no doubt to see a Hercules ?—well, he is altogether the reverse. He is almost a boy in look, with fair, sweet face, and light, curling locks. I left him a cloak to cover him, for he had nothing on but his shirt, black knee-breeches, and a pair of black worsted stockings— which struck me as singular.'

' Why, it was certainly not a sailor's dress.'

' Besides, though the ship was English, I believe my hero is a Frenchman, for he speaks our language as well as we do. What brought the tears to my eyes, was to see the young girls, when they came to themselves. As soon as they saw him, they threw themselves at his feet, and seemed to look up to him and thank him, as one would pray. Then they cast their eyes around them, as if in search of some other person, and, having exchanged a few words, they fell sobbing into each other's arms.'

' What a dreadful thing it is ! How many poor creatures must have perished !'

' When we quitted the rocks, the sea had already cast ashore seven dead bodies, besides fragments of the wreck, and packages. I spoke to some of the coast-guard, and they will remain all day on the look-out ; and if, as I hope, any more should escape with life, they are to be brought here. But surely that is the sound of voices !—yes, it is our shipwrecked guests !'

The bailiff and his wife ran to the door of the room—that door, which opened on the long gallery—whilst Rodin, biting convulsively his flat nails, awaited with angry impatience the arrival of the strangers. A touching picture soon presented itself to his view.

From the end of the darksome gallery, only lighted on one side by several windows, three persons, conducted by a peasant, advanced slowly. This group consisted of the two maidens, and the intrepid young man to whom they owed their lives. Rose and Blanche were on either side of their deliverer, who, walking with great difficulty, supported himself lightly on their arms.

Though he was full twenty-five years of age, the juvenile countenance of this man made him appear younger. His long, fair hair, parted on the fore-head, streamed wet and smooth over the collar of a large brown cloak, with which he had been covered. It would be difficult to describe the adorable expression of goodness in his pale, mild face, as pure as the most ideal creations of Raphael's pencil—for that divine artist alone could have caught the melancholy grace of those exquisite features, the serenity of that celestial look, from eyes limpid and blue as those of an archangel, or of a martyr ascended to the skies.

Yes, of a martyr ! for a blood-red halo already encircled that beauteous head. Piteous sight to see ! just above his light eyebrows, and rendered still more visible by the effect of the cold, a narrow cicatrix, from a wound inflicted many months before, appeared to encompass his fair forehead with a purple band ; and (still more sad !) his hands had been cruelly pierced by a crucifixion—his feet had suffered the same injury—and, if he now walked with so much difficulty, it was that his wounds had reopened, as he struggled over the sharp rocks.

This young man was Gabriel, the priest attached to the foreign mission, the adopted son of Dagobert's wife. He was a priest and martyr—for, in our days, there are still martyrs, as in the time when the Cæsars flung the early Christians to the lions and tigers of the circus.

Yes, in our days, the children of the people—for it is almost always amongst them that heroic and disinterested devotion may still be found—the children of the people, led by an honourable conviction, because it is courageous and sincere, go to all parts of the world, to try and propagate their faith, and brave both torture and death with the most unpretending valour.

How many of them, victims of some barbarous tribe, have perished, obscure and unknown, in the midst of the solitudes of the two worlds !—And for these humble soldiers of the cross, who have nothing but their faith and their intrepidity, there is never reserved on their return (and they seldom do return) the rich and sumptuous dignities of the church. Never does the purple or the mitre conceal their scarred brows and mutilated limbs ; like the great majority of other soldiers, they die forgotten.[*]

In their ingenuous gratitude, the daughters of General Simon, as soon as they recovered their senses after the shipwreck, and felt themselves able to ascend the cliffs, would not leave to any other person the care of sustaining the faltering steps of him who had rescued them from certain death.

The black garments of Rose and Blanche streamed with water ; their faces were deadly pale, and expressive of deep grief ; the marks of recent tears were on their cheeks, and, with sad, downcast eyes, they trembled both from agitation and cold, as the agonising thought recurred to them, that they should never again see Dagobert, their friend and guide ; for it was to him that Gabriel had stretched forth a helping hand, to assist him to climb the rocks. Unfortunately, the strength of both had failed, and the soldier had been carried away by a retreating wave.

The sight of Gabriel was a fresh surprise for Rodin, who had retired on one side, in order to observe all ; but this surprise was of so pleasant a nature, and he felt so much joy in beholding the missionary safe after such

---

* We always remember with emotion the end of a letter written, two or three years ago, by one of these young and valiant missionaries, the son of poor parents in Beauce. He was writing to his mother from the heart of Japan, and thus concluded his letter : ' Adieu, my dear mother ! they say there is much danger where I am now sent to. Pray for me, and tell all our good neighbours that I think of them very often.'—These few words, addressed from the centre of Asia to poor peasants in a hamlet of France, are only the more touching from their very simplicity.—E.S.

imminent peril, that the painful impression, caused by the view of General Simon's daughters, was a little softened. It must not be forgotten, that the presence of Gabriel in Paris, on the 13th of February, was essential to the success of Rodin's projects.

The bailiff and his wife, who were greatly moved at sight of the orphans, approached them with eagerness. Just then a farm-boy entered the room, crying : ' Sir ! sir ! good news—two more saved from the wreck !'

' Blessing and praise to God for it !' said the missionary.

' Where are they ?' asked the bailiff, hastening towards the door.

' There is one who can walk, and is following behind me with Justin ; the other was wounded against the rocks, and they are carrying him on a litter made of branches.'

' I will run and have him placed in the room below,' said the bailiff, as he went out. ' Catherine, you can look to the young ladies.'

' And the shipwrecked man who can walk—where is he ?' asked the bailiff's wife.

' Here he is,' said the peasant, pointing to some one who came rapidly along the gallery ; ' when he heard that the two young ladies were safe in the château—though he is old, and wounded in the head, he took such great strides, that it was all I could do to get here before him."

Hardly had the peasant pronounced these words, when Rose and Blanche, springing up by a common impulse, flew to the door. They arrived there at the same moment as Dagobert.

The soldier, unable to utter a syllable, fell on his knees at the threshold, and extended his arms to the daughters of General Simon ; while Spoilsport, running to them, licked their hands.

But the emotion was too much for Dagobert ; and, when he had clasped the orphans in his arms, his head fell backward, and he would have sunk down altogether, but for the care of the peasants. In spite of the observations of the bailiff's wife, on their state of weakness and agitation, the two young girls insisted on accompanying Dagobert, who was carried fainting into an adjoining apartment.

At sight of the soldier, Rodin's face was again violently contracted, for he had till then believed that the guide of General Simon's daughters was dead. The missionary, worn out with fatigue, was leaning upon a chair, and had not yet perceived Rodin.

A new personage, a man with a dead yellow complexion, now entered the room, accompanied by another peasant, who pointed out Gabriel to him. This man, who had just borrowed a smock-frock and a pair of trousers, approached the missionary, and said to him in French, but with a foreign accent : ' Prince Djalma has just been brought in here. His first word was to ask for you.'

' What does that man say ?' cried Rodin, in a voice of thunder ; for, at the name of Djalma, he had sprung with one bound to Gabriel's side.

' M. Rodin !' exclaimed the missionary, falling back in surprise.

' M. Rodin,' cried the other shipwrecked person ; and, from that moment, he kept his eye fixed on the correspondent of M. Van Dael.

' You here, sir ?' said Gabriel, approaching Rodin with an air of deference, not unmixed with fear.

' What did that man say to you ?' repeated Rodin, in an excited tone. ' Did he not utter the name of Prince Djalma ?'

' Yes, sir ; Prince Djalma was one of the passengers on board the English ship, which came from Alexandria, and in which we have just been wrecked. This vessel touched at the Azores, where I then was ; the ship that brought me from Charlestown having been obliged to put in there, and being likely to remain for some time, on account of serious damage, I embarked on board the "Black Eagle," where I met Prince Djalma. We were bound to Portsmouth, and from thence my intention was to proceed to France.'

Rodin did not care to interrupt Gabriel. This new shock had completely paralysed his thoughts. At length, like a man who catches at a last hope, which he knows beforehand to be vain, he said to Gabriel : 'Can you tell me who this Prince Djalma is?'

'A young man as good as brave—the son of an East Indian king, dispossessed of his territory by the English.'

Then, turning towards the other shipwrecked man, the missionary said to him with anxious interest : 'How is the Prince? are his wounds dangerous?'

'They are serious contusions, but they will not be mortal,' answered the other.

'Heaven be praised !' said the missionary, addressing Rodin ; 'here, you see, is another saved.'

'So much the better,' observed Rodin, in a quick, imperious tone.

'I will go see him,' said Gabriel, submissively. 'You have no orders to give me ?'

'Will you be able to leave this place in two or three hours, notwithstanding your fatigues ?'

'If it be necessary—yes.'——'It is necessary. You will go with me.'

Gabriel only bowed in reply, and Rodin sank confounded into a chair, while the missionary went out with the peasant. The man with the sallow complexion still lingered in a corner of the room, unperceived by Rodin.

This man was Faringhea, the half caste, one of the three chiefs of the Stranglers. Having escaped the pursuit of the soldiers in the ruins of Tchandi, he had killed Mahal the Smuggler, and robbed him of the despatches written by M. Joshua Van Dael to Rodin, as also of the letter by which the smuggler was to have been received as passenger on board the 'Ruyter.' When Faringhea left the hut in the ruins of Tchandi, he had not been seen by Djalma ; and the latter, when he met him on shipboard, after his escape (which we shall explain by-and-by), not knowing that he belonged to the sect of Phansegars, treated him during the voyage as a fellow-countryman.

Rodin, with his eye fixed and haggard, his countenance of a livid hue, biting his nails to the quick in silent rage, did not perceive the half-caste, who quietly approached him, and laying his hand familiarly on his shoulder, said to him : 'Your name is Rodin ?'

'What now ?' asked the other, starting, and raising his head abruptly.

'Your name is Rodin ?' repeated Faringhea.

'Yes. What do you want ?'

'You live in the Rue du Milieu-des-Ursins, Paris ?'

'Yes. But, once more, what do you want ?'

'Nothing now, brother : hereafter, much !'

And Faringhea, retiring, with slow steps, left Rodin alarmed at what had passed ; for this man, who scarcely trembled at any thing, had quailed before the dark look and grim visage of the Strangler.

CHAPTER XXVI.

THE DEPARTURE FOR PARIS.

THE most profound silence reigns throughout Cardoville House. The tempest has lulled by degrees, and nothing is heard from afar but the hoarse murmur of the waves, as they wash heavily the shore.

Dagobert and the orphans have been lodged in warm and comfortable apartments on the first-floor of the château. Djalma, too severely hurt to be carried upstairs, has remained in a room below. At the moment of the shipwreck, a weeping mother had placed her child in his arms. He had failed in the attempt to snatch this unfortunate infant from certain death, but his generous devotion had hampered his movements, and when thrown upon the rocks, he was almost dashed to pieces. Faringhea, who has been able to convince him of his affection, remains to watch over him.

Gabriel, after administering consolation to Djalma, has reascended to the chamber allotted to him ; faithful to the promise he made to Rodin, to be ready to set out in two hours, he has not gone to bed ; but, having dried his clothes, he has fallen asleep in a large, high-backed arm-chair, placed in front of a bright coal-fire. His apartment is situated near those occupied by Dagobert and the two sisters.

Spoilsport, probably quite at his ease in so respectable a dwelling, has quitted the door of Rose and Blanche's chamber, to lie down and warm himself at the hearth, by the side of which the missionary is sleeping. There, with his nose resting on his outstretched paws, he enjoys a feeling of perfect comfort and repose, after so many perils by land and sea. We will not venture to affirm, that he thinks habitually of poor old Jovial ; unless we recognise as a token of remembrance on his part, his irresistible propensity to bite all the white horses he has met with, ever since the death of his venerable companion, though before, he was the most inoffensive of dogs with regard to horses of every colour.

Presently one of the doors of the chamber opened, and the two sisters entered timidly. Awake for some minutes, they had risen and dressed themselves, feeling still some uneasiness with respect to Dagobert ; though the bailiff's wife, after showing them to their room, had returned again to tell them that the village-doctor found nothing serious in the hurt of the old soldier, still they hoped to meet some one belonging to the château, of whom they could make further inquiries about him.

The high back of the old-fashioned arm-chair, in which Gabriel was sleeping, completely screened him from view ; but the orphans, seeing their canine friend lying quietly at his feet, thought it was Dagobert reposing there, and hastened towards him on tiptoe. To their great astonishment, they saw Gabriel fast asleep, and stood still in confusion, not daring to advance or recede, for fear of waking him.

The long, light hair of the missionary was no longer wet, and now curled naturally round his neck and shoulders ; the paleness of his complexion was the more striking, from the contrast afforded by the deep purple of the damask covering of the arm-chair. His beautiful countenance expressed a profound melancholy, either caused by the influence of some painful dream, or else that he was in the habit of keeping down, when awake, some sad regrets, which revealed themselves without his knowledge when he was sleeping. Notwithstanding this appearance of bitter grief, his features preserved their character of angelic sweetness, and seemed endowed with an inexpressible charm, for nothing is more touching than suffering goodness. The two young girls cast down their eyes, blushed simultaneously, and exchanged anxious glances, as if to point out to each other the slumbering missionary.

' He sleeps, sister,' said Rose in a low voice.

' So much the better,' replied Blanche, also in a whisper, making a sign of caution ; ' we shall now be able to observe him well.'

' Yes, for we durst not do so, in coming from the sea hither.'

' Look ! what a sweet countenance !'

' He is just the same as we saw him in our dreams.'

' When he promised he would protect us.'

'And he has not failed us.'

' But here, at least, he is visible.'

' Not as it was in the prison at Leipsic, during that dark night.'

' And so—he has again rescued us "

' Without him, we should have perished this morning.'

' And yet, sister, it seems to me, that in our dreams his countenance shone with light.'

' Yes, you know, it dazzled us to look at him.'

' And then he had not so sad a mien.'

'That was because he came then from heaven ; now he is upon earth.'

' But, sister, had he then that bright red scar round his forehead ?'

' Oh, no ! we should have certainly perceived it.'

' And these other marks on his hands ?'

' If he has been wounded, how can he be an archangel ?'

' Why not, sister ? If he received those wounds in preventing evil, or in helping the unfortunate, who, like us, were about to perish ?'

' You are right. If he did not run any danger for those he protects, it would be less noble.'

' What a pity that he does not open his eyes !'

' Their expression is so good, so tender !'

' Why did he not speak of our mother, by the way ?'

' We were not alone with him ; he did not like to do so.'

' But now we are alone.'

' If we were to pray to him to speak to us ?'

The orphans looked doubtingly at each other, with charming simplicity ; a bright glow suffused their cheeks, and their young bosoms heaved gently beneath their black dresses.

' You are right. Let us kneel down to him.'

' Oh, sister ! *our* hearts beat so !' said Blanche, believing rightly, that Rose felt exactly as she did. ' And yet it seems to do us good. It is as if some happiness were going to befal us.'

The sisters, having approached the arm-chair on tiptoe, knelt down with clasped hands, one to the right, the other to the left of the young priest. It was a charming picture. Turning their lovely faces towards him, they said in a low whisper, with a soft, sweet voice, well suited to their youthful appearance : ' Gabriel ! speak to us of our mother !'

On this appeal, the missionary gave a slight start, half-opened his eyes, and, still in a state of semi-consciousness, between sleep and waking, beheld those two beauteous faces turned towards him, and heard two gentle voices repeat his name.

' Who calls me ?' said he, rousing himself, and raising his head.

' It is Blanche and Rose.'

It was now Gabriel's turn to blush, for he recognised the young girls, he had saved. ' Rise, my sisters !' said he to them ; ' you should kneel only unto God.'

The orphans obeyed, and were soon beside him, holding each other by the hand. 'You know my name, it seems,' said the missionary with a smile.

' Oh, we have not forgotten it !'

' Who told it you ?'

' Yourself.'

' I ?——' Yes—when you came from our mother.'

' I, my sisters ?' said the missionary, unable to comprehend the words of the orphans. ' You are mistaken. I saw you to-day for the first time.'

'But in our dreams?'

'Yes—do you not remember?—in our dreams.'

'In Germany—three months ago, for the first time. Look at us well!'

Gabriel could not help smiling at the simplicity of Rose and Blanche, who expected him to remember a dream of theirs; growing more and more perplexed, he repeated : 'In your dreams?'

'Certainly ; when you gave us such good advice.'

'And when we were so sorrowful in prison, your words, which we remembered, consoled us, and gave us courage.'

'Was it not you, who delivered us from the prison at Leipsic, in that dark night, when we were not able to see you?'

'I?'

'What other but you would thus have come to our help, and to that of our old friend?'

'We told him, that you would love him, because he loved us, although he would not believe in angels.'

'And this morning, during the tempest, we had hardly any fear.'

'Because we expected you.'

'This morning—yes, my sisters—it pleased heaven to send me to your assistance. I was coming from America, but I have never been in Leipsic. I could not, therefore, have let you out of prison. Tell me, my sisters,' added he, with a benevolent smile, 'for whom do you take me?'

'For a good angel, whom we have seen already in dreams, sent by our mother from heaven to protect us.'

'My dear sisters, I am only a poor priest. It is by mere chance, no doubt, that I bear some resemblance to the angel you have seen in your dreams, and whom you could not see in any other manner—for angels are not visible to mortal eye.'

'Angels are not visible?' said the orphans, looking sorrowfully at each other.

'No matter, my dear sisters,' said Gabriel, taking them affectionately by the hand ; 'dreams, like everything else, come from above. Since the remembrance of your mother was mixed up with this dream, it is twice blessed.

At this moment a door opened, and Dagobert made his appearance. Up to this time, the orphans, in their innocent ambition to be protected by an archangel, had quite forgotten the circumstance that Dagobert's wife had adopted a forsaken child, who was called Gabriel, and who was now a priest and missionary.

The soldier, though obstinate in maintaining that his hurt was only a blank wound (to use a term of General Simon's), had allowed it to be carefully dressed by the surgeon of the village, and now wore a black bandage, which concealed one half of his forehead, and added to the natural grimness of his features. On entering the room, he was not a little surprised to see a stranger holding the hands of Rose and Blanche familiarly in his own. This surprise was natural, for Dagobert did not know that the missionary had saved the lives of the orphans, and had attempted to save his also.

In the midst of the storm, tossed about by the waves, and vainly striving to cling to the rocks, the soldier had only seen Gabriel very imperfectly, at the moment when, having snatched the sisters from certain death, the young priest had fruitlessly endeavoured to come to his aid. And when, after the shipwreck, Dagobert had found the orphans in safety beneath the roof of the Manor House, he fell, as we have already stated, into a swoon, caused by fatigue, emotion, and the effects of his wound—so that he had again no opportunity of observing the features of the missionary.

The veteran began to frown from beneath his black bandage and thick, grey brows, at beholding a stranger so familiar with Rose and Blanche; but the sisters ran to throw themselves into his arms, and to cover him with filial caresses. His anger was soon dissipated by these marks of affection, though he continued, from time to time, to cast a suspicious glance at the missionary, who had risen from his seat, but whose countenance he could not well distinguish.

'How is your wound?' asked Rose, anxiously. 'They told us it was not dangerous.'

'Does it still pain?' added Blanche.

'No children; the surgeon of the village would bandage me up in this manner. If my head was carbonadoed with sabre cuts, I could not have more wrappings. They will take me for an old milksop; it is only a blank wound, and I have a good mind to——' And therewith the soldier raised one of his hands to the bandage.

'Will you leave that alone?' cried Rose, catching his arm. 'How can you be so unreasonable—at your age?'

'Well, well! don't scold! I will do what you wish, and keep it on.' Then, drawing the sisters to one end of the room, he said to them in a low voice, whilst he looked at the young priest from the corner of his eye: 'Who is that gentleman who was holding your hands when I came in? He has very much the look of a curate. You see, my children, you must be on your guard; because——'

'*He?*' cried both sisters at once, turning towards Gabriel. 'Without him, we should not now be here to kiss you.'

'What's that?' cried the soldier, suddenly drawing up his tall figure, and gazing full at the missionary.

'It is our guardian angel,' resumed Blanche.

'Without him,' said Rose, 'we must have perished this morning in the shipwreck.'

'Ah! it is he, who——' Dagobert could say no more. With swelling heart, and tears in his eyes, he ran to the missionary, offered him both his hands, and exclaimed in a tone of gratitude impossible to describe: 'Sir, I owe you the lives of these two children. I feel what a debt that service lays upon me. I will not say more—because it includes everything!'

Then, as if struck with a sudden recollection, he cried: 'Stop! when I was trying to cling to a rock, so as not to be carried away by the waves, was it not you that held out your hand to me? Yes—that light hair—that youthful countenance—yes—it was certainly you—now I am sure of it!'

'Unhappily, sir, my strength failed me, and I had the anguish to see you fall back into the sea.'

'I can say nothing more in the way of thanks than what I have already said,' answered Dagobert, with touching simplicity; 'in preserving these children you have done more for me than if you had saved my own life. But what heart and courage!' added the soldier, with admiration; 'and so young, with such a girlish look!'

'And so,' cried Blanche, joyfully, 'our Gabriel came to your aid also?'

'Gabriel!' said Dagobert, interrupting Blanche, and addressing himself to the priest. 'Is your name Gabriel?'

'Yes, sir.'

'Gabriel!' repeated the soldier, more and more surprised. 'And a priest!' added he.

'A priest of the foreign missions.'

'Who—who brought you up?' asked the soldier, with increasing astonishment.

'An excellent and generous woman, whom I revere as the best of mothers: for she had pity on me, a deserted infant, and treated me ever as her son.'

' Frances Baudoin—was it not ?' said the soldier, with deep emotion.

' It was, sir,' answered Gabriel, astonished in his turn. ' But how do you know this ?'

' The wife of a soldier, eh ?' continued Dagobert.

' Yes, of a brave soldier—who, from the most admirable devotion, is even now passing his life in exile—far from his wife—far from his son, my dear brother—for I am proud to call him by that name——'

' My Agricola !—my wife !—when did you leave them ?'

' What ! is it possible ! You the father of Agricola ?—Oh ! I knew not, until now,' cried Gabriel, clasping his hands together, ' I knew not all the gratitude that I owed to heaven !'

' And my wife ! my child !' resumed Dagobert, in a trembling voice; ' how are they? have you news of them ?'

' The accounts I received, three months ago, were excellent.'

' No; it is too much,' cried Dagobert ; ' it is too much !' The veteran was unable to proceed ; his feelings stifled his words, and he fell back exhausted in a chair.

And now Rose and Blanche recalled to mind that portion of their father's letter which related to the child named Gabriel, whom the wife of Dagobert had adopted ; then they also yielded to transports of innocent joy.

' Our Gabriel is the same as yours—what happiness !' cried Rose.

' Yes, my children ! he belongs to you as well as to me. We have all our part in him.' Then, addressing Gabriel, the soldier added with affectionate warmth : ' Your hand, my brave boy ! give me your hand !'

' Oh, sir ! you are too good to me.'

' Yes—that's it—thank me !—after all thou hast done for us !'

' Does my adopted mother know of your return ?' asked Gabriel, anxious to escape from the praises of the soldier.

' I wrote to her five months since, but said that I should come alone; there was a reason for it, which I will explain by-and-by. Does she still live in the Rue Brise-Miche ? It was there Agricola was born.'

' She still lives there.'

' In that case, she must have received my letter. I wished to write to her from the prison at Leipsic, but it was impossible.'

' From prison ! Have you just come out of prison ?'

' Yes ; I come straight from Germany, by the Elbe and Hamburg, and I should be still at Leipsic, but for an event which the Devil must have had a hand in—a good sort of devil, though.'

' What do you mean ? Pray explain to me.'

' That would be difficult, for I cannot explain it to myself. These little ladies,' he added, pointing with a smile to Rose and Blanche, ' pretended to know more about it than I did, and were continually repeating : " It was the angel that came to our assistance, Dagobert—the good angel we told thee of—though you said you would rather have Spoilsport to defend us——" '

' Gabriel, I am waiting for you,' said a stern voice, which made the missionary start. They all turned round instantly, whilst the dog uttered a deep growl.

It was Rodin. He stood in the doorway leading to the corridor. His features were calm and impassive, but he darted a rapid, piercing glance at the soldier and the sisters.

' Who is that man ?' said Dagobert, very little prepossessed in favour of Rodin, whose countenance he found singularly repulsive. ' What the mischief does he want ?'

' I must go with him,' answered Gabriel, in a tone of sorrowful constraint.

Then, turning to Rodin, he added : 'A thousand pardons ! I shall be ready in a moment.'

'What !' cried Dagobert, stupefied with amazement, 'going the very instant we have just met ? No, by my faith ! you shall not go. I have too much to tell you, and to ask in return. We will make the journey together. It will be a real treat for me.'

'It is impossible. He is my superior, and I must obey him.'

'Your superior ?—why, he's in citizen's dress.'

'He is not obliged to wear the ecclesiastical garb.'

'Rubbish ! since he is not in uniform, and there is no provost-marshal in your troop, send him to the——'

'Believe me, I would not hesitate a minute, if it were possible to remain.'

'I was right in disliking the phis of that man,' muttered Dagobert between his teeth. Then he added, with an air of impatience and vexation : 'Shall I tell him that he will much oblige us by marching off by himself?'

'I beg you not to do so,' said Gabriel ; 'it would be useless ; I know my duty, and have no will but my superior's. As soon as you arrive in Paris, I will come and see you, as also my adopted mother, and my dear brother, Agricola.'

'Well—if it must be. I have been a soldier, and know what subordination is,' said Dagobert, much annoyed. 'One must put a good face on bad fortune. So, the day after to-morrow, in the Rue Brise-Miche, my boy; for they tell me I can be in Paris by to-morrow evening, and we set out almost immediately. But I say—there seems to be a strict discipline with you fellows !'

'Yes, it is strict and severe,' answered Gabriel, with a shudder, and a stifled sigh.

'Come, shake hands—and let's say farewell for the present. After all, twenty-four hours will soon pass away.'

'Adieu ! adieu !' replied the missionary, much moved, whilst he returned the friendly pressure of the veteran's hand.

'Adieu, Gabriel !' added the orphans, sighing also, and with tears in their eyes.

'Adieu, my sisters !' said Gabriel—and he left the room with Rodin, who had not lost a word or an incident of this scene.

Two hours after, Dagobert and the orphans had quitted the Castle for Paris, not knowing that Djalma was left at Cardoville, being still too much injured to proceed on his journey. The half-caste, Faringhea, remained with the young prince, not wishing, he said, to desert a fellow-countryman.

We now conduct the reader to the Rue Brise-Miche, the residence of Dagobert's wife.

CHAPTER XXVII.

DAGOBERT'S WIFE.

THE following scenes occur in Paris, on the morrow of the day when the shipwrecked travellers were received in Cardoville House.

Nothing can be more gloomy than the aspect of the Rue Brise-Miche, one end of which leads into the Rue Saint-Merry, and the other into the little square of the Cloister, near the church. At this end, the street, or rather alley—for it is not more than eight feet wide—is shut in between immense black, muddy, dilapidated walls, the excessive height of which excludes both air and light ; hardly, during the longest days of the year, is the sun able to throw into it a few straggling beams; whilst, during the cold damps of winter, a chilling fog, which seems to penetrate everything, hangs constantly above the miry pavement of this species of oblong well.

It was about eight o'clock in the evening; by the faint, reddish light of the street lamp, hardly visible through the haze, two men, stopping at the angle of one of those enormous walls, exchanged a few words together.

'So,' said one, 'you understand all about it. You are to watch in the street, till you see them enter No. 5.'

'All right!' answered the other.

'And when you see 'em enter, so as to make quite sure of the game, go up to Frances Baudoin's room ——'

'Under the cloak of asking where the little humpbacked workwoman lives—the sister of that gay girl, the Queen of the Bacchanals.'

'Yes—and you must try and find out her address also—from her humpbacked sister, if possible—for it is very important. Women of her feather change their nests like birds, and we have lost track of her.'

'Make yourself easy; I will do my best with Humpy, to learn where her sister hangs out.'

'And to give you steam, I'll wait for you at the tavern opposite the Cloister, and we'll have a go of hot wine on your return.'

'I'll not refuse, for the night is deucedly cold.'

'Don't mention it! This morning, the water friz on my sprinkling-brush, and I turned as stiff as a mummy in my chair at the church-door. Ah, my boy! a distributor of holy water is not always upon roses!'

'Luckily, you have the pickings——'

'Well, well—good luck to you! Don't forget the Fiver, the little passage next to the dyer's shop.'

'Yes, yes—all right!' and the two men separated.

One proceeded to the Cloister Square; the other towards the further end of the street, where it led into the Rue Saint Merry. This latter soon found the number of the house he sought—a tall, narrow building, having, like all the other houses in the street, a poor and wretched appearance. When he saw he was right, the man commenced walking backwards and forwards in front of the door of No. 5.

If the exterior of these buildings was uninviting, the gloom and squalor of the interior cannot be described. The house No. 5 was, in a special degree, dirty and dilapidated. The water, which oozed from the wall, trickled down the dark and filthy staircase. On the second floor, a wisp of straw had been laid on the narrow landing-place, for wiping the feet on; but this straw, being now quite rotten, only served to augment the sickening odour, which arose from want of air, from damp, and from the putrid exhalations of the drains. The few openings, cut at rare intervals in the walls of the staircase, could hardly admit more than some faint rays of glimmering light.

In this quarter, one of the most populous in Paris, such houses as these, poor, cheerless, and unhealthy, are generally inhabited by the working classes. The house in question was of the number. A dyer occupied the ground-floor; the deleterious vapours arising from his vats added to the stench of the whole building. On the upper stories, several artisans lodged with their families, or carried on their different trades. Up four flights of stairs was the lodging of Frances Baudoin, wife of Dagobert. It consisted of one room, with a closet adjoining, and was now lighted by a single candle. Agricola occupied a garret in the roof.

Old greyish paper, broken here and there by the cracks, covered the crazy wall, against which rested the bed; scanty curtains, running upon an iron rod, concealed the windows; the brick floor, not polished, but often washed, had preserved its natural colour. At one end of this room was a round iron stove, with a large pot for culinary purposes. On the wooden table, painted yellow, marbled with brown, stood a minature house made of iron—a master-piece of patience and skill, the work of Agricola Baudoin, Dagobert's son.

A plaster crucifix, hung up against the wall, surrounded by several branches of consecrated box-tree, and various images of saints, very coarsely coloured, bore witness to the habits of the soldier's wife. Between the windows stood one of those old walnut-wood presses, curiously fashioned, and almost black with time ; an old arm-chair, covered with green cotton velvet (Agricola's first present to his mother), a few rush-bottomed chairs, and a work-table on which lay several bags of coarse, brown cloth, completed the furniture of this room, badly secured by a worm-eaten door. The adjoining closet contained a few kitchen and household utensils.

Mean and poor as this interior may perhaps appear, it would not seem so to the greater number of artizans ; for the bed was supplied with two mattresses, clean sheets, and a warm counterpane ; the old-fashioned press contained linen ; and, moreover, Dagobert's wife occupied all to herself a room as large as those in which numerous families, belonging to honest and laborious workmen, often live and sleep huddled together—only too happy if the boys and girls can have separate beds, or if the sheets and blankets are not pledged at the pawnbroker's.

Frances Baudoin, seated beside the small stove, which, in the cold and damp weather, yielded but little warmth, was busied in preparing her son Agricola's evening meal.

Dagobert's wife was about fifty years of age ; she wore a close jacket of blue cotton, with white flowers on it, and a stuff petticoat ; a white handker-chief was tied round her head, and fastened under the chin. Her counte-nance was pale and meagre, the features regular, and expressive of resigna-tion and great kindness. It would have been difficult to find a better, a more courageous mother. With no resource but her labour, she had suc-ceeded, by unwearied energy, in bringing up not only her own son Agricola, but also Gabriel, the poor deserted child, of whom, with admirable devotion, she had ventured to take charge.

In her youth, she had, as it were, anticipated the strength of later life, by twelve years of incessant toil, rendered lucrative by the most violent exer-tions, and accompanied by such privations as made it almost suicidal. Then (for it was a time of splendid wages, compared to the present), by sleepless nights and constant labour, she contrived to earn about two shillings (fifty sous) a day, and with this she managed to educate her son and her adopted child.

At the end of these twelve years, her health was ruined, and her strength nearly exhausted ; but, at all events, her boys had wanted for nothing, and had received such an education as children of the people can obtain. About this time, M. François Hardy took Agricola as an apprentice, and Gabriel prepared to enter the priests' seminary, under the active patronage of M. Rodin, whose communications with the confessor of Frances Baudoin had become very frequent about the year 1820.

This woman (whose piety had always been excessive) was one of those simple natures, endowed with extreme goodness, whose self-denial ap-proaches to heroism, and who devote themselves in obscurity to a life of martyrdom—pure and heavenly minds, in whom the instincts of the heart supply the place of the intellect !

The only defect, or rather the necessary consequence of this extreme simplicity of character, was the invincible determination she displayed in yielding to the commands of her confessor, to whose influence she had now for many years been accustomed to submit. She regarded this influence as most venerable and sacred ; no mortal power, no human consideration, could have prevented her from obeying it. Did any dispute arise on the subject, nothing could move her on this point ; she opposed to every argument a resistance entirely free from passion—mild as her disposition, calm as her conscience—but, like the latter, not to be shaken. In a word, Frances Baudoin was one of those pure, but uninstructed and credulous beings, who may sometimes, in skilful and dangerous hands, become, without knowing it, the instruments of much evil.

For some time past, the bad state of her health, and particularly the increasing weakness of her sight, had condemned her to a forced repose ; unable to work more than two or three hours a day, she consumed the rest of her time at church.

Frances rose from her seat, pushed the coarse bags at which she had been working to the further end of the table, and proceeded to lay the cloth for her son's supper, with maternal care and solicitude. She took from the press a small leathern bag, containing an old silver cup, very much battered, and a fork and spoon, so worn and thin, that the latter cut like a knife. These, her only *plate* (the wedding-present of Dagobert) she rubbed and polished as well as she was able, and laid by the side of her son's plate. They were the most precious of her possessions, not so much for what little intrinsic value might attach to them, as for the associations they recalled ; and she had often shed bitter tears, when, under the pressure of illness or want of employment, she had been compelled to carry these sacred treasures to the pawnbroker's.

Frances next took, from the lower shelf of the press, a bottle of water, and one of wine about three-quarters full, which she also placed near her son's plate ; she then returned to the stove, to watch the cooking of the supper.

Though Agricola was not much later than usual, the countenance of his mother expressed both uneasiness and grief ; one might have seen, by the redness of her eyes, that she had been weeping a good deal. After long and painful uncertainty, the poor woman had just arrived at the conviction that her eye-sight, which had been growing weaker and weaker, would soon be so much impaired as to prevent her working even the two or three hours a day which had lately been the extent of her labours.

Originally an excellent hand at her needle, she had been obliged, as her eyesight gradually failed her, to abandon the finer for the coarser sorts of work, and her earnings had necessarily diminished in proportion ; she had at length been reduced to the necessity of making those coarse bags for the army, which took about four yards of sewing, and were paid at the rate of two sous each, she having to find her own thread. This work, being very hard, she could at most complete three such bags in a day, and her gains thus amounted to threepence (six sous) !

It makes one shudder to think of the great number of unhappy females, whose strength has been so much exhausted by privations, old age, or sickness, that all the labour of which they are capable, hardly suffices to bring them in daily this miserable pittance. Thus do their gains diminish in exact proportion to the increasing wants which age and infirmity must occasion.

Happily, Frances had an efficient support in her son. A first-rate workman, profiting by the just scale of wages adopted by M. Hardy, his labour brought him from four to five shillings a day—more than double what was gained by the workmen of many other establishments. Admitting therefore that his mother were to gain nothing, he could easily maintain both her and himself.

But the poor woman, so wonderfully economical that she denied herself even some of the necessaries of life, had of late become ruinously liberal on the score of the sacristy, since she had adopted the habit of visiting daily the parish church. Scarcely a day passed but she had masses sung, or tapers burnt, either for Dagobert, from whom she had been so long separated, or for the salvation of her son Agricola, whom she considered on the high road to perdition. Agricola had so excellent a heart, so loved and revered his mother, and considered her actions in this respect inspired by so touching a sentiment, that he never complained when he saw a great part of his week's wages (which he paid regularly over to his mother every Saturday) disappear in pious forms.

Yet now and then he ventured to remark to Frances, with as much respect as tenderness, that it pained him to see her enduring privations injurious at her age, because she preferred incurring these devotional expenses. But what answer could he make to this excellent mother, when she replied with tears : ' My child, 'tis for the salvation of your father, and yours too.'

To dispute the efficacy of masses, would have been venturing on a subject which Agricola, through respect for his mother's religious faith, never discussed. He contented himself, therefore, to seeing her dispense with comforts she might have enjoyed.

A discreet tap was heard at the door. 'Come in,' said Frances. The person came in.

CHAPTER XXVIII.

THE SISTER OF THE BACCHANAL QUEEN.

THE person who now entered was a girl of about eighteen, short, and very much deformed. Though not exactly a hunchback, her spine was curved ; her breast was sunken, and her head deeply set in the shoulders. Her face was regular, but long, thin, very pale, and pitted with the small-pox ; yet it expressed great sweetness and melancholy. Her blue eyes beamed with kindness and intelligence. By a strange freak of nature, the handsomest woman would have been proud of the magnificent hair twisted in a coarse net at the back of her head. She held an old basket in her hand. Though miserably clad, the care and neatness of her dress revealed a powerful struggle with her poverty. Notwithstanding the cold, she wore a scanty frock made of print of an indefinable colour, spotted with white ; but it had been so often washed, that its primitive design and colour had long since disappeared. In her resigned, yet suffering face, might be read a long familiarity with every form of suffering, every description of taunting. From her birth, ridicule had ever pursued her. We have said that she was very deformed, and she was vulgarly called ' Mother Bunch.' Indeed it was so usual to give her this grotesque name, which every moment reminded her of her infirmity, that Frances and Agricola, though they felt as much compassion as other people showed contempt for her, never called her, however, by any other name.

Mother Bunch, as we shall therefore call her in future, was born in the house in which Dagobert's wife had resided for more than twenty years ; and she had, as it were, been brought up with Agricola and Gabriel.

There are wretches fatally doomed to misery. Mother Bunch had a very pretty sister, on whom Perrine Soliveau, their common mother, the widow of a ruined tradesman, had concentrated all her affection, while she treated her deformed child with contempt and unkindness. The latter would often come, weeping, to Frances, on this account, who tried to console her, and in the long evenings amused her by teaching her to read and sew. Accustomed to pity her by their mother's example, instead of imitating other children, who always taunted and sometimes even beat her, Agricola and Gabriel liked her, and used to protect and defend her.

She was about fifteen, and her sister Cephyse was about seventeen, when their mother died, leaving them both in utter poverty. Cephyse was intelligent, active, clever, but different to her sister; she had the lively, alert, hoydenish character which requires air, exercise, and pleasures—·a good girl enough, but foolishly spoiled by her mother. Cephyse, listening at first to Frances's good advice, resigned herself to her lot; and, having learnt to sew, worked like her sister, for about a year. But, unable to endure any longer the bitter privations her insignificant earnings, notwithstanding her incessant toil, exposed her to—privations which often bordered on starvation —Cephyse, young, pretty, of warm temperament, and surrounded by brilliant offers and seductions—brilliant, indeed, for her, since they offered food to satisfy her hunger, shelter from the cold, and decent raiment, without being obliged to work fifteen hours a day in an obscure and unwholesome hovel— Cephyse listened to the vows of a young lawyer's clerk, who forsook her soon after. She formed a connection with another clerk, whom she (instructed by the examples set her) forsook in turn for a bagman, whom she afterwards cast off for other favourites. In a word, what with changing and being forsaken, Cephyse in the course of one or two years was the idol of a set of grisettes, students and clerks; and acquired such a reputation at the balls on the Hampstead Heaths of Paris, by her decision of character, original turn of mind, and unwearied ardour in all kinds of pleasures, and especially her wild noisy gaiety, that she was termed the Bacchanal Queen, and proved herself in every way worthy of this bewildering royalty.

From that time poor Mother Bunch only heard of her sister at rare intervals. She still mourned for her, and continued to toil hard to gain her three-and-six a week. The unfortunate girl, having been taught sewing by Frances, made coarse shirts for the common people and the army. For these she received half-a-crown a dozen. They had to be hemmed, stitched, provided with collars and wristbands, buttons, and button-holes; and at the most, when at work twelve and fifteen hours a day, she rarely succeeded in turning out more than fourteen or sixteen shirts a week—an excessive amount of toil that brought her in about three shillings and fourpence a week. And the case of this poor girl was neither accidental nor uncommon. And this, because the remuneration given for women's work is an example of revolting injustice and savage barbarism. They are paid not half as much as men who are employed at the needle : such as tailors, and makers of gloves, or waistcoats, etc.—no doubt because women can work as well as men—because they are more weak and delicate—and because their need may be two-fold as great when they become mothers.

Well, Mother Bunch fagged on, with three-and-four a week. That is to say, toiling hard for twelve or fifteen hours every day, she succeeded in keeping herself alive, in spite of exposure to hunger, cold, and poverty—so numerous were her privations. Privations? No ! The word privation expresses but weakly that constant and terrible want of all that is necessary to preserve the existence God gives ; namely, wholesome air and shelter, sufficient and nourishing food, and warm clothing. Mortification would be a better word to describe that total want of all that is essentially vital, which a justly organised state of society ought—yes—ought necessarily to bestow on every active honest workman and workwoman, since civilization has dispossessed them of all territorial right, and left them no other patrimony than their hands.

The savage does not enjoy the advantage of civilization ; but he has, at least, the beasts of the field, the fowls of the air, the fish of the sea, and the fruits of the earth, to feed him, and his native woods for shelter and for fuel. The civilized man, disinherited of these gifts, considering the rights of property as sacred, may, in return for his hard daily labour, which enriches his country, demand wages that will enable him to live in the enjoyment of health : nothing more, and nothing less. For is it living, to drag along on the extreme edge which separates life from the grave, and even there continually struggle against cold, hunger, and disease ? And to show how far the mortification which society imposes thus inexorably on its millions of honest, industrious labourers (by its careless disregard of all the questions which concern the just remuneration of labour), may extend, we will describe how this poor girl contrived to live on three shillings and sixpence a week.

Society, perhaps, may then feel its obligation to so many unfortunate wretches for supporting, with resignation, the horrible existence which leaves them just sufficient life to feel the worst pangs of humanity. Yes : to live at such a price is virtue ! Yes, society thus organised, whether it tolerates or imposes so much misery, loses all right to blame the poor wretches who sell themselves, not through debauchery, but because they are cold and famishing. This poor girl spent her wages as follows :—

Six pounds of bread, second quality	-		-	-	-	-	0	8½
Four pails of water	-	-	-	-	-	-	0	2
Lard or dripping (butter being out of the question)						-	0	5
Coarse salt	-	-	-	-	-	-	-	0	0¾
A bushel of charcoal	-	-	-	-	-	0	4
A quart of dried vegetables	-	-	-	-	0	3
Three quarts of potatoes	-	-	-	-	-	0	2
Dips -	-	-	-	-	-	-	-	0	3¼
Thread and needles	-	-	-	-	-	0	2½
							2	7

To save charcoal, Mother Bunch prepared soup only two or three times a week at most, on a stove that stood on the landing of the fourth storey. On other days she ate it cold. There remained nine or ten pence a week for clothes and lodging. By rare good fortune, her situation was in one respect an exception to the lot of many others. Agricola, that he might not wound her delicacy, had come to a secret arrangement with the housekeeper, and hired a garret for her, just large enough to hold a small bed, a chair, and a table ; for which the sempstress had to pay five shillings a year. But Agricola, in fulfilment of his agreement with the porter, paid the balance, to make up the actual rent of the garret, which was twelve and sixpence. The poor girl had thus about eighteenpence a month left for her other expenses. But many workwomen, whose position is less fortunate than hers, since they have neither home nor family, buy a piece of bread and some other food to keep them through the day ; and at night patronise the ' twopenny rope,' one with another, in a wretched room containing five or six beds, some of which are always engaged by men, as male lodgers are by far the most abundant. Yes ; and in spite of the disgust that a poor and virtuous girl must feel at this arrangement, she must submit to it ; for a lodging-house keeper cannot have separate rooms for females. To furnish a room, however meanly, the poor workwoman must possess three or four shillings in ready money. But how save this sum, out of weekly earnings of a couple of florins, which are scarcely sufficient to keep her from starving, and are still less sufficient to clothe her ? No ! no ! The poor wretch must resign herself to this repugnant cohabitation ; and so, gradually, the instinct of modesty becomes weakened ; the natural sentiment of chastity, that saved her from the 'gay life,' becomes extinct ; vice appears to be the only means of improving her intolerable condition ; she yields ; and the first 'man made of money,' who can afford a governess for his children, cries out against the depravity of the lower orders ! And yet, painful as the condition of the working woman is, it is relatively fortunate. Should work fail her for one day, two days, what then ? Should sickness come—sickness almost always occasioned by unwholesome food, want of fresh air, necessary attention, and good rest ; sickness, often so enervating as to render work impossible ; though not so dangerous as to procure the sufferer a bed in an hospital—what becomes of the hapless wretches then ? The mind hesitates, and shrinks from dwelling on such gloomy pictures.

This inadequacy of wages, one terrible source only of so many evils, and often of so many vices, is general, especially among women ; and, again, this is not private wretchedness, but the wretchedness which afflicts whole classes, the type of which we endeavour to develop in Mother Bunch. It exhibits the moral and physical condition of thousands of human creatures in Paris, obliged to subsist on a scanty four shillings a week. This poor workwoman, then, notwithstanding the advantages she unknowingly enjoyed through Agricola's generosity, lived very miserably ; and her health, already shattered, was now wholly undermined by these constant hardships. Yet, with extreme delicacy, though ignorant of the little sacrifice already made for her by Agricola, Mother Bunch pretended she earned more than she really did, in order to avoid offers of service which it would have pained her to accept, because she knew the limited means of Frances and her son, and because it would have wounded her natural delicacy, rendered still more sensitive by so many sorrows and humiliations.

   ✥   ✥   ✥   ✥   ✥

But, singular as it may appear, this deformed body contained a loving and generous soul—a mind cultivated even to poetry ; and let us add, that this was owing to the example of Agricola Baudoin, with whom she had been brought up, and who had naturally the gift. This poor girl was the first confident to whom our young mechanic imparted his literary essays ; and when he told her of the charm and extreme relief he found in poetic reverie, after a day of hard toil, the workwoman, gifted with strong natural intelligence, felt, in her turn, how great a resource this would be to her in her lonely and despised condition.

One day, to Agricola's great surprise, who had just read some verses to her, the sewing-girl, with smiles and blushes, timidly communicated to him also a poetic composition. Her verses wanted rhythm and harmony, perhaps ; but they were simple and affecting, as a non-envenomed complaint entrusted to a friendly hearer. From that day Agricola and she held frequent consultations ; they gave each other mutual encouragement : but with this exception, no one else knew anything of the girl's poetical essays, whose mild timidity made her often pass for a person of weak intellect. This soul must have been great and beautiful, for in all her unlettered strains there was not a word of murmuring respecting her hard lot : her note was sad, but gentle—desponding, but resigned ; it was especially the language of deep tenderness—of mournful sympathy—of angelic charity for all poor creatures consigned, like her, to bear the double burthen of poverty and deformity. Yet she often expressed a sincere free-spoken admiration of beauty, free from all envy or bitterness ; she admired beauty as she admired the sun. But, alas ! many were the verses of hers that Agricola had never seen, and which he was never to see.

The young mechanic, though not strictly handsome, had an open masculine face; was as courageous as kind; possessed a noble, glowing, generous heart, a superior mind, and a frank, pleasing gaiety of spirits. The young girl, brought up with him, loved him as an unfortunate creature can love, who, dreading cruel ridicule, is obliged to hide her affection in the depths of her heart, and adopt reserve and deep dissimulation. She did not seek to combat her love; to what purpose should she do so? No one would ever know it. Her well known sisterly affection for Agricola explained the interest she took in all that concerned him; so that no one was surprised at the extreme grief of the young workwoman, when, in 1830, Agricola, after fighting intrepidly for the people's flag, was brought bleeding home to his mother. Dagobert's son, deceived, like others, on this point, had never suspected, and was destined never to suspect, this love for him.

Such was the poorly-clad girl who entered the room in which Frances was preparing her son's supper.

'Is it you, my poor love,' said she; 'I have not seen you since morning: have you been ill? Come and kiss me.'

The young girl kissed Agricola's mother, and replied: 'I was very busy about some work, mother; I did not wish to lose a moment; I have only just finished it. I am going down to fetch some charcoal—do you want anything while I'm out?'

'No, no, my child, thank you. But I am very uneasy. It is half-past eight, and Agricola is not come home.' Then she added, after a sigh: 'He kills himself with work for me. Ah, I am very unhappy, my girl; my sight is quite going. In a quarter of an hour after I begin working, I cannot see at all—not even to sew sacks. The idea of being a burden to my son drives me distracted.'

'Oh, don't, ma'am, if Agricola heard you say that——'

'I know the poor boy thinks of nothing but me, and that augments my vexation. Only I think that rather than leave me, he gives up the advantages that his fellow-workmen enjoy at Hardy's, his good and worthy master —instead of living in this dull garret, where it is scarcely light at noon, he would enjoy, like the other workmen, at very little expense, a good light room, warm in winter, airy in summer, with a view of the garden. And he is so fond of trees! not to mention that this place is so far from his work, that it is quite a toil to him to get to it.'

'Oh, when he embraces you he forgets his fatigue, Mrs. Baudoin,' said Mother Bunch; 'besides, he knows how you cling to the house in which he was born. M. Hardy offered to settle you at Plessy with Agricola, in the building put up for the workmen.'

'Yes, my child; but then I must give up church. I can't do that.'

'But,——be easy, I hear him,' said the hunchback, blushing.

A sonorous, joyous voice was heard singing on the stairs.

'At least, I'll not let him see I have been crying,' said the good mother, drying her tears. 'This is the only moment of rest and ease from toil he has—I must not make it sad to him.'

CHAPTER XXIX.

AGRICOLA BAUDOIN.

OUR blacksmith poet, a tall young man, about four and twenty years of age, was alert and robust, with ruddy complexion, dark hair and eyes, and aquiline nose, and an open, expressive countenance. His resemblance to Dagobert was rendered more striking by the thick brown moustache which he wore according to the fashion ; and a sharp-pointed imperial covered his chin. His cheeks, however, were shaven. Olive colour velveteen trousers, a blue blouse, bronzed by the forge smoke, a black cravat, tied carelessly round his muscular neck, a cloth cap with a narrow vizor, composed his dress. The only thing which contrasted singularly with his working habiliments was a handsome purple flower, with silvery pistils, which he held in his hand.

' Good evening, mother,' said he, as he came to kiss Frances immediately. Then, with a friendly nod, he added, ' Good evening, Mother Bunch.'

' You are very late, my child,' said Frances, approaching the little stove on which her son's simple meal was simmering : ' I was getting very anxious.'

' Anxious about me, or about my supper, dear mother ?' said Agricola, gaily : ' the deuce ! you won't excuse me for keeping the nice little supper waiting that you get ready for me, for fear it should be spoilt, eh ?'

So saying, the blacksmith tried to kiss his mother again.

' Have done, you naughty boy ; you'll make me upset the pan.'

' That would be a pity, mother ; for it smells delightfully. Let's see what it is.'

' Wait half a moment.'

' I'll swear, now, you have some of the fried potatoes and bacon I'm so fond of.'

' Being Saturday, of course !' said Frances, in a tone of mild reproach.

' True,' rejoined Agricola, exchanging a smile of innocent cunning with Mother Bunch ; ' but, talking of Saturday, mother, here are my wages.'

' Thank ye, child ; put the money in the cupboard.'

' Yes, mother !'

' Oh, dear,' cried the young sempstress, just as Agricola was about to put away the money, ' what a handsome flower you have in your hand, Agricola. I never saw a finer. In winter, too ! Do look at it, Mrs. Baudoin.'

' See there, mother,' said Agricola, taking the flower to her ; ' look at it, admire it, and especially smell it. You can't have a sweeter perfume ; a blending of vanilla and orange blossom.'

' Indeed, it does smell nice, child. Goodness ! how handsome !' said Frances, admiringly ; ' where did you find it ?'

' Find it, my good mother !' repeated Agricola, smilingly : ' do you think folks pick up such things between the Barrière du Maine and the Rue Brise-Miche ?'

' How did you get it then ?' inquired the sewing-girl, sharing in Frances's curiosity.

' Oh ! you would like to know ? Well, I'll satisfy you, and explain why I came home so late ; for something else detained me. It has been an evening of adventures, I promise you. I was hurrying home, when I heard a low, gentle barking at the corner of the Rue de Babylone ; it was just about dusk, and I could see a very pretty little dog, scarce bigger than my fist, black and tan, with long silky hair, and ears that covered its paws.'

' Lost, poor thing, I warrant,' said Frances.

' You've hit it. I took up the poor thing, and it began to lick my hands. Round its neck was a red satin ribbon, tied in a large bow ; but as that did not bear the master's name, I looked beneath it, and saw a small collar, made of a gold plate and small gold chains. So I took a lucifer match from my 'bacco-box, and striking a light, I read, " FRISKY belongs to Hon. Miss Adrienne de Cardoville, No. 7, Rue de Babylone." '

' Why, you were just in the street,' said Mother Bunch.

' Just so. Taking the little animal under my arm, I looked about me till I came to a long garden wall, which seemed to have no end, and found a small door of a summer-house, belonging no doubt to the large mansion at the other end of the park ; for this garden looked just like a park. So, looking up, I saw " No. 7," newly painted over a little door with a grated slide. I rang ; and in a few minutes, spent, no doubt, in observing me through the bars (for I am sure I saw a pair of eyes peeping through), the gate opened. And now, you'll not believe a word I have to say.'

' Why not, my child ?'

' Because it seems like a fairy tale.'

' A fairy tale ?' said Mother Bunch, as if she was really her namesake of elfish history.

' For all the world it does. I am quite astounded, even now, at my adventure ; it is like the remembrance of a dream.'

' Well, let us have it,' said the worthy mother, so deeply interested, that she did not perceive her son's supper was beginning to burn.

' First,' said the blacksmith, smiling at the curiosity he had excited, ' a young lady opened the door to me, but so lovely, so beautifully and gracefully dressed, that you would have taken her for a beautiful portrait of past times. Before I could say a word, she exclaimed, " Ah ! dear me, sir, you have brought back Frisky ; how happy Miss Adrienne will be ! Come, pray come in instantly ; she would so regret not having an opportunity to thank you in person !" And without giving me time to reply, she beckoned me to follow her. Oh, dear mother, it is quite out of my power to tell you all the magnificence I saw, as I passed through a small saloon, partially lighted, and full of perfume ! It would be impossible. The young woman walked too quickly. A door opened,—Oh, such a sight ! I was so dazzled I can remember nothing but a great glare of gold and light, crystal and flowers ; and, amidst all this brilliancy, a young lady of extreme beauty— ideal beauty ; but she had red hair, or rather hair shining like gold ! Oh ! it was charming to look at ! I never saw such hair before. She had black eyes, ruddy lips, and her skin seemed white as snow. This is all I can recollect ; for, as I said before, I was so dazzled, I seemed to be looking through a veil. " Madame," said the young woman, whom I never should have taken for a lady's maid, she was dressed so elegantly, " here is Frisky, This gentleman found him, and brought him back." " Oh, sir," said the young lady with the golden hair, in a sweet silvery voice, " what thanks I owe you ! I am foolishly attached to Frisky." Then, no doubt, concluding from my dress that she ought to thank me in some other way than by words, she took up a silk purse, and said to me, though I must confess with some hesitation—" No doubt, sir, it gave you some trouble to bring my pet back. You, have, perhaps, lost some valuable time—allow me——" She held forth her purse.'

'Oh, Agricola,' said Mother Bunch, sadly ; ' how people may be deceived !'

' Hear the end, and you will perhaps forgive the young lady. Seeing by my looks that the offer of the purse hurt me, she took a magnificent porcelain vase that contained this flower, and, addressing me in a tone full of grace and kindness, that left me room to guess that she was vexed at having wounded me, she said—" At least, sir, you will accept this flower." '

' You are right, Agricola,' said the girl, smiling sadly, ' an involuntary error could not be repaired in a nicer way.'

' Worthy young lady,' said Frances, wiping her eyes ; ' how well she understood my Agricola !'

' Did she not, mother ? But just as I was taking the flower, without daring to raise my eyes (for, notwithstanding the young lady's kind manner, there was something very imposing about her) another handsome girl, tall and dark, and dressed to the top of fashion, came in and said to the red-haired young lady, " He is here, Madame." She immediately rose and said to me, " A thousand pardons, sir. I shall never forget that I am indebted to you for a moment of much pleasure. Pray remember, on all occasions, my address and name—Adrienne de Cardoville." Thereupon she disappeared. I could not find a word to say in reply. The same young woman showed me to the door, and curtseyed to me very politely. And there I stood in the Rue de Babylone, as dazzled and astonished as if I had come out of an enchanted palace.'

' Indeed, my child, it is like a fairy tale. Is it not, my poor girl ?'

' Yes, ma'am,' said Mother Bunch, in an absent manner that Agricola did not observe.

' What affected me most,' rejoined Agricola, ' was, that the young lady, on seeing her little dog, did not forget me for it, as many would have done in her place, and took no notice of it before me. That shows delicacy and feeling, does it not ? Indeed, I believe this young lady to be so kind and generous, that I should not hesitate to have recourse to her in any important case.'

' Yes, you are right,' replied the sempstress, more and more absent.

The poor girl suffered extremely. She felt no jealousy, no hatred, towards this young stranger, who, from her beauty, wealth, and delicacy, seemed to belong to a sphere too splendid and elevated to be even within the reach of a work-girl's vision ; but, making an involuntary comparison of this fortunate condition with her own, the poor thing had never felt more cruelly her deformity and poverty. Yet such were the humility and gentle resignation of this noble creature, that the only thing which made her feel ill-disposed towards Adrienne de Cardoville was the offer of the purse to Agricola ; but then the charming way in which the young lady had atoned for her error, affected the sempstress deeply. Yet her heart was ready to break. She could not restrain her tears as she contemplated the magnificent flower—so rich in colour and perfume, which, given by a charming hand, was doubtless very precious to Agricola.

' Now, mother,' resumed the young man smilingly, and unaware of the painful emotion of the other bystander, ' you have had the cream of my adventures first. I have told you one of the causes of my delay ; and now for the other. Just now, as I was coming in, I met the dyer at the foot of the stairs, his arms a beautiful pea-green. Stopping me, he said, with an air full of importance, that he thought he had seen a chap sneaking about the house like a spy. " Well, what is that to you, Daddy Loriot ?" said I : " are you afraid he will nose out the way to make the beautiful green, with which you are dyed up to the very elbows ?"'

' But who could that man be, Agricola ?' said Frances.

' On my word, mother, I don't know and scarcely care ; I tried to persuade Daddy Loriot, who chatters like a magpie, to return to his cellar, since it could signify as little to him as to me, whether a spy watched him or not.' So saying, Agricola went and placed the little leathern sack, containing his wages, on a shelf, in the cupboard.

As Frances put down the saucepan on the end of the table, Mother Bunch, recovering from her reverie, filled a basin with water, and, taking it to the blacksmith, said to him in a gentle tone—

' Agricola—for your hands.'

' Thank you, little sister. How kind you are !' Then with a most unaffected gesture and tone, he added, ' There is my fine flower for your trouble.'

' Do you give it me ?' cried the sempstress, with emotion, while a vivid blush coloured her pale and interesting face. ' Do you give me this handsome flower, which a lovely rich young lady so kindly and graciously gave you ?' And the poor thing repeated, with growing astonishment, 'Do you give it to me ?'

'What the deuce should I do with it ? Wear it on my heart, have it set as a pin ?' said Agricola, smiling. 'It is true I was very much impressed by the charming way in which the young lady thanked me. I am delighted to think I found her little dog, and very happy to be able to give you this flower, since it pleases you. You see the day has been a happy one.'

While Mother Bunch trembling with pleasure, emotion, and surprise, took the flower, the young blacksmith washed his hands, so black with smoke and steel filings that the water became dark in an instant. Agricola, pointing out this change to the sempstress, said to her in a whisper, laughing,—

'Here's cheap ink for us paper stainers ! I finished some verses yesterday, which I am rather satisfied with. I will read them to you.'

With this, Agricola wiped his hands naturally on the front of his blouse, while Mother Bunch replaced the basin on the chest of drawers, and laid the flower against the side of it.

'Can't you ask for a towel,' said Frances, shrugging her shoulders, 'instead of wiping your hands on your blouse ?'

'After being scorched all day long at the forge, it will be all the better for a little cooling to-night, won't it ? Am I disobedient, mother ? Scold me, then, if you dare ! Come, let us see you.'

Frances made no reply ; but, placing her hands on either side of her son's head, so beautiful in its candour, resolution and intelligence, she surveyed him for a moment with maternal pride, and kissed him repeatedly on the forehead.

'Come,' said she, 'sit down : you stand all day at your forge, and it is late.'

'So,—your arm-chair again !' said Agricola.——'Our usual quarrel every evening—take it away, I shall be quite as much at ease on another.'

'No, no ! You ought at least to rest after your hard toil.'

'What tyranny !' said Agricola gaily, sitting down. 'Well, I preach like a good apostle ; but I am quite at ease in your arm-chair, after all. Since I sat down on the throne in the Tuileries, I have never had a better seat.'

Frances Baudoin, standing on one side of the table, cut a slice of bread for her son, while Mother Bunch, on the other, filled his silver mug. There was something affecting in the attentive eagerness of the two excellent creatures, for him whom they loved so tenderly.

'Won't you sup with me ?' said Agricola to the girl.

'Thank you, Agricola,' replied the sempstress, looking down, 'I have only just dined.'

'Oh, I only ask you for form's sake—you have your whims—we can never prevail on you to eat with us—just like mother ; she prefers dining all alone ; and in that way she deprives herself without my knowing it.'

'Goodness, child ! It is better for my health to dine early. Well, do you find it nice ?'

'Nice !—call it excellent ! Stockfish and parsnips. Oh, I am very fond of stockfish ; I should have been born a Newfoundland fisherman.'

This worthy lad, on the contrary, was but poorly refreshed, after a hard day's toil, with this paltry stew,—a little burnt as it had been, too, during his story ; but he knew he pleased his mother by observing the fast without complaining. He affected to enjoy his meal ; and the good woman accordingly observed with satisfaction :

'Oh, I see you like it, my dear boy ; Friday and Saturday next we'll have some more.'

'Thank you, mother,—only not two days together. One gets tired of luxuries, you know ! And now, let us talk of what we shall do to-morrow—

Sunday. We must be very merry, for the last few days you seem very sad, dear mother, and I can't make it out—I fancy you are not satisfied with me.'

'Oh, my dear child !—you—the pattern of——'

'Well, well ! Prove to me that you are happy, then, by taking a little amusement. Perhaps you will do us the honour of accompanying us, as you did last time,' added Agricola, bowing to Mother Bunch.

The latter blushed and looked down ; her face assumed an expression of bitter grief, and she made no reply.

'I have the prayers to attend all day, you know, my dear child,' said Frances to her son.

'Well, in the evening, then ? I don't propose the theatre : but they say there is a conjuror to be seen whose tricks are very amusing.'

'I am obliged to you, my son ; but that is a kind of theatre.'

'Dear mother, this is unreasonable !'

'My dear child, do I ever hinder others from doing what they like ?'

'True, dear mother ; forgive me. Well, then, if it should be fine, we will simply take a walk with Mother Bunch on the Boulevards. It is nearly three months since she went out with us ; and she never goes out without us.'

'No, no ; go alone, my child. Enjoy your Sunday, 'tis little enough.'

'You know very well, Agricola,' said the sempstress, blushing up to the eyes, 'that I ought not to go out with you and your mother again.'

'Why not, madame ? May I ask, without impropriety, the cause of this refusal ?' said Agricola, gaily.

The poor girl smiled sadly, and replied, 'Because I will not expose you to a quarrel on my account, Agricola.'

'Forgive me,' said Agricola, in a tone of sincere grief, and he struck his forehead vexedly.

To this Mother Bunch alluded sometimes, but very rarely, for she observed punctilious discretion. The girl had gone out with Agricola and his mother. Such occasions were, indeed, holidays for her. Many days and nights had she toiled hard to procure a decent bonnet and shawl, that she might not do discredit to her friends. The five or six days of holidays, thus spent arm in arm with him whom she adored in secret, formed the sum of her happy days.

Taking their last walk, a coarse, vulgar man elbowed her so rudely that the poor girl could not refrain from a cry of terror, and the man retorted it by saying,—

'What are you rolling your hump in my way for, stoopid ?'

Agricola, like his father, had the patience which force and courage give to the truly brave ; but he was extremely quick when it became necessary to avenge an insult. Irritated at the vulgarity of this man, Agricola left his mother's arm, to inflict on the brute, who was of his own age, size, and force, two vigorous blows, such as the powerful arm and huge fist of a blacksmith never before inflicted on human face. The villain attempted to return it, and Agricola repeated the correction, to the amusement of the crowd, and the fellow slunk away amidst a deluge of hisses. This adventure made Mother Bunch say she would not go out with Agricola again, in order to save him any occasion of quarrel. We may conceive the blacksmith's regret at having thus unwittingly revived the memory of this circumstance,—more painful, alas ! for Mother Bunch than Agricola could imagine, for she loved him passionately, and her infirmity had been the cause of that quarrel. Notwithstanding his strength and resolution, Agricola was childishly sensitive ; and, thinking how painful that thought must be to the poor girl, a large tear filled his eyes, and, holding out his hands, he said, in a brotherly tone, 'Forgive my heedlessness ! Come, kiss me.' And he gave her thin, pale cheeks two hearty kisses.

The poor girl's lips turned pale at this cordial caress ; and her heart beat so violently that she was obliged to lean against the corner of the table.

'Come, you forgive me, do you not ?' said Agricola.

'Yes ! yes !' she said, trying to subdue her emotion ; 'but the recollection of that quarrel pains me—I was so alarmed on your account ; if the crowd had sided with that man !'

'Alas !' said Frances, coming to the sewing-girl's relief, without knowing it, 'I was never so afraid in all my life !'

'Oh, mother,' rejoined Agricola, trying to change a conversation which had now become disagreeable for the sempstress, 'for the wife of a horse grenadier of the Imperial Guard, you have not much courage. Oh, my brave father ; I can't believe he is really coming ! The very thought turns me topsyturvy !'

'Heaven grant he may come,' said Frances, with a sigh.

'God grant it, mother. He will grant it, I should think. Lord knows, you have had masses enough said for his return.'

'Agricola, my child,' said Frances, interrupting her son, and shaking her head sadly, 'do not speak in that way. Besides, you are talking of your father.'

'Well, I'm in for it this evening. 'Tis your turn now ; positively, I am growing stupid, or going crazy. Forgive me, mother ! forgive ! That's the only word I can get out to-night. You know that, when I do let out on certain subjects, it is because I can't help it ; for I know well the pain it gives you.'

'You do not offend me, my poor, dear, misguided boy.'

'It comes to the same thing ; and there is nothing so bad as to offend one's mother ; and, with respect to what I said about father's return, I do not see that we have any cause to doubt it.'

'But we have not heard from him for four months.'

'You know, mother, in his letter—that is, in the letter which he dictated (for you remember that, with the candour of an old soldier, he told us that, if he could read tolerably well, he could not write) ; well, in that letter he said we were not to be anxious about him ; that he expected to be in Paris about the end of January, and would send us word, three or four days before, by what road he expected to arrive, that I might go and meet him.'

'True, my child ; and February is come, and no news yet.'

'The greater reason why we should wait patiently. But I'll tell you more : I should not be surprised if our good Gabriel were to come back about the same time. His last letter from America makes me hope so. What pleasure, mother, should all the family be together !'

'Oh, yes, my child ! It would be a happy day for me.'

'And that day will soon come, trust me.'

'Do you remember your father, Agricola ?' inquired Mother Bunch.

'To tell the truth, I remember most his great grenadier's shako and moustache, which used to frighten me so, that nothing but the red ribbon of his cross of honour, on the white facings of his uniform, and the shining handle of his sabre, could pacify me ; could it, mother ? But what is the matter ? You are weeping !'

'Alas ! poor Baudoin ! What he must suffer at being separated from us at his age—sixty and past ! Alas ! my child, my heart breaks, when I think that he comes home only to change one kind of poverty for another.'

'What do you mean ?'

'Alas ! I earn nothing now.'

'Why, what's become of me ? Isn't there a room here for you and for him ; and a table for you too ? Only, my good mother, since we are talking of domestic affairs,' added the blacksmith, imparting increased tenderness to his tone, that he might not shock his mother, 'when he and Gabriel come home, you won't want to have any more masses said, and tapers burned for them, will you? Well, that saving will enable father to have tobacco to smoke, and his bottle of wine every day. Then, on Sundays, we will take a nice dinner at the eating-house.'

A knocking at the door disturbed Agricola.

'Come in,' said he. Instead of doing so, some one half-opened the door, and, thrusting in an arm of a pea-green colour, made signs to the blacksmith.

''Tis old Loriot, the pattern of dyers,' said Agricola; 'come in, Daddy, no ceremony.'

'Impossible, my lad; I am dripping with dye from head to foot; I should cover missus's floor with green.'

'So much the better. It will remind me of the fields I like so much.'

'Without joking, Agricola, I must speak to you immediately.'

'About the spy, eh? Oh, be easy; what's he to us?'

'No; I think he's gone; at any rate, the fog is so thick I can't see him. But that's not it—come, come quickly! It is very important,' said the dyer, with a mysterious look; 'and only concerns you.'

'Me, only?' said Agricola, with surprise. 'What can it be?'

'Go and see, my child,' said Frances.

'Yes, mother; but the deuce take me if I can make it out.'

And the blacksmith left the room, leaving his mother with Mother Bunch.

CHAPTER XXX.

THE RETURN.

IN five minutes Agricola returned; his face was pale and agitated—his eyes glistened with tears, and his hands trembled; but his countenance expressed extraordinary happiness and emotion. He stood at the door for a moment, as if too much affected to accost his mother.

Frances's sight was so bad that she did not immediately perceive the change her son's countenance had undergone.

'Well, my child—what is it?' she inquired.

Before the blacksmith could reply, Mother Bunch, who had more discernment, exclaimed: 'Goodness, Agricola—how pale you are! Whatever is the matter?'

'Mother,' said the artisan, hastening to Frances, without replying to the sempstress,—'mother, expect news that will astonish you; but promise me you will be calm.'

'What do you mean? How you tremble! Look at me! Mother Bunch was right—you are quite pale.'

'My kind mother!' and Agricola, kneeling before Frances, took both her hands in his—'you must—you do not know,—but——'

The blacksmith could not go on. Tears of joy interrupted his speech.

'You weep, my dear child! Your tears alarm me! What is the matter?—you terrify me!'

'Oh, no, I would not terrify you; on the contrary,' said Agricola, drying his eyes—'you will be so happy. But, again, you must try and command your feelings, for too much joy is as hurtful as too much grief.'

'What?'

'Did I not say true, when I said he would come?'

'Father!' cried Frances. She rose from her seat; but her surprise and emotion were so great that she put one hand to her heart to still its beating, and then she felt her strength fail. Her son sustained her, and assisted her to sit down.

Mother Bunch, till now, had stood discreetly apart, witnessing from a distance the scene which completely engrossed Agricola and his mother. But she now drew near timidly, thinking she might be useful; for Frances changed colour more and more.

'Come, courage, mother,' said the blacksmith; 'now the shock is over, you have only to enjoy the pleasure of seeing my father.'

'My poor man! after eighteen years' absence. Oh, I cannot believe it,' said Frances, bursting into tears. 'Is it true? Is it, indeed, true?'

'So true, that if you will promise me to keep as calm as you can, I will tell you when you may see him.'

'Soon—may I not?'

'Yes; soon.'

'But when will he arrive?'

'He may arrive any minute—to-morrow—perhaps to-day.'

'To-day!'

Yes, mother! Well, I must tell you all—he has arrived.'

'He—he is——' Frances could not articulate the word. 'He was down stairs just now. Before coming up, he sent the dyer to apprise me that I might prepare you; for my brave father feared the surprise might hurt you.'

'Oh, heaven!'

'And now,' cried the blacksmith, in an accent of indescribable joy—'he is there, waiting! Oh, mother! for the last ten minutes I have scarcely been able to contain myself—my heart is bursting with joy.' And running to the door, he threw it open.

Dagobert, holding Rose and Blanche by the hand, stood on the threshold. Instead of rushing to her husband's arms, Frances fell on her knees in prayer. She thanked heaven with profound gratitude for hearing her prayers, and thus accepting her offerings. During a second, the actors of this scene stood silent and motionless. Agricola, by a sentiment of respect and delicacy, which struggled violently with his affection, did not dare to fall on his father's neck. He waited with constrained impatience till his mother had finished her prayer.

The soldier experienced the same feeling as the blacksmith; they understood each other. The first glance exchanged by father and son expressed their affection—their veneration for that excellent woman, who, in the fulness of her religious fervour, forgot, perhaps, too much the creature for the Creator.

Rose and Blanche, confused and affected, looked with interest on the kneeling woman; while Mother Bunch, shedding in silence tears of joy at the thought of Agricola's happiness, withdrew into the most obscure corner of the room, feeling that she was a stranger, and necessarily out of place in that family meeting. Frances rose, and took a step towards her husband, who received her in his arms. There was a moment of solemn silence. Dagobert and Frances said not a word. Nothing could be heard but a few sighs, mingled with sighs of joy. And, when the aged couple looked up, their expression was calm, radiant, serene; for the full and complete enjoyment of simple and pure sentiments never leaves behind a feverish and violent agitation.

'My children,' said the soldier, in tones of emotion, presenting the orphans to Frances, who, after her first agitation, had surveyed them with astonishment, 'this is my good and worthy wife; she will be to the daughters of General Simon what I have been to them.'

Then, madame, you will treat us as your children,' said Rose, approaching Frances with her sister,

'The daughters of General Simon !' cried Dagobert's wife, more and more astonished.

'Yes, my dear Frances; I have brought them from afar—not without some difficulty; but I will tell you that by-and-by.'

'Poor little things ! One would take them for two angels, exactly alike !' said Frances, contemplating the orphans with as much interest as admiration.

'Now—for us,' cried Dagobert, turning to his son.

'At last,' rejoined the latter.

We must renounce all attempts to describe the wild joy of Dagobert and his son, and the crushing grip of their hands, which Dagobert interrupted only to look in Agricola's face ; while he rested his hands on the young blacksmith's broad shoulders, that he might see to more advantage his frank masculine countenance, and robust frame. Then he shook his hand again, exclaiming, ' He's a fine fellow—well built—what a good-hearted look he has !'

From a corner of the room Mother Bunch enjoyed Agricola's happiness ; but she feared that her presence, till then unheeded, would be an intrusion. She wished to withdraw unnoticed, but could not do so. Dagobert and his son were between her and the door ; and she stood unable to take her eyes from the charming faces of Rose and Blanche. She had never seen anything so winsome ; and the extraordinary resemblance of the sisters increased her surprise. Then, their humble mourning revealing that they were poor, Mother Bunch involuntarily felt more sympathy towards them.

'Dear children ! They are cold ; their little hands are frozen, and, unfortunately, the fire is out,' said Frances. She tried to warm the orphans' hands in hers, while Dagobert and his son gave themselves up to the feelings of affection, so long restrained.

As soon as Frances said that the fire was out, Mother Bunch hastened to make herself useful, as an excuse for her presence ; and, going to the cupboard, where the charcoal and wood were kept, she took some small pieces, and, kneeling before the stove, succeeded, by the aid of a few embers that remained, in relighting the fire, which soon began to draw and blaze. Filling a coffee-pot with water, she placed it on the stove, presuming that the orphans required some warm drink. The sempstress did all this with so much dexterity and so little noise—she was naturally so forgotten amidst the emotions of the scene—that Frances, entirely occupied with Rose and Blanche, only perceived the fire when she felt its warmth diffusing round, and heard the boiling water singing in the coffee-pot. This phenomenon—fire rekindling of itself—did not astonish Dagobert's wife then, so wholly was she taken up in devising how she could lodge the maidens ; for Dagobert, as we have seen, had not given her notice of their arrival.

Suddenly a loud bark was heard three or four times at the door.

'Hallo ! there's Spoilsport,' said Dagobert, letting in his dog ; ' he wants to come in to brush acquaintance with the family too.'

The dog came in with a bound, and in a second was quite at home. After having rubbed Dagobert's hand with his muzzle, he went in turns to greet Rose and Blanche, and also Frances and Agricola ; but, seeing that they took but little notice of him, he perceived Mother Bunch, who stood apart, in an obscure corner of the room, and carrying out the popular saying, 'the friends of our friends are our friends,' he went and licked the hands of the young work-woman, who was just then forgotten by all. By a singular impulse, this action affected the girl to tears ; she patted her long, thin, white hand several times on the head of the intelligent dog. Then, finding that she could be no longer useful (for she had done all the little services she deemed in her power), she took the handsome flower Agricola had given her, opened the door gently, and went away so discreetly that no one noticed her departure. After this exchange of mutual affection, Dagobert, his wife, and son, began to think of the realities of life.

'Poor Frances,' said the soldier, glancing at Rose and Blanche, 'you did not expect such a pretty surprise !'

'I am only sorry, my friend,' replied Frances, 'that the daughters of General Simon will not have a better lodging than this poor room ; for with Agricola's garret——'

'It composes our mansion,' interrupted Dagobert ; 'there are handsomer, it must be confessed. But be at ease ; these young ladies are drilled into not being hard to suit on that score. To-morrow, I and my boy will go arm and arm, and I'll answer for it he won't walk the more upright and straight of the two, and find out General Simon's father, at M. Hardy's factory, to talk about business.'

'To-morrow, father,' said Agricola to Dagobert, 'you will not find at the factory either M. Hardy or Marshal Simon's father.'

'What is that you say, my lad ?' cried Dagobert, hastily, 'the Marshal !'

'To be sure ; since 1830, General Simon's friends have secured him the title and rank which the emperor gave him at the battle of Ligny.'

'Indeed !' cried Dagobert, with emotion, 'but that ought not to surprise me ; for, after all, it is just ; and when the emperor said a thing, the least they can do is to let it abide. But it goes all the same to my heart; it makes me jump again.'

Addressing the sisters, he said : 'Do you hear that, my children ? You arrive in Paris the daughters of a Duke and Marshal of France. One would hardly think it, indeed, to see you in this room, my poor little duchesses ! But patience ; all will go well. Ah, father Simon must have been very glad to hear that his son was restored to his rank ! eh, my lad ?'

'He told us he would renounce all kinds of ranks and titles to see his son again ; for it was during the general's absence that his friends obtained this act of justice. But they expect Marshal Simon every moment, for the last letters from India announced his departure.'

At these words Rose and Blanche looked at each other ; and their eyes filled with tears.

'Heaven be praised ! These children rely on his return ; but why shall we not find M. Hardy and father Simon at the factory to-morrow ?'

'Ten days ago, they went to examine and study an English mill established in the south ; but we expect them back every day.'

'The deuce ! that's vexing ; I relied on seeing the general's father, to talk over some important matters with him. At any rate, they know where to write to him. So to-morrow you will let him know, my lad, that his grand-daughters are arrived. In the meantime, children,' added the soldier, to Rose and Blanche, 'my good wife will give you her bed, and you must put up with the chances of war.' Poor things ! they will not be worse off here than they were on the journey.'

'You know we shall always be well off with you and madame,' said Rose.

'Besides, we only think of the pleasure of being at length in Paris, since here we are to find our father,' added Blanche.

'That hope gives you patience, I know,' said Dagobert, 'but no matter ! After all you have heard about it, you ought to be finely surprised, my children. As yet, you have not found it the golden city of your dreams, by any means. But patience, patience ; you'll find Paris not so bad as it looks.'

'Besides,' said Agricola, 'I am sure the arrival of Marshal Simon in Paris will change it for you into a golden city.'

'You are right, Agricola,' said Rose, with a smile, 'you have, indeed, guessed us.'

'What ! do you know my name ?'

'Certainly, Agricola, we often talked about you with Dagobert ; and latterly, too, with Gabriel,' added Blanche.

'Gabriel !' cried Agricola and his mother, at the same time.

'Yes,' replied Dagobert, making a sign of intelligence to the orphans, 'we have lots to tell you for a fortnight to come ; and, among other things, how we chanced to meet with Gabriel. All I can now say is that, in his way, he is quite as good as my boy (I shall never be tired of saying "my boy") ; and they ought to love each other like brothers. Oh, my brave, brave wife !' said Dagobert, with emotion, 'you did a good thing, poor as you were, taking the unfortunate child—and bringing him up with your own.'

'Don't talk so much about it, my dear ; it was such a simple thing.'

'You are right ; but I'll make you amends for it by-and-by. 'Tis down to your account ; in the meantime, you will be sure to see him to-morrow morning.'

'My dear brother arrived too !' cried the blacksmith ; 'who'll say, after this, that there are not days set apart for happiness ? How came you to meet him, father ?'

'I'll tell you all, by-and-by, about when and how we met Gabriel ; for if you expect to sleep, you are mistaken. You'll give me half your room, and a fine chat we'll have. Spoilsport will stay outside of this door ; he is accustomed to sleep at the children's door.'

'Dear me, love, I think of nothing. But, at such a moment, if you and the young ladies wish to sup, Agricola will fetch something from the cookshop.'

'What do you say, children ?'

'No, thank you, Dagobert, we are not hungry ; we are too happy.'

'You will take a little wine and water, sweetened, nice and hot, to warm you a little, my dear young ladies,' said Frances ; 'unfortunately, I have nothing else to offer you.'

'You are right, Frances ; the dear children are tired, and want to go to bed ; while they do so, I'll go to my boy's room, and, before Rose and Blanche are awake, I will come down and converse with you, just to give Agricola a respite.'

A knock was now heard at the door.

'It is good Mother Bunch come to see if we want her,' said Agricola.

'But I think she was here when my husband came in,' added Frances.

'Right, mother, ; and the good girl left lest she should be an intruder : she is so thoughtful. But no—no—it is not she who knocks so loud.'

'Go and see who it is, then, Agricola.'

Before the blacksmith could reach the door, a man, decently dressed, with a respectable air, entered the room, and glanced rapidly round, looking for a moment at Rose and Blanche.

'Allow me to observe, sir,' said Agricola, 'that after knocking, you might have waited till the door was opened, before you entered. Pray, what is your business ?'

'Pray excuse me, sir,' said the man, very politely, and speaking slowly, perhaps to prolong his stay in the room : 'I beg a thousand pardons—I regret my intrusion—I am ashamed——'

'Well, you ought to be, sir,' said Agricola, with impatience, 'what do you want ?'

'Pray, sir, does not Miss Soliveau, a deformed needle-woman, live here ?'

'No, sir ; upstairs,' said Agricola.

'Really, sir,' cried the polite man, with low bows, 'I am quite abroad at my blunder : I thought this was the room of that young person. I brought her proposals for work from a very respectable party.'

'It is very late, sir,' said Agricola, with surprise. 'But that young person is as one of our family. Call to-morrow ; you cannot see her to-night ; she's gone to bed.'

'Then, sir, I again beg you to excuse——'

'Enough, sir,' said Agricola, taking a step towards the door.

'I hope madame and the young ladies, as well as this gent, will be assured that——'

'If you go on much longer making excuses, sir, you will have to excuse the length of your excuses ; and it is time this came to an end !'

Rose and Blanche smiled at these words of Agricola ; while Dagobert rubbed his moustache with pride.

'What wit the boy has !' said he aside to his wife. 'But that does not astonish you—you are used to it.'

During this speech, the ceremonious person withdrew, having again directed a long inquiring glance to the sisters, and to Agricola, and Dagobert.

In a few minutes after, Frances having spread a mattress on the ground for herself, and put the whitest sheets on her bed for the orphans, assisted them to undress with maternal solicitude, Dagobert and Agricola having previously withdrawn to their garret. Just as the blacksmith, who preceded his father with a light, passed before the door of Mother Bunch's room, the latter, half concealed in the shade, said to him rapidly, in a low tone :

'Agricola, great danger threatens you : I must speak to you.'

These words were uttered in so hasty and low a voice, that Dagobert did not hear them ; but as Agricola stopped suddenly, with a start, the old soldier said to him,—

'Well, boy, what is it ?'

'Nothing, father,' said the blacksmith, turning round; 'I feared I did not light you well.'

'Oh, stand at ease about that ; I have the legs and eyes of fifteen to-night ;' and the soldier, not noticing his son's surprise, went into the little room where they were both to pass the night.

❀   ❀   ❀   ❀   ❀   ❀

On leaving the house, after his inquiries about Mother Bunch, the over-polite Paul Pry slunk along to the end of Brise-Miche Street. He advanced towards a hackney-coach drawn up on the Cloître Saint Méry Square.

In this carriage lounged Rodin, wrapped in a cloak.

'Well ?' said he, in an inquiring tone.

'The two girls and the man with grey moustache went directly to Frances Baudoin's ; by listening at the door, I learnt that the sisters will sleep with her, in that room, to-night ; the old man with grey moustache will share the young blacksmith's room.'

'Very well,' said Rodin.

'I did not dare insist on seeing the deformed workwoman this evening on the subject of the Bacchanal Queen ; I intend returning to-morrow, to learn the effect of the letter she must have received this evening by the post about the young blacksmith.'

'Do not fail ! And now you will call, for me, on Frances Baudoin's con-fessor, late as it is ; you will tell him that I am waiting for him at Rue du Milieu des Ursins—he must not lose a moment. Do you come with him. Should I not be returned, he will wait for me. You will tell him it is on a matter of great moment.'

'All shall be faithfully executed,' said the ceremonious man, cringing to Rodin, as the coach drove quickly away.

CHAPTER XXXI.

AGRICOLA AND MOTHER BUNCH.

WITHIN one hour after the different scenes which have just been described, the most profound silence reigned in the soldier's humble dwelling. A flickering light, which played through two panes of glass in a door, betrayed that Mother Bunch had not yet gone to sleep; for her gloomy recess, without air or light, was impenetrable to the rays of day, except by this door, opening upon a narrow and obscure passage, connected with the roof. A sorry bed, a table, an old portmanteau, and a chair, so nearly filled this chilling abode, that two persons could not possibly be seated within it, unless one of them sat upon the side of the bed.

The magnificent and precious flower that Agricola had given to the girl, was carefully stood up in a vessel of water, placed upon the table on a linen cloth, diffusing its sweet odour around, and expanding its purple calix in the very closet, whose plastered walls, grey and damp, were feebly lighted by the rays of an attenuated candle. The sempstress, who had taken off no part of her dress, was seated upon her bed—her looks were downcast, and her eyes full of tears. She supported herself with one hand resting on the bolster; and, inclining towards the door, listened with painful eagerness, every instant hoping to hear the footstep of Agricola. The heart of the young sempstress beat violently: her face, usually very pale, was now partially flushed,—so exciting was the emotion by which she was agitated. Sometimes she cast her eyes with terror upon a letter which she held in her hand, a letter that had been delivered by post in the course of the evening, and which had been placed by the housekeeper (the dyer) upon the table, while she was rendering some trivial domestic services during the recognitions of Dagobert and his family.

After some seconds, Mother Bunch heard a door, very near her own, softly opened.

'There he is at last!' she exclaimed; and Agricola immediately entered.

'I waited till my father went to sleep,' said the blacksmith, in a low voice, his physiognomy evincing much more curiosity than uneasiness. 'But what is the matter, my good sister? How your countenance is changed! You weep! What has happened? About what danger would you speak to me?'

'Hush! Read this!' said she, her voice trembling with emotion, while she hastily presented to him the open letter. Agricola held it towards the light, and read what follows:

'A person who has reasons for concealing himself, but who knows the sisterly interest you take in the welfare of Agricola Baudoin, warns you. That young and worthy workman will probably be arrested in the course of to-morrow.'

'I!' exclaimed Agricola, looking at Mother Bunch with an air of stupefied amazement. 'What is the meaning of all this?'

'Read on!' quickly replied the sempstress, clasping her hands.

Agricola resumed reading, scarcely believing the evidence of his eyes:—

'The song, entitled, "Working-men Freed," has been declared libellous. Numerous copies of it have been found among the papers of a secret society, the leaders of which are about to be incarcerated, as being concerned in the Rue des Prouvaires conspiracy.'

'Alas!' said the girl, melting into tears, 'now I see it all. The man who was lurking about below, this evening, who was observed by the dyer, was, doubtless, a spy, lying in wait for you coming home.'

'Nonsense!' exclaimed Agricola. 'This accusation is quite ridiculous!

Do not torment yourself. I never trouble myself with politics. My verses breathe nothing but philanthropy. Am I to blame, if they have been found among the papers of a secret society?' Agricola disdainfully threw the letter upon the table.

'Read ! pray read !' said the other ; 'read on.'

'If you wish it,' said Agricola, 'I will : no time is lost.'

He resumed the reading of the letter :

'A warrant is about to be issued against Agricola Baudoin. There is no doubt of his innocence being sooner or later made clear ; but it will be well if he screen himself for a time as much as possible from pursuit, in order that he may escape a confinement of two or three months previous to trial— an imprisonment which would be a terrible blow for his mother, whose sole support he is.

'A SINCERE FRIEND, who is compelled to remain unknown.'

After a moment's silence, the blacksmith raised his head ; his countenance resumed its serenity ; and laughing, he said : 'Reassure yourself, good Mother Bunch, these jokers have made a mistake by trying their games on me. It is plainly an attempt at making an April-fool of me before the time.'

'Agricola, for the love of heaven !' said the girl, in a supplicating tone ; 'treat not the warning thus lightly. Believe in my forebodings, and listen to my advice.'

'I tell you again, my good girl,' replied Agricola, 'that it is two months since my song was published. It is not in any way political ; indeed, if it were, they would not have waited till now before coming down on me.'

'But,' said the other, 'you forget that new events have arisen. It is scarcely two days since the conspiracy was discovered, in this very neigh- bourhood, in the Rue des Prouvaires. And,' continued she, 'if the verses, though perhaps hitherto unnoticed, have now been found in the possession of the persons apprehended for this conspiracy, nothing more is necessary to compromise you in the plot.'

'Compromise me !' said Agricola ; 'my verses ! in which I only praise the love of labour and of goodness ! To arrest me for that ! If so, justice would be but a blind noodle. That she might grope her way, it would be necessary to furnish her with a dog and a pilgrim's staff to guide her steps.'

'Agricola,' resumed Mother Bunch, overwhelmed with anxiety and terror on hearing the blacksmith jest at such a moment, 'I conjure you to listen to me ! No doubt, you uphold in the verses the sacred love of labour ; but you do also grievously deplore and deprecate the unjust lot of the poor labourers, devoted, as they are, without hope, to all the miseries of life; you recommend, indeed, only fraternity among men ; but your good and noble heart vents its indignation, at the same time, against the selfish and the wicked. In fine, you fervently hasten on, with the ardour of your wishes, the emanci- pation of all the artisans who, less fortunate than you, have not generous M. Hardy for employer. Say, Agricola, in these times of trouble, is there anything more necessary to compromise you than that numerous copies of your song have been found in possession of the persons who have been apprehended ?'

Agricola was moved by these affectionate and judicious expressions of an excellent creature, who reasoned from her heart ; and he began to view with more seriousness the advice which she had given him.

Perceiving that she had shaken him, the sewing-girl went on to say : 'And then, bear your fellow-workman, Remi, in recollection.'

'Remi !' said Agricola, anxiously.

'Yes,' resumed the sempstress ; 'a letter of his, a letter in itself quite insignificant, was found in the house of a person arrested last year for con- spiracy ; and Remi, in consequence, remained a month in prison.'

'That is true, but the injustice of his implication was easily shown, and he was set at liberty.'

'Yes, Agricola : but not till he had lain a month in prison ; and that has furnished the motive of the person who advised you to conceal yourself ! A month in prison ! Good heavens ! Agricola, think of that ! and your mother.'

These words made a powerful impression upon Agricola. He took up the letter and again read it attentively.

'And the man who has been lurking all this evening about the house?' proceeded she. 'I constantly recall that circumstance, which cannot be naturally accounted for. Alas ! what a blow it would be for your father, and poor mother, who is incapable of earning anything. Are you not now their only resource ? Oh ! consider, then, what would become of them without you—without your labour !'

'It would indeed be terrible,' said Agricola, impatiently casting the letter upon the table. 'What you have said concerning Remi is too true. He was as innocent as I am : yet an error of justice, an involuntary error though it be, is not the less cruel. But they don't commit a man without hearing him.'

'But they arrest him first, and hear him afterwards,' said Mother Bunch, bitterly ; 'and then, after a month or two, they restore him his liberty. And if he have a wife and children, whose only means of living is his daily labour, what becomes of them while their only supporter is in prison ? They suffer hunger, they endure cold, and they weep !'

At these simple and pathetic words, Agricola trembled.

'A month without work,' he said, with a sad and thoughtful air. 'And my mother, and father, and the two young ladies who make part of our family until the arrival in Paris of their father, Marshal Simon. Oh ! you are right. That thought, in spite of myself, affrights me !'

'Agricola !' exclaimed the girl impetuously ; 'suppose you apply to M. Hardy ; he is so good, and his character is so much esteemed and honoured, that, if he offered bail for you, perhaps they would give up their persecution ?'

'Unfortunately,' replied Agricola, 'M. Hardy is absent; he is on a journey with Marshal Simon.'

After a silence of some time, Agricola, striving to surmount his fears, added : 'But no ! I cannot give credence to this letter. After all, I had rather await what may come. I'll at least have the chance of proving my innocence on my first examination ; for indeed, my good sister, whether it be that I am in prison, or that I fly to conceal myself, my working for my family will be equally prevented.'

'Alas ! that is true,' said the poor girl ; 'what is to be done ! Oh, what is to be done ?'

'My brave father,' said Agricola to himself, 'if this misfortune happen to-morrow, what an awakening it will be for him, who came here to sleep so joyously !' The blacksmith buried his face in his hands.

Unhappily Mother Bunch's fears were too well-founded, for it will be re-collected that at that epoch of the year 1832, before and after the Rue des Prouvaires' conspiracy, a very great number of arrests had been made among the working classes, in consequence of a violent reaction against demo-cratical ideas.

Suddenly, the girl broke the silence which had been maintained for some seconds. A blush coloured her features, which bore the impressions of an indefinable expression of constraint, grief, and hope.

'Agricola, you are saved !'

'What say you ?' he asked.

'The young lady, so beautiful, so good, who gave you this flower' (she showed it to the blacksmith) 'who has known to make reparation with so much delicacy for having made a painful offer, cannot but have a generous heart. You must apply to her——'

With these words which seem to be wrung from her by a violent effort over herself, great tears rolled down her cheeks. For the first time in her life she experienced a feeling of grievous jealousy. Another woman was so happy as to have the power of coming to the relief of him whom she idolised ; while she herself, poor creature, was powerless and wretched.

'Do you think so ?' exclaimed Agricola surprised. 'But what could be done with this young lady ?'

'Did she not say to you,' answered Mother Bunch, '" Remember my name ; and in all circumstances address yourself to me ?"'

'She did indeed !' replied Agricola.

'This young lady, in her exalted position, ought to have powerful connections who will be able to protect and defend you. Go to her to-morrow morning ; tell her frankly what has happened, and request her support.'

'But tell me, my good sister, what it is you wish me to do ?'

'Listen. I remember that, in former times, my father told us that he had saved one of his friends from being put in prison, by becoming surety for him. It will be easy for you so to convince this young lady of your innocence, that she will be induced to become surety ; and after that, you will have nothing more to fear.'

'My poor child !' said Agricola, 'to ask so great a service from a person to whom one is almost unknown is hard.'

'Believe me, Agricola,' said the other sadly, 'I would never counsel what could possibly lower you in the eyes of any one, and above all—do you understand ?—above all, in the eyes of this young lady. I do not propose that you should ask money from her ; but only that she should give surety for you, in order that you may have the liberty of continuing at your employment, so that the family may not be without resources. Believe me, Agricola, that such a request is in no respect inconsistent with what is noble and becoming upon your part. The heart of the young lady is generous. She will comprehend your position. The required surety will be as nothing to her ; while to you it will be everything, and will even be the very life to those who depend upon you.'

'You are right, my good sister,' said Agricola, with sadness and dejection. 'It is perhaps worth while to risk taking this step. If the young lady consent to render me this service, and if giving surety will indeed preserve me from prison, I shall be prepared for every event. But no, no !' added he, rising, 'I'd never dare to make the request to her ! What right have I to do so ? What is the insignificant service that I rendered her, when compared with that which I should solicit from her.'

'Do you imagine then, Agricola, that a generous spirit measures the services which ought to be rendered, by those previously received ? Trust to me respecting a matter which is an affair of the heart. I am, it is true, but a lowly creature, and ought not to compare myself with any other person. I am nothing, and I can do nothing. Nevertheless, I am sure— yes, Agricola, I am sure—that this young lady, who is so very far above me, will experience the same feelings that I do in this affair ; yes, like me, she will at once comprehend that your position is a cruel one ; and she will do with joy, with happiness, with thankfulness, that which I would do, if, alas ! I could do anything more than uselessly consume myself with regrets.'

In spite of herself, she pronounced the last words with an expression so heart-breaking—there was something so moving in the comparison which this unfortunate creature, obscure and disdained, infirm and miserable, made of herself with Adrienne de Cardoville, the very type of resplendent youth, beauty, and opulence—that Agricola was moved even to tears ; and, holding out one of his hands to the speaker, he said to her, tenderly, ' How very good you are ; how full of nobleness, good feeling, and delicacy !'

' Unhappily,' said the weeping girl, ' I can do nothing more than advise.'

' And your counsels shall be followed out, my sister dear. They are those of a soul the most elevated I have ever known. Yes, you have won me over into making this experiment, by persuading me that the heart of Miss de Cardoville is perhaps equal in value to your own !'

At this charming and sincere assimilation of herself to Miss Adrienne, the sempstress forgot almost everything she had suffered, so exquisitely sweet and consoling were her emotions. If some poor creatures, fatally de-voted to sufferings, experience griefs of which the world knows nought, they sometimes, too, are cheered by humble and timid joys, of which the world is equally ignorant. The least word of true tenderness and affection, which elevates them in their own estimation, is ineffably blissful for these unfor-tunate beings, habitually consigned, not only to hardships and to disdain, but even to desolating doubts, and distrust of themselves.

' Then it is agreed that you will go, to-morrow morning, to this young lady's house ?' exclaimed Mother Bunch, trembling with a new-born hope. ' And,' she quickly added, ' at break of day I'll go down to watch at the street-door, to see if there be anything suspicious, and to apprize you of what I perceive.'

' Good, excellent girl !' exclaimed Agricola, with increasing emotion.

' It will be necessary to endeavour to set off before the wakening of your father,' said the hunchback. ' The quarter in which the young lady dwells, is so deserted, that the mere going there will almost serve for your present concealment.'

' I think I hear the voice of my father,' said Agricola, suddenly.

In truth, the little apartment was so near Agricola's garret, that he and the sempstress, listening, heard Dagobert say in the dark :

' Agricola, is it thus that you sleep, my boy? Why, my first sleep is over; and my tongue itches deucedly.'

' Go quick, Agricola !' said Mother Bunch ; ' your absence would dis-quiet him. On no account go out to-morrow morning, before I inform you whether or not I shall have seen anything suspicious.'

' Why, Agricola, you are not here ?' resumed Dagobert, in a louder voice.

' Here I am, father,' said the smith, while going out of the sempstress's apartment, and entering the garret to his father.

' I have been to fasten the shutter of a loft that the wind agitated, lest its noise should disturb you.'

' Thanks, my boy ; but it is not noise that wakes me,' said Dagobert, gaily ; ' it is an appetite, quite furious, for a chat with you. Oh, my dear boy, it is the hungering of a proud old man of a father, who has not seen his son for eighteen years.'

' Shall I light a candle, father ?'

' No, no ; that would be luxurious ; let us chat in the dark. It will be a new pleasure for me to see you to-morrow morning at day-break. It will be like seeing you for the first time twice.' The door of Agricola's garret being now closed, Mother Bunch heard nothing more.

The poor girl, without undressing, threw herself upon the bed, and closed not an eye during the night, painfully awaiting the appearance of day, in order that she might watch over the safety of Agricola. However, in spite of her vivid anxieties for the morrow, she sometimes allowed herself to sink into the reveries of a bitter melancholy. She compared the conversation she had just had in the silence of night, with the man whom she secretly adored, with what that conversation might have been, had she possessed some share of charms and beauty—had she been loved as she loved, with a chaste and devoted flame ! But soon sinking into belief that she should never know the ravishing sweets of a mutual passion, she found consolation in the hope of being useful to Agricola. At the dawn of day, she rose softly, and descended the staircase with little noise, in order to see if anything menaced Agricola from without.

CHAPTER XXXII.

THE AWAKENING.

THE weather, damp and foggy during a portion of the night, became clear and cold towards morning. Through the glazed skylight of Agricola's garret, where he lay with his father, a corner of the blue sky could be seen.

The apartment of the young blacksmith had an aspect as poor as the sewing-girl's. For its sole ornament, over the deal table upon which Agricola wrote his poetical inspirations, there hung suspended from a nail in the wall a portrait of Beranger—that immortal poet whom the people revere and cherish, because his rare and transcendent genius has delighted to enlighten the people, and to sing their glories and their reserves.

Although the day had only begun to dawn, Dagobert and Agricola had already risen. The latter had sufficient self-command to conceal his inquietude, for renewed reflection had again increased his fears.

The recent outbreak in the Rue des Prouvaires had caused a great number of precautionary arrests ; and the discovery of numerous copies of Agricola's song, in the possession of one of the chiefs of the disconcerted plot, was, in truth, calculated slightly to compromise the young blacksmith. His father, however, as we have already mentioned, suspected not his secret anguish. Seated by the side of his son, upon the edge of their mean little bed, the old soldier, by break of day, had dressed and shaved with military care; he now held between his hands both those of Agricola, his countenance radiant with joy, and unable to discontinue the contemplation of his boy.

'You will laugh at me, my dear boy,' said Dagobert to his son ; 'but I wished the night to the devil, in order that I might gaze upon you in full day, as I now see you. But all in good time ; I have lost nothing. Here is another silliness of mine ; it delights me to see you wear moustaches. What a splendid horse-grenadier you would have made ! Tell me ; have you never had a wish to be a soldier ?'

'I thought of mother !'

'That's right,' said Dagobert : 'and besides, I believe, after all, look ye, that the time of the sword has gone by. We old fellows are now good for nothing, but to be put in a corner of the chimney. Like rusty old carbines, we have had our day.'

'Yes ; your days of heroism and of glory,' said Agricola with excitement ; and then he added, with a voice profoundly softened and agitated, 'it is something good and cheering to be your son !'

'As to the good, I know nothing of that,' replied Dagobert ; 'but as for the cheering, it ought to be so ; for I love you proudly. And I think this is but the beginning ! What say you, Agricola ? I am like the famished wretches who have been some days without food. It is but by little and little that they recover themselves, and can eat. Now, you may expect to be tasted, my boy, morning and evening, and devoured during the day.

No, I wish not to think that—not all the day—no, that thought dazzles and perplexes me ; and I am no longer myself.'

These words of Dagobert caused a painful feeling to Agricola. He be‑ lieved that they sprang from a presentiment of the separation with which he was menaced.

'Well,' continued Dagobert ; 'you are quite happy ; M. Hardy is always good to you.'

'Oh !' replied Agricola : 'there is none in the world better, or more equitable and generous ! If you knew what wonders he has brought about in his factory ! Compared to all others, it is a paradise beside the stithies of Lucifer !'

'Indeed !' said Dagobert.

'You shall see,' resumed Agricola, 'what welfare, what joy, what affection, are displayed upon the countenances of all whom he employs ; who work with an ardent pleasure.'

'This M. Hardy of yours must be an out-and-out magician,' said Dago‑ bert.

'He is, father, a very great magician. He has known how to render labour pleasant and attractive. As for the pleasure, over and above good wages, he accords to us a portion of his profits according to our deserts ; whence you may judge of the eagerness with which we go to work. And that is not all : he has caused large, handsome buildings to be erected, in which all his workpeople find, at less expense than elsewhere, cheerful and salubrious lodgings, in which they enjoy all the advantages of an association. But you shall see—I repeat—you shall see !'

'They have good reason to say, that Paris is the region of wonders,' ob‑ served Dagobert.

'Well, behold me here again at last, never more to quit you, nor good mother !

No, father, we will never separate again,' said Agricola, stifling a sigh. 'My mother and I will both try to make you forget all that you have suffered.'

'Suffered !' exclaimed Dagobert, 'who the deuce has suffered ? Look me well in the face ; and see if I have a look of suffering ! Bombs and bayonets ! Since I have put my foot here, I feel myself quite a young man again ! You shall see me march soon : I bet that I tire you out ! You must rig yourself up something extra ! Lord, how they will stare at us ! I wager that in beholding your black moustache and my grey one, folks will say, behold father and son ! But let us settle what we are to do with the day. You will write to the father of Marshal Simon, informing him that his grand-daughters have arrived, and that it is necessary that he should hasten his return to Paris ; for he has charged himself with matters which are of great importance for them. While you are writing, I will go down to say good-morning to my wife, and to the dear little ones. We will then eat a morsel. Your mother will go to mass ; for I perceive that she likes to be regular at that : the good soul ! no great harm, if it amuse her ! and during her absence, we will make a raid together.'

'Father,' said Agricola, with embarrassment, 'this morning it is out of my power to accompany you.'

'How ! out of your power ?' said Dagobert ; 'recollect this is Monday !'

'Yes, father,' said Agricola, hesitatingly ; 'but I have promised to attend all the morning in the workshop, to finish a job that is required in a hurry. If I fail to do so, I shall inflict some injury upon M. Hardy. But I'll soon be at liberty.'

'That alters the case,' said Dagobert, with a sigh of regret. 'I thought to make my first parade through Paris with you this morning ; but it must be deferred in favour of your work. It is sacred : since it is that which sustains your mother. Nevertheless, it is vexatious, devilish vexatious. And yet no—I am unjust. See how quickly one gets habituated to and spoilt by happiness. I grow like a true grumbler, at a walk being put off for a few hours ! I do this ! I who, during eighteen years, have only hoped to see you once more, without daring to reckon very much upon it ! Oh ! I am but a silly old fool ! Vive l'amour et cogni—I mean—my Agricola !' And, to console himself, the old soldier gaily slapped his son's shoulder.

This seemed another omen of evil to the blacksmith ; for he dreaded one moment to another lest the fears of Mother Bunch should be realised. ' Now that I have recovered myself,' said Dagobert, laughing, ' let us speak of business. Know you where I find the addresses of all the notaries in Paris ?'

' I don't know ; but nothing is more easy than to discover it.'

' My reason is,' resumed Dagobert, ' that I sent from Russia by post, and by order of the mother of the two children that I have brought here, some important papers to a Parisian notary. As it was my duty to see this notary immediately upon my arrival, I had written his name and his address in a portfolio, of which, however, I have been robbed during my journey ; and as I have forgotten his devil of a name, it seems to me, that if I should see it again in the list of notaries, I might recollect it.'

Two knocks at the door of the garret made Agricola start. He involuntarily thought of a warrant for his apprehension.

His father, who, at the sound of the knocking turned round his head, had not perceived his emotion, and said with a loud voice : ' Come in !' The door opened. It was Gabriel. He wore a black cassock and a broad-brimmed hat.

To recognise his brother by adoption, and to throw himself into his arms, were two movements performed at once by Agricola—as quick as thought. —' My brother !' exclaimed Agricola.

' Agricola !' cried Gabriel.

' Gabriel !' responded the blacksmith.

' After so long an absence !' said the one.

' To behold you again !' rejoined the other.

Such were the words exchanged between the blacksmith and the missionary, while they were locked in a close embrace.

Dagobert, moved and charmed by these fraternal endearments, felt his eyes become moist. There was something truly touching in the affection of the young men—in their hearts so much alike, and yet of characters and aspects so very different—for the manly countenance of Agricola contrasted strongly with the delicacy and angelic physiognomy of Gabriel.

' I was forewarned by my father of your arrival,' said the blacksmith, at length. ' I have been expecting to see you ; and my happiness has been a hundred times the greater, because I have had all the pleasures of hoping for it.'

' And my good mother ?' asked Gabriel, in affectionately grasping the hands of Dagobert. ' I trust that you have found her in good health.'

' Yes, my brave boy !' replied Dagobert ; ' and her health will have become a hundred times better, now that we are all together. Nothing is so healthful as joy.' Then addressing himself to Agricola, who, forgetting his fear of being arrested, regarded the missionary with an expression of ineffable affection, Dagobert added :

' Let it be remembered, that, with the soft cheek of a young girl, Gabriel has the courage of a lion ; I have already told with what intrepidity he saved the lives of Marshal Simon's daughters, and tried to save mine also.'

'But, Gabriel! what has happened to your forehead?' suddenly exclaimed Agricola, who for a few seconds had been attentively examining the missionary.

Gabriel, having thrown aside his hat on entering, was now directly beneath the skylight of the garret apartment, the bright light through which shone upon his sweet, pale countenance : and the round scar, which extended from one eyebrow to the other, was therefore distinctly visible.

In the midst of the powerful and diversified emotions, and of the exciting events which so rapidly followed the shipwreck on the rocky coast near Cardoville House, Dagobert, during the short interview he then had with Gabriel, had not perceived the scar which seamed the forehead of the young missionary. Now, partaking, however, of the surprise of his son, Dagobert said :

'Aye, indeed ! how came this scar upon your brow?'

'And on his hands too ; see, dear father !' exclaimed the blacksmith, with renewed surprise, while he seized one of the hands which the young priest held out towards him in order to tranquillise his fears.

'Gabriel, my brave boy, explain this to us !' added Dagobert ; 'who has wounded you thus?' and in his turn, taking the other hand of the missionary, he examined the scar upon it with the eye of a judge of wounds, and then added, 'In Spain, one of my comrades was found and taken down alive from a cross, erected at the junction of several roads, upon which the monks had crucified, and left him to die of hunger, thirst, and agony. Ever afterwards he bore scars upon his hands, exactly similar to this upon your hand.'

'My father is right !' exclaimed Agricola. 'It is evident that your hands have been pierced through ! My poor brother !' and Agricola became grievously agitated.

'Do not think about it,' said Gabriel, reddening with the embarrassment of modesty. 'Having gone as a missionary amongst the savages of the Rocky Mountains, they crucified me, and they had begun to scalp me, when Providence snatched me from their hands.'

'Unfortunate youth,' said Dagobert ; 'without arms, then? You had not a sufficient escort for your protection?'

'It is not for such as me to carry arms,' said Gabriel, sweetly smiling ; and we are never accompanied by any escort.'

'Well, but your companions, those who were along with you, how came it that they did not defend you?' impetuously asked Agricola.

'I was alone, my dear brother.'

'Alone !'

'Yes, alone ; without even a guide.'

'You alone ! unarmed ! in a barbarous country !' exclaimed Dagobert, scarcely crediting a step so unmilitary, and almost distrusting his own sense of hearing.

'It was sublime !' said the young blacksmith and poet.

'The Christian faith,' said Gabriel, with mild simplicity, 'cannot be implanted by force or violence. It is only by the power of persuasion that the gospel can be spread amongst poor savages.'

'But when persuasions fail?' said Agricola.

'Why, then, dear brother, one has but to die for the belief that is in him, pitying those who have rejected it, and who have refused the blessings it offers to mankind.'

There was a period of profound silence after the reply of Gabriel, which was uttered with simple and touching pathos,

Dagobert was in his own nature too courageous not to comprehend a heroism thus calm and resigned ; and the old soldier, as well as his son, now contemplated Gabriel with the most earnest feelings of mingled admiration and respect.

Gabriel, entirely free from the affectation of false modesty, seemed quite unconscious of the emotions which he had excited in the breasts of his two friends ; and he therefore said to Dagobert, ' What ails you ?'

' What ails me !' exclaimed the brave old soldier, with great emotion : ' After having been for thirty years in the wars, I had imagined myself to be about as courageous as any man. And now I find I have a master ! And that master is yourself !'

' I !' said Gabriel : ' what do you mean ? What have I done ?'

' Thunder, don't you know that the brave wounds there' (the veteran took with transport both of Gabriel's hands), ' that these wounds are as glorious,—are more glorious,—than ours,—than all ours, as warriors by profession !'

' Yes ! yes ! my father speaks truth !' exclaimed Agricola ; and he added, with enthusiasm, ' Oh, for such priests ! How I love them ! How I venerate them ! how I am elevated by their charity, their courage, their resignation !'

' I entreat you not to extol me thus,' said Gabriel with embarrassment.

' Not extol you !' replied Dagobert. ' Hanged if I shouldn't. When I have gone into the heat of action, did I rush into it alone ? Was I not under the eyes of my commanding officer ? Were not my comrades there along with me ? In default of true courage, had I not the instinct of self-preservation to spur me on, without reckoning the excitement of the shouts and tumult of battle, the smell of the gunpowder, the flourishes of the trumpets, the thundering of the cannon, the ardour of my horse, which bounded beneath me as if the devil were at his tail ? Need I state that I also knew that the emperor was present, with his eye upon every one – the emperor, who, in recompense for a hole being made in my tough hide, would give me a bit of lace or a ribbon, as plaster for the wound. Thanks to all these causes, I passed for game. Fair enough ! But are you not a thousand times more game than I, my brave boy ; going alone, unarmed, to confront enemies a hundred times more ferocious than those whom we attacked,—we, who fought in whole squadrons, supported by artillery, bomb-shells, and case-shot ?'

' Excellent father !' cried Agricola, ' how noble of you to render to Gabriel this justice !'

' Oh, dear brother,' said Gabriel, ' his kindness to me makes him magnify what was quite natural and simple !'

' Natural !' said the veteran soldier ; ' yes, natural for gallants who have hearts of the true temper : but that temper is rare.'

' Oh, yes, very rare,' said Agricola ; ' for that kind of courage is the most admirable of all. Most bravely did you seek almost certain death, alone, bearing the cross in hand as your only weapon, to preach charity and Christian brotherhood. They seized you, tortured you ; and you await death and partly endure it, without complaint, without remonstrance, without hatred, without anger, without a wish for vengeance : forgiveness issuing from your mouth, and a smile of pity beaming upon your lips ; and this in the depths of forests, where no one could witness your magnanimity,—none could behold you,—and without other desire, after you were rescued, than modestly to conceal blessed wounds under your black robe ! My father is right, by Jove ! can you still contend that you are not as brave as he ?'

' And besides, too,' resumed Dagobert, ' the dear boy did all that for a thankless pay-master ; for it is true, Agricola, that his wounds will never change his humble black robe of a priest into the rich robe of a bishop !'

'I am not so disinterested as I may seem to be,' said Gabriel to Dagobert, smiling meekly. 'If I am deemed worthy, a great recompense awaits me on high.'

'As to all that, my boy,' said Dagobert, 'I do not understand it ; and I will not argue about it. I maintain it, that my old cross of honour would be at least as deservedly affixed to your cassock as upon my uniform.'

'But these recompenses are never conferred upon humble priests like Gabriel,' said Agricola, 'and if you did know, dear father, how much virtue and valour is among those whom the highest orders in the priesthood insolently call the inferior clergy,—the unseen merit and the blind devotedness to be found amongst worthy, but obscure, country curates, who are inhuma͏̈ treated and subjugated to a pitiless yoke by the lordly lawnsleeves ! Like us, those poor priests are worthy labourers in their vocation ; and for them, also, all generous hearts ought to demand enfranchisement ! Sons of common people, like ourselves, and useful as we are, justice ought to be rendered both to them and to us. Do I say right, Gabriel ? You will not contradict it ; for you have told me, that your ambition would have been to obtain a small country curacy ; because you understand the good that you could work within it.'

'My desire is still the same,' said Gabriel sadly : 'but, unfortunately——' and then, as if he wished to escape from a painful thought, and to change the conversation, he, addressing himself to Dagobert, added : 'Believe me : be more just than to undervalue your own courage by exalting mine. Your courage must be very great—very great ; for, after a battle, the spectacle of the carnage must be truly terrible to a generous and feeling heart. We, at least, though we may be killed, do not kill !'

At these words of the missionary, the soldier drew himself up erect, looked upon Gabriel with astonishment, and said, 'This is most surprising !'

'What is ?' inquired Agricola.

'What Gabriel has just told us,' replied Dagobert, 'brings to my mind what I experienced in warfare on the battle-field in proportion as I advanced in years. Listen, my children : more than once, on the night after a general engagement, I have been mounted as a vidette,—alone,—by night,—amid the moonlight, on the field of battle which remained in our possession, and upon which lay the bodies of seven or eight thousand of the slain, amongst whom were mingled the slaughtered remains of some of my old comrades: and then this sad scene, when the profound silence has restored me to my senses from the thirst for bloodshed and the delirious whirling of my sword (intoxicated like the rest), I have said to myself, "for what have these men been killed?— FOR WHAT—FOR WHAT?" But this feeling, well understood as it was, hindered me not, on the following morning, when the trumpets again sounded the charge, from rushing once more to the slaughter. But the same thought always recurred when my arm became weary with carnage: and after wiping my sabre upon the mane of my horse, I have said to myself, "I have killed !—killed ! !—killed ! ! ! and, FOR WHAT ! ! !"'

The missionary and the blacksmith exchanged looks on hearing the old soldier give utterance to this singular retrospection of the past.

'Alas !' said Gabriel to him, 'all generous hearts feel as you did during the solemn moments, when the intoxication of glory has subsided, and man is left alone to the influence of the good instincts planted in his bosom.'

'And that should prove, my brave boy,' rejoined Dagobert, 'that you are greatly better than I ; for those noble instincts, as you call them, have never abandoned you. * * * * But how the deuce did you escape from the claws of the infuriated savages who had already crucified you ?'

At this question of Dagobert, Gabriel started and reddened so visibly, that the soldier said to him : 'If you ought not or cannot answer my request, let us say no more about it.'

'I have nothing to conceal, either from you or from my brother,' replied the missionary with altered voice. 'Only, it will be difficult for me to make you comprehend what I cannot comprehend myself.'

'How is that ?' asked Agricola with surprise.

'Surely,' said Gabriel, reddening more deeply, 'I must have been deceived by a fallacy of my senses, during that abstracted moment in which I awaited death with resignation. My enfeebled mind, in spite of me, must have been cheated by an illusion ; or that, which to the present hour has remained inexplicable, would have been more slowly developed ; and I should have known with greater certainty that it was the strange woman——'

Dagobert, while listening to the missionary, was perfectly amazed ; for he also had vainly tried to account for the unexpected succour which had freed him and the two orphans from the prison at Leipsic.

'Of what woman do you speak ?' asked Agricola.

'Of her who saved me,' was the reply.

'A woman saved you from the hands of the savages !' said Dagobert.

'Yes,' replied Gabriel, though absorbed in his reflections, 'a woman, young and beautiful !'

'And who was this woman ?' asked Agricola.

'I know not. When I asked her, she replied, "I am the sister of the distressed !"'

'And whence came she? Whither went she?' asked Dagobert, singularly interested.

'"I go wheresoever there is suffering," she replied,' answered the missionary ; 'and she departed, going towards the north of America,—towards those desolate regions in which there is eternal snow, where the nights are without end.'

'As in Siberia,' said Dagobert, who had become very thoughtful.

'But,' resumed Agricola, addressing himself to Gabriel, who seemed also to have become more and more absorbed, 'in what manner or by what means did this woman come to your assistance ?'

    ✿   ✿   ✿   ✿   ✿

The missionary was about to reply to the last question, when there was heard a gentle tap at the door of the garret apartment, which renewed the fears that Agricola had forgotten since the arrival of his adopted brother. 'Agricola,' said a sweet voice outside the door, 'I wish to speak with you as soon as possible.'

The blacksmith recognised Mother Bunch's voice, and opened the door. But the young sempstress, instead of entering, drew back into the dark passage, and said, with a voice of anxiety : 'Agricola, it is an hour since broad day, and you have not yet departed ! How imprudent ! I have been watching below, in the street, until now, and have seen nothing alarming ; but they may come any instant to arrest you. Hasten, I conjure you, your departure for the abode of Miss de Cardoville. Not a minute should be lost.'

'Had it not been for the arrival of Gabriel, I should have been gone. But I could not resist the happiness of remaining some little time with him.'

'Gabriel here !' said Mother Bunch, with sweet surprise ; for, as has been stated, she had been brought up with him and Agricola.

'Yes,' answered Agricola, 'for half an hour he has been with my father and me.'

'What happiness I shall have in seeing him again,' said the sewing-girl. 'He doubtless came upstairs while I had gone for a brief space to your mother, to ask if I could be useful in any way on account of the young ladies ;

but they have been so fatigued that they still sleep. Your mother has requested me to give you this letter for your father. She has just received it.'

' Thanks.'

' Well,' resumed Mother Bunch, ' now that you have seen Gabriel, do not delay long. Think what a blow it would be for your father, if they came to arrest you in his very presence—*mon Dieu!*'

' You are right,' said Agricola ; ' it is indispensable that I should depart—while near Gabriel, in spite of my anxiety, my fears were forgotten.'

' Go quickly, then ; and if Miss de Cardoville should grant this favour, perhaps in a couple of hours you will return, quite at ease both as to yourself and us.'

' True ! a very few minutes more ; and I'll come down.'

' I return to watch at the door. If I perceive anything, I'll come up again to apprise you. But, pray, do not delay.'

' Be easy, good sister.' Mother Bunch hurriedly descended the staircase, to resume her watch at the street door, and Agricola re-entered his garret. ' Dear father,' he said to Dagobert, ' my mother has just received this letter, and she requests you to read it.'

' Very well ; read it for me, my boy.' And Agricola read as follows :

' MADAME,—I understand that your husband has been charged by General Simon with an affair of very great importance. Will you, as soon as your husband arrives in Paris, request him to come to my office at Chartres without a moment's delay. I am instructed to deliver to himself, and to no other person, some documents indispensable to the interests of General Simon.
' DURAND, Notary at Chartres.'

Dagobert looked at his son with astonishment, and said to him, ' Who can have told this gentleman already of my arrival in Paris ?'

' Perhaps, father,' said Agricola, ' this is the notary to whom you transmitted some papers, and whose address you have lost.'

' But his name was not Durand ; and I distinctly recollect that his address was Paris, not Chartres. And, besides,' said the soldier, thoughtfully, ' if he has some important documents, why didn't he transmit them to me ?'

' It seems to me that you ought not to neglect going to him as soon as possible,' said Agricola, secretly rejoiced that this circumstance would withdraw his father for about two days, during which time his (Agricola's) fate would be decided in one way or other.

' Your counsel is good,' replied his father.

' This thwarts your intentions in some degree ?' asked Gabriel.

' Rather, my lads ; for I counted upon passing the day with you. However, " duty before everything." Having come happily from Siberia to Paris, it is not for me to fear a journey from Paris to Chartres, when it is required on an affair of importance. In twice twenty-four hours I shall be back again. But the deuce take me if I expected to leave Paris for Chartres to-day. Luckily, I leave Rose and Blanche with my good wife ; and Gabriel, their angel, as they call him, will be here to keep them company.'

' That is, unfortunately, impossible,' said the missionary, sadly. ' This visit on my arrival is also a farewell visit.'

' A farewell visit ! Now !' exclaimed Dagobert and Agricola both at once.

' Alas, yes !'

' You start already on another mission ?' said Dagobert ; ' surely it is not possible ?'

' I must answer no question upon this subject,' said Gabriel, suppressing a sigh ; ' but from now, for some time, I cannot, and ought not, come again into this house.'

'Why, my brave boy,' resumed Dagobert with emotion, 'there is something in thy conduct that savours of constraint, of oppression. I know something of men. He you call superior, whom I saw for some moments after the shipwreck at Cardoville Castle, has a bad look ; and I am sorry to see you enrolled under such a commander.'

'At Cardoville Castle !' exclaimed Agricola, struck with the identity of the name with that of the young lady of the golden hair ; 'was it in Cardoville Castle that you were received after your shipwreck ?'

'Yes, my boy ; why, does that astonish you ?' asked Dagobert.

'Nothing, father ; but were the owners of the castle there at the time ?'

'No ; for the steward, when I applied to him for an opportunity to return thanks for the kind hospitality we had experienced, informed me that the person to whom the house belonged was resident at Paris.'

'What a singular coincidence,' thought Agricola, 'if the young lady should be the proprietor of the dwelling which bears her name !'

This reflection having recalled to Agricola the promise which he had made to Mother Bunch, he said to Dagobert : 'Dear father, excuse me ; but it is already late, and I ought to be in the workshop by eight o'clock.'

'That is too true, my boy. Let us go. This party is adjourned till my return from Chartres. Embrace me once more, and take care of yourself.

Since Dagobert had spoken of constraint and oppression to Gabriel, the latter had continued pensive. At the moment when Agricola approached him to shake hands, and to bid him adieu, the missionary said to him solemnly, with a grave voice, and in a tone of decision that astonished both the blacksmith and the soldier : 'My dear brother, one word more. I have come here to say to you also, that within a few days hence I shall have need of you ; and of you also, my father (permit me so to call you),' added Gabriel, with emotion, as he turned round to Dagobert.

'How ! you speak thus to us !' exclaimed Agricola ; 'what is the matter?'

'Yes,' replied Gabriel, 'I need the advice and assistance of two men of honour—of two men of resolution ;—and I can reckon upon you two—can I not ? At any hour, on whatever day it may be, upon a word from me, will you come ?'

Dagobert and his son regarded each other in silence, astonished at the accents of the missionary. Agricola felt an oppression of the heart. If he should be a prisoner when his brother should require his assistance, what could be done ?

'At every hour, by night or by day, my brave boy, you may depend upon us,' said Dagobert, as much surprised as interested —'You have a father and a brother ; make your own use of them.'

'Thanks, thanks,' said Gabriel, 'you set me quite at ease.'

'I'll tell you what,' resumed the soldier, 'were it not for your priest's robe, I should believe, from the manner in which you have spoken to us, that you are about to be engaged in a duel—in a mortal combat.'

'In a duel ?' said Gabriel, starting ; 'Yes ; it may be a duel—uncommon and fearful—at which it is necessary to have two witnesses such as you— A FATHER and A BROTHER !'

    ✿   ✿   ✿   ✿   ✿   ✿

Some instants afterwards, Agricola, whose anxiety was continually increasing, set off in haste for the dwelling of Mademoiselle de Cardoville, to which we now beg leave to take the reader.

CHAPTER XXXIII.

THE PAVILION.

DIZIER HOUSE was one of the largest and handsomest in the Rue Babylone, in Paris. Nothing could be more severe, more imposing, or more depressing than the aspect of this old mansion. Several immense windows, filled with small squares of glass, painted a greyish white, increased the sombre effect of the massive layers of huge stones, blackened by time, of which the fabric was composed.

This dwelling bore a resemblance to all the others that had been erected in the same quarter towards the middle of the last century. It was surmounted in front by a pediment : it had an elevated ground-floor which was reached from the outside by a circular flight of broad stone steps. One of the fronts looked on an immense court-yard, on each side of which an arcade led to the vast inferior apartments. The other front overlooked the garden, or rather park, of twelve or fifteen roods ; and, on this side, wings, approaching the principal part of the structure, formed a couple of lateral galleries. Like nearly all the other great habitations of this quarter, there might be seen at the extremity of the garden, what the owners and occupiers of each called the lesser mansion.

This extension was a Pompadour summer-house, built in the form of a rotunda, with the charming though incorrect taste of the era of its erection. It presented, in every part where it was possible for the stones to be cut, a profusion of endives, knots of ribands, garlands of flowers, and chubby cupids This pavilion, inhabited by Adrienne de Cardoville, was composed of a ground-floor, which was reached by a peristyle of several steps. A small vestibule led to a circular hall, lighted from the roof. Four principal apartments met here ; and ranges of smaller rooms, concealed in the upper story, served for minor purposes.

These dependencies of great habitations are in our days disused, or transformed into irregular conservatories ; but, by an uncommon exception, the black exterior of the pavilion had been scraped and renewed, and the entire structure repaired. The white stones of which it was built glistened like Parian marble ; and its renovated, coquettish aspect contrasted singularly with the gloomy mansion seen at the other extremity of an extensive lawn, on which were planted here and there gigantic clumps of verdant trees.

The following scene occurred at this residence on the morning following that of the arrival of Dagobert, with the daughters of Marshal Simon, in the Rue Brise-Miche. The hour of eight had sounded from the steeple of a neighbouring church ; a brilliant winter sun arose to brighten a pure blue sky behind the tall leafless trees, which in summer formed a dome of verdure over the summer-house. The door in the vestibule opened, and the rays of the morning sun beamed upon a charming creature, or rather upon two charming creatures, for the second one, though filling a modest place in the scale of creation, was not less distinguished by a beauty of its own, which was very striking. In plain terms, two individuals, one of them a young girl, and the other a tiny English dog, of great beauty, of that breed of spaniels called King Charles's, made their appearance under the peristyle of the rotunda. The name of the young girl was Georgette ; the beautiful little spaniel's was Frisky. Georgette was in her eighteenth year. Never had Florine or Manton, never had a lady's maid of Marivaux, a more mischievous face, an eye more quick, a smile more roguish, teeth more white, cheeks more roseate, figure more coquettish, feet smaller, or form smarter, attractive, and enticing. Though it was yet very early, Georgette was carefully and tastefully dressed. A tiny Valenciennes cap, with flaps and flap-band, of half-peasant fashion, decked with rose-coloured ribbons, and stuck a little backward upon bands of beautiful fair hair, surrounded her fresh and piquant face ; a robe of grey levantine, and a cambric neck-kerchief, fastened to her bosom by a large tuft of rose-coloured ribbons, displayed her figure, elegantly rounded ; a hollands apron, white as snow, trimmed below by three large hems surmounted by a Vandyke-row, encircled her waist, which was as round and flexible as a reed; her short, plain sleeves, edged with bone-lace, allowed her plump arms to be seen, which her long Swedish gloves, reaching to the elbow, defended from the rigour of the cold. When Georgette raised the bottom of her dress, in order to descend more quickly the steps, she exhibited to Frisky's indifferent eyes a beautiful ankle, and the beginning of the plump calf of a fine leg, incased in white silk, and a charming little foot, in a laced half-boot of Turkish satin. When a blonde like Georgette sets herself to be ensnaring ; when vivid glances sparkle from her eyes of bright yet tender blue ; when a joyous excitement suffuses her transparent skin, she is more resistless for the conquest of everything before her than a brunette.

This bewitching and nimble lady's-maid, who on the previous evening had introduced Agricola to the pavilion, was first waiting-woman to the Honourable Miss Adrienne de Cardoville, niece of the Princess Saint-Dizier.

Frisky, so happily found and brought back by the blacksmith, uttered weak but joyful barks, and bounded, ran, and frolicked upon the turf. She was not much bigger than one's fist ; her curled hair, of lustrous black, shone like ebony, under the broad, red satin ribbon which encircled her neck ; her paws, fringed with long silken fur, were of a bright and fiery tan, as well as her muzzle, the nose of which was inconceivably pug; her large eyes were full of intelligence ; and her curly ears so long that they trailed upon the ground. Georgette seemed to be as brisk and petulant as Frisky, and shared her sportiveness,—now scampering after the happy little spaniel, and now retreating, in order to be pursued upon the greensward in her turn. All at once, at the sight of a second person, who advanced with deliberate gravity, Georgette and Frisky were suddenly stopped in their diversion. The little King Charles, some steps in advance of Georgette, faithful to her name, and bold as the devil, held herself firmly upon her nervous paws, and fiercely awaited the coming up of the enemy, displaying at the same time rows of little teeth, which, though of ivory, were none the less pointed and sharp. The enemy consisted of a woman of mature age, accompanied by a very fat dog, of the colour of coffee and milk ; his tail was twisted like a corkscrew ; he was pot-bellied ; his skin was sleek ; his neck was turned a little to one side ; he walked with his legs inordinately spread out, and stepped with the air of a doctor. His black muzzle, quarrelsome and scowling, showed two fangs sallying forth, and turning up from the left side of the mouth ; and altogether he had an expression singularly forbidding and vindictive. This disagreeable animal, a perfect type of what might be called 'a church goer's pug,' answered to the name of 'My Lord.' His mistress, a woman of about fifty years of age, corpulent and of middle size, was dressed in a costume as gloomy and severe as that of Georgette was gay and showy. It consisted of a brown robe, a black silk mantle, and a hat of the same dye. The features of this woman might have been agreeable in her youth : and her florid cheeks, her correct eyebrows, her black eyes, which were still very lively, scarcely accorded with the peevish and austere physiognomy which she tried to assume. This matron, of slow and discreet gait, was Madame Augustine Grivois, first woman to the Princess Saint Dizier. Not only did the age, the face, and the dress of these two women present a striking contrast; but the contrast extended itself even to the animals which attended them. There were similar differences between Frisky and My

Lord, as between Georgette and Mrs. Grivois. When the latter perceived the little King Charles, she could not restrain a movement of surprise and repugnance, which escaped not the notice of the young lady's maid. Frisky, who had not retreated one inch, since the apparition of My Lord, regarded him valiantly, with a look of defiance, and even advanced towards him with an air so decidedly hostile, that the cur, though thrice as big as the little King Charles, uttered a howl of distress and terror, and sought refuge behind Mrs. Grivois, who bitterly said to Georgette :

'It seems to me, miss, that you might dispense with exciting your dog thus, and setting him upon mine.'

'It was, doubtless, for the purpose of protecting this respectable but ugly animal from similar alarms, that you tried to make us lose Frisky yesterday, by driving her into the street through the little garden gate. But fortunately an honest young man found Frisky in the Rue de Babylone, and brought her back to my mistress. However,' continued Georgette, 'to what, madame, do I owe the pleasure of seeing you this morning ?'

'I am commanded by the princess,' replied Mrs. Grivois, unable to conceal a smile of triumphant satisfaction, 'immediately to see Miss Adrienne. It regards a very important affair, which I am to communicate only to herself.'

At these words Georgette became purple, and could not repress a slight start of disquietude, which happily escaped Grivois, who was occupied with watching over the safety of her pet, whom Frisky continued to snarl at with a very menacing aspect ; and Georgette, having quickly overcome her temporary emotion, firmly answered : 'Miss Adrienne went to rest very late last night. She has forbidden me to enter her apartment before mid-day.'

'That is very possible: but as the present business is to obey an order of the Princess her aunt, you will do well if you please, miss, to awaken your mistress immediately.'

'My mistress is subject to no one's orders in her own house; and I will not disturb her till mid-day, in pursuance of her commands,' replied Georgette.

'Then I shall go myself,' said Mrs. Grivois.

'Florine and Hebe will not admit you. Indeed, here is the key of the saloon ; and through the saloon only can the apartments of Miss Adrienne be entered.'

'How ! do you dare refuse me permission to execute the orders of the princess ?'

'Yes ; I dare to commit the great crime of being unwilling to awaken my mistress !'

'Ah ! such are the results of the blind affection of the Princess for her niece,' said the matron, with affected grief : 'Miss Adrienne no longer respects her aunt's orders ; and she is surrounded by young hare-brained persons, who, from the first dawn of morning, dress themselves out as if for ball-going.'

'Oh, madame ! how came you to revile dress, who were formerly the greatest coquette and the most frisky and fluttering of all the princess's women. At least, that is what is still spoken of you in the hotel, as having been handed down from time out of mind, by generation to generation, even unto ours !'

'How ! from generation to generation ! do you mean to insinuate that I am a hundred years old, Miss Impertinence ?'

'I speak of the generations of waiting-women ; for, except you, it is the utmost if they remain two or three years in the Princess's house, who has too many tempers for the poor girls !'

'I forbid you to speak thus of my mistress, whose name some people ought not to pronounce but on their knees.'

' However,' said Georgette, ' if one wished to speak ill of——

' Do you dare ?'

' No longer ago than last night, at half-past eleven o'clock——'

' Last night ?'

' A four-wheeler,' continued Georgette, ' stopped at a few paces from the house. A mysterious personage, wrapped up in a cloak, alighted from it, and directly tapped, not at the door, but on the glass of the porter's lodge window ; and at one o'clock in the morning, the cab was still stationed in the street, waiting for the mysterious personage in the cloak, who, doubtless, during all that time, was, as you say, pronouncing the name of her Highness the Princess on his knees.'

Whether Mrs. Grivois had not been instructed as to a visit made to the Princess Saint-Dizier by Rodin (for he was the man in the cloak), in the middle of the night, after he had become certain of the arrival in Paris of General Simon's daughters ; or whether Mrs. Grivois thought it necessary to appear ignorant of the visit, she replied, shrugging her shoulders disdainfully ; ' I know not what you mean, madame. I have not come here to listen to your impertinent stuff. Once again I ask you—will you, or will you not, introduce me to the presence of Miss Adrienne ?'

' I repeat, madame, that my mistress sleeps, and that she has forbidden me to enter her bed-chamber before mid-day.'

This conversation took place at some distance from the summer-house, at a spot from which the peristyle could be seen at the end of a grand avenue, terminating in trees arranged in form of a V. All at once Mrs. Grivois, extending her hand in that direction, exclaimed : ' Great heavens ! is it possible ? what have I seen ?'

' What have you seen ?' said Georgette, turning round.

' What have I seen ?' repeated Mrs. Grivois, with amazement.

' Yes : what was it ?'

' Miss Adrienne.'

' Where ?' asked Georgette.

' I saw her run up the porch steps. I perfectly recognised her by her gait, by her hat, and by her mantle. To come home at eight o'clock in the morning !' cried Mrs. Grivois : ' it is perfectly incredible !'

' See my lady ? Why, you came to see her !' and Georgette burst out into fits of laughter ; and then said : ' Oh ! I understand ! you wish to out-do my story of the four-wheeler last night ! It is very neat of you !'

' I repeat,' said Mrs. Grivois, ' that I have this moment seen——'

' Oh ! adone, Mrs. Grivois : if you speak seriously, you are mad !'

' I am mad, am I ? because I have a pair of good eyes ! The little gate that opens on the street lets one into the *quincunx* near the pavilion. It is by that door, doubtless, that mademoiselle has re-entered. Oh, what shameful conduct ! what will the Princess say to it ! Ah ! her presentiments have not yet been mistaken. See to what her weak indulgence of her niece's caprices has led her ! It is monstrous !—so monstrous, that, though I have seen her with my own eyes, still I can scarcely believe it !'

' Since you've gone so far, ma'am, I now insist upon conducting you into the apartment of my lady, in order that you may convince yourself, by your own senses, that your eyes have deceived you !'

' Oh, you are very cunning, my dear, but not more cunning than I ! You propose my going now ! Yes, yes, I believe you : you are certain that by this time I shall find her in her apartment !'

' But, madame, I assure you——'

' All that I can say to you is this : that neither you, nor Florine, nor Hebe, shall remain here twenty-four hours. The Princess will put an end to this horrible scandal ; for I shall immediately inform her of what has passed. To go out in the night ! Re-enter at eight o'clock in the morning ! Why, I am all in a whirl ! Certainly, if I had not seen it with my own eyes, I could not have believed it ! Still, it is only what was to be expected. It will astonish nobody. Assuredly not ! All those to whom I am going to relate it, will say, I am quite sure, that it is not at all astonishing ! Oh ! what a blow to our respectable Princess ! What a blow for her !'

Mrs. Grivois returned precipitately towards the mansion, followed by her fat pug, who appeared to be as embittered as herself.

Georgette, active and light, ran, on her part, towards the pavilion, in order to apprise Miss de Cardoville that Mrs. Grivois had seen her, or fancied she had seen her, furtively enter by the little garden gate.

CHAPTER XXXIV.

ADRIENNE AT HER TOILET.

ABOUT an hour had elapsed since Mrs. Grivois had seen or pretended to have seen Adrienne de Cardoville re-enter in the morning the extension of Saint-Dizier House.

It is for the purpose, not of excusing, but of rendering intelligible, the following scenes, that it is deemed necessary to bring out into the light some striking peculiarities in the truly original character of Miss de Cardoville.

This originality consisted in an excessive independence of mind, joined to a natural horror of whatsoever is repulsive or deformed, and to an insatiable desire of being surrounded by everything attractive and beautiful. The painter most delighted with colouring and beauty, the sculptor most charmed by proportions of form, feel not more than Adrienne did the noble enthusiasm which the view of perfect beauty always excites in the chosen favourites of nature.

And it was not only the pleasures of sight which this young lady loved to gratify : the harmonious modulations of song, the melody of instruments, the cadences of poetry, afforded her infinite pleasures ; while a harsh voice or a discordant noise made her feel the same painful impression, or one nearly as painful, as that which she involuntarily experienced from the sight of a hideous object. Passionately fond of flowers, too, and of their sweet scents, there are some perfumes which she enjoyed equally with the delights of music or those of plastic beauty. It is necessary, alas, to acknowledge one enormity : Adrienne was dainty in her food ! She valued more than any one else the fresh pulp of handsome fruit, the delicate savour of a golden pheasant, cooked to a turn, and the odorous cluster of a generous vine.

But Adrienne enjoyed all these pleasures with an exquisite reserve. She sought religiously to cultivate and refine the senses given her. She would have deemed it black ingratitude to blunt those divine gifts by excesses, or to debase them by unworthy selections of objects upon which to exercise them ; a fault from which, indeed, she was preserved by the excessive and imperious delicacy of her taste.

The BEAUTIFUL and the UGLY occupied for her the places which GOOD and EVIL hold for others.

Her devotion to grace, elegance, and physical beauty, had led her also to the adoration of moral beauty ; for if the expression of a low and bad passion render uncomely the most beautiful countenances, those which are in themselves the most ugly are ennobled, on the contrary, by the expression of good feelings and generous sentiments.

In a word, Adrienne was the most complete, the most ideal personification of SENSUALITY—not of vulgar, ignorant, non-intelligent, mistaken sen-suousness which is always deceitful and corrupted by habit or by the necessity for gross and ill-regulated enjoyments, but that exquisite sensuality which is to the senses what intelligence is to the soul.

The independence of this young lady's character was extreme. Certain humiliating subjections imposed upon her success by its social position, above all things were revolting to her, and she had the hardihood to resolve to withdraw herself from them. She was a woman, the most womanish that it is possible to imagine—a woman in her timidity as well as in her audacity —a woman in her hatred of the brutal despotism of men, as well as in her intense disposition to self-devoting herself, madly even and blindly, to him who should merit such a devotion from her—a woman whose piquant wit was occasionally paradoxical—a superior woman, in brief, who entertained a well-grounded disdain and contempt for certain men either placed very high or greatly adulated, whom she had from time to time met in the draw-ing-room of her aunt, the Princess Saint-Dizier, when she resided with her.

These indispensable explanations being given, we usher the reader into the presence of Adrienne de Cardoville, who had just come out of the bath.

It would require all the brilliant colourings of the Venetian school to re-present that charming scene, which would rather seem to have occurred in the sixteenth century, in some palace of Florence or Bologna, than in Paris, in the Faubourg Saint-German, in the month of February, 1832.

Adrienne's dressing-room was a kind of miniature temple, seemingly one erected and dedicated to the worship of beauty, in gratitude to the Maker who has lavished so many charms upon woman, not to be neglected by her, or to cover and conceal them with ashes, or to destroy them by the contact of her person with sordid and harsh haircloth ; but in order that, with fervent gratitude for the divine gifts wherewith she is en-dowed, she may enhance her charms with all the illusions of grace and all the splendours of apparel, so as to glorify the divine work of her own per-fections in the eyes of all. Daylight was admitted into this semi-circular apartment, through one of those double windows, contrived for the preser-vation of heat, so happily imported from Germany. The walls of the pavilion being constructed of stone of great thickness, the depth of the aperture for the windows was therefore very great. That of Adrienne's dressing-room was closed on the outside by a sash containing a single large pane of plate glass, and within, by another large plate of ground glass. In the interval or space of about three feet left between these two transparent enclosures, there was a case or box filled with furze mould, whence sprung forth climbing plants, which, directed round the ground glass, formed a rich garland of leaves and flowers. A garnet damask tapestry, rich with har-moniously blended arabesques, in the purest style, covered the walls ; and a thick carpet of similar colour was extended over the floor : and this sombre ground, presented by the floor and walls, marvellously enhanced the effects of all the harmonious ornaments and decorations of the chamber.

Under the window, opposite to the south, was placed Adrienne's dressing-case, a real master-piece of the skill of the goldsmith. Upon a large tablet of *lapis-lazuli*, there were scattered boxes of jewels, their lids preciously enamelled ; several scent boxes of rock crystal, and other implements and utensils of the toilet, some formed of shells, some of mother-of-pearl, and others of ivory, covered with ornaments of gold in extraordinary taste. Two large figures, modelled in silver with antique purity, supported an oval swing mirror, which had for its rim, in place of a frame curiously carved, a fresh garland of natural flowers, renewed every day like a nosegay for a ball.

Two enormous Japanese vases, of purple and gold, three feet each in diameter, were placed upon the carpet on each side of the toilet, and, filled with camellias, ibiscures, and cape jasmin, in full flower, formed a sort of grove, diversified with the most brilliant colours. At the farther end of the apartment, opposite the casement, was to be seen, surrounded by another mass of flowers, a reduction in white marble of the enchanting group of Daphnis and Chloe, the more chaste ideal of graceful modesty and youthful beauty.

Two golden lamps burned perfumes upon the same pedestal which supported those two charming figures. A coffer of frosted silver, set off with small figures in jewellery and precious stones, and supported on four feet of gilt bronze, contained various necessaries for the toilette ; two frosted Psyches, decorated with diamond ear-rings ; some excellent drawings from Raphael and Titian, painted by Adrienne herself, consisting of portraits of both men and women of exquisite beauty ; several consoles of oriental jaspar, supporting ewers and basins of silver and of silver gilt, richly chased and filled with scented waters ; a voluptuously rich divan, some seats, and an illuminated gilt table, completed the furniture of this chamber, the atmosphere of which was impregnated with the sweetest perfumes.

Adrienne, whom her attendants had just helped from the bath, was seated before her toilette, her three women surrounding her. By a caprice, or rather by a necessary and logical impulse of her soul, filled as it was with the love of beauty and of harmony in all things, Adrienne had wished the young women who served her to be very pretty, and be dressed with attention and with a charming originality. We have already seen Georgette, a piquante blonde, attired in her attractive costume of an intriguing lady's maid of Marivaux ; and her two companions were quite equal to her both in gracefulness and gentility.

One of them, named Florine, a tall, delicately slender, and elegant girl, with the air and form of Diana Huntress, was of a pale brown complexion. Her thick black hair was turned up behind, where it was fastened with a long golden pin. Like the two other girls, her arms were uncovered to facilitate the performance of her duties about and upon the person of her charming mistress. She wore a dress of that gay green so familiar to the Venetian painters. Her petticoat was very ample. Her slender waist curved in from under the plaits of a tucker of white cambric, plaited in five minute folds, and fastened by five gold buttons. The third of Adrienne's women had a face so fresh and ingenuous, a waist so delicate, so pleasing, and so finished, that her mistress had given her the name of Hebe. Her dress, of a delicate rose colour, and Grecian cut, displayed her charming neck, and her beautiful arms up to the very shoulders. The physiognomy of these three young women was laughter-loving and happy. On their features there was no expression of that bitter sullenness, willing and hated obedience, or offensive familiarity, or base and degraded deference, which are the ordinary results of a state of servitude. In the zealous eagerness of the cares and attentions which they lavished upon Adrienne, there seemed to be at least as much of affection as of deference and respect. They appeared to derive an ardent pleasure from the services which they rendered to their lovely mistress. One would have thought that they attached to the dressing and embellishment of her person all the merits and the enjoyment arising from the execution of a work of art, in the accomplishing of which, fruitful of delights, they were stimulated by the passions of love, of pride, and of joy.

The sun beamed brightly upon the toilet-case, placed in front of the window. Adrienne was seated on a chair, its back elevated a little more than usual. She was enveloped in a long morning gown of blue silk, embroidered with a leaf of the same colour, which was fitted close to her waist, as exquisitely slender and delicate as that of a child of twelve years, by a girdle with floating tags. Her neck, delicately slender and flexible as a bird's, was uncovered, as were also her shoulders and arms, and all were of incomparable beauty. Despite the vulgarity of the comparison, the purest ivory alone can give an idea of the dazzling whiteness of her polished satin skin, of a texture so fresh and so firm, that some drops of water, collected and still remaining about the roots of her hair from the bath, rolled in serpentine lines over her shoulders, like pearls, or beads, of crystal, over white marble.

And what gave enhanced lustre to this wondrous carnation, known but to auburn-headed beauties, was the deep purple of her humid lips,—the roseate transparency of her small ears, of her dilated nostrils, and her nails, as bright and glossy, as if they had been varnished. In every spot, indeed, where her pure arterial blood, full of animation and heat, could make its way to the skin and shine through the surface, it proclaimed her high health and the vivid life and joyous buoyancy of her glorious youth. Her eyes were very large, and of a velvet softness. Now they glanced, sparkling and shining with comic humour or intelligence and wit ; and now they widened and extended themselves, languishing and swimming between their double fringes of long crisp eyelashes, of as deep a black as her finely drawn and exquisitely arched eyebrows ; for, by a delightful freak of nature, she had black eyebrows and eyelashes to contrast with the golden red of her hair. Her forehead, small like those of ancient Grecian statues, formed with the rest of her face a perfect oval. Her nose, delicately curved, was slightly aquiline ; the enamel of her teeth glistened when the light fell upon them ; and her vermeil mouth, voluptuously sensual, seemed to call for sweet kisses, and the gay smiles and delectations of dainty and delicious pleasure. It is impossible to behold or to conceive a carriage of the head freer, more noble, or more elegant than hers ; thanks to the great distance which separated the neck and the ear from their attachment to her outspread and dimpled shoulders. We have already said that Adrienne was red-haired ; but it was the redness of many of the admirable portraits of women by Titian and Leonardi da Vinci,—that is to say, molten gold presents not reflections more delightfully agreeable or more glittering, than the naturally undulating mass of her very long hair, as soft and fine as silk, so long, that, when let loose, it reached the floor ; in it, she could wholly envelop herself, like another Venus arising from the sea. At the present moment, Adrienne's tresses were ravishing to behold. Georgette, her arms bare, stood behind her mistress, and had carefully collected into one of her small white hands, those splendid threads whose naturally ardent brightness was doubled in the sunshine. When the pretty lady's maid plunged a comb of ivory into the midst of the undulating and golden waves of that enormously magnificent skein of silk, one might have said that a thousand sparks of fire darted forth and coruscated away from it in all directions. The sunshine, too, reflected not less golden and fiery rays from numerous clusters of spiral ringlets, which, divided upon Adrienne's forehead, fell over her cheeks, and in their elastic flexibility caressed the risings of her snowy bosom, to whose charming undulations they adapted and applied themselves. Whilst Georgette, standing, combed the beautiful locks of her mistress, Hebe, with one knee upon the floor, and having upon the other the sweet little foot of Miss Cardoville, busied herself in fitting it with a remarkably small shoe of black satin, and crossed its slender ties over a silk stocking of a pale yet rosy flesh colour, which imprisoned the smallest and finest ankle in the world. Florine, a little farther back, presented to her mistress, in a jewelled box, a perfumed paste, with which Adrienne slightly rubbed her dazzling hands and outspread fingers, which seemed tinted with carmine to their extremities.

Let us not forget Frisky, who, couched in the lap of her mistress, opened her great eyes with all her might, and seemed to observe the different operations of Adrienne's toilet with grave and reflective attention. A silver bell being sounded from without, Florine, at a sign from her mistress, went out and presently returned, bearing a letter upon a small silver-gilt salver. Adrienne, while her women continued fitting on her shoes, dressing her hair, and arranging her in her habiliments, took the letter, which was written by the steward of the estate of Cardoville, and read aloud as follows :

'HONOURED MADAME,—

'Knowing your goodness of heart and generosity, I venture to address you with respectful confidence. During twenty years I served the late Count and Duke of Cardoville, your noble father, I believe I may truly say, with probity and zeal. The castle is now sold ; so that I and my wife, in our old age, behold ourselves about to be dismissed, and left destitute of all resources ; which, alas ! is very hard at our time of life.'

'Poor creatures !' said Adrienne, interrupting herself in reading : 'my father, certainly, always prided himself upon their devotion to him, and their probity.' She continued :

'There does, indeed, remain to us a means of retaining our place here ; but it would constrain us to be guilty of baseness ; and be the consequences to us what they may, neither I nor my wife wish to purchase our bread at such a price.'

'Good, very good,' said Adrienne, 'always the same—dignity even in poverty—it is the sweet perfume of a flower, not the less sweet because it has bloomed in a meadow.'

'In order to explain to you, honoured madame, the unworthy task exacted from us, it is necessary to inform you, in the first place, that M. Rodin came here from Paris two days ago.'

'Ah ! M. Rodin !' said Mademoiselle de Cardoville, interrupting herself anew ; 'the secretary of Abbe d'Aigrigny ! I am not at all surprised at him being engaged in a perfidious or black intrigue. But let us see.'

'M. Rodin came from Paris to announce to us that the estate was sold, and that he was sure of being able to obtain our continuance in our place, if we would assist him in imposing a priest not of good character upon the new proprietor as her future confessor ; and if, the better to attain this end, we would consent to calumniate another priest, a deserving and excellent man, much loved and much respected in the country. Even that is not all. I was required to write twice or thrice a week to M. Rodin, and to relate to him everything that should occur in the house. I ought to acknowledge, honoured madame, that these infamous proposals were as much as possible disguised and dissimulated under sufficiently specious pretexts : but, notwithstanding the aspect which with more or less skill it was attempted to give to the affair, it was precisely and substantially what I have now had the honour of stating to you.'

'Corruption, calumny, and false and treacherous impeachment !' said Adrienne, with disgust : 'I cannot think of such wretches without involuntarily feeling my mind shocked by dismal ideas of black, venomous, and vile reptiles, of aspects most hideous indeed. How much more do I love to dwell upon the consoling thought of honest Dupont and his wife !' Adrienne proceeded :

'Believe me, we hesitated not an instant. We quit Cardoville, which has been our home for the last twenty years ;—but we shall quit it like honest people, and with the consciousness of our integrity. And now, honoured madame, if, in the brilliant circle in which you move—you, who are so benevolent and amiable—could find a place for us by your recommendation, then, with endless gratitude to you, we shall escape from a position of most cruel embarrassment.'

' Surely, surely,' said Adrienne, ' they shall not in vain appeal to me.   To wrest excellent persons from the gripe of M. Rodin, is not only a duty but a pleasure ; for it is at once a righteous and a dangerous enterprise ; and dearly do I love to brave powerful oppressors !'   Adrienne again went on reading :

' After having thus spoken to you of ourselves, honoured madame, permit us to implore your protection for other unfortunates ; for it would be wicked to think only of one's self.   Three days ago, two shipwrecks took place upon our ironbound coast.   A few passengers only were saved, and were conducted hither, where I and my wife gave them all necessary attentions. All these passengers have departed for Paris, except one, who still remains, his wounds having hitherto prevented him from leaving the house, and, indeed, they will constrain him to remain for some days to come.   He is a young East Indian prince, of about twenty years of age, and he appears to be as amiable and good as he is handsome, which is not a little to say, though he has a tawny skin, like the rest of his countrymen, as I understand.'

' An Indian prince! twenty years of age ! young, amiable, and hand-some !' exclaimed Adrienne, gaily ; ' this is quite delightful, and not at all of an ordinary or vulgar nature !   Oh ! this Indian prince has already awakened all my sympathies !   But what can I do with this Adonis from the banks of the Ganges, who has come to wreck himself upon the Picardy coast ?'

Adrienne's three women looked at her with much astonishment, though they were accustomed to the singular eccentricities of her character.

Georgette and Hebe even indulged in discreet and restrained smiles. Florine, the tall and beautiful pale brown girl, also smiled like her pretty companions ; but it was after a short pause of seeming reflection, as if she had previously been entirely engrossed in listening to and recollecting the minutest words of her mistress, who, though powerfully interested by the situation of the ' Adonis from Ganges' banks,' as she had called him, continued to read Dupont's letter :

' One of the countrymen of the Indian prince, who has also remained to attend upon him, has given me to understand that the youthful prince has lost in the shipwreck all he possessed, and knows not how to get to Paris, where his speedy presence is required by some affairs of the very greatest importance.   It is not from the prince himself that I have obtained this information : no ; he appears to be too dignified and proud to complain of his fate ; but his countryman, more communicative, has confidentially told me what I have stated, adding, that his young compatriot has already been subjected to great calamities, and that his father, who was the sovereign of an Indian kingdom, has been killed by the English, who have also dis-possessed his son of his crown.'

' This is very singular,' said Adrienne thoughtfully.   ' These circumstances recall to my mind that my father often mentioned that one of our relations was espoused in India by a native monarch ; and that General Simon (whom they have created a marshal) had entered into his service.'   Then interrupting herself to indulge in a smile, she added, ' Gracious ! this affair will be quite odd and fantastical !   Such things happen to nobody but me ; and then people say that I am the uncommon creature !   But it seems to me that it is not I, but Providence, which, in truth, sometimes shows itself very eccentric !   But let us see if worthy Dupont gives the name of this handsome prince !'

'We trust, honoured madame, that you will pardon our boldness : but we should have thought ourselves very selfish, if, while stating to you our own griefs, we had not also informed you that there is with us a brave and estimable prince involved in so much distress. In fine, lady, trust to me ; I am old; and I have had much experience of men ; and it was only necessary to see the nobleness of expression and the sweetness of countenance of this young Indian, to enable me to judge that he is worthy of the interest which I have taken the liberty to request in his behalf. It would be sufficient to transmit to him a small sum of money for the purchase of some European clothing ; for he has lost all his Indian vestments in the shipwreck.'

'Good heavens ! European clothing !' exclaimed Adrienne, gaily. 'Poor young prince ! Heaven preserve him from that ; and me also ! Chance has sent hither, from the heart of India, a mortal so far favoured as never to have worn the abominable European costume—those hideous habits, and frightful hats, which render the men so ridiculous, so ugly, that in truth there is not a single good quality to be discovered in them, nor one spark of what can either captivate or attract ! There comes to me at last a handsome young prince from the East, where the men are clothed in silk and cashmere. Most assuredly I'll not miss this rare and unique opportunity of exposing myself to a very serious and formidable temptation ! No, no ! not a European dress from me, though poor Dupont requests it ! But the name—the name of this dear prince ! Once more, what a singular event is this ! If it should turn out to be that cousin from beyond the Ganges ! During my childhood, I have heard so much in praise of his royal father ! Oh ! I shall be quite ravished to give his son the kind reception which he merits !' And then she read on :

'If, besides this small sum, honoured madame, you are so kind as to give him, and also his companion, the means of reaching Paris, you will confer a very great service upon this poor young prince, who is at present so unfortunate.

'To conclude, I know enough of your delicacy to be aware that it would perhaps be agreeable to you to afford this succour to the prince without being known as his benefactress ; in which case, I beg that you will be pleased to command me ; and you may rely upon my discretion. If, on the contrary, you wish to address it directly to himself, his name is, as it has been written for me by his countryman, "Prince Djalma, son of Radja-sing, King of Mundi."'

'Djalma !' said Adrienne, quickly, and appearing to call up her recollections, 'Radja-sing ! Yes—that is it ! These are the very names that my father so often repeated, while telling me that there was nothing more chivalric or heroic in the world than the old king, our relation by marriage ; and the son has not derogated, it would seem, from that character. Yes, Djalma, Radja-sing—once more, that is it—such names are not so common,' she added, smiling, 'that one should either forget or confound them with others. This Djalma is my cousin ! Brave and good—young and charming! above all, he has never worn the horrid European dress ! And destitute of every resource ! This is quite ravishing ! It is too much happiness at once ! Quick, quick ! let us improvise a pretty fairy tale, of which the handsome and beloved prince shall be the hero ! The poor bird of the golden and azure plumage has wandered into our dismal climate ; but he will find here, at least, something to remind him of his native region of sunshine and perfumes !' Then, addressing one of her women, she said : 'Georgette, take paper and write, my child.' The young girl went to the gilt, illuminated table, which contained materials for writing ; and, having seated herself, she said to her mistress : 'I await orders.'

Adrienne de Cardoville, whose charming countenance was radiant with the gaiety of happiness and joy, proceeded to dictate the following letter to a meritorious old painter, who had long since taught her the arts of drawing and designing; in which arts she excelled, as indeed she did in all others:

'MY DEAR TITIAN, MY GOOD VERONESE, MY WORTHY RAPHAEL,— 'You can render me a very great service,—and you will do it, I am sure, with that perfect and obliging complaisance by which you are ever distinguished.

'It is to go immediately and apply yourself to the skilful hand who designed my last costumes of the fifteenth century. But the present affair is to procure modern East Indian dresses for a young man,—yes, sir,—for a young man, —and according to what I imagine of him, I fancy that you can cause his measure to be taken from the Antinous, or, rather, from the Indian Bacchus; yes—that will be more likely.

'It is necessary that these vestments be at once of perfect propriety and correctness, magnificently rich, and of the greatest elegance. You will choose the most beautiful stuffs possible; and endeavour, above all things, that they be, or resemble, tissues of Indian manufacture; and you will add to them, for turbans and sashes, six splendid long cashmere shawls, two of them white, two red, and two orange; as nothing suits brown complexions better than those colours.

'This done (and I allow you at the utmost only two or three days), you will depart post in my carriage for Cardoville Manor House, which you know so well. The steward, the excellent Dupont, one of your old friends, will there introduce you to a young Indian Prince, named Djalma; and you will tell that most potent, grave, and reverend signior, of another quarter of the globe, that you have come on the part of an unknown friend, who, taking upon himself the duty of a brother, sends him what is necessary to preserve him from the odious fashions of Europe. You will add, that his friend expects him with so much impatience that he conjures him to come to Paris immediately. If he objects, that he is suffering, you will tell him that my carriage is an excellent bed-closet; and you will cause the bedding, etc., which it contains, to be fitted up, till he finds it quite commodious. Remember to make very humble excuses for the unknown friend not sending to the prince either rich palanquins, or even, modestly, a single elephant; for alas! palanquins are only to be seen at the opera; and there are no elephants but those in the menagerie,—though this must make us seem strangely barbarous in his eyes.

'As soon as you shall have decided on your departure, perform the journey as rapidly as possible, and bring here, into my house, in the Rue de Babylone (what predestination! that I should dwell in the street of BABYLON, —a name which must at least accord with the ear of an Oriental),—you will bring hither, I say, this dear prince, who is so happy as to have been born in a country of flowers, diamonds, and sun!

'Above all, you will have the kindness, my old and worthy friend, not to be at all astonished at this new freak, and refrain from indulging in extravagant conjectures. Seriously, the choice which I have made of you in this affair,—of you, whom I esteem and most sincerely honour,—is because it is sufficient to say to you that, at the bottom of all this, there is something more than a seeming act of folly.'

In uttering these last words, the tone of Adrienne was as serious and dignified as it had been previously comic and jocose. But she quickly resumed, more gaily, dictating to Georgette.

'Adieu, my old friend. I am something like that commander of ancient days, whose heroic nose and conquering chin you have so often made me draw: I jest with the utmost freedom of spirit even in the moment of battle : yes, for within an hour I shall give battle, a pitched battle—to my dear pew-dwelling aunt. Fortunately, audacity and courage never failed me ; and I burn with impatience for the engagement with my austere princess.

' A kiss, and a thousand heartfelt recollections to your excellent wife. If I speak of her here, who is so justly respected, you will please to understand, it is to make you quite at ease as to the consequences of this running away with, for my sake, a charming young prince,—for it is proper to finish well, where I should have begun, by avowing to you that he is charming indeed !

' Once more, adieu !'

Then, addressing Georgette, she said, ' Have you done writing, chit ?'

' Yes, madame.'

' Oh ! add this postscript :

' P.S.— I send you draft on sight on my banker for all expenses. Spare nothing. You know I am quite a grand seigneur ! I must use this masculine expression, since your sex have exclusively appropriated to yourselves (tyrants as you are) a term, so significant as it is of noble generosity.'

' Now, Georgette,' said Adrienne, ' bring me an envelope, and the letter, that I may sign it.' Mademoiselle de Cardoville took the pen that Georgette presented to her, signed the letter, and inclosed in it an order upon her banker, which was expressed thus :

' Please pay M. Norval, on demand without grace, the sum of money he may require for expenses incurred on my account.

' ADRIENNE DE CARDOVILLE.'

During all this scene, while Georgette wrote, Florine and Hebe had continued to busy themselves with the duties of their mistress's toilette, who had put off her morning gown, and was now in full dress, in order to wait upon the princess, her aunt. From the sustained and immovably fixed attention with which Florine had listened to Adrienne's dictating to Georgette her letter to M. Norval, it might easily have been seen that, as was her habit indeed, she endeavoured to retain in her memory even the slightest words of her mistress.

' Now, chit,' said Adrienne to Hebe, ' send this letter immediately to M. Norval.'

The same silver bell was again rung from without. Hebe moved towards the door of the dressing-room, to go and inquire what it was, and also to execute the order of her mistress as to the letter. But Florine precipitated herself, so to speak, before her, and so as to prevent her leaving the apartment ; and said to Adrienne :

' Will it please my lady for me to send this letter ? I have occasion to go to the mansion.'

' Go, Florine, then,' said Adrienne, ' seeing that you wish it. Georgette, seal the letter.'

At the end of a second or two, during which Georgette had sealed the letter, Hebe returned.

' Madame,' said she, re-entering, ' the working man who brought back Frisky yesterday, entreats you to admit him for an instant. He is very pale, and he appears quite sad.'

' Would that he may already have need of me ! I should be too happy !' said Adrienne gaily. ' Show the excellent young man into the little saloon. And, Florine, despatch this letter immediately.'

Florine went out. Miss de Cardoville, followed by Frisky, entered the little reception-room, where Agricola awaited her.

CHAPTER XXXV.

THE INTERVIEW.

WHEN Adrienne de Cardoville entered the saloon where Agricola expected her, she was dressed with extremely elegant simplicity. A robe of deep blue, perfectly fitted to her shape, embroidered in front with interlacings of black silk, according to the then fashion, outlined her nymph-like figure and her rounded bosom. A French cambric collar, fastened by a large Scotch pebble, set as a brooch, served her for necklace. Her magnificent golden hair formed a framework for her fair countenance, with an incredible profusion of long and light spiral tresses, which reached nearly to her waist.

Agricola, in order to save explanations with his father, and to make him believe that he had indeed gone to the workshop of M. Hardy, had been obliged to array himself in his working dress ; he had put on a new blouse though, and the collar of his shirt, of stout linen, very white, fell over upon a black cravat, negligently tied ; his grey trousers allowed his well-polished boots to be seen ; and he held between his muscular hands a cap of fine woollen cloth, quite new. To sum up, his blue blouse, embroidered with red, showing off the nervous chest of the young blacksmith, and indicating his robust shoulders, falling down in graceful folds, put not the least constraint upon his free and easy gait, and became him much better than either frock-coat or dress-coat would have done. While awaiting Miss de Cardoville, Agricola mechanically examined a magnificent silver vase, admirably graven. A small tablet, of the same metal, fitted into a cavity of its antique stand, bore the words—' Chased by JEAN MARIE, working chaser, 1831.'

Adrienne had stepped so lightly upon the carpet of her saloon, only separated from another apartment by the doors, that Agricola had not perceived the young lady's entrance. He started, and turned quickly round, upon hearing a silvery and brilliant voice say to him—

' That is a beautiful vase, is it not, sir ?'

' Very beautiful, madame,' answered Agricola greatly embarrassed.

' You may see from it that I like what is equitable,' added Miss de Cardoville, pointing with her finger to the little silver tablet ;—' an artist puts his name upon his painting ; an author publishes his on the title page of his book : and I contend that an artizan ought also to have his name connected with his workmanship.'

' Oh, madame, so this name ?'

' Is that of the poor chaser who executed this masterpiece, at the order of a rich goldsmith. When the latter sold me the vase, he was amazed at my eccentricity, he would have almost said at my injustice, when, after having made him tell me the name of the author of this production, I ordered his name to be inscribed upon it, instead of that of the goldsmith, which had already been affixed to the stand. In the absence of the rich profits, let the artizan enjoy the fame of his skill. Is it not just, sir ?'

It would have been impossible for Adrienne to commence the conversation more graciously : so that the blacksmith, already beginning to feel a little more at ease, answered :

' Being a mechanic myself, madame, I cannot but be doubly affected by such a proof of your sense of equity and justice.'

' Since you are a mechanic, sir,' resumed Adrienne, ' I cannot but felicitate myself on having so suitable a hearer. But please to be seated.'

With a gesture full of affability, she pointed to an arm-chair of purple silk embroidered with gold, sitting down herself upon a *tête-à-tête* of the same materials.

Seeing Agricola's hesitation, who again cast down his eyes with embarrassment, Adrienne, to encourage him, showed him Frisky, and said to him gaily : 'This poor little animal, to which I am very much attached, will always afford me a lively remembrance of your obliging complaisance, sir. And this visit seems to me to be of happy augury ; I know not what good presentiment whispers to me, that perhaps I shall have the pleasure of being useful to you in some affair.'

'Madame,' said Agricola, resolutely, 'my name is Baudoin : a blacksmith in the employment of M. Hardy, at Plessy, near the city. Yesterday you offered me your purse, and I refused it : to-day, I have come to request of you perhaps ten or twenty times the sum that you had generously proposed. I have said thus much all at once, madame, because it costs me the greatest effort. The words blistered my lips, but now I shall be more at ease.'

'I appreciate the delicacy of your scruples, sir,' said Adrienne; 'but if you knew me, you would address me without fear. How much do you require?'

'I do not know, madame,' answered Agricola.

'I beg your pardon. You don't know what sum ?'

'No, madame ; and I come to you to request, not only the sum necessary to me, but also information as to what that sum is.'

'Let us see, sir,' said Adrienne, smiling, 'explain this to me. In spite of my good will, you feel that I cannot divine, all at once, what it is that is required.'

'Madame, in two words, I can state the truth. I have a good old mother, who, in her youth, broke her health by excessive labour, to enable her to bring me up ; and not only me, but a poor abandoned child whom she had picked up. It is my turn now to maintain her ; and that I have the happiness of doing. But in order to do so, I have only my labour. If I am dragged from my employment, my mother will be without support.'

'Your mother cannot want for anything now, sir, since I interest myself for her.'

'You will interest yourself for her, madame ?' said Agricola.

'Certainly,' replied Adrienne.

'But you don't know her,' exclaimed the blacksmith.

'Now I do ; yes.'

'Oh, madame !' said Agricola, with emotion, after a moment's silence. 'I understand you. But indeed you have a noble heart. Mother Bunch was right.'

'Mother Bunch ?' said Adrienne, looking at Agricola with a very surprised air ; for what he said to her was an enigma.

The blacksmith, who blushed not for his friends, replied frankly :

'Madame, permit me to explain to you. Mother Bunch is a poor and very industrous young workwoman, with whom I have been brought up. She is deformed, which is the reason why she is called Mother Bunch. But though, on the one hand, she is sunk, as low as you are highly elevated on the other, yet, as regards the heart—as to delicacy--oh, lady, I am certain that your heart is of equal worth with hers ! That was at once her own thought, after I had related to her in what manner, yesterday, you had presented me with that beautiful flower.'

'I can assure you, sir,' said Adrienne, sincerely touched, 'that this comparison flatters and honours me more than anything else that you could say to me,—a heart that remains good and delicate, in spite of cruel misfortunes, is so rare a treasure ; while it is very easy to be good, when we have youth and beauty, and to be delicate and generous, when we are rich. I accept, then, your comparison ; but on condition that you will quickly put me in a situation to deserve it. Pray go on, therefore.'

In spite of the gracious cordiality of Miss de Cardoville, there was always observable in her so much of that natural dignity which arises from independence of character, so much elevation of soul and nobleness of sentiment that Agricola, forgetting the ideal physical beauty of his protectress, rather experienced for her the emotions of an affectionate and kindly, though profound respect, which offered a singular and striking contrast with the youth and gaiety of the lovely being who inspired him with this sentiment.

'If my mother alone, madame, were exposed to the rigour which I dread, I should not be so greatly disquieted with the fear of a compulsory suspension of my employment. Among poor people, the poor help one another ; and my mother is worshipped by all the inmates of our house, our excellent neighbours, who would willingly succour her. But they themselves are far from being well off ; and as they would incur privations by assisting her, their little benefits would be still more painful to my mother than the endurance even of misery by herself. And besides, it is not only for my mother that my exertions are required, but for my father, whom we have not seen for eighteen years, and who has just arrived from Siberia, where he remained during all that time, from zealous devotion to his former general, now Marshal Simon.'

'Marshal Simon !' said Adrienne, quickly, with an expression of much surprise.

'Do you know the marshal, madame ?'

'I do not personally know him ; but he married a lady of our family.'

'What joy !' exclaimed the blacksmith, 'then the two young ladies, his daughters, whom my father has brought from Russia, are your relations !'

'Has Marshal Simon two daughters ?' asked Adrienne, more and more astonished and interested.

'Yes, madame, two little angels of fifteen or sixteen ; and so pretty, so sweet ; they are twins so very much alike, as to be mistaken for one another. Their mother died in exile ; and the little she possessed having been confiscated, they have come hither with my father, from the depths of Siberia, travelling very wretchedly ; but he tried to make them forget so many privations by the fervency of his devotion and his tenderness. My excellent father ! you will not believe, madame, that, with the courage of a lion, he has all the love and tenderness of a mother.'

'And where are the dear children, sir ?' asked Adrienne.

'At our home, madame. It is that which renders my position so very hard ; that which has given me courage to come to you ; it is not but that my labour would be sufficient for our little household, even thus augmented ; but that I am about to be arrested.'

'About to be arrested ? For what ?'

'Pray, madame, have the goodness to read this letter, which has been sent by some one to Mother Bunch.'

Agricola gave to Miss de Cardoville the anonymous letter which had been received by the workwoman.

After having read the letter, Adrienne said to the blacksmith, with surprise, 'It appears, sir, you are a poet !'

'I have neither the ambition nor the pretension to be one, madame. Only, when I return to my mother after a day's toil, and often, even while forging my iron, in order to divert and relax my attention, I amuse myself with rhymes, sometimes composing an ode, sometimes a song.'

'And your song of the Freed Workingman, which is mentioned in this letter, is, therefore, very disaffected—very dangerous ?'

'Oh, no, madame ; quite the contrary. For myself, I have the good fortune to be employed in the factory of M. Hardy, who renders the condition of his workpeople as happy as that of their less fortunate comrades is the reverse; and I had limited myself to attempt, in favour of the great mass of the working classes, an equitable, sincere, warm, and earnest claim—nothing more. But you are aware, perhaps, madame, that in times of conspiracy and commotion, people are often incriminated and imprisoned on very slight grounds. Should such a misfortune befal me, what will become of my mother, my father, and the two orphans whom we are bound to regard as part of our family until the return of their father, Marshal Simon? It is on this account, madame, that, if I remain, I run the risk of being arrested. I have come to you to request you to provide surety for me; so that I should not be compelled to exchange the workshop for the prison, in which case I can answer for it that the fruits of my labour will suffice for all.'

'Thank the stars!' said Adrienne, gaily, 'this affair will arrange itself quite easily. Henceforth, Mr. Poet, you shall draw your inspirations in the midst of good fortune instead of adversity. Sad muse! But first of all, bonds shall be given for you.'

'Oh, madame, you have saved us!'

'To continue,' said Adrienne, 'the physician of our family is intimately connected with a very important minister (understand that, as you like,' said she, smiling, 'you will not deceive yourself much). The doctor exercises very great influence over this great statesman; for he has always had the happiness of recommending to him, on account of his health, the sweets and repose of private life, to the very eve of the day on which his portfolio was taken from him. Keep yourself, then, perfectly at ease. If the surety be insufficient, we shall be able to devise some other means.'

'Madame,' said Agricola, with great emotion, 'I am indebted to you for the repose, perhaps for the life of my mother. Believe that I shall ever be grateful.'

'That is all quite simple. Now for another thing. It is proper that those who have too much should have the right of coming to the aid of those who have too little. Marshal Simon's daughters are members of my family, and they will reside here with me, which will be more suitable. You will apprise your worthy mother of this; and in the evening, besides going to thank her for the hospitality which she has shown to my young relations, I shall fetch them home.'

    ✿   ✿   ✿   ✿   ✿   ✿

At this moment Georgette, throwing open the door which separated the room from an adjacent apartment, hurriedly entered, with an affrighted look, exclaiming:

'Oh, madame, something extraordinary is going on in the street.'

'How so? Explain yourself,' said Adrienne.

'I went to conduct my dress-maker to the little garden-gate,' said Georgette; 'where I saw some ill-looking men, attentively examining the walls and windows of the little out-building belonging to the pavilion, as if they wished to spy out some one.'

'Madame,' said Agricola, with chagrin, 'I have not been deceived. They are after me.'

'What say you?'

'I thought I was followed, from the moment when I left the Rue St. Méry: and now it is beyond doubt. They must have seen me enter your house; and are on the watch to arrest me. Well, now that your interest has been acquired for my mother,—now that I have no farther uneasiness for Marshal Simon's daughters,—rather than hazard your exposure to anything the least unpleasant, I run to deliver myself up.'

'Beware of that,' sir, said Adrienne quickly. 'Liberty is too precious to be voluntarily sacrificed. Besides, Georgette may have been mistaken,

But in any case, I entreat you not to surrender yourself. Take my advice; and escape being arrested. That, I think, will greatly facilitate my measures; for I am of opinion that justice evinces a great desire to keep possession of those upon whom she has once pounced.'

' Madame,' said Hebe, now also entering with a terrified look, ' a man knocked at the little door, and inquired if a young man in a blue blouse has not entered here. He added, that the person whom he seeks is named Agricola Baudoin, and that he has something to tell him of great importance.'

' That's my name,' said Agricola ; ' but the important information is a trick to draw me out.'

' Evidently,' said Adrienne ; ' and therefore we must play off trick for trick. What did you answer, child ?' added she, addressing herself to Hebe.

' I answered, that I didn't know what he was talking about.'

' Quite right,' said Adrienne : ' and the man who put the question ?'

' He went away, madame.'

' Without doubt to come back again, soon,' said Agricola.

' That is very probable,' said Adrienne, ' and therefore, sir, it is necessary for you to remain here some hours with resignation. I am unfortunately obliged to go immediately to the Princess Saint-Dizier, my aunt, for an important interview, which can no longer be delayed, and is rendered more pressing still by what you have told me concerning the daughters of Marshal Simon. Remain here, then, sir ; since if you go out, you will certainly be arrested.'

' Madame, pardon my refusal ; but I must say once more that I ought not to accept this generous offer.'

' Why ?'

' They have tried to draw me out, in order to avoid penetrating with the power of the law into your dwelling ; but if I go not out, they will come in ; and never will I expose you to anything so disagreeable. Now that I am no longer uneasy about my mother, what signifies prison ?'

' And the grief that your mother will feel, her uneasiness, and her fears,—nothing ? Think of your father ; and that poor work-woman who loves you as a brother, and whom I value as a sister ;—say, sir, do you forget them also ? Believe me, it is better to spare those torments to your family. Remain here ; and before the evening I am certain, either by giving surety, or some other means, of delivering you from these annoyances.'

' But, madame, supposing that I do accept your generous offer, they will come and find me here.'

' Not at all. There is in this pavilion, which was formerly the abode of a nobleman's left-handed wife,—you see, sir,' said Adrienne smiling, ' that I live in a very profane place—there is here a secret place of concealment, so wonderfully well-contrived, that it can defy all searches. Georgette will conduct you to it. You will be very well accommodated. You will even be able to write some verses for me, if the place inspire you.'

' Oh, madame ! how great is your goodness ! how have I merited it ?'

' Oh, sir, I will tell you. Admitting that your character and your position do not entitle you to any interest ;—admitting that I may not owe a sacred debt to your father for the touching regards and cares he has bestowed upon the daughters of Marshal Simon, my relations—do you forget Frisky, sir ?' asked Adrienne, laughing,—' Frisky, there, whom you have restored to my fondlings ? Seriously, if I laugh,' continued this singular and extravagant creature, ' it is because I know that you are entirely out of danger, and that I feel an increase of happiness. Therefore, sir, write for me quickly your address, and your mother's, in this pocket-book ; follow Georgette ; and spin me some pretty verses, if you do not bore yourself too much in that prison to which you fly.'

While Georgette conducted the blacksmith to the hiding-place, Hebe brought her mistress a small grey beaver hat with a grey feather ; for Adrienne had to cross the park to reach the house occupied by the Princess Saint-Dizier.

  ◦   ◦   ◦   ◦   ◦   ◦

A quarter of an hour after this scene, Florine entered mysteriously the apartment of Mrs. Grivois, the first woman of the princess.

'Well ?' demanded Mrs. Grivois of the young woman.

'Here are the notes which I have taken this morning,' said Florine, putting a paper into the duenna's hand. 'Happily, I have a good memory.'

'At what time exactly did she return home this morning?' asked the duenna, quickly.

'Who, madame ?'

'Miss Adrienne.'

'She did not go out, madame. We put her in the bath at nine o'clock.'

'But before nine o'clock she came home, after having passed the night out of her house. Eight o'clock was the time at which she returned, however.'

Florine looked at Mrs. Grivois with profound astonishment, and said—

'I do not understand you, madame.'

'What's that? Madame did not come home this morning at eight o'clock? Dare you lie ?'

'I was ill yesterday, and did not come down till nine this morning, in order to assist Georgette and Hebe help our young lady from the bath. I know nothing of what passed previously, I swear to you, madame.'

'That alters the case. You must ferret out what I allude to from your companions. They don't distrust you, and will tell you all.'

'Yes, madame.'

'What has your mistress done this morning since you saw her ?'

'Madame dictated a letter to Georgette for M. Norval. I requested permission to send it off, as a pretext for going out, and for writing down all I recollected.'

'Very well. And this letter ?'

'Jerome had to go out, and I gave it him to put in the post-office.'

'Idiot !' exclaimed Mrs. Grivois ; 'couldn't you bring it to me !'

'But, as madame dictated it aloud to Georgette, as is her custom, I knew the contents of the letter ; and I have written it in my notes.'

'That's not the same thing. It is likely there was need to delay sending off this letter. The princess will be very much displeased.'

'I thought I did right, madame.'

'I know that it is not good will that fails you. For these six months I have been satisfied with you. But this time you have committed a very great mistake.'

'Be indulgent, madame ! what I do is sufficiently painful !' The girl stifled a sigh.

Mrs. Grivois looked fixedly at her, and said in a sardonic tone :

'Very well, my dear, do not continue it. If you have scruples, you are free. Go your way.'

'You well know that I am not free, madame,' said Florine, reddening ; and with tears in her eyes she added :—'I am dependent upon M. Rodin, who placed me here.'

'Wherefore these regrets, then ?'

'In spite of one's self, one feels remorse. Madame is so good, and so confiding.'

'She is all perfection, certainly ! But you are not here to sing her praises. What occurred afterwards ?'

'The working-man who yesterday found and brought back Frisk, came early this morning and requested permission to speak with my young lady.'

'And is this working-man still in her house?'

'I don't know. He came in when I was going out with the letter.'

'You must contrive to learn what it was this working-man came about.'

'Yes, madame.'

'Has your mistress seemed pre-occupied, uneasy, or afraid of the interview which she is to have to-day with the princess? She conceals so little of what she thinks, that you ought to know.'

'She has been as gay as usual. She has even jested about the interview!'

'Oh! jested, has she?' said the tire-woman, muttering between her teeth, without Florine being able to hear her: '"They laugh most who laugh last." In spite of her audacious and diabolical character, she would tremble and would pray for mercy, if she knew what awaits her this day.' Then addressing Florine, she continued—

'Return, and keep yourself, I advise you, from those fine scruples, which will be quite enough to do you a bad turn. Do not forget!'

'I cannot forget that I belong not to myself, madame.'

'Any way, let it be so. Farewell.'

Florine quitted the mansion and crossed the park to regain the summer-house, while Mrs. Grivois went immediately to the Princess Saint-Dizier.

CHAPTER XXXVI.

A FEMALE JESUIT.

DURING the preceding scenes which occurred in the Pompadour rotunda, occupied by Miss de Cardoville, other events took place in the residence of the Princess Saint-Dizier. The elegance and sumptuousness of the former dwelling presented a strong contrast to the gloomy interior of the latter, the first floor of which was inhabited by the princess, for the plan of the ground floor rendered it only fit for giving parties; and, for a long time past, Madame de Saint-Dizier had renounced all worldly splendours. The gravity of her domestics, all aged and dressed in black; the profound silence which reigned in her abode, where everything was spoken, if it could be called speaking, in undertone; and the almost monastic regularity and order of this immense mansion, communicated to everything around the princess a sad and chilling character. A man of the world, who joined great courage to rare independence of spirit, speaking of the princess (to whom Adrienne de Cardoville went, according to her expression, to fight a pitched battle), said of her as follows: 'In order to avoid having Madame de Saint-Dizier for an enemy, I, who am neither bashful nor cowardly, have, for the first time in my life, been both a noodle and a coward.' This man spoke sincerely. But Madame de Saint-Dizier had not all at once arrived at this high degree of importance.

Some words are necessary for the purpose of exhibiting distinctly some phases in the life of this dangerous and implacable woman who, by her affiliation with the Order of Jesuits, had acquired an occult and formidable power. For there is something even more menacing than a Jesuit: it is a Jesuitess; and, when one has seen certain circles, it becomes evident that there exist, unhappily, many of those affiliated, who, more or less, uniformly dress (for the lay members of the Order call themselves 'Jesuits of the short robe').

Madame de Saint-Dizier, once very beautiful, had been, during the last years of the Empire, and the early years of the Restoration, one of the most fashionable women of Paris, of a stirring, active, adventurous, and commanding spirit, of cold heart, but lively imagination. She was greatly given to amorous adventures, not from tenderness of heart, but from a passion for intrigue, which she loved as men love play—for the sake of the emotions it excites. Unhappily, such had always been the blindness or the carelessness of her husband, the Prince of Saint-Dizier (eldest brother of the Count of Rennepont and Duke of Cardoville, father of Adrienne), that during his life he had never said one word that could make it be thought that he suspected the actions of his wife. Attaching herself to Napoleon, to dig a mine under the feet of the Colossus, that design at least afforded emotions sufficient to gratify the humour of the most insatiable. During some time, all went well. The princess was beautiful and spirited, dexterous and false, perfidious and seductive. She was surrounded by fanatical adorers, upon whom she played off a kind of ferocious coquetry, to induce them to run their heads into grave conspiracies. She hoped to resuscitate the *Frondeur* party, and carried on a very active secret correspondence with some influential personages abroad, well known for their hatred against the emperor and France. Hence arose her first epistolary relations with the Marquis d'Aigrigny, then colonel in the Russian service and aide-de-camp to General Moreau. But one day all these pretty intrigues were discovered. Many knights of Madame de Saint-Dizier were sent to Vincennes ; but the emperor, who might have punished her terribly, contented himself with exiling the princess to one of her estates near Dunkirk.

Upon the Restoration, the persecutions which Madame de Saint-Dizier had suffered for the Good Cause were entered to her credit, and she acquired even then very considerable influence, in spite of the lightness of her behaviour. The Marquis d'Aigrigny, having entered the military service of France, remained there. He was handsome, and of fashionable manners and address. He had corresponded and conspired with the princess, without knowing her ; and these circumstances necessarily led to a close connection between them.

Excessive self-love, a taste for exciting pleasures, aspirations of hatred, pride, and lordliness, a species of evil sympathy, the perfidious attraction of which brings together perverse natures without mingling them, had made of the princess and the Marquis accomplices rather than lovers. This connexion, based upon selfish and bitter feelings, and upon the support which two characters of this dangerous temper could lend to each other against a world in which their spirit of intrigue, of gallantry, and of contempt had made them many enemies, this connection endured till the moment when, after his duel with General Simon, the marquis entered a religious house, without any one understanding the cause of his unexpected and sudden resolution.

The princess, having not yet heard the hour of her conversion strike, continued to whirl round the vortex of the world with a greedy, jealous, and hateful ardour, for she saw that the last years of her beauty were dying out.

An estimate of the character of this woman may be formed from the following fact :

Still very agreeable, she wished to close her worldly and volatile career with some brilliant and final triumph, as a great actress knows the proper time to withdraw from the stage so as to leave regrets behind. Desirous of offering up this final incense to her own vanity, the princess skilfully selected her victims. She spied out in the world a young couple who idolised each other ; and, by dint of cunning and address she succeeded in taking away the lover from his mistress, a charming woman of eighteen, by whom he was adored. This triumph being achieved, Madame Saint-Dizier retired from the fashionable world in the full blaze of her exploit. After many long conversations with the Abbé-Marquis d'Aigrigny, who had become a renowned preacher, she departed suddenly from Paris, and spent two years upon her estate near Dunkirk, to which she took only one of her female attendants, viz., Mrs. Grivois.

When the princess afterwards returned to Paris, it was impossible to recognise the frivolous, intriguing, and dissipated woman she had formerly been. The metamorphosis was as complete as it was extraordinary and even startling. Saint-Dizier House, heretofore open to the banquets and festivals of every kind of pleasure, became gloomily silent and austere. Instead of the world of elegance and fashion, the princess now received in her mansion only women of ostentatious piety, and men of consequence, who were remarkably exemplary by the extravagant rigour of their religious and monarchical principles. Above all, she drew around her several noted members of the higher orders of the clergy. She was appointed patroness of a body of religious females. She had her own confessor, chaplain, almoner, and even spiritual director ; but this last performed his functions *in partibus.* The Marquis-Abbé d'Aigrigny continued in reality to be her spiritual guide ; and it is almost unnecessary to say that for a long time past their mutual relations as to flirting had entirely ceased.

This sudden and complete conversion of a gay and distinguished woman, especially as it was loudly trumpeted forth, struck the greater number of persons with wonder and respect. Others, more discerning, only smiled.

A single anecdote, from amongst a thousand, will suffice to show the alarming influence and power which the princess had acquired since her affiliation with the Jesuits. This anecdote will also exhibit the deep, vindictive, and pitiless character of this woman, whom Adrienne de Cardoville had so imprudently made herself ready to brave.

Amongst the persons who smiled more or less at the conversion of Madame de Saint-Dizier were the young and charming couple whom she had so cruelly disunited before she quitted for ever the scenes of revelry in which she had lived. The young couple became more impassioned and devoted to each other than ever ; they were reconciled and married, after the passing storm which had hurled them asunder ; and they indulged in no other vengeance against the author of their temporary infelicity than that of mildly jesting at the pious conversion of the woman who had done them so much injury.

Some time after, a terrible fatality overtook the loving pair. The husband, until then blindly unsuspicious, was suddenly inflamed by anonymous communications. A dreadful rupture ensued, and the young wife perished.

. As for the husband, certain vague rumours, far from distinct, yet pregnant with secret meanings, perfidiously contrived, and a thousand times more detestable than formal accusation, which can, at least, be met and destroyed, were strewn about him with so much perseverance, with a skill so diabolical, and by means and ways so very various, that his best friends, by little and little, withdrew themselves from him, thus yielding to the slow, irresistible influence of that incessant whispering and buzzing, confused as indistinct, amounting to some such result as this—

'Well ! you know !' says one.

'No !' replies another.

'People say very vile things about him !'

'Do they ? really ! What then ?'

'I don't know ! Bad reports ! Rumours grievously affecting his honour !'

'The deuce ! That's very serious. It accounts for the coldness with which he is now everywhere received !'

'I shall avoid him in future!'

'So will I,' etc.

Such is the world, that very often nothing more than groundless surmises are necessary to brand a man whose very happiness may have incurred envy. So it was with the gentleman of whom we speak. The unfortunate man, seeing the void around him extending itself,—feeling (so to speak) the earth crumbling from beneath his feet, knew not where to find or grasp the impalpable enemy whose blows he felt; for not once had the idea occurred to him of suspecting the princess, whom he had not seen since his adventure with her. Anxiously desiring to learn why he was so much shunned and despised, he at length sought an explanation from an old friend; but he received only a disdainfully evasive answer; at which, being exasperated, he demanded satisfaction. His adversary replied—"If you can find two persons of *our* acquaintance, I will fight you!" The unhappy man could not find one!

Finally, forsaken by all, without having ever obtained any explanation of the reason for forsaking him—suffering keenly for the fate of the wife whom he had lost, he became mad with grief, rage, and despair, and killed himself.

  ✿   ✿   ✿   ✿   ✿   ✿

On the day of his death, Madame de Saint-Dizier remarked that it was fit and necessary that one who had lived so shamefully should come to an equally shameful end, and that he who had so long jested at all laws, human and divine, could not seemly otherwise terminate his wretched life than by perpetrating a last crime—suicide! And the friends of Madame de Saint-Dizier hawked about and everywhere repeated these terrible words, with a contrite air, as if beatified and convinced! But this was not all. Along with chastisements there were rewards.

Observant people remarked that the favourites of the religious clan of Madame de Saint-Dizier rose to high distinctions with singular rapidity. The virtuous young men, such as were religiously attentive to tiresome sermons, were married to rich orphans of the Sacred Heart Convents, who were held in reserve for the purpose; poor young girls, who, learning too late what it is to have a pious husband selected and imposed upon them by a set of devotees, often expiated by very bitter tears the deceitful favour of being thus admitted into a world of hypocrisy and falsehood, in which they found themselves strangers without support, crushed by it if they dared to complain of the marriages to which they had been condemned.

In the parlour of Madame de Saint-Dizier were appointed prefects, colonels, treasurers, deputies, academicians, bishops and peers of the realm, from whom nothing more was required in return for the all-powerful support bestowed upon them, but to wear a pious gloss, sometimes publicly take the communion, swear furious war against everything impious or revolutionary, —and above all, correspond confidentially upon 'different subjects of his choosing' with the Abbé d'Aigrigny,—an amusement, moreover, which was very agreeable; for the abbé was the most amiable man in the world, the most witty, and, above all, the most obliging. The following is an historical fact, which requires the bitter and vengeful irony of Molière or Pascal to do it justice.

During the last year of the Restoration, there was one of the mighty dignitaries of the court, a firm and independent man, who did not make profession (as the holy fathers call it), that is, who did not communicate at the altar. The splendour amid which he moved was calculated to give the weight of a very injurious example to his indifference. The Abbé-Marquis d'Aigrigny was therefore despatched to him; and he, knowing the honourable and elevated character of the non-communicant, thought that if he could only bring him to profess by any means (whatever the means might be) the effect would be what was desired.   Like a man of intellect, the abbé prized the dogma but cheaply himself.   He only spoke of the suitableness of the step, and of the highly salutary example which the resolution to adopt it would afford to the public.

' M. Abbé,' replied the person sought to be influenced, ' I have a greater respect for religion than you have.   I should consider it an infamous mockery to go to the communion table without feeling the proper conviction.'

' Nonsense ! you inflexible man ! you frowning Alcestes,' said the marquis-abbé, smiling slyly.   ' Your profit and your scruples will go together, believe me, by listening to me.   In short, we shall manage to make a BLANK COMMUNION for you ; for after all, what is it that we ask ?—only the APPEARANCE !'

Now, a BLANK COMMUNION means, breaking an unconsecrated wafer !

The abbé-marquis retired with his offers, which were rejected with indignation ;—but then, the refractory man was dismissed from his place at court. This was but a single isolated fact.   Woe to all who found themselves opposed to the interest and principles of Madame de Saint-Dizier or her friends !   Sooner or later, directly or indirectly, they felt themselves cruelly stabbed, generally irremediably—some in their dearest connections, others in their credit ; some in their honour ; others in their official functions ; and all by secret action, noiseless, continuous, and latent, in time becoming a terrible and mysterious dissolvent, which invisibly undermined reputations, fortunes, positions the most solidly established. until the moment when all sunk for ever into the abyss, amid the surprise and terror of the beholders.

It will now be conceived how under the Restoration the Princess de Saint-Dizier had become singularly influential and formidable.   At the time of the Revolution of July (1830) she had 'rallied ;' and, strangely enough, by preserving some relation of family and of society with persons faithful to the worship of decayed monarchy, people still attributed to the princess much influence and power.   Let us mention, at last, that the Prince of Saint-Dizier, having died many years since, his very large personal fortune had descended to his younger brother, the father of Adrienne de Cardoville ; and he, having died eighteen months ago, that young lady found herself to be the last and only representative of that branch of the family of the Renneponts.

The Princess of Saint-Dizier awaited her niece in a very large room, rendered dismal by its gloomy green damask.   The chairs, etc., covered with similar stuff, were of carved ebony.   Paintings of scriptural and other religious subjects, and an ivory crucifix thrown up from a back-ground of black velvet, contributed to give the apartment a lugubrious and austere aspect.

Madame de Saint-Dizier, seated before a large desk, has just finished putting the seals on numerous letters ; for she had a very extensive and very diversified correspondence.   Though then aged about forty-five, she was still fair.   Advancing years had somewhat thickened her shape, which, formerly of distinguished elegance, was still sufficiently handsome to be seen to advantage under the straight folds of her black dress.   Her head-dress, very simple, decorated with grey ribbons, allowed her fair sleek hair to be seen, arranged in broad bands.   At first look, people were struck with her dignified though unassuming appearance ; and would have vainly tried to discover in her physiognomy, now marked with repentant calmness, any trace of the agitations of her past life.   So naturally grave and reserved was she, that people could not believe her the heroine of so many intrigues and adventures and gallantry.   Moreover, if by chance she ever heard any lightness in conversation, her countenance, since she had come to believe herself a kind of ' mother in the Church,' immediately expressed candid but grieved astonishment, which soon changed into an air of offended chastity and disdainful pity.

For the rest, her smile, when requisite, was still full of grace, and even of the seducing and resistless sweetness of seeming good-nature. Her large blue eyes, on fit occasions, became affectionate and caressing. But if any one dared to wound or ruffle her pride, gainsay her orders or harm her interests, her countenance, usually placid and serene, betrayed a cold but implacable malignity. Mrs. Grivois entered the cabinet, holding in her hand Florine's report of the manner in which Adrienne de Cardoville had spent the morning.

Mrs. Grivois had been about twenty years in the service of Madame de Saint-Dizier. She knew everything that a lady's-maid could or ought to have known of her mistress in the days of her sowing of wild (being a lady) flowers. Was it from choice that the princess had still retained about her person this so-well-informed witness of the numerous follies of her youth ? The world was kept in ignorance of the motive ; but one thing was evident, viz., that Mrs. Grivois enjoyed great privileges under the princess, and was treated by her rather as a companion than as a tiring-woman.

' Here are Florine's notes, madame,' said Mrs. Grivois, giving the paper to the princess.

' I will examine them presently,' said the princess ; ' but tell me, is my niece coming ? Pending the conference at which she is to be present, you will conduct into her house a person who will soon be here, to inquire for you by my desire.'

' Well, madame ?'

' This man will make an exact inventory of everything contained in Adrienne's residence. You will take care that nothing is omitted ; for that is of very great importance.'

' Yes, madame. But should Georgette or Hebe make any opposition ?'

' There is no fear ; the man charged with taking the inventory is of such a stamp, that when they know him, they will not dare to oppose either his making the inventory, or his other steps. It will be necessary not to fail, as you go along with him, to be careful to obtain certain peculiarities destined to confirm the reports which you have spread for some time past.'

' Do not have the slightest doubt, madame. The reports have all the consistency of truth.'

' Very soon, then, this Adrienne, so insolent and so haughty, will be crushed and compelled to pray for pardon ; and from me !'

   ✲   ✲   ✲   ✲   ✲   ✲

An old footman opened both of the folding doors, and announced the Marquis-Abbé d'Aigrigny.

' If Miss de Cardoville present herself,' said the princess to Mrs. Grivois, ' you will request her to wait an instant.'

' Yes, madame,' said the duenna, going out with the servant.

Madame de Saint-Dizier and D'Aigrigny remained alone.

CHAPTER XXXVII.

THE PLOT.

THE Abbé-Marquis d'Aigrigny, as the reader has easily divined, was the person already seen in the Rue du Milieu-des-Ursins ; whence he had departed for Rome, in which city he had remained about three months. The marquis was dressed in deep mourning, but with his usual elegance. His was not a priestly robe ; his black coat, and his waistcoat, tightly gathered in at the waist, set off to great advantage the elegance of his figure : his black cassimere pantaloons disclosed his feet, exactly fitted with laced boots, brilliantly polished. And all traces of his tonsure disappeared in the midst of the slight baldness which whitened slightly the back part of his head. There was nothing in his entire costume, or aspect, that revealed the priest, except, perhaps, the entire absence of beard, the more remarkable upon so manly a countenance. His chin, newly shaved, rested on a large and elevated black cravat, tied with a military ostentation which reminded the beholder that this abbé-marquis—this celebrated preacher—now one of the most active and influential chiefs of his order, had commanded a regiment of hussars upon the Restoration, and had fought in aid of the Russians against France.

Returned to Paris only this morning, the marquis had not seen the princess since his mother, the Dowager Marchioness d'Aigrigny, had died near Dunkirk, upon an estate belonging to Madame de Saint-Dizier, while vainly calling for her son to alleviate her last moments ; but the order to which M. d'Aigrigny had thought fit to sacrifice the most sacred feelings and duties of nature, having been suddenly transmitted to him from Rome, he had immediately set out for that city, though not without hesitation, which was remarked and denounced by Rodin ; for the love of M. d'Aigrigny for his mother had been the only pure feeling that had invariably distinguished his life.

When the servant had discreetly withdrawn with Mrs. Grivois, the marquis quickly approached the princess, held out his hand to her, and said with a voice of emotion :

'Hermina, have you not concealed something in your letters ? In her last moments, did not my mother curse me ?'

'No, no, Frederick, compose yourself. She had anxiously desired your presence. Her ideas soon became confused. But in her delirium it was still for you that she called.'

'Yes,' said the marquis, bitterly ; 'her maternal instinct doubtless assured her that my presence could have saved her life.'

'I entreat you to banish these sad recollections,' said the princess, 'this misfortune is irreparable.'

'Tell me for the last time, truly, did not my absence cruelly affect my mother ? Had she no suspicion that a more imperious duty called me elsewhere ?'

'No, no, I assure you. Even when her reason was shaken, she believed that you had not yet had time to come to her. All the sad details which I wrote to you upon this painful subject are strictly true. Again, I beg of you to compose yourself.'

'Yes, my conscience ought to be easy ; for I have fulfilled my duty in sacrificing my mother. Yet I have never been able to arrive at that complete detachment from natural affection, which is commanded to us by those awful words : " He who hates not his father and his mother, even with his soul, cannot be my disciple." '*

'Doubtless, Frederick,' said the princess, 'these renunciations are painful. But, in return, what influence, what power !'

* With regard to this text, a commentary upon it will be found in the *Constitutions of the Jesuits*, as follows :—' In order that the habit of language may come to the help of the sentiments, it is wise not to say, " I *have* parents, or I *have* brothers ;" but to say, " I *had* parents ; I *had* brothers." '—*General Examination*, p. 29 ; *Constitutions*.—Paulin, 1843. Paris.

'It is true,' said the marquis, after a moment's silence. 'What ought not to be sacrificed in order to reign in secret over the all-powerful of the earth, who lord it in full day ? This journey to Rome, from which I have just returned, has given me a new idea of our formidable power. For, Hermina, it is Rome which is the culminating point, overlooking the fairest and broadest quarters of the globe, made so by custom, by tradition, or by faith. Thence can our workings be embraced in their full extent. It is an uncommon view to see from its height the myriad tools, whose personality is continually absorbed into the immovable personality of our Order. What a might we possess ! Verily, I am always swayed with admiration, aye, almost frightened, that man once thinks, wishes, believes, and acts as he alone lists, until, soon ours, he becomes but a human shell ; its kernel of intelligence, mind, reason, conscience, and free will, shrivelled within him, dry and withered by the habit of mutely, fearingly bowing under mysterious tasks, which shatter and slay everything spontaneous in the human soul ! Then do we infuse in such spiritless clay, speechless, cold, and motionless as corpses, the breath of our Order, and, lo ! the dry bones stand up and walk, acting and executing, though only within the limits which are circled round them evermore. Thus do they become mere limbs of the gigantic trunk, whose impulses they mechanically carry out, while ignorant of the design, like the stone-cutter who shapes out a stone, unaware if it be for cathedral or bagnio.'

In so speaking, the marquis's features wore an incredible air of proud and domineering haughtiness.

'Oh, yes ! this power is great, most great,' observed the princess ; 'all the more formidable because it moves in a mysterious way over minds and consciences.'

'Aye, Hermina,' said the marquis : ' I have had under my command a magnificent regiment. Very often have I experienced the energetic and exquisite enjoyment of command ! At my word, my squadrons put themselves in action ; bugles blared, my officers, glittering in golden embroidery, galloped everywhere to repeat my orders : all my brave soldiers, burning with courage, and cicatrized by battles, obeyed my signal ; and I felt proud and strong, holding as I did (so to speak) in my hands, the force and valour of each and all combined into one being of resistless strength and invincible intrepidity,—of all of which I was as much the master, as I mastered the rage and fire of my war-horse ! Aye ! that was greatness. But now, in spite of the misfortunes which have befallen our Order, I feel myself a thousand times more ready for action, more authoritative, more strong, and more daring, at the head of our mute and black-robed militia, who only think and wish, or move and obey, mechanically, according to my will. On a sign, they scatter over the surface of the globe, gliding stealthily into households under guise of confessing the wife or teaching the children, into family affairs by hearing the dying avowals,—up to the throne through the quaking conscience of a credulous crowned coward ;—aye, even to the chair of the Pope himself, living manifesto of the Godhead though he is, by the services rendered him or imposed by him. Is not this secret rule, made to kindle or glut the wildest ambition, as it reaches from the cradle to the grave, from the labourer's hovel to the royal palace, from palace to the papal chair ? What career in all the world presents such splendid openings ? what unutterable scorn ought I not feel for the bright butterfly life of early days, when we made so many envy us? Don't you remember, Hermina?' he added, with a bitter smile.

'You are right, perfectly right, Frederick !' replied the princess quickly. 'How little soever we may reflect, with what contempt do we not think upon the past! I, like you, often compare it with the present; and then what satisfaction I feel at having followed your counsels! For, indeed, without you, I should have played the miserable and ridiculous part which a woman always plays in her decline from having been beautiful and surrounded by admirers. What could I have done at this hour? I should have vainly striven to retain around me a selfish and ungrateful world of gross and shameful men who court women only that they may turn them to the service of their passions, or to the gratification of their vanity. It is true that there would have remained to me the resource of what is called keeping an agreeable house for all others,—yes, in order to entertain them, be visited by a crowd of the indifferent, to afford opportunities of meeting to amorous young couples, who, following each other from parlour to parlour, come not to your house but for the purpose of being together; a very pretty pleasure, truly, that of harbouring those blooming, laughing, amorous youths, who look upon the luxury and brilliancy with which one surrounds them, as if they were their due upon bonds to minister to their pleasure, and to their impudent amours!'

Her words were so stinging, and such hateful envy sat upon her face, that she betrayed the intense bitterness of her regrets in spite of herself.

'No, no; thanks to you, Frederick,' she continued, 'after a last and brilliant triumph, I broke for ever with the world, which would soon have abandoned me, though I was so long its idol and its queen. And I have only changed my queendom. Instead of the dissipated men whom I ruled with a frivolity superior to their own, I now find myself surrounded by men of high consideration, of redoubtable character, and all-powerful, many of whom have governed the state; to them I have devoted myself, as they have devoted themselves to me! It is now only that I really enjoy that happiness, of which I ever dreamt. I have taken an active part, and have exercised a powerful influence over the greatest interests of the world; I have been initiated into the most important secrets; I have been able to strike, surely, whosoever scoffed at or hated me; and I have been able to elevate beyond their hopes those who have served or respected and obeyed me.'

'There are some madmen, and some so blind, that they imagine that we are struck down, because we ourselves have had to struggle against some misfortunes,' said M. d'Aigrigny, disdainfully, 'as if we were not, above all others, securely founded, organised for every struggle, and drew not from our very struggles a new and more vigorous activity. Doubtless the times are bad. But they will become better; and, as you know, it is nearly certain that in a few days (the 13th of February), we shall have at our disposal a means of action sufficiently powerful for re-establishing our influence, which has been temporarily shaken.'

'Yes, doubtless this affair of the medals is most important,' said the princess.

'I should not have made so much haste to return hither,' resumed the abbé, 'were it not to act in what will be, perhaps, for us, a very great event.'

'But you are aware of the fatality which has once again overthrown projects the most laboriously conceived and matured?'

'Yes; immediately on arriving I saw Rodin.'

'And he told you——?'

'The inconceivable arrival of the Indian, and of General Simon's daughters at Cardoville Castle, after a double shipwreck, which threw them upon the coast of Picardy; though it was deemed certain that the young girls were at Leipsic, and the Indian in Java. Precautions were so well taken, indeed,' added the marquis in vexation, 'that one would think an invisible power protects this family.'

'Happily, Rodin is a man of resources and activity, resumed the princess. 'He came here last night, and we had a long conversation.'

'And the result of your consultation is excellent,' added the marquis : 'the old soldier is to be kept out of the way for two days ; and his wife's confessor has been posted ; the rest will proceed of itself. To-morrow, the girls need no longer be feared ; and the Indian remains at Cardoville, wounded dangerously. We have plenty of time for action.'

'But that is not all,' continued the princess : 'there are still, without reckoning my niece, two persons, who, for our interests, ought not to be found in Paris on the 13th of February.'

'Yes, M. Hardy : but his most dear and intimate friend has betrayed him ; for, by means of that friend, we have drawn M. Hardy into the South, whence it is impossible for him to return before a month. As for that miserable vagabond workman, surnamed "Sleepinbuff !"——'

'Fie !' exclaimed the princess, with an expression of outraged modesty.

'That man,' resumed the marquis, 'is no longer an object of inquietude. Lastly, Gabriel, upon whom our vast and certain hope reposes, will not be left by himself for a single minute until the great day. Everything seems, you see, to promise success ; indeed, more so than ever ; and it is necessary to obtain this success at any price. It is for us a question of life or death ; for, in returning, I stopped at Forli, and there saw the Duke d'Orbano. His influence over the mind of the king is all-powerful—indeed, absolute ; and he has completely prepossessed the royal mind. It is with the duke alone, then, that it is possible to treat.'

'Well ?'

'D'Orbano has gained strength ; and he can, I know it, assure to us a legal existence, highly protected, in the dominions of his master, with full charge of popular education. Thanks to such advantages, after two or three years in that country we shall become so deeply rooted, that this very Duke d'Orbano, in his turn, will have to solicit support and protection from us. But at present he has everything in his power ; and he puts an absolute condition upon his services.'

'What is the condition ?'

'Five millions down ; and an annual pension of a hundred thousand francs.'

'It is very much.'

'Nay, but little if it be considered that our foot once planted in that country, we shall promptly repossess ourselves of that sum, which, after all, is scarcely an eighth part of what the affair of the medals, if happily brought to an issue, ought to assure to the Order.'

'Yes, nearly forty millions,' said the princess, thoughtfully.

'And again : these five millions that Orbano demands will be but an advance. They will be returned to us in voluntary gifts, by reason even of the increase of influence that we shall acquire from the education of children ; through whom we have their families. And yet, the fools hesitate ! those who govern see not, that in doing our own business, we do theirs also ;—that in abandoning education to us (which is what we wish for above all things) we mould the people into that mute and quiet obedience, that servile and brutal submission, which assures the repose of states by the immobility of the mind. They don't reflect that most of the upper and middle classes fear and hate us ; don't understand that (when we have persuaded the mass that their wretchedness is an eternal law, that sufferers must give up hope of relief, that it is a crime to sigh for welfare in this world, since the crown of glory on high is the only reward for misery here), then the stupefied people will resignedly wallow in the mire, all their impatient aspirations for better days smothered, and the volcano-blasts blown aside, which made the future of rulers so horrid and so dark ! They see not, in truth, that this blind and passive faith which we demand from the mass, furnishes their rulers with a bridle with which both to conduct and curb them ; whilst we ask from the happy of the world only some appearances which ought, if they had only the knowledge of their own corruption, to give an increased stimulant to their pleasures.

' It signifies not,' resumed the princess ; 'since, as you say, a great day is at hand, bringing nearly forty millions, of which the Order can become possessed by the happy success of the affair of the medals. We certainly can attempt very great things. Like a lever in your hands, such a means of action would be of incalculable power, in times during which all men buy and sell one another.'

' And then,' resumed M. d'Aigrigny, with a thoughtful air, 'here the re-action continues : the example of France is everything. In Austria and Holland we can rarely maintain ourselves ; while the resources of the Order diminish from day to day. We have arrived at a crisis ; but it can be made to prolong itself. Thus, thanks to the immense resource of the affair of the medals, we can not only brave all eventualities, but we can again powerfully establish ourselves, thanks to the offer of the Duke d'Orbano, which we accept ; and then, from that inassailable centre, our radiations will be incalculable. Ah ! the 13th of February !' added M. d'Aigrigny, after a moment of silence, and shaking his head : 'the 13th of February, a date perhaps fortunate and famous for our power as that of the council which gave to us (so to say) a new life !'

' And nothing must be spared,' resumed the princess, 'in order to succeed at any price. Of the six persons whom we have to fear, five are or will be out of any condition to hurt us. There remains then only my niece ; and you know that I have waited but for your arrival in order to take my last resolution. All my preparations are completed ; and this very morning we will begin to act.'

' Have your suspicions increased since your last letter?'

' Yes ; I am certain that she is more instructed than she wishes to appear ; and if so, we shall not have a more dangerous enemy.'

' Such has always been my opinion. Thus it is six months since I advised you to take in all cases the measures which you have adopted, in order to provoke, on her part, that demand of emancipation, the consequences of which now render quite easy that which would have been impossible with-out it.'

' At last,' said the princess, with an expression of joy, hateful and bitter, ' this indomitable spirit will be broken. I am at length about to be avenged of the many insolent sarcasms which I have been compelled to swallow, lest I should awaken her suspicions. I ! I to have borne so much till now ! for this Adrienne has made it her business (imprudent as she is !) to irritate me against herself !'

' Whosoever offends you, offends me : you know it,' said D'Aigrigny, 'my hatreds are yours.'

' And you yourself !' said the princess, 'how many times have you been the butt of her poignant irony !'

' My instincts seldom deceive me. I am certain that this young girl may become a dangerous enemy for us,' said the marquis, with a voice painfully broken into short monosyllables.

' And, therefore, it is necessary that she may be rendered incapable of ex-citing further fear,' responded Madame de Saint-Dizier, fixedly regarding the marquis.

' Have you seen Dr. Baleinier, and the sub-guardian, M. Tripeaud?' asked he.

'They will be here this morning. I have informed them of everything.'

'Did you find them well disposed to act against her?'

'Perfectly so—and the best is, Adrienne does not at all suspect the doctor, who has known how, up to a certain point, to preserve her confidence. Moreover, a circumstance which appears to me inexplicable has come to our aid.'

'What do you allude to?'

'This morning, Mrs. Grivois went, according to my orders, to remind Adrienne that I expected her at noon, upon important business. As she approached the pavilion, Mrs. Grivois saw, or thought she saw, Adrienne come in by the little garden-gate.'

'What do you tell me? Is it possible? Is there any positive proof of it? cried the marquis.

'Till now, there is no other proof than the spontaneous declaration of Mrs. Grivois : but whilst I think of it,' said the Princess, taking up a paper that lay before her, 'here is the report which, every day, one of Adrienne's women makes to me.'

'The one that Rodin succeeded in introducing into your niece's service?'.

'The same ; as this creature is entirely in Rodin's hands, she has hitherto answered our purpose very well. In this report, we shall perhaps find the confirmation of what Mrs. Grivois affirms she saw.'

Hardly had the Princess glanced at the note, than she exclaimed almost in terror : 'What do I see? Why, Adrienne is a very demon !'

'What now?'

'The bailiff at Cardoville, having written to my niece to ask her recommendation, informed her at the same time of the stay of the Indian prince at the castle. She knows that he is her relation, and has just written to her old drawing-master, Norval, to set out post with Eastern dresses, and bring Prince Djalma hither—the man that must be kept away from Paris at any cost.'

The marquis grew pale, and said to Mme. de Saint-Dizier: 'If this be not merely one of her whims, the eagerness she displays in sending for this relation hither, proves that she knows more than you even suspected. She is "posted" on the affair of the medals. Have a care—she may ruin all.'

'In that case,' said the princess, resolutely, 'there is no room to hesitate. We must carry things further than we thought, and make an end this very morning.'

'Yes, though it is almost impossible.'

'Nay, all is possible. The doctor and M. Tripeaud are ours,' said the princess, hastily.

'Though I am as sure as you are of the doctor, or of M. Tripeaud, under present circumstances, we must not touch on the question of acting—which will be sure to frighten them at first—until after our interview with your niece. It will be easy, notwithstanding her cleverness, to find out her armour's defect. If our suspicions should be realised—if she is really informed of what it would be so dangerous for her to know—then we must have no scruples, and above all no delay. This very day must see all set at rest. The time for wavering is past.'

'Have you been able to send for the person agreed on?' asked the princess, after a moment's silence.

'He was to be here at noon. He cannot be long.'

'I thought this room would do very well for our purpose. It is separated from the smaller parlour by a curtain only, behind which your man may be stationed.'

'Capital !'

' Is he a man to be depended on ?'

' Quite so—we have often employed him in similar matters.   He is as skilful as discreet.'

At this moment a low knock was heard at the door.

' Come in,' said the princess.

' Dr. Baleinier wishes to know if her Highness the Princess can receive him,' asked the valet-de-chambre.

' Certainly.   Beg him to walk in.'

' There is also a gentleman that M. l'Abbé appointed to be here at noon, by whose orders I have left him waiting in the oratory.'

' 'Tis the person in question,' said the marquis to the princess. 'We must have him in first.   'Twould be useless for Dr. Baleinier to see him at present.'

' Show this person in first,' said the princess ; ' next when I ring the bell, you will beg Dr. Baleinier to walk this way ; and, if Baron Tripeaud should call, you will bring him here also.   After that, I am at home to no one, except Mdlle. Adrienne.'——The servant went out.

CHAPTER XXXVIII.

ADRIENNE'S ENEMIES.

THE Princess de Saint-Dizier's valet soon returned, showing in a little, pale man, dressed in black, and wearing spectacles.   He carried under his left arm a long black morocco writing-case.

The princess said to this man : ' M. l'Abbé, I suppose, has already informed you of what is to be done ?'

' Yes, your highness,' said the man in a faint, shrill, piping voice, making at the same time a low bow.

' Shall you be conveniently placed in this room?' asked the princess, conducting him to the adjoining apartment, which was only separated from the other by a curtain hung before a doorway.

' I shall do nicely here, your highness,' answered the man in spectacles, with a second and still lower bow.

' In that case, sir, please to step in here; I will let you know when it is time.'

' I shall wait your highness's order.'

' And pray remember my instructions,' added the marquis, as he unfastened the loops of the curtain.

' You may be perfectly tranquil, M. l'Abbé.' The heavy drapery, as it fell, completely concealed the man in spectacles.

The princess touched the bell; some moments after, the door opened, and the servant announced a very important personage in this work.

Dr. Baleinier was about fifty years of age, middling size, rather plump, with a full shining, ruddy countenance.   His grey hair, very smooth and rather long, parted by a straight line in the middle, fell flat over his temples. He had retained the fashion of wearing short, black silk breeches, perhaps because he had a well-formed leg ; his garters were fastened with small, golden buckles, as were his shoes of polished morocco leather ; his coat, waistcoat, and cravat were black, which gave him rather a clerical appearance ; his sleek, white hand was half hidden beneath a cambric ruffle, very closely plaited ; on the whole, the gravity of his costume did not seem to exclude a shade of foppery.

His face was acute and smiling ; his small grey eye announced rare penetration and sagacity. A man of the world and a man of pleasure, a delicate epicure, witty in conversation, polite to obsequiousness, supple, adroit, insinuating, Baleinier was one of the oldest favourites of the congregational set of the Princess de Saint-Dizier. Thanks to this powerful support, its cause unknown, the doctor, who had been long neglected, in spite of real skill and incontestable merit, found himself, under the Restoration, suddenly provided with two medical sinecures most valuable, and soon after with numerous patients. We must add, that, once under the patronage of the princess, the doctor began scrupulously to observe his religious duties ; he communicated once a week, with great publicity, at the high mass in Saint Thomas Aquinas Church.

At the year's end, a certain class of patients, led by the example and enthusiasm of Madame de Saint-Dizier's followers, would have no other physician than Doctor Baleinier, and his practice was now increased to an extraordinary degree. It may be conceived how important it was for the order, to have amongst its 'plain clothes members' one of the most popular practitioners of Paris.

A doctor has in some sort a priesthood of his own. Admitted at all hours to the most secret intimacy of families, he knows, guesses, and is able to effect much. Like the priest, in short, he has the ear of the sick and the dying. Now, when he who cares for the health of the body, and he who takes charge of the health of the soul, understand each other, and render mutual aid for the advancement of a common interest, there is nothing (with certain exceptions), which they may not extract from the weakness and fears of a sick man at the last gasp—not for themselves (the laws forbid it) —but for third parties belonging more or less to the very convenient class of men of straw. Doctor Baleinier was therefore one of the most active and valuable assistant members of the Paris Jesuits.

When he entered the room, he hastened to kiss the princess's hand with the most finished gallantry.

'Always punctual, my dear M. Baleinier.'

'Always eager and happy to attend to your highness's orders.' Then, turning towards the marquis, whose hand he pressed cordially, he added : 'Here we have you then at last. Do you know, that three months' absence appears very long to your friends?'

'The time is as long to the absent as to those who remain, my dear doctor. Well ! here is the great day. Mdlle. de Cardoville is coming.'

'I am not quite easy,' said the princess; 'suppose she had any suspicion?'

'That's impossible,' said M. Baleinier ; 'we are the best friends in the world. You know, that Mdlle. Adrienne has always had great confidence in me. The day before yesterday, we laughed a good deal, and as I made some observations to her, as usual, on her eccentric mode of life, and on the singular state of excitement in which I sometimes found her——'

'M. Baleinier never fails to insist on these circumstances, in appearance so insignificant,' said Madame de Saint-Dizier to the marquis with a meaning look.

'They are indeed very essential,' replied the other.

'Mdlle. Adrienne answered my observations,' resumed the doctor, 'by laughing at me in the gayest and most witty manner; for I must confess, that this young lady has one of the aptest and most accomplished minds I know.'

'Doctor, doctor !' said Madame de Saint-Dizier, 'no weakness!'

Instead of answering immediately, M. Baleinier drew his gold snuff-box from his waistcoat pocket, opened it, and took slowly a pinch of snuff, looking all the time at the princess with so significant an air, that she appeared quite re-assured. 'Weakness, madame?' observed he at last, brushing some grains of snuff from his shirt-front with his plump white hand ; 'did I not have the honour of volunteering to extricate you from this embarrassment?'

'And you are the only person in the world that could render us this important service,' said D'Aigrigny.

'Your highness sees, therefore,' resumed the doctor, 'that I am not likely to show any weakness. I perfectly understand the responsibility of what I undertake ; but such immense interests, you told me, were at stake——'

'Yes,' said D'Aigrigny, 'interests of the first consequence.'

'Therefore I did not hesitate,' proceeded M. Baleinier ; 'and you need not be at all uneasy. As a man of taste, accustomed to good society, allow me to render homage to the charming qualities of Mdlle. Adrienne ; when the time for action comes, you will find me quite as willing to do my work.'

'Perhaps, that moment may be nearer than we thought,' said Madame de Saint-Dizier, exchanging a glance with D'Aigrigny.

'I am, and will be, always ready,' said the doctor. 'I answer for everything that concerns myself. I wish I could be as tranquil on every other point.'

'Is not your asylum still as fashionable—as an asylum can well be ?' asked Madame de Saint-Dizier, with a half smile.

'On the contrary. I might almost complain of having too many boarders. It is not that. But, whilst we are waiting for Mdlle. Adrienne, I will mention another subject, which only relates to her indirectly, for it concerns the person who bought Cardoville Manor, one Madame de la Sainte Colombe, who has taken me for a doctor, thanks to Rodin's able management.'

'True,' said D'Aigrigny ; 'Rodin wrote to me on the subject—but without entering into details.'

'These are the facts,' resumed the doctor. 'This Madame de la Sainte Colombe, who was at first considered easy enough to lead, has shown herself very refractory on the head of her conversion. Two spiritual directors have already renounced the task of saving her soul. In despair, Rodin unslipped little Philippon on her. He is adroit, tenacious, and above all patient in the extreme—the very man that was wanted. When I got Madame de la Sainte Colombe for a patient, Philippon asked my aid, which he was naturally entitled to. We agreed upon our plan. I was not to appear to know him the least in the world ; and he was to keep me informed of the variations in the moral state of his penitent, so that I might be able, by the use of very inoffensive medicines—for there was nothing dangerous in the illness—to keep my patient in alternate states of improvement or the reverse, according as her director had reason to be satisfied or displeased—so that he might say to her : " You see, madame, you are in the good way ! Spiritual grace acts upon your bodily health, and you are already better. If, on the contrary, you fall back into evil courses, you feel immediately some physical ail, which is a certain proof of the powerful influence of faith, not only on the soul, but on the body also." '

'It is doubtless painful,' said D'Aigrigny, with perfect coolness, 'to be obliged to have recourse to such means, to rescue perverse souls from perdition—but we must needs proportion our modes of action to the intelligence and the character of the individual.'

'By-the-by, the princess knows,' resumed the doctor, 'that I have often pursued this plan at St. Mary's Convent, to the great advantage of the soul's peace and health of some of our patients, being extremely innocent. These alternations never exceed the difference between " pretty well," and " not quite so well." Yet small as are the variations, they act most efficaciously on certain minds. It was thus with Madame de la Sainte Colombe. She was in such a fair way of recovery, both moral and physical, that Rodin thought he might get Philippon to advise the country for his penitent, fearing that Paris air might occasion a relapse. This advice, added to the desire the woman had to play "lady of the parish," induced her to buy Cardoville Manor, a good investment in any respects. But yesterday, unfortunate Philippon came to tell me, that Madame de la Sainte Colombe was about to have an awful relapse—moral, of course—for her physical health is now desperately good. The said relapse appears to have been occasioned by an interview she has had with one Jacques Dumoulin, whom they tell me you know, my dear abbé ; he has introduced himself to her, nobody can guess how.'

'This Jacques Dumoulin,' said the marquis, with disgust, 'is one of those men, that we employ while we despise. He is a writer full of gall, envy, and hate, qualities that give him a certain unmercifully cutting eloquence. We pay him largely to attack our enemies, though it is often painful to see principles we respect defended by such a pen. For this wretch lives like a vagabond—is constantly in taverns—almost always intoxicated—but, I must own, his power of abuse is inexhaustible, and he is well versed in the most abstruse theological controversies, so that he is sometimes very useful to us.'

'Well ! though Madame de la Sainte Colombe is hard upon sixty, it appears that Dumoulin has matrimonial views on her large fortune. You will do well to inform Rodin, so that he may be on his guard against the dark designs of this rascal. I really beg a thousand pardons for having so long occupied you with such a paltry affair—but, talking of St. Mary's Convent,' added the doctor, addressing the princess, 'may I take the liberty of asking if your highness has been there lately ?'

The princess exchanged a rapid glance with D'Aigrigny, and answered : 'Oh, let me see ! Yes, I was there about a week ago.'

'You will find great changes then. The wall that was next to my asylum has been taken down, for they are going to build a new wing and a chapel, the old one being too small. I must say, in praise of Mdlle. Adrienne,' continued the doctor, with a singular smile aside, 'that she promised me a copy of one of Raphael's Madonnas for this chapel.'

'Really ? very appropriate !' said the princess. 'But here it is almost noon, and M. Tripeaud has not come.'

'He is the deputy-guardian of Mdlle. de Cardoville, whose property he has managed, as former agent of the count-duke,' said the marquis, with evident anxiety, 'and his presence here is absolutely indispensable. It is greatly to be desired that his coming should precede that of Mdlle. de Cardoville, who may be here at any moment.'

'It is unlucky that his portrait will not do as well,' said the doctor, smiling maliciously, and drawing a small pamphlet from his pocket.

'What is that, doctor ?' asked the princess.

'One of those anonymous sheets, which are published from time to time. It is called the " Scourge," and Baron Tripeaud's portrait is drawn with such faithfulness, that it ceases to be satire. It is really quite life-like ; you have only to listen. The sketch is entitled : "TYPE OF THE LYNX-SPECIES."

'" The Baron Tripeaud.—This man, who is as basely humble towards his social superiors, as he is insolent and coarse to those who depend upon him —is the living, frightful incarnation of the worse portion of the moneyed and commercial aristocracy—one of the rich and cynical speculators, without heart, faith, or conscience, who would speculate for a rise or fall on the death of his mother, if the death of his mother could influence the price of stocks.

'" Such persons have all the odious vices of men suddenly elevated, not like those whom honest and patient labour has nobly enriched, but like those who owe their wealth to some blind caprice of fortune, or some lucky cast of the net in the miry waters of stock-jobbing.

'" Once up in the world, they hate the people—because the people remind them of a mushroom origin of which they are ashamed. Without pity for the dreadful misery of the masses, they ascribe it wholly to idleness or debauchery, because this calumny forms an excuse for their barbarous selfishness.

'" And this is not all. On the strength of his well-filled safe, mounted on his right of the candidate, Baron Tripeaud insults the poverty and political disfranchisement—

'" Of the officer, who, after forty years of wars and hard service, is just able to live on a scanty pension—

'" Of the magistrate, who has consumed his strength in the discharge of stern and sad duties, and who is not better remunerated in his latter days—

'" Of the learned man, who has made his country illustrious by useful labours; or the professor, who has initiated entire generations in the various branches of human knowledge—

'" Of the modest and virtuous country curate, the pure representative of the gospel, in its charitable, fraternal, and democratic tendencies, etc.

'" In such a state of things, how should our shoddy baron of *in-dust-ry* not feel the most sovereign contempt for all that stupid mob of honest folk, who, having given to their country their youth, their mature age, their blood, their intelligence, their learning, see themselves deprived of the rights which he enjoys, because he has gained a million by unfair and illegal transactions?

'" It is true, that your optimists say to these pariahs of civilisation, whose proud and noble poverty cannot be too much revered and honoured: ' Buy an estate, and you too may be electors and candidates !'

'" But to come to the biography of our worthy baron—Andrew Tripeaud, the son of an ostler, at a roadside inn——"'

At this instant, the folding-doors were thrown open, and the valet announced : 'The Baron Tripeaud !'

Dr. Baleinier put his pamphlet into his pocket, made the most cordial bow to the financier, and even rose to give him his hand. The baron entered the room, overwhelming every one with salutations. 'I have the honour to attend the orders of your highness the princess. She knows that she may always count upon me.'

'I do indeed rely upon you, M. Tripeaud, and particularly under present circumstances.'

'If the intentions of your highness the princess are still the same with regard to Mdlle. de Cardoville——"

'They are still the same, M. Tripeaud, and we meet to-day on that subject.'

'Your highness may be assured of my concurrence, as, indeed, I have already promised. I think that the greatest severity must at length be employed, and that even if it were necessary——'

'That is also our opinion,' said the marquis, hastily making a sign to the princess, and glancing at the place where the man in spectacles was hidden; 'we are all perfectly in harmony. Still, we must not leave any point doubtful, for the sake of the young lady herself, whose interest alone guides us in this affair. We must draw out her sincerity by every possible means.'

'Mademoiselle has just arrived from the summer-house, and wishes to see your highness,' said the valet, again entering, after having knocked at the door.

'Say that I wait for her,' answered the princess ; 'and now I am at home to no one—without exception. You understand me ; absolutely to no one.'

Thereupon, approaching the curtain behind which the man was concealed, Mme. de Saint-Dizier gave him the cue—after which she returned to her seat.

It is singular, but during the short space which preceded Adrienne's arrival, the different actors in this scene appeared uneasy and embarrassed, as if they had a vague fear of her coming. In about a minute, Mdlle. de Cardoville entered the presence of her aunt.

CHAPTER XXXIX.

THE SKIRMISH.

On entering, Mdlle. de Cardoville threw down upon a chair the grey beaver hat she had worn to cross the garden, and displayed her fine, golden hair, falling on either side of her face in long, light ringlets, and twisted in a broad knot behind her head. She presented herself without boldness, but with perfect ease : her countenance was gay and smiling ; her large black eyes appeared even more brilliant than usual. When she perceived Abbé d'Aigrigny, she started in surprise, and her rosy lips were just touched with a mocking smile. After nodding graciously to the doctor, she passed Baron Tripeaud by without looking at him, and saluted the princess with a stately obeisance, in the most fashionable style.

Though the walk and bearing of Mdlle. de Cardoville were extremely elegant, and full of propriety and truly feminine grace, there was about her an air of resolution and independence by no means common in women, and particularly in girls of her age. Her movements, without being abrupt, bore no traces of restraint, stiffness, or formality. They were frank and free as her character, full of life, youth, and freshness ; and one could easily divine that so buoyant, straightforward, and decided a nature had never been able to conform itself to the rules of an affected rigour.

Strangely enough, though he was a man of the world, a man of great talent, a churchman distinguished for his eloquence, and, above all, a person of influence and authority, Marquis d'Aigrigny experienced an involuntary, incredible, almost painful uneasiness, in presence of Adrienne de Cardoville. He—generally so much the master of himself, so accustomed to exercise great power—who (in the name of his Order) had often treated with crowned heads on the footing of an equal, felt himself abashed and lowered in the presence of this girl, as remarkable for her frankness as for her biting irony. Now, as men who are accustomed to impose their will upon others generally hate those who, far from submitting to their influence, hamper it, and make sport of them, it was no great degree of affection that the marquis bore towards the Princess de Saint-Dizier's niece.

For a long time past, contrary to his usual habit, he had ceased to try upon Adrienne that fascinating address to which he had often owed an irresistible charm ; towards her he had become dry, curt, serious, taking refuge in that icy sphere of haughty dignity and rigid austerity which completely hid all those amiable qualities with which he was endowed, and of which, in general, he made such efficient use. Adrienne was much amused at all this, and thereby showed her imprudence—for the most vulgar motives often engender the most implacable hatreds.

From these preliminary observations, the reader will understand the divers sentiments and interests which animated the different actors in the following scene.

Madame de Saint-Dizier was seated in a large arm-chair by one side of the hearth. Marquis d'Aigrigny was standing before the fire. Dr. Baleinier, seated near a bureau, was again turning over the leaves of Baron Tripeaud's biography, whilst the baron appeared to be very attentively examining one of the pictures of sacred subjects suspended from the wall.

'You sent for me, aunt, to talk upon matters of importance?' said Adrienne, breaking the silence which had reigned in the reception-room since her entrance.

'Yes, madame,' answered the princess, with a cold and severe mien ; 'upon matters of the gravest importance.'

'I am at your service, aunt. Perhaps we had better walk into your library?'

'It is not necessary. We can talk here.' Then, addressing the marquis, the doctor, and the baron, she said to them, 'Pray, be seated, gentlemen,' and they all took their places round the table.

'How can the subject of our interview interest these gentlemen, aunt?' asked Mdlle. de Cardoville, with surprise.

'These gentlemen are old family friends; all that concerns you must interest them, and their advice ought to be heard and accepted by you with respect.'

'I have no doubt, aunt, of the bosom friendship of M. d'Aigrigny for our family: I have still less of the profound and disinterested devotion of M. Tripeaud; M. Baleinier is one of my old friends; still, before accepting these gentlemen as spectators, or, if you will, as confidants of our interview, I wish to know what we are going to talk of before them.'

'I thought that, among your many singular pretensions, you had at least those of frankness and courage.'

'Really, aunt,' said Adrienne, smiling with mock humility, 'I have no more pretensions to frankness and courage than you have to sincerity and goodness. Let us admit, once for all, that we are what we are—without pretension.'

'Be it so,' said Madame de Saint-Dizier, in a dry tone; 'I have long been accustomed to the freaks of your independent spirit. I suppose, then, that, courageous and frank as you say you are, you will not be afraid to speak before such grave and respectable persons as these gentlemen what you would speak to me alone?'

'Is it a formal examination that I am to submit to? if so, upon what subject?'

'It is not an examination; but, as I have a right to watch over you, and as you take advantage of my weak compliance with your caprices, I mean to put an end to what has lasted too long, and tell you my irrevocable resolutions for the future, in presence of friends of the family. And, first, you have hitherto had a very false and imperfect notion of my power over you.'

'I assure you, aunt, that I have never had any notion, true or false, on the subject—for I have never even dreamt about it.'

'That is my own fault; for, instead of yielding to your fancies, I should have made you sooner feel my authority; but the moment is come to submit yourself; the severe censures of my friends have enlightened me in time. Your character is self-willed, independent, stubborn; it must change—either by fair means or by force, understand me, it *shall* change.'

At these words, pronounced harshly before strangers, with a severity which did not seem at all justified by circumstances, Adrienne tossed her head proudly; but, restraining herself, she answered with a smile: 'You say, aunt, that I·shall change. I should not be astonished at it. We hear of such odd conversions.'——The princess bit her lips.

'A sincere conversion can never be called odd, as you term it, madame,' said Abbé d'Aigrigny, coldly. 'It is, on the contrary, meritorious, and forms an excellent example.'

'Excellent?' answered Adrienne: 'that depends! For instance, what if one converts defects into vices?'

'What do you mean, madame?' cried the princess.

'I am speaking of myself, aunt; you reproach me with being independent and resolute—suppose I were to become hypocritical and wicked? In truth, I prefer keeping my dear little faults, which I love like spoiled children. I know what I am; I do not know what I might be.'

'But you must acknowledge, Mdlle. Adrienne,' said Baron Tripeaud, with a self-conceited and sententious air, 'that a conversion——'

' I believe,' said Adrienne, disdainfully, ' that M. Tripeaud is well versed in the conversion of all sorts of property into all sorts of profit, by all sorts of means—but he knows nothing of this matter.'

' But, madame,' resumed the financier, gathering courage from a glance of the princess, ' you forget that I have the honour to be your deputy guardian, and that——'

' It is true that M. Tripeaud has that honour,' said Adrienne, with still more haughtiness, and not even looking at the baron ; ' I could never tell exactly why. But as it is not now the time to guess enigmas, I wish to know, aunt, the object and end of this meeting ?'

' You shall be satisfied, madame. I will explain myself in a very clear and precise manner. You shall know the plan of conduct that you will have henceforth to pursue ; and if you refuse to submit thereto, with the obedience and respect that is due to my orders, I shall at once see what course to take.'

It is impossible to give an idea of the imperious tone and stern look of the princess, as she pronounced these words, which were calculated to startle a girl, until now accustomed to live in a great measure as she pleased : yet, contrary perhaps to the expectation of Madame de Saint-Dizier, instead of answering impetuously, Adrienne looked her full in the face, and said, laughing : ' This is a perfect declaration of war. It's becoming very amusing.'

' We are not talking of declarations of war,' said the Abbé d'Aigrigny, harshly, as if offended by the expressions of Mdlle. de Cardoville.

' Now, M. l'Abbé !' returned Adrienne, ' for an old colonel, you are really too severe upon a jest !—you are so much indebted to " war," which gave you a French regiment after fighting so long against France—in order to learn, of course, the strength and the weakness of her enemies.'

On these words, which recalled painful remembrances, the marquis coloured : he was going to answer, but the princess exclaimed : ' Really, madame, your behaviour is quite intolerable !'

' Well, aunt, I acknowledge I was wrong. I ought not to have said this is very amusing—for it is not so, at all ; but it is at least very curious—and perhaps,' added the young girl, after a moment's silence, ' perhaps very audacious—and audacity pleases me. As we are upon this subject, and you talk of a plan of conduct to which I must conform myself, under pain of (interrupting herself)—under pain of what, I should like to know, aunt ?'

' You shall know. Proceed.'

' I will, in the presence of these gentlemen, also declare, in a very plain and precise manner, the determination that I have come to. As it required some time to prepare for its execution, I have not spoken of it sooner, for you know I am not in the habit of saying, " I will do so and so !" but I do it.'

' Certainly ; and it is just this habit of culpable independence of which you must break yourself.'

' Well, I had intended only to inform you of my determination at a later period ; but I cannot resist the pleasure of doing so to-day, you seem so well disposed to hear and receive it. Still, I would beg of you to speak first : it may just so happen, that our views are precisely the same.'

' I like better to see you thus,' said the princess. ' I acknowledge at least the courage of your pride, and your defiance of all authority. You speak of audacity—yours is indeed great.'

' I am at least decided to do that which others in their weakness dare not —but which I dare. This, I hope, is clear and precise.'

' Very clear, very precise,' said the princess, exchanging a glance of satisfaction with the other actors in this scene. ' The positions being thus established, matters will be much simplified. I have only to give you notice, in your own interest, that this is a very serious affair—much more so than you imagine—and that the only way to dispose me to indulgence, is to substitute, for the habitual arrogance and irony of your language, the modesty and respect becoming a young lady.'

Adrienne smiled, but made no reply. Some moments of silence, and some rapid glances exchanged between the princess and her three friends, showed that these encounters, more or less brilliant in themselves, were to be followed by a serious combat.

Mdlle. de Cardoville had too much penetration and sagacity, not to remark, that the Princess de Saint-Dizier attached the greatest importance to this decisive interview. But she could not understand how her aunt could hope to impose her absolute will upon her : the threat of coercive measures appearing with reason a mere ridiculous menace: Yet, knowing the vindictive character of her aunt, the secret power at her disposal, and the terrible vengeance she had sometimes exacted—reflecting, moreover, that men in the position of the marquis and the doctor would not have come to attend this interview without some weighty motive—the young lady paused for a moment before she plunged into the strife.

But soon, the very presentiment of some vague danger, far from weakening her, gave her new courage to brave the worst, to exaggerate, if that were possible, the independence of her ideas, and uphold, come what might, the determination that she was about to signify to the Princess de Saint-Dizier.

CHAPTER XL.

THE REVOLT.

' MADAME,' said the princess to Adrienne de Cardoville, in a cold, severe tone, ' I owe it to myself, as well as to these gentlemen, to recapitulate, in a few words, the events that have taken place for some time past. Six months ago, at the end of the mourning for your father, you, being eighteen years old, asked for the management of your fortune, and for emancipation from control. Unfortunately, I had the weakness to consent. You quitted the house, and established yourself in the extension, far from all superintendence. Then began a train of expenditures, each one more extravagant than the last. Instead of being satisfied with one or two waiting-women, taken from that class from which they are generally selected, you chose governesses for lady-companions, whom you dressed in the most ridiculous and costly fashion. It is true, that, in the solitude of your pavilion, you yourself chose to wear, one after another, costumes of different ages. Your foolish fancies and unreasonable whims have been without end and without limit : not only have you never fulfilled your religious duties, but you have actually had the audacity to profane one of your rooms, by rearing in the centre of it a species of pagan altar, on which is a group in marble representing a youth and a girl'—the princess uttered these words as if they would burn her lips—' a work of art, if you will, but a work in the highest degree unsuitable to a person of your age. You pass whole days entirely secluded in your pavilion, refusing to see any one ; and Dr. Baleinier, the only one of my friends in whom you seem to have retained some confidence, having succeeded by much persuasion in gaining admittance, has frequently found you in so very excited a state, that he has felt seriously uneasy with regard to your health. You have always insisted on going out alone, without rendering any account of your actions to any one. You have taken delight in opposing, in every possible way, your will to my authority. Is all this true ?'

"'The picture of my past is not much flattered,' said Adrienne, smiling, 'but it is not altogether unlike.'

'So you admit, madame,' said Abbé d'Aigrigny, laying stress on his words, 'that all the facts stated by your aunt are scrupulously true?'

Every eye was turned towards Adrienne, as if her answer would be of extreme importance.

'Yes, M. l'Abbé,' said she; 'I live openly enough to render this question superfluous.'

'These facts are therefore admitted,' said Abbé d'Aigrigny, turning towards the doctor and the baron.

'These facts are completely established,' said M. Tripeaud, in a pompous voice.

'Will you tell me, aunt,' asked Adrienne, 'what is the good of this long preamble?'

'This long preamble, madame,' resumed the princess with dignity, 'exposes the past in order to justify the future.'

'Really, aunt, such mysterious proceedings are a little in the style of the answers of the Cumæan Sybil. They must be intended to cover something formidable.'

'Perhaps, mademoiselle—for to certain characters nothing is so formidable as duty and obedience. Your character is one of those inclined to revolt——'

'I freely acknowledge it, aunt—and it will always be so, until duty and obedience come to me in a shape that I can respect and love.'

'Whether you respect and love my orders or not, madame,' said the princess, in a curt harsh voice, 'you will, from to-day, from this moment, learn to submit blindly and absolutely to my will. In one word, you will do nothing without my permission: it is necessary, I insist upon it, and so I am determined it shall be.'

Adrienne looked at her aunt for a second, and then burst into so free and sonorous a laugh, that it rang for quite a time through the vast apartment. D'Aigrigny and Baron Tripeaud started in indignation. The princess looked angrily at her niece. The doctor raised his eyes to heaven, and clasped his hand over his waistcoat with a sanctimonious sigh.

'Madame,' said Abbé d'Aigrigny, 'such fits of laughter are highly unbecoming. Your aunt's words are serious, and deserve a different reception.'

'Oh, sir!' said Adrienne, recovering herself, 'it is not my fault if I laugh. How can I maintain my gravity, when I hear my aunt talking of blind submission to her orders? Is the swallow, accustomed to fly upwards and enjoy the sunshine, fledged to live with the mole in darkness?'

At this answer, D'Aigrigny affected to stare at the other members of this kind of family council with blank astonishment.

'A swallow? what does she mean?' asked the abbé of the baron, making a sign, which the latter understood.

'I do not know,' answered Tripeaud, staring in his turn at the doctor. 'She spoke too of a mole. It is quite unheard-of—incomprehensible.'

'And so, madame,' said the princess, appearing to share in the surprise of the others, 'this is the reply that you make to me?'

'Certainly,' answered Adrienne, astonished herself that they should pretend not to understand the simile of which she had made use, accustomed as she was to speak in figurative language.

'Come, come, madame,' said Dr. Baleinier, smiling good-humouredly, 'we must be indulgent. My dear Mdlle. Adrienne has naturally so uncommon and excitable a nature! She is really the most charming mad woman I know ; I have told her so a hundred times, in my position of an old friend, which allows such freedom.'

' I can conceive that your attachment makes you indulgent—but it is not the less true, doctor,' said D'Aigrigny, as if reproaching him for taking the part of Mdlle. de Cardoville, ' that such answers to serious questions are most extravagant.'

' The evil is, that mademoiselle does not seem to comprehend the serious nature of this conference,' said the princess, harshly. ' She will perhaps understand it better when I have given her my orders.'

' Let us hear these orders, aunt,' replied Adrienne, as, seated on the other side of the table, opposite to the princess, she leaned her small, dimpled chin in the hollow of her pretty hand, with an air of graceful mockery, charming to behold.

' From to-morrow forward,' resumed the princess, ' you will quit the summer-house that you at present inhabit, you will discharge your women, and come and occupy two rooms in this house, to which there will be no access except through my apartment. You will never go out alone. You will accompany me to the services of the church. Your emancipation terminates, in consequence of your prodigality duly proven. I will take charge of all your expenses, even to the ordering of your clothes, so that you may be properly and modestly dressed. Until your majority (which will be indefinitely postponed, by means of the intervention of a family-council), you will have no money at your own disposal. Such is my resolution.'

' And certainly your resolution can only be applauded, madame,' said Baron Tripeaud ; ' we can but encourage you to show the greatest firmness, for such disorders must have an end.'

' It is more than time to put a stop to such scandals,' added the abbé.

' Eccentricity and exaltation of temperament—may excuse many things,' ventured to observe the smooth-tongued doctor.

' No doubt,' replied the princess dryly to Baleinier, who played his part to perfection ; ' but then, doctor, the requisite measures must be taken with such characters.'

Madame de Saint-Dizier had expressed herself in a firm and precise manner ; she appeared convinced of the possibility of putting her threats into execution. M. Tripeaud and D'Aigrigny had just now given their full consent to the words of the princess. Adrienne began to perceive that something very serious was in contemplation, and her gaiety was at once replaced by an air of bitter irony and offended independence.

She rose abruptly, and coloured a little ; her rosy nostrils dilated, her eyes flashed fire, and, as she raised her head, she gently shook the fine, wavy, golden hair, with a movement of pride that was natural to her. After a moment's silence, she said to her aunt in a cutting tone : ' You have spoken of the past, madame ; I also will speak a few words concerning it, since you force me to do so, though I may regret the necessity. I quitted your dwelling, because it was impossible for me to live longer in this atmosphere of dark hypocrisy and black treachery.'

' Madame,' said D'Aigrigny, ' such words are as violent as they are unreasonable.'

' Since you interrupt me, sir,' said Adrienne, hastily, as she fixed her eyes on the abbé, ' tell me what examples did I meet with in my aunt's house ?'

' Excellent examples, madame.'

' Excellent, sir ? Was it because I saw there, every day, her conversion keep pace with your own ?'

' Madame, you forget yourself !' cried the princess, becoming pale with rage.

'Madame, I do not forget—I remember, like other people : that is all. I had no relation of whom I could ask an asylum. I wished to live alone. I wished to enjoy my revenues—because I chose rather to spend them myself, than to see them wasted by M. Tripeaud.'

'Madame,' cried the baron, 'I cannot imagine how you can presume——'

'Sir !' said Adrienne, reducing him to silence by a gesture of overwhelming lordliness, 'I speak of you—not to you. I wished to spend my income,' she continued, 'according to my own tastes. I embellished the retreat that I had chosen. Instead of ugly, ill-taught servants, I selected girls, pretty and well brought up, though poor. Their education forbade their being subjected to any humiliating servitude, though I have endeavoured to make their situation easy and agreeable. They do not serve me, but render me service—I pay them, but I am obliged to them—nice distinctions that your highness will not understand, I know. Instead of seeing them badly or ungracefully dressed, I have given them clothes that suit their charming faces well, because I like whatever is young and fair. Whether I dress myself one way or the other, concerns only my looking-glass. I go out alone, because I like to follow my fancy. I do not go to mass—but, if I had still a mother, I would explain to her my devotions, and she would kiss me none the less tenderly. It is true, that I have raised a pagan altar to youth and beauty, because I adore God in all that He has made fair and good, noble and grand—because, morn and evening, my heart repeats the fervent and sincere prayer : "Thanks, my Creator ! thanks !"—Your highness says that M. Baleinier has often found me in my solitude, a prey to a strange excitement : yes, it is true ; for it is then that, escaping in thought from all that renders the present odious and painful to me, I find refuge in the future—it is then that magical horizons spread far before me—it is then that such splendid visions appear to me, as make me feel myself rapt in a sublime and heavenly ecstasy, as if I no longer appertained to earth !' ·

As Adrienne pronounced these last words with enthusiasm, her countenance appeared transfigured, so resplendent did it become. In that moment, she had lost sight of all that surrounded her.

'It is then,' she resumed, with spirit soaring higher and higher, 'that I breathe a pure air, reviving and free—yes, free—above all, free—and so salubrious, so grateful to the soul !—Yes, instead of seeing my sisters painfully submit to a selfish, humiliating, brutal dominion, which entails upon them the seductive vices of slavery, the graceful fraud, the enchanting perfidy, the caressing falsehood, the contemptuous resignation, the hateful obedience—I behold them, my noble sisters ! worthy and sincere because they are free, faithful and devoted because they have liberty to choose—neither imperious nor base, because they have no master to govern or to flatter—cherished and respected, because they can withdraw from a disloyal hand their hand, loyally bestowed. Oh, my sisters ! my sisters ! I feel it. These are not merely consoling visions—they are sacred hopes.'

Carried away, in spite of herself, by the excitement of her feelings, Adrienne paused for a moment, in order to return to earth ; she did not perceive that the other actors in this scene were looking at each other with an air of delight.

'What she says there is excellent,' murmured the doctor in the princess's ear, next to whom he was seated ; 'were she in league with us, she would not speak differently.'

'It is only by excessive harshness,' added D'Aigrigny, 'that we shall bring her to the desired point.'

But it seemed as if the vexed emotion of Adrienne had been dissipated by the contact of the generous sentiments she had just uttered. Addressing

Baleinier with a smile, she said : ' I must own, doctor, that there is nothing more ridiculous, than to yield to the current of certain thoughts, in the presence of persons incapable of understanding them. This would give you a fine opportunity to make game of that exaltation of mind for which you sometimes reproach me. To let myself be carried away by transports at so serious a moment !—for, verily, the matter in hand seems to be serious. But you see, good M. Baleinier, when an idea comes into my head, I can no more help following it out, than I could refrain from running after butterflies when I was a little girl.'

' And heaven only knows whither these brilliant butterflies of all colours,' said M. Baleinier, smiling with an air of paternal indulgence, ' that are passing through your brain, are likely to lead you. Oh, madcap, when will she be as reasonable as she is charming ?'

' This very instant, my good doctor,' replied Adrienne. ' I am about to cast off my reveries for realities, and speak plain and positive language, as you shall hear.'

Upon which, addressing her aunt, she continued : ' You have imparted to me your resolution, madame ; I will now tell you mine. Within a week, I shall quit the pavilion that I inhabit, for a house which I have arranged to my taste, where I shall live after my own fashion. I have neither father nor mother, and I owe no account of my actions to any but myself.'

' Upon my word, mademoiselle,' said the princess, shrugging her shoulders, ' you talk nonsense. You forget that society has inalienable moral rights, which we are bound to enforce. And we shall not neglect them, depend upon it.'

' So, madame, it is you, and M. d'Aigrigny, and M. Tripeaud, that represent the morality of society ! This appears to me very fine. Is it because M. Tripeaud has considered (I must acknowledge it) my fortune as his own ? Is it because——'

' Now, really, madame,' began Tripeaud.

' In good time, madame,' said Adrienne to her aunt, without noticing the baron, ' as the occasion offers, I shall have to ask you for explanations with regard to certain interests, which have hitherto, I think, been concealed from me.'

These words of Adrienne made D'Aigrigny and the princess start, and then rapidly exchange a glance of uneasiness and anxiety. Adrienne did not seem to perceive it, but thus continued : ' To have done with your demands, madame, here is my final resolve. I shall live where and how I please. I think that, if I were a man, no one would impose on me, at my age, the harsh and humiliating guardianship you have in view, for living as I have lived till now—honestly, freely, and generously, in the sight of all.'

' This idea is absurd ! is madness !' cried the princess. ' To wish to live thus alone, is to carry immorality and immodesty to their utmost limits.'

' If so, madame,' said Adrienne, ' what opinion must you entertain of so many poor girls, orphans like myself, who live alone and free, as I wish to live ? They have not received, as I have, a refined education, calculated to raise the soul, and purify the heart. They have not wealth, as I have, to protect them from the evil temptations of misery ; and yet they live honestly and proudly in their distress.'

' Vice and virtue do not exist for such tag-rag vermin !' cried Baron Tripeaud, with an expression of anger and hideous disdain.

' Madame, you would turn away a lackey, that would venture to speak thus before you,' said Adrienne to her aunt, unable to conceal her disgust, ' and yet you oblige me to listen to such speeches !'

The Marquis d'Aigrigny touched M. Tripeaud with his knee under the table, to remind him that he must not express himself in the princess's parlours in the same manner as he would in the lobbies of the Exchange. To repair the baron's coarseness, the abbé thus continued : 'There is no comparison, mademoiselle, between people of the class you name, and a young lady of your rank.'

'For a Catholic priest, M. l'Abbé, that distinction is not very Christian,' replied Adrienne.

'I know the purport of my words, madame,' answered the abbé, dryly ; 'besides, the independent life that you wish to lead, in opposition to all reason, may tend to very serious consequences for you. Your family may one day wish to see you married——'

'I will spare my family that trouble, sir ; if I marry at all, I will choose for myself, which also appears to me reasonable enough. But, in truth, I am very little tempted by that heavy chain, which selfishness and brutality rivet for ever about our necks.'

'It is indecent, madame,' said the princess, 'to speak so lightly of such an institution.'

'Before you, especially, madame, I beg pardon for having shocked your highness ! You fear that my independent manner of living will frighten away all wooers ; but that is another reason for persisting in my inde- pendence, for I detest wooers. I only hope that they may have the very worst opinion of me. and there is no better means of effecting that object, than to appear to live as they live themselves. I rely upon my whims, my follies, my sweet faults, to preserve me from the annoyance of any matri- monial hunting.'

'You will be quite satisfied on that head,' resumed Madame de Saint- Dizier, 'if unfortunately the report should gain credit, that you have carried the forgetfulness of all duty, and decency, to such a height, as to return home at eight o'clock in the morning. So I am told is the case—but I cannot bring myself to believe such an enormity.'

'You are wrong, madame, for it is quite true.'

'So you confess it ?' cried the princess.

'I confess all that I do, madame. I came home this morning at eight o'clock.'

'You hear, gentlemen ?' ejaculated the princess.

'Oh !' said M. d'Aigrigny, in a bass voice.

'Ah !' said the baron, in a treble key.

'Oh !' muttered the doctor, with a deep sigh.

On hearing these lamentable exclamations, Adrienne seemed about to speak, perhaps to justify herself ; but her lip speedily assumed a curl of contempt, which showed that she disdained to stoop to any explanation.

'So it is true,' said the princess. ' Oh, wretched girl, you had accustomed me to be astonished at nothing ; but, nevertheless, I doubted the possibility of such conduct. It required your impudent and audacious reply to con- vince me of the fact.'

'Madame, lying has always appeared to me more impudent than to speak the truth.'

'And where had you been, madame ? and for what ?'

'Madame,' said Adrienne, interrupting her aunt, 'I never speak false— but neither do I speak more than I choose ; and then again, it were cowardice to defend myself from a revolting accusation. Let us say no more about it : your importunities on this head will be altogether vain. To resume : you wish to impose upon me a harsh and humiliating restraint ; I wish to quit the house I inhabit, to go and live where I please, at my own fancy. Which of us two will yield, remains to be seen. Now for another matter :

this mansion belongs to me ! As I am about to leave it, I am indifferent whether you continue to live here or not : but the ground-floor is uninhabited. It contains, besides the reception-rooms, two complete sets of apartments ; I have let them for some time.'

' Indeed !' said the princess, looking at D'Aigrigny with intense surprise. 'And to whom,' she added ironically, ' have you disposed of them ?'

' To three members of my family.'

' What does all this mean ?' said Mme. de Saint-Dizier, more and more astonished.

' It means, madame, that I wish to offer a generous hospitality to a young Indian prince, my kinsman on my mother's side. He will arrive in two or three days, and I wish to have the rooms ready to receive him.'

' You hear, gentlemen ?' said D'Aigrigny to the doctor and Tripeaud, with an affectation of profound stupor.

' It surpasses all one could imagine !' exclaimed the baron.

' Alas !' observed the doctor, benignantly, ' the impulse is generous in itself—but the mad little head crops out !'

' Excellent !' said the princess. ' I cannot prevent you, madame, from announcing the most extravagant designs ; but it is presumable that you will not stop short in so fair a path. Is that all ?'

' Not quite, your highness. I learned this morning, that two of my female relations, also on my mother's side—poor children of fifteen—orphan daughters of Marshal Simon—arrived yesterday from a long journey, and are now with the wife of the brave soldier who brought them to France from the depths of Siberia.'

At these words from Adrienne, D'Aigrigny and the princess could not help starting suddenly, and staring at each other with affright, so far were they from expecting that Mdlle. de Cardoville was informed of the coming of Marshal Simon's daughters. This discovery was like a thunder clap to them.

' You are no doubt astonished at seeing me so well informed,' said Adrienne : ' fortunately, before I have done, I hope to astonish you still more. But to return to these daughters of Marshal Simon : your highness will understand, that it is impossible for me to leave them in charge of the good people who have afforded them a temporary asylum. Though this family is honest, and hard-working, it is not the place for them. I shall go and fetch them hither, and lodge them in apartments on the ground-floor, along with the soldier's wife, who will do very well to take care of them.'

Upon these words, D'Aigrigny and the baron looked at each other, and the baron exclaimed : 'Decidedly, she's out of her head.'

Without a word to Tripeaud, Adrienne continued : ' Marshal Simon cannot fail to arrive at Paris shortly. Your highness perceives how pleasant it will be, to be able to present his daughters to him, and prove that they have been treated as they deserve. To-morrow morning I shall send for milliners and mantua makers, so that they may want for nothing. I desire their surprised father, on his return, to find them every way beautiful. They are pretty, I am told, as angels—but I will endeavour to make little Cupids of them.'

' At last, madame, you must have finished?' said the princess, in a sardonic and deeply irritated tone, whilst D'Aigrigny, calm and cold in appearance, could hardly dissemble his mental anguish.

' Try again !' continued the princess, addressing Adrienne. ' Are there no more relations that you wish to add to this interesting family-group ? Really a queen could not act with more magnificence.'

' Right ! I wish to give my family a royal reception—such as is due to the son of a king, and the daughters of the Duke de Ligny. It is well to unite other luxuries of life with the luxury of the hospitable heart,'

'The maxim is assuredly generous,' said the princess, becoming more and more agitated ; 'it is only a pity that you do not possess the mines of El Dorado to make it practicable.'

'It was on the subject of a mine, said to be a rich one, that I also wished to speak to your highness. Could I find a better opportunity ? Though my fortune is already considerable, it is nothing to what may come to our family at any moment. You will perhaps excuse, therefore, what you are pleased to call my royal prodigalities.'

D'Aigrigny's dilemma became momentarily more and more thorny. The affair of the medals was so important, that he had concealed it even from Dr. Baleinier, though he had called in his services to forward immense interests. Neither had Tripeaud been informed of it, for the princess believed that she had destroyed every vestige of those papers of Adrienne's father, which might have put him on the scent of this discovery. The abbé, therefore, was not only greatly alarmed that Mdlle. de Cardoville might be informed of this secret, but he trembled lest she should divulge it.

The princess, sharing the alarms of D'Aigrigny, interrupted her niece by exclaiming : 'Madame, there are certain family affairs which ought to be kept secret, and, without exactly understanding to what you allude, I must request you to change the subject.'

'What, madame ! are we not here a family party? Is that not sufficiently evident by the somewhat ungracious things that have been here said?'

'No matter, madame ! when affairs of interest are concerned, which are more or less disputable, it is perfectly useless to speak of them without the documents laid before every one.'

'And of what have we been speaking this hour, madame, if not of affairs of interest ? I really do not understand your surprise and embarrassment.'

'I am neither surprised nor embarrassed, madame ; but for the last two hours, you have obliged me to listen to so many new and extravagant things, that a little amaze is very permissible.'

'I beg your highness's pardon, but you are very much embarrassed,' said Adrienne, looking fixedly at her aunt, 'and M. d'Agrigny also—which confirms certain suspicions that I have not had the time to clear up. Have I then guessed rightly ?' she added, after a pause. 'We will see——'

'Madame, I command you to be silent,' cried the princess, no longer mistress of herself.

'Oh, madame !' said Adrienne, 'for a person who has in general so much command of her feelings, you compromise yourself strangely.'

Providence (as some will have it) came to the aid of the princess and the Abbé d'Aigrigny at this critical juncture. A valet entered the room ; his countenance bore such marks of fright and agitation, that the princess exclaimed as soon as she saw him : 'Why, Dubois ! what is the matter ?'

'I have to beg pardon, your highness, for interrupting you against your express orders, but a police inspector demands to speak with you instantly. He is below stairs, and the yard is full of policemen and soldiers.'

Notwithstanding the profound surprise which this new incident occasioned her, the princess, determining to profit by the opportunity thus afforded, to concert prompt measures with D'Aigrigny on the subject of Adrienne's threatened revelations, rose, and said to the abbé : 'Will you be so obliging as to accompany me, M. d'Aigrigny, for I do not know what the presence of this commissary of police may signify.'

D'Aigrigny followed the speaker into the next room,

CHAPTER XLI.

TREACHERY.

THE Princess de Saint-Dizier, accompanied by D'Aigrigny, and followed by the servant, stopped short in the next room to that in which had remained Adrienne, Tripeaud and the doctor.

'Where is the commissary?' asked the princess of the servant, who had just before announced to her the arrival of that magistrate.'

'In the blue saloon, madame.'

'My compliments, and beg him to wait for me a few moments.'

The man bowed and withdrew. As soon as he was gone, Madame de Saint-Dizier approached hastily M. d'Aigrigny, whose countenance, usually firm and haughty, was now pale and agitated.

'You see,' cried the princess in a hurried voice, 'Adrienne knows all. What shall we do?—what?'

'I cannot tell,' said the abbé, with a fixed and absent look. 'This disclosure is a terrible blow to us.'

'Is all, then, lost?'

'There is only one means of safety,' said M. d'Aigrigny;—'the doctor.'

'But how?' cried the princess. 'So, sudden? this very day?'

'Two hours hence, it will be too late; ere then, this infernal girl will have seen Marshal Simon's daughters.'

'But— Frederick!—it is impossible ! M. Baleinier will never consent. I ought to have been prepared beforehand—as we intended, after to-day's examination.'

'No matter,' replied the abbé, quickly; 'the doctor must try at any hazard.'

'But under what pretext?'——' I will try and find one.'

'Suppose you were to find a pretext, Frederick, and we could act immediately—nothing would be ready down there.'

'Be satisfied : they are always ready there, by habitual foresight.'

'How instruct the doctor on the instant?' resumed the princess.

'To send for him would be to rouse the suspicions of your niece,' said M. d'Aigrigny, thoughtfully ; 'and we must avoid that before everything.'

'Of course,' answered the princess ; 'her confidence in the doctor is one of our greatest resources.'

'There is a way,' said the abbé quickly ; 'I will write a few words in haste to Baleinier ; one of your people can take the note to him, as if it came from without—from a patient dangerously ill.'

'An excellent idea !' cried the princess. 'You are right. Here—upon this table—there is everything necessary for writing. Quick ! quick—But will the doctor succeed ?'

'In truth, I scarcely dare to hope it,' said the marquis, sitting down at the table with repressed rage. 'Thanks to this examination, going beyond our hopes, which our man, hidden behind the curtain, has faithfully taken down in shorthand—thanks to the violent scenes, which would necessarily have occurred to-morrow and the day after—the doctor, by fencing himself round with all sorts of clever precautions, would have been able to act with the most complete certainty. But to ask this of him to-day, on the instant ! —Hermina—it is folly to think of !'—The marquis threw down the pen which he held in his hand ; then he added, in a tone of bitter and profound irritation : ' At the very moment of success—to see all our hopes destroyed ! —Oh, the consequences of all this are incalculable. Your niece will be the cause of the greatest mischief—oh ! the greatest injury to us.'

It is impossible to describe the expression of deep rage and implacable hatred with which D'Aigrigny uttered these last words.

'Frederick,' cried the princess with anxiety, as she clasped her hands strongly around the abbé's, ' I conjure you, do not despair!—The doctor is fertile in resources, and he is *so* devoted to us. Let us at least make the attempt.'

' Well—it is at least a chance,' said the abbé, taking up the pen again.

' Should it come to the worst,' said the princess, ' and Adrienne go this evening to fetch General Simon's daughters, she may perhaps no longer find them.'

' We cannot hope for that. It is impossible that Rodin's orders should have been so quickly executed. We should have been informed of it.'

' It is true. Write then to the doctor; I will send you Dubois, to carry your letter. Courage, Frederick! we shall yet be too much for that ungovernable girl.' Madame de Saint-Dizier added, with concentrated rage : ' Oh, Adrienne! Adrienne! you shall pay dearly for your insolent sarcasms, and the anxiety you have caused us.'

As she went out, the princess turned towards M. d'Aigrigny, and said to him : ' Wait for me here. I will tell you the meaning of this visit of the police, and we will go in together.'

The princess disappeared. D'Aigrigny dashed off a few words, with a trembling hand.

CHAPTER XLII.

THE SNARE.

AFTER the departure of Madame de Saint-Dizier and the marquis, Adrienne had remained in her aunt's apartment with M. Baleinier and Baron Tripeaud.

On hearing of the commissary's arrival, Mdlle. de Cardoville had felt considerable uneasiness ; for there could be no doubt that, as Agricola had apprehended, this magistrate was come to search the hotel and extension, in order to find the smith, whom he believed to be concealed there.

Though she looked upon Agricola's hiding place as a very safe one, Adrienne was not quite tranquil on his account ; so in the event of any unfortunate accident, she thought it a good opportunity to recommend the refugee to the doctor, an intimate friend, as we have said, of one of the most influential ministers of the day. So, drawing near to the physician, who was conversing in a low voice with the baron, she said to him in her softest and most coaxing manner : 'My good M. Baleinier, I wish to speak a few words with you.' She pointed to the deep recess of one of the windows.

' I am at your orders, madame,' answered the doctor, as he rose to follow Adrienne to the recess.

M. Tripeaud, who, no longer sustained by the abbé's presence, dreaded the young lady as he did fire, was not sorry for this diversion. To keep up appearances, he stationed himself before one of the sacred pictures, and began again to contemplate it, as if there were no bounds to his admiration.

When Mdlle. de Cardoville was far enough from the baron, not to be overheard by him, she said to the physician, who, all smiles and benevolence, waited for her to explain : 'My good doctor, you are my friend, as you were my father's. Just now, notwithstanding the difficulty of your position, you had the courage to show yourself my only partisan.'

' Not at all, madame ; do not go and say such things !' cried the doctor, affecting a pleasant kind of anger. ' Plague on't ! you would get me into a pretty scrape ; so pray be silent on that subject. *Vade retro Satanas!—* which means : Get thee behind me, charming little demon that you are !'

' Do not be afraid,' answered Adrienne, with a smile ; ' I will not compromise you. Only allow me to remind you, that you have often made me offers of service, and spoken to me of your devotion.'

'Put me to the test—and you will see if I do not keep my promises.'

'Well, then ! give me a proof on the instant,' said Adrienne, quickly.

'Capital ! this is how I like to be taken at my word. What can I do for you ?'

'Are you still very intimate with your friend the minister ?'

'Yes ; I am just treating him for a loss of voice, which he always has, the day they put questions to him in the house. He likes it better.'

'I want you to obtain from him something very important for me.'

'For you ? pray, what is it ?'

At this instant, the valet entered the room, delivered a letter to M. Baleinier, and said to him : 'A footman just brought this letter for you, sir ; it is very pressing.'

The physician took the letter, and the servant went out.

'This is one of the inconveniences of merit,' said Adrienne, smiling ; 'they do not leave you a moment's rest, my poor doctor.'

'Do not speak of it, madame,' said the physician, who could not conceal a start of amazement, as he recognised the writing of D'Aigrigny ; 'these patients think we are made of iron, and have monopolised the health which they so much need. They have really no mercy. With your permission, madame,' added M. Baleinier, looking at Adrienne before he unsealed the letter.

Mdlle. de Cardoville answered by a graceful nod. Marquis d'Aigrigny's letter was not long; the doctor read it at a single glance, and, notwithstanding his habitual prudence, he shrugged his shoulders, and said hastily : 'To-day !—why, it's impossible. He is mad.'

'You speak no doubt of some poor patient, who has placed all his hopes in you—who waits and calls for you at this moment. Come, my dear M. Baleinier, do not reject his prayer. It is so sweet to justify the confidence we inspire.'

There was at once so much analogy, and such contradiction, between the object of this letter, written just before by Adrienne's most implacable enemy, and these words of commiseration which she spoke in a touching voice, that Dr. Baleinier himself could not help being struck with it. He looked at Mdlle. de Cardoville with an almost embarrassed air, as he replied : ' I am indeed speaking of one of my patients, who counts much upon me—a great deal too much—for he asks me to do an impossibility. But why do you feel so interested in an unknown person ?'

'If he is unfortunate, I know enough to interest me. The person for whom I ask your assistance with the minister, was quite as little known to me ; and now I take the deepest interest in him. I must tell you, that he is the son of the worthy soldier who brought Marshal Simon's daughters from the heart of Siberia.'

'What ! he is——'

'An honest workman, the support of his family ; but I must tell you all about it—this is how the affair took place.'

The confidential communication which Adrienne was going to make to the doctor, was cut short by Madame de Saint-Dizier, who, followed by M. d'Aigrigny, opened abruptly the door. An expression of infernal joy, hardly concealed beneath a semblance of extreme indignation, was visible in her countenance.

M. d'Aigrigny threw rapidly, as he entered the apartment, an inquiring and anxious glance at M. Baleinier. The doctor answered by a shake of the head. The abbé bit his lips with silent rage ; he had built his last hopes upon the doctor, and his projects seemed now for ever annihilated, notwithstanding the new blow which the princess had in reserve for Adrienne.

' Gentlemen,' said Madame de Saint-Dizier, in a sharp, hurried voice, for she was nearly choking with wicked pleasure, ' gentlemen, pray be seated ! I have some new and curious things to tell you, on the subject of this young lady.' She pointed to her niece, with a look of ineffable hatred and disdain.

' My poor child, what is the matter now ?' said M. Baleinier, in a soft, wheedling tone, before he left the window where he was standing with Adrienne. ' Whatever happens, count upon me !'—And the physician went to seat himself between M. d'Aigrigny and Mr. Tripeaud.

At her aunt's insolent address, Mdlle. de Cardoville had proudly lifted her head. The blood rushed to her face, and irritated at the new attacks with which she was menaced, she advanced to the table where the princess was seated, and said in an agitated voice to M. Baleinier : ' I shall expect you to call on me as soon as possible, my dear doctor. You know that I wish particularly to speak with you.'

Adrienne made one step towards the arm-chair, on which she had left her hat. The princess rose abruptly, and exclaimed : ' What are you doing, madame ?'

' I am about to retire. Your highness has expressed to me your will, and I have told you mine. It is enough.'

She took her hat. Madame de Saint-Dizier, seeing her prey about to escape, hastened towards her niece, and, in defiance of all propriety, seized her violently by the arm with a convulsive grasp, and bade her, ' Remain !'

' Fie, madame !' exclaimed Adrienne, with an accent of painful contempt, ' have we sunk so low ?'

' You wish to escape—you are afraid !' resumed Madame de Saint-Dizier, looking at her disdainfully from head to foot.

With these words ' you are afraid,' you could have made Adrienne de Cardoville walk into a fiery furnace. Disengaging her arm from her aunt's grasp, with a gesture full of nobleness and pride, she threw down the hat upon the chair, and, returning to the table, said imperiously to the princess : ' There is something even stronger than the disgust with which all this inspires me—the fear of being accused of cowardice. Go on, madame ! I am listening !'

With her head raised, her colour somewhat heightened, her glance half veiled by a tear of indignation, her arms folded over her bosom, which heaved in spite of herself with deep emotion, and her little foot beating convulsively on the carpet, Adrienne looked steadily at her aunt. The princess wished to infuse, drop by drop, the poison with which she was swelling, and make her victim suffer as long as possible, feeling certain that she could not escape. ' Gentlemen,' said Madame de Saint-Dizier, in a forced voice, ' this has occurred : I was told that the commissary of police wished to speak with me ; I went to receive this magistrate ; he excused himself, with a troubled air, for the nature of the duty he had to perform. A man, against whom a warrant was out, had been seen to enter the garden-house.'

Adrienne started; there could be no doubt that Agricola was meant. But she recovered her tranquillity, when she thought of the security of the hiding-place she had given him.

' The magistrate,' continued the princess, ' asked my consent to search the hotel and extension, to discover this man. It was his right. I begged him to commence with the garden-house, and accompanied him. Notwithstanding the improper conduct of Mademoiselle, it never, I confess, entered my head for a moment, that she was in any way mixed up with this police business. I was deceived.'

'What do you mean, madame?' cried Adrienne.

'You shall know all, madame,' said the princess, with a triumphant air, 'in good time. You were in rather too great a hurry just now, to show yourself so proud and satirical. Well! I accompanied the commissary in his search; we came to the summer-house; I leave you to imagine the stupor and astonishment of the magistrate, on seeing three creatures dressed up like actresses. At my request, the fact was noted in the official report; for it is well to reveal such extravagances to all whom it may concern.'

'The princess acted very wisely,' said Tripeaud, bowing; 'it is well that the authorities should be informed of such matters.'

Adrienne, too much interested in the fate of the workman to think of answering Tripeaud or the princess, listened in silence, and strove to conceal her uneasiness.

'The magistrate,' resumed Madame de Saint-Dizier, 'began by a severe examination of these young girls, to learn if any man had, with their knowledge, been introduced into the house; with incredible effrontery, they answered that they had seen nobody enter.'

'The true-hearted, honest girls!' thought Mademoisellle de Cardoville, full of joy; 'the poor workman is safe! the protection of Dr. Baleinier will do the rest.'

'Fortunately,' continued the princess, 'one of my women, Mrs. Grivois, had accompanied me. This excellent person, remembering to have seen Mademoiselle return home at eight o'clock in the morning, remarked with much simplicity to the magistrate, that the man, whom they sought, might probably have entered by the little garden gate, left open, accidentally, by Mademoiselle.'

'It would have been well, madame,' said Tripeaud, 'to have caused to be noted also in the report, that Mademoiselle had returned home at eight o'clock in the morning.'

'I do not see the necessity for this,' said the doctor, faithful to his part: 'it would have been quite foreign to the search carried on by the commissary.'

'But, doctor,' said Tripeaud.

'But, baron,' resumed M. Baleinier, in a firm voice, 'that is my opinion.'

'It was not mine, doctor,' said the princess; 'like M. Tripeaud, I considered it important to establish the fact by an entry in the report, and I saw, by the confused and troubled countenance of the magistrate, how painful it was to register the scandalous conduct of a young person placed in so high a position in society.'

'Certainly, madame,' said Adrienne, losing patience, 'I believe your modesty to be about equal to that of this candid commissary of police; but it seems to me, that your mutual innocence was alarmed a little too soon. You might, and ought to have reflected, that there was nothing extraordinary in my coming home at eight o'clock, if I had gone out at six.'

'The excuse, though somewhat tardy, is at least cunning,' said the princess, spitefully.

'I do not excuse myself, madame,' said Adrienne; 'but as M. Baleinier has been kind enough to speak a word in my favour, I give the possible interpretation of a fact, which it would not become me to explain in your presence.'

'The fact will stand, however, in the report,' said Tripeaud, 'until the explanation is given.'

Abbé d'Aigrigny, his forehead resting on his hand, remained as if a stranger to this scene; he was too much occupied with his fears at the consequences of the approaching interview between Mdlle. de Cardoville and

Marshal Simon's daughters—for there seemed no possibility of using force to prevent Adrienne from going out that evening.

Madame de Saint-Dizier went on : ' The fact which so greatly scandalised the commissary is nothing compared to what I yet have to tell you, gentlemen. We had searched all parts of the pavilion without finding any one, and were just about to quit the bedchamber, for we had taken this room the last, when Mrs. Grivois pointed out to us that one of the golden mouldings of a panel did not appear to come quite home to the wall. We drew the attention of the magistrate to this circumstance ; his men examined, touched, felt—the panel flew open !—and then—can you guess what we discovered ? But, no ! it is too odious, too revolting ; I dare not even——'

' Then I dare, madame,' said Adrienne, resolutely, though she saw with the utmost grief the retreat of Agricola was discovered ; ' I will spare your highness's candour the recital of this new scandal, and yet what I am about to say is in nowise intended as a justification.'

' It requires one, however,' said Madame de Saint-Dizier, with a disdainful smile ; ' a man concealed by you in your own bedroom.'

' A man concealed in her bedroom !' cried the Marquis d'Aigrigny, raising his head with apparent indignation, which only covered a cruel joy.

' A man ! in the bedroom of Mademoiselle !' added Baron Tripeaud. ' I hope this also was inserted in the report.'

' Yes, yes, baron,' said the princess with a triumphant air.

' But this man,' said the doctor, in a hypocritical tone, ' must have been a robber ? Any other supposition would be in the highest degree improbable. This explains itself.'

' Your indulgence deceives you, M. Baleinier,' answered the princess, dryly.

' We know the sort of thieves,' said Tripeaud ; ' they are generally young men, handsome, and very rich.'

' You are wrong, sir,' resumed Madame de Saint-Dizier. ' Mademoiselle does not raise her views so high. She proves that a dereliction from duty may be ignoble as well as criminal. I am no longer astonished at the sympathy which was just now professed for the lower orders. It is the more touching and affecting, as the man concealed by her was dressed in a blouse.'

' A blouse !' cried the baron, with an air of extreme disgust ; ' then he is one of the common people ? It really makes one's hair stand on end.'

' The man is a working smith—he confessed it,' said the princess ; ' but not to be unjust—he is really a good-looking fellow. It was doubtless that singular worship which Mademoiselle pays to the beautiful——'

' Enough, madame, enough !' said Adrienne suddenly, for, hitherto disdaining to answer, she had listened to her aunt with growing and painful indignation ; ' I was just now on the point of defending myself against one of your odious insinuations—but I will not a second time descend to any such weakness. One word only, madame ; has this honest and worthy artisan been arrested ?'

' To be sure, he has been arrested and taken to prison, under a strong escort. Does not that pierce your heart ?' sneered the princess, with a triumphant air. ' Your tender pity for this interesting smith must indeed be very great, since it deprives you of your sarcastic assurance.'

' Yes, madame ; for I have something better to do than to satirise that which is utterly odious and ridiculous,' replied Adrienne, whose eyes grew dim with tears at the thought of the cruel hurt to Agricola's family. Then, putting her hat on, and tying the strings, she said to the doctor : ' M. Baleinier, I asked you just now for your interest with the minister.'

'Yes, madame; and it will give me great pleasure to act on your behalf.'

'Is your carriage below?'

'Yes, madame,' said the doctor, much surprised.

'You will be good enough to accompany me immediately to the minister's. Introduced by you, he will not refuse me the favour, or rather the act of justice, that I have to solicit.'

'What, mademoiselle,' said the princess; 'do you dare take such a course, without my orders, after what has just passed? It is really quite unheard-of.'

'It confounds one,' added Tripeaud; 'but we must not be surprised at any thing.'

The moment Adrienne asked the doctor if his carriage was below, D'Aigrigny started. A look of intense satisfaction flashed across his countenance, and he could hardly repress the violence of his delight, when, darting a rapid and significant glance at the doctor, he saw the latter respond to it by twice closing his eyelids in token of comprehension and assent.

When therefore the princess resumed, in an angry tone, addressing herself to Adrienne: 'Madame, I forbid you leaving the house!'—D'Aigrigny said to the speaker, with a peculiar inflection of the voice: 'I think, your highness, we may trust the lady to the doctor's care.'

The marquis pronounced these words in so significant a manner, that the princess, having looked by turns at the physician and D'Aigrigny, understood it all, and her countenance grew radiant with joy.

Not only did this pass with extreme rapidity, but the night was already almost come, so that Adrienne, absorbed in painful thoughts with regard to Agricola, did not perceive the different signals exchanged between the princess, the doctor, and the abbé. Even had she done so, they would have been incomprehensible to her.

Not wishing to have the appearance of yielding too readily to the suggestion of the marquis, Madame de Saint-Dizier resumed: 'Though the doctor seems to me to be far too indulgent to Mademoiselle, I might not see any great objection to trusting her with him; but that I do not wish to establish such a precedent, for henceforward she must have no will but mine.'

'Madame,' said the physician gravely, feigning to be somewhat shocked by the words of the Princess de Saint-Dizier, 'I do not think I have been too indulgent to mademoiselle—but only just. I am at her orders, to take her to the minister if she wishes it. I do not know what she intends to solicit, but I believe her incapable of abusing the confidence I repose in her, or of making me support a recommendation undeserved.'

Adrienne, much moved, extended her hand cordially to the doctor, and said to him: 'Rest assured, my excellent friend, that you will thank me for the step I am taking, for you will assist in a noble action.'

Tripeaud, who was not in the secret of the new plans of the doctor and the abbé, in a low voice faltered to the latter, with a stupefied air, 'What! will you let her go?'

'Yes, yes,' answered D'Aigrigny abruptly, making a sign that he should listen to the princess, who was about to speak. Advancing towards her niece, she said to her in a slow and measured tone, laying a peculiar emphasis on every word: 'One moment more, mademoiselle—one last word in presence of these gentlemen. Answer me! Notwithstanding the heavy charges impending over you, are you still determined to resist my formal commands?'

'Yes, madame.

'Notwithstanding the scandalous exposure which has just taken place, you still persist in withdrawing yourself from my authority?'

' Yes, madame.'

' You refuse positively to submit to the regular and decent mode of life which I would impose upon you ?'

' I have already told you, madame, that I am about to quit this dwelling, in order to live alone and after my own fashion.'

' Is that your final decision ?'

' It is my last word.'

' Reflect ! the matter is serious. Beware !'

' I have given your highness my last word, and I never speak it twice.'

' Gentlemen, you hear all this ?' resumed the princess ; ' I have tried in vain all that was possible to conciliate. Mademoiselle will have only herself to thank for the measures to which this audacious revolt will oblige me to have recourse.'

' Be it so, madame,' replied Adrienne. Then, addressing M. Baleinier, she said quickly to him : ' Come, my dear doctor ; I am dying with impatience. Let us set out immediately. Every minute lost may occasion bitter tears to an honest family.'

So saying, Adrienne left the room precipitately with the physician. One of the servants called for M. Baleinier's carriage. Assisted by the doctor, Adrienne mounted the step, without perceiving that he said something in a low whisper to the footman that opened the coach-door.

When, however, he was seated by the side of Mdlle. de Cardoville, and the door was closed upon them, he waited for about a second, and then called out in a loud voice to the coachman : ' To the house of the minister, by the private entrance !' The horses started at a gallop.

- - -

CHAPTER XLIII.

A FALSE FRIEND.

NIGHT had set in dark and cold. The sky, which had been clear till the sun went down, was now covered with grey and lurid clouds ; a strong wind raised here and there, in circling eddies, the snow that was beginning to fall thick and fast.

The lamps threw a dubious light into the interior of Dr. Baleinier's carriage, in which he was seated alone with Adrienne de Cardoville. The charming countenance of the latter, faintly illumined by the lamps beneath the shade of her little grey hat, looked doubly white and pure in contrast with the dark lining of the carriage, which was now filled with that sweet, delicious, and almost voluptuous perfume which hangs about the garments of young women of taste. The attitude of the girl, seated next to the doctor, was full of grace. Her slight and elegant figure, imprisoned in her high-necked dress of blue cloth, imprinted its wavy outline on the soft cushion against which she leaned ; her little feet, crossed one upon the other, and stretched rather forward, rested upon a thick bear-skin, which carpeted the bottom of the carriage. In her hand, which was ungloved and dazzlingle white, she held a magnificently embroidered handkerchief, with which, to the great astonishment of M. Baleinier, she dried her eyes, now filled with tears.

Yes ; Adrienne wept, for she now felt the reaction from the painful scenes through which she had passed at Saint-Dizier House ; to the feverish and nervous excitement, which had till then sustained her, had succeeded a sorrowful dejection. Resolute in her independence, proud in her disdain, implacable in her irony, audacious in her resistance to unjust oppression, Adrienne was yet endowed with the most acute sensibility, which she always dissembled, however, in the presence of her aunt and those who surrounded her.

Notwithstanding her courage, no one could have been less masculine, less of a virago, than Mdlle. de Cardoville. She was essentially womanly, but as a woman, she knew how to exercise great empire over herself, the moment that the least mark of weakness on her part would have rejoiced or emboldened her enemies.

The carriage had rolled onwards for some minutes ; but Adrienne, drying her tears in silence, to the doctor's great astonishment, had not yet uttered a word.

'What, my dear Mdlle. Adrienne?' said M. Baleinier, truly surprised at her emotion ; 'what ! you, that were just now so courageous, weeping?'

'Yes,' answered Adrienne, in an agitated voice ; 'I weep in presence of a friend ; but, before my aunt—oh ! never.'

'And yet, in that long interview, your stinging replies——'

'Ah me ! do you think that I resigned myself with pleasure to that war of sarcasm? Nothing is more painful to me than such combats of bitter irony, to which I am forced by the necessity of defending myself from this woman and her friends. You speak of my courage : it does not consist, I assure you, in the display of wicked feelings—but in the power to repress and hide all that I suffer, when I hear myself treated so grossly—in the presence too of people that I hate and despise—when, after all, I have never done them any harm, and have only asked to be allowed to live alone, freely and quietly, and see those about me happy.'

'That's where it is : they envy your happiness, and that which you bestow upon others.'

'And it is my aunt,' cried Adrienne, with indignation, 'my aunt, whose whole life has been one long scandal, that accuses me in this revolting manner !—as if she did not know me proud and honest enough never to make a choice of which I should be ashamed ! Oh ! if I ever love, I shall proclaim it, I shall be proud of it ; for love, as I understand it, is the most glorious feeling in the world. But, alas !' continued Adrienne, with redoubled bitterness, 'of what use are truth and honour, if they do not secure you from suspicions, which are as absurd as they are odious?' So saying, she again pressed her handkerchief to her eyes.

'Come, my dear Mdlle. Adrienne,' said M. Baleinier, in a voice full of the softest unction, ' be calm—it is all over now. You have in me a devoted friend.' As he pronounced these last words, he blushed in spite of his diabolical craft.

'I know you are my friend,' said Adrienne ; 'I shall never forget that, by taking my part to-day; you exposed yourself to the resentment of my aunt— for I am not ignorant of her power, which is very great, alas ! for evil.'

'As for that,' said the doctor, affecting a profound indifference, ' we medical men are pretty safe from personal enmities.'

'Nay, my dear M. Baleinier ! Mme. de Saint-Dizier and her friends never forgive,' said the young girl, with a shudder. ' It needed all my invincible aversion, my innate horror for all that is base, cowardly, and perfidious, to induce me to break so openly with her. But if death itself were the penalty, I could not hesitate ; and yet,' she added, with one of those graceful smiles which gave such a charm to her beautiful countenance, ' yet I am fond of life ; if I have to reproach myself with anything, it is that I would have it too bright, too fair, too harmonious ; but then, you know, I am resigned to my faults.'

'Well, come, I am more tranquil,' said the doctor, gaily ; 'for you smile —that is a good sign.'

'It is often the wisest course; and yet, ought I smile, after the threats that my aunt has held out to me? Still, what can she do? what is the meaning of this kind of family council? Did she seriously think that the advice of a M. d'Aigrigny or a M. Tripeaud could have influenced me? And then she talked of rigorous measures. What measures can she take; do you know?'

'I think, between ourselves, that the princess only wished to frighten you, and hopes to succeed by persuasion. She has the misfortune to fancy herself a mother of the Church, and dreams of your conversion,' said the doctor maliciously, for he now wished to tranquillise Adrienne at any cost; 'but let us think no more about it. Your fine eyes must shine with all their lustre, to fascinate the minister that we are going to see.'

'You are right, dear doctor; we ought always avoid grief, for it has the disadvantage of making us forget the sorrows of others. But here am I, availing myself of your kindness, without even telling you what I require.'

'Luckily, we shall have plenty of time to talk over it, for our statesman lives at some distance.'

'In two words, here's the mystery,' answered Adrienne. 'I told you what reasons I had to interest myself in that honest workman. This morning he came to me in great grief, to inform me that he was compromised by some songs he had written (for he is a poet), and that, though innocent, he was threatened with an arrest; and if they put him into prison, his family, whose sole support he is, would die of hunger. Therefore he came to beg me to procure bail for him, so that he might be left at liberty to work. I promised, immediately, thinking of your interest with the minister; for, as they were already in pursuit of the poor lad, I chose to conceal him in my residence, and you know how my aunt has twisted that action. Now tell me, do you think, that, by means of your recommendation, the minister will grant me the freedom of this workman, bail being given for the same?'

'No doubt of it. There will not be the shadow of a difficulty—especially when you have explained the facts to him, with that eloquence of the heart which you possess in perfection.'

'Do you know, my dear Dr. Baleinier, why I have taken the resolution (which is perhaps a strange one) to ask you to accompany me to the minister's?'

'Why, doubtless, to recommend your friend in a more effective manner.'

'Yes—but also to put an end, by a decisive step, to the calumnies which my aunt will be sure to spread with regard to me, and which she has already, you know, had inserted in the report of the commissary of police. I have preferred to address myself at once, frankly and openly, to a man placed in a high social position. I will explain all to him, who will believe me, because truth has an accent of its own.'

'All this, my dear Mdlle. Adrienne, is wisely planned. You will, as the saw says, kill two birds with one stone—or rather, you will obtain by one act of kindness two acts of justice; you will destroy a dangerous calumny, and restore a worthy youth to liberty.'

'Come,' said Adrienne, laughing, 'thanks to this pleasing prospect, my light heart has returned.'

'How true that in life,' said the doctor, philosophically, 'everything depends on the point of view.'

Adrienne was so completely ignorant of the forms of a constitutional government, and had so blind a confidence in the doctor, that she did not doubt for an instant what he told her. She therefore resumed with joy: 'What happiness it will be! when I go to fetch the daughters of Marshal

Simon, to be able to console this workman's mother, who is now perhaps in a state of cruel anxiety, at not seeing her son return home !'

' Yes, you will have this pleasure,' said M. Baleinier, with a smile ; ' for we will solicit and intrigue to such purpose, that the good mother may learn from you the release of her son before she even knows that he has been arrested.'

' How kind, how obliging you are !' said Adrienne. ' Really, if the motive were not so serious, I should be ashamed of making you lose so much precious time, my dear M. Baleinier. But I know your heart.'

' I have no other wish, than to prove to you my profound devotion, my sincere attachment,' said the doctor, inhaling a pinch of snuff. But at the same time, he cast an uneasy glance through the window, for the carriage was just crossing the Place de l'Odéon, and, in spite of the snow, he could see the front of the Odéon theatre brilliantly illuminated. Now Adrienne, who had just turned her head towards that side, might perhaps be astonished at the singular road they were taking.

In order to draw off her attention by a skilful diversion, the doctor exclaimed suddenly : ' Bless me ! I had almost forgotten.'

' What is the matter, M. Baleinier ?' said Adrienne, turning hastily towards him.

' I had forgotten a thing of the highest importance, in regard to the success of our petition.'

' What is it, please ?' asked the young girl, anxiously.

M. Baleinier gave a cunning smile. ' Every man,' said he, ' has his weakness—ministers even more than others. The one we are going to visit has the folly to attach the utmost importance to his title, and the first impression would be unfavourable, if you did not lay great stress on the *Minister.*'

' Is that all, my dear M. Baleinier ?' said Adrienne, smiling in her turn. ' I will even go as far as Your Excellency, which is, I believe, one of his adopted titles.'

' Not now—but that is no matter ; if you could even slide in a My Lord or two, our business would be done at once.'

' Be satisfied ! since there are upstart ministers as well as City-turned gentlemen, I will remember Molière's M. Jourdain, and feed full the gluttonous vanity of your friend.'

' I give him up to you, for I know he will be in good hands,' replied the physician, who rejoiced to see that the carriage had now entered those dark streets which lead from the Place de l'Odéon to the Pantheon district ; ' I do not wish to find fault with the minister for being proud, since his pride may be of service to us on this occasion.'

' These petty devices are innocent enough,' said Mdlle. de Cardoville, ' and I confess, that I do not scruple to have recourse to them.' Then, leaning towards the door-sash, she added : ' Gracious ! how sad and dark are these streets. What wind, what snow ! In which quarter are we ?'

' What ! are you so ungrateful, that you do not recognise, by the absence of shops, your dear quarter of the Faubourg Saint Germain ?'

' I imagined we had quitted it long ago.'

' I thought so too,' said the physician, leaning forward as if to ascertain where they were, ' but we are still there. My poor coachman, blinded by the snow, which is beating against his face, must have gone wrong just now —but we are all right again. Yes, I perceive we are in the Rue Saint Guillaume—not the gayest of streets by the way—but, in ten minutes, we shall arrive at the minister's private entrance, for intimate friends like myself enjoy the privilege of escaping the honours of a grand reception,'

Mdlle. de Cardoville, like most carriage-people, was so little acquainted with certain streets of Paris, as well as with the customs of men in office, that she did not doubt for a moment the statements of Baleinier, in whom she reposed the utmost confidence.

When they left the Saint-Dizier House, the doctor had upon his lips a question which he hesitated to put, for fear of endangering himself in the eyes of Adrienne. The latter had spoken of important interests, the existence of which had been concealed from her. The doctor, who was an acute and skilful observer, had quite clearly remarked the embarrassment and anxiety of the princess and D'Aigrigny. He no longer doubted, that the plot directed against Adrienne—one in which he was the blind agent, in submission to the will of the Order—related to interests which had been concealed from him, and which, for that very reason, he burned to discover; for every member of the dark conspiracy to which he belonged had necessarily acquired the odious vices inherent to spies and informers—envy, suspicion, and jealous curiosity.

It is easy to understand, therefore, that Dr. Baleinier, though quite determined to serve the projects of D'Aigrigny, was yet very anxious to learn what had been kept from him. Conquering his irresolution, and finding the opportunity favourable, and no time to be lost, he said to Adrienne, after a moment's silence : ' I am going perhaps to ask you a very indiscreet question. If you think it such, pray do not answer.'

' Nay—go on, I entreat you.'

' Just now—a few minutes before the arrival of the commissary of police was announced to your aunt—you spoke, I think, of some great interests, which had hitherto been concealed from you.'

' Yes, I did so.'

' These words,' continued M. Baleinier, speaking slowly and emphatically, ' appeared to make a deep impression on the princess.'

' An impression so deep,' said Adrienne, ' that sundry suspicions of mine were changed to certainty.'

' I need not tell you, my charming friend,' resumed M. Baleinier, in a bland tone, ' that if I remind you of this circumstance, it is only to offer you my services, in case they should be required. If not—and there is the shadow of impropriety in letting me know more—forget that I have said a word.'

Adrienne became serious and pensive, and, after a silence of some moments, she thus answered Dr. Baleinier : ' On this subject, there are some things that I do not know—others that I may tell you—others again that I must keep from you : but you are so kind to-day, that I am happy to be able to give you a new mark of confidence.'

' Then I wish to know nothing,' said the doctor, with an air of humble deprecation, ' for I should have the appearance of accepting a kind of reward ; whilst I am paid a thousand times over, by the pleasure I feel in serving you.'

' Listen,' said Adrienne, without attending to the delicate scruples of Dr. Baleinier ; ' I have powerful reasons for believing that an immense inheritance must, at no very distant period, be divided between the members of my family, all of whom I do not know—for, after the Revocation of the Edict of Nantes, those from whom we are descended were dispersed in foreign countries, and experienced a great variety of fortunes.'

' Really !' cried the doctor, becoming extremely interested. ' Where is this inheritance, in whose hands ?'

' I do not know.'

' Now how will you assert your rights ?'

' That I shall learn soon.'

' Who will inform you of it ?'

' That I may not tell you.'

' But how did you find out the existence of this inheritance ?'

' That also I may not tell you,' returned Adrienne, in a soft and melancholy tone, which remarkably contrasted with the habitual vivacity of her conversation. ' It is a secret—a strange secret—and in those moments of excitement, in which you have sometimes surprised me, I have been thinking of extraordinary circumstances connected with this secret, which awakened within me lofty and magnificent ideas.'

Adrienne paused and was silent, absorbed in her own reflections. Baleinier did not seek to disturb her. In the first place, Mdlle. de Cardoville did not perceive the direction the coach was taking ; secondly, the doctor was not sorry to ponder over what he had just heard. With his usual perspicuity, he saw that the Abbé d'Aigrigny was concerned in this inheritance, and he resolved instantly to make a secret report on the subject ; either M. d'Agrigny was acting under the instructions of the Order, or by his own impulse ; in the one event, the report of the doctor would confirm a fact ; in the other, it would reveal one.

For some time, therefore, the lady and Dr. Baleinier remained perfectly silent, no longer even disturbed by the noise of the wheels, for the carriage now rolled over a thick carpet of snow, and the streets had become more and more deserted. Notwithstanding his crafty treachery, notwithstanding his audacity and the blindness of his dupe, the doctor was not quite tranquil as to the result of his machinations. The critical moment approached, and the least suspicion roused in the mind of Adrienne by any inadvertence on his part, might ruin all his projects.

Adrienne, already fatigued by the painful emotions of the day, shuddered from time to time, as the cold became more and more piercing ; in her haste to accompany Dr. Baleinier, she had neglected to take either shawl or mantle.

For some minutes the coach had followed the line of a very high wall, which, seen through the snow, looked white against a black sky. The silence was deep and mournful. Suddenly the carriage stopped, and the footman went to knock at a large gateway ; he first gave two rapid knocks, and then one other at a long interval. Adrienne did not notice the circumstance, for the noise was not loud, and the doctor had immediately begun to speak, to drown with his voice this species of signal.

' Here we are at last,' said he gaily to Adrienne ; ' you must be very winning—that is, you must be yourself.'

' Be sure I will do my best,' replied Adrienne, with a smile ; then she added, shivering in spite of herself : ' How dreadfully cold it is ! I must confess, my dear Dr. Baleinier, that when I have been to fetch my poor little relations from the house of our workman's mother, I shall be truly glad to find myself once more in the warmth and light of my own cheerful rooms for you know my aversion to cold and darkness.'

' It is quite natural,' said the doctor, gallantly ; ' the most charming flowers require the most light and heat.'

Whilst the doctor and Mdlle. de Cardoville exchanged these few words, a heavy gate had turned creaking upon its hinges, and the carriage had entered a court-yard. The physician got down first, to offer his arm to Adrienne.

CHAPTER XLIV.

THE MINISTER'S CABINET.

THE carriage had stopped before some steps covered with snow, which led to a vestibule lighted by a lamp. The better to ascend the steps, which were somewhat slippery, Adrienne leaned upon the doctor's arm.

'Dear me! how you tremble,' said he.

'Yes,' replied she, shuddering, 'I feel deadly cold. In my haste, I came out without a shawl. But how gloomy this house appears!' she added, pointing to the entrance.

'It is what you call the minister's private house, the sanctum sanctorum, whither our statesman retires far from the sound of the profane,' said Dr. Baleinier, with a smile. 'Pray come in!' and he pushed open the door of a large hall, completely empty.

'They are right in saying,' resumed Dr. Baleinier, who covered his secret agitation with an appearance of gaiety, 'that a minister's house is like nobody else's. Not a footman—not a page, I should say—to be found in the ante-chamber. Luckily,' added he, opening the door of a room which communicated with the vestibule:

' " In this seraglio reared, I know the secret ways." '

Mdlle. de Cardoville was now introduced into an apartment hung with green embossed paper, and very simply furnished with mahogany chairs, covered with yellow velvet; the floor was carefully polished, and a globe lamp, which gave at most a third of its proper light, was suspended (at a much greater height than usual) from the ceiling. Finding the appearance of this habitation singularly plain for the dwelling of a minister, Adrienne, though she had no suspicion, could not suppress a movement of surprise and paused a moment on the threshold of the door. M. Baleinier, by whose arm she held, guessed the cause of her astonishment, and said to her with a smile:

'This place appears to you very paltry for "his excellency," does it not? If you knew what a thing constitutional economy is!—Moreover, you will see a "my lord," who has almost as little pretension as his furniture. But please to wait for me an instant. I will go and inform the minister you are here, and return immediately.'

Gently disengaging himself from the grasp of Adrienne, who had involuntarily pressed close to him, the physician opened a small side-door, by which he instantly disappeared. Adrienne de Cardoville was left alone.

Though she could not have explained the cause of her impression, there was something awe-inspiring to the young lady in this large, cold, naked, curtainless room; and as, by degrees, she noticed certain peculiarities in the furniture, which she had not at first perceived, she was seized with an indefinable feeling of uneasiness.

Approaching the cheerless hearth, she perceived with surprise that an iron grating completely enclosed the opening of the chimney, and that the tongs and shovel were fastened with iron chains. Already astonished by this singularity, she was about mechanically to draw towards her an armchair placed against the wall, when she found that it remained motionless. She then discovered that the back of this piece of furniture, as well as that of all the other chairs, was fastened to the wainscoting by iron clamps. Unable to repress a smile, she exclaimed: 'Have they so little confidence in the statesman in whose house I am, that they are obliged to fasten the furniture to the walls?'

Adrienne had recourse to this somewhat forced pleasantry, as a kind of effort to resist the painful feeling of apprehension that was gradually creeping over her ; for the most profound and mournful silence reigned in this habitation, where nothing indicated the life, the movement, and the activity, which usually surround a great centre of business.   Only, from time to time, the young lady heard the violent gusts of wind from without.

More than a quarter of an hour had elapsed, and M. Baleinier did not return.   In her impatient anxiety, Adrienne wished to call some one to inquire about the doctor and the minister.   She raised her eyes to look for a bell-rope by the side of the chimney-glass ; she found none, but she perceived, that what she had hitherto taken for a glass, thanks to the half obscurity of the room, was in reality a large sheet of shining tin.   Drawing nearer to it, she accidentally touched a bronzed candlestick ; and this, as well as a clock, was fixed to the marble of the chimney-piece.

In certain dispositions of mind, the most insignificant circumstances often assume terrific proportions.   This immovable candlestick, this furniture fastened to the wainscot, this glass replaced by a tin sheet, this profound silence, and the prolonged absence of M. Baleinier, had such an effect upon Adrienne, that she was struck with a vague terror.   Yet such was her implicit confidence in the doctor, that she reproached herself with her own fears, persuading herself that the causes of them were after all of no real importance, and that it was unreasonable to feel uneasy at such trifles.

Still, though she thus strove to regain courage, her anxiety induced her to do what otherwise she would never have attempted.   She approached the little door by which the doctor had disappeared, and applied her ear to it. She held her breath, and listened, but heard nothing.

Suddenly, a dull, heavy sound, like that of a falling body, was audible just above her head ; she thought she could even distinguish a stifled moaning. Raising her eyes, hastily, she saw some particles of the plaster fall from the ceiling, loosened, no doubt, by the shaking of the floor above.

No longer able to resist the feeling of terror, Adrienne ran to the door by which she had entered with the doctor, in order to call some one.   To her great surprise, she found it was fastened on the outside.   Yet, since her arrival, she had heard no sound of a key turning in the lock.

More and more alarmed, the young girl flew to the little door by which the physician had disappeared, and at which she had just been listening. This door also was fastened on the outside.

Still, wishing to struggle with the terror which was gaining invincibly upon her, Adrienne called to her aid all the firmness of her character, and tried to argue away her fears.

' I must have been deceived,' she said ; ' it was only a fall that I heard. The moaning had no existence, except in my imagination.   There are a thousand reasons for believing that it was not a person who fell down.   But, then, these locked doors ?   They, perhaps, do not know that I am here ; they may have thought that there was nobody in this room.'

As she uttered these words, Adrienne looked round with anxiety ; then she added, in a firm voice : ' No weakness ! it is useless to try to blind myself to my real situation.   On the contrary, I must look it well in the face.   It is evident that I am not here at a minister's house ; no end of reasons prove it beyond a doubt ; M. Baleinier has therefore deceived me.   But for what end ?   Why has he brought me hither ?   Where am I ?'

The last two questions appeared to Adrienne both equally insoluble.   It only remained clear, that she was the victim of M. Baleinier's perfidy.   But this certainly seemed so horrible to the young girl's truthful and generous soul, that she still tried to combat the idea by the recollection of the confiding friendship which she had always shown this man.   She said to herself with bitterness : 'See how weakness and fear may lead one to unjust and odious suspicions ! Yes ; for until the last extremity, it is not justifiable to believe in so infernal a deception—and then only upon the clearest evidence. I will call some one ; it is the only way of completely satisfying these doubts.' Then, remembering that there was no bell, she added : 'No matter ; I will knock, and some one will doubtless answer.' With her little, delicate hand, Adrienne struck the door several times.

The dull, heavy sound which came from the door showed that it was very thick. No answer was returned to the young girl. She ran to the other door. There was the same appeal on her part, the same profound silence without—only interrupted from time to time by the howling of the wind.

'I am not more timid than other people,' said Adrienne, shuddering ; 'I do not know if it is the excessive cold, but I tremble in spite of myself. I endeavour to guard against all weakness ; yet I think that any one in my position would find all this very strange and frightful.'

At this instant, loud cries, or rather savage and dreadful howlings, burst furiously from the room just above, and soon after a sort of stamping of feet, like the noise of a violent struggle, shook the ceiling of the apartment. Struck with consternation, Adrienne uttered a loud cry of terror, became deadly pale, stood for a moment motionless with affright, and then rushed to one of the windows, and abruptly threw it open.

A violent gust of wind, mixed with melted snow, beat against Adrienne's face, swept roughly into the room, and soon extinguished the flickering and smoky light of the lamp. Thus, plunged in profound darkness, with her hands clinging to the bars that were placed across the window, Mdlle. de Cardoville yielded at length to the full influence of her fears, so long restrained, and was about to call aloud for help, when an unexpected apparition rendered her for some minutes absolutely mute with terror.

Another wing of the building, opposite to that in which she was, stood at no great distance. Through the midst of the black darkness, which filled the space between, one large, lighted window was distinctly visible. Through the curtainless panes, Adrienne perceived a white figure, gaunt and ghastly, dragging after it a sort of shroud, and passing and repassing continually before the window, with an abrupt and restless motion. Her eyes fixed upon this window, shining through the darkness, Adrienne remained as if fascinated by that fatal vision : and, as the spectacle filled up the measure of her fears, she called for help with all her might, without quitting the bars of the window to which she clung. After a few seconds, whilst she was thus crying out, two tall women entered the room in silence, unperceived by Mdlle. de Cardoville, who was still clinging to the window.

These women, of about forty to fifty years of age, robust and masculine, were negligently and shabbily dressed, like chambermaids of the lower sort ; over their clothes they wore large aprons of blue cotton, cut sloping from their necks, and reaching down to their feet. One of them, who held a lamp in her hand, had a broad, red, shining face, a large pimpled nose, small green eyes, and tow hair, which straggled rough and shaggy from beneath her dirty white cap. The other, sallow, withered, and bony, wore a mourning-cap over a parchment visage, pitted with the small-pox, and rendered still more repulsive by thick black eyebrows, and some long grey hairs that overshadowed the upper lip. This woman carried, half unfolded in her hand, a garment of strange form, made of thick grey stuff.

They both entered silently by the little door, at the moment when Adrienne, in the excess of her terror, was grasping the bars of the window, and crying out : 'Help ! help !'

Pointing out the young lady to each other, one of them went to place the lamp on the chimney-piece, whilst the other (she who wore the mourning-cap) approached the window, and laid her great bony hand upon Mdlle. de Cardoville's shoulder.

Turning round, Adrienne uttered a new cry of terror at the sight of this grim figure. Then, the first moment of stupor over, she began to feel less afraid ; hideous as was this woman, it was at least some one to speak to ; she exclaimed, therefore, in an agitated voice : 'Where is M. Baleinier?'

The two women looked at each other, exchanged a leer of mutual intelligence, but did not answer.

'I ask you, madame,' resumed Adrienne, 'where is M. Baleinier, who brought me hither ? I wish to see him instantly.'

'He is gone,' said the big woman.

'Gone !' cried Adrienne ; 'gone without me !—Gracious heaven ! what can be the meaning of all this?' Then, after a moment's reflection, she resumed : 'Please to fetch me a coach.'

The two women looked at each other, and shrugged their shoulders. 'I entreat you, madame,' continued Adrienne, with forced calmness in her voice, 'to fetch me a coach--since M. Baleinier is gone without me. I wish to leave this place.'

'Come, come, madame,' said the tall woman, who was called 'Tomboy,' without appearing to listen to what Adrienne asked, 'it is time for you to go to bed.'

'To go to bed !' cried Mdlle. Cardoville, in alarm. 'This is really enough to drive one mad.' Then, addressing the two women, she added : 'What is this house? where am I ? answer !'

'You are in a house,' said Tomboy, in a rough voice, 'where you must not make a row from the window, as you did just now.'

'And where you must not put out the lamp as you have done,' added the other woman, who was called Gervaise, 'or else we shall have a crow to pick with you.'

Adrienne, unable to utter a word, and trembling with fear, looked in a kind of stupor from one to the other of these horrible women ; her reason strove in vain to comprehend what was passing around her. Suddenly she thought she had guessed it, and exclaimed : 'I see there is a mistake here. I do not understand how, but there is a mistake. You take me for some one else. Do you know who I am? My name is Adrienne de Cardoville ! You see, therefore, that I am at liberty to leave this house ; no one in the world has the right to detain me. I command you, then, to fetch me a coach immediately. If there are none in this quarter, let me have some one to accompany me home to the Rue de Babylone, Saint-Dizier House. I will reward such a person liberally, and you also.'

'Well, have you finished?' said Tomboy. 'What is the use of telling us all this rubbish?'

'Take care,' resumed Adrienne, who wished to try every means ; 'if you detain me here by force, it will be very serious. You do not know to what you expose yourselves.'

'Will you come to bed ; yes or no?' said Gervaise, in a tone of harsh impatience.

'Listen to me, madame,' resumed Adrienne, precipitately ; let me out of this place, and I will give each of you two thousand francs. Is it not enough? I will give you ten—twenty—whatever you ask. I am rich—only let me out —for heaven's sake, let me out !—I cannot remain here—I am afraid.' As she said this, the tone of the poor girl's voice was heart-rending.

'Twenty thousand francs !—that's the usual figure, ain't it, Tommy ?'

'Let be, Gervaise ! they all sing the same song.'

'Well, then! since reasons, prayers, and menaces are all in vain,' said Adrienne, gathering energy from her desperate position, 'I declare to you that I will go out, and that instantly. We will see if you are bold enough to employ force against me.'

So saying, Adrienne advanced resolutely towards the door. But, at this moment, the wild, hoarse cries, which had preceded the noise of the struggle that had so frightened her, again resounded; only, this time, they were not accompanied by the movement of feet.

'Oh! what screams!' said Adrienne, stopping short, and in her terror drawing nigh to the two women. 'Do you not hear those cries? What, then, is this house, in which one hears such things? And over there, too,' added she, almost beside herself, as she pointed to the other wing, where the lighted window shone through the darkness, and the white figure continued to pass and repass before it; 'over there! do you see? What is it?'

'Oh! that 'un,' said Tomboy; 'one of the folks who, like you, have not behaved well.'

'What do you say?' cried Mdlle. de Cardoville, clasping her hands in terror. 'Heavens! what is this house? What do they do to them?'

'What will be done to you, if you are naughty, and refuse to come to bed,' answered Gervaise.

'They put this on them,' said Tomboy, showing the garment that she had held under her arm, 'they clap 'em into the strait-waistcoat.'

'Oh!' cried Adrienne, hiding her hands in her face with horror. A terrible discovery had flashed suddenly upon her. She understood it all.

Capping the violent emotions of the day, the effect of this last blow was dreadful. The young girl felt her strength give way. Her hands fell powerless, her face became fearfully pale, all her limbs trembled, and sinking upon her knees, and casting a terrified·glance at the strait-waistcoat, she was just able to falter in a feeble voice, 'Oh, no :—not that—for pity's sake, madame. I will do—whatever you wish.' And, her strength quite failing, she would have fallen upon the ground if the two women had not run towards her, and received her fainting into their arms.

'A fainting fit,' said Tomboy; 'that's not dangerous. Let us carry her to bed. We can undress her, and this will be all nothing.'

'Carry her, then,' said Gervaise. 'I will take the lamp.'

The tall and robust Tomboy took up Mdlle. de Cardoville as if she had been a sleeping child, carried her in her arms, and followed her companion into the chamber through which M. Baleinier had made his exit.

This chamber, though perfectly clean, was cold and bare. A greenish paper covered the walls, and a low, little iron bedstead, the head of which formed a kind of shelf, stood in one corner; a stove, fixed in the chimney-place, was surrounded by an iron grating, which forbade a near approach; a table fastened to the wall, a chair placed before this table, and also clamped to the floor, a mahogany chest of drawers, and a rush-bottomed arm-chair completed the scanty furniture. The curtainless window was furnished on the inside with an iron grating, which served to protect the panes from being broken.

It was into this gloomy retreat, which formed so painful a contrast with the charming little summer-house in the Rue de Babylone, that Adrienne was carried by Tomboy, who, with the assistance of Gervaise, placed the inanimate form on the bed. The lamp was deposited on the shelf at the head of the couch. Whilst one of the nurses held her up, the other unfastened and took off the cloth dress of the young girl, whose head drooped languidly on her bosom. Though in a swoon, large tears trickled slowly from her closed eyes, whose long black lashes threw their shadows on the transparent whiteness of her cheeks. Over her neck and breast of ivory flowed the golden waves of her magnificent hair, which had come down at the time of her fall. When, as they unlaced her satin corset, less soft, less fresh, less white than the virgin form beneath, which lay like a statue of ala-baster in its covering of lace and lawn, one of the horrible hags felt the arms and shoulders of the young girl with her large, red, horny, and chapped hands. Though she did not completely recover the use of her senses, she started involuntarily from the rude and brutal touch.

'Hasn't she little feet?' said the nurse, who, kneeling down, was employed in drawing off Adrienne's stockings. 'I could hold them both in the hollow of my hand.' In fact, a small, rosy foot, smooth as a child's, here and there veined with azure, was soon exposed to view, as was also a leg with pink knee and ankle, of as pure and exquisite a form as that of Diana Huntress.

'And what hair!' said Tomboy; 'so long and soft!—She might almost walk upon it. 'Twould be a pity to cut it off, to put ice upon her skull!' As she spoke, she gathered up Adrienne's magnificent hair, and twisted it as well as she could behind her head. Alas! it was no longer the fair, light hand of Georgette, Florine, or Hebe that arranged the beauteous locks of their mistress with so much love and pride!

And as she again felt the rude touch of the nurse's hand, the young girl was once more seized with the same nervous trembling, only more frequently and strongly than before. And soon, whether by a sort of instinctive repul-sion, magnetically excited during her swoon, or from the effect of the cold night air, Adrienne again started and slowly came to herself.

It is impossible to describe her alarm, horror, and chaste indignation, as, thrusting aside with both her hands the numerous curls that covered her face, bathed in tears, she saw herself half-naked between these filthy hags. At first, she uttered a cry of shame and terror ; then, to escape from the looks of the women, by a movement, rapid as thought, she threw down the lamp placed on the shelf at the head of her bed, so that it was extinguished and broken to pieces on the floor. After which, in the midst of the darkness, the unfortunate girl, covering herself with the bed-clothes, burst into pas-sionate sobs.

The nurses attributed Adrienne's cry and violent action to a fit of furious madness. 'Oh! you begin again to break the lamps—that's your partickler fancy, is it?' cried Tomboy, angrily, as she felt her way in the dark. 'Well! I gave you fair warning. You shall have the strait-waistcoat on this very night, like the mad gal upstairs.'

'That's it,' said the other ; 'hold her fast, Tommy, while I go and fetch a light. Between us, we'll soon master her.'

'Make haste, for, in spite of her soft look, she must be a regular fury. We shall have to sit up all night with her, I suppose.'

　　　※　　　　　　※　　　　　　※　　　　　　※　　　　　　※　　　　　　※

Sad and painful contrast! That morning, Adrienne had risen free, smiling, happy, in the midst of all the wonders of luxury and art, and surrounded by the delicate attentions of the three charming girls whom she had chosen to serve her. In her generous and fantastic mood, she had prepared a magni-ficent and fairy-like surprise for the young Indian prince, her relation ; she had also taken a noble resolution with regard to the two orphans brought home by Dagobert ; in her interview with Mme. de Saint-Dizier, she had shown herself by turns proud and sensitive, melancholy and gay, ironical and serious, loyal and courageous ; finally, she had come to this accursed house to plead in favour of an honest and laborious artisan.

And now, in the evening—delivered over by an atrocious piece of treachery to the ignoble hands of two coarse-minded nurses in a madhouse—Mdlle. de

Cardoville felt her delicate limbs imprisoned in that abominable garment, which is called a strait-waistcoat.

☼   ☼   ☼   ☼   ☼   ☼

Mdlle. de Cardoville passed a horrible night in company with the two hags. The next morning, at nine o'clock, what was the young lady's stupor to see Dr. Baleinier enter the room, still smiling with an air at once benevolent and paternal.

' Well, my dear child !' said he, in a bland, affectionate voice ; ' how have we spent the night ?'

———

CHAPTER XLV.

THE VISIT.

THE keepers, yielding to Mdlle. de Cardoville's prayers, and, above all, to her promises of good behaviour, had only left on the canvas jacket a portion of the time. Towards morning, they had allowed her to rise and dress herself, without interfering.

Adrienne was seated on the edge of her bed. The alteration in her features, her dreadful paleness, the lurid fire of fever shining in her eyes, the convulsive trembling which ever and anon shook her frame, showed already the fatal effects of this terrible night upon a susceptible and high-strung organisation. At sight of Dr. Baleinier, who, with a sign, made Gervaise and her mate leave the room, Adrienne remained petrified.

She felt a kind of giddiness at the thought of the audacity of the man, who dared to present himself to her ! But when the physician repeated, in the softest tone of affectionate interest : ' Well, my poor child ! how have we spent the night ?' she pressed her hands to her burning forehead, as if in doubt whether she was awake or sleeping. Then, staring at the doctor, she half opened her lips ; but they trembled so much that it was impossible for her to utter a word. Anger, indignation, contempt, and, above all, the bitter and acutely painful feeling of a generous heart, whose confidence has been basely betrayed, so overpowered Adrienne that she was unable to break the silence.

' Come, come ! I see how it is,' said the doctor, shaking his head sorrowfully ; ' you are very much displeased with me—is it not so ? Well ! I expected it, my dear child.'

These words, pronounced with the most hypocritical effrontery, made Adrienne start up. Her pale cheek flushed, her large eyes sparkled, she lifted proudly her beautiful head, whilst her upper lip curled slightly with a smile of disdainful bitterness ; then, passing in angry silence before M. Baleinier, who retained his seat, she directed her swift and firm steps towards the door. This door, in which was a little wicket, was fastened on the outside. Adrienne turned towards the doctor, and said to him, with an imperious gesture : ' Open that door for me !'

' Come, my dear Mdlle. Adrienne,' said the physician, ' be calm. Let us talk like good friends—for you know I am your friend.' And he inhaled slowly a pinch of snuff.

' It appears, sir,' said Adrienne, in a voice trembling with indignation, ' I am not to leave this place to-day ?'

' Alas ! no. In such a state of excitement—if you knew how inflamed your face is, and your eyes so feverish, your pulse must be at least eighty to the minute—I conjure you, my dear child, not to aggravate your symptoms by this fatal agitation.'

After looking fixedly at the doctor, Adrienne returned with a slow step, and again took her seat on the edge of the bed. 'That is right,' resumed M. Baleinier; 'only be reasonable; and, as I said before, let us talk together like good friends.'

'You say well, sir,' replied Adrienne, in a collected and perfectly calm voice; 'let us talk like friends. You wish to make me pass for mad—is it not so?'

'I wish, my dear child, that one day you may feel towards me as much gratitude as you now do aversion. The latter I had fully foreseen—but, however painful may be the performance of certain duties, we must resign ourselves to it.'

M. Baleinier sighed, as he said this, with such a natural air of conviction, that for a moment Adrienne could not repress a movement of surprise; then, while her lip curled with a bitter laugh, she answered: 'Oh, it's very clear, you have done all this for my good?'

'Really, my dear young lady—have I ever had any design than to be useful to you?'

'I do not know, sir, if your impudence be not still more odious than your cowardly treachery!'

'Treachery!' said M. Baleinier, shrugging his shoulders with a grieved air; 'treachery, indeed! Only reflect, my poor child—do you think, if I were not acting with good faith, conscientiously, in your interest, I should return this morning to meet your indignation, for which I was fully prepared? I am the head physician of this asylum, which belongs to me—but I have two of my pupils here, doctors, like myself—and might have left them to take care of you—but, no—I could not consent to it—I knew your character, your nature, your previous history, and (leaving out of the question the interest I feel for you) I can treat your case better than any one.'

Adrienne had heard M. Baleinier without interrupting him; she now looked at him fixedly, and said: 'Pray, sir, how much do they pay you to make me pass for mad?'

'Madame!' cried M. Baleinier, who felt stung in spite of himself.

'You know I am rich,' continued Adrienne, with overwhelming disdain; 'I will double the sum that they give you. Come, sir—in the name of friendship, as you call it—let me have the pleasure of outbidding them.'

'Your keepers,' said M. Baleinier, recovering all his coolness, 'have informed me, in their report of the night's proceedings, that you made similar propositions to them.'

'Pardon me, sir; I offered them what might be acceptable to poor women, without education, whom misfortune has forced to undertake a painful employment—but to you, sir—a man of the world, a man of science, a man of great abilities—that is quite different—the pay must be a great deal higher. There is treachery at all prices; so do not found your refusal on the smallness of my offer to those wretched women. Tell me—how much do you want?'

'Your keepers, in their report of the night, have also spoken of threats,' resumed M. Baleinier, with the same coolness; 'have you any of those likewise to address me? Believe me, my poor child, you will do well to exhaust at once your attempts at corruption, and your vain threats of vengeance. We shall then come to the true state of the case.'

'So you deem my threats vain!' cried Mdlle. de Cardoville, at length giving way to the full tide of her indignation, till then restrained. 'Do you think, sir, that when I leave this place—for this outrage must have an end —that I will not proclaim aloud your infamous treachery? Do you think that I will not denounce to the contempt and horror of all, your base conspiracy with Madame de Saint-Dizier? Oh! do you think that I will conceal the frightful treatment I have received! But, mad as I may be, I know that there are laws in this country, by which I will demand a full reparation for myself, and shame, disgrace, and punishment, for you, and for those who have employed you ! Henceforth, between you and me will be hate and war to the death ; and all my strength, all my intelligence——'

'Permit me to interrupt you, my dear Mdlle. Adrienne,' said the doctor, still perfectly calm and affectionate ; 'nothing can be more unfavourable to your cure, than to cherish idle hopes : they will only tend to keep up a state of deplorable excitement : it is best to put the facts fairly before you, that you may understand clearly your position. 1. It is impossible for you to leave this house. 2. You can have no communication with any one beyond its walls. 3. No one enters here that I cannot perfectly depend upon. 4. I am completely indifferent to your threats of vengeance, because law and reason are both in my favour.'

' What ! have you the right to shut me up here ?

' We should never have come to that determination, without a number of reasons of the most serious kind.'

' Oh ! there are reasons for it, it seems.'

' Unfortunately, too many.'

' You will perhaps inform me of them ?'

'Alas ! they are only too conclusive ; and if you should ever apply to the protection of the laws, as you threatened me just now, we should be obliged to state them. The fantastical eccentricity of your manner of living, your whimsical mode of dressing up your maids, your extravagant expenditure, the story of the Indian prince, to whom you offered a royal hospitality, your unprecedented resolution of going to live by yourself, like a young bachelor, the adventure of the man found concealed in your bed-chamber ; finally, the report of your yesterday's conversation, which was faithfully taken down in shorthand, by a person employed for that surprise.'

' Yesterday ?' cried Adrienne, with as much indignation as surprise.

' Oh, yes ! to be prepared for every event, in case you should misinterpret the interest we take in you, we had all your answers reported by a man who was conce iled behind a curtain in the next room ; and really, one day, in a calmer state of mind, when you come to read over quietly the particulars of what took place, you will no longer be astonished at the resolution we have been forced to adopt.'

' Go on, sir,' said Adrienne, with contempt.

' The facts I have cited being thus confirmed and acknowledged, you will understand, my dear Mdlle. Adrienne, that your friends are perfectly free from responsibility. It was their duty to endeavour to cure this derange-ment of mind, which at present only shows itself in idle whims, but which, were it to increase, might seriously compromise the happiness of your future life. Now, in my opinion, we may hope to see a radical cure, by means of a treatment at once physical and moral ; but the first condition of this attempt was to remove you from the scenes which so dangerously ex-cited your imagination ; whilst a calm retreat, the repose of a simple and solitary life, combined with my anxious, I may say, paternal care, will gradually bring about a complete recovery——'

' So, sir,' said Adrienne, with a bitter laugh, 'the love of a noble indepen-dence, generosity, the worship of the beautiful, detestation of what is base and odious, such are the maladies of which you wish to cure me ; I fear that my case is desperate, for my aunt has long ago tried to effect that benevolent purpose.'

' Well, we may perhaps not succeed ; but at least we will attempt it.' You see then, there is a mass of serious facts, quite enough to justify the determination come to by the family-council, which puts' me completely at my ease with regard to your menaces. It is to that I wish to return: a man of my age and condition never acts lightly in such circumstances, and you can readily understand what I was saying to you just now. In a word, do not hope to leave this place before your complete recovery, and rest assured, that I am and shall ever be safe from your resentment. This being once admitted, let us talk of your actual state with all the interest that you naturally inspire.'

'I think, sir, that, considering I am mad, you speak to me very reasonably.'

'Mad! no, thank heaven, my poor child, you are not mad yet—and I hope that, by my care, you will never be so. It is to prevent your becoming mad, that one must take it in time; and believe me, it is full time. You look at me with such an air of surprise—now tell me, what interest can I have in talking to you thus? Is it the hatred of your aunt that I wish to favour? To what end, I would ask? What can she do for me or against me? I think of her at this moment neither more nor less than I thought yesterday. Is it a new language that I hold to yourself? Did I not speak to you yesterday many times, of the dangerous excitement of mind in which you were, and of your singular whims and fancies? It is true, I made use of stratagem to bring you hither. No doubt, I did so. I hastened to avail myself of the opportunity, which you yourself offered, my poor, dear child; for you would never have come hither with your own good will. One day or the other, we must have found some pretext to get you here; and I said to myself; "Her interest before all! Do your duty, let whatever will betide!"——'

Whilst M. Baleinier was speaking, Adrienne's countenance, which had hitherto expressed alternately indignation and disdain, assumed an indefinable look of anguish and horror. On hearing this man talk in such a natural manner, and with such an appearance of sincerity, justice, and reason, she felt herself more alarmed than ever. An atrocious deception, clothed in such forms, frightened her a hundred times more than the avowed hatred of Madame de Saint-Dizier. This audacious hypocrisy seemed to her so monstrous, that she almost believed it impossible.

Adrienne had so little the art of hiding her emotions, that the doctor, a skilful and profound physiognomist, instantly perceived the impression he had produced. 'Come,' said he to himself, 'that is a great step. Fright has succeeded to disdain and anger. Doubt will come next. I shall not leave this place, till she has said to me: "Return soon, my good M. Baleinier!"' With a voice of sorrowful emotion, which seemed to come from the very depths of his heart, the doctor thus continued: 'I see, you are still suspicious of me. All I can say to you is falsehood, fraud, hypocrisy, hate—is it not so?—*Hate* you? why, in heaven's name, should I hate you? What have you done to me? or rather—you will perhaps attach more value to this reason from a man of my sort,' added M. Baleinier, bitterly, 'or rather, what interest have I to hate you?—You, that have only been reduced to the state in which you are by an over-abundance of the most generous instincts—you, that are suffering, as it were, from an excess of good qualities—you can bring yourself coolly and deliberately to accuse an honest man, who has never given you any but marks of affection, of the basest, the blackest, the most abominable crime, of ich a human being could be guilty. Yes, I call it a crime; because the atrocious deception of which you accuse me would not deserve any other name. Really, my poor child, it is hard—very hard—and I now see, that an independent spirit may sometimes exhibit as much injustice and intolerance as the most narrow mind. It does not incense me—no—it only pains me: yes, I assure you—it pains me cruelly.' And the doctor drew his hand across his moist eyes.

It is impossible to give the accent, the look, the gesture of M. Baleinier, as he thus expressed himself. The most able and practised lawyer, or the greatest actor in the world, could not have played this scene with more effect than the doctor—or rather, no one could have played it so well—for M. Baleinier, carried away by the influence of the situation, was himself half convinced of what he said.

In few words, he felt all the horror of his own perfidy ; but he felt also that Adrienne could not believe it ; for there are combinations of such nefarious character, that pure and upright minds are unable to comprehend them as possible. If a lofty spirit looks down into the abyss of evil, beyond a certain depth, it is seized with giddiness, and no longer able to distinguish one object from the other.

And then the most perverse of men have a day, an hour, a moment, in which the good instincts, planted in the heart of every creature, appear in spite of themselves. Adrienne was too interesting, was in too cruel a position, for the doctor not to feel some pity for her in his heart ; the tone of sympathy, which for some time past he had been obliged to assume towards her, and the sweet confidence of the young girl in return, had become for this man habitual and necessary gratifications. But sympathy and habit were now to yield to implacable necessity.

Thus the Marquis d'Aigrigny had idolised his mother ; dying, she called him to her—and he turned away from the last prayer of a parent in the agony of death. After such an example, how could M. Baleinier hesitate to sacrifice Adrienne? The members of the Order, of which he formed a part, were bound to him—but he was perhaps still more strongly bound to them, for a long partnership in evil creates terrible and indissoluble ties.

The moment M. Baleinier finished his fervid address to Mdlle. de Cardoville, the slide of the wicket in the door was softly pushed back, and a pair of eyes peered attentively into the chamber, unperceived by the doctor.

Adrienne could not withdraw her gaze from the physician's, which seemed to fascinate her. Mute, overpowered, seized with a vague terror, unable to penetrate the dark depths of this man's soul, moved in spite of herself by the accent of sorrow, half feigned and half real—the young lady had a momentary feeling of doubt. For the first time, it came into her mind, that M. Baleinier might perhaps be committing a frightful error—committing it in good faith.

Besides, the anguish of the past night, the dangers of her position, her feverish agitation, all concurred to fill her mind with trouble and indecision. She looked at the physician with ever increasing surprise, and making a violent effort not to yield to a weakness, of which she partly foresaw the dreadful consequences, she exclaimed : ' No, no, sir ; I will not, I cannot believe it. You have too much skill, too much experience, to commit such an error.'

' An error !' said M. Baleinier, in a grave and sorrowful tone. ' Let me speak to you in the name of that skill and experience, which you are pleased to ascribe to me. Hear me but for a moment, my dear child ; and then I will appeal to yourself.'

' To me !' replied the young girl, in a kind of stupor ; ' you wish to persuade me, that——' Then, interrupting herself, she added, with a convulsive laugh : ' This only is wanting to your triumph—to bring me to confess that I am mad—that my proper place is here—that I owe you——'

' Gratitude. Yes, you do owe it me, even as I told you at the commencement of this conversation. Listen to me then : my words may be cruel, but there are wounds which can only be cured with steel and fire. I conjure you, my dear child—reflect—throw back one impartial glance at your past life—weigh your own thoughts—and you will be afraid of yourself. Remember those moments of strange excitement, during which, as you have told me, you seemed to soar above the earth—and, above all, while it is yet time—while you preserve enough clearness of mind to compare and judge—compare, I entreat, your manner of living with that of other ladies of your age? Is there a single one who acts as you act? who thinks as you think? unless, indeed, you imagine yourself so superior to other women, that, in virtue of that supremacy, you can justify a life and habits that have no parallel in the world.'

'I have never had such stupid pride, you know it well,' said Adrienne, looking at the doctor with growing terror.

'Then, my dear child, to what are we to attribute your strange and inexplicable mode of life? Can you even persuade yourself that it is founded on reason? Oh, my child! take care!—As yet, you only indulge in charming originalities of conduct, poetical eccentricities, sweet and vague reveries—but the tendency is fatal, the downward course irresistible. Take care, take care!—The healthful, graceful, spiritual portion of your intelligence has yet the upper hand, and imprints its stamp upon all your extravagances; but you do not know, believe me, with what frightful force the insane portion of the mind, at a given moment, develops itself and strangles up the rest. Then we have no longer graceful eccentricities, like yours; but ridiculous, sordid, hideous delusions.'

'Oh! you frighten me,' said the unfortunate girl, as she passed her trembling hands across her burning brow.

'Then,' continued M. Baleinier, in an agitated voice, 'then the last rays of intelligence are extinguished; then madness—for we must pronounce the dreaded word—gets the upper hand, and displays itself in furious and savage transports.'

'Like the woman upstairs,' murmured Adrienne, as, with fixed and eager look, she raised her finger towards the ceiling.

'Sometimes,' continued the doctor, alarmed himself at the terrible consequences of his own words, but yielding to the inexorable fatality of his situation, 'sometimes madness takes a stupid and brutal form; the unfortunate creature, who is attacked by it, preserves nothing human but the shape—has only the instincts of the lower animals—eats with voracity, and moves ever backwards and forwards in the cell, in which such a being is obliged to be confined. That is all its life—all.'

'Like the woman yonder,' cried Adrienne, with a still wilder look, as she slowly raised her arm towards the window that was visible on the other side of the building.

'Why—yes,' said M. Baleinier. 'Like you, unhappy child, those women were young, fair, and sensible, but like you, alas! they had in them the fatal germ of insanity, which, not having been destroyed in time, grew, and grew, larger and ever larger, until it overspread and destroyed their reason.'

'Oh, mercy!' cried Mdlle. de Cardoville, whose head was getting confused with terror; 'mercy! do not tell me such things!—I am afraid. Take me from this place—oh! take me from this place!' she added, with a heart-rending accent; 'for, if I remain here, I shall end by going mad! No,' added she, struggling with the terrible agony which assailed her, 'no, do not hope it! I shall not become mad. I have all my reason. I am not blind enough to believe what you tell me. Doubtless, I live differently from others: think differently from others; am shocked by things that do not offend others; but what does all this prove? Only that I am different from others. Have I a bad heart? Am I envious or selfish? My ideas are singular, I know—yes, I confess it—but then, M. Baleinier, is not their tendency good, generous, noble!—Oh!' cried Adrienne's supplicating voice, while her tears flowed abundantly, 'I have never in my life done one malicious action ; my worst errors have arisen from excess of generosity. Is it madness to wish to see everybody about one too happy? And again, if you are mad, you must feel it yourself—and I do not feel it—and yet—I scarcely know—you tell me such terrible things of those two women ! You ought to know these things better than I. But then,' added Mdlle. de Cardoville, with an accent of the deepest despair, ' something ought to have been done. Why, if you felt an interest for me, did you wait so long ? Why did you not take pity on me sooner ? But the most frightful fact is, that I do not know whether I ought to believe you—for all this may be a snare—but no, no ! you weep—it is true, then !—you weep !' She looked anxiously at M. Baleinier, who, notwithstanding his cynical philosophy, could not restrain his tears at the sight of these nameless tortures.

' You weep over me,' she continued ; ' so it is true ! But (good heaven !) must there not be something done ? I will do all that you wish—all—so that I may not be like those women. But if it should be too late ? no, it is not too late—say it is not too late, my good M. Baleinier ! Oh, now I ask your pardon for what I said when you came in—but then I did not know, you see—I did not know !'

To these few broken words, interrupted by sobs, and rushing forth in a sort of feverish excitement, succeeded a silence of some minutes, during which the deeply affected physician dried his tears. His resolution had almost failed him. Adrienne hid her face in her hands. Suddenly she again lifted her head ; her countenance was calmer than before, though agitated by a nervous trembling.

' M. Baleinier,' she resumed, with touching dignity, ' I hardly know what I said to you just now. Terror, I think, made me wander; I have again collected myself. Hear me ! I know that I am in your power ; I know that nothing can deliver me from it. Are you an implacable enemy ? or are you a friend ? I am not able to determine. Do you really apprehend, as you assure me, that what is now eccentricity will hereafter become madness—or are you rather the accomplice in some infernal machination ? You alone can answer. In spite of my boasted courage, I confess myself conquered. Whatever is required of me—you understand, whatever it may be, I will subscribe to, I give you my word, and you know that I hold it sacred—you have therefore no longer any interest to keep me here. If, on the contrary, you really think my reason in danger—and I own that you have awakened in my mind vague, but frightful doubts—tell it me, and I will believe you. I am alone, at your mercy, without friends, without counsel. I trust myself blindly to you. I know not whether I address myself to a deliverer or a destroyer—but I say to you—here is my happiness—here is my life—take it—I have no strength to dispute it with you !'

These touching words, full of mournful resignation and almost hopeless reliance, gave the finishing stroke to the indecision of M. Baleinier. Already deeply moved by this scene, and without reflecting on the consequences of what he was about to do, he determined at all events to dissipate the terrible and unjust fears with which he had inspired Adrienne. Sentiments of remorse and pity, which now animated the physician, were visible in his countenance.

Alas ! they were too visible. The moment he approached to take the hand of Mdlle. de Cardoville, a low but sharp voice exclaimed from behind the wicket : ' M. Baleinier !'

' Rodin !' muttered the startled doctor to himself ; ' he's been spying me !'

' Who calls you ?' asked the lady of the physician.

' A person that I promised to meet here this morning,' replied he, with the utmost depression, ' to go with him to St. Mary's Convent, which is close at hand.'

'And what answer have you to give me?' said Adrienne, with mortal anguish.

After a moment's solemn silence, during which he turned his face towards the wicket, the doctor replied, in a voice of deep emotion : ' I am—what I have always been—a friend incapable of deceiving you.'

Adrienne became deadly pale. Then, extending her hand to M. Baleinier, she said to him in a voice that she endeavoured to render calm : ' Thank you—I will have courage—but will it be very long ?'

' Perhaps a month. Solitude, reflection, a proper regimen, my attentive care, may do much. You will be allowed everything that is compatible with your situation. Every attention will be paid you. If this room displeases you, I will see you have another.'

' No—this or another—it is of little consequence,' answered Adrienne, with an air of the deepest dejection.

' Come, come ! be of good courage. There is no reason to despair.'

' Perhaps you flatter me,' said Adrienne, with the shadow of a smile. ' Return soon,' she added, ' my dear M. Baleinier ! my only hope rests in you now.'

Her head fell upon her bosom, her hands upon her knees, and she remained sitting on the edge of the bed, pale, motionless, overwhelmed with woe.

' Mad !' she said, when M. Baleinier had disappeared. ' Perhaps mad !'

We have enlarged upon this episode, much less romantic than it may appear. Many times have motives of interest or vengeance, or perfidious machination, led to the abuse of the imprudent facility with which inmates are received in certain private lunatic asylums, from the hands of their families or friends.

We shall subsequently explain our views, as to the establishment of a system of inspection, by the crown or the civil magistrates, for the periodical survey of these institutions, and others of no less importance, at present placed beyond the reach of all superintendence. These latter are the nunneries of which we will presently have an example.

CHAPTER XLVI.

PRESENTIMENTS.

WHILST the preceding events took place in Dr. Baleinier's asylum, other scenes were passing about the same hour, at Frances Baudoin's, in the Rue Brise-Miche.

Seven o'clock in the morning had just struck at St. Méry church ; the day was dark and gloomy, and the sleet rattled against the windows of the joyless chamber of Dagobert's wife.

As yet ignorant of her son's arrest, Frances had waited for him the whole of the preceding evening, and a good part of the night, with the most anxious uneasiness ; yielding at length to fatigue and sleep, about three o'clock in the morning, she had thrown herself on a mattress beside the bed of Rose and Blanche. But she rose with the first dawn of day, to ascend to Agricola's garret, in the very faint hope that he might have returned home some hours before.

Rose and Blanche had just risen, and dressed themselves. They were alone in the sad, chilly apartment. Spoilsport, whom Dagobert had left in

Paris, was stretched at full length near the cold stove ; with his long muzzle resting on his forepaws, he kept his eyes fixed on the sisters.

Having slept but little during the night, they had perceived the agitation and anguish of Dagobert's wife. They had seen her walk up and down, now talking to herself, now listening to the least noise that came up the staircase, and now kneeling before the crucifix placed at one extremity of the room. The orphans were not aware, that, whilst she prayed with fervour on behalf of her son, this excellent woman was praying for them also. For the state of their souls filled her with anxiety and alarm.

The day before, when Dagobert had set out for Chartres, Frances, having assisted Rose and Blanche to rise, had invited them to say their morning prayer : they answered with the utmost simplicity, that they did not know any, and that they never more than addressed their mother, who was in heaven. When Frances, struck with painful surprise, spoke to them of catechism, confirmation, communion, the sisters opened widely their large eyes with astonishment, understanding nothing of such talk.

According to her simple faith, terrified at the ignorance of the young girls in matters of religion, Dagobert's wife believed their souls to be in the greatest peril, the more so as, having asked them if they had ever been baptised (at the same time explaining to them the nature of that sacrament), the orphans answered they did not think they had, since there was neither church nor priest in the village where they were born, during their mother's exile in Siberia.

Placing one's self in the position of Frances, you may understand how much she was grieved and alarmed ; for, in her eyes, these young girls, whom she already loved tenderly, so charmed was she with their sweet disposition, were nothing but poor heathens, innocently doomed to eternal damnation. So, unable to restrain her tears, or conceal her horrors, she had clasped them in her arms, promising immediately to attend to their salvation, and regretting that Dagobert had not thought of having them baptised by the way. Now, it must be confessed, that this notion had never once occurred to the ex-grenadier.

When she went to her usual Sunday devotions, Frances had not dared to take Rose and Blanche with her, as their complete ignorance of sacred things would have rendered their presence at church, if not useless, scandalous ; but, in her own fervent prayers she implored celestial mercy for these orphans, who did not themselves know the desperate position of their souls.

Rose and Blanche were now left alone, in the absence of Dagobert's wife. They were still dressed in mourning, their charming faces seeming even more pensive than usual. Though they were accustomed to a life of misfortune, they had been struck, since their arrival in the Rue Brise-Miche, with the painful contrast between the poor dwelling which they had come to inhabit, and the wonders which their young imagination had conceived of Paris, that golden city of their dreams. But soon this natural astonishment was replaced by thoughts of singular gravity for their age. The contemplation of such honest and laborious poverty made the orphans have reflections no longer those of children, but of young women. Assisted by their admirable spirit of justice, and of sympathy for all that is good, by their noble heart, by a character at once delicate and courageous, they had observed and meditated much during the last twenty-four hours.

' Sister,' said Rose to Blanche, when Frances had quitted the room, ' Dagobert's poor wife is very uneasy. Did you remark in the night,—how agitated she was ? how she wept and prayed ?'

' I was grieved to see it, sister, and wondered what could be the cause.'

' I am almost afraid to guess. Perhaps we may be the cause of her uneasiness?'

' Why so, sister? Because we cannot say prayers, nor tell if we have ever been baptised?'

' That seemed to give her a good deal of pain, it is true: I was quite touched by it, for it proves that she loves us tenderly. But I could not understand how we ran such terrible danger as she said we did.'

' Nor I either, sister. We have always tried not to displease our mother, who sees and hears us.'

' We love those who love us; we hate nobody; we are resigned to whatever may happen to us. So, who can reproach us with any harm?'

' No one. But, perhaps, we may do some without meaning it.'

' We?'

' Yes, and therefore I thought: We may perhaps be the cause of her uneasiness.'

' How so?'

' Listen, sister! yesterday Madame Baudoin tried to work at those sacks of coarse cloth there on the table."

' Yes; but in about half an hour, she told us sorrowfully, that she could not go on, because her eyes failed her, and she could not see clearly.'

' So that she is not able to earn her living.'

' No—but her son, M. Agricola, works for her. He looks so good, so gay, so frank, and so happy to devote himself for his mother. Oh, indeed! he is the worthy brother of our angel Gabriel!'

' You will see my reason for speaking of this. Our good old Dagobert told us, that, when we arrived here, he had only a few pieces of money left.'

' That is true.'

' Now both he and his wife are unable to earn their living: what can a poor old soldier like him do?'

' You are right; he only knows how to love us, and take care of us, like his children.'

' It must then be M. Agricola who will have to support his father; for Gabriel is a poor priest, who possesses nothing, and can render no assistance to those who have brought him up. So M. Agricola will have to support the whole family by himself.'

' Doubtless—he owes it to father and mother—it is his duty, and he will do it with a good will.'

' Yes, sister—but he owes us nothing.'

' What do you say, Blanche?'

' He is obliged to work for us also, as we possess nothing in the world.'

' I had not thought of that. True.'

' It is all very well, sister, for our father to be Duke and Marshal of France, as Dagobert tells us, it is all very well for us to hope great things from this medal, but as long as father is not here, and our hopes are not realised, we shall be merely poor orphans, obliged to remain a burden to this honest family, to whom we already owe so much, and who find it so hard to live, that——'

' Why do you pause, sister?'

' What I am about to say would make other people laugh; but you will understand it. Yesterday, when Dagobert's wife saw poor Spoilsport at his dinner, she said, sorrowfully: " Alas! he eats as much as a man!"—so that I could almost have cried to hear her. They must be very poor, and yet we ave come to increase their poverty.'

The sisters looked sadly at each other, while Spoilsport pretended not to know they were talking of his voracity.

'Sister, I understand,' said Rose, after a moment's silence. 'Well, we must not be at the charge of any one. We are young, and have courage. Till our fate is decided, let us fancy ourselves daughters of workmen. After all, is not our grandfather a workman? Let us find some employment, and earn our own living. It must be so proud and happy to earn one's living!'

'Good little sister,' said Blanche, kissing Rose. 'What happiness! You have forestalled my thought; kiss me!'

'How so!'

'Your project is mine exactly. Yesterday, when I heard Dagobert's wife complain so sadly that she had lost her sight, I looked into your large eyes, which reminded me of my own, and said to myself: " Well! this poor old woman may have lost her sight, but Rose and Blanche Simon can see pretty clearly "—which is a compensation,' added Blanche, with a smile.

'And, after all,' resumed Rose, smiling in her turn, 'the young ladies in question are not so very awkward, as not to be able to sew up great sacks of coarse cloth—though it may chafe their fingers a little.'

'So we had both the same thought, as usual; only I wished to surprise you, and waited till we were alone, to tell you my plan.'

'Yes, but there is something teases me.'

'What is that?'

'First of all, Dagobert and his wife will be sure to say to us: " Young ladies, you are not fitted for such work. What, daughters of a Marshal of France sewing up great ugly bags!" And then, if we insist upon it, they will add: "Well, we have no work to give you. If you want any, you must hunt for it." What would Misses Simon do then?'

'The fact is, that when Dagobert has made up his mind to anything——'

'Oh! even then, if we coax him well——'

'Yes, in certain things; but in others he is immovable. It is just as when upon the journey, we wished to prevent his doing so much for us.'

'Sister, an idea strikes me,' cried Rose, 'an excellent idea!'

'What is it? quick!'

'You know the young woman they call Mother Bunch, who appears to be so serviceable and persevering?'

'Oh yes! and so timid and discreet. She seems always to be afraid of giving offence, even if she looks at one. Yesterday, she did not perceive that I saw her; but her eyes were fixed on you with so good and sweet an expression, that tears came into mine at the very sight of it.'

'Well, we must ask her how she gets work, for certainly she lives by her labour.'

'You are right. She will tell us all about it; and when we know, Dagobert may scold us, or try to make great ladies of us, but we will be as obstinate as he is.'

'That is it; we must show some spirit! We will prove to him, as he says himself, that we have soldier's blood in our veins.'

'We will say to him: " Suppose, as you say, we should one day be rich, my good Dagobert, we shall only remember this time with the more pleasure."

'It is agreed then, is it not, Rose? The first time we are alone with Mother Bunch, we must make her our confidant, and ask her for information. She is so good a person, that she will not refuse us.'

'And when father comes home, he will be pleased, I am sure, with our courage.'

'And will approve our wish to support ourselves, as if we were alone in the world.'

On these words of her sister, Rose started. A cloud of sadness, almost of alarm, passed over her charming countenance, as she exclaimed: 'Oh, sister, what a horrible idea!'

' What is the matter? your look frightens me.'

' At the moment I heard you say, that our father would approve our wish to support ourselves, as if we were alone in the world—a frightful thought struck me—I know not why—but feel how my heart beats—just as if some misfortune were about to happen to us.'

' It is true; your poor heart beats violently. But what was this thought? You alarm me.'

' When we were prisoners, they did not at least separate us, and, besides, the prison was a kind of shelter——'

' A sad one, though shared with you.'

' But if, when arrived here, any accident had parted us from Dagobert— if we had been left alone, without help, in this great town?'

' Oh, sister! do not speak of that. It would indeed be terrible. What would become of us, kind heaven?'

This cruel thought made the girls remain for a moment speechless with emotion. Their sweet faces, which had just before glowed with a noble hope, grew pale and sad. After a pretty long silence, Rose uplifted her eyes, now filled with tears, ' Why does this thought,' she said, trembling, ' affect us so deeply, sister? My heart sinks within me, as if it were really to happen to us.'

' I feel as frightened as you yourself. Alas! were we both to be lost in this immense city, what would become of us?'

' Do not let us give way to such ideas, Blanche! Are we not here in Dagobert's house, in the midst of good people?'

' And yet, sister,' said Rose, with a pensive air, ' it is perhaps good for us to have had this thought.'

' Why so?'

' Because we shall now find this poor lodging all the better, as it affords a shelter from all our fears. And when, thanks to our labour, we are no longer a burden to any one, what more can we need until the arrival of our father?'

' We shall want for nothing—there you are right—but still, why did this thought occur to us, and why does it weigh so heavily on our minds?'

' Yes, indeed—why? Are we not here in the midst of friends that love us? How could we suppose that we should ever be left alone in Paris? It is impossible that such a misfortune should happen to us—is it not, my dear sister?'

' Impossible!' said Rose, shuddering. ' If the day before we reached that village in Germany, where poor Jovial was killed, any one had said to us: " To-morrow, you will be in prison"—we should have answered as now: " It is impossible. Is not Dagobert here to protect us; what have we to fear?" And yet, sister, the day after we were in prison at Leipsic.'

' Oh! do not speak thus, my dear sister! It frightens me.'

By a sympathetic impulse, the orphans took one another by the hand, while they pressed close together, and looked around with involuntary fear. The sensation they felt was in fact deep, strange, inexplicable, and yet lowering—one of those dark presentiments which come over us, in spite of ourselves—those fatal gleams of prescience, which throw a lurid light on the mysterious profundities of the future.

Unaccountable glimpses of divination! often no sooner perceived than forgotten—but, when justified by the event, appearing with all the attributes of an awful fatality!

The daughters of Marshal Simon were still absorbed in the mournful reverie which these singular thoughts had awakened, when Dagobert's wife, returning from her son's chamber, entered the room with a painfully agitated countenance.

CHAPTER XLVII.

THE LETTER.

FRANCES' agitation was so perceptible that Rose could not help exclaiming : ' Good gracious, what is the matter ?'

' Alas, my dear young ladies ! I can no longer conceal it from you,' said Frances, bursting into tears. ' Since yesterday, I have not seen him. I expected my son to supper as usual, and he never came ; but I would not let you see how much I suffered. I continued to expect him, minute after minute ; for ten years he has never gone up to bed without coming to kiss me ; so I spent a good part of the night close to the door, listening if I could hear his step. But he did not come ; and, at last, about three o'clock in the morning, I threw myself down upon the mattress. I have just been to see (for I still had a faint hope) if my son had come in this morning ——'

' Well, madame ?'

' There is no sign of him !' said the poor mother, drying her eyes.

Rose and Blanche looked at each other with emotion ; the same thought filled the minds of both ; if Agricola should not return, how would this family live ? would they not, in such an event, become doubly burdensome ?

' But, perhaps, madame,' said Blanche, ' M. Agricola remained too late at his work to return home last night.'

' Oh ! no, no ! he would have returned in the middle of the night, because he knew what uneasiness he would cause me by stopping out. Alas ! some misfortune must have happened to him ! Perhaps he has been injured at the forge, he is so persevering at his work. Oh, my poor boy ! and, as if I did not feel enough anxiety about him, I am also uneasy about the poor young woman who lives upstairs.'

' Why so, madame ?'

' When I left my son's room, I went into hers, to tell her my grief, for she is almost a daughter to me ; but I did not find her in the little closet where she lives, and the bed had not even been slept in. Where can she have gone so early—she, that never goes out ?'

Rose and Blanche looked at each other with fresh uneasiness, for they counted much upon Mother Bunch to help them in the resolution they had taken. Fortunately, both they and Frances were soon to be satisfied on this head, for they heard two low knocks at the door, and the sempstress's voice, saying : ' Can I come in, Mrs. Baudoin ?'

By a spontaneous impulse, Rose and Blanche ran to the door, and opened it to the young girl. Sleet and snow had been falling incessantly since the evening before ; the gingham dress of the young sempstress, her scanty cotton shawl, and the black net cap, which, leaving uncovered two thick bands of chestnut hair, encircled her pale and interesting countenance, were all dripping wet ; the cold had given a livid appearance to her thin, white hands ; it was only in the fire of her blue eyes, generally so soft and timid, that one perceived the extraordinary energy which this frail and fear-full creature had gathered from the emergency of the occasion.

' Dear me ! where do you come from, my good mother Bunch ?' said Frances. ' Just now, in going to see if my son had returned, I opened your door, and was astonished to find you gone out so early.'

' I bring you news of Agricola.'

' Of my son !' cried Frances, trembling all over. ' What has happened to him ? Did you see him ?—Did you speak to him ?—Where is he ?'

' I did not see him, but I know where he is.' Then, perceiving that Frances grew very pale, the girl added : ' He is well ; he is in no danger.'

' Blessed be God, who has pity on a poor sinner !—who yesterday restored me my husband, and to-day, after a night of cruel anguish, assures me of the safety of my child !' So saying, Frances knelt down upon the floor, and crossed herself with fervour.

During the moment of silence caused by this pious action, Rose and Blanche approached Mother Bunch, and said to her in a low voice, with an expression of touching interest : 'How wet you are ! you must be very cold. Take care you do not get ill. We did not venture to ask Madame Frances to light the fire in the stove, but now we will do so.'

Surprised and affected by the kindness of Marshal Simon's daughters, the hunchback, who was more sensible than others to the least mark of kindness, answered them with a look of ineffable gratitude : 'I am much obliged to you, young ladies ; but I am accustomed to the cold, and am moreover so anxious that I do not feel it.'

'And my son ?' said Frances, rising after she had remained some moments on her knees ; 'why did he stay out all night ? And could you tell me where to find him, my good girl ? Will he soon come ? why is he so long ?'

'I assure you, Agricola is well ; but I must inform you, that for some time——'

'Well ?'

'You must have courage, mother.'

'Oh ! the blood runs cold in my veins. What has happened ? why shall I not see him ?'

'Alas, he is arrested.'

'Arrested !' cried Rose and Blanche, with affright.

'Father ! Thy will be done !' said Frances ; 'but it is a great misfortune. Arrested ! for what ? He is so good and honest, that there must be some mistake.'

'The day before yesterday,' resumed Mother Bunch, 'I received an anonymous letter, by which I was informed that Agricola might be arrested at any moment, on account of his song. We agreed together that he should go to the rich young lady in the Rue de Babylone, who had offered him her services, and ask her to procure bail for him, to prevent his going to prison. Yesterday morning he set out to go to the young lady's.'

'And neither of you told me anything of all this—why did you hide it from me ?'

'That we might not make you uneasy, mother ; for, counting on the generosity of that young lady, I expected Agricola back every moment. When he did not come yesterday evening, I said to myself : "Perhaps the necessary formalities with regard to the bail have detained him." But the time passed on, and he did not make his appearance. So, I watched all night, expecting him.'

'So you did not go to bed either, my good girl ?'

'No, I was too uneasy. This morning, not being able to conquer my fears, I went out before dawn. I remembered the address of the young lady in the Rue de Babylone, and I ran thither.'

'Oh, well !' said Frances, with anxiety ; 'you were in the right. According to what my son told us, that young lady appeared very good and generous.'

Mother Bunch shook her head sorrowfully ; a tear glittered in her eyes; as she continued : 'It was still dark when I arrived at the Rue de Babylone; I waited till daylight was come.'

'Poor child ! you, who are so weak and timid,' said Frances, with deep feeling, 'to go so far, and in this dreadful weather !—Oh, you have been a real daughter to me !'

'Has not Agricola been like a brother to me !' said Mother Bunch, softly, with a slight blush.

'When it was daylight,' she resumed : 'I ventured to ring at the door of the little summer-house ; a charming young girl, but with a sad, pale countenance, opened the door to me. " I come in the name of an unfortunate mother in despair," said I to her immediately, for I was so poorly dressed that I feared to be sent away as a beggar ; but seeing, on the contrary, that the young girl listened to me with kindness, I asked her if, the day before, a young workman had not come to solicit a great favour of her mistress. " Alas ! yes," answered the young girl ; " my mistress was going to interest herself for him, and, hearing that he was in danger of being arrested, she concealed him here ; unfortunately, his retreat was discovered, and yesterday afternoon, at four o'clock, he was arrested and taken to prison." '

Though the orphans took no part in this melancholy conversation, the sorrow and anxiety depicted in their countenances, showed how much they felt for the sufferings of Dagobert's wife.

' But the young lady ?' cried Frances. ' You should have tried to see her, my good Mother Bunch, and begged her not to abandon my son. She is so rich that she must have influence, and her protection might save us from great calamities.'

' Alas !' said Mother Bunch, with bitter grief, ' we must renounce this last hope.'

' Why ?' said Frances. ' If this young lady is so good, she will have pity upon us, when she knows that my son is the only support of a whole family, and that for him to go to prison is worse than for another, because it will reduce us all to the greatest misery.'

' But this young lady,' replied the girl, ' according to what I learned from her weeping maid, was taken last evening to a lunatic asylum : it appears she is mad.'

' Mad ! Oh ! it is horrible for her, and for us also—for now there is no hope. What will become of us without my son ? Oh, merciful heaven !' The unfortunate woman hid her face in her hands.

A profound silence followed this heartrending outburst. Rose and Blanche exchanged mournful glances, for they perceived that their presence augmented the weighty embarrassments of this family. Mother Bunch, worn out with fatigue, a prey to painful emotions, and trembling with cold in her wet clothes, sank exhausted on a chair, and reflected on their desperate position.

That position was indeed a cruel one !

Often, in times of political disturbances, or of agitation amongst the labouring classes, caused by want of work, or by the unjust reduction of wages (the result of the powerful coalition of the capitalists)—often are whole families reduced, by a measure of preventive imprisonment, to as deplorable a position as that of Dagobert's household by Agricola's arrest—an arrest, which, as will afterwards appear, was entirely owing to Rodin's arts.

Now, with regard to this ' precautionary imprisonment,' of which the victims are almost always honest and industrious mechanics, driven to the necessity of combining together by the Inorganization of Labour and the Insufficiency of Wages, it is painful to see the law, which ought to be equal for all, refuse to strikers what it grants to masters—because the latter can dispose of a certain sum of money. Thus, under many circumstances, the rich man, by giving bail, can escape the annoyance and inconveniences of a preventive incarceration ; he deposits a sum of money, pledges his word to appear on a certain day, and goes back to his pleasures, his occupations, and the sweet delights of his family. Nothing can be better ; an accused person is innocent till he is proved guilty : we cannot be too much impressed with that indulgent maxim. It is well for the rich man that he can avail himself of the mercy of the law. But how is it with the poor ?

Not only has he no bail to give, for his whole capital consists of his daily labour ; but it is upon him chiefly that the rigours of preventive measures must fall with a terrible and fatal force.

For the rich man, imprisonment is merely the privation of ease and comfort, tedious hours, and the pain of separation from his family—distresses not unworthy of interest, for all suffering deserves pity, and the tears of the rich man separated from his children are as bitter as those of the poor. But the absence of the rich man does not condemn his family to hunger and cold, and the incurable maladies caused by exhaustion and misery.

For the workman, on the contrary, imprisonment means want, misery, sometimes death, to those most dear to him. Possessing nothing, he is unable to find bail, and he goes to prison. But if he have, as it often happens, an old, infirm father or mother, a sick wife, or children in the cradle ? What will become of this unfortunate family ? They could hardly manage to live from day to day upon the wages of this man, wages almost always insufficient, and suddenly this only resource will be wanting for three or four months together.

What will this family do ? To whom will they have recourse?

What will become of these infirm old men, these sickly wives, these little children, unable to gain their daily bread ? If they chance to have a little linen and a few spare clothes, these will be carried to the pawnbroker's, and thus they will exist for a week or so—but afterwards ?

And if winter adds the rigours of the season to this frightful and inevitable misery ?

Then will the imprisoned artisan see in his mind's eye, during the long and sleepless nights, those who are dear to him, wan, gaunt, haggard, exhausted, stretched almost naked upon filthy straw, or huddled close together to warm their frozen limbs. And, should he afterwards be acquitted, it is ruin and desolation that he finds on his return to his poor dwelling.

And then, after that long cessation from labour, he will find it difficult to return to his old employers. How many days will be lost in seeking for work ! and a day without employment is a day without bread !

Let us repeat our opinion, that if, under various circumstances, the law did not afford to the rich the facility of giving bail, we could only lament over all such victims of individual and inevitable misfortune. But since the law does provide the means of setting provisionally at liberty those who possess a certain sum of money, why should it deprive of this advantage those very persons, for whom liberty is indeed indispensable, as it involves the existence of themselves and families?

Is there any remedy for this deplorable state of things ? We believe there is.

The law has fixed the minimum of bail at five hundred francs. Now five hundred francs represent, upon the average, six months' labour of an industrious workman.

If he have a wife and two children (which is also about the average), it is evidently quite impossible for him to have saved any such sum.

So, to ask of such a man five hundred francs, to enable him to continue to support his family, is in fact to put him beyond the pale of the law, though, more than any one else, he requires its protection, because of the disastrous consequences which his imprisonment entails upon others.

Would it not be equitable and humane, a noble and salutary example, to accept, in every case where bail is allowed (and where the good character of the accused could be honourably established), moral guarantees, in the absence of material ones, from those who have no capital but their labour and their integrity—to accept the word of an honest man to appear upon the day of trial? Would it not be great and moral, in these days, to raise the value of the plighted word, and exalt man in his own eyes, by showing him that his promise was held to be sufficient security?

Will you so degrade the dignity of man, as to treat this proposition as an impossible and Utopian dream? We ask, how many prisoners of war have ever broken their parole, and if officers and soldiers are not brothers of the working-man?

Without exaggerating the virtue of promise-keeping in the honest and laborious poor, we feel certain, that an engagement taken by the accused to appear on the day of trial would be always fulfilled, not only with fidelity, but with the warmest gratitude—for his family would not have suffered by his absence, thanks to the indulgence of the law.

There is also another fact, of which France may well be proud. It is, that her magistrates (although miserably paid as the army itself) are generally wise, upright, humane, and independent; they have the true feeling of their own useful and sacred mission; they know how to appreciate the wants and distresses of the working classes, with whom they are so often brought in contact; to them might be safely granted the power of fixing those cases in which a moral security, the only one that can be given by the honest and necessitous man, should be received as sufficient.*

Finally, if those who make the laws have so low an opinion of the people as to reject with disdain the suggestions we have ventured to throw out, let them at least so reduce the minimum of bail, as to render it available for those who have most need to escape the fruitless rigours of imprisonment. Let them take, as their lowest limit, the month's wages of an artisan—say *eighty francs.*

This sum would still be exorbitant; but, with the aid of friends, the pawnbroker's, and some little advances, eighty francs might perhaps be found—not always, it is true—but still sometimes—and, at all events, many families would be rescued from frightful misery.

Having made these observations, let us return to Dagobert's family, who, in consequence of the preventive arrest of Agricola, were now reduced to an almost hopeless state.

    ✧   ✧   ✧   ✧   ✧   ✧

The anguish of Dagobert's wife increased, the more she reflected on her situation, for, including the marshal's daughters, four persons were left absolutely without resource. It must be confessed, however, that the excellent mother thought less of herself, than of the grief which her son must feel in thinking over her deplorable position.

At this moment there was a knock at the door.

'Who is there?' said Frances.

'It is me—Father Loriot.'

'Come in,' said Dagobert's wife.

The dyer, who also performed the functions of a porter, appeared at the door of the room. This time, his arms were no longer of a bright apple-green, but of a magnificent violet.

'Mrs. Baudoin,' said Father Loriot, 'here is a letter, that the giver of holy water at Saint Méry's has just brought from Abbé Dubois, with a request that I would bring it up to you immediately, as it is very pressing.'

'A letter from my confessor?' said Frances, in astonishment; and, as she took it, added: 'Thank you, Father Loriot.'

---

* In another work, we have mentioned, with respect and sympathy, the excellent book of M. Prosper Tarbé, Procureur du Roi, upon 'Work and Wages'—one of the best and most sterling productions that an enlightened love of humanity ever called forth from generous heart, and clear, practical intellect.

'You do not want anything?'

'No, Father Loriot.'

'My respects to the ladies!' and the dyer went out.

'Mother Bunch, will you read this letter for me?' said Frances, anxious to learn the contents of the missive in question.

'Yes, mother'—and the young girl read as follows :

'"MY DEAR MADAME BAUDOIN,—I am in the habit of hearing you Tuesday and Saturday, but I shall not be at liberty either to-morrow or the last day of the week ; you must then come to me this morning, unless you wish to remain a whole week without approaching the tribunal of penance."'

'Good heavens! a week!' cried Dagobert's wife. 'Alas! I am only too conscious of the necessity of going there to-day, notwithstanding the trouble and grief in which I am plunged.'

Then, addressing herself to the orphans, she continued : 'Heaven has heard the prayers that I made for you, my dear young ladies ; this very day I shall be able to consult a good and holy man with regard to the great dangers to which you are exposed. Poor dear souls, that are so innocent, and yet so guilty, without any fault of your own! Heaven is my witness, that my heart bleeds for you as much as for my son.'

Rose and Blanche looked at each other in confusion ; they could not understand the fears with which the state of their souls inspired the wife of Dagobert. The latter soon resumed, addressing the young sempstress : 'My good girl, will you render me yet another service?'

'Certainly.'

'My husband took Agricola's week's wages with him to pay his journey to Chartres. It was all the money I had in the house ; I am sure that my poor child had none about him, and in prison he will perhaps want some. Therefore take my silver cup, fork, and spoon, the two pair of sheets that remain over, and my wadded silk shawl, that Agricola gave me on my birthday, and carry them all to the pawnbroker's. I will try and find out in which prison my son is confined, and will send him half of the little sum we get upon the things ; the rest will serve us till my husband comes home. And then, what shall we do? What a blow for him—and only more misery in prospect—since my son is in prison, and I have lost my sight. Almighty Father!' cried the unfortunate mother, with an expression of impatient and bitter grief, 'why am I thus afflicted? Have I not done enough to deserve some pity, if not for myself, at least for those belonging to me?' But immediately reproaching herself for this outburst, she added, 'No, no! I ought to accept with thankfulness all that Thou sendest me. Forgive me for these complaints, or punish only myself!'

'Be of good courage, mother!' said Mother Bunch. 'Agricola is innocent, and will not remain long in prison.'

'But now I think of it,' resumed Dagobert's wife, 'to go to the pawnbroker's will make you lose much time, my poor girl.'

'I can make up that in the night, Madame Frances ; I could not sleep, knowing you in such trouble. Work will amuse me.'

'Yes, but the candles——'

'Never mind, I am a little beforehand with my work,' said the poor girl, telling a falsehood.

'Kiss me, at least,' said Frances, with moist eyes, 'for you are the very best creature in the world.' So saying, she hastened out of the room.

Rose and Blanche were left alone with Mother Bunch ; at length had arrived the moment for which they had waited with so much impatience. Dagobert's wife proceeded to St. Méry Church, where her confessor was expecting to see her.

CHAPTER XLVIII.

THE CONFESSIONAL.

NOTHING could be more gloomy than the appearance of St. Méry Church, on this dark and snowy winter's day. Frances stopped a moment beneath the porch, to behold a lugubrious spectacle.

While a priest was mumbling some words in a low voice, two or three dirty choristers, in soiled surplices, were chanting the prayers for the dead, with an absent and sullen air, round a plain deal coffin, followed only by a sobbing old man and a child, miserably clad. The beadle and the sacristan, very much displeased at being disturbed for so wretched a funeral, had not deigned to put on their liveries, but, yawning with impatience, waited for the end of the ceremony, so useless to the interests of the establishment. At length, a few drops of holy water being sprinkled on the coffin, the priest handed the brush to the beadle, and retired.

Then took place one of those shameful scenes, the necessary consequence of an ignoble and sacrilegious traffic, so frequent with regard to the burials of the poor, who cannot afford to pay for tapers, high mass, or violins—for now St. Thomas Aquinas' Church has violins even for the dead.

The old man stretched forth his hand to the sacristan to receive the brush. 'Come, look sharp!' said that official, blowing on his fingers.

The emotion of the old man was profound, and his weakness extreme; he remained for a moment without stirring, while the brush was clasped tightly in his trembling hand. In that coffin was his daughter, the mother of the ragged child who wept by his side—his heart was breaking at the thought of that last farewell; he stood motionless, and his bosom heaved with convulsive sobs.

'Now, will you make haste?' said the brutal beadle. 'Do you think we are going to sleep here?'

The old man quickened his movements. He made the sign of the cross over the corpse, and, stooping down, was about to place the brush in the hand of his grandson, when the sacristan, thinking the affair had lasted long enough, snatched the sprinkling-brush from the child, and made a sign to the bearers to carry away the coffin—which was immediately done.

'Wasn't that old beggar a slow coach?' said the beadle to his companion, as they went back to the sacristy. 'We shall hardly have time to get breakfast, and to dress ourselves for the bang-up funeral of this morning. That will be something like a dead man, that's worth the trouble. I shall shoulder my halberd in style!'

'And mount your colonel's epaulets, to throw dust in the eyes of the women that let out the chairs—eh, you old rascal?' said the other, with a sly look.

'What can I do, Catillard? When one has a fine figure, it must be seen,' answered the beadle, with a triumphant air. 'I cannot blind the women to prevent their losing their hearts!'

Thus conversing, the two men reached the sacristy. The sight of the funeral had only increased the gloom of Frances. When she entered the church, seven or eight persons, scattered about upon chairs, alone occupied the damp and icy building. One of the distributors of holy water, an old fellow with a rubicund, joyous, wine-bibbing face, seeing Frances approach the little font, said to her in a low voice : 'Abbé Dubois is not yet in his box. Be quick, and you will have the first wag of his beard.'

Though shocked at this pleasantry, Frances thanked the irreverent speaker, made devoutly the sign of the cross, advanced some steps into the church, and knelt down upon the stones to repeat the prayer, which she always offered up before approaching the tribunal of penance. Having said this prayer, she went towards a dark corner of the church, in which was an oaken confessional, with a black curtain drawn across the grated door. The places on each side were vacant ; so Frances knelt down in that upon the right hand, and remained there for some time absorbed in bitter reflections.

In a few minutes, a priest of tall stature, with grey hair and a stern countenance, clad in a long black cassock, stalked slowly along one of the aisles of the church. A short, old, mis-shapen man, badly dressed, leaning upon an umbrella, accompanied him, and from time to time whispered in his ear, when the priest would stop to listen with a profound and respectful deference.

As they approached the confessional, the short old man, perceiving Frances on her knees, looked at the priest with an air of interrogation. ' It is she,' said the clergyman.

' Well, in two or three hours, they will expect the two girls at St. Mary's Convent. I count upon it,' said the old man.

' I hope so, for the sake of their souls,' answered the priest ; and, bowing gravely, he entered the confessional. The short old man quitted the church.

This old man was Rodin. It was on leaving Saint Méry's that he went to the lunatic asylum, to assure himself that Dr. Baleinier had faithfully executed his instructions with regard to Adrienne de Cardoville.

Frances was still kneeling in the interior of the confessional. One of the slides opened, and a voice began to speak. It was that of the priest, who, for the last twenty years had been the confessor of Dagobert's wife, and exercised over her an irresistible and all-powerful influence.

' You received my letter ?' said the voice.

' Yes, father.'

' Very well—I listen to you.'

' Bless me, father—for I have sinned !' said Frances.

The voice pronounced the formula of the benediction. Dagobert's wife answered ' amen,' as was proper, said her *confiteor* to ' It is my fault,' gave an account of the manner in which she had performed her last penance, and then proceeded to the enumeration of the new sins, committed since she had received absolution.

For this excellent woman, a glorious martyr of industry and maternal love, always fancied herself sinning : her conscience was incessantly tormented by the fear that she had committed some incomprehensible offence. This mild and courageous creature, who, after a whole life of devotion, ought to have passed what time remained to her in calm serenity of soul, looked upon herself as a great sinner, and lived in continual anxiety, doubting much her ultimate salvation.

' Father,' said Frances, in a trembling voice, ' I accuse myself of omitting my evening prayer the day before yesterday. My husband, from whom I had been separated for many years, returned home. The joy and the agitation caused by his arrival, made me commit this great sin.'

' What next ?' said the voice, in a severe tone, which redoubled the poor woman's uneasiness.

' Father, I accuse myself of falling into the same sin yesterday evening. I was in a state of mortal anxiety, for my son did not come home as usual, and I waited for him minute after minute, till the hour had passed over.'

' What next ?' said the voice.

' Father, I accuse myself of having told a falsehood all this week to my son, by letting him think that on account of his reproaching me for neglecting my health, I had taken a little wine for my dinner—whereas I had left it for him, who has more need of it, because he works so much.'

' Go on ! said the voice.

' Father, I accuse myself of a momentary want of resignation this morning, when I learned that my poor son was arrested ; instead of submitting with respect and gratitude to this new trial which the Lord hath sent me—alas ! I rebelled against it in my grief—and of this I accuse myself.'

' A bad week,' said the priest, in a tone of still greater severity, ' a bad week—for you have always put the creature before the Creator. But proceed !'

' Alas, father !' resumed Frances, much dejected, ' I know that I am a great sinner; and I fear that I am on the road to sins of a still graver kind.'

' Speak !'

' My husband brought with him from Siberia two young orphans, daughters of Marshal Simon. Yesterday morning, I asked them to say their prayers, and I learned from them, with as much fright as sorrow, that they know none of the mysteries of our holy faith, though they are fifteen years old. They have never received the sacrament, nor are they even baptised, father—not even baptised !'

' They must be heathens !' cried the voice, in a tone of angry surprise.

' That is what so much grieves me, father ; for, as I and my husband are in the room of parents to these young orphans, we should be guilty of the sins which they might commit—should we not, father ?'

' Certainly,—since you take the place of those who ought to watch over their souls. The shepherd must answer for his flock,' said the voice.

' And if they should happen to be in mortal sin, father, I and my husband would be in mortal sin ?'

' Yes,' said the voice ; ' you take the place of their parents ; and fathers and mothers are guilty of all the sins which their children commit when those sins arise from the want of a Christian education.'

' Alas, father ! what am I to do ? I address myself to you as I would to heaven itself. Every day, every hour, that these poor young girls remain heathens, may contribute to bring about their eternal damnation, may it not, father ?' said Frances, in a tone of the deepest emotion.

' Yes,' answered the voice ; ' and the weight of this terrible responsibility rests upon you and your husband ; you have the charge of souls !'

' Lord, have mercy upon me !' said Frances, weeping.

' You must not grieve yourself thus,' answered the voice, in a softer tone ; ' happily for these unfortunates, they have met you upon the way. They will have in you and your husband good and pious examples—for I suppose that your husband, though formerly an ungodly person, now practises his religious duties ?'

' We must pray for him, father,' said Frances, sorrowfully ; ' grace has not yet touched his heart. He is like my poor child, who has also not been called to holiness. Ah, father !' said Frances, drying her tears, ' these thoughts are my heaviest cross.'

' So neither your husband nor your son practises,' resumed the voice, in a tone of reflection ; ' this is serious—very serious. The religious education of these two unfortunate girls has yet to begin. In your house, they will have ever before them the most deplorable examples. Take care ! I have warned you. You have the charge of souls—your responsibility is immense !'

' Father, it is that which makes me wretched—I am at a loss what to do. Help me, and give me your counsels : for twenty years your voice has been to me as the voice of the Lord.'

' Well ! you must agree with your husband to send these unfortunate girls to some religious house where they may be instructed.'

' We are too poor, father, to pay for their schooling, and unfortunately my son has just been put in prison for songs that he wrote.'

'Behold the fruit of impiety,' said the voice, severely ; 'look at Gabriel ! he has followed my counsels, and is now the model of every Christian virtue.'

'My son, Agricola, has had good qualities, father ; he is so kind, so devoted !'

'Without religion,' said the voice, with redoubled severity, 'what you call good qualities are only vain appearances ; at the least breath of the devil they will disappear—for the devil lurks in every soul that has no religion.'

'Oh ! my poor son !' said Frances, weeping ; 'I pray for him every day, that faith may enlighten him.'

'I have always told you,' resumed the voice, 'that you have been too weak with him. God now punishes you for it. You should have parted from this irreligious son, and not sanctioned his impiety by loving him as you do. "If thy right hand offend thee, cut it off," saith the Scripture.'

'Alas, father ! you know it is the only time I have disobeyed you ; but I could not bring myself to part from my son.'

'Therefore is your salvation uncertain—but God is merciful. Do not fall into the same fault with regard to these young girls, whom Providence has sent you, that you might save them from eternal damnation. Do not plunge them into it by your own culpable indifference.'

'Oh, father ! I have wept and prayed for them.'

'That is not sufficient. These unfortunate children cannot have any notion of good or evil. Their souls must be an abyss of scandal and impurity—brought up as they have been, by an impious mother, and a soldier devoid of religion.'

'As for that, father,' said Frances, with simplicity, 'they are gentle as angels, and my husband, who has not quitted them since their birth. declares they have the best hearts in the world.'

'Your husband has dwelt all his life in mortal sin,' said the voice, harshly ; 'how can he judge of the state of souls ? I repeat to you, that as you represent the parents of these unfortunates, it is not to-morrow, but it is to-day, and on the instant, that you must labour for their salvation, if you would not incur a terrible responsibility.'

'It is true—I know it well, father—and I suffer as much from this fear as from grief at my son's arrest. But what is to be done ? I could not instruct these young girls at home—for I have not the knowledge—I have only faith —and then my poor husband, in his blindness, makes game of sacred things, which my son, at least, respects in my presence, out of regard for me. Then, once more, father, come to my aid, I conjure you ! Advise me : what is to be done ?'

'We cannot abandon these two young souls to frightful perdition,' said the voice, after a moment's silence : 'there are not two ways of saving them: there is only one, and that is to place them in a religious house, where they may be surrounded by good and pious examples.'

'Oh, father ! if we were not so poor, or if I could still work, I would try to gain sufficient to pay for their board, and do for them as I did for Gabriel. Unfortunately, I have quite lost my sight ; but you, father, know some charitable souls, and if you could get any of them to interest themselves for these poor orphans ——'

'Where is their father ?'

'He was in India ; but, my husband tells me, he will soon be in France. That, however, is uncertain. Besides, it would make my heart bleed to see those poor children share our misery—which will soon be extreme—for we only live by my son's labour.'

'Have these girls no relation here ?' asked the voice.

'I believe not, father.'

' It was their mother who entrusted them to your husband, to bring them to France ?'

' Yes, father ; he was obliged to set out yesterday for Chartres, on some very pressing business, as he told me.'

It will be remembered that Dagobert had not thought fit to inform his wife of the hopes which the daughters of Marshal Simon founded on the possession of the medal, and that he had particularly charged them not to mention these hopes, even to Frances.

' So,' resumed the voice, after a pause of some moments' duration, ' your husband is not in Paris.'

' No, father ; but he will doubtless return this evening or to-morrow morning.'

' Listen to me,' said the voice, after another pause. ' Every minute lost for those two young girls is a new step on the road to perdition. At any moment the hand of God may smite them, for He alone knows the hour of our death ; and were they to die in the state in which they now are, they would most probably be lost to all eternity. This very day, therefore, you must open their eyes to the divine light, and place them in a religious house. It is your duty—it should be your desire !'

' Oh, yes, father ! but, unfortunately, I am too poor, as I have already told you.'

' I know it—you do not want for zeal or faith—but even were you capable of directing these young girls, the impious examples of your husband and son would daily destroy your work. Others must do for these orphans, in the name of Christian charity, that which you cannot do, though you are answerable for them before heaven.'

' Oh, father ! if, thanks to you, this good work could be accomplished, how grateful I should be !'

' It is not impossible. I know the superior of a convent, where these young girls would be instructed as they ought. The charge for their board would be diminished in consideration of their poverty ; but, however small, it must be paid, and there would be also an outfit to furnish. All that would be too dear for you.'

' Alas ! yes, father.'

' But, by taking a little from my poor-box, and by applying to one or two generous persons, I think I shall be able to complete the necessary sum, and so get the young girls received at the convent.'

' Ah, father ! you are my deliverer, and these children's.'

' I wish to be so—but, in the interest of their salvation, and to make these measures really efficacious, I must attach some conditions to the support I offer you.'

' Name them, father ; they are accepted beforehand. Your commands shall be obeyed in everything.'

' First of all, then, the children must be taken this very morning to the convent, by my housekeeper, to whom you must bring them almost immediately.'

' Nay, father ; that is impossible !' cried Frances.

' Impossible ? why ?'

In the absence of my husband——'

' Well ?'

' I dare not take such a step without consulting him.'

' Not only must you abstain from consulting him, but the thing must be done during his absence.'

' What, father ? should I not wait for his return ?'

' No, for two reasons,' answered the priest, sternly : first, because his hardened impiety would certainly lead him to oppose your pious resolution ; secondly, because it is indispensable that these young girls should break off all connexion with your husband, who, therefore, must be left in ignorance of the place of their retreat.'

' But, father,' said Frances, a prey to cruel doubt and embarrassment, ' it is to my husband that these children were entrusted—and to dispose of them without his consent would be——'

' Can you instruct these children at your house—yes or no ?' interrupted the voice.

' No, father, I cannot.'

' Are they exposed to fall into a state of final impenitence by remaining with you—yes or no ?'

' Yes, father, they are so exposed.'

' Are you responsible, as you take the place of their parents, for the mortal sins they may commit—yes or no ?'

' Alas, father ! I am responsible before God.'

' Is it in the interest of their eternal salvation that I enjoin you to place them this very day in a convent ?'

' It is for their salvation, father.'

' Well, then, choose !'

' But tell me, I entreat you, father, if I have the right to dispose of them without the consent of my husband ?'

' The right ! you have not only the right, but it is your sacred duty. Would you not be bound, I ask you, to rescue these unfortunate creatures from a fire, against the will of your husband, or during his absence ? Well ! you must now rescue them, not from a fire that will only consume the body, but from one in which their souls would burn to all eternity.'

' Forgive me, I implore you, father,' said the poor woman, whose indecision and anguish increased every minute ; ' satisfy my doubts !—How can I act thus, when I have sworn obedience to my husband ?'

' Obedience for good—yes—but never for evil. You confess, that, were it left to him, the salvation of these orphans would be doubtful, and perhaps impossible.'

' But, father,' said Frances, trembling, ' when my husband returns, he will ask me where are these children ? Must I tell him a falsehood ?'

' Silence is not falsehood ; you will tell him that you cannot answer his question.'

' My husband is the kindest of men ; but such an answer will drive him almost mad. He has been a soldier, and his anger will be terrible, father,' said Frances, shuddering at the thought.

' And were his anger a hundred times more terrible, you should be proud to brave it in so sacred a cause !' cried the voice, with indignation. ' Do you think that salvation is to be so easily gained on earth ? Since when does the sinner, that would walk in the way of the Lord, turn aside for the stones and briars that may bruise and tear him ?'

' Pardon, father, pardon !' said Frances, with the resignation of despair. ' Permit me to ask one more question, one only. Alas ! if you do not guide me, how shall I find the way ?'

' Speak !'

' When Marshal Simon arrives, he will ask his children of my husband. What answer can he then give to their father ?'

' When Marshal Simon arrives, you will let me know immediately, and then—I will see what is to be done. The rights of a father are only sacred in so far as he makes use of them for the salvation of his children. Before and above the father on earth, is the Father in Heaven, whom we must first serve. Reflect upon all this. By accepting what I propose to you, these young girls will be saved from perdition ; they will not be at your charge ; they will not partake of your misery ; they will be brought up in a sacred institution, as, after all, the daughters of a Marshal of France ought to be— and, when their father arrives at Paris, if he be found worthy of seeing them again, instead of finding poor, ignorant, half-savage heathens, he will behold two girls, pious, modest, and well-informed, who, being acceptable with the Almighty, may invoke His mercy for their father, who, it must be owned, has great need of it—being a man of violence, war, and battle. Now decide ! Will you, on peril of your soul, sacrifice the welfare of these girls in this world and the next, because of an impious dread of your husband's anger ?'

Though rude and fettered by intolerance, the confessor's language was (taking his view of the case) reasonable and just, because the honest priest was himself convinced of what he said ; a blind instrument of Rodin, ignorant of the end in view, he believed firmly, that, in forcing Frances to place these young girls in a convent, he was performing a pious duty. Such was, and is, one of the most wonderful resources of the order to which Rodin belonged—to have for accomplices good and sincere people, who are ignorant of the nature of the plots in which they are the principal actors.

Frances, long accustomed to submit to the influence of her confessor, could find nothing to object to his last words. She resigned herself to follow his directions, though she trembled to think of the furious anger of Dagobert, when he should no longer find the children that a dying mother had confided to his care. But, according to the priest's opinion, the more terrible this anger might appear to her, the more she would show her pious humility by exposing herself to it.

' God's will be done, father !' said she, in reply to her confessor. ' Whatever may happen, I will do my duty as a Christian—in obedience to your commands.'

' And the Lord will reward you for what you may have to suffer in the accomplishment of this meritorious act. You promise then, before God, that you will not answer any of your husband's questions, when he asks you for the daughters of Marshal Simon ?'

' Yes, father, I promise !' said Frances, with a shudder.

' And will preserve the same silence towards Marshal Simon himself, in case he should return, before his daughters appear to me sufficiently grounded in the faith to be restored to him ?'

' Yes, father,' said Frances, in a still fainter voice.

' You will come and give me an account of the scene that takes place between you and your husband, upon his return ?'

' Yes, father ; when must I bring the orphans to your house ?'

' In an hour. I will write to the superior, and leave the letter with my housekeeper. She is a trusty person, and will conduct the young girls to the convent.'

After she had listened to the exhortations of her confessor, and received absolution for her late sins, on condition of performing penance, Dagobert's wife left the confessional.

The church was no longer deserted. An immense crowd pressed into it, drawn thither by the pomp of the grand funeral, of which the beadle had spoken to the sacristan two hours before. It was with the greatest difficulty that Frances could reach the door of the church, now hung with sumptuous drapery.

What a contrast to the poor and humble train, which had that morning so timidly presented themselves beneath the porch !

The numerous clergy of the parish, in full procession, advanced majestically to receive the coffin covered with a velvet pall ; the watered silks and stuffs of their copes and stoles, their splendid silvered embroideries, sparkled in the light of a thousand tapers. The beadle strutted in all the glory of his brilliant uniform and flashing epaulets; on the opposite side walked in high glee the sacristan, carrying his whalebone staff with a magisterial air ; the voice of the choristers, now clad in fresh, white surplices, rolled out in bursts of thunder : the trumpets' blare shook the windows ; and upon the countenances of all those who were to have a share in the spoils of this rich corpse, this excellent corpse, this first-class corpse, a look of satisfaction was visible, intense and yet subdued, which suited admirably with the air and attitude of the two heirs, tall, vigorous fellows with florid complexions, who, without overstepping the limits of a charming modesty of enjoyment, seemed to cuddle and hug themselves most comfortably in their mourning cloaks.

Notwithstanding her simplicity and pious faith, Dagobert's wife was painfully impressed with this revolting difference between the reception of the rich and the poor man's coffin at the door of the house of God—for surely, if equality be ever real, it is in the presence of death and eternity !

The two sad spectacles she had witnessed, tended still further to depress the spirits of Frances. Having succeeded with no small trouble in making her way out of the church, she hastened to return to the Rue Brise-Miche, in order to fetch the orphans and conduct them to the housekeeper of her confessor, who was in her turn to take them to St. Mary's Convent, situated, as we know, next door to Dr. Baleinier's lunatic-asylum, in which Adrienne de Cardoville was confined.

CHAPTER XLIX.

MY LORD AND SPOILSPORT.

THE wife of Dagobert, having quitted the church, arrived at the corner of the Rue Brise-Miche, when she was accosted by the distributor of holy water; he came running out of breath, to beg her to return to Saint-Méry's, where the Abbé Dubois had yet something of importance to say to her.

The moment Frances turned to go back, a hackney-coach stopped in front of the house she inhabited. The coachman quitted his box to open the door.

' Driver,' said a stout woman dressed in black, who was seated in the carriage, and held a pug-dog upon her knees, ' ask if Mrs. Frances Baudoin lives in this house.'

' Yes, ma'am,' said the coachman.

The reader will no doubt have recognised Mrs. Grivois, head waiting-woman to the Princess de Saint-Dizier, accompanied by My Lord, who exercised a real tyranny over his mistress. The dyer, whom we have already seen performing the duties of a porter, being questioned by the coachman as to the dwelling of Frances, came out of his workshop, and advanced gallantly to the coach-door, to inform Mrs. Grivois, that Frances Baudoin did in fact live in the house, but that she was at present from home.

The arms, hands, and part of the face of Father Loriot were now of a superb gold-colour. The sight of this yellow personage singularly provoked My Lord, and at the moment the dyer rested his hand upon the edge of the coach-window, the cur began to yelp frightfully, and bit him in the wrist.

' Oh ! gracious heaven !' cried Mrs. Grivois, in an agony, whilst Father Loriot, withdrew his hand with precipitation ; ' I hope there is nothing poisonous in the dye that you have about you—my dog is so delicate !'

So saying, she carefully wiped the pug-nose, spotted with yellow. Father

Loriot, not at all satisfied with this speech, when he had expected to receive some apology from Mrs. Grivois on account of her dog's behaviour, said to her, as with difficulty he restrained his anger: 'If you did not belong to the fair sex, which obliges me to respect you in the person of that wretched animal, I would have the pleasure of taking him by the tail, and making him in one minute a dog of the brightest orange colour, by plunging him into my cauldron, which is already on the fire.'

' Dye my pet yellow!' cried Mrs. Grivois, in great wrath, as she descended from the hackney-coach, clasping My Lord tenderly to her bosom, and surveying Father Loriot with a savage look.

'I told you, Mrs. Baudoin is not at home,' said the dyer, as he saw the pug-dog's mistress advance in the direction of the dark staircase.

' Never mind ; I will wait for her,' said Mrs. Grivois tartly. ' On which story does she live ?'

' Up four pair !' answered Father Loriot, returning abruptly to his shop. And he added to himself, with a chuckle at the anticipation : 'I hope Father Dagobert's big growler will be in a bad humour, and give that villainous pug a shaking by the skin of his neck.'

Mrs. Grivois mounted the steep staircase with some difficulty, stopping at every landing-place to take breath, and looking about her with profound disgust. At length she reached the fourth story, and paused an instant at the door of the humble chamber, in which the two sisters and Mother Bunch then were.

The young semptress was occupied in collecting the different articles that she was about to carry to the pawnbroker's. Rose and Blanche seemed happier, and somewhat less uneasy about the future ; for they had learned from Mother Bunch, that, when they knew how to sew, they might between them earn eight francs a week, which would at least afford some assistance to the family.

The presence of Mrs. Grivois in Baudoin's dwelling was occasioned by a new resolution of Abbé d'Aigrigny and the Princess de Saint-Dizier ; they had thought it more prudent to send Mrs. Grivois, on whom they could blindly depend, to fetch the young girls ; and the confessor was charged to inform Frances, that it was not to his housekeeper, but to a lady that would call on her with a note from him, that she was to deliver the orphans, to be taken to a religious establishment.

Having knocked at the door, the waiting-woman of the Princess de Saint-Dizier entered the room, and asked for Frances Baudoin.

' She is not at home, madame,' said Mother Bunch timidly, not a little astonished at so unexpected a visit, and casting down her eyes before the gaze of this woman.

' Then I will wait for her, as I have important affairs to speak of,' answered Mrs. Grivois, examining with curiosity and attention the faces of the two orphans, who also cast down their eyes with an air of confusion.

So saying, Madame Grivois sat down, not without some repugnance, in the old arm-chair of Dagobert's wife, and believing that she might now leave her favourite at liberty, she laid him carefully on the floor. Immediately, a low growl, deep and hollow, sounding from behind the arm-chair, made Mrs. Grivois jump from her seat, and sent the pug-dog, yelping with affright, and trembling through his fat, to take refuge close to his mistress, with all the symptoms of angry alarm.

' What ! is there a dog here ?' cried Mrs. Grivois, stooping precipitately to catch up My Lord, whilst, as if he wished himself to answer the question, Spoilsport rose leisurely from his place behind the arm-chair, and appeared suddenly, yawning and stretching himself.

At sight of this powerful animal, with his double row of formidable pointed fangs, which he seemed to take delight in displaying as he opened his large jaws, Mrs. Grivois could not help giving utterance to a cry of terror. The snappish pug had at first trembled in all his limbs at the Siberian's approach; but, finding himself in safety on the lap of his mistress, he began to growl insolently, and to throw the most provoking glances at Spoilsport. These the worthy companion of the deceased Jovial answered disdainfully by gaping anew; after which he went smelling round Mrs. Grivois with a sort of uneasiness, turned his back upon My Lord, and stretched himself at the feet of Rose and Blanche, keeping his large, intelligent eyes fixed upon them, as if he foresaw that they were menaced with some danger.

'Turn out that beast,' said Mrs. Grivois, imperiously; 'he frightens my dog, and may do him some harm.'

'Do not be afraid, madame,' replied Rose, with a smile; 'Spoilsport will do no harm, if he is not attacked.'

'Never mind!' cried Mrs. Grivois; 'an accident soon happens. The very sight of that enormous dog, with his wolf's head and terrible teeth, is enough to make one tremble at the injuries he might do one. I tell you to turn him out.'

Mrs. Grivois had pronounced these last words in a tone of irritation, which did not sound at all satisfactory in Spoilsport's ears; so he growled and showed his teeth, turning his head in the direction of the stranger.

'Be quiet, Spoilsport!' said Blanche, sternly.

A new personage here entered the room, and put an end to this situation, which was embarrassing enough for the two young girls. It was a commissionaire, with a letter in his hand.

'What is it, sir?' asked Mother Bunch.

'A very pressing letter from the good man of the house; the dyer below stairs told me to bring it up here.'

'A letter from Dagobert!' cried Rose and Blanche, with a lively expression of pleasure. 'He is returned, then? where is he?'

'I do not know whether the good man is called Dagobert or not,' said the porter; 'but he is an old trooper, with a grey moustache, and may be found close by, at the office of the Chartres coaches.'

'That is he!' cried Blanche. 'Give me the letter.'

The porter handed it to the young girl, who opened it in all haste.

Mrs. Grivois was struck dumb with dismay; she knew that Dagobert had been decoyed from Paris, that the Abbé Dubois might have an opportunity to act with safety upon Frances. Hitherto, all had succeeded; the good woman had consented to place the young girls in the hands of a religious community—and now arrives this soldier, who was thought to be absent from Paris for two or three days at least, and whose sudden return might easily ruin this laborious machination, at the very moment when it seemed to promise success.

'Oh!' said Blanche, when she had read the letter. 'What a misfortune!'

'What is it, then, sister?' cried Rose.

'Yesterday, half way to Chartres, Dagobert perceived that he had lost his purse. He was unable to continue his journey; he took a place upon credit, to return, and he asks his wife to send him some money to the office, to pay what he owes.'

'That's it,' said the porter; 'for the good man told me to make haste, because he was there in pledge.'

'And nothing in the house!' cried Blanche. 'Dear me! what is to be done?'

At these words, Mrs. Grivois felt her hopes revive for a moment; they were soon, however, dispelled by Mother Bunch, who exclaimed, as she pointed to the parcel she had just made up : ' Be satisfied, dear young ladies ! here is a resource. The pawnbroker's, to which I am going, is not far off, and I will take the money direct to M. Dagobert : in half an hour, at latest, he will be here.'

' Oh, my dear friend ! you are right,' said Rose. ' How good you are ! you think of everything.'

' And here,' said Blanche, ' is the letter, with the address upon it. Take that with you.'

' Thank you,' answered Mother Bunch ; then, addressing the porter, she added : ' Return to the person who sent you, and tell him I shall be at the coach-office very shortly.'

' Infernal hunchback !' thought Mrs. Grivois, with suppressed rage, ' she thinks of everything. Without her, we should have escaped the plague of this man's return. What is to be done now ? The girls would not go with me, before the arrival of the soldier's wife : to propose it to them would expose me to a refusal, and might compromise all. Once more, what is to be done ?'

' Do not be uneasy, ladies,' said the porter as he went out ; ' I will go and assure the good man that he will not have to remain long in pledge.'

Whilst Mother Bunch was occupied in tying her parcel, in which she had placed the silver cup, fork, and spoon, Mrs. Grivois seemed to reflect deeply. Suddenly she started. Her countenance, which had been for some moments expressive of anxiety and rage, brightened up on the instant. She rose, still holding My Lord in her arms, and said to the young girls : ' As Mrs. Baudoin does not come in, I am going to pay a visit in the neighbourhood, and will return immediately. Pray tell her so !'

With these words, Mrs. Grivois took her departure, a few minutes before Mother Bunch left.

CHAPTER L.

APPEARANCES.

AFTER she had again endeavoured to cheer up the orphans, the sewing-girl descended the stairs, not without difficulty, for, in addition to the parcel, which was already heavy, she had fetched down from her own room the only blanket she possessed—thus leaving herself without protection from the cold of her icy garret.

The evening before, tortured with anxiety as to Agricola's fate, the girl had been unable to work ; the miseries of expectation and hope delayed had prevented her from doing so ; now another day would be lost, and yet it was necessary to live. Those overwhelming sorrows, which deprive the poor of the faculty of labour, are doubly dreaded ; they paralyse the strength, and, with that forced cessation from toil, want and destitution are often added to grief.

But Mother Bunch, that complete incarnation of holiest duty, had yet strength enough to devote herself for the service of others. Some of the most frail and feeble creatures are endowed with extraordinary vigour of soul ; it would seem as if, in these weak, infirm organizations, the spirit reigned absolute over the body, and knew how to inspire it with a factitious energy.

Thus, for the last twenty-four hours, Mother Bunch had neither slept nor eaten ; she had suffered from the cold, through the whole of a frosty night. In the morning she had endured great fatigue, in going, amid rain and snow, to the Rue de Babylone and back, twice crossing Paris—and yet her strength was not exhausted—so immense is the power of the human heart!

She had just arrived at the corner of the Rue Saint Méry. Since the recent Rue des Prouvaires conspiracy, there were stationed in this populous quarter of the town a much larger number of police-officers than usual. Now the young sempstress, though bending beneath the weight of her parcel, had quickened her pace almost to a run, when, just as she passed in front of one of the police, two five-franc pieces fell on the ground behind her, thrown there by a stout woman in black, who followed her closely.

Immediately after, the stout woman pointed out the two pieces to the policeman, and said something hastily to him with regard to Mother Bunch. Then she withdrew at all speed in the direction of the Rue Brise-Miche.

The policeman, struck with what Mrs. Grivois had said to him (for it was that person), picked up the money, and, running after the humpback, cried out to her : ' Hi, there ! young woman, I say—stop! stop !'

On this outcry, several persons turned round suddenly, and, as always happens in those quarters of the town, a nucleus of five or six persons soon grew to a considerable crowd.

Not knowing that the policeman was calling to her, Mother Bunch only quickened her speed, wishing to get to the pawnbroker's as soon as possible, and trying to avoid touching any of the passers by, so much did she dread the brutal and cruel railleries, to which her infirmity so often exposed her.

Suddenly, she heard many persons running after her, and at the same instant a hand was laid rudely on her shoulder. It was the policeman, followed by another officer, who had been drawn to the spot by the noise. Mother Bunch turned round, struck with as much surprise as fear.

She found herself in the centre of a crowd, composed chiefly of that hideous scum, idle and in rags, insolent and malicious, besotted with ignorance, brutalised by want, and always loafing about the corners. Workmen are scarcely ever met with in these mobs, for they are for the most part engaged in their daily labours.

' Come, can't you hear ? you are deaf as Punch's dog,' said the policeman, seizing Mother Bunch so rudely by the arm, that she let her parcel fall at her feet.

When the unfortunate girl, looking round in terror, saw herself exposed to all those insolent, mocking, malicious glances, when she beheld the cynical and coarse grimace on so many ignoble and filthy countenances, she trembled in all her limbs, and became fearfully pale. No doubt the policeman had spoken roughly to her ; but how could he speak otherwise to a poor deformed girl, pale and trembling, with her features agitated by grief and fear—to a wretched creature, miserably clad, who wore in winter a thin cotton gown, soiled with mud, and wet with melted snow—for the poor sempstress had walked much and far that morning. So the policeman resumed, with great severity, following that supreme law of appearances which makes poverty always suspected : ' Stop a bit, young woman ! it seems you are in a mighty hurry, to let your money fall without picking it up.'

' Was her blunt hid in her hump?' said the hoarse voice of a match-boy, a hideous and repulsive specimen of precocious depravity.

This sally was received with laughter, shouts, and hooting, which served to complete the sewing-girl's dismay and terror. She was hardly able to answer, in a feeble voice, as the policeman handed her the two pieces of silver : ' This money, sir, is not mine.'

' You lie,' said the other officer, approaching ; ' a respectable lady saw it drop from your pocket.'

'I assure you, sir, it is not so,' answered Mother Bunch, trembling.

'I tell you that you lie,' resumed the officer; 'for the lady, struck with your guilty and frightened air, said to me: "Look at yonder little hunchback, running away with that large parcel, and letting her money fall without even stopping to pick it up—it is not natural."'

'Bobby,' resumed the match-vendor in his hoarse voice, 'be on your guard! Feel her hump, for that is her luggage-van. I'm sure that you'll find boots, and cloaks, and umbrellas, and clocks in it—for I just heard the hour strike in the bend of her back.'

Then came fresh bursts of laughter and shouts and hooting, for this horrible mob has no pity for those who implore and suffer. The crowd increased more and more, and now they indulged in hoarse cries, piercing whistles, and all kinds of horse play.

'Let a fellow see her; it's free gratis.'

'Don't push so; I've paid for my place!'

'Make her stand up on something, that all may have a look.'

'My corns are being ground; it was not worth coming.'

'Show her properly—or return the money.'

'That's fair, ain't it?'

'Give it us in the "garden" style.'

'Trot her out in all her paces! Kim up!'

Fancy the feelings of this unfortunate creature, with her delicate mind, good heart, and lofty soul, and yet with so timid and nervous a character, as she stood alone with the two policemen in the thick of the crowd, and was forced to listen to all these coarse and savage insults.

But the young sempstress did not yet understand of what crime she was accused. She soon discovered it, however, for the policeman, seizing the parcel which she had picked up, and now held in her trembling hands, said to her rudely: 'What is there in that bundle?'

'Sir—it is—I am going——' The unfortunate girl hesitated—unable, in her terror, to find the word.

'If that's all you have to answer,' said the policeman, 'it's no great shakes. Come, make haste! turn your bundle inside out.'

So saying, the policeman snatched the parcel from her, half opened it, and repeated, as he enumerated the divers articles it contained: 'The devil!— sheets—a spoon and fork—a silver mug—a shawl—a blanket—you're a downy mot! it was not so bad a move. Dressed like a beggar, and with silver plate about you. Oh, yes! you're a deep 'un.'

'Those articles do not belong to you,' said the other officer.

'No, sir,' replied Mother Bunch, whose strength was failing her; 'but——'

'Oh, vile hunchback! you have stolen more than you are big!'

'Stolen!' cried Mother Bunch, clasping her hands in horror, for she now understood it all. 'Stolen!'

'The guard! make way for the sogers!' cried several persons at once.

'Oh, ho! here's the lobsters!'

'The fire-eaters!'

'The Arab-devourers!'

'Come for their dromedary!'

In the midst of these noisy jests, two soldiers and a corporal advanced with much difficulty. Their bayonets and the barrels of their guns were alone visible above the heads of this hideous and compact crowd. Some officious person had been to inform the officer at the nearest guard-house, that a considerable crowd obstructed the public way.

'Come, here is the guard—so march to the guard-house!' said the police-man, taking Mother Bunch by the arm.

'Sir,' said the poor girl, in a voice stifled by sobs, clasping her hands in terror, and sinking upon her knees on the pavement ; 'sir,—have pity—let me explain——'

'You will explain at the guard-house ; so come on !'

'But, sir—I am not a thief,' cried Mother Bunch, in a heart-rending tone ; have pity upon me—do not take me away like a thief, before all this crowd. Oh ! mercy ! mercy !'

'I tell you, there will be time to explain at the guard-house. The street is blocked up ; so come along ! Grasping the unfortunate creature by both her hands, he set her, as it were, on her feet again.

At this instant, the corporal and his two soldiers, having succeeded in making their way through the crowd, approached the policeman. 'Corporal,' said the latter, 'take this girl to the guard-house. I am an officer of the police.'

'Oh, gentlemen !' cried the girl, weeping hot tears, and wringing her hands, 'do not take me away, before you let me explain myself. I am not a thief—indeed, indeed, I am not a thief ! I will tell you—it was to render service to others—only let me tell you——'

'I tell you, you should give your explanations at the guard-house ; if you will not walk, we must drag you along,' said the policeman.

We must renounce the attempt to paint this scene, at once ignoble and terrible.

Weak, overpowered, filled with alarm, the unfortunate girl was dragged along by the soldiers, her knees sinking under her at every step. The two police-officers had each to lend an arm to support her, and mechanically she accepted their assistance. Then the vociferations and hootings burst forth with redoubled fury. Half-swooning between the two men, the hapless creature seemed to drain the cup of bitterness to the dregs.

Beneath that foggy sky, in that dirty street, under the shadow of the tall black houses, those hideous masses of people reminded one of the wildest fancies of Callot and of Goya : children in rags, drunken women, grim and blighted figures of men, rushed against each other, pushed, fought, struggled, to follow with howls and hisses an almost inanimate victim—the victim of a deplorable mistake.

Of a mistake ! How one shudders to think, that such arrests may often take place, founded upon nothing but the suspicion caused by the appearance of misery, or by some inaccurate description. Can we forget the case of that young girl, who, wrongfully accused of participating in a shameful traffic, found means to escape from the persons who were leading her to prison, and, rushing up the stairs of a house, threw herself from a window, in her despair, and was crushed to death upon the paving-stones.

Meanwhile, after the abominable denunciation of which Mother Bunch was the victim, Mrs. Grivois had returned precipitately to the Rue Brise-Miche. She ascended in haste to the fourth story, opened the door of Frances Baudoin's room, and saw—Dagobert in company with his wife and the two orphans !

CHAPTER LI.

THE CONVENT.

LET us explain in a few words the presence of Dagobert. His countenance was impressed with such an air of military frankness that the manager of the coach-office would have been satisfied with his promise to return and pay the money ; but the soldier had obstinately insisted on remaining in pledge, as he called it, till his wife had answered his letter. When, however, on the return of the porter, he found that the money was coming, his scruples were satisfied, and he hastened to run home.

We may imagine the stupor of Mrs. Grivois, when, upon entering the chamber, she perceived Dagobert (whom she easily recognised by the description she had heard of him) seated beside his wife and the orphans. The anxiety of Frances at sight of Mrs. Grivois was equally striking. Rose and Blanche had told her of the visit of a lady, during her absence, upon important business ; and, judging by the information received from her confessor, Frances had no doubt that this was the person charged to conduct the orphans to a religious establishment.

Her anxiety was terrible. Resolved to follow the counsels of Abbé Dubois, she dreaded lest a word from Mrs. Grivois should put Dagobert on the scent —in which case all would be lost, and the orphans would remain in their present state of ignorance and mortal sin, for which she believed herself responsible.

Dagobert, who held the hands of Rose and Blanche, left his seat as the Princess de Saint-Dizier's waiting-woman entered the room, and cast an inquiring glance on Frances.

The moment was critical—nay, decisive ; but Mrs. Grivois had profited by the example of the Princess de Saint-Dizier. So, taking her resolution at once, and turning to account the precipitation with which she had mounted the stairs, after the odious charge she had brought against poor Mother Bunch, and even the emotion caused by the unexpected sight of Dagobert, which gave to her features an expression of uneasiness and alarm—she exclaimed, in an agitated voice, after the moment's silence necessary to collect her thoughts : ' Oh, madame ! I have just been the spectator of a great misfortune. Excuse my agitation ! but I am so excited——'

' Dear me ! what is the matter?' said Frances, in a trembling voice, for she dreaded every moment some indiscretion on the part of Mrs. Grivois.

' I called just now,' resumed the other, ' to speak to you on some important business; whilst I was waiting for you, a poor young woman, rather deformed, put up sundry articles in a parcel——'

' Yes,' said Frances ; ' it was Mother Bunch, an excellent, worthy creature.'

' I thought as much, madame ; well, you shall hear what has happened. As you did not come in, I resolved to pay a visit in the neighbourhood. I go out, and get as far as the Rue St. Méry, when——Oh, madame !'

' Well?' said Dagobert, ' what then ?'

' I see a crowd—I inquire what is the matter—I learn that a policeman has just arrested a young girl as a thief, because she had been seen carrying a bundle, composed of different articles which did not appear to belong to her—I approached—what do I behold?—the same young woman that I had met just before in this room.'

' Oh ! the poor child !' exclaimed Frances, growing pale, and clasping her hands together. ' What a dreadful thing !'

' Explain, then,' said Dagobert to his wife. ' What was in this bundle ?'

' Well, my dear—to confess the truth—I was a little short, and I asked our poor friend to take some things for me to the pawnbroker's——'

' What ! and they thought she had robbed us !' cried Dagobert ; ' she, the most honest girl in the world ! it is dreadful—you ought to have interfered, madame ; you ought to have said that you knew her.'

' I tried to do so, sir ; but, unfortunately, they would not hear me. The crowd increased every moment, till the guard came up, and carried her off.'

' She might die of it, she is so sensitive and timid !' exclaimed Frances.

' Ah, good Mother Bunch ! so gentle ! so considerate !' said Blanche, turning with tearful eyes towards her sister.

' Not being able to help her,' resumed Mrs. Grivois, ' I hastened hither to inform you of this misadventure—which may, indeed, easily be repaired—as it will only be necessary to go and claim the young girl as soon as possible.'

At these words, Dagobert hastily seized his hat, and said abruptly to Mrs. Grivois : ' Zounds, madam ! you should have begun by telling us that. Where is the poor child ? Do you know ?'

' I do not, sir ; but there are still so many excited people in the street that, if you will have the kindness to step out, you will be sure to learn.'

' Why the devil do you talk of kindness ? It is my duty, madame. Poor child !' repeated Dagobert. ' Taken up as a thief !—it is really horrible. I will go to the guard-house, and to the commissary of police for this neighbourhood, and, by hook or crook, I will find her, and have her out, and bring her home with me.'

So saying, Dagobert hastily departed. Frances, now that she felt more tranquil as to the fate of Mother Bunch, thanked the Lord that this circumstance had obliged her husband to go out, for his presence at this juncture caused her a terrible embarrassment.

Mrs. Grivois had left My Lord in the coach below, for the moments were precious. Casting a significant glance at Frances, she handed her Abbé Dubois' letter, and said to her, with strong emphasis on every word : ' You will see by this letter, madame, what was the object of my visit, which I have not before been able to explain to you, but on which I truly congratulate myself, as it brings me into connexion with these two charming young ladies.'

Rose and Blanche looked at each other in surprise. Frances took the letter with a trembling hand. It required all the pressing and threatening injunctions of her confessor to conquer the last scruples of the poor woman, for she shuddered at the thought of Dagobert's terrible indignation. Moreover, in her simplicity, she knew not how to announce to the young girls that they were to accompany this lady.

Mrs. Grivois guessed her embarrassment, made a sign to her to be at her ease, and said to Rose, whilst Frances was reading the letter of her confessor : ' How happy your relation will be to see you, my dear young lady !'

' Our relation, madame ?' said Rose, more and more astonished.

' Certainly. She knew of your arrival here, but, as she is still suffering from the effects of a long illness, she was not able to come herself to-day, and has sent me to fetch you to her. Unfortunately,' added Mrs. Grivois, perceiving a movement of uneasiness on the part of the two sisters, ' it will not be in her power, as she tells Mrs. Baudoin in her letter, to see you for more than a very short time—so you may be back here in about an hour. But to-morrow, or the next day after, she will be well enough to leave home, and then she will come and make arrangements with Mrs. Baudoin and her husband, to take you into her house—for she could not bear to leave you at the charge of the worthy people who have been so kind to you.'

These last words of Mrs. Grivois made a favourable impression upon the two sisters, and banished their fears of becoming a heavy burden to Dagobert's family. If it had been proposed to them to quit altogether the house in the Rue Brise-Miche, without first asking the consent of their old friend, they would certainly have hesitated ; but Mrs. Grivois had only spoken of an hour's visit. They felt no suspicion, therefore, and Rose said to Frances : ' We may go and see our relation, I suppose, madame. without waiting for Dagobert's return ?'

' Certainly,' said Frances, in a feeble voice, ' since you are to be back almost directly.'

' Then, madame, I would beg these dear young ladies to come with me as soon as possible, as I should like to bring them back before noon.'

' We are ready, madame,' said Rose.

' Well, then, young ladies, embrace your second mother, and come,' said Mrs. Grivois, who was hardly able to control her uneasiness, for she trembled lest Dagobert should return from one moment to the other.

Rose and Blanche embraced Frances, who, clasping in her arms the two charming and innocent creatures that she was about to deliver up, could with difficulty restrain her tears, though she was fully convinced that she was acting for their salvation.

' Come, young ladies,' said Mrs. Grivois, in the most affable tone, ' let us make haste—you will excuse my impatience, I am sure—but it is in the name of your relation that I speak.'

Having once more tenderly kissed the wife of Dagobert, the sisters quitted the room hand in hand, and descended the staircase close behind Mrs. Grivois, followed (without their being aware of it) by Spoilsport. The intelligent animal cautiously watched their movements, for, in the absence of his master, he never let them out of his sight.

For greater security, no doubt, the waiting-woman of Madame de Saint-Dizier had ordered the hackney-coach to wait for her at a little distance from the Rue Brise-Miche, in the cloister square. In a few seconds, the orphans and their conductress reached the carriage.

' Oh, missus !' said the coachman, opening the door ; ' no offence, I hope —but you have the most ill-tempered rascal of a dog ! Since you put him into my coach, he has never ceased howling like a roasted cat, and looks as if he would eat us all up alive !' In fact, My Lord, who detested solitude, was yelling in the most deplorable manner.

' Be quiet, My Lord ! here I am,' said Mrs. Grivois ; then, addressing the two sisters, she added : ' Pray get in, my dear young ladies.'

Rose and Blanche got into the coach. Before she followed them, Mrs. Grivois was giving to the coachman in a low voice the direction to St. Mary's Convent, and was adding other instructions, when suddenly the pug-dog, who had growled savagely when the sisters took their seats in the coach, began to bark with fury. The cause of this anger was clear enough ; Spoilsport, until now unperceived, had with one bound entered the carriage.

The pug, exasperated by this boldness, forgetting his ordinary prudence, and excited to the utmost by rage and ugliness of temper, sprang at his muzzle, and bit him so cruelly, that, in his turn, the brave Siberian dog, maddened by the pain, threw himself upon the teaser, seized him by the throat, and fairly strangled him with two grips of his powerful jaws—as appeared by one stifled groan of the pug, previously half suffocated with fat.

All this took place in less time than is occupied by the description. Rose and Blanche had hardly opportunity to exclaim twice : ' Here, Spoilsport ! down !'

' Oh, good gracious !' said Mrs. Grivois, turning round at the noise. ' There again is that monster of a dog—he will certainly hurt my love. Send him away, young ladies—make him get down—it is impossible to take him with us.'

Ignorant of the degree of Spoilsport's criminality, for his paltry foe was stretched lifeless under a seat, the young girls yet felt that it would be improper to take the dog with them, and they therefore said to him in an angry tone, at the same time slightly touching him with their feet : ' Get down, Spoilsport ! go away !'

The faithful animal hesitated at first to obey this order. Sad and supplicatingly looked he at the orphans, and with an air of mild reproach, as if blaming them for sending away their only defender. But upon the stern repetition of the command, he got down from the coach, with his tail between his legs, feeling perhaps that he had been somewhat over-hasty with regard to the pug.

Mrs. Grivois, who was in a great hurry to leave that quarter of the town, seated herself with precipitation in the carriage; the coachman closed the door, and mounted his box; and then the coach started at a rapid rate, whilst Mrs. Grivois prudently let down the blinds, for fear of meeting Dagobert by the way.

Having taken these indispensable precautions, she was able to turn her attention to her pet, whom she loved with all that deep, exaggerated affection, which people of a bad disposition sometimes entertain for animals, as if they concentrated and lavished upon them all those feelings in which they are deficient with regard to their fellow-creatures. In a word, Mrs. Grivois was passionately attached to this peevish, cowardly, spiteful dog, partly perhaps from a secret sympathy with his vices. This attachment had lasted for six years, and only seemed to increase as My Lord advanced in age.

We have laid some stress on this apparently puerile detail, because the most trifling causes have often disastrous effects, and because we wish the reader to understand what must have been the despair, fury, and exasperation of this woman, when she discovered the death of her dog—a despair, a fury, and an exasperation, of which the orphans might yet feel the cruel consequences.

The hackney-coach had proceeded rapidly for some seconds, when Mrs. Grivois, who was seated with her back to the horses, called My Lord. The dog had very good reasons for not replying.

'Well, you sulky beauty!' said Mrs. Grivois, soothingly; 'you have taken offence, have you? It was not my fault if that great ugly dog came into the coach, was it, young ladies? Come and kiss your mistress, and let us make peace, old obstinate!'

The same obstinate silence continued on the part of the canine noble. Rose and Blanche began to look anxiously at each other, for they knew that Spoilsport was somewhat rough in his ways, though they were far from suspecting what had really happened. But Mrs. Grivois, rather surprised than uneasy at her pug-dog's insensibility to her affectionate appeals, and believing him to be sullenly crouching beneath the seat, stooped down to take him up, and feeling one of his paws, drew it impatiently towards her, whilst she said to him in a half-jesting, half-angry tone: 'Come, naughty fellow! you will give a pretty notion of your temper to these young ladies.'

So saying, she took up the dog, much astonished at his unresisting torpor; but what was her fright, when, having placed him upon her lap, she saw that he was quite motionless.

'An apoplexy!' cried she. 'The dear creature ate too much—I was always afraid of it.'

Turning round hastily, she exclaimed: 'Stop coachman! stop!' without reflecting, that the coachman could not hear her. Then raising the cur's head, still thinking that he was only in a fit, she perceived with horror the bloody holes imprinted by five or six sharp fangs, which left no doubt of the cause of his deplorable end.

Her first impulse was one of grief and despair. 'Dead!' she exclaimed; 'dead! and already cold! Oh, goodness!'—And this woman burst into tears.

The tears of the wicked are ominous. For a bad man to weep, he must have suffered much; and, with him, the reaction of suffering, instead of softening the soul, inflames it to a dangerous anger.

Thus, after yielding to that first painful emotion, the mistress of My Lord felt herself transported with rage and hate—yes, hate—violent hate for the young girls, who had been the involuntary cause of the dog's death. Her countenance so plainly betrayed her resentment, that Blanche and Rose were frightened at the expression of her face, which had now grown purple with fury, as with agitated voice and wrathful glance she exclaimed : 'It was your dog that killed him !'

' Oh, madame !' said Rose ; ' we had nothing to do with it.'

' It was your dog that bit Spoilsport first,' added Blanche, in a plaintive voice.

The look of terror impressed on the features of the orphans recalled Mrs. Grivois to herself. She saw the fatal consequences that might arise from yielding imprudently to her anger. For the very sake of vengeance, she had to restrain herself, in order not to awaken suspicion in the minds of Marshal Simon's daughters. But not to appear to recover too soon from her first impression, she continued for some minutes to cast irritated glances at the young girls ; then, little by little, her anger seemed to give way to violent grief ; she covered her face with her hands, heaved a long sigh, and appeared to weep bitterly.

' Poor lady !' whispered Rose to Blanche. ' How she weeps !—No doubt, she loved her dog as much as we love Spoilsport.'

'Alas ! yes,' replied Blanche. ' We also wept when our old Jovial was killed.'

After a few minutes, Mrs. Grivois raised her head, dried her eyes definitively, and said in a gentle, and almost affectionate voice : 'Forgive me, young ladies ! I was unable to repress the first movement of irritation, or rather of deep sorrow—for I was tenderly attached to this poor dog—he has never left me for six years.'

' We are very sorry for this misfortune, madame,' resumed Rose ; ' and we regret it the more, that it seems to be irreparable.'

' I was just saying to my sister, that we can the better fancy your grief, as we have had to mourn the death of our old horse, that carried us all the way from Siberia.'

' Well, my dear young ladies, let us think no more about it. It was my fault ; I should not have brought him with me ; but he was always so miserable, whenever I left him. You will make allowances for my weakness. A good heart feels for animals as well as people ; so I must trust to your sensibility to excuse my hastiness.'

' Do not think of it, madame ; it is only your grief that afflicts us.'

' I shall get over it, my dear young ladies—I shall get over it. The joy of the meeting between you and your relation will help to console me. She will be so happy. You are so charming ! and then the singular circumstance of your exact likeness to each other adds to the interest you inspire.'

' You are too kind to us, madame.'

' Oh, no—I am sure you resemble each other as much in disposition as in face.'

' That is quite natural, madame,' said Rose, ' for since our birth we have never left each other a minute, whether by night or by day. It would be strange, if we were not like in character.'

' Really, my dear young ladies ! you have never left each other a minute ?'

' Never, madame.' The sisters joined hands with an expressive smile.

' Then, how unhappy you would be, and how much to be pitied, if ever you were separated.'

' Oh, madame ! it is impossible,' said Blanche, smiling.

' How impossible ?'

' Who would have the heart to separate us ?'

' No doubt, my dear young ladies, it would be very cruel.'

'Oh, madame,' resumed Blanche, 'even very wicked people would not think of separating us.'

'So much the better, my dear young ladies—pray, why ?'

'Because it would cause us too much grief.'

'Because it would kill us.'

'Poor little dears !'

'Three months ago, we were shut up in prison. Well, when the governor of the prison saw us, though he looked a very stern man, he could not help saying : ' It would be killing these children to separate them ;' and so we remained together, and were as happy as one can be in prison.'

'It shows your excellent heart, and also that of the persons who knew how to appreciate it.

The carriage stopped, and they heard the coachman call out : ' Any one at the gate there ?'

'Oh ! here we are at your relation's,' said Mrs. Grivois. Two wings of a gate flew open, and the carriage rolled over the gravel of a court-yard

Mrs. Grivois having drawn up one of the blinds, they found themselves in a vast court, across the centre of which ran a high wall, with a kind of porch upon columns, under which was a little door. Behind this wall, they could see the upper part of a very large building in freestone. Compared with the house in the Rue Brise-Miche, this building appeared a palace ; so Blanche said to Mrs. Grivois, with an expression of artless admiration : ' Dear me, madame, what a fine residence !'

'That is nothing,' replied Madame Grivois; 'wait till you see the interior, which is much finer.'

When the coachman opened the door of the carriage, what was the rage of Mrs. Grivois, and the surprise of the girls, to see Spoilsport, who had been clever enough to follow the coach. Pricking up his ears, and wagging his tail, he seemed to have forgotten his late offences, and to expect to be praised for his intelligent fidelity.

'What !' cried Mrs. Grivois, whose sorrows were renewed at the sight ; ' has that abominable dog followed the coach.'

'A famous dog, mum,' answered the coachman : ' he never once left the heels of my horses. He must have been trained to it. He's a powerful beast, and two men couldn't scare him. Look at the throat of him now !'

The mistress of the deceased pug, enraged at the somewhat unseasonable praises bestowed upon the Siberian, said to the orphans, 'I will announce your arrival, wait for me an instant in the coach.'

So saying, she went with a rapid step towards the porch, and rang the bell. A woman, clad in a monastic garb, appeared at the door, and bowed respectfully to Mrs. Grivois, who addressed her in these few words : ' I have brought you the two young girls ; the orders of Abbé d'Aigrigny and the Princess are, that they be instantly separated, and kept apart in solitary cells—you understand, sister—and subjected to the rule for *impenitents.*'

'I will go and inform the superior, and it will be done,' said the portress, with another bend.

'Now, will you come, my dear young ladies ?' resumed Mrs. Grivois, addressing the two girls, who had secretly bestowed a few caresses upon Spoilsport, so deeply were they touched by his instinctive attachment ; ' you will be introduced to your relation, and I will return and fetch you in half an hour. Coachman, keep that dog back.'

Rose and Blanche, in getting out of the coach, were so much occupied with Spoilsport, that they did not perceive the portress, who was half hidden behind the little door. Neither did they remark, that the person who was to introduce them was dressed as a nun, till, taking them by the hand, she had led them across the threshold, when the door was immediately closed behind them.

As soon as Mrs. Grivois had seen the orphans safe into the convent, she told the coachman to leave the court-yard, and wait for her at the outer-gate. The coachman obeyed ; but Spoilsport, who had seen Rose and Blanche enter by the little door, ran to it, and remained there.

Mrs. Grivois then called the porter of the main entrance,—a tall, vigorous fellow, and said to him : ' Here are ten francs for you, Nicholas, if you will beat out the brains of that great dog, who is crouching under the porch.'

Nicholas shook his head, as he observed Spoilsport's size and strength. ' Devil take me, madame !' said he ; ''tis not so easy to tackle a dog of that build.'

' I will give you twenty francs ; only kill him before me.

' One ought to have a gun, and I have only an iron hammer.'

' That will do ; you can knock him down at a blow.'

' Well, madame—I will try—but I have my doubts.' And Nicholas went to fetch his mallet.

' Oh ! if I had the strength !' said Mrs. Grivois.

The porter returned with his weapon, and advanced slowly and treacherously towards Spoilsport, who was still crouching beneath the porch. ' Here, old fellow ! here, my good dog !' said Nicholas, striking his left hand on his thigh, and keeping his right behind him, with the crowbar grasped in it.

Spoilsport rose, examined Nicholas attentively, and no doubt perceiving by his manner that the porter meditated some evil design, bounded away from him, outflanked the enemy, saw clearly what was intended, and kept himself at a respectful distance.

' He smells a rat,' said Nicholas ; ' the rascal's on his guard. He will not let me come near him. It's no go.'

' You are an awkward fellow,' said Mrs. Grivois, in a passion, as she threw a five-franc piece to Nicholas : 'at all events, drive him away.'

' That will be easier than to kill him, madame,' said the porter. Indeed, finding himself pursued, and conscious probably that it would be useless to attempt an open resistance, Spoilsport fled from the court-yard into the street ; but once there, he felt himself, as it were, upon neutral ground, and notwithstanding all the threats of Nicholas, refused to withdraw an inch further than just sufficient to keep out of reach of the sledge-hammer. So that when Mrs. Grivois, pale with rage, again stepped into her hackney-coach, in which were My Lord's lifeless remains, she saw with the utmost vexation that Spoilsport was lying at a few steps from the gate, which Nicholas had just closed, having given up the chase in despair.

The Siberian dog, sure of finding his way back to the Rue Brise-Miche, had determined, with the sagacity peculiar to his race, to wait for the orphans on the spot where he then was.

Thus were the two sisters confined in St. Mary's Convent, which, as we have already said, was next door to the lunatic asylum in which Adrienne de Cardoville was immured.

   ❁   ❁   ❁   ❁   ❁   ❁

We now conduct the reader to the dwelling of Dagobert's wife, who was waiting with dreadful anxiety for the return of her husband, knowing that he would call her to account for the disappearance of Marshal Simon's daughters.

CHAPTER LII.

THE INFLUENCE OF A CONFESSOR.

HARDLY had the orphans quitted Dagobert's wife, when the poor woman, kneeling down, began to pray with fervour. Her tears, long restrained, now flowed abundantly ; notwithstanding her sincere conviction that she had performed a religious duty in delivering up the girls, she waited with extreme fear her husband's return. Though blinded by her pious zeal, she could not hide from herself, that Dagobert would have good reason to be angry ; and then this poor mother had also, under these untoward circumstances, to tell him of Agricola's arrest.

Every noise upon the stairs made Frances start with trembling anxiety ; after which, she would resume her fervent prayers, supplicating strength to support this new and arduous trial. At length, she heard a step upon the landing-place below, and, feeling sure this time that it was Dagobert, she hastily seated herself, dried her tears, and taking a sack of coarse cloth upon her lap, appeared to be occupied with sewing—though her aged hands trembled so much, that she could hardly hold the needle.

After some minutes the door opened, and Dagobert appeared. The soldier's rough countenance was stern and sad ; as he entered, he flung his hat violently upon the table, so full of painful thought, that he did not at first perceive the absence of the orphans.

' Poor girl !' cried he. ' It is really terrible !'

' Didst see Mother Bunch ? didst claim her ?' said Frances hastily, forgetting for a moment her own fears.

' Yes, I have seen her—but in what a state !—'twas enough to break one's heart. I claimed her, and pretty loud too, I can tell you ; but they said to me, that the commissary must first come to our place in order——' Here Dagobert paused, threw a glance of surprise round the room, and exclaimed abruptly : ' Where are the children ?'

Frances felt herself seized with an icy shudder. ' My dear,' she began, in a feeble voice—but she was unable to continue.

' Where are Rose and Blanche ! Answer me then ! And Spoilsport, who is not here either !'

' Do not be angry.'

' Come,' said Dagobert, abruptly, ' I see you have let them go out with a neighbour—why not have accompanied them yourself, or let them wait for me, if they wished to take a walk; which is natural enough, this room being so dull. But I am astonished that they should have gone out, before they had news of good Mother Bunch—they have such kind hearts. But how pale you are !' added the soldier, looking nearer at Frances ; ' what is the matter, my poor wife ? Are you ill ?'

Dagobert took Frances's hand affectionately in his own ; but the latter, painfully agitated by these words, pronounced with touching goodness, bowed her head, and wept as she kissed her husband's hand. The soldier, growing more and more uneasy, as he felt the scalding tears of his wife, exclaimed : ' You weep, you do not answer—tell me, then, the cause of your grief, poor wife ! Is it because I spoke a little loud, in asking you how you could let the dear children go out with a neighbour ? Remember their dying mother entrusted them to my care—'tis sacred, you see—and with them, I am like an old hen after her chickens,' added he, laughing to enliven Frances.

' Yes, you are right in loving them !'

' Come, then—be calm—you know me of old. With my great, hoarse voice, I am not so bad a fellow at bottom. As you can trust to this neighbour, there is no great harm done ; but, in future, my good Frances, do not take any step with regard to the children without consulting me. They asked, I suppose, to go out for a little stroll with Spoilsport?'

'No, my dear——I——'

'No! Who is this neighbour, to whom you have entrusted them? Where has she taken them? What time will she bring them back?'

'I do not know,' murmured Frances, in a failing voice.

'You do not know!' cried Dagobert, with indignation; but restraining himself, he added, in a tone of friendly reproach: 'You do not know? You cannot even fix an hour, or, better still, not entrust them to any one? The children must have been very anxious to go out. They knew that I should return at any moment, so why not wait for me—eh, Frances? I ask you, why did they not wait for me? Answer me, will you!—Zounds! you would make a saint swear!' cried Dagobert, stamping his foot; 'answer me, I say!'

The courage of Frances was fast failing. These pressing and reiterated questions, which might end by the discovery of the truth, made her endure a thousand slow and poignant tortures. She preferred coming at once to the point, and determined to bear the full weight of her husband's anger, like a humble and resigned victim, obstinately faithful to the promise she had sworn to her confessor.

Not having the strength to rise, she bowed her head, allowed her arms to fall on either side of the chair, and said to her husband in a tone of the deepest despondency: 'Do with me what you will—but do not ask what is become of the children—I cannot answer you.'

If a thunderbolt had fallen at the feet of the soldier, he would not have been more violently, more deeply moved; he became deadly pale; his bald forehead was covered with cold sweat; with fixed and staring look, he remained for some moments motionless, mute, and petrified. Then, as if roused with a start from this momentary torpor, and filled with a terrific energy, he seized his wife by the shoulders, lifted her like a feather, placed her on her feet before him, and, leaning over her, exclaimed in a tone of mingled fury and despair: 'The children!'

'Mercy! mercy!' gasped Frances, in a faint voice.

'Where are the children?' repeated Dagobert, as he shook with his powerful hands that poor frail body, and added in a voice of thunder: 'Will you answer? the children!'

'Kill me, or forgive me, I cannot answer you,' replied the unhappy woman, with that inflexible, yet mild obstinacy, peculiar to timid characters, when they act from convictions of doing right.

'Wretch!' cried the soldier; wild with rage, grief, despair, he lifted up his wife as if he would have dashed her upon the floor—but he was too brave a man to commit such cowardly cruelty, and, after that first burst of involuntary fury, he let her go.

Overpowered, Frances sank upon her knees, clasped her hands, and, by the faint motion of her lips, it was clear that she was praying. Dagobert had then a moment of stunning giddiness; his thoughts wandered; what had just happened was so sudden, so incomprehensible, that it required some minutes to convince himself that his wife (that angel of goodness, whose life had been one course of heroic self-devotion, and who knew what the daughters of Marshal Simon were to him) should say to him: 'Do not ask me about them—I cannot answer you.'

The firmest, the strongest mind would have been shaken by this inexplicable fact. But, when the soldier had a little recovered himself, he began to look coolly at the circumstances, and reasoned thus sensibly with himself: 'My wife alone can explain to me this inconceivable mystery—I do not mean either to beat or kill her—let us try every possible method, therefore, to induce her to speak, and above all, let me try to control myself.'

He took a chair, handed another to his wife, who was still on her knees, and said to her : ' Sit down.' With an air of the utmost dejection, Frances obeyed.

' Listen to me, wife,' resumed Dagobert in a broken voice, interrupted by involuntary starts, which betrayed the boiling impatience he could hardly restrain. ' Understand me—this cannot pass over in this manner—you know. I will never use violence towards you—just now, I gave way to a first moment of hastiness—I am sorry for it. Be sure, I shall not do so again : but, after all, I must know what has become of these children. Their mother entrusted them to my care, and I did not bring them all the way from Siberia, for you to say to me ; " Do not ask me—I cannot tell you what I have done with them." There is no reason in that. Suppose Marshal Simon were to arrive, and say to me, " Dagobert, my children ?" what answer am I to give him ? See, I am calm—judge for yourself—I am calm—but just put yourself in my place, and tell me—what answer am I to give to the marshal ? Well—what say you ! Will you speak ?'

' Alas ! my dear——'

' It is of no use crying *alas !*' said the soldier wiping his forehead, on which the veins were swollen as if they would burst ; ' what am I to answer to the marshal ?'

' Accuse me to him—I will bear it all—I will say——'

' What will you say ?'

' That, on going out, you entrusted the two girls to me, and that not finding them on return you asked me about them—and that my answer was, that I could not tell you what had become of them.'

' And you think the marshal will be satisfied with such reasons ?' cried Dagobert, clenching his fists convulsively upon his knees.

' Unfortunately, I can give no other—either to him or you—no—not if I were to die for it.'

Dagobert bounded from his chair at this answer, which was given with hopeless resignation. His patience was exhausted ; but determined not to yield to new bursts of anger, or to spend his breath in useless menaces, he abruptly opened one of the windows, and exposed his burning forehead to the cool air. A little calmer, he walked up and down for a few moments, and then returned to seat himself beside his wife. She, with her eyes bathed in tears, fixed her gaze upon the crucifix, thinking that she also had to bear a heavy cross.

Dagobert resumed : ' By the manner in which you speak, I see that no accident has happened, which might endanger the health of the children.'

' No, oh no ! thank God, they are quite well—that is all I can say to you.'

' Did they go out alone ?'

' I cannot answer you.'

' Has any one taken them away ?'

' Alas, my dear ! why ask me these questions ? I cannot answer you.'

' Will they come back here ?'

' I do not know.'

Dagobert started up ; his patience was once more exhausted. But, after taking a few turns in the room, he again seated himself as before.

' After all,' said he to his wife, ' you have no interest to conceal from me what is become of the children. Why refuse to let me know ?'

' I cannot do otherwise.'

' I think you will change your opinion, when you know something that I am now forced to tell you. Listen to me well !' added Dagobert, in an agitated voice ; ' if these children are not restored to me before the 13th of February—a day close at hand—I am in the position of a man that would rob the daughters of Marshal Simon—rob them, d'ye understand ?' said the soldier, becoming more and more agitated. Then, with an accent of despair which pierced Frances's heart, he continued : ' And yet I have done all that an honest man could do for those poor children—you cannot tell what I have had to suffer on the road—my cares, my anxieties—I, a soldier, with the charge of two girls. It was only by strength of heart, by devotion, that I could go through with it—and when, for my reward, I hoped to be able to say to their father : ' Here are your children !——' The soldier paused. To the violence of his first emotions had succeeded a mournful tenderness ; he wept.

At sight of the tears rolling slowly down Dagobert's grey moustache, Frances felt for a moment her resolution give way ; but, recalling the oath which she had made to her confessor, and reflecting that the eternal salvation of the orphans was at stake, she reproached herself inwardly with this evil temptation, which would no doubt be severely blamed by Abbé Dubois. She answered, therefore, in a trembling voice : ' How can they accuse you of robbing these children !'

' Know,' resumed Dagobert, drawing his hand across his eyes, ' that if these young girls have braved so many dangers, to come hither, all the way from Siberia, it is that great interests are concerned—perhaps an immense fortune—and that, if they are not present on the 13th February—here, in Paris, Rue Saint François—all will be lost—and through my fault—for I am responsible for your actions.'

' The 13th February ? Rue Saint François ?' cried Frances, looking at her husband with surprise. ' Like Gabriel !'

' What do you say about Gabriel ?'

' When I took him in (poor deserted child !), he wore a bronze medal about his neck.'

' A bronze medal !' cried the soldier, struck with amazement ; ' a bronze medal with these words, "At Paris you will be, the 13th of February, 1832, Rue Saint François ?"'

' Yes—how do you know ?'

' Gabriel, too !' said the soldier, speaking to himself. Then he added hastily : ' Does Gabriel know that this medal was found upon him ?'

' I spoke to him of it at some time. He had also about him a portfolio, filled with papers in a foreign tongue. I gave them to Abbé Dubois, my confessor, to look over. He told me afterwards, that they were of little consequence ; and, at a later period, when a charitable person, named M. Rodin, undertook the education of Gabriel, and to get him into the seminary, Abbé Dubois handed both papers and medal to him. Since then, I have heard nothing of them.'

When Frances spoke of her confessor, a sudden light flashed across the mind of the soldier, though he was far from suspecting the machinations which had so long been at work with regard to Gabriel and the orphans. But he had a vague feeling that his wife was acting in obedience to some secret influence of the confessional—an influence of which he could not understand the aim or object, but which explained, in part at least, Frances's inconceivable obstinacy with regard to the disappearance of the orphans.

After a moment's reflection, he rose, and said sternly to his wife, looking fixedly at her : ' There is a priest at the bottom of all this.'

' What do you mean, my dear ?'

' You have no interest to conceal these children. You are one of the best of women. You see that I suffer ; if you only were concerned, you would have pity upon me.'

' My dear——'

' I tell you, all this smacks of the confessional,' resumed Dagobert.   ' You would sacrifice me and these children to your confessor ; but take care--I shall find out where he lives—and a thousand thunders !   I will go and ask him who is master in my house, he or I—and if he does not answer,' added the soldier, with a threatening expression of countenance, ' I shall know how to make him speak.'

' Gracious heaven !' cried Frances, clasping her hands in horror at these sacrilegious words ; ' remember he is a priest !'

' A priest, who causes discord, treachery, and misfortune in my house, is as much of a wretch as any other, whom I have a right to call to account for the evil he does to me and mine.   Therefore, tell me immediately where are the children—or else, I give you fair warning, I will go and demand them of the confessor.   Some crime is here hatching, of which you are an accomplice without knowing it, unhappy woman !   Well, I prefer having to do with another than you.'

' My dear,' said Frances, in a mild, firm voice, ' you cannot think to impose by violence on a venerable man, who for twenty years has had the care of my soul.   His age alone should be respected.'

' No age shall prevent me !'

' Heavens ! where are you going ?   You alarm me !'

' I am going to your church.   They must know you there—I will ask for your confessor—and we shall see !'

' I entreat you, my dear,' cried Frances, throwing herself in a fright before Dagobert, who was hastening towards the door ; ' only think, to what you will expose yourself !   Heavens ! insult a priest ?   Why, it is one of the reserved cases !'

These last words, which appeared most alarming to the simplicity of Dagobert's wife, did not make any impression upon the soldier.   He disengaged himself from her grasp, and was going to rush out bareheaded, so high was his exasperation, when the door opened, and the commissary of police entered, followed by Mother Bunch and a policeman, carrying the bundle which he had taken from the young girl.

' The commissary !' cried Dagobert, who recognised him by his official scarf.   ' Ah ! so much the better—he could not have come at a fitter moment.'

CHAPTER LIII.

THE EXAMINATION.

' Mistress Frances Baudoin ?' asked the magistrate.

' Yes, sir—it is I,' said Frances.   Then, perceiving the pale and trembling sewing-girl, who did not dare to come forward, she stretched out her arms to her.   ' Oh, my poor child !' she exclaimed, bursting into tears ; ' forgive—forgive us—since it is for our sake you have suffered this humiliation !'

When Dagobert's wife had tenderly embraced the young sempstress, the latter, turning towards the commissary, said to him with an expression of sad and touching dignity : ' You see, sir, that I am not a thief.'

' Madame,' said the magistrate, addressing Frances, ' am I to understand that the silver mug, the shawl, the sheets contained in this bundle——'

' Belong to me, sir.   It was to render me a service that this dear girl, who is the best and most honest creature in the world, undertook to carry these articles to the pawnbroker's.'

' Sir,' said the magistrate sternly to the policeman, ' you have committed a deplorable error.   I shall take care to report you, and see that you are punished. You may go, sir.' Then, addressing Mother Bunch, with an air of real regret, he added : 'I can only express my sorrow for what has happened. Believe me, I deeply feel for the cruel position in which you have been placed.'

'I believe it, sir,' said Mother Bunch, 'and I thank you.' Overcome by so many emotions, she sank upon a chair.

The magistrate was about to retire, when Dagobert, who had been seriously reflecting for some minutes, said to him in a firm voice : 'Please to hear me, sir ; I have a deposition to make.'

'Speak, sir.'

'What I am about to say is very important ; it is to you, in your quality of a magistrate, that I make this declaration.'

'And as a magistrate I will hear you, sir.'

'I arrived here two days ago, bringing with me from Russia two girls who had been entrusted to me by their mother—the wife of Marshal Simon.'

'Of Marshal Simon, Duke de Ligny?' said the commissary, very much surprised.

'Yes, sir. Well, I left them here, being obliged to go out on pressing business. This morning, during my absence, they disappeared—and I am certain I know the man who has been the cause of it.'

'Now, my dear,' said Frances, much alarmed.

'Sir,' said the magistrate, 'your declaration is a very serious one. Disappearance of persons—sequestration, perhaps. But are you quite sure ?'

'These young ladies were here an hour ago ; I repeat, sir, that, during my absence, they have been taken away.'

'I do not doubt the sincerity of your declaration, sir ; but still it is difficult to explain so strange an abduction. Who tells you that these young girls will not return ? Besides, whom do you suspect ? One word, before you make your accusation. Remember, it is the magistrate who hears you. On leaving this place, the law will take its course in this affair.'

'That is what I wish, sir ; I am responsible for those young ladies to their father. He may arrive at any moment, and I must be prepared to justify myself.'

'I understand all these reasons, sir ; but still have a care you are not deceived by unfounded suspicions. Your denunciation once made, I may have to act provisionally against the person accused. Now, if you should be under a mistake, the consequences would be very serious for you ; and, without going further,' said the magistrate, pointing to Mother Bunch, with emotion, 'you see what are the results of a false accusation.'

'You hear, my dear,' cried Frances, terrified at the resolution of Dagobert to accuse Abbé Dubois ; 'do not say a word more, I entreat you.'

But the more the soldier reflected, the more he felt convinced that nothing but the influence of her confessor could have induced Frances to act as she had done ; so he resumed, with assurance : 'I accuse my wife's confessor of being the principal or the accomplice in the abduction of Marshal Simon's daughters.'

Frances uttered a deep groan, and hid her face in her hands ; while Mother Bunch, who had drawn nigh, endeavoured to console her. The magistrate had listened to Dagobert with extreme astonishment, and he now said to him with some severity : 'Pray, sir, do not accuse unjustly a man whose position is in the highest degree respectable—a priest, sir?—yes, a priest ? I warned you beforehand to reflect upon what you advanced. All this becomes very serious ; and, at your age, any levity in such matters would be unpardonable.'

'Bless me, sir !' said Dagobert, with impatience ; 'at my age, one has common sense. These are the facts. My wife is one of the best and most honourable of human creatures—ask any one in the neighbourhood, and they will tell you so—but she is a devotee ; and, for twenty years, she has always seen with her confessor's eyes. She adores her son, she loves me also ; but she puts the confessor before us both.'

' Sir,' said the commissary, ' these family details——'

' Are indispensable, as you shall see. I go out an hour ago, to look after this poor girl here. When I come back, the young ladies have disappeared. I ask my wife to whom she has entrusted them, and where they are ; she falls at my feet weeping, and says : " Do what you will with me, but do not ask me what is become of the children. I cannot answer you."'

' Is this true, madame?' cried the commissary, looking at Frances with surprise.

' Anger, threats, entreaties, had no effect,' resumed Dagobert ; ' to everything she answered as mildly as a saint : " I can tell you nothing !" Now, sir, I maintain that my wife has no interest to take away these children ; she is under the absolute dominion of her confessor; she has acted by his orders and for his purposes ; he is the guilty party.'

Whilst Dagobert spoke, the commissary looked more and more attentively at Frances, who, supported by the hunchback, continued to weep bitterly. After a moment's reflection, the magistrate advanced towards Dagobert's wife, and said to her : ' Madame, you have heard what your husband has just declared.'——' Yes, sir.'

' What have you to say in your justification ?'

' But, sir,' cried Dagobert, ' it is not my wife that I accuse—I do not mean that : it is her confessor.'

' Sir, you have applied to a magistrate ; and the magistrate must act as he thinks best for the discovery of the truth. Once more, madame,' he resumed, addressing Frances, ' what have you to say in your justification ?'

' Alas! nothing, sir.'

' Is it true that your husband left these young girls in your charge when he went out ?'

' Yes, sir.'

' Is it true that, on his return, they were no longer to be found ?'

' Yes, sir.'

' Is it true that, when he asked you where they were, you told him that you could give him no information on the subject ?'

The commissary appeared to wait for Frances's reply with a kind of anxious curiosity.

' Yes, sir,' said she, with the utmost simplicity, ' that was the answer I made my husband.'

' What, madame !' said the magistrate, with an air of painful astonishment ; ' that was your only answer to all the prayers and commands of your husband ? What ! you refused to give him the least information ? It is neither probable nor possible.'

' It is the truth, sir.'

' Well, but, after all, madame, what have you done with the young ladies that were entrusted to your care ?'

' I can tell you nothing about it, sir. If I would not answer my poor husband, I certainly will not answer any one else.'

' Well, sir,' resumed Dagobert, ' was I wrong ? An honest, excellent woman like that, who was always full of good sense and affection, to talk in this way—is it natural ? I repeat to you, sir, that it is the work of her confessor ; act against him promptly and decidedly, we shall soon know all, and my poor children will be restored to me.'

'Madame,' continued the commissary, without being able to repress a certain degree of emotion, 'I am about to speak to you very severely. My duty obliges me to do so. This affair becomes so serious and complicated, that I must instantly commence judicial proceedings on the subject. You acknowledge that these young ladies have been left in your charge, and that you cannot produce them. Now, listen to me ; if you refuse to give any explanation in the matter, it is you alone that will be accused of their disappearance. I shall be obliged, though with great regret, to take you into custody.'

'Me !' cried Frances, with the utmost alarm.

'Her !' exclaimed Dagobert ; 'never ! It is her confessor that I accuse, not my poor wife. Take her into custody, indeed !' He ran towards her, as if he would protect her.

'It is too late, sir,' said the commissary. 'You have made your charge for the abduction of these two young ladies. According to your wife's own declaration, she alone is compromised up to this point. I must take her before the Public Prosecutor, who will decide what course to pursue.'

'And I say, sir,' cried Dagobert, in a menacing tone, 'that my wife shall not stir from this room.'

'Sir,' said the commissary, coolly, 'I can appreciate your feelings ; but, in the interest of justice, I would beg you not to oppose a necessary measure —a measure which, moreover, in ten minutes it would be quite impossible for you to prevent.'

These words, spoken with calmness, recalled the soldier to himself. 'But, sir,' said he, ' I do not accuse my wife.'

'Never mind, my dear--do not think of me !' said Frances, with the angelic resignation of a martyr. 'The Lord is still pleased to try me sorely ; but I am his unworthy servant, and must gratefully resign myself to His will. Let them arrest me, if they choose ; I will say no more in prison than I have said already on the subject of those poor children.'

'But, sir,' cried Dagobert, 'you see that my wife is out of her head. You cannot arrest her.'

'There is no charge, proof, or indication against the other person whom you accuse, and whose character should be his protection. If I take your wife, she may perhaps be restored to you after a preliminary examination. I regret,' added the commissary, in a tone of pity, 'to have to execute such a mission, at the very moment when your son's arrest——'

'What !' cried Dagobert, looking with speechless astonishment at his wife and Mother Bunch ; 'what does he say ? my son ?'

'You were not then aware of it?' Oh, sir ! a thousand pardons !' said the magistrate, with painful emotion. 'It is distressing to make you such a communication.'

'My son !' repeated Dagobert, pressing his two hands to his forehead. 'My son ! arrested !'

'For a political offence of no great moment,' said the commissary.

'Oh ! this is too much. All comes on me at once !' cried the soldier, falling overpowered into a chair, and hiding his face with his hands.

* * * * * *

After a touching farewell, during which, in spite of her terror, Frances remained faithful to the vow she had made to the Abbé Dubois—Dagobert, who had refused to give evidence against his wife, was left leaning upon a table, exhausted by contending emotions, and could not help exclaiming : 'Yesterday, I had with me my wife, my son, my two poor orphans—and now—I am alone—alone !'

The moment he pronounced these words, in a despairing tone, a mild, sad voice was heard close behind him, saying timidly : 'M. Dagobert, I am here ; if you will allow me, I will remain and wait upon you.'

It was Mother Bunch !

Trusting that the reader's sympathy is with the old soldier thus left desolate, with Agricola in his prison, Adrienne in hers, the madhouse, and Rose and Blanche Simon in theirs, the nunnery ; we hasten to assure him (or her, as the case may be), that not only will their future steps be traced, but the dark machinations of the Jesuits, and the thrilling scenes in which new characters will perform their varied parts, pervaded by the watching spirit of the Wandering Jew, will be revealed in Part Second of this work, entitled : THE CHASTISEMENT.

PART SECOND.—THE CHASTISEMENT.

PROLOGUE.

THE BIRD'S-EYE VIEW OF TWO WORLDS.

As the eagle, perched upon the cliff, commands an all-comprehensive view —not only of what happens on the plains and in the woodlands, but of matters occurring upon the heights, which its aerie overlooks, so may the reader have sights pointed out to him, which lie below the level of the unassisted eye.

In the year 1831, the powerful Order of the Jesuits saw fit to begin to act upon information which had for some time been digesting in their hands.

As it related to a sum estimated at no less than thirty or forty millions of francs, it is no wonder that they should redouble all exertions to obtain it from the rightful owners.

These were, presumably, the descendants of Marius, Count of Rennepont, in the reign of Louis XIV. of France.

They were distinguished from other men by a simple token, which all, in the year above named, had in their hands.

It was a bronze medal, bearing these legends on reverse and obverse :

VICTIM	IN PARIS,
of	Rue Saint François, No. 3,
L. C. D. J.	In a century and a half
Pray for me !	you will be.
	February the 13th, 1832.
PARIS,	
February the 13th, 1682.	PRAY FOR ME !

Those who had this token were descendants of a family whom, a hundred and fifty years ago, persecution scattered through the world, in emigration and exile ; in changes of religion, fortune and name. For this family—what grandeur, what reverses, what obscurity, what lustre, what penury, what glory ! How many crimes sullied, how many virtues honoured it ! The history of this single family is the history of humanity ! Passing through many generations, throbbing in the veins of the poor and the rich, the sovereign and the bandit, the wise and the simple, the coward and the brave, the saint and the atheist, the blood flowed on to the year we have named.

Seven representatives summed up the virtue, courage, degradation, splendour, and poverty of the race. Seven: two orphan twin daughters of exiled parents, a dethroned prince, a humble missionary priest, a man of the middle class, a young lady of high name and large fortune, and a working man.

Fate scattered them in Russia, India, France, and America.

The orphans, Rose and Blanche Simon, had left their dead mother's grave in Siberia, under charge of a trooper named Francis Baudoin, *alias* Dagobert, who was as much attached to them as he had been devoted to their father, his commanding general.

On the road to France, this little party had met the first check, in the only tavern of Mockern village. Not only had a wild beast showman, known as Morok the lion-tamer, sought to pick a quarrel with the inoffensive veteran, but that failing, had let a panther of his menagerie loose upon the soldier's horse. That horse had carried Dagobert, under General Simon's and the Great Napoleon's eyes, through many battles ; had borne the General's wife (a Polish lady under the Czar's ban) to her home of exile in Siberia, and their children now across Russia and Germany, but only to perish thus cruelly. An unseen hand appeared in a manifestation of spite otherwise unaccountable. Dagobert, denounced as a French spy, and his fair young companions accused of being adventuresses to help his designs, had so kindled at the insult, not less to him than to his old commander's daughters, that he had taught the pompous burgomaster of Mockern a lesson, which, however, resulted in the imprisonment of the three in Leipsic jail.

General Simon, who had vainly sought to share his master's St. Helena captivity, had gone to fight the English in India. But notwithstanding his drilling of Radja-sing's sepoys, they had been beaten by the troops taught by Clive, and not only was the old king of Mundi slain, and the realm added to the Company's lands, but his son, Prince Djalma, taken prisoner. However, at length released, he had gone to Batavia, with General Simon. The prince's mother was a Frenchwoman, and among the property she left him in the capital of Java, the general was delighted to find just such another medal as he knew was in his wife's possession.

The unseen hand of enmity had reached to him ; for letters miscarried, and he did not know either his wife's decease or that he had twin daughters.

By a trick, on the eve of the steamship leaving Batavia for the Isthmus of Suez, Djalma was separated from his friend, and sailing for Europe alone, the latter had to follow in another vessel.

The missionary priest trod the war trails of the wilderness, with that faith and fearlessness which true soldiers of the cross should evince. In one of these heroic undertakings, Indians had captured him, and dragging him to their village under the shadow of the Rocky Mountains, they had nailed him in derision to a cross, and prepared to scalp him.

But if an unseen hand of a foe smote or stabbed at the sons of Rennepont, a visible interpositor had often shielded them, in various parts of the globe.

A man, seeming of thirty years of age, very tall, with a countenance as lofty as mournful, marked by the black eyebrows meeting, had thrown himself—during a battle's height—between a gun of a park which General Simon was charging and that officer. The cannon vomited its hail of death, but when the flame and smoke had passed, the tall man stood erect as before, smiling pityingly on the gunner, who fell on his knees as frightened as if he beheld Satan himself. Again, as General Simon lay upon the lost field of Waterloo, raging with his wounds, eager to die after such a defeat, this same man staunched his hurts, and bade him live for his wife's sake.

Years after, wearing the same unalterable look, this man accosted Dagobert in Siberia, and gave him for General Simon's wife, the diary and letters of her husband, written in India, in little hope of them ever reaching her hands. And at the year our story opens, this man unbarred the cell-door of Leipsic jail, and let Dagobert and the orphans out, free to continue their way into France.

On the other hand, when the scalping-knife had traced its mark around the head of Gabriel the missionary, and when only the dexterous turn and tug would have removed the trophy, a sudden apparition had terrified the superstitious savages. It was a woman of thirty, whose brown tresses formed a rich frame around a royal face, toned down by endless sorrowing. The red-skins shrank from her steady advance, and when her hand was stretched out between them and their young victim, they uttered a howl of alarm, and fled as if a host of their foemen were on their track. Gabriel was saved, but all his life he was doomed to bear that halo of martyrdom, the circling sweep of the scalper's knife.

He was a Jesuit. By the orders of his society he embarked for Europe. We should say here, that he, though owning a medal of the seven described, was unaware that he should have worn it. His vessel was driven by storms to refit at the Azores, where he had changed ship into the same as was bearing Prince Djalma to France, *viâ* Portsmouth.

But the gales followed him, and sated their fury by wrecking the " Black Eagle" on the Picardy coast. This was at the same point as where a disabled Hamburg steamer, among whose passengers were Dagobert and his two charges, was destroyed the same night. Happily the tempest did not annihilate them all. There were saved, Prince Djalma and a countryman of his, one Faringhea, a Thuggee chief, hunted out of British India ; Dagobert, and Rose and Blanche Simon, whom Gabriel had rescued. These survivors had recovered, thanks to the care they had received in Cardoville House, a country mansion which had sheltered them, and except the prince and the Strangler chief, the others were speedily able to go on to Paris.

The old grenadier and the orphans—until General Simon should be heard from—dwelt in the former's house. His son had kept it, from his mother's love for the life-long home. It was such a mean habitation as a workman like Agricola Baudoin could afford to pay the rent of, and far from the fit abode of the daughters of the Duke de Ligny and Marshal of France, which Napoleon had created General Simon, though the rank had only recently been approved by the restoration.

But in Paris the unknown hostile hand showed itself more malignant than ever.

The young lady of high name and large fortune was Adrienne de Cardoville, whose aunt, the Princess de Saint-Dizier, was a Jesuit. Through her and her accomplices' machinations, the young lady's forward yet virtuous, wildly aspiring but sensible, romantic but just, character was twisted into a passable reason for her immurement in a mad-house.

This asylum adjoined St. Mary's Convent, into which Rose and Blanche Simon were deceitfully conducted. To secure their removal, Dagobert had been decoyed into the country, under pretence of showing some of General Simon's documents to a lawyer ; his son Agricola arrested for treason, on account of some idle verses the blacksmith poet was guilty of, and his wife rendered powerless, or, rather, a passive assistant, by the influence of the confessional ! When Dagobert hurried back from his wild-goose chase, he found the orphans gone : Mother Bunch (a fellow-tenant of the house, who had been brought up in the family) ignorant, and his wife stubbornly refusing to break the promise she had given her confessor, and acquaint a single soul where she had permitted the girls to be taken. In his rage, the soldier rashly accused that confessor, but instead of arresting the Abbé Dubois, it was Mrs. Baudoin whom the magistrate felt compelled to arrest, as the person whom alone he ventured to commit for examination in regard to the orphans' disappearance. Thus triumphs, for the time being, the unseen foe.

The orphans in a nunnery; the dethroned prince a poor castaway in a foreign land; the noble young lady in a madhouse; the missionary priest under the thumb of his superiors.

As for the man of the middle class, and the working man, who conclude the list of this family, we are to read of them, as well as of the others, in the pages which now succeed these.

CHAPTER I.

THE MASQUERADE.

THE following day to that on which Dagobert's wife (arrested for not account-ing for the disappearance of General Simon's daughters) was led away before a magistrate, a noisy and animated scene was transpiring on the Place du Châtelet, in front of a building whose first floor and basement were used as the tap-rooms of the ' Sucking Calf' public-house.

A carnival night was dying out.

Quite a number of maskers, grotesquely and shabbily bedecked, had rushed out of the low dance-houses in the Guildhall Ward, and were roaring out staves of songs as they crossed the square. But on catching sight of a second troop of mummers running about the water-side, the first party stopped to wait for the others to come up, rejoicing, with many a shout, in hopes of one of those verbal battles of slang and smutty talk which made Vadé so illustrious.

This mob—nearly all its members half-seas over, soon swollen by the many people who have to be up early to follow their crafts—suddenly concentrated in one of the corners of the square, so that a pale, deformed girl, who was going that way, was caught in the human tide. This was Mother Bunch. Up with the lark, she was hurrying to receive some work from her employer. Remembering how a mob had treated her when she had been arrested in the streets only the day before, by mistake, the poor work-girl's fears may be imagined when she was now surrounded by the revellers against her will. But, spite of all her efforts—very feeble, alas!—she could not stir a step, for the band of merry-makers, newly arriving, had rushed in among the others, shoving some of them aside, pushing far into the mass, and sweeping Mother Bunch—who was in their way—clear over to the crowd around the public-house.

The new comers were much finer rigged out than the others, for they be-longed to the gay, turbulent class which goes frequently to the Chaumière, the Prado, the Colisée, and other more or less rowdyish haunts of waltzers, made up generally of students, shop-girls, and counter-skippers, clerks, un-fortunates, etc., etc.

This set, while retorting to the chaff of the other party, seemed to be very impatiently expecting some singularly desired person to put in her appearance.

The following snatches of conversation, passing between clowns and colum-bines, pantaloons and fairies, Turks and sultans, débardeurs and débardeuses, paired off more or less properly, will give an idea of the importance of the wished-for personage.

'They ordered the spread to be for seven in the morning, so their car-riages ought to have come up afore now.'

'Werry like, but the Bacchanal Queen has got to lead off the last dance in the Prado.'

'I wish to thunder I'd 'a known that, and I'd 'a stayed there to see her—my beloved Queen !'

'Gobinet! if you call her your beloved Queen again, I'll scratch you? Here's a pinch for you, anyhow !'

'Ow, wow, Celeste ! hands off ! You are black-spotting the be-yutiful white satin jacket my mamma gave me when I first came out as Don *Passqually!'*

'Why do you call the Bacchanal Queen your beloved, then ? What am I, I'd like to know?'

'You are my beloved, but not my Queen, for there is only one moon in the nights of nature, and only one Bacchanal Queen in the nights at the Prado.'

'That's a bit from a valentine ! You can't come over me with such rubbish.'

'Gobinet ! the Queen was an out-and-outer to-night !'

'In prime feather !'

'I never saw her more on the go !'

'And, my eyes ! wasn't her dress stunning ?'

'Took your breath away !'

'Crushing !'

'Heavy !'

'Im-mense !'

'The last kick !'

'No one but she can get up such dresses.'

'And, then, the dance !'

'Oh, yes ! it was at once bounding, waving, twisting ! There is not such another bayadere under the night-cap of the sky !'

'Gobinet, give me back my shawl directly. You have already spoilt it by rolling it round your great body. I don't choose to have my things ruined for hulking beasts who call other women bayaderes !'

'Celeste, simmer down. I am disguised as a Turk, and, when I talk of bayaderes, I am only in character.'

'Your Celeste is like them all, Gobinet ; she's jealous of the Bacchanal Queen.'——'Jealous !—do you think me jealous ? Well now ! that's too bad. If I chose to be as showy as she is they would talk of me as much. After all, it's only a nickname that makes her reputation ! *nickname !'*

'In that you have nothing to envy her—since you are called Celeste !

'You know well enough, Gobinet, that Celeste is my *real* name.'

'Yes ; but it's fancied a nickname—when one looks in your face.'

'Gobinet, I will put that down to your account.'

'And Oscar will help you to add it up, eh ?'

'Yes ; and you shall see the total. When I carry one, the remainder will not be you.'

'Celeste, you make me cry ! I only meant to say that your celestial name does not go well with your charming little face, which is still more mischievous than that of the Bacchanal Queen.'

'That's right ; wheedle me now, wretch !'

'I swear by the accursed head of my landlord, that, if you liked, you could spread yourself as much as the Bacchanal Queen—which is saying a great deal.'

'The fact is, that the Bacchanal has cheek enough, in all conscience.'

'Not to speak of her fascinating the bobbies !'

'And magnetising the beaks.'

'They may get as angry as they please · she always finishes by making them laugh.'

'And they all call her : Queen !'

' Last night, she charmed a slop (as modest as a country girl) whose purity took up arms against the famous dance of the Storm-blown Tulip.'

' What a quadrille ! Sleepinbuff and the Bacchanal Queen, having oppo-site to them Rose-Pompon and Ninny Moulin !'

' And all four making tulips as full-blown as could be !'

' By-the-by, is it true what they say of Ninny Moulin ?'

' What ?'

' Why that he is a writer, and scribbles pamphlets on religion.'

' Yes, it is true. I have often seen him at my employer's, with whom he deals ; a bad paymaster, but a jolly fellow !'

' And pretends to be devout, eh ?'

' I believe you, my boy—when it is necessary ; then he is my Lord Dumoulin, as large as life. He rolls his eyes, walks with his head on one side, and his toes turned in ; but, when the piece is played out, he slips away to the balls of which he is so fond. The girls christened him Ninny Moulin. Add, that he drinks like a fish, and you have the photo of the cove. All this doesn't prevent his writing for the religious newspapers ; and the saints, whom he lets in even oftener than himself, are ready to swear by him. You should see his articles and his tracts—only see, not read !—every page is full of the devil and his horns, and the desperate fryings which await your im-pious revolutionists—and then the authority of the bishops, the power of the Pope—hang it ! how could I know it all ? This toper, Ninny Moulin, gives good measure enough for their money !'

' The fact is, that he is both a heavy drinker and a heavy swell. How he rattled on with little Rose-Pompon in the dance of the full-blown tulip !'

' And what a rum chap he looked in his Roman helmet and top-boots.'

' Rose-Pompon dances divinely, too ; she has the poetic twist.'

' And don't show her heels a bit !'

' Yes ; but the Bacchanal Queen is six thousand feet above the level of any common leg-shaker. I always come back to her step last night in the full-blown tulip.'

' It was huge !'

' It was serene !'

' If I were father of a family, I would entrust her with the education of my sons !'

' It was that step, however, which offended the bobby's modesty.'

' The fact is, it was a little free.'

' Free as air—so the policeman comes up to her, and says : " Well, my Queen, is your foot to keep on a-goin' up for ever ?" " No, modest warrior !" replies the Queen ; " I practise the step only once every evening, to be able to dance it when I am old. I made a vow of it, that you might become an inspector." '

' What a comic card !'

' I don't believe she will remain always with Sleepinbuff.'

'Because he has been a workman ?'

' What nonsense ! it would preciously become us, students and shopboys, to give ourselves airs ! No ; but I am astonished at the Queen's fidelity.'

' Yes—they've been a team three or four good months.'

' She's wild upon him, and he on her.'

' They must lead a gay life.'

' Sometimes I ask myself where the devil Sleepinbuff gets all the money he spends. It appears that he pays all last night's expenses, three coaches-and-four, and a breakfast this morning for twenty, at ten francs a-head.'

' They say he has come into some property. That's why Ninny Moulin, who has a good nose for eating and drinking, made acquaintance with him last night—leaving out of the question that he may have some designs on the Bacchanal Queen.'

'He! In a lot! He's rather too ugly. The girls like to dance with him because he make's people laugh—but that's all. Little Rose-Pompon, who is such a pretty creature, has taken him as a harmless *chap-her-own*, in the absence of her student.'

'The coaches! the coaches!' exclaimed the crowd, all with one voice.

Forced to stop in the midst of the maskers, Mother Bunch had not lost a word of this conversation, which was deeply painful to her, as it concerned her sister, whom she had not seen for a long time. Not that the Bacchanal Queen had a bad heart; but the sight of the wretched poverty of Mother Bunch—a poverty which she had herself shared, but which she had not had strength of mind to bear any longer—caused such bitter grief to the gay, thoughtless girl, that she would no more expose herself to it, after she had in vain tried to induce her sister to accept assistance, which the latter always refused, knowing that its source could not be honourable.

'The coaches! the coaches!' once more exclaimed the crowd, as they pressed forward with enthusiasm, so that Mother Bunch, carried on against her will, was thrust into the foremost rank of the people assembled to see the show.

It was, indeed, a curious sight. A man on horseback, disguised as a postilion, his blue jacket embroidered with silver, an enormous tail from which the powder escaped in puffs, and a hat adorned with long ribbons, preceded the first carriage, cracking his whip, and crying with all his might: 'Make way for the Bacchanal Queen and her court!'

In an open carriage, drawn by four lean horses, on which rode two old postilions dressed as devils, was raised a downright pyramid of men and women, sitting, standing, leaning, in every possible variety of odd, extravagant, and grotesque costume; altogether an indescribable mass of bright colours, flowers, ribbons, tinsel, and spangles. Amid this heap of strange forms and dresses appeared wild or graceful countenances, ugly or handsome features —but all animated by the feverish excitement of a jovial frenzy—all turned with an expression of fanatical admiration towards the second carriage, in which the Queen was enthroned, whilst they united with the multitude in reiterated shouts of 'Long live the Bacchanal Queen.'

This second carriage, open like the first, contained only the four dancers of the famous step of the Storm-blown Tulip—Ninny Moulin, Rose-Pompon, Sleepinbuff, and the Bacchanal Queen.

Dumoulin, the religious writer, who wished to dispute possession of Mme. de la Sainte Colombe with his patron, M. Rodin—Dumoulin, surnamed Ninny Moulin, standing on the front cushions, would have presented a magnificent study for Callot or Gavarni, that eminent artist, who unites with the biting strength and marvellous fancy of an illustrious caricaturist, the grace, the poetry, and the depth of Hogarth.

Ninny Moulin, who was about thirty-five years of age, wore very much back upon his head a Roman helmet of silver paper. A voluminous plume of black feathers, rising from a red wood holder, was stuck on one side of this head-gear, breaking the too classic regularity of its outline. Beneath this casque, shone forth the most rubicund and jovial face, that ever was purpled by the fumes of generous wine. A prominent nose, with its primitive shape modestly concealed beneath a luxuriant growth of pimples, half red, half violet, gave a funny expression to a perfectly beardless face; while a large mouth, with thick lips turning their insides outwards, added to the air of mirth and jollity which beamed from his large grey eyes, set flat in his head.

On seeing this joyous fellow, with a paunch like Silenus, one could not help asking how it was, that he had not drowned in wine, a hundred times over, the gall, bile, and venom which flowed from his pamphlets against the enemies of Ultramontanism, and how his Catholic beliefs could float upwards in the midst of these mad excesses of drink and dancing. The question would have appeared insoluble, if one had not remembered how many actors, who play the blackest and most hateful first robbers on the stage, are, when off it, the best fellows in the world.

The weather being cold, Ninny Moulin wore a kind of box-coat, which, being half-open, displayed his cuirass of scales, and his flesh-coloured pantaloons, finishing just below the calf in a pair of yellow tops to his boots. Leaning forward in front of the carriage, he uttered wild shouts of delight, mingled with the words : 'Long live the Bacchanal Queen !'—after which, he shook and whirled the enormous rattle he held in his hand. Standing beside him, Sleepinbuff waved on high a banner of white silk, on which were the words : ' Love and joy to the Bacchanal Queen !'

Sleepinbuff was about twenty-five years of age. His countenance was gay and intelligent, surrounded by a collar of chestnut-coloured whiskers; but, worn with late hours and excesses, it expressed a singular mixture of carelessness and hardihood, recklessness and mockery ; still, no base or wicked passion had yet stamped there its fatal impress. He was the perfect type of the *Parisian*, as the term is generally applied, whether in the army, in the provinces, on board a king's ship, or a merchantman. It is not a compliment, and yet it is far from being an insult ; it is an epithet which partakes at once of blame, admiration, and fear ; for if, in this sense, the *Parisian* is often idle and rebellious, he is also quick at his work, resolute in danger, and always terribly satirical and fond of practical jokes.

He was dressed in a very flashy style. He wore a black velvet jacket with silver buttons, a scarlet waistcoat, trousers with broad blue stripes, a Cashmere shawl for a girdle with ends loosely floating, and a chimney-pot hat covered with flowers and streamers. This disguise set off his light, easy figure to great advantage.

At the back of the carriage, standing up on the cushions, were Rose-Pompon and the Bacchanal Queen.

Rose-Pompon, formerly a fringe-maker, was about seventeen years old, and had the prettiest and most winning little face imaginable. She was gaily dressed in débardeur costume. Her powdered wig, over which was smartly cocked on one side an orange and green cap, laced with silver, increased the effect of her bright black eyes, and of her round, carnation cheeks. She wore about her neck an orange-coloured cravat, of the same material as her loose sash. Her tight jacket and narrow vest of light green velvet, with silver ornaments, displayed to the best advantage a charming figure, the pliancy of which must have well suited the evolutions of the Storm-blown Tulip. Her large trousers, of the same stuff and colour as the jacket, were not calculated to hide any of her attractions.

The Bacchanal Queen, being at the least a head taller, leaned with one hand on the shoulder of Rose-Pompon. Mother Bunch's sister ruled, like a true monarch, over this mad revelry, which her very presence seemed to inspire, such influence had her own mirth and animation over all that surrounded her.

She was a tall girl of about twenty years of age, light and graceful, with regular features, and a merry, racketing air. Like her sister, she had magnificent chestnut hair, and large blue eyes ; but instead of being soft and timid, like those of the young sempstress, the latter shone with indefatigable ardour in the pursuit of pleasure. Such was the energy of her vivacious constitution, that, notwithstanding many nights and days passed in one continued revel, her complexion was as pure, her cheeks as rosy, her neck as fresh and fair, as if she had that morning issued from some peaceful home. Her costume, though singular and fantastic, suited her admirably. It was composed of a tight, long-waisted bodice in cloth of gold, trimmed with great bunches of scarlet ribbon, the ends of which streamed over her naked arms, and a short petticoat of scarlet velvet, ornamented with golden beads and spangles. This petticoat reached half-way down a leg, at once trim and strong, in a white silk stocking, and red buskin with brass heel.

Never had any Spanish dancer a more supple, elastic, and tempting form, than this singular girl, who seemed possessed with the spirit of dancing and perpetual motion, for, almost every moment, a slight undulation of head, hips, and shoulders seemed to follow the music of an invisible orchestra ; while the tip of her right foot, placed on the carriage door in the most alluring manner, continued to beat time—for the Bacchanal Queen stood proudly erect upon the cushions.

A sort of gilt diadem, the emblem of her noisy sovereignty, hung with little bells, adorned her forehead. Her long hair, in two thick braids, was drawn back from her rosy cheeks, and twisted behind her head. Her left hand rested on little Rose-Pompon's shoulder, and in her right she held an enormous nosegay, which she waved to the crowd, accompanying each salute with bursts of laughter.

It would be difficult to give a complete idea of this noisily animated and fantastic scene, which included also a third carriage, filled, like the first, with a pyramid of grotesque and extravagant masks. Amongst the delighted crowd, one person alone contemplated the picture with deep sorrow. It was Mother Bunch, who was still kept, in spite of herself, in the first rank of spectators.

Separated from her sister for a long time, she now beheld her in all the pomp of her singular triumph, in the midst of the cries of joy, and the applause of her companions in pleasure. Yet the eyes of the young sempstress grew dim with tears ; for, though the Bacchanal Queen seemed to share in the stunning gaiety of all around her—though her face was radiant with smiles, and she appeared fully to enjoy the splendours of her temporary elevation—yet she had the sincere pity of the poor workwoman, almost in rags, who was seeking, with the first dawn of morning, the means of earning her daily bread.

Mother Bunch had forgotten the crowd, to look only at her sister, whom she tenderly loved—only the more tenderly, that she thought her situation to be pitied. With her eyes fixed on the joyous and beautiful girl, her pale and gentle countenance expressed the most touching and painful interest.

All at once, as the brilliant glance of the Bacchanal Queen travelled along the crowd, it lighted on the sad features of Mother Bunch.

'My sister !' exclaimed Cephyse—such was the name of the Bacchanal Queen—'My sister !'—and with one bound, light as a ballet-dancer, she sprang from her movable throne (which fortunately just happened to be stopping), and, rushing up to the hunchback, embraced her affectionately.

All this had passed so rapidly, that the companions of the Bacchanal Queen, still stupefied by the boldness of her perilous leap, knew not how to account for it ; whilst the masks who surrounded Mother Bunch drew back in surprise, and the latter, absorbed in the delight of embracing her sister, whose caresses she returned, did not even think of the singular contrast between them, which was sure to soon excite the astonishment and hilarity of the crowd.

Cephyse was the first to think of this, and wishing to save her sister at least one humiliation, she turned towards the carriage, and said : ' Rose-Pompon, throw me down my cloak ; and, Ninny Moulin, open the door directly !'

Having received the cloak, the Bacchanal Queen hastily wrapped it round her sister, before the latter could speak or move. Then, taking her by the hand, she said to her : ' Come ! come !'

' I !' cried Mother Bunch, in alarm. ' Do not think of it !'

' I must speak with you. I will get a private room, where we shall be alone. So make haste, dear little sister ! Do not resist before all these people—but come !'

The fear of becoming a public sight decided Mother Bunch, who, confused moreover with the adventure, trembling and frightened, followed her sister almost mechanically, and was dragged by her into the carriage, of which Ninny Moulin had just opened the door. And so, with the cloak of the Bacchanal Queen covering Mother Bunch's poor garments and deformed figure, the crowd had nothing to laugh at, and only wondered what this meeting could mean, while the coaches pursued their way to the eating-house in the Place du Châtelet.

CHAPTER II.

THE CONTRAST.

SOME m nutes after the meeting of Mother Bunch with the Bacchanal Queen, the two sisters were alone together in a small room in the tavern.

' Let me kiss you again,' said Cephyse to the young sempstress ; ' at least now we are alone, you will not be afraid ?'

In the effort of the Bacchanal Queen to clasp Mother Bunch in her arms, the cloak fell from the form of the latter. At sight of those miserable garments, which she had hardly had time to observe on the Place du Châtelet, in the midst of the crowd, Cephyse clasped her hands, and could not repress an exclamation of painful surprise. Then, approaching her sister, that she might contemplate her more closely, she took her thin, icy palms between her own plump hands, and examined for some minutes, with increasing grief, the suffering, pale, unhappy creature, ground down by watching and privations, and half-clothed in a poor, patched cotton gown.

' Oh, sister ! to see you thus !' Unable to articulate another word, the Bacchanal Queen threw herself on the other's neck, and burst into tears. Then, in the midst of her sobs, she added : ' Pardon ! pardon !'

' What is the matter, my dear Cephyse?' said the young sewing-girl, deeply moved, and gently disengaging herself from the embrace of her sister. ' Why do you ask my pardon ?'

' Why ?' resumed Cephyse, raising her countenance, bathed in tears, and purple with shame ; ' is it not shameful of me, to be dressed in all this frippery, and throwing away so much money in follies, while you are thus miserably clad, and in need of everything—perhaps dying of want, for I have never seen your poor face look so pale and worn.'

' Be at ease, dear sister ! I am not ill. I was up rather late last night, and that makes me a little pale—but pray do not cry—it grieves me.'

The Bacchanal Queen had but just arrived, radiant in the midst of the intoxicated crowd, and yet it was Mother Bunch who was now employed in consoling her !

An incident occurred, which made the contrast still more striking. Joyous cries were heard suddenly in the next apartment, and these words were repeated with enthusiasm · ' Long live the Bacchanal Queen !'

Mother Bunch trembled, and her eyes filled with tears, as she saw her sister with her face buried in her hands, as if overwhelmed with shame. 'Cephyse,' she said, ' I entreat you not to grieve so. You will make me regret the delight of this meeting, which is indeed happiness to me ! It is so long since I saw you ! But tell me—what ails you ?'

'You despise me perhaps—you are right,' said the Bacchanal Queen, drying her tears.

' Despise you ? for what ?'

' Because I lead the life I do, instead of having the courage to support misery along with you.'

The grief of Cephyse was so heart-breaking, that Mother Bunch, always good and indulgent, wishing to console her, and raise her a little in her own estimation, said to her tenderly : 'In supporting it bravely for a whole year, my good Cephyse, you have had more merit and courage than I should have in bearing with it my whole life.'

'Oh, sister ! do not say that.'

'In simple truth,' returned Mother Bunch, ' to what temptations is a creature like me exposed ? Do I not naturally seek solitude, even as you seek a noisy life of pleasure ? What wants have I ? A very little suffices.'

' But you have not always that little ?'

' No—but, weak and sickly as I seem, I can endure some privations better than you could. Thus hunger produces in me a sort of numbness, which leaves me very feeble—but for you, robust and full of life, hunger is fury, is madness. Alas ! you must remember how many times I have seen you suffering from those painful attacks, when work failed us in our wretched garret, and we could not even earn our four francs a week—so that we had nothing—absolutely nothing to eat—for our pride prevented us from applying to the neighbours.'

' You have preserved the right to that honest pride.'

' And you as well ! Did you not struggle as much as a human creature could? But strength fails at last—I know you well, Cephyse—it was hunger that conquered you, and the painful necessity of constant labour, which was yet insufficient to supply our common wants.'

' But you could endure those privations—you endure them still.'

' Can you compare me with yourself ? Look,' said Mother Bunch, taking her sister by the hand, and leading her to a mirror placed above a couch, 'look !—Dost think that God made you so beautiful, endowed you with such quick and ardent blood, with so joyous, animated, grasping a nature, and with such taste and fondness for pleasure, that your youth might be spent in a freezing garret, hid from the sun, nailed constantly to your chair, clad almost in rags, and working without rest and without hope ? No ! for He has given us other wants than those of eating and drinking. Even in our humble condition, does not beauty require some little ornament ? Does not youth require some movement, pleasure, gaiety ? Do not all ages call for relaxation and rest ? Had you gained sufficient wages to satisfy hunger, to have a day or so's amusement in the week, after working every other day for twelve or fifteen hours, and to procure the neat and modest dress which so charming a face might naturally claim—you would never have asked for more, I am sure of it—you have told me as much a hundred times. You have yielded, therefore, to an irresistible necessity, because your wants are greater than mine.'

' It is true,' replied the Bacchanal Queen, with a pensive air ; 'if I could but have gained eighteenpence a day, my life would have been quite different ; for, in the beginning, sister, I felt cruelly humiliated to live at a man's expense.'

'Yes, yes—it was inevitable, my dear Cephyse ; I must pity, but cannot blame you. You did not choose your destiny ; but, like me, you have sub-mitted to it.'

'Poor sister !' said Cephyse, embracing the speaker tenderly ; 'you can encourage and console me in the midst of your own misfortunes, when I ought to be pitying you.'

'Be satisfied !' said Mother Bunch ; 'God is just and good. If He has denied me many advantages, He has given me my joys, as you have yours.'

'Joys ?'

'Yes, and great ones—without which life would be too burdensome, and I should not have the courage to go through with it.'

'I understand you,' said Cephyse, with emotion ; 'you still know how to devote yourself for others, and that lightens your own sorrows.'

'I do what I can, but, alas ! it is very little ; yet when I succeed,' added Mother Bunch, with a faint smile, 'I am as proud and happy as a poor little ant, who, after a great deal of trouble, has brought a big straw to the com-mon nest. But do not let us talk any more of me.'

'Yes, but I must, even at the risk of making you angry,' resumed the Bacchanal Queen, timidly ; 'I have something to propose to you which you once before refused. Jacques Rennepont has still, I think, some money left—we are spending it in follies—now and then giving a little to poor people we may happen to meet—I beg of you, let me come to your assistance —I see in your poor face, you cannot conceal it from me, that you are wearing yourself out with toil.'

'Thanks, my dear Cephyse, I know your good heart ; but I am not in want of anything. The little I gain is sufficient for me.'

'You refuse me,' said the Bacchanal Queen, sadly, 'because you know that my claim to this money is not honourable—be it so—I respect your scruples. But you will not refuse a service from Jacques ; he has been a workman, like ourselves, and comrades should help each other. Accept it, I beseech you, or I shall think you despise me.'

'And I shall think you despise me, if you insist any more upon it, my dear Cephyse,' said Mother Bunch, in a tone at once so mild and firm that the Bacchanal Queen saw that all persuasion would be in vain. She hung her head sorrowfully, and a tear again trickled down her cheek.

'My refusal grieves you,' said the other, taking her hand ; ' I am truly sorry—but reflect—and you will understand me.'

'You are right,' said the Bacchanal-Queen, bitterly, after a moment's silence ; 'you cannot accept assistance from my lover—it was an insult to propose it to you. There are positions in life so humiliating, that they soil even the good one wishes to do.'

'Cephyse, I did not mean to hurt you—you know it well.'

'Oh ! believe me,' replied the Bacchanal Queen, 'gay and giddy as I am, I have sometimes moments of reflection, even in the midst of my maddest joy. Happily, such moments are rare.'

'And what do you think of, then !'

'Why, that the life I lead is hardly the thing ; then I resolve to ask Jacques for a small sum of money, just enough to subsist on for a year, and form the plan of joining you, and gradually getting to work again.'

'The idea is a good one ; why not act upon it ?'

'Because, when about to execute this project, I examined myself sincerely, and my courage failed. I feel that I could never resume the habit of labour, and renounce this mode of life, sometimes rich, as to-day, sometimes pre-carious,—but at least free and full of leisure, joyous and without care, and at worst a thousand times preferable to living upon four francs a week.

Not that interest has guided me. Many times have I refused to exchange a lover, who had little or nothing, for a rich man, that I did not like. Nor have I ever asked anything for myself. Jacques has spent perhaps ten thousand francs the last three or four months, yet we only occupy two half-furnished rooms, because we always live out of doors, like the birds : fortunately, when I first loved him, he had nothing at all, and I had just sold some jewels that had been given me, for a hundred francs, and put this sum in the lottery. As mad people and fools are always lucky, I gained a prize of four thousand francs. Jacques was as gay, and light-headed, and full of fun as myself, so we said : " We love each other very much, and, as long as this money lasts, we will keep up the racket ; when we have no more, one of two things will happen—either we shall be tired of one another, and so part—or else we shall love each other still, and then, to remain together, we shall try and get work again ; and, if we cannot do so, and yet will not part—a bushel of charcoal will do our business !" '

'Good heaven !' cried Mother Bunch, turning pale.

' Be satisfied ! we have not come to that. We had still something left, when a kind of agent, who had paid court to me, but who was so ugly that I could not bear him for all his riches, knowing that I was living with Jacques, asked me to—— But why should I trouble you with all these details ? In one word, he leant Jacques money, on some sort of a doubtful claim he had, as was thought, to inherit some property. It is with this money that we are amusing ourselves—as long as it lasts.'

' But, my dear Cephyse, instead of spending this money so foolishly, why not put it out to interest, and marry Jacques, since you love him ?'

' Oh ! in the first place,' replied the Bacchanal Queen, laughing, as her gay and thoughtless character resumed its ascendancy, 'to put money out to interest gives one no pleasure. All the amusement one has is to look at a little bit of paper, which one gets in exchange for the nice little pieces of gold, with which one can purchase a thousand pleasures. As for marrying, I certainly like Jacques better than I ever liked any one ; but it seems to me, that, if we were married, all our happiness would end—for while he is only my lover, he cannot reproach me with what has passed—but, as my husband, he would be sure to upbraid me, sooner or later, and, if my conduct deserves blame, I prefer giving it to myself, because I shall do it more tenderly.'

' Mad girl that you are ! But this money will not last for ever. What is to be done next ?'

' Afterwards !—Oh ! that's all in the moon. To-morrow seems to me as if it would not come for a hundred years. If we were always saying : " We must die one day or the other"—would life be worth having ?'

The conversation between Cephyse and her sister was here again interrupted by a terrible uproar, above which sounded the sharp, shrill noise of Ninny Moulin's rattle. To this tumult succeeded a chorus of barbarous cries, in the midst of which were distinguishable these words, which shook the very windows : ' The Queen ! the Bacchanal Queen !'

Mother Bunch started at this sudden noise.

' It is only my court, who are getting impatient,' said Cephyse—and this time she could laugh.

' Heavens !' cried the sewing-girl, in alarm ; 'if they were to come here in search of you ?'

' No, no—never fear.'

' But listen ! do you not hear those steps ? they are coming along the passage—they are approaching. Pray, sister, let me go out alone, without being seen by all these people.'

That moment the door was opened, and Cephyse ran towards it. She saw in the passage a deputation headed by Ninny Moulin, who was armed with his formidable rattle, and followed by Rose-Pompon and Sleepinbuff.

'The Bacchanal Queen! or I poison myself with a glass of water!' cried Ninny Moulin.

'The Bacchanal Queen! or I publish my banns of marriage with Ninny Moulin!' cried little Rose-Pompon, with a determined air.

'The Bacchanal Queen! or the court will rise in arms, and carry her off by force!' said another voice.

'Yes, yes—let us carry her off!' repeated a formidable chorus.

'Jacques, enter alone!' said the Bacchanal Queen, notwithstanding these pressing summonses; then, addressing her court in a majestic tone, she added: 'In ten minutes, I shall be at your service—and then for a —— of a time!'

'Long live the Bacchanal Queen,' cried Dumoulin, shaking his rattle as he retired, followed by the deputation, whilst Sleepinbuff entered the room alone.

'Jacques,' said Cephyse, 'this is my good sister.'

'Enchanted to see you,' said Jacques, cordially; 'the more so as you will give me some news of my friend Agricola. Since I began to play the rich man, we have not seen each other, but I like him as much as ever, and think him a good and worthy fellow. You live in the same house. How is he?'

'Alas, sir! he and his family have had many misfortunes. He is in prison.'

'In prison!' cried Cephyse.

'Agricola in prison! what for?' said Sleepinbuff.

'For a trifling political offence. We had hoped to get him out on bail.'

'Certainly; for five hundred francs it could be done,' said Sleepinbuff.

'Unfortunately, we have not been able; the person upon whom we relied——'

The Bacchanal Queen interrupted the speaker by saying to her lover · 'Do you hear, Jacques? Agricola in prison, for want of five hundred francs!'

'To be sure! I hear and understand all about it. No need of your winking. Poor fellow! he was the support of his mother.'

'Alas! yes, sir—and it is the more distressing, as his father has but just returned from Russia, and his mother——'

'Here,' said Sleepinbuff, interrupting, and giving Mother Bunch a purse; 'take this—all the expenses here have been paid beforehand—this is what remains of my last bag. You will find here some twenty-five or thirty Napoleons, and I cannot make a better use of them than to serve a comrade in distress. Give them to Agricola's father; he will take the necessary steps, and to-morrow Agricola will be at his forge, where I had much rather he should be than myself.'

'Jacques, give me a kiss!' said the Bacchanal Queen.

'Now, and afterwards, and again and again!' said Jacques, joyously embracing the queen.

Mother Bunch hesitated for a moment; but reflecting that, after all, this sum of money, which was about to be spent in follies, would restore life and happiness to the family of Agricola, and that hereafter these very five hundred francs, when returned to Jacques, might be of the greatest use to him, she resolved to accept this offer. She took the purse, and, with tearful eyes, said to him: 'I will not refuse your kindness, M. Jacques; you are so good and generous. Agricola's father will thus at least have one consolation, in the midst of heavy sorrows. Thanks! many thanks!'

'There is no need to thank me ; money was made for others as well as ourselves.'

Here, without, the noise re-commenced more furiously than ever, and Ninny Moulin's rattle sent forth the most doleful sounds.

'Cephyse,' said Sleepinbuff, 'they will break everything to pieces, if you do not return to them, and I have nothing left to pay for the damage. Excuse us,' added he, laughing, 'but you see that royalty has its duties.'

Cephyse, deeply moved, extended her arms to Mother Bunch, who threw herself into them, shedding sweet tears. 'And now,' said she to her sister, 'when shall I see you again ?'

'Soon—though nothing grieves me more than to see you in want, out of which I am not allowed to help you.'

'You will come, then, to see me ? It is a promise ?'

'I promise you in her name,' said Jacques ; 'we will pay a visit to you and your neighbour Agricola.'

'Return to the company, Cephyse, and amuse yourself with a light heart ; for M. Jacques has made a whole family happy.'

So saying, and after Sleepinbuff had ascertained that she could go down without being seen by his noisy and joyous companions, Mother Bunch quietly withdrew, eager to carry one piece of good news at least to Dagobert ; but intending, first of all, to go to the Rue de Babylone, to the garden-house formerly occupied by Adrienne de Cardoville. We shall explain hereafter the cause of this determination.

As the girl quitted the eating-house, three men, plainly and comfortably dressed, were watching before it, and talking in a low voice. Soon after, they were joined by a fourth person, who rapidly descended the stairs of the tavern.

'Well ?' said the three first, with anxiety.

'He is there.'

'Are you sure of it ?'

'Are there two Sleepers-in-buff on earth ?' replied the other. 'I have just seen him ; he is togged out like one of the swell mob. They will be at table for three hours at least.'

'Then wait for me, you others. Keep as quiet as possible. I will go and fetch the *captain*, and the game is bagged.' So saying, one of the three men walked off quickly, and disappeared in a street leading from the square.

✿   ✿   ✿   ✿   ✿   ✿

At this same instant the Bacchanal Queen entered the banqueting-room, accompanied by Jacques, and was received with the most frenzied acclamations from all sides.

'Now then,' cried Cephyse, with a sort of feverish excitement, as if she wished to stun herself ; 'now then, friends—noise and tumult, hurricane and tempest, thunder and earthquake—as much as you please !' Then, holding out her glass to Ninny Moulin, she added : 'Pour out ! pour out !'

'Long live the Queen !' cried they all, with one voice.

CHAPTER III.

THE CAROUSE.

THE Bacchanal Queen, having Sleepinbuff and Rose-Pompon opposite her, and Ninny Moulin on her right hand, presided at the repast, called a réveille-matin (wake-morning), generously offered by Jacques to his companions in pleasure.

Both young men and girls seemed to have forgotten the fatigues of a ball, begun at eleven o'clock in the evening, and finished at six in the morning; and all these couples, joyous as they were amorous and indefatigable, laughed, ate, and drank, with youthful and Pantagruelian ardour, so that, during the first part of the feast, there was less chatter than clatter of plates and glasses.

The Bacchanal Queen's countenance was less gay, but much more animated than usual; her flushed cheeks and sparkling eyes announced a feverish excitement; she wished to drown reflection, cost what it might. Her conversation with her sister often recurred to her, and she tried to escape from such sad remembrances.

Jacques regarded Cephyse from time to time with passionate adoration; for, thanks to the singular conformity of character, mind, and taste between him and the Bacchanal Queen, their attachment had deeper and stronger roots than generally belong to ephemeral connexions founded upon pleasure. Cephyse and Jacques were themselves not aware of all the power of a passion which till now had been surrounded only by joys and festivities, and not yet been tried by any untoward event.

Little Rose-Pompon, left a widow a few days before by a student, who, in order to end the carnival in style, had gone into the country to raise supplies from his family, under one of those fabulous pretences which tradition carefully preserves in colleges of law and medicine—Rose-Pompon, we repeat, an example of rare fidelity, determined not to compromise herself, had taken for a chaperon the inoffensive Ninny Moulin.

This latter, having doffed his helmet, exhibited a bald head, encircled by a border of black, curling hair, pretty long at the back of the head. By a remarkable Bacchic phenomenon, in proportion as intoxication gained upon him, a sort of zone, as purple as his jovial face, crept by degrees over his brow, till it obscured even the shining whiteness of his crown. Rose-Pompon, who knew the meaning of this symptom, pointed it out to the company, and exclaimed with a loud burst of laughter : 'Take care, Ninny Moulin ! the tide of the wine is coming in.'

'When it rises above his head, he will be drowned,' added the Bacchanal Queen.

'Oh, Queen ! don't disturb me ; I am meditating,' answered Dumoulin, who was getting tipsy. He held in his hand, in the fashion of an antique goblet, a punch-bowl filled with wine, for he despised the ordinary glasses, because of their small size.

'Meditating,' echoed Rose-Pompon, 'Ninny Moulin is meditating. Be attentive !'

'He is meditating ; he must be ill then !'

'What is he meditating ? an illegal dance ?'

'A forbidden Anacreontic attitude ?'

'Yes, I am meditating,' returned Dumoulin, gravely ; 'I am meditating upon wine, generally and in particular—wine, of which the immortal Bossuet'—Dumoulin had the very bad habit of quoting Bossuet when he was drunk—'of which the immortal Bossuet says (and he was a judge of good liquor) : "In wine is courage, strength, joy, and spiritual fervour"—when one has any brains,' added Ninny Moulin, by way of parenthesis.

'Oh, my ! how I adore your Bossuet !' said Rose-Pompon.

'As for my particular meditation, it concerns the question, whether the wine at the marriage of Cana was red or white. Sometimes I incline to one side, sometimes to the other—and sometimes to both at once.'

'That is going to the bottom of the question,' said Sleepinbuff.

'And, above all, to the bottom of the bottles,' added the Bacchanal Queen.

'As your Majesty is pleased to observe ; and already, by dint of reflection and research, I have made a great discovery—namely, that, if the vine at the marriage of Cana was red——'

'It couldn't 'a' been white,' said Rose-Pompon, judiciously.

'And if I had arrived at the conviction that it was neither white nor red?' asked Dumoulin, with a magisterial air.

'That could only be when you had drunk till all was *blue*,' observed Sleepinbuff.

'The partner of the Queen says well. One may be too athirst for science; but never mind! From all my studies on this question, to which I have devoted my life—I shall await the end of my respectable career with the sense of having emptied tuns with a historical—theological—and archæological tone !'

It is impossible to describe the jovial grimace and tone with which Dumoulin pronounced and accentuated these last words, which provoked a general laugh.

'*Archieolopically ?*' said Rose-Pompon. 'What sawnee is that? Has he a tail? does he live in the water?'

'Never mind,' observed the Bacchanal Queen; 'these are words of wise men and conjurors; they are like horse-hair bustles—they serve for filling-out—that's all. I like better to drink; so fill the glasses, Ninny Moulin; some champagne, Rose-Pompon; here's to the health of your Philemon, and his speedy return !'

'And to the success of his plant upon his stupid and stingy family !' added Rose-Pompon.——The toast was received with unanimous applause.

'With the permission of her majesty and her court,' said Dumoulin, 'I propose a toast to the success of a project which greatly interests me, and has some resemblance to Philemon's jockeying. I fancy that the toast will bring me luck.'

'Let's have it, by all means !'

'Well, then—success to my marriage !' said Dumoulin, rising.

These words provoked an explosion of shouts, applause, and laughter. Ninny Moulin shouted, applauded, laughed even louder than the rest, opening wide his enormous mouth, and adding to the stunning noise the harsh springing of his rattle, which he had taken up from under his chair.

When the storm had somewhat subsided, the Bacchanal Queen rose and said : ' I drink to the health of the future Madame Ninny Moulin.'

'Oh, Queen! your courtesy touches me so sensibly that I must allow you to read in the depths of my heart the name of my future spouse,' exclaimed Dumoulin. ' She is called Madame Honorée-Modeste-Messaline-Angèle de la Sainte-Colombe, widow.'

'Bravo ! bravo !'

'She is sixty years old, and has more thousands of francs a-year than she has hairs in her grey moustache or wrinkles on her face ; she is so superbly fat that one of her gowns would serve as a tent for this honourable company. I hope to present my future spouse to you on Shrove-Tuesday, in the costume of a shepherdess that has just devoured her flock. Some of them wish to *con*vert her—but I have undertaken to *di*vert her, which she will like better. You must help me to plunge her headlong into all sorts of skylarking jollity.'

'We will plunge her into anything you please.'

'" She shall dance like *sixty !*"' said Rose-Pompon, humming a popular tune.

'She will overawe the police.'

'We can say to them · " Respect this lady ; your mother will perhaps be as old some day !"'

Suddenly, the Bacchanal Queen rose ; her countenance wore a singular expression of bitter and sardonic delight. In one hand she held a glass full to the brim. ' I hear the Cholera is approaching in his seven-league boots,' she cried. ' I drink luck to the Cholera !' And she emptied the bumper.

Notwithstanding the general gaiety, these words made a gloomy impression ; a sort of electric shudder ran through the assemblage, and nearly every countenance became suddenly serious.

' Oh, Cephyse !' said Jacques, in a tone of reproach.

' Luck to the Cholera,' repeated the Queen, fearlessly. ' Let him spare those who wish to live, and kill together those who dread to part !'

Jacques and Cephyse exchanged a rapid glance, unnoticed by their joyous companions, and for some time the Bacchanal Queen remained silent and thoughtful.

' If you put it that way, it is different,' cried Rose-Pompon, boldly. ' To the Cholera ! may none but good fellows be left on earth !'

In spite of this variation, the impression was still painfully impressive. Dumoulin, wishing to cut short this gloomy subject, exclaimed : ' Devil take the dead, and long live the living ! And, talking of chaps who both live and live well, I ask you to drink a health most dear to our joyous queen, the health of our Amphitryon. Unfortunately, I do not know his respectable name, having only had the advantage of making his acquaintance this night ; he will excuse me, then, if I confine myself to proposing the health of Sleepin-buff—a name by no means offensive to my modesty, as Adam never slept in any other manner. I drink to Sleepinbuff.'

' Thanks, old son !' said Jacques, gaily ; ' were I to forget your name, I should call you " Have-a-sip ?" and I am sure that you would answer : " I will." '

' I will directly !' said Dumoulin, making the military salute with one hand, and holding out the bowl with the other.

' As we have drunk together,' resumed Sleepinbuff, cordially, ' we ought to know each other thoroughly. I am Jacques Rennepont.'

' Rennepont !' cried Dumoulin, who appeared struck by the name, in spite of his half-drunkenness : ' you are Rennepont ?'

' Rennepont in the fullest sense of the word. Does that astonish you ?'

' There is a very ancient family of that name—the Counts of Rennepont.'

' The deuce there is !' said the other, laughing.

' The Counts of Rennepont are also Dukes of Cardoville,' added Dumoulin.

' Now, come, old fellow ! do I look as if I belonged to such a family ?—I, a workman out for a spree ?'

' You a workman ? why, we are getting into the Arabian Nights !' cried Dumoulin, more and more surprised. ' You give us a Belshazzar's banquet, with accompaniment of carriages and four, and yet are a workman ? Only tell me your trade, and I will join you, leaving the Vine of the Divine to take care of itself.'

' Come, I say ! don't think that I am a printer of flimsies, and a smasher !' replied Jacques, laughing.

' Oh, comrade ! no such suspicion——'

' It would be excusable, seeing the rigs I run. But I'll make you easy on that point. I am spending an inheritance.'

' Eating and drinking an uncle, no doubt ?' said Dumoulin, benevolently.

' Faith, I don't know.'

' What ! you don't know whom you are eating and drinking ?'

' Why, you see, in the first place, my father was a bonegrubber.'

' The devil he was !' said Dumoulin, somewhat out of countenance, though in general not over-scrupulous in the choice of his bottle-companions ; but, after the first surprise, he resumed, with the most charming amenity: 'There are some rag-pickers very high by scent—I mean descent!'

'To be sure! you may think to laugh at me,' said Jacques, 'but you are right in this respect, for my father was a man of very great merit. He spoke Greek and Latin like a scholar, and often told me that he had not his equal in mathematics; besides, he had travelled a good deal.'

'Well, then,' resumed Dumoulin, whom surprise had partly sobered, 'you may belong to the family of the Counts of Rennepont, after all.'

'In which case,' said Rose-Pompon, laughing, 'your father was not a gutter-snipe by trade, but only for the honour of the thing.'

'No, no—worse luck! it was to earn his living,' replied Jacques; 'but, in his youth, he had been well off. By what appeared, or rather by what did not appear, he had applied to some rich relation, and the rich relation had said to him: "Much obliged! try the work'us." Then he wished to make use of his Greek, and Latin, and mathematics. Impossible to do anything—Paris, it seems, being choke-full of learned men—so my father had to look for his bread at the end of a hooked stick, and there, too, he must have found it, for I ate of it during two years, when I came to live with him after the death of an aunt, with whom I had been staying in the country.'

'Your respectable father must have been a sort of philosopher,' said Dumoulin; 'but, unless found an inheritance in a dustbin, I don't see how you came into your property.'

'Wait for the end of the song. At twelve years of age I was an apprentice at the factory of M. Tripeaud; two years afterwards, my father died of an accident, leaving me the furniture of our garret—a mattress, a chair, and a table—and, moreover, in an old Eau de Cologne box, some papers (written, it seems, in English), and a bronze medal, worth about ten sous, chain and all. He had never spoken to me of these papers, so, not knowing if they were good for anything, I left them at the bottom of an old trunk, instead of burning them—which was well for me, since it is upon these papers that I have had money advanced.'

'What a godsend!' said Dumoulin. 'But somebody must have known that you had them?'

'Yes; one of those people that are always looking out for old debts came to Cephyse, who told me all about it; and, after he had read the papers, he said that the affair was doubtful, but that he would lend me ten thousand francs on it, if I liked. Ten thousand francs was a large sum, so I snapped him up!'

'But you must have supposed that these old papers were of great value?'

'Faith, no! since my father, who ought to have known their value, had never realised on them—and then, you see, ten thousand francs in good, bright coin, falling as it were from the clouds, are not to be sneezed at—so I took them—only the man made me do a bit of stiff, a guarantee, or something of that kind.'

'Did you sign it?'

'Of course—what did I care about it? The man told me it was only a matter of form. He spoke the truth, for the bill fell due a fortnight ago, and I have heard nothing of it. I have still about a thousand francs in his hands, for I have taken him for my banker. And that's the way, old pal, that I'm able to flourish and be jolly all day long, as pleased as Punch to have left my old grinder of a master, M. Tripeaud.'

As he pronounced this name, the joyous countenance of Jacques became suddenly overcast. Cephyse, no longer under the influence of the painful impression she had felt for a moment, looked uneasily at Jacques, for she knew the irritation which the name of M. Tripeaud produced within him.

'M. Tripeaud,' resumed Sleepinbuff, 'is one that would make the good bad, and the bad worse. They say that a good rider makes a good horse ; they ought to say that a good master makes a good workman. Zounds ! when I think of that fellow !' cried Sleepinbuff, striking his hand violently on the table.

'Come, Jacques—think of something else !' said the Bacchanal Queen. 'Make him laugh, Rose-Pompon.'

'I am not in a humour to laugh,' replied Jacques, abruptly, for he was getting excited from the effects of the wine ; 'it is more than I can bear to think of that man. It exasperates me ! it drives me mad ! You should have heard him saying : "Beggarly workmen ! rascally workmen ! they grumble that they have no food in their bellies ; well, then, we'll give them bayonets to stop their hunger."* And there's the children in his factory— you should see them, poor little creatures ! —working as long as the men— wasting away, and dying by the dozen—what odds ? as soon as they were dead plenty of others came to take their places—not like horses, which can only be replaced with money.'

'Well, it is clear, that you do not like your old master,' said Dumoulin, more and more surprised at his Amphitryon's gloomy and thoughtful air, and, regretting that the conversation had taken this serious turn, he whispered a few words in the ear of the Bacchanal Queen, who answered by a sign of intelligence.

'I don't like M. Tripeaud !' exclaimed Jacques. 'I hate him—and shall I tell you why ? Because it is as much his fault as mine, that I have become a good-for-nothing loafer. I don't say it to screen myself; but it is the truth. When I was 'prenticed to him as a lad, I was all heart and ardour, and so bent upon work, that I used to take my shirt off to my task, which, by the way, was the reason that I was first called Sleepinbuff. Well ! I might have toiled myself to death ; not one word of encourage- ment did I receive. I came first to my work, and was the last to leave off ; what matter ? it was not even noticed. One day, I was injured by the machinery. I was taken to the hospital. When I came out, weak as I was, I went straight to my work ; I was not to be frightened ; the others, who knew their master well, would often say to me : "What a muff you must be, little one ! What good will you get by working so hard ?"—still I went on. But, one day, a worthy old man, called Father Arsène, who had worked in the house many years, and was a model of good conduct, was suddenly turned away, because he was getting too feeble. It was a death-blow to him ; his wife was infirm, and, at his age, he could not get another place. When the foreman told him he was dismissed, he could not believe it, and he began to cry for grief. At that moment, M. Tripeaud passes ; Father Arsène begs him with clasped hands to keep him at half-wages. " What !" says M. Tripeaud, shrugging his shoulders ; " do you think that I will turn my factory into a house of invalids? You are no longer able to work—so be off !" " But I have worked forty years of my life ; what is to become of me ?" cried poor Father Arsène. " That is not my business," answered M. Tripeaud ; and, addressing his clerk, he added : " Pay what is due for the week, and let him cut his stick." Father Arsène did cut his stick ; that evening, he and his old wife suffocated themselves with charcoal. Now, you see, I was then a lad ; but that story of Father Arsène taught me, that, however hard you might work, it would only profit your master, who would not even thank you for it, and leave you to die on the flags in your old age. So all my fire was damped, and I said to myself : "What's the use of doing more than I just need ? If I gain heaps of gold for M. Tripeaud, shall I

* These atrocious words were actually spoken during the Lyons Riots.

get an atom of it?" Therefore, finding neither pride nor profit in my work, I took a disgust for it—just did barely enough to earn my wages—became an idler and a rake—and said to myself : "When I get too tired of labour, I can always follow the example of Father Arsène and his wife." '

Whilst Jacques resigned himself to the current of these bitter thoughts, the other guests, incited by the expressive pantomine of Dumoulin and the Bacchanal Queen, had tacitly agreed together ; and, on a signal from the Queen, who leaped upon the table, and threw down the bottles and glasses with her foot, all rose and shouted, with the accompaniment of Ninny Moulin's rattle : 'The Storm-blown Tulip ! the quadrille of the Storm-blown Tulip !'

At these joyous cries, which burst suddenly, like shell, Jacques started ; then gazing with astonishment at his guests, he drew his hand across his brow, as if to chase away the painful ideas that oppressed him, and exclaimed : ' You are right. Forward, the first couple ! Let us be merry !'

In a moment, the table, lifted by vigorous arms, was removed to the extremity of the banqueting-room ; the spectators, mounted upon chairs, benches, and window-ledges, began to sing in chorus the well-known air of les Etudiants, so as to serve instead of orchestra, and accompany the quadrille formed by Sleepinbuff, the Queen, Ninny Moulin, and Rose-Pompon.

Dumoulin, having entrusted his rattle to one of the guests, resumed his extravagant Roman helmet and plume ; he had taken off his great-coat at the commencement of the feast, so that he now appeared in all the splendour of his costume. His cuirass of bright scales ended in a tunic of feathers, not unlike those worn by the savages, who form the oxen's escort on Mardi Gras. Ninny Moulin had a huge paunch and thin legs, so that the latter moved about at pleasure in the gaping mouths of his large top boots.

Little Rose-Pompon, with her pinched-up cocked-hat stuck on one side, her hands in the pockets of her trousers, her bust a little inclined forward, and undulating from right to left, advanced to meet Ninny Moulin ; the latter danced, or rather leaped towards her, his left leg bent under him, his right leg stretched forward, with the toe raised, and the heel gliding on the floor ; moreover, he struck his neck with his left hand, and by a simultaneous movement, stretched forth his right, as if he would have thrown dust in the eyes of his opposite partner.

This first figure met with great success, and the applause was vociferous, though it was only the innocent prelude to the step of the Storm-blown Tulip—when suddenly the door opened, and one of the waiters, after looking about for an instant, in search of Sleepinbuff, ran to him, and whispered some words in his ear.

' Me !' cried Jacques, laughing ; 'here's a go !'

The waiter added a few more words, when Sleepinbuff's face assumed an expression of uneasiness, as he answered : ' Very well ! I come directly,'— and he made a step towards the door.

' What's the matter, Jacques?' asked the Bacchanal-Queen, in some surprise.

' I'll be back immediately. Some one take my place. Go on with the dance,' said Sleepinbuff, as he hastily left the room.

' Something, that was not put down in the bill,' said Dumoulin ; 'he will soon be back.'

' That's it,' said Cephyse. ' Now *cavalier seul !*' she added, as she took Jacques's place, and the dance continued.

Ninny Moulin had just taken hold of Rose-Pompon with his right hand, and of the Queen with his left, in order to advance between the two, in which figure he showed off his buffoonery to the utmost extent, when the door again opened, and the same waiter, who had called out Jacques, approached Cephyse with an air of consternation, and whispered in her ear, as he had before done to Sleepinbuff.

The Bacchanal Queen grew pale, uttered a piercing scream, and rushed out of the room without a word, leaving her guests in stupefaction.

CHAPTER IV.

THE FAREWELL.

THE Bacchanal Queen, following the waiter, arrived at the bottom of the staircase. A coach was standing before the door of the house. In it she saw Sleepinbuff, with one of the men who, two hours before, had been waiting on the Place du Châtelet.

On the arrival of Cephyse, the man got down, and said to Jacques, as he drew out his watch: 'I give you a quarter of an hour; it is all that I can do for you, my good fellow; after that we must start. Do not try to escape, for we'll be watching at the coach doors.'

With one spring, Cephyse was in the coach. Too much overcome to speak before, she now exclaimed, as she took her seat by Jacques, and remarked the paleness of his countenance : 'What is it ? What do they want with you ?'

'I am arrested for debt,' said Jacques, in a mournful voice.

'You !' exclaimed Cephyse, with a heart-rending sob.

'Yes, for that bill, or guarantee, they made me sign. And yet the man said it was only a form—the rascal !'

'But you have money in his hands ; let him take that on account.'

'I have not a copper ; he sends me word by the bailiff, that not having paid the bill, I shall not have the last thousand francs.'

'Then let us go to him, and entreat him to leave you at liberty. It was he who came to propose to lend you this money. I know it well, as he first addressed himself to me. He will have pity on you.'

'Pity ?—a money broker pity ? No ! no !'

'Is there then no hope ? none ?' cried Cephyse, clasping her hands in anguish. 'But there must be something done,' she resumed. 'He promised you——'

'You can see how he keeps his promises,' answered Jacques, with bitterness. 'I signed, without even knowing what I signed. The bill is over-due; everything is in order; it would be vain to resist. They have just explained all that to me.'

'But they cannot keep you long in prison. It is impossible.'

'Five years, if I do not pay. As I'll never be able to do so, my fate is certain.'

'Oh ! what a misfortune ! and not to be able to do anything !' said Cephyse, hiding her face in her hands.

'Listen to me, Cephyse,' resumed Jacques, in a voice of mournful emotion; 'since I am here, I have thought only of one thing—what is to become of you?'

'Never mind me !'

'Not mind you ?—art mad? What will you do? The furniture of our two rooms is not worth two hundred francs. We have squandered our money so foolishly, that we have not even paid our rent. We owe three quarters, and we must not therefore count upon the furniture. I leave you without a coin. At least *I* shall be fed in prison—but how will you manage to live ?'

' What is the use of grieving beforehand ?'

' I ask you, how you will live to-morrow ?' cried Jacques.

' I will sell my costume, and some other clothes. I will send you half the money, and keep the rest. That will last some days.'

' And afterwards ?—afterwards ?'

' Afterwards ?—why, then—I don't know—how can I tell you ! Afterwards—I'll look about me.'

' Hear me, Cephyse,' resumed Jacques, with bitter agony. 'It is now that I first know how much I love you. My heart is pressed as in a vice, at the thought of leaving you—and I shudder to think what is to become of you.' Then—drawing his hand across his forehead, Jacques added : ' You see we have been ruined by saying—"To-morrow will never come !"—for to-morrow *has* come. When I am no longer with you, and you have spent the last penny of the money gained by the sale of your clothes—unfit for work as you have become—what will you do next? Must I tell you what you will do !—you will forget me and——' Then, as if he recoiled from his own thoughts, Jacques exclaimed, with a burst of rage and despair—' Great Heaven ! if that were to happen, I should dash my brains out against the stones !'

Cephyse guessed the half-told meaning of Jacques, and throwing her arms around his neck, she said to him : ' I take another lover ?—never ! I am like you, for I now first know how much I love you.'

' But my poor Cephyse—how will you live ?'

' Well, I shall take courage. I will go back and dwell with my sister, as in old times ; we will work together, and so earn our bread. I'll never go out, except to visit you. In a few days your creditor will reflect, that, as you can't pay him ten thousand francs, he may as well set you free. By that time I shall have once more acquired the habit of working. You shall see, you shall see !—and you also will again acquire this habit. We shall live poor, but content. After all, we have had plenty of amusement for six months, while so many others have never known pleasure all their lives. And believe me, my dear Jacques, when I say to you—I shall profit by this lesson. If you love me, do not feel the least uneasiness ; I tell you, that I would rather die a hundred times, than have another lover.'

' Kiss me,' said Jacques, with eyes full of tears. ' I believe you—yes, I believe you—and you give me back my courage, both for now and hereafter. You are right ; we must try and get to work again, or else nothing remains but Father Arsène's bushel of charcoal ; for, my girl,' added Jacques, in a low and trembling voice, ' I have been like a drunken man these six months, and now I am getting sober, and see whither we were going. Our means once exhausted, I might perhaps have become a robber, and you——'

' Oh, Jacques ! don't talk so—it is frightful,' interrupted Cephyse ; ' I swear to you that I will return to my sister—that I will work—that I will have courage !'

Thus saying, the Bacchanal Queen was very sincere ; she fully intended to keep her word, for her heart was not yet completely corrupted. Misery and want had been with her, as with so many others, the cause and the excuse of her worst errors. Until now, she had at least followed the instincts of her heart, without regard to any base or venal motive. The cruel position in which she beheld Jacques had so far exalted her love, that she believed herself capable of resuming, along with Mother Bunch, that life of sterile and incessant toil, full of painful sacrifices and privations, which once had been impossible for her to bear, and which the habits of a life of leisure and dissipation would now render still more difficult.

Still, the assurances which she had just given Jacques calmed his grief and anxiety a little ; he had sense and feeling enough to perceive that the fatal track which he had hitherto so blindly followed was leading both him and Cephyse directly to infamy.

One of the bailiffs, having knocked at the coach-door, said to Jacques : 'My lad, you have only five minutes left—so make haste.'

'So, courage, my girl—courage !' said Jacques.

'I will ; you may rely upon me.'

'Are you going upstairs again ?'

'No—oh no !' said Cephyse. 'I have now a horror of this festivity.'

'Everything is paid for, and the waiter will tell them not to expect us back. They will be much astonished,' continued Jacques, 'but it's all the same now.'

'If you could only go with me to our lodging,' said Cephyse, 'this man would perhaps permit it, so as not to enter Sainte-Pélagie in that dress.'

'Oh ! he will not forbid you to accompany me ; but, as he will be with us in the coach, we shall not be able to talk freely in his presence. Therefore, let me speak reason to you for the first time in my life. Remember what I say, my dear Cephyse—and the counsel will apply to me as well as to yourself,' continued Jacques, in a grave and feeling tone—'resume from to-day the habit of labour. It may be painful, unprofitable—never mind—do not hesitate, for too soon will the influence of this lesson be forgotten. By-and-by it will be too late, and then you will end like so many unfortunate creatures——'

'I understand,' said Cephyse, blushing ; 'but I will rather die than lead such a life.'

'And there you will do well—for in that case,' added Jacques, in a deep and hollow voice, 'I will myself show you how to die.'

'I count upon you, Jacques,' answered Cephyse, embracing her lover with excited feeling ; then she added, sorrowfully : 'It was a kind of presentiment, when just now I felt so sad, without knowing why, in the midst of all our gaiety—and drank to the Cholera, so that we might die together.'

'Well ! perhaps the Cholera will come,' resumed Jacques, with a gloomy air ; 'that would save us the charcoal, which we may not even be able to buy.'

'I can only tell you one thing, Jacques, that to live and die together, you will always find me ready.'

'Come, dry your eyes,' said he, with profound emotion. 'Do not let us play the children before these men.'

   ✿   ✿   ✿   ✿   ✿   ✿

Some minutes after, the coach took the direction to Jacques' lodging, where he was to change his clothes, before proceeding to the debtors' prison.

   ✿   ✿   ✿   ✿   ✿   ✿

Let us repeat, with regard to the hunchback's sister—for there are things which cannot be too often repeated—that one of the most fatal consequences of the Inorganization of Labour is the Insufficiency of Wages.

The insufficiency of wages forces inevitably the greater number of young girls, thus badly paid, to seek their means of subsistence in connexions which deprave them.

Sometimes they receive a small allowance from their lovers, which, joined to the produce of their labour, enables them to live. Sometimes, like the sempstress's sister, they throw aside their work altogether, and take up their abode with the man of their choice, should he be able to support the expense. It is during this season of pleasure and idleness that the incurable leprosy of sloth takes lasting possession of these unfortunate creatures.

This is the first phase of degradation that the guilty carelessness of Society imposes on an immense number of workwomen, born with instincts of modesty, and honesty, and uprightness.

After a certain time they are deserted by their seducers—perhaps when they are mothers. Or, it may be, that foolish extravagance consigns the imprudent lover to prison, and the young girl finds herself alone, abandoned, without the means of subsistence.

Those who have still preserved courage and energy go back to their work —but the examples are very rare. The others, impelled by misery, and by habits of indolence, fall into the lowest depths.

And yet we must pity, rather than blame them, for the first and virtual cause of their fall has been the insufficient remuneration of labour and sudden reduction of pay.

Another deplorable consequence of this inorganization is the disgust which workmen feel for their employment, in addition to the insufficiency of their wages. And this is quite conceivable, for nothing is done to render their labour attractive, either by variety of occupations, or by honorary rewards, or by proper care, or by remuneration proportionate to the benefits which their toil provides, or by the hope of rest after long years of industry. No— the country thinks not, cares not, either for their wants or their rights.

And yet, to take only one example, machinists and workers in foundries, exposed to boiler explosions, and the contact of formidable engines, run every day greater dangers than soldiers in time of war, display rare practical sagacity, and render to industry—and, consequently, to their country—the most incontestable service, during a long and honourable career, if they do not perish by the bursting of a boiler, or have not their limbs crushed by the iron teeth of a machine.

In this last case, does the workman receive a recompense equal to that which awaits the soldier's praiseworthy, but sterile courage—a place in an asylum for invalids? No.

What does the country care about it? And if the master should happen to be ungrateful, the mutilated workman, incapable of further service, may die of want in some corner.

Finally, in our pompous festivals of commerce, do we ever assemble any of the skilful workmen who alone have woven those admirable stuffs, forged and damascened those shining weapons, chiselled those goblets of gold and silver, carved the wood and ivory of that costly furniture, and set those dazzling jewels with such exquisite art? No.

In the obscurity of their garrets, in the midst of a miserable and starving family, hardly able to subsist on their scanty wages, these workmen have contributed, at least, one half to bestow those wonders upon their country, which make its wealth, its glory, and its pride.

A minister of commerce, who had the least intelligence of his high functions and duties, would require of every factory that exhibits on these occasions, the selection by vote of a certain number of candidates, amongst whom the manufacturer would point out the one that appeared most worthy to represent the working classes in these great industrial solemnities.

Would it not be a noble and encouraging example to see the master propose for public recompense and distinction the workman, deputed by his peers, as amongst the most honest, laborious, and intelligent of his profession? Then one most grievous injustice would disappear, and the virtues of the workman would be stimulated by a generous and noble ambition—he would have an interest in doing well.

Doubtless, the manufacturer himself, because of the intelligence he displays, the capital he risks, the establishment he founds, and the good he sometimes does, has a legitimate right to the prizes bestowed upon him. But why is the workman to be rigorously excluded from these rewards, which have so powerful an influence upon the people? Are generals and officers the only ones that receive rewards in the army ? And when we have remunerated the captains of this great and powerful army of industry, why should we neglect the privates ?

Why for them is there no sign of public gratitude ? no kind or consoling word from august lips ? Why do we not see, in France, a single workman wearing a medal as a reward for his courageous industry, his long and laborious career ? The token, and the little pension attached to it, would be to him a double recompense, justly deserved. But, no ! for humble labour that sustains the State, there is only forgetfulness, injustice, indifference, and disdain !

By this neglect of the public, often aggravated by individual selfishness and ingratitude, our workmen are placed in a deplorable situation.

Some of them, notwithstanding their incessant toil, lead a life of privations, and die before their time, cursing the social system that rides over them. Others find a temporary oblivion of their ills in destructive intoxication. Others, again—in great number—having no interest, no advantage, no moral or physical inducement to do more or better, confine themselves strictly to just that amount of labour which will suffice to earn their wages. Nothing attaches them to their work, because nothing elevates, honours, glorifies it in their eyes. They have no defence against the seductions of indolence ; and if, by some chance, they find the means of living awhile in repose, they give way by degrees to habits of laziness and debauchery, and sometimes the worst passions soil for ever natures originally willing, healthy and honest—and all for want of that protecting and equitable superintendence which should have sustained, encouraged, and recompensed their first worthy and laborious tendencies.

    ❁   ❁   ❁   ❁   ❁   ❁

We now follow Mother Bunch, who, after seeking for work from the person that usually employed her, went to the Rue de Babylone, to the lodge lately occupied by Adrienne de Cardoville.

CHAPTER V.

FLORINE.

WHILE the Bacchanal Queen and Sleepinbuff terminated so sadly the most joyous portion of their existence, the sempstress arrived at the door of the summer-house in the Rue de Babylone.

Before ringing, she dried her tears ; a new grief weighed upon her spirits. On quitting the tavern, she had gone to the house of the person who usually found her in work ; but she was told that she could not have any, because it could be done a third more cheaply by women in prison. Mother Bunch, rather than lose her last resource, offered to take it at the third less ; but the linen had been already sent out, and the girl could not hope for employment for a fortnight to come, even if submitting to this reduction of wages. One may conceive the anguish of the poor creature ; the prospect before her was to die of hunger, if she would not beg or steal. As for her visit to the lodge in the Rue de Babylone, it will be explained presently.

She rang the bell timidly ; a few minutes after, Florine opened the door to her. The waiting-maid was no longer adorned after the charming taste of Adrienne ; on the contrary, she was dressed with an affectation of austere simplicity. She wore a high-necked dress of a dark colour, made full enough to conceal the light elegance of her figure. Her bands of jet-black hair were hardly visible beneath the flat border of a starched white cap, very much resembling the head-dress of a nun. Yet, in spite of this unornamental costume, Florine's pale countenance was still admirably beautiful.

We have said that, placed by former misconduct at the mercy of Rodin and M. d'Aigrigny, Florine had served them as a spy upon her mistress, notwithstanding the marks of kindness and confidence she had received from her. Yet Florine was not entirely corrupted; and she often suffered painful, but vain, remorse at the thought of the infamous part she was thus obliged to perform.

At sight of Mother Bunch, whom she recognised—for she had told her, the day before, of Agricola's arrest and Mdlle. de Cardoville's madness—Florine recoiled a step, so much was she moved with pity at the appearance of the young sempstress. In fact, the idea of being thrown out of work, in the midst of so many other painful circumstances, had made a terrible impression upon the young workwoman; the traces of recent tears furrowed her cheeks—without her knowing it, her features expressed the deepest despair—and she appeared so exhausted, so weak, so overcome, that Florine offered her arm to support her, and said to her kindly: 'Pray walk in and rest yourself; you are very pale, and seem to be ill and fatigued.'

So saying, Florine led her into a small room, with fireplace and carpet, and made her sit down in a tapestried arm-chair by the side of a good fire. Georgette and Hebe had been dismissed, and Florine was left alone in care of the house.

When her guest was seated, Florine said to her, with an air of interest: 'Will you not take anything? A little orange flower-water and sugar, warm.

'I thank you, mademoiselle,' said Mother Bunch, with emotion, so easily was her gratitude excited by the least mark of kindness; she felt, too, a pleasing surprise, that her poor garments had not been the cause of repugnance or disdain on the part of Florine.

'I thank you, mademoiselle,' said she, 'but I only require a little rest, for I come from a great distance. If you will permit me——'

'Pray rest yourself as long as you like, mademoiselle; I am alone in this pavilion since the departure of my poor mistress,'—here Florine blushed and sighed;—'so, pray, make yourself quite at home. Draw near the fire—you will be more comfortable—and, gracious! how wet your feet are!—place them upon this stool.'

The cordial reception given by Florine, her handsome face and agreeable manners, which were not those of an ordinary waiting-maid, forcibly struck Mother Bunch, who, notwithstanding her humble condition, was peculiarly susceptible to the influence of everything graceful and delicate. Yielding, therefore, to these attractions, the young sempstress, generally so timid and sensitive, felt herself almost at her ease with Florine.

'How obliging you are, mademoiselle!' said she, in a grateful tone. 'I am quite confused with your kindness.'

'I wish I could do you some greater service than offer you a place at the fire, mademoiselle. Your appearance is so good and interesting.'

'Oh, mademoiselle!' said the other, with simplicity, almost in spite of herself; 'it does one so much good to sit by a warm fire!' Then, fearing, in her extreme delicacy, that she might be thought capable of abusing the hospitality of her entertainer, by unreasonably prolonging her visit, she added: 'The motive that has brought me here is this. Yesterday, you informed me that a young workman, named Agricola Baudoin, had been arrested in this house.'

'Alas! yes, mademoiselle. At the moment, too, when my poor mistress was about to render him assistance.'

'I am Agricola's adopted sister,' resumed Mother Bunch, with a slight blush; 'he wrote to me yesterday evening from prison. He begged me to tell his father to come here as soon as possible, in order to inform Mdlle. de

Cardoville that he, Agricola, had important matters to communicate to her, or to any person that she might send ; but that he could not venture to mention them in a letter, as he did not know if the correspondence of prisoners might not be read by the governor of the prison.'

'What !' said Florine, with surprise ; 'to my mistress, M. Agricola has something of importance to communicate ?'

'Yes, mademoiselle ; for, up to this time, Agricola is ignorant of the great calamity that has befallen Mdlle. de Cardoville.'

'True ; the attack was indeed so sudden,' said Florine, casting down her eyes, 'that no one could have foreseen it.'

'It must have been so,' answered Mother Bunch ; 'for, when Agricola saw Mdlle. de Cardoville for the first time, he returned home, struck with her grace, and delicacy, and goodness.'

'As were all who approached my mistress,' said Florine, sorrowfully.

'This morning,' resumed the sewing-girl, ' when, according to Agricola's instructions, I wished to speak to his father on the subject, I found him already gone out, for he also is a prey to great anxieties ; but my adopted brother's letter appeared to me so pressing, and to involve something of such consequence to Mdlle. de Cardoville, who had shown herself so generous towards him, that I came here immediately.'

'Unfortunately, as you already know, my mistress is no longer here.'

'But is there no member of her family to whom, if I could not speak myself, I might at least send word by you, that Agricola has something to communicate of importance to this young lady ?'

'It is strange !' said Florine, reflecting, and without replying. Then, turning towards the sempstress, she added : ' You are quite ignorant of the nature of these revelations ?'

'Completely so, mademoiselle ; but I know Agricola. He is all honour and truth, and you may believe whatever he affirms. Besides, he would have no interest——'

'Good gracious !' interrupted Florine, suddenly, as if struck with a sudden light ; 'I have just remembered something. When he was arrested in a hiding-place where my mistress had concealed him, I happened to be close at hand, and M. Agricola said to me, in a quick whisper: " Tell your generous mistress that her goodness to me will not go unrewarded, and that my stay in that hiding-place may not be useless to her." That was all he could say to me, for they hurried him off instantly. I confess that I saw in those words only the expression of his gratitude, and his hope of proving it one day to my mistress ; but now that I connect them with the letter he has written you,——' said Florine, reflecting.

'Indeed !' remarked Mother Bunch, ' there is certainly some connexion between his hiding-place here and the important secrets which he wishes to communicate to your mistress, or one of her family.'

'The hiding-place had neither been inhabited nor visited for some time,' said Florine, with a thoughtful air ; ' M. Agricola may have found therein something of interest to my mistress.'

'If his letter had not appeared to me so pressing,' resumed the other, ' I should not have come hither ; but have left him to do so himself, on his release from prison, which now, thanks to the generosity of one of his old fellow-workmen, cannot be very distant. But, not knowing if bail would be accepted to-day, I have wished faithfully to perform his instructions. The generous kindness of your mistress made it my first duty.'

Like all persons whose better instincts are still roused from time to time, Florine felt a sort of consolation in doing good whenever she could with impunity—that is to say, without exposing herself to the inexorable resentments of those on whom she depended. Thanks to Mother Bunch, she might now have an opportunity of rendering a great service to her mistress. She knew enough of the Princess de Saint-Dizier's hatred of her niece, to feel certain that Agricola's communication could not, from its very importance, be made with safety to any but Mdlle. de Cardoville herself. She therefore said very gravely : ' Listen to me, mademoiselle ! I will give you a piece of advice which will, I think, be useful to my poor mistress—but which would be very fatal to me if you did not attend to my recommendations.'

' How so, mademoiselle ?' said the hunchback, looking at Florine with extreme surprise.

' For the sake of my mistress, M. Agricola must confide to no one, except herself, the important things he has to communicate.'

' But, if he cannot see Mdlle. Adrienne, may he not address himself to some of her family ?'

' It is from her family, above all, that he must conceal whatever he knows. Mdlle. Adrienne may recover, and then M. Agricola can speak to her. But should she never get well again, tell your adopted brother that it is better for him to keep his secret than to place it (which would infallibly happen) at the disposal of the enemies of my mistress.'

' I understand you, mademoiselle,' said Mother Bunch, sadly. ' The family of your generous mistress do not love her, and perhaps persecute her ?'

' I cannot tell you more on this subject now ; and, as regards myself, let me conjure you to obtain M. Agricola's promise that he will not mention to any one in the world the step you have taken, or the advice I have given you. The happiness—no, not the happiness,' resumed Florine, bitterly, as if that were a lost hope, ' not the happiness—but the peace of my life depends upon your discretion.'

' Oh ! be satisfied !' said the sewing-girl, both affected and amazed by the sorrowful expression of Florine's countenance ; ' I will not be ungrateful. No one in the world but Agricola shall know that I have seen you.'

' Thank you—thank you, mademoiselle,' cried Florine, with emotion.

' Do you thank me ?' said the other, astonished to see the large tears roll down her cheeks.

' Yes ! I am indebted to you for a moment of pure, unmixed happiness ; for I have perhaps rendered a service to my dear mistress, without risking the increase of the troubles that already overwhelm me.'

' You are not happy, then ?'

' That astonishes you ; but, believe me, whatever may be your fate, I would gladly change with you.'

' Alas, mademoiselle !' said the sempstress; ' you appear to have too good a heart, for me to let you entertain such a wish—particularly now.'

' What do you mean ?'

' I hope sincerely, mademoiselle,' proceeded Mother Bunch, with deep sadness, ' that you may never know what it is to want work, when labour is your only resource.'

' Are you reduced to that extremity ?' cried Florine, looking anxiously at the young sempstress, who hung her head, and made no answer. She reproached herself, in her excessive delicacy, with having made a communication which resembled a complaint, though it had only been wrung from her by the thought of her dreadful situation.

' If it is so,' went on Florine, ' I pity you with all my heart ; and yet I know not, if my misfortunes are not still greater than yours.'

Then, after a moment's reflection, Florine exclaimed, suddenly : ' But let me see ! If you are really in that position, I think I can procure you some work.'

'Is it possible, mademoiselle!' cried Mother Bunch. 'I should never have dared to ask you such a service ; but your generous offer commands my confidence, and may save me from destruction. I will confess to you, that, only this morning, I was thrown out of an employment which enabled me to earn four francs a week.'

'Four francs a week !' exclaimed Florine, hardly able to believe what she heard.

'It was little, doubtless,' replied the other; 'but enough for me. Unfortunately, the person who employed me, has found out where it can be done still cheaper.'

'Four francs a week !' repeated Florine, deeply touched by so much misery and resignation. 'Well ! I think I can introduce you to persons, who will secure you wages of at least two francs a day.'

'I could earn two francs a day ? ' Is it possible ?'

'Yes, there is no doubt of it ; only, you would have to go out by the day, unless you chose to take a place as servant.'

'In my position,' said Mother Bunch, with a mixture of timidity and pride, 'one has no right, I know, to be over-nice ; yet I should prefer to go out by the day, and still more to remain at home, if possible, even though I were to gain less.'

'To go out is unfortunately an indispensable condition,' said Florine.

'Then I must renounce this hope,' answered Mother Bunch, timidly ; 'not that I refuse to go out to work—but those who do so, are expected to be decently clad—and I confess without shame, because there is no disgrace in honest poverty, that I have no better clothes than these.'

'If that be all,' said Florine, hastily, 'they will find you the means of dressing yourself properly.'

Mother Bunch looked at Florine with increasing surprise. These offers were so much above what she could have hoped, and what indeed was generally earned by needlewomen, that she could hardly credit them.

'But,' resumed she, with hesitation, 'why should any one be so generous to me, mademoiselle ? How should I deserve such high wages ?'

Florine started. A natural impulse of the heart, a desire to be useful to the sempstress, whose mildness and resignation greatly interested her, had led her to make a hasty proposition ; she knew at what price would have to be purchased the advantages she proposed, and she now asked herself, if the hunchback would ever accept them on such terms. But Florine had gone too far to recede, and she durst not tell all. She resolved, therefore, to leave the future to chance ; and as those, who have themselves fallen, are little disposed to believe in the infallibility of others, Florine said to herself, that perhaps in the desperate position in which she was, Mother Bunch would not be so scrupulous after all. Therefore she said : 'I see, mademoiselle, that you are astonished at offers so much above what you usually gain ; but I must tell you, that I am now speaking of a pious institution, founded to procure work for deserving young women. This establishment, which is called St. Mary's Society, undertakes to place them out as servants, or by the day as needlewomen. Now this institution is managed by such charitable persons, that they themselves undertake to supply an outfit, when the young women received under their protection are not sufficiently well clothed to accept the places destined for them.'

This plausible explanation of Florine's magnificent offers appeared to satisfy the hearer. 'I can now understand the high wages of which you speak, mademoiselle,' resumed she ; 'only I have no claim to be patronised by the charitable persons who direct this establishment.'

'You suffer—you are laborious and honest—those are sufficient claims ;

only, I must tell you, they will ask if you perform regularly your religious duties.'

' No one loves and blesses God more fervently than I do, mademoiselle,' said the hunchback, with mild firmness ; ' but certain duties are an affair of conscience, and I would rather renounce this patronage, than be compelled——'

' Not the least in the world. Only, as I told you, there are very pious persons at the head of this institution, and you must not be astonished at their questions on such a subject. Make the trial, at all events ; what do you risk? If the propositions are suitable—accept them; if, on the contrary, they should appear to touch your liberty of conscience, you can always refuse—your position will not be the worse for it.'

Mother Bunch had nothing to object to this reasoning, which left her at perfect freedom, and disarmed her of all suspicion. ' On these terms, mademoiselle,' said she, ' I accept your offer, and thank you with all my heart. But who will introduce me ?'

' I will—to morrow, if you please.'

' But they will perhaps desire to make some inquiries about me.'

'The venerable Mother Sainte-Perpétue, superior of St. Mary's Convent, where the institution is established, will, I am sure, appreciate your good qualities without inquiry ; but, if otherwise, she will tell you, and you can easily satisfy her. It is then agreed—to-morrow.'

' Shall I call upon you here, mademoiselle ?'

' No ; as I told you before, they must not know that you came here on the part of M. Agricola, and a second visit might be discovered, and excite suspicion. I will come and fetch you in a coach ; where do you live ?'

' At No. 3, Rue Brise-Miche ; as you are pleased to give yourself so much trouble, mademoiselle, you have only to ask the dyer, who acts as porter. to call down Mother Bunch.'

' *Mother* Bunch ?' said Florine, with surprise.

'Yes, mademoiselle,' answered the sempstress, with a sad smile ; 'it is the name everyone gives me. And you see,' added the hunchback, unable to restrain a tear, ' it is because of my ridiculous infirmity, to which this name alludes, that I dread going out to work among strangers, because there are so many people who laugh at one, without knowing the pain they occasion. But,' continued she, drying her eyes, ' I have no choice, and must make up my mind to it.'

Florine, deeply affected, took the speaker's hand, and said to her : ' Do not fear. Misfortunes like yours must inspire compassion, not ridicule. May I not inquire for you by your real name ?'

' It is Magdalen Soliveau ; but I repeat, mademoiselle, that you had better ask for Mother Bunch, as I am hardly known by any other name.'

' I will, then, be in the Rue Brise-Miche to-morrow, at twelve o'clock.'

' Oh, mademoiselle ! how can I ever requite your goodness ?'

' Don't speak of it : I only hope my interference may be of use to you. But of this you must judge for yourself. As for M. Agricola, do not answer his letter ; wait till he is out of prison, and then tell him to keep his secret till he can see my poor mistress.'

' And where is the dear young lady now ?'

' I cannot tell you. I do not know where they took her, when she was attacked with this frenzy. You will expect me to-morrow ?'

' Yes—to-morrow,' said Mother Bunch.

      o   o   o   o   o

The convent whither Florine was to conduct the hunchback contained the daughters of Marshal Simon, and was next door to the lunatic asylum of Dr. Baleinier, in which Adrienne de Cardoville was confined.

CHAPTER VI.

MOTHER SAINTE-PERPETUE.

ST. MARY'S CONVENT, whither the daughters of Marshal Simon had been conveyed, was a large old building, the vast garden of which was on the Boulevard de l'Hôpital, one of the most retired places in Paris, particularly at this period. The following scenes took place on the 12th February, the eve of the fatal day, on which the members of the family of Rennepont, the last descendants of the sister of the Wandering Jew, were to meet together in the Rue St. François. St Mary's Convent was a model of perfect regularity. A superior council, composed of influential ecclesiastics, with Father d'Aigrigny for president, and of women of great reputed piety, at the head of whom was the Princess de Saint-Dizier, frequently assembled in deliberation, to consult on the means of extending and strengthening the secret and powerful influence of this establishment, which had already made remarkable progress.

Skilful combinations and deep foresight had presided at the foundation of St. Mary's Convent, which, in consequence of numerous donations, possessed already real estate to a great extent, and was daily augmenting its acquisitions. The religious community was only a pretext; but, thanks to an extensive connection, kept up by means of the most decided members of the ultramontane (*i.e.* high-church) party, a great number of rich orphans were placed in the convent, there to receive a solid, austere, religious education, very preferable, it was said, to the frivolous instruction which might be had in the fashionable boarding-schools, infected by the corruption of the age. To widows also, and lone women who happened moreover to be rich, the convent offered a sure asylum from the dangers and temptations of the world ; in this peaceful retreat, they enjoyed a delightful calm, and secured their salvation, whilst surrounded by the most tender and affectionate attentions. Nor was this all. Mother Sainte-Perpétue, the superior of the convent, undertook in the name of the institution to procure for the faithful, who wished to preserve the interior of their houses from the depravity of the age, companions for aged ladies, domestic servants, or needlewomen working by the day, all selected persons whose morality could be warranted. Nothing would seem more worthy of sympathy and encouragement than such an institution ; but we shall presently unveil the vast and dangerous network of intrigue concealed under these charitable and holy appearances. The lady-superior, Mother Sainte-Perpétue, was a tall woman of about forty years of age, clad in a stuff dress of the Carmelite tan colour, and wearing a long rosary at her waist ; a white cap under the chin, and a long black veil, closely encircled her thin, sallow face. A number of deep wrinkles had impressed their transverse furrows in her forehead of yellow ivory ; her marked and prominent nose was bent like the beak of a bird of prey ; her black eye was knowing and piercing ; the expression of her countenance was at once intelligent, cold, and firm.

In the general management of the pecuniary affairs of the community, Mother Sainte-Perpétue would have been a match for the most cunning attorney. When women are possessed of what is called a talent for business, and apply to it their keen penetration, their indefatigable perseverance, their prudent dissimulation, and, above all, that quick and exact insight, which is natural to them, the results are often prodigious. To Mother Sainte-Perpétue, a woman of the coolest and strongest intellect, the management of the vast transactions of the community was mere child's play. No one knew better how to purchase a depreciated property, to restore it to its former value. and then sell it with advantage ; the price of stock, the rate of exchange, the current value of the shares in the different companies, were all familiar to her ; she had never yet been known to make a bad speculation, when the question was to invest any of the funds which were given by pious souls for the purposes of the convent. She had established in the house the utmost order and discipline, and, above all, an extreme economy. The constant aim of all her efforts was to enrich, not herself, but the community she directed ; for the spirit of association, when become a collective egotism, gives to corporations the faults and vices of an individual. Thus a congregation may doat upon power and money, just as a miser loves them for their own sake. But it is chiefly with regard to estates that congregations act like a single man. They dream of landed property ; it is their fixed idea, their fruitful monomania. They pursue it with their most sincere, and warm, and tender wishes.

The first estate is to a rising little community what the wedding-trousseau is to a young bride, his first horse to a youth, his first success to a poet to a gay girl, her first fifty-guinea shawl ; because, after all, in this material age, an estate gives a certain rank to a society on the Religious Exchange, and has so much the more effect upon the simple-minded, that all these partnerships in the work of salvation, which end by becoming immensely rich, begin with modest poverty as social stock-in-trade, and charity towards their neighbours as security reserve fund. We may therefore imagine what bitter and ardent rivalry must exist between the different congregations with regard to the various estates that each can lay claim to ; with what ineffable satisfaction the richer society crushes the poorer beneath its inventory of houses, and farms, and paper securities ! Envy and hateful jealousy, rendered still more irritable by the leisure of a cloistered life, are the necessary consequences of such a comparison ; and yet nothing is less Christian—in the adorable acceptation of that divine word—nothing has less in common with the true, essential, and religiously social spirit of the gospel, than this insatiable ardour to acquire wealth by every possible means—this dangerous avidity. which is far from being atoned for, in the eyes of public opinion, by a few paltry alms, bestowed in the narrow spirit of exclusion and intolerance.

Mother Sainte-Perpétue was seated before a large cylindrical-fronted desk, in the centre of an apartment simply but comfortably furnished. An excellent fire burned within the marble chimney, and a soft carpet covered the floor. The superior, to whom all letters addressed to the sisters or the boarders were every day delivered, had just been opening the first, according to her acknowledged right, and carefully unsealing the second, without their knowing it, according to a right that she ascribed to herself, of course, with a view to the salvation of those dear creatures ; and partly, perhaps, a little to make herself acquainted with their correspondence, for she also had imposed on herself the duty of reading all letters that were sent from the convent, before they were put into the post. The traces of this pious and innocent inquisition were easily effaced, for the good mother possessed a whole arsenal of steel tools, some very sharp, to cut the paper imperceptibly round the seal—others, pretty little rods, to be slightly heated and rolled round the edge of the seal, when the letter had been read and replaced in its envelope, so that the wax, spreading as it melted, might cover the first incision. Moreover, from a praiseworthy feeling of justice and equality, there was in the arsenal of the good mother a little fumigator of the most ingenious construction, the damp and dissolving vapour of which was reserved for the letters humbly and modestly secured with wafers ; thus softened, they yielded to the least effort, without any tearing of the paper. According to the importance of the revelations, which she thus gleaned from the writers of the letters, the superior took notes more or less extensive. She was interrupted in this investigation by two gentle taps at the bolted door. Mother Sainte-Perpétue immediately let down the sliding cylinder of her cabinet, so as to cover the secret arsenal, and went to open the door with a grave and solemn air. A lay sister came to announce to her that the Princess de Saint-Dizier was waiting for her in the parlour, and that Mdlle. Florine, accompanied by a young girl, deformed and badly dressed, was waiting at the door of the little corridor.

'Introduce the princess first,' said Mother Sainte-Perpétue. And, with charming forethought, she drew an arm-chair to the fire. Mme. de Saint-Dizier entered.

Without pretensions to juvenile coquetry, still the princess was tastefully and elegantly dressed. She wore a black velvet bonnet of the most fashionable make, a large blue cashmere shawl, and a black satin dress, trimmed with sable, to match the fur of her muff.

'To what good fortune am I again to-day indebted for the honour of your visit, my dear daughter?' said the superior, graciously.

'A very important recommendation, my dear mother, though I am in a great hurry. I am expected at the house of his Eminence, and have, unfortunately, only a few minutes to spare. I have again to speak of the two orphans who occupied our attention so long yesterday.'

'They continue to be kept separate, according to your wish; and this separation has had such an effect upon them that I have been obliged to send this morning for Dr. Baleinier, from his asylum. He found much fever joined to great depression, and, singular enough, absolutely the same symptoms in both cases. I have again questioned these unfortunate creatures, and have been quite confounded and terrified to find them perfect heathens.'

'It was, you see, very urgent to place them in your care. But to the subject of my visit, my dear mother : we have just learned the unexpected return of the soldier who brought these girls to France, and was thought to be absent for some days ; but he is in Paris, and, notwithstanding his age, a man of extraordinary boldness, enterprise, and energy. Should he discover that the girls are here (which, however, is fortunately almost impossible), in his rage at seeing them removed from his impious influence, he would be capable of anything. Therefore let me entreat you, my dear mother, to redouble your precautions, that no one may effect an entrance by night. This quarter of the town is so deserted !'

'Be satisfied, my dear daughter ; we are sufficiently guarded. Our porter and gardeners, all well armed, make a round every night on the side of the Boulevard de l'Hôpital. The walls are high, and furnished with spikes at the more accessible places. But I thank you, my dear daughter, for having warned me. We will redouble our precautions.'

'Particularly this night, my dear mother.'

'Why so ?'

'Because if this infernal soldier has the audacity to attempt such a thing, it will be this very night.'

'How do you know, my dear daughter?'

'We have information which makes us certain of it,' replied the princess, with a slight embarrassment, which did not escape the notice of the Superior, though she was too crafty and reserved to appear to see it ; only she suspected that many things were concealed from her.

'This night, then,' resumed Mother Sainte-Perpétue, 'we will be more than ever on our guard. But as I have the pleasure of seeing you, my dear daughter, I will take the opportunity to say a word or two on the subject of that marriage we mentioned.'

'Yes, my dear mother,' said the princess, hastily, 'for it is very important.

The young Baron de Brisville is a man full of ardent devotion in these times of revolutionary impiety ; he practises openly, and is able to render us great services.   He is listened to in the Chamber, and does not want for a sort of aggressive and provoking eloquence ; I know not any one whose tone is more insolent with regard to his faith, and the plan is a good one, for this cavalier and open manner of speaking of sacred things raises and excites the curiosity of the indifferent.   Circumstances are happily such that he may show the most audacious violence towards our enemies, without the least danger to himself, which, of course, redoubles his ardour as a would-be martyr.   In a word, he is altogether ours, and we, in return, must bring about this marriage.   You know, besides, my dear mother, that he proposes to offer a donation of a hundred thousand francs to St. Mary's, the day he gains possession of the fortune of Mdlle. Baudricourt.'

' I have never doubted the excellent intentions of M. de Brisville with regard to an institution which merits the sympathy of all pious persons,' answered the Superior, discreetly ; ' but I did not expect to meet with so many obstacles on the part of the young lady.'

' How is that ?'

' This girl, whom I always believed a most simple, submissive, timid, almost idiotic person—instead of being delighted with this proposal of marriage, asks time to consider !'——' It is really pitiable !'

' She opposes to me an inert resistance.   It is in vain for me to speak severely, and tell her that, having no parents or friends, and being absolutely confided to my care, she ought to see with my eyes, hear with my ears, and, when I affirm that this union is suitable in all respects, give her adhesion to it without delay or reflection.'

' No doubt.   It would be impossible to speak more sensibly.'

' She answers that she wishes to see M. de Brisville, and know his character before being engaged.'

' It is absurd—since you undertake to answer for his morality, and esteem this a proper marriage.'

' Therefore, I remarked to Mdlle. Baudricourt, this morning, that till now I had only employed gentle persuasion, but that, if she forced me to it, I should be obliged, in her own interest, to act with rigour, to conquer so much obstinacy—that I should have to separate her from her companions, and to confine her closely in a cell, until she made up her mind, after all, to consult her own happiness, and—marry an honourable man.'

' And these menaces, my dear mother ?'

' Will, I hope, have a good effect.   She kept up a correspondence with an old school-friend in the country.   I have put a stop to this, for it appeared to me dangerous.   She is now under my sole influence, and I hope we shall attain our ends ; but you see, my dear daughter, it is never without crosses and difficulties that we succeed in doing good !'

' And I feel certain that M. de Brisville will even go beyond his first promise, and I will pledge myself for him, that, should he marry Mdlle. Baudricourt——'

' You know, my dear daughter,' said the superior, interrupting the princess, ' that if I were myself concerned, I would refuse everything ; but to give to this institution is to give to Heaven, and I cannot prevent M. de Brisville from augmenting the amount of his good works.   Then, you see, we are exposed to a sad disappointment.'

' What is that, my dear mother ?'

' The Sacred Heart Convent disputes an estate with us that would have suited us exactly.   Really, some people are quite insatiable !   I gave the lady superior my opinion upon it pretty freely.'

'She told me as much,' answered Mme. de Saint-Dizier, 'and laid the blame on the steward.'

'Oh ! so you see her, my dear daughter ?' exclaimed the superior, with an air of great surprise.

'I met her at the bishop's,' answered Mme. de Saint-Dizier, with a slight degree of hesitation, that Mother Sainte-Perpétue did not appear to notice.

'I really do not know,' resumed the latter, 'why our establishment should excite so violently the jealousy of the Sacred Heart. There is not an evil report that they have not spread with regard to St. Mary's Convent. Certain persons are always offended by the success of their neighbours !'

'Come, my dear mother,' said the princess, in a conciliating tone, 'we must hope that the donation of M. de Brisville will enable you to outbid the Sacred Heart. This marriage will have a double advantage, you see, my dear mother : it will place a large fortune at the disposal of a man who is devoted to us, and who will employ it as we wish ; and it will also greatly increase the importance of his position as our defender, by the addition to his income of 100,000 francs a year. We shall have at length an organ worthy of our cause, and shall no longer be obliged to look for defenders amongst such people as that Dumoulin.'

'There is great power and much learning in the writings of the man you name. It is the style of a Saint Bernard, in wrath at the impiety of the age.'

'Alas, my dear mother ! if you only knew what a strange Saint Bernard this Dumoulin is ! But I will not offend your ears ; all I can tell you is, that such defenders would compromise the most sacred cause. Adieu, my dear mother ! pray redouble your precautions to-night—the return of this soldier is alarming.'

'Be quite satisfied, my dear daughter ! Oh ! I forgot. Mdlle. Florine begged me to ask you a favour. It is, to let her enter your service. You know the fidelity she displayed in watching your unfortunate niece ; I think that, by rewarding her in this way, you will attach her to you completely, and I shall feel grateful on her account.'

'If you interest yourself the least in the world in Florine, my dear mother, the thing is done. I will take her into my service. And now it strikes me, she may be more useful to me than I thought.'

'A thousand thanks, my dear daughter, for such obliging attention to my request. I hope we shall soon meet again. The day after to-morrow, at two o'clock, we have a long conference with his Eminence and the Bishop ; do not forget !'

'No, my dear mother ; I shall take care to be exact. Only, pray, redouble your precautions to-night for fear of a great scandal !'

After respectfully kissing the hand of the superior, the princess went out by the great door, which led to an apartment opening on the principal stair-case. Some minutes after, Florine entered the room by another way. The superior was seated, and Florine approached her with timid humility.

'Did you meet the Princess de Saint-Dizier ?' asked Mother Sainte-Perpétue.

'No, mother ; I was waiting in the passage, where the windows look out on the garden.'

'The princess takes you into her service from to-day,' said the superior.

Florine made a movement of sorrowful surprise, and exclaimed : 'Me, mother ! but——'

'I asked her in your name, and you have only to accept,' answered the other imperiously.

'But, mother, I had entreated you——'

'I tell you, that you accept the offer,' said the superior, in so firm and positive a tone that Florine cast down her eyes, and replied in a low voice : ' I accept.'

' It is in M. Rodin's name that I give you this order.'

' I thought so, mother,' replied Florine, sadly ; ' on what conditions am I to serve the princess ?'

' On the same conditions as those on which you served her niece.'

Florine shuddered, and said : ' I am, then, to make frequent secret reports with regard to the princess ?'

' You will observe, you will remember, and you will give an account.'

' Yes, my mother.'

' You will above all direct your attention to the visits that the princess may receive from the lady superior of the Sacred Heart. You must try and listen —for we have to preserve the princess from evil influences.'

' I will obey, my mother.'

' You will also try and discover why two young orphans have been brought hither, and recommended to be severely treated by Mme. Grivois, the confidential waiting-woman of the princess.'

' Yes, mother.'

' Which must not prevent you from remembering anything else that may be worthy of remark. To-morrow I will give you particular instructions upon another subject.'

' It is well, mother.'

' If you conduct yourself in a satisfactory manner, and execute faithfully the instructions of which I speak, you will soon leave the princess to enter the service of a young bride ; it will be an excellent and lasting situation— always on the same conditions. It is, therefore, perfectly understood that you have asked me to recommend you to Madame de Saint-Dizier.'

' Yes, mother ; I shall remember.'

' Who is this deformed young girl that accompanies you ?'

A poor creature without any resource, very intelligent, and with an education above her class ; she works at her needle, but is at present without employment, and reduced to the last extremity. I have made inquiries about her this morning ; she has an excellent character.'

' She is ugly and deformed, you say ?'

' She has an interesting countenance, but she is deformed.'

The superior appeared pleased at this information, and added, after a moment's reflection : ' She appears intelligent ?'

' Very intelligent.'

' And is absolutely without resources ?'

' Yes, without any.'

' Is she pious ?'

' She does not practise.'

' No matter,' said the superior to herself ; ' if she be intelligent, that will suffice.' Then she resumed aloud : ' Do you know if she is a good workwoman ?'

' I believe so, mother.'

The superior rose, took a register from a shelf, appeared to be looking into it attentively for some time, and then said, as she replaced it : ' Fetch in this young girl, and go and wait for me in the press-room.'

' Deformed—intelligent—clever at her needle,' said the superior, reflecting ; ' she will excite no suspicion. We must see.'

In about a minute, Florine returned with Mother Bunch, whom she introduced to the superior, and then discreetly withdrew. The young sempstress was agitated, trembling, and much troubled, for she could, as it were, hardly believe a discovery which she had chanced to make during Florine's absence.

It was not without a vague sense of terror that the hunchback remained alone with the lady superior.

CHAPTER VII.

THE TEMPTATION

THIS was the cause of Mother Bunch's emotion. Florine, when she went to see the superior, had left the young sempstress in a passage supplied with benches, and forming a sort of ante-chamber on the first story. Being alone, the girl had mechanically approached a window which looked upon the convent garden, shut in by a half-demolished wall, and terminating at one end in an open paling. This wall was connected with a chapel that was still building, and bordered on the garden of a neighbouring house. The sewing-girl, at one of the windows on the ground floor of this house—a grated window, still more remarkable by the sort of tent-like awning above it— beheld a young female, with her eyes fixed upon the convent, making signs with her hand, at once encouraging and affectionate. From the window where she stood, Mother Bunch could not see to whom these signs were addressed; but she admired the rare beauty of the telegrapher, the brilliancy of her complexion, the shining blackness of her large eyes, the sweet and benevolent smile which lingered on her lips. There was, no doubt, some answer to her graceful and expressive pantomime, for, by a movement full of elegance, the girl laid her left hand on her bosom, and waved her right, which seemed to indicate that her heart flew towards the place on which she kept her eyes. One faint sunbeam, piercing the clouds, came at this moment to play with the tresses of the pale countenance, which, now held close to the bars of the window, was suddenly, as it were, illuminated by the dazzling reflection of her splendid golden hair. At sight of that charming face, set in its admirable frame of red curls, Mother Bunch started involuntarily ; the thought of Mdlle. de Cardoville crossed her mind, and she felt persuaded (nor was she, indeed, mistaken) that the protectress of Agricola was before her. On thus beholding, in that gloomy asylum, this young lady, so marvellously beautiful, and remembering the delicate kindness with which a few days before she had received Agricola in her luxurious little palace of dazzling splendour, the work-girl felt her heart sink within her. She believed Adrienne insane ; and yet, as she looked attentively at her, it seemed as if intelligence and grace animated that adorable countenance. Suddenly, Mdlle. de Cardoville laid her fingers upon her lips, blew a couple of kisses in the direction towards which she had been looking, and all at once disappeared. Reflecting upon the important revelations which Agricola had to make to Mdlle. de Cardoville, Mother Bunch regretted bitterly that she had no means of approaching her ; for she felt sure that, if the young lady were mad, the present was a lucid interval. She was yet absorbed in these uneasy reflections, when she saw Florine return, accompanied by one of the nuns. Mother Bunch was obliged, therefore, to keep silence with regard to the discovery she had made, and soon after she found herself in the superior's presence. This latter, after a rapid and searching examination of the countenance of the young workwoman, judged her appearance so timid, gentle, and honest, that she thought she might repose full confidence in the information given by Florine.

' My dear daughter,' said Mother Sainte-Perpétue, in an affectionate voice, ' Florine has told me in what a cruel situation you are placed. Is it true that you are entirely without work ?'

' Alas ! yes, madame.'

' Call me mother, my dear daughter ; that name is dearer to me, and it is the rule of our house. I need not ask you, what are your principles ?'

' I have always lived honestly by my labour, mother,' answered the girl, with a simplicity at once dignified and modest.

' I believe you, my dear daughter, and I have good reasons for so doing. We must thank the Lord, who has delivered you from temptation ; but tell me—are you clever at your trade ?'

' I do my best, mother, and have always satisfied my employers. If you please to try me, you will be able to judge.'

' Your affirmation is sufficient, my dear daughter. You prefer, I think, to go out by the day ?'

' Mdlle. Florine told me, mother, that I could not have work at home.'

' Why, no—not for the present, my child. If hereafter an opportunity should offer, I will think of it. Just now I have this to propose to you. A very respectable old lady has asked me to recommend to her a needlewoman by the day ; introduced by me, you would certainly suit her. The institution will undertake to clothe you becomingly, and this advance we shall retain by degrees out of your wages, for you will look to us for payment. We propose to give you two francs a day ; does that appear to you sufficient ?'

' Oh, mother ! it is much more than I could have expected.'

' You will, moreover, only be occupied from nine o'clock in the morning till six in the evening ; you will thus have still some off hours, of which you might make use. You see, the situation is not a hard one.'

' Oh ! quite the contrary, mother.'

' I must tell you, first of all, with whom the institution intends to place you. It is a widow lady, named Mme. de Brémont, a person of the most steadfast piety. In her house, I hope, you will meet with none but excellent examples. If it should be otherwise, you can come and inform me.'

' How so, mother ?' said the sewing-girl, with surprise.

' Listen to me, my dear daughter,' said Mother Sainte Perpétue, in a tone ever more and more affectionate ; ' the institution of St. Mary has a double end in view. You will perfectly understand that, if it is our duty to give to masters and mistresses every possible security as to the morality of the persons that we place in their families, we are likewise bound to give to the persons that we so place out every possible security as to the morality of their employers.'

' Nothing can be more just and of a wiser foresight, mother.'

' Naturally, my dear daughter ; for even as a servant of bad morals may cause the utmost trouble in a respectable family, so the bad conduct of a master or mistress may have the most baneful influence on the persons who serve them, or who come to work in their houses. Now, it is to offer a mutual guarantee to good masters and honest servants that we have founded this institution.'

' Oh, madame !' cried Mother Bunch, with simplicity ; ' such designs merit the thanks and blessings of every one.'

' And blessings do not fail us, my dear daughter, because we perform our promises. Thus, an interesting workwoman—such as you, for example—is placed with persons that we suppose irreproachable. Should she, however, perceive, on the part of her employers, or on that of the persons who frequent the house, any irregularity of morals, any tendency to what would offend her modesty, or shock her religious principles, she should immediately give us a detailed account of the circumstances that have caused her alarm. Nothing can be more proper—don't you think so ?'

' Yes, mother,' answered Mother Bunch, timidly, for she began to find this provision somewhat singular.

' Then, resumed the superior, ' if the case appears a serious one, we exhort our befriended one to observe what passes more attentively, so as to convince herself whether she had really reason to be alarmed. She makes a new report to us, and should it confirm our first fears, faithful to our pious guardianship, we withdraw her instantly from the house. Moreover, as the majority of our young people, notwithstanding their innocence and virtue, have not always sufficient experience to distinguish what may be injurious to their soul's health, we think it greatly to their interest that they should confide to us once a week, as a child would to her mother, either in person or by letter, whatever has chanced to occur in the house in which we have placed them. Then we can judge for them, whether to withdraw them or not. We have already about a hundred persons, companions to ladies, young women in shops, servants, and needlewomen by the day, whom we have placed in a great number of families, and, for the interest of all, we have every reason to congratulate ourselves on this mode of proceeding. You understand me, do you not, my dear daughter ?'

' Yes—yes, mother, said the sempstress, more and more embarrassed. She had too much uprightness and sagacity not to perceive that this plan of mutually insuring the morality of masters and servants resembled a vast spy-system, brought home to the domestic hearth, and carried on by the members of the institution almost without their knowledge, for it would have been difficult to disguise more skilfully the employment for which they were trained.

' If I have entered into these long details, my dear daughter,' resumed Mother Sainte-Perpétue, taking the hearer's silence for consent, ' it is that you may not suppose yourself obliged to remain in the house in question, if, against our expectation, you should not find there holy and pious examples. I believe Mme. de Brémont's house to be a pure and godly place ; only I have heard (though I will not believe it) that Mme. de Brémont's daughter, Mme. de Noisy, who has lately come to reside with her, is not so exemplary in her conduct as could be desired, that she does not fulfil regularly her religious duties, and that, during the absence of her husband, who is now in America, she receives visits, unfortunately too frequent, from one M. Hardy, a rich manufacturer.'

At the name of Agricola's master, Mother Bunch could not suppress a movement of surprise, and also blushed slightly. The superior naturally mistook this surprise and confusion for a proof of the modest susceptibility of the young sempstress, and added : ' I have told you all this, my dear daughter, that you might be on your guard. I have even mentioned reports that I believe to be completely erroneous, for the daughter of Mme. de Brémont has always had such good examples before her that she cannot have so forgotten them. But, being in the house from morning to night, you will be able, better than any one, to discover if these reports have any foundation in truth. Should it unfortunately so turn out, my dear daughter, you would come and confide to me all the circumstances that have led you to such a conclusion ; and, should I then agree in your opinion, I would withdraw you instantly from the house—for the piety of the mother would not compensate sufficiently for the deplorable example of the daughter's conduct. For, as soon as you form part of the institution, I am responsible for your salvation, and, in case your delicacy should oblige you to leave Mme. de Brémont's, as you might be some time without employment, the institution will allow you, if satisfied with your zeal and conduct, one franc a day till we could find you another place. You see, my dear daughter, that you have everything to gain with us. It is therefore agreed that the day after to-morrow you go to Mme. de Brémont's.' Mother Bunch found herself in a very hard position. Sometimes she thought that her first suspicions were confirmed, and, notwithstanding her timidity, her pride felt hurt at the supposition that, because they knew her poor, they should believe her capable of selling herself as a spy for the sake of high wages. Sometimes, on the contrary, her natural delicacy revolted at the idea that a woman of the age and condition of the superior could descend to make a proposition so disgraceful both to the accepter and the proposer, and she reproached herself with her first doubts, and asked herself if the superior had not wished to try her, before employing her, to see if her probity would enable her to resist a comparatively brilliant offer. Mother Bunch was naturally so inclined to think well of everyone, that she made up her mind to this last conclusion, saying to herself, that if, after all, she were deceived, it would be the least offensive mode of refusing these unworthy offers. With a movement, exempt from all haughtiness, but expressive of natural dignity, the young workwoman raised her head, which she had hitherto held humbly cast down, looked the superior full in the face, that the latter might read in her coun·tenance the sincerity of her words, and said to her in a slightly agitated voice, forgetting this time to call her 'mother :' ' Ah, madame ! I cannot blame you for exposing me to such a trial. You see that I am very poor, and I have yet done nothing to command your confidence. But, believe me, poor as I am, I would never stoop to so despicable an action as that which you have thought fit to propose to me, no doubt to assure yourself, by my refusal, that I am worthy of your kindness. No, no, madame—I could never bring myself to be a spy at any price.'

She pronounced these last words with so much animation that her cheeks became slightly flushed. The superior had too much tact and experience not to perceive the sincerity of the words. Thinking herself lucky that the young girl should put this construction upon the affair, she smiled upon her affectionately, and stretched out her arms to her, saying : ' It is well, my dear daughter. Come and embrace me !'

' Mother—I am really confused—with so much kindness——'

' No—you deserve it—your words are so full of truth and honesty. Only be persuaded that I have not put you to any trial, because there is no resemblance between the act of a spy and the marks of filial confidence that we require of our members for the sake of watching over their morals. But certain persons—I see you are of the number, my dear daughter—have such fixed principles, and so mature a judgment, that they can do without our advice and guardianship, and can appreciate themselves whatever might be dangerous to their salvation. I will therefore leave the entire responsibility to yourself, and only ask you for such communications as you may think proper to make.'

' Oh, madame ! how good you are !' said poor Mother Bunch, for she was not aware of the thousand devices of the monastic spirit, and thought herself already sure of gaining just wages honourably.

' It is not goodness—but justice !' answered Mother Saint-Perpétue, whose tone was becoming more and more affectionate. ' Too much tenderness cannot be shown to pious young women like you, whom poverty has only purified, because they have always faithfully observed the divine laws.'

' Mother——'

' One last question, my child ! how many times a month do you approach the Lord's table ?'

' Madame,' replied the hunchback, ' I have not taken the sacrament since my first communion, eight years ago. I am hardly able, by working every day, and all day long, to earn my bread. I have no time——'

' Gracious heaven !' cried the superior, interrupting, and clasping her hands with all the signs of painful astonishment. ' Is it possible? you do not practise?'

' Alas, madame! I tell you that I have no time,' answered Mother Bunch, looking disconcertedly at Mother Sainte-Perpétue.

' I am grieved, my dear daughter,' said the latter sorrowfully, after a moment's silence, ' but I told you that, as we place our friends in none but pious houses, so we are asked to recommend none but pious persons, who practise their religious duties. It is one of the indispensable conditions of our institution. It will therefore, to my great regret, be impossible for me to employ you as I had hoped. If, hereafter, you should renounce your present indifference to those duties, we will then see.'

' Madame,' said Mother Bunch, her heart swollen with tears, for she was thus forced to abandon a cheering hope, ' I beg pardon for having detained you so long—for nothing.'

' It is I, my dear daughter, who regret not to be able to attach you to the institution ; but I am not altogether hopeless, that a person, already so worthy of interest, will one day deserve by her piety the lasting support of religious people. Adieu, my dear daughter ! go in peace, and may God be merciful to you, until the day that you return with your whole heart to Him !'

So saying, the superior rose, and conducted her visitor to the door, with all the forms of the most maternal kindness. At the moment she crossed the threshold, she said to her : ' Follow the passage, go down a few steps, and knock at the second door on the right hand. It is the press-room, and there you will find Florine. She will show you the way out. Adieu, my dear daughter !'

As soon as Mother Bunch had left the presence of the superior, her tears, until now restrained, gushed forth abundantly. Not wishing to appear before Florine and the nuns in this state, she stopped a moment at one of the windows to dry her eyes. As she looked mechanically towards the window of the next house, where she fancied she had seen Adrienne de Cardoville, she beheld the latter come from a door in the building, and advance rapidly towards the open paling that separated the two gardens. At the same instant, and to her great astonishment, Mother Bunch saw one of the two sisters whose disappearance had caused the despair of Dagobert, with pale and dejected countenance, approach the fence that separated her from Mdlle. de Cardoville, trembling with fear and anxiety, as though she dreaded to be discovered.

CHAPTER VIII.

MOTHER BUNCH AND MDLLE. DE CARDOVILLE.

AGITATED, attentive, uneasy, leaning from one of the convent-windows, the work-girl followed with her eyes the movements of Mdlle. de Cardoville and Rose Simon, whom she so little expected to find together in such a place. The orphan, approaching close to the fence, which separated the nunnery-garden from that of Dr. Baleinier's asylum, spoke a few words to Adrienne, whose features at once expressed astonishment, indignation, and pity. At this juncture, a nun came running, and looking right and left, as though anxiously seeking for some one ; then, perceiving Rose, who timidly pressed close to the paling, she seized her by the arm, and seemed to scold her severely, and notwithstanding some energetic words addressed to her by Mdlle. de Cardoville, she hastily carried off the orphan, who, with weeping eyes, turned several times to look back at Adrienne ; whilst the latter, after showing the interest she took in her by expressive gestures, turned away suddenly, as if to conceal her tears.

The passage in which the witness stood, during this touching scene, was situated on the first story. The thought immediately occurred to the semp-stress, to go down to the ground-floor, and try to get into the garden, so that she might have an opportunity of speaking to the fair girl with the golden hair, and ascertaining if it were really Mdlle. de Cardoville, to whom, if she found her in a lucid interval, she might say, that Agricola had things of the greatest importance to communicate, but that he did not know how to inform her of them. The day was advancing, the sun was on its decline, and fearing that Florine would be tired of waiting for her, Mother Bunch made haste to act; with a light step, listening anxiously as she went, she reached the end of the passage, where three or four stairs led down to the landing-place of the press-room, and then formed a spiral descent to the ground-floor. Hearing voices in the press-room, the sempstress hastened down the stairs, and found herself in a long passage, in the centre of which was a glass-door, opening on that part of the garden reserved for the superior. A path, bordered by a high box-hedge, sheltered her from the gaze of curious eyes, and she crept along it, till she reached the open paling, which, at this spot, separated the convent-garden from that of Dr. Baleinier's asylum. She saw Mdlle. de Cardoville a few steps from her, seated, and with her arm resting upon a rustic bench. The firmness of Adrienne's character had for a moment been shaken by fatigue, astonishment, fright, despair, on the terrible night when she had been taken to the asylum by Dr. Baleinier; and the latter, taking a diabolical advantage of her weakness and despondency, had succeeded for a moment in making her doubt of her own sanity. But the calm, which necessarily follows the most painful and violent emotions, combined with the reflection and reasoning of a clear and subtle intellect, soon convinced Adrienne of the groundlessness of the fears inspired by the crafty doctor. She no longer believed that it could even be a mistake on the part of the man of science. She saw clearly in the conduct of this man, in which detestable hypocrisy was united with rare audacity, and both served by a skill no less remarkable, that M. Baleinier was, in fact, the blind instrument of the Princess de Saint-Dizier. From that moment, she remained silent and calm, but full of dignity; not a complaint, not a reproach was allowed to pass her lips. She waited. Yet, though they left her at liberty to walk about (carefully depriving her of all means of communicating with any one beyond the walls), Adrienne's situation was harsh and painful, particularly for her, who so loved to be surrounded by pleasant and harmonious objects. She felt, however, that this situation could not last long. She did not thoroughly understand the penetration and action of the laws; but her good sense taught her, that a confinement of a few days under the plea of some appearances of insanity, more or less plausible in themselves, might be attempted, and even executed with im-punity; but that it could not be prolonged beyond certain limits, because, after all, a young lady of her rank in society could not disappear suddenly from the world, without inquiries being made on the subject—and the pretence of a sudden attack of madness would lead to a serious investigation. Whether true or false, this conviction had restored Adrienne to her accustomed elasticity and energy of character. And yet she sometimes in vain asked herself the cause of this attempt on her liberty. She knew too well the Princess de Saint-Dizier, to believe her capable of acting in this way, without a certain end in view, and merely for the purpose of inflicting a momentary pang. In this, Mdlle. de Cardoville was not deceived: Father d'Aigrigny and the princess were both persuaded, that Adrienne, better in-formed than she wished to acknowledge, knew how important it was for her to find herself in the house in the Rue Saint-François on the 13th of

February, and was determined to maintain her rights. In shutting up Adrienne as mad, it was intended to strike a fatal blow at her future prospects ; but this last precaution was useless, for Adrienne, though upon the true scent of the family-secret they had wished to conceal from her, had not yet entirely penetrated its meaning, for want of certain documents, which had been lost or hidden.

Whatever had been the motives for the odious conduct of Mdlle. de Cardoville's enemies, she was not the less disgusted at it. No one could be more free from hatred or revenge, than was this generous young girl, but when she thought of all the sufferings which the Princess de Saint-Dizier, Abbé d'Aigrigny, and Dr. Baleinier had occasioned her, she promised herself, not reprisals, but a striking reparation. If it was refused her, she was resolved to combat— without truce or rest, this combination of craft, hypocrisy, and cruelty, not from resentment for what she had endured, but to preserve from the same torments other innocent victims, who might not, like her, be able to struggle and defend themselves. Adrienne, still under the painful impression which had been caused by her interview with Rose Simon, was leaning against one of the sides of the rustic bench on which she was seated, and held her left hand over her eyes. She had laid down her bonnet beside her, and the inclined position of her head brought the long golden curls over her fair, shining cheeks. In this recumbent attitude, so full of careless grace, the charming proportions of her figure were seen to advantage beneath a watered green dress, while a broad collar, fastened with a rose-coloured satin bow, and fine lace cuffs, prevented too strong a contrast between the hue of her dress and the dazzling whiteness of the swan-like neck and Raphaelesque hands, imperceptibly veined with tiny azure lines. Over the high and well-formed instep, were crossed the delicate strings of a little, black satin shoe—for Dr. Baleinier had allowed her to dress herself with her usual taste, and elegance of costume was not with Adrienne a mark of coquetry, but of duty towards herself, because she had been made so beautiful. At sight of this young lady, whose dress and appearance she admired in all simplicity, without any envious or bitter comparison with her own poor clothes and deformity of person, Mother Bunch said immediately to herself, with the good sense and sagacity peculiar to her, that it was strange a mad woman should dress so sanely and gracefully. It was therefore with a mixture of surprise and emotion that she approached the fence which separated her from Adrienne—reflecting, however, that the unfortunate girl might still be insane, and that this might turn out to be merely a lucid interval. And now, with a timid voice, but loud enough to be heard, Mother Bunch, in order to assure herself of Adrienne's identity, said, whilst her heart beat fast : ' Mdlle. de Cardoville !'

' Who calls me ?' said Adrienne. On hastily raising her head, and perceiving the hunchback, she could not suppress a slight cry of surprise, almost fright. For indeed this poor creature, pale, deformed, miserably clad, thus appearing suddenly before her, must have inspired Mdlle. de Cardoville, so passionately fond of grace and beauty, with a feeling of repugnance, if not of terror—and these two sentiments were both visible in her expressive countenance.

The other did not perceive the impression she had made. Motionless, with her eyes fixed, and her hands clasped in a sort of adoring admiration, she gazed on the dazzling beauty of Adrienne, whom she had only half seen through the grated window. All that Agricola had told her of the charms of his protectress, appeared to her a thousand times below the reality ; and never, even in her secret poetic visions, had she dreamed of such rare perfection. Thus, by a singular contrast, a feeling of mutual

surprise came over these two girls--extreme types of deformity and beauty,
wealth and wretchedness. After rendering as it were, this involuntary
homage to Adrienne, Mother Bunch advanced another step towards the fence.

'What do you want?' cried Mdlle. de Cardoville, rising with a sentiment
of repugnance, which could not escape the work-girl's notice; accordingly,
she held down her head timidly, and said in a soft voice: 'I beg your pardon, madame, to appear so suddenly before you. But moments are precious;
I come from Agricola.'

As she pronounced these words, the sempstress raised her eyes anxiously,
fearing that Mdlle. de Cardoville might have forgotten the name of the
workman. But, to her great surprise and joy, the fears of Adrienne seemed
to diminish at the name of Agricola, and approaching the fence, she looked
at the speaker with benevolent curiosity.

'You come from M. Agricola Baudoin?' said she. 'Who are you?'

'His adopted sister, madame—a poor needlewoman, who lives in the same
house.'

Adrienne appeared to collect her thoughts, and said, smiling kindly, after
a moment's silence: 'It was you, then, who persuaded M. Agricola to apply
to me to procure him bail?'

'Oh, madame, do you remember——'

'I never forget anything that is generous and noble. M. Agricola was
much affected when he spoke of your devotion. I remember it well; it
would be strange if I did not. But how came you here, in this convent?'

'They told me that I should perhaps be able to get some occupation
here, as I am out of work. Unfortunately, I have been refused by the lady
superior.'

'And how did you recognise me?'

'By your great beauty, madame, of which Agricola had told me.'

'Or rather by this,' said Adrienne, smiling, as she lifted, with the tips of
her rosy fingers, one end of a long, silky ringlet of golden hair.

'You must pardon Agricola, madame,' said the sewing-girl, with one of
those half smiles, which rarely settled on her lips: 'he is a poet, and omitted
no single perfection in the respectful and admiring description which he gave
of his protectress.'

'And what induced you to come and speak to me?'

'The hope of being useful to you, madame. You received Agricola with
so much goodness, that I have ventured to go shares in his gratitude.'

'You may well venture to do so, my dear girl,' said Adrienne, with ineffable grace; 'until now, unfortunately, I have only been able to serve your
adopted brother by intention.'

As they exchanged these words, Adrienne and Mother Bunch looked at each
other with increasing surprise. The latter was, first of all, astonished that a
person who passed for mad should express herself as Adrienne did; next, she
was amazed at the ease and freedom with which she herself answered the
questions of Mdlle. de Cardoville—not knowing that the latter was endowed
with the precious privilege of lofty and benevolent natures, to draw out from
those who approached her whatever sympathised with herself. On her side,
Mdlle. de Cardoville was deeply moved and astonished to hear this young,
low-born girl, dressed almost like a beggar, express herself in terms selected
with so much propriety. The more she looked at her, the more the feeling
of repugnance she at first experienced wore off, and was at length converted
into quite the opposite sentiment. With that rapid and minute power of
observation natural to women, she remarked beneath the black crape of
Mother Bunch's cap, the smoothness and brilliancy of the fair, chestnut
hair. She remarked, too, the whiteness of the long, thin hand, though it

displayed itself at the end of a patched and tattered sleeve—an infallible proof that care, and cleanliness, and self-respect were at least struggling against symptoms of fearful distress. Adrienne discovered, also, in the pale and melancholy features, in the expression of the blue eyes, at once intelligent, mild, and timid, a soft and modest dignity, which made one forget the deformed figure. Adrienne loved physical beauty, and admired it passionately; but she had too superior a mind, too noble a soul, too sensitive a heart, not to know how to appreciate moral beauty, even when it beamed from a humble and suffering countenance. Only, this kind of appreciation was new to Mdlle. de Cardoville; until now, her large fortune and elegant habits had kept her at a distance from persons of Mother Bunch's class. After a short silence, during which the fair patrician and the poor work-girl had closely examined each other, Adrienne said to the other : ' It is easy, I think, to explain the cause of our mutual astonishment. You have, no doubt, discovered that I speak pretty reasonably for a mad woman—if they have told you I am one. And I,' added Mdlle. de Cardoville, in a tone of respectful commiseration, ' find that the delicacy of your language and manners so singularly contrasts with the position in which you appear to be, that my surprise must be even greater than yours.'

' Ah, madame !' cried Mother Bunch, with a welling forth of such deep and sincere joy that the tears started to her eyes ; ' is it true ?—they have deceived me—you are not mad ! Just now, when I beheld you so kind and beautiful, when I heard the sweet tone of your voice, I could not believe that such a misfortune had happened to you. But, alas ! how is it then, madame, that you are in this place ?'

' Poor child !' said Adrienne, touched by the affectionate interest of this excellent creature ; ' and how is it that you, with such a heart and head, should be in such distress ? But be satisfied ! I shall not always be here—and that will suffice to tell you, that we shall both resume the place which becomes us. Believe me, I shall never forget how, in spite of the painful ideas which must needs occupy your mind, on seeing yourself deprived of work—your only resource—you have still thought of coming to me, and of trying to serve me. You may, indeed, be eminently useful to me, and I am delighted at it, for then I shall owe you much—and you shall see how I will take advantage of my gratitude !' said Adrienne, with a sweet smile. ' But,' resumed she, ' before talking of myself, let us think of others. Is your adopted brother still in prison ?'

' By this time, madame, I hope he has obtained his freedom ; thanks to the generosity of one of his comrades. His father went yesterday to offer bail for him, and they promised that he should be released to-day. But, from his prison, he wrote to me, that he had something of importance to reveal to you.'

' To me ?'

' Yes, madame. Should Agricola be released immediately, by what means can he communicate with you ?'

' He has secrets to tell me ?' resumed Mdlle. de Cardoville, with an air of thoughtful surprise. ' I seek in vain to imagine what they can be ; but so long as I am confined in this house, and secluded from every one, M. Agricola must not think of addressing himself directly or indirectly to me. He must wait till I am at liberty ; but that is not all, he must deliver from that convent two poor children, who are much more to be pitied than I am. The daughters of Marshal Simon are detained here against their will.'

' You know their name, madame ?'

' When M. Agricola informed me of their arrival in Paris, he told me they were fifteen years old, and that they resembled each other exactly—so that, the day before yesterday, when I took my accustomed walk, and observed two poor little weeping faces come close to the windows of their separate cells, one on the ground floor, the other on the first story a secret presentiment told me that I saw in them the orphans of whom M. Agricola had spoken, and in whom I already took a lively interest, as being my relations.'

'They are your relations, madame, then?'

'Yes, certainly. So, not being able to do more, I tried to express by signs how much I felt for them. Their tears, and the sadness of their charming faces, sufficiently told me that they were prisoners in the convent, as I am myself in this house.'

'Oh! I understand, madame—the victim of the animosity of your family?'

'Whatever may be my fate, I am much less to be pitied than these two children, whose despair is really alarming. Their separation is what chiefly oppresses them. By some words that one of them just now said to me, I see that they are, like me, the victims of an odious machination. But thanks to you, it will be possible to save them. Since I have been in this house I have had no communication with any one; they have not allowed me pen or paper, so it is impossible to write. Now listen to me attentively, and we shall be able to defeat an odious persecution.'

'Oh, speak! speak, madame!'

'The soldier, who brought these orphans to France, the father of M. Agricola, is still in town?'

'Yes, madame. Oh! if you only knew his fury, his despair, when, on his return home, he no longer found the children that a dying mother had confided to him!'

'He must take care not to act with the least violence. It would ruin all. Take this ring,' said Adrienne, drawing it from her finger, 'and give it to him. He must go instantly—are you sure that you can remember a name and address?'

'Oh! yes, madame. Be satisfied on that point. Agricola only mentioned your name once, and I have not forgotten it. There is a memory of the heart.'

'I perceive it, my dear girl. Remember, then, the name of the Count de Montbron.'

'The Count de Montbron—I shall not forget.'

'He is one of my good old friends, and lives on the Place Vendome, No. 7.'

'Place Vendome, No. 7—I shall remember.'

'M. Agricola's father must go to him this evening, and, if he is not at home, wait for his coming in. He must ask to speak to him, as if from me, and send him this ring as a proof of what he says. Once with him, he must tell him all—the abduction of the girls, the name of the convent where they are confined, and my own detention as a lunatic in the asylum of Dr. Baleinier. Truth has an accent of its own, which M. de Montbron will recognise. He is a man of much experience and judgment, and possessed of great influence. He will immediately take the necessary steps, and tomorrow, or the day after, these poor orphans and myself will be restored to liberty—all thanks to you! But moments are precious; we might be discovered; make haste, dear child!'

At the moment of drawing back, Adrienne said to Mother Bunch, with so sweet a smile and affectionate a tone, that it was impossible not to believe her sincere: 'M. Agricola told me that I had a heart like yours. I now understand how honourable, how flattering those words were for me. Pray give me your hand!' added Mdlle. de Cardoville, whose eyes were filling with tears; and, passing her beautiful hand through an opening in the fence, she offered it to the other. The words and the gesture of the fair patrician were full of so much real cordiality, that the sempstress, with no false shame, placed tremblingly her own poor thin hand in Adrienne's, while the latter, with a feeling of pious respect, lifted it spontaneously to her lips, and said : ' Since I cannot embrace you as my sister, let me at least kiss this hand, ennobled by labour !'

Suddenly, footsteps were heard in the garden of Dr. Baleinier ; Adrienne withdrew abruptly, and disappeared behind some trees, saying : ' Courage, memory, and hope !'

All this had passed so rapidly that the young workwoman had no time to speak or move ; tears. sweet tears. flowed abundantly down her pale cheeks. For a young lady, like Adrienne de Cardoville, to treat her as a sister, to kiss her hand, to tell her that she was proud to resemble her in heart—her, a poor creature, vegetating in the lowest abyss of misery—was to show a spirit of fraternal equality, divine as the gospel words.

There are words and impressions which make a noble soul forget years of suffering, and which, as by a sudden flash, reveal to it something of its own worth and grandeur. Thus it was with the hunchback. Thanks to this generous speech, she was for a moment conscious of her own value. And though this feeling was rapid as it was ineffable, she clasped her hands and raised her eyes to heaven with an expression of fervent gratitude ; for, if the poor sempstress did not practise, to use the jargon of ultramontane cant, no one was more richly endowed with that deep religious sentiment, which is to mere dogmas what the immensity of the starry heaven is to the vaulted roof of a church.

Five minutes after quitting Mdlle. de Cardoville, Mother Bunch, having left the garden without being perceived, reascended to the first story, and knocked gently at the door of the press-room. A sister came to open the door to her.

' Is not Mdlle. Florine, with whom I came, still here, sister ?' asked the needlewoman.

' She could not wait for you any longer. No doubt, you have come from our mother the superior ?'

' Yes, yes, sister,' answered the sempstress, casting down her eyes ; ' would you have the goodness to show me the way out ?'

' Come with me.'

The sewing-girl followed the nun, trembling at every step lest she should meet the superior, who would naturally have inquired the cause of her long stay in the convent.

At length the inner gate closed upon Mother Bunch. Passing rapidly across the vast court-yard and approaching the porter's lodge, to ask him to let her out, she heard these words pronounced in a gruff voice : ' It seems, old Jerome, that we are to be doubly on our guard to-night. Well, I shall put two extra balls in my gun. The superior says we are to make two rounds instead of one.'

' I want no gun, Nicholas,' said the other voice ; ' I have my sharp scythe, a true gardener's weapon—and none the worse for that.'

Feeling an involuntary uneasiness at these words, which she had heard by mere chance, Mother Bunch approached the porter's lodge, and asked him to open the outer gate.

' Where do you come from,' challenged the porter, leaning half-way out of his lodge, with a double-barrelled gun, which he was occupied in loading, in his hand, and at the same time examining the sempstress with a suspicious air.

' I come from speaking to the superior,' answered Mother Bunch timidly.

'Is that true?' said Nicholas roughly. 'You look like a sanctified scare-crow. Never mind. Make haste, and cut!'

The gate opened, and Mother Bunch went out. Hardly had she gone a few steps in the street, when, to her great surprise, she saw the dog Spoil-sport run up to her, and his master, Dagobert, a little way behind him, arriving also with precipitation. She was hastening to meet the soldier, when a full, sonorous voice exclaimed from a little distance: 'Oh, my good sister!' which caused the girl to turn round. From the opposite side to that whence Dagobert was coming, she saw Agricola hurrying towards the spot.

CHAPTER IX.

THE ENCOUNTERS.

AT the sight of Dagobert and Agricola, Mother Bunch remained motionless with surprise, a few steps from the convent-gate. The soldier had not yet perceived the sempstress. He advanced rapidly, following the dog, who, though lean, half-starved, rough-coated, and dirty, seemed to frisk with pleasure, as he turned his intelligent face towards his master, to whom he had gone back, after caressing Mother Bunch.

'Yes, yes; I understand you, old fellow!' said the soldier, with emotion. 'You are more faithful than I was; you did not leave the dear children for a minute. Yes; you followed them, and watched day and night, without food, at the door of the house to which they were taken—and, at length, weary of waiting to see them come forth, ran home to fetch me. Yes; whilst I was giving way to despair, like a furious madman, you were doing what I ought to have done—discovering their retreat. What does it all prove? Why, that beasts are better than men—which is well known. Well, at length I shall see them again. When I think that to-morrow is the 13th, and that without you, my old Spoilsport, all would be lost—it makes me shudder. But I say, shall we soon be there? What a deserted quarter! and night coming on!'

Dagobert had held this discourse to Spoilsport, as he walked along, following the good dog, who kept on at a rapid pace. Suddenly, seeing the faithful animal start aside with a bound, he raised his eyes, and perceived the dog frisking about the hunchback and Agricola, who had just met at a little distance from the convent-gate.

'Mother Bunch!' exclaimed both father and son, as they approached the young work-woman, and looked at her with extreme surprise.

'There is good hope, M. Dagobert,' said she, with inexpressible joy. 'Rose and Blanche are found!' Then, turning towards the smith, she added, 'There is good hope, Agricola: Mdlle. de Cardoville is not mad. I have just seen her.'

'She is not mad? what happiness!' exclaimed the smith.

'The children!' cried Dagobert, trembling with emotion, as he took the work-girl's hands in his own. 'You have seen them?'

'Yes; just now—very sad—very unhappy—but I was not able to speak to them.'

'Oh!' said Dagobert, stopping as if suffocated by the news, and pressing his hands on his bosom; 'I never thought that my old heart could beat so! —And yet, thanks to my dog, I almost expected what has taken place. Anyhow, I am quite dizzy with joy.'

'Well, father, 'tis a good day,' said Agricola, looking gratefully at the girl.

'Kiss me, my dear child!' added the soldier, as he pressed Mother Bunch affectionately in his arms; then, full of impatience, he added: 'Come, let us go and fetch the children.'

'Ah, my good sister !' said Agricola, deeply moved ; 'you will restore peace, perhaps life, to my father—and Mdlle. de Cardoville—but how do you know ?'

'A mere chance. And how did you come here ?'

'Spoilsport stops and barks,' cried Dagobert, who had already made several steps in advance.

Indeed the dog, who was as impatient as his master to see the orphans, and far better informed as to the place of their retreat, had posted himself at the convent gate, and was beginning to bark, to attract the attention of Dagobert. Understanding his dog, the latter said to the hunchback, as he pointed in that direction with his finger : 'The children are there ?'

'Yes, M. Dagobert.'

'I was sure of it. Good dog !—Oh, yes ! beasts are better than men— except you, my dear girl, who are better than either man or beast. But my poor children ! I shall see them, I shall have them once more !'

So saying, Dagobert, in spite of his age, began to run very fast towards Spoilsport. 'Agricola,' cried Mother Bunch, 'prevent thy father from knocking at that door. He would ruin all.'

In two strides, the smith had reached his father, just as the latter was raising his hand to the knocker. 'Stop, father !' cried the smith, as he seized Dagobert by the arm.

'What the devil is it now ?'

'Mother Bunch says that to knock would ruin all.'

'How so ?'

'She will explain it to you.' Although not so nimble as Agricola, Mother Bunch soon came up, and said to the soldier : 'M. Dagobert, do not let us remain before this gate. They might open it, and see us ; and that would excite suspicion. Let us rather go away——'

'Suspicion !' cried the veteran, much surprised, but without moving from the gate ; 'what suspicion ?'

'I conjure you, do not remain there !' said Mother Bunch, with so much earnestness, that Agricola joined her, and said to his father : 'Since sister wishes it, father, she has some reason for it. The Boulevard de l'Hôpital is a few steps from here ; nobody passes that way ; we can talk there without being interrupted.'

'Devil take me if I understand a word of all this !' cried Dagobert, with-out moving from his post. 'The children are here, and I will fetch them away with me. It is an affair of ten minutes.'

'Do not think that, M. Dagobert,' said Mother Bunch. 'It is much more difficult than you imagine. But come !—come !—I can hear them talk in the court-yard.'

In fact, the sound of voices was now distinctly audible. 'Come, father !' said Agricola, forcing away the soldier, almost in spite of himself. Spoil-sport, who appeared much astonished at these hesitations, barked two or three times without quitting his post, as if to protest against this humiliating retreat ; but, being called by Dagobert, he hastened to rejoin the main body.

It was now about five o'clock in the evening. A high wind swept thick masses of greyish, rainy cloud rapidly across the sky. The Boulevard de l'Hôpital, which bordered on this portion of the convent-garden, was, as we before said, almost deserted. Dagobert, Agricola, and the sewing-girl could hold a private conference in this solitary place.

The soldier did not disguise the extreme impatience that these delays occasioned in him. Hardly had they turned the corner of the street, when he said to Mother Bunch : 'Come, my child, explain yourself. I am upon hot coals.'

'The house in which the daughters of Marshal Simon are confined is a convent, M. Dagobert.'

'A convent !' cried the soldier : 'I might have suspected it.' Then he added : 'Well, what then ? I will fetch them from a convent as soon as from any other place. Once is not always.'

'But, M. Dagobert, they are confined against their will and against yours. They will not give them up.'

'They will not give them up ? Zounds ! we will see about that.' And he made a step towards the street.

'Father,' said Agricola, holding him back, 'one moment's patience ; let us hear all.'

'I will hear nothing. What ! the children are there—two steps from me —I know it—and I shall not have them, either by fair means or foul? Oh ! that would indeed be curious.' Let me go.'

'Listen to me, I beseech you, M. Dagobert,' said Mother Bunch, taking his hand : 'there is another way to deliver these poor children. And that without violence—for violence, as Mdlle. de Cardoville told me, would ruin all.'

'If there is any other way—quick—let me know it !'

'Here is a ring of Mdlle. de Cardoville's.'

'And who is this Mdlle. de Cardoville ?'

'Father,' said Agricola, 'it is the generous young lady, who offered to be my bail, and to whom I have very important matters to communicate.'

'Good, good,' replied Dagobert ; 'we will talk of that presently. Well, my dear girl—this ring ?'

'You must take it directly, M. Dagobert, to the Count de Montbron, No. 7, Place Vendôme. He appears to be a person of influence, and is a friend of Mdlle. de Cardoville's. This ring will prove that you come on her behalf, and you will tell him, that she is confined as a lunatic in the asylum next door to this convent, in which the daughters of Marshal Simon are detained against their will.'

'Well, well—what next ?'

'Then the Count de Montbron will take the proper steps with persons in authority, to restore both Mdlle. de Cardoville and the daughters of Marshal Simon to liberty—and perhaps, to-morrow, or the day after——'

'To-morrow or the day after !' cried Dagobert ; 'perhaps ?—It is to-day, on the instant, that I *must* have them. The day after to-morrow would be of much use ! Thanks, my good girl, but keep your ring : I will manage my own business. Wait for me here, my boy.'

'What are you going to do, father ?' cried Agricola, still holding back the soldier. 'It is a convent, remember.'

'You are only a raw recruit ; I have my theory of convents at my fingers' end. In Spain, I have put it in practice a hundred times. Here is what will happen. I knock ; a portress opens the door to me ; she asks me what I want, but I make no answer ; she tries to stop me, but I pass on ; once in the convent, I walk over it from top to bottom, calling my children with all my might.'

'But, M. Dagobert, the nuns ?' said Mother Bunch, still trying to detain the soldier.

'The nuns run after me, screaming like so many magpies. I know them. At Seville I fetched out an Andalusian girl, whom they were trying to keep by force. Well, I walk about the convent, calling for Rose and Blanche. They hear me, and answer. If they are shut in, I take the first piece of furniture that comes to hand, and break open the door.'

'But, M. Dagobert—the nuns—the nuns ?'

'The nuns, with all their squalling, will not prevent my breaking open the door, seizing my children in my arms, and carrying them off. Should the outer door be shut, there will be a second smash—that's all. So,' added Dagobert, disengaging himself from the grasp, 'wait for me here. In ten minutes I shall be back again. Go and get a hackney-coach ready, my boy.'

More calm than Dagobert, and, above all, better informed as to the provisions of the Penal Code, Agricola was alarmed at the consequences that might attend the veteran's strange mode of proceeding. So, throwing himself before him, he exclaimed: 'One word more, I entreat you.'

'Zounds! make haste!'

'If you attempt to enter the convent by force, you will ruin all.'

'How so?'

'First of all, M. Dagobert,' said Mother Bunch, 'there are men in the convent. As I came out just now, I saw the porter loading his gun, and heard the gardener talking of his sharp scythe, and the rounds he was to make at night.'

'Much I care for a porter's gun and a gardener's scythe!'

'Well, father; but listen to me a moment, I conjure you. Suppose you knock, and the door is opened—the porter will ask you what you want.'

'I tell him that I wish to speak to the superior, and so walk into the convent.'

'But, M. Dagobert,' said Mother Bunch, 'when once you have crossed the court-yard, you reach a second door, with a wicket. A nun comes to it, to see who rings, and does not open the door till she knows the object of the visit.'

'I will tell her that I wish to see the lady superior.'

'Then, father, as you are not known in the convent, they will go and inform the superior.'

'Well, what then?'—'She will come down.'

'What next?'

'She will ask you what you want, M. Dagobert.'

'What I want?—the devil! my children!'

'One minute's patience, father. You cannot doubt, from the precautions they have taken, that they wish to detain these young ladies against their will, and against yours.'

'Doubt! I am sure of it. To come to that point, they began by turning the head of my poor wife.'

'Then, father, the superior will reply to you, that she does not know what you mean, and that the young ladies are not in the convent.'

'And I will reply to her, that they are in the convent—witness Mother Bunch and Spoilsport.'

'The superior will answer, that she does not know you; that she has no explanations to give you; and will close the wicket.'

'Then I break it open—since one must come to that in the end—so leave me alone, I tell you! 'sblood! leave me alone!'

'And, on this noise and violence, the porter will run and fetch the guard, and they will begin by arresting you.'

'And what will become of your poor children then, M. Dagobert?' said Mother Bunch.

Agricola's father had too much good sense not to feel the truth of these observations of the girl and his son; but he knew also, that, cost what it might, the orphans must be delivered before the morrow. The alternative was terrible—so terrible, that, pressing his two hands to his burning forehead, Dagobert sunk back upon a stone bench, as if struck down by the inexorable fatality of the dilemma.

Agricola and the workwoman, deeply moved by this mute despair, exchanged a sad look. The smith, seating himself beside the soldier, said to him : ' Do not be down-hearted father. Remember what's been told you. By going with this ring of Mdlle. de Cardoville's to the influential gentleman she named, the young ladies may be free by to-morrow, or, at worst, by the day after.'

' Blood and thunder ! you want to drive me mad !' exclaimed Dagobert, starting up from the bench, and looking at Mother Bunch and his son with so savage an expression that Agricola and the sempstress drew back, with an air of surprise and uneasiness.

' Pardon me, my children !' said Dagobert, recovering himself after a long silence. ' I am wrong to get in a passion, for we do not understand one another. What you say is true ; and yet I am right to speak as I do. Listen to me. You are an honest man, Agricola : you an honest girl ; what I tell you is meant for you alone. I have brought these children from the depths of Siberia—do you know why? That they may be to-morrow morning in the Rue Saint-François. If they are not there, I have failed to execute the last wish of their dying mother.'

' No. 3, Rue Saint-François ?' cried Agricola, interrupting his father.

' Yes ; how do you know the number ?' said Dagobert.

' Is not the date inscribed on a bronze medal ?'

' Yes,' replied Dagobert, more and more surprised ; ' who told you ?'

'One instant, father !' exclaimed Agricola ; ' let me reflect. I think I guess it. Did you not tell me, my good sister, that Mdlle. de Cardoville was not mad ?'

' Not mad. They detain her in this asylum to prevent her communicating with any one. She believes herself, like the daughters of Marshal Simon, the victim of an odious machination.'

' No doubt of it,' cried the smith ; ' I understand all now. Mdlle. de Cardoville has the same interest as the orphans to appear to-morrow at the Rue Saint-François. But she does not perhaps know it.'

' How so ?'

' One word more, my good girl. Did Mdlle. de Cardoville tell you that she had a powerful motive to obtain her freedom by to-morrow ?'

' No ; for when she gave me this ring for the Count de Montbron, she said to me : " By his means both I and Marshal Simon's daughters will be at liberty either to-morrow or the day after——" '

' But explain yourself, then,' said Dagobert to his son, with impatience.

' Just now,' replied the smith, ' when you came to seek me in prison, I told you, father, that I had a sacred duty to perform, and that I would rejoin you at home.'

' Yes ; and I went, on my side, to take some measures, of which I will speak to you presently.'

' I ran instantly to the house in the Rue de Babylone, not knowing that Mdlle. de Cardoville was mad, or passed for mad. A servant, who opened the door to me, informed me that the young lady had been seized with a sudden attack of madness. You may conceive, father, what a blow that was to me ! I asked where she was : they answered, that they did not know. I asked if I could speak to any of the family ; as my jacket did not inspire any great confidence, they replied that none of her family were at present there. I was in despair, but an idea occurred to me. I said to myself : " If she is mad, her family physician must know where they have taken her ; if she is in a state to hear me, he will take me to her ; if not, I will speak to her doctor, as I would to her relations. A doctor is often a friend." I asked the servant, therefore, to give me the doctor's address. I obtained it without difficulty— Dr. Baleinier, No. 12, Rue Taranne. I ran thither, but he had gone out ; they told me that I should find him about five o'clock at his asylum, which is next door to the convent. That is how we have met.'

' But the medal—the medal ?' said Dagobert, impatiently ; ' where did you see it ?'

' It is with regard to this and other things that I wished to make important communications to Mdlle. de Cardoville.'

' And what are these communications ?'

' The fact is, father, I had gone to her the day of your departure, to beg her to get me bail. I was followed ; and, when she learned this from her waiting-woman, she concealed me in a hiding-place. It was a sort of little vaulted room, in which no light was admitted, except through a tunnel, made like a chimney; yet, in a few minutes, I could see pretty clearly. Having nothing better to do, I looked all about me, and saw that the walls were covered with wainscoting. The entrance to this room was composed of a sliding panel, moving by means of weights and wheels admirably contrived. As these concern my trade, I was interested in them, so I examined the springs, spite of my emotion, with curiosity, and understood the nature of their play ; but there was one brass nob, of which I could not discover the use. It was in vain to pull and move it from right to left, none of the springs were touched. I said to myself : " This knob, no doubt, belongs to another piece of mechanism"—and the idea occurred to me, instead of drawing it towards me, to push it with force. Directly after, I heard a grating sound, and perceived, just above the entrance of the hiding-place, one of the panels, about two feet square, fly open like the door of a secretary. As I had, no doubt, pushed the spring rather too hard, a bronze medal and chain fell out with the shock.'

' And you saw the address—Rue Saint-François ?' cried Dagobert.

' Yes, father ; and, with this medal, a sealed letter fell to the ground. On picking it up, I saw that it was addressed, in large letters : " For Mdlle. de Cardoville. To be opened by her the moment it is delivered." Under these words, I saw the initials " R." and " C.," accompanied by a flourish, and this date : " Paris, November the 12th, 1830." On the other side of the envelope I perceived two seals, with the letters " R." and " C.," surmounted by a coronet.'

' And the seals were unbroken ?' asked Mother Bunch.

' Perfectly whole.'

' No doubt, then, Mdlle. de Cardoville was ignorant of the existence of these papers,' said the sempstress.

' That was my first idea, since she was recommended to open the letter immediately, and, notwithstanding this recommendation, which bore date two years back, the seals remained untouched.'

' It is evident,' said Dagobert. ' What did you do ?'

' I replaced the whole where it was before, promising myself to inform Mdlle. de Cardoville of it. But, a few minutes after, they entered my hiding-place, which had been discovered, and I did not see her again. I was only able to whisper a few words of doubtful meaning to one of her waiting-women, on the subject of what I had found, hoping thereby to arouse the attention of her mistress ; and, as soon as I was able to write to you, my good sister, I begged you to go and call upon Mdlle. de Cardoville.'

' But this medal,' said Dagobert, ' is exactly like that possessed by the daughters of Marshal Simon. How can you account for that ?'

' Nothing so plain, father. Mdlle. de Cardoville is their relation. I remember now, that she told me so.'

' A relation of Rose and Blanche ?'

' Yes,' added Mother Bunch ; ' she told that also to me just now.

'Well, then,' resumed Dagobert, looking anxiously at his son, 'do you now understand why I must have my children this very day? Do you now understand, as their poor mother told me on her death-bed, that one day's delay might ruin all? Do you now see that I cannot be satisfied with a perhaps to-morrow, when I have come all the way from Siberia, only that those children might be to-morrow in the Rue Saint-François? Do you at last perceive that I must have them this night, even if I have to set fire to the convent?'

'But, father, if you employ violence——'

'Zounds! do you know what the commissary of police answered me this morning, when I went to renew my charge against your mother's confessor? He said to me that there was no proof, and that they could do nothing.'

'But now there is proof, father, for at least we know where the young girls are. With that certainty we shall be strong. The law is more powerful than all the superiors of convents in the world.'

'And the Count de Montbron, to whom Mdlle. de Cardoville begs you to apply,' said Mother Bunch, 'is a man of influence. Tell him the reasons that make it so important for these young ladies, as well as Mdlle. de Cardoville, to be at liberty this evening, and he will certainly hasten the course of justice, and to-night your children will be restored to you.'

'Sister is in the right, father. Go to the count. Meanwhile, I will run to the commissary, and tell him that we now know where the young girls are confined. Do you go home, and wait for us, my good girl. We will meet at our own house!'

Dagobert had remained plunged in thought; suddenly, he said to Agricola: 'Be it so. I will follow your counsel. But suppose the commissary says to you: "We cannot act before to-morrow"—suppose the Count de Montbron says to me the same thing—do not think I shall stand with my arms folded till the morning.'——'But, father——'

'It is enough,' resumed the soldier, in an abrupt voice: 'I have made up my mind. Run to the commissary, my boy; wait for us at home, my good girl; I will go to the count. Give me the ring. Now for the address!'

'The Count de Montbron, No. 7, Place Vendôme,' said she; 'you come on behalf of Mdlle. de Cardoville.'

'I have a good memory,' answered the soldier. 'We will meet as soon as possible in the Rue Brise-Miche.'

'Yes, father; have good courage. You will see that the law protects and defends honest people.'

'So much the better,' said the soldier; 'because, otherwise, honest people would be obliged to protect and defend themselves. Farewell, my children! we will meet soon in the Rue Brise-Miche.'

   ❀   ❀   ❀   ❀   ❀   ❀

When Dagobert, Agricola, and Mother Bunch separated, it was already dark night.

CHAPTER X.

THE MEETING.

IT is eight o'clock in the evening, the rain dashes against the windows of Frances Baudoin's apartment in the Rue Brise-Miche, while violent squalls of wind shake the badly-closed doors and casements. The disorder and confusion of this humble abode, usually kept with so much care and neatness, bore testimony to the serious nature of the sad events which had thus disturbed existences hitherto peaceful in their obscurity.

The paved floor was soiled with mud, and a thick layer of dust covered the furniture, once so bright and clean. Since Frances was taken away by the commissary, the bed had not been made ; at night Dagobert had thrown himself upon it for a few hours in his clothes, when, worn out with fatigue, and crushed by despair, he had returned from new and vain attempts to discover Rose and Blanche's prison-house. Upon the drawers stood a bottle, a glass, and some fragments of dry bread, proving the frugality of the soldier, whose means of subsistence were reduced to the money lent by the pawnbroker upon the things pledged by Mother Bunch, after the arrest of Frances.

By the faint glimmer of a candle, placed upon the little stove, now cold as marble, for the stock of wood had long been exhausted, one might have seen the hunchback sleeping upon a chair, her head resting on her bosom, her hands concealed beneath her cotton apron, and her feet resting on the lowest rung of the chair ; from time to time, she shivered in her damp, chill garments.

After that long day of fatigue and diverse emotions, the poor creature had eaten nothing. Had she even thought of it, she would have been at a loss for bread. Waiting for the return of Dagobert and Agricola, she had sunk into an agitated sleep—very different, alas ! from calm and refreshing slumber. From time to time, she half opened her eyes uneasily, and looked around her. Then, again, overcome by irresistible heaviness, her head fell upon her bosom.

After some minutes of silence, only interrupted by the noise of the wind, a slow and heavy step was heard on the landing-place. The door opened, and Dagobert entered, followed by Spoilsport.

Waking with a start, Mother Bunch raised her head hastily, sprang from her chair, and, advancing rapidly to meet Agricola's father, said to him : ' Well, M. Dagobert ! have you good news ? Have you——'

She could not continue, she was so struck with the gloomy expression of the soldier's features. Absorbed in his reflections, he did not at first appear to perceive the speaker, but threw himself despondingly on a chair, rested his elbows upon the table, and hid his face in his hands. After a long meditation, he rose, and said in a low voice : ' It must—yes, it must be done !'

Taking a few steps up and down the room, Dagobert looked around him, as if in search of something. At length, after about a minute's examination, he perceived, near the stove, a bar of iron, perhaps two feet long, serving to lift the covers, when too hot for the fingers. Taking this in his hand, he looked at it closely, poised it to judge of its weight, and then laid it down upon the drawers with an air of satisfaction. Surprised at the long silence of Dagobert, the needlewoman followed his movements with timid and uneasy curiosity. But soon her surprise gave way to fright, when she saw the soldier take down his knapsack, place it upon a chair, open it, and draw from it a pair of pocket-pistols, the locks of which he tried with the utmost caution.

Seized with terror, the sempstress could not forbear exclaiming : ' Good gracious, M. Dagobert ! what are you going to do ?'

The soldier looked at her as if he only now perceived her for the first time, and said to her in a cordial, but abrupt voice : ' Good evening, my good girl ! What is the time ?'

' Eight o'clock has just struck at Saint-Merri's, M. Dagobert.'

' Eight o'clock,' said the soldier, speaking to himself ; ' only eight !'

Placing the pistols by the side of the iron bar, he appeared again to reflect, while he cast his eyes round him.

' M. Dagobert,' ventured the girl, ' you have not, then, good news ?'

' No.'

That single word was uttered by the soldier in so sharp a tone, that, not daring to question him further, Mother Bunch sat down in silence. Spoil-sport came to lean his head on the knees of the girl, and followed the movements of Dagobert with as much curiosity as herself.

After remaining for some moments pensive and silent, the soldier approached the bed, took a sheet from it, appeared to measure its length, and then said, turning towards Mother Bunch : ' The scissors !'

' But, M. Dagobert——'

' Come, my good girl ! the scissors !' replied Dagobert, in a kind tone, but one that commanded obedience. The sempstress took the scissors from Frances' work-basket, and presented them to the soldier.

' Now, hold the other end of the sheet, my girl, and draw it out tight.'

In a few minutes, Dagobert had cut the sheet into four strips, which he twisted in the fashion of cords, fastening them here and there with bits of tape, so as to preserve the twist, and tying them strongly together, so as to make a rope of about twenty feet long. This, however, did not suffice him, for he said to himself : ' Now I must have a hook.'

Again he looked around him, and Mother Bunch, more and more frightened, for she now no longer doubted Dagobert's designs, said to him timidly : ' M. Dagobert, Agricola has not yet come in. It may be some good news that makes him so late.'

' Yes,' said the soldier, bitterly, as he continued to cast round his eyes in search of something he wanted ; ' good news like mine ! But I must have a strong iron hook.'

Still looking about, he found one of the coarse, grey sacks, that Frances was accustomed to make. He took it, opened it, and said to the work-girl : ' Put me the iron bar and the cord into this bag, my girl. It will be easier to carry.'

' Heavens !' cried she, obeying his directions ; ' you will not go without seeing Agricola, M. Dagobert ? He may perhaps have some good news to tell you.'

' Be satisfied ! I shall wait for my boy. I need not start before ten o'clock —so I have time.'

' Alas, M. Dagobert ! have you lost all hope ?'

' On the contrary. I have good hope—but in myself.'

So saying, Dagobert twisted the upper end of the sack, for the purpose of closing it, and placed it on the drawers, by the side of his pistols.

' At all events, you will wait for Agricola, M. Dagobert ?'

' Yes, if he arrive before ten o'clock.'

' Alas ! you have then quite made up your mind ?'

' Quite. And yet, if I were weak enough to believe in bad omens——'

' Sometimes, M. Dagobert, omens do not deceive one,' said the girl, hoping to induce the soldier to abandon his dangerous resolution.

' Yes,' resumed Dagobert ; ' old women say so—and, although I am not an old woman, what I saw just now weighed heavily on my heart. After all, I may have taken a feeling of anger for a presentiment.'

' What have you seen ?'

' I will tell it you, my good girl ; it may help to pass the time, which appears long enough.' Then, interrupting himself, he exclaimed : ' Was it the half-hour that just struck ?'——' Yes, M. Dagobert ; it is half-past eight.'

' Still an hour and a half,' said Dagobert, in a hollow voice. ' This,' he added, ' is what I saw. As I came along the street, my notice was attracted by a large red placard, at the head of which was a black panther devouring a white horse. That sight gave me a turn, for you must know, my good girl, that a black panther destroyed a poor old white horse that I had, Spoil-sport's companion, whose name was Iovial.'

At the sound of this name, once so familiar, Spoilsport, who was crouching at the work-woman's feet, raised his head hastily, and looked at Dagobert.

'You see that beasts have memory—he recollects,' said the soldier, sighing himself at the remembrance. Then, addressing his dog, he added: 'Dost remember Jovia'?'

On hearing this name a second time pronounced by his master, in a voice of emotion, Spoilsport gave a low whine, as if to indicate that he had not forgotten his old travelling-companion.

'It was indeed a melancholy incident, M. Dagobert,' said Mother Bunch, 'to find upon this placard a panther devouring a horse.'

'That is nothing to what's to come ; you shall hear the rest. I drew near the bill, and read in it, that one Morok, just arrived from Germany, is about to exhibit in a theatre different wild beasts that he tamed, among others a splendid lion, a tiger, and a black Java panther, named *Death*.'

'What an awful name !' said the hearer.

'You will think it more awful, my child, when I tell you, that this is the very panther which strangled my horse at Leipsic, four months ago.'

'Good Heaven ! you are right, M. Dagobert,' said the girl, 'it is awful.'

'Wait a little,' said Dagobert, whose countenance was growing more and more gloomy : 'that is not all. It was by means of this very Morok, the owner of the panther, that I and my poor children were imprisoned in Leipsic.'

'And this wicked man is in Paris, and wishes you evil?' said Mother Bunch. 'Oh ! you are right, M. Dagobert ; you must take care of yourself ; it is a bad omen.'

'For *him*, if I catch him,' said Dagobert, in a hollow tone. 'We have old accounts to settle.'

'M. Dagobert,' cried Mother Bunch, listening ; 'some one is running up the stairs. It is Agricola's footstep. I am sure he has good news.'

'That will just do,' said the soldier, hastily, without answering. 'Agricola is a smith. He will be able to find me the iron hook.'

A few moments after, Agricola entered the room ; but, alas ! the sempstress perceived at the first glance, in the dejected countenance of the workman, the ruin of her cherished hopes.

'Well !' said Dagobert to his son, in a tone which clearly announced the little faith he attached to the steps taken by Agricola ; 'well, what news?'

'Father, it is enough to drive one mad—to make one dash one's brains out against the wall !' cried the smith in a rage.

Dagobert turned towards Mother Bunch, and said : 'You see, my poor child—I was sure of it.'

'Well, father,' cried Agricola ; 'have you seen the Count de Montbron ?'

'The Count de Montbron set out for Lorraine three days ago. That is *my* good news,' continued the soldier, with bitter irony ; 'let us have yours —I long to know all. I need to know, if, on appealing to the laws, which, as you told me, protect and defend honest people, it ever happens that the rogues get the best of it. I want to know this, and *then* I want an iron hook —so I count upon you for both.'

'What do you mean, father ?'

'First, tell me what you have done. We have time. It is not much more than half-past eight. On leaving me, where did you go first ?'

'To the commissary, who had already received your depositions.'

'What did he say to you ?'

'After having very kindly listened to all I had to state, he answered, that these young girls were placed in a respectable house, a convent—so that there did not appear any urgent necessity for their immediate removal—and besides, he could not take upon himself to violate the sanctity of a religious dwelling, upon your simple testimony; to-morrow, he will make his report to the proper authorities, and steps will be taken accordingly.'

'Yes, yes—plenty of put offs,' said the soldier.

'"But, sir," answered I to him,' resumed Agricola, '"it is now, this very night, that you ought to act, for if these young girls should not be present to-morrow morning in the Rue Saint-François, their interests may suffer incalculable damage."—"I am very sorry for it," replied he, "but I cannot, upon your simple declaration, or that of your father, who—like yourself—is no relation or connection of these young persons, act in direct opposition to forms, which could not be set aside, even on the demand of a family. The law has its delays and its formalities, to which we are obliged to submit."'

'Certainly!' said Dagobert. 'We must submit to them, at the risk of becoming cowardly, ungrateful traitors!'

'Didst speak also of Mdlle. de Cardoville to him?' asked the work-girl.

'Yes—but he answered me on this subject in much the same manner: "It was very serious; there was no proof in support of my deposition. A third party had told me that Mdlle. de Cardoville affirms she was not mad; but all mad people pretend to be sane. He could not therefore, upon my sole testimony, take upon himself to enter the house of a respectable physician. But he would report upon it, and the law would have its course——"

'When I wished to act just now for myself,' said Dagobert, 'did I not foresee all this? And yet I was weak enough to listen to you.'

'But, father, what you wished to attempt was impossible, and you agreed that it would expose you to far too dangerous consequences.'

'So,' resumed the soldier, without answering his son, 'they told you in plain terms, that we must not think of obtaining legally the release of Rose and Blanche this evening, or even to-morrow morning?'

'Yes, father. In the eyes of the law, there is no special urgency. The question may not be decided for two or three days.'

'That is all I wished to know,' said Dagobert, rising, and walking up and down the room.

'And yet,' resumed his son, 'I did not consider myself beaten. In despair, but believing that justice could not remain deaf to such equitable claims, I ran to the *Palais de Justice*, hoping to find there a judge, a magistrate, who would receive my complaint, and act upon it.'

'Well?' said the soldier, stopping him.

'I was told that the courts shut every day at five o'clock, and do not open again till ten in the morning. Thinking of your despair, and of the position of poor Mdlle. de Cardoville, I determined to make one more attempt. I entered a guard-house of troops of the line, commanded by a lieutenant. I told him all. He saw that I was so much moved, and I spoke with such warmth and conviction, that he became interested.—"Lieutenant," said I to him, "grant me one favour: let a petty officer and two soldiers go to the convent, to obtain a legal entrance. Let them ask to see the daughters of Marshal Simon, and learn whether it is their choice to remain, or return to my father, who brought them from Russia. You will then see if they are not detained against their will——"'

'And what answer did he give you, Agricola?' asked Mother Bunch, while Dagobert shrugged his shoulders, and continued to walk up and down.

'"My good fellow," said he, "what you ask me is impossible. I understand your motives, but I cannot take upon myself so serious a measure. I should be broke were I to enter a convent by force."—"Then, sir, what am I to do? It is enough to turn one's head."—"Faith, I don't know," said the lieutenant; "it will be safest, I think, to wait."—Then, believing I had done all that was possible, father, I resolved to come back, in the hope that you might have been more fortunate than I—but, alas ! I was deceived !'

So saying, the smith sank upon a chair, for he was worn out with anxiety and fatigue. There was a moment of profound silence after these words of Agricola, which destroyed the last hopes of the three, mute and crushed beneath the strokes of inexorable fatality.

A new incident came to deepen the sad and painful character of this scene.

CHAPTER XI.

DISCOVERIES.

THE door—which Agricola had not thought of fastening—opened, as it were, timidly, and Frances Baudoin, Dagobert's wife, pale, sinking, hardly able to support herself, appeared on the threshold.

The soldier, Agricola, and Mother Bunch, were plunged in such deep dejection, that neither of them at first perceived the entrance. Frances advanced two steps into the room, fell upon her knees, clasped her hands together, and said in a weak and humble voice : 'My poor husband—pardon !'

At these words, Agricola and the work-girl—whose backs were towards the door—turned round suddenly, and Dagobert hastily raised his head.

' My mother !' cried Agricola, running to Frances.

' My wife !' cried Dagobert, as he also rose, and advanced to meet the unfortunate woman.

' On your knees, dear mother !' said Agricola, stooping down to embrace her affectionately. ' Get up, I entreat you !'

' No, my child,' said Frances, in her mild, firm accents, ' I will not rise, till your father has forgiven me. I have wronged him much—now I know it.'

' Forgive you, my poor wife ?' said the soldier, as he drew near with emotion. 'Have I ever accused you, except in my first transport of despair? No, no; it was the bad priests that I accused, and there I was right. Well ! I have you again,' added he, assisting his son to raise Frances ; ' one grief the less. They have then restored you to liberty ? Yesterday, I could not even learn in what prison they had put you. I have so many cares that I could not think of you only. But come, dear wife : sit down !'

' How feeble you are, dear mother!—how cold—how pale !' said Agricola with anguish, his eyes filling with tears. ' Why did you not let us know ?' added he. ' We would have gone to fetch you. But how you tremble ! Your hands are frozen !' continued the smith, as he knelt down before Frances. Then, turning towards Mother Bunch : ' Pray, make a little fire directly.'

' I thought of it, as soon as your father came in, Agricola, but there is no wood nor charcoal left.'

' Then pray borrow some of Father Loriot, my dear sister. He is too good a fellow to refuse. My poor mother trembles so—she might fall ill.'

Hardly had he said the words, than Mother Bunch went out. The smith rose from the ground, took the blanket from the bed, and carefully wrapped it about the knees and feet of his mother. Then, again kneeling down, he said to her : ' Your hands, dear mother !' and, taking those feeble palms in his own, he tried to warm them with his breath.

Nothing could be more touching than this picture : the robust young man, with his energetic and resolute countenance, expressing by his looks the greatest tenderness, and paying the most delicate attentions to his poor, pale, trembling old mother.

Dagobert, kind-hearted as his son, went to fetch a pillow, and brought it to his wife, saying : ' Lean forward a little, and I will put this pillow behind you ; you will be more comfortable, and warmer.'

' How you both spoil me !' said Frances, trying to smile. 'And you to be so kind, after all the ill I have done !' added she to Dagobert, as, disengaging one of her hands from those of her son, she took the soldier's hand and pressed it to her tearful eyes. ' In prison,' said she in a low voice, ' I had time to repent.'

Agricola's heart was near breaking at the thought that his pious and good mother, with her angelic purity, should for a moment have been confined in prison with so many miserable creatures. He would have made some attempt to console her on the subject of the painful past, but he feared to give a new shock to Dagobert, and was silent.

' Where is Gabriel, dear mother?' inquired he. ' How is he? As you have seen him, tell us all about him.'

' I have seen Gabriel,' said Frances, drying her tears ; ' he is confined at home. His superiors have rigorously forbidden his going out. Luckily, they did not prevent his receiving me, for his words and counsels have opened my eyes to many things. It is from him that I learned how guilty I had been to you, my poor husband.'

' How so ?' asked Dagobert.

' Why, you know that if I caused you so much grief, it was not from wickedness. When I saw you in such despair, I suffered almost as much myself ; but I durst not tell you so, for fear of breaking my oath. I had resolved to keep it, believing that I did well, believing that it was my duty. And yet something told me that it could not be my duty to cause you so much pain. " Alas, my God ! enlighten me !" I exclaimed in my prison, as I knelt down and prayed, in spite of the mockeries of the other women. " Why should a just and pious work, commanded by my confessor, the most respectable of men, overwhelm me and mine with so much misery ? Have mercy on me, my God, and teach me if I have done wrong without knowing it !" As I prayed with fervour, God heard me, and inspired me with the idea of applying to Gabriel. " I thank Thee, Father ! I will obey !" said I within myself. " Gabriel is like my own child ; but he is also a priest, a martyr—almost a saint. If any one in the world imitates the charity of our blessed Saviour, it is surely he. When I leave this prison, I will go and consult him, and he will clear up my doubts." '

' You are right, dear mother,' cried Agricola ; ' it was a thought from heaven. Gabriel is an angel of purity, courage, nobleness—the type of the true and good priest !'

' Ah, poor wife !' said Dagobert, with bitterness ; ' if you had never had any confessor but Gabriel !'

' I thought of it before he went on his journey,' said Frances, with simplicity. ' I should have liked to confess to the dear boy—but I fancied Abbé Dubois would be offended, and that Gabriel would be too indulgent with regard to my sins.'

' Your sins, poor dear mother?' said Agricola. ' As if you ever committed any !'

' And what did Gabriel tell you ?' asked the soldier.

' Alas, my dear ! had I but had such an interview with him sooner ! What I told him of Abbé Dubois roused his suspicions, and he questioned me, dear child, as to many things of which he had never spoken to me before. Then I opened to him my whole heart, and he did the same to me, and we both made sad discoveries with regard to persons whom we had always thought very respectable, and who yet had deceived each of us, unknown to the other.'

'How so?'

'Why, they used to tell him, under the seal of secrecy, things that were supposed to come from me; and they used to tell me, under the same seal of secrecy, things that were supposed to come from him. Thus, he confessed to me, that he did not feel at first any vocation for the priesthood; but they told him that I should not believe myself safe in this world or in the next, if he did not take orders, because I felt persuaded that I could best serve the Lord by giving Him so good a servant; and that yet I had never dared to ask Gabriel himself to give me this proof of his attachment, though I had taken him from the street, a deserted orphan, and brought him up as my own son, at the cost of labour and privations. Then, how could it be otherwise? The poor dear child, thinking he could please me, sacrificed himself. He entered the seminary.'

'Horrible,' said Agricola; ''tis an infamous snare, and, for the priests who were guilty of it, a sacrilegious lie!'

'During all that time,' resumed Frances, 'they were holding very different language to me. I was told that Gabriel felt his vocation, but that he durst not avow it to me, for fear of my being jealous on account of Agricola, who, being brought up as a workman, would not enjoy the same advantages as those which the priesthood would secure to Gabriel. So when he asked my permission to enter the seminary—dear child! he entered it with regret, but he thought he was making me so happy!—instead of discouraging this idea, I did all in my power to persuade him to follow it, assuring him that he could not do better, and that it would occasion me great joy. You understand, I exaggerated, for fear he should think me jealous on account of Agricola.'

'What an odious machination!' said Agricola, in amazement. 'They were speculating in this unworthy manner upon your mutual devotion. Thus Gabriel saw the expression of your dearest wish in the almost forced encouragement given to his resolution.'

'Little by little, however, as Gabriel has the best heart in the world, the vocation really came to him. That was natural enough—he was born to console those who suffer, and devote himself for the unfortunate. He would never have spoken to me of the past, had it not been for this morning's interview. But then I beheld him, who is usually so mild and gentle, become indignant, exasperated, against M. Rodin and another person whom he accuses. He had serious complaints against them already, but these discoveries, he says, will make up the measure.'

At these words of Frances, Dagobert pressed his hand to his forehead, as if to recall something to his memory. For some minutes he had listened with surprise, and almost terror, to the account of these secret plots, conducted with such deep and crafty dissimulation.

Frances continued: 'When at last I acknowledged to Gabriel, that, by the advice of Abbé Dubois, my confessor, I had delivered to a stranger the children confided to my husband—General Simon's daughters—the dear boy blamed me, though with great regret, not for having wished to instruct the poor orphans in the truths of our holy religion, but for having acted without the consent of my husband, who alone was answerable before God and man for the charge entrusted to him. Gabriel severely censured Abbé Dubois' conduct, who had given me, he said, bad and perfidious counsels; and then, with the sweetness of an angel, the dear boy consoled me, and exhorted me to come and tell you all. My poor husband! he would fain have accompanied me, for I had scarcely courage to come hither, so strongly did I feel the wrong I had done you; but, unfortunately, Gabriel is confined at the seminary by strict order of his superiors; he could not come with me, and——'

Here Dagobert, who seemed much agitated, abruptly interrupted his wife. 'One word, Frances,' said he ; 'for, in truth, in the midst of so many cares, and black, diabolical plots, one loses one's memory, and the head begins to wander. Didst not tell me, the day the children disappeared, that Gabriel, when taken in by you, had round his neck a bronze medal, and in his pocket a book filled with papers in a foreign language ?'

'Yes, my dear.'

'And this medal and these papers were afterwards delivered to your confessor ?'

'Yes, my dear.'

'And Gabriel never spoke of them since ?'

'Never.'

Agricola, hearing this from his mother, looked at her with surprise, and exclaimed : 'Then Gabriel has the same interest as the daughters of General Simon, or Mdlle. de Cardoville, to be in the Rue Saint-François to-morrow ?'

'Certainly,' said Dagobert. 'And now do you remember what he said to us, just after my arrival—that, in a few days, he would need our support in a serious matter ?'

'Yes, father.'

'And he is kept a prisoner at his seminary ! And he tells your mother that he has to complain of his superiors ! and he asked us for our support with so sad and grave an air, that I said to him——'

'He would speak so, if about to engage in a deadly duel,' interrupted Agricola. 'True, father ! and yet you, who are a good judge of valour, acknowledged that Gabriel's courage was equal to yours. For him so to fear his superiors, the danger must be great indeed.'

'Now that I have heard your mother, I understand it all,' said Dagobert. 'Gabriel is like Rose and Blanche, like Mdlle. de Cardoville, like your mother, like all of us, perhaps—the victim of a secret conspiracy of wicked priests. Now that I know their dark machinations, their infernal perseverance, I see,' added the soldier, in a whisper, 'that it requires strength to struggle against them. I had not the least idea of their power.'

'You are right, father ; for those who are hypocritical and wicked do as much harm as those who are good and charitable, like Gabriel, do good. There is no more implacable enemy than a bad priest.'

'I know it, and that's what frightens me ; for my poor children are in their hands. But is all-lost ? Shall I bring myself to give them up without an effort ? Oh, no, no ! I will not show any weakness—and yet, since your mother told us of these diabolical plots, I do not know how it is—but I seem less strong, less resolute. What is passing around me appears so terrible. The spiriting-away of these children is no longer an isolated fact—it is one of the ramifications of a vast conspiracy, which surrounds and threatens us all. It seems to me as if I and those I love walked together in darkness, in the midst of serpents, in the midst of snares that we can neither see nor struggle against. Well ! I'll speak out ! I have never feared death—I am not a coward—and yet I confess—yes, I confess it—these black robes frighten me——'

Dagobert pronounced these words in so sincere a tone, that his son started, for he shared the same impression. And it was quite natural. Frank, energetic, resolute characters, accustomed to act and fight in the light of day, never feel but one fear—and that is, to be ensnared and struck in the dark by enemies that escape their grasp. Thus, Dagobert had encountered death twenty times ; and yet, on hearing his wife's simple revelation of this dark tissue of lies, and treachery, and crime, the soldier felt a vague sense of fear ; and, though nothing was changed in the conditions of his nocturnal enterprise against the convent, it now appeared to him in a darker and more dangerous light.

The silence, which had reigned for some moments, was interrupted by Mother Bunch's return. The latter, knowing that the interview between Dagobert, his wife, and Agricola, ought not to have any importunate witness, knocked lightly at the door, and remained in the passage with Father Loriot.

' Can we come in, Mme. Frances?' asked the sempstress. ' Here is Father Loriot, bringing some wood.'

'Yes, yes ; come in, my good girl,' said Agricola, whilst his father wiped the cold sweat from his forehead.

The door opened, and the worthy dyer appeared, with his hands and arms of an amaranthine colour ; on one side, he carried a basket of wood, and on the other some live coal in a shovel.

' Good evening to the company !' said Daddy Loriot. ' Thank you for having thought of me, Mme. Frances. You know that my shop and everything in it are at your service. Neighbours should help one another ; that's my motto ! You were kind enough, I should think, to my late wife !'

Then, placing the wood in a corner, and giving the shovel to Agricola, the worthy dyer, guessing from the sorrowful appearance of the different actors in this scene, that it would be impolite to prolong his visit, added : ' You don't want anything else, Mme. Frances ?'

' No, thank you, Father Loriot.'

'Then, good evening to the company !' said the dyer ; and, addressing Mother Bunch, he added : ' Don't forget the letter for M. Dagobert. I durstn't touch it for fear of leaving the marks of my four fingers and thumb in amaranthine ! But, good evening to the company !' and Father Loriot went out.

' M. Dagobert, here is a letter,· said Mother Bunch. She set herself to light the fire in the stove, while Agricola drew his mother's arm-chair to the hearth.

' See what it is, my boy,' said Dagobert to his son ; ' my head is so heavy that I cannot see clear ' Agricola took the letter, which contained only a few lines, and read it, before he looked at the signature :

' " At Sea, December 25th, 1831.

' " I avail myself of a few minutes' communication with a ship bound direct for Europe, to write to you, my old comrade, a few hasty lines, which will reach you probably by way of Havre, before the arrival of my last letters from India. You must by this time be at Paris, with my wife and child— tell them——

' " I am unable to say more—the boat is departing. Only one word : I shall soon be in France. Do not forget the 13th February ; the future of my wife and child depends upon it.

' " Adieu, my friend ! Believe in my eternal gratitude. SIMON."'

'Agricola—quick ! look to your father !' cried the hunchback.

From the first words of this letter, which present circumstances made so cruelly applicable, Dagobert had become deadly pale. Emotion, fatigue, exhaustion, joined to this last blow, made him stagger.

His son hastened to him, and supported him in his arms. But soon the momentary weakness passed away, and Dagobert, drawing his hand across his brow, raised his tall figure to its full height. Then, whilst his eye sparkled, his rough countenance took an expression of determined resolution, and he exclaimed, in wild excitement : ' No, no ! I will not be a traitor ; I will not be a coward. The black robes shall not frighten me ; and, this night, Rose and Blanche Simon shall be free !'

CHAPTER XII.

THE PENAL CODE.

STARTLED for a moment by the dark and secret machinations of the black robes, as he called them, against the persons he most loved, Dagobert might have hesitated an instant to attempt the deliverance of Rose and Blanche ; but his indecision ceased directly on the reading of Marshal Simon's letter, which came so timely to remind him of his sacred duties.

To the soldier's passing dejection had succeeded a resolution full of calm and collected energy.

'Agricola, what o'clock is it ?' asked he of his son.

'Just struck nine, father.'

'You must make me, directly, an iron hook—strong enough to support my weight, and wide enough to hold on the coping of a wall. This stove will be forge and anvil ; you will find a hammer in the house ; and, as for iron,' said the soldier, hesitating, and looking around him, 'as for iron—here is some !'

So saying, the soldier took from the hearth a strong pair of tongs, and presented them to his son, adding : ' Come, my boy ! blow up the fire, blow it to a white heat, and forge me this iron !'

On these words, Frances and Agricola looked at each other with surprise ; the smith remained mute and confounded, not knowing the resolution of his father, and the preparations he had already commenced with the needle-woman's aid.

'Don't you hear me, Agricola,' repeated Dagobert, still holding the pair of tongs in his hand ; ' you must make me a hook directly.'

'A hook, father ?—for what purpose ?'

'To tie to the end of a cord that I have here. There must be a loop at one end large enough to fix it securely.'

'But this cord—this hook—for what purpose are they ?'

'To scale the walls of the convent, if I cannot get in by the door.'

'What convent ?' asked Frances of her son.

'How, father ?' cried the latter, rising abruptly. ' You still think of that ?'

'Why ! what else should I think of ?'

'But, father, it is impossible ; you will never attempt such an enterprise.'

'What is it, my child ?' asked Frances, with anxiety. ' Where is father going ?'

'He is going to break into the convent where Marshal Simon's daughters are confined, and carry them off.'

'Great God ! my poor husband—a sacrilege !' cried Frances, faithful to her pious traditions, and, clasping her hands together, she endeavoured to rise and approach Dagobert.

The soldier, foreseeing that he would have to contend with observations and prayers of all sorts, and resolved not to yield, determined to cut short all useless supplications, which would only make him lose precious time. He said, therefore, with a grave, severe, and almost solemn air, which showed the inflexibility of his determination : 'Listen to me, wife—and you also, my son—when, at my age, a man makes up his mind to anything, he knows the reason why. And when a man has once made up his mind, neither wife nor child can alter it. I have resolved to do my duty ; so spare yourselves useless words. It may be your duty to talk to me as you have done ; but it is over now, and we will say no more about it. This evening I must be master in my own house.'

Timid and alarmed, Frances did not dare to utter a word, but she turned a supplicating glance towards her son.

' Father,' said the latter, ' one word more—only one.'

' Let us hear,' replied Dagobert, impatiently.

' I will not combat your resolution ; but I will prove to you that you do not know to what you expose yourself.'

' I know it all,' replied the soldier, in an abrupt tone. ' The undertaking is a serious one ; but it shall not be said that I neglected any means to accomplish what I promised to do.'

' But, father, you do not know to what danger you expose yourself,' said the smith, much alarmed.

' Talk of danger ! talk of the porter's gun and the gardener's scythe !' said Dagobert, shrugging his shoulders contemptuously. ' Talk of them, and have done with it—for, after all, suppose I were to leave my carcass in the convent, would not you remain to your mother ? For twenty years, you were accustomed to do without me. It will be all the less trying to you.'

' And I, alas ! am the cause of these misfortunes !' cried the poor mother. ' Ah ! Gabriel had good reason to blame me.'

' Mme. Frances be comforted,' whispered the sempstress, who had drawn near to Dagobert's wife. ' Agricola will not suffer his father to expose himself thus.'

After a moment's hesitation, the smith resumed, in an agitated voice : ' I know you too well, father, to think of stopping you by the fear of death.'

' Of what danger, then, do you speak ?'

' Of a danger from which even you will shrink, brave as you are,' said the young man, in a voice of emotion, that forcibly struck his father.

' Agricola,' said the soldier, roughly and severely, 'that remark is cowardly, you are insulting.'

' Father——'

' Cowardly !' resumed the soldier, angrily ; ' because it is cowardice to wish to frighten a man from his duty—insulting ! because you think me capable of being so frightened.'

' Oh, M Dagobert !' exclaimed the sewing-girl, ' you do not understand Agricola.'

' I understand him too well,' answered the soldier, harshly.

Painfully affected by the severity of his father, but firm in his resolution, which sprang from love and respect, Agricola resumed, whilst his heart beat violently : ' Forgive me, if I disobey you, father ; but, were you to hate me for it, I must tell you to what you expose yourself by scaling at night the walls of a convent——'

' My son ! do you dare ?' cried Dagobert, his countenance inflamed with rage——

' Agricola !' exclaimed Frances, in tears. ' My husband !'

' M. Dagobert, listen to Agricola !' exclaimed Mother Bunch. ' It is only in your interest that he speaks.'

' Not one word more !' replied the soldier, stamping his foot with anger.

' I tell you, father,' exclaimed the smith, growing fearfully pale as he spoke, ' that you risk being sent to the galleys !'

' Unhappy boy !' cried Dagobert, seizing his son by the arm ; ' could you not keep that from me—rather than expose me to become a traitor and a coward ?' And the soldier shuddered, as he repeated : ' The galleys !'—and, bending down his head, remained mute, pensive, withered, as it were, by those blasting words.

' Yes, to enter an inhabited place by night, in such a manner, is what the law calls burglary, and punishes with the galleys,' cried Agricola, at once grieved and rejoicing at his father's depression of mind—'yes, father, the galleys, if you are taken in the act ; and there are ten chances to one that you would be so. Mother Bunch has told you, the convent is guarded. This morning, had you attempted to carry off the two young ladies in broad daylight, you would have been arrested ; but, at least, the attempt would have been an open one, with a character of honest audacity about it, that hereafter might have procured your acquittal. But to enter by night, and by scaling the walls—I tell you, the galleys would be the consequence. Now, father, decide. Whatever you do, I will do also—for you shall not go alone. Say but the word, and I will forge the hook for you—I have here hammer and pincers—and in an hour we will set out.'

A profound silence followed these words—a silence that was only interrupted by the stifled sobs of Frances, who muttered to herself in despair : 'Alas ! this is the consequence of listening to Abbé Dubois !'

It was in vain that Mother Bunch tried to console Frances. She was herself alarmed, for the soldier was capable of braving even infamy, and Agricola had determined to share the perils of his father.

In spite of his energetic and resolute character, Dagobert remained for some time in a kind of stupor. According to his military habits, he had looked at this nocturnal enterprise only as a *ruse de guerre*, authorised by his good cause. and by the inexorable fatality of his position ; but the words of his son brought him back to the fearful reality, and left him the choice of a terrible alternative—either to betray the confidence of Marshal Simon, and set at nought the last wishes of the mother of the orphans—or else to expose himself, and above all his son, to lasting disgrace—without even the certainty of delivering the orphans after all.

Drying her eyes, bathed in tears, Frances exclaimed, as if by a sudden inspiration . ' Dear me ! I have just thought of it. There is perhaps a way of getting these dear children from the convent without violence.'

' How so, mother ?' said Agricola, hastily.

' It is Abbé Dubois, who had them conveyed thither ; but Gabriel supposes, that he probably acted by the advice of M. Rodin.'

' And if that were so, mother, it would be in vain to apply to M. Rodin. We should get nothing from him.'

' Not from him—but perhaps from that powerful abbé, who is Gabriel's superior, and has always patronised him since his first entrance at the seminary '

' What abbé, mother ?'

' Abbé d'Aigrigny.'

' True, mother ; before being a priest, he was a soldier—he may be more accessible than others—and yet——'

. ' D'Aigrigny !' cried Dagobert, with an expression of hate and horror 'There is then mixed up with these treasons, a man, who was a soldier before being a priest, and whose name is D Aigrigny ?'

' Yes, father ; the Marquis d Aigrigny—before the Restoration, in the service of Russia—but, in 1815, the Bourbons gave him a regiment.'

' It is he !' said Dagobert, in a hollow voice. 'Always the same ! like an evil spirit—to the mother, father, children.'

' What do you mean, father ?'

' The Marquis d'Aigrigny !' replied Dagobert. ' Do you know what is this man ? Before he was a priest, he was the murderer of Rose and Blanche's mother, because she despised his love Before he was a priest, he fought against his country, and twice met General Simon face to face in war Yes ; while the general was prisoner at Leipsic, covered with wounds at Waterloo, the turncoat marquis triumphed with the Russians and English !—Under the Bourbons, this same renegade, loaded with honours, found himself once more face to face with the persecuted soldier of the empire. Between them, this time, there was a mortal duel—the marquis was wounded—General Simon was proscribed, condemned, driven into exile. The renegade, you say, has become a priest. Well! I am now certain, that it is he who has carried off Rose and Blanche, in order to wreak on them his hatred of their father and mother. It is the infamous D'Aigrigny, who holds them in his power. It is no longer the fortune of these children that I have to defend; it is their life—do you hear what I say?—their very life!'

'What, father! do you think this man capable——'

'A traitor to his country, who finishes by becoming a mock priest, is capable of anything. I tell you, that, perhaps at this moment, he may be killing those children by a slow-fire!' exclaimed the soldier, in a voice of agony. 'To separate them from one another was to begin to kill them. Yes!' added Dagobert, with an exasperation impossible to describe; 'the daughters of Marshal Simon are in the power of the Marquis d'Aigrigny and his band, and I hesitate to attempt their rescue, for fear of the galleys! The galleys!' added he, with a convulsive burst of laughter; 'what do I care for the galleys? Can they send a corpse there? If this last attempt fail, shall I not have the right to blow my brains out?—Put the iron in the fire, my boy—quick! time presses—and strike while the iron's hot!'

'But your son goes with you!' exclaimed Frances, with a cry of maternal despair. Then rising, she threw herself at the feet of Dagobert, and said: 'If you are arrested, he will be arrested also.'

'To escape the galleys, he will do as I do. I have two pistols.'

'And without you—without him,' cried the unhappy mother, extending her hands in supplication, 'what will become of me?'

'You are right—I was too selfish,' said Dagobert. 'I will go alone.'

'You shall not go alone, father,' replied Agricola.

'But your mother?'

'Mother Bunch sees what is passing; she will go to Mr. Hardy, my master, and tell him all. He is the most generous of men, and my mother will have food and shelter for the rest of her days.'

'And *I* am the cause of all!' cried Frances, wringing her hands in despair. 'Punish me, oh, heaven! for it is my fault. I gave up those children. I shall be punished be the death of my child!'

'Agricola, you shall not go with me—I forbid it!' said Dagobert, clasping his son closely to his breast.

'What! when I have pointed out the danger, am I to be the first to shrink from it? you cannot think thus lowly of me, father! Have I not also some one to deliver? The good, the generous Mdlle. de Cardoville, who tried to save me from a prison, is a captive in her turn! I will follow you, father. It is my right, my duty, my determination.'

So saying, Agricola put into the heated stove the tongs that were intended to form the hook. 'Alas! may heaven have pity upon us!' cried his poor mother, sobbing as she still knelt, whilst the soldier seemed a prey to the most violent internal struggle.

'Do not cry so, dear mother; you will break my heart,' said Agricola, as he raised her with the sempstress's help. 'Be comforted! I have exaggerated the danger of my father. By acting prudently, we two may succeed in our enterprise, without much risk—eh, father?' added he, with a significant glance at Dagobert. 'Once more, be comforted, dear mother. I will answer for everything. We will deliver Marshal Simon's daughters, and Mdlle. de Cardoville too. Sister, give me the hammer and pincers, there in the press.'

The sempstress, drying her tears, did as desired, while Agricola, by the help of bellows, revived the fire in which the tongs were heating.

'Here are your tools, Agricola,' said the hunchback, in a deeply-agitated voice, as she presented them with trembling hands to the smith, who, with the aid of the pincers, soon drew from the fire the white-hot tongs, and, with vigorous blows of the hammer, formed them into a hook, taking the stove for his anvil.

Dagobert had remained silent and pensive. Suddenly he said to Frances, taking her by the hand : 'You know what metal your son is. To prevent his following me would now be impossible. But do not be afraid, dear wife; we shall succeed—at least, I hope so And if we should not succeed—if Agricola and me should be arrested—well ! we are not cowards ; we shall not commit suicide ; but father and son will go arm in arm to prison, with heads high and proud, look, like two brave men who have done their duty. The day of trial must come, and we will explain all, honestly, openly—we will say, that, driven to the last extremity, finding no support, no protection in the law, we were forced to have recourse to violence. So hammer away, my boy !' added Dagobert, addressing his son, pounding the hot iron ; 'forge, forge, without fear. Honest judges will absolve honest men.'

'Yes, father, you are right ; be at ease, dear mother ! The judges will see the difference between rascals who scale walls in order to rob, and an old soldier and his son, who, at peril of their liberty, their life, their honour, have sought only to deliver unhappy victims.'

'And if this language should not be heard,' resumed Dagobert, 'so much the worse for them ! It will not be your son, or husband, who will be dishonoured in the eyes of honest people. If they send us to the galleys, and we have courage to survive—the young and the old convict will wear their chains proudly—and the renegade marquis, the traitor priest, will bear more shame than we. So, forge without fear, my boy ! There are things which the galleys themselves cannot disgrace—our good conscience and our honour ! But now,' he added, 'two words with my good Mother Bunch. It grows late, and time presses. On entering the garden, did you remark if the windows of the convent were far from the ground ?'

'No, not very far, M. Dagobert—particularly on that side which is opposite to the madhouse, where Mdlle. de Cardoville is confined.'

'How did you manage to speak to that young lady ?'

'She was on the other side of an open pailing, which separates the two gardens.'

'Excellent !' said Agricola, as he continued to hammer the iron : 'we can easily pass from one garden to the other. The madhouse may perhaps be the readier way out Unfortunately, you do not know Mdlle. de Cardoville's chamber.'

'Yes, I do,' returned the work-girl, recollecting herself. 'She is lodged in one of the wings, and there is a shade over her window, painted like canvas, with blue and white stripes.'

'Good ! I shall not forget that.'

'And can you form no guess as to where are the rooms of my poor children ?' said Dagobert

After a moment's reflection, Mother Bunch answered ; 'They are opposite to the chamber occupied by Mdlle. de Cardoville, for she makes signs to them from her window ; and I now remember she told me, that their two rooms are on different stories, one on the ground-floor, and the other up one pair of stairs.'

'Are these windows grated ?' asked the smith.

'I do not know.'

Never mind, my good girl ; with these indications, we shall do very well,' said Dagobert. 'For the rest, I have my plans,'

'Some water, my little sister,' said Agricola, 'that I may cool my iron.' Then, addressing his father : 'Will this hook do ?'

'Yes, my boy ; as soon as it is cold we will fasten the cord.'

For some time, Frances Baudoin had remained upon her knees, praying with fervour. She implored Heaven to have pity on Agricola and Dagobert, who, in their ignorance, were about to commit a great crime ; and she entreated that the celestial vengeance might fall upon her only, as she alone had been the cause of the fatal resolution of her son and husband.

Dagobert and Agricola finished their preparations in silence. They were both very pale, and solemnly grave. They felt all the danger of so desperate an enterprise.

The clock at Saint-Méry's struck ten. The sound of the bell was faint, and almost drowned by the lashing of the wind and rain, which had not ceased for a moment.

'Ten o'clock !' said Dagobert, with a start. 'There is not a minute to lose. Take the sack, Agricola.'——'Yes, father.'

As he went to fetch the sack, Agricola approached Mother Bunch, who was hardly able to sustain herself, and said to her in a rapid whisper : 'If we are not here to-morrow, take care of my mother. Go to M. Hardy, who will perhaps have returned from his journey. Courage, my sister ! embrace me. I leave poor mother to you.' The smith, deeply affected, pressed the almost fainting girl in his arms.

'Come, old Spoilsport,' said Dagobert ; 'you shall be our scout.' Approaching his wife, who, just risen from the ground, was clasping her son's head to her bosom, and covering it with tears and kisses, he said to her, with a semblance of calmness and serenity : 'Come, my dear wife, be reasonable ! Make us a good fire. In two or three hours we will bring home the two poor children, and a fine young lady. Kiss me ! that will bring me luck.

Frances threw herself on her husband's neck, without uttering a word. This mute despair, mingled with convulsive sobs, was heart-rending. Dagobert was obliged to tear himself from his wife's arms, and striving to conceal his emotion, he said to his son, in an agitated voice : 'Let us go—she unmans me. Take care of her, my good Mother Bunch. Agricola—come !'

The soldier slipped the pistols into the pocket of his great coat, and rushed towards the door, followed by Spoilsport.

'My son, let me embrace you once more—alas ! it is perhaps for the last time !' cried the unfortunate mother, incapable of rising, but stretching out her arms to Agricola. 'Forgive me ! it is all my fault.'

The smith turned back, mingled his tears with those of his mother—for he also wept—and murmured, in a stifled voice : 'Adieu, dear mother ! Be comforted. We shall soon meet again.'

Then, escaping from the embrace, he joined his father upon the stairs.

Frances Baudoin heaved a long sigh, and fell almost lifeless into the needlewoman's arms.

Dagobert and Agricola left the Rue Brise-Miche in the height of the storm, and hastened with great strides towards the Boulevard de l'Hôpital, followed by the dog.

CHAPTER XIII.

BURGLARY.

HALF-PAST eleven had just struck, when Dagobert and his son arrived on the Boulevard de l'Hôpital.

The wind blew violently, and the rain fell down in torrents, but notwith-standing the thickness of the watery clouds, it was tolerably light, thanks to the late rising of the moon. The tall, dark trees, and the white walls of the convent-garden, were distinguishable in the midst of the pale glimmer. Afar off, a street lamp, acted on by the wind, with its red light hardly visible through the mist and rain, swung backwards and forwards over the dirty causeway of the solitary boulevard.

At rare intervals, they heard, at a very great distance, the rattle and rumble of a coach, returning home late ; then all was again silent.

Since their departure from the Rue Brise-Miche, Dagobert and his son had hardly exchanged a word. The design of these two brave men was noble and generous, and yet, resolute but pensive, they glided through the dark-ness like bandits, at the hour of nocturnal crimes.

Agricola carried on his shoulders the sack containing the cord, the hook, and the iron bar ; Dagobert leaned upon the arm of his son, and Spoilsport followed his master.

' The bench, where we sat down, must be close by,' said Dagobert, stopping.

' Yes,' said Agricola, looking round ; ' here it is, father.'

' It is only half-past eleven—we must wait for midnight,' resumed Dago-bert. ' Let us be seated for an instant, to rest ourselves, and decide upon our plan.'

After a moment's silence, the soldier took his son's hands between his own, and thus continued : ' Agricola, my child—it is yet time. Let me go alone, I entreat you. I shall know very well how to get through the business ; but the nearer the moment comes, the more I fear to drag you into this dangerous enterprise.'

' And the nearer the moment comes, father, the more I feel I may be of some use ; but, be it good or bad, I will share the fortune of your adventure. Our object is praiseworthy ; it is a debt of honour that you have to pay, and I will take one half of it. Do not fancy that I will now draw back. And so, dear father, let us think of our plan of action.'

' Then you *will* come ?' said Dagobert, stifling a sigh.

' We must do everything,' proceeded Agricola, ' to secure success. You have already noticed the little garden-door, near the angle of the wall—that is excellent.'

' We shall get by that way into the garden, and look immediately for the open pailing.'

' Yes ; for on one side of this paling is the wing inhabited by Mdlle. de Cardoville, and on the other that part of the convent in which the general's daughters are confined.'

At this moment, Spoilsport, who was crouching at Dagobert's feet, rose suddenly, and pricked up his ears, as if to listen.

' One would think that Spoilsport heard something,' said Agricola. They listened—but heard only the wind, sounding through the tall trees of the boulevard.

' Now I think of it, father—when the garden-door is once open, shall we take Spoilsport with us ?'

' Yes ; for if there is a watch-dog, he will settle him. And then he will give us notice of the approach of those who go the rounds. Besides, he is so intelligent, so attached to Rose and Blanche, that (who knows ?) he may help to discover the place where they are. Twenty times I have seen him find them in the woods, by the most extraordinary instinct.'

A slow and solemn knell here rose above the noise of the wind : it was the first stroke of twelve.

That note seemed to echo mournfully through the souls of Agricola and his father. Mute with emotion, they shuddered, and by a spontaneous movement, each grasped the hand of the other. In spite of themselves, their hearts kept time to every stroke of the clock, as each successive vibration was prolonged through the gloomy silence of the night.

At the last stroke, Dagobert said to his son, in a firm voice : 'It is midnight. Shake hands, and let us forward !'

The moment was decisive and solemn. ' Now, father,' said Agricola, 'we will act with as much craft and daring as thieves going to pillage a strong box.'

So saying, the smith took from the sack the cord and hook ; Dagobert armed himself with the iron bar, and both advanced cautiously, following the wall in the direction of the little door, situated not far from the angle formed by the street and the boulevard. They stopped from time to time, to listen attentively, trying to distinguish those noises which were not caused either by the high wind or the rain.

It continued light enough for them to be able to see surrounding objects, and the smith and the soldier soon gained the little door, which appeared much decayed, and not very strong.

' Good !' said Agricola to his father. ' It will yield at one blow.'

The smith was about to apply his shoulder vigorously to the door, when Spoilsport growled hoarsely, and made a 'point.' Dagobert silenced the dog with a word, and grasping his son's arm, said to him in a whisper : 'Do not stir. The dog has scented some one in the garden.'

Agricola and his father remained for some minutes motionless, holding their breath and listening. The dog, in obedience to his master, no longer growled, but his uneasiness and agitation were displayed more and more. Yet they heard nothing.

' The dog must have been deceived, father,' whispered Agricola.

' I am sure of the contrary. Do not move.'

After some seconds of expectation, Spoilsport crouched down abruptly, and pushed his nose as far as possible under the door, snuffing up the air.

' They are coming,' said Dagobert hastily, to his son.

' Let us draw off a little distance,' replied Agricola.

' No,' said his father ; ' we must listen. It will be time to retire, if they open the door. Here, Spoilsport ! down !'

The dog obeyed, and withdrawing from the door, crouched down at the feet of his master. Some seconds after, they heard a sort of splashing on the damp ground, caused by heavy footsteps in puddles of water, and then the sound of words, which, carried away by the wind, did not reach distinctly the ears of the soldier and the smith.

' They are the people of whom Mother Bunch told us, going their round,' said Agricola to his father.

' So much the better. There will be an interval before they come round again, and we shall have some two hours 'before us, without interruption. Our affair is all right now.'

By degrees, the sound of the footsteps became less and less distinct, and at last died away altogether.

' Now, quick ! we must not lose any time,' said Dagobert to his son, after waiting about ten minutes ; ' they are far enough. Let us try to open the door.'

Agricola leaned his powerful shoulder against it, and pushed vigorously ; but the door did not give way, notwithstanding its age.

' Confound it !' said Agricola ; ' there is a bar on the inside. I am sure of it, or these old planks would not have resisted my weight.'

'What is to be done?'

'I will scale the wall by means of the cord and hook, and open the door from the other side.'

So saying, Agricola took the cord, and after several attempts, succeeded in fixing the hook on the coping of the wall.

'Now, father, give me a leg up; I will help myself up with the cord; once astride on the wall, I can easily turn the hook, and get down into the garden.'

The soldier leaned against the wall, and joined his two hands, in the hollow of which his son placed one of his feet, then mounting upon the robust shoulders of his father, he was able, by help of the cord, and some irregularities in the wall, to reach the top. Unfortunately, the smith had not perceived that the coping of the wall was strewed with broken bottles, so that he wounded his knees and hands; but, for fear of alarming Dagobert, he repressed every exclamation of pain, and replacing the hook, he glided down the cord to the ground. The door was close by, and he hastened to it; a strong wooden bar had indeed secured it on the inside. This was removed, and the lock was in so bad a state, that it offered no resistance to a violent effort from Agricola. The door was opened, and Dagobert entered the garden with Spoilsport.

'Now,' said the soldier to his son, 'thanks to you, the worst is over. Here is a means of escape for the poor children, and Mdlle. de Cardoville. The thing is now to find them, without accident or delay. Spoilsport will go before as a scout. Come, my good dog!' added Dagobert, 'above all—fair and softly!'

Immediately, the intelligent animal advanced a few steps, sniffing and listening with the care and caution of a hound searching for the game.

By the half-light of the clouded moon, Dagobert and his son perceived round them a V-shaped grove of tall trees, at which several paths met. Uncertain which to chose, Agricola said to his father : 'Let us take the path that runs alongside the wall. It will surely lead to some building.'

'Right! Let us walk on the strips of grass, instead of through the mud. It will make less noise.'

The father and son, preceded by the Siberian dog, kept for some time in a winding path, at no great distance from the wall. They stopped now and then to listen, or to satisfy themselves, before continuing their advance, with regard to the changing aspects of the trees and bushes, which, shaken by the wind, and faintly illumined by the pale light of the moon, often took strange and doubtful forms.

Half-past twelve struck as Agricola and his father reached a large iron gate which shut in that part of the garden reserved for the superior—the same into which Mother Bunch had intruded herself, after seeing Rose Simon converse with Adrienne de Cardoville.

Through the bars of this gate, Agricola and his father perceived at a little distance an open paling, which joined a half-finished chapel, and beyond it a little square building.

'That is no doubt the building occupied by Mdlle. de Cardoville,' said Agricola.

'And the building which contains the chambers of Rose and Blanche, but which we cannot see from here, is no doubt opposite it,' said Dagobert. 'Poor children! they are there, weeping tears of despair,' added he, with profound emotion.

'Provided the gate be but open,' said Agricola.

'It will probably be so—being within the walls.'

'Let us go on gently.'

The gate was only fastened by the catch of the lock. Dagobert was about to open it, when Agricola said to him : ' Take care ! do not make it creak on its hinges.'

' Shall I push it slowly or suddenly ?'

' Let me manage it,' said Agricola ; and he opened the gate so quickly, that it creaked very little ; still the noise might have been plainly heard, in the silence of the night, during one of the lulls between the squalls of wind.

Agricola and his father remained motionless for a moment, listening uneasily, before they ventured to pass through the gate. Nothing stirred, however ; all remained calm and still. With fresh courage, they entered the reserved garden.

Hardly had the dog arrived on this spot, when he exhibited tokens of extraordinary delight. Pricking up his ears, wagging his tail, bounding rather than running, he had soon reached the paling where, in the morning, Rose Simon had for a moment conversed with Mdlle. de Cardoville. He stopped an instant at this place, as if at fault, and turned round and round like a dog seeking the scent.

Dagobert and his son, leaving Spoilsport to his instinct, followed his least movements with intense interest, hoping everything from his intelligence and his attachment to the orphans.

' It was no doubt near this paling that Rose stood when Mother Bunch saw her,' said Dagobert. 'Spoilsport is on her track. Let him alone.'

After a few seconds, the dog turned his head towards Dagobert, and started at full trot in the direction of a door on the ground-floor of a building, opposite to that occupied by Adrienne. Arrived at this door, the dog lay down, seemingly waiting for Dagobert.

' No doubt of it ! the children are there !' said Dagobert, hastening to rejoin Spoilsport ; ' it was by this door that they took Rose into the house.'

'We must see if the windows are grated,' said Agricola, following his father.

' Well, old fellow !' whispered the soldier, as he came up to the dog and pointed to the building ; ' are Rose and Blanche there ?'

The dog lifted his head, and answered by a joyful bark. Dagobert had just time to seize the mouth of the animal with his hands.

' He will ruin all !' exclaimed the smith. 'They have, perhaps, heard him.'

' No,' said Dagobert. ' But there is no longer any doubt—the children are here.'

At this instant, the iron gate, by which the soldier and his son had entered the reserved garden, and which they had left open, fell to with a loud noise.

'They've shut us in,' said Agricola, hastily ; ' and there is no other issue.'

For a moment, the father and son looked in dismay at each other ; but Agricola instantly resumed : ' The gate has perhaps shut of itself. I will make haste to assure myself of this, and to open it again if possible.'

' Go quickly ; I will examine the windows.'

Agricola flew towards the gate, whilst Dagobert, gliding along the wall, soon reached the windows on the ground floor. They were four in number, and two of them were not grated. He looked up at the first story ; it was not very far from the ground, and none of the windows had bars. It would then be easy for that one of the two sisters, who inhabited this story, once informed of their presence, to let herself down by means of a sheet, as the orphans had already done to escape from the inn of the White Falcon. But the difficult thing was to know which room she occupied. Dagobert thought they might learn this from the sister on the ground floor ; but then there was another difficulty—at which of the four windows should they knock?

Agricola returned precipitately. ' It was the wind, no doubt, which shut the gate,' said he. ' I have opened it again, and made it fast with a stone. But we have no time to lose.'

'And how shall we know the windows of the poor children?' said Dagobert, anxiously.

'That is true,' said Agricola, with uneasiness. 'What is to be done?'

'To call them at hap-hazard,' continued Dagobert, 'would be to give the alarm.'

'Oh, heavens!' cried Agricola, with increasing anguish. 'To have arrived here, under their windows, and yet not to know!'

'Time presses,' said Dagobert, hastily, interrupting his son; 'we must run all risks.'

'But how, father?'

'I will call out loud, "Rose and Blanche"—in their state of despair, I am sure they do not sleep. They will be stirring at my first summons. By means of a sheet, fastened to the window, she who is on the first story will in five minutes be in our arms. As for the one on the ground floor—if her window is not grated, we can have her in a second. If it is, we shall soon loosen one of the bars.'

'But, father—this calling out aloud?'

'Will not perhaps be heard.'

'But if it is heard—all will be lost.'

'Who knows? Before they have time to call the watcn, and open several doors, the children may be delivered. Once at the entrance of the boulevard, and we shall be safe.'

'It is a dangerous course; but I see no other.'

'If there are only two men, I and Spoilsport will keep them in check, while you will have time to carry off the children.'

'Father, there is a better way—a surer one,' cried Agricola, suddenly. 'From what Mother Bunch told us, Mdlle. de Cardoville has corresponded by signs with Rose and Blanche.'

'Yes.'

'Hence she knows where they are lodged, as the poor children answered her from their windows.'

'You are right. There is only that course to take. But how find her room?'

'Mother Bunch told me there was a shade over the window.'

'Quick! we have only to break through a wooden fence. Have you the iron bar?'

'Here it is.'

'Then, quick!'

In a few steps, Dagobert and his son had reached the paling. Three planks, torn away by Agricola, opened an easy passage.

'Remain here, father, and keep watch,' said he to Dagobert, as he entered Dr. Baleinier's garden.

The indicated window was easily recognised. It was high and broad; a sort of shade surmounted it, for this window had once been a door, since walled in to the third of its height. It was protected by bars of iron, pretty far apart. Since some minutes, the rain had ceased. The moon, breaking through the clouds, shone full upon the building. Agricola, approaching the window, saw that the room was perfectly dark; but light came from a room beyond, through a door left half open. The smith, hoping that Mdlle. de Cardoville might be still awake, tapped lightly at the window. Soon after, the door in the background opened entirely, and Mdlle. de Cardoville, who had not yet gone to bed, came from the other chamber, dressed as she had been at her interview with Mother Bunch. Her charming features were visible by the light of the taper she held in her hand. Their present expression was that of surprise and anxiety. The young girl set down the candlestick on the table, and appeared to listen attentively as she approached the window. Suddenly she started, and stopped abruptly. She had just discerned the face of a man, looking at her through the window. Agricola, fearing that Mdlle. de Cardoville would retire in terror to the next room, again tapped on the glass, and running the risk of being heard by others, said in a pretty loud voice : ' It is Agricola Baudoin.'

These words reached the ears of Adrienne. Instantly remembering her interview with Mother Bunch, she thought that Agricola and Dagobert must have entered the convent for the purpose of carrying off Rose and Blanche. She ran to the window, recognised Agricola in the clear moonlight, and cautiously opened the casement.

' Madame,' said the smith, hastily ; ' there is not an instant to lose. The Count de Montbron is not in Paris. My father and myself have come to deliver you.'

' Thanks, thanks, M. Agricola !' said Mdlle. de Cardoville, in a tone expressive of the most touching gratitude ; ' but think first of the daughters of General Simon.'

' We do think of them, madame, I have come to ask you which are their windows.'

' One is on the ground floor, the last on the garden-side ; the other is exactly over it, on the first story.'

' Then they are saved !' cried the smith.

' But let me see !' resumed Adrienne, hastily ; ' the first story is pretty high. You will find, near the chapel they are building, some long poles belonging to the scaffolding. They may be of use to you.'

' They will be as good as a ladder, to reach the upstairs window. But now to think of you, madame.'

' Think only of the dear orphans. Time presses. Provided they are delivered to-night, it makes little difference to me to remain a day or two longer in this house.'

' No, mademoiselle,' cried the smith, ' it is of the first importance that you should leave this place to-night. Interests are concerned, of which you know nothing. I am now sure of it.'

' What do you mean ?'

' I have not time to explain myself further ; but I conjure you, madame, to come. I can wrench out two of these bars : I will fetch a piece of iron——'

' It is not necessary. They are satisfied with locking the outer door of this building, which I inhabit alone. You can easily break open the lock.'

' And, in ten minutes, we shall be on the boulevard,' said the smith. ' Make yourself ready, madame ; take a shawl, a bonnet, for the night is cold. I will return instantly.'

' M. Agricola,' said Adrienne, with tears in her eyes, ' I know what you risk for my sake. I shall prove to you, I hope, that I have as good a memory as you have. You and your adopted sister are noble and valiant creatures, and I am proud to be indebted to you. But do not return for me till the daughters of Marshal Simon are in safety.'

' Thanks to your directions, the thing will be done directly, madame. I fly to rejoin my father, and we will come together to fetch you.'

Following the excellent advice of Mdlle. de Cardoville, Agricola took one of the long, strong poles that rested against the wall of the chapel, and, bearing it on his robust shoulders, hastened to rejoin his father. Hardly had Agricola passed the fence, to direct his steps towards the chapel, obscured in shadow, than Mdlle. de Cardoville thought she perceived a human form issue from one of the clumps of trees in the convent-garden, cross the path hastily, and disappear behind a high hedge of box. Alarmed at the sight, Adrienne in vain called to Agricola in a low voice, to bid him beware. He could not hear her ; he had already rejoined his father, who, devoured by impatience, went from window to window with ever-increasing anguish.

'We are saved,' whispered Agricola. 'Those are the windows of the poor children—one on the ground floor, the other on the first story.'

'At last !' said Dagobert, with a burst of joy impossible to describe. He ran to examine the windows. 'They are not grated !' he exclaimed.

'Let us make sure, that one of them is there,' said Agricola ; 'then, by placing this pole against the wall, I will climb up to the first story, which is not so very high.'

'Right, my boy !—once there, tap at the window, and call Rose or Blanche. When she answers, come down. We will rest the pole against the window, and the poor child will slide along it. They are bold and active. Quick, quick ! to work !'

'And then we will deliver Mdlle. de Cardoville.'

Whilst Agricola placed his pole against the wall, and prepared to mount, Dagobert tapped at the panes of the last window on the ground floor, and said aloud : 'It is I—Dagobert.'

Rose Simon indeed occupied the chamber. The unhappy child, in despair at being separated from her sister, was a prey to a burning fever, and, unable to sleep, watered her pillow with her tears. At the sound of the tapping on the glass, she started up affrighted ; then, hearing the voice of the soldier— that voice so familiar and so dear—she sat up in bed, pressed her hands across her forehead, to assure herself that she was not the plaything of a dream, and, wrapped in her long night-dress, ran to the window with a cry of joy. But suddenly—and before she could open the casement—two reports of fire-arms were heard, accompanied by loud cries of 'Help ! thieves !'

The orphan stood petrified with terror, her eyes mechanically fixed upon the window, through which she saw confusedly, by the light of the moon, several men engaged in a mortal struggle, whilst the furious barking of Spoilsport was heard above all the incessant cries of 'Help ! help! Thieves! Murder !'

CHAPTER XIV.

THE EVE OF A GREAT DAY.

ABOUT two hours before the event last related took place at St. Mary's Convent, Rodin and Abbé d'Aigrigny met in the room where we have already seen them, in the Rue du Milieu-des-Ursins. Since the Revolution of July, Father d'Aigrigny had thought proper to remove for the moment to this temporary habitation all the secret archives and correspondence of his Order—a prudent measure, since he had every reason to fear that the reverend fathers would be expelled by the state from that magnificent establishment, with which the restoration had so liberally endowed their society.*

---

* This was an idle fear, for we read in the *Constitutionnel*, Feb. 1st, 1832, as follows: 'When, in 1822, M. de Corbiere abruptly abolished that splendid Normal School, which, during its few years existence, had called forth or developed such a variety of talent, it was decided, as some compensation, that a house in the Rue des Postes should be purchased, where the congregation of the Holy Ghost should be located and endowed. The Minister of Marine supplied the funds for this purpose, and its management was placed at the disposal of the Society, which then reigned over France. From that period it has held quiet possession of the place, which at once became a sort of house of entertainment, where Jesuitism sheltered, and provided for, the numerous noviciates that flocked from all parts of the country, to receive instruc-

Rodin, dressed in his usual sordid style, mean and dirty as ever, was writing modestly at his desk, faithful to his humble part of secretary, which

---

tions from Father Ronsin. Matters were in this state when the Revolution of July broke out, which threatened to deprive the Society of this establishment. But it will hardly be believed; this was not done. It is true that they suppressed their practice, but they left them in possession of the house in the Rue des Postes; and to this very day, the 31st of January, 1832, the members of the Sacred Heart are housed at the expense of government, during the whole of which time the Normal School has been without a shelter—and, on its reorganisation, thrust into a dirty hole, in a narrow corner of the College of Louis the Great.'

The above appeared in the *Constitutionnel*, respecting the house in the Rue des Postes. We are certainly ignorant as to the nature of the transactions, since that period, that have taken place between the reverend fathers and the government; but we read further, in a recently published article that appeared in a journal, in reference to the Society of Jesus, that the house in the Rue des Postes still forms a part of their landed property. We will here give some portions of the article in question.

'The following is a list of the property belonging to this branch of Jesuits:

	Fr.
House in the Rue des Postes, worth about	500,000
One in the Rue de Sèvres, estimated at	300,000
Farm, two leagues from Paris	150,000
House and church at Bourges	100,000
Nôtre Dame de Liesse, donation in 1843	60,000
Saint Acheul, House for Noviciates	400,000
Nantes, a house	100,000
Quimper, ditto	40,000
Laval, house and church	150,000
Rennes, a house	20,000
Vannes, ditto	20,000
Metz, ditto	40,000
Strasbourg	60,000
Rouen, ditto	15,000

By this it appears that these various items amount to little less than two millions. Teaching, moreover, is another important source of revenue to the Jesuits. The college at Broyclette alone brings in 200,000 francs. The two provinces in France (for the General of the Jesuits at Rome has divided France into two provinces, Lyons and Paris) possess, besides a large sum in ready money, Austrian bonds of more than 200,000 francs. Their Propagation of Faith furnishes annually some 50,000 francs; and the harvest which the priests collect by their sermons amounts to 150,000 francs. The alms given for charity may be estimated at the same figure, producing together a revenue of 540,000 francs. Now, to this revenue may be added the produce of the sale of the Society's works, and the profit obtained by hawking pictures. Each plate costs, design and engraving included, about 600 francs, off which are struck about 10,000 copies, at 40 francs per thousand, and there is a further expense of 250 francs to their publisher; and they obtain a net profit of 210 francs on every thousand. This indeed is working to advantage. And it can easily be imagined with what rapidity all these are sold. The fathers themselves are the travellers for the Society, and it would be difficult to find more zealous or persevering ones. They are always well received, and do not know what it is to meet with a refusal. They always take care that the publisher should be one of their own body. The first person whom they selected for this occupation was one of their members, possessing some money; but they were obliged, notwithstanding, to make certain advances to enable him to defray the expenses of its first establishment. But when they became fully convinced of the success of their undertaking, they suddenly called in these advances, which the publisher was not in a condition to pay. They were perfectly aware of this, and superseded him by a wealthy successor, with whom they could make a better bargain; and thus, without remorse, they ruined the man, by thrusting him from an appointment of which they had morally guaranteed the continuance.'

concealed, as we have already seen, a far more important office—that of Socius—a function which, according to the constitutions of the Order, consists in never quitting his superior, watching his least actions, spying into his very thoughts, and reporting all to Rome.

In spite of his usual impassibility, Rodin appeared visibly uneasy and absent in mind; he answered even more briefly than usual to the commands and questions of Father d'Aigrigny, who had but just entered the room.

'Has anything new occurred during my absence?' asked he. 'Are the reports still favourable?'

'Very favourable.'

'Read them to me.'

'Before giving this account to your reverence,' said Rodin, ' I must inform you that Morok has been two days in Paris.'

'Morok?' said Abbé d'Aigrigny, with surprise. ' I thought, on leaving Germany and Switzerland, he had received from Friburg the order to proceed southward. At Nismes, or Avignon, he would at this moment be useful as an agent; for the Protestants begin to move, and we fear a re-action against the Catholics.'

' I do not know,' said Rodin, ' if Morok may not have had private reasons for changing his route. His ostensible reasons are, that he comes here to give performances.'

'How so?'

'A dramatic agent, passing through Lyons, engaged him and his menagerie for the Port-Saint-Martin Theatre at a very high price. He says that he did not like to refuse such an offer.'

'Well,' said Father d'Aigrigny, shrugging his shoulders, 'but, by distributing his little books, and selling prints and chaplets, as well as by the influence he would certainly exercise over the pious and ignorant people of the South or of Brittany, he might render services, such as he can never perform in Paris.'

' He is now below, with a kind of giant, who travels about with him. In his capacity of your reverence's old servant, Morok hoped to have the honour of kissing your hand this evening.'

'Impossible—impossible—you know how much I am occupied. Have you sent to the Rue Saint-François?'

'Yes, I have. The old Jew guardian has had notice from the notary. To-morrow, at six in the morning, the masons will unwall the door, and, for the first time since one hundred and fifty years, the house will be opened.'

Father d'Aigrigny remained in thought for a moment, and then said to Rodin : 'On the eve of such a decisive day, we must neglect nothing, and call every circumstance to memory. Read me the copy of the note, inserted in the archives of the society, a century and a half ago, on the subject of Rennepont.'

The secretary took the note from the case, and read as follows

' "This 19th day of February, 1682, the Reverend Father-Provincial Alexander Bourdon sent the following advice, with these words in the margin : Of extreme importance for the future.

' " We have just discovered, by the confession of a dying person to one of our fathers, a very close secret.

' " Marius de Rennepont, one of the most active and redoubtable partisans of the Reformed Religion, and one of the most determined enemies of our Holy Society, had apparently re-entered the pale of our Mother-Church, but with the sole design of saving his worldly goods, threatened with confiscation because of his irreligious and damnable errors. Evidence having been furnished by different persons of our company to prove that the conversion of Rennepont was not sincere, and in reality covered a sacrilegious lure, the possessions of the said gentleman, now considered a relapsed heretic, were confiscated by our gracious sovereign, his Majesty King Louis XIV, and the said Rennepont was condemned to the galleys for life.[*] He escaped his doom by a voluntary death; in consequence of which abominable crime, his body was dragged upon a hurdle, and flung to the dogs on the highway.

' " From these preliminaries, we come to the great secret, which is of such importance to the future interests of our Society.

'" His Majesty Louis XIV., in his paternal and Catholic goodness towards the Church in general, and our Order in particular, had granted to us the profit of this confiscation, in acknowledgment of our services in discovering the infamous and sacrilegious relapse of the said Rennepont

' " But we have just learned, for certain, that a house situated in Paris, No. 3, Rue Saint-François, and a sum of fifty thousand gold crowns, have escaped this confiscation, and have consequently been stolen from our Society.

" ' The house was conveyed, before the confiscation, by means of a feigned purchase, to a friend of Rennepont's—a good Catholic, unfortunately, as against him we cannot take any severe measures. Thanks to the culpable, but secure connivance of his friend, the house has been walled-up, and is only to be opened in a century and a half, according to the last will of Rennepont. As for the fifty thousand gold crowns, they have been placed in hands which, unfortunately, are hitherto unknown to us, in order to be invested and put out to use for one hundred and fifty years, at the expiration of which time they are to be divided between the then existing descendants of the said Rennepont ; and it is calculated that this sum, increased by so many accumulations, will by then have become enormous, and will amount to at least forty or fifty millions of livres *tournois*. From motives which are not known, but which are duly stated in a testamentary document, the said Rennepont has concealed from his family, whom the edicts against the Protestants have driven out of France, the investment of these fifty thousand crowns ; and has only desired his relations to preserve in their line, from generation to generation, the charge to the last survivors, to meet in Paris, Rue Saint-François, a hundred and fifty years hence, on February the 13th, 1832. And that this charge might not be forgotten, he employed a person, whose description is known, but not his real occupation, to cause to be manufactured sundry bronze medals, on which the request and date are engraved, and to deliver one to each member of the family—a measure the more necessary, as, from some other motive equally unknown, but probably explained in the testament, the heirs are to present themselves on the day in question, before noon, in person, and not by any attorney or representative, or to forfeit all claim to the inheritance. The stranger who undertook to distribute the medals to the different members of the family of Rennepont is a man of thirty to thirty-six years of age, of tall stature, and with a proud and sad expression of countenance. He has black eyebrows, very thick, and singularly joined together. He is known as JOSEPH, and is much suspected of being an active and dangerous emissary of the wretched republicans and heretics of the Seven United Provinces. It results from these premises, that this sum, surreptitiously confided by a relapsed heretic to unknown hands,

---

* Louis XIV., the great king, punished with the galleys those Protestants who, once converted, often by force, afterwards returned to their first belief. As for those Protestants who remained in France, notwithstanding the rigour of the edicts against them, they were deprived of burial, dragged upon a hurdle, and given to the dogs.—E, S,

has escaped the confiscation decreed in our favour by our well-beloved king. A serious fraud and injury has therefore been committed, and we are bound to take every means to recover this our right, if not immediately, at least in some future time. Our Society being (for the greater glory of God and our Holy Father) imperishable, it will be easy, thanks to the connexion we keep up with all parts of the world, by means of missions and other establishments, to follow the line of this family of Rennepont from generation to generation, without ever losing sight of it—so that, a hundred and fifty years hence, at the moment of the division of this immense accumulation of property, our Company may claim the inheritance of which it has been so treacherously deprived, and recover it by any means in its power, *fas aut nefas*, even by craft or violence—our Company not being bound to act tenderly with the future detainers of our goods, of which we have been maliciously deprived by an infamous and sacrilegious heretic—and because it is right to defend, preserve, and recover one's own property by every means which the Lord may place within one's reach. Until, therefore, the complete restitution of this wealth, the family of Rennepont must be considered as reprobate and damnable, as the cursed seed of a Cain, and always to be watched with the utmost caution. And it is to be recommended, that, every year from this present date, a sort of inquisition should be held as to the situation of the successive members of this family "'

Rodin paused, and said to Father d'Aigrigny : ' Here follows the account, year by year, of the history of this family, from the year 1682, to our own day. It will be useless to read this to your reverence.'

' Quite useless,' said Abbé d'Aigrigny. ' The note contains all the important facts.' Then, after a moment's silence, he exclaimed, with an expression of triumphant pride : ' How great is the power of the Association, when founded upon tradition and perpetuity ! Thanks to this note, inserted in our archives a century and a half ago, this family has been watched from generation to generation—our Order has always had its eyes upon them, following them to all points of the globe, to which exile had distributed them—and at last, to-morrow, we shall obtain possession of this property, at first inconsiderable, but which a hundred and fifty years have raised to a royal fortune. Yes, we shall succeed, for we have foreseen every eventuality. One thing only troubles me.'

' What is that ?' asked Rodin.

' The information that we have in vain tried to obtain from the guardian of the house in the Rue Saint-François. Has the attempt been once more made, as I directed ?'

' It has been made.'

' Well ?'

' This time, as always before, the old Jew has remained impenetrable. Besides, he is almost in his second childhood, and his wife not much better.'

' When I think,' resumed Father d'Aigrigny, ' that for a century and a half, this house in the Rue Saint-François has remained walled up, and that the care of it has been transmitted from generation to generation in this family of the Samuels—I cannot suppose that they have all been ignorant as to who were and are the successive holders of these funds, now become immense by accumulation.'

' You have seen,' said Rodin, ' by the notes upon this affair, that the Order has always carefully followed it up ever since 1682. At different periods attempts have been made to obtain information upon subjects not fully explained in the note of Father Bourdon. But this race of Jew guardians has ever remained dumb, and we must therefore conclude that they know nothing about it,'

'That has always struck me as impossible; for the ancestor of these Samuels was present at the closing of the house, a hundred and fifty years ago. He was, according to the file, a servant or confidential clerk of De Rennepont. It is impossible that he should not have known many things, the tradition of which must have been preserved in the family.'

'If I were allowed to hazard a brief observation,' began Rodin, humbly.

'Speak.'

'A few years ago we obtained certain information through the confessional, that the funds were in existence, and that they had risen to an enormous amount.'

'Doubtless; and it was that which called the attention of the Reverend Father-General so strongly to this affair.'

'We know, then, what probably the descendants of the family do not— the immense value of this inheritance?'

'Yes,' answered Father d'Aigrigny, 'the person who certified this fact in confession is worthy of all belief. Only lately, the same declaration was renewed; but all the efforts of the confessor could not obtain the name of the trustee, or anything beyond the assertion, that the money could not be in more honest hands.'

'It seems to me, then,' resumed Rodin, 'that we are certain of what is most important.'

'And who knows if the holder of this enormous sum will appear to-morrow, in spite of the honesty ascribed to him? The nearer the moment, the more my anxiety increases. Ah!' continued Father d'Aigrigny, after a moment's silence, 'the interests concerned are so immense that the consequences of success are quite incalculable. However, all that it was possible to do, has been at least tried.'

To these words, which Father d'Aigrigny addressed to Rodin, as if asking for his assent, the *socius* returned no answer.

The abbé looked at him with surprise, and said: 'Are you not of my opinion—could more have been attempted? Have we not gone to the extreme limit of the possible?'

Rodin bowed respectfully, but remained mute.

'If you think we have omitted some precaution,' cried Father d'Aigrigny, with a sort of uneasy impatience, 'speak out! We have still time. Once more, do you think it is possible to do more than I have done? All the other descendants being removed, when Gabriel appears to-morrow in the Rue Saint-François, will he not be the only representative of this family, and consequently the rightful possessor of this immense fortune? Now, according to his act of renunciation, and the provisions of our statutes, it is not to him, but to the Order, that these possessions must fall. Could I have acted better, or in any other manner? Speak frankly!'

'I cannot permit myself to offer an opinion on this subject,' replied Rodin, humbly, and again bowing; 'the success of the measures taken must answer your reverence.'

Father d'Aigrigny shrugged his shoulders, and reproached himself for having asked advice of this writing-machine, that served him for a secretary, and to whom he only ascribed three qualities—memory, discretion, and exactness.

CHAPTER XV.

THE THUG.

AFTER a moment's silence, Father d'Aigrigny resumed: 'Read me to-day's report on the situation of each of the persons designated'

' Here is that of this evening ; it has just come.'

' Let us hear.'

Rodin read as follows : ' Jacques Rennepont, *alias* Sleepinbuff, was seen in the interior of the debtors' prison at eight o'clock this evening.'

' He will not disturb us to-morrow. One ; go on.'

' The lady superior of St. Mary's Convent, warned by the Princess de Saint-Dizier, has thought fit to confine still more strictly the Demoiselles Rose and Blanche Simon. This evening, at nine o'clock, they have been carefully locked in their cells, and armed men will make their round in the convent garden during the night.'

' Thanks to these precautions, there is nothing to fear from that side,' said Father d'Aigrigny. ' Go on.'

' Dr. Baleinier, also warned by the Princess de Saint-Dizier, continues to have Mdlle. de Cardoville very closely watched. At a quarter to nine, the door of the building in which she is lodged was locked and bolted.'

' That is still another cause the less for uneasiness.'

' As for M. Hardy,' resumed Rodin, ' I have received this morning, from Toulouse, a letter from his intimate friend, M. de Bressac, who has been of such service to us in keeping the manufacturer away for some days longer. This letter contains a note, addressed by M. Hardy to a confidential person, which M. de Bressac has thought fit to intercept, and send to us as another proof of the success of the steps he has taken, and for which he hopes we shall give him credit—as to serve us, he adds, he betrays his friend in the most shameful manner, and acts a part in an odious comedy. M. de Bressac trusts that, in return for these good offices, we will deliver up to him those papers, which place him in our absolute dependence, as they might ruin for ever a woman he loves with an adulterous passion. He says that we ought to have pity on the horrible alternative in which he is placed—either to dishonour and ruin the woman he adores, or infamously to betray the confidence of his bosom friend.'

' These adulterous lamentations are not deserving of pity,' answered Father d'Aigrigny, with contempt. ' We will see about that ; M. de Bressac may still be useful to us. But let us hear this letter of M. Hardy, that impious and republican manufacturer, worthy descendant of an accursed race, whom it is of the first importance to keep away.'

' Here is M. Hardy's letter,' resumed Rodin. ' To-morrow, we will send it to the person to whom it is addressed.'

Rodin read as follows :

' " Toulouse, February the 10th.

' " At length I find a moment to write to you, and to explain the cause of the sudden departure which, without alarming, must at least have astonished you. I write also to ask you a service ; the facts may be stated in a few words. I have often spoken to you of Felix de Bressac, one of my boyhood mates, though not nearly so old as myself. We have always loved each other tenderly, and have shown too many proofs of mutual affection not to count upon one another. He is a brother to me. You know all I mean by that expression. Well—a few days ago, he wrote to me from Toulouse, where he was to spend some time : ' If you love me, come ; I have the greatest need of you. At once ! Your consolations may perhaps give me the courage to live. If you arrive too late—why, forgive me—and think sometimes of him who will be yours to the last.' Judge of my grief and fear, on receipt of the above. I sent instantly for post-horses. My old foreman, whom I esteem and revere (the father of General Simon), hearing that I was going to the south, begged me to take him with me, and to leave him for some days in the department of the Creuse, to examine some ironworks recently founded there. I consented willingly to this proposition, as I should thus at least have some one to whom I could pour out the grief and anxiety which had been caused me by this letter from Bressac. I arrive at Toulouse ; they tell me that he left the evening before, taking arms with him, a prey to the most violent despair. It was impossible at first to tell whither he had gone ; after two days, some indications, collected with great trouble, put me upon his track. At last, after a thousand adventures, I found him in a miserable village. Never--no, never, have I seen despair like this. No violence, but a dreadful dejection, a savage silence. At first, he almost repulsed me ; then, this horrible agony having reached its height, he softened by degrees, and, in about a quarter of an hour, threw himself into my arms, bathed in tears. Beside him were his loaded pistols ; one day later, and all would have been over. I cannot tell you the reason of his despair ; I am not at liberty to do so ; but it did not greatly astonish me. Now there is a complete cure to effect. We must calm, and soothe, and heal this poor soul, which has been cruelly wounded. The hand of friendship is alone equal to this delicate task, and I have good hope of success. I have therefore persuaded him to travel for some time ; movement and change of scene will be favourable to him. I shall take him first to Nice ; we set out to-morrow. If he wishes to prolong this excursion, I shall do so too, for my affairs do not imperiously demand my presence in Paris before the end of March. As for the service I have to ask of you, it is conditional. These are the facts. According to some family papers that belonged to my mother, it seems I have a certain interest to present myself at No. 3, Rue Saint-François, in Paris, on the 13th of February. I had inquired about it, and could learn nothing, except that this house, of very antique appearance, has been shut up for the last hundred and fifty years, through a whim of one of my maternal ancestors, and that it is to be opened on the 13th of this month, in presence of the co-heirs, who, if I have any, are quite unknown to me. Not being able to attend myself, I have written to my foreman, the father of General Simon, in whom I have the greatest confidence, and whom I had left behind in the department of the Creuse, to set out for Paris, and to be present at the opening of this house, not as an agent (which would be useless), but as a spectator, and inform me at Nice what has been the result of this romantic notion of my ancestor's. As it is possible that my foreman may arrive too late to accomplish this mission, I should be much obliged if you would inquire at my house at Plessy, if he has yet come, and, in case of his still being absent, if you would take his place at the opening of the house in the Rue Saint-François. I believe that I have made a very small sacrifice for my friend Bressac, in not being in Paris on that day. But had the sacrifice been immense, I should have made it with pleasure, for my care and friendship are at present most necessary to the man whom I look upon as a brother. I count upon your compliance with my request, and, begging you to be kind enough to write to me, 'to be called for,' at Nice, the result of your visit of inquiry, I remain, &c., &c.,   ' " FRANCIS HARDY." '

' Though his presence cannot be of any great importance, it would be pre-ferable that Marshal Simon's father should not attend at the opening of this house to-morrow,' said Father d'Aigrigny. ' But no matter. M. Hardy him-self is out of the way. There only remains the young Indian.'

' As for him,' continued the abbé, with a thoughtful air, ' we acted wisely in letting M. Norval set out with the presents of Mdlle. de Cardoville. The doctor who accompanies M. Norval, and who was chosen by M. Baleinier, will inspire no suspicion ?'

' None,' answered Rodin. ' His letter of yesterday is completely satisfactory.'

'There is nothing, then, to fear from the Indian prince,' said D'Aigrigny. 'All goes well.'

'As for Gabriel,' resumed Rodin, 'he has again written this morning, to obtain from your reverence the interview that he has vainly solicited for the last three days. He is affected by the rigour exercised towards him, in forbidding him to leave the house for these five days past.'

'To-morrow, when we take him to the Rue Saint-François, I will hear what he has to say. It will be time enough. Thus, at this hour,' said Father d'Aigrigny, with an air of triumphant satisfaction, 'all the descendants of this family, whose presence might ruin our projects, are so placed that it is absolutely impossible for them to be at the Rue Saint-François to-morrow before noon, while Gabriel will be sure to be there. At last our end is gained.'

Two cautious knocks at the door interrupted Father d'Aigrigny. 'Come in,' said he.

An old servant in black presented himself, and said: 'There is a man down stairs who wishes to speak instantly to M. Rodin on very urgent business.'

'His name?' asked Father d'Aigrigny.

'He would not tell his name; but he says that he comes from M. Van Daël, a merchant in Java.'

Father d'Aigrigny and Rodin exchanged a glance of surprise, almost of alarm.

'See what this man is,' said D'Aigrigny to Rodin, unable to conceal his uneasiness, 'and then come and give me an account of it.' Then, addressing the servant, he added: 'Show him in'—and exchanging another expressive sign with Rodin, Father d'Aigrigny disappeared by a side-door.

A minute after, Faringhea, the ex-chief of the Stranglers, appeared before Rodin, who instantly remembered having seen him at Cardoville Castle.

The *socius* started, but he did not wish to appear to recollect his visitor. Still bending over his desk, he seemed not to see Faringhea, but wrote hastily some words on a sheet of paper that lay before him.

'Sir,' said the servant, astonished at the silence of Rodin, 'here is the person.'

Rodin folded the note that he had so precipitately written, and said to the servant: 'Let this be taken to its address. Wait for an answer.'

The servant bowed, and went out. Then Rodin, without rising, fixed his little reptile-eyes on Faringhea, and said to him courteously: 'To whom, sir, have I the honour of speaking?'

CHAPTER XVI.

THE TWO BROTHERS OF THE GOOD WORK.

FARINGHEA, as we have before stated, though born in India, had travelled a good deal, and frequented the European factories in different parts of Asia. Speaking well both English and French, and full of intelligence and sagacity, he was perfectly civilised.

Instead of answering Rodin's question, he turned upon him a fixed and searching look. The *socius*, provoked by this silence, and foreseeing vaguely that Faringhea's arrival had some connexion—direct or indirect—with Djalma, repeated, though still with the greatest coolness: 'To whom, sir, have I the honour of speaking?'

'Do you not recognise me,' said Faringhea, advancing two steps nearer to Rodin's chair.

'I do not think I have ever had the honour of seeing you,' answered the other, coldly.

'But I recognise you,' said Faringhea; 'I saw you at Cardoville Castle the day that a ship and a steamer were wrecked together.'

'At Cardoville Castle? It is very possible, sir. I was there when a ship-wreck took place.'

'And that day I called you by your name, and you asked me what I wanted. I replied: "Nothing *now*, brother—hereafter, much." The time has arrived. I have come to ask for much.'

'My dear sir,' said Rodin, still impassible, 'before we continue this conversation, which appears hitherto tolerably obscure, I must repeat my wish to be informed to whom I have the advantage of speaking. You have introduced yourself here under pretext of a commission from Mynheer Joshua Van Dael, a respectable merchant of Batavia, and——'

'You know the writing of M. Van Dael?' said Faringhea, interrupting Rodin.

'I know it perfectly.'

'Look!' The half-caste drew from his pocket (he was shabbily dressed in European clothes) a long despatch, which he had taken from one Mahal the Smuggler, after strangling him on the beach near Batavia. These papers he placed before Rodin's eyes, but without quitting his hold of them.

'It is, indeed, M. Van Dael's writing,' said Rodin, and he stretched out his hand towards the letter, which Faringhea quickly and prudently returned to his pocket.

'Allow me to observe, my dear sir, that you have a singular manner of executing a commission,' said Rodin. 'This letter, being to my address, and having been entrusted to you by M. Van Dael, you ought——'

'This letter was not entrusted to me by M. Van Dael,' said Faringhea, interrupting Rodin.

'How, then, is it in your possession?'

'A Javanese smuggler betrayed me. Van Dael had secured a passage to Alexandria for this man, and had given him this letter to carry with him for the European mail. I strangled the smuggler, took the letter, made the passage—and here I am.'

The Thug had pronounced these words with an air of savage boasting; his wild, intrepid glance did not quail before the piercing look of Rodin, who, at this strange confession, had hastily raised his head to observe the speaker.

Faringhea thought to astonish or intimidate Rodin by these ferocious words; but, to his great surprise, the *socius*, impassible as a corpse, said to him, quite simply: 'Oh! they strangle people in Java?'

'Yes, there *and* elsewhere,' answered Faringhea, with a bitter smile.

'I would prefer to disbelieve you; but I am surprised at your sincerity ——, what is your name?'

'Faringhea.'

'Well, then, M. Faringhea, what do you wish to come to? You have obtained, by an abominable crime, a letter addressed to me, and now you hesitate to deliver it——'

'Because I have read it, and it may be useful to me.'

'Oh! you have read it?' said Rodin, disconcerted for a moment. Then he resumed: 'It is true, that judging by your mode of possessing yourself of other people's correspondence, we cannot expect any great amount of honesty on your part. And pray what have you found so useful to you in this letter?'

'I have found, brother, that you are, like myself, a son of the Good Work.'

'Of what good work do you speak?' asked Rodin, not a little surprised.

Faringhea replied with an expression of bitter irony. 'Joshua says to you in his letter—"Obedience and courage, secrecy and patience, craft and' audacity, union between us, who have the world for our country, the brethren for our family, Rome for our queen." '

' It is possible that M. Van Dael has written thus to me. Pray, sir, what do you conclude from it ?'

' We, too, have the world for our country, brother, our accomplices for our family, and for our queen Bowanee.'

' I do not know that saint,' said Rodin, humbly.

' It is *our* Rome,' answered the Strangler. ' Van Dael speaks to you of those of your Order, who, scattered over all the earth, labour for the glory of Rome, your queen. Those of our band labour also in divers countries, for the glory of Bowanee.'

' And who are these sons of Bowanee, M. Faringhea ?'

' Men of resolution, audacious, patient, crafty, obstinate, who, to make the Good Work succeed, would sacrifice country and parents, and sister and brother, and who regard as enemies all not of their band !'

' There seems to be much that is good in the persevering and exclusively religious spirit of such an order,' said Rodin, with a modest and sanctified air ; ' only, one must know your ends and objects.'

' The same as your own, brother—we make corpses.'[*]

' Corpses !' cried Rodin.

' In his letter,' resumed Faringhea, ' Van Dael tells you that the greatest glory of your order is to make "a corpse of man." Our work also is to make corpses of men. Man's death is sweet to Bowanee.'

' But, sir,' cried Rodin, 'M. Van Dael speaks of the soul, of the will, of the mind, which are to be brought down by discipline.'

' It is true—you kill the soul, and we the body. Give me your hand, brother, for you also are hunters of men.'

' But once more, sir—understand, that we only meddle with the will, the mind,' said Rodin.

'And what are bodies deprived of soul, will, thought, but mere corpses? Come—come, brother ; the dead we make by the cord are not more icy and inanimate than those you make by your discipline. Take my hand, brother ; Rome and Bowanee are sisters.'

Notwithstanding his apparent calmness, Rodin could not behold, without some secret alarm, a wretch like Faringhea in possession of a long letter from Van Dael, wherein mention must necessarily have been made of Djalma. Rodin believed, indeed, that he had rendered it impossible for the young Indian to be at Paris on the morrow, but not knowing what con nexion might have been formed, since the shipwreck, between the prince and the half-caste, he looked upon Faringhea as a man who might probably be very dangerous. But the more uneasy the *socius* felt in himself, the more he affected to appear calm and disdainful. He replied, therefore : ' This comparison between Rome and Bowanee is no doubt very amusing ; but what, sir, do you deduce from it ?'

' I wish to show you, brother, what I am, and of what I am capable, to convince you that it is better to have me for a friend than an enemy.'

' In other terms, sir,' said Rodin, with contemptuous irony, 'you belong to a murderous sect in India, and, you wish, by a transparent allegory, to lead me to reflect on the fate of the man from whom you have stolen the letter addressed to me. In my turn, I will take the freedom just to observe to you, in all humility, M. Faringhea, that here it is not permitted to strangle

---

[*] The doctrine of passive and absolute obedience, the principal tool in the hands of the Jesuits, as summed up in these terrible words of the dying Loyola—*that every member of the order should be in the hands of his superiors as a dead body—perinde ac cadaver.*

anybody, and that if you were to think fit to make any corpses for the love of Bowanee, your goddess, we should make you a head shorter, for the love of another divinity commonly called Justice.'

'And what would they do to me, if I tried to poison any one?'

'I will again humbly observe to you, M. Faringhea, that I have no time to give you a course of criminal jurisprudence ; but, believe me, you had better resist the temptation to strangle or poison anyone.   One word more : will you deliver up to me the letters of M. Van Dael, or not?'

'The letters relative to Prince Djalma?' said the half-caste, looking fixedly at Rodin, who, notwithstanding a sharp and sudden twinge, remained impenetrable, and answered with the utmost simplicity : 'Not knowing what the letters which you, sir, are pleased to keep from me, may contain, it is impossible for me to answer your question.   I beg, and if necessary, I demand, that you will hand me those letters—or that you will retire.'

'In a few minutes, brother, you will entreat me to remain.'

'I doubt it.'

'A few words will operate this miracle.   If just now I spoke to you about poisoning, brother, it was because you sent a doctor to Cardoville Castle, to poison (at least for a time) Prince Djalma.'

In spite of himself, Rodin started almost imperceptibly, as he replied : 'I do not understand you.'

'It is true, that I am a poor foreigner, and doubtless speak with an accent ; I will try and explain myself better.   I know, by Van Dael's letters, the interest you have that Prince Djalma should not be here to-morrow, and all that you have done with this view.   Do you understand me now?'

'I have no answer for you.'

Two cautious taps at the door here interrupted the conversation.   'Come in,' said Rodin.

'The letter has been taken to its address, sir,' said the old servant, bowing, 'and here is the answer.'

Rodin took the paper, and, before he opened it, said courteously to Faringhea : 'With your permission, sir?'

'Make no ceremonies,' said the half-caste.

'You are very kind,' replied Rodin, as, having read the letter he received, he wrote hastily some words at the bottom, saying : 'Send this back to the same address.'

The servant bowed respectfully, and withdrew.

'Now can I continue?' asked the half-caste of Rodin.

'Certainly.'

'I will continue, then,' resumed Faringhea :

The day before yesterday, just as the prince, all wounded as he was, was about, by my advice, to take his departure for Paris, a fine carriage arrived, with superb presents for Djalma, from an unknown friend.   In this carriage were two men—one sent by the unknown friend—the other a doctor, sent by you to attend upon Djalma, and accompany him to Paris.   It was a charitable act, brother—was it not so?'

'Go on with your story, sir.'

'Djalma set out yesterday.   By declaring that the prince's wound would grow seriously worse, if he did not lie down in the carriage during all the journey, the doctor got rid of the envoy of the unknown friend, who went away by himself.   The doctor wished to get rid of me too ; but Djalma so strongly insisted upon it, that I accompanied the prince and doctor.   Yesterday evening, we had come about half the distance.   The doctor proposed we should pass the night at an inn.   "We have plenty of time," said he,

" to reach Paris by to-morrow evening"—the prince having told him, that he must absolutely be in Paris by the evening of the 12th. The doctor had been very pressing to set out alone with the prince. I knew by Van Dael's letter, that it was of great importance to you for Djalma not to be here on the 13th; I had my suspicions, and I asked the doctor if he knew you; he answered with an embarrassed air, and then my suspicion became certainty. When we reached the inn, whilst the doctor was occupied with Djalma, I went up to the room of the former, and examined a box full of phials that he had brought with him. One of them contained opium—and then I guessed——'

'What did you guess, sir?'

'You shall know. The doctor said to Djalma, before he left him: "Your wound is doing well, but the fatigue of the journey might bring on inflammation; it will be good for you, in the course of to-morrow, to take a soothing potion, that I will make ready this evening, to have with us in the carriage." The doctor's plan was a simple one,' added Faringhea; 'to-day, the prince was to take the potion at four or five o'clock in the afternoon—and fall into a deep sleep—the doctor to grow uneasy, and stop the carriage —to declare that it would be dangerous to continue the journey—to pass the night at an inn, and keep close watch over the prince, whose stupor was only to cease when it suited your purposes. That was your design—it was cleverly planned—I chose to make use of it for myself, and I have succeeded.'

'All that you are talking about, my dear sir,' said Rodin, biting his nails, 'is pure Hebrew to me.'

'No doubt, because of my accent. But tell me, have you heard speak of array-mow?'

'No.'

'Your loss! It is an admirable production of the Island of Java, so fertile in poisons.'

'What is that to me?' said Rodin, in a sharp voice, but hardly able to dissemble his growing anxiety.

'It concerns you nearly. We sons of Bowanee have a horror of shedding blood,' resumed Faringhea; 'to pass the cord round the neck of our victims, we wait till they are asleep. When their sleep is not deep enough, we know how to make it deeper. We are skilful at our work; the serpent is not more cunning, or the lion more valiant. Djalma himself bears our mark. The array-mow is an impalpable powder, and, by letting the sleeper inhale a few grains of it, or by mixing it with the tobacco to be smoked by a waking man, we can throw our victim into a stupor, from which nothing will rouse him. If we fear to administer too strong a dose at once, we let the sleeper inhale a little at different times, and we can thus prolong the trance at pleasure, and without any danger, as long as a man does not require meat and drink—say, thirty or forty hours. You see, that opium is mere trash compared to this divine narcotic. I had brought some of this with me from Java—as a mere curiosity, you know—without forgetting the counter poison.'

'Oh! there is a counter-poison, then?' said Rodin, mechanically.

'Just as there are people quite contrary to what we are, brother of the good work. The Javanese call the juice of this root tooboe; it dissipates the stupor caused by the array-mow, as the sun disperses the clouds. Now, yesterday evening, being certain of the projects of your emissary against Djalma, I waited till the doctor was in bed and asleep. I crept into his room, and made him inhale such a dose of array-mow—that he is probably sleeping still.'

'Miscreant!' cried Rodin, more and more alarmed by this narrative, for Faringhea had dealt a terrible blow at the machinations of the socius and his friends. 'You risk poisoning the doctor.'

'Yes, brother ; just as he ran the risk of poisoning Djalma. This morning we set out, leaving your doctor at the inn, plunged in a deep sleep. I was alone in the carriage with Djalma. He smoked, like a true Indian ; some grains of array-mow, mixed with the tobacco in his long pipe, first made him drowsy ; a second dose, that he inhaled, sent him to sleep ; and so I left him at the inn where we stopped. Now, brother, it depends upon me, to leave Djalma in his trance, which will last till to-morrow evening, or to rouse him from it on the instant. Exactly as you comply with my demands or not, Djalma will or will not be in the Rue Saint-François to-morrow.'

So saying, Faringhea drew from his pocket the medal belonging to Djalma, and observed, as he showed it to Rodin : 'You see, that I tell you the truth. During Djalma's sleep, I took from him this medal, the only indication he has of the place where he ought to be to-morrow. I finish, then, as I began : Brother, I have come to ask you for a great deal.'

For some minutes, Rodin had been biting his nails to the quick, as was his custom when seized with a fit of dumb and concentrated rage. Just then, the bell of the porter's lodge rang three times in a particular manner. Rodin did not appear to notice it, and yet a sudden light sparkled in his small reptile-eyes ; while Faringhea, with his arms folded, looked at him with an expression of triumph and disdainful superiority. The socius bent down his head, remained silent for some seconds, took mechanically a pen from his desk, and began to gnaw the feather, as if in deep reflection upon what Faringhea had just said. Then, throwing down the pen upon the desk, he turned suddenly towards the half-caste, and addressed him with an air of profound contempt : 'Now, really, M Faringhea—do you think to make game of us with your cock-and-bull stories ?'

Amazed, in spite of his audacity, the half-caste recoiled a step.

'What, sir !' resumed Rodin. 'You come here, into a respectable house, to boast that you have stolen letters, strangled this man, drugged that other? —Why, sir, it is downright madness. I wished to hear you to the end, to see to what extent you would carry your audacity—for none but a monstrous rascal would venture to plume himself on such infamous crimes. But I prefer believing, that they exist only in your imagination.'

As he barked out these words, with a degree of animation not usual in him, Rodin rose from his seat, and approached the chimney, while Faringhea, who had not yet recovered from his surprise, looked at him in silence. In a few seconds, however, the half-caste returned, with a gloomy and savage mien : 'Take care, brother; do not force me to prove to you that I have told the truth.'

'Come, come, sir ; you must be fresh from the Antipodes, to believe us Frenchmen such easy dupes. You have, you say, the prudence of a serpent, and the courage of a lion. I do not know if you are a courageous lion, but you are certainly not a prudent serpent. What! you have about you a letter from M Van Dael, by which I might be compromised—supposing all this not to be a fable—you have left Prince Djalma in a stupor, which would serve my projects, and from which you alone can rouse him—you are able, you say, to strike a terrible blow at my interests—and yet you do not consider (bold lion ! crafty serpent as you are !) that I only want to gain twenty-four hours upon you. Now, you come from the ends of India to Paris, an unknown stranger—you believe me to be as great a scoundrel as yourself, since you call me brother—and do not once consider, that you are here in my power—that this street and house are solitary, and that I could have three or four persons to bind you in à second, savage Strangler though you are !—and that just by pulling this bell-rope,' said Rodin, as he took it in his hand. ' Do not be alarmed,' added he, with a diabolical smile, as he saw Faringhea make an abrupt movement of surprise and fright ; ' would I give you notice, if I meant to act in this manner ?—But just answer me. Once bound and put in confinement for twenty-four hours, how could you injure me ? Would it not be easy for me to possess myself of Van Dael's letter, and Djalma's medal ? and the latter, plunged in a stupor till to-morrow evening, need not trouble me at all. You see, therefore, that your threats are vain— because they rest upon falsehood—because it is not true, that Prince Djalma is here and in your power. Begone, sir—leave the house ; and, when next you wish to make dupes, show more judgment in the selection.'

Faringhea seemed struck with astonishment. All that he had just heard seemed very probable. Rodin might seize upon him, the letter, and the medal, and, by keeping him prisoner, prevent Djalma from being awakened. And yet Rodin ordered him to leave the house, at the moment when Faringhea had imagined himself so formidable. As he thought for the motives of this inexplicable conduct, it struck him, that Rodin, notwithstanding the proofs he had brought him, did not yet believe that Djalma was in his power. On that theory, the contempt of Van Dael's correspondent admitted of a natural explanation. But Rodin was playing a bold and skilful game ; and, while he appeared to mutter to himself, as in anger, he was observing, with intense anxiety, the Strangler's countenance.

The latter, almost certain that he had divined the secret motive of Rodin, replied : ' I am going—but one word more. You think I deceive you ?'

' I am certain of it. You have told me nothing but a tissue of fables, and I have lost much time in listening to them. Spare me the rest ; it is late—and I should like to be alone.'

' One minute more : you are a man, I see, from whom nothing should be hid,' said Faringhea. ' From Djalma, I could now only expect alms and disdain—for, with a character like this, to say to him . " Pay me, because I might have betrayed you, and did not," would be to provoke his anger and contempt. I could have killed him twenty times over, but his day is not yet come,' said the Thug, with a gloomy air ; ' and to wait for that and other fatal days, I must have gold, much gold. You alone can pay me for the betrayal of Djalma, for you alone profit by it. You refuse to hear me, because you think I am deceiving you. But I took the direction of the inn where we stopped—and here it is. Send some one to ascertain the truth of what I tell you, and then you will believe me. But the price of my services will be high ; for I told you that I wanted much.'

So saying, Faringhea offered a printed card to Rodin ; the socius, who, out of the corner of his eye, followed all the half-caste's movements, appeared to be absorbed in thought, and taking no heed of anything.

' Here is the address,' repeated Faringhea, as he held out the card to Rodin ; ' assure yourself that I do not lie.'

' Eh ? what is it ?' said the other, casting a rapid but stolen glance at the address, which he read greedily, without touching the card.

' Take this address,' repeated the half-caste, ' and you may then assure yourself——'

' Really, sir,' cried Rodin, pushing back the card with his hand, ' your impudence confounds me. I repeat, that I wish to have nothing in common with you. For the last time, I tell you to leave the house. I know nothing about your Prince Djalma. You say you can injure me—do so—make no ceremonies—but, in heaven's name, leave me to myself '

So saying, Rodin rang the bell violently. Faringhea made a movement as if to stand upon the defensive ; but only the old servant, with his quiet and placid mien, appeared at the door.

' Lapierre, light the gentleman out,' said Rodin, pointing to Faringhea.

Terrified at Rodin's calmness, the half-caste hesitated to leave the room.

' What do you wait, sir ?' said Rodin, remarking his hesitation. ' I wish to be alone.'

' So, sir,' said Faringhea, as he withdrew, slowly, ' you refuse my offers ? Take care ! to-morrow it will be too late.'

' I have the honour to be your most humble servant, sir,' said Rodin, bowing courteously. The Strangler went out, and the door closed upon him.

Immediately, Father d'Aigrigny entered from the next room. His countenance was pale and agitated.

' What have you done ?' exclaimed he, addressing Rodin. ' I have heard all. I am unfortunately too sure that this wretch spoke the truth. The Indian is in his power, and he goes to rejoin him.'

' I think not,' said Rodin, humbly, as, bowing, he reassumed his dull and submissive countenance.

' What will prevent this man from rejoining the prince ?'

' Allow me. As soon as the rascal was shown in, I knew him ; and so, before speaking a word to him, I wrote a few lines to Morok, who was waiting below with Goliath till your reverence should be at leisure. Afterwards, in the course of the conversation, when they brought me Morok's answer, I added some fresh instructions, seeing the turn that affairs were taking '

' And what was the use of all this, since you have let the man leave the house ?'

' Your reverence will perhaps deign to observe that he did not leave it, till he had given me the direction of the hotel where the Indian now is, thanks to my innocent stratagem of appearing to despise him. But, if it had failed, Faringhea would still have fallen into the hands of Goliath and Morok, who are waiting for him in the street, a few steps from the door. Only we should have been rather embarrassed, as we should not have known where to find Prince Djalma.'

' More violence !' said Father d'Aigrigny, with repugnance.

' It is to be regretted, very much regretted,' replied Rodin ; ' but it was necessary to follow out the system already adopted.'

' Is that meant for a reproach ?' said Father d'Aigrigny, who began to think that Rodin was something more than a mere writing-machine.

' I could not permit myself to blame your reverence,' said Rodin, cringing almost to the ground. ' But all that will be required is to confine this man for twenty-four hours.'

' And afterwards—his complaints ?'

' Such a scoundrel as he is will not dare to complain. Besides, he left this house in freedom. Morok and Goliath will bandage his eyes when they seize him. The house has another entrance in the Rue Vieille-des-Ursins. At this hour, and in such a storm, no one will be passing through this deserted quarter of the town. The knave will be confused by the change of place ; they will put him into a cellar of the new building, and to-morrow night, about the same hour, they will restore him to liberty with the like precautions. As for the East Indian, we now know where to find him ; we must send to him a confidential person, and, if he recovers from his trance, there would be, in my humble opinion,' said Rodin, modestly, ' a very simple and quiet manner of keeping him away from the Rue Saint-François all day to-morrow.'

The same servant with the mild countenance, who had introduced and shown out Faringhea, here entered the room, after knocking discreetly at the door. He held in his hand a sort of game-bag, which he gave to Rodin, saying : 'Here is what M. Morok has just brought ; he came in by the Rue Vieille.'

The servant withdrew, and Rodin, opening the bag, said to Father d'Aigrigny, as he showed him the contents : ' The medal, and Van Dael's letter. Morok has been quick at his work.'

' One more danger avoided,' said the marquis ; ' it is a pity to be forced to such measures.'

' We must only blame the rascal who has obliged us to have recourse to them. I will send instantly to the hotel where the Indian lodges.'

' And, at seven in the morning, you will conduct Gabriel to the Rue Saint-François. It is there that I must have with him the interview which he has so earnestly demanded these three days.'

' I informed him of it this evening, and he awaits your orders.'

' At last, then,' said Father d'Aigrigny, ' after so many struggles, and fears, and crosses, only a few hours separate us from the moment which we have so long desired!'

    ✿   ✿   ✿   ✿   ✿   ✿

We now conduct the reader to the house in the Rue Saint-François.

CHAPTER XVII.

THE HOUSE IN THE RUE SAINT-FRANÇOIS.

ON entering the Rue Saint-Gervais, by the Rue Doré (in the Marais), you would have found yourself, at the epoch of this narrative, directly opposite to an enormously high wall, the stones of which were black and worm-eaten with age. This wall, which extended nearly the whole length of that solitary street, served to support a terrace shaded by trees of some hundred years old, which thus grew about forty feet above the causeway. Through their thick branches appeared the stone front, peaked roof, and tall brick chimneys of an antique house, the entrance of which was situated in the Rue Saint-François, not far from the Rue Saint-Gervais corner. Nothing could be more gloomy than the exterior of this abode. On the entrance-side also was a very high wall, pierced with two or three loop-holes, strongly grated. A carriage gateway in massive oak, barred with iron, and studded with large nail-heads, whose primitive colour disappeared beneath a thick layer of mud, dust, and rust, fitted close into the arch of a deep recess, forming the swell of a bay window above. In one of these massive gates was a smaller door, which served for ingress and egress to Samuel the Jew, the guardian of this dreary abode. On passing the threshold, you came to a passage, formed in the building which faced in the street. In this building was the lodging of Samuel, with its windows opening upon the rather spacious inner courtyard, through the railing of which you perceived the garden. In the middle of this garden stood a two-storied stone house, so strangely built, that you had to mount a flight of steps, or rather a double flight of at least twenty steps, to reach the door, which had been walled-up a hundred and fifty years before. The window-blinds of this habitation had been replaced by large thick plates of lead, hermetically soldered, and kept in by frames of iron clamped in the stone. Moreover, completely to intercept air and light, and thus to guard against decay within and without, the roof had been covered with thick sheets of lead, as well as the vents of the tall chimneys, which had previously been bricked up. The same precautions had been taken with respect to a small square belvidere, situated on the top of the house ; this glass cage was covered with a sort of dome, soldered to the roof. Only, in consequence of some singular fancy, in every one of the leaden plates, which concealed the four sides of the belvidere, corresponding to the cardinal points, seven little round holes had been bored in the form of a cross, and were easily distinguishable from the outside. Everywhere else the plates of lead were completely unpierced. Thanks to these precautions, and to the substantial structure of the building, nothing but a few outward repairs had been necessary; and the apartments, entirely removed from the influence of the external air, no doubt remained, during a century and a half, exactly in the same state as at the time of their being shut up. The aspect of walls in crevices, of broken, worm-eaten shutters, of a roof half fallen in, and windows covered with wallflowers, would perhaps have been less sad than the appearance of this stone house, plated with iron and lead, and preserved like a mausoleum. The garden, completely deserted, and only regularly visited once a week by Samuel, presented to the view, particularly in summer, an incredible confusion of parasites and brambles. The trees, left to themselves, had shot forth and mingled their branches in all directions; some straggling vines, reproduced from offshoots, had crept along the ground to the foot of the trees, and, climbing up their trunks, had twined themselves about them, and encircled their highest branches with their inextricable net. You could only pass through this virgin forest by following the path made by the guardian, to go from the grating to the house, the approaches to which were a little sloped to let the water run off, and carefully paved to the width of about ten feet. Another narrow path, which extended all round the enclosure, was every night perambulated by two or three Pyrenees dogs—a faithful race, which had been perpetuated in the house during a century and a half. Such was the habitation destined for the meeting of the descendants of the family of Rennepont. The night which separated the 12th from the 13th day of February was near its close. A calm had succeeded the storm, and the rain had ceased: the sky was clear and full of stars; the moon, on its decline, shone with a mild lustre, and threw a melancholy light over that deserted, silent house, whose threshold for so many years no human footstep had crossed.

A bright gleam of light, issuing from one of the windows of the guardian's dwelling, announced that Samuel was awake. Figure to yourself a tolerably large room, lined from top to bottom with old walnut wainscoting, browned to an almost black, with age. Two half-extinguished brands were smoking amid the cinders on the hearth. On the stone mantelpiece, painted to resemble grey granite, stands an old iron candlestick, furnished with a meagre candle, capped by an extinguisher. Near it one sees a pair of double-barrelled pistols, and a sharp cutlass, with a hilt of carved bronze, belonging to the seventeenth century. Moreover, a heavy rifle rests against one of the chimney jambs. Four stools, an old oak press, and a square table with twisted legs, formed the sole furniture of this apartment. Against the wall were systematically suspended a number of keys of different sizes, the shape of which bore evidence to their antiquity, whilst to their rings were affixed divers labels. The back of the old press, which moved by a secret spring, had been pushed aside, and discovered, built in the wall, a large and deep iron chest, the lid of which, being open, displayed the wondrous mechanism of one of those Florentine locks of the sixteenth century, which, better than any modern invention, set all picklocks at defiance; and, moreover, according to the notions of that age, are supplied with a thick lining of asbestos cloth, suspended by gold wire at a distance from the sides of the chest, for the purpose of rendering incombustible the articles contained in it. A large cedar-wood box had been taken from this chest, and placed upon a stool; it contained numerous papers, carefully arranged and docketed. By the light of a brass lamp, the old keeper Samuel was writing in a small register, whilst Bathsheba, his wife, was dictating to him from an account. Samuel was about eighty-two years old, and, notwithstanding his advanced age, a mass of grey curling hair covered his head. He was short, thin, nervous, and the involuntary petulance of his movements proved that years had not weakened his energy and activity ; though, out of doors, where, however, he made his appearance very seldom, he affected a sort of second childhood, as had been remarked by Rodin to Father d'Aigrigny. An old dressing-gown, of maroon-coloured camlet, with large sleeves, completely enveloped the old man, and reached to his feet.

Samuel's features were cast in the pure, Eastern mould of his race. His complexion was of a dead yellow, his nose aquiline, his chin shaded by a little tuft of white beard, while projecting cheek-bones threw a harsh shadow upon the hollow and wrinkled cheeks. His countenance was full of intelligence, fine sharpness, and sagacity. On his broad, high forehead one might read frankness, honesty, and firmness ; his eyes, black and brilliant as an Arab's, were at once mild and piercing.

His wife, Bathsheba, some fifteen years younger than himself, was of tall stature, and dressed entirely in black. A low cap, of starched lawn, which reminded one of the grave headdresses of Dutch matrons, encircled a pale and austere countenance, formerly of a rare and haughty beauty, and impressed with the Scriptural character. Some lines in the forehead, caused by the almost continual knitting of her grey brows, showed that this woman had often suffered from the pressure of intense grief.

At this very moment her countenance betrayed inexpressible sorrow. Her look was fixed, her head resting on her bosom. She had let her right hand, which held a small account-book, fall upon her lap, while the other hand grasped convulsively a long tress of jet-black hair, which she bore about her neck. It was fastened by a golden clasp, about an inch square, in which, under a plate of crystal, that shut in one side of it like a relic-case, could be seen a piece of linen, folded square, and almost entirely covered with dark red spots that resembled blood a long time dried.

After a short silence, during which Samuel was occupied with his register, he read aloud what he had just been writing : ' Per contra, 5,000 Austrian Metallics of 1,000 florins, under date of October 19th, 1826.'

After which enumeration, Samuel raised his head, and said to his wife : ' Well, is it right, Bathsheba? Have you compared it with the account-book?'

Bathsheba did not answer. Samuel looked at her, and, seeing that she was absorbed in grief, said to her, with an expression of tender anxiety : ' What is the matter ? Good heaven ! what is the matter with you ?'

' The 19th of October, 1826,' said she, slowly, with her eyes still fixed, and pressing yet more closely the lock of black hair which she wore about her neck ; ' it was a fatal day—for, Samuel, it was the date of the last letter which we received from——'

Bathsheba was unable to proceed. She uttered a long sigh, and concealed her face in her hands.

' Oh ! I understand you,' observed the old man, in a tremulous voice ; ' a father may be taken up by the thought of other cares ; but the heart of a mother is ever wakeful.' Throwing his pen down upon the table, Samuel leaned his forehead upon his hands in sorrow.

Bathsheba resumed, as if she found a melancholy pleasure in these cruel remembrances : ' Yes ; that was the last day on which our son, Abel, wrote to us from Germany, to announce to us that he had invested the funds according to your desire, and was going thence into Poland, to effect another operation.'

' And in Poland he met the death of a martyr,' added Samuel. ' With no motive and no proof, they accused him falsely of coming to organise smuggling, and the Russian governor, treating him as they treat our brothers in that land of cruel tyranny, condemned him to the dreadful punishment of the knout, without even hearing him in his defence. Why should they hear a Jew? What is a Jew? A creature below a serf, whom they reproach for all the vices that a degrading slavery has engendered. A Jew beaten to death! Who would trouble themselves about it?'

' And poor Abel, so good, so faithful, died beneath their stripes, partly from shame, partly from the wounds,' said Bathsheba, shuddering. ' One of our Polish brethren obtained with great difficulty permission to bury him. He cut off this lock of beautiful black hair—which, with this scrap of linen, bathed in the blood of our dear son, is all that now remains to us of him.' Bathsheba covered the hair and clasp with convulsive kisses.

' Alas !' said Samuel, drying his tears, which had burst forth at these sad recollections, ' the Lord did not at last remove our child, until the task which our family has accomplished faithfully for a century and a half was nearly at an end. Of what use will our race be henceforth upon earth?' added Samuel, most bitterly. ' Our duty is performed. This casket contains a royal fortune—and yonder house, walled up for a hundred and fifty years, will be opened to-morrow to the descendants of my ancestor's benefactor.' So saying, Samuel turned his face sorrowfully towards the house, which he could see through the window. The dawn was just about to appear. The moon had set ; belvidere, roof, and chimneys formed a black mass upon the dark blue of the starry firmament.

Suddenly, Samuel grew pale, and, rising abruptly, said to his wife in a tremulous tone, whilst he still pointed to the house : ' Bathsheba ! the seven points of light—just as it was thirty years ago. Look ! look !'

Indeed, the seven round holes, bored in the form of a cross in the leaden plates which covered the window of the belvidere, sparkled like so many luminous points, as if some one in the house ascended with a light to the roof.

CHAPTER XVIII.

DEBIT AND CREDI

FOR some seconds, Samuel and Bathsheba remained motionless, with their eyes fixed in fear and uneasiness on the seven luminous points, which shone through the darkness of the night from the summit of the belvidere ; while, on the horizon, behind the house, a pale, rosy hue announced the dawn of day.

Samuel was the first to break silence, and he said to his wife, as he drew his hand across his brow : ' The grief caused by the remembrance of our poor child has prevented us from reflecting that, after all, there should be nothing to alarm us in what we see.'

' How so, Samuel ?'

' My father always told me that he, and my grandfather before him, had seen such lights at long intervals.'

' Yes, Samuel—but without being able, any more than ourselves, to explain the cause.'

' Like my father and grandfather, we can only suppose that some secret passage gives admittance to persons who, like us, have some mysterious duty to fulfil in this dwelling. Besides, my father warned me not to be uneasy at these appearances, foretold by him, and now visible for the second time in thirty years.'

' No matter for that, Samuel, it does strike one as if it was something supernatural.'

'The days of miracles are over,' said the Jew, shaking his head sorrowfully; 'many of the old houses in this quarter have subterraneous communications with distant places—some extending even to the Seine and the Catacombs. Doubtless, this house is so situated, and the persons who make these rare visits enter by some such means.'

'But that the belvidere should be thus lighted up?'

'According to the plan of the building, you know that the belvidere forms a kind of skylight to the apartment called the Great Hall of Mourning, situated on the upper story. As it is completely dark, in consequence of the closing of all the windows, they must use a light to visit this Hall of Mourning—a room which is said to contain some very strange and gloomy things,' added the Jew, with a shudder.

Bathsheba, as well as her husband, gazed attentively on the seven luminous points, which diminished in brightness as the daylight gradually increased.

'As you say, Samuel, the mystery may be thus explained,' resumed the Hebrew's wife. 'Besides, the day is so important a one for the family of Rennepont, that this apparition ought not to astonish us under the circumstances.'

'Only to think,' remarked Samuel, 'that these lights have appeared at several different times throughout a century and a half! There must, therefore, be another family that, like ours, has devoted itself, from generation to generation, to accomplish a pious duty.'

'But what is this duty? It will perhaps be explained to-day.

'Come, come, Bathsheba,' suddenly exclaimed Samuel, as if roused from his reverie, and reproaching himself with idleness ; 'this is the day, and, before eight o'clock, our cash account must be in order, and these titles to immense property arranged, so that they may be delivered to the rightful owners'—and he pointed to the cedar-wood box.

'You are right, Samuel ; this day does not belong to us. It is a solemn day—one that would have been sweet, oh ! very sweet to you and me—if now any days could be sweet to us,' said Bathsheba bitterly, for she was thinking of her son.

'Bathsheba,' said Samuel, mournfully, as he laid his hand on his wife's ; 'we shall at least have the stern satisfaction of having done our duty. And has not the Lord been very favourable to us, though He has thus severely tried us by the death of our son? Is it not thanks to His providence that three generations of my family have been able to commence, continue, and finish this great work?'

'Yes, Samuel,' said the Jewess, affectionately, 'and for you at least this satisfaction will be combined with calm and quietness, for on the stroke of noon you will be delivered from a very terrible responsibility.'

So saying, Bathsheba pointed to the box.

'It is true,' replied the old man ; 'I had rather these immense riches were in the hands of those to whom they belong, than in mine ; but, to-day, I shall cease to be their trustee. Once more then, I will check the account for the last time, and compare the register with the cash-book that you hold in your hand.'

Bathsheba bowed her head affirmatively, and Samuel, taking up his pen, occupied himself once more with his calculations. His wife, in spite of herself, again yielded to the sad thoughts which that fatal date had awakened, by reminding her of the death of her son.

Let us now trace rapidly the history, in appearance so romantic and marvellous, in reality so simple, of the fifty thousand crowns, which, thanks to the law of accumulation, and to a prudent, intelligent and faithful investment, had naturally, and necessarily, been transformed, in the space of a century and a half, into a sum far more important than the forty millions estimated by Father d'Aigrigny—who, partially informed on this subject, and reckoning the disastrous accidents, losses, and bankruptcies which might have occurred during so long a period, believed that forty millions might well be considered enormous.

The history of this fortune being closely connected with that of the Samuel family, by whom it had been managed for three generations, we shall give it again in a few words.

About the period 1670, some years before his death, Marius de Rennepont, then travelling in Portugal, had been enabled, by means of powerful interest, to save the life of an unfortunate Jew, condemned to be burnt alive by the Inquisition, because of his religion. This Jew was Isaac Samuel, grandfather of the present guardian of the house in the Rue Saint-François.

Generous men often attach themselves to those they have served, as much, at least, as the obliged parties are attached to their benefactors. Having ascertained that Isaac, who at that time carried on a petty broker's business at Lisbon, was industrious, honest, active, laborious, and intelligent, M. de Rennepont, who then possessed large property in France, proposed to the Jew to accompany him, and undertake the management of his affairs. The same hatred and suspicion with which the Israelites have always been followed, was then at its height. Isaac was therefore doubly grateful for this mark of confidence on the part of M. de Rennepont. He accepted the offer, and promised from that day to devote his existence to the service of him who had first saved his life, and then trusted implicitly to his good faith and uprightness, although he was a Jew, and belonged to a race generally suspected and despised. M. de Rennepont, a man of great soul, endowed with a good spirit, was not deceived in his choice. Until he was deprived of his fortune, it prospered wonderfully in the hands of Isaac Samuel, who, gifted with an admirable aptitude for business, applied himself exclusively to advance the interests of his benefactor.

Then came the persecution and ruin of M. de Rennepont, whose property was confiscated and given up to the reverend fathers of the Company of Jesus only a few days before his death. Concealed in the retreat he had chosen, therein to put a violent end to his life, he sent secretly for Isaac Samuel, and delivered to him fifty thousand crowns in gold, the last remains of his fortune. This faithful servant was to invest the money to the best advantage, and, if he should have a son, transmit to him the same obligation ; or, should he have no child, he was to seek out some relation worthy of continuing this trust, to which would moreover be annexed a fair reward. It was thus to be transmitted and perpetuated from relative to relative, until the expiration of a century and a half. M. de Rennepont also begged Isaac to take charge, during his life, of the house in the Rue Saint-François, where he would be lodged gratis, and to leave this function likewise to his descendants, if it were possible.

If even Isaac Samuel had not had children, the powerful bond of union which exists between certain Jewish families, would have rendered practicable the last will of De Rennepont. The relations of Isaac would have become partners in his gratitude to his benefactor, and they, and their succeeding generations, would have religiously accomplished the task imposed upon one of their race. But, several years after the death of De Rennepont, Isaac had a son.

This son, Levy Samuel, born in 1689, not having had any children by his first wife, married again at nearly sixty years of age, and, in 1750, he also had a son—David Samuel, the guardian of the house in the Rue Saint-

François, who, in 1832 (the date of this narrative), was eighty-two years old, and seemed likely to live as long as his father, who had died at the age of ninety-three. Finally, Abel Samuel, the son whom Bathsheba so bitterly regretted, born in 1790, had perished under the Russian knout, at the age of thirty-six.

Having established this humble genealogy, we easily understand how this successive longevity of three members of the Samuel family, all of whom had been guardians of the walled house, by uniting, as it were, the nineteenth with the seventeenth century, simplified and facilitated the execution of M. de Rennepont's will ; the latter having declared his desire to the grandfather of the Samuels, that the capital should only be augmented by interest at five per cent.—so that the fortune might come to his descendants free from all taint of usurious speculation.

The fellow men of the Samuel family, the first inventors of the bill of exchange, which served them in the Middle Ages to transport mysteriously considerable amounts from one end of the world to the other, to conceal their fortune, and to shield it from the rapacity of their enemies—the Jews, we say, having almost the monopoly of the trade in money and exchanges, until the end of the eighteenth century, aided the secret transactions and financial operations of this family, which, up to about 1820, placed their different securities, which had become progressively immense, in the hands of the principal Israelitish bankers and merchants of Europe. This sure and secret manner of acting had enabled the present guardian of the house in the Rue Saint-François, to effect enormous investments, unknown to all ; and it was more especially during the period of his management, that the capital sum had acquired, by the mere fact of compound interest, an almost incalculable development. Compared with him, his father and grandfather had only small amounts to manage. Though it had only been necessary to find successively sure and immediate investments, so that the money might not remain as it were one day without bearing interest, it had acquired financial capacity to attain this result, when so many millions were in question. The last of the Samuels, brought up in the school of his father, had exhibited this capacity in a very high degree, as will be seen immediately by the results. Nothing could be more touching, noble, and respectable, than the conduct of the members of this Jewish family, who, partners in the engagement of gratitude taken by their ancestor, devote themselves for long years, with as much disinterestedness as intelligence and honesty, to the slow acquisition of a kingly fortune, of which they expect no part themselves, but which, thanks to them, would come pure, as immense, to the hands of the descendants of their benefactor ! Nor could anything be more honourable to him who made, and him who received this deposit, than the simple promise by word of mouth, unaccompanied by any security save mutual confidence and reciprocal esteem, when the result was only to be produced at the end of a century and a half !

    ❂   ❂   ❂   ❂   ❂   ❂

After once more reading his inventory with attention, Samuel said to his wife : " I am certain of the correctness of my additions. Now please to compare with the account-book in your hand the summary of the investments that I have just entered in the register. I will assure myself, at the same time, that the bonds and vouchers are properly arranged in this casket, that, on the opening of the will, they may be delivered in order to the notary.'

' Begin, my dear, and I will check you,' said Bathsheba.

Samuel read as follows, examining as he went on, the contents of his casket :—

Statement of the Account of the Heirs of M. DE RENNEPONT, *delivered by*
DAVID SAMUELS.

DEBIT.		CREDIT.
2,000,000 francs per annum, in the French 5 P. C., bought from 1825 to 1832, at an average price of 99f. 50c.	39,800,000	150,000 francs received from M. de Rennepont, in 1682, by Isaac Samuel,
900,000 francs, ditto, in the French 3 P. C., bought during the same years, at an average of 74f. 25c.	22,275,000	my grandfather; and invested by him, my father, and
5,000 shares in the Bank of France, bought at 1,900	9,500,000	myself, in different securities,
3,000 shares in the Four Canals, in a certificate from the Company, bought at 1,115f.	3,345,000	at Five per Cent. Interest, with a settlement of account
125,000 ducats of Neapolitans, at an average of 82. 2,050,000 ducats, at 4f. 400.	9,020,000	and investment of interest every six months, producing, as by annexed vouchers
5,000 Austrian Metallics, of 1,000 florins, at 93—say 4,650,000 florins, at 2f. 50c.	11,625,000	225,950,000
75,000 pounds sterling per annum, English Consolidated 3 P. C., at 88¾—say £2,218,750, at 25f.	55,468,750	Less losses sustained by failures, expenses of commission and brokerage, and salary of
1,200,000 florins, Dutch 2½ P. C., at 60—28,860,000 florins, at 2f. 100.	60,606,000	three generations of trustees, as per statement
Cash in bank notes, gold and silver	535,250	annexed - - 13,775,000
		————— 212,175,000
Francs	212,175,000	Francs 212,175,000

Paris, 12*th February,* 1832.

'It is quite right,' said Samuel, after examining the papers, contained in the cedar-wood box. 'There remains in hand, at the absolute disposal of the heirs of the Rennepont family, the sum of TWO HUNDRED AND TWELVE MILLIONS, ONE HUNDRED AND SEVENTY-FIVE THOUSAND FRANCS.' And the old man looked at his wife with an expression of legitimate pride.

'It is hardly credible!' cried Bathsheba, struck with surprise. 'I knew that you had immense property in your hands; but I could never have believed, that one hundred and fifty thousand francs, left a century and a half ago, should be the only source of this immense fortune.'

'It is even so, Bathsheba,' answered the old man, proudly. 'Doubtless, my grandfather, my father, and myself, have all been exact and faithful in the management of these funds; doubtless, we have required some sagacity in the choice of investments, in times of revolution and commercial panics; but all this was easy to us, thanks to our relations with our brethren in all countries—and never have I, or any of mine, made an usurious investment, or even taken the full advantage of the legal rate of interest. Such were not the positive demands of M. de Rennepont, given to my grandfather; nor is there in the world a fortune that has been obtained by purer means. Had it not been for this disinterestedness, we might have much augmented this two hundred and twelve millions, only by taking advantage of a few favourable circumstances.'

'Dear me ! is it possible?'

'Nothing is more simple, Bathsheba. Every one knows, that in fourteen years a capital will be doubled, by the mere accumulation of interest and compound interest at five per cent. Now reflect, that in a century and a half there are ten times fourteen years, and that these one hundred and fifty thousand francs have thus been doubled and redoubled, over and over again. All that astonishes you will then appear plain enough. In 1682, M. de Rennepont entrusted my grandfather with a hundred and fifty thousand francs ; this sum, invested as I have told you, would have produced in 1696, fourteen years after, three hundred thousand francs. These last, doubled in 1710, would produce six hundred thousand. On the death of my grandfather in 1719, the amount was already near a million; in 1724, it would be twelve hundred thousand francs ; in 1738, two millions four hundred thousand ; in 1752, about two years after my birth, four millions eight hundred thousand ; in 1766, nine millions six hundred thousand ; in 1780, nineteen millions two hundred thousand ; in 1794, twelve years after the death of my father, thirty-eight millions four hundred thousand ; in 1808, seventy-six millions eight hundred thousand ; in 1822, one hundred and fifty-three millions six hundred thousand ; and, at this time, taking the compound interest for ten years, it should be at least two hundred and twenty-five millions. But losses and inevitable charges, of which the account has been strictly kept, have reduced the sum to two hundred and twelve millions one hundred and seventy-five thousand francs, the securities for which are in this box.'

'I now understand you, my dear,' answered Bathsheba, thoughtfully ; 'but how wonderful is this power of accumulation ! and what admirable provision may be made for the future, with the smallest present resources !'

'Such, no doubt, was the idea of M. de Rennepont ; for my father has often told me, and he derived it from his father, that M. de Rennepont was one of the soundest intellects of his time,' said Samuel, as he closed the cedar-box.

'God grant his descendants may be worthy of this kingly fortune, and make a noble use of it !' said Bathsheba, rising.

It was now broad day, and the clock had just struck seven.

'The masons will soon be here,' said Samuel, as he replaced the cedar-box in the iron safe, concealed behind the antique press. 'Like you, Bath-Isheba, am curious and anxious to know, what descendants of M. de Rennepont will now present themselves.'

Two or three loud knocks on the outer gate resounded through the house. The barking of the watch-dogs responded to this summons.

Samuel said to his wife : 'It is no doubt the masons, whom the notary has sent with his clerk. Tie all the keys and their labels together ; I will come back and fetch them.'

So saying, Samuel went down to the door, with much nimbleness, considering his age, prudently opened a small wicket, and saw three workmen, in the garb of masons, accompanied by a young man dressed in black.

'What may you want, gentlemen?' said the Jew, before opening the door, as he wished first to make sure of the identity of the personages.

'I am sent by M. Dumesnil, the notary,' answered the clerk, 'to be present at the unwalling of a door. Here is a letter from my master, addressed to M. Samuel, guardian of the house.'

'I am he, sir,' said the Jew : 'please to put the letter through the slide, and I will take it.'

The clerk did as Samuel desired, but shrugged his shoulders at what he considered the ridiculous precautions of a suspicious old man. The housekeeper opened the box, took the letter, went to the end of the vaulted passage in order to read it, and carefully compared the signature with that of another letter which he drew from the pocket of his long coat ; then, after all these precautions, he chained up his dogs, and returned to open the gate to the clerk and masons.

'What the devil, my good man !' said the clerk, as he entered ; 'there would not be more formalities in opening the gates of a fortress !'

The Jew bowed, but without answering.

'Are you deaf, my good fellow ?' cried the clerk, close to his ears.

'No, sir,' said Samuel, with a quiet smile, as he advanced several steps beyond the passage. Then pointing to the old house, he added : ' That, sir, is the door which you will have to open ; you will also have to remove the lead and iron from the second window to the right.'

'Why not open all the windows ?' asked the clerk.

'Because, sir, as guardian of this house, I have received particular orders on the subject.'——'Who gave you these orders ?'

'My father, sir, who received them from his father, who transmitted them from the master of this house. When I cease to have the care of it, the new proprietor will do as he pleases.'

'Oh ! very well,' said the clerk, not a little surprised. Then, addressing himself to the masons, he added : 'This is your business, my fine fellows ; you are to unwall the door, and remove the iron frame-work of the second window to the right.'

Whilst the masons set to work, under the inspection of the notary's clerk, a coach stopped before the outer gate, and Rodin, accompanied by Gabriel, entered the house in the Rue Saint François.

CHAPTER XIX.

THE HEIR.

SAMUEL opened the door to Gabriel and Rodin.

The latter said to the Jew, ' You, sir, are the keeper of this house ?'

'Yes, sir,' replied Samuel.

'This is Abbé Gabriel de Rennepont' said Rodin, as he introduced his companion, 'one of the descendants of the family of the Renneponts.'

'Happy to hear it, sir.' said the Jew, almost involuntarily, struck with the angelic countenance of Gabriel—for nobleness and serenity of soul were visible in the glance of the young priest, and were written upon his pure, white brow, already crowned with the halo of martyrdom. Samuel looked at Gabriel with curiosity and benevolent interest ; but feeling that this silent contemplation must cause some embarrassment to his guest, he said to him, 'M. l'Abbé, the notary will not be here before ten o'clock.'

Gabriel looked at him in turn, with an air of surprise, and answered, 'What notary, sir ?'

'Father d'Aigrigny will explain all this to you,' said Rodin, hastily. Then addressing Samuel, he added, ' We are a little before the time. Will you allow us to wait for the arrival of the notary ?'

'Certainly,' said Samuel, 'if you please to walk into my house.'

'I thank you, sir,' answered Rodin, 'and accept your offer.'

'Follow me, then, gentlemen,' said the old man.

A few moments after, the young priest and the socius, preceded by Samuel, entered one of the rooms occupied by the latter, on the ground-floor of the building, looking out upon the courtyard.

'The Abbé d'Aigrigny, who has been the guardian of M. Gabriel, will soon be coming to ask for us,' added Rodin ; 'will you have the kindness, sir to show him into this room ?'

' I will not fail to do so, sir,' said Samuel, as he went out.

The socius and Gabriel were left alone. To the adorable gentleness which usually gave to the fine features of the missionary so touching a charm, there had succeeded in this moment a remarkable expression of sadness, resolution, and severity. Rodin not having seen Gabriel for some days, was greatly struck by the change he remarked in him. He had watched him silently all the way from the Rue des Postes to the Rue Saint François. The young priest wore, as usual, a long black cassock, which made still more visible the transparent paleness of his countenance. When the Jew had left the room, Gabriel said to Rodin, in a firm voice, ' Will you at length inform me, sir, why, for some days past, I have been prevented from speaking to his reverence Father d'Aigrigny ? Why has he chosen this house to grant me an interview ?'

' It is impossible for me to answer these questions,' replied Rodin, coldly. ' His reverence will soon arrive, and will listen to you. All I can tell you is, that the reverend father lays as much stress upon this meeting as you do. If he has chosen this house for the interview, it is because you have an interest to be here. You know it well—though you affected astonishment on hearing the guardian speak of a notary.'

So saying, Rodin fixed a scrutinising, anxious look upon Gabriel, whose countenance expressed only surprise.

' I do not understand you,' said he, in reply to Rodin. ' What have I to do with this house ?'

' It is impossible that you should not know it,' answered Rodin, still looking at him with attention.

' I have told you, sir, that I do not know it,' replied the other, almost offended by the pertinacity of the socius.

' What, then, did your adopted mother come to tell you yesterday ? Why did you presume to receive her without permission from Father d'Aigrigny, as I have heard this morning ? Did she not speak with you of certain family papers, found upon you when she took you in ?'

' No, sir,' said Gabriel ; ' those papers were delivered at the time to my adopted mother's confessor, and they afterwards passed into Father d'Aigrigny's hands. This is the first I hear for a long time of these papers.'

' So you affirm that Frances Baudoin did not come to speak to you on this subject ?' resumed Rodin, obstinately, laying great emphasis on his words.

' This is the second time, sir, that you seem to doubt my affirmation,' said the young priest, mildly, while he repressed a movement of impatience ; ' I assure you that I speak the truth.'

' He knows nothing,' thought Rodin ; for he was too well convinced of Gabriel's sincerity to retain the least doubt after so positive a declaration. ' I believe you,' went on he. ' The idea only occurred to me in reflecting what could be the reason of sufficient weight to induce you to transgress Father d'Aigrigny's orders with regard to the absolute retirement he had commanded, which was to exclude all communication with those without. Much more, contrary to all the rules of our house, you ventured to shut the door of your room, whereas it ought to remain half-open, that the mutual inspection enjoined us might be the more easily practised. I could only explain these sins against discipline, by the necessity of some very important conversation with your adopted mother.'

' It was to a priest, and not to her adopted son, that Madame Baudoin wished to speak,' replied Gabriel, in a tone of deep seriousness. ' I closed my door because I was to hear a confession.'

' And what had Frances Baudoin of such importance to confess ?'

' You will know that by-and-bye, when I speak to his reverence—if it be his pleasure that you should hear me.'

These words were so firmly spoken, that a long silence ensued. Let us remind the reader that Gabriel had hitherto been kept by his superiors in the most complete ignorance of the importance of the family interests which required his presence in the Rue Saint-François. The day before, Frances Baudoin, absorbed in her own grief, had forgotten to tell him that the two orphans also should be present at this meeting, and had she even thought of it, Dagobert would have prevented her mentioning this circumstance to the young priest.

Gabriel was therefore quite ignorant of the family ties which united him with the daughters of Marshal Simon, with Mdlle. de Cardoville, with M. Hardy, Prince Djalma, and Sleepinbuff. In a word, if it had then been revealed to him that he was the heir of Marius de Rennepont, he would have believed himself the only descendant of the family. During the moment's silence which succeeded his conversation with Rodin, Gabriel observed through the windows the masons at their work of unwalling the door. Having finished this first operation, they set about removing the bars of iron by which a plate of lead was fixed over the same entrance.

At this juncture, Father d'Aigrigny, conducted by Samuel, entered the room. Before Gabriel could turn round, Rodin had time to whisper to the reverend father, 'He knows nothing—and we have no longer anything to fear from the Indian.'

Notwithstanding his affected calmness, Father d'Aigrigny's countenance was pale and contracted, like that of a player who is about to stake all on a last, decisive game. Hitherto, all had favoured the designs of the Society ; but he could not think without alarm of the four hours which still remained before they should reach the fatal moment. Gabriel having turned towards him, Father d'Aigrigny offered him his hand with a smile, and said to him in an affectionate and cordial tone, 'My dear son, it has pained me a good deal to have been obliged to refuse you till now the interview that you so much desired. It has been no less distressing to me to impose on you a confinement of some days. Though I cannot give any explanation of what I may think fit to order, I will just observe to you that I have acted only for your interest.'

'I am bound to believe your reverence,' answered Gabriel, bowing his head.

In spite of himself, the young priest felt a vague sense of fear, for until his departure for his American mission, Father d'Aigrigny, at whose feet he had pronounced the formidable vows which bound him irrevocably to the Society of Jesus, had exercised over him that frightful species of influence which, acting only by despotism, suppression, and intimidation, breaks down all the living forces of the soul, and leaves it inert, trembling, and terrified. Impressions of early youth are indelible, and this was the first time, since his return from America, that Gabriel found himself in presence of Father d'Aigrigny ; and although he did not shrink from the resolution he had taken, he regretted not to have been able, as he had hoped, to gather new strength and courage from an interview with Agricola and Dagobert. Father d'Aigrigny knew mankind too well not to have remarked the emotion of the young priest, and to have endeavoured to explain its cause. This emotion appeared to him a favourable omen ; he redoubled, therefore, his seductive arts, his air of tenderness and amenity, reserving to himself, if necessary, the choice of assuming another mask. He sat down, while Gabriel and Rodin remained standing in a respectful position, and said to the former : 'You desire, my dear son, to have an important interview with me ?'

'Yes, father,' said Gabriel, involuntarily casting down his eyes before the large, glittering grey pupil of his superior.

'And I also have matters of great importance to communicate to you. Listen to me first ; you can speak afterwards.'

'I listen, father.'

'It is about twelve years ago, my dear son,' said Father d'Aigrigny, affectionately, 'that the confessor of your adopted mother, addressing himself to me through M. Rodin, called my attention to yourself, by reporting the astonishing progress you had made at the school of the Brothers. I soon found, indeed, that your excellent conduct, your gentle, modest character, and your precocious intelligence, were worthy of the most tender interest. From that moment I kept my eyes upon you, and at the end of some time, seeing that you did not fall off, it appeared to me that there was something more in you than the stuff that makes a workman. We agreed with your adopted mother, and through my intervention, you were admitted gratuitously to one of the schools of our Company. Thus one burden the less weighed upon the excellent woman who had taken charge of you, and you received from our paternal care all the benefits of a religious education. Is not this true, my dear son ?'

'It is true, father,' answered Gabriel, casting down his eyes.

'As you grew up, excellent and rare virtues displayed themselves in your character. Your obedience and mildness were above all exemplary. You made rapid progress in your studies. I knew not then to what career you wished to devote yourself, but I felt certain that, in every station of life, you would remain a faithful son of the Church. I was not deceived in my hopes, or rather, my dear son, you surpassed them all. Learning, by a friendly communication, that your adopted mother ardently desired to see you take orders, you acceded generously and religiously to the wish of the excellent woman to whom you owed so much. But as the Lord is always just in His recompenses, He willed that the most touching work of gratitude you could show to your adopted mother, should at the same time be divinely profitable, by making you one of the militant members of our holy Church.'

At these words, Gabriel could not repress a significant start, as he remembered Frances' sad confidences. But he restrained himself, whilst Rodin stood leaning with his elbow on the corner of the chimney-piece, continuing to examine him with singular and obstinate attention.

Father d'Aigrigny resumed : 'I do not conceal from you, my dear son, that your resolution filled me with joy. I saw in you one of the future lights of the Church, and I was anxious to see it shine in the midst of our Company. You submitted courageously to our painful and difficult tests ; you were judged worthy of belonging to us, and, after taking in my presence the irrevocable and sacred oath, which binds you for ever to our Company for the greater glory of God, you answered the appeal of our Holy Father* to willing souls, and offered yourself as a missionary, to preach to savages the one Catholic faith. Though it was painful to us to part with our dear son, we could not refuse to accede to such pious wishes. You set out a humble missionary—you return a glorious martyr—and we are justly proud to reckon you amongst our number. This rapid sketch of the past was necessary, my dear son, to arrive at what follows, for we wish now, if it be possible, to draw still closer the bonds that unite us. Listen to me, my dear son ; what I am about to say is confidential, and of the highest importance, not only for you, but the whole Company.'

'Then, father,' cried Gabriel hastily, interrupting the Abbé d'Aigrigny, 'I cannot—I ought not to hear you.'

* It is only in respect to Missions that the Jesuits acknowledge the papal supremacy.

The young priest became deadly pale ; one saw, by the alteration of his features, that a violent struggle was taking place within him, but recovering his first resolution, he raised his head, and casting an assured look on Father d'Aigrigny and Rodin, who glanced at each other in mute surprise, he resumed : 'I repeat to you, father, that if it concerns confidential matters of the Company, I must not hear you.'

'Really, my dear son, you occasion me the greatest astonishment. What is the matter ?—Your countenance changes, your emotion is visible. Speak without fear ; why can you not hear me ?'

'I cannot tell you, father, until I also have, in my turn, rapidly sketched the past—such as I have learned to judge it of late. You will then under-stand, father, that I am no longer entitled to your confidence, for an abyss will doubtlessly soon separate us.'

At these words, it is impossible to paint the look rapidly exchanged be-tween Rodin and Father d'Aigrigny. The socius began to bite his nails, fixing his reptile eye angrily upon Gabriel ; Father d'Aigrigny grew livid, and his brow was bathed in cold sweat. He asked himself with terror, if, at the moment of reaching the goal, the obstacle was going to come from Gabriel, in favour of whom all other obstacles had been removed. This thought filled him with despair. Yet the reverend father contained himself admirably, remained calm, and answered with affectionate unction : 'It is impossible to believe, my dear son, that you and I can ever be separated by an abyss—unless by the abyss of grief, which would be caused by any serious danger to your salvation. But speak ; I listen to you.'

'It is true, that, twelve years ago, father.' proceeded Gabriel, in a firm voice, growing more animated as he proceeded, 'I entered, through your intervention, a college of the Company of Jesus. I entered it loving, truthful, confiding. How did they encourage those precious instincts of childhood ? I will tell you. The day of my entrance, the superior said to me, as he pointed out two children a little older than myself: "These are the com-panions that you will prefer. You will always walk three together. The rules of the house forbid all intercourse between two persons only. They also require, that you should listen attentively to what your companions say, so that you may report it to me ; for these dear children may have, without knowing it, bad thoughts or evil projects. Now, if you love your comrades, you must inform me of these evil tendencies, that my paternal remonstrances may save them from punishment ; it is better to prevent evil than to punish it "——'

'Such are, indeed, my dear son,' said Father d'Aigrigny, 'the rules of our house, and the language we hold to all our pupils on their entrance.'

'I know it, father,' answered Gabriel, bitterly ; 'three days after, a poor, submissive, and credulous child, I was already a spy upon my comrades, hearing and remembering their conversation, and reporting it to the superior, who congratulated me on my zeal. What they thus made me do was shame-ful, and yet, God knows ! I thought I was accomplishing a charitable duty. I was happy in obeying the commands of a superior whom I respected, and to whose words I listened, in my childish faith, as I should have listened to those of heaven. One day, that I had broken some rule of the house, the superior said to me : "My child, you have deserved a severe punish-ment ; but you will be pardoned, if you succeed in surprising one of your comrades in the same fault that you have committed." And for fear that, notwithstanding my faith and blind obedience, this encouragement to turn informer, from the motive of personal interest, might appear odious to me, the superior added : "I speak to you, my child, for the sake of your com-rade's salvation. Were he to escape punishment, his evil habits would become habitual. But, by detecting him in a fault, and exposing him to salutary correction, you will have the double advantage of aiding in his salvation, and escaping yourself a merited punishment, which will have been remitted because of your zeal for your neighbour "——'

'Doubtless,' answered Father d'Aigrigny, more and more terrified by Gabriel's language ; 'and in truth, my dear son, all this is conformable to the rule followed in our colleges, and to the habits of the members of our Company, "who may denounce each other without prejudice to mutual love and charity, and only for their greater spiritual advancement, particularly when questioned by their superior, or commanded for the greater glory of God," as our Constitution has it.'

'I know it,' cried Gabriel ; 'I know it. 'Tis in the name of all that is most sacred amongst men, that we are encouraged to do evil.'

'My dear son,' said Father d'Aigrigny, trying to conceal his secret and growing terror beneath an appearance of wounded dignity, 'from you to me, these words are at least strange.'

At this, Rodin, quitting the mantelpiece, on which he had been leaning, began to walk up and down the room, with a meditative air, and without ceasing to bite his nails.

'It is cruel to be obliged to remind you, my dear son, that you are indebted to us for the education you have received, added Father d'Aigrigny.

'Such were its fruits, father,' replied Gabriel 'Until then I had been a spy on the other children, from a sort of disinterestedness ; but the orders of the superior made me advance another step on that shameful road. I had become an informer, to escape a merited punishment. And yet, such was my faith, my humility, my confidence, that I performed with innocence and candour this doubly odious part. Once, indeed, tormented by vague scruples, the last remains of generous aspirations that they were stifling within me, I asked myself if the charitable and religious end could justify the means, and I communicated my doubts to the superior. He replied, that I had not to judge, but to obey, and that to him alone belonged the responsibility of my acts.'

'Go on, my dear son,' said Father d'Aigrigny, yielding, in spite of himself, to the deepest dejection. 'Alas ! I was right in opposing your travel to America.'

'And yet it was the will of Providence, in that new, productive, and free country, that, enlightened by a singular chance, on past and present, my eyes were at length opened. Yes !' cried Gabriel, 'it was in America that, released from the gloomy abode where I had spent so many years of my youth, and finding myself for the first time face to face with the divine majesty of Nature, in the heart of immense solitudes through which I journeyed—it was there that, overcome by so much magnificence and grandeur, I made a vow——' Here Gabriel interrupted himself, to continue : 'Presently, father, I will explain to you that vow ; but believe me,' added the missionary, with an accent of deep sorrow, 'it was a fatal day to me when I first learned to fear and condemn all that I had hitherto most revered and blessed. Oh ! I assure you, father,' added Gabriel, with moist eyes, 'it was not for myself alone, that I then wept.'

'I know the goodness of your heart, my dear son,' replied Father d'Aigrigny, catching a glimpse of hope, on seeing Gabriel's emotion ; 'I fear that you have been led astray. But trust yourself to us, as to your spiritual fathers, and I doubt not we shall confirm your faith, so unfortunately shaken, and disperse the darkness which at present obscures your sight. Alas, my dear son, in your vain illusions, you have mistaken some false glimmer for the pure light of day. But go on !'.

Whilst Father d'Aigrigny was thus speaking, Rodin stopped, took a pocket-book from his coat, and wrote down several notes. Gabriel was becoming more and more pale and agitated. It required no small courage in him, to speak as he was speaking, for, since his journey to America, he had learned to estimate the formidable power of the Company. But this revelation of the past, looked at from the vantage-ground of a more enlightened present, was for the young priest the excuse, or rather the cause of the determination he had just signified to his superior, and he wished to explain all faithfully, notwithstanding the danger he knowingly encountered. He continued therefore, in an agitated voice : 'You know, father, that the last days of my childhood, that happy age of frankness and innocent joy, were spent in an atmosphere of terror, suspicion, and restraint. Alas ! how could I resign myself to the least impulse of confiding trust, when I was recommended to shun the looks of him who spoke with me, in order to hide the impression that his words might cause—to conceal whatever I felt, and to observe and listen to everything ? Thus I reached the age of fifteen ; by degrees, the rare visits that I was allowed to pay, but always in presence of one of our fathers, to my adopted mother and brother, were quite suppressed, so as to shut my heart against all soft and tender emotions. Sad and fearful in that large, old, noiseless, gloomy house, I felt that I became more and more isolated from the affections and the freedom of the world. My time was divided between mutilated studies, without connexion and without object, and long hours of minute devotional exercises. I ask you, father, did they ever seek to warm our young souls by words of tenderness or evangelic love ? Alas, no ! For the words of the divine Saviour—Love ye one another, they had substituted the command : Suspect ye one another. Did they ever, father, speak to us of our country or of liberty ?— No ! ah, no ! for those words make the heart beat high ; and with them, the heart must not beat at all. To our long hours of study and devotion, there only succeeded a few walks, three by three—never two and two—because by threes, the spy-system is more practicable, and because intimacies are more easily formed by two alone ; and thus might have arisen some of those generous friendships, which also make the heart beat more than it should.* And so, by the habitual repression of every feeling, there came a time when I could not feel at all. For six months, I had not seen my adopted mother and brother ; they came to visit me at the college ; a few years before, I should have received them with transports and tears ; this time my eyes were dry, my heart was cold. My mother and brother quitted me weeping. The sight of this grief struck me, and I became conscious of the icy insensibility which had been creeping upon me since I inhabited this tomb. Frightened at myself, I wished to leave it, while I had still strength to do so. Then, father, I spoke to you of the choice of a profession ; for sometimes, in waking moments, I seemed to catch from afar the sound of an active and useful life, laborious and free, surrounded by family affections. Oh ! then I felt the want of movement and liberty, of noble and warm emotions—of that life of the soul, which fled before me. I told it you, father, on my knees, bathing your hands with my tears. The life of a workman or a soldier—anything would have suited me. It was then you informed me, that my adopted mother, to whom I owed my life—for she had taken me in, dying of want, and, poor herself, had shared with me the scanty bread of her child—admirable sacrifice for a mother !— that she,' continued Gabriel, hesitating and casting down his eyes, for noble

---

* This rule is so strict in Jesuit Colleges, that if one of three pupils leaves the other two, they separate out of earshot till the first comes back.

natures blush for the guilt of others, and are ashamed of the infamies of which they are themselves victims, 'that she, that my adopted mother, had but one wish, one desire——'

'That of seeing you take orders, my dear son,' replied Father d'Aigrigny; 'for this pious and perfect creature hoped, that, in securing your salvation, she would provide for her own : but she did not venture to inform you of this thought, for fear you might ascribe it to an interested motive.'

'Enough, father !' said Gabriel, interrupting the Abbé d'Aigrigny, with a movement of involuntary indignation ; 'it is painful for me to hear you assert an error. Frances Baudoin never had such a thought.'

'My dear son, you are too hasty in your judgments,' replied Father d'Aigrigny, mildly. 'I tell you, that such was the one, sole thought of your adopted mother.'

'Yesterday, father, she told me all. She and I were equally deceived.'

'Then, my dear son,' said Father d'Aigrigny, sternly, 'you take the word of your adopted mother before mine ?'

'Spare me an answer painful for both of us, father,' said Gabriel, casting down his eyes.

'Will you now tell me,' resumed Father d'Aigrigny, with anxiety, 'what you mean to——'

The reverend father was unable to finish. Samuel entered the room, and said : 'A rather old man wishes to speak to M. Rodin.'

'That is my name, sir,' answered the *socius*, in surprise ; 'I am much obliged to you.' But, before following the Jew, he gave to Father d'Aigrigny a few words written with a pencil upon one of the leaves of his pocket-book.

Rodin went out in very uneasy mood, to learn who could have come to seek him in the Rue Saint-François. Father d'Aigrigny and Gabriel were left alone together.

CHAPTER XX.

THE RUPTURE.

PLUNGED into a state of mortal anxiety, Father d'Aigrigny had taken mechanically the note written by Rodin, and held it in his hand without thinking of opening it. The reverend father asked himself in alarm, what conclusion Gabriel would draw from these recriminations upon the past ; and he durst not make any answer to his reproaches, for fear of irritating the young priest, upon whose head such immense interests now reposed. Gabriel could possess nothing for himself, according to the constitutions of the Society of Jesus. Moreover, the reverend father had obtained from him, in favour of the Order, an express renunciation of all property that might ever come to him. But the commencement of this conversation seemed to announce so serious a change in Gabriel's views with regard to the Company, that he might choose to break through the ties which attached him to it ; and in that case, he would not be legally bound to fulfil any of his engage-ments.* The donation would thus be cancelled *de facto*, just at the moment of being so marvellously realized by the possession of the immense fortune of the Rennepont family, and D'Aigrigny's hopes would thus be completely and for ever frustrated. Of all the perplexities which the reverend father had experienced for some time past, with regard to this inheritance, none

---

* The statutes formally state that the Company can expel all drones and wasps, but that no man can break his ties, if the Order wishes to retain him.

had been more unexpected and terrible than this. Fearing to interrupt or question Gabriel, Father d'Aigrigny waited, in mute terror, the end of this interview, which already bore so threatening an aspect.

The missionary resumed : 'It is my duty, father, to continue this sketch of my past life, until the moment of my departure for America. You will understand, presently, why I have imposed on myself this obligation.'

Father d'Aigrigny nodded for him to proceed.

'Once informed of the pretended wishes of my adopted mother, I resigned myself to them, though at some cost of feeling. I left the gloomy abode, in which I had passed my childhood and part of my youth, to enter one of the seminaries of the Company. My resolution was not caused by an irresistible religious vocation, but by a wish to discharge the sacred debt I owed my adopted mother. Yet the true spirit of the religion of Christ is so vivifying, that I felt myself animated and warmed by the idea of carrying out the adorable precepts of our Blessed Saviour. To my imagination, a seminary, instead of resembling the college where I had lived in painful restraint, appeared like a holy place, where all that was pure and warm in the fraternity of the Gospel would be applied to common life—where, for example, the lessons most frequently taught would be the ardent love of humanity, and the ineffable sweets of commiseration and tolerance—where the everlasting words of Christ would be interpreted in their broadest sense—and where, in fine, by the habitual exercise and expansion of the most generous sentiments, men were prepared for the magnificent apostolic mission of making the rich and happy sympathise with the sufferings of their brethren, by unveiling the frightful miseries of humanity—a sublime and sacred morality, which none are able to withstand, when it is preached with eyes full of tears, and hearts overflowing with tenderness and charity !'

As he delivered these last words with profound emotion, Gabriel's eyes became moist, and his countenance shone with angelic beauty.

'Such is, indeed, my dear son, the spirit of Christianity ; but one must also study and explain the letter,' answered Father d'Aigrigny, coldly. 'It is to this study that the seminaries of our Company are specially destined. Now the interpretation of the letter is a work of analysis, discipline, and submission—and not one of heart and sentiment.'

'I perceived that only too well, father. On entering this new house, I found, alas ! all my hopes defeated. Dilating for a moment, my heart soon sunk within me. Instead of this centre of life, affection, youth, of which I had dreamed, I found, in the silent and ice-cold seminary, the same suppression of every generous emotion, the same inexorable discipline, the same system of mutual prying, the same suspicion, the same invincible obstacles to all ties of friendship. The ardour which had warmed my soul for an instant soon died out ; little by little, I fell back into the habits of a stagnant, passive, mechanical life, governed by a pitiless power with mechanical precision, just like the inanimate works of a watch.'

'But order, submission, and regularity are the first foundations of our Company, my dear son.'

'Alas, father ! it was death, not life, that I found thus organized. In the midst of this destruction of every generous principle, I devoted myself to scholastic and theological studies—gloomy studies—a wily, menacing, and hostile science which, always awake to ideas of peril, contest, and war, is opposed to all those of peace, progress, and liberty.'

'Theology, my dear son,' said Father d'Aigrigny, sternly, 'is at once a buckler and a sword ; a buckler, to protect and cover the Catholic faith—a sword, to attack and combat heresy.'

'And yet, father, Christ and His apostles knew not this subtle science ;

though their simple and touching words regenerated mankind, and set freedom over slavery. Does not the divine code of the Gospel suffice to teach men to love one another? But, alas! far from speaking to us this language, our attention was too often occupied with wars of religion, the rivers of blood that had flowed in honour of the Lord, and for the destruction of heresy. These terrible lessons made our life still more melancholy. As we grew near to manhood, our relations at the seminary assumed a growing character of bitterness, jealousy, and suspicion. The habit of tale-bearing against each other, applied to more serious subjects, engendered silent hate and profound resentments. I was neither better nor worse than the others. All of us, bowed down for years beneath the iron yoke of passive obedience, unaccustomed to reflection or free-will, humble and trembling before our superiors, had the same pale, dull, colourless disposition. At last I took orders; once a priest, you invited me, father, to enter the Company of Jesus, or rather I found myself insensibly brought to this determination. How, I do not know. For a long time before, my will was not my own. I went through all my proofs; the most terrible was decisive; for some months, I lived in the silence of my cell, practising with resignation the strange and mechanical exercises that you ordered me. With the exception of your reverence, nobody approached me during that long space of time; no human voice but yours sounded in my ear. Sometimes, in the night, I felt vague terrors; my mind, weakened by fasting, austerity, and solitude, was impressed with frightful visions. At other times, on the contrary, I felt a sort of quiescence, in the idea that, having once pronounced my vows, I should be delivered for ever from the burden of thought and will. Then I abandoned myself to an insurmountable torpor, like those unfortunate wretches, who, surprised by a snow-storm, yield to a suicidal repose. Thus I awaited the fatal moment. At last, according to the rule of discipline, *choking with the death rattle,*[*] I hastened the moment of accomplishing the final act of my expiring will—the vow to renounce it for ever.'

'Remember, my dear son,' replied Father d'Aigrigny, pale and tortured by increasing anguish, 'remember, that, on the eve of the day fixed for the completion of your vows, I offered, according to the rule of our Company, to absolve you from joining us—leaving you completely free, for we accept none but voluntary vocations.'

'It is true, father,' answered Gabriel, with sorrowful bitterness; 'when, worn out and broken by three months of solitude and trial, I was completely exhausted, and unable to move a step, you opened the door of my cell, and said to me : "If you like, rise and walk; you are free !" Alas ! I had no more strength. The only desire of my soul, inert and paralyzed for so long a period, was the repose of the grave; and, pronouncing those irrevocable vows, I fell, like a corpse, into your hands.'

'And, till now, my dear son, you have never failed in this corpse-like obedience,—to use the expression of our glorious founder—because, the more absolute this obedience, the more meritorious it must be.'

After a moment's silence, Gabriel resumed : 'You had always concealed from me, father, the true ends of the Society into which I entered. I was asked to abandon my free-will to my superiors, in the name of the Greater Glory of God. My vows once pronounced, I was to be in your hands a docile and obedient instrument ; but I was to be employed, you told me, in a holy, great, and beauteous work. I believed you, father—how should I not have believed you ?—but a fatal event changed my destiny—a painful malady caused by——'

---

[*] This is their own command. The constitution expressly bids the novice wait for this decisive climax of the ordeal before taking the vows.

'My son,' cried Father d'Aigrigny, interrupting Gabriel, 'it is useless to recall these circumstances.'

'Pardon me, father, I must recall them. I have the right to be heard. I cannot pass over in silence any of the facts, which have led me to take the immutable resolution that I am about to announce to you.'

'Speak on, my son,' said Father d'Aigrigny, frowning ; for he was much alarmed at the words of the young priest, whose cheeks, until now pale, were covered with a deep blush.

'Six months before my departure for America,' resumed Gabriel, casting down his eyes, 'you informed me, that I was destined to confess penitents ; and, to prepare me for that sacred ministry, you gave me a book.'

Gabriel again hesitated. His blushes increased. Father d'Aigrigny could scarcely restrain a start of impatience and anger.

'You gave me a book,' resumed the young priest, with a great effort to control himself, ' a book containing questions to be addressed by a confessor to youths, and young ,girls, and married women, when they present themselves at the tribunal of penance. My God !' added Gabriel, shuddering at the remembrance. ' I shall never forget that awful moment. It was night. I had retired to my chamber, taking with me this book, composed, you told me, by one of our fathers, and completed by a holy bishop.* Full of respect, faith, and confidence, I opened those pages. At first, I did not understand them—afterwards I understood—and then I was seized with shame and horror—struck with stupor—and had hardly strength to close, with trembling hand, this abominable volume. I ran to you, father, to accuse myself of having involuntarily cast my eyes on those nameless pages, which, by mistake, you had placed in my hands.'

'Remember, also, my dear son,' said Father d'Aigrigny, gravely, ' that I calmed your scruples, and told you that a priest, who is bound to hear everything under the seal of confession, must be able to know and appreciate everything ; and that our Company imposes the task of reading this Compendium, as a classical work, upon young deacons, seminarists, and priests, who are destined to be confessors.'

'I believed you, father. In me the habit of inert obedience was so powerful, and I was so unaccustomed to independent reflection, that, notwithstanding my horror (with which I now reproached myself as with a crime), I took the volume back into my chamber, and read. Oh, father ! what a dreadful revelation of criminal fancies, guilty of guiltiest in their refinement !'

      ✧   ✧   ✧   ✧   ✧   ✧

'You speak of this book in blameable terms,' said Father d'Aigrigny, severely ; 'you were the victim of a too lively imagination. It is to it that you must attribute this fatal impression, and not to an excellent work, irreproachable for its special purpose, and duly authorized by the Church. You are not able to judge of such a production.'

      ✧   ✧   ✧   ✧   ✧   ✧

'I will speak of it no more, father,' said Gabriel ; and he thus resumed : 'A long illness followed that terrible night. Many times, they feared for my reason. When I recovered, the past appeared to me like a painful dream. You told me then, father, that I was not yet ripe for certain functions ; and it was then that I earnestly entreated you to be allowed to go on the American missions. After having long refused my prayer, you at length consented. From my childhood, I had always lived in the college

---

* It is impossible, even in Latin, to give· our readers an idea of this infamous work.

or seminary, in a state of continual restraint and subjection. By constantly holding down my head and eyes, I had lost the habit of contemplating the heavens and the splendours of nature. But, oh! what deep, religious happiness I felt, when I found myself suddenly transported to the centre of the imposing grandeur of the seas—half-way between the ocean and the sky!—I seemed to come forth from a place of thick darkness; for the first time, for many years, I felt my heart beat freely in my bosom; for the first time, I felt myself master of my own thoughts, and ventured to examine my past life, as from the summit of a mountain, one looks down into a gloomy vale. Then strange doubts rose within me. I asked myself, by what right, and for what end, any beings had so long repressed, almost annihilated, the exercise of my will, of my liberty, of my reason, since God had endowed me with these gifts. But I said to myself, that perhaps, one day, the great, beauteous, and holy work, in which I was to have my share, would be revealed to me, and would recompense my obedience and resignation.'

At this moment, Rodin re-entered the room. Father d'Aigrigny questioned him with a significant look. The *socius* approached, and said to him in a low voice, so that Gabriel could not hear: 'Nothing serious. It was only to inform me, that Marshal Simon's father is arrived at M. Hardy's factory.'

Then, glancing at Gabriel, Rodin appeared to interrogate Father d'Aigrigny, who hung his head with a desponding air. Yet he resumed, again addressing Gabriel, whilst Rodin took his old place, with his elbow on the chimney-piece: 'Go on, my dear son. I am anxious to learn what resolution you have adopted.'

'I will tell you in a moment, father. I arrived at Charleston. The superior of our establishment in that place, to whom I imparted my doubts as to the objects of our Society, took upon himself to clear them up, and unveiled it all to me with alarming frankness. He told me the tendency—not perhaps of all the members of the Company, for a great number must have shared my ignorance—but the objects which our leaders have pertinaciously kept in view, ever since the foundation of the Order. I was terrified. I read the casuists. Oh, father! that was a new and dreadful revelation, when, at every page, I read the excuse and justification of robbery, slander, adultery, perjury, murder, regicide. When I considered that I, the priest of a God of charity, justice, pardon, and love, was to belong henceforth to a Company, whose chiefs professed and gloried in such doctrines, I made a solemn oath to break for ever the ties which bound me to it!'*

On these words of Gabriel, Father d'Aigrigny and Rodin exchanged a look of terror. All was lost; their prey had escaped them. Deeply moved by the remembrances he recalled, Gabriel did not perceive the action of the reverend father and the socius, and thus continued: 'In spite of my resolution, father, to quit the Company, the discovery I had made was very painful to me. Oh! believe me, for the honest and loving soul, nothing is more frightful than to have to renounce what it has long respected!—I suffered so much, that, when I thought of the dangers of my mission, I hoped, with a secret joy, that God would perhaps take me to Himself under these circumstances; but, on the contrary, He watched over me with providential solicitude.'

As he said this, Gabriel felt a thrill, for he remembered a Mysterious

---

* This is true. See the extracts from the Compendium for the use of Schools, published under the title of 'Discoveries by a Bibliophilist,' Strasburg, 1843. For regicide, see Sanchez and others.

Woman, who had saved his life in America. After a moment's silence, he resumed : ' My mission terminated, I returned hither to beg, father, that you would release me from my vows. Many times, but in vain, I solicited an interview. Yesterday, it pleased Providence that I should have a long conversation with my adopted mother ; from her I learned the trick by which my vocation had been forced upon me—and the sacrilegious abuse of the confessional, by which she had been induced to entrust to other persons the orphans that a dying mother had confided to the care of an honest soldier. You understand, father, that, if even I had before hesitated to break these bonds, what I have heard yesterday must have rendered my decision irrevocable. But at this solemn moment, father, I am bound to tell you, that I do not accuse the whole Society ; many simple, credulous, and confiding men, like myself, must no doubt form part of it. Docile instruments, they see not in their blindness the work to which they are destined. I pity them, and pray God to enlighten them, as He has enlightened me.'

' So, my son,' said Father d'Aigrigny, rising with livid and despairing look, ' you come to ask of me to break the ties which attach you to the Society ?'

' Yes, father ; you received my vows—it is for you to release me from them.'

' So, my son, you understand that engagements once freely taken by you, are now to be considered as null and void ?'

' Yes, father.'

' So, my son, there is to be henceforth nothing in common between you and our Company?'

' No, father—since I request you to absolve me of my vows.'

' But, you know, my son, that the Society may release you—but that you cannot release yourself.'

' The step I take proves to you, father, the importance I attach to an oath, since I come to you to release me from it. Nevertheless, were you to refuse me, I should not think myself bound in the eyes of God or man.'

' It is perfectly clear,' said Father d'Aigrigny to Rodin, his voice expiring upon his lips, so deep was his despair.

Suddenly, whilst Gabriel, with downcast eyes, waited for the answer of Father d'Aigrigny, who remained mute and motionless, Rodin appeared struck with a new idea, on perceiving that the reverend father still held in his hand the note written in pencil. The socius hastily approached Father d'Aigrigny, and said to him in a whisper, with a look of doubt and alarm : ' Have you not read my note ?'

' I did not think of it,' answered the reverend father, mechanically.

Rodin appeared to make a great effort to repress a movement of violent rage. Then he said to Father d'Aigrigny, in a calm voice : ' Read it now.'

Hardly had the reverend father cast his eyes upon this note, than a sudden ray of hope illumined his hitherto despairing countenance. Pressing the hand of the socius with an expression of deep gratitude, he said to him in a low voice : ' You are right. Gabriel is ours.'

CHAPTER XXI.

THE CHANGE.

BEFORE again addressing Gabriel, Father d'Aigrigny carefully reflected ; and his countenance, lately so disturbed, became, gradually, once more serene. He appeared to meditate and calculate the effects of the eloquence he was about to employ, upon an excellent and safe theme, which the socius, struck with the danger of the situation, had suggested in a few lines rapidly written with a pencil, and which, in his despair, the reverend father had at first neglected. Rodin resumed his post of observation near the mantelpiece, on which he leaned his elbow, after casting at Father d'Aigrigny a glance of disdainful and angry superiority, accompanied by a significant shrug of the shoulders.

After this involuntary manifestation, which was luckily not perceived by Father d'Aigrigny, the cadaverous face of the socius resumed its icy calmness, and his flabby eyelids, raised a moment with anger and impatience, fell, and half-veiled his little, dull eyes. It must be confessed that Father d'Aigrigny, notwithstanding the ease and elegance of his speech, notwithstanding the seduction of his exquisite manners, his agreeable features, and the exterior of an accomplished and refined man of the world, was often subdued and governed by the unpitying firmness, the diabolical craft and depth of Rodin, the old, repulsive, dirty, miserably dressed man, who seldom abandoned his humble part of secretary and mute auditor. The influence of education is so powerful, that Gabriel, notwithstanding the formal rupture he had just provoked, felt himself still intimidated in presence of Father d'Aigrigny, and waited with painful anxiety for the answer of the reverend father to his express demand to be released from his old vows. His reverence having, doubtless, regularly laid his plan of attack, at length broke silence, heaved a deep sigh, gave to his countenance, lately so severe and irritated, a touching expression of kindness, and said to Gabriel, in an affectionate voice, 'Forgive me, my dear son, for having kept silence so long ; but your abrupt determination has so stunned me, and has raised within me so many painful thoughts, that I have had to reflect for some moments, to try and penetrate the cause of this rupture, and I think I have succeeded. You have well considered, my dear son, the serious nature of the step you are taking ?'

'Yes, father.'

'And you have absolutely decided to abandon the Society, even against my will ?'

'It would be painful to me, father—but I must resign myself to it.'

'It should be very painful to you, indeed, my dear son ; for you took the irrevocable vow freely, and this vow, according to our statutes, binds you not to quit the Society, unless with the consent of your superiors.'

'I did not then know, father, the nature of the engagement I took. More enlightened now, I ask to withdraw myself ; my only desire is to obtain a curacy in some village far from Paris. I feel an irresistible vocation for such humble and useful functions. In the country, there is so much misery. and such ignorance of all that could contribute to ameliorate the condition of the agricultural labourer, that his existence is as unhappy as that of a negro slave ; for what liberty has he ? and what instruction ? Oh ! it seems to me, that, with God's help, I might, as a village curate, render some services to humanity. It would therefore be painful to me, father, to see you refuse——'

'Be satisfied, my son,' answered Father d'Aigrigny ; 'I will no longer seek to combat your desire to separate yourself from us.'

'Then, father, you release me from my vows ?'

'I have not the power to do so, my dear son ; but I will write immediately to Rome, to ask the necessary authority from our general.'

'I thank you, father.'

'Soon, my dear son, you will be delivered from these bonds, which you deem so heavy ; and the men you abandon will not the less continue to pray for you, that God may preserve you from still greater wanderings. You think yourself released with regard to us, my dear son ; but we do not think ourselves released with regard to you. It is not thus that we can get rid of the habit of paternal attachment. What would you have? We look upon ourselves as bound to our children, by the very benefits with which we have loaded them. You were poor, and an orphan ; we stretched out our arms to you, as much from the interest which you deserved, my dear son, as to spare your excellent adopted mother too great a burden.'

' Father,' said Gabriel, with suppressed emotion, ' I am not ungrateful.'

' I wish to believe so, my dear son. For long years, we gave to you, as to our beloved child, food for the body and the soul. It pleases you now to renounce and abandon us. Not only do we consent to it—but now that I have penetrated the true motives of your rupture with us, it is my duty to release you from your vow.'

' Of what motives do you speak, father ?'

'Alas ! my dear son, I understand your fears. Dangers menace us—you know it well.'

'Dangers, father ?' cried Gabriel.

' It is impossible, my dear son, that you should not be aware that, since the fall of our legitimate sovereigns, our natural protectors, revolutionary impiety becomes daily more and more threatening. We are oppressed with persecutions. I can, therefore, comprehend and appreciate, my dear son, the motive which, under such circumstances, induces you to separate from us.'

'Father !' cried Gabriel, with as much indignation as grief, ' you do not think that of me—you cannot think it.'

Without noticing the protestation of Gabriel, Father d'Aigrigny continued his imaginary picture of the dangers of the Company, which, far from being really in peril, was already beginning secretly to recover its influence.

' Oh ! if our Company were now as powerful as it was some years ago,' resumed the reverend father ; ' if it were still surrounded by the respect and homage which are due to it from all true believers—in spite of the abominable calumnies with which we are assailed—then, my dear son, we should perhaps have hesitated to release you from your vows, and have rather endeavoured to open your eyes to the light, and save you from the fatal delusion to which you are a prey. But now that we are weak, oppressed, threatened on every side, it is our duty, it is an act of charity, not to force you to share in perils from which you have the prudence to wish to withdraw yourself.'

So saying, Father d'Aigrigny cast a rapid glance at his socius, who answered with a nod of approbation, accompanied by a movement of impatience that seemed to say : ' Go on ! go on !'

Gabriel was quite overcome. There was not in the whole world a heart more generous, loyal, and brave than his. We may judge of what he must have suffered, on hearing the resolution he had come to thus misinterpreted.

'Father,' he resumed, in an agitated voice, whilst his eyes filled with tears, ' your words are cruel and unjust. You know that I am not a coward.'

' No,' said Rodin, in his sharp, cutting voice, addressing Father d'Aigrigny, and pointing to Gabriel with a disdainful look ; ' your dear son is only prudent.'

These words from Rodin made Gabriel start ; a slight blush coloured his pale cheeks ; his large and blue eyes sparkled with a generous anger ; then, faithful to the precepts of Christian humility and resignation, he conquered this irritable impulse, hung down his head, and, too much agitated to reply, remained silent, and brushed away an unseen tear. This tear did not escape the notice of the socius. He saw in it no doubt a favourable symptom, for he exchanged a glance of satisfaction with Father d'Aigrigny. The latter was about to touch on a question of great interest, so, notwithstanding his self-command, his voice trembled slightly ; but encouraged, or rather pushed on by a look from Rodin, who had become extremely attentive, he said to Gabriel : 'Another motive obliges us not to hesitate in releasing you from your vow, my dear son. It is a question of pure delicacy. You probably learned yesterday from your adopted mother, that you will perhaps be called upon to take possession of an inheritance, of which the value is unknown.'

Gabriel raised his head hastily, and said to Father d'Aigrigny : 'As I have already stated to M. Rodin, my adopted mother only talked of her scruples of conscience, and I was completely ignorant of the existence of the inheritance of which you speak.'

The expression of indifference with which the young priest pronounced these last words, was remarked by Rodin.

'Be it so,' replied Father d'Aigrigny. ' You were not aware of it—I be· lieve you—though all appearances would tend to prove the contrary—to prove, indeed, that the knowledge of this inheritance was not unconnected with your resolution to separate from us.'

' I do not understand you, father.'

' It is very simple. Your rupture with us would then have two motives. First, we are in danger, and you think it prudent to leave us——'

' Father ! ——'

'Allow me to finish, my dear son, and come to the second motive. If I am deceived, you can tell me so. These are the facts : Formerly, on the hypothesis that your family, of which you knew nothing, might one day leave you some property, you made, in return for the care bestowed on you by the Company, a free gift of all you might hereafter possess, not to us—but to the poor, of whom we are the born shepherds.'

' Well, father ?' asked Gabriel, not seeing to what this preamble tended.

' Well, my dear son—now that you are sure of enjoying a competence, you wish, no doubt, by separating from us, to annul this donation made under other circumstances.'

' To speak plainly, you violate your oath, because we are persecuted, and because you wish to take back your gifts,' added Rodin, in a sharp voice, as if to describe in the clearest and plainest manner the situation of Gabriel with regard to the Society.

At this infamous accusation, Gabriel could only raise his hands and eyes to heaven, and exclaim, with an expression of despair, ' Oh, heaven !'

Once more exchanging a look of intelligence with Rodin, Father d'Aigrigny said to him, in a severe tone, as if reproaching him for his too savage frank· ness : ' I think you go too far. Our dear son could only have acted in the base and cowardly manner you suggest, had he known his position as an heir ; but, since he affirms the contrary, we are bound to believe him—in spite of appearances.'

' Father,' said Gabriel, pale, agitated, trembling, and with half-suppressed grief and indignation, ' I thank you, at least, for having suspended your judgment. No, I am not a coward ; for heaven is my witness, that I knew of no danger to which the Society was exposed. Nor am I base and avaricious ; for heaven is also my witness, that only at this moment I learn from you, father, that I may be destined to inherit property, and——'

' One word, my dear son. It is quite lately that I became informed of this circumstance, by the greatest chance in the world,' said Father d'Aigrigny, interrupting Gabriel ; 'and that was thanks to some family papers which your adopted mother had given to her confessor, and which were entrusted to us when you entered our college. A little before your return from America, in arranging the archives of the Company, your file of papers fell into the hands of our father-attorney. It was examined, and we thus learned that one of your paternal ancestors, to whom the house in which we now are belonged, left a will which is to be opened to-day at noon. Yesterday, we believed you one of us ; our statutes command that we should possess nothing of our own ; you had corroborated those statutes, by a donation in favour of the patrimony of the poor—which we administer. It was no longer you, therefore, but the Company, which, in my person, presented itself as the inheritor in your place, furnished with your titles, which I have here ready in order. But now, my dear son, that you separate from us, you must present yourself in your own name. We came here as the representatives of the poor, to whom in former days you piously abandoned whatever goods might fall to your share. Now, on the contrary, the hope of a fortune changes your sentiments. You are free to resume your gifts.'

Gabriel had listened to Father d'Aigrigny with painful impatience. At length he exclaimed : 'Do you mean to say, father, that you think me capable of cancelling a donation freely made, in favour of the Company, to which I am indebted for my education ? You believe me infamous enough to break my word, in the hope of possessing a modest patrimony ?'

'This patrimony, my dear son, may be small ; but it may also be considerable.'

'Well, father ! if it were a king's fortune,' cried Gabriel, with proud and noble indifference, 'I should not speak otherwise—and I have, I think, the right to be believed. Listen to my fixed resolution. The Company to which I belong runs, you say, great dangers. I will inquire into these dangers. Should they prove threatening—strong in the determination which morally separates me from you—I will not leave you till I see the end of your perils. As for the inheritance, of which you believe me so desirous, I resign it to you formally, father, as I once freely promised. My only wish is, that this property may be employed for the relief of the poor. I do not know what may be the amount of this fortune, but large or small, it belongs to the Company, because I have thereto pledged my word. I have told you, father, that my chief desire is to obtain a humble curacy in some poor village—poor, above all—because there my services will be most useful. Thus, father, when a man, who never spoke falsehood in his life, affirms to you, that he only sighs for so humble an existence, you ought, I think, to believe him incapable of snatching back, from motives of avarice, gifts already made.'

Father d'Aigrigny had now as much trouble to restrain his joy, as he before had to conceal his terror. He appeared, however, tolerably calm, and said to Gabriel : 'I did not expect less from you, my dear son.'

Then he made a sign to Rodin, to invite him to interpose. The latter perfectly understood his superior. He left the chimney, drew near to Gabriel, and leaned against the table, upon which stood paper and inkstand. Then, beginning mechanically to beat the tattoo with the tips of his coarse fingers, in all their array of flat and dirty nails, he said to Father d'Aigrigny : 'All this is very fine ! but your dear son gives you no security for the fulfilment of his promise—except an oath—and that, we know, is of little value.'

'Sir !' cried Gabriel.

'Allow me,' said Rodin, coldly. 'The law does not acknowledge our existence, and therefore can take no cognizance of donations made in favour of the Company. You might resume to-morrow what you are pleased to give us to-day.'

'But my oath, sir !' cried Gabriel.

Rodin looked at him fixedly, as he answered : 'Your oath ? Did you not swear eternal obedience to the Company, and never to separate from us ? —and of what weight now are these oaths ?'

For a moment Gabriel was embarrassed ; but, feeling how false was this logic, he rose, calm and dignified, went to seat himself at the desk, took up a pen, and wrote as follows :

'Before God, who sees and hears me, and in presence of you, Father d'Aigrigny and M. Rodin. I renew and confirm, freely and voluntarily, the absolute donation made by me to the Society of Jesus, in the person of the said Father d'Aigrigny, of all the property which may hereafter belong to me, whatever may be its value. I swear, on pain of infamy, to perform this irrevocable promise, whose accomplishment I regard, in my soul and conscience, as the discharge of a debt, and the fulfilment of a pious duty.

'This donation having for its object the acknowledgment of past services, and the relief of the poor, no future occurrences can at all modify it. For the very reason that I know I could one day legally cancel the present free and deliberate act, I declare, that if ever I were to attempt such a thing, under any possible circumstances, I should deserve the contempt and horror of all honest people.

'In witness whereof I have written this paper, on the 13th of February, 1832, in Paris, immediately before the opening of the testament of one of my paternal ancestors.

'GABRIEL DE RENNEPONT.'

As he rose, the young priest delivered this document to Rodin, without uttering a word. The socius read it attentively, and, still impassible, answered, as he looked at Gabriel : ' Well, it is a written oath—that is all.'

Gabriel dwelt stupefied at the audacity of Rodin, who ventured to tell him, that this document, in which he renewed his donation in so noble, generous, and spontaneous a manner, was not all sufficient. The socius was the first again to break the silence, and he said to Father d'Aigrigny, with his usual cool impudence : ' One of two things must be. Either your dear son means to render this donation absolutely valuable and irrevocable,— or——'

'Sir,' exclaimed Gabriel, interrupting him, and hardly able to restrain himself, ' spare yourself and me such a shameful supposition.'

'Well, then,' resumed Rodin, impassible as ever, ' as you are perfectly decided to make this donation a serious reality, what objection can you have to secure it legally ?'

'None, sir,' said Gabriel bitterly, ' since my written and sworn promise will not suffice you.'

'My dear son,' said Father d'Aigrigny, affectionately, 'if this were a donation for my own advantage, believe me I should require no better security than your word. But here I am, as it were, the agent of the Society, or rather the trustee of the poor, who will profit by your generosity. For the sake of humanity, therefore, we cannot secure this gift by too many legal precautions, so that the unfortunate objects of our care may have certainty instead of vague hopes to depend upon. God may call you to him at any moment, and who shall say that your heirs will be so ready to keep the oath you have taken ?'

'You are right, father,' said Gabriel, sadly ; 'I had not thought of the case of death, which is yet so probable.'

Hereupon, Samuel opened the door of the room, and said : 'Gentlemen.

the notary has just arrived. Shall I show him in? At ten o'clock precisely, the door of the house will be opened.'

'We are the more glad to see the notary,' said Rodin, 'as we just happen to have some business with him. Pray ask him to walk in.'

'I will bring him to you instantly,' replied Samuel, as he went out.

'Here is a notary,' said Rodin to Gabriel. 'If you have still the same intentions, you can legalise your donation in presence of this public officer, and thus save yourself from a great burden for the future.'

'Sir,' said Gabriel, 'happen what may, I am 'as irrevocably engaged by this written promise, which I beg you to keep, father'—and he handed the paper to Father d'Aigrigny—'as by the legal document, which I am about to sign,' he added, turning to Rodin.

'Silence, my dear son,' said Father d'Aigrigny ; 'here is the notary,' just as the latter entered the room.

During the interview of the administrative officer with Rodin, Gabriel, and Father d'Aigrigny, we shall conduct the reader to the interior of the walled-up house.

CHAPTER XXII.

THE RED ROOM.

As Samuel had said, the door of the walled-up house had just been disencumbered of the bricks, lead, and iron, which had kept it from view, and its panels of carved oak appeared as fresh and sound, as on the day when they had first been withdrawn from the influence of the air and time. The labourers, having completed their work, stood waiting upon the steps, as impatient and curious as the notary's clerk, who had superintended the operation, when they saw Samuel slowly advancing across the garden, with a great bunch of keys in his hand.

'Now, my friends,' said the old man, when he had reached the steps, 'your work is finished. The master of this gentleman will pay you, and I have only to show you out by the street-door.'

'Come, come, my good fellow,' cried the clerk, 'you don't think. We are just at the most interesting and curious moment ; I and these honest masons are burning to see the interior of this mysterious house, and you would be cruel enough to send us away? Impossible !'

'I regret the necessity, sir, but so it must be. I must be the first to enter this dwelling, absolutely alone, before introducing the heirs, in order to read the testament.'

'And who gave you such ridiculous and barbarous orders?' cried the clerk, singularly disappointed.

'My father, sir.'

'A most respectable authority, no doubt ; but come, my worthy guardian, my excellent guardian,' resumed the clerk, 'be a good fellow, and let us just take a peep in at the door.'

'Yes, yes, sir, only a peep !' cried the heroes of the trowel, with a supplicating air.

'It is disagreeable to have to refuse you, gentlemen,' answered Samuel ; 'but I cannot open this door, until I am alone.'

The masons, seeing the inflexibility of the old man, unwillingly descended the steps ; but the clerk had resolved to dispute the ground inch by inch, and exclaimed : 'I shall wait for my master. I do not leave the house without him. He may want me—and whether I remain on these steps or elsewhere, can be of little consequence to you, my worthy keeper.'

The clerk was interrupted in his appeal by his master himself, who called out, from the further side of the court-yard, with an air of business : 'M. Piston ! quick, M. Piston—come directly !'

'What the devil does he want with me ?' cried the clerk, in a passion. ' He calls me just at the moment when I might have seen something.'

' M. Piston,' resumed the voice, approaching, ' do you not hear ?'

While Samuel let out the masons, the clerk saw, through a clump of trees, his master running towards him bareheaded, and with an air of singular haste and importance. The clerk was therefore obliged to leave the steps, to answer the notary's summons, towards whom he went with a very bad grace.

'Sir, sir,' said M. Dumesnil, 'I have been calling you this hour, with all my might.'

' I did not hear you, sir,' said M. Piston.

'You must be deaf, then. Have you any change about you ?'

'Yes, sir,' answered the clerk, with some surprise.

'Well, then, you must go instantly to the nearest stamp-office, and fetch me three or four large sheets of stamped paper, to draw up a deed. Run ! it is wanted directly.'

'Yes, sir,' said the clerk, casting a rueful and regretful glance at the door of the walled-up house.

'But make haste, will you, M. Piston,' said the notary.

' I do not know, sir, where to get any stamped paper.'

' Here is the guardian,' replied M. Dumesnil. 'He will no doubt be able to tell you.'

At this instant, Samuel was returning, after showing the masons out by the street-door.

' Sir,' said the notary to him, ' will you please to tell me where we can get stamped paper ?'

'Close by, sir,' answered Samuel ; 'in the tobacconist's, No. 17, Rue Vieille-du-Temple.'

'You hear, M. Piston ?' said the notary to his clerk. ' You can get the stamps at the tobacconist's, No. 17, Rue Vieille-du-Temple. Be quick ! for this deed must be executed immediately, before the opening of the will. Time presses.'

'Very well, sir ; I will make haste,' answered the clerk, discontentedly, as he followed his master, who hurried back into the room where he had left Rodin, Gabriel, and Father d'Aigrigny.

During this time, Samuel, ascending the steps, had reached the door, now disencumbered of the stone, iron, and lead, with which it had been blocked up. It was with deep emotion that the old man, having selected from his bunch of keys the one he wanted, inserted it in the key-hole, and made the door turn upon its hinges. Immediately he felt on his face a current of damp, cold air, like that which exhales from a cellar suddenly opened. Having carefully reclosed and double-locked the door, the Jew advanced along the hall, lighted by a glass trefoil over the arch of the door. The panes had lost their transparency by the effect of time, and now had the appearance of ground-glass. This hall, paved with alternate squares of black and white marble, was vast, sonorous, and contained a broad stair-case leading to the first story. The walls of smooth stone offered not the least appearance of decay or dampness ; the stair-rail of wrought iron presented no traces of rust ; it was inserted, just above the bottom step, into a column of grey granite, which sustained a statue of black marble, representing a negro bearing a flambeau. This statue had a strange countenance, the pupils of the eyes being made of white marble.

The Jew's heavy tread echoed beneath the lofty dome of the hall. The grandson of Isaac Samuel experienced a melancholy feeling, as he reflected that the footsteps of his ancestor had probably been the last which had resounded through this dwelling, of which he had closed the doors a hundred and fifty years before ; for the faithful friend, in favour of whom M. de Rennepont had made a feigned transfer of the property, had afterwards parted with the same, to place it in the name of Samuel's grandfather, who had transmitted it to his descendants, as if it had been his own inheritance.

To these thoughts, in which Samuel was wholly absorbed, was joined the remembrance of the light seen that morning through the seven openings in the leaden cover of the belvedere ; and, in spite of the firmness of his character, the old man could not repress a shudder, as, taking a second key from his bunch, and reading upon the label : The Key of the Red Room, he opened a pair of large folding doors, leading to the inner apartments. The window which, of all those in the house, had alone been opened, lighted this large room, hung with damask, the deep purple of which had undergone no alteration. A thick Turkey carpet covered the floor, and large arm-chairs of gilded wood, in the severe Louis XIV. style, were symmetrically arranged along the wall. A second door, leading to the next room, was just opposite the entrance. The wainscoting and the cornice were white, relieved with fillets and mouldings of burnished gold. On each side of this door was a large piece of buhl-furniture, inlaid with brass and porcelain, supporting ornamental sets of sea-crackle vases. The window was hung with heavy, deep-fringed damask curtains, surmounted by scolloped drapery, with silk tassels, directly opposite the chimney-piece of dark-grey marble, adorned with carved brass-work. Rich chandeliers, and a clock in the same style as the furniture, were reflected in a large Venice glass, with basiled edges. A round table, covered with a cloth of crimson velvet, was placed in the centre of this saloon.

As he approached this table, Samuel perceived a piece of white vellum, on which were inscribed these words : 'My testament is to be opened in this saloon. The other apartments are to remain closed, until after the reading of my last will.—M. DE R.'

'Yes,' said the Jew, as he perused with emotion these lines traced so long ago ; 'this is the same recommendation as that which I received from my father ; for it would seem that the other apartments of this house are filled with objects, on which M. de Rennepont set a high value, not for their intrinsic worth, but because of their origin. The Hall of Mourning must be a strange and mysterious chamber. Well,' added Samuel, as he drew from his pocket a register bound in black shagreen, with a brass lock, from which he drew the key, after placing it upon the table, 'here is the statement of the property in hand, which I have been ordered to bring hither, before the arrival of the heirs.'

The deepest silence reigned in the room, at the moment when Samuel placed the register on the table. Suddenly, a simple and yet most startling occurrence roused him from his reverie. In the next apartment was heard the clear, silvery tone of a clock, striking slowly ten. And the hour was ten ! Samuel had too much sense to believe in perpetual motion, or in the possibility of constructing a clock to go for one hundred and fifty years. He asked himself, therefore, with surprise and alarm, how this clock could still be going, and how it could mark so exactly the hour of the day. Urged with restless curiosity, the old man was about to enter the room ; but, recollecting the recommendation of his father, which had now been confirmed by the few lines he had just read from De Rennepont's pen, he stopped at the door, and listened with extreme attention.

He heard nothing—absolutely nothing, but the last dying vibration of the clock. After having long reflected upon this strange fact, Samuel, comparing it with the no less extraordinary circumstance of the light perceived that morning through the apertures in the belvedere, concluded that there must be some connexion between these two incidents. If the old man could not penetrate the true cause of these extraordinary appearances, he at least explained them to himself, by remembering the subterraneous communications, which, according to tradition, were said to exist between the cellars of this house and distant places ; and he conjectured that unknown and mysterious personages thus gained access to it two or three times in a century. Absorbed in these thoughts, Samuel approached the fireplace, which, as we have said, was directly opposite the window. Just then, a bright ray of sunlight, piercing the clouds, shone full upon two large portraits, hung upon either side of the fireplace, and not before remarked by the Jew. They were painted life-size, and represented one a woman, the other a man. By the sober yet powerful colouring of these paintings, by the large and vigorous style, it was easy to recognise a master's hand. It would have been difficult to find models more fitted to inspire a great painter. The woman appeared to be from five-and-twenty to thirty years of age. Magnificent brown hair, with golden tints, crowned a forehead, white, noble, and lofty. Her head-dress, far from recalling the fashion, which Madame de Sévigné brought in during the age of Louis XIV., reminded one rather of some of the portraits of Paul Veronese, in which the hair encircles the face in broad, undulating bands, surmounted by a thick plait, like a crown, at the back of the head. The eye-brows, finely pencilled, were arched over large eyes of bright, sapphire blue. Their gaze, at once proud and mournful, had something fatal about it. The nose, finely formed, terminated in slight dilated nostrils : a half smile, almost of pain, contracted the mouth ; the face was a long oval, and the complexion, extremely pale, was hardly shaded on the cheek by a light rose-colour. The position of the head and neck announced a rare mixture of grace and dignity. A sort of tunic or robe, of glossy black material, came as high as the commencement of her shoulders, and just marking her lithe and tall figure, reached down to her feet, which were almost entirely concealed by the folds of this garment.

The attitude was full of nobleness and simplicity. The head looked white and luminous, standing out from a dark grey sky, marbled at the horizon by purple clouds, upon which were visible the bluish summits of distant hills, in deep shadow. The arrangement of the picture, as well as the warm tints of the foreground, contrasting strongly with these distant objects, showed that the woman was placed upon an eminence, from which she could view the whole horizon. The countenance was deeply pensive and desponding. There was an expression of supplicating and resigned grief, particularly in her look, half raised to heaven, which one would have thought impossible to picture. On the left side of the fireplace was the other portrait, painted with like vigour. It represented a man, between thirty and thirty-five years of age, of tall stature. A large brown cloak, which hung round him in graceful folds, did not quite conceal a black doublet, buttoned up to the neck, over which fell a square white collar. The handsome and expressive head was marked with stern powerful lines, which did not exclude an admirable air of suffering, resignation, and ineffable goodness. The hair, as well as the beard and eyebrows, was black ; and the latter, by some singular caprice of nature, instead of being separated and forming two distinct arches, extended from one temple to the other, in a single bow, and seemed to mark the forehead of this man with a black line,

The background of this picture also represented a stormy sky ; but, beyond some rocks in the distance, the sea was visible, and appeared to mingle with the dark clouds. The sun, just now shining upon these two remarkable figures (which it appeared impossible to forget, after once seeing them), augmented their brilliancy.

Starting from his reverie, and casting his eyes by chance upon these portraits, Samuel was greatly struck with them. They appeared almost alive. 'What noble and handsome faces !' he exclaimed, as he approached to examine them more closely. 'Whose are these portraits ? They are not those of any of the Rennepont family, for my father told me that they are all in the Hall of Mourning. Alas !' added the old man, 'one might think, from the great sorrow expressed in their countenances, that they ought to have a place in that mourning-chamber.'

After a moment's silence, Samuel resumed : 'Let me prepare everything for this solemn assembly, for it has struck ten.' So saying, he placed the gilded arm-chairs round the table, and then continued, with a pensive air : 'The hour approaches, and of the descendants of my grandfather's benefactor, we have seen only this young priest, with the angelic countenance. Can he be the sole representative of the Rennepont family ? He is a priest, and this family will finish with him ! Well ! the moment is come when I must open this door, that the will may be read. Bathsheba is bringing hither the notary. They knock at the door ; it is time !' And Samuel, after casting a last glance towards the place where the clock had struck ten, hastened to the outer door, behind which voices were now audible.

He turned the key twice in the lock, and threw the portals open. To his great regret, he saw only Gabriel on the steps, between Rodin and Father d'Aigrigny. The notary, and Bathsheba, who had served them as a guide, waited a little behind the principal group.

Samuel could not repress a sigh, as he stood bowing on the threshold, and said to them : 'All is ready, gentlemen. You may walk in.'

CHAPTER XXIII.

THE TESTAMENT.

WHEN Gabriel, Rodin, and Father d'Aigrigny entered the Red Room, they were differently affected. Gabriel, pale and sad, felt a kind of painful impatience. He was anxious to quit this house, though he had already relieved himself of a great weight, by executing before the notary, secured by every legal formality, a deed making over all his rights of inheritance to Father d'Aigrigny. Until now it had not occurred to the young priest, that in bestowing the care upon him, which he was about to reward so generously, and in forcing his vocation by a sacrilegious falsehood, the only object of Father d'Aigrigny might have been to secure the success of a dark intrigue. In acting as he did, Gabriel was not yielding, in his view of the question, to a sentiment of exaggerated delicacy. He had made this donation freely, many years before. He would have looked upon it as infamy now to withdraw it. It was hard enough to be suspected of cowardice : for nothing in the world would he have incurred the least reproach of cupidity.

The missionary must have been endowed with a very rare and excellent nature, or this flower of scrupulous probity would have withered beneath the deleterious and demoralising influence of his education ; but happily, as cold sometimes preserves from corruption, the icy atmosphere in which he had passed a portion of his childhood and youth had benumbed, but not vitiated, his generous qualities, which had indeed soon revived in the warm air of liberty. Father d'Aigrigny, much paler and more agitated than Gabriel, strove to excuse and explain his anxiety by attributing it to the sorrow he experienced at the rupture of his dear son with the Order. Rodin, calm, and perfectly master of himself, saw with secret rage the strong emotion of Father d'Aigrigny, which might have inspired a man less con-fiding than Gabriel with strange suspicions. Yet, notwithstanding his apparent indifference, the socius was perhaps still more ardently impatient than his superior for the success of this important affair. Samuel appeared quite desponding, no other heir but Gabriel having presented himself. No doubt the old man felt a lively sympathy for the young priest ; but then *he* was a priest, and with him would finish the line of Rennepont ; and this immense fortune, accumulated with so much labour, would either be again distributed, or employed otherwise than the testator had desired. The different actors in this scene were standing round the table. As they were about to seat themselves, at the invitation of the notary, Samuel pointed to the register bound in black shagreen, and said : ' I was ordered, sir, to de-posit here this register It is locked. I will deliver up the key, immediately after the reading of the will.'

' This course is, in fact, directed by the note which accompanies the will,' said M. Dumesnil, ' as it was deposited, in the year 1682, in the hands of Master Thomas Le Semelier, king's counsel, and notary of the Chatelet of Paris, then living at No. 13, Place Royale.'

So saying, M. Dumesnil drew from a portfolio of red morocco a large parchment envelope, grown yellow with time ; to this envelope was annexed, by a silken thread, a note also upon vellum.

' Gentlemen,' said the notary, ' if you please to sit down, I will read the subjoined note, to regulate the formalities at the opening of the will.'

The notary, Rodin, Father d'Aigrigny, and Gabriel, took seats. The young priest, having his back turned to the fireplace, could not see the two portraits. In spite of the notary's invitation, Samuel remained standing behind the chair of that functionary, who read as follows :

' " On the 13th February, 1832, my will shall be carried to No. 3, in the Rue Saint-François.

' " At ten o'clock precisely, the door of the Red Room shall be opened to my heirs, who will no doubt have arrived long before at Paris, in anticipation of this day, and will have had time to establish their line of descent.

' " As soon as they are assembled, the will shall be read, and, at the last stroke of noon, the inheritance shall be finally settled in favour of those of my kindred, who, according to my recommendation (preserved, I hope, by tradition in my family, during a century and a half), shall present themselves in person, and not by agents, before twelve o'clock, on the 13th of February, in the Rue Saint-François." '

Having read these words in a sonorous voice, the notary stopped an in-stant, and resumed, in a solemn tone : ' M. Gabriel François Marie de Rennepont, priest, having established, by legal documents, his descent on the father's side, and his relationship to the testator, and being at this hour the only one of the descendants of the Rennepont family here present, I open the testament in his presence, as it has been ordered.'

So saying, the notary drew from its envelope the will, which had been previously opened by the President of the Tribunal, with the formalities re-quired by law. Father d'Aigrigny leaned forward, and resting his elbow on the table, seemed to pant for breath. Gabriel prepared himself to listen with more curiosity than interest. Rodin was seated at some distance from the table, with his old hat between his knees, in the bottom of which, half hidden by the folds of a shabby blue cotton handkerchief, he had placed his watch. The attention of the socius was divided between the least noise from without, and the slow evolution of the hands of the watch, which he followed with his little, wrathful eye, as if hastening their progress, so great was his impatience for the hour of noon.

The notary, unfolding the sheet of parchment, read what follows, in the midst of profound attention :

> ' " Hameau de Villetaneuse,
> ' " February 13th, 1682.

' " I am about to escape, by death, from the disgrace of the galleys, to which the implacable enemies of my family have caused me to be condemned as a relapsed heretic.

' " Moreover, life is too bitter for me since the death of my son, the victim of a mysterious crime.

' " At nineteen years of age—poor Henry !—and his murderers unknown—no, not unknown—if I may trust my presentiments.

' " To preserve my fortune for my son, I had feigned to abjure the Protestant faith. As long as that beloved boy lived, I scrupulously kept up Catholic appearances. The imposture revolted me, but the interest of my son was concerned.

' " When they killed him, this deceit became insupportable to me. I was watched, accused, and condemned as relapsed. My property has been confiscated, and I am sentenced to the galleys.

' " 'Tis a terrible time we live in ! Misery and servitude ! sanguinary despotism and religious intolerance ! Oh, it is sweet to abandon life ! sweet to rest, and see no more such evils and such sorrows !

' " In a few hours, I shall enjoy that rest. I shall die. Let me think of those who will survive—or rather, of those who will live perhaps in better times.

' " Out of all my fortune, there remains to me a sum of fifty thousand crowns, deposited in a friend's hands.

' " I have no longer a son ; but I have numerous relations, exiled in various parts of Europe. This sum of fifty thousand crowns, divided between them, would profit each of them very little. I have disposed of it differently.

' " In this I have followed the wise counsels of a man, whom I venerate as the image of God on earth, for his intelligence, wisdom, and goodness are almost divine.

' " Twice in the course of my life have I seen this man, under very fatal circumstances—twice have I owed him safety, once of the soul, once of the body.

' " Alas ! he might perhaps have saved my poor child, but he came too late—too late !

' " Before he left me, he wished to divert me from the intention of dying—for he knew all. But his voice was powerless. My grief, my regret, my discouragement, were too much for him.

' " It is strange ! when he was convinced of my resolution to finish my days by violence, some words of terrible bitterness escaped him, making me believe that he envied me—my fate—my death !

' " Is he perhaps condemned to live ?

' " Yes ; he has, no doubt, condemned himself to be useful to humanity, and yet life is heavy on him, for I heard him repeat one day, with an expression of despair and weariness that I have never forgotten ; ' Life ! life ! who will deliver me from it ?'

' " Is life then so very burdensome to him ?

'" He is gone. His last words have made me look for my departure with sereni y. Thanks to him, my death shall not be without fruit.

'" Thanks to him, these lines, written at this moment by a man who, in a few hours, will have ceased to live, may perhaps be the parents of great things a century and a half hence—yes ! great and noble things, if my last will is piously followed by my descendants, for it is to them that I here address myself.

'" That they may understand and appreciate this last will—which I commend to the care of the unborn, who dwell in the future whither I am hastening—they must know the persecutors of my family and avenge their ancestor, but by a noble vengeance.

'" My grandfather was a Catholic. Induced by perfidious counsels rather than religious zeal, he attached himself, though a layman, to a Society whose power has always been terrible and mysterious— the Society of Jesus——"

At these words of the testament, Father d'Aigrigny, Rodin, and Gabriel looked involuntarily at each other. The notary, who had not perceived this action, continued to read :

'" After some years, during which he had never ceased to profess the most absolute devotion to this Society, he was suddenly enlightened by fearful revelations as to the secret ends it pursued, and the means it employed.

'" This was in 1610, a month before the assassination of Henry IV.

'" My grandfather, terrified at the secret of which he had become the unwilling depositary, and which was to be fully explained by the death of the best of kings, not only broke with the Society, but, as if Catholicism itself had been answerable for the crimes of its members, he abandoned the Romish religion, in which he had hitherto lived, and became a Protestant.

'" Undeniable proofs, attesting the connivance of two members of the Company with Ravaillac, a connivance also proved in the case of Jean Chatel, the regicide, were in my grandfather's possession.

'" This was the first cause of the violent hatred of the Society for our family. Thank Heaven, these papers have been placed in safety, and if my last will is executed, will be found marked A. M. C. D. G., in the ebony casket in the Hall of Mourning, in the house in the Rue Saint François.

'" My father was also exposed to these secret persecutions. His ruin, and perhaps his death, would have been the consequence, had it not been for the intervention of an angelic woman, towards whom he felt an almost religious veneration.

'" The portrait of this woman, whom I saw a few years ago, as well as that of the man whom I hold in the greatest reverence, were painted by me from memory, and have been placed in the Red Room in the Rue Saint-François—to be gratefully valued, I hope, by the descendants of my family." '

For some moments Gabriel had become more and more attentive to the reading of this testament. He thought within himself by how strange a coincidence one of his ancestors had, two centuries before, broken with the Society of Jesus, as he himself had just done ; and that from this rupture, two centuries old, dated also that species of hatred with which the Society of Jesus had always pursued his family. Nor did the young priest find it less strange that this inheritance, transmitted to him after a lapse of a hundred and fifty years from one of his kindred (the victim of the Society of Jesus), should return by a voluntary act to the coffers of this same society. When the notary read the passage relative to the two portraits, Gabriel, who, like Father d'Aigrigny, sat with his back towards the pictures, turned round to look at them. Hardly had the missionary cast his eyes on the portrait of the woman, than he uttered a loud cry of surprise, and almost terror. The notary paused in his reading, and looked uneasily at the young priest.

CHAPTER XXIV.

THE LAST STROKE OF NOON.

AT the cry uttered by Gabriel, the notary had stopped reading the testament, and Father d'Aigrigny hastily drew near the young priest. The latter rose trembling from his seat, and gazed with increasing stupor at the female portrait.

Then he said in a low voice, as if speaking to himself, ' Good Heaven ! is it possible that nature can produce such resemblances ? Those eyes—so proud and yet so sad—that forehead—that pale complexion—yes, all her features are the same—all of them !'

' My dear son, what is the matter ?' said Father d'Aigrigny, as astonished as Samuel and the notary.

' Eight months ago,' replied the missionary, in a voice of deep emotion, without once taking his eyes from the picture, 'I was in the power of the Indians, in the heart of the Rocky Mountains. They had crucified, and were beginning to scalp me ; I was on the point of death, when Divine Providence sent me unexpected aid—sent me this woman for a deliverer.'

' That woman !' cried Samuel, Father d'Aigrigny, and the notary, all together.

Rodin alone appeared completely indifferent to this episode of the picture. His face contracted with angry impatience, he bit his nails to the quick, as he contemplated with agony the slow progress of the hands of his watch.

' What ! that woman saved your life ?' resumed Father d'Aigrigny.

'Yes, this woman,' replied Gabriel, in a still lower and more trembling voice ; 'this woman—or rather a woman so much resembling her, that if this picture had not been here for a century and a half, I should have felt sure it was the same—nor can I explain to myself that so striking a resemblance could be the effect of chance. Well,' added he, after a moment's silence, as he heaved a profound sigh, ' the mysteries of Nature, and the will of God, are impenetrable.'

Gabriel fell back into his chair, in the midst of a general silence, which was broken by Father d'Aigrigny saying, ' It is a case of extraordinary resemblance ; that is all, my dear son. Only, the natural gratitude which you feel towards your benefactress, makes you take a deep interest in this singular concidence.'

Rodin, bursting with impatience, here said to the notary, by whose side he stood, ' It seems to me, sir, that all this little romance has nothing to do with the testament.'

' You are right,' answered the notary, resuming his seat ; ' but the fact is so extraordinary, and, as you say, romantic, that one cannot help sharing in this gentleman's astonishment.'

He pointed to Gabriel, who, with his elbow resting on the arms of the chair, leaned his forehead upon his hand, apparently quite absorbed in thought. The notary continued the reading of the will, as follows :—

' " Such are the persecutions to which my family has been exposed on the part of the Society of Jesus.

' " The Society possesses at this hour the whole of my confiscated property. I am about to die. May its hatred perish with me, and spare my kindred, whose fate at this solemn moment is my last and only thought.

' " This morning I sent for a man of long-tried probity—Isaac Samuel. He owes his life to me, and every day I congratulate myself on having been able to preserve to the world so honest and excellent a creature.

' " Before the confiscation of my property, Isaac Samuel had long managed it with as much intelligence as uprightness. I have entrusted him with the fifty thousand crowns, returned to me by a faithful friend. Isaac Samuel, and his descendants after him, to whom he will leave this debt of gratitude, will invest the above sum, and allow it to accumulate, until the expiration of the hundred-and-fiftieth year from this time.

' "The amount thus accumulated may become enormous, and constitute a royal fortune, if no unfavourable event should occur. May my descendants attend to my wishes, as to the division and employment of this immense sum !

' "In a century and a half, there happen so many changes, so many varieties of fortunes, such a rise and fall in the condition of the successive generations of a family, that probably, a hundred-and-fifty years hence, my descendants will belong to various classes of society, and thus represent the divers social elements of their time.

' "There may, perhaps, be among them men of great intelligence, great courage, or great virtue—learned men, or names illustrious in arts and arms. There may, perhaps, also be obscure workmen, or humble citizens—perhaps, also, alas ! great criminals.

' " However this may be, my most earnest desire is that my descendants should combine together, and, reconstituting one family, by a close and sincere union, put into practice the divine words of Christ, ' Love ye one another.'

' "This union would have a salutary tendency ; for it seems to me that upon union, upon the association of men together, must depend the future happiness of mankind.

' " The Company, which so long persecuted my family, is one of the most striking examples of the power of association, even when applied to evil.

' " There is something so fruitful and divine in this principle, that it sometimes forces to good the worst and most dangerous combinations.

' " Thus, the missions have thrown a scanty but pure and generous light on the darkness of this Company of Jesus—founded with the detestable and impious aim of destroying, by a homicidal education, all will, thought, liberty, and intelligence, in the people, so as to deliver them, trembling, superstitious, brutal, and helpless, to the despotism of kings, governed in their turn by confessors belonging to the Society."'

At this passage of the will, there was another strange look exchanged between Gabriel and Father d'Aigrigny. The notary continued :—

' " If a perverse association, based upon the degradation of humanity, upon fear and despotism, and followed by the maledictions of the people, has survived for centuries, and often governed the world by craft and terror —how would it be with an association, which, taking fraternity and evangelic love for its means, had for its end to deliver man and woman from all degrading slavery, to invite to the enjoyment of terrestrial happiness those who have hitherto known nothing of life but its sorrows and miseries, and to glorify and enrich the labour that feeds the state?—to enlighten those whom ignorance has depraved ?—to favour the free expansion of all the passions, which God, in His infinite wisdom, and inexhaustible goodness, gave to man as so many powerful levers ?—to sanctify all the gifts of Heaven : love, maternity, strength, intelligence, beauty, genius?—to make men truly religious, and deeply grateful to their Creator, by making them understand the splendours of Nature, and bestowing on them their rightful share in the treasures which have been poured upon us ?

' " Oh ! if it be Heaven's will that, in a century and a half, the descendants of my family, faithful to the last wishes of a heart that loved humanity, meet in this sacred union!—if it be Heaven's will that amongst them be found charitable and passionate souls, full of commiseration for those who suffer, and lofty minds, ardent for liberty! warm and eloquent natures! resolute characters! women, who unite beauty and wit with goodness—oh! then, how fruitful, how powerful will be the harmonious union of all these ideas, and influences, and forces—of all these attractions grouped round that princely fortune, which, concentrated by association, and wisely managed, would render practicable the most admirable Utopias!

'"What a wondrous centre of fertile and generous thoughts! what precious and life-giving rays would stream incessantly from this focus of charity, emancipation, and love! What great things might be attempted, what magnificent examples given to the world! What a divine mission! What an irresistible tendency towards good might be impressed on the whole human race by a family thus situated, and in possession of such means!

'"And, then, such a beneficent association would be able to combat the fatal conspiracy of which I am the victim, and which, in a century and a half, may have lost none of its formidable power.

'"So, to this work of darkness, restraint, and despotism, which weighs heavily on the Christian world, my family would oppose their work of light, expansion, and liberty!

'"The genii of good and evil would stand face to face. The struggle would commence, and God would protect the right.

'"And that these immense pecuniary resources, which will give so much power to my family, may not be exhausted by the course of years, my heirs, following my last will, are to place out, upon the same conditions, double the sum that I have invested—so that, a century and a half later, a new source of power and action will be at the disposal of their descendants. What a perpetuity of good!

'"In the ebony cabinet of the Hall of Mourning will be found some practical suggestions on the subject of this association.

'"Such is my last will—or rather, such are my last hopes.

'"When I require absolutely that the members of my family should appear in person in the Rue Saint-François, on the day of the opening of this testament, it is so that, united in that solemn moment, they may see and know each other. My words may then, perhaps, have some effect upon them; and, instead of living divided, they will combine together. It will be for their own interest, and my wishes will thus be accomplished.

'"When I sent, a few days ago, to those of my family whom exile has dispersed over Europe, a medal on which is engraven the date of the convocation of my heirs, a century and a half from this time, I was forced to keep secret my true motive, and only to tell them, that my descendants would find it greatly to their interest to attend this meeting.

'"I have acted thus, because I know the craft and perseverance of the society of which I have been the victim. If they could guess that my descendants would hereafter have to divide immense sums between them, my family would run the risk of much fraud and malice, through the fatal recommendations handed down from age to age in the Society of Jesus.

'"May these precautions be successful! May the wish, expressed upon these medals, be faithfully transmitted from generation to generation!

'"If I fix a day and hour, in which my inheritance shall irrevocably fall to those of my descendants who shall appear in the Rue Saint-François on the 13th February, 1832, it is that all delays must have a term, and that my heirs will have been sufficiently informed years before of the great importance of this meeting.

'"After the reading of my testament, the person who shall then be the trustee of the accumulated funds, shall make known their amount, so that, with the last stroke of noon, they may be divided between my heirs then and there present.

' " The different apartments of the house shall then be opened to them. They will see in them divers objects, well worthy of interest, pity, and respect—particularly in the Hall of Mourning.

' " My desire is, that the house may not be sold, but that it may remain furnished as it is, and serve as a place of meeting for my descendants, if, as I hope, they attend to my last wishes.

' " If, on the contrary, they are divided amongst themselves—if, instead of uniting for one of the most generous enterprises that ever signalized an age, they yield to the influence of selfish passions—if they prefer a sterile individuality to a fruitful association—if, in this immense fortune, they see only an opportunity for frivolous dissipation, or sordid interest—may they be accursed by all those whom they might have loved, succoured, and disfettered !—and then let this house be utterly demolished and destroyed, and the papers, of which Isaac Samuel possesses the inventory, as well as the two portraits in the Red Room, be burnt by the guardian of the the property.

' " I have spoken. My duty is accomplished. In all this, I have followed the counsels of the man whom I revere and love as the image of God upon earth.

' " The faithful friend, who preserved for me the fifty thousand crowns, the wreck of my fortune, knows the use I mean to make of them. I could not refuse his friendship this mark of confidence. But I have concealed from him the name of Isaac Samuel—for to have mentioned it might have exposed this latter and his descendants to great dangers.

' " In a short time, this friend, who knows not that my resolution to die is so near its accomplishment, will come hither with my notary. Into their hands, after the usual formalities, I shall deliver my sealed testament.

' " Such is my last will. I leave its execution to the superintending care of Providence. God will protect the cause of love, peace, union, and liberty.

' " This mystic testament,* having been freely made by me, and written entirely with my own hand, I intend and will its scrupulous execution both in spirit and the letter.

' " This 13th day of February, 1682, at one o'clock in the afternoon.

' " MARIUS DE RENNEPONT." '

As the notary had proceeded with the reading of the testament, Gabriel was successively agitated by divers painful impressions. At first, as we have before said, he was struck with the singular fatality which restored this immense fortune, derived from a victim of the Society of Jesus, to the hands of that very association, by the renewal of his deed of gift. Then, as his charitable and lofty soul began fully to comprehend the admirable tendency of the association so earnestly recommended by Marius de Rennepont, he reflected with bitter remorse, that, in consequence of his act of renunciation, and of the absence of any other heir, this great idea would never be realized, and a fortune, far more considerable than had even been expected, would fall to the share of an ill-omened society, in whose hands it would become a terrible means of action. At the same time, it must be said that the soul of Gabriel was too pure and noble to feel the slightest personal regret, on hearing the great probable value of the property he had renounced. He rejoiced rather in withdrawing his mind, by a touching contrast, from

---

* This term is sanctioned by legal usage.

the thought of the wealth he had abandoned, to the humble parsonage, where he hoped to pass the remainder of his life, in the practice of most evangelical virtue.

These ideas passed confusedly through his brain. The sight of that woman's portrait, the dark revelations contained in the testament, the grandeur of the views exhibited in this last will of M. de Rennepont, all these extraordinary incidents had thrown Gabriel into a sort of stupor, in which he was still plunged, when Samuel offered the key of the register to the notary, saying : 'You will find, sir, in this register, the exact statement of the sums in my possession, derived from the investment and accumulation of the one hundred and fifty thousand francs, entrusted to my grandfather by M. Marius de Rennepont.'

'Your grandfather !' cried Father d'Aigrigny, with the utmost surprise ; 'it is then your family that has always had the management of this property.'

'Yes, sir ; and, in a few minutes, my wife will bring hither the casket which contains the vouchers.'

'And to what sum does this property amount ?' asked Rodin, with an air of the most complete indifference.

'As M. Notary may convince himself by this statement,' replied Samuel, with perfect frankness, and as if he were only talking of the original one hundred and fifty thousand francs, ' I have in my possession various current securities to the amount of two hundred and twelve millions, one hundred and seventy——'

'You say, sir ?' cried Father d'Aigrigny, without giving Samuel time to finish, for the odd money did not at all interest his reverence.

'Yes, the sum !' added Rodin, in an agitated voice, and, for the first time, perhaps, in his life, losing his presence of mind ; 'the sum—the sum—the sum !'

'I say, sir,' resumed the old man 'that I hold securities for two hundred and twelve millions, one hundred and seventy-five thousand francs, payable to self or bearer—as you may soon convince yourself, M. Notary, for here is my wife with the casket.'

Indeed, at this moment, Bathsheba entered, holding in her arms the cedar-wood chest, which contained the securities in question ; she placed it upon the table, and withdrew, after exchanging an affectionate glance with Samuel. When the latter declared the enormous amount of the sum in hand, his words were received with silent stupor. All the actors in this scene, except himself, believed that they were the sport of some delusion. Father d'Aigrigny and Rodin had counted upon forty millions. This sum, in itself enormous, was more than quintupled. Gabriel, when he heard the notary read those passages in the testament, which spoke of a princely fortune, being quite ignorant of the prodigious effects of eligible investments, had valued the property at some three or four millions. He was, therefore, struck dumb with amazement at the exorbitant amount named. Notwithstanding his admirable disinterestedness and scrupulous honour, he felt dazzled and giddy at the thought, that all these immense riches might have belonged to him—alone. The notary, almost as much amazed as Gabriel, examined the statement, and could hardly believe his eyes. The Jew also remained mute, and seemed painfully absorbed in thought, that no other heir made his appearance.

In the depth of this profound silence, the clock in the next room began slowly to strike twelve. Samuel started, and heaved a deep sigh. A few seconds more, and the fatal term would be at an end. Rodin, Father d'Aigrigny, Gabriel, and the notary, were all under the influence of such complete surprise, that not one of them even remarked how strange it was to hear the sound of this clock.

' Noon !' cried Rodin, as, by an involuntary movement, he hastily placed his two hands upon the casket, as if to take possession of it.

'At last !' cried Father d'Aigrigny, with an expression of joy, triumph, transport, which it is impossible to describe. Then he added, as he threw himself into Gabriel's arms, whom he embraced warmly : ' Oh, my dear son ! how the poor will bless you ! You will be a second Vincent de Paul. You will be canonised, I promise you.'

' Let us first thank Providence,' said Rodin, in a grave and solemn tone, as he fell upon his knees, 'let us thank Providence, that He has permitted so much wealth to be employed for His glory !'

Father d'Aigrigny, having again embraced Gabriel, took him by the hand, and said : ' Rodin is right. Let us kneel, my dear son, and render thanks to Providence !'

So saying, Father d'Aigrigny knelt down, dragging Gabriel with him, and the latter, confused and giddy with so many precipitate events, yielded mechanically to the impulse. It was the last stroke of twelve when they all rose together.

Then said the notary, in a slightly agitated voice, for there was something extraordinary and solemn in this scene : ' No other heir of M. Marius de Rennepont having presented himself, before noon on this day, I execute the will of the testator, by declaring, in the name of law and justice, that M. François Marie Gabriel de Rennepont, here present, is the sole heir and possessor of all the estate, real and personal, bequeathed under the said will ; all which estate the said Gabriel de Rennepont, priest, has freely and voluntarily made over by deed of gift to Frederic Emanuel de Bordeville, Marquis d'Aigrigny, priest, who has accepted the same, and is, therefore, the only legal holder of such property, in the room of the said Gabriel de Rennepont, by virtue of the said deed, drawn up and engrossed by me this morning, and signed in my presence by the said Gabriel de Rennepont and Frederic d'Aigrigny.'

At this moment, the sound of loud voices was heard from the garden. Bathsheba entered hastily, and said to her husband with an agitated air : ' Samuel—a soldier—who insists ——'

She had not time to finish. Dagobert appeared at the door of the Red Room. The soldier was fearfully pale. He seemed almost fainting ; his left arm was in a sling, and he leaned upon Agricola. At sight of Dagobert, the pale and flabby eyelids of Rodin were suddenly distended, as if all the blood in his body had flowed towards the head. Then the socius threw himself upon the casket, with the haste of ferocious rage and avidity, as if he were resolved to cover it with his body, and defend it at the peril of his life.

CHAPTER XXV.

THE DEED OF GIFT.

FATHER D'AIGRIGNY did not recognise Dagobert, and had never seen Agricola. He could not, therefore, at first explain the kind of angry alarm exhibited by Rodin. But the reverend father understood it all, when he heard Gabriel utter a cry of joy, and saw him rush into the arms of the smith, exclaiming : ' My brother ! my second father—oh ! it is heaven that sends you to me.'

Having pressed Gabriel's hand, Dagobert advanced towards Father d'Aigrigny, with a rapid but unsteady step. As he remarked the soldier's threatening countenance, the reverend father, strong in his acquired rights, and feeling that, since noon, he was at home here, drew back a little, and said imperiously to the veteran : 'Who are you, sir !—What do you want here ?'

Instead of answering, the soldier continued to advance ; then, stopping just facing Father d'Aigrigny, he looked at him for a second with such an astounding mixture of curiosity, disdain, aversion, and audacity, that the ex-colonel of hussars quailed before the pale face and glowing eye of the veteran. The notary and Samuel, struck with surprise, remained mute spectators of this scene, while Agricola and Gabriel followed with anxiety Dagobert's least movements. As for Rodin, he pretended to be leaning on the casket, in order still to cover it with his body.

Surmounting at length the embarrassment caused by the steadfast look of the soldier, Father d'Aigrigny raised his head, and repeated : 'I ask you, sir, who you are, and what you want ?'

'Do you not recognise me?' said Dagobert, hardly able to restrain himself.

'No, sir——'

'In truth,' returned the soldier, with profound contempt, 'you cast down your eyes for shame, when, at Leipsic, you fought for the Russians against the French, and when General Simon, covered with wounds, answered you, renegade that you were, when you asked him for his sword : "I do not surrender to a traitor!"—and dragged himself along to one of the Russian grenadiers, to whom he yielded up his weapon. Well ! there was then a wounded soldier by the side of General Simon—I am he.'

'In brief, sir, what do you want ?' said Father d'Aigrigny, hardly able to control himself.

'I have come to unmask you—you, that are as false and hateful a priest, as Gabriel is admirable and beloved by all.'

'Sir !' cried the marquis, becoming livid with rage and emotion.

'I tell you, that you are infamous,' resumed the soldier, with still greater force. 'To rob Marshal Simon's daughters, and Gabriel, and Mdlle. de Cardoville of their inheritance, you have had recourse to the most shameful means.'

'What do you say ?' cried Gabriel. 'The daughters of Marshal Simon ?'

'Are your relations, my dear boy ; as is also that worthy Mdlle. de Cardoville, the benefactress of Agricola. Now, this priest,' he added, pointing to Father d'Aigrigny, 'has had them shut up—the one as mad, in a lunatic asylum—the others in a convent. As for you, my dear boy, I did not hope to find you here, believing that they would have prevented you, like the others, from coming hither this morning. But, thank God, you are here, and I arrive in time. I should have been sooner, but for my wound. I have lost so much blood, that I have done nothing but faint all the morning.'

'Truly !' cried Gabriel, with uneasiness. 'I had not remarked your arm in a sling. What is the wound ?'

At a sign from Agricola, Dagobert answered : 'Nothing ; the consequence of a fall. But here I am, to unveil many infamies.'

It is impossible to paint the curiosity, anguish, surprise, or fear, of the different actors in this scene, as they listened to Dagobert's threatening words. But the most overcome was Gabriel. His angelic countenance was distorted, his knees trembled under him. Struck by the communication of Dagobert, which revealed the existence of other heirs, he was unable to speak for some time ; at length, he cried out, in a tone of despair :

'And it is I—oh, God! I—who am the cause of the spoliation of this family!'

'You, brother?' exclaimed Agricola.

'Did they not wish to rob you also?' added Dagobert.

'The will,' cried Gabriel, with increasing agony, 'gave the property to those of the heirs that should appear before noon.'

'Well?' said Dagobert, alarmed at the emotion of the young priest.

'Twelve o'clock has struck,' resumed the latter. 'Of all the family, I alone was present. Do you understand it now? The term is expired. The heirs have been thrust aside by me!'

'By you!' said Dagobert, stammering with joy. 'By you, my brave boy! then all is well.'

'But——'

'All is well,' resumed Dagobert, radiant with delight. 'You will share with the others—I know you.'

'But all this property I have irrevocably made over to another,' cried Gabriel, in despair.

'Made over the property!' cried Dagobert, quite petrified. 'To whom, then?—to whom?'

'To this gentleman,' said Gabriel, pointing to Father d'Aigrigny.

'To him!' exclaimed Dagobert, overwhelmed by the news; 'to him—the renegade—who has always been the evil genius of this family!'

'But, brother,' cried Agricola, 'did you then know your claim to this inheritance?'

'No,' answered the young priest, with deep dejection; 'no—I only learned it this morning, from Father d'Aigrigny. He told me, that he had only recently been informed of my rights, by family papers long ago found upon me, and sent by our mother to her confessor.'

A sudden light seemed to dawn upon the mind of the smith, as he exclaimed: I understand it all now. They discovered in these papers, that you would one day have a chance of becoming rich. Therefore, they interested themselves about you—therefore, they took you into their college, where we could never see you—therefore, they deceived you in your vocation by shameful falsehoods, to force you to become a priest, and to lead you to make this deed of gift. Oh, sir!' resumed Agricola, turning towards Father d'Aigrigny, with indignation, 'my father is right—such machinations are indeed infamous!'

During this scene, the reverend father and his socius, at first alarmed and shaken in their audacity, had by degrees recovered all their coolness. Rodin, still leaning upon the casket, had said a few words in a low voice to Father d'Aigrigny. So that when Agricola, carried away by his indignation, reproached the latter with his infamous machinations, he bowed his head humbly, and answered: 'We are bound to forgive injuries, and offer them to the Lord as a mark of our humility.'

Dagobert, confounded at all he had just heard, felt his reason begin to wander. After so much anxiety, his strength failed beneath this new and terrible blow. Agricola's just and sensible words, in connexion with certain passages of the testament, at once enlightened Gabriel as to the views of Father d'Aigrigny, in taking charge of his education, and leading him to join the Society of Jesus. For the first time in his life, Gabriel was able to take in at a glance all the secret springs of the dark intrigue, of which he had been the victim. Then, indignation and despair surmounting his natural timidity, the missionary, with flashing eye, and cheeks inflamed with noble wrath, exclaimed, as he addressed Father d'Aigrigny: 'So, father, when you placed me in one of your colleges, it was not from any feeling of kindness or commiseration, but only in the hope of bringing me one day to renounce in favour of your order my share in this inheritance ; and it did not even suffice you to sacrifice me to your cupidity, but I must also be rendered the involuntary instrument of a shameful spoliation ! If only I were concerned—if you only coveted my claim to all this wealth, I should not complain. I am the minister of a religion which honours and sanctifies poverty ; I have consented to the donation in your favour, and I have not, I could never have any claim upon it. But property is concerned which belongs to poor orphans, brought from a distant exile by my adopted father, and I will not see them wronged. But the benefactress of my adopted brother is concerned, and I will not see her wronged. But the last will of a dying man is concerned, who, in his ardent love of humanity, bequeathed to his descendants an evangelic mission—an admirable mission of progress, love, union, liberty—and I will not see this mission blighted in its bud. No, no ; I tell you, that this mission shall be accomplished, though I have to cancel the donation I have made.'

On these words, Father d'Aigrigny and Rodin looked at each other with a slight shrug of the shoulders. At a sign from the socius, the reverend father began to speak with immovable calmness, in a slow and sanctified voice, keeping his eyes constantly cast down : 'There are many incidents connected with this inheritance of M. de Rennepont, which appear very complicated—many phantoms, which seem unusually menacing—and yet, nothing could be really more simple and natural. Let us proceed in regular order. Let us put aside all these calumnious imputations ; we will return to them afterwards. M. Gabriel de Rennepont—and I humbly beg him to contradict me, if I depart in the least instance from the exact truth—M. Gabriel de Rennepont, in acknowledgment of the care formerly bestowed on him by the society to which I have the honour to belong, made over to me, as its representative, freely and voluntarily, all the property that might come to him one day, the value of which was unknown to him, as well as to myself.'

Father d'Aigrigny here looked at Gabriel, as if appealing to him for the truth of this statement.

'It is true, said the young priest ; 'I made this donation freely.'

'This morning, in consequence of a private conversation, which I will not repeat—and in this, I am certain beforehand, of the Abbé Gabriel——'

'True, replied Gabriel, generously ; 'the subject of this conversation is of little importance.'

'It was then, in consequence of this conversation that the Abbé Gabriel manifested the desire to confirm this donation—not in my favour, for I have little to do with earthly wealth—but in favour of the sacred and charitable works of which our Company is the trustee. I appeal to the honour of M. Gabriel to declare if he have not engaged himself towards us, not only by a solemn oath, but by a perfectly legal act, executed in presence of M. Dumesnil, here present ?'

'It is all true,' answered Gabriel.

'The deed was prepared by me,' added the notary.

'But Gabriel could only give you what belonged to him,' cried Dagobert. 'The dear boy never supposed that you would make use of him to rob other people.'

'Do me the favour, sir, to allow me to explain myself,' replied Father d'Aigrigny, courteously ; 'you can afterwards make answer.'

Dagobert repressed with difficulty his painful impatience. The reverend father continued : 'The Abbé Gabriel has therefore, by the double engagement of an oath and a legal act, confirmed his donation. Much more,' resumed Father d'Aigrigny ; ' when. to his great astonishment and to ours, the enormous amount of the inheritance became known, the Abbé Gabriel, faithful to his own admirable generosity, far from repenting of his gifts, consecrated them once more by a pious movement of gratitude to Providence—for M. Notary will doubtless remember, that, after embracing the Abbé Gabriel with transport, and telling him that he was a second Vincent de Paul in charity, I took him by the hand, and we both knelt down together, to thank heaven for having inspired him with the thought to offer these immense riches to the Greater Glory of the Lord.'

' That is true, also,' answered Gabriel, honestly ; ' so long as myself was concerned, though I might be astounded for a moment by the revelation of so enormous a fortune, I did not think for an instant of cancelling the donation I had freely made.'

' Under these circumstances,' resumed Father d'Aigrigny, ' the hour fixed for the settlement of the inheritance having struck, and Abbé Gabriel being the only heir that presented himself, he became necessarily the only legitimate possessor of this immense wealth—enormous, no doubt—and charity makes me rejoice that it is enormous ; for, thanks to it, many miseries will be relieved, and many tears wiped away   But, all on a sudden, here comes this gentleman,' said Father d'Aigrigny, pointing to Dagobert ; ' and, under some delusion, which I forgive from the bottom of my soul, and which I am sure he will himself regret, accuses me, with insults and threats, with having carried off (I know not where) some persons (I know not whom), in order to prevent their being here at the proper time——'

' Yes, I accuse you of this infamy !' cried the soldier, exasperated by the calmness and audacity of the reverend father ; ' yes—and I will——'

' Once, again, sir, I conjure you to be so good as to let me finish ; you can reply afterwards, said Father d'Aigrigny, humbly, in the softest and most honied accents.

' Yes, I will reply, and confound you ! cried Dagobert.

' Let him finish, father : you can speak presently, said Agricola.

The soldier was silent, as Father d'Aigrigny continued with new assurance : ' Doubtless, if there should really be any other heirs, besides the Abbé Gabriel, it is unfortunate for them that they have not appeared in proper time.   And if, instead of defending the cause of the poor and needy, I had only to look to my own interest, I should be far from availing myself of this advantage, due only to chance ; but, as a trustee for the great family of the poor, I am obliged to maintain my absolute right to this inheritance ; and I do not doubt that M. Notary will acknowledge the validity of my claim, and deliver to me these securities, which are now my legitimate property.'

' My only mission,' replied the notary, in an agitated voice, ' is faithfully to execute the will of the testator.   The Abbé Gabriel de Rennepont alone presented himself, within the term fixed by the testament.   The deed of gift is in due form ; I cannot refuse, therefore to deliver to the person named in the deed the amount of the heritage——'

On these words, Samuel hid his face in his hands, and heaved a deep sigh ; he was obliged to acknowledge the rigorous justice of the notary's observations.

' But, sir,' cried Dagobert, addressing the man of law, ' this cannot be. You will not allow two poor orphans to be despoiled.   It is in the name of their father and mother, that I speak to you.   I give you my honour—the honour of a soldier !—that they took advantage of the weakness of my wife to carry the daughters of Marshal Simon to a convent, and thus prevent me bringing them here this morning.   It is so true, that I have already laid my charge before a magistrate.'

'And what answer did you receive?' said the notary.

'That my deposition was not sufficient for the law to remove these young girls from the convent in which they were, and that inquiries would be made——'

'Yes, sir,' added Agricola, 'and it was the same with regard to Mdlle. de Cardoville, detained as mad in a lunatic asylum, though in the full enjoyment of her reason. Like Marshal Simon's daughters, she too has a claim to this inheritance. I took the same steps for her, as my father took for Marshal Simon's daughters.'

'Well?' asked the notary.

'Unfortunately, sir,' answered Agricola, 'they told me, as they did my father, that my deposition would not suffice, and that they must make inquiries.'

At this moment, Bathsheba, having heard the street-bell ring, left the Red Room at a sign from Samuel. The notary resumed, addressing Agricola and his father : 'Far be it from me, gentlemen, to call in question your good faith ; but I cannot, to my great regret, attach such importance to your accusations, which are not supported by proof, as to suspend the regular legal course. According to your own confession, gentlemen, the authorities, to whom you addressed yourselves, did not see fit to interfere on your depositions, and told you they would inquire further. Now, really, gentlemen, I appeal to you : how can I, in so serious a matter, take upon myself a responsibility, which the magistrates themselves have refused to take?'

'Yes, you should do so, in the name of justice and honour!' cried Dagobert.

'It may be so, sir, in your opinion ; but, in my view of the case, I remain faithful to justice and honour, by executing with exactness the last will of the dead. For the rest, you have no occasion to despair. If the persons, whose interests you represent, consider themselves injured, they may hereafter have recourse to an action at law, against the person receiving as *donee* of the Abbé Gabriel—but in the meanwhile, it is my duty to put him in immediate possession of the securities. I should be gravely injured, were I to act in any other manner.'

The notary's observations seemed so reasonable, that Samuel, Dagobert, and Agricola were quite confounded. After a moment's thought, Gabriel appeared to take a desperate resolution, and said to the notary, in a firm voice : 'Since, under these circumstances, the law is powerless to obtain the right, I must adopt, sir, an extreme course. Before doing so, I will ask M. l'Abbé d'Aigrigny, for the last time, if he will content himself with that portion of the property which falls justly to me, on condition that the rest shall be placed in safe hands, till the heirs, whose names have been brought forward, shall prove their claim?'

'To this proposition I must answer as I have done already,' replied Father d'Aigrigny ; 'it is not I who am concerned, but an immense work of charity I am, therefore, obliged to refuse the part-offer of the Abbé Gabriel, and to remind him of his engagements of every kind.'

'Then you refuse this arrangement?' asked Gabriel, in an agitated voice.

'Charity commands me to do so.'

'You refuse it—absolutely?'

'I think of all the good and pious institutions that these treasures will enable us to establish for the Greater Glory of the Lord, and I have neither the courage nor the desire to make the least concession.'

'Then, sir,' resumed the good priest, in a still more agitated manner, 'since you force me to it, I revoke my donation. I only intended to dispose of my own property, and not of that which did not belong to me.'

'Take care, M. l'Abbé,' said Father d'Aigrigny; 'I would observe that *I* hold in my hand a written, formal promise.'

'I know it, sir; you have a written paper, in which I take an oath never to revoke this donation, upon any pretext whatever, and on pain of incurring the aversion and contempt of all honest men. Well, sir! be it so,' said Gabriel, with deep bitterness; 'I will expose myself to all the consequences of perjury; you may proclaim it everywhere. I may be hated and despised by all—but God will judge me!' The young priest dried a tear, which trickled from his eye.

'Oh! do not be afraid, my dear boy!' cried Dagobert, with reviving hope. 'All honest men will be on your side!'

'Well done, brother!' said Agricola.

'M. Notary,' said Rodin, in his little sharp voice, 'please to explain to Abbé Gabriel, that he may perjure himself as much as he thinks fit, but that the Civil Code is much less easy to violate than a mere promise, which is only—sacred!'

'Speak, sir,' said Gabriel.

'Please to inform Abbé Gabriel,' resumed Rodin, 'that a deed of gift, like that made in favour of Father d'Aigrigny, can only be cancelled for one of three reasons—is it not so?'

'Yes, sir, for three reasons,' said the notary.

'The first is in case of the birth of a child,' said Rodin, 'and I should blush to mention such a contingency to the Abbé Gabriel. The second is the ingratitude of the *donee*—and the Abbé Gabriel may be certain of our deep and lasting gratitude. The last case is the non-fulfilment of the wishes of the *donor*, with regard to the employment of his gifts. Now, although the Abbé Gabriel may have suddenly conceived a very bad opinion of us, he will at least give us some time to show that his gifts have been disposed of according to his wishes, and applied to the Greater Glory of the Lord.'

'Now, M. Notary,' added Father d'Aigrigny, 'it is for you to decide and say, if Abbé Gabriel *can* revoke the donation he has made.'

Just as the notary was going to answer, Bathsheba re-entered the room, followed by two more personages, who appeared in the Red Room at a little distance from each other.

CHAPTER XXVI.

A GOOD GENIUS.

THE first of the two, whose arrival had interrupted the answer of the notary, was Faringhea. At sight of this man's forbidding countenance, Samuel approached, and said to him: 'Who are you, sir?'

After casting a piercing glance at Rodin, who started but soon recovered his habitual coolness, Faringhea replied to Samuel: 'Prince Djalma arrived lately from India, in order to be present here this day, as it was recommended to him by an inscription on a medal, which he wore about his neck.'

'He, also!' cried Gabriel, who had been the shipmate of the Indian Prince from the Azores, where the vessel in which he came from Alexandria had been driven into port; 'he also one of the heirs! In fact, the prince told me during the voyage that his mother was of French origin. But, doubtless, he thought it right to conceal from me the object of his journey. Oh! that Indian is a noble and courageous young man. Where is he?'

The Strangler again looked at Rodin, and said, laying strong emphasis upon his words : 'I left the prince yesterday evening. He informed me that, although he had a great interest to be here, he might possibly sacrifice that interest to other motives. I passed the night in the same hotel, and this morning, when I went to call on him, they told me he was already gone out. My friendship for him led me to come hither, hoping the information I should be able to give might be of use to the prince.'

In making no mention of the snare into which he had fallen the day before, in concealing Rodin's machinations with regard to Djalma, and in attributing the absence of this latter to a voluntary cause, the Strangler evidently wished to serve the socius, trusting that Rodin would know how to recompense his discretion. It is useless to observe, that all this story was impudently false. Having succeeded that morning in escaping from his prison by a prodigious effort of cunning, audacity, and skill, he had run to the hotel where he had left Djalma ; there he had learned that a man and woman, of an advanced age, and most respectable appearance, calling themselves relations of the young Indian, had asked to see him—and that, alarmed at the dangerous state of somnolency in which he seemed to be plunged, they had taken him home in their carriage, in order to pay him the necessary attention.

' It is unfortunate,' said the notary, 'that this heir also did not make his appearance—but he has, unhappily, forfeited his right to the immense inheritance that is in question.'

' Oh ! an immense inheritance is in question,' said Faringhea, looking fixedly at Rodin, who prudently turned away his eyes.

The second of the two personages we have mentioned entered at this moment. It was the father of Marshal Simon, an old man of tall stature, still active and vigorous for his age. His hair was white and thin. His countenance, rather fresh-coloured, was expressive at once of quickness, mildness, and energy.

Agricola advanced hastily to meet him. ' You here, M. Simon !' he exclaimed.

'Yes, my boy,' said the marshal's father, cordially pressing Agricola's hand, ' I have just arrived from my journey. M. Hardy was to have been here, about some matter of inheritance, as he supposed ; but, as he will still be absent from Paris for some time, he has charged me——'

' He also an heir !—M. Francis Hardy !' cried Agricola, interrupting the old workman.

' But how pale and agitated you are, my boy !' said the marshal's father, looking round with astonishment. ' What is the matter ?'

' What is the matter ?' cried Dagobert, in despair, as he approached the foreman. ' The matter is that they would rob your granddaughters, and that I have brought them from the depths of Siberia only to witness this shameful deed !'

' Eh ?' cried the old workman, trying to recognise the soldier's face, ' you are then——'

' Dagobert.'

'You—the generous, devoted friend of my son !' cried the marshal's father, pressing the hands of Dagobert in his own with strong emotion ; ' but did you not speak of Simon's daughter ?'

' Of his daughters ; for he is more fortunate than he imagines,' said Dagobert. ' The poor children are twins.'

' And where are they ?' asked the old man.

' In a convent.'

' In a convent ?'——' Yes ; by the treachery of this man, who keeps them there in order to disinherit them.'

' What man ?'

' The Marquis d'Aigrigny.'

' My son's mortal enemy !' cried the old workman, as he threw a glance of aversion at Father d'Aigrigny, whose audacity did not fail him.

' And that is not all,' added Agricola. ' M. Hardy, my worthy and excellent master, has also lost his right to this immense inheritance.'

' What ?' cried Marshal Simon's father ; ' but M. Hardy did not know that such important interests were concerned. He set out hastily to join one of his friends who was in want of him.'

At each of these successive revelations, Samuel felt his trouble increase ; but he could only sigh over it, for the will of the testator was couched, unhappily, in precise and positive terms.

Father d'Aigrigny, impatient to end this scene, which caused him cruel embarrassment, in spite of his apparent calmness, said to the notary, in a grave and expressive voice : ' It is necessary, sir, that all this should have an end. If calumny could reach me, I would answer victoriously by the facts that have just come to light. Why attribute to odious conspiracies the absence of the heirs, in whose names this soldier and his son have so uncourteously urged their demands ? Why should such absence be less explicable than the young Indian's, or than M. Hardy's, who, as his confidential man has just told us, did not even know the importance of the interests that called him hither ? Is it not probable, that the daughters of Marshal Simon, and Mdlle. de Cardoville have been prevented from coming here to-day by some very natural reasons ? But, once again, this has lasted too long. I think M. Notary will agree with me, that this discovery of new heirs does not at all affect the question, which I had the honour to propose to him just now ; namely, whether, as trustee for the poor, to whom Abbé Gabriel made a free gift of all he possessed, I remain, notwithstanding his tardy and illegal opposition, the only possessor of this property, which I have promised, and which I now again promise, in presence of all here assembled, to employ for the Greater Glory of the Lord ? Please to answer me plainly, M. Notary ; and thus terminate a scene which must needs be painful to us all.'

' Sir,' replied the notary, in a solemn tone, ' on my soul and conscience, and in the name of law and justice, as a faithful and impartial executor of the last will of M. Marius de Rennepont, I declare that, by virtue of the deed of gift of Abbé Gabriel de Rennepont, you, M. l'Abbé d'Aigrigny, are the only possessor of this property, which I place at your immediate disposal, that you may employ the same according to the intention of the donor.'

These words, pronounced with conviction and gravity, destroyed the last vague hopes that the representatives of the heirs might till then have entertained. Samuel became paler than usual, and pressed convulsively the hand of Bathsheba, who had drawn near to him. Large tears rolled down the cheeks of the two old people. Dagobert and Agricola were plunged into the deepest dejection. Struck with the reasoning of the notary, who refused to give more credence and authority to their remonstrances than the magistrates had done before him, they saw themselves forced to abandon every hope. But Gabriel suffered more than any one ; he felt the most terrible remorse, in reflecting that, by his blindness, he had been the involuntary cause and instrument of this abominable theft.

So, when the notary, after having examined and verified the amount of securities contained in the cedar box, said to Father d'Aigrigny : ' Take possession, sir, of this casket——' Gabriel exclaimed, with bitter disappointment and profound despair : ' Alas ! one would fancy, under these circumstances, that an inexorable fatality pursues all those who are worthy of interest, affection or respect. Oh, my God !' added the young priest, clasping his hands with fervour, ' Thy sovereign justice will never permit the triumph of such iniquity !'

It was as if heaven had listened to the prayer of the missionary. Hardly had he spoken, when a strange event took place.

Without waiting for the end of Gabriel's invocation, Rodin, profiting by the decision of the notary, had seized the casket in his arms, unable to repress a deep aspiration of joy and triumph. At the very moment when Father d Aigrigny and his socius thought themselves at last in safe possession of the treasure, the door of the apartment in which the clock had been heard striking was suddenly opened.

A woman appeared upon the threshold.

At sight of her, Gabriel uttered a loud cry, and remained as if thunderstruck. Samuel and Bathsheba fell on their knees together, and raised their clasped hands. The Jew and Jewess felt inexplicable hopes reviving within them.

All the other actors in this scene appeared struck with stupor. Rodin— Rodin himself—recoiled two steps, and replaced the casket on the table with a trembling hand. Though the incident might appear natural enough --a woman appearing on the threshold of a door, which she had just thrown open—there was a pause of deep and solemn silence. Every bosom seemed oppressed, and as if struggling for breath. All experienced, at sight of this woman, surprise mingled with fear, and indefinable anxiety—for this woman was the living original of the portrait, which had been placed in the room a hundred and fifty years ago. The same head-dress, the same flowing robe, the same countenance, so full of poignant and resigned grief ! She advanced slowly, and without appearing to perceive the deep impression she had caused She approached one of the pieces of furniture, inlaid with brass, touched a spring concealed in the moulding of gilded bronze, so that an upper drawer flew open, and taking from it a sealed parchment envelope, she walked up to the table, and placed this packet before the notary, who, hitherto silent and motionless, received it mechanically from her.

Then, casting upon Gabriel, who seemed fascinated by her presence, a long, mild, melancholy look, this woman directed her steps towards the hall, the door of which had remained open. As she passed near Samuel and Bathsheba, who were still kneeling, she stopped an instant, bowed her fair head towards them, and looked at them with tender solicitude. Then, giving them her hands to kiss, she glided away as slowly as she had entered—throwing a last glance upon Gabriel. The departure of this woman seemed to break the spell under which all present had remained for the last few minutes. Gabriel was the first to speak, exclaiming, in an agitated voice : ' It is she—again—here—in this house !'

' Who, brother ?' said Agricola, uneasy at the pale and almost wild looks of the missionary ; for the smith had not yet remarked the strange resemblance of the woman to the portrait, though he shared in the general feeling of amazement, without being able to explain it to himself. Dagobert and Faringhea were in a similar state of mind.

' Who is this woman ?' resumed Agricola, as he took the hand of Gabriel, which felt damp and icy cold.

' Look !' said the young priest. ' Those portraits have been there for more than a century and a half.'

He pointed to the paintings, before which he was now seated, and Agricola, Dagobert, and Faringhea raised their eyes to either side of the fireplace. Three exclamations were now heard at once,

'It is she—it is the same woman !' cried the smith, in amazement ; 'and her portrait has been here for a hundred and fifty years !'

'What do I see ?' cried Dagobert, as he gazed at the portrait of the man. 'The friend and emissary of Marshal Simon. Yes ! it is the same face that I saw last year in Siberia. Oh, yes ! I recognise that 'd and sorrowful air—those black eye-brows, which make only one !'

'My eyes do not deceive me,' muttered Faringhea to himself, shuddering with horror 'It is the same man, with the black mark on his forehead, that we strangled and buried on the banks of the Ganges—the same man, that one of the sons of Bowanee told me, in the ruins of Tchandi, had been met by him afterwards at one of the gates of Bombay—the man of the fatal curse, who scatters death upon his passage—and his picture has existed for a hundred and fifty years !'

And, like Dagobert and Agricola, the Strangler could not withdraw his eyes from that strange portrait.

'What a mysterious resemblance !' thought Father d'Aigrigny. Then, as if struck with a sudden idea, he said to Gabriel : 'But this woman is the same that saved your life in America ?'

'It is the same,' answered Gabriel, with emotion ; 'and yet she told me she was going towards the North,' added the young priest, speaking to himself.

'But how came she in this house ?' said Father d Aigrigny, addressing Samuel. 'Answer me ! did this woman come in with you, or before you ?'

'I came in first, and alone, when this door was first opened since a century and half,' said Samuel, gravely.

'Then how can you explain the presence of this woman here ?' said Father d'Aigrigny

'I do not try to explain it,' said the Jew. 'I see, I believe, and now I hope,' added he, looking at Bathsheba with an indefinable expression.

'But you ought to explain the presence of this woman !' said Father d'Aigrigny, with vague uneasiness. 'Who is she ? How came she hither ?'

'All I know is, sir, that my father has often told me, there are subterraneous communications between this house and distant parts of the quarter.'

'Oh ! then nothing can be clearer,' said Father d Aigrigny ; 'it only remains to be known what this woman intends by coming hither. As for her singular resemblance to this portrait, it is one of the freaks of nature.'

Rodin had shared in the general emotion, at the apparition of this mysterious woman. But when he saw that she had delivered a sealed packet to the notary, the socius, instead of thinking of the strangeness of this unexpected vision, was only occupied with a violent desire to quit the house with the treasure which had just fallen to the Company. He felt a vague anxiety at sight of the envelope with the black seal, which the protectress of Gabriel had delivered to the notary, and was still held mechanically in his hands. The socius, therefore, judging this a very good opportunity to walk off with the casket, during the general silence and stupor which still continued, slightly touched Father d'Aigrigny's elbow, made him a sign of intelligence, and, tucking the cedar-wood chest under his arm, was hastening towards the door.

'One moment, sir,' said Samuel, rising, and standing in his path ; 'I request M. Notary to examine the envelope, that has just been delivered to him. You may then go out.'

'But, sir,' said Rodin, trying to force a passage, 'the question is definitively decided in favour of Father d'Aigrigny. Therefore, with your permission——'

'I tell you, sir,' answered the old man, in a loud voice : 'that this **casket** *shall* not leave the house, until M. Notary has examined the envelope just delivered to him !'

These words drew the attention of all. Rodin was forced to retrace his steps. Notwithstanding the firmness of his character, the Jew shuddered at the look of implacable hate which Rodin turned upon him at this moment.

Yielding to the wish of Samuel, the notary examined the envelope with attention. 'Good Heaven !' he cried, suddenly ; 'what do I see ?—Ah ! so much the better !'

At this exclamation, all eyes turned upon the notary. Oh ! read, read, sir !' cried Samuel, clasping his hands together. 'My presentiments have not then deceived me !'

'But, sir,' said Father d'Aigrigny to the notary, for he began to share in the anxiety of Rodin, 'what is this paper ?'

'A codicil,' answered the notary ; 'a codicil, which re-opens the whole question.'

'How, sir ?' cried Father d'Aigrigny, in a fury, as he hastily drew nearer to the notary, 're-opens the whole question ! By what right ?'

'It is impossible,' added Rodin. 'We protest against it.'

'Gabriel ! father ! listen,' cried Agricola, 'all is not lost. There is yet hope. Do you hear Gabriel ? There is yet hope.'

'What do you say ?' exclaimed the young priest, rising, and hardly believing the words of his adopted brother.

'Gentlemen,' said the notary, 'I will read to you the superscription of this envelope. It changes, or rather, it adjourns, the whole of the testamentary provisions.'

'Gabriel !' cried Agricola, throwing himself on the neck of the missionary, 'all is adjourned, nothing is lost !'

'Listen, gentlemen,' said the notary ; and he read as follows :

'"This is a Codicil, which, for reasons herein stated, adjourns and prorogues to the 1st day of June, 1832, though without any other change, all the provisions contained in the testament made by me, at one o'clock this afternoon. The house shall be reclosed, and the funds left in the hands of the same trustee. to be distributed to the rightful claimants on the 1st of June, 1832.

'"Villetaneuse, this 13th of February, 1682, eleven o'clock at night.
'"MARIUS DE RENNEPONT."'

'I protest against this codicil as a forgery !' cried Father d'Aigrigny livid with rage and despair.

'The woman who delivered it to the notary is a suspicious character,' added Rodin. 'The codicil has been forged.'

'No, sir,' said the notary, severely ; 'I have just compared the two signatures, and they are absolutely alike. For the rest—what I said this morning, with regard to the absent heirs, is now applicable to you—the law is open ; you may dispute the authenticity of this codicil. Meanwhile, everything will remain suspended—since the term for the adjustment of the inheritance is prolonged for three months and a half.'

When the notary had uttered these last words, Rodin's nails dripped blood ; for the first time, his wan lips became red.

'Oh, God ! Thou hast heard and granted my prayer !' cried Gabriel, kneeling down with religious fervour, and turning his angelic face towards heaven. 'Thy sovereign justice has not let iniquity triumph !'

'What do you say, my brave boy ?' cried Dagobert, who, in the first tumult of joy, had not exactly understood the meaning of the codicil.

'All is put off, father!' exclaimed the smith ; 'the heirs will have three months and a half more to make their claim. And now that these people are unmasked,' added Agricola, pointing to Rodin and Father d'Aigrigny, 'we have nothing more to fear from them. We shall be on our guard ; and the orphans, Mdlle. de Cardoville, my worthy master, M. Hardy, and this young Indian, will all recover their own.'

We must renounce the attempt to paint the delight, the transport of Gabriel and Agricola, of Dagobert, and Marshal Simon's father, of Samuel and Bathsheba. Faringhea alone remained in gloomy silence, before the portrait of the man with the black-barred forehead. As for the fury of Father d'Aigrigny and Rodin, when they saw Samuel retake possession of the casket, we must also renounce any attempt to describe it. On the notary's suggestion, who took with him the codicil, to have it opened according to the formalities of the law, Samuel agreed that it would be more prudent to deposit in the Bank of France the securities of immense value that were now known to be in his possession.

While all the generous hearts, which had for a moment suffered so much, were overflowing with happiness, hope, and joy, Father d'Aigrigny and Rodin quitted the house with rage and death in their souls. The reverend father got into his carriage, and said to his servants · 'To Saint-Dizier House!'—Then, worn out and crushed, he fell back upon the seat, and hid his face in his hands, while he uttered a deep groan Rodin sat next to him, and looked with a mixture of anger and disdain at this so dejected and broken-spirited man.

'The coward!' said he to himself. 'He despairs—and yet——'

A quarter of an hour later, the carriage stopped in the Rue de Babylone, in the courtyard of Saint-Dizier House.

CHAPTER XXVII.

THE FIRST LAST, AND THE LAST FIRST

THE carriage had travelled rapidly to Saint-Dizier House. During all the way, Rodin remained mute, contenting himself with observing Father d'Aigrigny, and listening to him, as he poured forth his grief and fury in a long monologue, interrupted by exclamations, lamentations, and bursts of rage, directed against the strokes of that inexorable destiny, which had ruined in a moment the best founded hopes. When the carriage entered the courtyard, and stopped before the portico, the princess's face could be seen through one of the windows, half hidden by the folds of a curtain ; in her burning anxiety, she came to see if it was really Father d'Aigrigny who arrived at the house. Still more, in defiance of all ordinary rules, this great lady, generally so scrupulous as to appearances, hurried from her apartment, and descended several steps of the staircase, to meet Father d'Aigrigny, who was coming up with a dejected air. At sight of the livid and agitated countenance of the reverend father, the princess stopped suddenly, and grew pale. She suspected that all was lost. A look rapidly exchanged with her old lover left her no doubt of the issue she so much feared. Rodin humbly followed the reverend father, and both, preceded by the princess, entered the room. The door once closed, the princess, addressing Father d'Aigrigny, exclaimed with unspeakable anguish : 'What has happened ?'

Instead of answering this question, the reverend father, his eyes sparkling with rage, his lips white, his features contracted, looked fixedly at the princess, and said to her : 'Do you know the amount of this inheritance, that we estimated at forty millions ?'

'I understand,' cried the princess ; 'we have been deceived. The inheritance amounts to nothing, and all you have done has been in vain.'

'Yes, it has indeed been in vain,' answered the reverend father, grinding his teeth with rage ; 'it was no question of forty millions, but of two hundred and twelve millions.'

'Two hundred and twelve millions !' repeated the princess in amazement, as she drew back a step. 'It is impossible !'

'I tell you I saw the vouchers, which were examined by the notary.

'Two hundred and twelve millions ?' resumed the princess, with deep dejection. 'It is an immense and sovereign power—and you have renounced —you have not struggled for it, by every possible means, and till the last moment ?'

'Madame, I have done all that I could !—notwithstanding the treachery of Gabriel, who this very morning declared that he renounced us, and separated from the Society.'

'Ungrateful !' said the princess, unaffectedly.

'The deed of gift, which I had the precaution to have prepared by the notary, was in such good, legal form, that in spite of the objections of that accursed soldier and his son, the notary had put me in possession of the treasure.'

'Two hundred and twelve millions !' repeated the princess, clasping her hands. 'Verily, it is like a dream !'

'Yes,' replied Father d'Aigrigny, bitterly, 'for us, this possession is indeed a dream, for a codicil has been discovered, which puts off for three months and a half all the testamentary provisions. Now that our very precautions have roused the suspicion of all these heirs—now that they know the enormous amount at stake—they will be upon their guard ; and all is lost.'

'But who is the wretch that produced this codicil ?'

'A woman.'——'What woman ?'

'Some wandering creature, that Gabriel says he met in America, where she saved his life.'

'And how could this woman be there—how could she know the existence of this codicil ?'

'I think it was all arranged with a miserable Jew, the guardian of the house, whose family has had charge of the funds for three generations ; he had no doubt some secret instructions, in case he suspected the detention of any of the heirs, for this Marius de Rennepont had foreseen that our Company would keep their eyes upon his race.'

'But can you not dispute the validity of this codicil ?'

'What, go to law in these times—litigate about a will—incur the certainty of a thousand clamours, with no security for success ?—It is bad enough, that even this should get wind. Alas ! it is terrible. So near the goal ! after so much care and trouble. An affair that had been followed up with so much perseverance during a century and a half !'

'Two hundred and twelve millions !' said the princess. 'The Order would have had no need to look for establishments in foreign countries ; with such resources, it would have been able to impose itself upon France.'

'Yes,' resumed Father d'Aigrigny, with bitterness ; 'by means of education, we might have possessed ourselves of the rising generation. The power is altogether incalculable.' Then, stamping with his foot, he resumed : 'I tell you, that it is enough to drive one mad with rage ! an affair so wisely, ably, patiently conducted !'

'Is there no hope?'

'Only that Gabriel may not revoke his donation, in as far as concerns himself. That alone would be a considerable sum—not less than thirty millions.'

'It is enormous—it is almost what you hoped,' said the princess ; 'then why despair?'

'Because it is evident that Gabriel will dispute this donation. However legal it may be, he will find means to annul it, now that he is free, informed as to our designs, and surrounded by his adopted family. I tell you, that all is lost. There is no hope left. I think it will even be prudent to write to Rome, to obtain permission to leave Paris for a while. This town is odious to me !'

'Oh, yes ! I see that no hope is left—since you, my friend, have decided almost to fly.'

Father d'Aigrigny was completely discouraged and broken down ; this terrible blow had destroyed all life and energy within him. He threw himself back in an arm-chair, quite overcome. During the preceding dialogue, Rodin was standing humbly near the door, with his old hat in his hand. Two or three times, at certain passages in the conversation between Father d'Aigrigny and the princess, the cadaverous face of the socius, whose wrath appeared to be concentrated, was slightly flushed, and his flabby eyelids were tinged with red, as if the blood mounted in consequence of an interior struggle ; but, immediately after, his dull countenance resumed its pallid hue.

'I must write instantly to Rome, to announce this defeat, which has become an event of the first importance, because it overthrows immense hopes,' said Father d'Aigrigny, much depressed.

The reverend father had remained seated ; pointing to a table, he said to Rodin, with an abrupt and haughty air : 'Write !'

The socius placed his hat on the ground, answered with a respectful bow the command, and with stooping head and slanting walk, went to seat himself on a chair, that stood before a desk. Then, taking pen and paper, he waited, silent and motionless, for the dictation of his superior.

'With your permission, princess?' said Father d'Aigrigny to Madame de Saint-Dizier. The latter answered by an impatient wave of the hand, as if she reproached him for the formal demand at such a time. The reverend father bowed, and dictated these words in a hoarse and hollow voice : 'All our hopes, which of late had become almost certainties, have been suddenly defeated. The affair of the Rennepont inheritance, in spite of all the care and skill employed upon it, has completely and finally failed. At the point to which matters had been brought, it is unfortunately worse than a failure ; it is a most disastrous event for the Society, which was clearly entitled to this property, fraudulently withdrawn from a confiscation made in our favour. My conscience at least bears witness, that, to the last moment, I did all that was possible to defend and secure our rights. But I repeat, we must consider this important affair as lost absolutely and for ever, and think no more about it.'

Thus dictating, Father d'Aigrigny's back was turned towards Rodin. At a sudden movement made by the socius, in rising and throwing his pen upon the table, instead of continuing to write, the reverend father turned round, and, looking at Rodin with profound astonishment, said to him : 'Well ! what are you doing?'

'It is time to end this—the man is mad !' said Rodin to himself, as he advanced slowly towards the fire-place.

'What ! you quit your place—you cease writing?' said the reverend father, in amazement. Then, addressing the princess, who shared in his astonishment, he added, as he glanced contemptuously at the socius : 'He is losing his senses.'

' Forgive him,' replied Mme. de Saint-Dizier ; ' it is, no doubt, the emotion caused by the ruin of this affair.'

'Thank the princess, return to your place, and continue to write,' said Father d'Aigrigny to Rodin, in a tone of disdainful compassion, as, with imperious finger, he pointed to the table.

The socius, perfectly indifferent to this new order, approached the fire-place, drew himself up to his full height as he turned his arched back, planted himself firmly on his legs, stamped on the carpet with the heel of his clumsy, greasy shoes, crossed his hands beneath the flaps of his old, spotted coat, and, lifting his head, looked fixedly at Father d'Aigrigny. The socius had not spoken a word, but his hideous countenance, now flushed, suddenly revealed such a sense of his superiority, and such sovereign con-tempt for Father d'Aigrigny, mingled with so calm and serene a daring, that the reverend father and the princess were quite confounded by it. They felt themselves overawed by this little old man, so sordid and so ugly. Father d'Aigrigny knew too well the customs of the Company, to believe his humble secretary capable of assuming so suddenly these airs of transcendant superiority without a motive, or rather, without a positive right. Late, too late, the reverend father perceived, that this subordinate agent might be partly a spy, partly an experienced assistant, who, according to the consti-tutions of the Order, had the power and mission to depose and provisionally replace, in certain urgent cases, the incapable person over whom he was stationed as a guard. The reverend father was not deceived. From the general to the provincials, and to the rectors of the colleges, all the superior members of the Order have stationed near them, often without their know-ledge, and in apparently the lowest capacities, men able to assume their functions at any given moment, and who, with this view, constantly keep up a direct correspondence with Rome.

From the moment Rodin had assumed this position, the manners of Father d'Aigrigny, generally so haughty, underwent a change. Though it cost him a good deal, he said with hesitation, mingled with deference : ' You have, no doubt, the right to command me—who hitherto have com-manded.' Rodin, without answering, drew from his well-rubbed and greasy pocket-book a slip of paper, stamped upon both sides, on which were written several lines in Latin. When he had read it, Father d'Aigrigny pressed this paper respectfully, even religiously, to his lips : then returned it to Rodin, with a low bow. When he again raised his head, he was purple with shame and vexation. Notwithstanding his habits of passive obedience and immutable respect for the will of the Order, he felt a bitter and violent rage at seeing himself thus abruptly deposed from power. That was not all. Though, for a long time past, all relations in gallantry had ceased be-tween him and Mme. de Saint-Dizier, the latter was not the less a woman ; and for him to suffer this humiliation in presence of a woman was, un-doubtedly, cruel, as, notwithstanding his entrance into the Order, he had not wholly laid aside the character of man of the world. Moreover, the princess, instead of appearing hurt and offended by this sudden transformation of the superior into a subaltern, and of the subaltern into a superior, looked at Rodin with a sort of curiosity mingled with interest. As a woman—as a woman, intensely ambitious, seeking to connect herself with every powerful influence—the princess loved this strange species of contrast. She found it curious and interesting to see this man, almost in rags, mean in appear-ance, and ignobly ugly, and but lately the most humble of subordinates, look down from the height of his superior intelligence upon the nobleman by birth, distinguished for the elegance of his manners, and just before so considerable a personage in the Society. From that moment, as the more important personage of the two, Rodin completely took the place of Father d'Aigrigny in the princess's mind. The first pang of humiliation over, the reverend father, though his pride bled inwardly, applied all his knowledge of the world to behave with redoubled courtesy towards Rodin, who had become his superior by this abrupt change of fortune. But the ex-socius, incapable of appreciating, or rather of acknowledging, such delicate shades of manner, established himself at once, firmly, imperiously, brutally, in his new position, not from any reaction of offended pride, but from a consciousness of what he was really worth. A long acquaintance with Father d'Aigrigny had revealed to him the inferiority of the latter.

'You threw away your pen,' said Father d'Aigrigny to Rodin with extreme deference, 'while I was dictating a note for Rome. Will you do me the favour to tell me how I have acted wrong?'

'Directly,' replied Rodin, in his sharp, cutting voice. 'For a long time this affair appeared to me above your strength ; but I abstained from interfering. And yet what mistakes ! what poverty of invention ; what coarseness in the means employed to bring it to bear !'

'I can hardly understand your reproaches,' answered Father d'Aigrigny, mildly, though a secret bitterness made its way through his apparent submission. 'Was not the success certain, had it not been for this codicil? Did you not yourself assist in the measures that you now blame?'

'You commanded, then, and it was my duty to obey. Besides, you were just on the point of succeeding—not because of the means you had taken—but in spite of those means, with all their awkward and revolting brutality.'

'Sir—you are severe,' said Father d'Aigrigny.

'I am just. One has to be prodigiously clever, truly, to shut up any one in a room, and then lock the door ! And yet, what else have you done ? The daughters of General Simon?—imprisoned at Leipsic, shut up in a convent at Paris ! Adrienne de Cardoville?—placed in confinement. Sleepinbuff?—put in prison. Djalma?—quieted by a narcotic. One only ingenious method, and a thousand times safer, because it acted morally, not materially, was employed to remove M. Hardy. As for your other proceedings—they were all bad, uncertain, dangerous. Why? Because they were violent, and violence provokes violence. Then it is no longer a struggle of keen, skilful, persevering men, seeing through the darkness in which they walk, but a match of fisticuffs in broad day. Though we should be always in action, we should always shrink from view ; and yet you could find no better plan than to draw universal attention to us by proceedings at once open and deplorably notorious. To make them more secret, you call in the guard, the commissary of police, the gaolers, for your accomplices. It is pitiable, sir ; nothing but the most brilliant success could cover such wretched folly ; and this success has been wanting.'

'Sir,' said Father d'Aigrigny, deeply hurt, for the Princess de Saint-Dizier, unable to conceal the sort of admiration caused in her by the plain, decisive words of Rodin, looked at her old lover with an air that seemed to say, 'He is right ;'—'sir, you are more than severe in your judgment ; and, notwithstanding the deference I owe to you, I must observe, that I am not accustomed——'

'There are many other things to which you are not accustomed,' said Rodin, harshly interrupting the reverend father ; 'but you will accustom yourself to them. You have hitherto had a false idea of your own value. There is the old leaven of the soldier and the worldling fermenting within you, which deprives your reason of the coolness, lucidity, and penetration that it ought to possess. You have been a fine military officer, brisk and gay, foremost in wars and festivals, with pleasures and women. These things have half worn you out. You will never be anything but a subaltern ; you have been thoroughly tested. You will always want that vigour and concentration of mind which governs men and events. That vigour and concentration of mind I have—and do you know why ? It is because solely devoted to the service of the Company, I have always been ugly, dirty, unloved, unloving—I have all my manhood about me !'

In pronouncing these words, full of cynical pride, Rodin was truly fearful. The Princess de Saint-Dizier thought him almost handsome by his energy and audacity.

Father d'Aigrigny, feeling himself overawed, invincibly and inexorably, by this diabolical being, made a last effort to resist, and exclaimed, ' Oh ! sir, these boastings are no proofs of valour and power. We must see you at work.'

' Yes,' replied Rodin, coldly ; ' do you know at what work ?' Rodin was fond of this interrogative mode of expression. ' Why, at the work that you so basely abandon.'

' What !' cried the Princess de Saint-Dizier ; for Father d'Aigrigny, stupefied at Rodin's audacity, was unable to utter a word.

' I say,' resumed Rodin, slowly, ' that I undertake to bring to a good issue this affair of the Rennepont inheritance, which appears to you so desperate.'

' You ?' cried Father d'Aigrigny. ' You ?'

' I.'

' But they have unmasked our manœuvres.'

' So much the better ; we shall be obliged to invent others.'

' But they will suspect us in everything.'

' So much the better ; the success that is difficult is the most certain.'

' What ! do you hope to make Gabriel consent not to revoke his donation, which is perhaps illegal.'

' I mean to bring in to the coffers of the Company the whole of the two hundred and twelve millions, of which they wish to cheat us. Is that clear ?'

' It is clear—but impossible.'

' And I tell you that it is, and must be, possible. Do you not understand, short-sighted as you are !' cried Rodin, animated to such a degree that his cadaverous face became slightly flushed ; ' do you not understand that it is no longer in our choice to hesitate ? Either these two hundred and twelve millions must be ours—and then the re-establishment of our sovereign influence in France is sure—for, in these venal times, with such a sum at command, you may bribe or overthrow a government, or light up the flame of civil war, and restore legitimacy, which is our natural ally, and, owing all to us, would give us all in return——'

' That is clear,' cried the princess, clasping her hands in admiration.

' If, on the contrary,' resumed Rodin, ' these two hundred and twelve millions fall into the hands of the family of the Renneponts, it will be our ruin and our destruction. We shall create a stock of bitter and implacable enemies. Have you not heard the execrable designs of that Rennepont, with regard to the association he recommends, and which, by an accursed fatality, his race are just in a condition to realize ? Think of the forces that would rally round these millions. There would be Marshal Simon, acting in the name of his daughters—that is, the man of the people become a duke, without being the vainer for it, which secures his influence with the mob, because military spirit and Bonapartism still represent, in the eyes of the

French populace, the traditions of national honour ana glory. There would be Francis Hardy, the liberal, independent, enlightened citizen, the type of the great manufacturer, the friend of progress, the benefactor of his workmen. There would be Gabriel—"the good priest," as they say!—the apostle of the primitive gospel, the representative of the democracy of the church, of the poor country curate as opposed to the rich bishop, the tiller of the vine as opposed to him who sits in the shade of it ; the propagator of all the ideas of fraternity, emancipation, progress—to use their own jargon—and that, not in the name of revolutionary and incendiary politics, but in the name of a religion of charity, love, and peace--to speak as they speak. There, too, would be Adrienne de Cardoville, the type of elegance, grace, and beauty, the priestess of the senses, which she deifies by refining and cultivating them. I need not tell you of her wit and audacity ; you know them but too well. No one could be more dangerous to us than this creature, a patrician in blood, a plebeian in heart, a poet in imagination. Then, too, there would be Prince Djalma, chivalrous, bold, ready for adventure, knowing nothing of civilised life, implacable in his hate as in his affection, a terrible instrument for whoever can make use of him. In this detestable family, even such a wretch as Sleepinbuff, who in himself is of no value, raised and purified by the contact of these generous and far from narrow natures (as they call them), might represent the working class, and take a large share in the influence of that association. Now do you not think that if all these people, already exasperated against us, because (as they say) we have wished to rob them, should follow the detestable counsels of this Rennepont—should unite their forces around this immense fortune, which would strengthen them a hundred-fold—do you not think that, if they declare a deadly war against us, they will be the most dangerous enemies that we have ever had ? I tell you that the Company has never been in such serious peril ; yes, it is now a question of life and death. We must no longer defend ourselves, but lead the attack, so as to annihilate this accursed race of Rennepont, and obtain possession of these millions.'

At this picture, drawn by Rodin with a feverish animation, which had only the more influence from its unexpectedness, the princess and Father d'Aigrigny looked at each other in confusion.

' I confess,' said the reverend father to Rodin, ' I had not considered all the dangerous consequences of this association, recommended by M. de Rennepont. I believe that the heirs, from the characters we know them to be possessed of, would wish to realise this Utopia. The peril is great and pressing ; what is to be done ?'

' What, sir ? You have to act upon ignorant, heroic, enthusiastic natures like Djalma's—sensual and eccentric characters like Adrienne de Cardoville's—simple and ingenuous minds like Rose and Blanche Simon's—honest and frank dispositions like Francis Hardy's—angelic and pure souls like Gabriel's—brutal and stupid instincts like Jacques'—and can you ask, "What is to be done ?"'

' In truth, I do not understand you,' said Father d'Aigrigny.

' I believe it. Your past conduct shows as much,' replied Rodin, contemptuously. ' You have had recourse to the lowest and most mechanical contrivances, instead of acting upon the noble and generous passions, which, once united, would constitute so formidable a bond ; but which, now divided and isolated, are open to every surprise, every seduction, every attack ! Do you at length understand me ? Not yet ?' added Rodin, shrugging his shoulders. ' Answer me—do people die of despair ?——' Yes.'

' May not the gratitude of successful love reach the last limits of insane generosity ?'

' Yes.'

' May there not be such horrible deceptions, that suicide is the only refuge from frightful realities ?'

' Yes.'

' May not the excess of sensuality lead to the grave by a slow and voluptuous agony ?'

' Yes.'

' Are there not in life such terrible circumstances that the most worldly, the firmest, the most impious characters, throw themselves blindly, overwhelmed with despair, into the arms of religion, and abandon all earthly greatness for sackcloth, and prayers, and solitude ?'

' Yes.'

' Are there not a thousand occasions in which the reaction of the passions works the most extraordinary changes, and brings about the most tragic catastrophes in the life of man and woman ?'——' No doubt.'

' Well, then ! why ask me, " What is to be done ?" What would you say, for example, if, before three months are over, the most dangerous members of this family of the Renneponts should come to implore, upon their knees, admission to that very Society which they now hold in horror, and from which Gabriel has just separated ?'

' Such a conversion is impossible,' cried Father d Aigrigny.

' Impossible ? What were you, sir, fifteen years ago ?' said Rodin. ' An impious and debauched man of the world. And yet you came to us, and your wealth became ours. What ! we have conquered princes, kings, popes; we have absorbed and extinguished in our unity magnificent intelligences, which, from afar, shone with too dazzling a light ; we have all but governed two worlds ; we have perpetuated our Society, full of life, rich, and formidable, even to this day, through all the hate, and all the persecutions that have assailed us : and yet we shall not be able to get the better of a single family, which threatens our Company, and has despoiled us of a large fortune ? What ! we are not skilful enough to obtain this result without having recourse to awkward and dangerous violence ? You do not know, then, the immense field that is thrown open by the mutually destructive power of human passions, skilfully combined, opposed, restrained, excited ?—particularly,' added Rodin, with a strange smile, ' when, thanks to a powerful ally, these passions are sure to be redoubled in ardour and energy.'

' What ally ?' asked Father d'Aigrigny, who, as well as the Princess de Saint-Dizier, felt a sort of admiration mixed with terror.

' Yes, resumed Rodin, without answering the reverend father ; ' this formidable ally, who comes to our assistance, may bring about the most astonishing transformations—make the coward brave, and the impious credulous, and the gentle ferocious——'

' But this ally !' cried the Princess, oppressed with a vague sense of fear. ' This great and formidable ally—who is he ?'

' If he comes, resumed Rodin, still impassible, ' the youngest and most vigorous, every moment in danger of death, will have no advantage over the sick man at his last gasp.'

' But who is this ally ?" exclaimed Father d'Aigrigny, more and more alarmed, for as the picture became darker, Rodin's face became more cadaverous.

' This ally, who can decimate a population, may carry away with him in the shroud that he drags at his heels, the whole of an accursed race ; but even he must respect the life of that great intangible body, which does not perish with the death of its members—for the spirit of the Society of Jesus is immortal !'

'And this ally?'

'Oh! this ally,' resumed Rodin, 'who advances with slow steps, and whose terrible coming is announced by mournful presentiments——'

'Is——'

'The Cholera!'

These words, pronounced by Rodin in an abrupt voice, made the Princess and Father d'Aigrigny grow pale and tremble. Rodin's look was gloomy and chilling, like a spectre's. For some moments, the silence of the tomb reigned in the saloon. Rodin was the first to break it. Still impassible, he pointed with imperious gesture to the table, where a few minutes before he had himself been humbly seated, and said in a sharp voice to Father d'Aigrigny, 'Write!'

The reverend father started at first with surprise; then, remembering that from a superior he had become an inferior, he rose, bowed lowly to Rodin, as he passed before him, seated himself at the table, took the pen, and said, 'I am ready.'

Rodin dictated, and the reverend father wrote as follows: 'By the mismanagement of the Reverend Father d'Aigrigny, the affair of the inheritance of the Rennepont family has been seriously compromised. The sum amounts to two hundred and twelve millions. Notwithstanding the check we have received, we believe we may safely promise to prevent these Renneponts from injuring the Society, and to restore the two hundred and twelve millions to their legitimate possessors. We only ask for the most complete and extensive powers.'

   ✿   ✿   ✿   ✿   ✿   ✿

A quarter of an hour after this scene, Rodin left Saint-Dizier House, brushing with his sleeve the old greasy hat, which he had pulled off to return the salute of the porter by a very low bow.

CHAPTER XXVIII.

THE STRANGER.

THE following scene took place on the morrow of the day in which Father d'Aigrigny had been so rudely degraded by Rodin to the subaltern position formerly occupied by the socius.

   ✳   ✳   ✳   ✳   ✳   ✳

It is well known that the Rue Clovis is one of the most solitary streets in the Montagne St. Geneviève district. At the epoch of this narrative, the house No. 4, in this street, was composed of one principal building, through which ran a dark passage, leading to a little, gloomy court, at the end of which was a second building, in a singularly miserable and dilapidated condition. On the ground-floor, in front of the house, was a half-subterraneous shop, in which was sold charcoal, faggots, vegetables, and milk. Nine o'clock in the morning had just struck. The mistress of the shop, one Mother Arsène, an old woman of a mild, sickly countenance, clad in a brown stuff dress, with a red bandanna round her head, was mounted on the top step of the stairs which led down to her door, and was employed in setting out her goods—that is, on one side of the door she placed a tin milk-can, and on the other some bunches of stale vegetables, flanked with yellowed cabbages. At the bottom of the steps, in the shadowy depths of the cellar, one could see the light of the burning charcoal in a little stove. This shop, situated at the side of the passage, served as a porter's lodge, and the old woman acted as portress. On a sudden, a pretty little creature, coming from the house, entered lightly and merrily the shop. This young girl was

Rose-Pompon, the intimate friend of the Bacchanal Queen.—Rose-Pompon, a *widow* for the moment, whose bacchanalian *cicisbeo* was Ninny Moulin, the orthodox scapegrace, who, on occasion, after drinking his fill, could transform himself into Jacques Dumoulin, the religious writer, and pass gaily from dishevelled dances to ultramontane polemics, from Storm-blown Tulips to Catholic pamphlets.

Rose-Pompon had just quitted her bed, as appeared by the negligence of her strange morning costume ; no doubt for want of any other head-dress, on her beautiful light hair, smooth and well-combed, was stuck jauntily a foraging-cap, borrowed from her masquerading costume. Nothing could be more sprightly than that face, seventeen years old, rosy, fresh, dimpled, and brilliantly lighted up by a pair of gay, sparkling blue eyes. Rose-Pompon was so closely enveloped from the neck to the feet in a red and green plaid cloak, rather faded, that one could guess the cause of her modest embarrassment. Her naked feet, so white that one could not tell if she wore stockings or not, were slipped into little morocco shoes, with plated buckles. It was easy to perceive that her cloak concealed some article which she held in her hand.

'Good day, Rose-Pompon,' said Mother Arsène with a kindly air ; 'you are early this morning. Had you no dance last night ?'

'Don't talk of it, Mother Arsène ; I had no heart to dance. Poor Cephyse —the Bacchanal Queen—has done nothing but cry all night. She cannot console herself, that her lover should be in prison.'

'Now, look here, my girl,' said the old woman, 'I must speak to you about your friend Cephyse. You won't be angry ?'

'Am I ever angry ?' said Rose-Pompon, shrugging her shoulders.

'Don't you think that M. Philemon will scold me on his return ?'

'Scold you ! what for ?'

'Because of his rooms, that you occupy.'

'Why, Mother Arsène, did not Philemon tell you, that, in his absence, I was to be as much mistress of his two rooms as I am of himself ?'

'I do not speak of you, but of your friend Cephyse, whom you have also brought to occupy M. Philemon's lodgings.'

'And where would she have gone without me, my good Mother Arsène ? Since her lover was arrested, she has not dared to return home, because she owes ever so many quarters. Seeing her troubles, I said to her : " Come, lodge at Philemon's. When he returns, we must find another place for you.' "

'Well, little lovely—if you only assure me that M. Philemon will not be angry——'

'Angry ! for what ? That we spoil his things ? A fine set of things he has to spoil ! I broke his last cup yesterday—and am forced to fetch the milk in this comic concern.'

So saying, laughing with all her might, Rose-Pompon drew her pretty little white arm from under her cloak, and presented to Mother Arsène one of those champagne glasses of colossal capacity, which hold about a bottle.

'Oh, dear !' said the greengrocer in amazement ; 'it is like a glass trumpet.'

'It is Philemon's grand gala-glass, which they gave him when he took his degrees in boating,' said Rose-Pompon, gravely.

'And to think you must put your milk in it—I am really ashamed,' said Mother Arsène.

'So am I ! If I were to meet any one on the stairs, holding this glass in my hand like a Roman candlestick, I should burst out laughing, and break the last remnant of Philemon's bazaar, and he would give me his malediction.'

'There is no danger that you will meet any one. The first-floor is gone out, and the second gets up very late.'

'Talking of lodgers,' said Rose-Pompon, 'is there not a room to let on the second-floor in the rear house? It might do for Cephyse, when Philemon comes back.'

'Yes, there is a little closet in the roof—just over the two rooms of the mysterious old fellow,' said Mother Arsène.

'Oh, yes! Father Charlemagne. Have you found out anything more about him?'

'Dear me, no, my girl! only that he came this morning at break of day, and knocked at my shutters. "Have you received a letter for me, my good lady?" said he—for he is always so polite, the dear man!—"No, sir," said I.—"Well, then, pray don't disturb yourself, my good lady!" said he; "I will call again." And so he went away.'

'Does he never sleep in the house?'

'Never. No doubt, he lodges somewhere else—but he passes some hours here, once every four or five days.'

'And always comes alone?'

'Always.'

'Are you quite sure? Does he never manage to slip in some little puss of a woman? Take care, or Philemon will give you notice to quit,' said Rose-Pompon, with an air of mock-modesty.

'M. Charlemagne with a woman! Oh, poor dear man!' said the green-grocer, raising her hands to heaven; 'if you saw him, with his greasy hat, his old grey coat, his patched umbrella, and his simple face, he looks more like a saint than anything else.'

'But then, Mother Arsène, what does the saint do here, all alone for hours, in that hole at the bottom of the court, where one can hardly see at noonday?'

'That's what I ask myself, my dovey, what can he be doing? It can't be that he comes to look at his furniture, for he has nothing but a flock-bed, a table, a stove, a chair, and an old trunk.'

'Somewhat in the style of Philemon's establishment,' said Rose-Pompon.

'Well, notwithstanding that, Rosey, he is as much afraid that any one should come into his room, as if we were all thieves, and his furniture was made of massy gold. He has had a patent lock put on the door, at his own expense; he never leaves me his key; and he lights his fire himself, rather than let anybody into his room.'

'And you say he is old?'

'Yes, fifty or sixty.'

'And ugly?'

'Just fancy, little viper's eyes, looking as if they had been bored with a gimlet, in a face as pale as death—so pale, that the lips are white. That's for his appearance. As for his character, the good old man is so polite!—he pulls off his hat so often, and makes you such low bows, that it is quite embarrassing.'

'But, to come back to the point,' resumed Rose-Pompon, 'what can he do all alone in those two rooms? If Cephyse should take the closet, on Philemon's return, we may amuse ourselves by finding out something about it. How much do they want for the little room?'

'Why, it is in such bad condition, that I think the landlord would let it go for fifty or fifty-five francs a-year, for there is no room for a stove, and the only light comes through a small pane in the roof.'

'Poor Cephyse!' said Rose, sighing, and shaking her head sorrowfully. 'After having amused herself so well, and flung away so much money with

Jacques Rennepont, to live in such a place, and support herself by hard work ! She must have courage !'

'Why, indeed, there is a great difference between that closet and the coach-and-four in which Cephyse came to fetch you the other day, with all the fine masks, that looked so gay—particularly the fat man in the silver paper helmet, with the plume and the top boots. What a jolly fellow !'

'Yes, Ninny Moulin. There is no one like him to dance the forbidden fruit. You should see him with Cephyse, the Bacchanal Queen. Poor laughing, noisy thing !—the only noise she makes now is crying.'

'Oh ! these young people—these young people !' said the greengrocer.

'Easy, Mother Arsène ; you were young once.'

'I hardly know. I have always thought myself much the same as I am now.'

'And your lovers, Mother Arsène ?'

'Lovers ! Oh, yes ! I was too ugly for that—and too well taken care of.'

'Your mother looked after you, then ?'

'No, my girl ; but I was harnessed.'

'Harnessed !' cried Rose Pompon, in amazement, interrupting the dealer.

'Yes,—harnessed to a water-cart, along with my brother. So, you see, when we had drawn like a pair of horses for eight or ten hours a day, I had no heart to think of nonsense.'

'Poor Mother Arsène, what a hard life,' said Rose-Pompon, with interest.

'In the winter, when it froze, it was hard enough. I and my brother were obliged to be rough-shod, for fear of slipping.'

'What a trade for a woman ! It breaks one's heart. And they forbid people to harness dogs !' added Rose-Pompon, sententiously.*

'Why, 'tis true,' resumed Mother Arsène. 'Animals are sometimes better off than people. But what would you have ? One must live, you know. As you make your bed, you must lie. It was hard enough, and I got a disease of the lungs by it—which was not my fault. The strap, with which I was harnessed, pressed so hard against my chest, that I could scarcely breathe : so I left the trade, and took to a shop, which is just to tell you, that if I had had a pretty face and opportunity, I might have done like so many other young people, who begin with laughter and finish——'

'With a laugh t'other side of the mouth—you would say ; it is true, Mother Arsène. But, you see, everyone has not the courage to go into harness, in order to remain virtuous. A body says to herself, you must have some amusement while you are young and pretty—you will not always be seventeen years old—and then—and then—the world will end, or you will get married.'

'But, perhaps, it would have been better to begin by that.'

'Yes, but one is too stupid ; one does not know how to catch the men, or to frighten them. One is simple, confiding, and they only laugh at us. Why, Mother Arsène, I am myself an example that would make you shudder; but 'tis quite enough to have had one's sorrows, without fretting one's self at the remembrance.'

'What, my beauty ! you, so young and gay, have had sorrows ?'

'Ah, Mother Arsène ! I believe you. At fifteen and a half I began to cry, and never left off till I was sixteen. That was enough, I think.'

'They deceived you, mademoiselle ?'

'They did worse. They treated me as they have treated many a poor

---

* There are, really, ordinances, full of a touching interest for the canine race, which forbid the harnessing of dogs.

girl, who had no more wish to go wrong than I had. My story is not a three volume one. My father and mother are peasants near Saint-Valéry, but so poor—so poor, that having five children to provide for, they were obliged to send me, at eight years old, to my aunt, who was a charwoman here in Paris. The good woman took me out of charity, and very kind it was of her, for I earned but little. At eleven years of age she sent me to work in one of the factories of the Faubourg Saint-Antoine. I don't wish to speak ill of the masters of these factories ; but what do they care, if little boys and girls are mixed up pell-mell with young men and women of eighteen to twenty ? Now you see, there, as everywhere, some are no better than they should be ; they are not particular in word or deed, and I ask you, what an example for the children, who hear and see more than you think for. Then, what happens ? They get accustomed as they grow older, to hear and see things, that afterwards will not shock them at all.'

'What you say there is true, Rose-Pompon. Poor children ! who takes any trouble about them ?—not their father or mother, for they are at their daily work.'

'Yes, yes, Mother Arsène, it is all very well ; it is easy to cry down a young girl that has gone wrong ; but if they knew all the ins and outs, they would perhaps pity rather than blame her. To come back to myself—at fifteen years old I was tolerably pretty. One day I had something to ask of the head clerk. I went to him in his private room. He told me he would grant what I wanted, and even take me under his patronage, if I would listen to him ; and he began by trying to kiss me. I resisted. Then he said to me—" You refuse my offer ? You shall have no more work ; I discharge you from the factory." '

'Oh, the wicked man !' said Mother Arsène.

'I went home all in tears, and my poor aunt encouraged me not to yield, and she would try to place me elsewhere. Yes—but it was impossible ; the factories were all full. Misfortunes never come single ; my aunt fell ill, and there was not a sou in the house ; I plucked up my courage, and returned to entreat the mercy of the clerk at the factory. Nothing would do. "So much the worse," said he ; "you are throwing away your luck. If you had been more complying, I should perhaps have married you." What could I do, Mother Arsène ?—misery was staring me in the face ; I had no work ; my aunt was ill ; the clerk said he would marry me—I did like so many others.'

'And when, afterwards, you spoke to him about marriage ?'

'Of course he laughed at me, and in six months left me. Then I wept all the tears in my body, till none remained—then I was very ill—and then—I consoled myself, as one may console one's self for anything. After some changes, I met with Philemon. It is upon him that I revenge myself for what others have done to me. I am his tyrant,' added Rose-Pompon, with a tragic air, as the cloud passed away which had darkened her pretty face during her recital to Mother Arsène.

'It is true,' said the latter thoughtfully. 'They deceive a poor girl—who is there to protect or defend her ? Oh ! the evil we do does not always come from ourselves, and then——'

'I spy Ninny Moulin !' cried Rose-Pompon, interrupting the greengrocer, and pointing to the other side of the street. 'How early abroad ! What can he want with me ?' and Rose wrapped herself still more closely and modestly in her cloak.

It was indeed Jacques Dumoulin, who advanced with his hat stuck on one side, with rubicund nose and sparkling eye, dressed in a loose coat, which displayed the rotundity of his abdomen. His hands, one of which held a huge cane shouldered like a musket, were plunged into the vast pockets of his outer garment.

Just as he reached the threshold of the door, no doubt with the intention of speaking to the portress, he perceived Rose-Pompon. 'What!' he exclaimed, 'my pupil already stirring! That is fortunate. I came on purpose to bless her at the rise of morn!'

So saying, Ninny Moulin advanced with open arms towards Rose-Pompon, who drew back a step.

'What, ungrateful child!' resumed the writer on divinity. 'Will you refuse me the morning's paternal kiss?'

'I accept paternal kisses from none but Philemon. I had a letter from him yesterday, with a jar of preserves, two geese, a bottle of home-made brandy, and an eel. What ridiculous presents! I kept the drink, and changed the rest for two darling live pigeons, which I have installed in Philemon's cabinet, and a very pretty dove-cote it makes me. For the rest, my husband is coming back with seven hundred francs, which he got from his respectable family, under pretence of learning the bass viol, the cornet-à-piston, and the speaking trumpet, so as to make his way in society, and a slap-up marriage—to use your expression—my good child.'

'Well, my dear pupil, we will taste the family brandy, and enjoy ourselves in expectation of Philemon and his seven hundred francs.'

So saying, Ninny Moulin slapped the pockets of his waistcoat, which gave forth a metallic sound, and added : 'I come to propose to you to embellish my life, to-day and to-morrow, and even the day after, if your heart is willing.'

'If the amusements are decent and paternal, my heart does not say no.'

'Be satisfied ; I will act by you as your grandfather, your great-grand-father, your family portrait. We will have a ride, a dinner, the play, a fancy-dress ball, and a supper afterwards. Will that suit you?'

'On condition that poor Cephyse is to go with us. It will raise her spirits.'

'Well, Cephyse shall be of the party.

'Have you come into a fortune, great apostle?'

'Better than that, most rosy and pompous of all Rose-Pompons ! I am head editor of a religious journal ; and as I must make some appearance in so respectable a concern, I ask every month for four weeks in advance, and three days of liberty. On this condition, I consent to play the saint for twenty-seven days out of thirty, and to be always as grave and heavy as the paper itself.'

'A journal ! that will be something droll, and dance forbidden steps all alone on the tables of the cafés.'

'Yes, it will be droll enough ; but not for everybody. They are rich sacristans, who pay the expenses. They don't look to money, provided the journal bites, tears, burns, pounds, exterminates and destroys. On my word of honour, I shall never have been in such a fury !' added Ninny Moulin, with a loud, hoarse laugh. 'I shall wash the wounds of my adversaries with venom of the finest vintage, and gall of the first quality.'

For his peroration, Ninny Moulin imitated the pop of uncorking a bottle of champagne—which made Rose-Pompon laugh heartily.

'And what,' resumed she, 'will be the name of your journal of sacristans?'

'It will be called "Neighbourly Love."'

'Come ! that is a very pretty name.'

'Wait a little ! there is a second title.'

'Let us hear it.'

"Neighbourly Love ; or, the Exterminator of the Incredulous, the Indifferent, the Lukewarm, and Others," with this motto from the great Bossuet: " Those who are not for us are against us." '

' That is what Philemon says in the battles at the Chaumière, when he shakes his cane.'

' Which proves, that the genius of the Eagle of Meaux is universal. I only reproach him for having been jealous of Molière.'

' Bah ! actor's jealousy,' said Rose-Pompon.

' Naughty girl !' cried Ninny Moulin, threatening her with his finger.

' But if you are going to exterminate Madame de la Sainte-Colombe, who is somewhat lukewarm—how about your marriage ?'

' My journal will advance it, on the contrary. Only think ! editor-in-chief is a superb position ; the sacristans will praise, and push, and support, and bless me ; I shall get La Sainte-Colombe—and then, what a life I'll lead !'

At this moment, a postman entered the shop, and delivered a letter to the greengrocer, saying : ' For M. Charlemagne, post-paid !'

' My !' said Rose-Pompon ; ' it is for the little mysterious old man, who has such extraordinary ways. Does it come from far ?'

' I believe you ; it comes from Italy, from Rome,' said Ninny Moulin, looking in his turn at the letter, which the greengrocer held in her hand. ' Who is the astonishing little old man of whom you speak ?'

' Just imagine to yourself, my great apostle,' said Rose-Pompon, ' a little old man, who has two rooms at the bottom of that court. He never sleeps there, but comes from time to time, and shuts himself up for hours, without ever allowing any one to enter his lodging, and without any one knowing what he does there.'

' He is a conspirator,' said Ninny Moulin, laughing, ' or else a coiner.'

' Poor dear man,' said Mother Arsène, ' what has he done with his false money? He pays me always in sous for the bit of bread and the radish I furnish him for his breakfast.'

' And what is the name of this mysterious chap ?' asked Dumoulin.

' M. Charlemagne,' said the greengrocer. ' But look, when one speaks of the devil, one is sure to see his horns.'

' Where's the horns ?'

' There, by the side of the house—that little old man, who walks with his neck awry, and his umbrella under his arm.'

' M. Rodin !' ejaculated Ninny Moulin, retreating hastily, and descending three steps into the shop, in order not to be seen. Then he added : ' You say, that this gentleman calls himself——'

' M. Charlemagne—do you know him ?' asked the greengrocer.

' What the devil does he do here, under a false name ?' said Jacques Dumoulin to himself.

' You know him?' said Rose-Pompon, with impatience. ' You are quite confused.'

' And this gentleman has two rooms in this house, and comes here mysteriously,' said Jacques Dumoulin, more and more surprised.

' Yes,' resumed Rose-Pompon ; ' you can see his windows from Philemon's dove-cote.'

' Quick ! quick ! let me go into the passage, that I may not meet him,' said Dumoulin.

And, without having been perceived by Rodin, he glided from the shop into the passage, and thence mounted to the stairs, which led to the apartment occupied by Rose-Pompon.

' Good-morning, M. Charlemagne,' said Mother Arsène to Rodin, who made his appearance on the threshold. ' You come twice in a day ; that is right, for your visits are extremely rare.'

'You are too polite, my good lady,' said Rodin, with a very courteous bow ; and he entered the shop of the greengrocer.

CHAPTER XXIX.

THE DEN.

RODIN'S countenance, when he entered Mother Arsène's shop, was expressive of the most simple candour. He leaned his hands on the knob of his umbrella, and said ; 'I much regret, my good lady, that I roused you so early this morning.'

'You do not come often enough, my dear sir, for me to find fault with you.'

'How can I help it, my good lady ? I live in the country, and only come hither from time to time to settle my little affairs.'

'Talking of that, sir, the letter you expected yesterday has arrived this morning. It is large, and comes from far. Here it is,' said the greengrocer, drawing it from her pocket ; 'it cost nothing for postage.'

'Thank you, my good lady,' said Rodin, taking the letter with apparent indifference, and putting it into the side-pocket of his great coat, which he carefully buttoned over.

'Are you going up to your rooms, sir ?'

'Yes, my good lady.'

'Then I will get ready your little provisions,' said Mother Arsène ; 'as usual, I suppose, my dear sir ?'

'Just as usual.'

'It shall be ready in the twinkling of an eye, sir.'

So saying, the greengrocer took down an old basket ; after throwing into it three or four pieces of turf, a little bundle of wood, and some charcoal, she covered all this fuel with a cabbage leaf ; then, going to the further end of the shop, she took from a chest a large round loaf, cut off a slice, and selecting a magnificent radish with the eye of a connoisseur, divided it in two, made a hole in it, which she filled with grey salt, joined the two pieces together again, and placed it carefully by the side of the bread, on the cabbage leaf which separated the eatables from the combustibles. Finally, taking some embers from her stove, she put them into a little earthern pot, containing ashes, which she placed also in the basket.

Then, reascending to her top step, Mother Arsène said to Rodin : 'Here is your basket, sir.'

'A thousand thanks, my good lady,' answered Rodin, and, plunging his hand into the pocket of his trousers, he drew forth eight sous, which he counted out one by one to the greengrocer, and said to her, as he carried off his store : 'Presently, when I come down again, I will return your basket as usual.'

'Quite at your service, my dear sir, quite at your service,' said Mother Arsène.

Rodin tucked his umbrella under his left arm, took up the greengrocer's basket with his right hand, entered the dark passage, crossed the little court, and mounted with light step to the second storey of a dilapidated building ; there, drawing a key from his pocket, he opened a door, which he locked carefully after him. The first of the two rooms which he occupied was completely unfurnished ; as for the second, it is impossible to imagine a more gloomy and miserable den. Papering so much worn, torn and faded, that no one could recognise its primitive colour, bedecked the walls. A wretched flock-bed, covered with a moth-fretted blanket ; a stool, and a little table of worm-eaten wood ; an earthenware stove, as cracked as old china ; a trunk, with a padlock, placed under the bed—such was the furni-ture of this desolate hole. A narrow window, with dirty panes, hardly gave any light to this room, which was almost deprived of air by the height of the building in front ; two old cotton pocket-handkerchiefs, fastened to-gether with pins, and made to slide upon a string stretched across the window, served for curtains. The plaster of the roof, coming through the broken and disjointed tiles, showed the extreme neglect of the inhabitant of this abode. After locking his door, Rodin threw his hat and umbrella on the bed, placed his basket on the ground, set the radish and bread on the table, and, kneeling down before his stove, stuffed it with fuel, and lighted it by blowing with vigorous lungs on the embers contained in his earthen pot.

When, to use the consecrated expression, the stove began to draw, Rodin spread out the handkerchiefs, which served him for curtains ; then, thinking himself quite safe from every eye, he took from the side pocket of his great coat the letter that Mother Arsène had given him. In doing so, he brought out several papers and different articles ; one of these papers, folded into a thick and rumpled packet, fell upon the table, and flew open. It contained a silver cross of the Legion of Honour, black with time. The red ribbon of this cross had almost entirely lost its original colour. At sight of this cross, which he replaced in his pocket with the medal of which Faringhea had despoiled Djalma, Rodin shrugged his shoulders with a contemptuous and sardonic air ; then, producing his large silver watch, he laid it on the table by the side of the letter from Rome. He looked at this letter with a singular mixture of suspicion and hope, of fear and impatient curiosity. After a moment's reflection, he prepared to unseal the envelope ; but suddenly he threw it down again upon the table, as if, by a strange caprice, he had wished to prolong for a few minutes that agony of uncertainty, as poignant and irritating as the emotion of the gambler.

Looking at his watch, Rodin resolved not to open the letter, until the hand should mark half-past nine, of which it still wanted seven minutes. In one of those whims of puerile fatalism, from which great minds have not been exempt, Rodin said to himself : ' I burn with impatience to open this letter. If I do not open it till half-past nine, the news will be favour-able.' To employ these minutes, Rodin took several turns up and down the room, and stood in admiring contemplation before two old prints, stained with damp and age, and fastened to the wall by rusty nails. The first of these works of art—the only ornaments with which Rodin had decorated this hole—was one of those coarse pictures, illuminated with red, yellow, green, and blue, such as are sold at fairs ; an Italian inscription announced that this print had been manufactured at Rome. It represented a woman covered with rags, bearing a wallet, and having a little child upon her knees ; a hor-rible hag of a fortune-teller held in her hands the hand of the little child, and seemed to read there his future fate, for these words in large blue letters issued from her mouth : ' Sara Papa ' (he shall be Pope).

The second of these works of art, which appeared to inspire Rodin with deep meditations, was an excellent etching, whose careful finish and bold, correct drawing, contrasted singularly with the coarse colouring of the other picture. This rare and splendid engraving, which had cost Rodin six louis (an enormous expense for him), represented a young boy dressed in rags. The ugliness of his features was compensated by the intellectual expression of his strongly marked countenance. Seated on a stone, surrounded by a herd of swine, that he seemed employed in keeping, he was seen in front, with his elbow resting on his knee, and his chin in the palm of his hand,

The pensive and reflective attitude of this young man, dressed as a beggar, the power expressed in his large forehead, the acuteness of his penetrating glance, and the firm lines of the mouth, seemed to reveal indomitable resolution, combined with superior intelligence and ready craft. Beneath this figure, the emblems of the papacy encircled a medallion, in the centre of which was the head of an old man, the lines of which, strongly marked, recalled in a striking manner, notwithstanding their look of advanced age, the features of the young swineherd. This engraving was entitled THE YOUTH OF SIXTUS V.; the coloured print was entitled The Prediction.*

In contemplating these prints more and more nearly, with ardent and inquiring eye, as though he had asked for hopes or inspirations from them, Rodin had come so close that, still standing, with his right arm bent behind his head, he rested, as it were, against the wall, whilst, hiding his left hand in the pocket of his black trousers, he thus held back one of the flaps of his olive great coat. For some minutes, he remained in this meditative attitude.

    ✿   ✿   ✿   ✿   ✿   ✿

Rodin, as we have said, came seldom to this lodging; according to the rules of his Order, he had till now lived with Father d'Aigrigny, whom he was specially charged to watch. No member of the Society, particularly in the subaltern position which Rodin had hitherto held, could either shut himself in, or possess an article of furniture made to lock. By this means nothing interferes with the mutual spy-system, incessantly carried on, which forms one of the most powerful resources of the Company of Jesus. It was on account of certain combinations, purely personal to himself, though connected on some points with the interests of the Order, that Rodin, unknown to all, had taken these rooms in the Rue Clovis. And it was from the depths of this obscure den that the socius corresponded directly with the most eminent and influential personages of the sacred college. On one occasion, when Rodin wrote to Rome, that Father d'Aigrigny, having received orders to quit France without seeing his dying mother, had hesitated to set out, the socius had added, in form of postscriptum, at the bottom of the letter denouncing to the General of the Order the hesitation of Father d'Aigrigny:

'Tell the Prince Cardinal that he may rely upon me, but I hope for his active aid in return.'

This familiar manner of corresponding with the most powerful dignitary of the Order, the almost patronising tone of the recommendation that Rodin addressed to the Prince Cardinal, proved that the socius, notwithstanding his apparently subaltern position, was looked upon, at that epoch, as a very important personage, by many of the princes of the Church, who wrote to him at Paris under a false name, making use of a cipher and other customary precautions. After some moments passed in contemplation, before the portrait of Sixtus V., Rodin returned slowly to the table, on which lay the letter, which, by a sort of superstitious delay, he had deferred opening, notwithstanding his extreme curiosity. As it still wanted some minutes of half-past nine, Rodin, in order not to lose time, set about making preparations for his frugal breakfast. He placed on the table, by the side of an inkstand, furnished with pens, the slice of bread and the radish; then, seating himself on his stool, with the stove, as it were, between his legs, he drew a horn-handled knife from his pocket, and, cutting alternately a morsel of bread and a morsel of radish, with the sharp, well-worn blade, he began his tem-

* According to the tradition, it was predicted to the mother of Sixtus V. that he would be pope; and, in his youth, he is said to have kept swine.

perate repast with a vigorous appetite, keeping his eye fixed on the hand of his watch. When it reached the momentous hour, he unsealed the envelope with a trembling hand.

It contained two letters. The first appeared to give him little satisfaction ; for, after some minutes, he shrugged his shoulders, struck the table impatiently with the handle of his knife, disdainfully pushed aside the letter with the back of his dirty hand, and perused the second epistle, holding his bread in one hand, and with the other mechanically dipping a slice of radish into the grey salt spilt on a corner of the table. Suddenly, Rodin's hand remained motionless. As he progressed in his reading, he appeared more and more interested, surprised, and struck. Rising abruptly, he ran to the window, as if to assure himself, by a second examination of the cipher, that he was not deceived. The news announced to him in the letter seemed to be unexpected. No doubt, Rodin found that he had deciphered correctly, for, letting fall his arms, not in dejection, but with the stupor of a satisfaction as unforeseen as extraordinary, he remained for some time with his head down, and his eye fixed—the only mark of joy that he gave being manifested by a loud, frequent, and prolonged respiration. Men who are as audacious in their ambition, as they are patient and obstinate in their mining and countermining, are surprised at their own success, when this latter precedes and surpasses their wise and prudent expectations. Rodin was now in this case. Thanks to prodigies of craft, address, and dissimulation, thanks to mighty promises of corruption, thanks to the singular mixture of admiration, fear, and confidence, with which his genius inspired many influential persons, Rodin now learned from members of the pontifical government, that, in case of a possible and probable occurrence, he might, within a given time, aspire, with a good chance of success, to a position which has too often excited the fear, the hate, or the envy of many sovereigns, and which has, in turn, been occupied by great, good men, by abominable scoundrels, and by persons risen from the lowest grades of society. But for Rodin to attain this end with certainty, it was absolutely necessary for him to succeed in that project, which he had undertaken to accomplish without violence, and only by the play and the rebound of passions skilfully managed. The project was : To secure for the Society of Jesus the fortune of the Rennepont family.

This possession would thus have a double and immense result ; for Rodin, acting in accordance with his personal views, intended to make of his Order (whose chief was at his discretion) a stepping-stone and a means of intimidation. When his first impression of surprise had passed away— an impression that was only a sort of modesty of ambition and self-diffidence, not uncommon with men of really superior powers—Rodin looked more coldly and logically on the matter, and almost reproached himself for his surprise. But soon after, by a singular contradiction, yielding to one of those puerile and absurd ideas, by which men are often carried away when they think themselves alone and unobserved, Rodin rose abruptly, took the letter which had caused him such glad surprise, and went to display it, as it were, before the eyes of the young swineherd in the picture ; then, shaking his head proudly and triumphantly, casting his reptile-glance on the portrait, he muttered between his teeth, as he placed his dirty finger on the pontifical emblem : ' Eh, brother ? and I also—perhaps !'

After this ridiculous interpolation, Rodin returned to his seat, and, as if the happy news he had just received had increased his appetite, he placed the letter before him, to read it once more, whilst he exercised his teeth, with a sort of joyous fury, on his hard bread and radish, chanting an old Litany.

There was something strange, great, and, above all, frightful, in the contrast afforded by this immense ambition, already almost justified by events, and contained, as it were, in so miserable an abode. Father d'Aigrigny (who, if not a very superior man, had at least some real value, was a person of high birth, very haughty, and placed in the best society) would never have ventured to aspire to what Rodin thus looked to from the first. The only aim of Father d'Aigrigny, and even this he thought presumptuous, was to be one day elected General of his Order—that Order which embraced the world. The difference of the ambitious aptitudes of these two personages is conceivable. When a man of eminent abilities, of a healthy and vivacious nature, concentrates all the strength of his mind and body upon a single point, remaining, like Rodin, obstinately chaste and frugal, and renouncing every gratification of the heart and the senses—the man, who revolts against the sacred designs of his Creator, does so almost always in favour of some monstrous and devouring passion—some infernal divinity, which, by a sacrilegious pact, asks of him, in return for the bestowal of formidable power, the destruction of every noble sentiment, and of all those ineffable attractions and tender instincts with which the Maker, in His eternal wisdom and inexhaustible munificence, has so paternally endowed His creatures.

* * * * *

During the scene that we have just described, Rodin had not perceived that the curtain of a window on the third story of the building opposite had been partially drawn aside, and had half-revealed the sprightly face of Rose Pompon, and the Silenus-like countenance of Ninny Moulin. It ensued that Rodin, notwithstanding his barricade of cotton handkerchiefs, had not been completely sheltered from the indiscreet and curious examination of the two dancers of the Storm-blown Tulip.

CHAPTER XXX.

AN UNEXPECTED VISIT.

THOUGH Rodin had experienced much surprise on reading the second letter from Rome, he did not choose that his answer should betray any such amazement. Having finished his frugal breakfast, he took a sheet of paper, and rapidly wrote in cipher the following note, in the short, abrupt style that was natural to him when not obliged to restrain himself :

'The information does not surprise me. I had foreseen it all. Indecision and cowardice always bear such fruit. This is not enough. Heretical Russia murders Catholic Poland. Rome blesses the murderers, and curses the victims.*

'Let it pass.

'In return, Russia guarantees to Rome, by Austria, the bloody suppression of the patriots of Romagna.

* On page 110 of Lamennais' *Affaires de Rome,* will be seen the following admirable scathing of Rome by the most truly evangelical spirit of our age : 'So long as the issue of the conflict between Poland and her oppressors remained in the balances, the papal official organ contained not one word to offend the so long victorious nation ; but hardly had she gone down under the Czar's atrocious vengeance, and the long torture of a whole land doomed to rack, exile, and servitude began, than this same journal found no language black enough to stain those whom fortune had fled. Yet it is wrong to charge this unworthy insult to papal power ; it only cringes to the law which Russia lays down to it, when it says :

' "If you want to keep your own bones unbroken, bide where you are, beside the scaffold, and, as the victims pass, hoot at them !" '

'That, too, is well.

'The cut-throat band of good Cardinal Albani is not sufficient for the massacre of the impious liberals.   They are weary of the task.

'Not so well.   They must go on.'

When Rodin had written these last words, his attention was suddenly attracted by the clear and sonorous voice of Rose-Pompon, who, knowing her Béranger by heart, had opened Philemon's window, and, seated on the sill, sang with much grace and prettiness this verse of the immortal song-writer :

> 'How wrong you are !   Is't you dare say
>   That heaven ever scowls on earth ?
> The earth that laughs up to its blue,
>   The earth that owes it joy and birth ?
> Oh, may the wine from vines it warms,
>   May holy love thence flutt'ring down,
> Lend my philosophy their charms,
>   To drive away care's direful frown !
>   So, firm let's stand,
>   Full glass in hand,
>   And all evoke
>   The God of honest folk !'

This song, in its divine gentleness, contrasted so strangely with the cold cruelty of the few lines written by Rodin, that he started and bit his lips with rage, as he recognised the words of the great poet, truly Christian, who had dealt such rude blows to the false Church.   Rodin waited for some moments with angry impatience, thinking the voice would continue ; but Rose-Pompon was silent, or only continued to hum, and soon changed to another air, that of the Good Pope, which she entoned, but without words. Rodin, not venturing to look out of his window to see who was this trouble-some warbler, shrugged his shoulders, resumed his pen, and continued :

'To it again.   We must exasperate the independent spirits in all countries—excite *philosophic* rage all over Europe—make liberalism foam at the mouth—raise all that is wild and noisy against Rome.   To effect this, we must proclaim in the face of the world these three propositions :   1. It is abominable to assert that a man may be saved in any faith whatever, provided his morals be pure.   2. It is odious and absurd to grant liberty of conscience to the people.   3. The liberty of the press cannot be held in too much horror.*

'We must bring the *Pap-fed man* to declare these propositions in every respect orthodox—show him their good effect upon despotic governments —upon true Catholics, the muzzlers of the people.   He will fall into the snare.   The propositions once published, the storm will burst forth.   A general rising against Rome—a wide schism—the sacred college divided into three parties.   One approves—the other blames—the third trembles. The *Sick Man*, still more frightened than he is now at having allowed the destruction of Poland, will shrink from the clamours, reproaches, threats, and violent ruptures that he has occasioned.

'That is well—and goes far.

'Then, set the Pope to shaking the conscience of the *Sick Man*, to disturb his mind, and terrify his soul.

'To sum up.   Make everything bitter to him—divide his council—isolate him—frighten him—redouble the ferocious ardour of good Albani—revive the appetite of the Sanfedists †—give them a glut of liberals—let there be

---

* *See* Pope Gregory XVI.'s Encyclical Letter to the Bishops in France, 1832.

† Hardly had the Sixteenth Gregory ascended the pontifical throne, than news came of the rising in Bologna.   His first idea was to call the Austrians, and incite

pillage, rape, massacre, as at Cesena—a downright river of Carbonaro blood —the *Sick Man* will have a surfeit of it. So many butcheries in his name —he will shrink, be sure he will shrink—every day will have its remorse, every night its terror, every minute its anguish; and the abdication he already threatens will come at last—perhaps too soon. That is now the only danger; you must provide against it.

'In case of an abdication, the grand penitentiary has understood me. Instead of confiding to a general the direction of our Order, the best militia of the Holy See, I should command it myself. Thenceforward this militia would give me no uneasiness. For instance: the Janissaries and the Prætorian Guards were always fatal to authority—why?—because they were able to organise themselves as defenders of the government, independently of the government; hence their power of intimidation.

'Clement XIV. was a fool. To brand and abolish our Company was an absurd fault. To protect and make it harmless, by declaring himself the General of the Order, is what he should have done. The Company, then at his mercy, would have consented to anything. He would have absorbed us, made us vassals of the Holy See, and would no longer have had to fear *our services*. Clement XIV. died of the cholic. Let him heed who hears. In a similar case, I should not die the same death.'

Just then, the clear and liquid voice of Rose-Pompon was again heard. Rodin bounded with rage upon his seat; but soon, as he listened to the following verse, new to him (for, unlike Philemon's widow, he had not his Béranger at his fingers' ends), the Jesuit, accessible to certain odd, superstitious notions, was confused and almost frightened at so singular a coincidence. It is Béranger's Good Pope who speaks:—

> 'What are monarchs? sheepish sots!
>   Or they're robbers, puffed with pride,
> Wearing badges of crime blots,
>   Till their certain graves gape wide.
> If they'll pour out coin for me,
>   I'll absolve them—skin and bone!
> If they haggle—they shall see,
>   My *nieces* dancing on their throne!
>   So laugh away!
>   Leap, my fay!
> Only watch *me* hurl the thunder
> First of all, but Zeus under,
> I'm the Pope, the whole world's wonder!'

Rodin, half-risen from his chair, with outstretched neck and attentive eye, was still listening, when Rose-Pompon, flitting like a bee from flower to flower of her *repertoire*, had already begun the delightful air of Colibri. Hearing no more, the Jesuit reseated himself, in a sort of stupor; but, after some minutes' reflection, his countenance again brightened up, and he seemed

---

the Sanfedist volunteer bands of fanatics. Cardinal Albini defeated the liberals at Cesena, where his followers pillaged churches, sacked the town, and ill-treated women. At Forli, cold-blooded murders were committed. In 1832 the Sanfedists (*Holy Faithites*) openly paraded their medals, bearing the heads of the Duke of Modena and the Pope; letters issued by the apostolic confederation; privileges and indulgences. They took the following oath:—" I, A. B., vow to rear the throne and altar over the bones of infamous freedom-shriekers, and exterminate these latter without pity for children's cries and women's tears." The disorders perpetrated by these marauders went beyond all bounds; the Romish Court regularised anarchy and organised the Sanfedists into volunteer corps, to which fresh privileges were granted.'
[Revue des Deux Mondes, Nov. 15th, 1844.—'La Revolution en Italie.']

to see a lucky omen in this singular incident. He resumed his pen, and the first words he wrote partook, as it were, of this strange confidence in fate.

'I have never had more hope of success than at this moment. Another reason to neglect nothing. Every presentiment demands redoubled zeal. A new thought occurred to me yesterday.

'We shall act here in concert. I have founded an ultra-Catholic paper, called *Neighbourly Love.* From its ultramontane, tyrannical, liberticidal fury, it will be thought the organ of Rome. I will confirm these reports. They will cause new terrors.

'That will be well.

'I shall raise the question of the liberty of instruction. The raw liberals will support us. Like fools, they admit us to equal rights ; when our privileges, our influence of the confessional, our obedience to Rome, all place us beyond the circle of equal rights, by the advantages which we enjoy. Double fools ! they think us disarmed, because they have disarmed themselves towards us.

'A burning question—irritating clamours—new cause of disgust for the *Weak Man.* Every little makes a mickle.

'That also is very well.

'To sum up all in two words. The end is abdication—the means, vexation, incessant torture. The Rennepont inheritance will pay for the election. The price agreed, the merchandise will be sold.'

Rodin here paused abruptly, thinking he had heard some noise at that door of his, which opened on the staircase ; therefore he listened with suspended breath ; but all remaining silent, he thought he must have been deceived, and took up his pen :

'I will take care of the Rennepont business—the hinge on which will turn our temporal operations. We must begin from the foundation—substitute the play of interests, and the springs of passion, for the stupid club-law of Father d'Aigrigny.' He nearly compromised everything—and yet he has good parts, knows the world, has powers of seduction, quick insight—but plays ever in a single key, and is not great enough to make himself little. In his stead, I shall know how to make use of him. There is good stuff in the man. I availed myself in time of the full powers given by the R. F. G. ; I may inform Father d'Aigrigny, in case of need, of the secret engagements taken by the General towards myself. Until now, I have let him invent for this inheritance the destination that you know of. A good thought, but unseasonable. The same end, by other means.

'The information was false. There are over two hundred millions. Should the eventuality occur, what was doubtful must become certain. An immense latitude is left us. The Rennepont business is now doubly mine, and within three months, the two hundred millions will be ours, by the free will of the heirs themselves. It must be so ; for this failing, the temporal part would escape me, and my chances be diminished by one half. I have asked for full powers ; time presses, and I act as if I had them. One piece of information is indispensable for the success of my projects. I expect it from you, and I must have it ; do you understand me ? The powerful influence of your brother at the Court of Vienna will serve you in this. I wish to have the most precise details as to the present position of the Duke de Reichstadt—the Napoleon II. of the Imperialists. Is it possible, by means of your brother, to open a secret correspondence with the prince, unknown to his attendants ?

'Look to this promptly. It is urgent. This note will be sent off to-day. I shall complete it to-morrow. It will reach you, as usual, by the hands of the petty shop-keeper.'

At the moment when Rodin was sealing this letter within a double envelope, he thought that he again heard a noise at the door. He listened. After some silence, several knocks were distinctly audible. Rodin started. It was the first time any one had knocked at his door, since nearly a twelvemonth that he occupied this room. Hastily placing the letter in his great coat pocket, the Jesuit opened the old trunk under his bed, took from it a packet of papers wrapped in a tattered cotton handkerchief, added to them the two letters in cipher he had just received, and carefully relocke d he trunk. The knocking continued without, and seemed to show more and more impatience. Rodin took the greengrocer's basket in his hand, tucked his umbrella under his arm, and went with some uneasiness to ascertain who was this unexpected visitor. He opened the door, and found himself face to face with Rose-Pompon, the troublesome singer, and who now, with a light and pretty courtesy, said to him in the most guileless manner in the world, ' M. Rodin, if you please ?'

CHAPTER XXXI.

FRIENDLY SERVICES.

NOTWITHSTANDING his surprise and uneasiness, Rodin did not frown. He began by locking his door after him, as he noticed the young girl's inquisitive glance. Then he said to her good-naturedly, ' Who do you want, my dear ?'

' M. Rodin,' repeated Rose-Pompon, stoutly, opening her bright blue eyes to their full extent, and looking Rodin full in the face.

' It's not here,' said he, moving towards the stairs. ' I do not know him. Inquire above or below.'

' No, you don't ! giving yourself airs at your age !' said Rose-Pompon, shrugging her shoulders. ' As if we did not know that you are M. Rodin.'

' Charlemagne,' said the socius, bowing ; ' Charlemagne, to serve you—if I am able.'

' You are not able,' answered Rose-Pompon, majestically ; then she added with a mocking air, ' So, we have our little pussy-cat hiding-places ; we change our name ; we are afraid Mamma Rodin will find us out.'

' Come, my dear child,' said the socius, with a paternal smile ; ' you have come to the right quarter. I am an old man, but I love youth—happy, joyous youth ! Amuse yourself, pray, at my expense. Only let me pass, for I am in a hurry.' And Rodin again advanced towards the stairs.

' M. Rodin,' said Rose-Pompon, in a solemn voice, ' I have very important things to say to you, and advice to ask about a love affair.'

' Why, little madcap that you are ! have you nobody to tease in your own house, that you must come here ?'

' I lodge in this house, M. Rodin,' answered Rose-Pompon, laying a malicious stress on the name of her victim.

' You ? Oh, dear, only to think I did not know I had such a pretty neighbour.'

' Yes, I have lodged here six months, M. Rodin.'

' Really ! where ?'

' On the third story, front, M. Rodin.'

' It was you, then, that sang so well just now ?'

' Rather.'

' You gave me great pleasure, I must say.'

' You are very polite, M. Rodin.'

' You lodge, I suppose, with your respectable family ?'

'I believe you, M. Rodin,' said Rose-Pompon, casting down her eyes with a timid air. 'I lodge with Grandpapa Philemon, and Grandmama Bacchanal—who is a queen, and no mistake.'

Rodin had hitherto been seriously uneasy, not knowing in what manner Rose had discovered his real name. But on hearing her mention the Bacchanal Queen, with the information that she lodged in the house, he found something to compensate for the disagreeable incident of Rose-Pompon's appearance. It was, indeed, important to Rodin to find out the Bacchanal Queen, the mistress of Sleepinbuff, and the sister of Mother Bunch, who had been noted as dangerous since her interview with the superior of the convent, and the part she had taken in the projected escape of Mdlle. de Cardoville. Moreover, Rodin hoped—thanks to what he had just heard—to bring Rose-Pompon to confess to him the name of the person from whom she had learned that 'Charlemagne' masked 'Rodin.'

Hardly had the young girl pronounced the name of the Bacchanal Queen, than Rodin clasped his hands, and appeared as much surprised as interested.

'Oh, my dear child,' she exclaimed, 'I conjure you not to jest on this subject. Are you speaking of a young girl who bears that nick-name, the sister of a deformed needlewoman?'

'Yes, sir, the Bacchanal Queen is her nick-name,' said Rose-Pompon, astonished in her turn ; 'she is really Cephyse Soliveau, and she is my friend.'

'Oh ! she is your friend ?' said Rodin, reflecting.

'Yes, sir, my bosom friend.'

'So you love her ?'

'Like a sister. Poor girl ! I do what I can for her, and that's not much. But how comes it that a respectable man of your age should know the Bacchanal Queen ?—Ah ! that shows you have a false name !'

'My dear child, I am no longer inclined to laugh,' said Rodin, with so sorrowful an air, that Rose-Pompon, reproaching herself with her pleasantry, said to him : 'But how comes it that you know Cephyse ?'

'Alas ! I do not know her—but a young fellow, that I like excessively——'

'Jacques Rennepont ?'

'Otherwise called Sleepinbuff. He is now in prison for debt,' sighed Rodin. 'I saw him yesterday.'

'You saw him yesterday ?—how strange !' said Rose-Pompon, clapping her hands. 'Quick ! quick !—come over to Philemon's, to give Cephyse news of her lover. She is so uneasy about him.'

'My dear child, I should like to give her good news of that worthy fellow, whom I like in spite of his follies, for who has not been guilty of follies ?' added Rodin, with indulgent good-nature.

'To be sure,' said Rose-Pompon, twisting about as if she still wore the costume of a débardeur.

'I will say more,' added Rodin : 'I love him because of his follies ; for, talk as we may, my dear child, there is always something good at bottom, a good heart, or something, in those who spend generously their money for other people.'

'Well, come ! you are a very good sort of man,' said Rose-Pompon, enchanted with Rodin's philosophy. 'But why will you not come and see Cephyse, and talk to her of Jacques ?'

'Of what use would it be to tell her what she knows already—that Jacques is in prison ? What I should like, would be to get the worthy fellow out of his scrape.'

'Oh, sir! only do that, only get Jacques out of prison,' cried Rose-Pompon, warmly, 'and we will both give you a kiss—me and Cephyse!'

'It would be throwing kisses away, dear little madcap!' said Rodin, smiling. 'But be satisfied; I want no reward to induce me to do good when I can.'

'Then you hope to get Jacques out of prison?'

Rodin shook his head, and answered with a grieved and disappointed air. 'I did hope it. Certainly, I did hope it; but now all is changed.'

'How's that?' asked Rose Pompon, with surprise.

'That foolish joke of calling me M. Rodin may appear very amusing to you, my dear child. I understand it, you being only an echo. Some one has said to you: " Go and tell M. Charlemagne that he is one M. Rodin. That will be very funny." '

'Certainly, I should never myself have thought of calling you M. Rodin. One does not invent such names,' answered Rose-Pompon.

'Well! that person, with his foolish jokes, has done, without knowing it, a great injury to Jacques Rennepont.'

'What! because I called you Rodin instead of Charlemagne?' cried Rose Pompon, much regretting the pleasantry which she had carried on at the instigation of Ninny Moulin. 'But really, sir,' she added, 'what can this joke have to do with the service that you were about to render Jacques?'

'I am not at liberty to tell you, my child. In truth, I am very sorry for poor Jacques. Believe me, I am; but do let me pass.'

'Listen to me, sir, I beg,' said Rose-Pompon; 'if I told you the name of the person who told me to call you Rodin, would you interest yourself again for Jacques?'

'I do not wish to know any one's secrets, my dear child. In all this, you have been the echo of persons who are, perhaps, very dangerous; and, notwithstanding the interest I feel for Jacques Rennepont, I do not wish, you understand, to make myself enemies. Heaven forbid!'

Rose-Pompon did not at all comprehend Rodin's fears, and upon this he had counted; for, after a second's reflection, the young girl resumed: 'Well, sir—this is too deep for me; I do not understand it. All I know is, that I am truly sorry if I have injured a good young man by a mere joke. I will tell you exactly how it happened. My frankness may be of some use.'

'Frankness will often clear up the most obscure matters,' said Rodin, sententiously.

'After all,' said Rose-Pompon, 'it's Ninny's fault. Why does he tell me nonsense, that might injure poor Cephyse's lover? You see, sir, it happened in this way. Ninny Moulin, who is fond of a joke, saw you just now in the street. The portress told him that your name was Charlemagne. He said to me: " No; his name is Rodin. We must play him a trick. Go to his room, Rose-Pompon, knock at the door, and call him M. Rodin. You will see what a rum face he will make." I promised Ninny Moulin not to name him; but I do it rather than run the risk of injuring Jacques.'

At Ninny Moulin's name Rodin had not been able to repress a movement of surprise. This pamphleteer, whom he had employed to edit the 'Neighbourly Love,' was not personally formidable; but, being fond of talking in his drink, he might become troublesome, particularly if Rodin, as was probable, had often to visit this house, to execute his project upon Sleepinbuff, through the medium of the Bacchanal Queen. The socius resolved, therefore, to provide against this inconvenience.

'So, my dear child,' said he to Rose-Pompon, 'it is a M. Desmoulins that persuaded you to play off this silly joke?'

'Not Desmoulins, but Dumoulin,' corrected Rose. 'He writes in the pewholders' papers, and defends the saints for money; for, if Ninny Moulin is a saint, his patrons are Saint Drinkard and Saint Flashette, as he himself declares.'

'This gentleman appears to be very gay.'

'Oh! a very good fellow.'

'But stop,' resumed Rodin, appearing to recollect himself; 'aint he a man about thirty-six or forty, fat, with a ruddy complexion?'

Ruddy as a glass of red wine,' said Rose-Pompon, 'and with a pimpled nose like a mulberry.'

'That's the man—M. Dumoulin. Oh! in that case, I am quite satisfied, my dear child. The jest no longer makes me uneasy; for M. Dumoulin is a very worthy man—only perhaps a little too fond of his joke.'

'Then, sir, you will try to be useful to Jacques? The stupid pleasantry of Ninny Moulin will not prevent you?'

'I hope not.'

'But I must not tell Ninny Moulin that you know it was he who sent me to call you M. Rodin—eh, sir?'

'Why not? In every case, my dear child, it is always better to speak frankly the truth.'

'But, sir, Ninny Moulin so strongly recommended me not to name him to you——'

'If you have named him, it is from a very good motive; why not avow it? However, my dear child, this concerns you, not me. Do as you think best.'

'And may I tell Cephyse of your good intentions towards Jacques?"

'The truth, my dear child, always the truth. One need never hesitate to say what is.'

'Poor Cephyse! how happy she will be!' cried Rose-Pompon, cheerfully; 'and the news will come just in time.'

'Only you must not exaggerate; I do not promise positively to get this good fellow out of prison; I say, that I will do what I can. But what I promise positively is—for, since the imprisonment of poor Jacques, your friend most be very much straitened——'

'Alas, sir!'

'What I promise positively is, some little assistance, which your friend will receive to-day, to enable her to live honestly; and if she behaves well—hereafter—why, hereafter, we shall see.'

'Oh, sir! you do not know how welcome will be your assistance to poor Cephyse! One might fancy you were her actual good angel. Faith! you may call yourself Rodin, or Charlemagne; all I know is, that you are a nice, sweet——"

'Come, come, do not exaggerate,' said Rodin; 'Say a good sort of old fellow; nothing more, my dear child. But see how things fall out, sometimes! Who could have told me, when I heard you knock at my door—which, I must say, vexed me a great deal—that it was a pretty little neighbour of mine, who, under the pretext of playing off a joke, was to put me in the way of doing a good action? Go and comfort your friend; this evening she will receive some assistance; and let us have hope and confidence. Thanks be, there are still some good people in the world!'

'Oh, sir! you prove it yourself.'

'Not at all! The happiness of the old is to see the young happy.'

This was said by Rodin with so much apparent kindness, that Rose-Pompon felt the tears well up to her eyes, and answered with much emotion; 'Sir, Cephyse and me are only poor girls; there are many more virtuous in the world ; but I venture to say, we have good hearts. Now, if ever you should be ill, only send for us ; there are no Sisters of Charity that will take better care of you. It is all that we can offer you, without reckoning Philemon, who shall go through fire and water for you, I give you my word for it—and Cephyse, I am sure, will answer for Jacques also, that he will be yours in life and death '

'You see, my dear child. that I was right in saying—a fitful head and a good heart. Adieu, till we meet again.'

Thereupon Rodin, taking up the basket, which he had placed on the ground by the side of his umbrella, prepared to descend the stairs.

'First of all, you must give me this basket ; it will be in your way going down,' said Rose-Pompon, taking the basket from the hands of Rodin, notwithstanding his resistance. Then she added : ' Lean upon my arm. The stairs are so dark. You might slip.'

'I will accept your offer, my dear child, for I am not very courageous.' Leaning paternally on the right arm of Rose-Pompon, who held the basket in her left hand, Rodin descended the stairs, and crossed the court-yard.

'Up there, on the third story, do you see that big face close to the window-frame ?' said Rose-Pompon suddenly to Rodin, stopping in the centre of the little court. ' That is my Ninny Moulin. Do you know him? Is he the same as yours ?'

'The same as mine,' said Rodin, raising his head, and waving his hand very affectionately to Jacques Dumoulin, who, stupefied thereat, retired abruptly from the window.

'The poor fellow ! I am sure he is afraid of me since his foolish joke,' said Rodin, smiling. ' He is very wrong.'

And he accompanied these last words with a sinister nipping of the lips, not perceived by Rose-Pompon.

'And now, my dear child,' said he, as they both entered the passage, ' I no longer need your assistance ; return to your friend, and tell her the good news you have heard.'

'Yes, sir, you are right. I burn with impatience to tell her what a good man you are.' And Rose-Pompon sprung towards the stairs.

'Stop, stop ! how about my basket that the little madcap carries off with her !' said Rodin.

'Oh, true ! I beg your pardon,. sir. Poor Cephyse ! how pleased she will be. Adieu, sir !' And Rose-Pompon's pretty figure disappeared in the darkness of the staircase, which she mounted with an alert and impatient step.

Rodin issued from the entry. ' Here is your basket, my good lady,' said he, stopping at the threshold of Mother Arsène's shop. ' I give you my humble thanks for your kindness.'

'For nothing, my dear sir, for nothing. It is all at your service. Well ! was the radish good ?'

'Succulent, my dear madame, and excellent.'

'Oh ! I am glad of it. Shall we soon see you again ?'

'I hope so. But could you tell me where is the nearest post-office ?'

'Turn to the left, the third house, at the grocer's.'

'A thousand thanks.'

'I wager it's a love letter for your sweetheart,' said Mother Arsène, enlivened probably by Rose-Pompon's and Ninny Moulin's proximity.

'Ha ! ha ! ha ! the good lady !' said Rodin, with a titter. Then, suddenly resuming his serious aspect, he made a low bow to the green-grocer, adding : 'Your most obedient, humble servant !' and walked out into the street.

We now usher the reader into Dr. Baleinier's asylum, in which Mdlle. de Cardoville was confined.

CHAPTER XXXII.

THE ADVICE.

ADRIENNE DE CARDOVILLE had been still more strictly confined in Dr. Baleinier's house, since the double nocturnal attempt of Agricola and Dagobert, in which the soldier, though severely wounded, had succeeded, thanks to the intrepid devotion of his son, seconded by the heroic Spoilsport, in gaining the little garden gate of the convent, and escaping by way of the boulevard, along with the young smith. Four o'clock had just struck. Adrienne, since the previous day, had been removed to a chamber on the second story of the asylum. The grated window, with closed shutters, only admitted a faint light to this apartment. The young lady, since her interview with Mother Bunch, expected to be delivered any day by the intervention of her friends. But she felt painful uneasiness on the subject of Agricola and Dagobert, being absolutely ignorant of the issue of the struggle in which her intended liberators had been engaged with the people of the asylum and convent. She had in vain questioned her keepers on the subject ; they had remained perfectly mute. These new incidents had augmented the bitter resentment of Adrienne against the Princess de Saint-Dizier, Father d'Aigrigny, and their creatures. The slight paleness of Mdlle. de Cardoville's charming face, and her fine eyes a little drooping, betrayed her recent sufferings ; seated before a little table, with her forehead resting upon one of her hands, half veiled by the long curls of her golden hair, she was turning over the leaves of a book. Suddenly, the door opened, and M. Baleinier entered. The doctor, a Jesuit, in lay attire, a docile and passive instrument of the will of his Order, was only half in the confidence of Father d'Aigrigny and the Princess de Saint-Dizier. He was ignorant of the object of the imprisonment of Mdlle. de Cardoville ; he was ignorant also of the sudden change which had taken place in the relative position of Father d'Aigrigny and Rodin, after the reading of the testament of Marius de Rennepont. The doctor had, only the day before, received orders from Father d'Aigrigny (now acting under the directions of Rodin) to confine Mdlle. de Cardoville still more strictly, to act towards her with redoubled severity, and to endeavour to force her, it will be seen by what expedients, to renounce the judicial proceedings, which she promised herself to take hereafter against her persecutors. At sight of the docter, Mdlle. de Cardoville could not hide the aversion and disdain with which this man inspired her. M. Baleinier, on the contrary, always smiling, always courteous, approached Adrienne with perfect ease and confidence, stopped a few steps from her, as if to study her features more attentively, and then added, like a man who is satisfied with the observations he had made : 'Come ! the unfortunate events of the night before last have had a less injurious influence than I feared. There is some improvement ; the complexion is less flushed, the look calmer, the eyes still somewhat too bright, but no longer shining with such unnatural fire. You were getting on so well ! Now the cure must be prolonged—for this unfortunate night affair threw you into a state of excitement, that was only the more dangerous from your not being conscious of it. Happily, with care, your recovery will not, I hope, be very much delayed.' Accustomed though she was to the audacity of this tool of the Congregation, Mdlle. de Cardoville could not forbear saying to him, with a smile of bitter disdain : 'What impudence, sir, there is in your probity ! What effrontery in your zeal to earn your hire ! Never for a moment do you lay aside your mask ; craft and falsehood are ever on your lips. Really, if this shameful comedy causes you as much fatigue as it does me disgust and contempt, they can never pay you enough.'

'Alas !' said the doctor, in a sorrowful tone ; 'always this unfortunate delusion, that you are not in want of our care !—that I am playing a part, when I talk to you of the sad state in which you were, when we were obliged to bring you hither by stratagem. Still, with the exception of this little sign of rebellious insanity, your condition has marvellously improved. You are on the high road to a complete cure. By and by, your excellent heart will render me the justice that is due to me ; and, one day, I shall be judged as I deserve.'

'I believe it, sir ; the day approaches, in which you *will* be judged as *you* deserve,' said Adrienne, laying great stress upon the two words.

'Always that other fixed idea,' said the doctor, with a sort of commiseration. 'Come, be reasonable. Do not think of this childishness.'

'What ! renounce my intention to demand at the hands of justice reparation for myself, and disgrace for you and your accomplices ? Never, sir— never !'

'Well !' said the doctor, shrugging his shoulders ; 'once at liberty, thank heaven, you will have many other things to think of, my fair enemy.'

'You forget piously the evil that you do ; but I, sir, have a better memory.'

'Let us talk seriously. Have you really the intention of applying to the courts ?' inquired Dr. Baleinier, in a grave tone.

'Yes, sir : and you know that what I intend, I firmly carry out.'

'Well ! I can only conjure you not to follow out this idea,' replied the doctor, in a still more solemn tone ; 'I ask it as a favour, in the name of your own interest.'

'I think, sir, that you are a little too ready to confound your interest with mine.'

'Now come,' said Dr. Baleinier, with a feigned impatience, as if quite certain of convincing Mdlle. de Cardoville on the instant ; 'would you have the melancholy courage to plunge into despair two persons full of goodness and generosity ?'

'Only two ? The jest would be complete, if you were to reckon three : you, sir, and my aunt, and Abbé d'Aigrigny ; for these are no doubt the generous persons in whose name you implore my pity.'

'No, madame ; I speak neither of myself, nor of your aunt, nor of Abbé d'Aigrigny.'

'Of whom, then, sir ?' asked Mdlle. de Cardoville, with surprise.

'Of two poor fellows, who, no doubt sent by those whom you call your friends, got into the neighbouring convent the other night, and thence into this garden. The guns which you heard go off were fired at them.'

'Alas ! I thought so. They refused to tell me if either of them was wounded,' said Adrienne, with painful emotion.

'One of them received a wound, but not very serious, since he was able to fly and escape pursuit.'

'Thank God !' cried Mdlle. de Cardoville, clasping her hands with fervour.

'It is quite natural that you should rejoice at their escape ; but by what strange contradiction do you now wish to put the officers of justice on their track ? A singular manner, truly, of rewarding their devotion !'

'What do you say, sir ?' asked Mdlle. de Cardoville.

'For if they should be arrested,' resumed Dr. Baleinier, without answering her, 'as they have been guilty of house-breaking and attempted burglary, they would be sent to the galleys.'

'Heavens! and for my sake!'

'Yes; it would be *for* you, and what is worse, *by* you, that they would be condemned.'

'By *me*, sir?'

'Certainly; that is, if you follow up your vengeance against your aunt and Abbé d'Aigrigny—I do not speak of myself, for I am quite safe; in a word, if you persist in laying your complaint before the magistrates, that you have been unjustly confined in this house.'

'I do not understand you, sir. Explain yourself,' said Adrienne, with growing uneasiness.

'Child that you are!' cried the Jesuit of the short robe, with an air of conviction; 'do you think that if the law once takes cognizance of this affair, you can stop short its action where and when you please? When you leave this house, you lodge a complaint against me and against your family; well, what happens? The law interferes, inquires, calls witnesses, enters into the most minute investigations. Then, what follows? Why, that this nocturnal escalade, which the superior of the convent has some interest in hushing up, for fear of scandal—that this nocturnal attempt, I say, which I also would keep quiet, is necessarily divulged, and as it involves a serious crime, to which a heavy penalty is attached, the law will ferret into it, and find out these unfortunate men and if, as is probable, they are detained in Paris by their duties or occupations, or even by a false security, arising from the honourable motives which they know to have actuated them, they will be arrested. And who will be the cause of this arrest? You, by your deposition against us.'

'Oh, sir! that would be horrible; but it is impossible.'

'It is very possible, on the contrary,' returned M. Baleinier; 'so that, while I and the superior of the convent, who alone are really entitled to complain, only wish to keep quiet this unpleasant affair, it is you—you, for whom these unfortunate men have risked the galleys—that will deliver them up to justice.'

Though Mdlle. de Cardoville was not completely duped by the lay Jesuit, she guessed that the merciful intentions which he expressed with regard to Dagobert and his son would be absolutely subordinate to the course she might take in pressing or abandoning the legitimate vengeance which she meant to claim of authority. Indeed, Rodin, whose instructions the doctor was following without knowing it, was too cunning to have it said to Mdlle. de Cardoville: 'If you attempt any proceedings, we denounce Dagobert and his son,' but he attained the same end, by inspiring Adrienne with fears on the subject of her two liberators, so as to prevent her taking any hostile measures. Without knowing the exact law on the subject, Mdlle. de Cardoville had too much good sense not to understand, that Dagobert and Agricola might be very seriously involved in consequence of their nocturnal adventure, and might even find themselves in a terrible position. And yet, when she thought of all she had suffered in that house, and of all the just resentment she entertained in the bottom of her heart, Adrienne felt unwilling to renounce the stern pleasure of exposing such odious machinations to the light of day. Dr. Baleinier watched with sullen attention her whom he considered his dupe, for he thought he could divine the cause of the silence and hesitation of Mdlle. de Cardoville.

'But, sir,' resumed the latter, unable to conceal her anxiety, 'if I were disposed, for whatever reason, to make no complaint, and to forget the wrongs I have suffered, when should I leave this place?'

'I cannot tell; for I do not know when you will be radically cured,' said the doctor, benignantly. 'You are in a very good way, but——'

'Still this insolent and stupid acting !' broke forth Mdlle. de Cardoville, interrupting the doctor with indignation. 'I ask, and if it must be, I entreat you, to tell me how long I am to be shut up in this dreadful house, for I shall leave it some day, I suppose?'

'I hope so, certainly,' said the Jesuit of the short robe, with unction; 'but when, I am unable to say. Moreover, I must tell you frankly, that every precaution is taken against such attempts as those of the other night ; and the most vigorous watch will be maintained, to prevent your communicating with any one. And all this in your own interest, that your poor head may not again be dangerously excited.'

'So, sir,' said Adrienne, almost terrified, 'compared with what awaits me, the last few days have been days of liberty.'

'Your interest before everything,' answered the doctor, in a fervent tone.

Mdlle. de Cardoville, feeling the impotence of her indignation and despair, heaved a deep sigh, and hid her face in her hands.

At this moment, quick footsteps were heard in the passage, and one of the nurses entered, after having knocked at the door.

'Sir,' said she to the doctor, with a frightened air, 'there are two gentlemen below, who wish to see you instantly, and the lady also.'

Adrienne raised her head hastily ; her eyes were bathed in tears.

'What are the names of these persons?' said M. Baleinier, much astonished.

'One of them said to me,' answered the nurse : '"Go and inform Dr. Baleinier that I am a magistrate, and that I come on a duty regarding Mdlle. de Cardoville."'

'A magistrate !' exclaimed the Jesuit of the short robe, growing purple in the face, and unable to hide his surprise and uneasiness.

'Heaven be praised !' cried Adrienne, rising with vivacity, her countenance beaming through her tears with hope and joy ; 'my friends have been informed in time, and the hour of justice is arrived !'

'Ask these persons to walk up,' said Dr. Baleinier, after a moment's reflection. Then, with a still more agitated expression of countenance, he approached Adrienne with a harsh, and almost menacing air, which contrasted with the habitual placidity of his hypocritical smile, and said to her in a low voice : 'Take care, madame ! do not rejoice too soon.'

'I no longer fear you,' answered Mdlle. de Cardoville, with a bright, flashing eye. 'M. de Montbron is no doubt returned to Paris, and has been informed in time. He accompanies the magistrate, and comes to deliver me. I pity you, sir— both you and yours,' added Adrienne, with an accent of bitter irony.

'Madame,' cried M. Baleinier, no longer able to dissemble his growing alarm, 'I repeat to you, take care ! Remember what I have told you. Your accusations would necessarily involve the discovery of what took place the other night. Beware ! the fate of the soldier and his son is in your hands. Recollect they are in danger of the convict's chains.'

'Oh ! I am not your dupe, sir. You are holding out a covert menace. Have at least the courage to say to me, that, if I complain to the magistrates, you will denounce the soldier and his son.'

'I repeat, that, if you make any complaint, those two people are lost,' answered the doctor, ambiguously.

Startled by what was really dangerous in the doctor's threats, Adrienne asked : 'Sir, if this magistrate questions me, do you think I will tell him a falsehood?'

'You will answer what is true,' said M. Baleinier, hastily, in the hope of still attaining his end. 'You will answer that you were in so excited a state of mind a few days ago, that it was thought advisable, for your own sake, to bring you hither, without your knowing it. But you are now so much better, that you acknowledge the utility of the measures taken with regard to you. I will confirm these words ; for, after all, it is the truth.'

'Never !' cried Mdlle. de Cardoville, with indignation ; 'never will I be the accomplice of so infamous a falsehood ; never will I be base enough to justify the indignities that I have suffered !'

'Here is the magistrate,' said M. Baleinier, as he caught the sound of approaching footsteps. 'Beware !'

The door opened, and, to the indescribable amazement of the doctor, Rodin appeared on the threshold, accompanied by a man dressed in black, with a dignified and severe countenance. In the interest of his projects, and from motives of craft and prudence that will hereafter be known, Rodin had not informed Father d'Aigrigny, and consequently the doctor, of the unexpected visit he intended to pay to the asylum, accompanied by a magistrate. On the contrary, he had only the day before given orders to M. Baleinier to confine Mdlle. de Cardoville still more strictly. Therefore, imagine the stupor of the doctor when he saw the judicial officer, whose un-expected presence and imposing aspect were otherwise sufficiently alarming, enter the room, accompanied by Rodin, Abbé d'Aigrigny's humble and obscure secretary. From the door, Rodin, who was very shabbily dressed, as usual, pointed out Mdlle. de Cardoville to the magistrate, by a gesture at once respectful and compassionate. Then, while the latter, who had not been able to repress a movement of admiration at sight of the rare beauty of Adrienne, seemed to examine her with as much surprise as interest, the Jesuit modestly receded several steps.

Dr. Baleinier, in his extreme astonishment, hoping to be understood by Rodin, made suddenly several private signals, as if to interrogate him on the cause of the magistrate's visit. But this was only productive of fresh amazement to M. Baleinier ; for Rodin did not appear to recognize him, or to understand his expressive pantomime, and looked at him with affected bewilderment. At length, as the doctor, growing impatient, redoubled his mute questionings, Rodin advanced with a stride, stretched forward his crooked neck, and said, in a loud voice : ' What is your pleasure, doctor ?'

These words, which completely disconcerted Baleinier, broke the silence which had reigned for some seconds, and the magistrate turned round. Rodin added, with imperturbable coolness : ' Since our arrival, the doctor has been making all sorts of mysterious signs to me. I suppose he has something private to communicate, but, as I have no secrets, I must beg him to speak out loud.'

This reply, so embarrassing for M. Baleinier, uttered in a tone of aggression, and with an air of icy coldness, plunged the doctor into such new and deep amazement, that he remained for some moments without answering. No doubt the magistrate was struck with this incident, and with the silence which followed it, for he cast a look of great severity on the doctor. Mdlle. de Cardoville, who had expected to have seen M. de Montbron, was also singularly surprised.

CHAPTER XXXIII.

THE ACCUSER.

BALEINIER, disconcerted for a moment by the unexpected presence of a magistrate, and by Rodin's inexplicable attitude, soon recovered his presence of mind, and addressing his colleague of the longer robe, said to him : ' If

I made signs to you, sir, it was that, while I wished to respect the silence which this gentleman'—glancing at the magistrate—'has preserved since his entrance, I desired to express my surprise at the unexpected honour of this visit.'

' It is to the lady that I will explain the reason for my silence, and beg her to excuse it,' replied the magistrate, as he made a half-bow to Adrienne, whom he thus continued to address : ' I have just received so serious a declaration with regard to you, madame, that I could not forbear looking at you for a moment in silence, to see if I could read in your countenance or in your attitude, the truth or falsehood of the accusation that has been placed in my hands ; and I have every reason to believe that it is but too well founded.'

' May I at length be informed, sir,' said Dr. Baleinier, in a polite but firm tone, ' to whom I have the honour of speaking ?'

' Sir, I am juge d'instruction, and I have come to inform myself as to a fact which has been pointed out to me——'

' Will you do me the honour to explain yourself, sir ?' said the doctor, bowing.

' Sir,' resumed the magistrate, M. de Gernande, a man of about fifty years of age, full of firmness and straightforwardness, and knowing how to unite the austere duties of his position with benevolent politeness, ' you are accused of having committed—a very great error, not to use a harsher expression. As for the nature of that error, I prefer believing, sir, that you (a first rate man of science) may have been deceived in the calculation of a medical case, rather than suspect you of having forgotten all that is sacred in the exercise of a profession that is almost a priesthood.'

' When you specify the facts, sir,' answered the Jesuit of the short robe, with a degree of haughtiness, ' it will be easy for me to prove that my reputation as a man of science is no less free from reproach, than my conscience as a man of honour.'

' Madame,' said M. de Gernande, addressing Adrienne, ' is it true that you were conveyed to this house by stratagem ?'

' Sir,' cried M. Baleinier, ' permit me to observe, that the manner in which you open this question is an insult to me.'

' Sir, it is to the lady that I have the honour of addressing myself,' replied M. de Gernande, sternly ; ' and I am the sole judge of the propriety of *my* questions.'

Adrienne was about to answer affirmatively to the magistrate, when an expressive look from Dr. Baleinier reminded her that she would perhaps expose Dagobert and his son to cruel dangers. It was no base and vulgar feeling of vengeance by which Adrienne was animated, but a legitimate indignation, inspired by odious hypocrisy. She would have thought it cowardly not to unmask the criminals ; but wishing to avoid compromising others, she said to the magistrate, with an accent full of mildness and dignity : ' Permit me, sir, in my turn, rather to ask you a question.'

' Speak, madame.'

' Will the answer I make be considered a formal accusation ?'

' I have come hither, madame, to ascertain the truth, and no consideration should induce you to dissemble it."

' So be it, sir,' resumed Adrienne ; ' but suppose, having just causes of complaint, I lay them before you, in order to be allowed to leave this house, shall I afterwards be at liberty not to press the accusations I have made ?'

' You may abandon proceedings, madame, but the law will take up your cause in the name of society, if its rights have been injured in your person.'

' Shall I then not be allowed to pardon ? Should I not be sufficiently avenged by a contemptuous forgetfulness of the wrongs I have suffered ?'

' Personally, madame, you may forgive and forget ; but I have the honour to repeat to you, that society cannot show the same indulgence, if it should turn out that you have been the victim of a criminal machination—and I have every reason to fear it is so. The manner in which you express yourself, the generosity of your sentiments, the calmness and dignity of your attitude, convince me that I have been well informed.'

' I hope, sir,' said Dr. Baleinier, recovering his coolness, 'that you will at least communicate the declaration that has been made to you.'

' It has been declared to me, sir,' said the magistrate, in a stern voice, 'that Mdlle. de Cardoville was brought here by stratagem.'

' By stratagem ?'——' Yes, sir.'

' It is true. The lady *was* brought here by stratagem,' answered the Jesuit of the short robe, after a moment's silence.

' You confess it, then ?' said M. de Gernande.

' Certainly I do, sir. I admit that I had recourse to means which we are unfortunately too often obliged to employ, when persons who most need our assistance are unconscious of their own sad state.'

' But, sir,' replied the magistrate, 'it has also been declared to me, that Mdlle. de Cardoville never required such aid.'

' That, sir, is a question of medical jurisprudence, which has to be examined and discussed, said M Baleinier, recovering his assurance.

' It will, *indeed*, sir, be seriously discussed ; for you are accused of confining Mdlle. de Cardoville, while in the full possession of all her faculties.'

' And may I ask you for what purpose ?' said M. Baleinier, with a slight shrug of the shoulders, and in a tone of irony. ' What interest had I to commit such a crime, even admitting that my reputation did not place me above so odious and absurd a charge ?'

' You are said to have acted, sir, in furtherance of a family plot, devised against Mdlle. de Cardoville for a pecuniary motive.'

' And who has dared, sir, to make so calumnious a charge ?' cried Dr. Baleinier, with indignant warmth. ' Who has had the audacity to accuse a respectable, and I dare to say, respected man, of having been the ac-complice in such infamy ?'

' I,' said Rodin, coldly.

' You ! cried Dr. Baleinier, falling back two steps, as if thunderstruck.

' Yes, I accuse you,' repeated Rodin, in a clear sharp voice.

' Yes, it was this gentleman who came to me this morning, with ample proofs, to demand my interference in favour of Mdlle. de Cardoville,' said the magistrate, drawing back a little, to give Adrienne the opportunity of seeing her defender.

Throughout this scene, Rodin's name had not hitherto been mentioned. Mdlle. de Cardoville had often heard speak of the Abbé d'Aigrigny's secretary in no very favourable terms ; but, never having seen him, she did not know that her liberator was this very Jesuit. She therefore looked towards him, with a glance in which were mingled curiosity, interest, surprise and gratitude. Rodin's cadaverous countenance, his repulsive ugliness, his sordid dress, would a few days before have occasioned Adrienne a perhaps invincible feeling of disgust. But the young lady, remembering how the sempstress, poor, feeble, deformed, and dressed almost in rags, was endowed, notwithstanding her wretched exterior, with one of the noblest and most admirable hearts, recalled this recollection in favour of the Jesuit. She forgot that he was ugly and sordid, only to remember that he was old, that he seemed poor, and that he had come to her assistance. Dr. Baleinier, notwithstanding his craft, notwithstanding his audacious hypocrisy, in spite even of his presence of mind, could not conceal how much he was disturbed by Rodin's denunciation. His head became troubled as he remembered how, on the first day of Adrienne's confinement in this house, the implacable appeal of Rodin, through the hole in the door, had prevented him (Baleinier) from yielding to emotions of pity, inspired by the despair of this unfortunate young girl, driven almost to doubt of her own reason. And yet it was this very Rodin, so cruel, so inexorable, the devoted agent of Father d'Aigrigny, who denounced him (Baleinier), and brought a magistrate to set Adrienne at liberty—when, only the day before, Father d'Aigrigny had ordered an increase of severity towards her !

The lay Jesuit felt persuaded that Rodin was betraying Father d'Aigrigny in the most shameful manner, and that Mdlle. de Cardoville's friends had bribed and bought over this scoundrelly secretary. Exasperated by what he considered a monstrous piece of treachery, the doctor exclaimed, in a voice broken with rage : 'And it is you, sir, that have the impudence to accuse me—you, who only a few days ago——'

Then, reflecting that the retort upon Rodin would be self-accusation, he appeared to give way to an excess of emotion, and resumed with bitterness: ' Ah, sir, you are the last person that I should have thought capable of this odious denunciation. It is shameful !'

' And who had a better right than I to denounce this infamy ?' answered Rodin, in a rude, overbearing tone. ' Was I not in a position to learn—unfortunately, too late—the nature of the conspiracy of which Mdlle. de Cardoville and others have been the victims ? Then, what was my duty as an honest man ? Why, to inform the magistrate, to prove what I set forth, and to accompany him hither. That is what I have done.'

' So, sir,· said the doctor, addressing the magistrate, 'it is not only myself that this man accuses, but he dares also——'

' I accuse the Abbé d'Aigrigny,' resumed Rodin, in a still louder and more imperative tone, interrupting the doctor, ' I accuse the Princess de Saint Dizier, I accuse you, sir—of having, from a vile motive of self-interest, confined Mdlle. de Cardoville in this house, and the two daughters of Marshal Simon in the neighbouring convent. Is that clear ?'

' Alas ! it is only too true,· said Adrienne, hastily. ' I have seen those poor children all in tears, making signs of distress to me.'

The accusation of Rodin, with regard to the orphans, was a new and fearful blow for Dr Baleinier He felt perfectly convinced that the traitor had passed clear over to the enemy's camp. Wishing therefore to put an end to this embarrassing scene, he tried to put a good face on the matter, in spite of his emotion, and said to the magistrate : ' I might confine myself, sir, to silence—disdaining to answer such accusations, till a judicial decision had given them some kind of authority. But, strong in a good conscience, I address myself to Mdlle. de Cardoville, and I beg her to say if this very morning I did not inform her, that her health would soon be sufficiently restored to allow her to leave this house. I conjure her, in the name of her well-known love of truth, to state if such was not my language, when I was alone with her——'

' Come, sir !· said Rodin, interrupting Baleinier with an insolent air ; ' suppose that, from pure generosity, this dear young lady were to admit as much—what will it prove in your favour ?—why, nothing at all.'

' What, sir,' cried the doctor, ' do you presume——'

' I presume to unmask you, without asking your leave. What have you just told us ? Why, that being alone with Mdlle de Cardoville, you talked to her as if she were really mad. How very conclusive !'

' But, sir——' cried the doctor.

'But, sir,' resumed Rodin, without allowing him to continue, ' it is evident that, foreseeing the possibility of what has occurred to-day, and, to provide yourself with a hole to creep out at, you have pretended to believe your own execrable falsehood, in presence of this poor young lady, that you might afterwards call in aid the evidence of your own assumed conviction. Come, sir ! such stories will not go down with people of common sense or common humanity.'

'Come now, sir !' exclaimed Baleinier, angrily.

'Well, sir,' resumed Rodin, in a still louder voice, which completely drowned that of the doctor ; 'is it true, or is it not, that you have recourse to the mean evasion of ascribing this odious imprisonment to a scientific error ? I affirm that you do so, and that you think yourself safe, because you can now say : "Thanks to my care, the young lady has recovered her reason. What more would you have ?"'

'Yes, I do say that, sir, and I maintain it."

'You maintain a falsehood ; for it is proven that the lady never lost her reason for a moment.'

'But I, sir, maintain that she did lose it.'

'And I, sir, will prove the contrary,' said Rodin.

'You ? How will you do that ?' cried the doctor.

'That I shall take care not to tell you at present, as you may well suppose,' answered Rodin, with an ironical smile, adding, with indignation : 'But, really, sir, you ought to die for shame, to dare to raise such a question in presence of the lady. You should at least have spared her this discussion.'——'Sir !'

'Oh, fie, sir ! I say, fie ! It is odious to maintain this argument before her—odious if you speak truth, doubly odious if you lie,' said Rodin, with disgust.

'This violence is inconceivable !' cried the Jesuit of the short robe, exasperated ; 'and I think the magistrate shows great partiality in allowing such gross calumnies to be heaped upon me !'

'Sir,' answered M. de Gernande, severely, 'I am entitled not only to hear, but to provoke any contradictory discussion that may enlighten me in the execution of my duty ; it results from all this, that, even in your opinion, sir, Mdlle. de Cardoville's health is sufficiently good to allow her to return home immediately.'

'At least, I do not see any very serious inconvenience likely to arise from it, sir,' said the doctor : 'only I maintain that the cure is not so complete as it might have been, and, on this subject, I decline all responsibility for the future.'

'You can do so, safely,' said Rodin ; 'it is not likely that the young lady will ever again have recourse to your honest assistance.'

'It is useless, therefore, to employ my official authority, to demand the immediate liberation of Mdlle. de Cardoville,' said the magistrate.

'She is free,' said Baleinier, 'perfectly free.'

'As for the question whether you have imprisoned her on the plea or a supposititious madness, the law will inquire into it, sir, and you will be heard.'

'I am quite easy, sir,' answered M. Baleinier, trying to look so ; 'my conscience reproaches me with nothing.'

. 'I hope it may turn out well, sir,' said M. de Gernande. 'However bad appearances may be, more especially when persons of your station in society are concerned, we should always wish to be convinced of their innocence.' Then, turning to Adrienne, he added : 'I understand, madame, how painful this scene must be to all your feelings of delicacy and generosity ; hereafter, it will depend upon yourself, either to proceed for damages against Mr. Baleinier, or to let the law take its course. One word more. The bold and upright man'—here the magistrate pointed to Rodin—'who has taken up your cause in so frank and disinterested a manner, expressed a belief that you would, perhaps, take charge for the present of Marshal Simon's daughters, whose liberation I am about to demand from the convent where they also are confined by stratagem.'

'The fact is, sir,' replied Adrienne, 'that, as soon as I learned the arrival of Marshal Simon's daughters in Paris, my intention was to offer them apartments in my house. These young ladies are my near relations. It is at once a duty and a pleasure for me to treat them as sisters. I shall, therefore, be doubly grateful to you, sir, if you will trust them to my care.'

'I think that I cannot serve them better,' answered M. de Gernande. Then, addressing Baleinier, he added, 'Will you consent, sir, to my bringing these two ladies hither? I will go and fetch them, while Mdlle. de Cardoville prepares for her departure. They will then be able to leave this house with their relation.'

'I entreat the lady to make use of this house as her own, until she leaves it,' replied M. Baleinier. 'My carriage shall be at her orders to take her home.'

'Madame,' said the magistrate, approaching Adrienne, 'without prejudging the question, which must soon be decided by a court of law, I may at least regret that I was not called in sooner. Your situation must have been a very cruel one.'

'There will at least remain to me, sir, from this mournful time,' said Adrienne, with graceful dignity, 'one precious and touching remembrance —that of the interest which you have shown me. I hope that you will one day permit me to thank you, at my own home, not for the justice you have done me, but for the benevolent and paternal manner in which you have done it. And moreover, sir,' added Mdlle. de Cardoville, with a sweet smile, 'I should like to prove to you, that what they call my cure is complete.'

M. de Gernande bowed respectfully in reply. During the short dialogue of the magistrate with Adrienne, their backs were both turned to Baleinier and Rodin. The latter, profiting by this moment's opportunity, hastily slipped into the doctor's hand a note just written with a pencil in the bottom of his hat. Baleinier looked at Rodin in stupefied amazement. But the latter made a peculiar sign, by raising his thumb to his forehead, and drawing it twice across his brow. Then he remained impassible. This had passed so rapidly, that when M. de Gernande turned round, Rodin was at a distance of several steps from Dr. Baleinier, and looking at Mdlle. de Cardoville with respectful interest.

'Permit me to accompany you, sir,' said the doctor, preceding the magistrate, whom Mdlle. de Cardoville saluted with much affability. Then both went out, and Rodin remained alone with the young lady.

After conducting M. de Gernande to the outer door of the house, M. Baleinier made haste to read the pencil-note written by Rodin; it ran as follows: 'The magistrate is going to the convent, by way of the street. Run round by the garden, and tell the superior to obey the order I have given with regard to the two young girls. It is of the utmost importance.'

The peculiar sign which Rodin had made, and the tenor of this note, proved to Dr. Baleinier, who was passing from surprise to amazement, that the secretary, far from betraying the reverend father, was still acting for the Greater Glory of the Lord. However, whilst he obeyed the orders, M. Baleinier sought in vain to penetrate the motives of Rodin's inexplicable conduct, who had himself informed the authorities of an affair that was to have been hushed up, and that might have the most disastrous consequences for Father d'Aigrigny, Madame de Saint-Dizier, and Baleinier himself. But let us return to Rodin, left alone with Mdlle. de Cardoville.

CHAPTER XXXI\

FATHER D'AIGRIGNY'S SECRETARY.

HARDLY had the magistrate and Dr. Baleinier disappeared, than Mdlle. de Cardoville, whose countenance was beaming with joy, exclaimed, as she looked at Rodin with a mixture of respect and gratitude, ' At length, thanks to you, sir, I am free—free ! Oh, I had never before felt how much happiness, expansion, delight, there is in that adorable word—liberty !'

Her bosom rose and fell, her rosy nostrils dilated, her vermilion lips were half open, as if she again inhaled with rapture pure and vivifying air.

' I have been only a few days in this horrible place,' she resumed, ' but I have suffered enough from my captivity to make me resolve never to let a year pass without restoring to liberty some poor prisoners for debt. This vow no doubt appears to belong a little to the Middle Ages,' added she, with a smile ; ' but I would fain borrow from that noble epoch something more than its old windows and furniture. So, doubly thanks, sir !—for I take you as a partner in that project of deliverance, which has just (you see) unfolded itself in the midst of the happiness I owe to you, and by which you seem so much affected. Oh ! let my joy speak my gratitude, and pay you for your generous aid !' exclaimed the young girl, with enthusiasm.

Mdlle. de Cardoville had truly remarked a complete transfiguration in the countenance of Rodin. This man, lately so harsh, severe, inflexible, with regard to Dr. Baleinier, appeared now under the influence of the mildest and most tender sentiments. His little, half-veiled eyes were fixed upon Adrienne with an expression of ineffable interest. Then, as if he wished to tear himself from these impressions, he said, speaking to himself, ' Come, come no weakness. Time is too precious ; my mission is not fulfilled. My dear young lady,' added he, addressing himself to Adrienne, ' believe what I say —we will talk hereafter of gratitude—but we have now to talk of the present so important for you and your family. Do you know what is taking place ?

Adrienne looked at the Jesuit with surprise, and said . ' What is taking place, sir ?'

' Do you know the real motive of your imprisonment in this house ? Do you know what influenced the Princess de Saint-Dizier and Abbé d'Aigrigny ?'

At the sound of those detested names, Mdlle. de Cardoville's face, now so full of happiness, became suddenly sad, and she answered with bitterness : ' It is hatred, sir, that no doubt animated Madame de Saint-Dizier against me.'

' Yes, hatred ; and, moreover, the desire to rob you with impunity of an immense fortune.'

' Me, sir ! how ?'

' You must be ignorant, my dear young lady, of the interest you had to be in the Rue Saint-François on the 13th February, for an inheritance ?'

' I was ignorant, sir, of the date and details : but I knew by some family papers, and thanks to an extraordinary circumstance, that one of our ancestors——'

' Had left an enormous sum to be divided between his descendants ; is it not so ?'——' Yes, sir.'

' But what unfortunately you did not know, my dear young lady, was that the heirs were all bound to be present at a certain hour on the 13th February. This day and hour once past, the absent would forfeit their claim. Do you now understand why you have been imprisoned here, my dear young lady?'

'Yes, yes; I understand it,' cried Mdlle. de Cardoville; 'cupidity was added to the hatred which my aunt felt for me. All is explained. Marshal Simon's daughters, having the same right as I had, have, like me, been imprisoned.'

'And yet,' cried Rodin, 'you and they were not the only victims.'

'Who, then, are the others, sir?'——'A young East Indian.'

'Prince Djalma?' said Adrienne, hastily.

'For the same reason he has been nearly poisoned with a narcotic.'

'Great God!' cried the young girl, clasping her hands in horror. 'It is fearful. That young prince, who was said to have so noble and generous a character! But I had sent to Cardoville Castle——'

'A confidential person, to fetch the prince to Paris—I know it, my dear young lady; but, by means of a trick, your friend was got out of the way, and the young Oriental delivered to his enemies.'

'And where is he now?'

'I have only vague information on the subject. I know that he is in Paris, and do not despair of finding him. I shall pursue my researches with an almost paternal ardour, for we cannot too much love the rare qualities of that poor king's son. What a heart, my dear young lady! what a heart! Oh, it is a heart of gold, pure and bright as the gold of his country!'

'We must find the prince, sir,' said Adrienne with emotion; 'let me entreat you to neglect nothing for that end. He is my relation—alone here—without support—without assistance.'

'Certainly,' replied Rodin, with commiseration. 'Poor boy!—for he is almost a boy—eighteen or nineteen years of age—thrown into the heart of Paris, of this hell—with his fresh, ardent, half-savage passions—with his simplicity and confidence—to what perils may he not be exposed?'

'Well, we must first find him, sir,' said Adrienne, hastily; 'and then we will save him from these dangers. Before I was confined here, I learned his arrival in France, and sent a confidential person to offer him the services of an unknown friend. I now see that this mad idea, with which I have been so much reproached, was a very sensible one. I am more convinced of it than ever. The prince belongs to my family, and I owe him a generous hospitality. I had destined for him the lodge I occupied at my aunt's.'

'And you, my dear young lady?'

'To-day, I shall remove to a house, which I had prepared some time ago, with the determination of quitting Madame de Saint-Dizier, and living alone as I pleased. Then, sir, as you seem bent upon being the good genius of our family, be as generous with regard to Prince Djalma, as you have been to me and Marshal Simon's daughters. I entreat you to discover the hiding-place of this poor king's son, as you call him; keep my secret for me, and conduct him to the house offered by the unknown friend. Let him not disquiet himself about anything; all his wants shall be provided for; he shall live—like a prince.'

'Yes; he will indeed live like a prince, thanks to your royal munificence. But never was such kind interest better deserved. It is enough to see (as I have seen) his fine, melancholy countenance——'

'You have seen him then, sir?' said Adrienne, interrupting Rodin.

'Yes, my dear young lady; I was with him for about two hours. It was quite enough to judge of him. His charming features are the mirror of his soul.'

'And where did you see him, sir?'

'At your old Château de Cardoville, my dear young lady, near which he had been shipwrecked in a storm, and whither I had gone to——' Rodin hesitated for a moment, and then, as if yielding to the frankness of his disposition, added : ' Whither I had gone to commit a bad action—a shameful, miserable action, I must confess !'

'You, sir?—at Cardoville House—to commit a bad action?' cried Adrienne, much surprised.

'Alas ! yes, my dear young lady,' answered Rodin with simplicity. ' In one word, I had orders from Abbé d'Aigrigny, to place your former bailiff in the alternative either of losing his situation or lending himself to a mean action—something, in fact, that resembled spying and calumny ; but the honest, worthy man refused.'

'Why, who are you, sir?' said Mdlle. de Cardoville, more and more astonished.

'I am Rodin, lately secretary of the Abbé d'Aigrigny—a person of very little importance, as you see.'

It is impossible to describe the accent, at once humble and ingenuous, of the Jesuit, as he pronounced these words, which he accompanied with a respectful bow. On this revelation, Mdlle. de Cardoville drew back abruptly. We have said that Adrienne had sometimes heard talk of Rodin, the humble secretary of the Abbé d'Aigrigny, as a sort of obedient and passive machine. That was not all ; the bailiff of Cardoville Manor, writing to Adrienne on the subject of Prince Djalma, had complained of the perfidious and dishonest propositions of Rodin. She felt, therefore, a vague suspicion, when she heard that her liberator was the man who had played so odious a part. Yet this unfavourable feeling was balanced by the sense of what she owed to Rodin, and by his frank denunciation of Abbé d'Aigrigny before the magistrate. And then the Jesuit, by his own confession, had anticipated, as it were, the reproaches that might have been addressed to him. Still, it was with a kind of cold reserve that Mdlle. de Cardoville resumed this dialogue, which she had commenced with as much frankness as warmth and sympathy.

Rodin perceived the impression he had made. He expected it. He was not the least disconcerted when Mdlle. de Cardoville said to him, as she fixed upon him a piercing glance, ' Ah ! you are M. Rodin—secretary to the Abbé d'Aigrigny?'

'Say ex-secretary, if you please, my dear young lady,' answered the Jesuit ; 'for you see clearly that I can never again enter the house of the Abbé d'Aigrigny. I have made of him an implacable enemy, and I am now without employment—but no matter—nay, so much the better—since, at this price, the wicked are unmasked, and honest people rescued.'

These words, spoken with much simplicity and dignity, revived a feeling of pity in Adrienne's heart. She thought within herself that, after all, the poor old man spoke the truth. Abbé d'Aigrigny's hate, after this exposure, would be inexorable, and Rodin had braved it for the sake of a generous action.

Still Mdlle. de Cardoville answered coldly, ' Since you knew, sir, that the propositions you were charged to make to the bailiff of Cardoville were shameful and perfidious, how could you undertake the mission?'

'How?' replied Rodin, with a sort of painful impatience ; 'why, because I was completely under Abbé d'Aigrigny's charm, one of the most prodigiously clever men I have ever known, and, as I only discovered the day before yesterday, one of the most prodigiously dangerous men there is in the world. He had conquered my scruples, by persuading me that the End justifies the Means. I must confess that the end he seemed to propose to himself was great and beautiful ; but the day before yesterday I was cruelly undeceived. I was awakened, as it were, by a thunder-peal. Oh, my dear young lady !' added Rodin, with a sort of embarrassment and confusion, 'let us talk no more of my fatal journey to Cardoville. Though I was only an ignorant and blind instrument, I feel as ashamed and grieved at it as if I had acted for myself. It weighs upon me, it oppresses me. I entreat you, let us speak rather of yourself, and of what interests you—for the soul expands with generous thoughts, even as the breast is dilated in pure and healthful air.'

Rodin had confessed his fault so spontaneously, he explained it so naturally, he appeared to regret it so sincerely, that Adrienne, whose suspicions had no other grounds, felt her distrust a good deal diminished.

'So,' she resumed, still looking attentively at Rodin, 'it was at Cardoville that you saw Prince Djalma ?'

'Yes, madame ; and my affection for him dates from that interview. Therefore, I will accomplish my task. Be satisfied, my dear young lady ; like you, like Marshal Simon's daughters, the prince shall avoid being the victim of this detestable plot, which unhappily does not stop there.'

'And who besides, then, is threatened ?'

'M. Hardy, a man full of honour and probity, who is also your relation, and interested in this inheritance, but kept away from Paris by infamous treachery. And another heir, an unfortunate artisan, who, falling into a trap cleverly baited, has been thrown into a prison for debt.'

'But, sir,' said Adrienne, suddenly, ' for whose advantage was this abominable plot, which really alarms me, first devised ?'

'For the advantage of Abbé d'Aigrigny,' answered Rodin.

'How, and by what right ! Was he also an heir ?'

'It would take too long to explain it to you, my dear young lady. You will know all one day. Only be convinced that your family has no more bitter enemy than Abbé d'Aigrigny.'

'Sir,' said Adrienne, giving way to one last suspicion, 'I will speak frankly to you. How can I have deserved the interest that you seem to take in me, and that you even extend to all the members of my family ?'

'My dear young lady,' answered Rodin, with a smile, ' were I to tell you the cause, you would only laugh at, or misapprehend me.'

'Speak, I beg of you, sir. Do not mistrust me or yourself.'

'Well, then, I became interested in you—devoted to you—because your heart is generous, your mind lofty, your character independent and proud. Once attached to you, those of your race, who are indeed themselves worthy of interest, were no longer indifferent to me. To serve them was to serve you also.'

'But, sir—admitting that you suppose me worthy of the too flattering praises you bestow upon me—how could you judge of my heart, my mind, my character ?'

'I will tell you, my dear young lady ; but first I must make another confession, that fills me with shame. If you were not even so wonderfully endowed, what you have suffered in this house should suffice to command the interest of every honest man—don't you think so ?'

'I do think it should, sir.'

'I might thus explain the interest I feel in you. But no—I confess it—that would not have sufficed with me. Had you been only Mdlle. de Cardoville—a rich, noble, beautiful young lady—I should doubtless have pitied your misfortune ; but I should have said to myself, " This poor young lady is certainly much to be pitied ; but what can I, poor man, do in it ? My only resource is my post of secretary to the Abbé d'Aigrigny, and he would be the first that must be attacked. He is all-powerful, and I am nothing. To engage in a struggle with him would be to ruin myself, without the hope of saving this unfortunate person." But when I learnt what you were, my dear young lady, I revolted, in spite of my inferiority. " No," I said, " a thousand times, no ! So fine an intellect, so great a heart, shall not be the victims of an abominable plot. I may perish in the struggle, but I will at least make the attempt." '

No words can paint the mixture of delicacy, energy, and sensibility with which Rodin uttered these sentiments. As it often happens with people singu-larly repulsive and ill-favoured, if they can once bring you to forget their ugli-ness, their very deformity becomes a source of interest and commiseration, and you say to yourself, ' What a pity that such a mind, such a soul, should in-habit so poor a body !'—and you are touched and softened by the contrast.

It was thus that Mdlle. de Cardoville began to look upon Rodin. He had shown himself as simple and affectionate towards her as he had been brutal and insolent to Dr. Baleinier. One thing only excited the lively curiosity of Mdlle. de Cardoville—she wished to know how Rodin had conceived the de-votion and admiration which she seemed to inspire.

' Forgive my indiscreet and obstinate curiosity, sir, but I wish to know——'

' How you were morally revealed to me—is it not so ? Oh, my dear young lady ! nothing is more simple. I will explain it to you in two words. The Abbé d'Aigrigny saw in me nothing but a writing-machine, an obtuse, mute, blind instrument——'

' I thought M. d'Aigrigny had more penetration.'

' And you are right, my dear young lady ; he is a man of unparalleled sagacity ; but I deceived him by affecting more than simplicity. Do not, therefore, think me false. No ; I am proud in my manner—and my pride consists in never appearing above my position, however subaltern it may be ! Do you know why ? It is that, however haughty may be my superiors, I can say to myself, " They do not know my value. It is the inferiority of my condition, not me, that they humiliate." By this I gain doubly—my self-love is spared, and I hate no one.'

' Yes, I understand that sort of pride,' said Adrienne, more and more struck with Rodin's original turn of mind.

' But let us return to what concerns you, my dear young lady. On the eve of the 13th of February, the Abbé d'Aigrigny delivered to me a paper in shorthand, and said to me, " Transcribe this examination ; you may add that it is to support the decision of a family-council, which has declared, in accordance with the report of Dr. Baleinier, the state of mind of Mdlle. de Cardoville to be sufficiently alarming to render it necessary to confine her in a lunatic asylum." '

' Yes,' said Adrienne, with bitterness ; ' it related to a long interview, which I had with the Princess de Saint-Dizier, my aunt, and which was taken down without my knowledge.'

' Behold me, then, poring over my shorthand report, and beginning to transcribe it. At the end of the first ten lines, I was struck with stupor. I knew not if I were awake or dreaming. " What ! mad ?" They must be themselves insane who dare assert so monstrous a proposition !—More and more interested, I continued my reading—I finished it—Oh ! then, what shall I say ? What I felt, my dear young lady, it is impossible to express. It was sympathy, delight, enthusiasm !'

' Sir,' said Adrienne.

' Yes, my dear young lady, enthusiasm ! Let not the words shock your modesty, Know that these ideas, so new, so independent, so courageous which you expressed to your aunt with so much brilliancy, are, without your being aware of it, common to you and another person, for whom you will one day feel the most tender and religious respect.'

'Of whom do you speak, sir?' cried Mdlle de Cardoville, more and more interested.

After a moment's apparent hesitation, Rodin resumed, 'No, no—it is useless now to inform you of it. All I can tell you, my dear young lady, is that, when I had finished my reading, I ran to Abbé d'Aigrigny's, to convince him of the error into which he had fallen with regard to you. It was impossible then to find him; but yesterday morning I told him plainly what I thought He only appeared surprised to find that I could think at all. He received my communications with contemptuous silence. I thought him deceived; I continued my remonstrances, but quite in vain. He ordered me to follow him to the house, where the testament of your ancestor was to be opened. I was so blind with regard to the Abbé d'Aigrigny, that it required the successive arrivals of the soldier, of his son, and of Marshal Simon's father, to open my eyes thoroughly. Their indignation unveiled to me the extent of a conspiracy, plotted long ago, and carried on with terrible ability. Then, I understood why you were confined here as a lunatic; why the daughters of Marshal Simon were imprisoned in a convent. Then a thousand recollections returned to my mind; fragments of letters and statements, which had been given me to copy or decipher, and of which I had never been able to find the explanation, put me on the track of this odious machination. To express then and there the sudden horror I felt at these crimes, would have been to ruin all. I did not make this mistake. I opposed cunning to cunning; I appeared even more eager than Abbé d'Aigrigny. Had this immense inheritance been destined for me alone, I could not have shown myself more grasping and merciless. Thanks to this stratagem, Abbé d'Aigrigny had no suspicion. A providential accident having rescued the inheritance from his hands, he left the house in a state of profound consternation. For my part, I felt indescribable joy; for I had now the means of saving and avenging you, my dear young lady As usual, I went yesterday evening to my place of business. During the absence of the abbé, it was easy for me to peruse the correspondence relative to the inheritance. In this way I was able to unite all the threads of this immense plot. Oh! then, my dear young lady, I remained, struck with horror, in presence of the discoveries that I made, and that I never should have made under any other circumstances.'

'What discoveries, sir?'

'There are some secrets which are terrible to those who possess them. Do not ask me to explain, my dear young lady; but, in this examination, the league formed against you and your relations, from motives of insatiable cupidity, appeared to me in all its dark audacity. Thereupon, the lively and deep interest which I already felt for you, my dear young lady, was augmented greatly, and extended itself to the other innocent victims of this infernal conspiracy. In spite of my weakness, I determined to risk all, to unmask the Abbé d'Aigrigny. I collected the necessary proofs, to give my declaration before the magistrate the needful authority; and, this morning, I left the abbé's house without revealing to him my projects. He might have employed some violent method to detain me; yet it would have been cowardly to attack him without warning. Once out of his house, I wrote to him, that I had in my hands proofs enough of his crimes, to attack him openly in the face of day. I would accuse, and he must defend himself. I went directly to a magistrate, and you know the rest.'

At this juncture, the door opened, and one of the nurses appeared, and said to Rodin : ' Sir, the messenger that you and the magistrate sent to the Rue Brise-Miche has just come back.'

' Has he left the letter ?'

'Yes, sir ; and it was taken upstairs directly.'

'Very well. Leave us !' The nurse went out.

CHAPTER XXXV.

SYMPATHY.

IF it had been possible for Mdlle. de Cardoville to harbour any suspicion of the sincerity of Rodin's devotion, it must have given way before this reasoning, unfortunately so simple and undeniable. How could she suppose the faintest complicity between the Abbé d'Aigrigny and his secretary, when it was the latter who completely unveiled the machinations of his master, and exposed them to the tribunals ? when in this, Rodin went even further than Mdlle. de Cardoville would herself have gone ? Of what secret design could she suspect the Jesuit ? At worst, of a desire to earn by his services the profitable patronage of the young lady. And then, had he not just now protested against this supposition, by declaring his devotion, not to Mdlle. de Cardoville—not to the fair, rich, noble lady—but to the high-souled and generous girl ? Finally, as Rodin had said himself, could any but a miserable wretch fail to be interested in Adrienne's fate. A strange mixture of curiosity, surprise, and interest, was joined with Mdlle. de Cardoville's feelings of gratitude towards Rodin. Yet, as she recognised the superior mind under that humble exterior, she was suddenly struck with a grave suspicion. ' Sir,' said she to Rodin, ' I always confess to the persons I esteem the doubts they may have inspired, so that they may justify themselves, and excuse me, if I am wrong.'

Rodin looked at Mdlle. de Cardoville with surprise, as if mentally calculating the suspicions that she might entertain, and replied, after a moment's silence : ' You are perhaps thinking of my journey to Cardoville, of my base proposals to your good and worthy bailiff ? Oh ! if you ——'

' No, no, sir,' said Adrienne, interrupting him ; ' you made that confession spontaneously, and I quite understand, that, blinded with regard to M. d'Aigrigny, you passively executed instructions repugnant to your delicacy. But how comes it, that, with your incontestable merits, you have so long occupied so mean a position in his service ?'

' It is true,' said Rodin, with a smile ; ' that must impress you unfavourably, my dear young lady ; for a man of any capacity, who remains long in an inferior condition, has evidently some radical vice, some bad or base passion ——'

' It is generally true, sir.'

' And personally true—with regard to myself.'

' What, sir ! do you make this avowal ?'

' Alas ! I confess that I have a bad passion, to which, for forty years, I have sacrificed all chances of attaining to a better position.'

' And this passion, sir ?'

' Since I must make the unpleasant avowal, this passion is indolence— yes, indolence—the horror of all activity of mind, of all moral responsibility, of taking the lead in anything. With the twelve hundred francs that Abbé d'Aigrigny gave me, I was the happiest man in the world ; I trusted in the nobleness of his views ; his thoughts became mine, his wishes mine. My work once finished, I returned to my poor little chamber, I lighted my fire, I dined on vegetables—then, taking up some book of philosophy, little known, and dreaming over it, I gave free course to my imagination, which, restrained all the day long, carried me through numberless theories to a delicious Utopia. Then, from the eminences of my intelligence, lifted up, Lord knows whither, by the audacity of my thoughts, I seemed to look down upon my master, and upon the great men of the earth. This fever lasted for three or four hours, after which I had a good sleep ; and, the next morning, I went lightly to my work, secure of my daily bread, without cares for the future, living content with little, waiting with impatience for the delights of my solitary evening, and saying to myself as I went on writing like a stupid machine : 'And yet—and yet—if I chose !'——

'Doubtless, you could, like others, surer than others, have reached a higher position,' said Adrienne, greatly struck with Rodin's practical philosophy.

'Yes, I think I could have done so ; but for what purpose?—You see, my dear young lady, what often renders people of some merit puzzles to the vulgar, is that they are frequently content to say : "'If I chose !"'

'But sir, without attaching much importance to the luxuries of life, there is a certain degree of comfort, which age renders almost indispensable, and which you seem to have utterly renounced.'

'Undeceive yourself, if you please, my dear young lady,' said Rodin, with a playful smile. 'I am a true Sybarite ; I require absolutely warm clothes, a good stove, a soft mattress, a good piece of bread, a fresh radish, flavoured with good cheap salt, and some good, clear water ; and, notwithstanding this complication of wants, my twelve hundred francs have always more than sufficed, for I have been able to make some little savings.'

'But now that you are without employment, how will you manage to live, sir ?' said Adrienne, more and more interested by the singularities of this man, and wishing to put his disinterestedness to the proof.

'I have laid by a little, which will serve me till I have unravelled the last thread of Father d'Aigrigny's dark designs. I owe myself this reparation, for having been his dupe ; three or four days, I hope, will complete the work. After that, I have the certainty of meeting with a situation, in my native province, under a collector of taxes : some time ago, the offer was made me by a friend ; but then I would not leave Father d'Aigrigny, notwithstanding the advantages proposed. Fancy, my dear young lady—eight hundred francs, with board and lodging ! As I am a little of the roughest, I should have preferred lodging apart ; but, as they give me so much, I must submit to this little inconvenience.'

Nothing could exceed Rodin's ingenuity, in making these little household confidences (so abominably false) to Mdlle. de Cardoville, who felt her last suspicions give way.

'What, sir ?' said she to the Jesuit, with interest ; 'in three or four days, you mean to quit Paris ?'

'I hope to do so, my dear young lady ; and that,' added he, in a mysterious tone, 'and that for many reasons. But what would be very precious to me,' he resumed, in a serious voice, as he looked at Adrienne with emotion, 'would be to carry with me the conviction, that you did me the justice to believe, that, on merely reading your interview with the Princess de Saint-Dizier, I recognised at once qualities quite unexampled in our day, in a young person of your age and condition.'

'Ah, sir !' said Adrienne, with a smile, 'do not think yourself obliged to return so soon the sincere praises that I bestowed on your superiority of mind. I should be better pleased with ingratitude.'

'Oh, no ! I do not flatter you, my dear young lady. Why should I ? We may probably never meet again. I do not flatter you ; I understand you—that's all—and what will seem strange to you, is, that your appearance completes the idea which I had already formed of you, my dear young lady, in reading your interview with your aunt ; and some parts of your character, hitherto obscure to me, are now fully displayed.'

'Really, sir, you astonish me more and more.'

'I can't help it ! I merely describe my impressions. I can now explain perfectly, for example, your passionate love of the beautiful, your eager worship of the refinements of the senses, your ardent aspirations for a better state of things, your courageous contempt of many degrading and servile customs, to which woman is condemned ; yes, now I understand the noble pride with which you contemplate the mob of vain, self-sufficient, ridiculous men, who look upon woman as a creature destined for their service, according to the laws made after their own not very handsome image. In the eyes of these hedge-tyrants, woman, a kind of inferior being, to whom a council of cardinals deigned to grant a soul by a majority of two voices, ought to think herself supremely happy in being the servant of these petty pachas, old at thirty, worn-out, used-up, weary with excesses, wishing only for repose, and seeking, as they say, to make an end of it, which they set about by marrying some poor girl, who is on her side desirous to make a beginning.'

Mdlle. de Cardoville would certainly have smiled at these satirical remarks, if she had not been greatly struck by hearing Rodin express in such appropriate terms her own ideas, though it was the first time in her life that she saw this dangerous man. Adrienne forgot, or rather, she was not aware, that she had to deal with a Jesuit of rare intelligence, uniting the information and the mysterious resources of the police-spy with the profound sagacity of the confessor ; one of those diabolic priests, who, by the help of a few hints, avowals, letters, reconstruct a character, as Cuvier could reconstruct a body from zoological fragments. Far from interrupting Rodin, Adrienne listened to him with growing curiosity. Sure of the effect he produced, he continued, in a tone of indignation : 'And your aunt and the Abbé d'Aigrigny treated you as mad, because you revolted against the yoke of such tyrants ! because, hating the shameful vices of slavery, you chose to be independent with the suitable qualities of independence, free with the proud virtues of liberty ?'

'But, sir,' said Adrienne, more and more surprised, 'how can my thoughts be so familiar to you ?'

'First, I know you perfectly, thanks to your interview with the Princess de Saint-Dizier ; and next, if it should happen that we both pursue the same end, though by different means,' resumed Rodin, artfully, as he looked at Mdlle. de Cardoville with an air of intelligence, 'why should not our convictions be the same ?'

'I do not understand you, sir. Of what end do you speak ?'

'The end pursued incessantly by all lofty, generous, independent spirits—some acting, like you, my dear young lady, from passion, from instinct, without perhaps explaining to themselves the high mission they are called on to fulfil. Thus, for example, when you take pleasure in the most refined delights, when you surround yourself with all that charms the senses, do you think that you only yield to the attraction of the beautiful, to the desire of exquisite enjoyments ? No ! ah, no ! for then you would be incomplete, odiously selfish, a dry egotist, with a fine taste—nothing more—and at your age, it would be hideous, my dear young lady, it would be hideous !'

'And do you really think thus severely of me ?' said Adrienne, with uneasiness, so much influence had this man irresistibly attained over her.

'Certainly, I should think thus of you, if you loved luxury for luxury's sake ;—but, no—quite another sentiment animates you,' resumed the Jesuit. 'Let us reason a little. Feeling a passionate desire for all these enjoyments, you know their value and their need more than any one—is it not so ?'

'It is so,' replied Adrienne, deeply interested.

'Your gratitude and favour are then necessarily acquired by those who, poor, laborious, and unknown, have procured for you these marvels of luxury, which you could not do without ?'

'This feeling of gratitude is so strong in me, sir,' replied Adrienne, more and more pleased to find herself so well understood, 'that I once had inscribed on a masterpiece of goldsmith's work, instead of the name of the seller, that of the poor unknown artist who designed it, and who has since risen to his true place.'

'There, you see, I was not deceived,' went on Rodin ; 'the taste for enjoyment renders you grateful to those who procure it for you ; and that is not all ; here am I, an example, neither better nor worse than my neighbours, but accustomed to privations, which cause me no suffering—so that the privations of others necessarily touch me less nearly than they do you, my dear young lady ; for your habits of comfort must needs render you more compassionate towards misfortune. You would yourself suffer too much from poverty, not to pity and succour those who are its victims.'

'Really, sir,' said Adrienne, who began to feel herself under the fatal charm of Rodin, 'the more I listen to you, the more I am convinced that you would defend a thousand times better than I could those ideas for which I was so harshly reproached by Madame de Saint-Dizier and Abbé d'Aigrigny. Oh ! speak, speak, sir ! I cannot tell you with what happiness, with what pride I listen.'

Attentive and moved, her eyes fixed on the Jesuit with as much interest as sympathy and curiosity, Adrienne, by a graceful toss of the head that was habitual to her, threw back her long, golden curls, the better to contemplate Rodin, who thus resumed : 'You are astonished, my dear young lady, that you were not understood by your aunt or by Abbé d'Aigrigny ! What point of contact had you with these hypocritical, jealous, crafty minds, such as I can judge them to be now? Do you wish a new proof of their hateful blindness ? Among what they called your monstrous follies, which was the worst, the most damnable ? Why, your resolution to live alone and in your own way, to dispose freely of the present and the future. They declared this to be odious, detestable, immoral. And yet—was this resolution dictated by a mad love of liberty ? no !—by a disordered aversion to all restraint ? no !— by the desire of singularity ?—no !—for then I, too, should have blamed you severely.'

'Other reasons have indeed guided me, sir, I assure you,' said Adrienne eagerly, for she had become very eager for the esteem with which her character might inspire Rodin.

'Oh ! I know it well ; your motives could only be excellent ones,' replied the Jesuit. 'Why then did you take this resolution, so much called in question ? Was it to brave established etiquette ? no ! for you respected them until the hate of Mme. de Saint-Dizier forced you to withdraw yourself from her unbearable guardianship. Was it to live alone, to escape the eyes of the world ? no ! you would be a hundred times more open to observation in this than any other condition. Was it to make a bad use of your liberty ? no, ah, no ! those who design evil seek for darkness and solitude ; while you place yourself right before the jealous and envious eyes of the vulgar crowd. Why then do you take this determination so courageous and rare, unexampled in a young person of your age? Shall I tell you, my dear young lady? It is, that you wish to prove, by your example, that a woman of pure heart and honest mind, with a firm character and independence of soul, may nobly and proudly throw off the humiliating guardianship that custom has imposed upon her. Yes, instead of accepting the fate of a revolted slave, a life only destined to hypocrisy or vice, you wish to live freely in presence of all the world, independent, honourable, and respected. You wish to have, like man, the exercise of your own free will, the entire responsibility of all your actions, so as to establish the fact, that a woman left completely to herself, may equal man in reason, wisdom, uprightness, and surpass him in delicacy and dignity. That is your design, my dear young lady. It is noble and great. Will your example be imitated? I hope it may; but whether it be so or not, your generous attempt, believe me, will place you in a high and worthy position.'

Mdlle. de Cardoville's eyes shone with a proud and gentle brightness, her cheeks were slightly coloured, her bosom heaved, she raised her charming head with a movement of involuntary pride; at length completely under the charm of that diabolical man, she exclaimed: 'But, sir, who are you that can thus know and analyse my most secret thoughts, and read my soul more clearly than myself, so as to give new life and action to those ideas of independence which have long stirred within me? Who are you, that can thus elevate me in my own eyes, for now I am conscious of accomplishing a mission, honourable to myself, and perhaps useful to my sisters immersed in slavery? Once again, sir, who are you?'

'Who am I, madame?' answered Rodin, with a smile of the greatest good-nature; 'I have already told you that I am a poor old man, who for the last forty years, having served in the day time as a writing machine to record the ideas of others, went home every evening to work out ideas of his own—a good kind of man who, from his garret, watches and even takes some little share in the movement of generous spirits, advancing towards an end that is nearer than is commonly thought. And thus, my dear young lady, as I told you just now, you and I are both tending towards the same objects, though you may do the same without reflection, and merely in obedience to your rare and divine instincts. So continue so to live, fair, free, and happy!—it is your mission—more providential than you may think it. Yes; continue to surround yourself with all the marvels of luxury and art; refine your senses, purify your tastes, by the exquisite choice of your enjoyments; by genius, grace, and purity raise yourself above the stupid and ill-favoured mob of men, that will instantly surround you, when they behold you alone and free; they will consider you an easy prey, destined to please their cupidity, their egotism, their folly. Laugh at them, and mock these idiotic and sordid pretensions. Be the queen of your own world, and make yourself respected as a queen. Love—shine—enjoy—it is your part upon earth. All the flowers, with which you are whelmed in profusion, will one day bear fruit. You think that you have lived only for pleasure; in reality, you will have lived for the noblest aims that could tempt a great and lofty soul. And so—some years hence—we may meet again, perhaps; you, fairer and more followed than ever; I, older and more obscure. But, no matter —a secret voice, I am sure, says to you at this moment, that between us two, however different, there exists an invisible bond, a mysterious communion, which nothing hereafter will ever be able to destroy!'

He uttered these final words in a tone of such profound emotion, that Adrienne started. Rodin had approached without her perceiving it, and without, as it were, walking at all, for he dragged his steps along the floor, with a sort of serpent motion; and he had spoken with so much warmth and enthusiasm, that his pale face had become slightly tinged, and his repulsive ugliness had almost disappeared before the brilliancy of his small sharp eyes, now wide open, and fixed full upon Adrienne. The latter leaned forward, with half-open lips and deep-drawn breath, nor could she take her eyes from the Jesuit's, he had ceased to speak, and yet she was still listening. The feelings of the fair young lady, in presence of this little old man, dirty, ugly, and poor, were inexplicable. That comparison so common, and yet so true, of the frightful fascination of the bird by the serpent, might give some idea of the singular impression made upon her. Rodin's tactics were skilful and sure. Until now, Mdlle. de Cardoville had never analyzed her tastes or instincts. She had followed them, because they were inoffensive and charming. How happy and proud she then was sure to be to hear a man of superior mind not only praise these tendencies, for which she had been heretofore so severely blamed, but congratulate her upon them, as upon something great, noble, and divine ! If Rodin had only addressed himself to Adrienne's self-conceit, he would have failed in his perfidious designs, for she had not the least spark of vanity. But he addressed himself to all that was enthusiastic and generous in her heart ; that which he appeared to encourage and admire in her was really worthy of encouragement and admiration. How could she fail to be the dupe of such language, concealing though it did such dark and fatal projects ?

Struck with the Jesuit's rare intelligence, feeling her curiosity greatly excited by some mysterious words that he had purposely uttered, hardly explaining to herself the strange influence which this pernicious counsellor already exercised over her, and animated by respectful compassion for a man of his age and talents placed in so precarious a position, Adrienne said to him, with all her natural cordiality : 'A man of your merit and character, sir, ought not to be at the mercy of the caprice of circumstances. Some of your words have opened a new horizon before me ; I feel that, on many points, your counsels may be of the greatest use to me. Moreover, in coming to fetch me from this house, and in devoting yourself to the service of other persons of my family, you have shown me marks of interest which I cannot forget without ingratitude. You have lost a humble but secure situation. Permit me——'

'Not a word more, my dear young lady,' said Rodin, interrupting Mdlle. de Cardoville, with an air of chagrin. 'I feel for you the deepest sympathy ; I am honoured by having ideas in common with you ; I believe firmly that some day you will have to ask advice of the poor old philosopher ; and, precisely because of all that, I must and ought to maintain towards you the most complete independence.'

'But, sir, it is I that would be the obliged party, if you deigned to accept what I offer.'

'Oh, my dear young lady,' said Rodin, with a smile ; 'I know that your generosity would always know how to make gratitude light and easy ; but, once more, I cannot accept anything from you. One day, perhaps, you will know why.'——'One day ?'

'It is impossible for me to tell you more. And then, supposing I were under an obligation to you, how could I tell you all that was good and beautiful in your actions ? Hereafter, if you are somewhat indebted to me for my advice, so much the better ; I shall be the more ready to blame you, if I find anything to blame.'

'In this way, sir, you would forbid me to be grateful to you.

'No, no,' said Rodin, with apparent emotion. 'Oh, believe me ! there will come a solemn moment, in which you may repay all, in a manner worthy of yourself and me.'

This conversation was here interrupted by the nurse, who said to Adrienne as she entered : ' Madame, there is a little humpbacked workwoman downstairs, who wishes to speak to you. As, according to the doctor's new orders, you are to do as you like, I have come to ask, if I am to bring her up to you. She is so badly dressed, that I did not venture.'

' Bring her up, by all means,' said Adrienne, hastily, for she had recognised Mother Bunch by the nurse's description. ' Bring her up directly.'

' The doctor has also left word, that his carriage is to be at your orders, madame ; are the horses to be put to ?'

' Yes, in a quarter of an hour,' answered Adrienne to the nurse, who went out ; then, addressing Rodin, she continued : ' I do not think the magistrate can now be long, before he returns with Marshal Simon's daughters.'

' I think not, my dear young lady ; but who is this deformed workwoman ?' asked Rodin, with an air of indifference.

' The adopted sister of a gallant fellow, who risked all in endeavouring to rescue me from this house. And, sir,' said Adrienne, with emotion, ' this young workwoman is a rare and excellent creature. Never was a nobler mind, a more generous heart, concealed beneath an exterior less——'

But reflecting, that Rodin seemed to unite in his own person the same moral and physical contrasts as the sewing-girl, Adrienne stopped short, and then added, with inimitable grace, as she looked at the Jesuit, who was somewhat astonished at the sudden pause : ' No ; this noble girl is not the only person who proves how loftiness of soul, and superiority of mind, can make us indifferent to the vain advantages which belong only to the accidents of birth or fortune.' At the moment of Adrienne speaking these last words, Mother Bunch entered the room.

––––

CHAPTER XXXVI.

SUSPICIONS.

MDLLE. DE CARDOVILLE sprang hastily to meet the visitor, and said to her, in a voice of emotion, as she extended her arms towards her : ' Come— come—there is no grating to separate us now !'

On this allusion, which reminded her how her poor, laborious hand had been respectfully kissed by the fair and rich patrician, the young workwoman felt a sentiment of gratitude, which was at once ineffable and proud. But, as she hesitated to respond to the cordial reception, Adrienne embraced her with touching affection. When Mother Bunch found herself clasped in the fair arms of Mdlle. de Cardoville, when she felt the fresh and rosy lips of the young lady fraternally pressed to her own pale and sickly cheek, she burst into tears without being able to utter a word. Rodin, retired in a corner of the chamber, looked on this scene with secret uneasiness. Informed of the refusal, so full of dignity, which Mother Bunch had opposed to the perfidious temptations of the superior of St. Mary's Convent, and knowing the deep devotion of this generous creature for Agricola—a devotion which for some days she had so bravely extended to Mdlle. de Cardoville —the Jesuit did not like to see the latter thus labouring to increase that affection. He thought, wisely, that one should never despise friend or enemy, however small they may appear. Now, devotion to Mdlle. de Cardoville constituted an enemy in his eyes ; and we know, moreover, that Rodin combined in his character rare firmness, with a certain degree of superstitious weakness, and he now felt uneasy at the singular impression of fear which Mother Bunch inspired in him. He determined to recollect this presentiment.

Delicate natures sometimes display in the smallest things the most charming instincts of grace and goodness. Thus, when the sewing-girl was
shedding abundant and sweet tears of gratitude, Adrienne took a richly
embroidered handkerchief, and dried the pale and melancholy face. This
action, so simple and spontaneous, spared the work-girl one humiliation ;
for, alas ! humiliation and suffering are the two gulfs, along the edge of
which misfortune continually passes. Therefore, the least kindness is in
general a double benefit to the unfortunate. Perhaps the reader may smile
in disdain at the puerile circumstance we mention. But poor Mother Bunch,
not venturing to take from her pocket her old ragged handkerchief, would
long have remained blinded by her tears, if Mdlle. de Cardoville had not
come to her aid.

'Oh ! you are so good—so nobly charitable, lady !' was all that the
sempstress could say, in a tone of deep emotion ; for she was still more
touched by the attention of the young lady, than she would perhaps have
been by a service rendered.

'Look there, sir,' said Adrienne to Rodin, who drew near hastily. 'Yes,'
added the young patrician, proudly, ' I have indeed discovered a treasure.
Look at her, sir ; and love her as I love her, honour as I honour. She has
one of those hearts for which we are seeking.'

'And which, thank heaven, we are still able to find, my dear young lady !'
said Rodin, as he bowed to the needlewoman.

The latter raised her eyes slowly, and looked at the Jesuit. At sight of
that cadaverous countenance, which was smiling benignantly upon her, the
young girl started. It was strange ! she had never seen this man, and yet
she felt instantly the same fear and repulsion that he had felt with regard to
her. Generally timid and confused, the work-girl could not withdraw her
eyes from Rodin's ; her heart beat violently, as at the coming of some great
danger, and, as the excellent creature feared only for those she loved, she
approached Adrienne involuntarily, keeping her eyes fixed on Rodin. The
Jesuit was too good a physiognomist not to perceive the formidable impression he had made, and he felt an increase of his instinctive aversion for the
sempstress. Instead of casting down his eyes, he appeared to examine her
with such sustained attention, that Mdlle. de Cardoville was astonished
at it.

'I beg your pardon, my dear girl,' said Rodin, as if recalling his recollections, and addressing himself to Mother Bunch, 'I beg your pardon—but I
think—if I am not deceived—did you not go a few days since to St. Mary's
Convent, hard by ?'

'Yes, sir.'

'No doubt, it was you. Where then was my head ?' cried Rodin. 'It
was you—I should have guessed it sooner.'

'Of what do you speak, sir ?' asked Adrienne.

'Oh ! you are right, my dear young lady,' said Rodin, pointing to the
hunchback. 'She has indeed a noble heart, such as we seek. If you knew
with what dignity, with what courage this poor girl, who was out of work—
and, for her, to want work is to want everything—if you knew, I say, with
what dignity she rejected the shameful wages, that the superior of the convent
was unprincipled enough to offer, on condition of her acting as a spy in a
family where it was proposed to place her.'

'Oh, that is infamous !' cried Mdlle. de Cardoville, with disgust. 'Such
a proposal to this poor girl—to her !'

'Madame,' said Mother Bunch, bitterly, 'I had no work, I was poor, they
did not know me—and they thought they might propose anything to the
likes of me.'

'And I tell you,' said Rodin, 'that it was a double baseness on the part of the superior, to offer such temptation to misery, and it was doubly noble in you to refuse.'

'Sir,' said the sewing-girl, with modest embarrassment.

'Oh ! I am not to be intimidated,' resumed Rodin. 'Praise or blame, I speak out roughly what I think. Ask this dear young lady,' he added, with a glance at Adrienne. 'I tell you plainly, that I think as well of you as she does herself.'

'Believe me, dear,' said Adrienne, 'there are some sorts of praise which honour, recompense, and encourage ; and M. Rodin's is of the number. I know it—yes, I know it.'

'Nay, my dear young lady, you must not ascribe to me all the honour of this judgment.'

'How so, sir ?'

'Is not this dear girl the adopted sister of Agricola Baudoin, the gallant workman, the energetic and popular poet ? Is not the affection of such a man the best of guarantees, and does it not enable us to judge, as it were, by the label ?' added Rodin, with a smile.

'You are right, sir,' said Adrienne ; 'for, before knowing this dear girl, I began to feel deeply interested in her, from the day that her adopted brother spoke to me about her. He expressed himself with so much warmth, so much enthusiasm, that I at once conceived an esteem for the person capable of inspiring so noble an attachment.'

These words of Adrienne, joined to another circumstance, had such an effect upon their hearer, that her pale face became crimson. The unfortu- nate hunchback loved Agricola, with a love as passionate as it was secret and painful ; the most indirect allusion to this fatal sentiment occasioned her the most cruel embarrassment. Now, the moment Mdlle. de Cardoville spoke of Agricola's attachment for Mother Bunch, the latter had encountered Rodin's observing and penetrating look fixed upon her. Alone with Adrienne, the sempstress would have felt only a momentary confusion on hearing the name of the smith ; but unfortunately she fancied that the Jesuit, who already filled her with involuntary fear, had seen into her heart, and read the secrets of that fatal love, of which she was the victim. Thence the deep blushes of the poor girl, and the embarrassment so painfully visible, that Adrienne was struck with it.

A subtle and prompt mind, like Rodin's, on perceiving the smallest effect, immediately seeks the cause. Proceeding by comparison, the Jesuit saw on one side a deformed, but intelligent young girl, capable of passionate devo- tion ; on the other, a young workman, handsome, bold, frank, and full of talent. 'Brought up together, sympathising with each other on many points, there must be some fraternal affection between them,' said he to himself ; 'but fraternal affection does not blush, and the hunchback blushed and grew troubled beneath my look ; does she, then, LOVE Agricola ?'

Once on the scent of this discovery, Rodin wished to pursue the investiga- tion. Remarking the surprise and visible uneasiness that Mother Bunch had caused in Adrienne, he said to the latter, with a smile, looking signifi- cantly at the needlewoman : 'You see, my dear young lady, how she blushes. The good girl is troubled by what we said of the attachment of this gallant workman.'

The needlewoman hung down her head, overcome with confusion. After the pause of a second, during which Rodin preserved silence, so as to give time for his cruel remark to pierce the heart of the victim, the savage resumed : 'Look at the dear girl ! how embarrassed she appears!'

Again, after another silence, perceiving that Mother Bunch from crimson haa become deadly pale, and was trembling in all her limbs, the Jesuit feared he had gone too far, whilst Adrienne said to her friend, with anxiety : 'Why, dear child, are you so agitated ?'

'Oh ! it is clear enough,' resumed Rodin, with an air of perfect simplicity ; for, having discovered what he wished to know, he now chose to appear unconscious. 'It is quite clear and plain. This good girl has the modesty of a kind and tender sister for a brother. When you praise him, she fancies that she is herself praised.'

'And she is as modest as she is excellent,' added Adrienne, taking both of the girl's hands, 'the least praise, either of her adopted brother or of herself, troubles her in this way. But it is mere childishness, and I must scold her for it.'

Mdlle. de Cardoville spoke sincerely, for the explanation given by Rodin appeared to her very plausible. Like all other persons who, dreading every moment the discovery of some painful secret have their courage as easily restored as shaken, Mother Bunch persuaded herself (and she needed to do so, to escape dying of shame), that the last words of Rodin were sincere, and that he had no idea of the love she felt for Agricola. So her agony diminished, and she found words to reply to Mdlle. de Cardoville.

'Excuse me, madame,' she said timidly, 'I am so little accustomed to such kindness as that with which you overwhelm me, that I make a sorry return for all your goodness.'

'Kindness, my poor girl?' said Adrienne. 'I have done nothing for you yet. But, thank heaven ! from this day I shall be able to keep my promise, and reward your devotion to me, your courageous resignation, your sacred love of labour, and the dignity of which you have given so many proofs, under the most cruel privations. In a word, from this day, if you do not object to it, we will part no more.'

'Madame, you are too kind,' said Mother Bunch, in a trembling voice ; 'but I——'

'Oh ! be satisfied,' said Adrienne, anticipating her meaning. 'If you accept my offer, I shall know how to reconcile with my desire (not a little selfish) of having you near me, the independence of your character, your habits of labour, your taste for retirement, and your anxiety to devote yourself to those who deserve commiseration ; it is, I confess, by affording you the means of satisfying these generous tendencies, that I hope to seduce and keep you by me.'

'But what have I done?' asked the other, simply, 'to merit any gratitude from you? Did you not begin, on the contrary, by acting so generously to my adopted brother?'

'Oh ! I do not speak of gratitude,' said Adrienne ; 'we are quits. I speak of friendship and sincere affection, which I now offer you.'

'Friendship to me, madame?'

'Come, come,' said Adrienne, with a charming smile, 'do not be proud because your position gives you the advantage. I have set my heart on having you for a friend, and you will see that it shall be so. But now that I think of it (a little late, you will say), what good wind brings you hither?'

'This morning, M. Dagobert received a letter, in which he was requested to come to this place, to learn some news that would be of the greatest interest to him. Thinking it concerned Marshal Simon's daughters, he said to me : "Mother Bunch, you have taken so much interest in those dear children, that you must come with me : you shall witness my joy on finding them, and that will be your reward——"'

Adrienne glanced at Rodin. The latter made an affirmative movement of the head, and answered : 'Yes, yes, my dear young lady ; it was I who wrote to the brave soldier, but without signing the letter, or giving any explanation. You shall know why.'

'Then, my dear girl, why did you come alone ?' said Adrienne.

'Alas, madame ! on arriving here, it was your kind reception that made me forget my fears.'

'What fears ?' asked Rodin.

'Knowing that you lived here, madame, I supposed the letter was from you ; I told M. Dagobert so, and he thought the same. When we arrived, his impatience was so great, that he asked at the door if the orphans were in this house, and he gave their description. They told him no. Then, in spite of my supplications, he insisted on going to the convent to inquire about them.'

'What imprudence !' cried Adrienne.

'After what took place the other night, when he broke in,' added Rodin, shrugging his shoulders.

'It was in vain to tell him,' returned Mother Bunch, 'that the letter did not announce positively, that the orphans would be delivered up to him ; but that, no doubt, he would gain some information about them. He refused to hear anything, but said to me : " If I cannot find them, I will rejoin you. But they were at the convent the day before yesterday, and now that all is discovered, they cannot refuse to give them up——"'

'And with such a man there is no disputing !' said Rodin, with a smile.

'I hope they will not recognise him !' said Adrienne, remembering Baleinier's threats.

'It is not likely,' replied Rodin ; 'they will only refuse him admittance. That will be, I hope, the worst misfortune that will happen. Besides, the magistrate will soon be here with the girls. I am no longer wanted : other cares require my attention. I must seek out Prince Djalma. Only tell me, my dear young lady, where I shall find you, to keep you informed of my discoveries, and to take measures with regard to the young prince, if my inquiries, as I hope, shall be attended with success.'

'You will find me in my new house, Rue d'Anjou, formerly Beaulieu House. But now I think of it,' said Adrienne, suddenly, after some moments of reflection, 'it would not be prudent or proper, on many accounts, to lodge the Prince Djalma in the pavilion I occupied at Saint-Dizier House. I saw, some time ago, a charming little house, all furnished and ready ; it only requires some embellishments, that could be completed in twenty-four hours, to make it a delightful residence. Yes, that will be a thousand times preferable,' added Mdlle. de Cardoville, after a new interval of silence ; 'and I shall thus be able to preserve the strictest incognito.'

'What !' cried Rodin, whose projects would be much impeded by this new resolution of the young lady ; 'you do not wish him to know who you are ?'

'I wish Prince Djalma to know absolutely nothing of the anonymous friend who comes to his aid ; I desire that my name should not be pronounced before him, and that he should not even know of my existence—at least, for the present. Hereafter—in a month, perhaps—I will see ; circumstances will guide me.'

'But this incognito,' said Rodin, hiding his disappointment, 'will be difficult to preserve.'

'If the prince had inhabited the lodge, I agree with you ; the neighbourhood of my aunt would have enlightened him, and this fear is one of the reasons that have induced me to renounce my first project. But the prince will inhabit a distant quarter—the Rue Blanche. Who will inform him of my secret? One of my old friends, M. Norval—you, sir—and this dear girl,' pointing to Mother Bunch, 'on whose discretion I can depend as on your own, will be my only confidants. My secret will then be quite safe. Besides, we will talk further on this subject to-morrow. You must begin by discovering the retreat of this unfortunate young prince.'

Rodin, though much vexed at Adrienne's subtle determination with regard to Djalma, put the best face on the matter, and replied : 'Your intentions shall be scrupulously fulfilled, my dear young lady ; and to-morrow, with your leave, I hope to give you a good account of what you are pleased to call my providential mission.'

'To-morrow, then, I shall expect you with impatience,' said Adrienne, to Rodin, affectionately. ' Permit me always to rely upon you, as from this day you may count upon me. You must be indulgent with me, sir ; for I see that I shall yet have many counsels, many services to ask of you—though I already owe you so much.'

'You will never owe me enough, my dear young lady, never enough,' said Rodin, as he moved discreetly towards the door, after bowing to Adrienne. At the very moment he was going out, he found himself face to face with Dagobert.

'Holloa ! at last I have caught one !' shouted the soldier, as he seized the Jesuit by the collar with a vigorous hand.

CHAPTER XXXVII.

EXCUSES.

ON seeing Dagobert grasp Rodin so roughly by the collar, Mdlle. de Cardoville exclaimed in terror, as she advanced several steps towards the soldier : ' In the name of Heaven, sir ! what are you doing ?'

'What am I doing ?' echoed the soldier, harshly, without relaxing his hold on Rodin, and turning his head towards Adrienne, whom he did not know ; 'I take this opportunity to squeeze the throat of one of the wretches in the band of that renegade, until he tells me where my poor children are.'

'You strangle me,' said the Jesuit, in a stifled voice, as he tried to escape from the soldier.

'Where are the orphans, since they are not here, and the convent door has been closed against me ?' cried Dagobert, in a voice of thunder.

'Help ! help !' gasped Rodin.

'Oh ! it is dreadful !' said Adrienne, as, pale and trembling, she held up her clasped hands to Dagobert. 'Have mercy, sir ! listen to me ! listen to him !'

'M. Dagobert !' cried Mother Bunch, seizing with her weak hands the soldier's arm, and showing him Adrienne, 'this is Mdlle. de Cardoville. What violence in her presence ! and then, you are deceived—doubtless !'

At the name of Mdlle. de Cardoville, the benefactress of his son, the soldier turned round suddenly, and loosened his hold on Rodin. The latter, crimson with rage and suffocation, set about adjusting his collar and his cravat.

'I beg your pardon, madame,' said Dagobert, going towards Adrienne, who was still pale with fright ; 'I did not know who you were, and the first impulse of anger quite carried me away.'

'But what has this gentleman done to you ?' said Adrienne. 'If you had listened to me, you would have learned——'

'Excuse me if I interrupt you, madame,' said the soldier to Adrienne, in a hollow voice. Then, addressing himself to Rodin, who had recovered his coolness, he added ; ' Thank the lady, and begone !—If you remain here, I will not answer for myself.'

One word only, my dear sir,' said Rodin

' I tell you, that if you remain, I will not answer for myself !' cried Dagobert, stamping his foot.

'But, for heaven's sake, tell me the cause of this anger,' resumed Adrienne ; ' above all, do not trust to appearances. Calm yourself, and listen.'

' Calm myself, madame !' cried Dagobert, in despair ; ' I can think only of one thing, madame—of the arrival of Marshal Simon—he will be in Paris to-day or to-morrow.'

" Is it possible ?' said Adrienne. Rodin started with surprise and joy.

' Yesterday evening,' proceeded Dagobert, ' I received a letter from the marshal ; he has landed at Havre. For three days I have taken step after step, hoping that the orphans would be restored to me, as the machinations of those wretches have failed.' He pointed to Rodin with a new gesture of impatience. ' Well ! it is not so. They are conspiring some new infamy. I am prepared for anything.'

' But, sir,' said Rodin, advancing, ' permit me——'

' Begone ! cried Dagobert, whose irritation and anxiety redoubled, as he thought how at any moment Marshal Simon might arrive in Paris. ' Begone ! Were it not for this lady, I would at least be revenged on some one.'

Rodin made a nod of intelligence to Adrienne, whom he approached prudently, and, pointing to Dagobert with a gesture of affectionate commiseration, he said to the latter : ' I will leave you, sir, and the more willingly, as I was about to withdraw when you entered.' Then, coming still closer to Mdlle. de Cardoville, the Jesuit whispered to her, ' Poor soldier ! he is beside himself with grief, and would be incapable of hearing me. Explain it all to him, my dear young lady ; he will be nicely caught,' added he, with a cunning air. ' But in the meantime,' resumed Rodin, feeling in the side pocket of his great coat, and taking out a small parcel, ' let me beg you to give him this, my dear young lady. It is my revenge, and a very good one.'

And while Adrienne, holding the little parcel in her hand, looked at the Jesuit with astonishment, the latter, laying his forefinger upon his lip, as if recommending silence, drew backward on tiptoe to the door, and went out after again pointing to Dagobert with a gesture of pity ; while the soldier, in sullen dejection, with his head drooping, and his arms crossed upon his bosom, remained deaf to the sewing girl's earnest consolations. When Rodin had left the room, Adrienne, approaching the soldier, said to him, in her mild voice, with an expression of deep interest, ' Your sudden entry prevented my asking you a question that greatly concerns me. How is your wound ?'

' Thank you, madame,' said Dagobert, starting from his painful lethargy, ' it is of no consequence, but I have not time to think of it. I am sorry to have been so rough in your presence, and to have driven away that wretch ; but 'tis more than I could master. At sight of those people, my blood is all up.'——' And yet, believe me, you have been too hasty in your judgment. The person who was just now here——'

' Too hasty, madame ! I do not see him to-day for the first time. He was with that renegade the Abbé d'Aigrigny——'

' No doubt—and yet he is an honest and excellent man.'

' He !' cried Dagobert.

' Yes, for at this moment he is busy about only one thing—restoring to you those dear children !'

'He !' repeated Dagobert, as if he could not believe what he heard.   He restore me my children ?'

'Yes ; and sooner, perhaps, than you think for.'

'Madame,' said Dagobert, abruptly, 'he deceives you. You are the dupe of that old rascal.'

'No,' said Adrienne, shaking her head, with a smile.   'I have proofs of his good faith. First of all, it is he who delivers me from this house.'

'Is it true ?' said Dagobert, quite confounded.

'Very true ; and here is, perhaps, something that will reconcile you to him,' said Adrienne, as she delivered the small parcel which Rodin had given her as she went out.   'Not wishing to exasperate you by his presence, he said to me : " Give this to that brave soldier ; it is my revenge."'

Dagobert looked at Mdlle. de Cardoville with surprise, as he mechanically opened the little parcel. When he had unfolded it, and discovered *his* own silver cross, black with age, and the old red, faded ribbon, treasures taken from him at the White Falcon Inn, at the same time as his papers, he exclaimed in a broken voice . 'My cross ! my cross ! It is my cross !' In the excitement of his joy, he pressed the silver star to his grey moustache.

Adrienne and the other were deeply affected by the emotion of the soldier, who continued, as he ran towards the door by which Rodin had gone out : 'Next to a service rendered to Marshal Simon, my wife, or son, nothing could be more precious to me. And you answer for this worthy man, madame, and I have ill used him in your presence ! Oh ! he is entitled to reparation, and he shall have it.'

So saying, Dagobert left the room precipitately, hastened through two other apartments, gained the staircase, and descending it rapidly, overtook Rodin on the lowest step.

'Sir,' said the soldier to him, in an agitated voice, as he seized him by the arm, 'you must come upstairs directly.'

'You should make up your mind to one thing or the other, my dear sir,' said Rodin, stopping good-naturedly ; 'one moment you tell me to begone, and the next to return. How are we to decide ?'

'Just now, sir, I was wrong ; and when I am wrong, I acknowledge it. I abused and ill-treated you before witnesses ; I will make you my apologies before witnesses.'

'But, my dear sir—I am much obliged to you—I am in a hurry.

'I cannot help your being in a hurry. I tell you, I must have you come upstairs, directly—or else—or else,' resumed Dagobert, taking the hand of the Jesuit. and pressing it with as much cordiality as emotion, 'or else the happiness you have caused me in returning my cross will not be complete.'

'Well, then, my good friend, let us go up.'

'And not only have you restored me my cross, for which I have wept many tears, believe me, unknown to any one,' cried Dagobert, much affected ; 'but the young lady told me, that, thanks to you, those poor children——but tell me—no false joy—is it really true ?—My God ! is it really true ?'

'Ah ! ah ! Mr. Inquisitive,' said Rodin, with a cunning smile.   Then he added : 'Be perfectly tranquil, my growler ; you shall have your two angels back again.' And the Jesuit began to ascend the stairs.

'Will they be restored to me to-day ?' cried Dagobert, stopping Rodin abruptly, by catching hold of his sleeve.

'Now, really, my good friend,' said the Jesuit, 'let us come to the point ! Are we to go up or down ? I do not find fault, but you turn me about like a teetotum.'

'You are right. We shall be better able to explain things upstairs. Come with me—quick! quick!' said Dagobert, as, taking the Jesuit by the arm, he hurried him along, and brought him triumphantly into the room, where Adrienne and Mother Bunch had remained in much surprise at the soldier's sudden disappearance.

'Here he is! here he is!' cried Dagobert, as he entered. 'Luckily, I caught him at the bottom of the stairs.'

'And you have made me come up at a fine pace!' added Rodin, pretty well out of breath

'Now, sir, said Dagobert, in a grave voice, 'I declare, in presence of all, that I was wrong to abuse and ill-treat you. I make you my apology for it, sir; and I acknowledge, with joy, that I owe you—much—oh! very much —and when I owe, I pay.'

So saying, Dagobert held out his honest hand to Rodin, who pressed it in a very affable manner, and replied: 'Now, really—what is all this about? What great service do you speak of?'

'This!' said Dagobert, holding up the cross before Rodin's eyes 'You do not know, then, what this cross is to me?'

'On the contrary, supposing you would set great store by it, I intended to have the pleasure of delivering it myself. I had brought it for that purpose; but, between ourselves, you gave me so warm a reception, that I had not the time——'

'Sir,' said Dagobert, in confusion, 'I assure you that I sincerely repent of what I have done'

'I know it, my good friend; do not say another word about it. You were then much attached to this cross?'

'Attached to it, sir!' cried Dagobert. 'Why, this cross,' and he kissed it as he spoke, 'is my relic. He from whom it came was my saint—my hero—and he had touched it with his hand!'

'Oh!' said Rodin, feigning to regard the cross with as much curiosity as respectful admiration; 'did Napoleon—the Great Napoleon—indeed touch with his own hand—that victorious hand!—this noble star of honour?'

'Yes, sir, with his own hand. He placed it there upon my bleeding breast, as a cure for my fifth wound. So that, you see, were I dying of hunger, I think I should not hesitate betwixt bread and my cross—that I might, in any case, have it on my heart in death But, enough—enough! —let us talk of something else. It is foolish in an old soldier, is it not?' added Dagobert, drawing his hand across his eyes, and then, as if ashamed to deny what he really felt: 'Well, then! yes, he resumed, raising his head proudly, and no longer seeking to conceal the tears that rolled down his cheek; 'yes, I weep for joy, to have found my cross—my cross, that the Emperor gave me with his *victorious* hand, as this worthy man has called it.'

'Then blessed be my poor old hand for having restored you the glorious treasure!' said Rodin, with emotion. 'In truth,' he added, 'the day will be a good one for everybody—as I announced to you this morning in my letter.'

'That letter without a signature?' asked the soldier, more and more astonished. 'Was it from you?'

'It was I who wrote it. Only, fearing some new snare of the Abbé d'Aigrigny, I did not choose, you understand, to explain myself more clearly.'——'Then—I shall see—my orphans?'

Rodin nodded affirmatively, with an expression of great good-nature.

'Presently—perhaps immediately,' said Adrienne, with a smile. 'Well! was I right in telling you that you had not judged this gentleman fairly?'

'Why did he not tell me all this when I came in?' cried Dagobert, almost beside himself with joy.

'There was one difficulty in the way, my good friend,' said Rodin; 'it was, that when you came in, you nearly throttled me.'

'True; I was too hasty. Once more, I ask your pardon. But was I to blame? I had only seen you with that Abbé d'Aigrigny, and in the first moment——'

'This dear young lady,' said Rodin, bowing to Adrienne, 'will tell you that I have been, without knowing it, the accomplice in many perfidious actions, but as soon as I began to see my way through the darkness, I quitted the evil course on which I had entered, and returned to that which is honest, just, and true.'

Adrienne nodded affirmatively to Dagobert, who appeared to consult her look.

'If I did not sign the letter that I wrote to you, my good friend, it was partly from fear that my name might inspire suspicion; and if I asked you to come hither, instead of to the convent, it was that I had some dread—like this dear young lady—lest you might be recognised by the porter or by the gardener, your affair of the other night rendering such a recognition somewhat dangerous.'

'But M. Baleinier knows all; I forgot that,' said Adrienne, with uneasiness. 'He threatened to denounce M. Dagobert and his son, if I made any complaint.'

'Do not be alarmed, my dear young lady; it will soon be for you to dictate conditions,' replied Rodin. 'Leave that to me; and as for you, my good friend, your torments are now finished.'

'Yes,' said Adrienne, 'an upright and worthy magistrate has gone to the convent, to fetch Marshal Simon's daughters. He will bring them hither; but he thought with me, that it would be most proper for them to take up their abode in my house. I cannot, however, come to this decision without your consent, for it is to you that these orphans were entrusted by their mother.'

'You wish to take her place with regard to them, madame?' replied Dagobert; 'I can only thank you with all my heart, for myself and for the children. But, as the lesson has been a sharp one, I must beg to remain at the door of their chamber, night and day. If they go out with you, I must be allowed to follow them at a little distance, so as to keep them in view, just like Spoilsport, who has proved himself a better guardian than myself. When the marshal is once here—it will be in a day or two—my post will be relieved. Heaven grant it may be soon!'

'Yes,' replied Rodin, in a firm voice, 'heaven grant he may arrive soon, for he will have to demand a terrible reckoning of the Abbé d'Aigrigny, for the persecution of his daughters; and yet the marshal does not know all.'

'And don't you tremble for the renegade?' asked Dagobert, as he thought how the marquis would soon find himself face to face with the marshal.

'I never care for cowards and traitors,' answered Rodin; 'and when Marshal Simon returns——' Then, after a pause of some seconds, he continued: 'If he will do me the honour to hear me, he shall be edified as to the conduct of the Abbé d'Aigrigny. The marshal knows that his dearest friends, as well as himself, have been victims of the hatred of that dangerous man.'——'How so?' said Dagobert.

'Why, yourself, for instance,' replied Rodin; you are an example of what I advance'——'I!'

Do you think it was mere chance, that brought about the scene at the White Falcon Inn, near Leipsic?'

'Who told you of that scene?' said Dagobert, in astonishment.

'Where you accepted the challenge of Morok,' continued the Jesuit, without answering Dagobert's question, 'and so fell into a trap, or else refused it, and were then arrested, for want of papers, and thrown into prison as a vagabond, with these poor children. Now, do you know the object of this violence? It was to prevent your being here on the 13th of February.'

'But the more I hear, sir,' said Adrienne, 'the more I am alarmed at the audacity of the Abbé d'Aigrigny, and the extent of the means he has at his command. Really,' she resumed, with increasing surprise, 'if your words were not entitled to absolute belief——'

'You would doubt their truth, madame?' said Dagobert. 'It is like me. Bad as he is, I cannot think that this renegade had relations with a wild-beast showman as far off as Saxony; and then, how could he know that I and the children were to pass through Leipsic? It is impossible, my good man.'

'In fact, sir,' resumed Adrienne, 'I fear that you are deceived by your dislike (a very legitimate one) of Abbé d'Aigrigny, and that you ascribe to him an almost fabulous degree of power and extent of influence.'

After a moment's silence, during which Rodin looked first at Adrienne and then at Dagobert, with a kind of pity, he resumed : 'How could the Abbé d'Aigrigny have your cross in his possession, if he had no connection with Morok?'

'That is true, sir,' said Dagobert; 'joy prevented me from reflecting. But how, indeed, did my cross come into your hands?'

'By means of the Abbé d'Aigrigny's having precisely those relations with Leipsic, of which you and the young lady seem to doubt.'

'But how did my cross get to Paris?'——'Tell me; you were arrested at Leipsic for want of papers—is it not so?'

'Yes; but I could never understand how my passports and money disappeared from my knapsack. I thought I must have had the misfortune to lose them.'

Rodin shrugged his shoulders, and replied : 'You were robbed of them at the White Falcon Inn, by Goliath, one of Morok's servants; and the latter sent the papers and the cross to the Abbé d'Aigrigny, to prove that he had succeeded in executing his orders with respect to the orphans and yourself. It was the day before yesterday, that I obtained the key of that dark machination. Cross and papers were amongst the stores of Abbé d'Aigrigny; the papers formed a considerable bundle, and he might have missed them; but, hoping to see you this morning, and knowing how a soldier of the Empire values his cross, his sacred relic, as you call it, my good friend—I did not hesitate. I put the relic into my pocket. "After all," said I, " it is only restitution, and my delicacy perhaps exaggerates this breach of trust."'

'You could not have done a better action,' said Adrienne; 'and, for my part, because of the interest I feel for M. Dagobert, I take it as a personal favour. But, sir, after a moment's silence, she resumed with anxiety : 'What terrible power must be at the command of M. d'Aigrigny, for him to have such extensive and formidable relations in a foreign country?'

'Silence!' said Rodin, in a low voice, and looking round him with an air of alarm. 'Silence! In heaven's name do not ask me about it!'

CHAPTER XXXVIII.

REVELATIONS.

MDLLE. DE CARDOVILLE, much astonished at the alarm displayed by Rodin, when she had asked him for some explanation of the formidable and far-reaching power of the Abbé d'Aigrigny, said to him : ' Why, sir, what is there so strange in the question that I have just asked you ?'

After a moment's silence, Rodin cast his looks all around, with well-feigned uneasiness, and replied in a whisper : ' Once more, madame, do not question me on so fearful a subject. The walls of this house may have ears.'

Adrienne and Dagobert looked at each other with growing surprise. Mother Bunch, by an instinct of incredible force, continued to regard Rodin with invincible suspicion. Sometimes she stole a glance at him, as if trying to penetrate the mask of this man, who filled her with fear. At one moment, the Jesuit encountered her anxious gaze, obstinately fixed upon him ; immediately he nodded to her with the greatest amenity. The young girl, alarmed at finding herself observed, turned away with a shudder.

' No, no, my dear young lady,' resumed Rodin, with a sigh, as he saw Mdlle. de Cardoville astonished at his silence ; ' do not question me on the subject of Abbé d'Aigrigny's power !'

' But, to persist, sir,' said Adrienne ; ' why this hesitation to answer ? What do you fear ?'

' Ah, my dear young lady,' said Rodin, shuddering, ' those people are so powerful ! their animosity is so terrible !'

' Be satisfied, sir ; I owe you too much, for my support ever to fail you.'

' Ah, my dear young lady,' cried Rodin, as if hurt by the supposition ; ' think better of me, I entreat you. Is it for myself that I fear ?—No, no ; I am too obscure, too inoffensive ; but it is for you, for Marshal Simon, for the other members of your family, that all is to be feared. Oh, my dear young lady ! let me beg you to ask no questions. There are secrets which are fatal to those who possess them.'

' But, sir, is it not better to know the perils with which one is threatened ?'

' When you know the manœuvres of your enemy, you may at least defend yourself,' said Dagobert. ' I prefer an attack in broad daylight to an ambuscade.'

' And I assure you,' resumed Adrienne, ' the few words you have spoken cause me a vague uneasiness.'

' Well, if I must, my dear young lady,' replied the Jesuit, appearing to make a great effort, ' since you do not understand my hints, I will be more explicit ; but remember,' added he, in a deeply serious tone, ' that you have persevered in forcing me to tell you what you had perhaps better not have known.'——' Speak, sir, I pray you speak,' said Adrienne.

Drawing about him Adrienne, Dagobert, and Mother Bunch, Rodin said to them in a low voice, and with a mysterious air : ' Have you never heard of a powerful association, which extends its net over all the earth, and counts its disciples, agents, and fanatics in every class of society—which has had, and often has still, the ear of kings and nobles—which, in a word, can raise its creatures to the highest positions, and with a word can reduce them again to the nothingness from which it alone could uplift them ?'

' Good heaven, sir !' said Adrienne, ' what formidable association ? Until now I never heard of it.'

' I believe you ; and yet your ignorance on this subject greatly astonishes me, my dear young lady.'

' And why should it astonish you ?' ——' Because you lived some time with your aunt, and must have often seen the Abbé d'Aigrigny.'

'I lived at the princess's, but not with her; for a thousand reasons she had inspired me with warrantable aversion.'

'In truth, my dear young lady, my remark was ill-judged. It was there, above all, and particularly in your presence, that they would keep silence with regard to this association—and yet to it alone did the Princess de Saint-Dizier owe her formidable influence in the world, during the last reign. Well, then; know this—it is the aid of that association which renders the Abbé d'Aigrigny so dangerous a man. By it he was enabled to follow and to reach divers members of your family, some in Siberia, some in India, others on the heights of the American mountains; but, as I have told you it was only the day before yesterday, and by chance, that, examining the papers of Abbé d'Aigrigny, I found the trace of his connexion with this Company, of which he is the most active and able chief.'

'But the name, sir, the name of this Company?' said Adrienne.

'Well! it is——', but Rodin stopped short.

'It is,' repeated Adrienne, who was now as much interested as Dagobert and the sempstress; 'it is——'

Rodin looked round him, beckoned all the actors in this scene to draw nearer, and said in a whisper, laying great stress upon the words. 'It is—the Society of Jesus!' and he again shuddered.

'The Jesuits!' cried Mdlle. de Cardoville, unable to restrain a burst of laughter, which was the more buoyant, as, from the mysterious precautions of Rodin, she had expected some very different revelation. 'The Jesuits! she resumed, still laughing. 'They have no existence, except in books; they are frightful historical personages, certainly; but why should you put forward Madame de Saint-Dizier and M. d'Aigrigny in that character? Such as they are, they have done quite enough to justify my aversion and disdain.'

After listening in silence to Mdlle. de Cardoville, Rodin continued, with a grave and agitated air: 'Your blindness frightens me, my dear young lady; the past should have given you some anxiety for the future, since, more than any one, you have already suffered from the fatal influence of this Company, whose existence you regard as a dream!'

'I, sir?' said Adrienne, with a smile, although a little surprised.——'You.'

'Under what circumstances?'

'You ask me this question, my dear young lady! you ask me this question!—and yet you have been confined here as a mad person! Is it not enough to tell you that the master of this house is one of the most devoted lay members of the Company, and therefore the blind instrument of the Abbé d'Aigrigny.'

'So,' said Adrienne, this time without smiling, 'Dr. Baleinier——'

'Obeyed the Abbé d'Aigrigny, the most formidable chief of that formidable society. He employs his genius for evil; but I must confess he is a man of genius. Therefore, it is upon him that you and yours must fix all your doubts and suspicions; it is against him that you must be upon your guard. For, believe me, I know him, and he does not look upon the game as lost. You must be prepared for new attacks, doubtless of another kind, but only the more dangerous on that account——'

'Luckily, you give us notice,' said Dagobert, 'and you will be on our side.'

'I can do very little, my good friends; but that little is at the service of honest people,' said Rodin.

'Now,' said Adrienne, with a thoughtful air, completely persuaded by Rodin's air of conviction, 'I can explain the inconceivable influence that my aunt exercised in the world. I ascribed it chiefly to her relations with persons in power; I thought that she, like the Abbé d'Aigrigny, was concerned in dark intrigues, for which religion served as a veil—but I was far from believing what you tell me.'

'How many things you have got to learn!' resumed Rodin. 'If you knew, my dear young lady, with what art these people surround you, without your being aware of it, by agents devoted to themselves! Every one of your steps is known to them, when they have any interest in such knowledge. Thus, little by little, they act upon you--slowly, cautiously, darkly. They circumvent you by every possible means, from flattery to terror—seduce or frighten, in order at last to rule you, without your being conscious of their authority. Such is their object, and I must confess they pursue it with detestable ability.'

Rodin had spoken with so much sincerity, that Adrienne trembled ; then, reproaching herself with these fears, she resumed : 'And yet, no—I can never believe in so infernal a power ; the might of priestly ambition belongs to another age. Heaven be praised, it has disappeared for ever!'

'Yes, certainly, it is out of sight ; for they now know how to disperse and disappear, when circumstances require it. But then are they the most dangerous ; for suspicion is laid asleep, and they keep watch in the dark. Oh ! my dear young lady, if you knew their frightful ability ! In my hatred of all that is oppressive, cowardly, and hypocritical, I had studied the history of that terrible society, before I knew that the Abbé d'Aigrigny belonged to it. Oh ! it is dreadful. If you knew what means they employ ! When I tell you that, thanks to their diabolical devices, the most pure and devoted appearances often conceal the most horrible snares.' Rodin's eye rested, as if by chance, on the hunchback ; but, seeing that Adrienne did not take the hint, the Jesuit continued : 'In a word—are you not exposed to their pursuits ?—have they any interest in gaining you over ?—oh ! from that moment, suspect all that surround you, suspect the most noble attachments, the most tender affections, for these monsters sometimes succeed in corrupting your best friends, and making a terrible use of them, in proportion to the blindness of your confidence.'

'Oh ! it is impossible,' cried Adrienne, in horror. 'You must exaggerate. No ! hell itself never dreamed of more frightful treachery!'

'Alas, my dear young lady ! one of your relations, M. Hardy— the most loyal and generous-hearted man that could be—has been the victim of some such infamous treachery. Do you know what we learned from the reading of your ancestor's will ? Why, that he died the victim of the malevolence of these people ; and now, at the lapse of a hundred and fifty years, his descendants are still exposed to the hate of that indestructible society.'

'Oh, sir ! it terrifies me,' said Adrienne, feeling her heart sink within her. 'But are there no weapons against such attacks ?'

'Prudence, my dear young lady—the most watchful caution—the most incessant study and suspicion of all that approach you.'

'But such a life would be frightful ! It is a torture to be the victim of continual suspicions, doubts, and fears.'

'Without doubt ! They know it well, the wretches ! That constitutes their strength. They often triumph by the very excess of the precautions taken against them. Thus, my dear young lady, and you, brave and worthy soldier, in the name of all that is dear to you, be on your guard, and do not lightly impart your confidence. Be on your guard, for you have nearly fallen the victims of those people. They will always be your implacable enemies. And you, also, poor, interesting girl!' added the Jesuit, speaking to Mother Bunch, 'follow my advice—fear these people. Sleep, as the proverb says, with one eye open.'

'I, sir!' said the workgirl, 'What have I done ? what have I to fear ?'

'What have you done ? Dear me ! Do not you tenderly love this young lady, your protectress ? have you not attempted to assist her ? Are you not the adopted sister of the son of this intrepid soldier, the brave Agricola ? Alas, poor girl ! are not these sufficient claims to their hatred, in spite of your obscurity ? Nay, my dear young lady ! do not think that I exaggerate. Reflect ! only reflect ! Think what I have just said to the faithful companion-in-arms of Marshal Simon, with regard to his imprisonment at Leipsic. Think what happened to yourself, when, against all law and reason, you were brought hither. Then you will see, that there is nothing exaggerated in the picture I have drawn of the secret power of this Company. Be always on your guard, and, in doubtful cases, do not fear to apply to me. In three days, I have learned enough by my own experience, with regard to their manner of acting, to be able to point out to you many a snare, device, and danger, and to protect you from them.'

'In any such case, sir,' replied Mdlle. de Cardoville, 'my interest, as well as gratitude, would point to you as my best counsellor.'

According to the skilful tactics of the sons of Loyola, who sometimes deny their own existence, in order to escape from an adversary—and sometimes proclaim with audacity the living power of their organization, in order to intimidate the feeble—Rodin had laughed in the face of the bailiff of Cardoville, when the latter had spoken of the existence of the Jesuits ; while now, at this moment, picturing their means of action, he endeavoured, and he succeeded in the endeavour, to impregnate the mind of Mdlle. de Cardoville with some germs of doubt, which were gradually to develop themselves by reflection, and serve hereafter the dark projects that he meditated. Mother Bunch still felt considerable alarm with regard to Rodin. Yet, since she had heard the fatal powers of the formidable Order revealed to Adrienne, the young sempstress, far from suspecting the Jesuit of having the audacity to speak thus of a society of which he was himself a member, felt grateful to him, in spite of herself, for the important advice that he had just given her patroness. The side-glance which she now cast upon him (which Rodin also detected, for he watched the young girl with sustained attention), was full of gratitude, mingled with surprise. Guessing the nature of this impression, and wishing entirely to remove her unfavourable opinion, and also to anticipate a revelation which would be made sooner or later, the Jesuit appeared to have forgotten something of great importance, and exclaimed, striking his forehead : ' What was I thinking of ?' Then, speaking to Mother Bunch, he added : ' Do you know where your sister is, my dear girl ?' Disconcerted and saddened by this unexpected question, the workwoman answered with a blush, for she remembered her last interview with the brilliant Bacchanal Queen : ' I have not seen my sister for some days, sir.'

'Well, my dear girl, she is not very comfortable,' said Rodin ; ' I promised one of her friends to send her some little assistance. I have applied to a charitable person, and that is what I received for her.' So saying, he drew from his pocket a sealed roll of coin, which he delivered to Mother Bunch, who was now both surprised and affected.

'You have a sister in trouble, and I know nothing of it ?' said Adrienne, hastily. ' This is not right of you, my child !'

'Do not blame her,' said Rodin. ' First of all, she did not know that her sister was in distress, and, secondly, she could not ask you, my dear young lady, to interest yourself about her.'

As Mdlle. de Cardoville looked at Rodin with astonishment, he added, again speaking to the hunchback : ' Is not that true, my dear girl ?'

'Yes, sir,' said the sempstress, casting down her eyes and blushing. Then she added, hastily and anxiously : ' But when did you see my sister, sir ? where is she ? how did she fall into distress ?'

'All that would take too long to tell you, my dear girl ; but go as soon as possible to the greengrocer's in the Rue Clovis, and ask to speak to your sister as from M. Charlemagne or M. Rodin, which you please, for I am equally well known in that house by my Christian name as by my surname, and then you will learn all about it.   Only tell your sister, that, if she behaves well, and keeps to her good resolutions, there are some who will continue to look after her.'

More and more surprised, Mother Bunch was about to answer Rodin, when the door opened, and M. de Gernande entered.   The countenance of the magistrate was grave and sad.

'Marshal Simon's daughters ?' cried Mdlle. de Cardoville.

'Unfortunately, they are not with me,' answered the judge.

'Then, where are they, sir ?   What have they done with them ?   The day before yesterday, they were in the convent ?' cried Dagobert, overwhelmed by this complete destruction of his hopes.

Hardly had the soldier pronounced these words, when, profiting by the impulse which gathered all the actors in this scene about the magistrate, Rodin withdrew discreetly towards the door, and disappeared without any one perceiving his absence.   Whilst the soldier, thus suddenly thrown back to the depths of his despair, looked at M. de Gernande, waiting with anxiety for the answer, Adrienne said to the magistrate : 'But, sir, when you applied at the convent, what explanation did the superior give on the subject of these young girls ?'

'The lady superior refused to give any explanation, madame.   "You pretend," said she, " that the young persons of whom you speak are detained here against their will.   Since the law gives you the right of entering this house, make your search."   " But, madame, please to answer me positively," said I to the superior ; "do you declare, that you know nothing of the young girls, whom I have come to claim."   " I have nothing to say on this subject, sir.   You assert, that you are authorised to make a search ; make it."   Not being able to get any other explanation,' continued the magistrate, ' I searched all parts of the convent, and had every door opened —but, unfortunately, I could find no trace of these young ladies.'

'They must have sent them elsewhere,' cried Dagobert ; 'who knows ? —perhaps, ill.   They will kill them—O God ! they will kill them !' cried he, in a heart-rending tone.

'After such a refusal, what is to be done ?   Pray, sir, give us your advice; you are our providence,' said Adrienne, turning to speak to Rodin, who she fancied was behind her.   'What is your——'

Then, perceiving that the Jesuit had suddenly disappeared, she said to Mother Bunch, with uneasiness : 'Where is M. Rodin ?'

'I do not know, madame,' answered the girl, looking round her ; 'he is no longer here.'

'It is strange,' said Adrienne, 'to disappear so abruptly !'

'I told you he was a traitor !' cried Dagobert, stamping with rage ; 'they are all in a plot together.'

'No, no,' said Mdlle. de Cardoville ; 'do not think that.   But the absence is not the less to be regretted, for, under these difficult circumstances, he might have given us very useful information, thanks to the position he occupied at M. d'Aigrigny's.'

'I confess, madame, that I rather reckoned upon it,' said M. de Gernande; 'and I returned hither, not only to inform you of the fruitless result of my search, but also to seek from the upright and honourable man, who so courageously unveiled these odious machinations, the aid of his counsels in this contingency.'

Strangely enough, for the last few moments Dagobert was so completely absorbed in thought, that he paid no attention to the words of the magistrate, however important to him. He did not even perceive the departure of M. de Gernande, who retired after promising Adrienne that he would neglect no means to arrive at the truth, in regard to the disappearance of the orphans. Uneasy at this silence, wishing to quit the house immediately, and induce Dagobert to accompany her, Adrienne, after exchanging a rapid glance with Mother Bunch, was advancing towards the soldier, when hasty steps were heard from without the chamber, and a manly sonorous voice, exclaiming, with impatience, 'Where is he—where is he?'

At the sound of this voice, Dagobert seemed to rouse himself with a start, made a sudden bound, and with a loud cry, rushed towards the door. It opened. Marshal Simon appeared on the threshold!

CHAPTER XXXIX.

PIERRE SIMON.

MARSHAL PIERRE SIMON, Duke de Ligny, was a man of tall stature, plainly dressed in a blue frock-coat, buttoned up to the throat, with a red ribbon tied to the top button-hole. You could not have wished to see a more frank, honest, and chivalrous cast of countenance than the marshal's. He had a broad forehead, an aquiline nose, a well formed chin, and a complexion bronzed by exposure to the Indian sun. His hair, cut very short, was inclined to grey about the temples ; but his eyebrows were still as black as his large, hanging moustache. His walk was free and bold, and his decided movements showed his military impetuosity. A man of the people, a man of war and action, the frank cordiality of his address invited friendliness and sympathy. As enlightened as he was intrepid, as generous as he was sincere, his manly, plebeian pride was the most remarkable part of his character. As others are proud of their high birth, so was he of his obscure origin, because it was ennobled by the fine qualities of his father, the rigid republican, the intelligent and laborious artisan, who, for the space of forty years, had been the example and the glory of his fellow-workmen. In accepting with gratitude the aristocratic title which the Emperor had bestowed upon him, Pierre Simon acted with that delicacy which receives from a friendly hand a perfectly useless gift, and estimates it according to the intention of the giver. The religious veneration of Pierre Simon for the Emperor had never been blind ; in proportion as his devotion and love for his idol were instructive and necessary, his admiration was serious, and founded upon reason. Far from resembling those swashbucklers who love fighting for its own sake, Marshal Simon not only admired his hero as the greatest captain in the world, but he admired him, above all, because he knew that the Emperor had only accepted war in the hope of one day being able to dictate universal peace ; for if peace obtained by glory and strength is great, fruitful, and magnificent, peace yielded by weakness and cowardice is sterile, disastrous, and dishonouring. The son of a workman, Pierre Simon still further admired the Emperor, because that imperial parvenu had always known how to make that popular heart beat nobly, and, remembering the people, from the masses of whom he first arose, had invited them fraternally to share in regal and aristocratic pomp.

When Marshal Simon entered the room, his countenance was much agitated. At sight of Dagobert, a flash of joy illumined his features ; he rushed towards the soldier, extending his arms, and exclaimed, ' My friend! my old friend !'

Dagobert answered this affectionate salute with silent emotion. Then the marshal, disengaging himself from his arms, and fixing his moist eyes upon him, said to him in so agitated a voice that his lips trembled, 'Well, didst arrive in time for the 13th of February?'

'Yes, general; but everything is postponed for four months.'

'And—my wife?—my child?' At this question Dagobert shuddered, hung down his head, and was silent.

'They are not, then, here?' asked Simon, with more surprise than uneasiness. 'They told me they were not at your house, but that I should find you here—and I came immediately. Are they not with you?'

'General,' said Dagobert, becoming deadly pale; 'general——' Drying the drops of cold sweat that stood upon his forehead, he was unable to articulate a word, for his voice was checked in his parched throat.

'You frighten me!' exclaimed Pierre Simon, becoming pale as the soldier, and seizing him by the arm.

At this, Adrienne advanced, with a countenance full of grief and sympathy; seeing the cruel embarrassment of Dagobert, she wished to come to his assistance, and she said to Pierre Simon, in a mild but agitated voice, 'Marshal, I am Mdlle. de Cardoville—a relation of your dear children.'

Pierre Simon turned round suddenly, as much struck with the dazzling beauty of Adrienne as with the words she had just pronounced. He stammered out in his surprise, 'You, madame—a relation—of *my children!*'

He laid a stress on the last words, and looked at Dagobert in a kind of stupor.

'Yes, marshal—*your children*,' hastily replied Adrienne; 'and the love of those charming twin sisters——'

'Twin sisters!' cried Pierre Simon, interrupting Mdlle. de Cardoville, with an outburst of joy impossible to describe. 'Two daughters instead of one! Oh! what happiness for their mother! Pardon me, madame, for being so impolite,' he continued; 'and so little grateful for what you tell me. But you will understand it; I have been seventeen years without seeing my wife; I come, and I find three loved beings, instead of two. Thanks, madame : would I could express all the gratitude I owe you! You are our relation : this is no doubt your house; my wife and children are with you. Is it so? You think that my sudden appearance might be prejudicial to them? I will wait—but, madame, you, that I am certain are good as fair —pity my impatience—will make haste to prepare them to receive me——'

More and more agitated, Dagobert avoided the marshal's gaze, and trembled like a leaf. Adrienne cast down her eyes without answering. Her heart sunk within her, at thought of dealing the terrible blow to Marshal Simon.

The latter, astonished at this silence, looking at Adrienne, then at the soldier, became first uneasy, and at last alarmed. 'Dagobert!' he exclaimed, 'something is concealed from me!'——'General!' stammered the soldier, 'I assure you—I—I——'

'Madame!' cried Pierre Simon, 'I conjure you, in pity, speak to me frankly!—my anxiety is horrible. My first fears return upon me. What is it? Are my wife and daughters ill? Are they in danger? Oh! speak! speak!'

'Your daughters, marshal,' said Adrienne, 'have been rather unwell, since their long journey—but they are in no danger.'——'Oh, heaven! it is my wife!'

'Have courage, sir!' said Mdlle. de Cardoville, sadly. 'Alas! you must seek consolation in the affection of the two angels that remain to you.'

'General!' said Dagobert, in a firm, grave tone, 'I returned from Siberia —alone with your two daughters.'

'And their mother ! their mother !' cried Simon, in a voice of despair.

'I set out with the two orphans the day after her death,' said the soldier.

'Dead ?' exclaimed Pierre Simon, overwhelmed by the stroke ; 'dead ?' A mournful silence was the only answer. The marshal staggered beneath this unexpected shock, leaned on the back of a chair for support, and then, sinking into the seat, concealed his face with his hands. For some minutes nothing was heard but stifled sobs, for not only had Pierre Simon idolised his wife, but by one of those singular compromises, that a man long cruelly tried sometimes makes with destiny, Pierre Simon, with the fatalism of loving souls, thought he had a right to reckon upon happiness after so many years of suffering, and had not for a moment doubted that he should find his wife and child—a double consolation reserved to him after going through so much. Very different from certain people, whom the habit of misfortune renders less exacting, Simon had reckoned upon happiness as complete as had been his misery. His wife and child were the sole, indispensable conditions of this felicity, and, had the mother survived her daughters, she would have no more replaced them in his eyes than they did her. Weakness or avarice of the heart, so it was ; we insist upon this singularity, because the consequences of these incessant and painful regrets exercised a great influence on the future life of Marshal Simon. Adrienne and Dagobert had respected the overwhelming grief of this unfortunate man. When he had given a free course to his tears, he raised his manly countenance, now of marble paleness, drew his hand across his blood-shot eyes, rose, and said to Adrienne, 'Pardon me, madame ; I could not conquer my first emotion. Permit me to retire. I have cruel details to ask of the worthy friend who only quitted my wife at the last moment. Have the kindness to let me see my children—my poor orphans !——' And the marshal's voice again broke.

'Marshal,' said Mdlle. de Cardoville, 'just now we were expecting your dear children : unfortunately, we have been deceived in our hopes.' Pierre Simon first looked at Adrienne without answering, as if he had not heard or understood.——' But console yourself,' resumed the young girl ; 'we have yet no reason to despair.'

'To despair ?' repeated the marshal, mechanically, looking by turns at Mdlle. de Cardoville and Dagobert ; 'to despair ?—of what, in heaven's name ?'

'Of seeing your children, marshal,' said Adrienne ; 'the presence of their father will facilitate the search.'

'The search !' cried Pierre Simon. 'Then, my daughters are not here ?'

'No, sir,' said Adrienne, at length ; 'they have been taken from the affectionate care of the excellent man who brought them from Russia, to be removed to a convent.'

'Wretch !' cried Pierre Simon, advancing towards Dagobert, with a menacing and terrible aspect ; 'you shall answer to me for all !'

'Oh, sir, do not blame him !' cried Mdlle. de Cardoville.

'General,' said Dagobert, in a tone of mournful resignation, ' I merit your anger. It is my fault. Forced to absent myself from Paris, I entrusted the children to my wife ; her confessor turned her head, and persuaded her that your daughters would be better in a convent than at our house. She believed him, and let them be conveyed there. Now, they say at the convent, that they do not know where they are. This is the truth : do what you will with me ; I have only to silently endure.'

'This is infamous !' cried Pierre Simon, pointing to Dagobert, with a gesture of despairing indignation. ' In whom can a man confide, if he has deceived me ? Oh, my God !'

'Stay, marshal! do not blame him,' repeated Mdlle. de Cardoville ; ' do not think so ! He has risked life and honour to rescue your children from the convent. He is not the only one who has failed in this attempt. Just now, a magistrate—despite his character and authority—was not more successful. His firmness towards the superior, his minute search of the convent, were all in vain. Up to this time, it has been impossible to find these unfortunate children.'

' But where's this convent !' cried Marshal Simon, raising his head, his face all pale and agitated with grief and rage. ' Where is it ? Do these vermin know what a father is, deprived of his children ?' At the moment when Marshal Simon, turning towards Dagobert, pronounced these words, Rodin, holding Rose and Blanche by the hand, appeared at the open door of the chamber. On hearing the marshal's exclamation, he started with surprise, and a flash of diabolical joy lit up his grim countenance—for he had not expected to meet Pierre Simon so opportunely.

Mdlle. de Cardoville was the first to perceive the presence of Rodin. She exclaimed, as she hastened towards him : ' Oh ! I was not deceived. He is still our providence.'

' My poor children !' said Rodin, in a low voice, to the young girls, as he pointed to Pierre Simon, ' this is your father !'

' Sir !' cried Adrienne, following close upon Rose and Blanche. ' Your children are here !'

As Simon turned round abruptly, his two daughters threw themselves into his arms. Here was a long silence, broken only by sobs, and kisses, and exclamations of joy.

' Come forward, at least, and enjoy the good you have done !' said Mdlle. de Cardoville, drying her eyes, and turning towards Rodin, who, leaning against the door, seemed to contemplate this scene with deep emotion.

Dagobert, at sight of Rodin bringing back the children, was at first struck with stupor, and unable to move a step ; but, hearing the words of Adrienne, and yielding to a burst of almost insane gratitude, he threw himself on his knees before the jesuit, joined his hands together, and exclaimed in a broken voice : ' You have saved me, by bringing back these children.'

' Oh, bless you, sir !' said Mother Bunch, yielding to the general current.

' My good friends, this is too much,' said Rodin, as if his emotions were beyond his strength ; ' this is really too much for me. Excuse me to the marshal, and tell him that I am repaid by the sight of his happiness.'

' Pray, sir,' said Adrienne, ' let the marshal at least have the opportunity to see and know you.'

' Oh, remain ! you that have saved us all !' cried Dagobert, trying to stop Rodin.

' Providence, you know, my dear young lady, does not trouble itself about the good that is done, but the good that remains to do,' said Rodin, with an accent of playful kindness. ' Must I not think of Prince Djalma ? My task is not finished, and moments are precious. Come,' he added, disengaging himself gently from Dagobert's hold, ' come—the day has been as good a one as I had hoped. The Abbé d'Aigrigny is unmasked ; you are free, my dear young lady ; you have recovered your cross, my brave soldier ; Mother Bunch is sure of a protectress ; the marshal has found his children. I have my share in all these joys ; it is a full share—my heart is satisfied. Adieu, my friends, till we meet again.' So saying, Rodin waved his hand affectionately to Adrienne, Dagobert, and the hunchback, and withdrew, waving his hand with a look of delight on Marshal Simon, who, seated between his daughters, held them in his arms, and covered them with tears and kisses, remaining quite indifferent to all that was passing around him.

An hour after this scene, Mdlle. de Cardoville and the sempstress, Marshal Simon, his two daughters, and Dagobert quitted Dr. Baleinier's asylum.

   ✿   ✿   ✿   ✿   ✿   ✿

In terminating this episode, a few words by way of moral, with regard to lunatic asylums and convents may not be out of place. We have said, and we repeat, that the laws which apply to the superintendence of lunatic asylums appear to us insufficient. Facts that have recently transpired before the courts, and other facts that have been privately communicated to us, evidently prove this insufficiency. Doubtless, magistrates have full power to visit lunatic asylums. They are even required to make such visits. But we know, from the best authority, that the numerous and pressing occupations of magistrates, whose number is often out of proportion with the labour imposed upon them, render these inspections so rare, that they are, so to speak, illusory. It appears, therefore, to us advisable to institute a system of inspections, at least twice a month, specially designed for lunatic asylums, and entrusted to a physician and a magistrate, so that every complaint may be submitted to a double examination. Doubtless, the law is sufficient when its ministers are fully informed ; but how many formalities, how many difficulties must be gone through, before they can be so, particularly when the unfortunate creature who needs their assistance, already suspected, isolated, and imprisoned, has no friend to come forward in defence, and demand, in his or her name, the protection of the authorities ! Is it not imperative, therefore, on the civil power, to meet these necessities by a periodical and well-organised system of inspection ?

What we here say of lunatic asylums will apply with still greater force to convents for women, seminaries, and houses inhabited by religious bodies. Recent and notorious facts, with which all France has rung, have unfortunately proved that violence, forcible detention, barbarous usage, abduction of minors, and illegal imprisonment, accompanied by torture, are occurrences which, if not frequent, are at least possible in religious houses. It required singular accidents, audacious and cynical brutalities, to bring these detestable actions to public knowledge. How many other victims have been, and perhaps still are, entombed in those large silent mansions, where no profane look may penetrate, and which, through the privileges of the clergy, escape the superintendance of the civil power Is it not deplorable that these dwellings should not also be subject to periodical inspection, by visitors consisting, if it be desired, of a priest, a magistrate, and some delegate of the municipal authorities ? If nothing takes place. but what is legal, humane, and charitable, in these establishments, which have all the character, and incur all the responsibility, of public institutions, why this resistance, this furious indignation of the church party, when any mention is made of touching what they call their privileges ? There is something higher than the constitutions devised at Rome · we mean the Law of France —the common law—which grants to all protection, but which, in return, exacts from all respect and obedience.

CHAPTER XL.

THE EAST INDIAN IN PARIS.

SINCE three days, Mdlle. de Cardoville had left Dr. Baleinier's. The following scene took place in a little dwelling in the Rue Blanche, to which Djalma had been conducted in the name of his unknown protector. Fancy to yourself a pretty, circular apartment, hung with Indian drapery, with purple figures on a grey ground, just relieved by a few threads of gold. The ceiling, towards the centre, is concealed by similar hangings, tied together by a thick, silken cord ; the two ends of this cord, unequal in length, terminated, instead of tassels, in two tiny Indian lamps of gold filigree-work, marvellously finished. By one of those ingenious combinations, so common in barbarous countries, these lamps served also to burn perfumes. Plates of blue crystal, let in between the openings of the arabesques, and illumined by the interior light, shone with so limpid an azure, that the golden lamps seemed starred with transparent sapphires. Light clouds of whitish vapour rose incessantly from these lamps, and spread all around their balmy odour.

Daylight was only admitted to this room (it was about two o'clock in the afternoon) through a little greenhouse, on the other side of a door of plate-glass, made to slide into the thickness of the wall, by means of a groove. A Chinese shade was arranged so as to hide or replace this glass at pleasure. Some dwarf palm trees, plantains, and other Indian productions, with thick leaves of a metallic green, arranged in clusters in this conservatory, formed, as it were, the background to two large variegated bushes of exotic flowers, which were separated by a narrow path, paved with yellow and blue Japanese tiles, running to the foot of the glass. The daylight, already much dimmed by the leaves through which it passed, took a hue of singular mildness as it mingled with the azure lustre of the perfumed lamps, and the crimson brightness of the fire in the tall chimney of oriental porphyry. In the semi-obscurity of this apartment, impregnated with sweet odours and the aromatic vapour of Persian tobacco, a man with brown, hanging locks, dressed in a long robe of dark green, fastened round the waist by a parti-coloured sash, was kneeling upon a magnificent Turkey carpet, carefully feeding the golden bowl of a hookah ; the long, flexible tube of this pipe, after rolling its folds upon the carpet, like a scarlet serpent with silver scales, rested between the slender fingers of Djalma, who was reclining negligently on a divan. The young prince was bareheaded ; his jet-black hair, parted on the middle of his forehead, streamed waving about his face and neck of antique beauty—their warm transparent colours resembling amber or topaz. Leaning his elbow on a cushion, he supported his chin with the palm of his right hand. The flowing sleeve of his robe, falling back from his arm, which was round as that of a woman, revealed mysterious signs formerly tattooed there in India by a Thug's needle. The son of Radja-sing held in his left hand the amber mouthpiece of his pipe. His robe of magnificent cashmere, with a border of a thousand hues, reaching to his knee, was fastened about his slim and well-formed figure by the large folds of an orange-coloured shawl. This robe was half withdrawn from one of the elegant legs of this Asiatic Antinous, clad in a kind of very close fitting gaiter of crimson velvet, embroidered with silver, and terminating in a small white morocco slipper, with a scarlet heel. At once mild and manly, the countenance of Djalma was expressive of that melancholy and contemplative calmness habitual to the Indian and the Arab, who possess the happy privilege of uniting, by a rare combination, the meditative indolence of the dreamer with the fiery energy of the man of action—now delicate, nervous, impressionable as women—now determined, ferocious, and sanguinary as bandits.

And this semi-feminine comparison, applicable to the moral nature of the Arab and the Indian, so long as they are not carried away by the ardour of battle and the excitement of carnage, is almost equally applicable to their physical constitution ; for if, like women of good blood, they have small extremities, slender limbs, fine and supple forms, this delicate and often charming exterior always covers muscles of steel, full of an elasticity, and vigour truly masculine. Djalma's oblong eyes, like black diamonds set in bluish mother-of-pearl, wandered mechanically from the exotic flowers to the ceiling ; from time to time he raised the amber mouthpiece of the hookah to his lips ; then, after a slow aspiration, half opening his rosy lips, strongly contrasted with the shining enamel of his teeth, he sent forth a little spiral line of smoke, freshly scented by the rose-water through which it had passed.

'Shall I put more tobacco in the hookah ?' said the kneeling figure, turning towards Djalma, and revealing the marked and sinister features of Faringhea the Strangler.

The young prince remained dumb, either that, from an oriental contempt for certain races, he disdained to answer the half-caste, or that, absorbed in his reverie, he did not even hear him. The Strangler became again silent ; crouching cross-legged upon the carpet, with his elbows resting on his knees, and his chin upon his hands, he kept his eyes fixed on Djalma, and seemed to await the reply or the orders of him whose sire had been surnamed the Father of the Generous. How had Faringhea, the sanguinary worshipper of Bowanee, the Divinity of Murder, been brought to seek or to accept such humble functions? How came this man, possessed of no vulgar talents, whose passionate eloquence and ferocious energy had recruited many assassins for the service of the Good Work, to resign himself to so base a condition ? Why, too, had this man, who, profiting by the young prince's blindness with regard to himself, might have so easily sacrificed him as an offering to Bowanee—why had he spared the life of Radja-sing's son ? Why, in fine, did he expose himself to such frequent encounters with Rodin, whom he had only known under the most unfavourable auspices ? The sequel of this story will answer all these questions. We can only say at present, that, after a long interview with Rodin, two nights before, the Thug had quitted him with downcast eyes and cautious bearing.

After having remained silent for some time, Djalma, following with his eye the cloud of whitish smoke that he had just sent forth into space, addressed Faringhea, without looking at him, and said to him in the language, as hyperbolical as concise, of orientals : 'Time passes. The old man with the good heart does not come. But he *will* come. His word *is* his word.'

'His word *is* his word, my lord,' repeated Faringhea, in an affirmative tone. 'When he came to fetch you, three days ago, from the house whither those wretches, in furtherance of their wicked designs, had conveyed you in a deep sleep—after throwing me, your watchful and devoted servant, into a similar state—he said to you : "The unknown friend, who sent for you to Cardoville Castle, bids me come to you, prince. Have confidence, and follow me. A worthy abode is prepared for you."—And again, he said to you, my lord : "Consent not to leave the house, until my return. Your interest requires it. In three days you will see me again, and then be restored to perfect freedom." You consented to those terms, my lord, and for three days you have not left the house.'

'And I wait for the old man with impatience,' said Djalma, 'for this solitude is heavy with me. There must be so many things to admire in Paris. Above all——'

Djalma did not finish the sentence, but relapsed into a reverie. After some moments' silence, the son of Radja-sing said suddenly to Faringhea, in the tone of an impatient yet indolent sultan : 'Speak to me !'

'Of what shall I speak, my lord ?'

'Of what you will,' said Djalma, with careless contempt, as he fixed on the ceiling his eyes, half-veiled with languor. 'One thought pursues me—I wish to be diverted from it. Speak to me.'

Faringhea threw a piercing glance on the countenance of the young Indian, and saw that his cheeks were coloured with a slight blush. 'My lord,' said the half-caste, 'I can guess your thought.'

Djalma shook his head, without looking at the Strangler. The latter resumed : 'You are thinking of the women of Paris, my lord.'

'Be silent, slave !' said Djalma, turning abruptly on the sofa, as if some painful wound had been touched to the quick. Faringhea obeyed.

After the lapse of some moments, Djalma broke forth again with impatience, throwing aside the tube of the hookah, and veiling both eyes with his hands : 'Your words are better than silence. Cursed be my thoughts, and the spirit which calls up these phantoms !'

'Why should you fly these thoughts, my lord ? You are nineteen years of age, and hitherto all your youth has been spent in war and captivity. Up to this time, you have remained as chaste as Gabriel, that young Christian priest, who accompanied us on our voyage.'

Though Faringhea did not at all depart from his respectful deference for the prince, the latter felt that there was something of irony in the tone of the half-caste, as he pronounced the word 'chaste.'

Djalma said to him with a mixture of pride and severity : 'I do not wish to pass for a barbarian, as they call us, with these civilised people ; therefore I glory in my chastity.'——'I do not understand, my lord.'

'I may perhaps love some woman, pure as was my mother, when she married my father ; and to ask for purity from a woman, a man must be chaste as she.'

At this, Faringhea could not refrain from a sardonic smile.

'Why do you laugh, slave?' said the young prince, imperiously.

'Among civilised people, as you call them, my lord, the man who married in the flower of his innocence would be mortally wounded with ridicule.'

'It is false, slave ! He would only be ridiculous if he married one that was not pure as himself.'

'Then, my lord, he would not only be wounded—he would be killed outright, for he would be doubly and unmercifully laughed at.'

'It is false ! it is false ! Where did you learn all this ?'

'I have seen Parisian women at the Isle of France, and at Pondicherry, my lord : moreover, I learned a good deal during our voyage ; I talked with a young officer, while you conversed with the young priest.'

'So, like the sultans of our harems, civilised men require of women the innocence they have themselves lost.'

'They require it the more, the less they have of it, my lord.'

'To require without any return, is to act as a master to his slave ; by what right ?'

'By the right of the strongest—as it is among us, my lord.'

'And what do the women do ?'——'They prevent the men from being too ridiculous, when they marry, in the eyes of the world.'

'But they kill a woman that is false ?' said Djalma, raising himself abruptly, and fixing upon Faringhea a savage look, that sparkled with lurid fire.

'They kill her, my lord, as with us—when they find her out.'

'Despots like ourselves ! Why then do these civilised men not shut up their women, to force them to a fidelity which they do not practise ?'

'Because their civilisation is barbarous, and their barbarism civilised, my lord.'

'All this is sad enough, if true,' observed Djalma, with a pensive air, adding, with a species of enthusiasm, employing, as usual, the mystic and figurative language familiar to the people of his country : 'Yes, your talk afflicts me, slave—for two drops of dew blending in the cup of a flower, are as hearts that mingle in a pure and virgin love ; and two rays of light united in one inextinguishable flame, are as the burning and eternal joys of lovers joined in wedlock.'

Djalma spoke of the pure enjoyments of the soul with inexpressible grace, yet it was when he painted less ideal happiness, that his eyes shone like stars ; he shuddered slightly, his nostrils swelled, the pale gold of his complexion became vermilion, and the young prince sank into a deep reverie.

Faringhea, having remarked this emotion, thus spoke : ' If, like the proud and brilliant king-bird of our woods, you prefer numerous and varied plea-sures to solitary and monotonous amours—handsome, young, rich as you are, my lord, were you to seek out the seductive Parisians—voluptuous phantoms of your nights—charming tormentors of your dreams—were you to cast upon them looks bold as a challenge, supplicating as prayers, ardent as desires—do you not think that many a half-veiled eye would borrow fire from your glance ? Then it would no longer be the monotonous delights of a single love, the heavy chain of our life—no, it would be the thousand pleasures of the harem—a harem peopled with free and proud beauties, whom happy love would make your slaves. So long constrained, there is no such thing as excess to you. Believe me, it would then be you, the ardent, the magnificent son of our country, that would become the love and pride of these women—the most seductive in the world, who would soon have for you no looks but those of languor and passion.'

Djalma had listened to Faringhea with silent eagerness. The expres-sion of his features had completely changed ; it was no longer the melan-choly and dreaming youth, invoking the sacred remembrance of his mother, and finding only in the dew of heaven, in the calyx of flowers, images suffi-ciently pure to paint the chastity of the love he dreamed of ; it was no longer even the young man, blushing with a modest ardour at the thought of the permitted joys of a legitimate union. No ! the incitements of Faringhea had kindled a subterraneous fire ; the inflamed countenance of Djalma, his eyes now sparkling and now veiled, his manly and sonorous respiration, announced the heat of his blood, the boiling up of the passions, only the more energetic, that they had been hitherto restrained.

So, springing suddenly from the divan, supple, vigorous, and light as a young tiger, Djalma clutched Faringhea by the throat, exclaiming : ' Thy words are burning poison !'

' My lord,' said Faringhea, without opposing the least resistance, ' your slave is your slave.' This submission disarmed the prince.

' My life belongs to you,' repeated the half-caste.

' I belong to you, slave !' cried Djalma, repulsing him. ' Just now, I hung upon your lips, devouring your dangerous lies.'

' Lies, my lord ? Only appear before these women, and their looks will confirm my words.'

' These women love me !—*me*, who have only lived in war and in the woods ?'

' The thought that you, so young, have already waged bloody war on men and tigers, will make them adore, my lord.'——' You lie !'

' I tell you, my lord, on seeing your hand, as delicate as theirs, but which has been so often bathed in hostile blood, they will wish to caress it ; and they will kiss it again, when they think that, in our forests, with loaded rifle, and a poniard between your teeth, you smiled at the roaring of lion or pan-ther, for whom you lay in wait.'

' But I am a savage—a barbarian.'

'And for that very reason you will have them at your feet. They will feel themselves both terrified and charmed by all the violence and fury, the rage of jealousy, the passion and the love, to which a man of your blood, your youth, your ardour, must be subject. To day mild and tender, to-morrow fierce and suspicious, another time ardent and passionate, such you will be—and such you ought to be, if you wish to win them. Yes ; let a hiss of rage be heard between two kisses : let a dagger glitter in the midst of caresses, and they will fall before you, palpitating with pleasure, love, and fear—and you will be to them, not a man, but a god.'

'Dost think so ?' cried Djalma, carried away in spite of himself by the Thug's wild eloquence.

'You know, you feel, that I speak the truth,' cried the latter, extending his arm towards the young Indian.

'Why, yes !' exclaimed Djalma, his eye sparkling, his nostrils swelling, as he moved about the apartment with savage bounds. ' I know not if I possess my reason, or if I am intoxicated, but it seems to me that you speak truth. Yes, I feel that they will love me with madness and fury, because my love will be mad and furious ; they will tremble with pleasure and fear, because the very thought of it makes me tremble with delight and terror. Slave, it is true ; there is something exciting and fearful in such a love !' As he spoke forth these words, Djalma was superb in his impetuous sensuality. It is a rare thing to see a young man arrive in his native purity, at the age in which are developed, in all their powerful energy, those admirable instincts of love, which God has implanted in the heart of his creatures, and which, repressed, disguised, or perverted, may unseat the reason, or generate mad excesses and frightful crimes—but which, directed towards a great and noble passion, may and must, by their very violence, elevate man, through devotion and tenderness, to the limits of the ideal.

' Oh ! this woman—this woman, before whom I am to tremble—and who, in turn, must tremble before me—where is she ?' cried Djalma, with redoubled excitement. ' Shall I ever find her ?'

' One is a good deal, my lord,' replied Faringhea, with his sardonic coolness ; ' he who looks for one woman, will rarely succeed in this country ; he who seeks women, is only at a loss to choose.'

*　　*　　*　　*　　*　　*　　*

As the half-caste made this impertinent answer to Djalma, a very elegant blue-and-white carriage stopped before the garden-gate of the house, which opened upon a deserted street. It was drawn by a pair of beautiful blood-horses, of a cream colour, with black manes and tails. The scutcheons on the harness were of silver, as were also the buttons of the servants' livery, which was blue with white collars. On the blue hammercloth, also laced with white, as well as on the panels of the doors, were lozenge-shaped coats of arms, without crest or coronet, as usually borne by unmarried daughters of noble families. Two women were in this carriage—Mdlle. de Cardoville and Florine.

CHAPTER XLI.

RISING.

To explain the arrival of Mdlle. de Cardoville at the garden-door of the house occupied by Djalma, we must cast a retrospective glance at previous events. On leaving Doctor Baleinier's, Mdlle. de Cardoville had gone to take up her residence in the Rue d'Anjou. During the last few months of her stay with her aunt, Adrienne had secretly caused this handsome dwelling to be repaired and furnished, and its luxury and elegance were now increased by all the wonders of the lodge of Saint-Dizier House. The world found it very strange, that a lady of the age and condition of Mdlle. de Cardoville should take the resolution of living completely alone and free, and, in fact, of keeping house exactly like a bachelor, a young widow, or an emancipated minor. The world pretended not to know that Mdlle. de Cardoville possessed what is often wanting in men, whether of age or twice of age—a firm character, a lofty mind, a generous heart, strong and vigorous good sense.

Judging that she would require faithful assistance in the internal management of her house, Adrienne had written to the bailiff of Cardoville, and his wife, old family servants, to come immediately to Paris : M. Dupont thus filled the office of steward, and Mme. Dupont that of housekeeper. An old friend of Adrienne's father, the Count de Montbron, an accomplished old man, once very much in fashion, and still a connoisseur in all sorts of elegances, had advised Adrienne to act like a princess, and take an equerry ; recommended for this office a man of good rearing and ripe age, who, himself an amateur in horses, had been ruined in England, at Newmarket, the Derby, and Tattersall's, and reduced, as sometimes happened to gentlemen in that country, to drive the stage-coaches, thus finding an honest method of earning his bread, and at the same time gratifying his taste for horses. Such was M. de Bonneville, M. de Montbron's choice. Both from age and habits, this equerry could accompany Mdlle. de Cardoville on horseback, and, better than anyone else, superintend the stable. He accepted, therefore, the employment with gratitude, and, thanks to his skill and attention, the equipages of Mdlle. de Cardoville were not eclipsed in style by anything of the kind in Paris. Mdlle. de Cardoville had taken back her women, Hebe, Georgette, and Florine. The latter was at first to have re-entered the service of the Princess de Saint-Dizier, to continue her part of spy for the superior of St. Mary's Convent ; but, in consequence of the new direction given by Rodin to the Rennepont affair, it was decided that Florine, if possible, should return to the service of Mdlle. de Cardoville. This confidential place, enabling this unfortunate creature to render important and mysterious services to the people who held her fate in their hands, forced her to infamous treachery. · Unfortunately, all things favoured this machination. We know that Florine, in her interview with Mother Bunch, a few days after Mdlle. de Cardoville was imprisoned at Dr. Baleinier's, had yielded to a twinge of remorse, and given to the sempstress advice likely to be of use to Adrienne's interests—sending word to Agricola not to deliver to Madame de Saint-Dizier the papers found in the hiding-place of the pavilion, but only to entrust them to Mdlle. de Cardoville herself. The latter, afterwards informed of these details by Mother Bunch, felt a double degree of confidence and interest in Florine, took her back into her service with gratitude, and almost immediately charged her with a confidential mission—that of superintending the arrangements of the house hired for Djalma's habitation. As for Mother Bunch (yielding to the solicitations of Mdlle. de Cardoville, and finding she was no longer of use to Dagobert's wife, of whom we shall speak hereafter), she had consented to take up her abode in the hotel on the Rue d'Anjou, along with Adrienne, who, with that rare sagacity of the heart peculiar to her, entrusted the young sempstress, who served her also as a secretary, with the department of alms-giving.

Mdlle. de Cardoville had at first thought of entertaining her merely as a friend, wishing to pay homage in her person to probity with labour, resignation in sorrow, and intelligence in poverty ; but, knowing the workgirl's natural dignity, she feared, with reason, that, notwithstanding the delicate circumspection with which the hospitality would be offered, Mother Bunch might perceive in it alms in disguise. Adrienne preferred, therefore, while she treated her as a friend, to give her a confidential employment. In this manner the great delicacy of the needlewoman would be spared, since she could earn her livelihood by performing duties which would at the same time satisfy her praiseworthy instincts of charity. In fact, she could fulfil, better than any one, the sacred mission confided to her by Adrienne. Her cruel experience in misfortune, the goodness of her angelic soul, the elevation of her mind, her rare activity, her penetration with regard to the painful secrets of poverty, her perfect knowledge of the industrial classes, were sufficient security for the tact and intelligence with which the excellent creature would second the generous intentions of Mdlle. de Cardoville.

❖   ❖   ❖   ❖   ❖   ❖

Let us now speak of the divers events which, on that day, preceded the coming of Mdlle. de Cardoville to the garden-gate of the house in the Rue Blanche. About ten o'clock in the morning, the blinds of Adrienne's bedchamber, closely shut, admitted no ray of daylight to this apartment, which was only lighted by a spherical lamp of oriental alabaster, suspended from the ceiling by three long silver chains. This apartment, terminating in a dome, was in the form of a tent with eight sides. From the ceiling to the floor, it was hung with white silk, covered with long draperies of muslin, fastened in large puffs to the wall, by bands caught in at regular distances by plates of ivory. Two doors, also of ivory, admirably encrusted with mother-of-pearl, led, one to the bath-room, the other to the toilet-chamber, a sort of little temple dedicated to the worship of beauty, and furnished as it had been at the pavilion of Saint-Dizier House. Two other compartments of the wall were occupied by windows, completely veiled with drapery. Opposite the bed, enclosing splendid fire-dogs of chased silver, was a chimney-piece of white marble, like crystallised snow, on which were sculptured two magnificent caryatides, and a frieze representing birds and flowers. Above this frieze, carved in open-work with extreme delicacy, was a marble basket, filled with red camellias. Their leaves of shining green, their flowers of a delicate rosy hue, were the only colours that disturbed the harmonious whiteness of this virgin retreat. Finally, half surrounded by waves of white muslin, which poured down from the dome like a mass of light clouds, the bed was visible—very low, and resting on feet of carved ivory, which stood upon the ermine carpet that covered the floor. With the exception of a plinth, also in ivory, admirably inlaid with mother-of-pearl, the bed was entirely covered with white satin, wadded and quilted like an immense scent-bag. The cambric sheets, trimmed with lace, being a little disturbed on one side, discovered the corner of a white taffeta mattress, and a light counterpane of watered stuff—for an equal temperature always reigned in this apartment, warm as a fine spring day.

From a singular scruple, arising from the same sentiment which had caused Adrienne to have inscribed on a masterpiece of goldsmith's work the name of the maker instead of that of the seller, she had wished all these articles, so costly and sumptuous, to be manufactured by workmen chosen amongst the most intelligent, honest, and industrious of their class, whom she had supplied with the necessary materials. In this manner she had been able to add to the price of the work the profit usually gained by the middle man, who speculates in such labour; this notable augmentation of wages had spread happiness and comfort through a hundred necessitous families, who, blessing the munificence of Adrienne, gave her, as she said, the right to enjoy her luxury as a good action. Nothing could be fresher or more charming than the interior of this bedchamber. Mdlle. de Cardoville had just awoke ; she reposed in the middle of this flood of muslin, lace, cambric, and white silk, in a position full of sweet grace. Never during the night did she cover that beautiful golden hair (a certain recipe, said the Greeks, for preserving it for a long while in magnificence). Every evening, her women arranged her long silky curls in flat tresses, forming two broad bands, which, descending sufficiently low almost entirely to conceal the small ear, the rosy lobe of which was alone visible, were joined to the large plait behind the head.

This head-dress, borrowed from Greek antiquity, set off to admiration the pure, fine features of Mdlle. de Cardoville, and made her look so much younger, that, instead of eighteen, one would hardly have given her fifteen years of age. Gathered thus closely about the temples, the hair lost its transparent and brilliant hues, and would have appeared almost brown, but for the golden tints which played here and there, amid the undulations of the tresses. Lulled in that morning torpor, the warm langour of which is so favourable to soft'reveries, Adrienne leaned with her elbow on the pillow, and her head a little on one side, which displayed to advantage the ideal contour of her bared neck and shoulders : her smiling lips, moist and rosy, were, like her cheeks, cold as if they had just been bathed in ice-water ; her snow-white lids half veiled the large, dark, soft eyes, which now gazed languidly upon vacancy, and now fixed themselves with pleasure upon the rosy flowers and green leaves in the basket of camellias. Who can paint the matchless serenity of Adrienne's awaking—when the fair and chaste soul roused itself in the fair and chaste body ? It was the awaking of a heart as pure as the fresh and balmy breath of youth, that made her bosom rise and fall in its white, immaculate purity. What creed, what dogma, what formula, what religious symbol, oh ! paternal and divine Creator ! can ever give a more complete idea of Thy harmonious and ineffable power, than the image of a young maiden awaking in the bloom of her beauty, and in all the grace of that modesty with which Thou hast endowed her, seeking, in her dreamy innocence, for the secret of that celestial instinct of love, which Thou hast placed in the bosom of all Thy creatures—oh ! Thou whose love is eternal, and goodness infinite !

The confused thoughts which, since her sleep, had appeared gently to agitate Adrienne, absorbed her more and more ; her head resting on her bosom, her beautiful arm upon the couch, her features, without becoming precisely sad, assumed an expression of touching melancholy. Her dearest desire was accomplished ; she was about to live independent and alone. But this affectionate, delicate, expansive, and marvellously complete nature, felt that God had not given her such rare treasures, to bury them in a cold and selfish solitude. She felt how much that was great and beautiful might be inspired by love, both in herself, and in him that should be worthy of her. Confiding in her courage, and the nobleness of her character, proud of the example that she wished to give to other women, knowing that all eyes would be fixed enviously upon her, she felt, as it were, only too sure of herself ; far from fearing that she should make a bad choice, she rather feared, that she should not find any from whom to choose, so pure and perfect was her taste. And, even had she met with her own ideal, she had views so singular and so just, so extraordinary and yet so sensible, with regard to the independence and dignity of woman, that, inexorably determined to make no concession upon this head, she asked herself if the man of her choice would ever accept the hitherto unheard-of conditions that she meant to impose. In recalling to her remembrance the possible suitors that she had met in the world, she remembered also the dark, but true picture, which Rodin had drawn with so much caustic bitterness. She remembered too, not without a certain pride, the encouragement this man had given her, not by flattery, but by advising her to follow out and accomplish a great, generous, and beautiful design. The current or the caprice of fancy soon brought Adrienne to think of Djalma. Whilst she congratulated herself on having paid to her royal kinsman the duties of a kingly hospitality, the young lady was far from regarding the prince as the hero of her future.

And first she said to herself, not unreasonably, that this half-savage boy, with passions, if not untameable, yet untamed, transported on a sudden into the midst of a refined civilisation, would be inevitably destined to fiery trials and violent transformations. Now Mdlle. de Cardoville, having nothing masculine or despotic in her character, had no wish to civilise the young savage. Therefore, notwithstanding the interest, or rather because of the interest, which she felt for the young Indian, she was firmly resolved, not to make herself known to him, till after the lapse of two or three months ; and she determined also, that, even if Djalma should learn by chance that she was his relation, she would not receive his visit. She desired, if not to try him, at least to leave him free in all his acts, so that he might expend the first fire of his passions, good or bad. But not wishing to abandon him quite without defence to the perils of a Parisian life, she requested the Count de Montbron, in confidence, to introduce Prince Djalma to the best company in Paris, and to enlighten him by the counsels of his long experience. M. de Montbron had received the request of Mdlle. de Cardoville with the greatest pleasure, taking delight, he said in starting his royal tiger in drawing-rooms, and bringing him into contact with the flower of the fine ladies and gentlemen of Paris, offering at the same time to wager any amount in favour of his half-savage pupil.

' As for myself, my dear Count,' said Adrienne to M. de Montbron, with her usual frankness, ' my resolution is not to be shaken. You have told me the effect that will be produced in the fashionable world, by the first appearance of Prince Djalma, an Indian nineteen years of age, of surprising beauty, proud and wild as a young lion arriving from his forest ; it is new, it is extraordinary, you added ; and, therefore, all the coquetries of civilised life will pursue him with an eagerness which makes me tremble for him. Now, seriously, my dear count, it will not suit me to appear as the rival of so many fine ladies, who are about to expose themselves intrepidly to the claws of the young tiger. I take great interest in him, because he is my cousin, because he is handsome, because he is brave, and above all because he does not wear that horrible European dress. No doubt, these are rare qualities—but not sufficient to make me change my mind. Besides, the good old philosopher, my new friend, has given me advice about this Indian, which you, my dear count, who are not a philosopher, will yet approve. It is, for some time, to receive visits at home, but not to visit other people— which will spare me the awkwardness of meeting my royal cousin, and allow me to make a careful choice, even amongst my usual society. As my house will be an excellent one, my position most unusual, and as I shall be suspected of all sorts of naughty secrets, I shall be in no want of inquisitive visitors, who will amuse me a good deal, I assure you.'

And as M. de Montbron asked, if the exile of the poor young Indian tiger was to last long, Adrienne answered : ' As I shall see most of the persons, to whom you will introduce him, I shall be pleased to hear different opinions about him. If certain men speak well of him, and certain women ill, I shall have good hope of him. In a word, the opinion that I come to, in sifting the true from the false (you may leave that to my sagacity), will shorten or prolong the exile of my royal cousin.'

Such were the formal intentions of Mdlle. de Cardoville with regard to Djalma, even on the day she went with Florine to the house he occupied. In a word, she had positively resolved not to be known to him for some months to come.

    ✺   ✺   ✺   ✺   ✺   ✺

After long reflecting that morning, on the chances that might yet offer themselves to satisfy the wants of her heart, Adrienne fell into a new, deep reverie. This charming creature, so full of life and youth, heaved a low sigh, raised her arms above her head, turned her profile towards the pillow, and remained for some moments as if powerless and vanquished. Motionless beneath the white tissues that wrapped her round, she looked like a fair, marble statue, visible beneath a light layer of snow. Suddenly, Adrienne raised herself up, drew her hand across her brow, and rang for her women. At the first silver tone of the bell, the two ivory doors opened. Georgette appeared on the threshold of the dressing-room, from which Frisky, a little black-and-tan dog, with his golden collar, escaped with a joyful barking. Hebe appeared at the same time on the threshold of the bath-room. At the further end of this apartment, lighted from above, might be seen upon a green mat of Spanish leather, with golden ornaments, a crystal bath in the form of a long shell. The three only divisions in this masterpiece of glass-work, were concealed by the elegant device of several large reeds in silver, which rose from the wide base of the bath, also of wrought silver, representing children and dolphins playing among branches of natural coral, and azure shells. Nothing could be more pleasing than the effect of these purple reeds and ultramarine shells, upon a dull ground of silver ; the balsamic vapour, which rose from the warm, limpid, and perfumed water, that filled the crystal shell, spread through the bath-room, and floated like a light cloud into the sleeping-chamber.

Seeing Hebe in her fresh and pretty costume, bringing her a long bathing-gown, hanging upon a bare and dimpled arm, Adrienne said to her : ' Where is Florine, my child ?'

' Madame, she went downstairs two hours ago ; she was wanted for something very pressing.'——' Who wanted her ?'

' The young person who serves Madame as secretary. She went out this morning very early ; and, as soon as she returned, she sent for Florine, who has not come back since.'

' This absence no doubt relates to some important affair of my angelic minister of succour,' said Adrienne, smiling, and thinking of the hunchback. Then she made a sign to Hebe to approach her bed.

    ✳   ✳   ✳   ✳   ✳   ✳

About two hours after rising, Adrienne, having had herself dressed, as usual, with rare elegance, dismissed her women, and sent for Mother Bunch, whom she treated with marked deference, always receiving her alone. The young sempstress entered hastily, with a pale, agitated countenance, and said, in a trembling voice : ' Oh, madame ! my presentiments were justified. You are betrayed.'

' Of what presentiments do you speak, my dear child !' said Adrienne, with surprise. ' Who betrays me ?'——' M. Rodin !' answered the workgirl.

CHAPTER XLII.

DOUBTS.

On hearing the accusation brought against Rodin, Mdlle. de Cardoville looked at the denunciator with new astonishment. Before continuing this scene, we may say that Mother Bunch was no longer clad in her poor, old clothes, but was dressed in black, with as much simplicity as taste. The sad colour seemed to indicate her renunciation of all human vanity, the eternal mourning of her heart, and the austere duties imposed upon her by her devotion to misfortune. With her black gown, she wore a large falling collar, white and neat as her little gauze cap, with its grey ribbons, which, revealing her bands of fine brown hair, set off to advantage her pale and melancholy countenance, with its soft blue eyes. Her long, delicate hands, preserved from the cold by gloves, were no longer, as formerly, of a violet hue, but of an almost transparent whiteness.

Her agitated features expressed a lively uneasiness. Extremely surprised, Mdlle. de Cardoville exclaimed : 'What do you say ?'——' M. Rodin betrays you, madame.'

' M. Rodin ? Impossible !'——' Oh, madame ! my presentiments did not deceive me.'

' Your presentiments ?'——' The first time I saw M. Rodin, I was frightened in spite of myself. My heart sank within me, and I trembled—for you, madame.'

' For me ?' said Adrienne. ' Why did you not tremble for yourself, my poor friend ?'

' I do not know, madame ; but such was my first impression. And this fear was so invincible, that, notwithstanding the kindness that M. Rodin showed my sister, he frightened me, none the less.'

' That is strange. I can understand as well as any one the almost irresistible influence of sympathies or aversions ; but, in this instance——. However,' resumed Adrienne, after a moment's reflection, ' no matter for that ; how have these suspicions been changed to certainty ?'

' Yesterday, I went to take to my sister Cephyse, the assistance that M. Rodin had given me, in the name of a charitable person. I did not find Cephyse at the friend's who had taken care of her ; I therefore begged the portress to inform my sister that I would call again this morning. That is what I did ; but you must excuse me, madame, some necessary details.'

' Speak, speak, my dear.'——' The young girl who had received my sister,' said Mother Bunch, with embarrassment, casting down her eyes and blushing, ' does not lead a very regular life. A person, with whom she has gone on several parties of pleasure, one M. Dumoulin, had informed her of the real name of M. Rodin, who has a kind of lodging in that house, and there goes by the name of Charlemagne.'

' That is just what he told us at Dr. Baleinier's ; and, the day before yesterday, when I again alluded to the circumstance, he explained to me the necessity in which he was, for certain reasons, to have a humble retreat in that remote quarter—and I could not but approve of his motives.'

' Well, then ! yesterday, M. Rodin received a visit from the Abbé d'Aigrigny.'——' The Abbé d'Aigrigny !' exclaimed Mdlle. de Cardoville.

' Yes, madame ; he remained for two hours shut up with M. Rodin.'

' My child, you must have been deceived.'

' I was told, madame, that the Abbé d'Aigrigny had called in the morning to see M. Rodin ; not finding him at home, he had left with the portress his name written on a slip of paper, with the words, "I shall return in two hours." The girl of whom I spoke, madame, had seen this slip of paper. As all that concerns M. Rodin appears mysterious enough, she had the curiosity to wait for M. d'Aigrigny in the porter's lodge, and, about two hours afterwards, he indeed returned, and saw M. Rodin.'

' No, no,' said Adrienne, shuddering ; ' it is impossible. There must be some mistake.'

' I think not, madame ; for, knowing how serious such a discovery would be, I begged the young girl to describe to me the appearance of M. d'Aigrigny.'

' Well ?'——' The Abbé d'Aigrigny, she told me, is about forty years of age. He is tall and upright, dresses plainly, but with care ; has grey eyes, very large and piercing, thick eye-brows, chestnut-coloured hair, a face closely shaved, and a very decided aspect.'

' It is true,' said Adrienne, hardly able to believe what she heard. ' The description is exact.'

' Wishing to have all possible details,' resumed Mother Bunch, ' I asked the portress if M. Rodin and the Abbé d'Aigrigny appeared to be at variance when they quitted the house ? She replied no, but that the abbé said to M. Rodin, as they parted at the door : " I will write to you to-morrow, as agreed." '

' Is it a dream ? Good heaven !' said Adrienne, drawing her hands across her forehead in a sort of stupor. ' I cannot doubt your word, my poor friend ; and yet it is M. Rodin who himself sent you to that house, to give assistance to your sister : would he have wilfully laid open to you his secret interviews with the Abbé d'Aigrigny ? It would have been bad policy in a traitor.'

' That is true, and the same reflection occurred to me. And yet the meeting of these two men appeared so dangerous to you, madame, that I returned home full of terror.'

Characters of extreme honesty are very hard to convince of the treachery of others : the more infamous the deception, the more they are inclined to doubt it. Adrienne was one of these characters, rectitude being a prime quality of her mind. Though deeply impressed by the communication, she remarked : ' Come, my dear, do not let us frighten ourselves too soon, or be over-hasty in believing evil. Let us try to enlighten ourselves by reasoning, and first of all remember facts. M. Rodin opened for me the doors of Dr. Baleinier's asylum ; in my presence, he brought his charge against the Abbé d'Aigrigny ; he forced the superior of the convent to restore Marshal Simon's daughters, he succeeded in discovering the retreat of Prince Djalma—he faithfully executed my intentions with regard to my young cousin ; only yesterday, he gave me the most useful advice. All this is true—is it not ?'

' Certainly, madame.'

' Now suppose that M. Rodin, putting things in their worst light, had some after-thought—that he hopes to be liberally rewarded, for instance ; hitherto, at least, he has shown complete disinterestedness.'

' That also is true, madame,' said poor Mother Bunch, obliged, like Adrienne, to admit the evidence of fixed facts.

' Now let us look to the possibility of treachery. Unite with the Abbé d'Aigrigny to betray me ! Betray *me ?*—how ? and for what purpose ? What have I to fear ? Is it not the Abbé d'Aigrigny, on the contrary, is it not Madame de Saint-Dizier, who have to render an account for the injuries they have done me ?'

' But, then, madame, how do you explain the meeting of these two men, who have so many motives for mutual aversion ? May there not be some dark project still behind ? Besides, madame, I am not the only one to think so.'

' How is that ?'——' This morning, on my return, I was so much agitated, that Mdlle. Florine asked me the cause of my trouble. I know, madame, how much she is devoted to you.'

' Nobody could be more so ; only recently, you yourself informed me of the signal service she rendered, during my confinement at Dr. Baleinier's.'

' Well, madame, this morning, on my return, thinking it necessary to have you informed as soon as possible, I told all to Mdlle. Florine. Like me—even more, perhaps—she was terrified at the meeting of Rodin and M. d'Aigrigny. After a moment's reflection, she said to me : " It is, I think, useless to disturb my mistress at present ; it can be of no importance whether she is informed of this treachery two or three hours sooner or later ; during that time I may be able to discover something more. I have an idea, which I think a good one. Make my excuses to my mistress ; I shall soon be back." Then Florine sent for a hackney-coach, and went out.'

' Florine is an excellent girl,' said Mdlle. de Cardoville, with a smile, for further reflection had quite reassured her ; ' but, on this occasion, I think that her zeal and good heart have deceived her, as they have you, my poor friend. Do you know, that we are two madcaps, you and I, not to have thought of one thing, which would have put us quite at our ease ?'

' How so, madame ?'——' The Abbé d'Aigrigny fears M. Rodin ; he may have sought him out, to entreat his forbearance. Do you not find this explanation both satisfactory and reasonable ?'

' Perhaps so, madame,' said Mother Bunch, after a moment's reflection ; ' yes, it is probable.' But after another silence, and as if yielding to a conviction superior to every possible argument, she exclaimed : ' And yet, no ; believe me, madame, you are deceived. I feel it. All appearances may be against what I affirm ; yet, believe me, these presentiments are too strong not to be true. And have you not guessed the most secret instincts of my heart ? why should I not be able to guess the dangers with which you are menaced ?'

' What do you say ? what have I guessed ?' replied Mdlle. de Cardoville, involuntarily impressed by the other's tone of conviction and alarm.

' What have you guessed ?' resumed the latter. ' All the troublesome susceptibility of an unfortunate creature, to whom destiny has decreed a life apart. If I have hitherto been silent, it is not from ignorance of what I owe you. Who told you, madame, that the only way to make me accept your favours without blushing, was to give me some employment, that would enable me to soothe the misfortunes I had so long shared ? Who told you, when you wished me to have a seat at your table, and to treat as your friend the poor needlewoman, in whose person you sought to honour resignation and honest industry—who told you, when I answered with tears of gratitude and regret, that it was not false modesty, but a consciousness of my own ridiculous deformity, that made me refuse your offer ? Who told you, that, but for this, I should have accepted it proudly, in the name of all my low-born sisters ? But you replied to me with the touching words : " I understand your refusal, my friend ; it is not occasioned by false modesty, but by a sentiment of dignity that I love and respect." Who told you,' continued the workgirl, with increasing animation, ' that I should be so happy to find a little solitary retreat in this magnificent house, which dazzles me with its splendour ? Who guided you in the choice of the apartment (still far too good) that you have provided for me ? Who taught you, that, without envying the beauty of the charming creatures that surround you, and whom I love because they love you, I should always feel, by an involuntary comparison, embarrassed and ashamed before them ? Who told you therefore to send them away, whenever you wished to speak with me ? Yes ! who has revealed to you all the painful and secret susceptibilities of a position like mine ! Who has revealed them to you ? God, no doubt ! who in His infinite majesty creates worlds, and yet cares for the poor little insect hidden beneath the grass. And you think, that the gratitude of a heart you have understood so well, cannot rise in its turn to the knowledge of what may be hurtful to you ? No, no, lady ; some people have the instinct of self-preservation ; others have the still more precious instinct that enables them to preserve those they love. God has given me this instinct. I tell you, that you *are* betrayed !' And with animated look, and cheeks slightly coloured with emotion, the speaker laid such stress upon the last words, and accompanied them with such energetic gesture, that Mdlle. de Cardoville, already shaken by the girl's warmth, began almost to share in her apprehensions. Then, although she had before learned to appreciate the superior intelligence of this poor child of the people, Mdlle. de Cardoville had never till now heard her friend express herself with so much eloquence—an eloquence, too, that was inspired by the noblest sentiments. This circumstance added to the impression made upon Adrienne. But at the moment she was about to answer, a knock was heard at the door of the room, and Florine entered.

On seeing the alarmed countenance of her waiting-maid, Mdlle. de Cardoville said, hastily : ' Well, Florine ! what news ? Whence come you, my child ?'——' From Saint-Dizier House, madame.'

' And why did you go there ?' asked Mdlle. de Cardoville, with surprise.

' This morning,' said Florine, glancing at the workgirl, ' madame, there, confided to me her suspicions and uneasiness. I shared in them. The visit of the Abbé d'Aigrigny to M. Rodin appeared to me very serious. I thought, if it should turn out that M. Rodin had been during the last few days to Saint-Dizier House, there would be no longer any doubt of his treachery.'

' True,' said Adrienne, more and more uneasy. ' Well ?'

' As I had been charged to superintend the removal from the lodge, I knew that several things had remained there. To obtain admittance, I had to apply to Mrs. Grivois. I had thus a pretext for returning to the hotel.'

' What next, Florine, what next ?'——' I endeavoured to get Mrs. Grivois to talk of M. Rodin ; but it was in vain.'

' She suspected you,' said the workgirl. ' It was to be anticipated.'

' I asked her,' continued Florine, ' if they had seen M. Rodin at the hotel lately. She answered evasively. Then, despairing of getting anything out of her,' continued Florine, ' I left Mrs. Grivois, and that my visit might excite no suspicion, I went to the pavilion—when, as I turned down the avenue—whom do I see ?—why, M. Rodin himself, hastening towards the little garden-door, wishing no doubt to depart unnoticed by that way.'

' Madame, you hear,' cried Mother Bunch, clasping her hands with a supplicating air ; ' such evidence should convince you.'

' M. Rodin at the Princess de Saint-Dizier's !' cried Mdlle. de Cardoville, whose glance, generally so mild, now suddenly flashed with vehement indignation. Then she added, in a tone of considerable emotion, ' Continue, Florine.'

' At sight of M. Rodin, I stopped,' proceeded Florine, ' and keeping a little on one side, I gained the pavilion without being seen. I looked out into the street, through the closed blinds, and perceived a hackney-coach. It was waiting for M. Rodin, for, a minute after, he got into it, saying to the coachman, " No. 39, Rue Blanche "——'

' The prince's !' exclaimed Mdlle. de Cardoville.——' Yes, madame.'

' Yes, M. Rodin was to see him to-day,' said Adrienne, reflecting.

' No doubt he betrays you, madame, and the prince also ; the latter will be made his victim more easily than you.'

' Shame ! shame !' cried Mdlle. de Cardoville, on a sudden, as she rose, all her features contracted with painful anger. ' After such a piece of treachery, it is enough to make us doubt of everything—even of ourselves.'

' Oh, madame ! is it not dreadful ?' said Mother Bunch, shuddering.

' But, then, why did he rescue me and mine, and accuse the Abbé d'Aigrigny?' wondered Mdlle. de Cardoville. 'Of a truth, it is enough to make one lose one's reason. It is an abyss—but, oh ! how frightful is doubt !'

'As I returned,' said Florine, casting a look of affectionate devotion on her mistress, 'I thought of a way to make all clear ; but there is not a minute to lose.'

'What do you mean?' said Adrienne, looking at Florine with surprise.

'M. Rodin will soon be alone with the prince,' said Florine.

'No doubt,' replied Adrienne.——'The prince always sits in a little room that opens upon a greenhouse. It is there that he will receive M. Rodin.'

'What then?' resumed Adrienne.——'This greenhouse, which I had arranged according to your orders, has only one issue—by a door leading into a little lane. The gardener gets in that way every morning, so as not to have to pass through the apartments. Having finished his work, he does not return thither during the day.'

'What do you mean ? what is your project?' said Adrienne, looking at Florine with growing surprise.

'The plants are so disposed, that, I think, if even the shade were not there, which screens the glass that separates the saloon from the greenhouse, one might get near enough to hear what was passing in the room, without being seen. When I was superintending the arrangements, I always entered by this greenhouse door. The gardener had one key, and I another. Luckily, I have not yet parted with mine. Within an hour, you may know how far to trust M. Rodin. If he betrays the prince, he betrays you also.'

'What say you?' cried Mdlle. de Cardoville.——'Set out instantly with me ; we reach the side-door ; I enter alone, for precaution's sake—if all is right, I return——'

'You would have *me* turn spy ?' said Mdlle. de Cardoville, haughtily, interrupting Florine. 'You cannot think it.'

'I beg your pardon, madame,' said the girl, casting down her eyes, with a confused and sorrowful air ; 'you had suspicions, and meseems 'tis the only way to confirm or to destroy them.'

'Stoop to listen to a conversation—never !' replied Adrienne.

'Madame,' said Mother Bunch, suddenly, after some moments' thought, 'permit me to tell you that Mdlle. Florine is right. The plan proposed is a painful one, but it is the only way in which you can clear up, perhaps for ever, your doubts as to M. Rodin. Notwithstanding the evidence of facts, in spite of the almost certainty of my presentiments, appearances may deceive us. I was the first who accused M. Rodin to you. I should not forgive myself all the rest of my life, did I accuse him wrongfully. Beyond doubt, it is painful, as you say, madame, to listen to a conversation——' Then, with a violent effort to console herself, she added, as she strove to repress her tears, 'Yet, as your safety is at stake, madame—for, if this be treachery, the future prospect is dreadful—I will go in your place—to——'

'Not a word more, I entreat you,' cried Mdlle. de Cardoville, interrupting. 'Let you, my poor friend, do for me what I thought degrading to do myself? Never !'

Then, turning to Florine, she added, 'Tell M. de Bonneville to have the carriage got ready on the instant.'

'You consent, then !' cried Florine, clasping her hands, and not seeking to conceal her joy ; and her eyes also became full of tears.

'Yes, I consent,' answered Adrienne, with emotion. 'If it is to be war— a war to the knife, that they would wage with me—I must be prepared for it ; and, come to think of it, it would only be weakness and folly not to put myself on my guard. No doubt this step costs me much, and is very repugnant to me, but it is the only way to put an end to suspicions that would be a continual torment to me, and perhaps to prevent still greater evils. Yes! for many important reasons, this interview of M. Rodin with Prince Djalma may be doubly decisive with me—as to the confidence, or the inexorable hate, that I must henceforth feel for M. Rodin. So, Florine, quick! —my cloak and bonnet, and the carriage. You will go with me. As for you, my dear, pray wait for me here,' she added, turning to the work-girl.

Half an hour after this conversation, Adrienne's carriage stopped, as we have before seen, at the little garden-gate of the house in the Rue Blanche. Florine entered the greenhouse, and soon returned to her mistress. 'The shade is down, madame. M. Rodin has just entered the prince's room.' Mdlle. de Cardoville was, therefore, present, though invisible, at the following scene, which took place between Rodin and Djalma.

CHAPTER XLIII.

THE LETTER.

SOME minutes before the entrance of Mdlle. de Cardoville into the greenhouse, Rodin had been introduced by Faringhea into the presence of the prince, who, still under the influence of the burning excitement into which he had been plunged by the words of the half-caste, did not appear to perceive the Jesuit. The latter, surprised at the animated expression of Djalma's countenance, and his almost frantic air, made a sign of interrogation to Faringhea, who answered him privately in the following symbolical manner: —After laying his forefinger on his head and heart, he pointed to the fire burning in the chimney, signifying by his pantomimic action that the head and heart of Djalma were both in flames. No doubt Rodin understood him, for an imperceptible smile of satisfaction played upon his wan lips; then he said aloud to Faringhea, 'I wish to be alone with the prince. Let down the shade, and see that we are not interrupted.' The half-caste bowed, and touched a spring near the sheet of plate-glass, which slid into the wall as the blind descended; then, again bowing, Faringhea left the room. It was shortly after that Mdlle. de Cardoville and Florine entered the greenhouse, which was now only separated from the room in which was Djalma, by the transparent thickness of a shade of white silk, embroidered with large coloured birds. The noise of the door, which Faringhea closed as he went out, seemed to recall the young Indian to himself; his features, though still animated, recovered their habitual expression of mildness and gentleness; he started, drew his hand across his brow, looked round him, as if waking up from a deep reverie, and then, advancing towards Rodin, with an air as respectful as confused, he said to him, using the expression commonly applied to old men in his country, 'Pardon me, father.' Still following the customs of his nation, so full of deference towards age, he took Rodin's hand to raise it to his lips, but the Jesuit drew back a step, and refused this homage.

'For what do you ask pardon, my dear prince?' said he to Djalma.

'When you entered, I was in a dream; I did not come to meet you. Once more, pardon me, father!'

'Once more, I forgive you with all my heart, my dear prince. But let us have some talk. Pray resume your place on the couch, and your pipe, too, if you like it.'

But Djalma, instead of adopting the suggestion, and throwing himself on the divan, according to his custom, insisted on seating himself in a chair, notwithstanding all the persuasion of 'the Old Man with the Good Heart,' as he always called the Jesuit.

'Really, your politeness troubles me, my dear prince,' said Rodin ; 'you are here at home in India ; at least, we wish you to think so.'

'Many things remind me of my country,' said Djalma, in a mild, grave tone. 'Your goodness reminds me of my father, and of him who was a father to me,' added the Indian, as he thought of Marshal Simon, whose arrival in Paris had been purposely concealed from him.

After a moment's silence, he resumed in a tone full of affectionate warmth, as he stretched out his hand to Rodin, 'You are come, and I am happy !'

'I understand your joy, my dear prince, for I come to take you out of prison—to open your cage for you. I had begged you to submit to a brief seclusion, entirely for your own interest.'

'Can I go out to-morrow ?'——'To-day, my dear prince, if you please.'

The young Indian reflected for a moment, and then resumed, 'I must have friends, since I am here in a palace that does not belong to me.'

'Certainly you have friends—excellent friends,' answered Rodin. At these words, Djalma's countenance seemed to acquire fresh beauty. The most noble sentiments were expressed in his fine features : his large black eyes became slightly humid, and, after another interval of silence, he rose and said to Rodin with emotion : 'Come !'

'Whither, dear prince ?' said the other, much surprised.

'To thank my friends. I have waited three days. It is long.'

'Permit me, dear prince—I have much to tell you on this subject— please to be seated.'

Djalma resumed his seat with docility. Rodin continued : 'It is true, that you have friends ; or rather, you have a friend. Friends are rare.'

'What are you ?'——'Well, then, you have two friends, my dear prince— myself, whom you know, and one other, whom you do not know, and who desires to remain unknown to you.'

'Why ?'——'Why ?' answered Rodin, after a moment's embarrassment. 'Because the happiness he feels in giving you these proofs of his friendship and even his own tranquillity, depend upon preserving this mystery.'

'Why should there be concealment when we do good.'

'Sometimes, to conceal the good we do, my dear prince.'

'I profit by his friendship ; why should he conceal himself from me ?' These repeated questions of the young Indian appeared to puzzle Rodin, who, however, replied : 'I have told you, my dear prince, that your secret friend would perhaps have his tranquillity compromised, if he were known.'

'If he were known—as my friend ?'

'Exactly so, dear prince.'

The countenance of Djalma immediately assumed an appearance of sorrowful dignity ; he raised his head proudly, and said in a stern and haughty voice : 'Since this friend hides himself from me, he must either be ashamed of me, or there is reason for me to be ashamed of him. I only accept hospitality from those who are worthy of me, and who think me worthy of them. I leave this house.' So saying, Djalma rose with such an air of determination, that Rodin exclaimed : 'Listen to me, my dear prince. Allow me to tell you, that your petulance and touchiness are almost incredible. Though we have endeavoured to remind you of your beautiful country, we are here in Europe, in France, in the centre of Paris. This consideration may perhaps a little modify your views. Listen to me, I conjure you.'

Notwithstanding his complete ignorance of certain social conventionalisms, Djalma had too much good sense and uprightness, not to appreciate reason, when it appeared reasonable. The words of Rodin calmed him. With that ingenuous modesty, with which natures full of strength and generosity are almost always endowed, he answered mildly : 'You are right, father. I am no longer in my own country. Here the customs are different. I will reflect upon it.'

Notwithstanding his craft and suppleness, Rodin sometimes found himself perplexed by the wild and unforeseen ideas of the young Indian. Thus he saw, to his great surprise, that Djalma now remained pensive for some minutes, after which he resumed in a calm but firm tone : 'I have obeyed you, father : I have reflected.'——' Well, my dear prince ?'

'In no country in the world, under no pretext, should a man of honour conceal his friendship for another man of honour.'

'But suppose there should be danger in avowing this friendship ?' said Rodin, very uneasy at the turn the conversation was taking. Djalma eyed the Jesuit with contemptuous astonishment, and made no reply.

'I understand your silence, my dear prince : a brave man ought to defy danger. True ; but if it should be you that the danger threatens, in case this friendship were discovered, would not your man of honour be excusable, even praiseworthy, to persist in remaining unknown ?'——' I accept nothing from a friend, who thinks me capable of denying him from cowardice.'

'Dear prince—listen to me.'——' Adieu, father.'

'Yet reflect !'——' I have said it,' replied Djalma, in an abrupt and almost sovereign tone, as he walked towards the door.

'But suppose a woman were concerned,' cried Rodin, driven to extremity, and hastening after the young Indian, for he really feared that Djalma might rush from the house, and thus overthrow all his projects.

At the last words of Rodin, the Indian stopped abruptly. 'A woman !' said he, with a start, and turning red. 'A woman is concerned ?'

'Why, yes ! suppose it were a woman,' resumed Rodin, 'would you not then understand her reserve, and the secrecy with which she is obliged to surround the marks of affection she wishes to give you ?'

'A woman !' repeated Djalma, in a trembling voice, clasping his hands in adoration ; and his beautiful countenance was expressive of the deepest emotion. 'A woman !' said he again. 'A Parisian ?'

'Yes, my dear prince, as you force me to this indiscretion, I will confess to you that your friend is a real Parisian—a noble matron, endowed with the highest virtues—whose age alone merits all your respect.'

'She is very old, then ?' cried poor Djalma, whose charming dream was thus abruptly dispelled.

'She may be a few years older than I am,' answered Rodin, with an ironical smile, expecting to see the young man express a sort of comical disappointment or angry regret.

But it was not so. To the passionate enthusiasm of love, which had for a moment lighted up the prince's features, there now succeeded a respectful and touching expression. He looked at Rodin with emotion, and said to him in a broken voice : ' This woman is, then, a mother to me ?'

It is impossible to describe with what a pious, melancholy, and tender charm the Indian uttered the word mother.

'You have it, my dear prince ; this respectable lady wishes to be a mother to you. But I may not reveal to you the cause of the affection she feels for you. Only, believe me—this affection is sincere, and the cause honourable. If I do not tell you her secret, it is that, with us, the secrets of women, young or old, are equally sacred.'

'That is right, and I will respect it. Without seeing her, I will love her —as I love God, without seeing Him.'

'And now, my dear prince, let me tell you what are the intentions of your maternal friend. This house will remain at your disposal, as long as you like it ; French servants, a carriage, and horses, will be at your orders ; the charges of your housekeeping will be paid for you. Then, as the son of a king should live royally, I have left in the next room a casket containing five hundred louis ; every month a similar sum will be provided : if it should not be found sufficient for your little amusements, you will tell me, and it shall be augmented.'

At a movement of Djalma, Rodin hastened to add : 'I must tell you at once. my dear prince, that your delicacy may be quite at ease. First of all, you may accept anything from a mother ; next, as in about three months you will come into possession of an immense inheritance, it will be easy for you, if you feel the obligation a burden—and the sum cannot exceed, at the most, four or five thousand louis--to repay these advances. Spare nothing, then, but satisfy all your fancies. You are expected to appear in the great world of Paris, in a style becoming the son of a king who was called the Father of the Generous. So once again I conjure you not to be restrained by a false delicacy ; if this sum should not be sufficient——'

'I will ask for more. My mother is right ; the son of a monarch ought to live royally.'

Such was the answer of the Indian, made with perfect simplicity, and without any appearance of astonishment at these magnificent offers. This was natural. Djalma would have done for others what they were doing for him, for the traditions of the prodigal magnificence and splendid hospitality of Indian princes are well known. Djalma had been as moved as grateful, on hearing that a woman loved him with maternal affection. As for the luxury with which she sought to surround him, he accepted it without astonishment and without scruple. This resignation, again, somewhat disconcerted Rodin, who had prepared many excellent arguments to persuade the Indian to accept his offers.

'Well, then, it's all agreed, my dear prince,' resumed the Jesuit. 'Now, as you must see the world, it's just as well to enter by the best door, as we say. One of the friends of your maternal protectress, the Count de Montbron, an old nobleman of the greatest experience, and belonging to the first society, will introduce you in some of the best houses in Paris.'

'Will you not introduce me, father ?'

'Alas ! my dear prince, look at me. Tell me, if you think I am fitted for such an office. No, no ; I live alone and retired from the world. And then,' added Rodin, after a short silence, fixing a penetrating, attentive, and curious look upon the prince, as if he would have subjected him to a sort of experiment by what follows ; 'and then, you see, M. de Montbron will be better able than I should, in the world you are about to enter, to enlighten you as to the snares that will be laid for you. For if you have friends, you have also enemies—cowardly enemies, as you know, who have abused your confidence in an infamous manner, and have made sport of you. And as, unfortunately, their power is equal to their wickedness, it would perhaps be more prudent in you to try to avoid them—to fly, instead of resisting them openly.'

At the remembrance of his enemies, at the thought of flying from them, Djalma trembled in every limb ; his features became of a livid paleness ; his eyes wide open, so that the pupil was encircled with white, sparkled with lurid fire ; never had scorn, hatred, and the desire of vengeance, expressed themselves so terribly on a human face. His upper lip, blood-red, was curled convulsively, exposing a row of small, white, and close-set teeth, and giving to his countenance, lately so charming, an air of such animal ferocity, that Rodin started from his seat, and exclaimed : 'What is the matter, prince ? You frighten me.'

Djalma did not answer. Half leaning forward, with his hands clenched in rage, he seemed to cling to one of the arms of the chair, for tear of yielding to a burst of terrific fury.' At this moment, the amber mouthpiece of his pipe rolled, by chance, under one of his feet ; the violent tension, which contracted all the muscles of the young Indian, was so powerful, and, notwithstanding his youth and his light figure, he was endowed with such vigour, that with one abrupt stamp he powdered to dust the piece of amber, in spite of its extreme hardness.

'In the name of heaven, what is the matter prince?' cried Rodin.

'Thus would I crush my cowardly enemies !' exclaimed Djalma, with menacing and excited look. Then, as if these words had brought his rage to a climax, he bounded from his seat, and, with haggard eyes, strode about the room for some seconds in all directions, as if he sought for some weapon, and uttered from time to time a hoarse cry, which he endeavoured to stifle by thrusting his clenched fist against his mouth, whilst his jaws moved convulsively. It was the impotent rage of a wild beast, thirsting for blood. Yet, in all this, the young Indian preserved a great and savage beauty ; it was evident that these instincts of sanguinary ardour and blind intrepidity, now excited to this pitch by horror of treachery and cowardice, when applied to war, or to those gigantic Indian hunts, which are even more bloody than a battle, must make of Djalma what he really was—a hero.

Rodin admired, with deep and ominous joy, the fiery impetuosity of passion in the young Indian, for, under various conceivable circumstances, the effect must be terrible. Suddenly, to the Jesuit's great surprise, the tempest was appeased. Djalma's fury was calmed thus instantaneously, because reflection showed him how vain it was. Ashamed of his childish violence, he cast down his eyes. His countenance remained pale and gloomy ; and, with a cold tranquillity, far more formidable than the violence to which he had yielded, he said to Rodin : 'Father, you will this day lead me to meet my enemies.'

'In what end, my dear prince ? What would you do ?'

'Kill the cowards !'——' Kill them ! you must not think of it.'

'Faringhea will aid me.'

'Remember, you are not on the banks of the Ganges, and here one does not kill an enemy like a hunted tiger.'

'One fights with a loyal enemy, but one kills a traitor like an accursed dog,' replied Djalma, with as much conviction as tranquillity.

'Ah, prince, whose father was the Father of the Generous,' said Rodin, in a grave voice ; 'what pleasure can you find in striking down creatures as cowardly as they are wicked ?'——' To destroy what is dangerous, is a duty.'

'So prince, you seek for revenge ?'

'I do not revenge myself on a serpent,' said the Indian, with haughty bitterness ; 'I crush it.'

'But, my dear prince, here we cannot get rid of our enemies in that manner. If we have cause of complaint——'

'Women and children complain,' said Djalma, interrupting Rodin ; 'men strike.'

'Still on the banks of the Ganges, my dear prince. Here, society takes your cause into its own hands, examines, judges, and if there be good reason, punishes.'

'In my own quarrel, I am both judge and executioner.'

'Pray listen to me : you have escaped the odious snares of your enemies, have you not ?—Well ! suppose it were thanks to the devotion of the venerable woman who has for you the tenderness of a mother, and that she were to ask you to forgive them—she, who saved you from their hands—what would you do then ?'

The Indian hung his head, and was silent. Profiting by his hesitation, Rodin continued : ' I might say to you that I know your enemies, but that in the dread of seeing you commit some terrible imprudence, I would conceal their names from you for ever. But no ! I swear to you, that if the respectable person, who loves you as her son, should find it either right or useful that I should tell you their names, I will do so—until she has pronounced, I must be silent.'

Djalma looked at Rodin with a dark and wrathful air. At this moment, Faringhea entered, and said to Rodin : ' A man with a letter, not finding you at home, has been sent on here. Am I to receive it ? He says it comes from the Abbé d'Aigrigny.'

' Certainly,' answered Rodin. ' That is,' he added, ' with the prince's permission.'——Djalma nodded in reply ; Faringhea went out.

' You will excuse what I have done, dear prince. I expected this morning a very important letter. As it was late in coming to hand, I ordered it to be sent on.'

A few minutes after, Faringhea returned with the letter, which he delivered to Rodin—and the half-caste again withdrew.

CHAPTER XLIV.

ADRIENNE AND DJALMA.

WHEN Faringhea had quitted the room, Rodin took the letter from Abbé d'Aigrigny with one hand, and with the other appeared to be looking for something, first in the side pocket of his great coat, then in the pocket behind, then in that of his trousers ; and, not finding what he sought, he laid the letter on his knee, and felt himself all over with both hands, with an air of regret and uneasiness. The divers movements of this pantomime, performed in the most natural manner, were crowned by the exclamations : ' Oh ! dear me ! how vexatious !'

' What is the matter ?' asked Djalma, starting from the gloomy silence in which he had been plunged for some minutes.

' Alas ! my dear prince !' replied Rodin, ' the most vulgar and puerile accident may sometimes cause the greatest inconvenience. I have forgotten or lost my spectacles. Now, in this twilight, with the very poor eyesight that years of labour have left me, it will be absolutely impossible for me to read this most important letter—and an immediate answer is expected—most simple and categorical—a yes or a no. Time presses; it is really most annoying. If,' added Rodin, laying great stress on his words, without looking at Djalma, but so as the prince might remark it ; ' if only some one would render me the service to read it for me ; but there is no one—no one !'

' Father,' said Djalma, obligingly, ' shall I read it for you ? When I have finished it, I shall forget what I have read.'

' You ?' cried Rodin, as if the proposition of the Indian had appeared to him extravagant and dangerous ; ' it is impossible, prince, for you to read this letter.'——' Then excuse my having offered,' said Djalma, mildly.

' And yet,' resumed Rodin, after a moment's reflection, and as if speaking to himself, ' why not ?'

And he added, addressing Djalma : ' Would you really be so obliging, my dear prince ? I should not have ventured to ask you this service.'

So saying, Rodin delivered the letter to Djalma, who read aloud as follows : " ' Your visit this morning to Saint-Dizier House can only be considered, from what I hear, as a new act of aggression on your part.

' " Here is the last proposition I have to make. It may be as fruitless as the step I took yesterday, when I called upon you in the Rue Clovis.

' " After that long and painful explanation, I told you that I would write to you. I keep my promise, and here is my ultimatum.

' " First of all, a piece of advice. Beware ! If you are determined to maintain so unequal a struggle, you will be exposed even to the hatred of those whom you so foolishly seek to protect. There are a thousand ways to ruin you with them, by enlightening them as to your projects. It will be proved to them, that you have shared in the plot, which you now pretend to reveal, not from generosity, but from cupidity." ' Though Djalma had the delicacy to feel that the least question on the subject of this letter would be a serious indiscretion, he could not forbear turning his head suddenly towards the Jesuit, as he read the last passage.

' Oh, yes ! it relates to me. Such as you see me, my dear prince,' added he, glancing at his shabby clothes, ' I am accused of cupidity.'

' And who are these people that you protect ?'——' Those I protect ?' said Rodin, feigning some hesitation, as if he had been embarrassed to find an answer ; ' who are those I protect ? Hem—hem—I will tell you. They are poor devils without resources ; good people without a penny, having only a just cause on their side, in a law-suit in which they are engaged. They are threatened with destruction by powerful parties— very powerful parties ; but, happily, these latter are known to me, and I am able to unmask them. What else could have been ? Being myself poor and weak, I range myself naturally on the side of the poor and weak. But continue, I beg of you.'

Djalma resumed : ' " You have therefore everything to fear if you persist in your hostility, and nothing to gain by taking the side of those whom you call your friends. They might more justly be termed your dupes, for your disinterestedness would be inexplicable, were it sincere. It must therefore conceal some after-thought of cupidity.

' " Well ! in that view of the case, we can offer you ample compensa- tion—with this difference, that your hopes are now entirely founded on the probable gratitude of your friends, a very doubtful chance at the best, whereas our offers will be realized on the instant. To speak clearly, this is what we ask, what we exact of you. This very night, before twelve, you must have left Paris, and engage not to return for six months." ' Djalma could not repress a movement of surprise, and looked at Rodin.

' Quite natural,' said the latter ; ' the cause of my poor friends would be judged by that time, and I should be unable to watch over them. You see how it is, my dear prince,' added Rodin, with bitter indignation. ' But please continue, and excuse me for having interrupted you ; though, indeed, such impudence disgusts me.'

Djalma continued : ' " That we may be certain of your removal from Paris for six months, you will go to the house of one of our friends in Germany. You will there be received with generous hospitality, but forcibly detained until the expiration of the term." '——' Yes, yes ! a voluntary prison,' said Rodin.

' " On these conditions, you will receive a pension of one thousand francs a month, to begin from your departure from Paris, ten thousand francs down, and twenty thousand at the end of the six months—the whole to be completely secured to you. Finally, at the end of the six months, we will place you in a position both honourable and independent." '

Djalma having stopped short with involuntary indignation, Rodin said to him : ' Let me beg you to continue, my dear prince. Read to the end, and it will give you some idea of what passes in the midst of our civilization.'

Djalma resumed : ' " You know well enough the course of affairs, and what we are, to feel that in providing for your absence, we only wish to get rid of an enemy, not very dangerous, but rather troublesome. Do not be blinded by your first success. The results of your denunciation will be stifled, because they are calumnious. The judge who received your evidence will soon repent his odious partiality. You may make what use you please of this letter. We know what we write, to whom we write, and how we write. You will receive this letter at three o'clock ; if by four o'clock we have not your full and complete acceptance, written with your own hand at the bottom of this letter, war must commence between us—and not from to-morrow, but on the instant."'

Having finished reading the letter, Djalma looked at Rodin, who said to him : ' Permit me to summon Faringhea.'——He rang the bell, and the half-caste appeared. Rodin took the letter from the hands of Djalma, tore it into halves, rubbed it between his palms, so as to make a sort of a ball, and said to the half-caste, as he returned it to him : ' Give this paper to the person who waits for it, and tell him that is my only answer to his shameless and insolent letter ; you understand me—this shameless and insolent letter.'

' I understand,' said the half-caste ; and he went out.

' This will perhaps be a dangerous war for you, father,' said the Indian, with interest.

' Yes, dear prince, it may be dangerous, but I am not like you ; I have no wish to kill my enemies, because they are cowardly and wicked. I fight them under the shield of the law. Imitate me in this.' Then, seeing that the countenance of Djalma darkened, he added : ' I am wrong. I will advise you no more on this subject. Only, let us defer the decision to the judgment of your noble and motherly protectress. I shall see her to morrow ; if she consents, I will tell you the names of your enemies. If not—not.'

' And this woman, this second mother,' said Djalma, ' is her character such, that I can rely on her judgment ?'

' She !' cried Rodin, clasping his hands, and speaking with increased excitement. ' Why, she is the most noble, the most generous, the most valiant being upon earth !—why, if you were really her son, and she loved you with all the strength of maternal affection, and a case arose in which you had to choose between an act of baseness and death, she would say to you : " Die !" hough she might herself die with you.'

' Oh, noble woman ! so was my mother !' cried Djalma, with enthusiasm.

' Yes,' resumed Rodin, with growing energy, as he approached the window concealed by the shade, towards which he threw an oblique and anxious glance, ' if you would imagine your protectress, think only of courage, uprightness, and loyalty personified. Oh ! she has the chivalrous frankness of the brave man, joined with the high-souled dignity of the woman, who not only never in her life told a falsehood, never concealed a single thought, but who would rather die than give way to the least of those sentiments of craft and dissimulation, which are almost forced upon ordinary women by the situation in which they are placed.'

It is difficult to express the admiration which shone upon the countenance of Djalma, as he listened to this description. His eyes sparkled, his cheeks glowed, his heart palpitated with enthusiasm.

' That is well, noble heart !' said Rodin to him, drawing still nearer to the blind ; ' I love to see your soul sparkle through your eyes, on hearing me speak thus of your unknown protectress. Oh ! but she is worthy of the pious adoration which noble hearts and great characters inspire !'

' Oh ! I believe you,' cried Djalma, with enthusiasm ; ' my heart is full of admiration and also of astonishment ; for my mother is no more, and yet such a woman exists !'

'Yes, she exists. For the consolation of the afflicted, for the glory of her sex, she exists. For the honour of truth, and the shame of falsehood, she exists. No lie, no disguise, has ever tainted her loyalty, brilliant and heroic as the sword of a knight. It is but a few days ago that this noble woman spoke to me these admirable words, which, in all my life, I shall not forget : "Sir," said she, "if ever I suspect any one that I love or esteem——" '

Rodin did not finish. The shade, so violently shaken that the spring broke, was drawn up abruptly, and, to the great astonishment of Djalma, Mdlle. de Cardoville appeared before him. Adrienne's cloak had fallen from her shoulders, and in the violence of the movement with which she had approached the blind, her bonnet, the strings of which were untied, had also fallen. Having left home suddenly, with only just time to throw a mantle over the picturesque and charming costume which she often chose to wear when alone, she appeared so radiant with beauty to Djalma's dazzled eyes, in the centre of those leaves and flowers, that the Indian believed himself under the influence of a dream.

With clasped hands, eyes wide open, the body slightly bent forward, as if in the act of prayer, he stood petrified with admiration. Mdlle. de Cardoville, much agitated, and her countenance glowing with emotion, remained on the threshold of the greenhouse, without entering the room. All this had passed in less time than it takes to describe it. Hardly had the blind been raised, than Rodin, feigning surprise, exclaimed : ' You here, madame ?'

' Oh, sir !' said Adrienne, in an agitated voice, ' I come to terminate the phrase which you have commenced. I told you, that when a suspicion crossed my mind, I uttered it aloud to the person by whom it was inspired. Well ! I confess it : I have failed in this honesty. I came here as a spy upon you, when your answer to the Abbé d'Aigrigny was giving me a new pledge of your devotion and sincerity. I doubted your uprightness at the moment when you were bearing testimony to my frankness. For the first time in my life, I stooped to deceit ; this weakness merits punishment, and I submit to it—demands reparation, and I make it—calls for apologies, and I tender them to you.' Then, turning towards Djalma, she added : ' Now, prince, I am no longer mistress of my secret. I am your relation, Mdlle. de Cardoville ; and I hope you will accept from a sister the hospitality that you did not refuse from a mother.'

Djalma made no reply. Plunged in ecstatic contemplation of this sudden apparition, which surpassed his wildest and most dazzling visions, he felt a sort of intoxication, which, paralysing the power of thought, concentred all his faculties in the one sense of sight ; and just as we sometimes seek in vain to satisfy unquenchable thirst, the burning look of the Indian sought, as it were, with devouring avidity, to take in all the rare perfections of the young lady. Verily, never had two more divine types of beauty met face to face. Adrienne and Djalma were the very ideal of a handsome youth and maiden. There seemed to be something providential in the meeting of these two natures, so young and so vivacious, so generous and so full of passion, so heroic and so proud, who, before coming into contact, had, singularly enough, each learned the moral worth of the other : for if, at the words of Rodin, Djalma had felt arise in his heart an admiration, as lively as it was sudden, for the valiant and generous qualities of that unknown benefactress, whom he now discovered in Mdlle. de Cardoville, the latter had, in her turn, been moved, affected, almost terrified, by the interview she had just overheard, in which Djalma had displayed the nobleness of his soul, the delicate goodness of his heart, and the terrible transports of his temper. Then she had not been able to repress a movement of astonishment, almost admiration, at sight of the surprising beauty of the prince ; and soon after, a strange, painful sentiment, a sort of electric shock, seemed to penetrate all her being, as her eyes encountered Djalma's.

Cruelly agitated, and suffering deeply from this agitation, she tried to dissemble the impression she had received, by addressing Rodin, to apologise for having suspected him. But the obstinate silence of the Indian redoubled the lady's painful embarrassment. Again raising her eyes towards the prince, to invite him to respond to her fraternal offer, she met his ardent gaze wildly fixed upon her, and she looked once more with a mixture of fear, sadness, and wounded pride ; then she congratulated herself on having foreseen the inexorable necessity of keeping Djalma at a distance from her, such apprehension did this ardent and impetuous nature already inspire. Wishing to put an end to her present painful situation, she said to Rodin, in a low and trembling voice . ' Pray, sir, speak to the prince ; repeat to him my offers. I cannot remain longer.' So saying, Adrienne turned, as if to rejoin Florine. But, at the first step, Djalma sprang towards her with the bound of a tiger, about to be deprived of his prey. Terrified by the expression of wild excitement which inflamed the Indian's countenance, the young lady drew back with a loud scream.

At this, Djalma remembered himself, and all that had passed. Pale with regret and shame, trembling, dismayed, his eyes streaming with tears, and all his features marked with an expression of the most touching despair, he fell at Adrienne's feet, and lifting his clasped hands towards her, said in a soft, supplicating, timid voice : ' Oh, remain ! remain ! do not leave me. I have waited for you so long !' To this prayer, uttered with the timid simplicity of a child, and a resignation which contrasted strangely with the savage violence that had so frightened Adrienne, she replied, as she made a sign to Florine to prepare for their departure : ' Prince, it is impossible for me to remain longer here.'

' But you will return ?' said Djalma, striving to restrain his tears. ' I shall see you again ?'

' Oh, no ! never—never !' said Mdlle. de Cardoville, in a failing voice. Then, profiting by the stupor into which her answer had thrown Djalma, Adrienne disappeared rapidly behind the plants in the greenhouse.

Florine was hastening to rejoin her mistress, when, just at the moment she passed before Rodin, he said to her in a low, quick voice : ' To morrow we must finish with the hunchback.' Florine trembled in every limb, and, without answering Rodin, disappeared, like her mistress, behind the plants. Broken, overpowered, Djalma remained upon his knees, with his head resting on his breast. His countenance expressed neither rage nor excitement, but a painful stupor ; he wept silently. Seeing Rodin approach him, he rose, but with so tremulous a step, that he could hardly reach the divan, on which he sank down, hiding his face in his hands.

Then Rodin, advancing, said to him in a mild and insinuating tone : ' Alas ! I feared what has happened. I did not wish you to see your benefactress ; and if I told you she was old, do you know why, dear prince ?'

Djalma, without answering, let his hands fall upon his knees, and turned towards Rodin a countenance still bathed in tears.

' I knew that Mdlle. de Cardoville was charming, and at your age it is so easy to fall in love,' continued Rodin ; ' I wished to spare you that misfortune, my dear prince, for your beautiful protectress passionately loves a handsome young man of this town.'

Upon these words, Djalma suddenly pressed both hands to his heart, as if he felt a piercing stab, uttered a cry of savage grief, threw back his head, and fell fainting upon the divan.

Rodin looked at him coldly for some seconds, and then said as he went away, brushing his old hat with his elbow : 'Come ! it works—it works !'

CHAPTER XLV.

THE CONSULTATION.

It is night. It has just struck nine. It is the evening of that day on which Mdlle. de Cardoville first found herself in presence of Djalma. Florine, pale, agitated, trembling, with a candle in her hand, had just entered a bed-room, plainly but comfortably furnished. This room was one of the apartments occupied by Mother Bunch, in Adrienne's house. They were situated on the ground-floor, and had two entrances. One opened on the garden, and the other on the court-yard. From this side came the persons who applied to the workgirl for succour ; an ante-chamber in which they waited, a parlour in which they were received, constituted Mother Bunch's apartments, along with the bedroom, which Florine had just entered, looking about her with an anxious and alarmed air, scarcely touching the carpet with the tips of her satin shoes, holding her breath, and listening at the least noise.

Placing the candle upon the chimney-piece, she took a rapid survey of the chamber, and approached the mahogany desk, surmounted by a well-filled book-case. The key had been left in the drawers of this piece of furniture, and they were all three examined by Florine. They contained different petitions from persons in distress, and various notes in the girl's handwriting. That was not what Florine wanted. Three card-board boxes were placed in pigeon-holes beneath the bookcase. These also were vainly explored, and Florine, with a gesture of vexation, looked and listened anxiously ; then, seeing a chest of drawers, she made therein a fresh and useless search. Near the foot of the bed was a little door, leading to a dressing-room. Florine entered it, and looked—at first without success—into a large wardrobe, in which were suspended several black dresses, recently made for Mother Bunch, by order of Mdlle. de Cardoville. Perceiving, at the bottom of this wardrobe, half hidden beneath a cloak, a very shabby little trunk, Florine opened it hastily, and found there, carefully folded up, the poor old garments in which the work-girl had been clad when she first entered this opulent mansion.

Florine started—an involuntary emotion contracted her features ; but considering that she had not liberty to indulge her feelings, but only to obey Rodin's implacable orders, she hastily closed both trunk and wardrobe, and leaving the dressing-room, returned into the bed-chamber. After having again examined the writing-stand, a sudden idea occurred to her. Not content with once more searching the card-board boxes, she drew out one of them from the pigeon-hole, hoping to find what she sought behind the box : her first attempt failed, but the second was more successful. She found behind the middle box a copy-book of considerable thickness. She started in surprise, for she had expected something else ; yet she took the manuscript, opened it, and rapidly turned over the leaves. After having perused several pages, she manifested her satisfaction, and seemed as if about to put the book in her pocket ; but after a moment's reflection, she replaced it where she had found it, arranged everything in order, took her candle, and quitted the apartment without being discovered—of which, in-deed, she had felt pretty sure, knowing that Mother Bunch would be occupied with Mdlle. de Cardoville for some hours.

    ✿   ✿   ✿   ✿   ✿   ✿

The day after Florine's researches, Mother Bunch, alone in her bed-
chamber, was seated in an arm-chair, close to a good fire. A thick carpet
covered the floor ; through the window-curtains could be seen the lawn of
a large garden ; the deep silence was only interrupted by the regular ticking of a clock, and the crackling of the wood. Her hands resting on the
arms of the chair, she gave way to a feeling of happiness, such as she had
never so completely enjoyed since she took up her residence at the hotel.
For her, accustomed so long to cruel privations, there was a kind of inexpressible charm in the calm silence of this retreat—in the cheerful aspect
of the garden, and above all, in the consciousness that she was indebted
for this comfortable position, to the resignation and energy she had displayed, in the thick of the many severe trials which now ended so happily.
An old woman, with a mild and friendly countenance, who had been, by
express desire of Adrienne, attached to the hunchback's service, entered
the room, and said to her : ' Mademoiselle, a young man wishes to speak to
you on pressing business. He gives his name as Agricola Baudoin.'
At this name, Mother Bunch uttered an exclamation of surprise and joy,
blushed slightly, rose and ran to the door which led to the parlour in which
was Agricola.
' Good morning, dear sister,' said the smith, cordially embracing the
young girl, whose cheeks burned crimson beneath those fraternal kisses.
' Ah, me !' cried the sempstress on a sudden, as she looked anxiously at
Agricola ; ' what is that black band on your forehead? You have been
wounded !'
' A mere nothing,' said the smith, ' really nothing. Do not think of it. I
will tell you all about that presently. But first, I have things of importance
to communicate.'
' Come into my room, then ; we shall be alone,' said Mother Bunch, as
she went before Agricola.
Notwithstanding the expression of uneasiness which was visible on the
countenance of Agricola, he could not forbear smiling with pleasure as he
entered the room, and looked around him.
' Excellent, my poor sister ! this is how I would always have you lodged.
I recognise here the hand of Mdlle. de Cardoville. What a heart ! what a
noble mind !—Dost know, she wrote to me the day before yesterday, to
thank me for what I had done for her, and sent me a gold pin (very plain),
which she said I need not hesitate to accept, as it had no other value but
that of having been worn by her mother ! You can't tell how much I was
affected by the delicacy of this gift !'
' Nothing must astonish you from a heart like hers,' answered the hunchback. ' But the wound—the wound ?'
' Presently, my good sister ; I have so many things to tell you. Let us
begin by what is most pressing, for I want you to give me some good advice
in a very serious case. You know how much confidence I have in your
excellent heart and judgment. And then, I have to ask of you a service—
oh ! a great service,' added the smith, in an earnest, and almost solemn
tone, which astonished his hearer. ' Let us begin with what is not personal
to myself.'——' Speak quickly.'
' Since my mother went with Gabriel to the little country curacy he has
obtained, and since my father lodges with Marshal Simon and the young
ladies, I have resided, you know, with my mates, at M. Hardy's factory, in
the common dwelling-house. Now, this morning—but first, I must tell you
that M. Hardy, who has lately returned from a journey, is again absent for
a few days on business. This morning, then, at the hour of breakfast, I
remained at work a little after the last stroke of the bell ; I was leaving the

workshop to go to our eating-room, when I saw entering the court-yard, a lady who had just got out of a hackney-coach. I remarked that she was fair, though her veil was half down ; she had a mild and pretty countenance, and her dress was that of a fashionable lady. Struck with her paleness, and her anxious, frightened air, I asked her if she wanted anything. "Sir," said she to me, in a trembling voice, and as if with a great effort, "do you belong to this factory ?"—"Yes, madame."—"M. Hardy is then in danger ?" she exclaimed.—"M. Hardy, madame ? He has not yet returned home." —"What !" she went on, "M. Hardy did not come hither yesterday evening ? Was he not dangerously wounded by some of the machinery ?" As she said these words, the poor young lady's lips trembled, and I saw large tears standing in her eyes. "Thank God, madame ! all this is entirely false," said I, "for M. Hardy has not returned, and indeed is only expected by to-morrow or the day after."—"You are quite sure that he has not returned ! quite sure that he is not hurt ?" resumed the pretty young lady, drying her eyes.—"Quite sure, madame ; if M. Hardy were in danger, I should not be so quiet in talking to you about him."—"Oh ! thank God ! thank God !" cried the young lady. Then she expressed to me her gratitude, with so happy, so feeling an air, that I was quite touched by it. But suddenly, as if then only she felt ashamed of the step she had taken, she let down her veil, left me precipitately, went out of the court-yard, and got once more into the hackney coach that had brought her. I said to myself : "This is a lady who takes great interest in M. Hardy, and has been alarmed by a false report."'

'She loves him, doubtless,' said Mother Bunch, much moved, 'and, in her anxiety, she perhaps committed an act of imprudence, in coming to inquire after him.'

'It is only too true. I saw her get into the coach with interest, for her emotion had infected me. The coach started—and what did I see a few seconds after ? A cab, which the young lady could not have perceived, for it had been hidden by an angle of the wall ; and, as it turned round the corner, I distinguished perfectly a man seated by the driver's side, and making signs to him to take the same road as the hackney-coach.'

'The poor young lady was followed,' said Mother Bunch, anxiously.

'No doubt of it ; so I instantly hastened after the coach, reached it, and through the blinds that were let down, I said to the young lady, whilst I kept running by the side of the coach-door : "Take care, madame ; you are followed by a cab."'

'Well, Agricola ! and what did she answer ?'——'I heard her exclaim, "Great heaven !" with an accent of despair. The coach continued its course. The cab soon came up with me ; I saw, by the side of the driver, a great, fat, ruddy man, who, having watched me running after the coach, no doubt suspected something, for he looked at me somewhat uneasily.'

'And when does M. Hardy return ?' asked the hunchback.——'To-morrow, or the day after. Now, my good sister, advise me. It is evident that this young lady loves M. Hardy. She is probably married, for she looked so embarrassed when she spoke to me, and she uttered a cry of terror on learning that she was followed. What shall I do ? I wished to ask advice of Father Simon, but he is so very strict in such matters—and then a love affair, at his age !—while you are so delicate and sensible, my good sister, that you will understand it all.'

The girl started, and smiled bitterly ; Agricola did not perceive it, and thus continued : 'So I said to myself, "There is only Mother Bunch, who can give me good advice." Suppose M. Hardy returns to-morrow, shall I tell him what has passed or not ?'

'Wait a moment,' cried the other, suddenly interrupting Agricola, and appearing to recollect something ; 'when I went to St. Mary's Convent, to ask for work of the superior, she proposed that I should be employed by the day, in a house in which I was to watch, or, in other words, to act as a spy——'——'What a wretch !'

'And do you know,' said the girl, 'with whom I was to begin this odious trade ? Why, with a Madame de—Fremont, or de Bremont, I do not remember which, a very religious woman, whose daughter, a young married lady, received visits a great deal too frequent (according to the superior) from a certain manufacturer.'

'What do you say?' cried Agricola. 'This manufacturer must be——'

'M. Hardy. I had too many reasons to remember that name, when it was pronounced by the superior. Since that day, so many other events have taken place, that I had almost forgotten the circumstance. But it is probable that this young lady is the one of whom I heard speak at the convent.'

'And what interest had the superior of the convent to set a spy upon her ?' asked the smith.

'I do not know ; but it is clear that the same interest still exists, since the young lady was followed, and perhaps, at this hour, is discovered and dishonoured. Then ! it is dreadful !' Then, seeing Agricola start suddenly, Mother Bunch added : 'What, then, is the matter ?'

'Yes—why not ?' said the smith, speaking to himself ; 'why may not all this be the work of the same hand ? The superior of a convent may have a private understanding with an abbé—but, then, for what end ?'

'Explain yourself, Agricola,' said the girl. 'And then,—where did you get your wound ? Tell me that, I conjure you.'

'It is of my wound that I am just going to speak ; for, in truth, the more I think of it, the more this adventure of the young lady seems to connect itself with other facts.'

'How so ?'——'You must know that, for the last few days, singular things are passing in the neighbourhood of our factory. First, as we are in Lent, an abbé from Paris (a tall, fine-looking man, they say) has come to preach in the little village of Villiers, which is only a quarter of a league from our works. The abbé has found occasion to slander and attack M. Hardy in his sermons.'

'How is that ?'——'M. Hardy has printed certain rules with regard to our work, and the rights and benefits he grants us. These rules are followed by various maxims as noble as they are simple, with precepts of brotherly love such as all the word can understand, extracted from different philosophies and different religions. But because M. Hardy has chosen what is best in all religions, the abbé concludes that M. Hardy has no religion at all, and he has therefore not only attacked him for this in the pulpit, but has denounced our factory as a centre of perdition and damnable corruption, because, on Sundays, instead of going to listen to his sermons, or to drink at a tavern, our comrades, with their wives and children, pass their time in cultivating their little gardens, in reading, singing in chorus, or dancing together in the common dwelling-house. The abbé has even gone so far as to say, that the neighbourhood of such an assemblage of atheists, as he calls us, might draw down the anger of Heaven upon the country—that the hovering of Cholera was much talked of, and that very possibly, thanks to our impious presence, the plague might fall upon all our neighbourhood.'

'But to tell such things to ignorant people,' exclaimed Mother Bunch, 'is likely to excite them to fatal actions.'——'That is just what the abbé wants.'

'What do you tell me ?'——'The people of the environs, still more excited, no doubt, by other agitators, show themselves hostile to the workmen of our factory. Their hatred, or at least their envy, has been turned to account. Seeing us live all together, well lodged, well warmed, and comfortably clad, active, gay, and laborious, their jealousy has been embittered by the sermons, and by the secret manœuvres of some depraved characters, who are known to be bad workmen, in the employment of M. Tripeaud, our opposition. All this excitement is beginning to bear fruit; there have been already two or three fights between us and our neighbours. It was in one of these skirmishes that I received a blow with a stone on my head.'

'Is it not serious, Agricola?—are you quite sure?' said Mother Bunch, anxiously.

'It is nothing at all, I tell you. But the enemies of M. Hardy have not confined themselves to preaching. They have brought into play something far more dangerous.'

'What is that?'——'I, and nearly all my comrades, did our part in the three Revolutionary days of July; but we are not eager at present, for good reasons, to take up arms again. That is not everybody's opinion; well, we do not blame others, but we have our own ideas; and Father Simon, who is as brave as his son, and as good a patriot as any one, approves and directs us. Now, for some days past, we find all about the factory, in the garden, in the courts, printed papers to this effect : " You are selfish cowards; because chance has given you a good master, you remain indifferent to the misfortunes of your brothers, and to the means of freeing them; material comforts have enervated your hearts."'

'Dear me, Agricola! what frightful perseverance in wickedness !'

'Yes ! and unfortunately these devices have their effect on some of our younger mates. As the appeal was, after all, to proud and generous sentiments, it has had some influence. Already, seeds of division have shown themselves in our workshops, where, before, all were united as brothers. A secret agitation now reigns there. Cold suspicion takes the place, with some, of our accustomed cordiality. Now, if I tell you that I am nearly sure these printed papers, thrown over the walls of our factory, to raise these little sparks of discord amongst us, have been scattered about by the emissaries of this same preaching abbé—would it not seem from all this, taken in conjunction with what happened this morning to the young lady, that M. Hardy has of late numerous enemies?'

'Like you, I think it very fearful, Agricola,' said the girl; 'and it is so serious, that M. Hardy alone can take a proper decision on the subject. As for what happened this morning to the young lady, it appears to me that, immediately on M. Hardy's return, you should ask for an interview with him, and, however delicate such a communication may be, tell him all that passed.'

'There is the difficulty. Shall I not seem as if wishing to pry into his secrets?'

'If the young lady had not been followed, I should have shared your scruples. But she was watched, and is evidently in danger. It is therefore, in my opinion, your duty to warn M. Hardy. Suppose (which is not improbable) that the lady is married; would it not be better, for a thousand reasons, that M. Hardy should know all?'

'You are right, my good sister; I will follow your advice. M. Hardy shall know everything. But now that we have spoken of others, I have to speak of myself—yes, of myself—for it concerns a matter, on which may depend the happiness of my whole life,' added the smith, in a tone of seriousness, which struck his hearer. 'You know,' proceeded Agricola, after a moment's silence, 'that, from my childhood, I have never concealed anything from you—that I have told you everything—absolutely everything ?'

'I know it, Agricola, I know it,' said the hunchback, stretching out her white and slender hand to the smith, who grasped it cordially, and thus continued : 'When I say everything, I am not quite exact—for I have always concealed from you my little love-affairs—because, though we may tell almost anything to a sister, there are subjects of which we ought not to speak to a good and virtuous girl, such as you are.'

'I thank you, Agricola. I had remarked this reserve on your part,' observed the other, casting down her eyes, and heroically repressing the grief she felt ; 'I thank you.'

'But for the very reason, that I made it a duty never to speak to you of such love affairs, I said to myself, if ever it should happen that I have a serious passion—such a love as makes one think of marriage—oh ! then, just as we tell our sister even before our father and mother, my good sister shall be the first to be informed of it.'——'You are very kind, Agricola.'

'Well then ! the serious passion has come at last. I am over head and ears in love, and I think of marriage.'

At these words of Agricola, poor Mother Bunch felt herself for an instant paralysed. It seemed as if all her blood was suddenly frozen in her veins. For some seconds, she thought she was going to die. Her heart ceased to beat ; she felt it, not breaking, but melting away to nothing. Then, the first blasting emotion over, like those martyrs who found, in the very excitement of pain, the terrible power to smile in the midst of tortures, the unfortunate girl found, in the fear of betraying the secret of her fatal and ridiculous love, almost incredible energy. She raised her head, looked at the smith calmly, almost serenely, and said to him in a firm voice : 'Ah ! so, you truly love ?'

'That is to say, my good sister, that, for the last four days, I scarcely live at all—or live only upon this passion.'

'It is only since four days that you have been in love ?'

'Not more—but time has nothing to do with it.'

'And is *she* very pretty ?'——'Dark hair—the figure of a nymph—fair as a lily—blue eyes, as large as that—and as mild, as good as your own.'

'You flatter me, Agricola.'——'No, no, it is Angela that I flatter—for that's her name. What a pretty one ! Is it not, my good Mother Bunch ?'

'A charming name,' said the poor girl, contrasting bitterly that graceful appellation with her own nickname, which the thoughtless Agricola applied to her without thinking of it. Then she resumed, with fearful calmness : 'Angela ? yes, it is a charming name !'

'Well, then ! imagine to yourself, that this name is not only suited to her face, but to her heart. In a word, I believe her heart to be almost equal to yours.'

'She has my eyes—she has my heart,' said Mother Bunch, smiling. 'It is singular, how like we are.'

Agricola did not perceive the irony of despair contained in these words. He resumed, with a tenderness as sincere as it was inexorable : 'Do you think, my good girl, that I could ever have fallen seriously in love with any one, who had not in character, heart, and mind, much of you ?'

'Come, brother,' said the girl, smiling—yes, the unfortunate creature had the strength to smile ; 'come, brother, you are in a gallant vein to-day. Where did you make the acquaintance of this beautiful young person ?'

'She is only the sister of one of my mates. Her mother is the head laundress in our common dwelling, and as she was in want of assistance, and we always take in preference the relations of members of the association, Mrs. Bertin (that's the mother's name) sent for her daughter from Lille, where she had been stopping with one of her aunts, and, for the last five days, she has been in the laundry. The first evening I saw her, I passed three hours, after work was over, in talking with her, and her mother and brother ; and the next day, I felt that my heart was gone ; the day after that, the feeling was only stronger—and now I am quite mad about her, and resolved on marriage—according as you shall decide. Do not be surprised at this ; everything depends upon you. I shall only ask my father and mother's leave, after I have yours.'

' I do not understand you, Agricola.'——' You know the utter confidence I have in the incredible instinct of your heart. Many times, you have said to me : " Agricola, love this person, love that person, have confidence in that other "—and never yet were you deceived. Well ! you must now render me the same service. You will ask permission of Mdlle. de Cardoville to absent yourself ; I will take you to the factory : I have spoken of you to Mrs. Bertin and her daughter, as of a beloved sister ; and, according to your impression at sight of Angela, I will declare myself or not. This may be childishness, or superstition, on my part ; but I am so made.'

' Be it so,' answered Mother Bunch, with heroic courage ; ' I will see Mdlle. Angela ; I will tell you what I think of her—and that, mind you, sincerely.'

' I know it. When will you come ?'——' I must ask Mdlle. de Cardoville what day she can spare me. I will let you know '

' Thanks, my good sister !' said Agricola, warmly ; then he added, with a smile : ' Bring your best judgment with you—your full-dress judgment.'

' Do not make a jest of it, brother,' said Mother Bunch, in a mild, sad voice ; ' it is a serious matter, for it concerns the happiness of your whole life.'

At this moment, a modest knock was heard at the door. ' Come in,' said Mother Bunch. Florine appeared.

' My mistress begs that you will come to her, if you are not engaged,' said Florine to Mother Bunch.

The latter rose, and, addressing the smith, said to him : ' Please wait a moment, Agricola. I will ask Mdlle. de Cardoville what day I can dispose of, and I will come and tell you.' So saying, the girl went out, leaving Agricola with Florine.

' I should have much wished to pay my respects to Mdlle. de Cardoville,' said Agricola ; ' but I feared to intrude.'

' My lady is not quite well, sir,' said Florine, ' and receives no one to-day. I am sure, that as soon as she is better, she will be quite pleased to see you.'

Here Mother Bunch returned, and said to Agricola : ' If you can come for me to-morrow, about three o'clock, so as not to lose the whole day, we will go to the factory, and you can bring me back in the evening.'

' Then, at three o'clock to-morrow, my good sister.'——' At three, to-morrow, Agricola.'

    ❁   ❁   ❁   ❁   ❁   ❁

The evening of that same day, when all was quiet in the hotel, Mother Bunch, who had remained till ten o'clock with Mdlle. de Cardoville, re-entered her bedchamber, locked the door after her, and finding herself at length free and unrestrained, threw herself on her knees before a chair, and burst into tears. She wept long—very long. When her tears at length ceased to flow, she dried her eyes, approached the writing-desk, drew out one of the boxes from the pigeon-hole, and, taking from this hiding-place the manuscript which Florine had so rapidly glanced over the evening before, she wrote in it during a portion of the night.

CHAPTER XLVI.

MOTHER BUNCH'S DIARY.

WE have said that the hunchback wrote during a portion of the night, in the book discovered the previous evening by Florine, who had not ventured to take it away, until she had informed the persons who employed her of its contents, and until she had received their final orders on the subject. Let us explain the existence of this manuscript, before opening it to the reader. The day on which Mother Bunch first became aware of her love for Agricola, the first word of this manuscript had been written. Endowed with an essentially trusting character, yet always feeling herself restrained by the dread of ridicule—a dread which, in its painful exaggeration, was the workgirl's only weakness—to whom could the unfortunate creature have confided the secret of that fatal passion, if not to paper—that mute confidant of timid and suffering souls, that patient friend, silent and cold, who, if it makes no reply to heartrending complaints, at least always listens, and never forgets?

When her heart was overflowing with emotion, sometimes mild and sad, sometimes harsh and bitter, the poor workgirl, finding a melancholy charm in these dumb and solitary outpourings of the soul, now clothed in the form of simple and touching poetry, and now in unaffected prose, had accustomed herself by degrees not to confine her confidences to what immediately related to Agricola, for though he might be mixed up with all her thoughts, other reflections, which the sight of beauty, of happy love, of maternity, of wealth, of misfortune, called up within her, were so impressed with the influence of her unfortunate personal position, that she would not even have dared to communicate them to him. Such, then, was this journal of a poor daughter of the people, weak, deformed, and miserable, but endowed with an angelic soul, and a fine intellect, improved by reading, meditation, and solitude ; pages quite unknown, which yet contained many deep and striking views, both as regards men and things, taken from the peculiar standpoint in which fate had placed this unfortunate creature. The following lines, here and there abruptly interrupted or stained with tears, according to the current of her various emotions, on hearing of Agricola's deep love for Angela, formed the last pages of this journal :—

'Friday, March 3rd, 1832.

'I spent the night without any painful dreams. This morning, I rose with no sorrowful presentiment. I was calm and tranquil when Agricola came. He did not appear to me agitated. He was simple and affectionate as he always is. He spoke to me of events relating to M. Hardy, and then, without transition, without hesitation, he said to me : "The last four days I have been desperately in love. The sentiment is so serious, that I think of marriage. I have come to consult you about it." That was how this overwhelming revelation was made to me—naturally and cordially—I on one side of the hearth, and Agricola on the other, as if we had talked of indifferent things. And yet no more is needed to break one's heart. Some one enters, embraces you like a brother, sits down, talks—and then——Oh, merciful heaven ! my head wanders.

 * * * * * *

'I feel calmer now. Courage, my poor heart, courage !—Should a day of misfortune again overwhelm me, I will read these lines written under the impression of the most cruel grief I can ever feel, and I will say to myself : "What is the present woe compared to that past ?" My grief is indeed cruel ! it is illegitimate, ridiculous, shameful ; I should not dare to confess it, even to the most indulgent of mothers. Alas ! there are some fearful sorrows, which yet rightly make men shrug their shoulders in pity or contempt. Alas! these are forbidden misfortunes. Agricola has asked me to go to-morrow, to see this young girl to whom he is so passionately attached, and whom he will marry, if the instinct of my heart should approve the marriage. This thought is the most painful of all those which have tortured me, since he so pitilessly announced this love. Pitilessly? No, Agricola—no, my brother—forgive me this unjust cry of pain! Is it that you know, can even suspect, that I love you better than you love, better than you can ever love, this charming creature?

' "Dark-haired—the figure of a nymph—fair as a lily—with blue eyes—as large as that—and almost as mild as your own."

' That is the portrait he drew of her. Poor Agricola! how would he have suffered, had he known that every one of his words was tearing my heart! Never did I so strongly feel the deep commiseration and tender pity, inspired by a good, affectionate being, who, in the sincerity of his ignorance, gives you your death-wound with a smile. We do not blame him—no—we pity him to the full extent of the grief that he would feel on learning the pain he had caused us. It is strange! but never did Agricola appear to me more handsome than this morning. His manly countenance was slightly agitated, as he spoke of the uneasiness of that pretty young lady. As I listened to him describing the agony of a woman who runs the risk of ruin for the man she loves, I felt my heart beat violently, my hands were burning, a soft languor floated over me——Ridiculous folly! As if I had any right to feel thus!

*   *   *   *   *   *

' I remember that, while he spoke, I cast a rapid glance at the glass. I felt proud that I was so well dressed; he had not even remarked it: but no matter—it seemed to me that my cap became me, that my hair shone finely, my gaze beamed mild——I found Agricola so handsome, that I almost began to think myself less ugly—no doubt, to excuse myself in my own eyes for daring to love him. After all, what happened to-day would have happened one day or another! Yes, that is consoling—like the thoughts that death is nothing, because it must come at last—to those who are in love with life! I have been always preserved from suicide—the last resource of the unfortunate, who prefer trusting in God to remaining amongst his creatures—by the sense of duty. One must not only think of self. And I reflected also—" God is good—always good—since the most wretched beings find opportunities for love and devotion."—How is it that I, so weak and poor, have always found means to be helpful and useful to some one?

' This very day I felt tempted to make an end with life—Agricola and his mother had no longer need of me.—Yes, but the unfortunate creatures whom Mdlle. de Cardoville has commissioned me to watch over?—but my benefactress herself, though she has affectionately reproached me with the tenacity of my suspicions in regard to that man? I am more than ever alarmed for her—I feel that she is more than ever in danger—more than ever, I have faith in the value of my presence near her. Hence, I must live. Live—to go to-morrow to see this girl, whom Agricola passionately loves? Good heaven! why have I always known grief, and never hate? There must be a bitter pleasure in hating. So many people hate!—Perhaps I may hate this girl—Angela, as he called her, when he said, with so much simplicity: "A charming name, is it not, Mother Bunch?" Compare this name, which recalls an idea so full of grace, with the ironical symbol of my witch's deformity! Poor Agricola! poor brother! goodness is sometimes as blind as malice, I see. Should I hate this young girl?—Why? Did she deprive me of the beauty which charms Agricola? Can I find fault with

her for being beautiful ? When I was not yet accustomed to the consequences of my ugliness, I asked myself, with bitter curiosity, why the Creator
had endowed his creatures so unequally. The habit of pain has allowed me
to reflect calmly, and I have finished by persuading myself, that to beauty
and ugliness are attached the two most noble emotions of the soul—admiration and compassion. Those who are like me admire beautiful persons—
such as Angela, such as Agricola—and these in their turn feel a touching pity
for such as I am. Sometimes, in spite of one's self, one has very foolish hopes.
Because Agricola, from a feeling of propriety, had never spoken to me of
his love affairs, I sometimes persuaded myself that he had none—that he
loved me, and that the fear of ridicule alone was with him, as with me, an
obstacle in the way of confessing it. Yes, I have even made verses on that
subject—and those, I think, not the worst I have written.

'Mine is a singular position ! If I love, I am ridiculous ; if any love me,
he is still more ridiculous. How did I come so to forget that, as to have
suffered and to suffer what I do?—But blessed be that suffering, since it
has not engendered hate—no ; for I will not hate this girl—I will perform
a sister's part to the last ; I will follow the guidance of my heart ; I have
the instinct of preserving others—my heart will lead and enlighten me. My
only fear is, that I shall burst into tears when I see her, and not be able to
conquer my emotion. Oh, then ! what a revelation to Agricola—a discovery
of the mad love he has inspired !—Oh, never ! the day in which he knew
that, would be the last of my life. There would then be within me something stronger than duty—the longing to escape from shame—that incurable
shame, that burns me like a hot iron. No, no ; I will be calm. Besides,
did I not just now, when with him, bear courageously a terrible trial ? I
will be calm. My personal feelings must not darken the second-sight, so
clear for those I love. Oh ! painful, painful task ! for the fear of yielding
involuntarily to evil sentiments must not render me too indulgent towards
this girl. I might compromise Agricola's happiness, since my decision is
to guide his choice. Poor creature that I am ! How I deceive myself !
Agricola asks my advice, because he thinks that I shall not have the melancholy courage to oppose his passion : or else he would say to me : " No
matter—I love ; and I brave the future !"

'But then, if my advice, if the instincts of my heart, are not to guide him
—if his resolution is taken beforehand—of what use will be to-morrow's
painful mission ? Of what use ? To obey him. Did he not say—" Come !"
In thinking of my devotion for him, how many times, in the secret depths
of my heart, I have asked myself if the thought had ever occurred to him
to love me otherwise than as a sister ; if it had ever struck him, what a
devoted wife he would have in me ! And why should it have occurred to
him ? As long as he wished, as long as he may still wish, I have been, and
I shall be, as devoted to him, as if I were his wife, sister, or mother. Why
should he desire what he already possesses ?

'Married to him—oh, God !—the dream is mad as ineffable. Are not
such thoughts of celestial sweetness—which include all sentiments from
sisterly to maternal love—forbidden to me, on pain of ridicule as distressing
as if I wore dresses and ornaments, that my ugliness and deformity would
render absurd ? I wonder, if I were now plunged into the most cruel distress, whether I should suffer as much as I do, on hearing of Agricola's intended marriage ? Would hunger, cold, or misery diminish this dreadful
dolour ?—or is it the dread pain that would make me forget hunger, cold,
and misery ?

'No, no ; this irony is bitter. It is not well in me to speak thus. Why
such deep grief ? In what way have the affection, the esteem, the respect

of Agricola, changed towards me? I complain—but how would it be, kind heaven! if, as, alas! too often happens, I were beautiful, loving, devoted, and he had chosen another, less beautiful, less loving, less devoted?— Should I not be a thousand times more unhappy? for then I might, I would have to blame him—whilst now I can find no fault with him, for never having thought of a union which was impossible, because ridiculous. And had he wished it, could I ever have had the selfishness to consent to it? I began to write the first pages of this diary, as I began these last, with my heart steeped in bitterness—and as I went on, committing to paper what I could have intrusted to no one, my soul grew calm, till Resignation came —Resignation, my chosen saint, who, smiling through her tears, suffers and loves, but hopes—never!'

* * * * * *

These words were the last in the journal. It was clear, from the blots of abundant tears, that the unfortunate creature had often paused to weep.

In truth, worn out by so many emotions, Mother Bunch, late in the night, had replaced the book behind the card-board box, not that she thought it safer there than elsewhere (she had no suspicion of the slightest need for such precaution), but because it was more out of the way there than in any of the drawers, which she frequently opened in presence of other people. Determined to perform her courageous promise, and worthily accomplish her task to the end, she waited the next day for Agricola, and firm in her heroic resolution, went with the smith to M. Hardy's factory. Florine, informed of her departure, but detained a portion of the day in attendance on Mdlle. de Cardoville, preferred waiting for night to perform the new orders she had asked and received, since she had communicated by letter the contents of Mother Bunch's journal. Certain not to be surprised, she entered the workgirl's chamber, as soon as the night was come.

Knowing the place where she should find the manuscript, she went straight to the desk, took out the box, and then, drawing from her pocket a sealed letter, prepared to leave it in the place of the manuscript, which she was to carry away with her. So doing, she trembled so much, that she was obliged to support herself an instant by the table. Every good sentiment was not extinct in Florine's heart; she obeyed passively the orders she received, but she felt painfully how horrible and infamous was her conduct. If only herself had been concerned, she would no doubt have had the courage to risk all, rather than submit to this odious despotism; but unfortunately, it was not so, and her ruin would have caused the mortal despair of another person whom she loved better than life itself. She resigned herself, therefore, not without cruel anguish, to abominable treachery.

Though she hardly ever knew for what end she acted, and this was particularly the case with regard to the abstraction of the journal, she foresaw vaguely, that the substitution of this sealed letter for the manuscript would have fatal consequences for Mother Bunch, for she remembered Rodin's declaration, that 'it was time to finish with the young sempstress.'

What did he mean by those words? How would the letter that she was charged to put in the place of the diary contribute to bring about this result? She did not know—but she understood that the clear-sighted devotion of the hunchback justly alarmed the enemies of Mdlle. de Cardoville, and that she (Florine) herself daily risked having her perfidy detected by the young needlewoman. This last fear put an end to the hesitations of Florine; she placed the letter behind the box, and, hiding the manuscript under her apron, cautiously withdrew from the chamber.

CHAPTER XLVII.

THE DIARY CONTINUED.

RETURNED into her own room, some hours after she had concealed there the manuscript abstracted from Mother Bunch's apartment, Florine yielded to her curiosity, and determined to look through it. She soon felt a growing interest, an involuntary emotion, as she read more of these private thoughts of the young sempstress. Among many pieces of verse, which all breathed a passionate love for Agricola—a love so deep, simple, and sincere, that Florine was touched by it, and forgot the author's deformity—among many pieces of verse, we say, were divers other fragments, thoughts, and narratives, relating to a variety of facts. We shall quote some of them, in order to explain the profound impression that their perusal made upon Florine.

Fragments from the Diary.

'This is my birthday. Until this evening, I had cherished a foolish hope. Yesterday, I went down to Mrs. Baudoin's, to dress a little wound she had on her leg. When I entered the room, Agricola was there. No doubt he was talking of me to his mother, for they stopped when I came in, and exchanged a meaning smile. In passing the drawers, I saw a pasteboard box, with a pincushion-lid, and I felt myself blushing with joy, as I thought this little present was destined for me, but I pretended not to see it. While I was on my knees before his mother, Agricola went out. I remarked, that he took the little box with him. Never has Mrs. Baudoin been more tender and motherly than she was that morning. It appeared to me that she went to bed earlier than usual. "It is to send me away sooner," said I to myself, "that I may enjoy the surprise Agricola has prepared for me." How my heart beat, as I ran fast, very fast, up to my closet! I stopped a moment before opening the door, that my happiness might last the longer. At last I entered the room, my eyes swimming with tears of joy. I looked upon my table, my chair, my bed—there was nothing. The little box was not to be found. My heart sank within me. Then I said to myself: "It will be to-morrow—this is only the eve of my birthday." The day is gone. Evening is come. Nothing. The pretty box was not for me. It had a pincushion-cover. It was only suited for a woman. To whom has Agricola given it?

'I suffer a good deal just now. It was a childish idea that I connected with Agricola's wishing me many happy returns of the day. I am ashamed to confess it ; but it might have proved to me, that he has not forgotten I have another name besides that of Mother Bunch, which they always apply to me. My susceptibility on this head is unfortunately so stubborn, that I cannot help feeling a momentary pang of mingled shame and sorrow, every time that I am called by that fairy-tale name, and yet I have had no other from infancy. It is for that very reason that I should have been so happy if Agricola had taken this opportunity to call me for once by my own humble name—Magdalen. Happily, he will never know these wishes and regrets !'

Deeper and deeper touched by this page of simple grief, Florine turned over several leaves, and continued :

'I have just been to the funeral of poor little Victorine Herbin, our neighbour. Her father, a journeyman upholsterer, is gone to work by the month, far from Paris. She died at nineteen, without a relation near her. Her agony was not long. The good woman who attended her to the last, told us that she only pronounced these words : "At last, oh, at last !" and that with an air of satisfaction, added the nurse. Dear child! she had become so pitiful. At fifteen, she was a rosebud—so pretty, so fresh-looking, with her light hair as soft as silk; but she wasted away by degrees—her trade of renovating mattresses killed her. She was slowly poisoned by the emanations from the wool.[*] They were all the worse, that she worked almost entirely for the poor, who have cheap stuff to lie upon.

'She had the courage of a lion, and an angel's resignation. She always said to me, in her low, faint voice, broken by a dry and frequent cough : "I have not long to live, breathing, as I do, lime and vitriol all day long. I spit blood, and have spasms that make me faint."

'"Why not change your trade?" have I said to her.

'"Where will I find the time to make another apprenticeship?" she would answer; "and it is now too late. I feel that I am *done for*. It is not *my fault*," added the good creature, "for I did not choose my employment. My father would have it so; luckily he can do without me. And then, you see, when one is dead, one cares for nothing, and has no fear of 'slop wages.'"

'Victorine uttered that sad, common phrase very sincerely, and with a sort of satisfaction. Therefore she died, repeating : "At last!"

'It is painful to think that the labour by which the poor man earns his daily bread, often becomes a long suicide! I said this the other day to Agricola; he answered me, that there were many other fatal employments; those who prepare aquafortis, white lead, or minium, for instance, are sure to take incurable maladies of which they die.

'"Do you know," added Agricola, "what they say when they start for those fatal works?—Why, 'We are going to the slaughter-house.'"

'That made me tremble with its terrible truth.

'"And all this takes place in our day," said I to him, with an aching heart; "and it is well-known. And, out of so many of the rich and powerful, no one thinks of the mortality which decimates his brothers, thus forced to eat homicidal bread!"

'"What can you expect, my poor sister?" answered Agricola. "When men are to be incorporated, that they may get killed in war, all pains are taken with them. But when they are to be organised, so as to live in peace, no one cares about it, except M. Hardy, my master. People say, 'Pooh! hunger, misery, and suffering of the labouring classes—what is that to us? that is not politics.' They are *wrong*," added Agricola; "IT IS MORE THAN POLITICS."

'As Victorine had not left anything to pay for the church service, there was only the presentation of the body under the porch; for there is not

---

[*] In the *Ruche Populaire*, a working man's organ, are the following particulars :

"Carding Mattresses.—The dust which flies out of the wool makes carding destructive to health in any case, but trade adulterations enhance the danger. In sticking sheep, the skin gets blood-spotted; it has to be bleached to make it saleable. Lime is the main whitener, and some of it clings to the wool after the process. The dresser (female, most often) breathes in the fine dust, and, by lung and other complaints, is far from seldom deplorably situated; the majority sicken of it and give up the trade, while those who keep to it, at the very least, suffer with a catarrh or asthma that torments them until death.

"As for horsehair, the very best is not pure. You can judge what the inferior quality is, from the workgirls calling it *vitriol hair*, because it is the refuse or clippings from goats and swine, washed in vitriol, boiled in dyes, &c., to burn and disguise such foreign bodies as straw, thorns, splinters, and even bits of skin, not worth picking out. The dust rising when a mass of this is beaten, makes as many ravages as the lime-wool."

even a plain mass for the poor. Besides, as they could not give eighteen francs to the curate, no priest accompanied the pauper's coffin to the common grave. If funerals, thus abridged and cut short, are sufficient in a religious point of view, why invent other and longer forms? Is it from cupidity?— If, on the other hand, they are not sufficient, why make the poor man the only victim of this insufficiency? But why trouble ourselves about the pomp, the incense, the chants, of which they are either too sparing or too liberal? Of what use? and for what purpose? They are vain, terrestrial things, for which the soul recks nothing, when, radiant, it ascends towards its Creator. Yesterday, Agricola made me read an article in a newspaper, in which violent blame and bitter irony are by turns employed, to attack what they call the baneful tendencies of some of the lower orders, to improve themselves, to write, to read the poets, and sometimes to make verses. Material enjoyments are forbidden us by poverty. Is it humane to reproach us for seeking the enjoyments of the mind? What harm can it do any one if every evening, after a day's toil, remote from all pleasure, I amuse myself, unknown to all, in making a few verses, or in writing in this journal the good or bad impressions I have received? Is Agricola the worse workman, because, on returning home to his mother, he employs Sunday in composing some of those popular songs, which glorify the fruitful labours of the artisan, and say to all, *Hope and brotherhood?* Does he not make a more worthy use of his time than if he spent it in a tavern? Ah! those who blame us for these innocent and noble diversions, which relieve our painful toils and sufferings, deceive themselves when they think, that, in proportion as the intellect is raised and refined, it is more difficult to bear with privations and misery, and that so the irritation increases against the luckier few.

'Admitting even this to be the case—and it is not so—is it not better to have an intelligent, enlightened enemy, to whose heart and reason you may address yourself, than a stupid, ferocious, implacable foe? But no; enmities disappear as the mind becomes enlightened, and the horizon of compassion extends itself. We thus learn to understand moral afflictions. We discover that the rich also have to suffer intense pains, and that brotherhood in misfortune is already a link of sympathy. Alas! they also have to mourn bitterly for idolised children, beloved mistresses, reverend mothers; with them, also, especially amongst the women, there are, in the height of luxury and grandeur, many broken hearts, many suffering souls, many tears shed in secret. Let them not be alarmed. By becoming their equals in intelligence, the people will learn to pity the rich, if good and unhappy—and to pity them still more if rejoicing in wickedness.

'What happiness! what a joyful day! I am giddy with delight. Oh, truly, man is good, humane, charitable. Oh, yes! the Creator has implanted within him every generous instinct—and, unless he be a monstrous exception, he never does evil willingly. Here is what I saw just now. I will not wait for the evening to write it down, for my heart would, as it were, have time to cool. I had gone to carry home some work that was wanted in a hurry. I was passing the Place du Temple. A few steps from me I saw a child, about twelve years old at most, with bare head and feet, in spite of the severe weather, dressed in a shabby, ragged smock-frock and trousers, leading by the bridle a large cart-horse, with his harness still on. From time to time the horse stopped short and refused to advance. The child, who had no whip, tugged in vain at the bridle. The horse remained motionless. Then the poor little fellow cried out, " O dear! O dear!" and began to weep bitterly, looking round him as if to implore the assistance of the passers-by. His dear little face was impressed with so heart-piercing a sorrow, that, without reflecting, I made an attempt at which I can now only smile, I must have presented so grotesque a figure. I am horribly afraid of horses, and I am still more afraid of exposing myself to public gaze. Nevertheless, I took courage, and, having an umbrella in my hand, I approached the horse, and with the impetuosity of an ant that strives to move a large stone with a little piece of straw, I struck with all my strength on the croup of the rebellious animal. " Oh, thanks, my good lady !" exclaimed the child, drying his eyes ; " hit him again, if you please. Perhaps he will get up."

' I began again, heroically ; but, alas ! either from obstinacy or laziness, the horse bent his knees, and stretched himself out upon the ground ; then, getting entangled with his harness, he tore it, and broke his great wooden collar. I had drawn back quickly, for fear of receiving a kick. Upon this new disaster, the child could only throw himself on his knees in the middle of the street, clasping his hands and sobbing, and exclaiming in a voice of despair, " Help ! help !"

' The call was heard ; several of the passers-by gathered round, and a more efficacious correction than mine was administered to the restive horse, who rose in a vile state, and without harness.

' " My master will beat me," cried the poor child, as his tears redoubled ; " I am already two hours after time, for the horse would not go, and now he has broken his harness. My master will beat me, and turn me away. O dear ! what will become of me ! I have no father nor mother."

' At these words, uttered with a heartrending accent, a worthy old clothes-dealer of the Temple, who was amongst the spectators, exclaimed, with a kindly air, " No father nor mother ! Do not grieve so, my poor little fellow , the Temple can supply everything. We will mend the harness, and, if my gossips are like me, you shall not go away bareheaded or barefooted in such weather as this."

' This proposition was greeted with acclamation ; they led away both horse and child ; some were occupied in mending the harness, then one supplied a cap, another a pair of stockings, another some shoes, and another a good jacket ; in a quarter of an hour the child was warmly clad, the harness repaired, and a tall lad of eighteen, brandishing a whip, which he cracked close to the horse's ears, by way of warning, said to the little boy, who, gazing first at his new clothes, and then at the good woman, believed himself the hero of a fairy-tale. " Where does your governor live, little 'un ?"——' " On the Quai du Canal-Saint-Martin, sir," answered he, in a voice trembling with joy.

' " Very good," said the young man, " I will help you take home the horse, who will go well enough with me, and I will tell the master that the delay was no fault of your'n. A balky horse ought not to be trusted to a child of your age."

' At the moment of setting out, the poor little fellow said timidly to the good dame, as he took off his cap to her, " Will you let me kiss you, ma'am ?"

' His eyes were full of tears of gratitude. There was heart in that child. This scene of popular charity gave me delightful emotions. As long as I could, I followed with my eyes the tall young man and the child, who now could hardly keep up with the pace of the horse, rendered suddenly docile by fear of the whip.

' Yes ! I repeat it with pride ; man is naturally good and helpful. Nothing could have been more spontaneous than this movement of pity and tenderness in the crowd, when the poor little fellow exclaimed, " What will become of me ? I have no father or mother !"

' " Unfortunate child !" said I to myself. " No father nor mother. In the hands of a brutal master, who hardly covers him with a few rags, and ill-treats him into the bargain. Sleeping, no doubt, in the corner of a stable. Poor little fellow ! and yet so mild and good, in spite of misery and misfortune. I saw it—he was even more grateful than pleased at the service done him. But perhaps this good natural disposition, abandoned without support or counsel, or help, and exasperated by bad treatment, may become changed and embittered—and then will come the age of the passions—the bad temptations——"

' Oh ! in the deserted poor, virtue is doubly saintly and respectable !'

' This morning, after having (as usual) gently reproached me for not going to mass, Agricola's mother said to me these words, so touching in her simple and believing mouth, " Luckily, I pray for you and myself too, my poor girl ; the good God will hear me, and you will *only* go, I hope, to Purgatory."

' Good mother, angelic soul ! she spoke those words in so grave and mild a tone, with so strong a faith in the happy result of her pious intercession, that I felt my eyes become moist, and I threw myself on her neck, as sincerely grateful as if I had believed in Purgatory. This day has been a lucky one for me. I hope I have found work, which luck I shall owe to a young person full of heart and goodness. She is to take me to-morrow to St. Mary's Convent, where she thinks she can find me employment.'

Florine, already much moved by the reading, started at this passage in which Mother Bunch alluded to her, ere she continued as follows :

' Never shall I forget with what touching interest, what delicate benevolence, this handsome young girl received me, so poor, and so unfortunate. It does not astonish me, for she is attached to the person of Mdlle. de Cardoville. She must be worthy to reside with Agricola's benefactress. It will always be dear and pleasant to me to remember her name. It is graceful and pretty as her face ; it is Florine. I am nothing, I have nothing—but if the fervent prayers of a grateful heart might be heard, Mdlle. Florine would be happy, very happy. Alas ! I am reduced to say prayers for her—only prayers—for I can do nothing but remember and love her !'

These lines, expressing so simply the sincere gratitude of the hunchback, gave the last blow to Florine's hesitations. She could no longer resist the generous temptation she felt. As she read these last fragments of the journal, her affection and respect for Mother Bunch made new progress. More than ever she felt how infamous it was in her to expose to sarcasms and contempt the most secret thoughts of this unfortunate creature. Happily, good is often as contagious as evil. Electrified by all that was warm, noble, and magnanimous in the pages she had just read, Florine bathed her failing virtue in that pure and vivifying source, and, yielding at last to one of those good impulses which sometimes carried her away, she left the room with the manuscript in her hand, determined, if Mother Bunch had not yet returned, to replace it—resolved to tell Rodin that, this second time, her search for the journal had been vain, the sempstress having no doubt discovered the first attempt.

CHAPTER XLVIII.

THE DISCOVERY.

A LITTLE while before Florine made up her mind to atone for her shameful breach of confidence, Mother Bunch had returned from the factory, after accomplishing to the end her painful task. After a long interview with Angela, struck, like Agricola, with the ingenuous grace, sense, and goodness, with which the young girl was endowed, Mother Bunch had the courageous frankness to advise the smith to enter into this marriage. The following scene took place whilst Florine, still occupied in reading the journal, had not yet taken the praiseworthy resolution of replacing it. It was ten o'clock at night. The work-girl, returned to Cardoville House, had just entered her chamber. Worn out by so many emotions, she had thrown herself into a chair. The deepest silence reigned in the house. It was now and then interrupted by the soughing of a high wind, which raged without and shook the trees in the garden. A single candle lighted the room, which was papered with dark green. That peculiar tint, and the hunchback's black dress, increased her apparent paleness. Seated in an arm-chair by the side of the fire, with her head resting upon her bosom, her hands crossed upon her knees, the workgirl's countenance was melancholy and resigned ; on it was visible the austere satisfaction which is felt by the consciousness of a duty well performed.

Like all those who, brought up in the merciless school of misfortune, no longer exaggerate the sentiment of sorrow, too familiar and assiduous a guest to be treated us a stranger, Mother Bunch was incapable of long yielding to idle regrets and vain despair, with regard to what was already past. Beyond doubt, the blow had been sudden, dreadful ; doubtless it must leave a long and painful remembrance in the sufferer's soul ; but it was soon to pass, as it were, into that chronic state of pain-durance, which had become almost an integral part of her life. And then this noble creature, so indulgent to fate, found still some consolations in the intensity of her bitter pain. She had been deeply touched by the marks of affection shown her by Angela, Agricola's intended ; and she had felt a species of pride of the heart, in perceiving with what blind confidence, with what ineffable joy, the smith accepted the favourable presentiments which seemed to consecrate his happiness. Mother Bunch also said to herself : 'At least, henceforth I shall not be agitated by hopes, or rather by suppositions as ridiculous as they were senseless. Agricola's marriage puts a term to all the miserable reveries of my poor head.'

Finally, she found a real and deep consolation in the certainty that she had been able to go through this terrible trial, and conceal from Agricola the love she felt for him. We know how formidable to this unfortunate being were those ideas of ridicule and shame, which she believed would attach to the discovery of her mad passion. After having remained for some time absorbed in thought, Mother Bunch rose, and advanced slowly towards the desk.

'My only recompense,' said she, as she prepared the materials for writing, 'will be to entrust the mute witness of my pains with this new grief. I shall at least have kept the promise that I made to myself. Believing, from the bottom of my soul, that this girl is able to make Agricola happy, I told him so with the utmost sincerity. One day, a long time hence, when I shall read over these pages, I shall perhaps find in that a compensation for all that I now suffer.'

So saying, she drew the box from the pigeon-hole. Not finding her manuscript, she uttered a cry of surprise ; but what was her alarm, when she perceived a letter to her address in the place of the journal ! She became deadly pale ; her knees trembled ; she almost fainted away. But her increasing terror gave her a fictitious energy, and she had the strength to break the seal. A bank-note for five hundred francs fell from the letter on the table, and Mother Bunch read as follows ;

'MADEMOISELLE,—There is something so original and amusing in reading in your memoirs the story of your love for Agricola, that it is impossible to resist the pleasure of acquainting him with the extent of it, of which he is doubtless ignorant, but to which he cannot fail to show himself sensible. Advantage will be taken to forward it to a multitude of other persons who might, perhaps, otherwise be unfortunately deprived of the amusing contents of your diary. Should copies and extracts not be sufficient, we will have it printed, as one cannot too much diffuse such things. Some will weep—others will laugh—what appears superb to one set of people, will seem ridiculous to another ; such is life—but your journal will surely make a great sensation. 'As you are capable of wishing to avoid your triumph, and as you were only covered with rags when you were received out of charity into this house, where you wish to *figure* as the great lady, which does not suit your *shape* for more reasons than one, we enclose in the present five hundred francs to pay for your day-book, and prevent your being without resources, in case you should be modest enough to shrink from the congratulations which await you, certain to overwhelm you by to-morrow, for, at this hour, your journal is already in circulation.

'One of your brethren,

'A REAL MOTHER BUNCH.'

The vulgar, mocking, and insolent tone of this letter, which was purposely written in the character of a jealous lackey, dissatisfied with the admission of the unfortunate creature into the house, had been calculated with infernal skill, and was sure to produce the effect intended.

'Oh, good heaven !' were the only words the unfortunate girl could pronounce, in her stupor and alarm.

Now, if we remember in what passionate terms she had expressed her love for her adopted brother, if we recal many passages of this manuscript, in which she revealed the painful wounds often inflicted on her by Agricola without knowing it, and if we consider how great was her terror of ridicule, we shall understand her mad despair on reading this infamous letter. Mother Bunch did not think for a moment of all the noble words and touching narratives contained in her journal. The one horrible idea which weighed down the troubled spirit of the unfortunate creature, was, that on the morrow Agricola, Mdlle. de Cardoville, and an insolent and mocking crowd, would be informed of this ridiculous love, which would, she imagined, crush her with shame and confusion. This new blow was so stunning, that the recipient staggered a moment beneath the unexpected shock. For some minutes, she remained completely inert and helpless ; then, upon reflection, she suddenly felt conscious of a terrible necessity.

This hospitable mansion, where she had found a sure refuge after so many misfortunes, must be left for ever. The trembling timidity and sensitive delicacy of the poor creature did not permit her to remain a minute more in this dwelling, where the most secret recesses of her soul had been laid open, profaned, and exposed no doubt to sarcasm and contempt. She did not think of demanding justice and revenge from Mdlle. de Cardoville. To cause a ferment of trouble and irritation in this house, at the moment of quitting it, would have appeared to her ingratitude towards her benefactress. She did not seek to discover the author or the motive of this odious robbery and insulting letter. Why should she, resolved, as she was, to fly from the humiliations with which she was threatened ? She had a vague notion (as indeed was intended), that this infamy might be the work of some of the servants, jealous of the affectionate deference shown her by Mdlle. de Cardoville—and this thought filled her with despair. Those pages—so painfully confidential, which she would not have ventured to impart to the most tender and indulgent mother, because, written as it were with her heart's blood, they painted with too cruel a fidelity the thousand secret wounds of her soul —those pages were to serve, perhaps served even now, for the jest and laughing-stock of the lackeys of the mansion.

    ✿   ✿   ✿   ✿   ✿   ✿

The money which accompanied this letter, and the insulting way in which it was offered, rather tended to confirm her suspicions. It was intended that the fear of misery should not be the obstacle of her leaving the house. The workgirl's resolution was soon taken, with that calm and firm resignation which was familiar to her. She rose, with somewhat bright and haggard eyes, but without a tear in them. Since the day before, she had wept too much. With a trembling, icy hand, she wrote these words on a paper, which she left by the side of the bank-note : ‘ May Mdlle. de Cardoville be blessed for all that she has done for me, and forgive me for having left her house, where I can remain no longer.’

Having written this, Mother Bunch threw into the fire the infamous letter, which seemed to burn her hands. Then, taking a last look at her chamber, furnished so comfortably, she shuddered involuntarily as she thought of the misery that awaited her—a misery more frightful than that of which she had already been the victim, for Agricola's mother had departed with Gabriel, and the unfortunate girl could no longer, as formerly, be consoled in her distress by the almost maternal affection of Dagobert's wife. To live alone —quite alone—with the thought that her fatal passion for Agricola was laughed at by everybody, perhaps even by himself—such were the future prospects of the hunchback. This future terrified her—a dark desire crossed her mind—she shuddered, and an expression of bitter joy contracted her features. Resolved to go, she made some steps towards the door, when, in passing before the fireplace, she saw her own image in the glass, pale as death, and clothed in black ; then it struck her, that she wore a dress which did not belong to her, and she remembered a passage in the letter, which alluded to the rags she had on before she entered that house. ‘ True !’ said she, with a heart-breaking smile, as she looked at her black garments ; ‘ they would call me a thief.’

And, taking her candle, she entered the little dressing-room, and put on again the poor, old clothes, which she had preserved as a sort of pious remembrance of her misfortunes. Only at this instant did her tears flow abundantly. She wept—not in sorrow at resuming the garb of misery, but in gratitude ; for all the comforts around her, to which she was about to bid an eternal adieu, recalled to her mind at every step the delicacy and goodness of Mdlle. de Cardoville : therefore, yielding to an almost involuntary impulse, after she had put on her poor, old clothes, she fell on her knees in the middle of the room, and, addressing herself in thought to Mdlle. de Cardoville, she exclaimed, in a voice broken by convulsive sobs : ‘ Adieu ! oh, for ever, adieu !—You, that deigned to call me friend—and sister !’

Suddenly, she rose in alarm ; she heard steps in the corridor, which led from the garden to one of the doors of her apartment, the other door opening into the parlour. It was Florine, who (alas ! too late) was bringing back the manuscript. Alarmed at this noise of footsteps, and believing herself already the laughing-stock of the house, Mother Bunch rushed from the room, hastened across the parlour, gained the courtyard, and knocked at the window of the porter's lodge. The house-door opened, and immediately closed upon her. And so the workgirl left Cardoville House.

    ✿   ✿   ✿   ✿   ✿   ✿

Adrienne was thus deprived of a devoted, faithful, and vigilant guardian. Rodin was delivered from an active and sagacious antagonist, whom he had always, with good reason, feared. Having, as we have seen, guessed Mother Bunch's love for Agricola, and knowing her to be a poet, the Jesuit supposed, logically enough, that she must have written secretly some verses inspired by this fatal and concealed passion. Hence the order given to Florine, to try and discover some written evidence of this love; hence this letter, so horribly effective in its coarse ribaldry, of which, it must be observed, Florine did not know the contents, having received it after communicating a summary of the contents of the manuscript, which, the first time, she had only glanced through without taking it away. We have said, that Florine, yielding too late to a generous repentance, had reached Mother Bunch's apartment, just as the latter quitted the house in consternation.

Perceiving a light in the dressing-room, the waiting-maid hastened thither. She saw upon a chair the black dress that Mother Bunch had just taken off, and, a few steps further, the shabby little trunk, open and empty, in which she had hitherto preserved her poor garments. Florine's heart sank within her; she ran to the secretary; the disorder of the cardboard boxes, the note for five hundred francs left by the side of the two lines written to Mdlle. de Cardoville, all proved that her obedience to Rodin's orders had borne fatal fruit, and that Mother Bunch had quitted the house for ever. Finding the uselessness of her tardy resolution, Florine resigned herself with a sigh to the necessity of delivering the manuscript to Rodin. Then, forced by the fatality of her miserable position to console herself for evil by evil, she considered that the hunchback's departure would at least make her treachery less dangerous.

✿　　✿　　✿　　✿　　✿　　✿

Two days after these events, Adrienne received the following note from Rodin, in answer to a letter she had written him, to inform him of the workgirl's inexplicable departure :—

'MY DEAR YOUNG LADY,—Obliged to set out this morning for the factory of the excellent M. Hardy, whither I am called by an affair of importance, it is impossible for me to pay you my humble respects. You ask me what I think of the disappearance of this poor girl? I really do not know. The future will, I doubt not, explain all to her advantage. Only, remember what I told you at Dr. Baleinier's, with regard to a certain society and its secret emissaries, with whom it has the art of surrounding those it wishes to keep a watch on. I accuse no one; but let us only recal facts. This poor girl accused me; and I am, as you know, the most faithful of your servants. She possessed nothing; and yet five hundred francs were found in her secretary. You loaded her with favours; and she leaves your house without even explaining the cause of this extraordinary flight. I draw no conclusion, my dear young lady; I am always unwilling to condemn without evidence; but reflect upon all this, and be on your guard, for you have perhaps escaped a great danger. Be more circumspect and suspicious than ever; such at least is the respectful advice of your most obedient, humble servant,　　　　　　　　　　　'RODIN.'

CHAPTER XLIX.

THE TRYSTING-PLACE OF THE WOLVES.

IT was a Sunday morning—the very day on which Mdlle. de Cardoville had received Rodin's letter with regard to Mother Bunch's disappearance. Two men were talking together, seated at a table in one of the publichouses in the little village of Villiers, situated at no great distance from M.

Hardy's factory. The village was for the most part inhabited by quarry-men and stonecutters, employed in working the neighbouring quarries. Nothing can be ruder and more laborious, and at the same time less ade-quately paid, than the work of this class of people. Therefore, as Agricola had told Mother Bunch, they drew painful comparisons between their con-dition, almost always miserable, and the comfort and comparative ease, en-joyed by M. Hardy's workmen, thanks to his generous and intelligent man-agement, and to the principles of association and community, which he had put in practice amongst them. Misery and ignorance are always the cause of great evils. Misery is easily excited to anger, and ignorance soon yields to perfidious counsels. For a long time, the happiness of M. Hardy's workmen had been naturally envied, but not with a jealousy amounting to hatred. As soon, however, as the secret enemies of the manufacturer, uniting with his rival Baron Tripeaud, had an interest in changing this peaceful state of things—it changed accordingly.

With diabolical skill and perseverance, they succeeded in kindling the most evil passions. By means of chosen emissaries, they applied to those quarrymen and stonecutters of the neighbourhood, whose bad conduct had aggravated their misery. Notorious for their turbulence, audacity, and energy, these men might exercise a dangerous influence on the majority of their companions, who were peaceful, laborious, and honest, but easily in-timidated by violence. These turbulent leaders, previously embittered by misfortune, were soon impressed with an exaggerated idea of the happiness of M. Hardy's workmen, and excited to a jealous hatred of them. They went still further; the incendiary sermons of an abbé, a member of the Jesuits, who had come expressly from Paris to preach during Lent against M. Hardy, acted powerfully on the minds of the women, who filled the church, whilst their husbands were haunting the taverns. Profiting by the growing fear, which the approach of the Cholera then inspired, the preacher struck with terror these weak and credulous imaginations by pointing to M. Hardy's factory as a centre of corruption and damnation, capable of drawing down the vengeance of Heaven, and bringing the fatal scourge upon the country. Thus the men, already inflamed with envy, were still more excited by the incessant urgency of their wives, who, maddened by the abbé's sermons, poured their curses on that band of atheists, who might bring down so many misfortunes upon them and their children. Some bad characters, belonging to the factory of Baron Tripeaud, and paid by him (for it was a great interest the honourable manufacturer had in the ruin of M. Hardy), came to augment the general irritation, and to complete it by raising one of those alarming union-questions, which in our day have un-fortunately caused so much bloodshed. Many of M. Hardy's workmen, before they entered his employ, had belonged to a society or union, called the Devourers; while many of the stonecutters in the neighbouring quarries belonged to a society called the Wolves. Now, for a long time, an im-placable rivalry had existed between the Wolves and Devourers, and brought about many sanguinary struggles, which are the more to be de-plored, as, in some respects, the idea of these unions is excellent, being founded on the fruitful and mighty principle of association. But unfortu-nately, instead of embracing all trades in one fraternal communion, these unions break up the working-class into distinct and hostile societies, whose rivalry often leads to bloody collisions.* For the last week, the Wolves, excited by so many different importunities, burned to discover an occasion or a pretext to come to blows with the Devourers; but the latter, not

* Let it be noted, to the working man's credit, that such outrageous scenes become more and more rare as he is enlightened to the full consciousness of his worth.

frequenting the public-houses, and hardly leaving the factory during the week, had hitherto rendered such a meeting impossible, and the Wolves had been forced to wait for the Sunday with ferocious impatience.

Moreover, a great number of the quarrymen and stonecutters, being peaceable and hard working people, had refused, though Wolves themselves, to join this hostile manifestation against the Devourers of M. Hardy's factory; the leaders had been obliged to recruit their forces from the vagabonds and idlers of the barriers, whom the attraction of tumult and disorder had easily enlisted under the flag of the warlike Wolves. Such then was the dull fermentation, which agitated the little village of Villiers, whilst the two men of whom we have spoken were at table in the public-house.

These men had asked for a private room, that they might be alone. One of them was still young, and pretty well dressed. But the disorder in his clothes, his loose cravat, his shirt spotted with wine, his dishevelled hair, his look of fatigue, his marble complexion, his bloodshot eyes, announced that a night of debauch had preceded this morning; whilst his abrupt and heavy gesture, his hoarse voice, his look, sometimes brilliant, and sometimes stupid, proved that to the last fumes of the intoxication of the night before, were joined the first attacks of a new state of drunkenness. The companion of this man said to him, as he touched his glass with his own:
'Your health, my boy!'

'Yours!' answered the young man; 'though you look to me like the devil.'

'I!—the devil?'——'Yes.'

'Why?'——'How did you come to know me?'

'Do you repent that you ever knew me?'

'Who told you that I was a prisoner at Sainte-Pélagie?'

'Didn't I take you out of prison?'——'Why did you take me out?'

'Because I have a good heart.'——'You are very fond of me, perhaps— just as the butcher likes the ox that he drives to the slaughter-house.'

'Are you mad?'——'A man does not pay a hundred thousand francs for another without a motive.'

'I have a motive.'——'What is it? what do you want to do with me?'

'A jolly companion, that will spend his money like a man, and pass every night like the last. Good wine, good cheer, pretty girls, and gay songs. Is that such a bad trade?'

After he had remained a moment without answering, the young man replied with a gloomy air: 'Why, on the eve of my leaving prison, did you attach this condition to my freedom, that I should write to my mistress to tell her that I would never see her again! Why did you exact this letter from me?'

Such better tendencies are to be attributed to the just influence of an excellent tract on trades' unions, written by M. Agricole Perdiguier, and published in 1841, Paris. This author, a joiner, founded at his own expense an establishment in the Faubourg St. Antoine, where some forty or fifty of his trade lodged, and were given, after the day's work, a course of geometry, etc., applied to wood-carving. We went to one of the lectures, and found as much clearness in the professor as attention and intelligence in the audience. At ten, after reading selections, all the lodgers retire, forced by their scanty wages to sleep, perhaps, four in a room. M. Perdignier informed us that study and instruction are such powerful ameliorators, that, during six years, he had only one of his lodgers to expel. 'In a few days,' he remarked, 'the bad eggs find out this is no place for them to addle sound ones!' We are happy to here render public homage to a learned and upright man, devoted to his fellow-workmen.

'A sigh! what, are you still thinking of her?'——'Always.'

'You are wrong. Your mistress is far from Paris by this time. I saw her get into the stage-coach, before I came to take you out of Sainte-Pélagie.'

'Yes, I was stifled in that prison. To get out, I would have given my soul to the devil. You thought so, and therefore you came to me; only, instead of my soul, you took Cephyse from me. Poor Bacchanal-Queen! And why did you do it? Thousand thunders! Will you tell me?'

'A man as much attached to his mistress as you are is no longer a man. He wants energy, when the occasion requires.'——'What occasion?'

'Let us drink!'——'You make me drink too much brandy.'

'Bah! look at me!'——'That's what frightens me. It seems something devilish. A bottle of brandy does not even make you wink. You must have a stomach of iron and a head of marble.'

'I have long travelled in Russia. There we drink to roast ourselves.'

'And here to only warm. So—let's drink—but wine.'

'Nonsense! wine is fit for children. Brandy for men like us!'——'Well, then, brandy; but it burns, and sets the head on fire, and then we see all the flames of hell!'

'That's how I like to see you, hang it!'——'But when you told me that I was too much attached to my mistress, and that I should want energy when the occasion required, of what occasion did you speak?'

'Let us drink!'——'Stop a moment, comrade. I am no more of a fool than others. Your half-words have taught me something.'

'Well, what?'——'You know that I have been a workman, that I have many companions, and that, being a good fellow, I am much liked amongst them. You want me for a catspaw, to catch other chestnuts?'

'What then?'——'You must be some getter-up of riots—some speculator in revolts.'

'What next?'——'You are travelling for some anonymous society, that trades in musket-shots.'

'Are you a coward?'——'I burned powder in July, I can tell you—make no mistakes!'

'You would not mind burning some again?'——'Just as well that sort of fireworks as any other. Only I find revolutions more agreeable than useful; all that I got from the barricades of the three days was burnt breeches and a lost jacket. All the cause won by me, with its "Forward! March!" says.'

'You know many of Hardy's workmen?'——'Oh! that's why you have brought me down here?'

'Yes—you will meet with many of the workmen from the factory.'

'Men from Hardy's take part in a row? No, no; they are too well off for that. You have been sold.'

'You will see presently.'——'I tell you they are well off. What have they to complain of?'

'What of their brethren—those who have not so good a master, and die of hunger and misery, and call on them for assistance? Do you think they will remain deaf to such a summons? Hardy is only an exception. Let the people but give a good pull all together, and the exception will become the rule, and all the world be happy.'

'What you say there is true, but it would be a devil of a pull that would make an honest man out of my old master, Baron Tripeaud, who made me what I am—an out-and-out rip.'

'Hardy's workmen are coming; you are their comrade, and have no interest in deceiving them. They will believe you. Join with me in persuading them——'——'To what?'

'To leave this factory, in which they grow effeminate and selfish, and forget their brothers.'——'But if they leave the factory, how are they to live?'

'We will provide for that—on the great day.'——'And what's to be done till then?'

'What you have done last night—drink, laugh, sing, and, by way of work, exercise themselves privately in the use of arms.'——'Who will bring these workmen here?'

'Some one has already spoken to them. They have had printed papers, reproaching them with indifference to their brothers. Come, will you support me?'

'I'll support you—the more readily as I cannot very well support myself! I only cared for Cephyse in the world; I know that I am on a bad road; you are pushing me on further: let the ball roll!—Whether we go to the devil one way or the other is not of much consequence. Let's drink!'

'Drink to our next night's fun; the last was only apprenticeship.'

'Of what then are you made? I looked at you, and never saw you either blush or smile, or change countenance. You are like a man of iron.'

'I am not a lad of fifteen. It would take something more to make me laugh. I shall laugh to-night.'

'I don't know if it's the brandy; but, devil take me, if you don't frighten me when you say you shall laugh to-night!'

So saying, the young man rose, staggering; he began to be once more intoxicated.

There was a knock at the door. 'Come in!' The host made his appearance.

'What's the matter?'——'There's a young man below, who calls himself Olivier. He asks for M. Morok.'

'That's right. Let him come up.' The host went out.

'It is one of our men, but he is alone,' said Morok, whose savage countenance expressed disappointment. 'It astonishes me, for I expected a good number. Do you know him?'——'Olivier? Yes—a fair chap, I think.'

'We shall see him directly. Here he is.' A young man, with an open, bold, intelligent countenance, at this moment entered the room.

'What! old Sleepinbuff!' he exclaimed, at sight of Morok's companion.

'Myself. I have not seen you for an age, Olivier.'

'Simple enough, my boy. We do not work at the same place.'

'But you are alone!' cried Morok; and pointing to Sleepinbuff, he added 'You may speak before him—he is one of us. But why are you alone?'

'I come alone, but in the name of my comrades.'

'Oh!' said Morok, with a sigh of satisfaction, 'they consent.'

'They refuse—just as I do!'

'What, the devil! they refuse? Have they no more courage than women?' cried Morok, grinding his teeth with rage.——'Hark ye,' answered Olivier, coolly. 'We have received your letters, and seen your agent. We have had proof that he is really connected with great societies, many members of which are known to us.'

'Well! why do you hesitate?'——'First of all, nothing proves that these societes are ready to make a movement.'

'I tell you they are.'——'He—tells you—they are,' said Sleepinbuff, stammering; 'and I (hic!) affirm it. Forward! March!'

'That's not enough,' replied Olivier. 'Besides, we have reflected upon it. For a week the factory was divided. Even yesterday the discussion was too warm to be pleasant. But this morning Father Simon called us to him; we explained ourselves fully before him, and he brought us all to one mind. We mean to wait, and if any disturbance breaks out, we shall see.'

' Is that your final word ?'——' It is our last word.'

' Silence !' cried Sleepinbuff, suddenly, as he listened, balancing himself on his tottering legs. ' It is like the noise of a crowd not far off.' A dull sound was indeed audible, which became every moment more and more distinct, and at length grew formidable.

' What is that ?' said Olivier, in surprise. ——' Now,' replied Morok, smiling with a sinister air, ' I remember the host told me there was a great ferment in the village against the factory. If you and your other comrades had separated from Hardy's other workmen, as I hoped, these people who are beginning to howl would have been *for* you, instead of against you.'

' This was a trap, then, to set one half of M. Hardy's workmen against the other !' cried Olivier ; ' you hoped that we should make common cause with these people against the factory, and that——'

The young man had not time to finish. A terrible outburst of shouts, howls, and hisses shook the tavern. At the same instant the door was abruptly opened, and the host, pale and trembling, hurried into the chamber, exclaiming : ' Gentlemen ! do any of you work at M. Hardy's factory ?'

' I do,' said Olivier.

' Then you are lost. Here are the Wolves in a body, saying there are Devourers here from M. Hardy's, and offering them battle—unless the Devourers will give up the factory, and range themselves on their side.'

' It was a trap, there can be no doubt of it !' cried Olivier, looking at Morok and Sleepinbuff, with a threatening air ; ' if my mates had come, we were all to be let in.'——' I lay a trap, Olivier ?' stammered Jacques Rennepont. ' Never !'

' Battle to the Devourers ! or let them join the Wolves !' cried the angry crowd with one voice, as they appeared to invade the house.

' Come !' exclaimed the host. Without giving Olivier time to answer, he seized him by the arm, and opening a window which led to a roof at no very great height from the ground, he said to him : ' Make your escape by this window, let yourself slide down, and gain the fields ; it is time.'

As the young workman hesitated, the host added, with a look of terror : ' Alone, against a couple of hundred, what can you do ? A minute more, and you are lost. Do you not hear them ? They have entered the yard ; they are coming up.'

Indeed, at this moment, the groans, hisses, and cheers redoubled in violence ; the wooden staircase which led to the first storey shook beneath the quick steps of many persons, and the shout arose, loud and piercing : ' Battle to the Devourers !'

' Fly, Olivier !' cried Sleepinbuff, almost sobered by the danger.

Hardly had he pronounced the words when the door of the large room, which communicated with the small one in which they were, was burst open with a frightful crash.

' Here they are !' cried the host, clasping his hands in alarm. Then, running to Olivier, he pushed him, as it were, out of the window ; for, with one foot on the sill, the workman still hesitated.

The window once closed, the publican returned towards Morok the instant the latter entered the large room, into which the leaders of the Wolves had just forced an entry, whilst their companions were vociferating in the yard and on the staircase. Eight or ten of these madmen, urged by others to take part in these scenes of disorder, had rushed first into the room, with countenances inflamed by wine and anger ; most of them were armed with long sticks. A blaster, of Herculean strength and stature, with an old red handkerchief about his head, its ragged ends streaming over his shoulders, miserably dressed in a half-worn goat-skin, brandished an iron drilling-rod, and appeared to direct the movements. With bloodshot eyes, threatening and ferocious countenance, he advanced towards the small room, as if to drive back Morok, and exclaimed, in a voice of thunder : ' Where are the Devourers ?—the Wolves will eat 'em up !'

The host hastened to open the door of the small room, saying : ' There is no one here, my friends—no one. Look for yourselves.'

' It is true,' said the quarryman, surprised, after peeping into the room ; ' where are they, then ? We were told there were a dozen of them here. They should have marched with us against the factory, or there'd 'a been a battle, and the Wolves would have tried their teeth !'

' If they have not come,' said another, ' they will come. Let's wait.'

' Yes, yes ; we will wait for them.'

' We will look close at each other.'——' If the Wolves want to see the Devourers,' said Morok, 'why not go and howl round the factory of the miscreant atheists ? At the first howl of the Wolves they will come out, and give you battle.'

' They will give you—battle,' repeated Sleepinbuff, mechanically.

' Unless the Wolves are afraid of the Devourers,' added Morok.

' Since you talk of fear, you shall go with us, and see who's afraid !' cried the formidable blaster, in a thundering voice, as he advanced towards Morok.——A number of voices joined in with, ' Who says the Wolves are afraid of the Devourers ?'——' It would be the first time !'

' Battle ! battle ! and make an end of it !'——' We are tired of all this. Why should we be so miserable, and they so well off ?'

' They have said that quarrymen are brutes, only fit to turn wheels in a shaft, like dogs to turn spits,' cried an emissary of Baron Tripeaud's.

' And that the Devourers would make themselves caps with wolf-skin,' added another.

' Neither they nor their wives ever go to mass. They are pagans and dogs !' cried an emissary of the preaching abbé.——' The men might keep their Sunday as they pleased ; but their wives not to go to mass !—it is abominable.'

' And, therefore, the curate has said that their factory, because of its abominations, might bring down the cholera on the country.'——' True ! he said that in his sermon.'——' Our wives heard it.'——' Yes, yes ; down with the Devourers, who want to bring the cholera on the country !'

' Hooray, for a fight !' cried the crowd in chorus.——' To the factory, my brave Wolves !' cried Morok, with the voice of a Stentor ; ' on to the factory !'

' Yes ! to the factory ! to the factory !' repeated the crowd, with furious stamping ; for, little by little, all who could force their way into the room, or up the stairs, had there collected together.

These furious cries recalling Jacques for a moment to his senses, he whispered to Morok : ' It is slaughter you would provoke ? I wash my hands of it.'

' We shall have time to let them know at the factory. We can give these fellows the slip on the road,' answered Morok. Then he cried aloud, addressing the host, who was terrified at this disorder : ' Brandy !—let us drink to the health of the brave Wolves ! I will stand treat.' He threw some money to the host, who disappeared, and soon returned with several bottles of brandy, and some glasses.

' What ! glasses ?' cried Morok. ' Do jolly companions, like we are, drink out of glasses ?' So saying, he forced out one of the corks, raised the neck of the bottle to his lips, and, having drunk a deep draught, passed it to the gigantic quarryman,

'That's the thing!' said the latter. 'Here's in honour of the treat!—None but a sneak will refuse, for this stuff will sharpen the Wolves' teeth!

'Here's to your health, mates!' said Morok, distributing the bottles.

'There will be blood at the end of all this,' muttered Sleepinbuff, who, in spite of his intoxication, perceived all the danger of these fatal incitements. Indeed, a large portion of the crowd was already quitting the yard of the public-house, and advancing rapidly towards M. Hardy's factory.

Those of the workmen and inhabitants of the village, who had not chosen to take any part in this movement of hostility (they were the majority), did not make their appearance, as this threatening troop passed along the principal street; but a good number of women, excited to fanaticism by the sermons of the abbé, encouraged the warlike assemblage with their cries. At the head of the troop advanced the gigantic blaster, brandishing his formidable bar, followed by a motley mass, armed with sticks and stones. Their heads still warmed by their recent libations of brandy, they had now attained a frightful state of frenzy. Their countenances were ferocious, inflamed, terrible. This unchaining of the worst passions seemed to forbode the most deplorable consequences. Holding each other arm-in-arm, and walking four or five together, the Wolves gave vent to their excitement in war-songs, which closed with the following verse:

> 'Forward! full of assurance!
> Let us try our vigorous arms!
> They have wearied out our prudence;
> Let us show we've no alarms.
> Sprung from a monarch glorious,[*]
> To-day we'll not grow pale,
> Whether we win the fight, or fail,
> Whether we die, or are victorious!
> Children of Solomon, mighty king,
> All your efforts together bring,
> Till in triumph we shall sing!'

Morok and Jacques had disappeared whilst the tumultuous troop were leaving the tavern to hasten to the factory.

CHAPTER L.

THE COMMON DWELLING-HOUSE.

WHILST the Wolves, as we have just seen, prepared a savage attack on the Devourers, the factory of M. Hardy had that morning a festal air, perfectly in accordance with the serenity of the sky; for the wind was from the north, and pretty sharp for a fine day in March. The clock had just struck nine in the Common Dwelling-house of the workmen, separated from the workshops by a broad path planted with trees. The rising sun bathed in light this imposing mass of buildings, situated a league from Paris, in a gay and salubrious locality, from which were visible the woody and picturesque hills, that on this side overlook the great city. Nothing could be plainer, and yet more cheerful than the aspect of the Common Dwelling-house of the workmen. Its slanting roof of red tiles projected over white walls, divided here and there by broad rows of bricks, which contrasted agreeably with the green colour of the blinds on the first and second stories.

[*] The Wolves (among others) ascribe the institution of their company to King Solomon. See the curious work by M. Agricole Perdignier, from which the war-song is extracted.

These buildings, open to the south and east, were surrounded by a large garden of about ten acres, partly planted with trees, and partly laid out in fruit and kitchen-garden. Before continuing this description, which perhaps will appear a little like a fairy-tale, let us begin by saying, that the wonders, of which we are about to present the sketch, must not be considered Utopian dreams ; nothing, on the contrary, could be of a more positive character, and we are able to assert, and even to prove (what in our time is of great weight and interest), that these wonders were the result of an excellent speculation, and represented an investment as lucrative as it was secure. To undertake a vast, noble, and most useful enterprise ; to bestow on a considerable number of human creatures an ideal prosperity, compared with the frightful, almost homicidal doom, to which they are generally condemned ; to instruct them, and elevate them in their own esteem ; to make them prefer to the coarse pleasures of the tavern, or rather to the fatal oblivion which they find there, as an escape from the consciousness of their deplorable destiny, the pleasures of the intellect and the enjoyments of art ; in a word, to make men moral by making them happy ; and finally, thanks to this generous example, so easy of imitation, to take a place amongst the benefactors of humanity—and yet, at the same time, to do, as it were, without knowing it, an excellent stroke of business— may appear fabulous. And yet this was the secret of the wonders of which we speak.

Let us enter the interior of the factory. Ignorant of Mother Bunch's cruel disappearance, Agricola gave himself up to the most happy thoughts as he recalled Angela's image, and, having finished dressing with unusual care, went in search of his betrothed.

Let us say two words on the subject of the lodging, which the smith occupied in the Common Dwelling-house, at the incredibly low rate of seventy-five francs per annum, like the other bachelors on the establishment. This lodging, situated on the second story, was comprised of a capital chamber and bedroom, with a southern aspect, and looking on the garden ; the pine floor was perfectly white and clean ; the iron bedstead was supplied with a good mattress and warm coverings : a gas-burner and a warm-air pipe were also introduced into the rooms, to furnish light and heat as required ; the walls were hung with pretty fancy papering, and had curtains to match ; a chest of drawers, a walnut table, a few chairs, a small library, comprised Agricola's furniture. Finally, in the large and light closet, was a place for his clothes, a dressing-table, and large zinc basin, with an ample supply of water. If we compare this agreeable, salubrious, comfortable lodging, with the dark, icy, dilapidated garret, for which the worthy fellow paid ninety francs at his mother's, and to get to which he had more than a league and a half to go every evening, we shall understand the sacrifice he made to his affection for that excellent woman.

Agricola, after casting a last glance of tolerable satisfaction at his looking-glass, while he combed his moustache and imperial, quitted his chamber, to go and join Angela in the women's workroom. The corridor, along which he had to pass, was broad, well-lighted from above, floored with pine, and extremely clean. Notwithstanding some seeds of discord which had been lately sown by M. Hardy's enemies amongst his workmen, until now so fraternally united, joyous songs were heard in almost all the apartments which skirted the corridor, and, as Agricola passed before several open doors, he exchanged a cordial good-morrow with many of his comrades. The smith hastily descended the stairs, crossed the court-yard, in which was a grass-plot planted with trees, with a fountain in the centre, and gained the other wing of the building. There was the work-room, in which a portion of the wives and daughters of the associated artisans, who happened not to be employed in the factory, occupied themselves in making up the linen. This labour, joined to the enormous saving effected by the purchase of the materials wholesale, reduced to an incredible extent the price of each article. After passing through this workroom, a vast apartment looking on the garden, well-aired in summer,* and well-warmed in winter, Agricola knocked at the door of the rooms occupied by Angela's mother.

If we say a few words with regard to this lodging, situated on the first story, with an eastern aspect, and also looking on the garden, it is that we may take it as a specimen of the habitation of a family in this association, supplied at the incredibly small price of one hundred and twenty-five francs per annum.

A small entrance, opening on the corridor, led to a large room, on each side of which was a smaller chamber, destined for the family, when the boys and girls were too big to continue to sleep in the two dormitories, arranged after the fashion of a large school, and reserved for the children of both sexes. Every night, the superintendence of these dormitories was entrusted to a father and mother of a family, belonging to the association. The lodging of which we speak, being, like all the others, disencumbered of the paraphernalia of a kitchen—for the cooking was done in common, and on a large scale, in another part of the building—was kept extremely clean. A pretty large piece of carpet, a comfortable arm-chair, some pretty-looking china on a stand of well-polished wood, some prints hung against the walls, a clock of gilt bronze, a bed, a chest of drawers, and a mahogany secretary, announced that the inhabitants of this apartment enjoyed not only the necessaries, but some of the luxuries of life. Angela, who, from this time, might be called Agricola's betrothed, justified in every point the flattering portrait which the smith had drawn of her in his interview with poor Mother Bunch. The charming girl, seventeen years of age at most, dressed with as much simplicity as neatness, was seated by the side of her mother. When Agricola entered, she blushed slightly at seeing him.

'Mademoiselle,' said Agricola, 'I have come to keep my promise, if your mother has no objection.'

'Certainly, M. Agricola,' answered the mother of the young girl, cordially. 'She would not go over the Common Dwelling-house with her father, her brother, or me, because she wished to have that pleasure with you to-day. It is quite right that you, who can talk so well, should do the honours of the house to the new-comer. She has been waiting for you an hour, and with such impatience !'

'Pray excuse me, mademoiselle,' said Agricola, gaily ; 'in thinking of the pleasure of seeing you, I forgot the hour. That is my only excuse.'

'Oh, mother !' said the young girl, in a tone of mild reproach, and becoming red as a cherry, ' why did you say that ?'

'Is it true, yes or no ? I do not blame you for it ; on the contrary. Go with M. Agricola, child, and he will tell you, better than I can, what all the workmen of the factory owe to M. Hardy.'

'M. Agricola,' said Angela, tying the ribbons of her pretty cap, ' what a pity that your good little adopted sister is not with us.'

'Mother Bunch ?—yes, you are right, mademoiselle ; but that is only a pleasure put off, and the visit she paid us yesterday will not be the last.'

Having embraced her mother, the girl took Agricola's arm, and they went out together.

'Dear me, M. Agricola !' said Angela ; ' if you knew how much I was

* See Adolphe Bobierre ' On Air and Health,' Paris, 1844.

surprised on entering this fine house, after being accustomed to see so much misery amongst the poor workmen in our country, and in which I too have had my share, whilst here everybody seems happy and contented. It is really like fairy-land ; I think I am in a dream, and when I ask my mother the explanation of these wonders, she tells me, " M. Agricola will explain it all to you." '

' Do you know why I am so happy to undertake that delightful task, mademoiselle ?' said Agricola, with an accent at once grave and tender. ' Nothing could be more in season.'

' Why so, M. Agricola ?'——' Because, to show you this house, to make you acquainted with all the resources of our association, is to be able to say to you : " Here, the workman, sure of the present, sure of the future, is not, like so many of his poor brothers, obliged to renounce the sweetest joys of the heart—the desire of choosing a companion for life—in the fear of uniting misery to misery." ' Angela cast down her eyes, and blushed.

' Here the workman may safely yield to the hope of knowing the sweet joys of a family, sure of not having his heart torn hereafter by the sight of the horrible privations of those who are dear to him ; here, thanks to order and industry, and the wise employment of the strength of all, men, women, and children live happy and contented. In a word, to explain all this to you, mademoiselle,' added Agricola, smiling with a still more tender air, ' is to prove, that here we can do nothing more reasonable than love, nothing wiser than marry.'

' M. Agricola,' answered Angela, in a slightly agitated voice, and blushing still more as she spoke, ' suppose we were to begin our walk.'

' Directly, mademoiselle,' replied the smith, pleased at the trouble he had excited in that ingenuous soul. ' But, come ; we are near the dormitory of the little girls. The chirping birds have long left their nests. Let us go there.'

' Willingly, M. Agricola.'

The young smith and Angela soon entered a spacious dormitory, resembling that of a first-rate boarding school. The little iron bedsteads were arranged in symmetrical order ; at each end were the beds of the two mothers of families, who took the superintendence by turns.

' Dear me ! how well it is arranged, M. Agricola ; and how neat and clean ! Who is it that takes such good care of it ?'

' The children themselves ; we have no servants here. There is an extraordinary emulation between these urchins—as to who shall make her bed most neatly, and it amuses them quite as much as making a bed for their dolls. Little girls, you know, delight in playing at keeping house. Well, here they play at it in good earnest, and the house is admirably kept in consequence.'

' Oh ! I understand. They turn to account their natural taste for all such kinds of amusement.'

' That is the whole secret. You will see them everywhere usefully occupied, and delighted at the importance of the employments given them.'

' Oh, M. Agricola !' said Angela, timidly, ' only compare these fine dormitories, so warm and healthy, with the horrible icy garrets, where children are heaped pell-mell on a wretched straw-mattress, shivering with cold, as is the case with almost all the workmen's families in our country !'

' And in Paris, mademoiselle, it is even worse.'

' Oh ! how kind, generous, and rich must M. Hardy be, to spend so much money in doing good !'

' I am going to astonish you, mademoiselle !' said Agricola, with a smile ; ' to astonish you so much, that perhaps you will not believe me.'

' Why so, M. Agricola ?'——' There is not certainly in the world a man with a better and more generous heart that M. Hardy ; he does good for its own sake, and without thinking of his personal interest. And yet, Mdlle. Angela, were he the most selfish and avaricious of men, he would still find it greatly to his advantage to put us in a position to be as comfortable as we are.'

' Is it possible, M. Agricola ? You tell me so, and I believe it ; but if good can so easily be done, if there is even an advantage in doing it, why is it not more commonly attempted ?'——' Ah ! mademoiselle, it requires three gifts very rarely met with in the same person—knowledge, power, and will.'

' Alas ! yes. Those who have the knowledge, have not the power.'

' And those who have the power, have neither the knowledge nor the will.'

' But how does M. Hardy find any advantage in the good he does for you.'

' I will explain that presently, mademoiselle.'

' Oh ! what a nice, sweet smell of fruit !' said Angela, suddenly.——' Our common fruit-store is close at hand. I wager we shall find there some of the little birds from the dormitory—not occupied in picking and stealing, but hard at work.'

Opening a door, Agricola led Angela into a large room, furnished with shelves, on which the winter-fruits were arranged in order. A number of children, from seven to eight years old, neatly and warmly clad, and glowing with health, exerted themselves cheerfully, under the superintendence of a woman, in separating and sorting the spoilt fruit.

' You see,' said Agricola, ' wherever it is possible, we make use of the children. These occupations are amusements for them, answering to the need of movement and activity natural to their age ; and, in this way, we can employ the grown girls and the women to much better advantage.'

' True, M. Agricola ; how well it is all arranged.'

' And if you saw what services the urchins in the kitchen render ! Directed by one or two women, they do the work of eight or ten servants.'——' In fact,' said Angela, smiling, ' at their age, we like so much to play at cooking dinner. They must be delighted.'

' And, in the same way, under pretext of playing at gardening, they weed the ground, gather the fruit and vegetables, water the flowers, roll the paths, and so on. In a word, this army of infant-workers, who generally remain till ten or twelve years of age without being of any service, are here very useful. Except three hours of school, which is quite sufficient for them, from the age of six or seven their recreations are turned to good account, and the dear little creatures, by the saving of full-grown arms which they effect, actually gain more than they cost ; and then, mademoiselle, do you not think there is something in the presence of childhood thus mixed up with every labour—something mild, pure, almost sacred, which has its influence on our words and actions, and imposes a salutary reserve ? The coarsest man will respect the presence of children.'

' The more one reflects, the more one sees that everything here is really designed for the happiness of all !' said Angela, in admiration.

' It has not been done without trouble. It was necessary to conquer prejudices, and break through customs. But see, Mdlle. Angela ! here we are at the kitchen,' added the smith, smiling ; ' is it not as imposing as that of a barrack or a public school ?'

Indeed, the culinary department of the Common Dwelling-house was immense. All its utensils were bright and clean ; and thanks to the marvellous and economical inventions of modern science (which are always beyond the reach of the poorer classes, to whom they are most necessary, because they can only be practised on a large scale), not only the fire on the hearth, and in the stoves, was fed with half the quantity of fuel that would have been consumed by each family individually, but the excess of the caloric sufficed, with the aid of well-constructed tubes, to spread a mild and equal warmth through all parts of the house. And here also children, under the direction of two women, rendered numerous services. Nothing could be more comic than the serious manner in which they performed their culinary functions ; it was the same with the assistance they gave in the bakehouse, where, at an extraordinary saving in the price (for they bought flour wholesale), they made an excellent household bread, composed of pure wheat and rye, so preferable to that whiter bread, which too often owes its apparent qualities to some deleterious substance.

'Good-day, Dame Bertrand,' said Agricola, gaily, to a worthy matron, who was gravely contemplating the slow evolution of several spits, worthy of Gamache's Wedding, so heavily were they laden with pieces of beef, mutton, and veal, which began to assume a fine golden brown colour of the most attractive kind ; 'good day, Dame Bertrand. According to the rule, I do not pass the threshold of the kitchen. I only wish it to be admired by this young lady, who is a new-comer amongst us.'

'Admire, my lad, pray admire—and above all take notice, how good these brats are, and how well they work !' So saying, the matron pointed with the long ladle, which served her as a sceptre, to some fifteen children of both sexes, seated round a table, and deeply absorbed in the exercise of their functions, which consisted in peeling potatoes and picking herbs.

'We are, I see, to have a downright Belshazzar's feast, Dame Bertrand ?' said Agricola, laughing.

'Faith ! a feast like we have always, my lad. Here is our bill of fare for to-day. A good vegetable soup, roast beef with potatoes, salad, fruit, cheese ; and for extras, it being Sunday, some currant tarts made by Mother Denis at the bakehouse, where the oven is heating now.'

'What you tell me, Dame Bertrand, gives me a furious appetite,' said Agricola, gaily. 'One soon knows when it is *your* turn in the kitchen,' added he, with a flattering air.——'Get along, do !' said the female Soyer on service, merrily.

'What astonishes me so much, M. Agricola,' said Angela, as they continued their walk, 'is the comparison of the insufficient, unwholesome food of the workmen in our country, with that which is provided here.'

'And yet we do not spend more than twenty-five sous a day, for much better food than we should get for three francs in Paris.'

'But really it is hard to believe, M. Agricola. How is it possible ?'

'It is thanks to the magic wand of M. Hardy. I will explain it all presently.'

'Oh ! how impatient I am to see M. Hardy !'——'You will soon see him —perhaps to-day ; for he is expected every moment. But here is the re-fectory, which you do not yet know, as your family, like many others, prefer dining at home. See what a fine room, looking out on the garden, just opposite the fountain !'

It was indeed a vast hall, built in the form of a gallery, with ten windows opening on the garden. Tables, covered with shining oil-cloth, were ranged along the walls, so that, in winter, this apartment served in the evening, after work, as a place of meeting for those who preferred to pass an hour together, instead of remaining alone or with their families. Then, in this large hall, well warmed and brilliantly lighted with gas, some read, some played cards, some talked, and some occupied themselves with easy work.

'That is not all,' said Agricola to the young girl ; 'I am sure you will like this apartment still better when I tell you, that on Thursdays and Sundays we make a ball-room of it, and on Tuesdays and Saturdays a concert-room,'

' Really !'

' Yes,' continued the smith proudly, ' we have amongst us musicians, quite capable of tempting us to dance. Moreover, twice a week, nearly all of us sing in chorus—men, women, and children. Unfortunately, this week, some disputes that have arisen in the factory have prevented our concerts.'

' So many voices ! that must be superb.'

' It is very fine, I assure you. M. Hardy has always encouraged this amusement amongst us, which has, he says—and he is right—so powerful an effect on the mind and the manners. One winter, he sent for two pupils of the celebrated Wilhelm, and, since then, our school has made great progress. I assure you, Mdlle. Angela, that, without flattering ourselves, there is something truly exciting in the sound of two hundred voices, singing in chorus some hymn to Labour or Freedom. You shall hear it, and you will, I think, acknowledge that there is something great and elevating in the heart of man, in this fraternal harmony of voices, blending in one grave, sonorous, imposing sound.'

' Oh ! I believe it. But what happiness to inhabit here. It is a life of joy ; for labour, mixed with recreation, becomes itself a pleasure.'

' Alas ! here, as everywhere, there are tears and sorrows,' replied Agricola, sadly. ' Do you see that isolated building, in a very exposed situation ?'

' Yes ; what is it ?'——' That is our hospital for the sick. Happily, thanks to our healthy mode of life, it is not often full : an annual subscription enables us to have a good doctor. Moreover, a mutual benefit society is arranged in such a manner amongst us, that any one of us, in case of illness, receives two-thirds of what he would have gained in health.'

' How well it is all managed ! And there, M. Agricola, on the other side of the grass-plot ?'——' That is the wash-house, with water laid on, cold and hot ; and under yonder shed is the drying-place : further on, you see the stables, and the lofts and granaries for the provender of the factory horses.'

' But M. Agricola, will you tell me the secret of all these wonders ?'

' In ten minutes, you shall understand it all, mademoiselle.'

Unfortunately, Angela's curiosity was for a while disappointed. The girl was now standing with Agricola close to the iron gate, which shut in the garden from the broad avenue that separated the factory from the Common Dwelling-house. Suddenly, the wind brought from the distance the sound of trumpets and military music ; then was heard the gallop of two horses, approaching rapidly, and soon after a general officer made his appearance, mounted on a fine black charger, with a long flowing tail and crimson housings ; he wore cavalry boots and white breeches, after the fashion of the empire ; his uniform glittered with gold embroidery, the red ribbon of the Legion of Honour was passed over his right epaulet, with its four silver stars, and his hat had a broad gold border, and was crowned with a white plume, the distinctive sign reserved for the marshals of France. No warrior could have had a more martial and chivalrous air, or have sat more proudly on his war-horse. At the moment Marshal Simon (for it was he) arrived opposite the place where Angela and Agricola were standing, he drew up his horse suddenly, sprang lightly to the ground, and threw the golden reins to a servant in livery, who followed also on horseback.

' Where shall I wait for your grace ?' asked the groom.——' At the end of the avenue,' said the marshal.

And, uncovering his head respectfully, he advanced hastily with his hat in his hand, to meet a person whom Angela and Agricola had not previously perceived. This person soon appeared at a turn of the avenue ; he was an old man, with an energetic, intelligent countenance. He wore a very neat blouse, and a cloth cap over his long, white hair. With his hands in his pockets, he was quietly smoking an old meerschaum pipe.

'Good morning, father,' said the marshal, respectfully, as he affectionately embraced the old workman, who, having tenderly returned the pressure, said to him : 'Put on your hat, my boy. But how gay we are !' added he, with a smile.

'I have just been to a review, father, close by ; and I took the opportunity to call on you as soon as possible.'

'But shall I then not see my grand-daughters to-day, as I do every Sunday ?'——'They are coming in a carriage, father, and Dagobert accompanies them.'

'But what is the matter ? you appear full of thought.'——'Indeed, father,' said the marshal, with a somewhat agitated air, 'I have serious things to talk about.'

'Come in, then,' said the old man, with some anxiety. The marshal and his father disappeared at the turn of the avenue.

Angela had been struck with amazement at seeing this brilliant General, who was entitled 'your grace,' salute an old workman in a blouse as his father ; and, looking at Agricola with a confused air, she said to him : 'What, M. Agricola ! this old workman ——'

'Is the father of Marshal Duke de Ligny—the friend—yes, I may say the friend,' added Agricola, with emotion, 'of my father, who for twenty years served under him in war.'

'To be placed so high, and yet to be so respectful and tender to his father !' said Angela. 'The marshal must have a very noble heart ; but why does he let his father remain a workman ?'

'Because Father Simon will not quit his trade and the factory for anything in the world. He was born a workman, and he will die a workman, though he is the father of a duke and marshal of France.'

————

CHAPTER LI.

THE SECRET.

When the very natural astonishment which the arrival of Marshal Simon had caused in Angela had passed away, Agricola said to her with a smile : 'I do not wish to take advantage of this circumstance, Mdlle. Angela, to spare you the account of the secret, by which all the wonders of our Common Dwelling-house are brought to pass.'

'Oh ! I should not have let you forget your promise, M. Agricola,' answered Angela, 'what you have already told me interests me too much for that.'

'Listen, then. M. Hardy, like a true magician, has pronounced three cabalistic words : ASSOCIATION—COMMUNITY—FRATERNITY. We have understood the sense of these words, and the wonders you have seen have sprung from them, to our great advantage ; and also, I repeat, to the great advantage of M. Hardy.'

'It is that which appears so extraordinary, M. Agricola.'

'Suppose, mademoiselle, that M. Hardy, instead of being what he is, had only been a cold-hearted speculator, looking merely to the profit, and saying to himself : "To make the most of my factory, what is needed? Good work—great economy in the raw material—full employment of the workman's time ; in a word, cheapness of manufacture, in order to produce cheaply—excellence of the thing produced, in order to sell dear."'

'Truly, M. Agricola, no manufacturer could desire more.'

'Well, mademoiselle, these conditions might have been fulfilled, as they have been, but how ? Had M. Hardy only been a speculator, he might have said : "At a distance from my factory, my workmen might have trouble to get there ; rising earlier, they will sleep less ; it is a bad economy to take from the sleep so necessary to those who toil. When they get feeble, the work suffers for it ; then the inclemency of the seasons makes its worse ; the workman arrives wet, trembling with cold, enervated before he begins to work—and then, what work !"'

'It is unfortunately but too true, M. Agricola. At Lille, when I reacned the factory, wet through with a cold rain, I used sometimes to shiver all day long at my work.'

'Therefore, Mdlle. Angela, the speculator might say : "To lodge my workmen close to the door of my factory would obviate this inconvenience. Let us make the calculation. In Paris, the married workman pays about two hundred and fifty francs a-year,* for one or two wretched rooms and a closet, dark, small, unhealthy, in a narrow, miserable street ; there he lives pell-mell with his family. What ruined constitutions are the consequence ! and what sort of work can you expect from a feverish and diseased creature ? As for the single men, they pay for a smaller, and quite as unwholesome lodging, about one hundred and fifty francs a-year. Now, let us make the addition. I employ one hundred and forty-six married workmen, who pay together, for their wretched holes, thirty-six thousand five hundred francs ; I employ also one hundred and fifteen bachelors, who pay at the rate of seventeen thousand two hundred and eighty francs ; the total will amount to about fifty thousand francs per annum, the interest on a million "'

'Dear me, M. Agricola ! what a sum to be produced by uniting all these little rents together !'

'You see, mademoiselle, that fifty thousand francs a-year is a millionaire's rent. Now, what says our speculator : "To induce our workmen to leave Paris, I will offer them enormous advantages. I will reduce their rent one-half, and, instead of small, unwholesome rooms, they shall have large, airy apartments, well-warmed and lighted, at a trifling charge Thus, one hundred and forty-six families, paying me only one hundred and twenty-five francs a-year, and one hundred and fifteen bachelors, seventy-five francs, I shall have a total of twenty-six to twenty-seven thousand francs. Now, a building large enough to hold all these people would cost me at most five hundred thousand francs.† I shall then have invested my money at five per cent. at the least, and with perfect security, since the wages is a guarantee for the payment of the rent."'

"Ah, M. Agricola ! I begin to understand how it may sometimes be advantageous to do good, even in a pecuniary sense.'

'And I am almost certain, mademoiselle, that, in the long run, affairs conducted with uprightness and honesty turn out well. But to return to our speculator. "Here," will he say, "are my workmen, living close to my factory, well lodged, well warmed, and arriving always fresh at their work. That is not all ; the English workman who eats good beef, and drinks good

---

* The average price of a workman's lodging, composed of two small rooms and a closet at most, on the third or fourth story.

† This calculation is amply sufficient, if not excessive. A similar building, at one league from Paris, on the side of Montrouge, with all the necessary offices, kitchen, wash-houses, etc., with gas and water laid on, apparatus for warming, etc., and a garden of ten acres, cost, at the period of this narrative, hardly five hundred thousand francs. An experienced builder has obliged us with an estimate, which confirms what we advance. It is, therefore, evident, that, even at the same price which workmen are in the habit of paying, it would be possible to provide them with perfectly healthy lodgings, and yet invest one's money at ten per cent.

beer, does twice as much, in the same time, as the French workman,* reduced to a detestable kind of food, rather weakening than the reverse, thanks
to the poisonous adulteration of the articles he consumes. My workmen
will then labour much better, if they eat much better. How shall I manage
it without loss? Now I think of it, what is the food in barracks, schools,
even prisons? Is it not the union of individual resources which procures
an amount of comfort impossible to realise without such an association?
Now, if my two hundred and sixty workmen, instead of cooking two hundred and sixty detestable dinners, were to unite to prepare one good dinner
for all of them, which might be done, thanks to the savings of all sorts that
would ensue, what an advantage for me and them! Two or three women,
aided by children, would suffice to make ready the daily repasts; instead
of buying wood and charcoal in fractions,† and so paying for it double its
value, the association of my workmen would, upon my security (their wages
would be a sufficient security for me in return), lay in their own stock of
wood, flour, butter, oil, wine, etc., all which they would procure directly
from the producers. Thus, they would pay three or four sous for a bottle
of pure, wholesome wine, instead of paying twelve or fifteen sous for poison.
Every week the association would buy a whole ox, and some sheep, and
the women would make bread, as in the country. Finally, with these resources, and order, and economy, my workmen may have wholesome,
agreeable, and sufficient food, for from twenty to twenty-five sous a day." '

'Ah! this explains it, M. Agricola.'

'It is not all, mademoiselle. Our cool-headed speculator would continue:
"Here are my workmen well lodged, well warmed, well fed, with a saving
of at least half: why should they not also be warmly clad? Their health
will then have every chance of being good, and health is labour. The association will buy wholesale, and at the manufacturing price (still upon my
security, secured to me by their wages), warm, good, strong materials, which
a portion of the workmen's wives will be able to make into clothes as well
as any tailor. Finally, the consumption of caps and shoes being considerable, the association will obtain them at a great reduction in price." Well,
Mdlle. Angela! what do you say to our speculator?'

'I say, M. Agricola,' answered the young girl, with ingenuous admiration, 'that it is almost incredible, and yet so simple!'

'No doubt, nothing is more simple than the good and beautiful, and yet
we think of it so seldom. Observe, that our man has only been speaking
with a view to his own interest—only considering the material side of the
question—reckoning for nothing the habit of fraternity and mutual aid,
which inevitably springs from living together in common—not reflecting that
a better mode of life improves and softens the character of man—not thinking of the support and instruction which the strong owe to the weak—not
acknowledging, in fine, that the honest, active, and industrious man has a
positive right to demand employment from society, and wages proportionate
to the wants of his condition. No, our speculator only thinks of the gross
profits; and yet, you see, he invests his money in buildings at five per cent.,
and finds the greatest advantages in the material comfort of his workmen.'

'It is true, M. Agricola.'

'And what will you say, mademoiselle, when I prove to you that our

---

* The fact was proved in the works connected with the Rouen Railway. Those
French workmen who, having no families, were able to live like the English, did
at least as much work as the latter, being strengthened by wholesome and sufficient
nourishment.

† Buying pennyworths, like all other purchases at minute retail, are greatly to the
poor man's disadvantage.

speculator finds also a great advantage in giving to his workmen, in addition to their regular wages, a proportionate share of his profits?'

'That appears to me more difficult to prove, M. Agricola.'

'Yet I will convince you of it in a few minutes.'

Thus conversing, Angela and Agricola had reached the garden-gate of the Common Dwelling-house. An elderly woman, dressed plainly, but with care and neatness, approached Agricola, and asked him : 'Has M. Hardy returned to the factory, sir?'——'No, madame ; but we expect him hourly.'

'To-day, perhaps?'——'To-day or to-morrow, madame.'

'You cannot tell me at what hour he will be here?'——'I do not think it is known, madame, but the porter of the factory, who also belongs to M. Hardy's private house, may, perhaps, be able to inform you.'

'I thank you, sir.'——'Quite welcome, madame.'

'M. Agricola,' said Angela, when the woman who had just questioned him was gone, 'did you remark that this lady was very pale and agitated?'

'I noticed it as you did, mademoiselle ; I thought I saw tears standing in her eyes.'——'Yes, she seemed to have been crying. Poor woman ! perhaps she came to ask assistance of M. Hardy. But what ails you, M. Agricola? You appear quite pensive.'

Agricola had a vague presentiment that the visit of this elderly woman, with so sad a countenance, had some connection with the adventure of the young and pretty lady, who, three days before, had come all agitated and in tears to inquire after M. Hardy, and who had learned—perhaps too late—that she was watched and followed.

'Forgive me, mademoiselle,' said Agricola to Angela ; 'but the presence of this old lady reminded me of a circumstance, which, unfortunately, I cannot tell you, for it is a secret that does not belong to me alone.'

'Oh ! do not trouble yourself, M. Agricola,' answered the young girl, with a smile ; 'I am not inquisitive, and what we were talking of before interests me so much, that I do not wish to hear you speak of anything else.'

'Well, then, mademoiselle, I will say a few words more, and you will be as well informed as I am of the secrets of our association.'

'I am listening, M. Agricola.'

'Let us still keep in view the speculator from mere interest. "Here are my workmen," says he, "in the best possible condition to do a great deal of work. Now, what is to be done to obtain large profits ? Produce cheaply, and sell dear. But there will be no cheapness, without economy in the use of the raw material, perfection of the manufacturing process, and celerity of labour. Now, in spite of all my vigilance, how am I to prevent my workmen from wasting the materials ? How am I to induce them, each in his own province, to seek for the most simple and least irksome processes?"'

'True, M. Agricola ; how is that to be done?'——'"And that is not all," says our man ; "to sell my produce at high prices, it should be irreproachable, excellent. My workmen do pretty well ; but that is not enough. I want them to produce masterpieces."'——'But, M. Agricola, when they have once performed the task set them, what interest have workmen to give themselves a great deal of trouble to produce masterpieces?'

'There it is, Mdlle. Angela ; WHAT INTEREST have they? Therefore, our speculator soon says to himself : "That my workmen may have an *interest* to be economical in the use of the materials, an interest to employ their time well, an interest to invent new and better manufacturing processes, an interest to send out of their hands nothing but masterpieces—I must give them an interest in the profits earned by their economy, activity, zeal, and skill. The better they manufacture, the better I shall sell, and the larger will be their gain, and mine also."'

'Oh ! now I understand, M. Agricola.'

'And our speculator would make a good speculation. Before he was interested, the workman said : "What does it matter to me, that I do more or better in the course of the day ? What shall I gain by it ? Nothing. Well, then, little work for little wages. But now, on the contrary (he says), I have an interest in displaying zeal and economy. All is changed. I redouble my activity, and strive to excel the others. If a comrade is lazy, and likely to do harm to the factory, I have the right to say to him : ' Mate, we all suffer more or less from your laziness, and from the injury you are doing the common-weal.' "'——' And then, M. Agricola, with what ardour, courage, and hope, you must set to work !'

'That is what our speculator counts on ; and he may say to himself, further : " Treasures of experience and practical wisdom are often buried in workshops, for want of good-will, opportunity, or encouragement. Excellent workmen, instead of making all the improvements in their power, follow with indifference the old jog-trot. What a pity ! for an intelligent man, occupied all his life with some special employment, must discover, in the long run, a thousand ways of doing his work better and quicker. I will form, therefore, a sort of consulting committee ; I will summon to it my foremen and my most skilful workmen. Our interest is now the same. Light will necessarily spring from this centre of practical intelligence." Now, the speculator is not deceived in this, and soon struck with the incredible resources, the thousand new, ingenious, perfect inventions suddenly revealed by his workmen, " Why," he exclaims, " if you knew this, did you not tell it before ? What for the last ten years has cost me a hundred francs to make, would have cost me only fifty, without reckoning an enormous saving of time."—" Sir," answers the workman, who is not more stupid than others, " what interest had I, that you should effect a saving of fifty per cent. ? None. But now it is different. You give me, besides my wages, a share in your profits : you raise me in my own esteem, by consulting my experience and knowledge. Instead of treating me as an inferior being, you enter into communion with me. It is my interest, it is my duty, to tell you all I know, and to try to acquire more." And thus it is, Mdlle. Angela, that the speculator can organise his establishment, so as to shame his oppositionists, and provoke their envy. Now if, instead of a cold-hearted calculator, we take a man who unites with the knowledge of these facts the tender and generous sympathies of an evangelical heart, and the elevation of a superior mind, he will extend his ardent solicitude, not only to the material comfort, but to the moral emancipation, of his workmen. Seeking everywhere every possible means to develop their intelligence, to improve their hearts, and strong in the authority acquired by his beneficence, feelii g that he on whom depends the happiness or the misery of three hundred human creatures has also the care of souls, he will be the guide of those whom he no longer calls his workmen, but his brothers, in a straightforward and noble path, and will try to create in them the taste for knowledge and art, which will render them happy and proud of a condition of life, that is often accepted by others with tears and curses of despair. Well, Mdlle. Angela, such a man is——but, see ! he could not arrive amongst us except in the middle of a blessing. There he is—there is M. Hardy !'

'Oh, M. Agricola !' said Angela, deeply moved, and drying her tears ; 'we should receive him with our hands clasped in gratitude.'——'Look if that mild and noble countenance is not the image of his admirable soul !'

A carriage with post-horses, in which was M. Hardy, with M. de Blessac, the unworthy friend who was betraying him in so infamous a manner, entered at this moment the courtyard of the factory.

A little while after, a humble hackney-coach was seen advancing also towards the factory, from the direction of Paris. In this coach was Rodin.

CHAPTER LII.

REVELATIONS.

DURING the visit of Angela and Agricola to the Common Dwelling-house, the band of Wolves, joined upon the road by many of the haunters of taverns, continued to march towards the factory, which the hackney-coach, that brought Rodin from Paris, was also fast approaching. M. Hardy, on getting out of the carriage with his friend M. de Blessac, had entered the parlour of the house that he occupied next the factory. M. Hardy was of middle size, with an elegant and slight figure, which announced a nature essentially nervous and impressionable. His forehead was broad and open, his complexion pale, his eyes black, full at once of mildness and penetration, his countenance honest, intelligent, and attractive.

One word will paint the character of M. Hardy. His mother had called him her Sensitive Plant. His was indeed one of those fine and exquisitely delicate organisations, which are trusting, loving, noble, generous, but so susceptible, that the least touch makes them shrink into themselves. If we join to this excessive sensibility a passionate love for art, a first-rate intellect, tastes essentially refined, and then think of the thousand deceptions and numberless infamies of which M. Hardy must have been the victim in his career as a manufacturer, we shall wonder how this heart, so delicate and tender, had not been broken a thousand times, in its incessant struggle with merciless self-interest. M. Hardy had indeed suffered much. Forced to follow the career of productive industry, to honour the engagements of his father, a model of uprightness and probity, who had yet left his affairs somewhat embarrassed, in consequence of the events of 1815, he had succeeded, by perseverance and capacity, in attaining one of the most honourable positions in the commercial world. But, to arrive at this point, what ignoble annoyances had he to bear with, what perfidious opposition to combat, what hateful rivalries to tire out !

Sensitive as he was, M. Hardy would a thousand times have fallen a victim to his emotions of painful indignation against baseness, of bitter disgust at dishonesty, but for the wise and firm support of his mother. When he returned to her, after a day of painful struggles with odious deceptions, he found himself suddenly transported into an atmosphere of such beneficent purity, of such radiant serenity, that he lost almost on the instant the remembrance of the base things by which he had been so cruelly tortured during the day ; the pangs of his heart were appeased at the mere contact of her great and lofty soul ; and therefore his love for her resembled idolatry. When he lost her, he experienced one of those calm, deep sorrows, which have no end—which become, as it were, part of life, and have even sometimes their days of melancholy sweetness. A little while after this great misfortune, M. Hardy became more closely connected with his workmen. He had always been a just and good master ; but, although the place that his mother left in his heart would ever remain void, he felt as it were a redoubled overflowing of the affections, and the more he suffered, the more he craved to see happy faces around him. The wonderful ameliorations, which he now produced in the physical and moral condition of all about him, served, not to divert, but to occupy his grief. Little by little, he withdrew from the world, and concentrated his life in three affections : a tender and devoted friendship, which seemed to include all past friendships—a love ardent and sincere, like a last passion—and a paternal attachment to his workmen. His days therefore passed in the heart of that little world, so full of respect and gratitude towards him—a world, which he had, as it were, created after the image of his mind, that he might find there a refuge from the painful realities he dreaded, surrounded with good, intelligent, happy beings, capable of responding to the noble thoughts which had become more and more necessary to his existence. Thus, after many sorrows, M. Hardy, arrived at the maturity of age, possessing a sincere friend, a mistress worthy of his love, and knowing himself certain of the passionate devotion of his workmen, had attained, at the period of this history, all the happiness he could hope for since his mother's death.

    ❉   ❉   ❉   ❉   ❉   ❉

M. de Blessac, his bosom friend, had long been worthy of his touching and fraternal affection ; but we have seen by what diabolical means Father d'Aigrigny and Rodin had succeeded in making M. de Blessac, until then upright and sincere, the instrument of their machinations. The two friends, who had felt on their journey a little of the sharp influence of the north wind, were warming themselves at a good fire lighted in M. Hardy's parlour.

'Oh ! my dear Marcel, I begin really to get old,' said M. Hardy, with a smile, addressing M. de Blessac ; 'I feel more and more the want of being at home. To depart from my usual habits has become painful to me, and I execrate whatever obliges me to leave this happy little spot of ground.'

'And when I think,' answered M. de Blessac, unable to forbear blushing, 'when I think, my friend, that you undertook this long journey only for my sake !——'

'Well, my dear Marcel ! have you not just accompanied me in your turn, in an excursion which, without you, would have been as tiresome as it has been charming ?'

'What a difference, my friend ! I have contracted towards you a debt that I can never repay.'

'Nonsense, my dear Marcel ! Between us, there are no distinctions of meum and tuum. Besides, in matters of friendship, it is as sweet to give as to receive.'——'Noble heart ! noble heart !'

'Say, happy heart !—most happy, in the last affections for which it beats.'

'And who, gracious heaven ! could deserve happiness on earth, if it be not you, my friend ?'

'And to what do I owe that happiness ? To the affections which I found here, ready to sustain me, when, deprived of the support of my mother, who was all my strength, I felt myself (I confess my weakness) almost incapable of standing up against adversity.'

'You, my friend—with so firm and resolute a character in doing good— you, that I have seen struggle with so much energy and courage, to secure the triumph of some great and noble idea ?'

'Yes ; but the farther I advance in my career, the more am I disgusted with all base and shameful actions, and the less strength I feel to encounter them.'——'Were it necessary, you would have the courage, my friend.'

'My dear Marcel,' replied M. Hardy, with mild and restrained emotion, 'I have often said to you : My courage was my mother. You see, my friend, when I went to her, with my heart torn by some horrible ingratitude, or disgusted by some base deceit, she, taking my hands between her own venerable palms, would say to me in her grave and tender voice : " My dear child, it is for the ungrateful and dishonest to suffer ; let us pity the wicked, let us forget evil, and only think of good."—Then, my friend, this heart, painfully contracted, expanded beneath the sacred influence of the maternal words, and every day I gathered strength from her, to recommence on the morrow a cruel struggle with the sad necessities of my condition. Happily, it has pleased God, that, after losing that beloved mother, I have been able to bind up my life with affections, deprived of which, I confess, I should find myself feeble and disarmed—for you cannot tell, Marcel, the support, the strength that I have found in your friendship.'

' Do not speak of me, my dear friend,' replied M. de Blessac, dissembling his embarrassment. ' Let us talk of another affection, almost as sweet and tender as that of a mother.'

' I understand you, my good Marcel,' replied M. Hardy ; ' I have concealed nothing from you, since, under such serious circumstances, I had recourse to the counsels of your friendship. Well ! yes ; I think that every day I live augments my adoration for this woman, the only one that I have ever passionately loved, the only one that I shall now ever love. And then I must tell you, that my mother, not knowing what Margaret was to me, was often loud in her praise, and that circumstance renders this love almost sacred in my eyes.'

' And then there are such strange resemblances between Mme. de Noisy's character and yours, my friend ; above all, in her worship of her mother.'

' It is true, Marcel ; that affection has often caused me both admiration and torment. How often she has said to me, with her habitual frankness : " I have sacrificed all for you, but I would sacrifice you for my mother." '

' Thank Heaven, my friend, you will never see Mme. de Noisy exposed to that cruel choice. Her mother, you say, has long renounced her intention of returning to America, where M. de Noisy, perfectly careless of his wife, appears to have settled himself permanently. Thanks to the discreet devotion of the excellent woman by whom Margaret was brought up, your love is concealed in the deepest mystery. What could disturb it now ?'

' Nothing—oh ! nothing,' cried M. Hardy. ' I have almost security for its duration.'

' What do you mean, my friend ?'——' I do not know if I ought to tell you.'

' Have you ever found me indiscreet, my friend ?'——' You, good Marcel ! how can you suppose such a thing ?' said M. Hardy, in a tone of friendly reproach ; ' no ! but I do not like to tell you of my happiness, till it is complete ; and I am not yet quite certain——'

A servant entered at this moment and said to M. Hardy : ' Sir, there is an old gentleman who wishes to speak to you on very pressing business.'

' So soon !' said M. Hardy, with a slight movement of impatience. ' With your permission, my friend.' Then, as M. de Blessac seemed about to withdraw into the next room, M. Hardy added with a smile : ' No, no ; do not stir. Your presence will shorten the interview.'

' But if it be a matter of business, my friend ?'——' I do everything openly, as you know.' Then, addressing the servant, M. Hardy bade him : ' Ask the gentleman to walk in.'

' The postilion wishes to know if he is to wait ?'——' Certainly : he will take M. de Blessac back to Paris.'

The servant withdrew, and presently returned, introducing Rodin, with with whom M. de Blessac was not acquainted, his treacherous bargain having been negotiated through another agent.

' M. Hardy?' said Rodin, bowing respectfully to the two friends, and looking from one to the other with an air of inquiry.

' That is my name, sir ; what can I do to serve you ?' answered the manufacturer, kindly ; for, at first sight of the humble and ill-dressed old man, he expected an application for assistance.

' M. François Hardy,' repeated Rodin, as if he wished to make sure of the identity of the person.——' I have had the honour to tell you, that I am he.'

'I have a private communication to make to you, sir,' said Rodin.

'You may speak, sir. This gentleman is my friend,' said M. Hardy, pointing to M. de Blessac.

'But I wish to speak to you alone, sir,' resumed Rodin.

M. de Blessac was again about to withdraw, when M. Hardy retained him with a glance, and said to Rodin kindly, for he thought his feelings might be hurt by asking a favour in presence of a third party : 'Permit me to inquire if it is on your account or on mine, that you wish this interview to be secret ?'

'On your account entirely, sir,' answered Rodin.

'Then, sir,' said M. Hardy, with some surprise, 'you may speak out. I have no secrets from this gentleman.'

After a moment's silence, Rodin resumed, addressing himself to M. Hardy : 'Sir, you deserve, I know, all the good that is said of you ; and you therefore command the sympathy of every honest man.'

'I hope so, sir.'

'Now, as an honest man, I come to render you a service.'

'And this service, sir——'

'To reveal to you an infamous piece of treachery, of which you have been the victim.'——'I think, sir, you must be deceived.'

'I have the proofs of what I assert.'——'Proofs ?'

'The written proofs of the treachery that I come to reveal : I have them here,' answered Rodin. 'In a word, a man whom you believed your friend, has shamefully deceived you, sir.'

'And the name of this man ?'——'M. Marcel de Blessac,' replied Rodin.

On these words, M. de Blessac started, and became pale as death. He could hardly murmur : 'Sir——'

But, without looking at his friend, or perceiving his agitation, M. Hardy seized his hand, and exclaimed hastily : 'Silence, my friend !' Then, whilst his eye flashed with indignation, he turned towards Rodin, who had not ceased to look him full in the face, and said to him, with an air of lofty disdain : 'What ! do you accuse M. de Blessac ?'——'Yes, I accuse him,' replied Rodin, briefly.

'Do you know him ?'——'I have never seen him.'

'Of what do you accuse him ? And how dare you say that he has betrayed me ?'

'Two words, if you please,' said Rodin, with an emotion which he appeared hardly able to restrain. 'If one man of honour sees another about to be slain by an assassin, ought he not give the alarm of murder ?'

'Yes, sir ; but what has that to do——'

'In my eyes, sir, certain treasons are as criminal as murders : I have come to place myself between the assassin and his victim.'

'The assassin ? the victim ?' said M. Hardy, more and more astonished.

'You doubtless know M. de Blessac's writing ?' said Rodin.——'Yes, sir.'

'Then read this,' said Rodin, drawing from his pocket a letter, which he handed to M. Hardy.

Casting now for the first time a glance at M. de Blessac, the manufac-·turer drew back a step, terrified at the deathlike paleness of this man, who, struck dumb with shame, could not find a word to justify himself ; for he was far from possessing the audacious effrontery necessary to carry him through his treachery.

'Marcel !' cried M. Hardy, in alarm, and deeply agitated by this unexpected blow. 'Marcel ! how pale you are ! you do not answer !'

'Marcel ! this, then, is M. de Blessac ?' cried Rodin, feigning the most painful surprise. 'Oh, sir, if I had known——'

'But don't you hear this man, Marcel?' cried M. Hardy. 'He says that you have betrayed me infamously.' He seized the hand of M. de Blessac. That hand was cold as ice. 'Oh, God! Oh, God!' said M. Hardy, drawing back in horror: 'he makes no answer!'

'Since I am in presence of M. de Blessac,' resumed Rodin, 'I am forced to ask him, if he can deny having addressed many letters to the Rue du Milieu des Ursins, at Paris, under cover of M. Rodin.'

M. de Blessac remained dumb. M. Hardy, still unwilling to believe what he saw and heard, convulsively tore open the letter, which Rodin had just delivered to him, and read the first few lines—interrupting the perusal with exclamations of grief and amazement. He did not require to finish the letter, to convince himself of the black treachery of M. de Blessac. He staggered; for a moment his senses seemed to abandon him. The horrible discovery made him giddy, and his head swam on his first look down into that abyss of infamy. The loathsome letter dropped from his trembling hands. But soon indignation, rage, and scorn succeeded this moment of despair, and rushing, pale and terrible, upon M. de Blessac: 'Wretch!' he exclaimed, with a threatening gesture. But, pausing as in the act to strike: 'No!' he added, with fearful calmness. 'It would be to soil my hand.'

He turned towards Rodin, who had approached hastily, as if to interpose. 'It is not worth while chastising a wretch,' said M. Hardy; 'but I will press your honest hand, sir—for you have had the courage to unmask a traitor and a coward.'

'Sir!' cried M. de Blessac, overcome with shame; 'I am at your orders —and——"

He could not finish. The sound of voices was heard behind the door, which opened violently, and an aged woman entered, in spite of the efforts of the servant, exclaiming in an agitated voice: 'I tell you, I must speak instantly to your master.'

On hearing this voice, and at sight of the pale, weeping woman, M. Hardy, forgetting M. de Blessac, Rodin, the infamous treachery, and all, fell back a step, and exclaimed: 'Madame Duparc! you here! What is the matter?'

'Oh, sir! a great misfortune——'

'Margaret!' cried M. Hardy, in a tone of despair.

'She is gone, sir!'——'Gone!' repeated M. Hardy, as horrorstruck as if a thunderbolt had fallen at his feet. 'Margaret gone!'

'All is discovered. Her mother took her away—three days ago!' said the unhappy woman, in a failing voice.

'Gone! Margaret! It is not true. You deceive me,' cried M. Hardy. Refusing to hear more, wild, despairing, he rushed out of the house, threw himself into his carriage, to which the post-horses were still harnessed, waiting for M. de Blessac, and said to the postilion: 'To Paris! as fast as you can go!'

❋　　　❋　　　❋　　　❋　　　❋　　　❋

As the carriage, rapid as lightning, started upon the road to Paris, the wind brought nearer the distant sound of the war-song of the Wolves, who were rushing towards the factory. In this impending destruction, see Rodin's subtle hand, administering his fatal blows to clear his way up to the chair of St. Peter, to which he aspired. His tireless, wily course can hardly be darker shadowed by aught save that dread coming horror, the Cholera, whose aid he evoked, and whose health the Bacchanal Queen wildly drank.

That once gay girl, and her poor famished sister; the fair patrician and her Oriental lover ; Agricola, the workman, and his veteran father ; the smiling Rose-Pompon, and the prematurely withered Jacques Rennepont ; Father d'Aigrigny, the mock priest ; and Gabriel, the true disciple ; with the rest that have been named, and others yet to be pictured, in the blaze or the blots of their life's paths, will be seen in the third and concluding part of this romance, entitled, 'THE WANDERING JEW : REDEMPTION.'

PART THIRD.—THE REDEMPTION.

CHAPTER I.

THE WANDERING JEW'S CHASTISEMENT.

'TIS night—the moon is brightly shining, the brilliant stars are sparkling in a sky of melancholy calmness, the shrill whistlings of a northerly wind— cold, bleak, and evil-bearing—are increasing : winding about, and bursting into violent blasts, with their harsh and hissing gusts, they are sweeping the heights of Montmartre. A man is standing on the very summit of the hill ; his lengthened shadow, thrown out by the moon's pale beams, darkens the rocky ground in the distance. The traveller is surveying the huge city lying at his feet—the City of Paris—from whose profundities are cast up its towers, cupolas, domes, and steeples, in the bluish moisture of the horizon ; while from the very centre of this sea of stones is rising a lumi- nous vapour, reddening the starry azure of the sky above. It is the distant light of a myriad lamps which at night, the season for pleasure, is illumi- nating the noisy capital.

' No !' said the traveller, ' it will not be. The Lord surely will not suffer it. Twice is quite enough. Five centuries ago, the avenging hand of the Almighty drove me hither from the depths of Asia. A solitary wanderer, I left in my track more mourning, despair, disaster, and death, than the in- numerable armies of a hundred devastating conquerors could have produced. I then entered this city, and it was decimated. Two centuries ago that inexorable hand which led me through the world again conducted me here; and on that occasion, as on the previous one, that scourge, which at inter- vals the Almighty binds to my footsteps, ravaged this city, attacking first my brethren, already wearied by wretchedness and toil. My brethren ! through me—the labourer of Jerusalem, cursed by the Lord, who in my per- son cursed the race of labourers—a race always suffering, always disin- herited, always slaves, who, like me, go on, on, on, without rest or intermis- sion, without recompense, or hope ; until at length, women, men, children, and old men, die under their iron yoke of self-murder, that others in their turn then take up, borne from age to age on their willing but aching shoulders. And here again, for the third time, in the course of five centu- ries, I have arrived at the summit of one of the hills which overlooks the city ; and perhaps I bring again with me terror, desolation, and death. And this unhappy city, intoxicated in a whirl of joys, and nocturnal revelries, knows nothing about it—oh ! it knows not that I am at its very gate. But no ! no ! my presence will not be a source of fresh calamity to it. The Lord, in His unsearchable wisdom, has brought me hither across France, making me avoid on my route all but the humblest villages, so that no in-crease of the funeral knell has marked my journey. And then, moreover, the spectre has left me—that spectre, livid and green, with its deep blood-shot eyes. When I touched the soil of France, its moist and icy hand abandoned mine—it disappeared. And yet I feel the atmosphere of death surrounding me still. There is no cessation ; the biting gusts of this sinister wind, which envelope me in their breath, seem by their envenomed breath to propagate the scourge. Doubtless the anger of the Lord is appeased. Maybe, my presence here is meant only as a threat, intending to bring those to their senses whom it ought to intimidate. It must be so ; for were it otherwise, it would, on the contrary, strike a loud-sounding blow of greater terror, casting at once dread and death into the very heart of the country, into the bosom of this immense city. Oh, no ! no ! the Lord will have mercy ; He will not condemn me to this new affliction. Alas ! in this city my brethren are more numerous and more wretched than in any other. And must I bring death to them ? No ! the Lord will have mercy ; for, alas ! the seven descendants of my sister are at last all united in this city. And must I bring death to them ? Death ! instead of that immediate assist-ance they stand so much in need of ? For that woman who, like myself, wanders from one end of the world into the other, has gone now on her ever-lasting journey, after having confounded their enemies' plots. In vain did she foretell that great evils still threatened those who are akin to me through my sister's blood. The unseen hand by which I am led, drives that woman away from me, even as though it were a whirlwind that swept her on. In vain she entreated and implored at the moment she was leaving those who are so dear to me.—At least, O Lord, permit me to stay until I shall have finished my task ! Onward ! A few days, for mercy's sake, only a few days ! Onward ! I leave these whom I am protecting on the very brink of an abyss ! Onward ! Onward ! ! And the wandering star is launched afresh on its perpetual course. But her voice traversed through space, call-ing me to the assistance of my own ! When her voice reached me I felt that the offspring of my sister were still exposed to fearful dangers : those dangers are still increasing. Oh, say, say, Lord ! shall the descendants of my sister escape those woes which for so many centuries have oppressed my race ? Wilt Thou pardon me in them ? Wilt Thou punish me in them ? Oh ! lead them, that they may obey the last wishes of their ancestor. Guide them, that they may join their charitable hearts, their powerful strength, their best wisdom, and their immense wealth, and work together for the future happiness of mankind, thereby, perhaps, enabled to ransom me from my eternal penalties. Let those divine words of the Son of Man, " *Love ye one another !*" be their only aim ; and by the assistance of their all-powerful words, let them contend against and vanquish those false priests who have trampled on the precepts of love, of peace, and hope commanded by the Saviour, setting up in their stead the precepts of hatred, violence, and despair. Those false shepherds, supported by the powerful and wealthy of the world, who in all times have been their accomplices, instead of ask-ing here below a little happiness for my brethren, who have been suffering and groaning for centuries, dare to utter, in Thy name, O Lord ! that the poor must always be doomed to the tortures of this world, and that it is criminal in Thine eyes that they should either wish for or hope a mitigation of their sufferings on earth, because the happiness of the few and the wretchedness of nearly all mankind is Thine almighty will. Blasphemies ! is it not the contrary of these homicidal words that is more worthy of the name of Divine will? Hear me, O Lord ! for mercy's sake. Snatch from their enemies the descendants of my sister, from the artisan up to the king's son. Do not permit them to crush the germ of a mighty and fruitful association, which, perhaps, under Thy protection, may take its place among the records of the happiness of mankind. Suffer me, O Lord! to unite those whom they are endeavouring to divide—to defend those whom they are attacking. Suffer me to bring hope to those from whom hope has fled, to give courage to those who are weak, to uphold those whom evil threatens, and to sustain those who would persevere in well-doing. And then, perhaps, their struggles, their devotedness, their virtues, their miseries might expiate my sin. Yes, mine—misfortune, misfortune alone, made me unjust and wicked. O Lord! since Thine almighty hand hath brought me hither, for some end unknown to me, disarm Thyself, I implore Thee, of Thine anger, and let not me be the instrument of Thy vengeance! There is enough of mourning in the earth these two years past—Thy creatures have fallen by millions in my footsteps. The world is decimated. A veil of mourning extends from one end of the globe to the other. I have travelled from Asia even to the Frozen Pole, and death has followed in my wake. Dost Thou not hear, O Lord! the universal wailings that mount up to Thee? Have mercy upon all, and upon me. One day, grant me but a single day, that I may collect the descendants of my sister together, and save them!' And uttering these words, the wanderer fell upon his knees, and raised his hands to heaven in a suppliant attitude.

Suddenly, the wind howled with redoubled violence; its sharp whistlings changed to a tempest. The Wanderer trembled, and exclaimed in a voice of terror, 'O Lord! the blast of death is howling in its rage. It appears as though a whirlwind were lifting me up. Lord, wilt Thou not, then, hear my prayer? The spectre! O! do I behold the spectre? Yes, there it is; its cadaverous countenance is agitated by convulsive throes, its red eyes are rolling in their orbits. Begone! begone! Oh! its hand—its icy hand has seized on mine! Mercy, Lord, have mercy! "Onward!" Oh, Lord! this scourge, this terrible avenging scourge! Must I, then, again carry it into this city, must my poor wretched brethren be the first to fall under it—though already so miserable? Mercy, mercy! "Onward!" And the descendants of my sister—oh, pray, have mercy, mercy! "Onward!" O Lord, have pity on me! I can no longer keep my footing on the ground; the spectre is dragging me over the brow of the hill; my course is as rapid as the death-bearing wind that whistles in my track; I already approach the walls of the city. Oh, mercy, Lord, mercy on the descendants of my sister—spare them! do not compel me to be their executioner, and let them triumph over their enemies. Onward, onward! The ground is fleeing from under me; I am already at the city gate; oh, yet, Lord, yet there is time; oh, have mercy on this slumbering city, that it may not even now awaken with lamentations of terror, of despair and death! O Lord, I touch the threshold of the gate; verily Thou willest it so, then. 'Tis done—Paris! the scourge is in thy bosom! oh, cursed, cursed evermore am I. *Onward! on! on!'* *

---

* In 1346, the celebrated Black Death ravaged the earth, presenting the same symptoms as the cholera, and the same inexplicable phenomena as to its progress and the results in its route. In 1660 a similar epidemic decimated the world. It is well known that when the cholera first broke out in Paris, it had taken a wide and unaccountable leap; and, also memorable, a north-east wind prevailed during its utmost fierceness.

CHAPTER II.

THE DESCENDANTS OF THE WANDERING JEW.

THAT lonely wayfarer whom we have heard so plaintively urging to be relieved of his gigantic burden of misery, spoke of 'his sister's descendants' being of all ranks, from the working man to the king's son. They were seven in number, who had, in the year 1832, been led to Paris, directly or indirectly, by a bronze medal which distinguished them from others, bearing these words :—

VICTIM of L. C. D. J. Pray for me ! ——— PARIS, February the 13th, 1682.	IN PARIS, Rue Saint François, No. 3, In a century and a half you will be. February the 13th, 1832. ——— PRAY FOR ME !

The son of the King of Mundi had lost his father and his domains in India by the irresistible march of the English, and was but in title Prince Djalma. Spite of attempts to make his departure from the East delayed until after the period when he could have obeyed his medal's command, he had reached France by the second month of 1832. Nevertheless, the results of shipwreck had detained him from Paris till after that date. A second possessor of this token had remained unaware of its existence, only discovered by accident. But an enemy who sought to thwart the union of these seven members, had shut her up in a mad-house, from which she was released only after that day. Not alone was she in imprisonment. An old Bonapartist, General Simon, Marshal of France, and Duke de Ligny, had left a wife in Russian exile, while he (unable to follow Napoleon to St. Helena) continued to fight the English in India by means of Prince Djalma's Sepoys, whom he drilled. On the latter's defeat, he had meant to accompany his young friend to Europe, induced the more by finding that the latter's mother, a Frenchwoman, had left him such another bronze medal as he knew his wife to have had.

Unhappily, his wife had perished in Siberia, without his knowing it, any more than he did, that she had left twin daughters, Rose and Blanche. Fortunately for them, one who had served their father in the Grenadiers of the Guard, Francis Baudoin, nicknamed Dagobert, undertook to fulfil the dying mother's wishes, inspired by the medal. Saving a check at Leipsic, where one Morok the lion tamer's panther had escaped from its cage and killed Dagobert's horse, and a subsequent imprisonment (which the Wandering Jew's succouring hand had terminated) the soldier and his orphan charges had reached Paris in safety and in time. But there, a renewal of the foe's attempts had gained its end. By skilful devices, Dagobert and his son Agricola were drawn out of the way while Rose and Blanche Simon were decoyed into a nunnery, under the eyes of Dagobert's wife. But she had been bound against interfering by the influence of the Jesuit confessional. The fourth was M. Hardy, a manufacturer, and the fifth, Jacques Rennepont, a drunken scamp of a workman, who were more easily fended off, the latter in a sponging house, the former by a friend's lure. Adrienne de Cardoville, daughter of the Count of Rennepont, who had also been Duke of Cardoville, was the lady who had been unwarrantably placed in the lunatic asylum. The fifth, unaware of the medal, was Gabriel, a youth, who had been brought up, though a foundling, in Dagobert's family, as a brother to Agricola. He had entered holy orders, and more, was a Jesuit, in name though not in heart. Unlike the others, his return from abroad had been smoothed. He had signed away all his future prospects, for the benefit of the order of Loyola, and, moreover, executed a more complete deed of transfer on the day, the 13th of February, 1832, when he, alone of the heirs, stood in the room of the house, No. 3, Rue St. François, claiming what was a vast surprise for the Jesuits, who, a hundred and fifty years before, had discovered that Count Marius de Rennepont had secreted a considerable amount of his wealth, all of which had been confiscated to them, in those painful days of dragoonings, and the revocation of the Edict of Nantes. They had bargained for some thirty or forty millions of francs to be theirs, by educating Gabriel into resigning his inheritance to them, but it was two hundred and twelve millions which the Jesuit representatives (Father d'Aigrigny and his secretary, Rodin) were amazed to hear their nursling placed in possession of. They had the treasure in their hands, in fact, when a woman of strangely sad beauty had mysteriously entered the room where the will had been read, and laid a paper before the notary. It was a codicil, duly drawn up and signed, deferring the carrying out of the testament until the first day of June the same year. The Jesuits fled from the house, in rage and intense disappointment. Father d'Aigrigny was so stupor-stricken at the defeat, that he bade his secretary at once write off to Rome, that the Rennepont inheritance had escaped them, and hopes to seize it again were utterly at an end. Upon this, Rodin had revolted, and shown that he had authority to command where he had, so far, most humbly obeyed. Many such spies hang about their superior's heels, with full powers to become the governor in turn, at a moment's notice. Thenceforward, he, Rodin, had taken the business into his own hands. He had let Rose and Blanche Simon out of the convent into their father's arms. He had gone in person to release Adrienne de Cardoville from the asylum. More, having led her to sigh for Prince Djalma, he prompted the latter to burn for her.

He let not M. Hardy escape. A friend whom the latter treated as a brother, had been shown up to him as a mere spy of the Jesuits ; the woman whom he adored, a wedded woman, alas ! who had loved him in spite of her vows, had been betrayed. Her mother had compelled her to hide her shame in America, and, as she had often said—' Much as you are endeared to me, I cannot waver between you and my mother !' so she had obeyed, without one farewell word to him. Confess, Rodin was a more dexterous man than his late master ! In the pages that ensue farther proofs of his superiority in baseness and satanic heartlessness will not be wanting.

CHAPTER III.

THE ATTACK.

On M. Hardy's learning from the confidential go-between of the lovers, that his mistress had been taken away by her mother, he turned from Rodin and dashed away in a post-carriage. At the same moment, as loud as the rattle of the wheels, there arose the shouts of a band of workmen and rioters, hired by the Jesuit's emissaries, coming to attack Hardy's operatives. An old grudge long existing between them and a rival manufacturer's—Baron Tripeaud—labourers, fanned the flames. When M. Hardy had left the factory, Rodin, who was not prepared for this sudden departure, returned slowly to his hackney-coach ; but he stopped suddenly, and started with pleasure and surprise, when he saw, at some distance, Marshal Simon and his father advancing towards one of the wings of the Common Dwelling-house ; for an accidental circumstance had so far delayed the interview of the father and son.

'Very well !' said Rodin. 'Better and better ! Now, only let my man have found out and persuaded little Rose-Pompon !'

And Rodin hastened towards his hackney-coach. At this moment, the wind, which continued to rise, brought to the ear of the Jesuit the war song of the approaching Wolves.

The workman was in the garden. The marshal said to him, in a voice of such deep emotion that the old man started ; 'Father, I am very unhappy.'

A painful expression, until then concealed, suddenly darkened the countenance of the marshal.

'You unhappy ?' cried Father Simon, anxiously, as he pressed nearer to the marshal.

'For some days, my daughters have appeared constrained in manner, and lost in thought. During the first moments of our re-union, they were mad with joy and happiness. Suddenly, all has changed ; they are becoming more and more sad. Yesterday, I detected tears in their eyes ; then, deeply moved, I clasped them in my arms, and implored them to tell me the cause of their sorrow. Without answering, they threw themselves on my neck, and covered my face with their tears.'

'It is strange. To what do you attribute this alteration ?'

'Sometimes, I think I have not sufficiently concealed from them the grief occasioned me by the loss of their mother, and they are perhaps miserable that they do not suffice for my happiness. And yet (inexplicable as it is) they seem not only to understand, but to share my sorrow. Yesterday, Blanche said to me : "How much happier still should we be, if our mother were with us !——" '

'Sharing your sorrow, they cannot reproach you with it. There must be some other cause for their grief.'

'Yes,' said the marshal, looking fixedly at his father ; 'yes—but to penetrate this secret—it would be necessary not to leave them.'

'What do you mean ?'——'First learn, father, what are the duties which would keep me here ; then you shall know those which may take me away from you, from my daughters, and from my other child.'

'What other child ?'

'The son of my old friend, the Indian prince.'

'Djalma ? Is there anything the matter with him ?'——'Father, he frightens me. I told you, father, of his mad and unhappy passion for Mdlle. de Cardoville.'

'Does that frighten you, my son ?' said the old man, looking at the marshal with surprise. 'Djalma is only eighteen, and, at that age, one love drives away another.'

'You have no idea of the ravages which the passion has already made in the ardent, indomitable boy ; sometimes, fits of savage ferocity follow the most painful dejection. Yesterday, I came suddenly upon him ; his eyes were bloodshot, his features contracted with rage ; yielding to an impulse of mad fury, he was piercing with his poniard a cushion of red cloth, whilst he exclaimed, panting for breath, "Ha ! blood !—I will have blood !" "Unhappy boy !" I said to him, "what means this insane passion ?" "I'm killing the man !" replied he, in a hollow and savage voice : it is thus he designates his supposed rival.'

'There is indeed something terrible,' said the old man, 'in such a passion, in such a heart '

'At other times,' resumed the marshal, 'it is against Mdlle. de Cardoville that his rage bursts forth ; and at others, against himself. I have been obliged to remove his weapons, for a man who came with him from Java, and who appears much attached to him, has informed me that he suspected him of entertaining some thoughts of suicide.'——' Unfortunate boy !'

' Well, father,' said Marshal Simon, with profound bitterness ; 'it is at the moment when my daughters and my adopted son require all my solicitude, that I am perhaps on the eve of quitting them.'——' Of quitting them ?'

' Yes, to fulfil a still more sacred duty than that imposed by friendship or family,' said the marshal, in so grave and solemn a tone, that his father exclaimed, with deep emotion : ' What can this duty be ?'

' Father,' said the marshal, after remaining a moment in thoughtful silence, ' who made me what I am ? Who gave me the ducal title, and the marshal's bâton ?'——' Napoleon.'

' For you, the stern republican, I know that he lost all his value, when, from the first citizen of a Republic, he became an emperor.'

' I cursed his weakness,' said Father Simon, sadly ; ' the demi-god sank into a man.'

' But for me, father—for me, the soldier, who have always fought beside him, or under his eye—for me, whom he raised from the lowest rank in the army to the highest—for me, whom he loaded with benefits and marks of affection—for me, he was more than a hero, he was a friend—and there was as much gratitude as admiration in my idolatry for him. When he was exiled, I would fain have shared his exile ; they refused me that favour ; then I conspired, then I drew my sword against those who had robbed his son of the crown which France had given him.'

' And, in your position, you did well, Pierre ; without sharing your admiration, I understood your gratitude. The projects of exile, the conspiracies —I approved them all—you know it.'

' Well, then that disinherited child, in whose name I conspired seventeen years ago, is now of an age to wield his father's sword.'

' Napoleon II. !' exclaimed the old man, looking at his son with surprise and extreme anxiety ; 'the king of Rome !'

' King ? no ; he is no longer king. Napoleon ? no ; he is no longer Napoleon. They have give him some Austrian name, because the other frightened them. Everything frightens them. Do you know what they are doing with the son of the Emperor ?' resumed the marshal, with painful excitement. ' They are torturing him—killing him by inches !'

' Who told you this ?'——' Somebody who knows, whose words are but too true. Yes ; the son of the Emperor struggles with all his strength against a premature death. With his eyes turned towards France, he waits —he waits—and no one comes—no one—out of all the men that his father made as great as they once were little, not one thinks of that crowned child, whom they are stifling, till he dies.'

' But you think of him ?'——' Yes ; but I had first to learn—oh ! there is no doubt of it, for I have not derived all my information from the same source—I had first to learn the cruel fate of this youth, to whom I also swore allegiance ; for one day, as I have told you, the Emperor, proud and loving father as he was, showed him to me in his cradle, and said : " My old friend, you will be to the son what you have been to the father : who loves us, loves our France." '

' Yes, I know it. Many times you have repeated those words to me, and, like yourself, I have been moved by them.'

' Well, father ! suppose, informed of the sufferings of the son of the Emperor, I had seen—with the positive certainty that I was not deceived—a letter from a person of high rank in the court of Vienna, offering to a man, that was still faithful to the Emperor's memory, the means of communicating with the King of Rome, and perhaps of saving him from his tormentors——'

'What next?' said the workman, looking fixedly at his son. 'Suppose Napoleon II. once at liberty——'

'What next?' exclaimed the marshal. Then he added, in a suppressed voice : ' Do you think, father, that France is insensible to the humiliations she endures ? Do you think that the memory of the Emperor is extinct ? No, no ; it is, above all, in the days of our country's degradation, that she whispers that sacred name. How would it be, then, were that na me to rise glorious on the frontier, reviving in his son ? Do you not think that the heart of all France would beat for him ?'

'This implies a conspiracy — against the present government — with Napoleon II. for a watchword,' said the workman. 'This is very serious.'

' I told you, father, that I was very unhappy ; judge if it be not so,' cried the marshal. ' Not only I ask myself, if I ought to abandon my children and you, to run the risk of so daring an enterprise, but I ask myself if I am not bound to the present government, which, in acknowledging my rank and title, if it bestowed no favour, at least did me an act of justice. How shall I decide ?—abandon all that I love, or remain insensible to the tortures of the son of the Emperor—of that Emperor to whom I owe everything—to whom I have sworn fidelity, both to himself and child ? Shall I lose this only opportunity, perhaps, of saving him, or shall I conspire in his favour ? Tell me, if I exaggerate what I owe to the memory of the Emperor ? Decide for me, father ! During a whole sleepless night, I strove to discover, in the midst of this chaos, the line prescribed by honour ; but I only wandered from indecision to indecision. You alone, father—you alone, I repeat, can direct me.'

After remaining for some moments in deep thought, the old man was about to answer, when some person, running across the little garden, opened the door hastily, and entered the room in which were the marshal and his father. It was Olivier, the young workman, who had been able to effect his escape from the village in which the Wolves had assembled.

' M. Simon ! M. Simon !' cried he, pale, and panting for breath. ' They are here—close at hand. They have come to attack the factory.'

'Who?' cried the old man, rising hastily. ——' The Wolves, quarrymen, and stonecutters, joined on the road by a crowd of people from the neighbourhood, and vagabonds from town. Do you not hear them ? They are shouting, " Death to the Devourers !" '

The clamour was indeed approaching, and grew more and more distinct.

' It is the same noise that I heard just now,' said the marshal, rising in his turn.

' There are more than two hundred of them, M. Simon,' said Olivier ; ' they are armed with clubs and stones, and unfortunately the greater part of our workmen are in Paris. We are not above forty here in all ; the women and children are already flying to their chambers, screaming for terror. Do you not hear them ?'

The ceiling shook beneath the tread of many hasty feet.

' Will this attack be a serious one ?' said the marshal to his father, who appeared more and more dejected.

' Very serious,' said the old man ; ' there is nothing more fierce than these combats between different unions ; and everything has been done lately to excite the people of the neighbourhood against the factory.'

' If you are so inferior in number,' said the marshal, ' you must begin by barricading all the doors — and then——'

He was unable to conclude. A burst of ferocious cries shook the windows of the room, and seemed so near and loud, that the marshal, his father, and the young workman, rushed out into the little gardan, which was bounded on one side by a wall that separated it from the fields. Suddenly, whilst the shouts redoubled in violence, a shower of large stones, intended to break the windows of the house, smashed some of the panes on the first story, struck against the wall, and fell into the garden, all around the marshal and his father. By a fatal chance, one of these large stones struck the old man on the head. He staggered, bent forward, and fell bleeding into the arms of Marshal Simon, just as arose from without, with increased fury, the savage cries of, 'Death to the Devourers!'

CHAPTER IV.

THE WOLVES AND THE DEVOURERS.

IT was a frightful thing to view the approach of the lawless crowd, whose first act of hostility had been so fatal to Marshal Simon's father. One wing of the Common Dwelling-house, which joined the garden-wall on that side, was next to the fields. It was there that the Wolves began their attack. The precipitation of their march, the halt they had made at two public-houses on the road, their ardent impatience for the approaching struggle, had inflamed these men to a high pitch of savage excitement. Having discharged their first shower of stones, most of the assailants stooped down to look for more ammunition. Some of them, to do so with greater ease, held their bludgeons between their teeth ; others had placed them against the wall ; here and there, groups had formed tumultuously round the principal leaders of the band ; the most neatly dressed of these men wore frocks, with caps, whilst others were almost in rags, for, as we have already said, many of the hangers-on at the barriers, and people without any profession, had joined the troop of the Wolves, whether welcome or not. Some hideous women, with tattered garments, who always seem to follow in the track of such people, accompanied them on this occasion, and, by their cries and fury, inflamed still more the general excitement. One of them, tall, robust, with purple complexion, blood-shot eyes, and toothless jaws, had a handkerchief over her head, from beneath which escaped her yellow, frowsy hair. Over her ragged gown, she wore an old plaid shawl, crossed over her bosom, and tied behind her back. This hag seemed possessed with a demon. She had tucked up her half-torn sleeves ; in one hand she brandished a stick, in the other she grasped a huge stone ; her companions called her Ciboule (scullion).

This horrible hag exclaimed, in a hoarse voice : ' I'll bite the women of the factory ; I'll make them bleed.'

The ferocious words were received with applause by her companions, and with savage cries of ' Ciboule for ever !' which excited her to frenzy.

Amongst the other leaders, was a small, dry, pale man, with the face of a ferret, and a black beard all round the chin ; he wore a scarlet Greek cap, and beneath his long blouse, perfectly new, appeared a pair of neat cloth trousers, strapped over thin boots. This man was evidently of a different condition of life from that of the other persons in the troop ; it was he, in particular, who ascribed the most irritating and insulting language to the workmen of the factory, with regard to the inhabitants of the neighbourhood. He howled a great deal, but he carried neither stick nor stone. A full-faced, fresh-coloured man, with a formidable bass voice, like a chorister's, asked him : ' Will you not have a shot at those impious dogs, who might bring down the Cholera on the country, as the curate told us ?'

' I will have a better shot than you,' said the little man, with a singular, sinister smile.——' And with what, I'd like to see ?'

' Probably, with this,' said the little man, stooping to pick up a large stone; but, as he bent, a well-filled though light bag, which he appeared to carry under his blouse, fell to the ground.

' Look, you are losing both bag and baggage,' said the other ; ' it does not seem very heavy.'

' They are samples of wool,' answered the man with the ferret's face, as he hastily picked up the bag, and replaced it under his blouse ; then he added: ' Attention ! the big blaster is going to speak.'

And, in fact, he who exercised the most complete ascendancy over this irritated crowd was the terrible quarryman. His gigantic form towered so much above the multitude, that his great head, bound in its ragged hand-kerchief, and his Herculean shoulders, covered with a fallow goat-skin, were always visible above the level of that dark and swarming crowd, only relieved here and there by a few women's caps, like so many white points. Seeing to what a degree of exasperation the minds of the crowd had reached, the small number of honest, but misguided workmen, who had allowed themselves to be drawn into this dangerous enterprise, under the pretext of a quarrel between rival unions, now fearing for the consequences of the struggle, tried, but too late, to abandon the main body. Pressed close, and as it were, girt in with the more hostile groups, dreading to pass for cowards, or to expose themselves to the bad treatment of the majority, they were forced to wait for a more favourable moment to effect their escape. To the savage cheers, which had accompanied the first discharge of stones, succeeded a deep silence commanded by the stentorian voice of the quarryman.

' The Wolves have howled,' he exclaimed ; 'let us wait and see how the Devourers will answer, and when they will begin the fight.'

' We must draw them out of their factory, and fight them on neutral ground,' said the little man with the ferret's face, who appeared to be the thieves' advocate ; ' otherwise there would be trespass.'

' What do we care about trespass ?' cried the horrible hag, Ciboule ; 'in or out, I will tear the chits of the factory.'

' Yes, yes,' cried other hideous creatures, as ragged as Ciboule herself ; ' we must not leave all to the men.'——' We must have our fun too !'

' The women of the factory say that all the women of the neighbourhood are drunken drabs,' cried the little man with the ferret's face.

' Good ! we'll pay them for it.'——'The women shall have their share.'

' That's our business.'——' They like to sing in their Common House,' cried Ciboule ; 'we will make them sing the wrong side of their mouths, in the key of " Oh, dear me !" '

This pleasantry was received with shouts, hootings, and furious stamping of feet, to which the stentorian voice of the quarryman put a term by roaring : ' Silence !'

' Silence ! silence !' repeated the crowd. ' Hear the blaster !'

' If the Devourers are cowards enough not to dare to show themselves, after a second volley of stones, there is a door down there which we can break open, and we will soon hunt them from their holes.'

' It would be better to draw them out, so that none might remain in the factory,' said the little old man with the ferret's face, who appeared to have some secret motive.

' A man fights where he can,' cried the quarryman, in a voice of thunder ; ' all right, if we can but once catch hold. We could fight on a sloping roof, or on the top of a wall—couldn't we, my Wolves ?'

Yes, yes !' cried the crowd, still more excited by those savage words ; 'if they don't come out, we will break in.'——'We will see their fine palace !'

'The pagans haven't even a chapel,' said the bass voice. 'The curate has damned them all !'——'Why should they have a palace, and we nothing but dog-kennels?'

'Hardy's workmen say that kennels are good enough for such as you,' said the little man with the ferret's face.——'Yes, yes ! they said so.'

'We'll break all their traps.'——'We'll pull down their bazaar.'

'We'll throw the house out of the windows.'——'When we have made the mealy-mouthed chits sing,' cried Ciboule, 'we will make them dance to the clatter of stones on their heads.'

'Come, my Wolves ! attention !' cried the quarryman, still in the same stentorian voice ; 'one more volley, and if the Devourers do not come out, down with the door !'

This proposition was received with cheers of savage ardour, and the quarryman, whose voice rose above the tumult, cried with all the strength of his herculean lungs : 'Attention, my Wolves. Make ready ! all together. Now, are you ready?'——'Yes, yes—all ready !'

'Then, present !—fire !' And, for the second time, a shower of enormous stones poured upon that side of the Common Dwelling-house which was turned towards the fields. A part of these projectiles broke such of the windows as had been spared by the first volley. To the sharp smashing and cracking of glass were joined the ferocious cries uttered in chorus by this formidable mob, drunk with its own excesses : 'Death to the Devourers !'

Soon these outcries became perfectly frantic, when, through the broken windows, the assailants perceived women running in terror, some with children in their arms, and others raising their hands to heaven, calling aloud for help ; whilst a few, bolder than the rest, leaned out of the windows, and tried to fasten the outside blinds.

'There come the ants out of their holes !' cried Ciboule, stooping to pick up a stone. 'We must have a fling at them for luck !' The stone, hurled by the steady, masculine hand of the virago, went straight to its mark, and struck an unfortunate woman who was trying to close one of the shutters.

'Hit in the white !' cried the hideous creature.——'Well done, Ciboule ! —you've rapped her *coker-nut !*' cried a voice.

'Ciboule for ever !'——'Come out, you Devourers, if you dare !'

'They have said a hundred times, that the neighbours were too cowardly even to come and look at their house,' squealed the little man with the ferret's face.——'And now they show the white feather !'

'If they will not come out,' cried the quarryman, in a voice of thunder, 'let us smoke them out !'——'Yes, yes !'

'Let's break open the door !'——'We are sure to find them !'

'Come on ! come on !'

The crowd, with the quarryman at their head, and Ciboule not far from him, brandishing a stick, advanced tumultuously towards one of the great doors. The ground shook beneath the rapid tread of the mob, which had now ceased shouting ; but the confused, and, as it were, subterraneous noise, sounded even more ominous than those savage outcries. The Wolves soon arrived opposite the massive oaken door. At the moment the blaster raised a sledge-hammer, the door opened suddenly. Some of the most determined of the assailants were about to rush in at this entrance ; but the quarryman stepped back, extending his arm as if to moderate their ardour and impose silence. Then his followers gathered round him.

The half-open door discovered a party of workmen, unfortunately by **no** means numerous, but with countenances full of resolution. They had armed themselves hastily with forks, iron bars, and clubs. Agricola, who was their leader, held in his hand a heavy sledge-hammer. The young workman was very pale; but the fire of his eye, his menacing look, and the intrepid assurance of his bearing, showed that his father's blood boiled in his veins, and that in such a struggle he might become fear-inspiring. Yet he succeeded in restraining himself, and challenged the quarryman, in a firm voice: 'What do you want?'——'A fight!' thundered the blaster.

'Yes, yes! a fight!' repeated the crowd.

'Silence, my Wolves!' cried the quarryman, as he turned round, and stretched forth his large hand towards the multitude. Then addressing Agricola, he said: 'The Wolves have come to ask for a fight.'

'With whom?'——'With the Devourers.'

'There are no Devourers here,' replied Agricola; 'we are only peaceable workmen. So begone.'——'Well! here are the Wolves, that will eat your quiet workmen.'

'The Wolves will eat no one here,' said Agricola, looking full at the quarryman, who approached him with a threatening air; 'they can only frighten little children.'

'Oh! you think so,' said the quarryman, with a savage sneer. Then, raising his weapon, he shook it in Agricola's face, exclaiming: 'Is that any laughing matter?'

'Is that?' answered Agricola, with a rapid movement, parrying the stone-sledge with his own hammer.

'Iron against iron—hammer against hammer—that suits me,' said the quarryman.

'It does not matter what suits you,' answered Agricola, hardly able to restrain himself. 'You have broken our windows, frightened our women, and wounded—perhaps killed—the oldest workman in the factory, who at this moment lies bleeding in the arms of his son.' Here Agricola's voice trembled in spite of himself. 'It is, I think, enough.'

'No; the Wolves are hungry for more,' answered the blaster; 'you must come out (cowards that you are!), and fight us on the plain.'

'Yes! yes! battle!—let them come out!' cried the crowd, howling, hissing, waving their sticks, and pushing further into the small space which separated them from the door.

'We will have no battle,' answered Agricola: 'we will not leave our home; but if you have the misfortune to pass this,' said Agricola, throwing his cap upon the threshold, and setting his foot on it with an intrepid air, 'if you pass this, you attack us in our own house, and you will be answerable for all that may happen.'

'There or elsewhere we will have the fight! the Wolves must eat the Devourers. Now for the attack!' cried the fierce quarryman, raising his hammer to strike Agricola.

But the latter, throwing himself on one side by a sudden leap, avoided the blow, and struck with his hammer full at the chest of the quarryman, who staggered for a moment, but instantly recovering his legs, rushed furiously on Agricola, crying: 'Follow me, Wolves!'

CHAPTER V.

THE RETURN.

As soon as the combat had begun between Agricola and the blaster, the general fight became terrible ardent, implacable. A flood of assailants, following the quarryman's steps, rushed into the house with irresistible fury ; others, unable to force their way through this dreadful crowd, where the more impetuous squeezed, stifled, and crushed those who were less so, went round in another direction, broke through some lattice-work, and thus placed the people of the factory, as it were, between two fires. Some resisted courageously ; others, seeing Ciboule, followed by some of her horrible companions, and by several of the most ill-looking ruffians, hastily enter that part of the Common Dwelling-house in which the women had taken refuge, hurried in pursuit of this band ; but some of the hag's companions, having faced about, and vigorously defended the entrance of the staircase against the workmen, Ciboule, with three or four like herself, and about the same number of no less ignoble men, rushed through the rooms, with the intention of robbing or destroying all that came in their way. A door, which at first resisted their efforts, was soon broken through ; Ciboule rushed into the apartment with a stick in her hand, her hair dishevelled, furious, and, as it were, maddened with the noise and tumult. A beautiful young girl (it was Angela), who appeared anxious to defend the entrance to a second chamber, threw herself on her knees, pale and supplicating, and raising her clasped hands, exclaimed : ' Do not hurt my mother !'

' I'll serve you out first, and your mother afterwards,' replied the horrible woman, throwing herself on the poor girl, and endeavouring to tear her face with her nails, whilst the rest of the ruffianly band broke the glass and the clock with their sticks, and possessed themselves of some articles of wearing apparel.

Angela, struggling with Ciboule, uttered loud cries of distress, and still attempted to guard the room in which her mother had taken refuge ; whilst the latter, leaning from the window, called Agricola to their assistance. The smith was now engaged with the huge blaster. In a close struggle, their hammers had become useless, and with bloodshot eyes and clenched teeth, chest to chest, and limbs twined together like two serpents, they made the most violent efforts to overthrow each other. Agricola, bent forward, held under his right arm the left leg of the quarryman, which he had seized in parrying a violent kick ; but such was the Herculean strength of the leader of the Wolves, that he remained firm as a tower, though resting only on one leg. With the hand that was still free (for the other was griped by Agricola as in a vice), he endeavoured with violent blows to break the jaws of the smith, who, leaning his head forward, pressed his forehead hard against the breast of his adversary.

' The Wolf will break the Devourer's teeth, and he shall devour no more,' said the quarryman.

' You are no true Wolf,' answered the smith, redoubling his efforts ; ' the true Wolves are honest fellows, and do not come ten against one.'

' True or false, I will break your teeth.'

' And I your paw,' said the smith, giving so violent a wrench to the leg of the quarryman, that the latter uttered a cry of acute pain, and, with the rage of a wild beast, butting suddenly forward with his head, succeeded in biting Agricola in the side of the neck.

The pang of this bite forced Agricola to make a movement, which enabled the quarryman to disengage his leg. Then, with a superhuman effort, he threw himself with his whole weight on Agricola, and brought him to the ground, falling himself upon him.

At this juncture, Angela's mother, leaning from one of the windows of the Common Dwelling-house, exclaimed in a heart-rending voice : ' Help, Agricola !--they are killing my child !'

'Let me go—and on my honour—I will fight you to-morrow, or when you will,' said Agricola, panting for breath.

'No warmed-up food for me; I eat all hot,' answered the quarryman, seizing the smith by the throat, whilst he tried to place one of his knees upon his chest.

'Help!—they are killing my child!' cried Angela's mother, in a voice of despair.

'Mercy! I ask mercy! Let me go!' said Agricola, making the most violent efforts to escape. 'I am too hungry,' answered the quarryman.

Exasperated by the terror which Angela's danger occasioned him, Agricola redoubled his efforts, when the quarryman suddenly felt his thigh seized by the sharp teeth of a dog, and at the same instant received from a vigorous hand three or four heavy blows with a stick upon his head. He relaxed his grasp, and fell stunned upon his hand and knee, whilst he mechanically raised his other arm to parry the blows, which ceased as soon as Agricola was delivered.

'Father, you have saved me!' cried the smith, springing up. 'If only I am in time to rescue Angela!'

'Run!—never mind me!' answered Dagobert; and Agricola rushed into the house.

Dagobert, accompanied by Spoilsport, had come, as we have already said, to bring Marshal Simon's daughters to their grandfather. Arriving in the midst of the tumult, the soldier had collected a few workmen to defend the entrance of the chamber, to which the marshal's father had been carried in a dying state. It was from this post that the soldier had seen Agricola's danger. Soon after, the rush of the conflict separated Dagobert from the quarryman, who remained for some moments insensible. Arrived in two bounds at the Common Dwelling-house, Agricola succeeded in forcing his way through the men who defended the staircase, and rushed into the corridor that led to Angela's chamber. At the moment he reached it, the unfortunate girl was mechanically guarding her face with both hands against Ciboule, who, furious as the hyena over its prey, was trying to scratch and disfigure her.

To spring upon the horrible hag, seize her by her yellow hair with irresistible hand, drag her backwards, and then with one cuff, stretch her full length upon the ground, was for Agricola an achievement as rapid as thought. Furious with rage, Ciboule rose again almost instantly; but at this moment, several workmen, who had followed close upon Agricola, were able to attack with advantage, and whilst the smith lifted the fainting form of Angela, and carried her into the next room, Ciboule and her band were driven from that part of the house.

After the first fire of the assault, the small number of real Wolves, who, as Agricola said, were in the main honest fellows, but had the weakness to let themselves be drawn into this enterprise, under the pretext of a quarrel between rival unions, seeing the excesses committed by the rabble who accompanied them, turned suddenly round, and ranged themselves on the side of the Devourers.

'There are no longer here either Wolves or Devourers,' said one of the most determined Wolves to Olivier, with whom he had been fighting roughly and fairly; 'there are none here but honest workmen, who must unite to drive out a set of scoundrels, that have come only to break and pillage.'

'Yes,' added another; 'it was against our will that they began by breaking your windows.'

'The big blaster did it all,' said another; 'the true Wolves wash their hands of him. We shall soon settle his account.'

'We may fight every day—but we ought to esteem each other.'*

This defection of a portion of the assailants (unfortunately but a small portion) gave new spirit to the workmen of the factory, and all together, Wolves and Devourers, though very inferior in number, opposed themselves to the band of vagabonds, who were proceeding to new excesses. Some of these wretches, still further excited by the little man with the ferret's face, a secret emissary of Baron Tripeaud, now rushed in a mass towards the workshops of M. Hardy. Then began a lamentable devastation. These people, seized with the mania of destruction, broke without remorse machines of the greatest value, and most delicate construction ; half-manufactured articles were pitilessly destroyed ; a savage emulation seemed to inspire these barbarians, and those workshops, so lately the model of order and well-regulated economy, were soon nothing but a wreck ; the courts were strewed with fragments of all kinds of wares, which were thrown from the windows with ferocious outcries, or savage bursts of laughter. Then, still thanks to the incitements of the little man with the ferret's face, the books of M. Hardy, archives of commercial industry, so indispensable to the trader, were scattered to the wind, torn, trampled under foot, in a sort of infernal dance, composed of all that was most impure in this assembly of low, filthy, and ragged men and women, who held each other by the hand, and whirled round and round with horrible clamour. Strange and painful contrast ! At the height of the stunning noise of these horrid deeds of tumult and devastation, a scene of imposing and mournful calm was taking place in the chamber of Marshal Simon's father, the door of which was guarded by a few devoted men. The old workman was stretched on his bed, with a bandage across his blood-stained white hair. His countenance was livid, his breathing oppressed, his look fixed and glazed.

Marshal Simon, standing at the head of the bed, bending over his father, watched in despairing anguish the least sign of consciousness on the part of the dying man, near whom was a physician, with his finger on the failing pulse. Rose and Blanche, brought hither by Dagobert, were kneeling beside the bed, their hands clasped, and their eyes bathed in tears ; a little further, half hidden in the shadows of the room, for the hours had passed quickly, and the night was at hand, stood Dagobert himself, with his arms crossed upon his breast, and his features painfully contracted. A profound and solemn silence reigned in this chamber, only interrupted by the broken sobs of Rose and Blanche, or by Father Simon's hard breathing. The eyes of the marshal were dry, gloomy, and full of fire. He only withdrew them from his father's face, to interrogate the physician by a look. There are strange coincidences in life. That physician was Dr. Baleinier. The asylum of the doctor being close to the barrier that was nearest to the factory, and his fame being widely spread in the neighbourhood, they had run to fetch him on the first call for medical assistance.

* We wish it to be understood, that the necessities of our story alone have made t' e Wolves the assailants. While endeavouring to paint the evils arising from the abuse of the spirit of association, we do not wish to ascribe a character of savage hostility to one sect rather than to the other—to the Wolves more than to the Devourers. The Wolves, a club of united stone-cutters, are generally industrious, intelligent workmen, whose situation is the more worthy of interest, as not only their labours, conducted with mathematical precision, are of the rudest and most wearisome kind, but they are likewise out of work during three or four months of the year, their profession being, unfortunately, one of those which the winter condemns to a forced cessation. A number of Wolves, in order to perfect themselves in their trade, attend every evening a course of linear geometry, applied to the cutting of stone, analogous to that given by M. Agricole Perdignier, for the benefit of carpenters. Several working stone-cutters sent an architectural model in plaster to the last exhibition.

Suddenly, Dr. Baleinier made a movement ; the marshal, who had not taken his eyes off him, exclaimed : 'Is there any hope ?'——'At least, my lord duke, the pulse revives a little.'

'He is saved !' said the marshal.——'Do not cherish false hopes, my lord duke,' answered the doctor, gravely ; 'the pulse revives, owing to the powerful applications to the feet, but I know not what will be the issue of the crisis.'

'Father ! father ! do you hear me ?' cried the marshal, seeing the old man slightly move his head, and feebly raise his eyelids. He soon opened his eyes, and this time their intelligence had returned.

'Father ! you live—you know me !' cried the marshal, giddy with joy and hope.——'Pierre ! are you there ?' said the old man, in a weak voice. 'Your hand—give it——' and he made a feeble movement.

'Here, father !' cried the marshal, as he pressed the hand of the old man in his own.

Then, yielding to an impulse of delight, he bent over his father, covered his hands, face, and hair with kisses, and repeated : 'He lives ! kind heaven, he lives ! he is saved !'

At this instant, the noise of the struggle which had recommenced between the rabble, the Wolves, and the Devourers, reached the ears of the dying man.

'That noise ! that noise !' said he ; 'they are fighting.'——'It is growing less, I think,' said the marshal, in order not to agitate his father.

'Pierre,' said the old man, in a weak and broken voice, 'I have not long to live.'——'Father——'

'Let me speak, child ; if I can but tell you all.'——'Sir,' said Baleinier piously, to the old workman, 'heaven may perhaps work a miracle in your favour ; show yourself grateful, and allow a priest ——'

'A priest ! Thank you, sir—I have my son,' said the old man ; 'in his arms, I will render up my soul—which has always been true and honest.'

'You die ?' exclaimed the marshal ; 'no ! no !'

'Pierre,' said the old man, in a voice which, firm at first, gradually grew fainter, 'just now—you asked my advice—in a very serious matter. I think, that the wish to tell you of your duty—has recalled me—for a moment—to life—for I should die miserable—if I thought you in a road unworthy of yourself and me. Listen to me, my son —my noble son—at this last hour, a father cannot deceive himself. You have a great duty to perform—under pain—of not acting like a man of honour—under pain of neglecting my last will. You ought, without hesitation ——'

Here the voice failed the old man. When he had pronounced the last sentence, he became quite unintelligible. The only words that Marshal Simon could distinguish, were these : 'Napoleon II.—oath—dishonour—my son !'

Then the old workman again moved his lips mechanically—and all was over. At the moment he expired, the night was quite come, and terrible shouts were heard from without, of 'Fire ! Fire !' The conflagration had broken out in one of the workshops, filled with inflammable stuff, into which had glided the little man with the ferret's face. At the same time, the roll of drums was heard in the distance, announcing the arrival of a detachment of troops from town.

    ✿   ✿   ✿   ✿   ✿   ✿

During an hour, in spite of every effort, the fire had been spreading through the factory. The night is clear, cold, starlight ; the wind blows keenly from the north, with a moaning sound. A man, walking across the fields, where the rising ground conceals the fire from him, advances with slow and unsteady steps

It is M. Hardy. He had chosen to return home on foot, across the country, hoping that a walk would calm the fever in his blood—an icy fever, more like the chill of death. He had not been deceived. His adored mistress— the noble woman, with whom he might have found refuge from the conse- quences of the fearful deception which had just been revealed to him—had quitted France. He could have no doubt of it. Margaret was gone to America. Her mother had exacted from her, in expiation of her fault, that she should not even write to him one word of farewell—to him, for whom she had sacrificed her duty as a wife. Margaret had obeyed.

Besides, she had often said to him : ' Between m·· mother and you, I should not hesitate.'

She had not hesitated. There was therefore no hope, not the slightest ; even if an ocean had not separated him from Margaret. he knew enough of her blind submission to her mother, to be certain that all relations between them were broken off for ever. It is well. He will no longer reckon upon this heart—his last refuge. The two roots of his life have been torn up and broken, with the same blow, the same day, almost at the same moment. What then remains for thee, poor sensitive plant, as thy tender mother used to call thee ? What remains to console thee for the loss of this last love— this last friendship, so infamously crushed ? Oh ! there remains for thee that one corner of the earth, created after the image of thy mind—that little colony, so peaceful and flourishing, where, thanks to thee, labour brings with it joy and recompense. Those worthy artisans, whom thou hast made happy, good, and grateful, will not fail thee. That also is a great and holy affection ; let it be thy shelter in the midst of this frightful wreck of all thy most sacred convictions ! The calm of that cheerful and pleasant retreat, the sight of the unequalled happiness of thy dependents, will soothe thy poor, suffering soul, which now seems to live only for suffering. Come ! you will soon reach the top of the hill, from which you can see afar, in the plain below, that paradise of workmen, of which you are the presiding divinity.

M. Hardy had reached the summit of the hill. At that moment the conflagration, repressed for a short time, burst forth with redoubled fury from the Common Dwelling-house, which it had now reached. A bright streak, at first white, then red, then copper-coloured, illuminated the distant horizon. M. Hardy looked at it with a sort of incredulous, almost idiotic stupor. Suddenly, an immense column of flame shot up in the thick of a cloud of smoke, accompanied by a shower of sparks, and streamed towards the sky, casting a bright reflection over all the country, even to M. Hardy's feet. The violence of the north-wind, driving the flames in waves before it, soon brought to the ears of M. Hardy the hurried clanging of the alarm- bell of the burning factory.

CHAPTER VI.

THE GO-BETWEEN.

A FEW days have elapsed since the conflagration of M. Hardy's factory. The following scene takes place in the Rue Clovis, in the house where Rodin had lodged, and which was still inhabited by Rose-Pompon, who, without the least scruple, availed herself of the household arrangements of her friend Philemon. It was about noon, and Rose-Pompon, alone in the chamber of the student, who was still absent, was breakfasting very gaily by the fire- side ; but how singular a breakfast ! what a queer fire ! how strange an apartment !

Imagine a large room, lighted by two windows without curtains—for as they looked on empty space, the lodger had no fear of being overlooked. One side of this apartment served as a wardrobe, for there was suspended Rose-Pompon's flashy costume of débardeur, not far from the boatman's jacket of Philemon, with his large trousers of coarse, grey stuff, covered with pitch (shiver my timbers !), just as if this intrepid mariner had bunked in the forecastle of a frigate, during a voyage round the globe. A gown of Rose-Pompon's hung gracefully over a pair of pantaloons, the legs of which seemed to come from beneath the petticoat. On the lowest of several book-shelves, very dusty and neglected, by the side of three old boots (wherefore *three* boots ?) and a number of empty bottles, stood a skull, a scientific and friendly souvenir, left to Philemon by one of his comrades, a medical student. With a species of pleasantry, very much to the taste of the student-world, a clay pipe with a very black bowl was placed between the magnificently white teeth of this skull ; moreover, its shining top was half hidden beneath an old hat, set knowingly on one side, and adorned with faded flowers and ribbons. When Philemon was drunk, he used to contemplate this bony emblem of mortality, and break out into the most poetical monologues, with regard to this philosophical contrast between death and the mad pleasures of life. Two or three plaster casts, with their noses and chins more or less injured, were fastened to the wall, and bore witness to the temporary curiosity which Philemon had felt with regard to phrenological science, from the patient and serious study of which he had drawn the following logical conclusion :—That, having to an alarming extent the bump of getting into debt, he ought to resign himself to the fatality of his organisation, and accept the inconvenience of creditors as a vital necessity. On the chimney-piece stood uninjured, in all its majesty, the magnificent rowing club drink-ing-glass, a china tea-pot without a spout, and an ink-stand of black wood, the glass mouth of which was covered by a coat of greenish and mossy mould. From time to time, the silence of this retreat was interrupted by the cooing of pigeons, which Rose-Pompon had established with cordial hospitality in the little study. Chilly as a quail, Rose-Pompon crept close to the fire, and at the same time seemed to enjoy the warmth of a bright ray of sunshine, which enveloped her in its golden light. This droll little creature was dressed in the oddest costume, which, however, displayed to advantage the freshness of her piquant and pretty countenance, crowned with its fine, fair hair, always neatly combed and arranged the first thing in the morning. By way of dressing-gown, Rose-Pompon had ingeniously drawn over her linen, the ample scarlet flannel skirt which belonged to Philemon's official garb in the rowing-club ; the collar, open and turned down, displayed the whiteness of the young girl's under garment, as also of her neck and shoulders, on whose firm and polished surface the scarlet shirt seemed to cast a rosy light. The grisette's fresh and dimpled arms half protruded from the large, turned-up sleeves ; and her charming legs were also half visible, crossed one over the other, and clothed in neat white stockings, and boots. A black silk cravat formed the girdle which fastened the shirt round the wasp-like waist of Rose-Pompon, just above those hips, worthy of the enthusiasm of a modern Phidias, and which gave to this style of dress a grace very original.

We have said, that the breakfast of Rose-Pompon was singular. You shall judge. On a little table placed before her, was a wash-hand-basin, into which she had recently plunged her fresh face, bathing it in pure water. From the bottom of this basin, now transformed into a salad-bowl, Rose-Pompon took with the tips of her fingers large green leaves, dripping with vinegar, and craunched them between her tiny white teeth, whose enamel was too hard to allow them to be set on edge. Her drink was a glass of water and syrup of gooseberries, which she stirred with a wooden mustard-spoon. Finally, as an extra dish, she had a dozen olives in one of those blue glass trinket-dishes sold for twenty-five sous. Her dessert was composed of nuts, which she prepared to roast on a red-hot shovel. That Rose-Pompon, with such an unaccountable savage choice of food, should retain a freshness of complexion worthy of her name, is one of those miracles, which reveal the mighty power of youth and health. When she had eaten her salad, Rose-Pompon was about to begin upon her olives, when a low knock was heard at the door, which was modestly bolted on the inside.

'Who is there?' said Rose-Pompon.

'A friend—the oldest of the old,' replied a sonorous, jovial voice. 'Why do you lock yourself in?'

'What! is it you, Ninny Moulin?'

'Yes, my beloved pupil. Open quickly. Time presses.'

'Open to you? Oh, I dare say!—that would be pretty, the figure I am!'

'I believe you! what does it matter what figure you are? It would be very pretty, thou rosiest of all the roses with which Cupid ever adorned his quiver!'

'Go and preach fasting and morality in your journal, fat apostle!' said Rose-Pompon, as she restored the scarlet shirt to its place, with Philemon's other garments.

'I say! are we to talk much longer through the door, for the greater edification of our neighbours?' cried Ninny Moulin. 'I have something of importance to tell you—something that will astonish you ——'

'Give me time to put on my gown, great plague that you are!'

'If it is because of my modesty, do not think of it. I am not over nice. I should like you very well as you are.'

'Only to think that such a monster is the favourite of all the church-goers!' said Rose-Pompon, opening the door as she finished fastening her dress.

'So! you have at last returned to the dovecot, you stray bird!' said Ninny Moulin, folding his arms, and looking at Rose-Pompon with comic seriousness. 'And where may you have been, I pray? For three days the naughty little bird has left its nest.'

'True; I only returned home last night. You must have called during my absence?'

'I came every day, and even twice a day, young lady, for I have very serious matters to communicate.'

'Very serious matters? Then we shall have a good laugh at them.'

'Not at all—they are really serious,' said Ninny Moulin, seating himself. 'But, first of all, what did you do during the three days that you left your conjugal and Philemonic home? I must know all about it, before I tell you more.'

'Will you have some olives?' said Rose-Pompon, as she nibbled one of them herself.

'Is that your answer?—I understand!—Unfortunate Philemon!'

'There is no unfortunate Philemon in the case, slanderer. Clara had a death in her house, and, for the first few days after the funeral she was afraid to sleep alone.'

'I thought Clara sufficiently provided against such fears.'

'There you are deceived, you great viper! I was obliged to go and keep the poor girl company.'

At this assertion, the religious pamphleteer hummed a tune, with an incredulous and mocking air.

'You think I have played Philemon tricks?' cried Rose-Pompon, cracking a nut with the indignation of injured innocence.

'I do not say tricks; but one little rose-coloured trick.'

'I tell you, that it was not for my pleasure I went out. On the contrary —for, during my absence, poor Cephyse disappeared.'

'Yes, Mother Arsène told me that the Bacchanal-Queen was gone on a journey. But when I talk of Philemon, you talk of Cephyse; we don't progress.'

'May I be eaten by the black panther that they are showing at the Porte-Saint-Martin if I do not tell you the truth. And, talking of that, you must get tickets to take me to see those animals, my little Ninny Moulin! They tell me there never were such darling wild beasts.'

'Now really, are you mad?'

'Why so?'——'That I should guide your youth, like a venerable patriarch, through the dangers of the *Storm-blown Tulip*, all well and good—I ran no risk of meeting my pastors and masters; but were I to take you to a Lent-Spectacle (since there are only beasts to be seen), I might just run against my sacristans—and how pretty I should look with you on my arm!'

'You can put on a false nose, and straps to your trousers, my big Ninny; they will never know you.'

'We must not think of false noses, but of what I have to tell you, since you assure me that you have no intrigue in hand.'

'I swear it!' said Rose-Pompon, solemnly, extending her left hand horizontally, whilst with her right she put a nut into her mouth. Then she added, with surprise, as she looked at the outside coat of Ninny Moulin, 'Goodness gracious! what full pockets you have got! What is there in them?'

'Something that concerns you, Rose-Pompon,' said Dumoulin, gravely.

'Me?'

'Rose-Pompon!' said Ninny Moulin, suddenly, with a majestic air; 'will you have a carriage? Will you inhabit a charming apartment, instead of living in this dreadful hole? Will you be dressed like a duchess?'

'Now for some more nonsense! Come, will you eat the olives? If not, I shall eat them all up. There is only one left.'

Without answering this gastronomic offer, Ninny Moulin felt in one of his pockets, and drew from it a case containing a very pretty bracelet, which he held up sparkling before the eyes of the young girl.

'Oh! what a sumptuous bracelet!' cried she, clapping her hands. 'A green-eyed serpent biting his tail—the emblem of my love for Philemon.'

'Do not talk of Philemon; it annoys me,' said Ninny Moulin, as he clasped the bracelet round the wrist of Rose-Pompon, who allowed him to do it, laughing all the while like mad, and saying to him, 'So you've been employed to make a purchase, big apostle, and you wish to see the effect of it. Well! it is charming!'

'Rose-Pompon,' resumed Ninny Moulin, 'would you like to have a servant, a box at the Opera, and a thousand francs a month for your pin-money?'

'Always the same nonsense. Get along!' said the young girl, as she held up the bracelet to the light, still continuing to eat her nuts. 'Why always the same farce, and no change of bills?'

Ninny Moulin again plunged his hand into his pocket, and this time drew forth an elegant chain, which he hung round Rose-Pompon's neck.

'Oh! what a beautiful chain!' cried the young girl, as she looked by turns at the sparkling ornament and the religious writer. 'If you chose that also, you have a very good taste. But am I not a good-natured girl to be your *dummy*, just to show off your jewels?'

'Rose-Pompon,' returned Ninny Moulin, with a still more majestic air, 'these trifles are nothing to what you may obtain, if you will but follow the advice of your old friend.'

Rose began to look at Dumoulin with surprise, and said to him, 'What does all this mean, Ninny Moulin? Explain yourself; what advice have you to give?'

Dumoulin did not answer, but replunging his hand into his inexhaustible pocket, he fished up a parcel, which he carefully unfolded, and in which was a magnificent mantilla of black lace. Rose-Pompon started up, full of new admiration, and Dumoulin threw the rich mantilla over the young gir''s shoulders.

'It is superb! I have never seen anything like it! What patterns! what work!' said Rose-Pompon, as she examined all with simple and per- fectly disinterested curiosity. Then she added, 'Your pocket is like a shop; where did you get all these pretty things?' Then, bursting into a fit of laughter, which brought the blood to her cheeks, she exclaimed, 'Oh, I have it! These are the wedding-presents for Madame de la Sainte-Colombe. I congratulate you; they are very choice.'

'And where do you suppose I should find money to buy these wonders?' said Ninny Moulin. 'I repeat to you, all this is yours if you will but listen to me!'

'How is this?' said Rose-Pompon, with the utmost amazement; 'is what you tell me in downright earnest?'——'In downright earnest.'

'This offer to make me a great lady?'——'The jewels might convince you of the reality of my offers.'

'And you propose all this to me for some one else, my poor Ninny Moulin?'

'One moment,' said the religious writer, with a comical air of modesty; 'you must know me well enough, my beloved pupil, to feel certain that I should be incapable of inducing you to commit an improper action. I re- spect myself too much for that—leaving out the consideration that it would be unfair to Philemon, who confided to me the guardianship of your virtue.'

'Then, Ninny Moulin,' said Rose-Pompon, more and more astonished, 'on my word of honour, I can make nothing of it.'

'Yet, 'tis all very simple, and I——'

'Oh! I've found it,' cried Rose-Pompon, interrupting Ninny Moulin; 'it is some gentleman who offers me his hand, his heart, and all the rest of it. Could you not tell me that directly?'

'A marriage? oh, laws, yes!' said Dumoulin, shrugging his shoulders.

'What! is it not a marriage?' said Rose-Pompon, again much surprised. 'No.'

'And the offers you make me are honest ones, my big apostle?'

'They could not be more so.' Here Dumoulin spoke the truth.

'I shall not have to be unfaithful to Philemon?'——'No.'

'Or faithful to any one else?'——'No.'

Rose-Pompon looked confounded. Then she rattled on: 'Come, do not let us have any joking! I am not foolish enough to imagine that I am to live just like a duchess, just for nothing. What, therefore, must I give in return?'——'Nothing at all.'

'Nothing?'——'Not even that,' said Ninny Moulin, biting his nail-tip.

'But what am I to do, then?'——'Dress yourself as handsomely as pos- sible, take your ease, amuse yourself, ride about in a carriage. You see, it is not very fatiguing—and you will, moreover, help to do a good action.'

'What! by living like a duchess?'——'Yes! so make up your mind. Do not ask me for any more details, for I cannot give them to you. For the rest, you will not be detained against your will. Just try the life I propose to you. If it suits you, go on with it; if not, return to your Philemonic household.'——'In fact——'

'Only try it. What can you risk?'

'Nothing; but I can hardly believe that all you say is true. And then,' added she, with hesitation, 'I do not know if I ought——'

Ninny Moulin went to the window, opened it, and said to Rose·Pompon, who ran up to it, 'Look there! before the door of the house.'

'What a pretty carriage! How comfortable a body'd be inside of it!'

'That carriage is yours. It is waiting for you.'

'Waiting for me!' exclaimed Rose-Pompon; 'am I to decide as short as that?'——'Or not at all.'

'To-day?'——'On the instant.'

'But where will they take me?'——'How should I know?'

'You do not know where they will take me?'——'Not I,'—and Dumoulin still spoke the truth—'the coachman has his orders.'

'Do you know all this is very funny, Ninny Moulin?'——'I believe you. If it were not funny, where would be the pleasure?'

'You are right.'——'Then you accept the offer? That is well. I am delighted both for you and myself.'

'For yourself?'

'Yes; because, in accepting, you render me a great service.'

'You? How so?'——'It matters little, as long as I feel obliged to you.'

'True.'——'Come, then; let us set out!'

'Bah! after all, they cannot eat me,' said Rose-Pompon, resolutely.

With a skip and a jump, she went to fetch a rose-coloured cap, and, going up to a broken looking-glass, placed the cap very much cocked on one side on her bands of light air. This left uncovered her snowy neck, with the silky roots of the hair behind, and gave to her pretty face a very mischievous, not to say licentious expression.

'My cloak!' said she to Ninny Moulin, who seemed to be relieved from a considerable amount of uneasiness, since she had accepted his offer.

'Fie! a cloak will not do,' answered her companion, feeling once more in his pocket, and drawing out a fine Cashmere shawl, which he threw over Rose-Pompon's shoulders.

'A Cashmere!' cried the young girl, trembling with pleasure and joyous surprise. Then she added, with an air of heroism: 'It is settled! I will run the gauntlet.' And with a light step she descended the stairs, followed by Ninny Moulin.

The worthy greengrocer was at her post. 'Good morning, mademoiselle; you are early to day,' said she to the young girl.——'Yes, Mother Arsène; there is my key.'

'Thank you, mademoiselle.'——'Oh! now I think of it,' said Rose-Pompon, suddenly, in a whisper, as she turned towards Ninny Moulin, and withdrew further from the portress, 'what is to become of Philemon?'

'Philemon?'——'If he should arrive——'

'Oh! the devil!' said Ninny Moulin, scratching his ear.——'Yes; if Philemon should arrive, what will they say to him? for I may be a long time absent.'

'Three or four months, I suppose.'——'Not more?'

'I should think not.'——'Oh! very good!' said Rose-Pompon. Then turning towards the greengrocer, she said to her, after a moment's reflection: 'Mother Arsène, if Philemon should come home, you will tell him I have gone out—on business.'

'Yes, mademoiselle.'——'And that he must not forget to feed my pigeons, which are in his study.'

'Yes, mademoiselle.'——'Good-bye, Mother Arsène.'

'Good-bye, mademoiselle.' And Rose-Pompon entered the carriage in triumph, along with Ninny Moulin.

'The devil take me if I know what is to come of all this,' said Jacques Dumoulin to himself, as the carriage drove rapidly down the Rue Clovis. 'I have repaired my error—and now I laugh at the rest.'

CHAPTER VII.

ANOTHER SECRET.

THE following scene took place a few days after the abduction of Rose-Pompon by Ninny Moulin. Mdlle. de Cardoville was seated, in a dreamy mood, in her cabinet, which was hung with green silk, and furnished with an ebony library, ornamented with large bronze caryatides. By some significant signs, one could perceive that Mdlle. de Cardoville had sought in the fine airs some relief from sad and serious thoughts. Near an open piano, was a harp, placed before a music-stand. A little further, on a table covered with boxes of oil and water-colour, were several brilliant sketches. Most of them represented Asiatic scenes, lighted by the fires of an oriental sun. Faithful to her fancy of dressing herself at home in a picturesque style, Mademoiselle de Cardoville resembled that day one of those proud portraits of Velasquez, with stern and noble aspect. Her gown was of black moire, with wide-swelling petticoat, long waist, and sleeve slashed with rose-coloured satin, fastened together with jet bugles. A very stiff Spanish ruff reached almost to her chin, and was secured round her neck by a broad rose-coloured ribbon. This frill, slightly heaving, sloped down as far as the graceful swell of the rose-coloured stomacher, laced with strings of jet beads, and terminating in a point at the waist. It is impossible to express how well this black garment, with its ample and shining folds, relieved with rose-colour and brilliant jet, harmonised with the shining whiteness of Adrienne's skin, and the golden flood of her beautiful hair, whose long, silky ringlets descended to her bosom.

· The young lady was in a half-recumbent posture, with her elbow resting on a couch covered with green silk. The back of this piece of furniture, which was pretty high towards the fire-place, sloped down insensibly towards the foot. A sort of light, semi-circular trellis-work, in gilded bronze, raised about five feet from the ground, covered with flowering plants (the admirable *passiflores quadrangulatæ*, planted in a deep ebony box, from the centre of which rose the trellis-work), surrounded this couch with a sort of screen of foliage, enamelled with large flowers, green without, purple within, and as brilliant as those flowers of porcelain, which we receive from Saxony. A sweet, faint perfume, like a faint mixture of jasmine with violet, rose from the cup of these admirable *passiflores*. Strange enough, a large quantity of new books (Adrienne having bought them since the last two or three days), and quite fresh-cut, were scattered around her on the couch, and on a little table ; whilst other larger volumes, amongst which were several atlases full of engravings, were piled on the sumptuous fur, which formed the carpet beneath the divan. Stranger still, these books, though of different forms, and by different authors, all treated of the same subject. The posture of Adrienne revealed a sort of melancholy dejection. Her cheeks were pale ; a light blue circle surrounded her large, black eyes, now half-closed, and gave to them an expression of profound grief. Many causes contributed to this sorrow—amongst others, the disappearance of Mother Bunch. Without absolutely believing the perfidious insinuations of Rodin, who gave her to understand that, in the fear of being unmasked by him, the hunchback had not dared to remain in the house, Adrienne felt a cruel sinking of the heart, when she thought how this young girl, in whom she had had so much confidence, had fled from her almost sisterly hospitality, without even uttering a word of gratitude ; for care had been taken not to show her the few lines written by the poor needlewoman to her benefactress, just before her departure. She had only been told of the note for five hundred francs found on her desk ; and this last inexplicable circumstance had contributed to awaken cruel suspicions in the breast of Mdlle. de Cardoville. She already felt the fatal effects of that mistrust of everything and everybody, which Rodin had recommended to her ; and this sentiment of suspicion and reserve had the more tendency to become powerful, that, for the first time in her life, Mdlle. de Cardoville, until then a stranger to all deception, had a secret to conceal—a secret, which was equally her happiness, her shame, and her torment.

Half-recumbent on her divan, pensive and depressed, Adrienne pursued, with a mind often absent, one of her newly purchased books. Suddenly, she uttered an exclamation of surprise ; the hand which held the book trembled like a leaf, and from that moment she appeared to read with passionate attention and devouring curiosity. Soon, her eyes sparkled with enthusiasm, her smile assumed ineffable sweetness, and she seemed at once proud, happy, delighted—but, as she turned over the last page, her countenance expressed disappointment and chagrin. Then she recommenced this reading, which had occasioned her such sweet emotion, and this time she read with the most deliberate slowness, going over each page twice, and spelling, as it were, every line, every word. From time to time, she paused, and in a pensive mood, with her forehead leaning on her fair hand, she seemed to reflect, in a deep reverie, on the passages she had read with such tender and religious love. Arriving at a passage which so affected her, that a tear started in her eye, she suddenly turned the volume, to see on the cover the name of the author. For a few seconds, she contemplated this name with a singular expression of gratitude, and could not forbear raising to her rosy lips the page on which it was printed. After reading many times over the lines with which she had been so much struck, forgetting, no doubt, the letter in the spirit, she began to reflect so deeply, that the book glided from her hand, and fell upon the carpet. During the course of this reverie, the eyes of the young girl rested, at first mechanically, upon an admirable bas-relief, placed on an ebony stand, near one of the windows. This magnificent bronze, recently cast after a plaster copy from the antique, represented the triumph of the Indian Bacchus. Never, perhaps, had Grecian art attained such rare perfection. The youthful conqueror, half-clad in a lion's skin, which displayed his juvenile grace and charming purity of form, shone with divine beauty. Standing up in a car, drawn by two tigers, with an air at once gentle and proud, he leaned with one hand upon a thyrsus, and with the other guided his savage steeds in tranquil majesty. By this rare mixture of grace, vigour, and serenity, it was easy to recognise the hero who had waged such desperate combats with men and with monsters of the forest. Thanks to the brownish tone of the figure, the light, falling from one side of the sculpture, admirably displayed the form of the youthful god, which, carved in relievo, and thus illumined, shone like a magnificent statue of pale gold upon the dark fretted background of the bronze.

When Adrienne's look first rested on this rare assemblage of divine per fections, her countenance was calm and thoughtful. But this contemplation, at first mechanical, became gradually more and more attentive and conscious, and the young lady, rising suddenly from her seat, slowly approached the bas-relief, as if yielding to the invincible attraction of an extraordinary resemblance. Then a slight blush appeared on the cheeks of Mdlle. de Cardoville, stole across her face, and spread rapidly to her neck and forehead. She approached still closer, threw round a hasty glance, as if half-ashamed, or as if she had feared to be surprised in a blameable action, and twice stretched forth her hand, trembling with emotion, to touch with the tips of her charming fingers the bronze forehead of the Indian Bacchus. And twice she stopped short, with a kind of modest hesitation. At last, the temptation became too strong for her. She yielded to it ; and her alabaster finger, after delicately caressing the features of pale gold, was pressed more boldly for an instant on the pure and noble brow of the youthful god. At this pressure, though so slight, Adrienne seemed to feel a sort of electric shock ; she trembled in every limb, her eyes languished, and, after swimming for an instant in their humid and brilliant crystal, were raised, half-closed, to heaven. Then her head was thrown a little way back, her knees bent insensibly, her rosy lips were half opened, as if to give a passage to her heated breath, for her bosom heaved violently, as though youth and life had accelerated the pulsations of her heart, and made her blood boil in her veins. Finally, the burning cheeks of Adrienne betrayed a species of ecstasy, timid and passionate, chaste and sensual, the expression of which was ineffably touching.

An affecting spectacle indeed is that of a young maiden, whose modest brow flushes with the first fires of a secret passion. Does not the Creator of all things animate the body as well as the soul, with a spark of divine energy ? Should He not be religiously glorified in the intellect as in the senses, with which He has so paternally endowed His creatures ? They are impious blasphemers who seek to stifle the celestial senses, instead of guiding and harmonising them in their divine flight. Suddenly, Mdlle. de Cardoville started, raised her head, opened her eyes as if awaking from a dream, withdrew abruptly from the sculptures, and walked several times up and down the room in an agitated manner, pressing her burning hands to her forehead. Then, falling, as it were, exhausted on her seat, her tears flowed in abundance. The most bitter grief was visible in her features, which revealed the fatal struggle that was passing within her. By degrees, her tears ceased. To this crisis of painful dejection, succeeded a species of violent scorn and indignation against herself, which were expressed by these words that escaped her : ' For the first time in my life, I feel weak and cowardly. Oh, yes ! cowardly—very cowardly !'

  *   *   *   *   *   *

The sound of a door, opening and closing, roused Mdlle. de Cardoville from her bitter reflections. Georgette entered the room, and said to her mistress : ' Madame, can you receive the Count de Montbron ?'

Adrienne, too well-bred to exhibit before her women the sort of impatience occasioned by this unseasonable visit, said to Georgette : ' You told M. de Montbron that I was at home ?'——' Yes, madame.'

' Then beg him to walk in.' Though Mdlle. de Cardoville felt at that moment much vexed at the arrival of Montbron, let us hasten to say, that she entertained for him an almost filial affection, and a profound esteem, though, by a not unfrequent contrast, she almost always differed from him in opinion. Hence arose, when Mdlle. de Cardoville had nothing to disturb her mind, the most gay and animated discussions, in which M. de Montbron, notwithstanding his mocking and sceptical humour, his long experience, his rare knowledge of men and things, his fashionable training, in a word, had not always the advantage, and even acknowledged his defeat gaily enough. Thus, to give an idea of the differences of the count and Adrienne, before, as he would say, laughingly, he had made himself her accomplice, he had always opposed (from other motives than those alleged by Madame de Saint-Dizier) Adrienne's wish to live alone and in her own way ; whilst Rodin, on the contrary, by investing the young girl's resolve on this subject with an ideal grandeur of intention, had acquired a species of influence over her. M. de Montbron, now upwards of sixty years of age, had been a most prominent character during the Directory, Consulate, and the Empire. His prodigal style of living, his wit, his gaiety, his duels, his amours, and his losses at play, had given him a leading influence in the best society of his day ; while his character, his kind-heartedness, and liberality, secured him the lasting friendship of nearly all his female friends. At the time we now present him to the reader, he was still a great gambler ; and, moreover, a very lucky gambler. He had, as we have stated, a very lordly style ; his manners were decided, but polished and lively ; his habits were such as belong to the higher classes of society, though he could be excessively sharp towards people whom he did not like. He was tall and thin, and his slim figure gave him an almost youthful appearance ; his forehead was high, and a little bald ; his hair was grey and short, his countenance long, his nose aquiline, his eyes blue and piercing, and his teeth white, and still very good.

' The Count de Montbron,' said Georgette, opening the door. The count entered, and hastened to kiss Adrienne's hand, with a sort of paternal familiarity.

' Come !' said M. de Montbron to himself ; ' let us try to discover the truth I am in search of, that we may escape a great misfortune.'

CHAPTER VIII.

THE CONFESSION.

MDLLE. DE CARDOVILLE, not wishing to betray the cause of the violent feelings which agitated her, received M. de Montbron with a feigned and forced gaiety. On the other hand, notwithstanding his tact and knowledge of the world, the count was much embarrassed how to enter upon the subject on which he wished to confer with Adrienne, and he resolved to feel his way, before seriously commencing the conversation. After looking at the young lady for some seconds, M. de Montbron shook his head, and said, with a sigh of regret : ' My dear child, I am not pleased.'

' Some affair of the heart, or of *hearts*, my dear count ?' returned Adrienne, smiling.——' Of the heart,' said M. de Montbron.

' What ! you, so great a player, think more of a woman's whim than a throw of the dice ?'——' I have a heavy heart, and you are the cause of it, my dear child.'

' M. de Montbron, you will make me very proud,' said Adrienne, with a smile.

' You would be wrong, for I tell you plainly, my trouble is caused by your neglect of your beauty. Yes, your countenance is pale, dejected, sorrowful ; you have been low-spirited for the last few days ; you have something on your mind, I am sure of it.'

' My dear M. de Montbron, you have so much penetration, that you may be allowed to fail for once, as now. I am not sad, I have nothing on my mind, and—I am about to utter a very silly piece of impertinence—I have never thought myself so pretty.'

'On the contrary, nothing could be more modest than such an assertion. Who told you that falsehood? a woman?'

'No; it was my heart, and it spoke the truth,' answered Adrienne, with a slight degree of emotion. 'Understand it, if you can,' she added.

'Do you mean that you are proud of the alteration in your features, because you are proud of the sufferings of your heart?' said M. de Montbron, looking at Adrienne with attention. 'Be it so; I am then right. You have some sorrow. I persist in it,' added the count, speaking with a tone of real feeling, 'because it is painful to me.'

'Be satisfied; I am as happy as possible—for every instant I take delight in repeating, how, at my age, I am free—absolutely free!'——'Yes; free to torment yourself, free to be miserable.'

'Come, come, my dear count!' said Adrienne, 'you are recommencing our old quarrel. I still find in you the ally of my aunt and the Abbé d'Aigrigny'

'Yes; as the republicans are the allies of the legitimists—to destroy each other in their turn. Talking of your abominable aunt, they say that she holds a sort of council at her house these last few days, a regular mitred conspiracy. She is certainly in a good way.'

'Why not? Formerly, she would have wished to be Goddess of Reason; now, we shall perhaps see her canonized. She has already performed the first part of the life of Mary Magdalen.'

'You can never speak worse of her than she deserves, my dear child. Still, though for quite opposite reasons, I agreed with her on the subject of your wish to reside alone.'——'I know it.'

'Yes; and because I wished to see you a thousand times freer than you really are, I advised you——.'——'To marry.'

'No doubt; you would have had your dear liberty, with its consequences, only, instead of Mdlle. de Cardoville, we should have called you Madame Somebody, having found an excellent husband to be responsible for your independence.'

'And who would have been responsible for this ridiculous husband? And who would bear a mocked and degraded name? I, perhaps?' said Adrienne, with animation. 'No, no, my dear count, good or ill, I will answer for my own actions; to my name shall attach the reputation, which I alone have formed. I am as incapable of basely dishonouring a name which is not mine, as of continually bearing it myself, if it were not held in esteem. And, as one can only answer for one's own actions, I prefer to keep my name.'——'You are the only person in the world that has such ideas.'

'Why?' said Adrienne, laughing. 'Because it appears to me horrible, to see a poor young girl lost and buried in some ugly and selfish man, and become, as they say seriously, the better half of the monster—yes! a fresh and blooming rose to become part of a frightful thistle!—Come, my dear count; confess there is something odious in this conjugal metempsychosis,' added Adrienne, with a burst of laughter.

The forced and somewhat feverish gaiety of Adrienne contrasted painfully with her pale and suffering countenance; it was so easy to see that she strove to stifle with laughter some deep sorrow, that M. de Montbron was much affected by it; but, dissembling his emotion, he appeared to reflect a moment, and took up mechanically one of the new, fresh-cut books, by which Adrienne was surrounded. After casting a careless glance at this volume, he continued, still dissembling his feelings: 'Come, my dear madcap: this is another folly. Suppose I were twenty years old, and that you did me the honour to marry me—you would be called Lady de Montbron, I imagine?'——'Perhaps.'

'How perhaps? Would you not bear my name, if you married me?'

'My dear count,' said Adrienne, with a smile, 'do not let us pursue this hypothesis, which can only leave us—regrets.'

Suddenly, M. de Montbron started, and looked at Mdlle. de Cardoville with an expression of surprise. For some moments, whilst talking to Adrienne, he had mechanically taken up two or three of the volumes scattered over the couch, and had glanced at their titles in the same careless manner. The first was the 'Modern History of India.' The second, 'Travels in India.' The third, 'Letters on India.' Much surprised, M. de Montbron had continued his investigation, and found that the fourth volume continued this Indian nomenclature, being 'Rambles in India.' The fifth was, 'Recollections of Hindostan.' The sixth, 'Notes of a Traveller in the East Indies.'

Hence the astonishment, which, for many serious reasons, M. de Montbron had no longer been able to conceal, and which his looks betrayed to Adrienne. The latter, having completely forgotten the presence of the accusing volumes by which she was surrounded, yielded to a movement of involuntary confusion, and blushed slightly; but, her firm and resolute character again coming to her aid, she looked full at M. de Montbron, and said to him: 'Well, my dear count! what surprises you?'

Instead of answering, M. de Montbron appeared still more absorbed in thought, and contemplating the young girl, he could not forbear saying to himself: 'No, no—it is impossible—and yet ——'

'It would, perhaps, be indiscreet in me to listen to your soliloquy, my dear count,' said Adrienne.

'Excuse me, my dear child; but what I see surprises me so much——'

'And pray what do you see?'

'The traces of so great and novel an interest in all that relates to India,' said M. de Montbron, laying a slight stress on his words, and fixing a piercing look upon the young girl.

'Well!' said Adrienne, stoutly.——'Well! I seek the cause of this sudden passion——'

'Geographical?' said Mdlle. de Cardoville, interrupting M. de Montbron: 'you may find this taste somewhat serious for my age, my dear count—but one must find occupation for leisure hours—and then, having a cousin, who is both an Indian and a prince, I should like to know something of the fortunate country from which I derive this savage relationship.'

These last words were pronounced with a bitterness that was not lost on M. de Montbron: watching Adrienne attentively, he observed: 'Meseems, you speak of the prince with some harshness.'

'No; I speak of him with indifference.'——'Yet he deserves a very different feeling.'

'On the part of some other person, perhaps,' replied Adrienne, drily.

'He is so unhappy!' said M. de Montbron, in a tone of sincere pity. 'When I saw him the other day, he made my heart ache.'

'What have I to do with it?' exclaimed Adrienne, with an accent of painful and almost angry impatience.

'I should have thought that his cruel torments at least deserved your pity,' answered the count, gravely.

'Pity—from me!' cried Adrienne, with an air of offended pride. Then, restraining herself, she added coldly: 'You are jesting, M. de Montbron. It is not in sober seriousness that you ask me to take interest in the amorous torments of your prince.'

There was so much cold disdain in these last words of Adrienne, her pale and agitated countenance betrayed such haughty bitterness, that M. de Montbron said, sorrowfully: 'It is then true; I have not been deceived.

I, who thought, from our old and constant friendship, that I had some claim to your confidence, have known nothing of it—while you told all to another. It is painful, very painful to me.'

' I do not understand you, M. de Montbron.'——' Well then, since I must speak plainly,' cried the count, 'there is, I see, no hope for this unhappy boy—you love another.'

As Adrienne started—' Oh ! you cannot deny it,' resumed the count ; 'your paleness and melancholy for the last few days, your implacable indifference to the prince—all prove to me that you are in love.'

Hurt by the manner in which the count spoke of the sentiment he attributed to her, Mdlle. de Cardoville answered with dignified stateliness ; ' You must know, M. de Montbron, that a secret discovered is not a confidence. Your language surprises me.'

' Oh, my dear friend, if I use the poor privilege of experience—if I guess that you are in love—if I tell you so, and even go so far as to reproach you with it—it is because the life or death of this poor prince is concerned ; and I feel for him as if he were my son, for it is impossible to know him without taking the warmest interest in him.'

' It would be singular,' returned Adrienne, with redoubled coldness, and still more bitter irony, 'if my love—admitting I were in love—could have any such strange influence on Prince Djalma. What can it matter to him ?' added she, with almost agonizing disdain.

' What can it matter to him ? Now really, my dear friend, permit me to tell you, that it is you who are jesting cruelly. What ! this unfortunate youth loves you with all the blind ardour of a first love— twice has attempted to terminate by suicide the horrible tortures of his passion—and you think it strange that your love for another should be with him a question of life or death !'

' He loves me then ?' cried the young girl, with an accent impossible to describe.——' He loves you to madness, I tell you ; I have seen it.'

Adrienne seemed overcome with amazement. From pale, she became crimson ; as the redness disappeared, her lips grew white, and trembled. Her emotion was so strong, that she remained for some moments unable to speak, and pressed her hand to her heart, as if to moderate its pulsations.

M. de Montbron, almost frightened at the sudden change in Adrienne's countenance, hastily approached her, exclaiming : 'Good heaven, my poor child ! what is the matter ?'

Instead of answering, Adrienne waved her hand to him, in sign that he should not be alarmed ; and, in fact, the count was speedily tranquillised, for the beautiful face, which had so lately been contracted with pain, irony, and scorn, seemed now expressive of the sweetest and most ineffable emotions ; Adrienne appeared to luxuriate in delight, and to fear losing the least particle of it ; then, as reflection told her, that she was, perhaps, the dupe of illusion or falsehood, she exclaimed suddenly, with anguish, addressing herself to M. de Montbron : ' But is what you tell me true ?'

' What I tell you !'——' Yes—that Prince Djalma—— '

' Loves you to madness ?—Alas ! it is only too true.'

' No, no,' cried Adrienne, with a charming expression of simplicity ; 'that could never be *too* true.'——'What do you say ?' cried the count.

' But that woman ?' asked Adrienne, as if the word scorched her lips.

' What woman ?'

' She who has been the cause of all these painful struggles.'

' That woman !—why, who should it be but you ?'

' What, I ? Oh ! tell me, was it I ?'——' On my word of honour. I trust my experience. I have never seen so ardent and sincere a passion.'

'Oh! is it really so? Has he never had any other love?'——'Never.'

'Yet I was told so.'——'By whom?'

'M. Rodin.'——'That Djalma——'

'Had fallen violently in love, two days after I saw him.'——'M. Rodin told you that!' cried M. de Montbron, as if struck with a sudden idea. 'Why, it is he who told Djalma that you were in love with some one else.'

'I!'——'And this it was which occasioned the poor youth's dreadful despair.'

'It was this which occasioned *my* despair.'——'You love him, then, just as he loves you!' exclaimed M. de Montbron, transported with joy.

'Love him!' said Mdlle. de Cardoville. A discreet knock at the door interrupted Adrienne.

'One of your servants, no doubt. Be calm,' said the count.

'Come in,' said Adrienne, in an agitated voice.——'What is it?' said Mdlle. de Cardoville. Florine entered the room.

'M. Rodin has just been. Fearing to disturb mademoiselle, he would not come in; but he will return in half an hour. Will mademoiselle receive him?'

'Yes, yes,' said the count to Florine; 'even if I am still here, show him in, by all means. Is not that your opinion?' asked M. de Montbron of Adrienne.——'Quite so,' answered the young girl; and a flash of indignation darted from her eyes, as she thought of Rodin's perfidy.

'Oho! the old knave!' said M. de Montbron, 'I always had my doubts of that crooked neck!' Florine withdrew, leaving the count with her mistress.

CHAPTER IX.

LOVE.

Mdlle. de Cardoville was transfigured. For the first time, her beauty shone forth in all its lustre. Until now overshadowed by indifference, or darkened by grief, she appeared suddenly illumined by a brilliant ray of sunshine. The slight irritation caused by Rodin's perfidy passed like an imperceptible shade from her brow. What cared she now for falsehood and perfidy? Had they not failed? And, for the future, what human power could interpose between her and Djalma, so sure of each other? Who would dare to cross the path of those two beings, resolute and strong with the irresistible power of youth, love, and liberty? Who would dare to follow them into that blazing sphere, whither they went, so beautiful and happy, to blend together in their inextinguishable love, protected by the proof-armour of their own happiness? Hardly had Florine left the room, when Adrienne approached M. de Montbron with a rapid step. She seemed to have become taller; and to watch her advancing, light, radiant, and triumphant, one might have fancied her a goddess walking upon the clouds.

'When shall I see him?' was her first word to M. de Montbron.

'Well—say to-morrow; he must be prepared for so much happiness; in so ardent a nature, such sudden, unexpected joy might be terrible.'

Adrienne remained pensive for a moment, and then said rapidly: 'To-morrow—yes—not before to-morrow. I have a superstition of the heart.'

'What is it?'——'You shall know. HE LOVES ME—that word says all, contains all, comprehends all, is all—and yet I have a thousand questions to ask with regard to him—but I will ask none before to-morrow, because, by a mysterious fatality, to-morrow is with me a sacred anniversary. It will be an age till then; but, happily, I can wait. Look here!'

Beckoning M. de Montbron, she led him to the Indian Bacchus. 'How much it is like him!' said she to the count.

'Indeed,' exclaimed the latter, 'it is strange!'——'Strange?' returned Adrienne, with a smile of gentle pride; 'strange, that a hero, a demi-god, an ideal of beauty, should resemble Djalma?'

'How you love him!' said M. de Montbron, deeply touched, and almost dazzled by the felicity which beamed from the countenance of Adrienne.

'I must have suffered a good deal, do you not think so?' said she, after a moment's silence.

'If I had not made up my mind to come here to-day, almost in despair, what would have happened?'

'I cannot tell; I should perhaps have died, for I am wounded mortally here'—she pressed her hand to her heart. 'But what might have been death to me, will now be life.'

'It was horrible,' said the count, shuddering. 'Such a passion, buried in your own breast, proud as you are——'

'Yes, proud—but not self-conceited. When I learned his love for another, and that the impression which I fancied I had made on him at our first interview had been immediately effaced, I renounced all hope, without being able to renounce my love. Instead of shunning his image, I surrounded myself with all that could remind me of him. In default of happiness, there is a bitter pleasure in suffering through what we love.'

'I can now understand your Indian library.'

Instead of answering the count, Adrienne took from the stand one of the freshly cut volumes, and, bringing it to M. de Montbron, said to him, with a smile and a celestial expression of joy and happiness : 'I was wrong—I am vain. Just read this—aloud, if you please. I tell you that I can wait for to-morrow.' Presenting the book to the count, she pointed out one passage with the tip of her charming finger. Then she sank down upon the couch, and, in an attitude of deep attention, with her body bent forward, her hands crossed upon the cushion, her chin resting upon her hands, her large eyes fixed with a sort of adoration on the Indian Bacchus, that was just opposite to her, she appeared by this impassioned contemplation to prepare herself to listen to M. de Montbron.

The latter, much astonished, began to read, after again looking at Adrienne, who said to him, in her most coaxing voice 'Very slowly, I beg of you.'

M. de Montbron then read the following passage from the journal of a traveller in India : ' " When I was at Bombay, in 1829, I constantly heard amongst the English there, of a young hero, the son of——" '

The count having paused a second, by reason of the barbarous spelling of the name of Djalma's father, Adrienne immediately said to him, in her soft voice : 'The son of Kadja-sing.'

'What a memory!' said the count, with a smile. And he resumed : ' " A young hero, the son of Kadja-sing, king of Mundi. On his return from a distant and sanguinary expedition amongst the mountains against this Indian king, Colonel Drake was filled with enthusiasm for this son of Kadja-sing, known as Djalma. Hardly beyond the age of childhood, this young prince has, in the course of this implacable war given proofs of such chivalrous intrepidity, and of so noble a character, that his father has been surnamed the Father of the Generous." '

'That is a touching custom,' said the count. 'To recompense the father, as it were, by giving him a surname in honour of his son, is a great idea. But how strange you should have met with this book!' added the count, in surprise. 'I can understand; there is matter here to inflame the coolest head,'

'Oh ! you will see, you will see,' said Adrienne.

The count continued to read : ' " Colonel Drake, one of the bravest and best officers of the English army, said yesterday, in my presence, that, having been dangerously wounded, and taken prisoner by Prince Djalma, after an energetic resistance, he had been conveyed to the camp established in the village of——" '

Here there was the same hesitation on the part of the count, on seeing a still more barbarous name than the first ; so, not wishing to try the adventure, he paused, and said to Adrienne, ' Now really, I give this up.'

' And yet it is so easy !' replied Adrienne ; and she pronounced with inexpressible softness, a name in itself soft, ' The village of Shumshabad.

' You appear to have an infallible process for remembering geographical names,' said the count, continuing : ' " Once arrived at the camp, Colonel Drake received the kindest hospitality, and Prince Djalma treated him with the respect of a son. It was there that the colonel became acquainted with some facts, which carried to the highest pitch his enthusiasm for Prince Djalma. I heard him relate the two following.

' " In one of the battles, the prince was accompanied by a young Indian of about twelve years of age, whom he loved tenderly, and who served him as a page, following him on horseback to carry his spare weapons. This child was idolised by its mother ; just as they set out on the expedition, she had entrusted her son to Prince Djalma's care, saying, with a stoicism worthy of antiquity, ' Let him be your brother.' ' He shall be my brother,' had replied the prince. In the height of a disastrous defeat, the child is severely wounded, and his horse killed ; the prince, at peril of his life, notwithstanding the precipitation of a forced retreat, disengages him, and places him on the croup of his own horse ; they are pursued ; a musket-ball strikes their steed, who is just able to reach a jungle, in the midst of which, after some vain efforts, he falls exhausted. The child is unable to walk, but the prince carries him in his arms, and hides with him in the thickest part of the jungle. The English arrive, and begin their search ; but the two victims escape. After a night and a day of marches, counter-marches, stratagems, fatigues, unheard-of perils, the prince, still carrying the child, one of whose legs is broken, arrives at his father's camp, and says, with the utmost simplicity, ' I had promised his mother that I would act a brother's part by him—and I have done so.' "

' That is admirable !' cried the count.——' Go on—pray go on !' said Adrienne, drying a tear, without removing her eyes from the bas-relief, which she continued to contemplate with growing adoration.

The count continued : ' " Another time, Prince Djalma, followed by two black slaves, went, before sunrise, to a very wild spot, to seize a couple of tiger cubs only a few days old. The den had been previously discovered. The two old tigers were still abroad. One of the blacks entered the den by a narrow aperture ; the other, aided by Djalma, cut down a tolerably large tree, to prepare a trap for one of the old tigers. On the side of the aperture, the cavern was exceedingly steep. The prince mounted to the top of it with agility, to set his trap, with the aid of the other black. Suddenly, a dreadful roar was heard ; and, in a few bounds, the tigress, returning from the chase, reached the opening of the den. The black who was laying the trap with the prince had his skull fractured by her bite ; the tree, falling across the entrance, prevented the female from penetrating the cavern, and at the same time stopped the exit of the black who had seized the cubs.

' " About twenty feet higher, upon a ledge of rock, the prince lay flat on the ground, looking down upon this frightful spectacle. The tigress, rendered furious by the cries of her little ones, gnawed the hands of the black, who, from the interior of the den, strove to support the trunk of the tree, his only rampart, whilst he uttered the most lamentable outcries." '

' It is horrible !' said the count.

' Oh ! go on ! pray go on !' exclaimed Adrienne, with excitement ; ' you will see what can be achieved by the heroism of goodness.'

The count pursued : ' " Suddenly the prince seized his dagger between his teeth, fastened his sash to a block of stone, took his axe in one hand, and with the other slid down this substitute for a rope ; falling a few steps from the wild beast, he sprang upon her, and, swift as lightning, dealt her two mortal strokes, just as the black, losing his strength, was about to drop the trunk of the tree, sure to have been torn to pieces." '

' And you are astonished at his resemblance with the demi-god, to whom fable itself ascribes no more generous devotion !' cried the young lady, with still increasing excitement.

' I am astonished no longer, I only admire,' said the count, in a voice of emotion ; ' and, at these two noble instances of heroism, my heart beats with enthusiasm, as if I were still twenty.'——' And the noble heart of this traveller beat like yours at the recital,' said Adrienne ; ' you will see.'

' " What renders so admirable the intrepidity of the prince, is, that, according to the principle of Indian castes, the life of a slave is of no importance ; thus a king's son, risking his life for the safety of a poor creature, so generally despised, obeyed an heroic and truly Christian instinct of charity, until then unheard of in this country.

' " ' Two such actions, said Colonel Drake, with good reason, 'are sufficient to paint the man ;' it is with a feeling of profound respect and admiration, therefore, that I, an obscure traveller, have written the name of Prince Djalma in my book ; and at the same time, I have experienced a kind of sorrow, when I have asked myself what would be the future fate of this prince, buried in the depths of a savage country, always devastated by war. However humble may be the homage that I pay to this character, worthy of the heroic age, his name will at least be repeated with generous enthusiasm by all those who have hearts that beat in sympathy with what is great and noble." '

' And just now, when I read those simple and touching lines,' resumed Adrienne, ' I could not forbear pressing my lips to the name of the traveller.'

' Yes ; he is such as I thought him,' cried the count, with still more emotion, as he returned the book to Adrienne, who rose, with a grave and touching air, and said to him : ' It was thus I wished you to know him, that you might understand my adoration ; for this courage, this heroic goodness, I had guessed beforehand, when I was an involuntary listener to his conversation. From that moment, I knew him to be generous as intrepid, tender and sensitive as energetic and resolute ; and when I saw him so marvellously beautiful—so different, in the noble character of his countenance, and even in the style of his garments, from all I had hitherto met with—when I saw the impression that I made upon him, and which I perhaps felt still more violently—I knew that my whole life was bound up with his love.'

' And now, what are your plans ?'——' Divine, radiant as my heart. When he learns his happiness, I wish that Djalma should feel dazzled as I do, so as to prevent my gazing on my sun ; for I repeat, that until to-morrow will be a century to me. Yes, it is strange ! I should have thought that after such a discovery, I should feel the want of being left alone, plunged in an ocean of delicious dreams. But no ! from this time till to-morrow—I dread solitude—I feel a kind of feverish impatience—uneasy—ardent—Oh ! where is the beneficent fairy, that, touching me with her wand, will lull me into slumber till to-morrow !'

' I will be that beneficent fairy,' said the count, smiling.——' You ?'

' Yes, I.'——' And how so ?'

' The power of my wand is this : I will relieve you from a portion of your houghts by making them materially visible.'

'Pray explain yourself.'——' And my plan will have another advantage for you. Listen to me ; you are so happy now that you can hear anything. Your odious aunt, and her equally odious friends, are spreading the report that your residence with Dr. Baleinier——'

'Was rendered necessary by the derangement of my mind,' said Adrienne, with a smile ; ' I expected that.'

' It is stupid enough ; but, as your resolution to live alone makes many envious of you, and many hostile, you must feel that there will be no want of persons ready to believe the most absurd calumny possible.'

' I hope as much. To pass for mad in the eyes of fools is very flattering.'

' Yes ; but to prove to fools that they are fools, and that in the face of all Paris, is much more amusing. Now, people begin to talk of your absence ; you have given up your daily rides ; for some time my niece has appeared alone in our box at the Opera ; you wish to kill the time till to-morrow— well ! here is an excellent opportunity. It is two o'clock ; at half-past three, my niece will come in the carriage ; the weather is splendid ; there is sure to be a crowd in the Bois de Boulogne. You can take a delightful ride, and be seen by everybody. Then, as the air and movement will have calmed your fever of happiness, I will commence my magic this evening, and take you to India.'

' To India ?'——' Into the midst of one of those wild forests, in which roar the lion, the panther, and the tiger. We will have this heroic combat, which so moved you just now, under our own eyes, in all its terrible reality.'

' Really, my dear count, you must be joking.'——' Not at all ; I promise to show you real wild beasts, formidable tenants of the country of our demigod—growling tigers—roaring lions—do you not think that will be better than books ?'

'But how ?'——' Come ! I must give you the secret of my supernatural power. On returning from your ride, you shall dine with my niece, and we will go together to a very curious spectacle, now exhibiting at the Porte-Saint-Martin Theatre. A most extraordinary lion-tamer there shows you a number of wild beasts, in a state of nature, in the midst of a forest (here only commences the illusion), and has fierce combats with them all—tigers, lions, and panthers. All Paris is crowding to these representations, and all Paris will see you there, more charming than ever.'

' I accept your offer,' said Adrienne, with childish delight. ' Yes, you are right. I shall feel a strange pleasure in beholding these ferocious monsters, who will remind me of those that my demi-god so heroically overcame. I accept also, because, for the first time in my life, I am anxious to be admired—even by everybody. I accept finally because——' Here Mdlle. de Cardoville was interrupted by a low knock at the door, and by the entrance of Florine, who announced M. Rodin.

CHAPTER X.

THE EXECUTION.

RODIN entered. A rapid glance at Mdlle. de Cardoville and M. de Montbron told him at once that he was in a dilemma. In fact, nothing could be less encouraging than the faces of Adrienne and the count. The latter, when he disliked people, exhibited his antipathy, as we have already said, by an impertinently aggressive manner, which had before now occasioned a good number of duels. At sight of Rodin, his countenance at once assumed a harsh and insolent expression ; resting his elbow on the chimney-piece, and conversing with Adrienne, he looked disdainfully over his shoulder, without taking the least notice of the Jesuit's low bow. On the other hand, at sight of this man, Mdlle. de Cardoville almost felt surprise, that she should experience no movement of anger or hatred. The brilliant flame which burned in her heart, purified it from every vindictive sentiment. She smiled, on the contrary ; for, glancing with gentle pride at the Indian Bacchus, and then at herself, she asked herself what two beings, so young, and fair, and free, and loving, could have to fear from this old, sordid man, with his ignoble and base countenance, now advancing towards her with the writhing of a reptile. In a word, far from feeling anger or aversion with regard to Rodin, the young lady seemed full of the spirit of mocking gaiety, and her large eyes, already lighted up with happiness, now sparkled with irony and mischief. Rodin felt himself ill at ease. People of his stamp greatly prefer violent to mocking enemies. They can encounter bursts of rage— sometimes by falling on their knees, weeping, groaning, and beating their breasts—sometimes by turning on their adversary, armed and implacable. But they are easily disconcerted by biting raillery ; and thus it was with Rodin. He saw that, between Adrienne de Cardoville and M. de Montbron, he was about to be placed in what is vulgarly termed a 'regular fix.'

The count opened the fire ; still glancing over his shoulder, he said to Rodin : 'Ah ! you are here, my benevolent gentleman !'

'Pray, sir, draw a little nearer,' said Adrienne, with a mocking smile. 'Best of friends and model of philosophers—as well as declared enemy of all fraud and falsehood—I have to pay you a thousand compliments.'

'I accept anything from you, my dear young lady, even though undeserved,' said the Jesuit, trying to smile, and thus exposing his vile yellow teeth ; 'but may I be informed how I have earned these compliments ?'

'Your penetration, sir, which is rare——' replied Adrienne.——'And your veracity, sir,' said the count, 'which is perhaps no less rare——'

'In what have I exhibited my penetration, my dear young lady ?' said Rodin, coldly. 'In what my veracity ?' added he, turning towards M. de Montbron.

'In what, sir ?' said Adrienne. 'Why, you have guessed a secret surrounded by difficulties and mystery. In a word, you have known how to read the depths of a woman's heart.'

'I, my dear young lady ?'——'You, sir ! rejoice at it, for your penetration has had the most fortunate results.'

'And your veracity has worked wonders,' added the count.

'It is pleasant to do good, even without knowing it,' said Rodin, still acting on the defensive, and throwing side glances by turns on the count and Adrienne ; 'but will you inform me what it is that deserves this praise——'

'Gratitude obliges me to inform you of it,' said Adrienne, maliciously ; 'you have discovered, and told Prince Djalma, that I was passionately in love. Well ! I admire your penetration ; it was true.'

'You have also discovered, and told this lady, that Prince Djalma was passionately in love,' resumed the count. 'Well ! I admire your penetration, my dear sir ; it was true.' Rodin looked confused, and at a loss for a reply.

'The person that I loved so passionately,' said Adrienne, 'was the prince.'

'The person that the prince loved so passionately,' resumed the coun!,
'was this lady.'

These revelations, so sudden and alarming, almost stunned Rodin ; he
remained mute and terrified, thinking of the future.

'Do you understand now, sir, the extent of our gratitude towards you ?
resumed Adrienne, in a still more mocking tone. 'Thanks to your sagacity,
thanks to the touching interest you take in us, the prince and I are indebted
to you for the knowledge of our mutual sentiments.'

The Jesuit had now gradually recovered his presence of mind, and his
apparent calmness greatly irritated M. de Montbron, who, but for Adrienne's
presence, would have assumed another tone than jests.

'There is some mistake,' said Rodin, ' in what you have done me the
honour to tell me, my dear young lady. I have never in my life spoken of
the sentiments, however worthy and respectable, that you may entertain for
Prince Djalma——'

'That is true,' replied Adrienne ; 'with scrupulous and exquisite discretion, whenever you spoke to me of the deep love felt by Prince Djalma, you
carried your reserve and delicacy so far as to inform me that it was not I
whom he loved.'

'And the same scruple induced you to tell the prince that Mdlle. de
Cardoville loved some one passionately—but that he was not the person,'
added the count.

'Sir,' answered Rodin, drily, ' I need hardly tell you that I have no desire
to mix myself up with amorous intrigues.'

'Come ! this is either pride or modesty,' said the count, insolently. 'For
your own interest, pray do not advance such things ; for, if we took you at
your word, and it became known, it might injure some of the nice little
trades that you carry on.'

'There is one at least,' said Rodin, drawing himself up as proudly as M.
de Montbron, 'whose rude apprenticeship I shall owe to you. It is the
wearisome one of listening to your discourse.'

'I tell you what, my good sir !' replied the count, disdainfully : 'you force
me to remind you that there are more ways than one of chastising impudent rogues.'

'My dear count !' said Adrienne to M. de Montbron, with an air of reproach.

With perfect coolness, Rodin replied : 'I do not exactly see, sir, first,
what courage is shown by threatening a poor old man like myself ; and,
secondly——'

'M. Rodin,' said the count, interrupting the Jesuit, 'first, a poor old man
like you, who does evil under the shelter of the age he dishonours, is both
cowardly and wicked, and deserves a double chastisement ; secondly, with
regard to this question of age, I am not aware that gamekeepers and policemen bow down respectfully to the grey coats of old wolves, and the grey
hairs of old thieves. What do you think, my good sir ?'

Still impassible, Rodin raised his flabby eyelid, fixed for hardly a second
his little reptile eye upon the count, and darted at him one of his rapid,
cold, and piercing glances—and then the livid eyelid again covered the dull
eye of that corpse-like face.

'Not having the disadvantage of being an old wolf, and still less an old
thief,' said Rodin, quietly, 'you will permit me, sir, to take no account of
the pursuit of hunters and police. As for the reproaches made me, I have
a very simple method of answering—I do not say of justifying myself—I
never justify myself——'——' You don't say !' said the count.

'Never,' resumed Rodin coolly ; 'my acts are sufficient for that. I will then simply answer, that seeing the deep, violent, almost fearful impression made by this lady on the prince——'

' Let this assurance which you give me of the prince's love,' said Adrienne, interrupting Rodin with an enchanting smile, 'absolve you of all the evil you wished to do me. The sight of our happiness be your only punishment !'

'It may be that I need neither absolution nor punishment, for, as I have already had the honour to observe to the count, my dear young lady, the future will justify my acts. Yes ; it was my duty to tell the prince that you loved another than himself, and to tell you that he loved another than yourself—all in your mutual interest. That my attachment for you may have misled me, is possible—I am not infallible ; but, after my past conduct towards you, my dear young lady, I have, perhaps, some right to be astonished at seeing myself thus treated. This is not a complaint. If I never justify myself, I never complain either.'

' Now really, there is something heroic in all this, my good sir,' said the count. ' You do not condescend to complain or justify yourself, with regard to the evil you have done.'

' The evil I have done ?' said Rodin, looking fixedly at the count. ' Are we playing at enigmas ?'

' What, sir !' cried the count, with indignation ; 'is it nothing, by your falsehoods, to have plunged the prince into so frightful a state of despair, that he has twice attempted his life ? Is it nothing, by similar falsehoods, to have induced this lady to believe so cruel and complete an error, that but for the resolution I have to-day taken, it might have led to the most fatal consequences ?'

' And will you do me the honour to tell me, sir, what interest I could have in all this despair and error, admitting even that I had wished to produce them ?'

' Some great interest, no doubt,' said the count, bluntly ; ' the more dangerous that it is concealed. You are one of those, I see, to whom the woes of others are pleasure and profit.'

' That is really too much, sir,' said Rodin, bowing ; ' I should be quite contented with the profit.'

' Your impudent coolness will not deceive me ; this is a serious matter,' said the count. ' It is impossible that so perfidious a piece of roguery can be an isolated act. Who knows but this may still be one of the fruits of Madame de Saint-Dizier's hatred for Mdlle. de Cardoville ?'

Adrienne had listened to the preceding discussion with deep attention. Suddenly she started, as if struck by a sudden revelation.

After a moment's silence, she said to Rodin, without anger, without bitterness, but with an expression of gentle and serene calmness : ' We are told, sir, that happy love works miracles. I should be tempted to believe it ; for, after some minutes' reflection, and when I recall certain circumstances, your conduct appears to me in quite a new light.'

' And what may this new perspective be, my dear young lady ?'——' That you may see it from my point of view, sir, allow me to remind you of a few facts. That sewing-girl was generously devoted to me ; she had given me unquestionable proofs of her attachment. Her mind was equal to her noble heart ; but she had an invincible dislike to you. All on a sudden she disappears mysteriously from my house, and you do your best to cast upon her odious suspicions. M. de Montbron has a paternal affection for me ; but, as I must confess, little sympathy for you ; and you have always tried to produce a coldness between us. Finally, Prince Djalma has a deep affection for me, and you employ the most perfidious treachery to kill that sentiment within him. For what end do you act thus? I do not know; but certainly with some hostile design.'

'It appears to me, madame,' said Rodin, severely, 'that you have forgotten services performed.'

'I do not deny, sir, that you took me from the house of Dr. Baleinier; but, a few days sooner or later, I must infallibly have been released by M. de Montbron.'

'You are right, my dear child,' said the count; 'it may be that your enemies wished to claim the merit of what must necessarily have happened through the exertions of your friends.'

'You are drowning, and I save you—it is all a mistake to feel grateful,' said Rodin, bitterly; 'some one else would no doubt have saved you a little later.'

'The comparison is wanting in exactness,' said Adrienne, with a smile; 'a lunatic asylum is not a river, and though, from what I see, I think you quite capable of diving, you have had no occasion to swim on this occasion. You merely opened a door for me, which would have opened of itself a little later.'

'Very good, my dear child!' said the count, laughing heartily at Adrienne's reply.

'I know, sir, that your care did not extend to me only. The daughters of Marshal Simon were brought back by you; but we may imagine that the claim of the Duke de Ligny to the possession of his daughters would not have been in vain. You returned to an old soldier his imperial cross, which he held to be a sacred relic; it is a very touching incident. Finally, you unmasked the Abbé d'Aigrigny and Dr. Baleinier; but I had already made up my mind to unmask them. However, all this proves that you are a very clever man——'——'Oh, madame!' said Rodin, humbly.

'Full of resources and invention——'——'Oh, madame!'

'It is not my fault if, in our long interview at Dr. Baleinier's, you betrayed that superiority of mind which struck me so forcibly, and which seems to embarrass you so much at present. What would you have, sir?—great minds like yours find it difficult to maintain their incognito. Yet, as by different ways—oh! very different,' added the young lady, maliciously, 'we are tending to the same end (still keeping in view our conversation at Dr. Baleinier's), I wish, for the sake of our future communion, as you call it, to give you a piece of advice, and speak frankly to you.'

Rodin had listened to Mdlle. de Cardoville with apparent impassibility, holding his hat under his arm, and twirling his thumbs, whilst his hands were crossed upon his waistcoat. The only external mark of the intense agitation into which he was thrown by the calm words of Adrienne, was that the livid eyelids of the Jesuit, which had been hypocritically closed, became gradually red, as the blood flowed into them. Nevertheless, he answered Mdlle. de Cardoville in a firm voice, and with a low bow: 'Good advice and frankness are always excellent things.'

'You see, sir,' resumed Adrienne, with some excitement, 'happy love bestows such penetration, such energy, such courage, as enables one to laugh at perils, to detect stratagems, and to defy hatred. Believe me, the divine light which surrounds two loving hearts will be sufficient to disperse all darkness, and reveal every snare. You see, in India—excuse my weakness, but I like to talk of India,' added the young girl, with a smile of indescribable grace and meaning—'in India, when travellers sleep at night, they kindle great fires round their ajoupa (excuse this touch of local colouring), and far as extends the luminous circle, it puts to flight by its mere brilliancy, all the impure and venomous reptiles that shun the day and live only in darkness,'

'The meaning of this comparison has quite escaped me,' said Rodin, continuing to twirl his thumbs, and half raising his eyelids, which were getting redder and redder.

'I will speak more plainly,' said Adrienne, with a smile. 'Suppose, sir, that the last is a service which you have rendered me and the prince—for you only proceed by way of services—that, I acknowledge, is novel and ingenious.'

'Bravo, my dear child!' said the count, joyfully. 'The execution will be complete.'

'Oh! this is meant for an execution?' said Rodin, still impassible.

'No, sir,' answered Adrienne, with a smile; 'it is a simple conversation between a poor young girl and an old philosopher, the friend of humanity. Suppose, then, that these frequent services that you have rendered to me and mine have suddenly opened my eyes; or, rather,' added the young girl, in a serious tone, 'suppose that heaven, who gives to the mother the instinct to defend her child, has given me, along with happiness, the instinct to preserve my happiness, and that a vague presentiment, by throwing light on a thousand circumstances until now obscure, has suddenly revealed to me that, instead of being the friend, you are, perhaps, the most dangerous enemy of myself and family.'

'So we pass from the execution to suppositions,' said Rodin, still immovable.

'And from suppositions, sir, if you must have it, to certainty,' resumed Adrienne, with dignified firmness; 'yes, now I believe that I was for awhile your dupe, and I tell you, without hate, without anger, but with regret—that it is painful to see a man of your sense and intelligence stoop to such machinations, and, after having recourse to so many diabolical manœuvres, finish at last by being ridiculous; for, believe me, there is nothing more ridiculous for a man like you, than to be vanquished by a young girl, who has no weapon, no defence, no instructor, but her love. In a word, sir, I look upon you from to-day as an implacable and dangerous enemy; for I half perceive your aim, without guessing by what means you will seek to accomplish it. No doubt your future means will be worthy of the past. Well! in spite of all this, I do not fear you. From to-morrow, my family will be informed of everything, and an active, intelligent, resolute union will keep us all upon our guard, for it doubtless concerns this enormous inheritance, of which they wish to deprive us. Now, what connexion can there be between the wrongs I reproach you with and the pecuniary end proposed? I do not at all know—but you have told me yourself that our enemies are so dangerously skilful, and their craft so far-reaching, that we must expect all, be prepared for all. I will remember the lesson. I have promised you frankness, sir, and now I suppose you have it.'

'It would be an imprudent frankness if I were your enemy,' said Rodin, still impassible; 'but you also promised me some advice, my dear young lady.'

'My advice will be short; do not attempt to continue the struggle, because, you see, there is something stronger than you and yours—it is a woman's resolve, defending her happiness.'

Adrienne pronounced these last words with so sovereign a confidence; her beautiful countenance shone, as it were, with such intrepid joy, that Rodin, notwithstanding his phlegmatic audacity, was for a moment frightened. Yet he did not appear in the least disconcerted; and, after a moment's silence, he resumed, with an air of almost contemptuous compassion: 'My dear young lady, we may perhaps never meet again; it is probable. Only remember one thing, which I now repeat to you: I never justify myself. The future will provide for that. Notwithstanding which, my dear young lady, I am your very humble servant; and he made her a low bow.

'Count, I beg to salute you most respectfully,' he added, bowing still more humbly to M. de Montbron; and he went out.

Hardly had Rodin left the room than Adrienne ran to her desk, and writing a few hasty lines, sealed the note, and said to M de Montbron : 'I shall not see the prince before to-morrow—as much from superstition of the heart as because it is necessary for my plans that this interview should be attended with some little solemnity. You shall know all ; but I write to him on the instant, for, with an enemy like M. Rodin, one must be prepared for all.'

'You are right, my dear child ; quick ! the letter.' Adrienne gave it to him.

'I tell him enough,' said she, 'to calm his grief ; and not enough to deprive me of the delicious happiness of the surprise I reserve for to-morrow.'

'All this has as much sense as heart in it ; I will hasten to the prince's abode, to deliver your letter. I shall not see him, for I could not answer for myself. But come ! our proposed drive, our evening's amusement, are still to hold good.'

'Certainly. I have more need than ever to divert my thoughts till to-morrow. I feel, too, that the fresh air will do me good, for this interview with M. Rodin has warmed me a little.'

'The old wretch ! but we will talk further of him. I will hasten to the prince's and return with Madame de Morinval, to fetch you to the Champs-Elysées.'

The Count de Montbron withdrew precipitately, as joyful at his departure as he had been sad on his arrival.

CHAPTER XI.

THE CHAMPS-ELYSEES.

It was about two hours after the interview of Rodin with Mdlle. de Cardoville. Numerous loungers, attracted to the Champs-Elysées by the serenity of a fine spring day (it was towards the end of the month of March), stopped to admire a very handsome equipage. A bright-blue open carriage, with white-and-blue wheels, drawn by four superb horses, of cream colour, with black manes, and harness glittering with silver ornaments, mounted by two boy postilions of equal size, with black velvet caps, light-blue cassi-mere jackets with white collars, buck-skin breeches, and top-boots ; two tall, powdered footmen, also in light-blue livery, with white collars and facings, being seated in the rumble behind. No equipage could have been turned out in better style. The horses, full of blood, spirit, and vigour, were skilfully managed by the postilions, and stepped with singular regularity, gracefully keeping time in their movements, champing their bits covered with foam, and ever and anon shaking their cockades of blue and white silk, with long floating ends, and a bright rose blooming in the midst.

A man on horseback, dressed with elegant simplicity, keeping at the other side of the avenue, contemplated with proud satisfaction this equipage which he had, as it were, created. It was M. de Bonneville—Adrienne's equerry, as M. de Montbron called him—for the carriage belonged to that young lady. A change had taken place in the plan for this magic day's amusement. M. de Montbron had not been able to deliver Mdlle. de Cardoville's note to Prince Djalma. Faringhea had told him that the prince had gone that morning into the country with Marshal Simon, and would not be back before evening. The letter should be given him on his arrival. Completely satisfied as to Djalma, knowing that he could find these few lines, which, without informing him of the happiness that awaited him, would at least give him some idea of it, Adrienne had followed the advice of M. de Montbron, and gone to the drive in her own carriage, to show all the world that she had quite made up her mind, in spite of the perfidious reports circulated by the Princess de Saint-Dizier, to keep to her resolution of living by herself in her own way. Adrienne wore a small white bonnet, with a fall of blonde, which well became her rosy face and golden hair ; her high dress of garnet-coloured velvet was almost hidden beneath a large green cashmere shawl. The young Marchioness de Morinval, who was also very pretty and elegant, was seated at her right. M. de Montbron occupied the front seat of the carriage.

Those who know the Parisian world, or, rather, that imperceptible fraction of the world of Paris which goes every fine, sunny day to the Champs-Elysées, to see and be seen, will understand that the presence of Mdlle. de Cardoville on that brilliant promenade was an extraordinary and interesting event.

The world (as it is called) could hardly believe its eyes, on seeing this lady of eighteen, possessed of princely wealth, and belonging to the highest nobility, thus prove to every one, by this appearance in public, that she was living completely free and independent, contrary to all custom and received notions of propriety. This kind of emancipation appeared something monstrous, and people were almost astonished that the graceful and dignified bearing of the young lady should belie so completely the calumnies circulated by Madame de Saint-Dizier and her friends, with regard to the pretended madness of her niece. Many beaux, profiting by their acquaintance with the Marchioness de Morinval or M. de Montbron, came by turns to pay their respects, and rode for a few minutes by the side of the carriage, so as to have an opportunity of seeing, admiring, and perhaps hearing, Mdlle. de Cardoville ; she surpassed their expectations, by talking with her usual grace and spirit. Then surprise and enthusiasm knew no bounds. What had at first been blamed as an almost insane caprice, was now voted a charming originality, and it only depended on Mdlle. de Cardoville herself, to be declared from that day the queen of elegance and fashion. The young lady understood very well the impression she had made ; she felt proud and happy, for she thought of Djalma ; when she compared him to all these men of fashion, her happiness was the more increased. And, verily, these young men, most of whom had never quitted Paris, or had ventured at most as far as Naples or Baden, looked insignificant enough by the side of Djalma, who, at his age, had so many times commanded and combated in bloody wars, and whose reputation for courage and generosity, mentioned by travellers with admiration, had already reached from India to Paris. And then, how could these charming exquisites, with their small hats, their scanty frock-coats, and their huge cravats, compare with the Indian prince, whose graceful and manly beauty was still heightened by the splendour of a costume, at once so rich and so picturesque ?

On this happy day, all was joy and love for Adrienne. The sun, setting in a splendidly serene sky, flooded the promenade with its golden light. The air was warm. Carriages and horsemen passed and repassed in rapid succession ; a light breeze played with the scarfs of the women, and the plumes in their bonnets ; all around was noise, movement, sunshine. Adrienne, leaning back in her carriage, amused herself with watching this busy scene, sparkling with Parisian luxury ; but, in the vortex of this brilliant chaos, she saw in thought the mild, melancholy countenance of

Djalma—when suddenly something fell into her lap, and she started. It was a bunch of half-faded violets. At the same instant she heard a child's voice following the carriage, and saying : 'For the love of heaven, my good lady, one little sou !' Adrienne turned her head, and saw a poor little girl, pale and wan, with mild, sorrowful features, scarcely covered with rags, holding out her hand, and raising her eyes in supplication. Though the striking contrast of extreme misery, side by side with extreme luxury, is so common, that it no longer excites attention, Adrienne was deeply affected by it. She thought of Mother Bunch, now, perhaps the victim of frightful destitution.

'Ah ! at least,' thought the young lady, 'let not this day be one of happiness for me alone !'

She leaned from the carriage-window, and said to the poor child : 'Have you a mother, my dear ?'

'No, my lady, I have neither father nor mother.'

'Who takes care of you ?'

'No one, my lady. They give me nosegays to sell, and I must bring home money—or they beat me.'

'Poor little thing.'

'A sou, my good lady—a sou, for the love of heaven !' said the child, continuing to follow the carriage, which was then moving slowly.

'My dear count,' said Adrienne, smiling, and addressing M. de Montbron, 'you are, unfortunately, no novice at an elopement. Please to stretch forth your arms, take up that child with both hands, and lift her into the carriage. We can hide her between Lady de Morinval and myself ; and we can drive away before any one perceives this audacious abduction.'

'What !' said the count, in surprise. 'You wish——'——'Yes ; I beg you to do it.'

'What a folly !'——'Yesterday, you might, perhaps, have treated this caprice as a folly ; but to-day,' said Adrienne, laying great stress upon the word, and glancing at M. de Montbron with a significant air, 'to-day, you should understand that it is almost a duty.'

'Yes, I understand you, good and noble heart !' said the count, with emotion ; while Lady de Morinval, who knew nothing of Mdlle. de Cardoville's love for Djalma, looked with as much surprise as curiosity at the count and the young lady.

M. de Montbron, leaning from the carriage, stretched out his arms towards the child, and said to her : 'Give me your hands, little girl.'

Though much astonished, the child obeyed mechanically, and held out both her little arms ; then the count took her by the wrists, and lifted her lightly from the ground, which he did the more easily, as the carriage was very low, and its progress by no means rapid. More stupefied than frightened, the child said not a word. Adrienne and Lady de Morinval made room for her to crouch down between them, and the little girl was soon hidden beneath the shawls of the two young women. All this was executed so quickly, that it was hardly perceived by a few persons passing in the side-avenues.

'Now, my dear count,' said Adrienne, radiant with pleasure, 'let us make off at once with our prey.'

M. de Montbron half rose, and called to the postilions, 'Home !' and the four horses started at once into a rapid and regular trot.

'This day of happiness now seems consecrated, and my luxury is excused,' thought Adrienne ; 'till I can again meet with that poor Mother Bunch, and from this day I will make every exertion to find her out ; her place will at least not be quite empty.'

There are often strange coincidences in life. At the moment when this thought of the hunchback crossed the mind of Adrienne, a crowd had collected in one of the side-avenues, and other persons soon ran to join the group.

'Look, uncle!' said Lady de Morinval; 'how many people are assembled yonder. What can it be? Shall we stop, and send to inquire?'

'I am sorry, my dear, but your curiosity cannot be satisfied,' said the count, drawing out his watch; 'it will soon be six o'clock, and the exhibition of the wild beasts begins at eight. We shall only just have time to go home and dine. Is not that your opinion, my dear child?' said he to Adrienne.

'And yours, Julia?' said Mdlle. de Cardoville to the marchioness.

'Oh, certainly!' answered her friend.

'I am the less inclined to delay,' resumed the count, 'as when I have taken you to the Porte-Saint-Martin, I shall be obliged to go for half-an-hour to my club, to ballot for Lord Campbell, whom I propose.'

'Then, Adrienne and I will be left alone at the play, uncle?'——'Your husband will go with you, I suppose.'

'True, dear uncle; but do not quite leave us, because of that.'

'Be sure I shall not: for I am curious as you are to see these terrible animals, and the famous Morok, the incomparable lion-tamer.'

A few minutes after, Mdlle. de Cardoville's carriage had left the Champs-Elysées, carrying with it the little girl, and directing its course towards the Rue d'Anjou. As the brilliant equipage disappeared from the scene, the crowd, of which we before have spoken, greatly increased about one of the large trees in the Champs-Elysées, and expressions of pity were heard here and there amongst the groups. A lounger approached a young man on the skirts of the crowd, and said to him: 'What is the matter, sir?'

'I hear it is a poor young girl, a hunchback, that has fallen from exhaustion.'

'A hunchback! is that all? There will always be enough hunchbacks,' said the lounger, brutally, with a coarse laugh.

'Hunchback or not, if she dies of hunger,' answered the young man, scarcely able to restrain his indignation, 'it will be no less sad—and there is really nothing to laugh at, sir.'

'Die of hunger! pooh!' said the lounger, shrugging his shoulders. 'It is only lazy scoundrels, that will not work, who die of hunger. And it serves them right.'

'I wager, sir, there is one death you will never die of,' cried the young man, incensed at the cruel insolence of the lounger.

'What do you mean?' answered the other, haughtily.——'I mean, sir, that your heart is not likely to kill you.'

'Sir!' cried the lounger, in an angry tone.——'Well! what, sir?' replied the young man, looking full in his face.

'Nothing,' said the lounger, turning abruptly on his heel, and grumbling as he sauntered towards an orange-coloured cabriolet, on which was emblazoned an enormous coat-of-arms, surmounted by a baron's crest. A servant in green livery, ridiculously laced with gold, was standing beside the horse, and did not perceive his master.

'Are you catching flies, fool?' said the latter, pushing him with his cane. The servant turned round in confusion. 'Sir,' said he.

'Will you never learn to call me Monsieur le Baron, rascal?' cried his master, in a rage.—'Open the door directly!'

The lounger was Baron Tripeaud, the manufacturing baron, the stock-jobber. The poor hunchback was Mother Bunch, who had, indeed, fallen

with hunger and fatigue, whilst on her way to Mdlle. de Cardoville's.   The
unfortunate creature had found courage to brave the shame of the ridicule
she so much feared, by returning to that house from which she was a voluntary exile ; but this time, it was not for herself, but for her sister Cephyse—
the Bacchanal Queen, who had returned to Paris the previous day, and
whom Mother Bunch now sought, through the means of Adrienne, to rescue
from a most dreadful fate.

       ✿   ✿   ✿   ✿   ✿   ✿

Two hours after these different scenes, an enormous crowd pressed round
the doors of the Porte-Saint-Martin, to witness the exercises of Morok, who
was about to perform a mock combat with the famous black panther of Java,
named Death.   Adrienne, accompanied by Lord and Lady de Morinval,
now stepped from a carriage at the entrance of the theatre.   They were to
be joined in the course of the evening by M. de Montbron, whom they had
dropped, in passing, at his club.

CHAPTER XII.

BEHIND THE SCENES.

THE large theatre of the Port-Saint-Martin was crowded by an impatient
multitude. All Paris had hurried with eager and burning curiosity to Morok's
exhibition.   It is quite unnecessary to say that the lion-tamer had completely abandoned his small taste in religious baubles, which he had so successfully carried on at the White Falcon Inn at Leipsic.   There were,
moreover, numerous tokens by which the surprising effects of Morok's
sudden conversion had been blazoned in the most extraordinary pictures :
the antiquated baubles in which he had formerly dealt would have found no
sale in Paris.   Morok had nearly finished dressing himself, in one of the
actor's rooms, which had been lent to him.   Over a coat of mail, with
cuishes and brassarts, he wore an ample pair of red trousers, fastened round
his ankles by broad rings of gilt brass.   His long caftan of black cloth, embroidered with scarlet and gold, was bound round his waist and wrist by
other large rings of gilt metal.   This sombre costume imparted to him an
aspect still more ferocious.   His thick and red-haired beard fell in large
quantities down to his chest, and a long piece of white muslin was folded
round his red head.   A devout missionary in Germany and an actor in
Paris, Morok knew as well as his employers, the Jesuits, how to accommo-
date himself to circumstances.

Seated in one corner of the room, and contemplating with a sort of stupid
admiration, was Jacques Rennepont, better known as ' Sleepinbuff' (from
the likelihood that he would end his days in rags, or his present antipathy
to great care in dress).   Since the day Hardy's factory had been destroyed
by fire, Jacques had not quitted Morok, passing the nights in excesses, which
had no baneful effects on the iron constitution of the lion-tamer.   On the
other's features, on the contrary, a great alteration was perceptible ; his
hollow cheeks, marble pallor, his eyes, by turns dull and heavy, or gleaming
with lurid fire, betrayed the ravages of debauchery ; his parched lips were
almost constantly curled by a bitter and sardonic smile.   His spirit, once
gay and sanguine, still struggled against the besotting influence of habitual
intoxication.   Unfitted for labour, no longer able to forego gross pleasures,
Jacques sought to drown in wine the few virtuous impulses which he still
possessed, and had sunk so low as to accept without shame the large dole
of sensual gratification proffered him by Morok, who paid all the expenses
of their orgies, but never gave him money, in order that he might be com-

pletely dependent on him. After gazing at Morok for some time in amazement, Jacques said to him, in a familiar tone : 'Well, yours is a famous trade ; you may boast that, at this moment, there are not two men like you in the whole world. That's flattering. It's a pity you don't stick to this fine trade.'

'What do you mean ?'——'Why, how is the conspiracy going on, in whose honour you make me keep it up all day and all night ?'

'It is working, but the time is not yet come ; that is why I wish to have you always at hand, till the great day. Do you complain ?'

'Hang it, no !' said Jacques. 'What could I do ? Burnt up with brandy as I am, if I wanted to work, I've no longer the strength to do so. I have not, like you, a head of marble, and a body of iron ; but as for fuddling myself with gunpowder, instead of anything else, that'll do for me ; I'm only fit for that work, now—and then, it will drive away thought.'

'Of what kind ?'——'You know that when I do think, I think only of one thing,' said Jacques, gloomily.

'The Bacchanal Queen ?—still ?' said Morok, in a disdainful tone.

'Still ! rather : when I shall think of her no longer, I shall be dead—or stupefied. Fiend !'

'You were never better or more intelligent, you fool !' replied Morok, fastening his turban. The conversation was here interrupted. Morok's aider entered hastily.

The gigantic form of this Hercules had increased in width. He was habited like Alcides ; his enormous limbs, furrowed with veins as thick as whipcord, were covered with a close-fitting flesh-coloured garment, to which a pair of red drawers formed a strong contrast.

'Why do you rush in like a storm, Goliath ?' said Morok.——'There's a pretty storm in the house ; they are beginning to get impatient, and are calling out like madmen. But if that were all !'

'Well, what else ?'——'*Death* will not be able to play this evening.'

Morok turned quickly round. He seemed uneasy. 'Why so ?' he exclaimed.——'I have just seen her ; she's crouching at the bottom of her cage ; her ears lie so close to her head, she looks as if they had been cut off. You know what that means.'

'Is that all ?' said Morok, turning to the glass to complete his head-dress.

'It's quite enough ; she's in one of her tearing fits. Since that night, in Germany, when she ripped up that old hack of a white horse, I've not seen her look so savage ! her eyes shine like burning candles.'

'Then she must have her fine collar on,' said Morok, quietly.——'Her fine collar ?'——'Yes ; her spring-collar.'

'And I must be lady's-maid,' said the giant. 'A nice toilet to attend to !'

'Hold your tongue !'——'That's not all——' continued Goliath, hesitating.

'What more ?'——'I might as well tell you at once.'

'Will you speak ?'——'Well !—he is here.'

'Who, you stupid brute ?'——'The Englishman !'

Morok started ; his arms fell powerless by his side. Jacques was struck with the lion-tamer's paleness and troubled countenance.

'The Englishman !—you have seen him ?' cried Morok, addressing Goliath. 'You are quite sure ?'

'Quite sure. I was looking through the peephole in the curtain ; I saw him in one of the stage-boxes—he wishes to see things close ; he's easy to recognise, with his pointed forehead, big nose, and goggle eyes.'

Morok shuddered again ; usually fierce and unmoved, he appeared to be more and more agitated, and so alarmed, that Jacques said to him : 'Who is this Englishman ?'

'He has followed me from Strasburg, where he fell in with me,' said Morok, with visible dejection. 'He travelled with his own horses, by short stages, as I did ; stopping where I stopped, so as never to miss one of my exhibitions. But two days before I arrived at Paris, he left me—I thought I was rid of him,' said Morok, with a sigh.

'Rid of him !—how you talk !' replied Jacques, surprised ; 'such a good customer, such an admirer !'

'Aye !' said Morok, becoming more and more agitated ; 'this wretch has wagered an enormous sum, that I will be devoured in his presence, during one of my performances : he hopes to win his wager—that is why he follows me about.'

Sleepinbuff found the John Bull's idea so amusingly eccentric, that, for the first time since a very long period, he burst into a peal of hearty laughter. Morok, pale with rage, rushed towards him with so menacing an air, that Goliath was obliged to interpose.

'Come, come,' said Jacques, 'don't be angry ; if it is serious, I will not laugh any more.'

Morok was appeased, and said to Sleepinbuff in a hoarse voice : 'Do you think me a coward ?'

'No, by heaven !'

'Well ! and yet this Englishman, with his grotesque face, frightens me more than my tiger or my panther !'

'You say so, and I believe it,' replied Jacques ; 'but I cannot understand why the presence of this man should alarm you.

'But, consider, you dull knave !' cried Morok, 'that, obliged to watch in-cessantly, the least movement of the ferocious beast, whom I keep in sub-jection by my action and my looks, there is something terrible in knowing that two eyes are there—always there—fixed—waiting till the least absence of mind shall expose me to be torn in pieces by the animals.'

'Now, I understand,' said Jacques, shuddering in his turn. 'It is terrible.'

'Yes ; for once there, though I may not see this cursed Englishman, I fancy I have his two round eyes, fixed and wide open, always before me. My tiger *Cain* once nearly mutilated my arm, when my attention was drawn away by this Englishman, whom the devil take ! Blood and thunder !' cried Morok : 'this man will be fatal to me.' And Morok paced the room in great agitation.

'Besides, *Death* lays her ears close to her skull,' said Goliath, brutally. 'If you persist—mind, I tell you—the Englishman will win his wager this evening.'

'Go away, you brute !—don't vex my head with your confounded pre-dictions,' cried Morok : 'go and prepare *Death's* collar.'

'Well, every one to his taste ; you wish the panther to *taste* you,' said the giant, stalking heavily away, after this joke.

'But if you feel these fears,' said Jacques, 'why do you not say that the panther is ill ?'

Morok shrugged his shoulders, and replied with a sort of feverish ferocity : 'Have you ever heard of the fierce pleasure of the gamester, who stakes his honour, his life, upon a card ? Well ! I too—in these daily exhibitions where my life is at stake—find a wild, fierce pleasure in braving death, before a crowded assembly, shuddering and terrified at my audacity. Yes, even in the fear with which this Englishman inspires me, I find, in spite of myself, a terrible excitement, which I abhor, and which yet subjugates me.'

At this moment, the stage-manager entered the room, and interrupted the beast-tamer. 'May we give the signal, M. Morok ?' said the stage-manager. 'The overture will not last above ten minutes.'

'I am ready,' said Morok.——'The police-inspector has just now given orders, that the double chain of the panther, and the iron ring riveted to the floor of the stage, at the end of the cavern in the foreground, shall be again examined ; and everything has been reported quite secure.'——'Yes —secure—except for me,' murmured the beast-tamer.

'So, M. Morok, the signal may be given ?'——'The signal may be given,' replied Morok. And the manager went out.

CHAPTER XIII.

UP WITH THE CURTAIN.

THE usual bell sounded with solemnity behind the scenes ; the overture began, and, to say the truth, but little attention was paid to it. The interior of the theatre offered a very animated view. With the exception of two stage-boxes even with the dress-circle, one to the left, the other to the right of the audience, every seat was occupied. A great number of very fashionable ladies, attracted, as is always the case, by the strange wildness of the spectacle, filled the boxes. The stalls were crowded by most of the young men who, in the morning, had walked their horses on the Champs-Elysées. The observations which passed from one stall to another will give some idea of their conversation.

'Do you know, my dear boy, there would not be so crowded or fashionable an audience to witness Racine's Athalie ?'

'Undoubtedly. What is the beggarly howling of an actor, compared to the roaring of the lion ?'

'I cannot understand how the authorities permit this Morok to fasten his panther with a chain to an iron ring in the corner of the stage. If the chain were to break ?'——'Talking of broken chains—there's little Mme. de Blinville, who is no tigress. Do you see her in the second tier, opposite ?'

'It becomes her very well to have broken, as you say, the marriage chain; she looks very well this season.'

'Oh ! there is the beautiful Duchess de Saint-Prix ; all the world is here to-night---I don't speak of ourselves.'——'It is a regular Opera-night—what a festive scene !'

'Well, after all, people do well to amuse themselves ; perhaps it will not be for long.'——'Why so ?'

'Suppose the cholera were to come to Paris ?'——'Oh ! nonsense !'

'Do *you* believe in the cholera ?'——'To be sure I do ! He's coming from the North, with his walking-stick under his arm.'

'The devil take him on the road ! don't let us see his green visage here.'

'They say he's at London.'

'A pleasant journey to him !'——'Come, let us talk of something else ; it may be a weakness, if you please, but I call this a dull subject.'

'I believe you.'

'Oh ! gentlemen—I am not mistaken—no—it is she !'

'Who then ?'——'Mdlle. de Cardoville ! She is coming into the stage-box with Morinval and his wife. It is a complete resuscitation ; this morning on the Champs-Elysées ; in the evening here.'

'Faith, you are right ! It is Mdlle. de Cardoville.

'Good heaven ! how lovely she is !'

'Lend me your eye-glass.'——'Well, what do you think of her ?'

'Exquisite—dazzling !'——'And in addition to her beauty, an inexhaustible flow of wit, three hundred thousand francs a year, high birth, eighteen years of age, and—free as air,'

' Yes, that is to say, that, provided it pleased her, I might be to-morrow—or even to-day—the happiest of men.'

' It is enough to turn one's brain.'——' I am told, that her mansion, Rue d'Anjou, is like an enchanted palace : a great deal is said about a bath-room and bed-room, worthy of the Arabian Nights.'

' And free as air—I come back to that.'——' Ah ! if I were in her place !'

' My levity would be quite shocking.'——' Oh ! gentlemen, what a happy man will he be who is loved first !'

' You think, then, that she will have many lovers ?'

' Being as free as air——'

' All the boxes are full, except the stage-box opposite to that in which Mdlle. de Cardoville is seated. Happy the occupiers of that box !'

' Did you see the English ambassador's lady in the dress-circle?'

' And the Princess d'Alvimar—what an enormous bouquet !'

' I should like to know the name—of that nosegay.'

' Oh !—it's Germigny.'——' How flattering for the lions and tigers, to attract so fashionable an audience.'

' Do you notice, gentlemen, how all the women are eye-glassing Mdlle. de Cardoville !'——' She makes a sensation.'

' She is right to show herself ; they gave her out as mad.'

' Oh ! gentlemen, what a capital phiz !'

' Where—where ?'

' There—in the omnibus-box beneath Mdlle. de Cardoville's.'

' It's a Nuremburg nutcracker.'——' An ourang-outang !'

' Did you ever see such round, staring eyes ?'——' And the nose !'

' And the forehead !'——' It's a caricature.'

' Order, order ! the curtain rises.'

And, in fact, the curtain rose. Some explanation is necessary for the clear understanding of what follows. In the lower stage-box, to the left of the audi-ence, were several persons, who had been referred to by the young men in the stalls. The omnibus-box was occupied by the Englishman, the eccen-tric and portentous bettor, whose presence inspired Morok with so much dread.

It would require Hoffman's rare and fantastic genius to describe worthily that countenance, at once grotesque and frightful, as it stood out from the dark background of the box. This Englishman was about fifty years old; his forehead was quite bald, and of a conical shape ; beneath this fore-head, surmounted by eyebrows like parenthesis marks, glittered large, green eyes, remarkably round and staring, and set very close to a hooked nose, extremely sharp and prominent ; a chin like that on the old-fashioned nut-crackers was half-hidden in a broad and ample white cravat, as stiffly starched as the round-cornered shirt-collar, which nearly touched his ears. The face was exceedingly thin and bony, and yet the complexion was high-coloured, approaching to purple, which made the bright green of the pupils, and the white of the other part of the eyes, still more conspicuous. The mouth, which was very wide, sometimes whistled inaudibly the tune of a Scotch jig (always the same tune), sometimes was slightly curled with a sardonic smile. The Englishman was dressed with extreme care ; his blue coat, with brass buttons, displayed his spotless waistcoat, snowy white as his ample cravat ; his shirt was fastened with two magnificent ruby studs, and his patrician hands were carefully kid-gloved.

To any one who knew the eccentric and cruel desire which attracted this man to every representation, his grotesque face became almost terrific, in-stead of exciting ridicule ; and it was easy to understand the dread experi-enced by Morok at sight of those great, staring round eyes, which appeared to watch for the death of the lion-tamer (what a horrible death !) with un-shaken confidence. Above the dark box of the Englishman, affording a graceful contrast, were seated the Morinvals and Mdlle. de Cardoville. The latter was placed nearest the stage. Her head was uncovered, and she wore a dress of sky-blue China crape, ornamented at the bosom with a brooch of the finest Oriental pearls—nothing more ; yet Adrienne, thus attired, was charming. She held in her hand an enormous bouquet, composed of the rarest flowers of India : the stephanotis and the gardenia mingled the dead white of their blossoms with the purple hibiscus and Java amaryllis.

Madame de Morinval, seated on the opposite side of the box, was dressed with equal taste and simplicity ; Morinval, a fair and very handsome young man, of elegant appearance, was behind the two ladies. M. de Montbron was expected to arrive every moment. The reader will please to recollect that the stage-box to the right of the audience, opposite Adrienne's, had re-mained till then quite empty. The stage represented one of the gigantic forests of India. In the background, tall exotic trees rose in spiral or spread-ing forms, among rugged masses of perpendicular rocks, with here and there glimpses of a tropical sky. The side-scenes formed tufts of trees, in-terspersed with rocks ; and at the side which was immediately beneath Adrienne's box appeared the irregular opening of a deep and gloomy cavern, round which were heaped huge blocks of granite, as if thrown together by some convulsion of nature. This scenery, full of a wild and savage grandeur, was wonderfully 'built up, so as to make the illusion as complete as possible ; the foot-lights were lowered, and, being covered with a purple shade, threw over this landscape a subdued reddish light, which increased the gloomy and startling effect of the whole. Adrienne, leaning forward from the box, with cheeks slightly flushed, sparkling eyes, and throbbing heart, sought to trace in this scene the solitary forest described by the traveller who had eulogised Djalma's generosity and courage, when he threw himself upon a ferocious tigress to save the life of a poor black slave. Chance coincided wonderfully indeed with her recollections. Ab-sorbed in the contemplation of the scenery and the thoughts it awakened in her heart, she paid no attention to what was passing in the house. And yet something calculated to excite curiosity was taking place in the opposite stage-box.

The door of this box opened. A man about forty years of age of a yellow complexion, entered ; he was clothed after the East Indian fashion, in a long robe of orange silk, bound round the waist with a green sash, and he wore a small white turban. He placed two chairs at the front of the box ; and, having glanced round the house for a moment, he started, his black eyes sparkled, and he went out quickly. That man was Faringhea. His apparition caused surprise and curiosity in the theatre ; the majority of the spectators not having, like Adrienne, a thousand reasons for being absorbed in the contemplation of a picturesque set scene. The public attention was still more excited when they saw the box, which Faringhea had just left, entered by a youth of rare beauty, also dressed Oriental fashion, in a long robe of white Cashmere with flowing sleeves, with a scarlet turban striped with gold on his head, and a sash to correspond, in which was stuck a long dagger, glittering with precious stones. This young man was Prince Djalma. For an instant he remained standing at the door, and cast a look of indiffe-rence upon the immense theatre, crowded with people ; then, stepping for-ward with a majestic and tranquil air, the prince seated himself negligently on one of the chairs, and, turning his head in a few moments towards the entrance, appeared surprised at not seeing some person whom he doubtless expected. This person appeared at length ; the boxkeeper had been assisting her to take off her cloak. She was a charming, fair-haired girl, attired with more show than taste, in a dress of white silk, with broad cherry-coloured stripes, made ultra-fashionably low, and with short sleeves ; a large bow of cherry-coloured ribbon was placed on each side of her light hair, and set off the prettiest, sprightliest, most wilful little face in the world.

It was Rose-Pompon. Her pretty arms were partly covered by long white gloves, and ridiculously loaded with bracelets ; in her hand she carried an enormous bouquet of roses.

Far from imitating the calm demeanour of Djalma, Rose-Pompon skipped into the box, moved the chairs about noisily, and fidgeted on her seat for some time, to display her fine dress ; then, without being in the least intimidated by the presence of the brilliant assembly, she, with a little coquettish air, held her bouquet towards Djalma, that he might smell it, and appeared finally to establish herself on her seat. Faringhea came in, shut the door of the box, and seated himself behind the prince. Adrienne, still completely absorbed in the contemplation of the Indian forest, and in her own sweet thoughts, had not observed the new-comers. As she was turning her head completely towards the stage, and Djalma could not, for the moment, see even her profile, he, on his side, had not recognised Mdlle. de Cardoville.

CHAPTER XIV.

DEATH.

THE pantomime opening, by which was introduced the combat of Morok with the black panther, was so unmeaning, that the majority of the audience paid no attention to it, reserving all their interest for the scene in which the lion-tamer was to make his appearance.

This indifference of the public explains the curiosity excited in the theatre by the arrival of Faringhea and Djalma—a curiosity which expressed itself (as at this day, when uncommon foreigners appear in public) by a slight murmur and general movement amongst the crowd. The sprightly, pretty face of Rose-Pompon, always charming, in spite of her singularly staring dress, in style sc ridiculous for such a theatre, and her light and familiar manner towards the handsome Indian who accompanied her, increased and animated the general surprise ; for, at this moment, Rose-Pompon, yielding without reserve to a movement of teasing coquetry, had held up, as we have already stated, her large bunch of roses to Djalma. But the prince, at sight of the landscape which reminded him of his country, instead of appearing sensible to this pretty provocation, remained for some minutes as in a dream, with his eyes fixed upon the stage. Then Rose-Pompon began to beat time on the front of the box with her bouquet, whilst the somewhat too visible movement of her pretty shoulders showed that this devoted dancer was thinking of fast-life dances, as the orchestra struck up a more lively strain.

Placed directly opposite the box in which Faringhea, Djalma, and Rose-Pompon had just taken their seats, Lady Morinval soon perceived the arrival of these two personages, and particularly the eccentric coquetries of Rose-Pompon. Immediately, the young marchioness, leaning over towards Mdlle. de Cardoville, who was still absorbed in memories ineffable, said to her, laughing : 'My dear, the most amusing part of the performance is not upon the stage. Look just opposite.'

' 'Just opposite ?' repeated Adrienne, mechanically ; and, turning towards Lady Morinval with an air of surprise, she glanced in the direction pointed out.

She looked—what did she see?—Djalma seated by the side of a young woman, who was familiarly offering to his sense of smell the perfume of her bouquet. Amazed, struck almost literally to the heart, as by an electric shock, swift, sharp, and painful, Adrienne became deadly pale. From instinct, she shut her eyes for a second, in order *not to see*—as men try to ward off the dagger, which, having once dealt the blow, threatens to strike again. Then suddenly, to this feeling of grief succeeded a reflection, terrible both to her love and to her wounded pride.

'Djalma is present with this woman, though he must have received my letter,' she said to herself,—' wherein he was informed of the happiness that awaited him.'

At the idea of so cruel an insult, a blush of shame and indignation displaced Adrienne's paleness, who, overwhelmed by this sad reality, said to herself: 'Rodin did not deceive me.'

We abandon all idea of picturing the lightning-like rapidity of certain emotions which in a moment may torture—may kill you in the space of a minute. Thus Adrienne was precipitated from the most radiant happiness to the lowest depths of an abyss of the most heart-rending grief, in less than a second; for a second hardly elapsed before she replied to Lady Morinval: 'What is there, then, so curious, opposite to us, my dear Julia?'

This evasive question gave Adrienne time to recover her self-possession. Fortunately, thanks to the thick folds of hair which almost entirely concealed her cheeks, the rapid and sudden changes from pallor to blush escaped the notice of Lady Morinval, who gaily replied: 'What, my dear, do you not perceive those East Indians who have just entered the box immediately opposite to ours? There, just before us!'

'Yes, I see them; but what then?' replied Adrienne, in a firm tone.

'And don't you observe anything remarkable?' said the marchioness.

'Don't be too hard, ladies,' laughingly interposed the marquis; 'we ought to allow the poor foreigners some little indulgence. They are ignorant of our manners and customs; were it not for that, they would never appear in the face of all Paris in such dubious company.'

'Indeed,' said Adrienne, with a bitter smile, 'their simplicity is touching; we must pity them.'

'And, unfortunately, the girl is charming, spite of her low dress and bare arms,' said the marchioness; 'she cannot be more than sixteen or seventeen at most. Look at her, my dear Adrienne; what a pity!'

'It is one of your charitable days, my dear Julia,' answered Adrienne; 'we are to pity the Indians, to pity this creature, and—pray, whom else are we to pity?'

'We will not pity that handsome Indian, in his red-and-gold turban,' said the marquis, laughing, 'for, if this goes on, the girl with the cherry-coloured ribbons will be giving him a kiss. See how she leans towards her sultan.'

'They are very amusing,' said the marchioness, sharing the hilarity of her husband, and looking at Rose-Pompon through her glass; then she resumed, in about a minute, addressing herself to Adrienne: 'I am quite certain of one thing. Notwithstanding her giddy airs, that girl is very fond of her Indian. I just saw a look that expresses a great deal.'

'Why so much penetration, my dear Julia?' said Adrienne, mildly; 'what interest have we to read the heart of that girl?'

'Why, if she loves her sultan, she is quite in the right,' said the marquis, looking through his opera-glass in turn; 'for, in my whole life, I never saw a more handsome fellow than that Indian. I can only catch his side-face, but the profile is pure and fine as an antique cameo. Do you not think so?'

added the marquis, leaning towards Adrienne. 'Of course, it is only as a matter of art, that I permit myself to ask you the question.'

'As a work of *art*,' answered Adrienne, 'it is certainly very fine.'

'But see !' said the marchioness ; 'how impertinent the little creature is ! —She is actually staring at us.'

'Well !' said the marquis ; 'and she is actually laying her hand quite unceremoniously on her sultan's shoulder, to make him share, no doubt, in her admiration of you ladies.'

In fact, Djalma, until now occupied with the contemplation of the scene which reminded him of his country, had remained insensible to the enticements of Rose-Pompon, and had not yet perceived Adrienne.

'Well now !' said Rose-Pompon, bustling herself about in front of the box, and continuing to stare at Mdlle. de Cardoville, for it was she, and not the marchioness, who now drew her attention ; 'that is something quite out of the common way—a pretty woman, with red hair ; but such a sweet red, it must be owned. Look, Prince Charming !'

And so saying, she tapped Djalma lightly on the shoulder ; he started at these words, turned round, and for the first time perceived Mdlle. de Cardoville.

Though he had been almost prepared for this meeting, the prince was so violently affected by it, that he was about involuntarily to rise, in a state of the utmost confusion ; but he felt the iron hand of Faringhea laid heavily on his shoulder, and heard him whisper in Hindostanee : 'Courage ! and by to-morrow she will be at your feet.'

As Djalma still struggled to rise, the half-caste added, to restrain him : 'Just now, she grew pale and red with jealousy. No weakness, or all is lost !'

'So ! there you are again, talking your dreadful gibberish,' said Rose-Pompon, turning round towards Faringhea. 'First of all, it is not polite ; and then the language is so odd, that one might suppose you were cracking nuts.'

'I spoke of you to my master,' said the half-caste ; 'he is preparing a surprise for you.'

'A surprise ? oh ! that is different. Only make haste—do you hear, Prince Charming !' added she, looking tenderly at Djalma.

'My heart is breaking,' said Djalma, in a hollow voice to Faringhea, still using the language of India.

'But to-morrow it will bound with joy and love,' answered the half-caste. 'It is only by disdain that you can conquer a proud woman. To-morrow, I tell you, she will be trembling, confused, supplicating, at your feet !'

'To-morrow, she will hate me like death !' replied the prince, mournfully.

'Yes, were she now to see you weak and cowardly. It is now too late to draw back ; look full at her, take the nosegay from this girl, and raise it to your lips. Instantly, you will see yonder woman, proud as she is, grow pale and red, as just now. Then will you believe me ?'

Reduced by despair to make almost any attempt, and fascinated, in spite of himself, by the diabolical hints of Faringhea, Djalma looked for a second full at Mdlle. de Cardoville ; then, with a trembling hand he took the bouquet from Rose-Pompon, and, again looking at Adrienne, pressed it to his lips.

Upon this insolent bravado, Mdlle. de Cardoville could not restrain so sudden and visible a pang, that the prince was struck by it.

'She is yours,' said the half-caste to him. 'Did you see, my lord, how she trembled with jealousy ?—Only have courage ! and she is yours. She will soon prefer you to that handsome young man behind her—for *it is he* whom she has hitherto fancied herself in love with.'

As if the half-caste had guessed the movement of rage and hatred, which this revelation would excite in the heart of the prince, he hastily added : 'Calmness and disdain ! Is it not his turn now to hate you ?'

The prince restrained himself, and drew his hand across his forehead, which glowed with anger.

'There now ! what are you telling him, that vexes him so ?' said Rose-Pompon to Faringhea, with pouting lip. Then, addressing Djalma, she continued : ' Come, Prince Charming, as they say in the fairy-tale, give me back my flowers.'

As she took it again, she added : ' You have kissed it, and I could almost eat it.' Then, with a sigh, and a passionate glance at Djalma, she said softly to herself : ' That monster Ninny Moulin did not deceive me. All this is *quite proper;* I have not even *that* to reproach myself with.' And with her little white teeth, she bit at a rosy nail of her right hand, from which she had just drawn the glove.

It is hardly necessary to say, that Adrienne's letter had not been delivered to the prince, and that he had not gone to pass the day in the country with Marshal Simon. During the three days in which Montbron had not seen Djalma, Faringhea had persuaded him, that, by affecting another passion, he would bring Mdlle. de Cardoville to terms. With regard to Djalma's presence at the theatre, Rodin had learned from her maid, Florine, that her mistress was to go in the evening to the Porte-Saint-Martin. Before Djalma had recognized her, Adrienne, who felt her strength failing her, was on the point of quitting the theatre ; the man, whom she had hitherto placed so high, whom she had regarded as a hero and a demi-god, and whom she had imagined plunged in such dreadful despair, that, led by the most tender pity, she had written to him with simple frankness, that a sweet hope might calm his grief—replied to a generous mark of sincerity and love, by making himself a ridiculous spectacle with a creature unworthy of him. What incurable wounds for Adrienne's pride ! It mattered little, whether Djalma knew or not, that she would be a spectator of the indignity. But when she saw herself recognised by the prince, when he carried the insult so far as to look full at her, and, at the same time, raise to his lips the creature's bouquet who accompanied him, Adrienne was seized with noble indignation, and felt sufficient courage to remain ; instead of closing her eyes to evidence, she found a sort of barbarous pleasure in assisting at the agony and death of her pure and divine love. With head erect, proud and flashing eye, flushed cheek, and curling lip, she looked in her turn at the prince with disdainful steadiness. It was with a sardonic smile that she said to the marchioness, who, like many others of the spectators, was occupied with what was passing in the stage-box : ' This revolting exhibition of savage manners is at least in accordance with the rest of the performance.'

' Certainly,' said the marchioness ; ' and my dear uncle will have lost, perhaps, the most amusing part.'

' Montbron ?' said Adrienne, hastily, with hardly repressed bitterness ; ' yes, he will regret not having *seen all.* I am impatient for his arrival. Is it not to him that I am indebted for this charming evening ?'

Perhaps Madame de Morinval would have remarked the expression of bitter irony, that Adrienne could not altogether dissemble, if suddenly a hoarse and prolonged roar had not attracted her attention, as well as that of the rest of the audience, who had hitherto been quite indifferent to the scenes intended for an introduction to the appearance of Morok. Every eye was now turned instinctively towards the cavern, situated to the left of the stage, just below Mdlle. de Cardoville's box ; a thrill of curiosity ran through the house. A second roar, deeper and more sonorous, and apparently expressive of more irritation than the first, now rose from the cave, the mouth of which was half-hidden by artificial brambles, made so as to be easily put on one side. At this sound, the Englishman stood up in his little box, leaned half over the front, and began to rub his hands with great energy ; then, remaining perfectly motionless, he fixed his large, green, glittering eyes on the mouth of the cavern.

At these ferocious howlings, Djalma also had started, notwithstanding the frenzy of love, hate, and jealousy, to which he was a prey. The sight of this forest, and the roarings of the panther, filled him with deep emotion, for they recalled the remembrance of his country, and of those great hunts which, like war, have their own terrible excitement. Had he suddenly heard the horns and gongs of his father's army sounding to the charge, he could not have been transported with more savage ardour. And now deep growls, like distant thunder, almost drowned the roar of the panther. The lion and tiger, Judas and Cain answered her from their dens at the back of the stage. On this frightful concert, with which his ears had been familiar in the midst of the solitudes of India, when he lay encamped, for the purposes of the chase or of war, Djalma's blood boiled in his veins. His eyes sparkled with a wild ardour. Leaning a little forward, with both hands pressed on the front of the box, his whole body trembled with a convulsive shudder. The audience, the theatre, Adrienne herself, no longer existed for him ; he was in a forest of his own lands, tracking the tiger.

Then there mingled with his beauty so intrepid and ferocious an expression, that Rose-Pompon looked at him with a sort of terror and passionate admiration. For the first time in her life, perhaps, her pretty blue eyes, generally so gay and mischievous, expressed a serious emotion. She could not explain what she felt ; but her heart seemed tightened, and beat violently, as though some calamity were at hand.

Yielding to a movement of involuntary fear, she seized Djalma by the arm, and said to him : ' Do not stare so into that cavern ; you frighten me.'

Djalma did not hear what she said.

' Here he is ! here he is !' murmured the crowd, almost with one voice, as Morok appeared at the back of the stage.

Dressed as we have described, Morok now carried in addition a bow and a long quiver full of arrows. He slowly descended the line of painted rocks, which came sloping down towards the centre of the stage. From time to time, he stopped as if to listen, and appeared to advance with caution. Looking from one side to the other, his eyes involuntarily encountered the large, green eyes of the Englishman, whose box was close to the cavern. Instantly the lion-tamer's countenance was contracted in so frightful a manner, that Lady Morinval, who was examining him closely with the aid of an excellent glass, said hastily to Adrienne : ' My dear, the man is afraid. Some misfortune will happen.'

' How can accidents happen,' said Adrienne, with a sardonic smile, ' in the midst of this brilliant crowd, so well dressed and full of animation ! Misfortunes here, this evening ! why, dear Julia, you do not think it. It is in darkness and solitude that misfortunes come—never in the midst of a joyous crowd, and in all this blaze of light.'

' Good gracious, Adrienne ! take care !' cried the marchioness, unable to repress an exclamation of alarm, and seizing her arm, as if to draw her closer ; ' do you not see it ?' And, with a trembling hand, she pointed to the cavern's mouth. Adrienne hastily bent forward, and looked in that direction. ' Take care ! do not lean so forward !' exclaimed Lady Morinval,

'Your terrors are nonsensical, my dear,' said the marquis to his wife. 'The panther is securely chained ; and even were it to break its chain (which is impossible), we are here beyond its reach.'

A long murmur of trembling curiosity here ran through the house, and every eye was intently fixed on the cavern. From amongst the artificial brambles, which she abruptly pushed aside with her broad chest, the black panther suddenly appeared. Twice she stretched forth her flat head, illumined by yellow, flaming eyes ; then, half-opening her blood-red jaws, she uttered another roar, and exhibited two rows of formidable fangs. A double iron chain, and a collar also of iron, painted black, blended with the ebon shades of her hide, and with the darkness of the cavern. The illusion was complete, and the terrible animal seemed to be at liberty in her den.

'Ladies,' said the marquis, suddenly, 'look at those Indians. Their emotion makes them superb !'

In fact, the sight of the panther had raised the wild ardour of Djalma to its utmost pitch. His eyes sparkled in their pearly orbits like two black diamonds : his upper lip was curled convulsively with an expression of animal ferocity, as if he were in a violent paroxysm of rage.

Faringhea, now leaning on the front of the box, was also greatly excited, by reason of a strange coincidence. 'That black panther of so rare a breed,' thought he, 'which I see here at Paris, upon a stage, must be the very one that the Malay'—the Thug who had tattooed Djalma at Java during his sleep—'took quite young from his den, and sold to a European captain. Bowanee's power is everywhere !' added the Thug, in his sanguinary superstition.

'Do you not think,' resumed the marquis, addressing Adrienne, 'that those Indians are really splendid in their present attitude ?'

'Perhaps they may have seen such a hunt in their own country,' said Adrienne, as if she would recall and brave the most cruel remembrances.

'Adrienne,' said the marchioness, suddenly, in an agitated voice, 'the lion-tamer has now come nearer—is not his countenance fearful to look at ? —I tell you he is afraid.'

'In truth,' observed the marquis, this time very seriously, 'he is dreadfully pale, and seems to grow worse every minute, the nearer he approaches this side. It is said that, were he to lose his presence of mind for a single moment, he would run the greatest danger.'

'O ! it would be horrible !' cried the marchioness, addressing Adrienne, 'if he were wounded—there—under our eyes !'

'Every wound does not kill,' replied her friend, with an accent of such cold indifference, that the marchioness looked at her with surprise, and said to her : 'My dear girl, what you say there is cruel !'

'It is the air of the place that acts on me,' answered Adrienne, with an icy smile.

'Look ! look ! the lion-tamer is about to shoot his arrow at the panther,' said the marquis, suddenly. 'No doubt, he will next perform the hand to hand grapple.'

Morok was at this moment in front of the stage, but he had yet to traverse its entire breadth to reach the cavern's mouth. He stopped an instant, adjusted an arrow to the string, knelt down behind a mass of rock, took deliberate aim—and then the arrow hissed across the stage, and was lost in the depths of the cavern, into which the panther had retired, after showing for a moment her threatening head to the audience. Hardly had the arrow disappeared, than Death, purposely irritated by Goliath (who was invisible) sent forth a howl of rage, as if she had been really wounded.

Morok's actions became so expressive, he evinced so naturally his joy at having hit the wild beast, that a tempest of applause burst from every quarter of the house. Then, throwing away his bow, he drew a dagger from his girdle, took it between his teeth, and began to crawl forward on hands and knees, as though he meant to surprise the wounded panther in his den. To render the illusion perfect, Death, again excited by Goliath, who struck him with an iron bar, sent forth frightful howlings from the depths of the cavern.

The gloomy aspect of the forest, only half-lighted with a reddish glare, was so effective—the howlings of the panther were so furious—the gestures, attitude, and countenance of Morok were so expressive of terror, that the audience, attentive and trembling, now maintained a profound silence. Every one held his breath, and a kind of shudder came over the spectators, as though they expected some horrible event. What gave such a fearful air of truth to the pantomime of Morok, was that, as he approached the cavern step by step, he approached also the Englishman's box. In spite of himself, the lion-tamer, fascinated by terror, could not take his eyes from the large green eyes of this man, and it seemed as if every one of the abrupt movements which he made in crawling along, was produced by a species of magnetic attraction, caused by the fixed gaze of the fatal wagerer. Therefore, the nearer Morok approached, the more ghastly and livid he became. At sight of this pantomime, which was no longer acting, but the real expression of intense fear, the deep and trembling silence which had reigned in the theatre was once more interrupted by acclamations, with which were mingled the roarings of the panther, and the distant growls of the lion and tiger.

The Englishman leaned almost out of his box, with a frightful sardonic smile on his lip, and with his large eyes still fixed, panted for breath. The perspiration ran down his bald red forehead, as if he had really expended an incredible amount of magnetic power in attracting Morok, whom he now saw close to the cavern entrance. The moment was decisive. Crouching down with his dagger in his hand, following with eye and gesture Death's every movement, who, roaring furiously, and opening wide her enormous jaws, seemed determined to guard the entrance of her den, Morok waited for the moment to rush upon her. There is such fascination in danger, that Adrienne shared, in spite of herself, the feeling of painful curiosity, mixed with terror, that thrilled through all the spectators. Leaning forward like the marchioness, and gazing upon this scene of fearful interest, the lady still held mechanically in her hand the Indian bouquet preserved since the morning. Suddenly, Morok raised a wild shout, as he rushed towards Death, who answered this exclamation by a dreadful roar, and threw herself upon her master with so much fury, that Adrienne, in alarm, believing the man lost, drew herself back, and covered her face with her hands. Her flowers slipped from her grasp, and, falling upon the stage, rolled into the cavern in which Morok was struggling with the panther.

Quick as lightning, supple and agile as a tiger, yielding to the intoxication of his love, and to the wild ardour excited in him by the roaring of the panther, Djalma sprang at one bound upon the stage, drew his dagger, and rushed into the cavern to recover Adrienne's nosegay. At that instant, Morok, being wounded, uttered a dreadful cry for help; the panther, rendered still more furious at sight of Djalma, made the most desperate efforts to break her chain. Unable to succeed in doing so, she rose upon her hind legs, in order to seize Djalma, then within reach of her sharp claws. It was only by bending down his head, throwing himself on his knees, and twice plunging his dagger into her belly with the rapidity of lightning, that Djalma escaped certain death. The panther gave a howl, and fell with her whole weight upon the prince. For a second, during which lasted her terrible agony, nothing was seen but a confused and convulsive mass of black limbs, and white garments stained with blood—and then Djalma rose, pale, bleeding, for he was wounded—and standing erect, his eye flashing with savage pride, his foot on the body of the panther, he held in his hand Adrienne's bouquet, and cast towards her a glance which told the intensity of his love. Then only did Adrienne feel her strength fail her—for only superhuman courage had enabled her to watch all the terrible incidents of the struggle.

CHAPTER XV.

THE CONSTANT WANDERER.

It is night. The moon shines and the stars glimmer in the midst of a serene but cheerless sky ; the sharp whistlings of the north-wind, that fatal, dry, and icy breeze, ever and anon burst forth in violent gusts. With its harsh and cutting breath, it sweeps Montmartre's Heights. On the highest point of the hills, a man is standing. His long shadow is cast upon the stony, moon-lit ground. He gazes on the immense city, which lies outspread beneath his feet. PARIS—with the dark outline of its towers, cupolas, domes, and steeples, standing out from the limpid blue of the horizon, while from the midst of the ocean of masonry, rises a luminous vapour, that reddens the starry azure of the sky. It is the distant reflection of the thousand fires, which at night, the hour of pleasures, light up so joyously the noisy capital.

' No,' said the wayfarer ; ' it is not to be. The Lord will not exact it. Is not *twice* enough ?'

' Five centuries ago, the avenging hand of the Almighty drove me hither from the uttermost confines of Asia. A solitary traveller, I had left behind me more grief, despair, disaster, and death, than the innumerable armies of a hundred devastating conquerors. I entered this town, and it too was decimated.

' Again, two centuries ago, the inexorable hand, which leads me through the world, brought me once more hither ; and then, as the time before, the plague, which the Almighty attaches to my steps, again ravaged this city, and fell first on my brethren, already worn out with labour and misery.

' My brethren—mine ?—the cobbler of Jerusalem, the artisan accursed by the Lord, who, in my person, condemned the whole race of workmen, ever suffering, ever disinherited, ever in slavery, toiling on like me without rest or pause, without recompense or hope, till men, women, and children, young and old, all die beneath the same iron yoke—that murderous yoke, which others take in their turn, thus to be borne from age to age on the submissive and bruised shoulders of the masses.

' And now, for the third time in five centuries, I reach the summit of one of the hills that overlook the city. And perhaps I again bring with me fear, desolation, and death.

' Yet this city, intoxicated with the sounds of its joys and its nocturnal revelries, does not know—oh ! does not know that *I* am at its gates.

' But no, no ! my presence will not be a new calamity. The Lord, in his impenetrable views, has hitherto led me through France, so as to avoid the humblest hamlet ; and the sound of the funeral knell has not accompanied my passage.

' And, moreover, the spectre has left me—the green, livid spectre, with its hollow, bloodshot eyes. When I touched the soil of France, its damp and icy hand was no longer clasped in mine—and it disappeared.

'And yet—I feel that the atmosphere of death is around me.

'The sharp whistlings of that fatal wind cease not, which, catching me in their whirl, seem to propagate blasting and mildew as they blow.

'But perhaps the wrath of the Lord is appeased, and my presence here is only a threat—to be communicated in some way to those whom it should intimidate.

'Yes ; for otherwise he would smite with a fearful blow, by first scattering terror and death here in the heart of the country, in the bosom of this immense city !

'Oh ! no, no ! the Lord will be merciful. No ! he will not condemn me to this new torture.

'Alas ! in this city, my brethren are more numerous and miserable than elsewhere. And should I be their messenger of death ?'

'No ! the Lord will have pity. For, alas ! the seven descendants of my sister have at length met in this town. And to them likewise should I be the messenger of death, instead of the help they so much need ?'

'For that woman, who like me wanders from one border of the earth to the other, after having once more rent asunder the nets of their enemies, has gone forth upon her endless journey.

'In vain she foresaw that new misfortunes threatened my sister's family. The invisible hand, that drives me on, drives *her* on also.

'Carried away, as of old, by the irresistible whirlwind, at the moment of leaving my kindred to their fate, she in vain cried with supplicating tone : "Let me at least, O Lord, complete my task !"—"Go on !"—"A few days, in mercy, only a few poor days !"—"Go on !"—"I leave those I love on the brink of the abyss !"—"Go on ! Go on !"

'And the wandering star again started on its eternal round. And her voice, passing through space, called me to the assistance of mine own.

'When that voice reached me, I knew that the descendants of my sister were still exposed to frightful perils. Those perils are even now on the increase.

'Tell me, O Lord ! will they escape the scourge, which for so many centuries has weighed down our race?

'Wilt thou pardon me in them? wilt thou punish me in them? Oh, that they might obey the last will of their ancestor !

'Oh, that they might join together their charitable hearts, their valour and their strength, their noble intelligence, and their great riches !

'They would then labour for the future happiness of humanity—they would thus, perhaps, redeem me from my eternal punishment !

'The words of the Son of Man, LOVE YE ONE ANOTHER, will be their only end, their only means.

'By the help of those all-powerful words, they will fight and conquer the false priests, who have renounced the precepts of love, peace, and hope, for lessons of hatred, violence, and despair.

'Those false priests, who, kept in pay by the powerful and happy of this world, their accomplices in every age, instead of asking here below for some slight share of well-being for my unfortunate brethren, dare in thy name, O Lord God, to assert that the poor are condemned to endless suffering in this world—and that the desire or the hope to suffer less is a crime in thine eyes— because the happiness of the few, and the misery of nearly the whole human race, is (O blasphemy !) according to thy will. Is not the very contrary of those murderous words alone worthy of divinity !

'In mercy, hear me, Lord ! Rescue from their enemies the descendants of my sister—the artisan as the king's son. Do not let them destroy the germ of so mighty and fruitful an association, which, with thy blessing, would make an epoch in the annals of human happiness!

'Let me unite them, O Lord, since others would divide them—defend them, since others attack; let me give hope to those who have ceased to hope, courage to those who are brought low with fear—let me raise up the falling, and sustain those who persevere in the way of the righteous!

'And, peradventure, their struggles, devotion, virtue, and grief, may expiate my fault—that of a man, whom misfortune alone rendered unjust and wicked.

'Oh! since thy Almighty hand hath led me hither—to what end I know not—lay aside Thy wrath, I beseech Thee—let me be no longer the instrument of Thy vengeance!

'Enough of woe upon the earth! for the last two years, Thy creatures have fallen by thousands upon my track. The world is decimated. A veil of mourning extends over all the globe.

'From Asia to the icy Pole, they died upon the path of the wanderer. Dost Thou not hear the long-drawn sigh that rises from the earth unto Thee, O Lord?

'Mercy for all! mercy for me!—Let me but unite the descendants of my sister for a single day, and they will be saved!'

As he pronounced these words, the wayfarer sank upon his knees, and raised to heaven his supplicating hands. Suddenly, the wind blew with redoubled violence; its sharp whistlings were changed into the roar of a tempest.

The traveller shuddered; in a voice of terror he exclaimed: 'The blast of death rises in its fury—the whirlwind carries me on—Lord! thou art then deaf to my prayer?

'The spectre! oh, the spectre! it is again here! its green face twitching with convulsive spasms—its red eyes rolling in their orbits. Begone! begone!—its hand, oh! its icy hand has again laid hold of mine. Have mercy, heaven!'——'Go on!'

'Oh, Lord! the pestilence—the terrible plague—must I carry it into this city?—And my brethren will perish the first—they, who are so sorely smitten even now! Mercy!'——'Go on!'

'And the descendants of my sister. Mercy! Mercy!'——'Go on!'

'Oh, Lord, have pity!—I can no longer keep my ground; the spectre drags me to the slope of the hill; my walk is rapid as the deadly blast that rages behind me; already do I behold the city-gates. Have mercy, Lord, on the descendants of my sister! Spare them; do not make me their executioner; let them triumph over their enemies!'——'Go on! Go on!'

'The ground flies beneath my feet; there is the city gate. Lord, it is yet time! Oh, mercy for that sleeping town! Let it not waken to cries of terror, despair, and death! Lord, I am on the threshold. Must it be?—Yes, it is done. Paris, the plague is in thy bosom. The curse—oh, the eternal curse!'——'Go on! Go on! Go on!'

CHAPTER XVI.

THE LUNCHEON.

THE morning after the doomed traveller, descending the heights of Montmartre, had entered the walls of Paris, great activity reigned in St. Dizier House. Though it was hardly noon, the Princess de St. Dizier, without being exactly in full dress (she had too much taste for that), was yet arrayed with more care than usual. Her light hair, instead of being merely banded, was arranged in two bunches of curls, which suited very well with her full and florid cheeks. Her cap was trimmed with bright rose-coloured ribbon, and whoever had seen the lady in her tight-fitting dress of grey watered silk would have easily guessed that Mrs. Grivois, her tire-woman, must have required the assistance and the efforts of another of the princess's women to achieve so remarkable a reduction in the ample figure of their mistress.

We shall explain the edifying cause of this partial return to the vanities of the world. The princess, attended by Mrs. Grivois, who acted as house-keeper, was giving her final orders with regard to some preparations that were going on in a vast parlour. In the midst of this room was a large round table, covered with crimson velvet, and near it stood several chairs, amongst which, in the place of honour, was an arm-chair of gilded wood. In one corner, not far from the chimney, in which burned an excellent fire, was a buffet. On it were the divers materials for a most dainty and exqui-site collation. Upon silver dishes were piled pyramids of sandwiches, com-posed of the roes of carp and anchovy paste, with slices of pickled tunny-fish and Lenigord truffles (it was in Lent) ; on silver dishes, placed over burning spirits of wine, so as to keep them very hot, tails of Meuse craw-fish boiled in cream, smoked in golden-coloured pastry, and seemed to challenge comparison with delicious little Marennes oyster-patties, stewed in Madeira, and flavoured with a seasoning of spiced sturgeon. By the side of these substantial dishes were some of a lighter character, such as pine-apple tarts, strawberry-creams (it was early for such fruit), and orange-jelly served in the peel, which had been artistically emptied for that purpose. Bordeaux, Madeira, and Alicant sparkled like rubies and topazes in large glass decanters, while two Sèvres ewers were filled, one with coffee *a la crême*, the other with vanilla chocolate, almost in the state of sherbet, from being plunged in a large cooler of chiselled silver, containing ice.

But what gave to this dainty collation a singularly apostolic and papal character were sundry symbols of religious worship carefully represented. Thus there were charming little Calvaries in apricot paste, sacerdotal mitres in burnt almonds, episcopal croziers in sweet cake, to which the princess added, as a mark of delicate attention, a little cardinal's hat in cherry sweet-meat, ornamented with bands in burnt sugar. The most important, how-ever, of these Catholic delicacies, the masterpiece of the cook, was a su-perb crucifix in angelica, with a crown of candied berries. These are strange profanations, which scandalise even the least devout. But, from the impudent juggle of the coat of Triers, down to the shameless jest of the shrine at Argenteuil, people, who are pious after the fashion of the princess, seem to take delight in bringing ridicule upon the most respect-able traditions.

After glancing with an air of satisfaction at these preparations for the collation, the lady said to Mrs. Grivois, as she pointed to the gilded arm-chair, which seemed destined for the president of the meeting : ' Is there a cushion under the table, for his Eminence to rest his feet on ? He always complains of cold.'

' Yes, your highness,' said Mrs. Grivois, when she had looked under the table ; ' the cushion is there.'

' Let also a pewter bottle be filled with boiling water, in case his Emi-nence should not find the cushion enough to keep his feet warm.'

' Yes, my lady.'

' And put some more wood on the fire.'——' But, my lady, it is already a very furnace. And if his Eminence is always too cold, my lord the Bishop of Halfagen is always too hot. He perspires dreadfully.'

The princess shrugged her shoulders, and said to Mrs. Grivois : ' Is not his Eminence Cardinal Malipieri the superior of his Lordship the Bishop of Halfagen ?'——' Yes, your highness.'

'Then, according to the rules of the hierarchy, it is for his Lordship to suffer from the heat, rather than his Eminence from the cold. Therefore, do as I tell you, and put more wood on the fire. Nothing is more natural; his Eminence being an Italian, and his Lordship coming from the north of Belgium, they are accustomed to different temperatures.'

'Just as your highness pleases,' said Mrs. Grivois, as she placed two enormous logs on the fire ; ' but in such a heat as there is here his Lordship might really be suffocated.'

'I also find it too warm ; but does not our holy religion teach us lessons of self-sacrifice and mortification?' said the princess, with a touching expression of devotion.

We have now explained the cause of the rather gay attire of the Princess. She was preparing for a reception of prelates, who, along with Father d'Aigrigny and other dignitaries of the Church, had already held at the princely house a sort of council on a small scale. A young bride who gives her first ball, an emancipated minor who gives his first bachelor's dinner, a woman of talent who reads aloud for the first time her first unpublished work, are not more joyous and proud, and, at the same time, more attentive to their guests, than was this lady with her prelates. To behold great interests discussed in her house, and in her presence, to hear men of acknowledged ability ask her advice upon certain practical matters relating to the influence of female congregations, filled the princess with pride, as her claims to consideration were thus sanctioned by Lordships and Eminences, and she took the position, as it were, of a mother of the Church. Therefore, to win these prelates, whether native or foreign, she had recourse to no end of saintly flatteries and sanctified coaxing. Nor could anything be more logical than these successive transfigurations of this heartless woman, who only loved sincerely and passionately the pursuit of intrigue and domination. With the progress of age, she passed naturally from the intrigues of love to those of politics, and from the latter to those of religion.

At the moment she finished inspecting her preparations, the sound of coaches was heard in the courtyard, apprising her of the arrival of the persons she had been expecting. Doubtless, these persons were of the highest rank, for, contrary to all custom, she went to receive them at the door of her outer saloon. It was, indeed, Cardinal Malipieri, who was always cold, with the Belgian Bishop of Halfagen, who was always hot. They were accompanied by Father d'Aigrigny. The Roman cardinal was a tall man, rather bony than thin, with a yellowish puffy countenance, haughty and full of craft ; he squinted a good deal, and his black eyes were surrounded by a deep brown circle. The Belgian Bishop was short, thick, and fat, with a prominent abdomen, an apoplectic complexion, a slow, deliberate look, and a soft, dimpled, delicate hand.

The company soon assembled in the great saloon. The cardinal instantly crept close to the fire, whilst the bishop, beginning to sweat and blow, cast longing glances at the iced chocolate and coffee, which were to aid him in sustaining the oppressive heat of the artificial dog-day. Father d'Aigrigny, approaching the princess, said to her in a low voice : 'Will you give orders for the admittance of Abbé Gabriel de Rennepont, when he arrives ?'

'Is that young priest then here?' asked the princess, with extreme surprise.

'Since the day before yesterday. We had him sent for to Paris, by his superiors. You shall know all. As for Father Rodin, let Mrs. Grivois admit him, as the other day, by the little door of the back-stairs.'

'He will come to-day.'——'He has very important matters to communicate. He desired that both the cardinal and the bishop should be present for they have been informed of everything at Rome by the Superior Gene‹ ral, in their quality of associates.'

The princess rang the bell, gave the necessary orders, and, returning towards the cardinal, said to him, in a tone of the most earnest solicitude ‹. ' Does your Eminence begin to feel a little warmer ? Would your Eminence like a bottle of hot water to your feet ? Shall we make a larger fire for your Eminence ?'

At this proposition, the Belgian bishop, who was wiping the perspiration from his forehead, heaved a despairing sigh.

' A thousand thanks, princess,' answered the cardinal to her, in very good French, but with an intolerable Italian accent ; ' I am really overcome with so much kindness.'

' Will not your Lordship take some refreshment ?' said the princess to the bishop, as she turned towards the sideboard.

' With your permission, madame, I will take a little iced coffee,' said the prelate, making a prudent circuit to approach the dishes without passing before the fire.

' And will not your Eminence try one of these little oyster-patties ? Th are quite hot,' said the princess.

' I know them already, princess,' said the cardinal, with the air and look of an epicure ; ' they are delicious, and I cannot resist the temptation.'

' What wine shall I have the honour to offer your Eminence ?' resumed the princess, graciously.

' A little claret, if you please, madame ;' and as Father d'Aigrigny prepared to fill the cardinal's glass, the princess disputed with him that pleasure.

' Your Eminence will doubtless approve what I have done,' said Father d'Aigrigny to the cardinal, whilst the latter was gravely despatching the oyster-patties, ' in not summoning for to-day the Bishop of Mogador, the Archbishop of Nanterre, and our holy Mother Perpétue, the lady-superior of St. Marie Convent, the interview we are about to have with his Reverence Father Rodin and Abbé Gabriel being altogether private and confidential.'

' Our good father was perfectly right,' said the cardinal ; ' for, though the possible consequences of this Rennepont affair may interest the whole Church, there are some things that are as well kept secret.'

' Then I must seize this opportunity to thank your Eminence for having deigned to make an exception in favour of a very obscure and humble servant of the Church,' said the princess to the cardinal, with a very deep and respectful curtsey.

' It is only just and right, madame,' replied the cardinal, bowing, as he replaced his empty glass upon the table ; ' we know how much the Church is indebted to you for the salutary direction you give to the religious institutions of which you are the patroness.'

' With regard to that, your Eminence may be assured that I always refuse assistance to any poor person who cannot produce a certificate from the confessional.'

' And it is only thus, madam,' resumed the cardinal, this time allowing himself to be tempted by the attractions of the crawfish's tails, ' it is only thus that charity has any meaning. I care little that the irreligious should feel hunger, but with the pious it is different ;' and the prelate gaily swallowed a mouthful. ' Moreover,' resumed he, ' it is well known with what ardent zeal you pursue the impious, and those who are rebels against the authority of our Holy Father.'

' Your Eminence may feel convinced that I am *Roman* in heart and soul ; I see no difference between a Gallican and a Turk, said the princess, bravely.

' The princess is right,' said the Belgian bishop : ' I will go further, and assert that a Gallican should be more odious to the church than a pagan. In this respect I am of the opinion of Louis XIV. They asked him a favour for a man about the court. "Never," said the great king ; "this person is a Jansenist."—" No, sire ; he is an atheist !"—" Oh ! that is different ; I will grant what he asks," said the king.'

This little episcopal jest made them all laugh. After which Father d'Aigrigny resumed seriously, addressing the cardinal : ' Unfortunately, as I was about to observe to your Eminence with regard to the Abbé Gabriel, unless they are very narrowly watched, the lower clergy have a tendency to become infected with dissenting views, and with ideas of rebellion against what they call the despotism of the bishops.'

'This young man must be a Catholic Luther !' said the bishop. And, walking on tip-toe, he went to pour himself out a glorious glass of Madeira, in which he soaked some sweet cake, made in the form of a crozier.

Led by his example, the cardinal, under pretence of warming his feet by drawing still closer to the fire, helped himself to an excellent glass of old Malaga, which he swallowed by mouthfuls, with an air of profound meditation ; after which he resumed : ' So this Abbé Gabriel starts as a reformer. He must be an ambitious man. Is he dangerous ?'

' By our advice his superiors have judged him to be so. They have ordered him to come hither. He will soon be here, and I will tell your Eminence why I have sent for him. But first, I have a note on the dangerous tendencies of the Abbé Gabriel. Certain questions were addressed to him, with regard to some of his acts, and it was in consequence of his answers that his superiors recalled him.'

So saying, Father d'Aigrigny took from his pocket-book a paper, which he read as follows :

' " *Question.*—Is it true that you performed religious rites for an inhabitant of your parish who died in final impenitence of the most detestable kind, since he had committed suicide ?

' " *Answer of Abbé Gabriel.*—I paid him the last duties, because, more than any one else, because of his guilty end, he required the prayers of the church. During the night which followed his interment I continually implored for him the divine mercy.

' " *Q.*—Is it true that you refused a set of silver-gilt sacramental vessels, and other ornaments, with which one of the faithful, in pious zeal, wished to endow your parish ?

' " *A.*—I refused the vessels and embellishments, because the house of the Lord should be plain and without ornament, so as to remind the faithful that the divine Saviour was born in a stable. I advised the person who wished to make these useless presents to my parish to employ the money in judicious almsgiving, assuring him it would be more agreeable to the Lord."'

'What a bitter and violent declamation against the adorning of our temples !' cried the cardinal. 'This young priest is most dangerous. Continue, my good father.'

And, in his indignation, his Eminence swallowed several mouthfuls of strawberry-cream. Father d'Aigrigny continued :

' " *Q.*—Is it true that you received in your parsonage, and kept there for some days, an inhabitant of the village, by birth a Swiss, belonging to the Protestant communion ? Is it true that not only you did not attempt to convert him to the one Catholic and Apostolic faith, but that you carried so far the neglect of your sacred duties as to inter this heretic in the ground consecrated for the repose of true believers ?

' " *A.*—One of my brethren was houseless. His life had been honest and laborious. In his old age his strength had failed him, and sickness had come at the back of it ; almost in a dying state, he had been driven from his humble dwelling by a pitiless landlord, to whom he owed a year's rent. I received the old man in my house, and soothed his last days. The poor creature had toiled and suffered all his life ; dying, he uttered no word of bitterness at his hard fate ; he recommended his soul to God, and piously kissed the crucifix. His pure and simple spirit returned to the bosom of its Creator. I closed his eyes with respect, I buried him, I prayed for him ; and, though he died in the Protestant faith, I thought him worthy of a place in consecrated ground." '

'Worse and worse !' said the cardinal. 'This tolerance is monstrous. It is a horrible attack on that maxim of Catholicism : " Out of the pale of the Church there is no salvation." '

'And all this is the more serious, my lord,' resumed Father d'Aigrigny, 'because the mildness, charity, and Christian devotion of Abbé Gabriel have excited, not only in his parish, but in all the surrounding districts, the greatest enthusiasm. The priests of the neighbouring parishes have yielded to the general impulse, and it must be confessed that but for his moderation a wide-spread schism would have commenced.'

'But what do you hope will result from bringing him here ?' said the prelate. ——'The position of Abbé Gabriel is complicated ; first of all, he is the heir of the Rennepont family.'

'But has he not ceded his rights ?' asked the cardinal.

'Yes, my lord ; and this cession, which was at first informal, has lately, with his free consent, been made perfectly regular in law ; for he had sworn, happen what might, to renounce his part of the inheritance in favour of the Society of Jesus. Nevertheless, his Reverence Father Rodin thinks, that if your Eminence, after explaining to Abbé Gabriel that he was about to be recalled by his superiors, were to propose to him some eminent position at Rome, he might be induced to leave France, and we might succeed in arousing within him those sentiments of ambition which are doubtless only sleeping for the present ; your Eminence having observed, very judiciously, that every reformer must be ambitious.'

'I approve of this idea,' said the cardinal, after a moment's reflection ; 'with his merit and power of acting on other men, Abbé Gabriel may rise very high, if he is docile ; and if he should not be so, it is better for the safety of the Church that he should be at Rome than here—for you know, my good father, we have securities that are unfortunately wanting in France.'*

After some moments of silence, the cardinal said suddenly to Father d'Aigrigny : 'As we were talking of Father Rodin, tell me frankly what you think of him.'

'Your Eminence knows his capacity,' said Father d'Aigrigny, with a constrained and suspicious air ; 'our reverend Father-General——'

'Commissioned him to take your place,' said the cardinal ; 'I know that. He told me so at Rome. But what do you think of the character of Father Rodin ? Can one have full confidence in him ?'

'He has so complete, so original, so secret, and so impenetrable a mind,' said Father d'Aigrigny, with hesitation, 'that it is difficult to form any certain judgment with respect to him.'

'Do you think him ambitious ?' said the cardinal, after another moment's pause. 'Do you not suppose him capable of having other views than those of the greater glory of his Order ?—Come, I have reasons for speaking thus,' added the prelate, with emphasis.

'Why,' resumed Father d'Aigrigny, not without suspicion, for the game

* It is known that, in 1845, the Inquisition, solitary confinement, &c., still existed at Rome.

is played cautiously between people of the same craft, 'what should your Eminence think of him, either from your own observation, or from the report of the Father-General ?'

'I think—that if his apparent devotion to his Order really concealed some after-thought—it would be well to discover it—for, with the influence that he has obtained at Rome (as I have found out), he might one day, and that shortly, become very formidable.'

'Well !' cried Father d'Aigrigny, impelled by his jealousy of Rodin ; 'I am, in this respect, of the same opinion as your eminence ; for I have sometimes perceived in him flashes of ambition, that were as alarming as they were extraordinary—and since I must tell all to your Eminence——'

Father d'Aigrigny was unable to continue ; at this moment Mrs. Grivois, who had been knocking at the door, half-opened it, and made a sign to her mistress. The princess answered by bowing her head, and Mrs. Grivois again withdrew. A second afterwards Rodin entered the room.

CHAPTER XVII.

RENDERING THE ACCOUNT.

AT sight of Rodin, the two prelates and Father d'Aigrigny rose spontaneously, so much were they overawed by the real superiority of this man ; their faces, just before contracted with suspicion and jealousy, suddenly brightened up, and seemed to smile on the reverend father with affectionate deference. The princess advanced some steps to meet him.

Rodin, badly dressed as ever, leaving on the soft carpet the muddy track of his clumsy shoes, put his umbrella into one corner, and advanced towards the table—not with his accustomed humility, but with slow step, uplifted head, and steady glance ; not only did he feel himself in the midst of his partisans, but he knew that he could rule them all by the power of his intellect.

'We were speaking of your reverence, my dear, good father,' said the cardinal, with charming affability.

'Ah !' said Rodin, looking fixedly at the prelate ; 'and what were you saying ?'

'Why,' replied the Belgian bishop, wiping his forehead, 'all the good that can be said of your reverence.'

'Will you not take something, my good father ?' said the princess to Rodin, as she pointed to the splendid sideboard.——'Thank you, madam, I have eaten my radish already this morning.'

'My secretary, Abbé Berlini, who was present at your repast, was, indeed, much astonished at your reverence's frugality,' said the prelate ; 'it is worthy of an anchorite.'

'Suppose we talk of business,' said Rodin, abruptly, like a man accustomed to lead and control the discussion.

'We shall always be most happy to hear you,' said the prelate. 'Your reverence yourself fixed to-day to talk over this great Rennepont affair. It is of such importance, that it was partly the cause of my journey to France ; for to support the interests of the glorious Company of Jesus, with which I have the honour of being associated, is to support the interests of Rome itself, and I promised the reverend Father-General that I would place myself entirely at your orders.'

'I can only repeat what his Eminence has just said,' added the bishop. 'We set out from Rome together, and our ideas are just the same.'

'Certainly,' said Rodin, addressing the cardinal, 'your Eminence may serve our cause, and that materially. I will tell you how presently.'

Then, addressing the princess, he continued : ' I have desired Dr. Balei-nier to come here, madam, for it will be well to inform him of certain things.'——' He will be admitted as usual,' said the princess.

Since Rodin's arrival Father d'Aigrigny had remained silent ; he seemed occupied with bitter thoughts, and with some violent internal struggle. At last, half rising, he said to the prelate, in a forced tone of voice : ' I will not ask your Eminence to judge between the reverend Father Rodin and myself. Our General has pronounced, and I have obeyed. But, as your Eminence will soon see our superior, I should wish that you would grant me the favour to report faithfully the answers of Father Rodin to one or two questions I am about to put to him.'

The prelate bowed. Rodin looked at Father d'Aigrigny with an air of surprise, and said to him, drily : ' The thing is decided. What is the use of questions ?'

' Not to justify myself,' answered Father d'Aigrigny, ' but to place matters in their true light before his eminence.'

' Speak, then ;. but let us have no useless speeches,' said Rodin, drawing out his large silver watch, and looking at it. ' By two o'clock I must be at Saint-Sulpice.'

' I will be as brief as possible,' said Father d'Aigrigny, with repressed re-sentment. Then, addressing Rodin, he resumed : ' When your reverence thought fit to take my place, and to blame, very severely perhaps, the manner in which I had managed the interests confided to my care, I confess honestly that these interests were gravely compromised.'

' Compromised ?' said Rodin, ironically ; ' you mean lost. Did you not order me to write to Rome, to bid them renounce all hope ?'

' That is true,' said Father d'Aigrigny.

' It was then a desperate case, given up by the best doctors,' continued Rodin, with irony, ' and yet I have undertaken to restore it to life. Go on.'

And, plunging both hands into the pockets of his trousers, he looked Father d'Aigrigny full in the face.

' Your reverence blamed me harshly,' resumed Father d'Aigrigny, ' not for having sought, by every possible means, to recover the property odiously diverted from our society——'

' All your casuists authorise you to do so,' said the cardinal ; ' the texts are clear and positive ; you have a right to recover, *per fas aut nefas,* what has been treacherously taken from you.'

' And therefore,' resumed Father d'Aigrigny, ' Father Rodin only reproached me with the military roughness of my means. " Their violence," he said, " was in dangerous opposition to the manners of the age." Be it so ; but, first of all, I could not be exposed to any legal proceedings, and, but for one fatal circumstance, success would have crowned the course I had taken, however rough and brutal it may appear. Now, may I ask your reverence, what——'

' What I have done more than you ?' said Rodin to Father d'Aigrigny, giving way to his impertinent habit of interrupting people ; ' what I have done better than you ?—what step I have taken in the Rennepont affair, since I received it from you in a desperate condition ? Is that what you wish to know ?'——' Precisely,' said Father d'Aigrigny, drily.

' Well, I confess,' resumed Rodin, in a sardonic tone, ' just as you did great things, coarse things, turbulent things, I have been doing little, puerile, secret things. Oh, heaven ! you cannot imagine what a foolish part I, who passed for a man of enlarged views, have been acting for the last six weeks.'

' I should never have allowed myself to address such a reproach to your reverence, however deserved it may appear,' said Father d'Aigrigny, with a bitter smile.

'A reproach?' said Rodin, shrugging his shoulders; 'a reproach? You shall be the judge. Do you know what I wrote about you, some six weeks ago? Here it is: "Father d'Aigrigny has excellent qualities. He will be of much service to me"—and from to-morrow I shall employ you very actively,' added Rodin, by way of parenthesis—"but he is not great enough to know how to make himself little on occasion." Do you understand?'

'Not very well,' said Father d'Aigrigny, blushing.

'So much the worse for you,' answered Rodin; 'it only proves that I was right. Well, since I must tell you, I have been wise enough to play the most foolish part for six whole weeks. Yes, I have chatted nonsense with a grisette—have talked of liberty, progress, humanity, emancipation of woman, with a young, excited girl; of Napoleon the Great, and all sorts of Bonapartist idolatry, with an old, imbecile soldier; of imperial glory, humiliation of France, hopes in the King of Rome, with a certain marshal of France, who, with a heart full of adoration for the robber of thrones, that was transported to Saint-Helena, has a head as hollow and sonorous as a trumpet, into which you have only to blow some warlike or patriotic notes, and it will flourish away of itself, without knowing why or how. More than all this, I have talked of love affairs with a young tiger. When I told you it was lamentable to see a man of any intelligence descend, as I have done, to all such petty ways of connecting the thousand threads of this dark web, was I not right? Is it not a fine spectacle to see the spider obstinately weaving its net?—to see the ugly little black animal crossing thread upon thread, fastening it here, strengthening it there, and again lengthening it in some other place? You shrug your shoulders in pity; but return two hours after —what will you find? The little black animal eating its fill, and in its web a dozen of the foolish flies, bound so securely, that the little black animal has only to choose the moment of its repast.'

As he uttered these words, Rodin smiled strangely; his eyes, gradually half closed, opened to their full width, and seemed to shine more than usual. The Jesuit felt a sort of feverish excitement, which he attributed to the contest in which he had engaged before these eminent personages, who already felt the influence of his original and cutting speech.

Father d'Aigrigny began to regret having entered on the contest. He resumed, however, with ill-repressed irony: 'I do not dispute the smallness of your means. I agree with you, they are very puerile—they are even very vulgar. But that is not quite sufficient to give an exalted notion of your merit. May I be allowed to ask——'

'What these means have produced?' resumed Rodin, with an excitement that was not usual with him. 'Look into my spider's web, and you will see there the beautiful and insolent young girl, so proud, six weeks ago, of her grace, mind, and audacity—now pale, trembling, mortally wounded at the heart.'

'But the act of chivalrous intrepidity of the Indian prince, with which all Paris is ringing,' said the princess, 'must surely have touched Mdlle. de Cardoville.'

'Yes; but I have paralysed the effect of that stupid and savage devotion, by demonstrating to the young lady that it is not sufficient to kill black panthers to prove one's self a susceptible, delicate, and faithful lover.'

'Be it so,' said Father d'Aigrigny; 'we will admit the fact that Mdlle. de Cardoville is wounded to the heart.'

'But what does this prove with regard to the Rennepont affair?' asked the cardinal, with curiosity, as he leaned his elbows on the table.

'There results from it,' said Rodin, 'that, when our most dangerous enemy is mortally wounded, she abandons the battlefield. That is something, I should imagine.'

'Indeed,' said the princess, 'the talents and audacity of Mdlle. de Cardoville would make her the soul of the coalition formed against us.'

'Be it so,' replied Father d'Aigrigny, obstinately ; 'she may be no longer formidable in that respect. But the wound in her heart will not prevent her from inheriting.'

'Who tells you so ?' asked Rodin, coldly, and with assurance. 'Do you know why I have taken such pains, first to bring her in contact with Djalma, and then to separate her from him ?'

'That is what I ask you,' said Father d'Aigrigny ; 'how can this storm of passion prevent Mdlle. de Cardoville and the prince from inheriting ?'

'Is it from the serene, or from the stormy sky, that darts the destroying thunderbolt ?' said Rodin, disdainfully. 'Be satisfied ; I shall know where to place the conductor. As for M. Hardy, the man lived for three things : his workmen, his friend, his mistress. He has been thrice wounded in the heart. I always take aim at the heart ; it is legal and sure.'

'It is legal, and sure, and praiseworthy,' said the bishop ; 'for, if I understand you rightly, this manufacturer had a concubine : now, it is well to make use of an evil passion for the punishment of the wicked.'

'True, quite true,' added the cardinal ; 'if they have evil passions for us to make use of, it is their own fault.'

'Our holy Mother Perpétue,' said the princess, 'took every means to discover this abominable adultery.'

'Well, then, M. Hardy is wounded in his dearest affections, I admit,' said Father d'Aigrigny, still disputing every inch of ground ; 'ruined too in his fortune, which will only make him the more eager after this inheritance.'

The argument appeared of weight to the two prelates and the princess ; all looked at Rodin with anxious curiosity. Instead of answering, he walked up to the sideboard, and, contrary to his habits of stoical sobriety, and in spite of his repugnance for wine, he examined the decanters, and said : 'What is there in them ?'

'Claret and sherry,' said the hostess, much astonished at the sudden taste of Rodin, 'and——'

The latter took a decanter at hazard, and poured out a glass of Madeira, which he drank off at a draught. Just before, he had felt a strange kind of shivering ; to this had succeeded a sort of weakness. He hoped the wine would revive him.

After wiping his mouth with the back of his dirty hand, he returned to the table, and said to Father d'Aigrigny : 'What did you tell me about M. Hardy ?'

'That, being ruined in fortune, he would be the more eager to obtain this immense inheritance,' answered Father d'Aigrigny, inwardly much offended at the imperious tone.

'M. Hardy think of money ?' said Rodin, shrugging his shoulders. 'He is indifferent to life, plunged in a stupor, from which he only starts to burst into tears. Then he speaks with mechanical kindness to those about him. I have placed him in good hands. He begins, however, to be sensible to the attentions shown him, for he is good, excellent, weak ; and it is to this excellence, Father d'Aigrigny, that you must appeal to finish the work in hand.'

'I ?' said Father d'Aigrigny, much surprised.——'Yes ; and then you will find that the result I have obtained is considerable, and——'

Rodin paused, and, pressing his hand to his forehead, said to himself : 'It is strange !'

'What is the matter ?' said the princess, with interest.——'Nothing, madame,' answered Rodin, with a shiver ; 'it is doubtless the wine I drank ; I am not accustomed to it. I feel a slight headache ; but it will pass.'

'Your eyes are very bloodshot, my good father,' said the princess.

'I have looked too closely into my web,' answered the Jesuit, with a sinister smile ; 'and I must look again, to make Father d'Aigrigny, who pretends to be blind, catch a glimpse of my other flies. The two daughters of Marshal Simon, for instance, growing sadder and more dejected every day, at the icy barrier raised between them and their father ; and the latter thinking himself one day dishonoured if he does this, another if he does that ; so that the hero of the Empire has become weaker and more irresolute than a child. What more remains of this impious family ? Jacques Rennepont ? Ask Morok, to what a state of debasement intemperance has reduced him, and towards what an abyss he is rushing !—There is my occurrence-sheet ; you see to what are reduced all the members of this family, who, six weeks ago, had each elements of strength and union ! Behold these Renneponts, who, by the will of their heretical ancestor, were to unite their forces to combat and crush our Society !—There was good reason to fear them ; but what did I say ? That I would act upon their passions. What have I done ? I have acted upon their passions. At this hour they are vainly struggling in my web—they are mine—they are mine——'

As he was speaking, Rodin's countenance and voice had undergone a singular alteration ; his complexion, generally so cadaverous, had become flushed, but unequally, and in patches ; then, strange phenomenon ! his eyes grew both more brilliant and more sunken, and his voice sharper and louder. The change in the countenance of Rodin, of which he did not appear to be conscious, was so remarkable, that the other actors in this scene looked at him with a sort of terror.

Deceived as to the cause of this impression, Rodin exclaimed with indignation, in a voice interrupted by deep gaspings for breath : 'Is it pity for this impious race, that I read upon your faces ? Pity for the young girl, who never enters a church, and erects pagan altars in her habitation ? Pity for Hardy, the sentimental blasphemer, the philanthropic atheist, who had no chapel in his factory, and dared to blend the names of Socrates, Marcus-Aurelius, and Plato, with our Saviour's ? Pity for the Indian worshipper of Brahma ? Pity for the two sisters, who have never even been baptized ? Pity for that brute, Jacques Rennepont ? Pity for the stupid imperial soldier, who has Napoleon for his god, and the bulletins of the Grand Army for his gospel ? Pity for this family of renegades, whose ancestor, a relapsed heretic, not content with robbing us of our property, excites from his tomb, at the end of a century and a half, his cursed race to lift their heads against us ? What ! to defend ourselves from these vipers, we shall not have the right to crush them in their own venom ?—I tell you, that it is to serve heaven, and to give a salutary example to the world, to devote, by unchaining their own passions, this impious family to grief and despair and death !'

As he spoke thus, Rodin was dreadful in his ferocity ; the fire of his eyes became still more brilliant ; his lips were dry and burning, a cold sweat bathed his temples, which could be seen throbbing ; an icy shudder ran through his frame. Attributing these symptoms to fatigue from writing through a portion of the night, and wishing to avoid fainting, he went to the sideboard, filled another glass with wine, which he drank off at a draught, and returned as the cardinal said to him : 'If your course with regard to this family needed justification, my good father, your last word would have victoriously justified it. Not only are you right, according to your own casuists, but there is nothing in your proceedings contrary to human laws. As for the divine law, it is pleasing to the Lord to destroy impiety with its own weapons.'

Conquered, as well as the others, by Rodin's diabolical assurance, and brought back to a kind of fearful admiration, Father d'Aigrigny said to him : ' I confess I was wrong in doubting the judgment of your reverence. Deceived by the appearance of the means employed, I could not judge of their connection, and above all, of their results. I now see, that, thanks to you, success is no longer doubtful.'

' This is an exaggeration,' replied Rodin, with feverish impatience ; ' all these passions are at work, but the moment is critical. As the alchemist bends over the crucible, which may give him either treasures or sudden death—I alone at this moment——'

Rodin did not finish the sentence. He pressed both his hands to his forehead, with a stifled cry of pain.

' What is the matter ?' said Father d'Aigrigny. ' For some moments you have been growing fearfully pale.'——' I do not know what is the matter,' said Rodin, in an altered voice ; 'my head-ache increases—I am seized with a sort of giddiness.'

' Sit down,' said the princess, with interest.——' Take something,' said the bishop.

' It will be nothing,' said Rodin, with an effort ; ' I am no milksop, thank heaven !—I had little sleep last night ; it is fatigue—nothing more. I was saying, that I alone could now direct this affair : but I cannot execute the plan myself. I must keep out of the way, and watch in the shade : I must hold the threads, which I alone can manage,' added Rodin, in a faint voice.

' My good father,' said the cardinal uneasily, ' I assure you that you are very unwell. Your paleness is becoming livid.'

' It is possible,' answered Rodin, courageously ; ' but I am not to be so soon conquered. To return to our affair—this is the time, in which your qualities, Father d'Aigrigny, will turn to good account. I have never denied them, and they may now be of the greatest use. You have the power of charming—grace—eloquence—you must——'

Rodin paused again. A cold sweat poured from his forehead. He felt his legs give way under him, notwithstanding his obstinate energy.

' I confess, I am not well,' he said ; ' yet, this morning, I was as well as ever. I shiver. I am icy cold.'

' Draw near the fire—it is a sudden indisposition,' said the bishop, offering his arm with heroic devotion ; ' it will not be anything of consequence.'

' If you were to take something warm, a cup of tea,' said the princess ; ' Dr. Baleinier will be here directly—he will reassure us as to this—indisposition.'

' It is really inexplicable,' said the prelate.

At these words of the cardinal, Rodin, who had advanced with difficulty towards the fire, turned his eyes upon the prelate, and looked at him fixedly in a strange manner, for about a second ; then, strong in his unconquerable energy, notwithstanding the change in his features, which were now visibly disfigured, Rodin said, in a broken voice, which he tried to make firm : ' The fire has warmed me ; it will be nothing. I have no time to coddle myself. It would be a pretty thing to fall ill just as the Rennepont affair can only succeed by my exertions ! Let us return to business. I told you, Father d'Aigrigny, that you might serve us a good deal ; and you also, princess, who have espoused this cause as if it were your own——'

Rodin again paused. This time he uttered a piercing cry, sank upon a chair placed near him, and, throwing himself back convulsively, he pressed his hands to his chest, and exclaimed : ' Oh ! what pain !'

Then (dreadful sight !) a cadaverous decomposition, rapid as thought, took place in Rodin's features. His hollow eyes were filled with blood, and seemed to shrink back in their orbits, which formed, as it were, two dark holes, in the centre of which blazed points of fire ; nervous convulsions drew the flabby, damp, and icy skin tight over the bony prominences of the face, which was becoming rapidly green. From the lips, writhing with pain, issued the struggling breath, mingled with the words : ' Oh ! I suffer ! I burn !'

Then, yielding to a transport of fury, Rodin tore with his nails his naked chest, for he had twisted off the buttons of his waistcoat, and rent his black and filthy shirt-front, as if the pressure of those garments augmented the violence of the pain under which he was writhing. The bishop, the cardinal, and Father d'Aigrigny, hastily approached Rodin, to try and hold him ; he was seized with horrible convulsions ; but, suddenly, collecting all his strength, he rose upon his feet stiff as a corpse. Then, with his garments in disorder, his thin, grey hair standing up all around his greenish face, fixing his red and flaming eyes upon the cardinal, he seized him with convulsive grasp, and exclaimed in a terrible voice, half stifled in his throat: 'Cardinal Malipieri—this illness is too sudden—they suspect me at Rome —you are of the race of the Borgias—and your secretary was with me this morning !'

'Unhappy man ! what does he dare insinuate?' cried the prelate, as amazed as he was indignant at the accusation. So saying, the cardinal strove to free himself from the grasp of Rodin, whose fingers were now as stiff as iron.

' I am poisoned !' muttered Rodin, and sinking back, he fell into the arms of Father d'Aigrigny.

Notwithstanding his alarm, the cardinal had time to whisper to the latter : ' He thinks himself poisoned. He must therefore be plotting something very dangerous.'

The door of the room opened. It was Dr. Baleinier.

' Oh, doctor !' cried the princess, as she ran pale and frightened towards him ; ' Father Rodin has been suddenly attacked with terrible convulsions. Quick ! quick !'

' Convulsions ? oh ! it will be nothing, madame,' said the doctor, throwing down his hat upon a chair, and hastily approaching the group which surrounded the sick man.

' Here is the doctor !' cried the princess. All stepped aside, except Father d'Aigrigny, who continued to support Rodin, leaning against a chair.

' Heavens ! what symptoms !' cried Dr. Baleinier, examining with growing terror the countenance of Rodin, which from green was turning blue.

' What is it ?' asked all the spectators, with one voice.——' What is it ?' repeated the doctor, drawing back as if he had trodden upon a serpent. ' It is the cholera ! and contagious !'

On this frightful, magic word, Father d'Aigrigny abandoned his hold of Rodin, who rolled upon the floor.

' He is lost !' cried Dr. Baleinier. ' But I will run to fetch the means for a last effort.' And he rushed towards the door.

The Princess de Saint-Dizier, Father d'Aigrigny, the bishop, and the cardinal followed in terror the flight of Dr. Baleinier. They all pressed to the door, which, in their consternation, they could not open. It opened at last—but from without—and Gabriel appeared upon the threshold. Gabriel, the type of the true priest, the holy, the evangelical minister, to whom we can never pay enough of respect and ardent sympathy, and tender admiration. His angelic countenance, in its mild serenity, offered a striking contrast to these faces, all disturbed and contracted with terror.

The young priest was nearly thrown down by the fugitives, who rushed through the now open doorway, exclaiming : ' Do not go in ! he is dying of the cholera. Fly !'

On these words, pushing back the bishop, who, being the last, was trying to force a passage, Gabriel ran towards Rodin, while the prelate succeeded in making his escape. Rodin, stretched upon the carpet, his limbs twisted with fearful cramps, was writhing in the extremity of pain. The violence of his fall had, no doubt, roused him to consciousness, for he moaned, in a sepulchral voice : 'They leave me to die—like a dog—the cowards !—Help !—no one——'

And the dying man, rolling on his back with a convulsive movement, turned towards the ceiling a face on which was branded the infernal despair of the damned, as he once more repeated : ' No one !——not one !'

His eyes, which suddenly flamed with fury, just then met the large blue eyes of the angelic and mild countenance of Gabriel, who, kneeling beside him, said to him, in his soft, grave tones : ' I am here, father—to help you, if help be possible—to pray for you, if God calls you to him.'

' Gabriel !' murmured Rodin, with failing voice ; ' forgive me for the evil I have done you—do not leave me—do not——'

Rodin could not finish ; he had succeeded in raising himself into a sitting posture ; he now uttered a loud cry, and fell back without sense or motion.

   ✿   ✿   ✿   ✿   ✿   ✿

The same day it was announced in the evening papers : ' The cholera has broken out in Paris. The first case declared itself this day, at half-past three, P.M., in the Rue de Babylone, at Saint-Dizier House.'

CHAPTER XVIII.

THE SQUARE OF NOTRE-DAME.

A WEEK had passed since Rodin was seized with the cholera, and its ravages had continually increased. That was an awful time ! A funeral pall was spread over Paris, once so gay. And yet, never had the sky been of a more settled, purer blue ; never had the sun shone more brilliantly. The inexorable serenity of nature, during the ravages of the deadly scourge, offered a strange and mysterious contrast. The flaunting light of the dazzling sunshine fell full upon the features, contracted by a thousand agonising fears. Each trembled for himself, or for those dear to him ; every countenance was stamped with an expression of feverish astonishment and dread. People walked with rapid steps, as if they would escape from the fate which threatened them ; besides, they were in haste to return to their homes, for often they left life, health, happiness, and, two hours later, they found agony, death, and despair.

At every moment, new dismal objects met the view. Sometimes carts passed along, filled with coffins, symmetrically piled ; they stopped before every house. Men in black and grey garments were in waiting before the door ; they held out their hands, and to some, one coffin was thrown, to some two, frequently three or four, from the same house. It sometimes happened that the store was quickly exhausted, and the cart, which had arrived full, went away empty, whilst many of the dead in the street were still unserved. In nearly every dwelling, upstairs and down, from the roof to the cellar, there was a stunning tapping of hammers : coffins were being nailed down, and so many, so very many were nailed, that sometimes those who worked stopped from sheer fatigue. Then broke forth laments, heartrending moans, despairing imprecations. They were uttered by those from whom the men in black and grey had taken someone to fill the coffins.

Unceasingly were the coffins filled, and day and night did those men work, but by day more than by night, for, as soon as it was dusk, came a gloomy file of vehicles of all kinds—the usual hearses were not sufficient ; but cars, carts, drays, hackney-coaches, and such like, swelled the funeral procession ; different to the other conveyances, which entered the streets full and went away empty—these came empty but soon returned full. During that period, the windows of many houses were illuminated, and often the lights remained burning till the morning. It was 'the season.' These illuminations resembled the gleaming rays which shine in the gay haunts of pleasure ; but there were tapers instead of wax candles, and the chanting of prayers for the dead replaced the murmur of the ball-room. In the streets, instead of the facetious transparencies which indicate the costumiers, there swung at intervals huge lanterns of a blood-red colour, with these words in black letters : 'Assistance for those attacked with the cholera.' The true places for revelry, during the night, were the churchyards ; they ran riot— they, usually so desolate and silent, during the dark, quiet hours, when the cypress trees rustle in the breeze, so lonely, that no human step dared to disturb the solemn silence which reigned there at night, became, on a sudden, animated, noisy, riotous, and resplendent with light. By the smoky flame of torches, which threw a red glare upon the dark fir-trees, and the white tomb-stones, many grave-diggers worked merrily, humming snatches of some favourite tune. Their laborious and hazardous industry then commanded a very high price ; they were in such request that it was necessary to humour them. They drank often and much ; they sang long and loud ; and this to keep up their strength and spirits good, absolute requisites in such an employment. If, by chance, any did not finish the grave they had began, some obliging comrade finished for it *them* (fitting expression !), and placed them in it with friendly care.

Other distant sounds responded to the joyous strains of the grave-diggers ; public-houses had sprung up in the neighbourhood of the churchyards, and the drivers of the dead, when they had 'set down their customers,' as they jocosely expressed themselves, enriched with their unusual gratuities, feasted and made merry like lords ; dawn often found them with a glass in their hand, and a jest on their lips ; and, strange to say, among these funeral satellites, who breathed the very atmosphere of the disease, the mortality was scarcely perceptible. In the dark, squalid quarters of the town, where, surrounded by infectious exhalations, the indigent population was crowded together, and miserable beings, exhausted by severe privation, were 'bespoke' by the cholera, as it was energetically said at the time, not only individuals, but whole families, were carried off in a few hours ; and yet, sometimes, oh, merciful Providence ! one or two little children were left in the cold and empty room, after father and mother, brother and sister, had been taken away in their shells.

Frequently, houses which had swarmed with hard working labourers, were obliged to be shut up for want of tenants ; in one day, they had been completely cleared by this terrible visitation, from the cellars, where little chimney sweepers slept upon straw, to the garret, on whose cold brick floor lay stretched some wan and half-naked being, without work and without bread. But, of all the wards of Paris, that which perhaps presented the most frightful spectacle during the progress of the cholera, was the City ; and in the City, the square before the cathedral of Nôtre-Dame was almost every day the theatre of dreadful scenes : for this locality was frequently thronged with those who conveyed the sick from the neighbouring streets to the Great Hospital. The cholera had not one aspect, but a thousand. So that one week after Rodin had been suddenly attacked, several events combining the horrible and the grotesque occurred in the square of Nôtre-Dame.

Instead of the Rue d'Arcole, which now leads directly to the square, it was then approached on one side, by a mean, narrow lane, like all the other streets of the City, and terminating in a dark, low archway. Upon entering the square, the principal door of the huge Cathedral was to the left of the spectator, and facing him were the Hospital buildings. A little beyond, was an opening, which gave to view a portion of the parapet of the Quay Nôtre-Dame. A placard had been recently stuck on the discoloured and sunken wall of the archway ; it contained these words, traced in large characters.*

'VENGEANCE !   VENGEANCE !

' The Working-men carried to the Hospitals are poisoned, because the number of Patients is too great ; every night, Boats filled with Corpses, drop down the Seine.

' Vengeance and Death to the murderers of the People !'

Two men, enveloped in cloaks, and half-hidden in the deep shadow of the vault, were listening with anxious curiosity to the threatening murmur, which rose with increasing force from among a tumultuous assembly, grouped around the Hospital. Soon, cries of ' Death to the doctors !—Vengeance !' reached the ears of the persons who were in ambush under the arch.

' The posters are working,' said one ; ' the train is on fire. When once the populace is roused, we can set them on whom we please.'

' I say,' replied the other man, ' look over there. That Hercules, whose athletic form towers above the mob, was one of the most frantic leaders when M. Hardy's factory was destroyed.'

' To be sure he was ; I know him again. Wherever mischief is to be done, you are sure to find those vagabonds.'

' Now, take my advice, do not let us remain under this archway,' said the other man ; ' the wind is as cold as ice, and though I am cased in flannel——'

' You are right, the cholera is confoundedly impolite. Besides, everything is going on well here ; I am likewise assured that the whole of the Faubourg St.-Antoine is ready to rise in the republican cause ; that will serve our ends, and our holy religion will triumph over revolutionary impiety. Let us rejoin Father d'Aigrigny.'

' Where shall we find him ?'——' Near here, come—come.' The two hastily disappeared.

The sun, beginning to decline, shed its golden rays upon the blackened sculptures of the porch of Nôtre-Dame, and upon its two massy towers, rising in imposing majesty against a perfectly blue sky, for during the last few days, a north-east wind, dry and cold, had driven away the lightest cloud. A considerable number of people, as we have already stated, obstructed the approach to the Hospital ; they crowded round the iron railings that protect the front of the building, behind which was stationed a detachment of infantry, the cries of ' Death to the doctors !' becoming every moment more threatening. The people who thus vociferated belonged to an idle, vagabond, and depraved populace—the dregs of the Paris mob ; and (terrible spectacle !) the unfortunate beings who were forcibly carried through the midst of these hideous groups entered the Hospital, whilst the air resounded with hoarse clamours, and cries of ' Death.' Every moment,

* It is well known that at the time of the cholera, such placards were numerou in Paris, and were alternately attributed to opposite parties. Among others, to the priests, many of the bishops having published mandatory letters, or stated openly in the churches of their diocese, that the Almighty had sent the cholera as a punishment to France for having driven away its lawful sovereign, and assimilated the Catholic to other forms of worship.

fresh victims were brought along in litters, and on stretchers ; the litters were frequently furnished with coarse curtains, and thus the sick occupants were concealed from the public gaze ; but the stretchers having no covering, the convulsive movements of the dying patients often thrust aside the sheet, and exposed to view their faces, livid as corpses. Far from inspiring with terror the wretches assembled round the Hospital, such spectacles became to them the signal for savage jests, and atrocious predictions upon the fate of these poor creatures, when once in the power of the doctors.

The big blaster and Ciboule, with a good many of their adherents, were among the mob. After the destruction of Hardy's factory, the quarryman was formally expelled from the union of the Wolves, who would have nothing more to do with this wretch ; since then, he had plunged into the grossest debauchery, and speculating on his herculean strength, had hired himself as the officious champion of Ciboule and her compeers. With the exception therefore of some chance passengers, the square of Nôtre-Dame was filled with a ragged crowd, composed of the refuse of the Parisian populace— wretches who call for pity as well as blame ; for misery, ignorance, and destitution, beget but too fatally vice and crime. These savages of civilization felt neither pity, improvement, nor terror, at the shocking sights with which they were surrounded ; careless of a life which was a daily struggle against hunger, or the allurements of guilt, they braved the pestilence with infernal audacity, or sank under it with blasphemy on their lips.

The tall form of the quarryman was conspicuous amongst the rest ; with inflamed eyes and swollen features, he yelled at the top of his voice : 'Death to the body snatchers ! they poison the people.'

'That is easier than to feed them,' added Ciboule. Then, addressing herself to an old man, who was being carried with great difficulty through the dense crowd, upon a chair, by two men, the hag continued : 'Hey ? don't go in there, old croaker ; die here in the open air, instead of dying in that den, where you'll be doctored like an old rat.'

'Yes,' added the quarryman ; 'and then they'll throw you into the water to feast the fishes, which you won't swallow any more.'

At these atrocious cries, the old man looked wildly around, and uttered faint groans. Ciboule wished to stop the persons who were carrying him, and they had much difficulty in getting rid of the hag. The number of cholera-patients arriving increased every moment, and soon neither litters nor stretchers could be obtained, so that they were borne along in the arms of the attendants. Several awful episodes bore witness to the startling rapidity of the infection. Two men were carrying a stretcher covered with a blood-stained sheet ; one of them suddenly felt himself attacked with the complaint ; he stopped short, his powerless arms let go the stretcher ; he turned pale, staggered, fell upon the patient, becoming as livid as him ; the other man, struck with terror, fled precipitately, leaving his companion and the dying man in the midst of the crowd. Some drew back in horror, others burst into a savage laugh.

'The horses have taken fright,' said the quarryman, 'and have left the turn-out in the lurch.'——'Help !' cried the dying man, with a despairing accent ; 'for pity's sake take me in.'

'There's no more room in the pit,' said one, in a jeering tone.——'And you've no legs left to reach the gallery,' added another.

The sick man made an effort to rise ; but his strength failed him ; he fell back exhausted on the mattress. A sudden movement took place among the crowd, the stretcher was overturned, the old man and his companion were trodden underfoot, and their groans were drowned in the cries of 'Death to the body-snatchers !' The yells were renewed with fresh fury, but the ferocious band, who respected nothing in their savage fury, were soon after obliged to open their ranks to several workmen, who vigorously cleared the way for two of their friends, carrying in their arms a poor artizan. He was still young, but his heavy and already livid head hung down upon the shoulder of one of them. A little child followed, sobbing, and holding by one of the workmen's coats. The measured and sonorous sound of several drums was now heard at a distance in the winding streets of the city; they were beating the call to arms, for sedition was rife in the Faubourg Saint-Antoine. The drummers emerged from under the archway, and were traversing the square, when one of them, a grey-haired veteran, suddenly slackened the rolling of his drum, and stood still: his companions turned round in surprise—he had turned green; his legs gave way, he stammered some unintelligible words, and had fallen upon the pavement before those in the front rank had time to pause. The overwhelming rapidity of this attack startled for a moment the most hardened among the surrounding spectators; for, wondering at the interruption, a part of the crowd had rushed towards the soldiers.

At sight of the dying man, supported in the arms of two of his comrades, one of the individuals, who, concealed under the arch, had watched the beginning of the popular excitement, said to the drummers: 'Your comrade drank, perhaps, at some fountain on the road?'

'Yes, sir,' replied one; 'he was very thirsty; he drank two mouthfuls of water on the Place du Chatelet.'

'Then he is poisoned,' said the man.——'Poisoned?' cried several voices.

'It is not surprising,' replied the man, in a mysterious tone; 'poison is thrown into the public fountains; and this very morning a man was massacred in the Rue Beaubourg, who was discovered emptying a paper of arsenic into a pot of wine at a public-house.'[*]

Having said these words, the man disappeared in the crowd. This report, no less absurd than the tales about the poisoning of the Hospital patients, was received with a general burst of indignation. Five or six ragged beings, regular ruffians, seized the body of the expiring drummer, hoisted it upon their shoulders, in spite of all the efforts of his comrades to prevent them, and paraded the square exhibiting the dismal trophy. Ciboule and the quarryman went before, crying: 'Make way for the corpse! This is how they poison the people!'

A fresh incident now attracted the attention of the crowd. A travelling-carriage, which had not been able to pass along the Quai-Napoleon, the pavement of which was up, had ventured among the intricate streets of the city, and now arrived in the square of Nôtre-Dame on its way to the other side of the Seine. Like many others, its owners were flying from Paris, to escape the pestilence which decimated it. A man-servant and a lady's-maid were in the rumble, and they exchanged a glance of alarm as they passed the Hospital, whilst a young man seated in the front part of the carriage let down the glass, and called to the postilions to go slowly, for fear of accident, as the crowd was very dense at that part of the square. This young man was Lord Morinval, and on the back seat were Lord Montbron and his niece, Lady Morinval. The pale and anxious countenance of the young lady showed the alarm which she felt; and Montbron, notwithstanding his firmness of mind, appeared to be very uneasy; he, as well as his niece, frequently had recourse to a smelling-bottle filled with camphor.

During the last few minutes, the carriage had advanced very slowly, the

[*] It is notorious, that at this unhappy period several persons were massacred, under a false accusation of poisoning the fountains, etc.

postilions managing their horses with great caution, when a sudden hubbub, at first distant and undefined, but soon more distinct, arose among the throng ; as it drew near, the ringing sound of chains and metal, peculiar to the artillery-wagons, was plainly audible, and presently one of these vehicles came towards the travelling-carriage, from the direction of the Quai Nôtre-Dame. It seemed strange, that though the crowd was so compact, yet, at the rapid approach of this wagon, the close ranks of human beings opened as if by enchantment, but the following words which were passed from mouth, to mouth soon accounted for the prodigy: 'A wagon full of dead ! the wagon of the dead !' As we have already stated, the usual funeral conveyances were no longer sufficient for the removal of the corpses ; a number of artillery-wagons had been put into requisition, and the coffins were hastily piled in these novel hearses.

Many of the spectators regarded this gloomy vehicle with dismay, but the quarryman and his band redoubled their horrible jokes.

'Make way for the omnibus of the departed !' cried Ciboule.——' No danger of having one's toes crushed in that omnibus,' said the quarryman.

' Doubtless, they're easy to please, the stiff-uns in there.'——'They never want to be set down, at all events.'

' I say, there's only one reg'lar on duty as postilion !'——' That's true, the leaders are driven by a man in a smock-frock.'

'Oh ! I daresay the other soldier was tired, lazy fellow ! and got into the omnibus with the others—they'll all get out at the same big hole.'

' Head foremost, you know.'——' Yes, they pitch them head first into a bed of lime.'

' Why, one might follow the dead-cart blind-fold, and no mistake. It's worse than Montfaucon knacker-yards !'

' Ha ! ha ! ha !—it's rather gamey !' said the quarryman, alluding to the infectious and cadaverous odour which this funeral conveyance left behind it.

'Here's sport !' exclaimed Ciboule : ' the omnibus of the dead will run against the fine coach. Hurrah !—the rich folks will smell death.'

Indeed, the wagon was now directly in front of the carriage, and at a very little distance from it. A man in a smock-frock and wooden shoes drove the two leaders, and an artilleryman the other horses. The coffins were so piled up within this wagon, that its semi-circular top did not shut down closely, so that, as it jolted heavily over the uneven pavement, the biers could be seen chafing against each other. The fiery eyes and inflamed countenance of the man in the smock-frock showed that he was half intoxicated ; urging on the horses with his voice, his heels, and his whip, he paid no attention to the remonstrances of the soldier, who had great difficulty in restraining his own animals, and was obliged to follow the irregular movements of the carman. Advancing in this disorderly manner, the wagon deviated from its course just as it should have passed the travelling-carriage, and ran against it. The shock forced open the top, one of the coffins was thrown out, and, after damaging the panels of the carriage, fell upon the pavement with a dull and heavy sound. The deal planks had been hastily nailed together, and were shivered in the fall, and from the wreck of the coffin rolled a livid corpse, half enveloped in a shroud.

At this horrible spectacle, Lady Morinval, who had mechanically leaned forward, gave a loud scream, and fainted. The crowd fell back in dismay ; the postilions, no less alarmed, took advantage of the space left open to them by the retreat of the multitude ; they whipped their horses, and the carriage dashed on towards the quay. As it disappeared behind the furthermost buildings of the Hospital, the shrill, joyous notes of distant trumpets were heard, and repeated shouts proclaimed : ' The Cholera Masquerade !' The words announced one of those episodes combining buffoonery with terror, which marked the period when the pestilence was on the increase, though now they can with difficulty be credited. If the evidence of eye-witnesses did not agree in every particular with the accounts given in the public papers of this masquerade, they might be regarded as the ravings of some diseased brain, and not as the notice of a fact which really occurred.

' The Masquerade of the Cholera ' appeared, we say, in the square of Nôtre-Dame, just as Morinval's carriage gained the quay, after disengaging itself from the death-wagon.

CHAPTER XIX.

THE CHOLERA MASQUERADE.*

A STREAM of people, who preceded the masquerade, made a sudden ir-ruption through the arch into the square, uttering loud cheers as they advanced. Children were also there, blowing horns, whilst some hooted and others hissed.

The quarryman, Ciboule, and their band, attracted by this new spectacle, rushed tumultuously towards the arch. Instead of the two eating-houses, which now (1845) stand on either side of the Rue d'Arcole, there was then only one, situated to the left of the vaulted passage, and much celebrated amongst the joyous community of students, for the excellence both of its cookery and its wines. At the first blare of the trumpets, sounded by the outriders in livery who preceded the masquerade, the windows of the great room of the eating-house were thrown open, and several waiters, with their napkins under their arms, leaned forward, impatient to witness the arrival of the singular guests they were expecting.

At length, the grotesque procession made its appearance in the thick of an immense uproar. The train comprised a chariot, escorted by men and women on horseback, clad in rich and elegant fancy dresses. Most of these maskers belonged to the middle and easy classes of society. The report had spread that a masquerade was in preparation, for the purpose of daring the cholera, and, by this joyous demonstration, to revive the courage of the affrighted populace. Immediately, artists, young men about town, students, and so on, responded to the appeal, and though till now unknown one to the other, they easily fraternised together. Many brought their mistresses, to complete the show. A subscription had been opened to defray the ex-penses, and, that morning, after a splendid breakfast at the other end of Paris, the joyous troop had started bravely on their march, to finish the day by a dinner in the square of Nôtre-Dame.

We say bravely, for it required a singular turn of mind, a rare firmness of character, in young women, to traverse, in this fashion, a great city plunged in consternation and terror—to fall in at every step with litters loaded with the dying, and carriages filled with the dead—to defy, as it were, in a spirit of strange pleasantry, the plague that was decimating the Parisians. It is certain that, in Paris alone, and there only amongst a peculiar class, could

---

* We read in the *Constitutionnel*, Saturday, March 31st, 1832 : ' The Parisians readily conform to that part of the official instructions with regard to the cholera, which prescribes, as a preservation from the disease, not to be afraid, to amuse one's self, etc. The pleasures of Mid-Lent have been as brilliant and as mad as those of the carnival itself. For a long time past there had not been so many balls at this period of the year. Even the cholera has been made the subject of an itinerant caricature.'

such an idea have ever been conceived or realised. Two men, grotesquely disguised as postilions at a funeral, with formidable false noses, rose-coloured crape hat-bands, and large favours of roses and crape bows at their button-holes, rode before the vehicle. Upon the platform of the car were groups of allegorical personages, representing WINE, PLEASURE, LOVE, PLAY. The mission of these symbolical beings was, by means of jokes, sarcasms, and mockeries, to plague the life out of Goodman Cholera, a sort of funereal and burlesque Cassander, whom they ridiculed and made game of in a hundred ways. The moral of the play was this : ' To brave Cholera in security, let us drink, laugh, game, and make love !'

WINE was represented by a huge, lusty Silenus, thick-set, and with swollen paunch, a crown of ivy on his brow, a panther's skin across his shoulder, and in his hand a large gilt goblet, wreathed with flowers. None other than Ninny Moulin, the famous moral and religious writer, could have exhibited to the astonished and delighted spectators an ear of so deep a scarlet, so majestic an abdomen, and a face of such triumphant and majestic fulness. Every moment, Ninny Moulin appeared to empty his cup—after which he burst out laughing in the face of Goodman Cholera. Goodman Cholera, a cadaverous pantaloon, was half-enveloped in a shroud ; his mask of greenish cardboard, with red, hollow eyes, seemed every moment to grin as in mockery of death ; from beneath his powdered peruke, surmounted by a pyramidical cotton night-cap, appeared his neck and arm, dyed of a bright green colour ; his lean hand, which shook almost always with a feverish trembling (not feigned, but natural), rested upon a crutch-handled cane ; finally, as was becoming in a pantaloon, he wore red stockings, with buckles at the knees, and high slippers of black beaver. This grotesque representative of the cholera was Sleepinbuff.

Notwithstanding a slow and dangerous fever, caused by the excessive use of brandy, and by constant debauchery, that was silently undermining his constitution, Jacques Rennepont had been induced by Morok to join the masquerade. The brute-tamer himself, dressed as the King of Diamonds, represented PLAY. His forehead was adorned with a diadem of gilded paper, his face was pale and impassible, and, as his long, yellow beard fell down the front of his party-coloured robe, Morok looked exactly the character he personated. From time to time, with an air of grave mockery, he shook close to the eyes of Goodman Cholera a large bag full of sounding counters, and on this bag were painted all sorts of playing-cards. A certain stiffness in the right arm showed that the lion-tamer had not yet quite recovered from the effects of the wound which the panther had inflicted before being stabbed by Djalma.

PLEASURE, who also represented Laughter, classically shook her rattle, with its sonorous gilded bells, close to the ears of Goodman Cholera. She was a quick, lively young girl, and her fine black hair was crowned with a scarlet cap of liberty. For Sleepinbuff's sake, she had taken the place of the poor Bacchanal Queen, who would not have failed to attend on such an occasion—she, who had been so valiant and gay, when she bore her part in a less philosophical, but not less amusing masquerade. Another pretty creature, Modeste Bornichoux, who served as a model to a painter of renown (one of the cavaliers of the procession), was eminently successful in her representation of LOVE. He could not have had a more charming face, and more graceful form. Clad in a light blue spangled tunic, with a blue and silver band across her chestnut hair, and little transparent wings affixed to her white shoulders, she placed one forefinger upon the other, and pointed with the prettiest impertinence at Goodman Cholera. Around the principal group, other maskers, more or less grotesque in appearance, waved each a banner, on which were inscriptions of a very anacreontic character, consider‹ ing the circumstances :

'Down with the Cholera !' 'Short and sweet !' 'Laugh away, laugh always !' 'We'll collar the Cholera !' 'Love for ever !' 'Wine for ever !' 'Come if you dare, old terror !'

There was really such audacious gaiety in this masquerade, that the greater number of the spectators, at the moment when it crossed the square, in the direction of the eating-house, where dinner was waiting, applauded it loudly and repeatedly. This sort of admiration, which courage, however mad and blind, almost always inspires, appeared to others (a small number, it must be confessed) a kind of defiance to the wrath of heaven ; and these received the procession with angry murmurs. This extraordinary spectacle, and the different impressions it produced, were too remote from all custo- mary facts to admit of a just appreciation. We hardly know if this daring bravado was deserving of praise or blame.

Besides, the appearance of those plagues, which from age to age decimate the population of whole countries, has almost always been accompanied by a sort of mental excitement, which none of those who have been spared by the contagion can hope to escape. It is a strange fever of the mind, which sometimes rouses the most stupid prejudices and the most ferocious pas- sions, and sometimes inspires, on the contrary, the most magnificent devo- tion, the most courageous actions—with some, driving the fear of death to a point of the wildest terror—with others, exciting the contempt of life to express itself in the most audacious bravadoes. Caring little for the praise or blame it might deserve, the masquerade arrived before the eating-house, and made its entry in the midst of universal acclamations. Everything seemed to combine to give full effect to this strange scene, by the opposi- tion of the most singular contrasts. Thus the tavern, in which was to be held this extraordinary feast, being situated at no great distance from the antique cathedral, and the gloomy hospital, the religious anthems of the ancient temple, the cries of the dying, and the bacchanalian songs of the banqueteers, must needs mingle, and by turns drown one another. The maskers now got down from their chariot, and from their horses, and went to take their places at the repast, which was waiting for them. The actors in the masquerade are at table in the great room of the tavern. They are joyous, noisy, even riotous. Yet their gaiety has a strange tone, peculiar to itself.

Sometimes, the most resolute involuntarily remember that their life is at stake in this mad and audacious game with destiny. That fatal thought is rapid as the icy fever-shudder, which chills you in an instant ; therefore, from time to time, an abrupt silence, lasting indeed only for a second, be- trays these passing emotions, which are almost immediately effaced by new bursts of joyful acclamation, for each one says to himself : 'No weakness ! my chum and my girl are looking at me !'

And all laugh, and knock glasses together, and challenge the next man, and drink out of the glass of the nearest woman. Jacques had taken off the mask and peruke of Goodman Cholera. His thin, leaden features, his deadly paleness, the lurid brilliancy of his hollow eyes, showed the inces- sant progress of the slow malady which was consuming this unfortunate man, brought by excesses to the last extremity of weakness. Though he felt the slow fire devouring his entrails, he concealed his pain beneath a forced and nervous smile.

To the left of Jacques was Morok, whose fatal influence was ever on the increase, and to his right the girl disguised as PLEASURE. She was named Mariette. By her side sat Ninny Moulin, in all his majestic bulk, who often pretended to be looking for his napkin under the table, in order to have the opportunity of pressing the knees of his other neighbour, Modeste, the representative of LOVE. Most of the guests were grouped according to their several tastes, each tender pair together, and the bachelors where they could. They had reached the second course, and the excellence of the wine, the good cheer, the gay speeches, and even the singularity of the occasion, had raised their spirits to a high degree of excitement, as may be gathered from the extraordinary incidents of the following scene.

CHAPTER XX.

THE DEFIANCE.

Two or three times, without being remarked by the guests, one of the waiters had come to whisper to his fellows, and point with expressive gesture to the ceiling. But his comrades had taken small account of his observations or fears, not wishing, doubtless, to disturb the guests, whose mad gaiety seemed ever on the increase.

'Who can doubt now of the superiority of our manner of treating this impertinent Cholera? Has he dared even to touch our sacred battalion?' said a magnificent mountebank-Turk, one of the standard-bearers of the masquerade.

'Here is all the mystery,' answered another. 'It is very simple. Only laugh in the face of the plague, and it will run away from you.'

'And right enough too, for very stupid work it does,' added a pretty little Columbine, emptying her glass.

'You are right, my darling; it is intolerably stupid work,' answered the Clown belonging to the Columbine; 'here you are, very quiet, enjoying life, and all on a sudden you die with an atrocious grimace. Well! what then? Clever, isn't it? I ask you, what does it prove?'

'It proves,' replied an illustrious painter of the romantic school, disguised like a Roman out of one of David's pictures, 'it proves that the Cholera is a wretched colourist, for he has nothing but a dirty green on his pallet. Evidently he is a pupil of Jacobus, that king of classical painters, who are another species of plagues.'

'And yet, master,' added respectfully a pupil of the great painter, 'I have seen some cholera patients whose convulsions were rather fine, and their dying looks first-rate!'

'Gentlemen,' cried a sculptor of no less celebrity, 'the question lies in a nutshell. The Cholera is a detestable colourist, but a good draughtsman. He shows you the skeleton in no time. By heaven! how he strips off the flesh!—Michael Angelo would be nothing to him.'

'True,' cried they all, with one voice; 'the Cholera is a bad colourist, but a good draughtsman.'

'Moreover, gentlemen,' added Ninny Moulin, with comic gravity, 'this plague brings with it a providential lesson, as the great Bossuet would have said.'——'The lesson! the lesson!'

'Yes, gentlemen; I seem to hear a voice from above, proclaiming: "Drink of the best, empty your purse, and kiss your neighbour's wife; for your hours are perhaps numbered, unhappy wretch!"'

So saying, the orthodox Silenus took advantage of a momentary absence of mind on the part of Modeste, his neighbour, to imprint on the blooming cheek of LOVE a long, loud kiss. The example was contagious, and a storm of kisses was mingled with bursts of laughter.

'Ha! blood and thunder!' cried the great painter, as he gaily threatened

Ninny Moulin ; 'you are very lucky that to-morrow will perhaps be the end of the world, or else I should pick a quarrel with you for having kissed my lovely LOVE.'

'Which proves to you, O Rubens ! O Raphael ! the thousand advantages of the Cholera, whom I declare to be essentially sociable and caressing.'

'And philanthropic,' said one of the guests ; 'thanks to him, creditors take care of the health of their debtors. This morning a usurer, who feels a particular interest in my existence, brought me all sorts of anti-choleraic drugs, and begged me to make use of them.'

'And I !' said the pupil of the great painter. 'My tailor wished to force me to wear a flannel band next to the skin, because I owe him a thousand crowns. But I answered, " Oh, tailor, give me a receipt in full, and I will wrap myself up in flannel, to preserve you my custom !"'

'O Cholera, I drink to thee !' said Ninny Moulin, by way of grotesque invocation. 'You are not Despair ; on the contrary, you are the emblem of Hope—yes, of Hope. How many husbands, how many wives, longed for a number (alas ! too uncertain chance) in the lottery of widowhood ! You appear, and their hearts are gladdened. Thanks to you, benevolent pest ! their chances of liberty are increased a hundredfold.'

'And how grateful heirs ought to be ! A cold—a heat—a trifle—and there, in an hour, some old uncle becomes a revered benefactor !'

'And those who are always looking out for other people's places—what an ally they must find in the Cholera !'

'And how true it will make many vows of constancy !' said Modeste, sentimentally. 'How many villains have sworn to a poor, weak woman, to love her all their lives, who never meant (the wretches !) to keep their word so well !'

'Gentlemen,' cried Ninny Moulin, 'since we are now, perhaps, at the eve of the end of the world, as yonder celebrated painter has expressed it, I propose to play the world topsy-turvy : I beg these ladies to make advances to us, to tease us, to excite us, to steal kisses from us, to take all sorts of liberties with us, and (we shall not die of it) even to insult us. Yes, I declare that I will allow myself to be insulted. So, LOVE, you may offer me the greatest insult that can be offered to a virtuous and modest bachelor,' added the religious writer, leaning over towards his neighbour, who repulsed him with peals of laughter ; and the proposal of Ninny Moulin being received with general hilarity, a new impulse was given to the mirth and riot.

In the midst of the uproar, the waiter, who had before entered the room several times, to whisper uneasily to his comrades, whilst he pointed to the ceiling, again appeared with a pale and agitated countenance ; approaching the man who performed the office of butler, he said to him, in a low voice, tremulous with emotion : ' They are come !'

' Who ?'——' You know—up there ;' and he pointed to the ceiling.

' Oh !' said the butler, becoming thoughtful ; ' where are they ?'

'They have just gone upstairs ; they are there now,' answered the waiter, shaking his head with an air of alarm ; ' yes, they are there !'

'What does master say ?'——' He is very vexed, because——' and the waiter glanced round at the guests. ' He does not know what to do ; he has sent me to you.'

' What the devil have I to do with it ?' said the other, wiping his forehead. ' It was to be expected, and cannot be helped.'

' I will not remain here till they begin.'

'You may as well go, for your long face already attracts attention. Tell master we must wait for the upshot.'

The above incident was scarcely perceived in the midst of the growing tumult of the joyous feast. But, among the guests, one alone laughed not, drank not. This was Jacques. With fixed and lurid eye, he gazed upon vacancy. A stranger to what was passing around him, the unhappy man thought of the Bacchanal Queen, who had been so gay and brilliant in the midst of similar saturnalia. The remembrance of that one being, whom he still loved with an extravagant love, was the only thought that from time to time roused him from his besotted state.

It is strange, but Jacques had only consented to join this masquerade because the mad scene reminded him of the merry day he had spent with Cephyse—that famous breakfast, after a night of dancing, in which the Bacchanal Queen, from some extraordinary presentiment, had proposed a lugubrious toast with regard to this very pestilence, which was then reported to be approaching France. ' To the Cholera !' had she said. ' Let him spare those who wish to live, and kill at the same moment those who dread to part !'

And now, at this time, remembering those mournful words, Jacques was absorbed in painful thought. Morok perceived his absence of mind, and said aloud to him, ' You have given over drinking, Jacques. Have you had enough wine ? Then you will want brandy. I will send for some.'

' I want neither wine nor brandy,' answered Jacques, abruptly, and he fell back into a sombre reverie.

' Well, you may be right,' resumed Morok, in a sardonic tone, and raising his voice still higher. ' You do well to take care of yourself. I was wrong to name brandy in these times. There would be as much temerity in facing a bottle of brandy as the barrel of a loaded pistol.'

On hearing his courage as a toper called in question, Sleepinbuff looked angrily at Morok. ' You think it is from cowardice that I will not drink brandy !' cried the unfortunate man, whose half-extinguished intellect was roused to defend what he called his dignity. ' Is it from cowardice that I refuse, d'ye think, Morok ? Answer me !'

' Come, my good fellow, we have all shown our pluck to-day,' said one of the guests to Jacques ; ' you, above all, who, being rather indisposed, yet had the courage to take the part of Goodman Cholera.'

' Gentlemen,' resumed Morok, seeing the general attention fixed upon himself and Sleepinbuff, ' I was only joking ; for if my comrade' (pointing to Jacques) ' had the imprudence to accept my offer, it would be an act, not of courage, but of foolhardiness. Luckily, he has sense enough to renounce a piece of boasting so dangerous at this time, and I——'

' Waiter !' cried Jacques, interrupting Morok with angry impatience, ' two bottles of brandy, and two glasses !'

' What are you going to do ?' said Morok, with pretended uneasiness. ' Why do you order two bottles of brandy ?'

' For a duel,' said Jacques, in a cool, resolute tone.

' A duel !' cried the spectators, in surprise.——' Yes,' resumed Jacques, ' a duel with brandy. You pretend there is as much danger in facing a bottle of brandy as a loaded pistol ; let us each take a full bottle, and see who will be the first to cry quarter.'

This strange proposition was received by some with shouts of joy, and by others with genuine uneasiness.

' Bravo ! the champions of the bottle !' cried the first.——' No, no ; there would be too much danger in such a contest,' said the others.

' Just now,' added one of the guests, ' this challenge is as serious as an invitation to fight to the death.'——' You hear,' said Morok, with a diabolical smile, ' you hear, Jacques ? Will you now retreat before the danger ?'

At these words, which reminded him of the peril to which he was about to expose himself, Jacques started, as if a sudden idea had occurred to him. He raised his head proudly, his cheeks were slightly flushed, his eye shone with a kind of gloomy satisfaction, and he exclaimed in a firm voice : ' Hang it, waiter ! are you deaf ? I asked you for two bottles of brandy.'

' Yes, sir,' said the waiter, going to fetch them, although himself frightened at what might be the result of this bacchanalian struggle. But the mad and perilous resolution of Jacques was applauded by the majority.

Ninny Moulin moved about on his chair, stamped his feet, and shouted with all his might : ' Bacchus and drink ! bottles and glasses ! the throats are dry ! brandy to the rescue ! Largess ! largess !'

And, like a true champion of the tournament, he embraced Modeste, adding, to excuse the liberty : ' Love, you shall be the Queen of Beauty, and I am only anticipating the victor's happiness !'

' Brandy to the rescue !' repeated they all, in chorus. ' Largess !'

' Gentlemen,' added Ninny Moulin, with enthusiasm, shall we remain indifferent to the noble example set us by Goodman Cholera ? He said in his pride, " brandy !" Let us gloriously answer, " punch !" '

' Yes, yes ! punch !——' Punch to the rescue !'

' Waiter !' shouted the religious writer, with the voice of a Stentor, ' waiter ! have you a pan, a cauldron, a hogshead, or any other immensity, in which we can brew a monster punch ?'

' A Babylonian punch !'——' A lake of punch !'——' An ocean of punch !'

Such was the ambitious crescendo that followed the proposition of Ninny Moulin.

' Sir,' answered the waiter, with an air of triumph, ' we just happen to have a large copper cauldron, quite new. It has never been used, and would hold at least thirty bottles.'

' Bring the cauldron !' said Ninny Moulin, majestically.

' The cauldron for ever !' shouted the chorus.

' Put in twenty bottles of brandy, six loaves of sugar, a dozen lemons, a pound of cinnamon, and then—fire ! fire !' shouted the religious writer, with the most vociferous exclamations.——' Yes, yes ! fire !' repeated the chorus.

The proposition of Ninny Moulin gave a new impetus to the general gaiety ; the most extravagant remarks were mingled with the sound of kisses, taken or given under the pretext that perhaps there would be no to-morrow, that one must make the most of the present, etc., etc. Suddenly, in one of the moments of silence which sometimes occur in the midst of the greatest tumult, a succession of slow and measured taps sounded above the ceiling of the banqueting-room. All remained silent, and listened.

CHAPTER XXI.

BRANDY TO THE RESCUE.

AFTER the lapse of some seconds, the singular rapping which had so much surprised the guests, was again heard, but this time louder and longer.

' Waiter !' cried one of the party, ' what in the devil's name is that knocking ?'

The waiter, exchanging with his comrades a look of uneasiness and alarm, stammered out in reply : ' Sir ——it is——it is——'

' Well ! I suppose it is some crabbed, cross-grained lodger, some animal, the enemy of joy, who is pounding on the floor of his room to warn us to sing less loud,' said Ninny Moulin.

' Then, by a general rule,' answered sententiously the pupil of the great painter, ' if lodger or landlord ask for silence, tradition bids us reply by an infernal uproar, destined to drown all his remonstrances. Such, at least,' added the scapegrace, modestly, 'are the foreign relations that I have always seen observed between neighbouring powers.'

This remark was received with general laughter and applause. During the tumult, Morok questioned one of the waiters, and then exclaimed in a shrill tone, which rose above the clamour : 'I demand a hearing !'

'Granted !' cried the others, gaily. During the silence which followed the exclamation of Morok, the noise was again heard ; it was this time quicker than before.

'The lodger is innocent,' said Morok, with a strange smile, 'and would be quite incapable of interfering with your enjoyment.'

'Then why does he keep up that knocking ?' said Ninny Moulin, empty-ing his glass.——'Like a deaf man who has lost his ear-horn ?' added the young artist.

'It is not the lodger who is knocking,' said Morok, in a sharp, quick tone ; 'for they are nailing him down in his coffin.' A sudden and mourn-ful silence followed these words.

'His coffin—no, I am wrong,' resumed Morok ; 'her coffin, I should say, or more properly their coffin ; for, in these pressing times, they put mother and child together.'

'A woman !' cried PLEASURE, addressing the waiter ; 'is it a woman that is dead ?'——'Yes, ma'am ; a poor young woman about twenty years of age,' answered the waiter in a sorrowful tone. 'Her little girl, that she was nursing, died soon after—all in less than two hours. My master is very sorry that you ladies and gents should be disturbed in this way ; but he could not foresee this misfortune, as yesterday morning the young woman was quite well, and singing with all her might—no one could have been gayer than she was.'

Upon these words, it was as if a funeral pall had been suddenly thrown over a scene lately so full of joy ; all the rubicund and jovial faces took an expression of sadness ; no one had the hardihood to make a jest of mother and child, nailed down together in the same coffin. The silence became so profound, that one could hear each breath oppressed by terror : the last blows of the hammer seemed to strike painfully on every heart ; it appeared as if each sad feeling, until now repressed, was about to replace that ani-mation and gaiety, which had been more factitious than sincere. The moment was decisive. It was necessary to strike an immediate blow, and to raise the spirits of the guests, for many pretty rosy faces began to grow pale, many scarlet ears became suddenly white ; Ninny Moulin's were of the number.

On the contrary, Sleepinbuff exhibited an increase of audacity ; he drew up his figure, bent down from the effects of exhaustion, and, with a cheek slightly flushed, he exclaimed : 'Well, waiter ? are those bottles of brandy coming ? and the punch ? Devil and all ! are the dead to frighten the living ?'

'He's right ! Down with sorrow, and let's have the punch !' cried several of the guests, who felt the necessity of reviving their courage.

'Forward, punch !'

'Begone, dull care !'——'Jollity for ever !'

'Gentlemen, here is the punch,' said a waiter, opening the door. At sight of the flaming beverage, which was to reanimate their enfeebled spirits, the room rang with the loudest applause.

The sun had just set. The room was large, being capable of dining a hundred guests ; and the windows were few, narrow, and half veiled by red cotton curtains. Though it was not yet night, some portions of this vast saloon were almost entirely dark. Two waiters brought the monster-punch, in an immense brass kettle, brilliant as gold, suspended from an iron bar, and crowned with flames of changing colour. The burning beverage was then placed upon the table, to the great joy of the guests, who began to forget their past alarms.

'Now,' said Jacques to Morok, in a taunting tone, 'while the punch is burning, we will have our duel. The company shall judge.' Then, pointing to the two bottles of brandy, which the waiter had brought, Jacques added : 'Choose your weapon !'——'Do you choose,' answered Morok.

'Well ! here's your bottle—and here's your glass. Ninny Moulin shall be umpire.'

'I do not refuse to be judge of the field,' answered the religious writer ; 'only I must warn you, comrade, that you are playing a desperate game, and that just now, as one of these gentlemen has said, the neck of a bottle of brandy in one's mouth, is perhaps more dangerous than the barrel of a loaded pistol.'

'Give the word, old fellow !' said Jacques, interrupting Ninny Moulin, 'or I will give it myself.'——'Since you will have it so—so be it !'

'The first who gives in is conquered,' said Jacques.

'Agreed !' answered Morok.

'Come, gentlemen, attention ! we must follow every movement,' resumed Ninny Moulin. ' Let us first see if the bottles are of the same size—equality of weapons being the foremost condition.'

During these preparations, profound silence reigned in the room. The courage of the majority of those present, animated for a moment by the arrival of the punch, was soon again depressed by gloomy thoughts, as they vaguely foresaw the danger of the contest between Morok and Jacques. This impression, joined to the sad thoughts occasioned by the incident of the coffin, darkened by degrees many a countenance. Some of the guests, indeed, continued to make a show of rejoicing, but their gaiety appeared forced. Under certain circumstances, the smallest things will have the most powerful effect. We have said that, after sunset, a portion of this large room was plunged in obscurity ; therefore, the guests who sat in the remote corners of the apartment, had no other light than the reflection of the flaming punch. Now it is well known, that the flame of burning spirit throws a livid, blueish tint over the countenance ; it was therefore a strange, almost frightful spectacle, to see a number of the guests, who happened to be at a distance from the windows, in this ghastly and fantastic light.

The painter, more struck than all the rest by this effect of colour, exclaimed : 'Look ! at this end of the table, we might fancy ourselves feasting with cholera-patients, we are such fine blues and greens.'

This jest was not much relished. Fortunately, the loud voice of Ninny Moulin demanded attention, and for a moment turned the thoughts of the company.

'The lists are open,' cried the religious writer, really more frightened than he chose to appear. 'Are you ready, brave champions ?' he added.

'We are ready,' said Morok and Jacques.

'Present ! fire !' cried Ninny Moulin, clapping his hands. And the two drinkers each emptied a tumbler full of brandy at a draught.

Morok did not even knit his brow ; his marble face remained impassible ; with a steady hand he replaced his glass upon the table. But Jacques, as he put down his glass, could not conceal a slight convulsive trembling, caused by internal suffering.

'Bravely done !' cried Ninny Moulin. 'The quarter of a bottle of brandy at a draught—it is glorious ! No one else here would be capable of such prowess. And now, worthy champions, if you believe me, you will stop where you are.'

'Give the word !' answered Jacques, intrepidly. And, with feverish and shaking hand, he seized the bottle ; then suddenly, instead of filling his glass, he said to Morok : ' Bah ! we want no glasses. It is braver to drink from the bottle. I dare you to it !'

Morok's only answer was to shrug his shoulders, and raise the neck of the bottle to his lips. Jacques hastened to imitate him. The thin, yellowish, transparent glass gave a perfect view of the progressive diminution of the liquor. The stony countenance of Morok, and the pale, thin face of Jacques, on which already stood large drops of cold sweat, were now, as well as the features of the other guests, illumined by the blueish light of the punch ; every eye was fixed upon Morok and Jacques, with that barbarous curiosity which cruel spectacles seem involuntarily to inspire.

Jacques continued to drink, holding the bottle in his left hand ; suddenly, he closed and tightened the fingers of his right hand with a convulsive movement ; his hair clung to his icy forehead, and his countenance revealed an agony of pain. Yet he continued to drink ; only, without removing his lips from the neck of the bottle, he lowered it for an instant, as if to recover breath. Just then, Jacques met the sardonic look of Morok, who continued to drink with his accustomed impassibility. Thinking that he saw the expression of insulting triumph in Morok's glance, Jacques raised his elbow abruptly, and drank with avidity a few drops more. But his strength was exhausted. A quenchless fire devoured his vitals. His sufferings were too intense, and he could no longer bear up against them. His head fell backwards, his jaws closed convulsively, he crushed the neck of the bottle between his teeth, his neck grew rigid, his limbs writhed with spasmodic action, and he became almost senseless.

' Jacques, my good fellow ! it is nothing,' cried Morok, whose ferocious glance now sparkled with diabolical joy. Then, replacing his bottle on the table, he rose to go to the aid of Ninny Moulin, who was vainly endeavouring to hold Sleepinbuff.

This sudden attack had none of the symptoms of cholera. Yet terror seized upon all present ; one of the women was taken with hysterics, and another uttered piercing cries and fainted away. Ninny Moulin, leaving Jacques in the hands of Morok, ran towards the door to seek for help,—when that door was suddenly opened, and the religious writer drew back in alarm, at the sight of the unexpected personage who appeared on the threshold.

CHAPTER XXII

MEMORIES.

THE person before whom Ninny Moulin stopped in such extreme astonishment was the Bacchanal Queen.

Pale and wan, with hair in disorder, hollow cheeks, sunken eyes, and clothed almost in rags, this brilliant and joyous heroine of so many mad orgies was now only the shadow of her former self. Misery and grief were impressed on that countenance, once so charming. Hardly had she entered the room, when Cephyse paused ; her mournful and unquiet gaze strove to penetrate the half-obscurity of the apartment, in search of him she longed to see. Suddenly the girl started, and uttered a loud scream. She had just perceived, at the other side of a long table, by the blueish light of the punch, Jacques struggling with Morok and one of the guests, who were hardly able to restrain his convulsive movements.

At this sight Cephyse, in her first alarm, carried away by her affection, did what she had so often done in the intoxication of joy and pleasure. Light and agile, instead of losing precious time in making a long circuit, she sprang at once upon the table, passed nimbly through the array of plates and bottles, and with one spring was by the side of the sufferer.

'Jacques!' she exclaimed, without yet remarking the lion-tamer, and throwing herself on the neck of her lover. 'Jacques! it is I—Cephyse!'

That well-known voice, that heart-piercing cry, which came from the bottom of the soul, seemed not unheard by Sleepinbuff. He turned his head mechanically towards the Bacchanal Queen, without opening his eyes, and heaved a deep sigh; his stiffened limbs relaxed, a slight trembling succeeded to the convulsions, and in a few seconds his heavy eyelids were raised with an effort, so as to uncover his dull and wandering gaze. Mute with astonishment, the spectators of this scene felt an uneasy curiosity. Cephyse, kneeling beside her lover, bathed his hands in her tears, covered them with kisses, and exclaimed, in a voice broken by sobs, 'It is I—Cephyse—I have found you again—it was not my fault that I abandoned you! Forgive me, forgive——'

'Wretched woman!' cried Morok, irritated at this meeting, which might, perhaps, be fatal to his projects; 'do you wish to kill him? In his present state, this agitation is death. Begone!' So saying, he seized Cephyse suddenly by the arm, just as Jacques, waking, as it were, from a painful dream, began to distinguish what was passing around him.

'You! it is you!' cried the Bacchanal Queen, in amazement, as she recognised Morok, 'who separated me from Jacques!'

She paused; for the dim eye of the victim, as it rested upon her, grew suddenly bright.

'Cephyse!' murmured Jacques; 'is it you?'——'Yes, it is I,' answered she, in a voice of deep emotion; 'who have come—I will tell you——'

She was unable to continue, and, as she clasped her hands together, her pale, agitated, tearful countenance expressed her astonishment and despair at the mortal change which had taken place in the features of Jacques. He understood the cause of her surprise, and as he contemplated, in his turn, the suffering and emaciated countenance of Cephyse, he said to her, 'Poor girl! you also have had to bear much grief, much misery—I should hardly have known you.'

'Yes,' replied Cephyse, 'much grief—much misery—and worse than misery,' she added, trembling, whilst a deep blush overspread her pale features.——'Worse than misery?' said Jacques, astonished.

'But it is you who have suffered,' hastily resumed Cephyse, without answering her lover.

'Just now, I was going to make an end of it—your voice has recalled me for an instant—but I feel something here,' and he laid his hand upon his breast, 'which never gives quarter. It is all the same now—I have seen you—I shall die happy.'

'You shall not die, Jacques; I am here——'

'Listen to me, my girl. If I had a bushel of live coal in my stomach, it could hardly burn me more. For more than a month, I have been consuming my body by a slow fire. This gentleman,' he added, glancing at Morok, 'this dear friend, always undertook to feed the flame. I do not regret life; I have lost the habit of work, and taken to drink and riot; I should have finished by becoming a thorough blackguard; I preferred that my friend here should amuse himself with lighting a furnace in my inside. Since what I drank just now, I am certain that it flames like yonder punch.'

'You are both foolish and ungrateful,' said Morok, shrugging his shoulders ; 'you held out your glass, and I filled it—and, faith, we shall drink long and often together yet.'

For some moments, Cephyse had not withdrawn her eyes from Morok. ' I tell you, that you have long blown the fire, in which I have burnt my skin,' resumed Jacques, addressing Morok in a feeble voice, 'so that they may not think I die of cholera. It would look as if I had been frightened by the part I played. I do not therefore reproach you, my affectionate friend,' added he, with a sardonic smile ; 'you dug my grave gaily—and sometimes, when, seeing the great dark hole, into which I was about to fall, I drew back a step—but you, my excellent friend, still pushed me forward, saying, "Go on, my boy, go on !"—and I went on—and here I am——'

So saying, Sleepinbuff burst into a bitter laugh, which sent an icy shudder through the spectators of this scene.

' My good fellow,' said Morok, coolly, 'listen to me, and follow my advice——'

'Thank you ! I know your advice—and, instead of listening to you, I prefer speaking to my poor Cephyse. Before I go down to the moles, I should like to tell her what weighs on my heart.'

' Jacques,' replied Cephyse, 'do not talk so. I tell you, you shall not die.'

' Why then, my brave Cephyse, I shall owe my life to you,' returned Jacques, in a tone of serious feeling, which surprised the spectators. 'Yes,' resumed he, ' when I came to myself, and saw you so poorly clad, I felt something good about my heart—do you know why ?—it was because I said to myself, "Poor girl ! she has kept her word bravely ; she has chosen to toil, and want, and suffer—rather than take another love—who would have given her what I gave her as long as I could "—and that thought, Cephyse, refreshed my soul. I needed it, for I was burning—and I burn still,' added he, clenching his fists with pain ; 'but that made me happy—it did me good—thanks, my good, brave Cephyse—yes, you are good and brave—and you were right ; for I never loved any but you in the wide world ; and if, in my degradation, I had one thought that raised me a little above the filth, and made me regret that I was not better—the thought was of you ! Thanks then, my poor, dear love,' said Jacques, whose hot and shining eyes were becoming moist ; 'thanks once again,' and he reached his cold hand to Cephyse ; 'if I die, I shall die happy—if I live, I shall live happy also. Give me your hand, my brave Cephyse !—you have acted like a good and honest creature.'

Instead of taking the hand which Jacques offered her, Cephyse, still kneeling, bowed her head, and dared not raise her eyes to her lover.

' You don't answer,' said he, leaning over towards the young girl ; ' you don't take my hand—why is this ?'

The unfortunate creature only answered by stifled sobs. Borne down with shame, she held herself in so humble, so supplicating an attitude, that her forehead almost touched the feet of her lover.

Amazed at the silence and conduct of the Bacchanal Queen, Jacques looked at her with increasing agitation ; suddenly he stammered out with trembling lips, 'Cephyse, I know you. If you do not take my hand, it is because——' Then, his voice failing, he added, in a dull tone, after a moment's silence, ' When, six weeks ago, I was taken to prison, did you not say to me, "Jacques, I swear that I will work—and if need be, live in horrible misery—but I will live true !" That was your promise. Now, I know you never speak false ; tell me you have kept your word, and I shall believe you.'

Cephyse only answered by a heartrending sob, as she pressed the knees of Jacques against her heaving bosom. By a strange contradiction, more common than is generally thought—this man, degraded by intoxication and debauchery, who, since he came out of prison, had plunged in every excess, and tamely yielded to all the fatal incitements of Morok, yet received a fearful blow, when he learned, by the mute avowal of Cephyse, the infidelity of this creature, whom he had loved in spite of degradation. The first impulse of Jacques was terrible. Notwithstanding his weakness and exhaustion, he succeeded in rising from his seat, and, with a countenance contracted by rage and despair, he seized a knife, before they had time to prevent him, and turned it upon Cephyse. But at the moment he was about to strike, shrinking from an act of murder, he hurled the knife far away from him, and falling back into the chair, covered his face with his hands.

At the cry of Ninny Moulin, who had, though late, thrown himself upon Jacques to take away the knife, Cephyse raised her head ; Jacques's woeful dejection wrung her heart ; she rose, and fell upon his neck, notwithstanding his resistance, exclaiming in a voice broken by sobs, 'Jacques, if you knew ! if you only knew—listen—do not condemn me without hearing me —I will tell you all, I swear to you—without falsehood—this man,' and she pointed to Morok, 'will not dare deny what I say ; he came, and told me to have the courage to——'

'I do not reproach you. I have no right to reproach you. Let me die in peace. I ask nothing but that now,' said Jacques, in a still weaker voice, as he repulsed Cephyse. Then he added, with a grievous and bitter smile, 'Luckily, I have my dose. I knew—what I was doing—when I accepted the duel with brandy.'

'No, you shall not die, and you shall hear me,' cried Cephyse, with a bewildered air ; 'you shall hear me, and everybody else shall hear me. They shall see that it is not my fault. Is it not so, gentlemen ? Do I not deserve pity ? You will entreat Jacques to forgive me ; for if driven by misery—finding no work—I was forced to this—not for the sake of any luxury—you see the rags I wear—but to get bread and shelter for my poor, sick sister—dying, and even more miserable than myself—would you not have pity upon me ? Do you think one finds pleasure in one's infamy ?' cried the unfortunate, with a burst of frightful laughter ; then she added, in a low voice, and with a shudder, 'Oh, if you knew, Jacques ! it is so infamous, so horrible, that I preferred death to fall so low a second time. I should have killed myself, had I not heard you were here.' Then, seeing that Jacques did not answer her, but shook his head mournfully as he sank down, though still supported by Ninny Moulin, Cephyse exclaimed, as she lifted her clasped hands towards him, 'Jacques ! one word—for pity's sake—forgive me !'

'Gentlemen, pray remove this woman,' cried Morok ; 'the sight of her causes my friend too painful emotions.'

'Come, my dear child, be reasonable,' said several of the guests, who, deeply moved by this scene, were endeavouring to withdraw Cephyse from it : 'leave him, and come with us ; he is not in any danger.'

'Gentlemen ! oh, gentlemen !' cried the unfortunate creature, bursting into tears, and raising her hands in supplication ; 'listen to me—I will do all that you wish me—I will go—but, in heaven's name, send for help, and do not let him die thus. Look, what pain he suffers ! what horrible convulsions !'

'She is right,' said one of the guests, hastening towards the door ; 'we must send for a doctor.'

'There is no doctor to be found,' said another ; 'they are all too busy.'

'We will do better than that,' cried a third ; 'the hospital is just opposite, and we can carry the poor fellow thither. They will give him instant help. A leaf of the table will make a litter, and the table-cloth a covering.'

'Yes, yes, that is it,' said several voices ; 'let us carry him over at once.'

Jacques, burnt up with brandy, and overcome by his interview with Cephyse, had again fallen into violent convulsions. It was the dying paroxysm of the unfortunate man. They were obliged to tie him with the ends of the cloth, so as to secure him to the leaf which was to serve for a litter, which two of the guests hastened to carry away. They yielded to the supplications of Cephyse, who asked, as a last favour, to accompany Jacques to the Hospital. When the mournful procession quitted the great room of the eating-house, there was a general flight among the guests. Men and women made haste to wrap themselves in their cloaks, in order to conceal their costume. The coaches, which had been ordered in tolerable number for the return of the masquerade, had luckily arrived. The defiance had been fully carried out, the audacious *bravado* accomplished, and they could now retire with the honours of war. Whilst a part of the guests were still in the room, an uproar, at first distant, but which soon drew nearer, broke out with incredible fury in the square of Nôtre-Dame.

Jacques had been carried to the outer door of the tavern. Morok and Ninny Moulin, striving to open a passage through the crowd in the direction of the Hospital, preceded the litter. A violent reflux of the multitude soon forced them to stop, whilst a new storm of savage outcries burst from the other extremity of the square, near the angle of the church.

'What is it then ?' asked Ninny Moulin of one of those ignoble figures that was leaping up before him. 'What are those cries ?'

'They are making mince-meat of a poisoner, like him they have thrown into the river,' replied the man. 'If you want to see the fun, follow me close,' added he, 'and peg away with your elbows, for fear you should be too late.' Hardly had the wretch pronounced these words than a dreadful shriek sounded above the roar of the crowd, through which the bearers of the litter, preceded by Morok, were with difficulty making their way. It was Cephyse who uttered that cry. Jacques (one of the seven heirs of the Rennepont family) had just expired in her arms ! By a strange fatality, at the very moment that the despairing exclamation of Cephyse announced that death, another cry rose from that part of the square where they were attacking the poisoner. That distant, supplicating cry, tremulous with horrible alarm, like the last appeal of a man staggering beneath the blows of his murderers, chilled the soul of Morok in the midst of his execrable triumph.

'Damnation !' cried the skilful assassin, who had selected drunkenness and debauchery for his murderous but legal weapons ; 'it is the voice of the Abbé d'Aigrigny, whom they have in their clutches !'

CHAPTER XXIII.

THE POISONER.

It is necessary to go back a little before relating the adventure of Father d'Aigrigny, whose cry of distress made so deep an impression upon Morok just at the moment of Jacques Rennepont's death. We have said that the most absurd and alarming reports were circulating in Paris ; not only did people talk of poison given to the sick, or thrown into the public fountains, but it was also said that wretches had been surprised in the act of putting arsenic into the pots which are usually kept all ready on the counters of wine-shops. Goliath was on his way to rejoin Morok, after delivering a message to Father d'Aigrigny, who was waiting in a house on the Place de l'Archévêché. He entered a wine-shop in the Rue de la Calandre, to get some refreshment, and having drunk two glasses of wine, he proceeded to pay for them. Whilst the woman of the house was looking for change, Goliath, mechanically and very innocently, rested his hand on the mouth of one of the pots that happened to be within his reach.

The tall stature of this man and his repulsive and savage countenance had already alarmed the good woman, whose fears and prejudices had previously been roused by the public rumours on the subject of poisoning ; but when she saw Goliath place his hand over the mouth of one of her pots, she cried out in dismay : 'Oh ! my gracious ! what are you throwing into that pot ?' At these words, spoken in a loud voice, and with the accent of terror, two or three of the drinkers at one of the tables rose precipitately, and ran to the counter, while one of them rashly exclaimed : 'It is a poisoner !'

Goliath, not aware of the reports circulated in the neighbourhood, did not at first understand of what he was accused. The men raised their voices as they called on him to answer the charge ; but he, trusting to his strength, shrugged his shoulders in disdain, and roughly demanded the change, which the pale and frightened hostess no longer thought of giving him.

'Rascal !' cried one of the men, with so much violence that several of the passers-by stopped to listen ; 'you shall have your change when you tell us what you threw in the pot !'

'Ha ! did he throw anything into the wine-pot ?' said one of the passers-by.

'It is, perhaps, a poisoner,' said another.

'He ought to be taken up,' added a third.——'Yes, yes,' cried those in the house—honest people, perhaps, but under the influence of the general panic ; 'he must be taken up, for he has been throwing poison into the wine-pots.'

The words 'He is a poisoner' soon spread through the group, which, at first composed of three or four persons, increased every instant around the door of the wine-shop. A dull, menacing clamour began to rise from the crowd ; the first accuser, seeing his fears thus shared and almost justified, thought he was acting like a good and courageous citizen in taking Goliath by the collar, and saying to him : 'Come and explain yourself at the guard-house, villain !'

The giant, already provoked at insults of which he did not perceive the real meaning, was exasperated at this sudden attack ; yielding to his natural brutality, he knocked his adversary down upon the counter, and began to hammer him with his fists. During this collision, several bottles and two or three panes of glass were broken with much noise, whilst the woman of the house, more and more frightened, cried out with all her might : 'Help ! a poisoner ! Help ! murder !'

At the sound of the breaking windows and these cries of distress, the passers-by, of whom the greater number believed in the stories about the poisoners, rushed into the shop to aid in securing Goliath. But the latter, thanks to his herculean strength, after struggling for some moments with seven or eight persons, knocked down two of his most furious assailants, disengaged himself from the others, drew near the counter, and, taking a vigorous spring, rushed head foremost, like a bull about to butt, upon the crowd that blocked up the door ; then, forcing a passage, by the help of his enormous shoulders and athletic arms, he made his way into the street, and ran with all speed in the direction of the square of Nôtre-Dame, his garments torn, his head bare, and his countenance pale and full of rage. Immediately, a number of persons from amongst the crowd started in pursuit of Goliath, and a hundred voices exclaimed : 'Stop—stop the poisoner !'

Hearing these cries, and seeing a man draw near with a wild and troubled look, a butcher, who happened to be passing with his large, empty tray on his head, threw it against Goliath's shins, and taken by surprise, he stumbled and fell. The butcher, thinking he had performed as heroic an action as if he had encountered a mad dog, flung himself on Goliath, and rolled over with him on the pavement, exclaiming : ' Help ! it is a poisoner ! Help ! help !' This scene took place not far from the Cathedral, but at some distance from the crowd which was pressing round the hospital gate, as well as from the eating-house in which the masquerade of the cholera then was. The day was now drawing to a close. On the piercing call of the butcher, several groups, at the head of which were Ciboule and the quarryman, flew towards the scene of the struggle, while those who had pursued the pretended poisoner from the Rue de la Calandre, reached the square on their side.

At sight of this threatening crowd advancing towards him, Goliath, whilst he continued to defend himself against the butcher, who held him with the tenacity of a bull-dog, felt that he was lost unless he could rid himself of this adversary before the arrival of the rest ; with a furious blow of the fist, therefore, he broke the jaw of the butcher, who just then was above him, and, disengaging himself from his hold, he rose, and staggered a few steps forward. Suddenly he stopped. He saw that he was surrounded. Behind him rose the walls of the cathedral ; to the right and left, and in front of him, advanced a hostile multitude. The groans uttered by the butcher, who had just been lifted from the ground covered with blood, augmented the fury of the populace.

This was a terrible moment for Goliath ; still standing alone in the centre of a ring that grew smaller every second, he saw on all sides angry enemies rushing towards him, and uttering cries of death. As the wild boar turns round once or twice, before resolving to stand at bay and face the devouring pack, Goliath, struck with terror, made one or two abrupt and wavering movements. Then, as he abandoned the possibility of flight, instinct told him that he had no mercy to expect from a crowd given up to blind and savage fury—a fury the more pitiless as it was believed to be legitimate. Goliath determined, therefore, at least to sell his life dearly ; he sought for a knife in his pocket, but, not finding it, he threw out his left leg in an athletic posture, and, holding up his muscular arms, hard and stiff as bars of iron, waited with intrepidity for the shock.

The first who approached Goliath was Ciboule. The hag, heated and out of breath, instead of rushing upon him, paused, stooped down, and taking off one of the large wooden shoes that she wore, hurled it at the giant's head with so much force and with so true an aim that it struck him right in the eye, which hung half out of its socket. Goliath pressed his hands to his face, and uttered a cry of excruciating pain.

' I've made him squint !' said Ciboule, with a burst of laughter.

Goliath, maddened by the pain, instead of waiting for the attack, which the mob still hesitated to begin, so greatly were they awed by his appearance of herculean strength—the only adversary worthy to cope with him being the quarryman, who had been borne to a distance by the surging of the crowd—Goliath, in his rage, rushed headlong upon the nearest. Such a struggle was too unequal to last long ; but despair redoubled the Colossus's strength, and the combat was for a moment terrible. The unfortunate man did not fall at once. For some seconds, almost buried amid a swarm of furious assailants, one saw now his mighty arm rise and fall like a sledge-hammer, beating upon sculls and faces, and now his enormous head, livid and bloody, drawn back by some of the combatants hanging to his tangled hair. Here and there sudden openings and violent oscillations of the crowd bore witness to the incredible energy of Goliath's defence. But when the quarryman succeeded in reaching him, Goliath was overpowered and thrown down. A long, savage cheer in triumph announced this fall; for, under such circumstances, to '*go under*' is 'to die.' Instantly a thousand breathless and angry voices repeated the cry of 'Death to the poisoner!'

Then began one of those scenes of massacre and torture, worthy of cannibals, horrible to relate, and the more incredible, that they happen almost always in the presence, and often with the aid, of honest and humane people, who, blinded by false notions and stupid prejudices, allow themselves to be led into all sorts of barbarity, under the idea of performing an act of inexorable justice. As it frequently happens, the sight of the blood which flowed in torrents from Goliath's wounds inflamed to madness the rage of his assailants. A hundred fists struck at the unhappy man; he was stamped under foot; his face and chest were beaten in. Ever and anon, in the midst of furious cries of 'Death to the poisoner!' heavy blows were audible, followed by stifled groans. It was a frightful butchery. Each individual, yielding to a sanguinary frenzy, came in turn to strike his blow, or to tear off his morsel of flesh. Women—yes, women—mothers!—came to spend their rage on this mutilated form.

There was one moment of frightful terror. With his face all bruised and covered with mud, his garments in rags, his chest bare, red, gaping with wounds—Goliath, availing himself of a moment's weariness on the part of his assassins, who believed him already finished, succeeded, by one of those convulsive starts frequent in the last agony, in raising himself to his feet for a few seconds; then, blind with wounds and loss of blood, striking about his arms in the air as if to parry blows that were no longer struck, he muttered these words, which came from his mouth, accompanied by a crimson torrent: 'Mercy! I am no poisoner. Mercy!' This sort of resurrection produced so great an effect on the crowd, that for an instant they fell back affrighted. The clamour ceased, and a small space was left around the victim. Some hearts began even to feel pity; when the quarryman, seeing Goliath blinded with blood, groping before him with his hands, exclaimed in ferocious allusion to a well known game: 'Now for blind man's buff.'

Then, with a violent kick, he again threw down the victim, whose head struck twice heavily on the pavement.

Just as the giant fell, a voice from amongst the crowd exclaimed: 'It is Goliath! stop! he is innocent.'

It was Father d'Aigrigny, who, yielding to a generous impulse, was making violent efforts to reach the foremost rank of the actors in this scene, and who cried out, as he came nearer, pale, indignant, menacing: 'You are cowards and murderers! This man is innocent. I know him. You shall answer for his life.'

These vehement words were received with loud murmurs.

'You know that poisoner,' cried the quarryman, seizing the Jesuit by the collar; 'then perhaps you are a poisoner too.'

'Wretch,' exclaimed Father d'Aigrigny, endeavouring to shake himself loose from the grasp, 'do you dare to lay hand upon me?'

'Yes, I dare do anything,' answered the quarryman.

'He knows him: he's a poisoner like the other,' cried the crowd, pressing round the two adversaries; whilst Goliath, who had fractured his skull in the fall, uttered a long death-rattle.

At a sudden movement of Father d'Aigrigny, who disengaged himself from the quarryman, a large glass phial of a peculiar form, very thick, and nlled with a greenish liquor, fell from his pocket, and rolled close to the dying Goliath. At sight of this phial, many voices exclaimed together: 'It is poison! Only see! He had poison upon him.'

The clamour redoubled at this accusation, and they pressed so close to Abbé d'Aigrigny, that he exclaimed: 'Do not touch me! do not approach me!'

'If he is a poisoner,' said a voice, 'no more mercy for him than for the other.'

'I a poisoner?' said the abbé, struck with horror.

Ciboule had darted upon the phial; the quarryman seized it from her, uncorked it, and presenting it to Father d'Aigrigny, said to him: 'Now tell us! what is that?'

'It is not poison,' cried Father d'Aigrigny.——'Then drink it!' returned the quarryman.

'Yes, yes! let him drink it!' cried the mob.——'Never,' answered Father d'Aigrigny, in extreme alarm. And he drew back as he spoke, pushing away the phial with his hand.

'Do you see? It *is* poison. He dares not drink it,' they exclaimed. Hemmed in on every side, Father d'Aigrigny stumbled against the body of Goliath.

'My friends,' cried the Jesuit, who, without being a poisoner, found himself exposed to a terrible alternative, for his phial contained aromatic salts of extraordinary strength, designed for a preservative against the cholera, and as dangerous to swallow as any poison, 'my good friends you are in error. I conjure you, in the name of heaven——'

'If that is not poison, drink it?' interrupted the quarryman, as he again offered the bottle to the Jesuit.

'If he does not drink it, death to the poisoner of the poor!'

'Yes!—death to him! death to him!'

'Unhappy men!' cried Father d'Aigrigny, whilst his hair stood on end with terror; 'do you mean to murder me?'

'What about all those, that you and your mate have killed, you wretch?'

'But it is not true—and——'

'Drink then!' repeated the inflexible quarryman; I ask you for the last time.'——'To drink that would be death,' cried Father d'Aigrigny.

'Oh! only hear the wretch!' cried the mob, pressing closer to him; 'he has confessed—he has confessed!'——'He has betrayed himself!'*

'He said, "to drink that would be death."'——'But listen to me!' cried the abbé, clasping his hands together; 'this phial is——'

Furious cries interrupted Father d'Aigrigny. 'Ciboule, make an end of that one!' cried the quarryman, spurning Goliath with his foot. 'I will begin this one!' And he seized Father d'Aigrigny by the throat.

At these words, two different groups formed themselves. One, led by Ciboule, 'made an end' of Goliath, with kicks and blows, stones and wooden shoes; his body was soon reduced to a horrible thing, mutilated, nameless, formless—a mere inert mass of filth and mangled flesh. Ciboule gave her cloak, which they tied to one of the dislocated ankles of the body, and thus dragged it to the parapet of the quay. There, with shouts of ferocious joy, they precipitated the bloody remains into the river. Now who does not shudder at the thought that, in a time of popular commotion, a word, a single word, spoken imprudently, even by an honest man, and without hatred, will suffice to provoke so horrible a murder.

* This fact is historical. A man was murdered because a phial full of ammonia was found upon him. On his refusal to drink it, the populace, persuaded that the bottle contained poison, tore him to pieces.

'Perhaps it is a poisoner!' said one of the drinkers in the tavern of the Rue de la Calandre—nothing more—and Goliath had been pitilessly murdered.

What imperious reasons for penetrating the lowest depths of the masses with instruction and with light—to enable unfortunate creatures to defend themselves from so many stupid prejudices, so many fatal superstitions, so much implacable fanaticism!—How can we ask for calmness, reflection, self-control, or the sentiment of justice from abandoned beings, whom ignorance has brutalised, and misery depraved, and suffering made ferocious, and of whom society takes no thought, except when it chains them to the galleys, or binds them ready for the executioner! The terrible cry which had so startled Morok was uttered by Father d'Aigrigny as the quarryman laid his formidable hand upon him, saying to Ciboule : 'Make an end of that one—I will begin this one!'

CHAPTER XXIV.

IN THE CATHEDRAL.

NIGHT was almost come, as the mutilated body of Goliath was thrown into the river. The oscillations of the mob had carried into the street, which runs along the left side of the cathedral, the group into whose power Father d'Aigrigny had fallen. Having succeeded in freeing himself from the grasp of the quarryman, but still closely pressed by the multitude that surrounded him, crying, 'Death to the poisoner!' he retreated step by step, trying to parry the blows that were dealt him. By presence of mind, address and courage, recovering at that critical moment his old military energy, he had hitherto been able to resist and to remain firm on his feet—knowing, by the example of Goliath, that to fall was to die. Though he had little hope of being heard to any purpose, the abbé continued to call for help with all his might. Disputing the ground inch by inch, he manœuvred so as to draw near one of the lateral walls of the church, and at length succeeded in ensconcing himself in a corner formed by the projection of a buttress, and close by a little door.

This position was rather favourable. Leaning with his back against the wall, Father d'Aigrigny was sheltered from the attacks of a portion of his assailants. But the quarryman, wishing to deprive him of this last chance of safety, rushed upon him, with the intention of dragging him out into the circle, where he would have been trampled under foot. The fear of death gave Father d'Aigrigny extraordinary strength, and he was able once more to repulse the quarryman, and remain entrenched in the corner where he had taken refuge. The resistance of the victim redoubled the rage of the assailants. Cries of murderous import resounded with new violence. The quarryman again rushed upon Father d'Aigrigny, saying, 'Follow me, friends! this lasts too long. Let us make an end of it.'

Father d'Aigrigny saw that he was lost. His strength was exhausted, and he felt himself sinking; his legs trembled under him, and a cloud obscured his sight; the howling of the furious mob began to sound dull upon his ear. The effects of violent contusions, received during the struggle, both on the head and chest, were now very perceptible. Two or three times, a mixture of blood and foam rose to the lips of the abbé; his position was a desperate one.

'To be slaughtered by these brutes, after escaping death so often in war!' Such was the thought of Father d'Aigrigny, as the quarryman rushed upon him.

Suddenly, at the very moment when the abbé, yielding to the instinct of self-preservation, uttered one last call for help, in a heart-piercing voice, the door against which he leaned opened behind him, and a firm hand caught hold of him, and pulled him into the church. Thanks to this movement, performed with the rapidity of lightning, the quarryman, thrown forward in his attempt to seize Father d'Aigrigny, could not check his progress, and found himself just opposite to the person who had come, as it were, to take the place of the victim.

The quarryman stopped short, and then fell back a couple of paces, so much was he amazed at this sudden apparition, and impressed, like the rest of the crowd, with a vague feeling of admiration and respect at sight of him who had come so miraculously to the aid of Father d'Aigrigny. It was Gabriel. The young missionary remained standing on the threshold of the door. His long black cassock was half lost in the shadows of the cathedral; whilst his angelic countenance, with its border of long light hair, now pale and agitated by pity and grief, was illumined by the last faint rays of twilight. This countenance shone with so divine a beauty, and expressed such touching and tender compassion, that the crowd felt awed, as, with his large blue eyes full of tears, and his hands clasped together, he exclaimed, in a sonorous voice : ' Have mercy, my brethren ! Be humane—be just !'

Recovering from his first feeling of surprise and involuntary emotion, the quarryman advanced a step towards Gabriel, and said to him : ' No mercy for the poisoner ! we must have him. Give him up to us, or we go and take him ?'——' You cannot think of it, my brethren,' answered Gabriel ; 'the church is a sacred place—a place of refuge for the persecuted.'

' We would drag our poisoner from the altar !' answered the quarryman, roughly ; ' so give him up to us.'

' Listen to me, my brethren,' said Gabriel, extending his arms towards them.——' Down with the shaveling !' cried the quarryman ; 'let us go in and hunt him up in the church !'

' Yes, yes !' cried the mob, again led away by the violence of this wretch, ' down with the blackgown ?'——' They are all of a piece !'

' Down with them !'——' Let us do as we did at the archbishop's !'

' Or at Saint-Germain-l'Auxerrois !'——' What do our likes care for a church ?'

' If the priests defend the poisoners, we'll pitch them into the water too !'

' Yes, yes !'

' I'll show you the lead !' cried the quarryman ; and, followed by Ciboule, and a good number of determined men, he rush towards Gabriel.

The missionary, who for some moments had watched the increasing fury of the crowd, had foreseen this movement ; hastily retreating into the church, he succeeded, in spite of the efforts of the assailants, in nearly closing the door, and in barricading it by the help of a wooden bar, which he held in such a manner as would enable the door to resist for a few minutes.

Whilst he thus defended the entrance, Gabriel shouted to Father d'Aigrigny : ' Fly, father ! fly through the vestry ! the other doors are fastened.'

The Jesuit, overpowered by fatigue, covered with contusions, bathed in cold sweat, feeling his strength altogether fail, and too soon fancying himself in safety, had sunk, half fainting, into a chair. At the voice of Gabriel, he rose with difficulty, and, with a trembling step, endeavoured to reach the choir, separated from the rest of the church by an iron railing.

' Quick, father !' added Gabriel, in alarm, using every effort to maintain the door, which was now vigorously assailed. ' Make haste ! In a few minutes it will be too late. All alone !' continued the missionary, in despair, ' alone, to arrest the progress of these madmen !'

He was indeed alone. At the first outbreak of the attack, three or four sacristans and other members of the establishment were in the church ; but, struck with terror, and remembering the sack of the archbishop's palace, and of Saint-Germain-l'Auxerrois, they had immediately taken flight. Some of them had concealed themselves in the organ-loft, and others fled into the vestry, the doors of which they locked after them, thus cutting off the retreat of Gabriel and Father d'Aigrigny. The latter, bent double by pain, yet roused by the missionary's portentive warning, helping himself on by means of the chairs he met with on his passage, made vain efforts to reach the choir railing. After advancing a few steps, vanquished by his suffering, he staggered and fell upon the pavement, deprived of sense and motion. At the same moment, Gabriel, in spite of the incredible energy with which the desire to save Father d'Aigrigny had inspired him, felt the door giving way beneath the formidable pressure from without.

Turning his head, to see if the Jesuit had at least quitted the church, Gabriel, to his great alarm, perceived that he was lying motionless at a few steps from the choir. To abandon the half-broken door, to run to Father d'Aigrigny, to lift him in his arms, and drag him within the railing of the choir, was for the young priest an action rapid as thought ; for he closed the gate of the choir just at the instant that the quarryman and his band, having finished breaking down the door, rushed in a body into the church.

Standing in front of the choir, with his arms crossed upon his breast, Gabriel waited calmly and intrepidly for this mob, still more exasperated by such unexpected resistance.

The door once forced, the assailants rushed in with great violence. But hardly had they entered the church, than a strange scene took place. It was nearly dark ; only a few silver lamps shed their pale light round the sanc‧tuary, whose far outlines disappeared in shadow. On suddenly entering the immense cathedral, dark, silent, and deserted, the most audacious were struck with awe, almost with fear, in presence of the imposing grandeur of that stony solitude. Outcries and threats died away on the lips of the most furious. They seemed to dread awaking the echoes of those enormous arches, those black vaults, from which oozed a sepulchral dampness, which chilled their brows, inflamed with anger, and fell upon their shoulders like a mantle of ice.

Religious tradition, routine, habit, the memories of childhood, have so much influence upon men, that hardly had they entered the church, than several of the quarryman's followers respectfully took off their hats, bowed their bare heads, and walked along cautiously, as if to check the noise of their footsteps on the sounding stones. Then they exchanged a few words in a low and fearful whisper. Others timidly raised their eyes to the far heights of the topmost arches of that gigantic building, now lost in obscurity, and felt almost frightened to see themselves so little in the midst of that immensity of darkness. But at the first joke of the quarryman, who broke this respectful silence, the emotion soon passed away.

'Blood and thunder !' cried he ; 'are you fetching breath to sing vespers ? If they had wine in the font, well and good !'

These words were received with a burst of savage laughter. 'All this time the villain will escape !' said one.

'And we shall be done,' added Ciboule.——'One would think we had cowards here, who are afraid of the sacristans !' cried the quarryman.

'Never !' replied the others in chorus ; 'we fear nobody.'——'Forward !'

'Yes, yes—forward !' was repeated on all sides. And the animation, which had been calmed down for a moment, was redoubled in the midst of renewed tumult. Some moments after, the eyes of the assailants, becoming accustomed to the twilight, were able to distinguish, in the midst of the faint halo shed around by a silver lamp, the imposing countenance of Gabriel, as he stood before the iron railing of the choir.

'The poisoner is here, hid in some corner,' cried the quarryman. 'We must force this parson to give us back the villain.'

'He shall answer for him !'

'He took him into the church.'

'He shall pay for both, if we do not find the other !'

As the first impression of involuntary respect was effaced from the minds of the crowd, their voices rose the louder, and their faces became the more savage and threatening, because they all felt ashamed of their momentary hesitation and weakness.

'Yes, yes !' cried many voices, trembling with rage, 'we must have the life of one or the other !'——'Or of both !'

'So much the worse for this priest, if he wants to prevent us from serving out our poisoner !'——'Death to him ! death to him !'

With this burst of ferocious yells, which were fearfully re-echoed from the groined arches of the cathedral, the mob, maddened by rage, rushed towards the choir, at the door of which Gabriel was standing. The young missionary, who, when placed on the cross by the savages of the Rocky Mountains, yet entreated Heaven to spare his executioners, had too much courage in his heart, too much charity in his soul, not to risk his life a thousand times over to save Father d'Aigrigny's—the very man who had betrayed him by such cowardly and cruel hypocrisy.

CHAPTER XXV.

THE MURDERERS.

THE quarryman, followed by his gang, ran towards Gabriel, who had advanced a few paces from the choir-railing, and exclaimed, his eyes sparkling with rage : 'Where is the poisoner ? We will have him !'

'Who has told you, my brethren, that he is a poisoner ?' replied Gabriel, with his deep, sonorous voice. 'A poisoner ! Where are the proofs—witnesses, or victims ?'

'Enough of that stuff ! we are not here for confession,' brutally answered the quarryman, advancing towards him in a threatening manner. 'Give up the man to us ; he shall be forthcoming, unless you choose to stand in his shoes ?'

'Yes, yes !' exclaimed several voices ; 'they are "in" with one another ! One or the other we will have !'

'Very well, then ; since it is so,' said Gabriel, raising his head, and advancing with calmness, resignation, and fearlessness ; 'he or me,' added he ; —'it seems to make no difference to you—you are determined to have blood—take mine, and I will pardon you, my friends ; for a fatal delusion has unsettled your reason.'

These words of Gabriel, his courage, the nobleness of his attitude, the beauty of his countenance, had made an impression on some of the assailants, when suddenly a voice exclaimed : 'Look ! there is the poisoner, behind the railing.'

'Where—where ?' cried they.

'There—don't you see ?—stretched on the floor.'

On hearing this, the mob, which had hitherto formed a compact mass, in the sort of passage separating the two sides of the nave, between the rows of chairs, dispersed in every direction to reach the railing of the choir, the last and only barrier that now sheltered Father d'Aigrigny. During this manœuvre, the quarryman, Ciboule, and others, advanced towards Gabriel, exclaiming, with ferocious joy : 'This time we have him. Death to the poisoner !'

To save Father d'Aigrigny, Gabriel would have allowed himself to be massacred at the entrance of the choir ; but, a little further on, the railing, not above four feet in height, would in another instant be scaled or broken through. The missionary lost all hope of saving the Jesuit from a frightful death. Yet he exclaimed : 'Stop, poor deluded people !'—and, extending his arms, he threw himself in front of the crowd.

His words, gesture, and countenance, were expressive of an authority at once so affectionate and so fraternal, that there was a momentary hesitation amongst the mob. But to this hesitation soon succeeded the most furious crys of 'Death ! death !'

'You cry for his death ?' cried Gabriel, growing still paler.

'Yes ! yes !'

'Well, let him die,' cried the missionary, inspired with a sudden thought; 'let him die on the instant !'

These words of the young priest struck the crowd with amazement. For a few moments they all stood mute, motionless, and as it were paralysed, looking at Gabriel in stupid astonishment.

'This man is guilty, you say,' resumed the young missionary, in a voice trembling with emotion. 'You have condemned him without proof, without witnesses—no matter ; he must die. You reproach him with being a poisoner ; where are his victims ? You cannot tell—but no matter ; he is condemned. You refuse to hear his defence, the sacred right of every accused person—no matter ; the sentence is pronounced. You are at once his accusers, judges, and executioners. Be it so !—You have never seen till now this unfortunate man, he has done you no harm, he has perhaps not done harm to any one—yet you take upon yourselves the terrible responsibility of his death—understand me well—of his death. Be it so then ! your conscience will absolve you—I will believe it. He must die ; the sacredness of God's house will not save him——'

'No, no !' cried many furious voices.——'No,' resumed Gabriel, with increasing warmth ; 'no, you have determined to shed his blood, and you will shed it, even in the Lord's temple. It is, you say, your right. You are doing an act of terrible justice. But why then so many vigorous arms to make an end of one dying man ? Why these outcries ? this fury ? this violence ? Is it thus that the people, the strong and equitable people, are wont to execute their judgments ? No, no ; when, sure of their right, they strike their enemies, it is with the calmness of the judge, who, in freedom of soul and conscience, passes sentence. No, the strong and equitable people do not deal their blows like men blind or mad, uttering cries of rage, as if to drown the sense of some cowardly and horrible murder. No, it is not thus that they exercise the formidable right, to which you now lay claim—for you will have it——'

'Yes, we will have it !' shouted the quarryman, Ciboule, and others of the more pitiless portion of the mob ; whilst a great number remained silent, struck with the words of Gabriel, who had just painted to them, in such lively colours, the frightful act they were about to commit.

'Yes,' resumed the quarryman, 'it is our right ; we have determined to kill the poisoner !'

So saying, and with bloodshot eyes, and flushed cheek, the wretch advanced at the head of a resolute group, making a gesture as though he would have pushed aside Gabriel, who was still standing in front of the railing. But, instead of resisting the bandit, the missionary advanced a couple of steps to meet him, took him by the arm, and said in a firm voice: 'Come !'

And dragging, as it were, with him the stupefied quarryman, whose companions did not venture to follow at the moment, struck dumb as they were by this new incident, Gabriel rapidly traversed the space which separated him from the choir, opened the iron gate, and, still holding the quarryman by the arm, led him up to the prostrate form of Father d'Aigrigny, and said to him : 'There is the victim. He is condemned. Strike !'

'I !' cried the quarryman, hesitating ; 'I—all alone !'

'Oh !' replied Gabriel, with bitterness, 'there is no danger. You can easily finish him. Look ! he is broken down with suffering ; he has hardly a breath of life left ; he will make no resistance. Do not be afraid !'

The quarryman remained motionless, whilst the crowd, strangely impressed with this incident, approached a little nearer the railing, without daring to come within the gate.

'Strike then !' resumed Gabriel, addressing the quarryman, whilst he pointed to the crowd with a solemn gesture ; 'there are the judges ; you are the executioner.'

'No !' cried the quarryman, drawing back, and turning away his eyes ; 'I'm not the executioner—not I !'

The crowd remained silent. For a few moments, not a word, not a cry, disturbed the stillness of the solemn cathedral. In a desperate case, Gabriel had acted with a profound knowledge of the human heart. When the multitude, inflamed with blind rage, rushes with ferocious clamour upon a single victim, and each man strikes his blow, this dreadful species of combined murder appears less horrible to each, because they all share in the common crime ; and then the shouts, the sight of blood, the desperate defence of the man they massacre, finish by producing a sort of ferocious intoxication ; but, amongst all those furious madmen, who take part in the homicide, select one, and place him face to face with the victim, no longer capable of resistance, and say to him, 'Strike !'—he will hardly ever dare to do so.

It was thus with the quarryman ; the wretch trembled at the idea of committing a murder in cold blood, 'all alone.' The preceding scene had passed very rapidly ; amongst the companions of the quarryman, nearest to the railing, some did not understand an impression, which they would themselves have felt as strongly as this bold man, if it had been said to them : 'Do the office of executioner !' These, therefore, began to murmur aloud at his weakness. 'He dares not finish the poisoner,' said one.

'The coward !'——'He is afraid.'

'He draws back.' Hearing these words, the quarryman ran to the gate, threw it wide open, and, pointing to Father d'Aigrigny, exclaimed : 'If there is one here braver than I am, let him go and finish the job—let him be the executioner—come !'

On this proposal the murmurs ceased. A deep silence reigned once more in the cathedral. All those countenances, but now so furious, became sad, confused, almost frightened. The deluded mob began to appreciate the ferocious cowardice of the action it had been about to commit. Not one durst go alone to strike the half-expiring man. Suddenly, Father d'Aigrigny uttered a dying rattle, his head and one of his arms stirred with a convulsive movement, and then fell back upon the stones as if he had just expired.

Gabriel uttered a cry of anguish, and threw himself on his knees close to Father d'Aigrigny, exclaiming : 'Great Heaven ! he is dead !'

There is a singular variableness in the mind of a crowd, susceptible alike to good or evil impressions. At the heart-piercing cry of Gabriel, all these people, who, a moment before, had demanded, with loud uproar, the massacre of this man, felt touched with a sudden pity. The words ' He is dead !' circulated in low whispers through the crowd, accompanied by a slight shudder, whilst Gabriel raised with one hand the victim's heavy head, and with the other sought to feel if the pulse still beat beneath the ice-cold skin.

' Mr. Curate,' said the quarryman, bending towards Gabriel, ' is there really no hope ?'

The answer was waited for with anxiety, in the midst of deep silence. The people hardly ventured to exchange a few words in whispers.

' Blessed be God !' exclaimed Gabriel, suddenly. ' His heart beats.'

' His heart beats,' repeated the quarryman, turning his head towards the crowd, to inform them of the good news.

' Oh ! his heart beats !' repeated the others, in whispers.

' There is hope. We may yet save him,' added Gabriel, with an expression of indescribable happiness.

' We may yet save him,' repeated the quarryman, mechanically.

' We may yet save him,' muttered the crowd.

' Quick, quick,' resumed Gabriel, addressing the quarryman ; ' help me, brother. Let us carry him to a neighbouring house, where he can have immediate aid.'

The quarryman obeyed with readiness. Whilst the missionary lifted Father d'Aigrigny by holding him under the arms, the quarryman took the legs of the almost inanimate body. Together, they carried him outside of the choir. At sight of the formidable quarryman, aiding the young priest to render assistance to the man whom he had just before pursued with menaces of death, the multitude felt a sudden thrill of compassion. Yielding to the powerful influence of the words and example of Gabriel, they felt themselves deeply moved, and each became anxious to offer his services.

' Mr. Curate, he would perhaps be better on a chair, that one could carry upright,' said Ciboule.

' Shall I go and fetch a stretcher from the hospital ?' asked another.

' Mr. Curate, let me take your place ; the body is too heavy for you.'

' Don't trouble yourself,' said a powerful man, approaching the missionary respectfully ; ' I can carry him alone.'

' Shall I run and fetch a coach, Mr. Curate ?' said a young vagabond, taking off his red cap.——' Right,' said the quarryman ; ' run away, my buck !'

' But first, ask Mr. Curate if you are to go for a coach,' said Ciboule, stopping the impatient messenger.——' True,' added one of the bystanders; ' we are here in a church, and Mr. Curate has the command. He is at home.'

' Yes, yes ; go at once, my child,' said Gabriel to the obliging young vagabond.

Whilst the latter was making his way through the crowd, a voice said : ' I've a little wicker-bottle of brandy ; will that be of any use ?'

' No doubt,' answered Gabriel, hastily ; ' pray give it here. We can rub his temples with the spirit, and make him inhale a little.'

' Pass the bottle,' cried Ciboule ; ' but don't put your noses in it !' And, passed with caution from hand to hand, the flask reached Gabriel in safety.

Whilst waiting for the coming of the coach, Father d'Aigrigny had been seated on a chair. Whilst several good-natured people carefully supported the abbé, the missionary made him inhale a little brandy. In a few minutes, the spirit had a powerful influence on the Jesuit ; he made some slight movements, and his oppressed bosom heaved with a deep sigh,

'He is saved—he will live,' cried Gabriel, in a triumphant voice ; he will live, my brothers !'

'Oh ! glad to hear it !' exclaimed many voices.

'Oh, yes ! be glad, my brothers !' repeated Gabriel ; 'for, instead of being weighed down with the remorse of crime, you will have a just and charitable action to remember. Let us thank God, that he has changed your blind fury into a sentiment of compassion ! Let us pray to Him, that neither you, nor those you love, may ever be exposed to such frightful danger as this unfortunate man has just escaped. Oh, my brothers !' added Gabriel, as he pointed to the image of Christ with touching emotion, which communicated itself the more easily to others from the expression of his angelic countenance ; 'oh, my brothers ! let us never forget, that HE, who died upon that cross for the defence of the oppressed, for the obscure children of the people like to ourselves, pronounced those affectionate words so sweet to the heart : " Love ye one another !"—Let us never forget it ; let us love and help one another, and we poor people shall then become better, happier, just. Love—yes, love ye one another—and fall prostrate before that Saviour, who is the God of all that are weak, oppressed, and suffering in this world !'

So saying, Gabriel knelt down. All present respectfully followed his example, such power was there in his simple and persuasive words. At this moment, a singular incident added to the grandeur of the scene. We have said that a few seconds before the quarryman and his band entered the body of the church, several persons had fled from it. Two of these had taken refuge in the organ-loft, from which retreat they had viewed the preceding scene, themselves remaining invisible. One of these persons was a young man charged with the care of the organ, and quite musician enough to play on it. Deeply moved by the unexpected turn of an event which at first appeared so tragical, and yielding to an artistical inspiration, this young man, at the moment when he saw the people kneeling with Gabriel, could not forbear striking the notes. Then a sort of harmonious sigh, at first almost insensible, seemed to rise from the midst of this immense cathedral, like a divine aspiration. As soft and aerial as the balmy vapour of incense, it mounted and spread through the lofty arches. Little by little, the faint, sweet sounds, though still as it were covered, changed to an exquisite melody, religious, melancholy, and affectionate, which rose to heaven like a song of ineffable gratitude and love. And the notes were at first so faint, so covered, that the kneeling multitude had scarcely felt surprise, and had yielded insensibly to the irresistible influence of that enchanting harmony.

Then many an eye, until now dry and ferocious, became wet with tears —many hard hearts beat gently, as they remembered the words pronounced by Gabriel with so tender an accent : 'Love ye one another !' It was at this moment that Father d'Aigrigny came to himself—and opened his eyes. He thought himself under the influence of a dream. He had lost his senses in sight of a furious populace, who, with insult and blasphemy on their lips, pursued him with cries of death even to the sanctuary of the temple. He opened his eyes—and, by the pale light of the sacred lamps, to the solemn music of the organ, he saw that crowd, just now so menacing and implacable, kneeling in mute and reverential emotion, and humbly bowing their heads before the majesty of the shrine.

Some minutes after, Gabriel, carried almost in triumph on the shoulders of the crowd, entered the coach, in which Father d'Aigrigny, who by degrees had completely recovered his senses, was already reclining. By the order of the Jesuit, the coach stopped before the door of a house in the Rue de Vaugirard ; he had the strength and courage to enter this dwelling alone ; Gabriel was not admitted, but we shall conduct the reader thither.

CHAPTER XXVI.

THE PATIENT.

AT the end of the Rue de Vaugirard, there was then a very high wall, with only one small doorway in all its length. On opening this door, you entered a yard surrounded by a railing, with screens like Venetian blinds, to prevent your seeing between the rails. Crossing this courtyard, you come to a fine large garden, symmetrically planted, at the end of which stood a building two stories high, looking perfectly comfortable, without luxury, but with all that cosy simplicity which betokens discreet opulence. A few days had elapsed since Father d'Aigrigny had been so courageously rescued by Gabriel from the popular fury. Three ecclesiastics, wearing black gowns, white bands, and square caps, were walking in the garden with a slow and measured step. The youngest seemed to be about thirty years of age ; his countenance was pale, hollow, and impressed with a certain ascetic austerity. His two companions, aged between fifty or sixty, had, on the contrary, faces at once hypocritical and cunning ; their round, rosy cheeks shone brightly in the sunshine, whilst their triple chins, buried in fat, descended in soft folds over the fine cambric of their bands. According to the rules of their order (they belonged to the Society of Jesus), which forbade their walking only two together, these three members of the brotherhood never quitted each other a moment.

'I fear,' said one of the two, continuing a conversation already begun, and speaking of an absent person, 'I fear, that the continual agitation to which the reverend father has been a prey, ever since he was attacked with the cholera, has exhausted his strength, and caused the dangerous relapse which now makes us fear for his life.'

'They say,' resumed the other, 'that never was there seen anxiety like to his.'

'And moreover,' remarked the young priest, bitterly, 'it is painful to think, that his reverence Father Rodin has given cause for scandal, by obstinately refusing to make a public confession, the day before yesterday, when his situation appeared so desperate, that, between two fits of delirium, it was thought right to propose to him to receive the last sacraments.'

'His reverence declared that he was not so ill as they supposed,' answered one of the fathers, 'and that he would have the last duties performed when he thought necessary.'

'The fact is, that for the last ten days, ever since he was brought here dying, his life has been, as it were, only a long and painful agony ; and yet he continues to live.'

'I watched by him during the first three days of his malady, with M. Rousselet, the pupil of Dr. Baleinier,' resumed the youngest father ; 'he had hardly a moment's consciousness, and when the Lord did grant him a lucid interval, he employed it in detestable execrations against the fate which had confined him to his bed.'

'It is said,' resumed the other, 'that Father Rodin made answer to his Eminence Cardinal Malipieri, who came to persuade him to die in an exemplary manner, worthy of a son of Loyola, our blessed founder'—at these words, the three Jesuits bowed their heads together, as if they had been all moved by the same spring—'it is said, that Father Rodin made answer to his eminence : " I do not need to confess publicly ; I WANT TO LIVE, AND I *will* LIVE." '

' I did not hear that,' said the young priest, with an indignant air ; ' but if Father Rodin really made use of such expressions, it is——'

Here, no doubt, reflection came to him just in time, for he stole a side-long glance at his two silent, impassible companions, and added : ' It is a great misfortune for his soul ; but I am certain, his reverence has been slandered.'

' It was only as a calumnious report, that I mentioned those words,' said the other priest, exchanging a glance with his companion.

One of the garden gates opened, and one of the three reverend fathers exclaimed, at sight of the personage who now entered : ' Oh ! here is his Eminence Cardinal Malipieri, coming to pay a visit to Father Rodin.'

' May this visit of his eminence,' said the young priest, calmly, ' be more profitable to Father Rodin than the last !'

Cardinal Malipieri was crossing the garden, on his way to the apartment occupied by Rodin.

   ❂   ❂   ❂   ❂   ❂   ❂

Cardinal Malipieri, whom we saw assisting at the sort of council held at the Princess de Saint-Dizier's, now on his way to Rodin's apartment, was dressed as a layman, but enveloped in an ample pelisse of puce-coloured satin, which exhaled a strong odour of camphor, for the prelate had taken care to surround himself with all sorts of anti-cholera specifics.   Having reached the second story of the house, the cardinal knocked at a little grey door.   Nobody answering, he opened it, and, like a man to whom the locality was well known, passed through a sort of antechamber, and entered a room in which was a turn-up bed.   On a black wood table were many phials, which had contained different medicines.   The prelate's countenance seemed uneasy and morose ; his complexion was still yellow and bilious ; the brown circle which surrounded his black, squinting eyes appeared still darker than usual.

Pausing a moment, he looked round him almost in fear, and several times stopped to smell at his anti-cholera bottle.   Then, seeing he was alone, he approached a glass over the chimney-piece, and examined with much atten-tion the colour of his tongue ; after some minutes spent in this careful investigation, with the result of which he appeared tolerably satisfied, he took some preservative lozenges out of a golden box, and allowed them to melt in his mouth, whilst he closed his eyes with a sanctified air.   Having taken these sanitary precautions, and again pressed his bottle to his nose, the prelate prepared to enter the third room, when he heard a tolerably loud noise through the thin partition which separated him from it, and, stopping to listen, all that was said in the next apartment easily reached his ear.

' Now that my wounds are dressed, I will get up,' said a weak, but sharp and imperious voice.

' Do not think of it, reverend father,' was answered in a stronger tone ; ' it is impossible.'

' You shall see if it is impossible,' replied the other voice.

' But, reverend father, you will kill yourself.   You are not in a state to get up.   You will expose yourself to a mortal relapse.   I cannot consent to it.'

To these words succeeded the noise of a faint struggle, mingled with groans more angry than plaintive, and the voice resumed : ' No, no, father ; for your own safety, I will not leave your clothes within your reach.   It is almost time for your medicine ; I will go and prepare it for you.'

Almost immediately after, the door opened, and the prelate saw enter a man of about twenty-five years of age, carrying on his arm an old olive great-coat and threadbare black trousers, which he threw down upon a chair.

This personage was Ange Modeste Rousselet, chief pupil of Dr. Baleinier; the countenance of the young practitioner was mild, humble, and reserved; his hair, very short in front, flowed down upon his neck behind. He made a slight start in surprise on perceiving the cardinal, and bowed twice very low, without raising his eyes.

'Before anything else,' said the prelate, with his marked Italian accent, still holding to his nose his bottle of camphor, 'have any choleraic symptoms returned?'

'No, my lord; the pernicious fever, which succeeded the attack of cholera, still continues.'

'Very good. But will not the reverend father be reasonable? What was the noise that I just heard?'

'His reverence wished absolutely to get up and dress himself; but his weakness is so great, that he could not have taken two steps from the bed. He is devoured by impatience, and we fear that this agitation will cause a mortal relapse.'

'Has Dr. Baleinier been here this morning?'

'He has just left, my lord.'

'What does he think of the patient?'

'He finds him in the most alarming state, my lord. The night was so bad, that he was extremely uneasy this morning. Father Rodin is at one of those critical junctures, when a few hours may decide the life or death of the patient. Dr. Baleinier is now gone to fetch what is necessary for a very painful operation, which he is about to perform on the reverend father.'

'Has Father d'Aigrigny been told of this?'

'Father d'Aigrigny is himself very unwell, as your eminence knows; he has not been able to leave his bed for the last three days.'

'I inquired about him as I came up,' answered the prelate, 'and I shall see him directly. But, to return to Father Rodin, have you sent for his confessor, since he is in a desperate state, and about to undergo a serious operation?'

'Dr. Baleinier spoke a word to him about it, as well as about the last sacraments; but Father Rodin exclaimed, with great irritation, that they did not leave him a moment's peace, that he had as much care as any one for his salvation, and that——'

'Per Bacco! I am not thinking of him,' cried the cardinal, interrupting Ange Modeste Rousselet with his pagan oath, and raising his sharp voice to a still higher key; 'I am not thinking of him, but of the interests of the Company. It is indispensable that the reverend father should receive the sacraments with the most splendid solemnity, and that his end should not only be Christian, but exemplary. All the people in the house, and even strangers, should be invited to the spectacle, so that his edifying death may produce an excellent sensation.'

'That is what Fathers Grison and Brunet have already endeavoured to persuade his reverence, my lord; but your eminence knows with what impatience Father Rodin received this advice, and Dr. Baleinier did not venture to persist, for fear of advancing a fatal crisis.'

'Well, I will venture to do it; for in these times of revolutionary impiety, a solemnly Christian death would produce a very salutary effect on the public. It would indeed be proper to make the necessary preparations to embalm the reverend father; he might then lie in state for some days, with lighted tapers, according to Romish custom. My secretary would furnish the design for the bier ; it would be very splendid and imposing ; from his position in the Order, Father Rodin is entitled to have everything in the most sumptuous style. He must have at least six hundred tapers, and a dozen funeral lamps, burning spirits of wine, to hang just over the body, and light it from above : the effect would be excellent. We must also distribute little tracts to the people, concerning the pious and ascetic life of his reverence——'

Here a sudden noise, like that of some piece of metal thrown angrily on the floor, was heard from the next room, in which was the sick man, and interrupted the prelate in his description.

'I hope Father Rodin has not heard you talk of embalming him, my lord,' said Rousselet, in a whisper : 'his bed touches the partition, and almost everything is audible through it.'

'If Father Rodin has heard me,' answered the cardinal, sinking his voice, and retiring to the other end of the room, 'this circumstance will enable me to enter at once on the business ; but, in any case, I persist in believing that the embalming and the lying in state are required to make a good effect upon the public. The people are already frightened at the cholera, and such funeral pomp would have no small influence on the imagination.'

'I would venture to observe to your Eminence, that here the laws are opposed to such exhibitions.'

'The laws—always the laws !' said the cardinal, angrily ; 'has not Rome also her laws ? And is not every priest a subject of Rome ? Is it not time——'

But, not choosing, doubtless, to begin a more explicit conversation with the young doctor, the prelate resumed, 'We will talk of this hereafter. But, tell me, since my last visit, has the reverend father had any fresh attacks of delirium ?'

'Yes, my lord ; here is the note, as your eminence commanded.' So saying, Rousselet delivered a paper to the prelate. We will inform the reader that this part of the conversation between Rousselet and the cardinal was carried on at a distance from the partition, so that Rodin could hear nothing of it, whilst that which related to the embalming had been perfectly audible to him.

The cardinal, having received the note from Rousselet, perused it with an expression of lively curiosity. When he had finished, he crumpled it in his hand, and said, without attempting to dissemble his vexation, 'Always nothing but incoherent expressions. Not two words together, from which you can draw any reasonable conclusion. One would really think this man had the power to control himself even in his delirium, and to rave about insignificant matters only.'

Then, addressing Rousselet, 'You are sure that you have reported everything that escaped from him during his delirium ?'

'With the exception of the same phrases, that he repeated over and over again, your eminence may be assured that I have not omitted a single word, however unmeaning.'

'Show me into Father Rodin's room,' said the prelate, after a moment's silence.——'But, my lord,' answered the young doctor, with some hesitation, 'the fit has only left him about an hour, and the reverend father is still very weak.'

'The more's the reason,' replied the prelate, somewhat indiscreetly. Then, recollecting himself, he added, 'He will the better appreciate the consolations I have to offer. Should he be asleep, awake him, and announce my visit.'

'I have only orders to receive from your eminence,' said Rousselet, bowing, and entering the next room.

Left alone, the cardinal said to himself, with a pensive air, 'I always come back to that. When he was suddenly attacked by the cholera, Father Rodin believed himself poisoned by order of the Holy See. He must then have been plotting something very formidable against Rome, to entertain so abominable a fear. Can our suspicions be well founded? Is he acting secretly and powerfully on the Sacred College? But then for what end? This it has been impossible to penetrate, so faithfully has the secret been kept by his accomplices. I had hoped that, during his delirium, he would let slip some word that would put us on the trace of what we are so much interested to discover. With so restless and active a mind, delirium is often the exaggeration of some dominant idea; yet here I have the report of five different fits—and nothing—no, nothing but vague, unconnected phrases.'

The return of Rousselet put an end to these reflections. 'I am sorry to inform my lord that the reverend father obstinately refuses to see any one. He says that he requires absolute repose. Though very weak, he has a savage and angry look, and I should not be surprised if he overheard your eminence talk about embalming him.'

The cardinal, interrupting Rousselet, said to him, 'Did Father Rodin have his last fit of delirium in the night?'

'Between three and half-past five this morning, my lord.'

'Between three and half-past five,' repeated the prelate, as if he wished to impress this circumstance on his memory: 'the attack presented no particular symptoms?'

'No, my lord; it consisted of rambling, incoherent talk, as your eminence may see by this note.'

Then, as he perceived the prelate approaching Father Rodin's door, Rousselet added, 'The reverend father will positively see no one, my lord; he requires rest, to prepare for the operation; it might be dangerous——'

Without attending to these observations, the cardinal entered Rodin's chamber. It was a tolerably large room, lighted by two windows, and simply but commodiously furnished. Two logs were burning slowly in the fire-place, in which stood a coffee-pot, a vessel containing mustard-poultice, etc. On the chimney-piece were several pieces of rag, and some linen bandages. The room was full of that faint, chemical odour peculiar to the chambers of the sick, mingled with so putrid a stench, that the cardinal stopped at the door a moment, before he ventured to advance further. As the three reverend fathers had mentioned in their walk, Rodin lived because he had said to himself, 'I want to live, and I will live.'

For, as men of timid imaginations and cowardly minds often die from the mere dread of dying, so a thousand facts prove that vigour of character and moral energy may often struggle successfully against disease, and triumph over the most desperate symptoms.

It was thus with the Jesuit. The unshaken firmness of his character, the formidable tenacity of his will (for the will has sometimes a mysterious and almost terrific power), aiding the skilful treatment of Dr. Baleinier, had saved him from the pestilence with which he had been so suddenly attacked. But the shock had been succeeded by a violent fever, which placed Rodin's life in the utmost peril. This increased danger had caused the greatest alarm to Father d'Aigrigny, who felt, in spite of his rivalry and jealousy, that Rodin was the master-spirit of the plot in which they were engaged, and could alone conduct it to a successful issue.

The curtains of the room were half closed, and admitted only a doubtful light to the bed on which Rodin was lying. The Jesuit's features had lost the greenish hue peculiar to cholera patients, but remained perfectly livid and cadaverous, and so thin, that the dry, rugged skin appeared to cling to the smallest prominence of bone. The muscles and veins of the long, lean, vulture-like neck resembled a bundle of cords. The head, covered with an old, black, filthy night-cap, from beneath which strayed a few thin, grey hairs, rested upon a dirty pillow ; for Rodin would not allow them to change his linen. His iron-grey beard had not been shaved for some time, and stood out like the hairs of a brush. Under his shirt he wore an old flannel waistcoat full of holes. He had one of his arms out of bed, and his bony hairy hand, with its blueish nails, held fast a cotton handkerchief of indescribable colour.

You might have taken him for a corpse, had it not been for the two brilliant sparks which still burned in the depths of his eyes. In that look, in which seemed concentred all the remaining life and energy of the man, you might read the most restless anxiety. Sometimes his features revealed the sharpest pangs ; sometimes the twisting of his hands, and his sudden starts, proclaimed his despair at being thus fettered to a bed of pain, whilst the serious interests which he had in charge required all the activity of his mind. Thus, with thoughts continually on the stretch, his mind often wandered, and he had fits of delirium, from which he woke as from a painful dream. By the prudent advice of Dr. Baleinier, who considered him not in a state to attend to matters of importance, Father d'Aigrigny had hitherto evaded Rodin's questions with regard to the Rennepont affair, which he dreaded to see lost and ruined in consequence of his forced inaction. The silence of Father d'Aigrigny on this head, and the ignorance in which they kept him, only augmented the sick man's exasperation. Such was the moral and physical state of Rodin, when Cardinal Malipieri entered his chamber against his will.

CHAPTER XXVII.

THE LURE.

To understand fully the tortures of Rodin, reduced to inactivity by sickness, and to explain the importance of Cardinal Malipieri's visit, we must remember the audacious views of the ambitious Jesuit, who believed himself following in the steps of Sixtus V., and expected to become his equal. By the success of the Rennepont affair, to attain to the generalship of his Order, by the corruption of the Sacred College to ascend the pontifical throne, and then, by means of a change in the statutes of the Company, to incorporate the Society of Jesus with the Holy See, instead of leaving it independent, to equal and almost always rule the Papacy—such were the secret projects of Rodin.

Their possibility was sanctioned by numerous precedents, for many mere monks and priests had been suddenly raised to the pontifical dignity. And as for their morality, the accession of the Borgias, of Julius II., and other dubious Vicars of Christ, might excuse and authorise the pretensions of the Jesuit.

Though the object of his secret intrigues at Rome had hitherto been enveloped in the greatest mystery, suspicions had been excited in regard to his private communications with many members of the Sacred College. A portion of that college, Cardinal Malipieri at the head of them, had become very uneasy on the subject, and, profiting by his journey to France, the cardinal had resolved to penetrate the Jesuit's dark designs. If, in the scene we have just painted, the cardinal showed himself so obstinately bent on having a conference with Rodin, in spite of the refusal of the latter, it was because the prelate hoped, as we shall soon see, to get by cunning at the secret, which had hitherto been so well concealed. It was, therefore, in the midst of all these extraordinary circumstances, that Rodin saw himself the victim of a malady, which paralysed his strength, at the moment when he had need of all his activity, and of all the resources of his mind. After remaining for some seconds motionless near the door, the cardinal, still holding his bottle under his nose, slowly approached the bed where Rodin lay.

The latter, enraged at this perseverance, and wishing to avoid an interview which for many reasons was singularly odious to him, turned his face towards the wall, and pretended to be asleep. Caring little for this feint, and determined to profit by Rodin's state of weakness, the prelate took a chair, and, conquering his repugnance, sat down close to the Jesuit's bed.

' My reverend and very dear father, how do you find yourself?' said he to him, in a honied tone, which his Italian accent seemed to render still more hypocritical. Rodin pretended not to hear, breathed hard, and made no answer. But the cardinal, not without disgust, shook with his gloved hand the arm of the Jesuit, and repeated in a louder voice : ' My reverend and very dear father, answer me, I conjure you !'

Rodin could not restrain a movement of angry impatience, but he continued silent. The cardinal was not a man to be discouraged by so little ; he again shook the arm of the Jesuit, somewhat more roughly, repeating, with a passionless tenacity that would have incensed the most patient person in the world : ' My reverend and very dear father, since you are not asleep, listen to me, I entreat of you.'

Irritable with pain, exasperated by the obstinacy of the prelate, Rodin abruptly turned his head, fixed on the Roman his hollow eyes, shining with lurid fire, and, with lips contracted by a sardonic smile, said to him, bitterly : ' You must be very anxious, my lord, to see me embalmed, and lie in state with tapers, as you were saying just now, for you thus to come to torment me in my last moments, and hasten my end !'

' Oh, my good father ! how can you talk so ?' cried the cardinal, raising his hands as if to call heaven to witness to the sincerity of the tender interest he felt for the Jesuit.

' I tell you that I heard all just now, my lord ; for the partition is thin,' added Rodin, with redoubled bitterness.

' If you mean that, from the bottom of my soul, I desired that you should make an exemplary and Christian end, you are perfectly right, my dear father. I did say so ; for, after a life so well employed, it would be sweet to see you an object of adoration for the faithful !'

' I tell you, my lord,' cried Rodin, in a weak and broken voice, ' that it is ferocious to express such wishes in the presence of a dying man. Yes,' he added, with growing animation, that contrasted strongly with his weakness, ' take care what you do ; for if I am too much plagued and pestered—if I am not allowed to breathe my last breath quietly—I give you notice that you will force me to die in anything but a Christian manner, and if you mean to profit by an edifying spectacle, you will be deceived.'

This burst of anger having greatly fatigued Rodin, his head fell back upon the pillow, and he wiped his cracked and bleeding lips with his old cotton handkerchief.

' Come, come, be calm, my very dear father,' resumed the cardinal, with a patronising air ; ' do not give way to such gloomy ideas. Doubtless, Providence reserves you for great designs, since you have been already delivered from so much peril. Let us hope that you will be likewise saved from your present danger.'

Rodin answered by a hoarse growl, and turned his face towards the wall.

The imperturbable prelate continued : 'The views of Providence are not confined to your salvation, my very dear father. Its power has been manifested in another way. What I am about to tell you is of the highest importance. Listen attentively.'

Without turning his head, Rodin muttered in a tone of angry bitterness, which betrayed his intense sufferings : 'They desire my death. My chest is on fire, my head racked with pain, and they have no pity. Oh, I suffer the tortures of the damned !'

'What ! *already ?*' thought the Roman, with a smile of sarcastic malice ; then he said aloud : 'Let me persuade you, my very dear father—make an effort to listen to me ; you will not regret it.'

Still stretched upon the bed, Rodin lifted his hands clasped upon his cotton handkerchief with a gesture of despair, and then let them fall again by his side.

The cardinal slightly shrugged his shoulders, and laid great stress on what follows, so that Rodin might not lose a word of it : 'My dear father, it has pleased Providence that, during your fit of raving, you have made, without knowing it, the most important revelations.'

The prelate waited with anxious curiosity for the effect of the pious trap he had laid for the Jesuit's weakened faculties. But the latter, still turned towards the wall, did not appear to have heard him and remained silent.

'You are, no doubt, reflecting on my words, my dear father,' resumed the cardinal; 'you are right, for it concerns a very serious affair. I repeat to you that Providence has allowed you, during your delirium, to betray your most secret thoughts—happily, to me alone. They are such as would compromise you in the highest degree. In short, during your delirium of last night, which lasted nearly two hours, you unveiled the secret objects of your intrigues at Rome with many of the members of the Sacred College.'

The cardinal, rising softly, stooped over the bed to watch the expression of Rodin's countenance. But the latter did not give him time. As a galvanised corpse starts into strange and sudden motion, Rodin sprang into a sitting posture at the last words of the prelate.

'He has betrayed himself,' said the cardinal, in a low voice, in Italian. Then, resuming his seat, he fixed on the Jesuit his eyes, that sparkled with triumphant joy.

Though he did not hear the exclamation of Malipieri, nor remark the expression of his countenance, Rodin, notwithstanding his state of weakness, instantly felt the imprudence of his start. He pressed his hand to his forehead, as though he had been seized with a giddiness ; then, looking wildly round him, he pressed to his trembling lips his old cotton handkerchief, and *gnawed* it mechanically for some seconds.

'Your emotion and alarm confirm the sad discoveries I have made,' resumed the cardinal, still more rejoicing at the success of his trick ; 'and now, my dear father,' added he, 'you will understand that it is for your best interest to enter into the most minute detail as to your projects and accomplices at Rome. You may then hope, my dear father, for the indulgence of the Holy See—that is, if your avowals are sufficiently explicit to fill up the chasms necessarily left in a confession made during delirium.'

Rodin, recovered from his first surprise, perceived, but too late, that he had fallen into a snare, not by any words he had spoken, but by his too significant movements. In fact, the Jesuit had feared for a moment that he might have betrayed himself during his delirium, when he heard himself accused of dark intrigues with Rome ; but, after some minutes of reflection, his common sense suggested : 'If this crafty Roman knew my secret, he would take care not to tell me so. He has only suspicions, confirmed by my involuntary start just now.'

Rodin wiped the cold sweat from his burning forehead. The emotion of this scene augmented his sufferings, and aggravated the danger of his condition. Worn out with fatigue, he could not remain long in a sitting posture, and soon fell back upon the bed.

'*Per Bacco !*' said the cardinal to himself, alarmed at the expression of the Jesuit's face ; 'if he were to die before he has spoken, and so escape the snare !'

Then, leaning over the bed, the prelate asked : 'What is the matter, my very dear father ?'

'I am weak, my lord—I am in pain—I cannot express what I suffer.'

'Let us hope, my very dear father, that this crisis will have no fatal results ; but the contrary may happen, and it behoves the salvation of your soul to make instantly the fullest confession. Were it even to exhaust your strength, what is this perishable body compared to eternal life ?'

'Of what confession do you speak, my lord ?' said Rodin, in a feeble and yet sarcastic tone.——'What confession !' cried the amazed cardinal ; 'why, with regard to your dangerous intrigues at Rome.'

'What intrigues ?' asked Rodin.——'The intrigues you revealed during your delirium,' replied the prelate, with still more angry impatience. 'Were not your avowals sufficiently explicit ? Why, then, this culpable hesitation to complete them ?'

'My avowals—were explicit—you assure me ?' said Rodin, pausing after each word for want of breath, but without losing his energy and presence of mind.

'Yes, I repeat it,' resumed the cardinal : 'with the exception of a few chasms, they were most explicit.'

'Then why repeat them ?' said Rodin, with the same sardonic smile on his violet lips.

'Why repeat them ?' cried the angry prelate. 'In order to gain pardon ; for if there is indulgence and mercy for the repentant sinner, there must be condemnation and curses for the hardened criminal !'

'Oh, what torture ! I am dying by slow fire !' murmured Rodin. 'Since I have told all,' he resumed, 'I have nothing more to tell. You know it already.'

'I know all—doubtless, I know all,' replied the prelate, in a voice of thunder ; 'but how have I learned it ? By confessions made in a state of unconsciousness. Do you think they will avail you anything ? No ; the moment is solemn—death is at hand ; tremble to die with a sacrilegious falsehood on your lips,' cried the prelate, shaking Rodin violently by the arm ; 'dread the eternal flames, if you dare deny what you know to be the truth. Do you deny it ?'

'I deny nothing,' murmured Rodin, with difficulty. 'Only leave me alone !'

'Then heaven inspires you,' said the cardinal, with a sigh of satisfaction ; and, thinking he had nearly attained his object, he resumed, 'Listen to the divine word, that will guide you, father. You deny nothing ?'

'I was—delirious—and cannot—(oh ! how I suffer !)' added Rodin, by way of parenthesis ; 'and cannot therefore—deny—the nonsense—I may have uttered !'

'But when this nonsense agrees with the truth,' cried the prelate, furious at being again deceived in his expectation ; 'but when raving is an involuntary, providential revelation——'

'Cardinal Malipieri—your craft is no match—for my agony,' answered

Rodin, in a failing voice. ' The proof—that I have not told my secret—if I have a secret—is—that you want to make me tell it !' In spite of his pain and weakness, the Jesuit had courage to raise himself in the bed, and look the cardinal full in the face, with a smile of bitter irony. After which he fell back on the pillow, and pressed his hands to his chest, with a long sigh of anguish.

' Damnation ! the infernal Jesuit has found me out !' said the cardinal to himself, as he stamped his foot with rage. ' He sees that he was compromised by his first movement ; he is now upon his guard ; I shall get nothing more from him—unless indeed, profiting by the state of weakness in which he is, I can, by entreaties, by threats, by terror——'

The prelate was unable to finish. The door opened abruptly, and Father d'Aigrigny entered the room, exclaiming with an explosion of joy : ' Excellent news !'

CHAPTER XXVIII.

GOOD NEWS.

BY the alteration in the countenance of Father d'Aigrigny, his pale cheek, and the feebleness of his walk, one might see that the terrible scene in the square of Nôtre-Dame, had violently reacted upon his health. Yet his face was radiant and triumphant, as he entered Rodin's chamber, exclaiming : ' Excellent news !'

On these words, Rodin started. In spite of his weakness, he raised his head, and his eyes shone with a curious, uneasy, piercing expression. With his lean hand, he beckoned Father d'Aigrigny to approach the bed, and said to him, in a broken voice, so weak that it was scarcely audible : ' I am very ill—the cardinal has nearly finished me—but if this excellent news—relates to the Rennepont affair—of which I hear nothing—it might save me yet !'

' Be saved then !' cried Father d'Aigrigny, forgetting the recommendations of Dr. Baleinier ; ' read, rejoice ! What you foretold is beginning to be realised !'

So saying, he drew a paper from his pocket, and delivered it to Rodin, who seized it with an eager and trembling hand. Some minutes before, Rodin would have been really incapable of continuing his conversation with the cardinal, even if prudence had allowed him to do so ; nor could he have read a single line, so dim had his sight become. But, at the words of Father d'Aigrigny, he felt such a renewal of hope and vigour, that, by a mighty effort of energy and will, he rose to a sitting posture, and, with clear head, and look of intelligent animation, he read rapidly the paper that Father d'Aigrigny had just delivered to him.

The cardinal amazed at this sudden transfiguration, asked himself if he beheld the same man, who, a few minutes before, had fallen back on his bed, almost insensible.

Hardly had Rodin finished reading, than he uttered a cry of stifled joy, saying, with an accent impossible to describe : ' ONE gone ! it works—'tis well !' And, closing his eyes in a kind of ecstatic transport, a smile of proud triumph overspread his face, and rendered him still more hideous, by discovering his yellow and gumless teeth. His emotion was so violent, that the paper fell from his trembling hand.

' He has fainted,' cried Father d'Aigrigny, with uneasiness, as he leaned over Rodin. ' It is my fault, I forgot that the doctor cautioned me not to talk to him of serious matters.'

'No ; do not reproach yourself,' said Rodin, in a low voice, half-raising himself in the bed. 'This unexpected joy may perhaps cure me. Yes—I scarce know what I feel—but look at my cheeks—it seems to me, that, for the first time since I have been stretched on this bed of pain, they are a little warm.'

Rodin spoke the truth. A slight colour appeared suddenly on his livid and icy cheeks ; his voice, though still very weak, became less tremulous, and he exclaimed, in a tone of conviction that startled Father d'Aigrigny and the prelate, 'This first success answers for the others. I read the future. Yes, yes ; our cause will triumph. Every member of the execrable Rennepont family will be crushed—and that soon—you will see——'

'Then, pausing, Rodin threw himself back on the pillow, exclaiming : 'Oh ! I am choked with joy. My voice fails me.'

'But what is it ?' asked the cardinal of Father d'Aigrigny.

The latter replied, in a tone of hypocritical sanctity : 'One of the heirs of the Rennepont family, a poor fellow, worn out with excesses and debauchery, died three days ago, at the close of some abominable orgies, in which he had braved the cholera with sacrilegious impiety. In consequence of the indisposition that kept me at home, and of another circumstance, I only received to-day the certificate of the death of this victim of intemperance and irreligion. I must proclaim it to the praise of his reverence'—pointing to Rodin—'that he told me, the worst enemies of the descendants of that infamous renegade would be their own bad passions, and that we might look to them as our allies against the whole impious race. And so it has happened with Jacques Rennepont.'

'You see,' said Rodin, in so faint a voice that it was almost unintelligible, 'the punishment begins already. One of the Renneponts is dead—and believe me—this certificate,' and he pointed to the paper that Father d'Aigrigny held in his hand, 'will one day be worth forty millions to the Society of Jesus—and that—because——'

The lips alone finished the sentence. During some seconds, Rodin's voice had become so faint, that it was at last quite imperceptible. His larynx, contracted by violent emotion, no longer emitted any sound. The Jesuit, far from being disconcerted by this incident, finished his phrase, as it were, by expressive pantomime. Raising his head proudly, he tapped his forehead with his forefinger, as if to express that it was to his ability this first success was owing. But he soon fell back again on the bed, exhausted, breathless, sinking, with his cotton handkerchief pressed once more to his parched lips. The good news, as Father d'Aigrigny called it, had not cured Rodin. For a moment only, he had had the courage to forget his pain. But the slight colour on his cheek soon disappeared ; his face became once more livid. His sufferings, suspended for a moment, were so much increased in violence, that he writhed beneath the coverlet, and buried his face in the pillow, extending his arms above his head, and holding them stiff as bars of iron. After this crisis, intense as it was rapid, during which Father d'Aigrigny and the prelate bent anxiously over him, Rodin, whose face was bathed in cold sweat, made a sign that he suffered less, and that he wished to drink of a potion to which he pointed. Father d'Aigrigny fetched it for him, and while the cardinal held him up with marked disgust, the abbé administered a few spoonfuls of the potion, which almost immediately produced a soothing effect.

'Shall I call M. Rousselet ?' said Father d'Aigrigny, when Rodin was once more laid down in bed.

Rodin shook his head ; then, with a fresh effort, he raised his right hand, opened it, and pointed with his forefinger to a desk in a corner of the room, to signify that, being no longer able to speak, he wished to write.

'I understand your reverence,' said Father d'Aigrigny; 'but first calm yourself. Presently, if you require it, I will give you writing materials.'

Two knocks at the outer door of the next room interrupted this scene. From motives of prudence, Father d'Aigrigny had begged Rousselet to remain in the first of the three rooms. He now went to open the door, and Rousselet handed him a voluminous packet, saying: 'I beg pardon for disturbing you, father, but I was told to let you have these papers instantly.'

'Thank you, M. Rousselet,' said Father d'Aigrigny; 'do you know at what hour Dr. Baleinier will return.'

'He will not be long, father, for he wishes to perform before night the painful operation, that will have a decisive effect on the condition of Father Rodin. I am preparing what is necessary for it,' added Rousselet, as he pointed to a singular and formidable apparatus, which Father d'Aigrigny examined with a kind of terror.

'I do not know if the symptom is a serious one,' said the Jesuit; 'but the reverend father has suddenly lost his voice.'

'It is the third time this has happened within the last week,' said Rousselet; 'the operation of Dr. Baleinier will act both on the larynx and on the lungs.'

'Is the operation a very painful one?' asked Father d'Aigrigny.

'There is, perhaps, none more cruel in surgery,' answered the young doctor; 'and Dr. Baleinier has partly concealed its nature from Father Rodin.'

'Please to wait here for Dr. Baleinier, and send him to us as soon as he arrives,' resumed Father d'Aigrigny; and, returning to the sick chamber, he sat down by the bed-side, and said to Rodin, as he showed him the letter: 'Here are different reports with regard to different members of the Rennepont family, whom I have had looked after by others, my indisposition having kept me at home for the last few days. I do not know, father, if the state of your health will permit you to hear——'

Rodin made a gesture, at once so supplicating and peremptory, that Father d'Aigrigny felt there would be at least as much danger in refusing as in granting his request; so, turning towards the cardinal, still inconsolable at not having discovered the Jesuit's secret, he said to him with respectful deference, pointing at the same time to the letter: 'Have I the permission of your Eminence?'

The prelate bowed, and replied: 'Your affairs are ours, my dear father. The Church must always rejoice in what rejoices your glorious Company.'

Father d'Aigrigny unsealed the packet, and found in it different notes in different handwritings. When he had read the first, his countenance darkened, and he said, in a grave tone: 'A misfortune—a great misfortune.'

Rodin turned his head abruptly, and looked at him with an air of uneasy questioning.

'Florine is dead of the cholera,' answered Father d'Aigrigny; 'and what is the worst,' added he, crumpling the note between his hands, 'before dying, the miserable creature confessed to Mdlle. de Cardoville that she long acted as a spy under the orders of your reverence.'

No doubt the death of Florine, and the confession she had made, crossed some of the plans of Rodin, for he uttered an inarticulate murmur, and his countenance expressed great vexation.

Passing to another note, Father d'Aigrigny continued: 'This relates to Marshal Simon, and is not absolutely bad, but still far from satisfactory, as it announces some amelioration in his position. We shall see if it merits belief, by information from another source.'

Rodin made a sign of impatience, to hasten Father d'Aigrigny to read the note, which he did as follows : ' " For some days, the mind of the marshal has appeared to be less sorrowful, anxious, and agitated. He lately passed two hours with his daughters, which had not been the case for some time before. The harsh countenance of the soldier Dagobert is becoming smoother—a sure sign of some amelioration in the condition of the marshal. Detected by their handwriting, the last anonymous letters were returned by Dagobert to the postman, without having been opened by the marshal. Some other method must be found to get them delivered." '

Looking at Rodin, Father d'Aigrigny said to him : ' Your reverence thinks with me that this note is not very satisfactory ?'

Rodin held down his head. One saw by the expression of his countenance how much he suffered by not being able to speak. Twice he put his hand to his throat, and looked at Father d'Aigrigny with anguish.

' Oh !' cried Father d'Aigrigny, angrily, when he had perused another note, ' for one lucky chance, to-day brings some very black ones.'

At these words, turning hastily to Father d'Aigrigny, and extending his trembling hands, Rodin questioned him with look and gesture. The cardinal, sharing his uneasiness, exclaimed : ' What do you learn by this note, my dear father ?'

' We thought the residence of M. Hardy in our house completely unknown,' replied Father d'Aigrigny, ' but we now fear that Agricola Baudoin has discovered the retreat of his old master, and that he has even communicated with him by letter, through a servant of the house. So,' added the reverend father, angrily, ' during the three days that I have not been able to visit the pavilion, one of my servants must have been bought over. There is one of them, a man blind of one eye, whom I have always suspected—the wretch ! But no ; I will not yet believe this treachery. The consequences would be too deplorable ; for I know how matters stand, and that such a correspondence might ruin everything By awaking in M. Hardy memories with difficulty laid asleep, they might destroy in a single day all that has been done since he inhabits our house. Luckily, this note contains only doubts and fears ; my other information will be more positive, and will not, I hope, confirm them.'

' My dear father,' said the cardinal, 'do not despair. The Lord will not abandon the good cause !'

Father d'Aigrigny seemed very little consoled by this assurance. He remained still and thoughtful, whilst Rodin writhed his head in a paroxysm of mute rage, as he reflected on this new check.

' Let us turn to the last note,' said Father d'Aigrigny, after a moment of thoughtful silence. ' I have so much confidence in the person who sends it, that I cannot doubt the correctness of the information it contains. May it contradict the others !'

In order not to break the chain of facts contained in this last note, which was to have so startling an effect on the actors in this scene, we shall leave it to the reader's imagination to supply the exclamations of surprise, hate, rage and fear of Father d'Aigrigny, and the terrific pantomime of Rodin, during the perusal of this formidable document, the result of the observations of a faithful and secret agent of the reverend fathers. Comparing this note with the other information received, the results appeared more distressing to the reverend fathers. Thus Gabriel had long and frequent conferences with Adrienne, who before was unknown to him. Agricola Baudoin had opened a communication with Francis Hardy, and the officers of justice were on the track of the authors and instigators of the riot which had led to the burning of the factory of Baron Tripeaud's rival. It seemed almost certain that Mdlle. de Cardoville had had an interview with Prince Djalma.

This combination of facts showed that, faithful to the threats she had uttered to Rodin, when she had unmasked the double perfidy of the reverend father, Mdlle. de Cardoville was actively engaged in uniting the scattered members of her family, to form a league against those dangerous enemies, whose detestable projects, once unveiled and boldly encountered, could hardly have a chance of success. The reader will now understand the tremendous effect of this note on Father d'Aigrigny and Rodin—on Rodin, stretched powerless on a bed of pain at the moment when the scaffolding, raised with so much labour, seemed to be tumbling around him.

CHAPTER XXIX.

THE OPERATION.

WE have given up the attempt to paint the countenance, attitude, and gesticulation of Rodin during the reading of this note, which seemed to ruin all his most cherished hopes. Everything was failing at once, at the moment when only superhuman trust in the success of his plans could give him sufficient energy to strive against mortal sickness. A single, absorbing thought had agitated him even to delirium : What progress, during his illness, had been made in this immense affair ? He had first heard a good piece of news, the death of Jacques Rennepont ; but now the advantages of this decease, which reduced the number of the heirs from seven to six, were entirely lost. To what purpose would be this death, if the other members of the family, dispersed and persecuted with such infernal perseverance, were to unite and discover the enemies who had so long aimed at them in darkness ? If all those wounded hearts were to console, enlighten, support each other, their cause would be gained, and the inheritance rescued from the reverend fathers. What was to be done ?

Strange power of the human will !—Rodin had one foot in the grave ; he was almost at the last gasp ; his voice had failed him. And yet that obstinate nature, so full of energy and resources, did not despair. Let but a miracle restore his health, and that firm confidence in the success of his projects, which has given him power to struggle against disease, tells him that he could yet save all—but then he must have health and life ! Health ! life ! His physician does not know if he will survive the shock —if he can bear the pain—of a terrible operation. Health ! life ! and just now Rodin heard talk of the solemn funeral they had prepared for him. And yet—health, life, he will have them. Yes ; he has willed to live— and he has lived—why should he not live longer? He will live—because he has willed it !

All that we have just written passed through Rodin's mind in a second. His features, convulsed by the mental torment he endured, must have assumed a very strange expression, for Father d'Aigrigny and the cardinal looked at him in silent consternation. Once resolved to live, and to sustain a desperate struggle with the Rennepont family, Rodin acted in consequence. For a few moments Father d'Aigrigny and the prelate believed themselves under the influence of a dream. By an effort of unparalleled energy, and as if moved by hidden mechanism, Rodin sprang from the bed, dragging the sheet with him, and trailing it, like a shroud, behind his livid and flesh-less body. The room was cold ; the face of the Jesuit was bathed in sweat ; his naked and bony feet left their moist print upon the stones.

'What are you doing? It is death!' cried Father d'Aigrigny, rushing towards Rodin, to force him to lie down again.

But the latter, extending one of his skeleton arms, as hard as iron, pushed aside Father d'Aigrigny with inconceivable vigour, considering the state of exhaustion in which he had so long been.

'He has the strength of a man in a fit of epilepsy,' said Father d'Aigrigny, recovering his balance.

With a steady step Rodin advanced to the desk on which Dr. Baleinier daily wrote his prescriptions. Seating himself before it, the Jesuit took pen and paper, and began to write in a firm hand. His calm, slow, and sure movements had in them something of the deliberateness remarked in somnambulists. Mute and motionless, hardly knowing whether they dreamed or not, the cardinal and Father d'Aigrigny remained staring at the incredible coolness of Rodin, who, half-naked, continued to write with perfect tranquillity.

'But, father,' said the Abbé d'Aigrigny, advancing towards him, 'this is madness!'

Rodin shrugged his shoulders, stopped him with a gesture, and made him a sign to read what he had just written.

The reverend father expected to see the ravings of a diseased brain ; but he took the note, whilst Rodin commenced another.

'My lord,' exclaimed Father d'Aigrigny, 'read this!'

The cardinal read the paper, and returning it to the reverend father with equal amazement, added : 'It is full of reason, ability, and resources. We shall thus be able to neutralise the dangerous combination of Abbé Gabriel and Mdlle. de Cardoville, who appear to be the most formidable leaders of the coalition.'

'It is really miraculous,' said Father d'Aigrigny.

'Oh, my dear father!' whispered the cardinal, shaking his head ; 'what a pity that we are the only witnesses of this scene! What an excellent MIRACLE we could have made of it! In one sense, it is another Raising of Lazarus!'

'What an idea, my lord!' answered Father d'Aigrigny, in a low voice. 'It is perfect—and we must not give it up——'

This innocent little plot was interrupted by Rodin, who, turning his head, made a sign to Father d'Aigrigny to approach, and delivered to him another sheet, with this note attached : 'To be executed within an hour.'

Having rapidly perused the paper, Father d'Aigrigny exclaimed : 'Right ! I had not thought of that. Instead of being fatal, the correspondence between Agricola and M. Hardy may thus have the best results. Really,' added the reverend father in a low voice to the prelate, while Rodin continued to write, 'I am quite confounded. I read—I see—and yet I can hardly believe my eyes. Just before, exhausted and dying—and now with his mind as clear and penetrating as ever. Can this be one of the phenomena of somnambulism, in which the mind alone governs and sustains the body?'

Suddenly the door opened, and Dr. Baleinier entered the room. At sight of Rodin, seated half-naked at the desk, with his feet upon the cold stones, the doctor exclaimed, in a tone of reproach and alarm : 'But, my lord—but, father—it is murder to let the unhappy man do this!—If he is delirious from fever, he must have the strait-waistcoat, and be tied down in bed.'

So saying, Dr. Baleinier hastily approached Rodin, and took him by the arm. Instead of finding the skin dry and chilly, as he expected, he found it flexible, almost damp. Struck with surprise, the doctor sought to feel the pulse of the left hand, which Rodin resigned to him, whilst he continued working with the right.

'What a prodigy !' cried the doctor, as he counted Rodin's pulse ; 'for a week past, and even this morning, the pulse has been abrupt, intermittent, almost insensible, and now it is firm, regular—I am really puzzled—what then has happened ? I can hardly believe what I see,' added the doctor, turning towards Father d'Aigrigny and the cardinal.

'The reverend father, who had first lost his voice, was next seized with such furious and violent despair, caused by the receipt of bad news,' answered Father d'Aigrigny, 'that we feared a moment for his life ; while now, on the contrary, the reverend father has gained sufficient strength to go to his desk, and write for some minutes, with a clearness of argument and expression, which has confounded both the cardinal and myself.'

'There is no longer any doubt of it,' cried the doctor. 'The violent despair has caused a degree of emotion, which will admirably prepare the reactive crisis, that I am now almost certain of producing by the operation.'

'You persist in the operation?' whispered Father d'Aigrigny, whilst Rodin continued to write.

'I might have hesitated this morning ; but, disposed as he now is for it, I must profit by the moment of excitement, which will be followed by greater depression.'

'Then, without the operation——' said the cardinal.

'This fortunate and unexpected crisis will soon be over, and the reaction may kill him, my lord.'

'Have you informed him of the serious nature of the operation ?'

'Pretty nearly, my lord.'

'But it is time to bring him to the point.'

'That is what I will do, my lord,' said Dr. Baleinier ; and approaching Rodin, who continued to write, he thus addressed him, in a firm voice : 'My reverend father, do you wish to be up and well in a week ?'

Rodin nodded, full of confidence, as much as to say : 'I am up already.'

'Do not deceive yourself,' replied the doctor. 'This crisis is excellent, but it will not last, and if we would profit by it, we must proceed with the operation of which I have spoken to you—or, I tell you plainly, I answer for nothing after such a shock.'

Rodin was the more struck with these words, as, half an hour ago, he had experienced the short duration of the improvement occasioned by Father d'Aigrigny's good news, and as already he felt increased oppression on the chest.

Dr. Baleinier, wishing to decide him, added : 'In a word, father, will you live or die ?'

Rodin wrote rapidly this answer, which he gave to the doctor : 'To live, I would let you cut me limb from limb. I am ready for anything.' And he made a movement to rise.

'I must tell you, reverend father, so as not to take you by surprise,' added Dr. Baleinier, 'that this operation is cruelly painful.'

Rodin shrugged his shoulders, and wrote with a firm hand : 'Leave me my head ; you may take all the rest.'

The doctor read these words aloud, and the cardinal and Father d'Aigrigny looked at each other in admiration of this dauntless courage.

'Reverend father,' said Dr. Baleinier, 'you must lie down.'

Rodin wrote : 'Get everything ready. I have still some orders to write. Let me know when it is time.'

Then folding up a paper, which he had sealed with a wafer, Rodin gave these words to Father d'Aigrigny : 'Send this note instantly to the agent who addressed the anonymous letters to Marshal Simon.'

'Instantly, reverend father,' replied the abbé ; 'I will employ a sure messenger.'

'Reverend father,' said Baleinier to Rodin, 'since you *must* write, lie down in bed, and write there, during our little preparations.'

Rodin made an affirmative gesture, and rose. But already the prognostics of the doctor were realised. The Jesuit could hardly remain standing for a second ; he fell back into a chair, and looked at Dr. Baleinier with anguish, whilst his breathing became more and more difficult.

The doctor said to him : 'Do not be uneasy. But we must make haste. Lean upon me and Father d'Aigrigny.'

Aided by these two supporters, Rodin was able to regain the bed. Once there, he made signs that they should bring him pen, ink, and paper. Then he continued to write upon his knees, pausing from time to time, to breathe with great difficulty.

'Reverend father,' said Baleinier to D'Aigrigny, 'are you capable of acting as one of my assistants in the operation ? Have you that sort of courage ?'

'No,' said the reverend father ; 'in the army, I could never assist at an amputation. The sight of blood is too much for me.'

'There will be no blood,' said the doctor, 'but it will be worse. Please send me three of our reverend fathers to assist me, and ask M. Rousselet to bring in the apparatus.'

Father d'Aigrigny went out. The prelate approached the doctor, and whispered, pointing to Rodin : 'Is he out of danger ?'

'If he stands the operation—yes, my lord.'

'Are you sure that he will stand it ?'

'To him I should say, "yes," to you, "I hope so."'

'And were he to die, would there be time to administer the sacraments in public, with a certain pomp, which always causes some little delay ?'

'His dying may continue, my lord—a quarter of an hour.'

'It is short, but we must be satisfied with that,' said the prelate.

And, going to one of the windows, he began to tap with his fingers on the glass, while he thought of the illumination effects, in the event of Rodin's lying-in-state. At this moment, Rousselet entered, with a large square box under his arm. He placed it on the drawers, and began to arrange his apparatus.

'How many have you prepared ?' said the doctor.——'Six, sir.'

'Four will do, but it is well to be fully provided. The cotton is not too thick ?'——'Look, sir.'

'Very good.'——'And how is the reverend father ?' asked the pupil.

'Humph !' answered the doctor, in a whisper. 'The chest is terribly clogged, the respiration hissing, the voice gone—still there is a change.'

'All my fear is, sir, that the reverend father will not be able to stand the dreadful pain.'

'It is another chance ; but, under the circumstances, we must risk all. Come, my dear boy, light the taper ; I hear our assistants.'

Just then Father d'Aigrigny entered the room, accompanied by the three Jesuits, who, in the morning, had walked in the garden. The two old men, with their rosy cheeks, and the young one, with the ascetic countenance, all three dressed in black, with their square caps and white bands, appeared perfectly ready to assist Dr. Baleinier in his formidable operation.

CHAPTER XXX.

THE TORTURE.

' Reverend fathers,' said Dr. Baleinier, graciously, to the three, 'I thank you for your kind aid. What you have to do is very simple, and, by the blessing of heaven, this operation will save the life of our dear Father Rodin.'

The three black-gowns cast up their eyes piously, and then bowed altogether, like one man. Rodin, indifferent to what was passing around him, never ceased an instant to write or reflect. Nevertheless, in spite of his apparent calmness, he felt such difficulty in breathing, that more than once Dr. Baleinier had turned round uneasily, as he heard the stifled rattling in the throat of the sick man. Making a sign to his pupil, the doctor approached Rodin, and said to him : 'Come, reverend father ; this is the important moment. Courage !'

No sign of alarm was expressed in the Jesuit's countenance. His features remained impassible as those of a corpse. Only, his little reptile-eyes sparkled still more brightly in their dark cavities. For a moment, he looked round at the spectators of this scene ; then, taking his pen between his teeth, he folded and wafered another letter, placed it on the table beside the bed, and nodded to Dr. Baleinier, as if to say, ' I am ready.'

'You must take off your flannel waistcoat, and your shirt, father.' Rodin hesitated an instant, and the doctor resumed : ' It is absolutely necessary, father.'

Aided by Baleinier, Rodin obeyed, whilst the doctor added, no doubt to spare his modesty : ' We shall only require the chest, right and left, my dear father.'

And now Rodin, stretched upon his back, with his dirty night-cap still on his head, exposed the upper part of a livid trunk, or rather, the bony cage of a skeleton, for the shadows of the ribs and cartilages encircled the skin with deep, black lines. As for the arms, they resembled bones twisted with cord, and covered with tanned parchment.

' Come, M. Rousselet, the apparatus !' said Baleinier.

Then addressing the three Jesuits, he added : ' Please draw near, gentlemen ; what you have to do is very simple, as you will see.'

It was indeed very simple. The doctor gave to each of his four assistants a sort of little steel tripod about two inches in diameter and three in height; the circular centre of this tripod was filled with cotton ; the instrument was held in the left hand by means of a wooden handle. In the right hand, each assistant held a small tin tube about eighteen inches long ; at one end was a mouthpiece to receive the lips of the operator, and the other spread out so as to form a cover to the little tripod. These preparations had nothing alarming in them. Father d'Aigrigny and the prelate, who looked on from a little distance, could not understand how this operation should be so painful. They soon understood it.

Dr. Baleinier, having thus provided his four assistants, made them approach Rodin, whose bed had been rolled into the middle of the room. Two of them were placed on one side, two on the other.

' Now, gentlemen,' said Dr. Baleinier, ' set light to the cotton ; place the lighted part on the skin of his reverence, by means of the tripod which contains the wick ; cover the tripod with the broad part of the tube, and then blow through the other end to keep up the fire. It is very simple, as you see.'

It was, in fact, full of the most patriarchal and primitive ingenuity. Four lighted cotton wicks, so disposed as to burn very slowly, were applied to the two sides of Rodin's chest. This is vulgarly called the *moxa.* The trick is done, when the whole thickness of the skin has been burnt slowly through. It lasts seven or eight minutes. They say that an amputation is nothing to it. Rodin had watched the preparations with intrepid curiosity. But, at the first touch of the four fires, he writhed like a serpent, without being able to utter a cry. Even the expression of pain was denied him. The four assistants being disturbed by the sudden start of Rodin, it was necessary to begin again.

'Courage, my dear father ! offer these sufferings to the Lord !' said Dr. Baleinier, in a sanctified tone. 'I told you the operation would be very painful ; but then it is salutary in proportion. Come ; you that have shown such decisive resolution, do not fail at the last moment !'

Rodin had closed his eyes, conquered by the first agony of pain. He now opened them, and looked at the doctor as if ashamed of such weakness. And yet on the sides of his chest were four large, bleeding wounds—so violent had been the first singe. As he again extended himself on the bed of torture, Rodin made a sign that he wished to write. The doctor gave him the pen, and he wrote as follows, by way of memorandum : 'It is better not to lose any time. Inform Baron Tripeaud of the warrant issued against Leonard, so that he may be on his guard.'

Having written this note, the Jesuit gave it to Dr. Baleinier, to hand it to Father d'Aigrigny, who was as much amazed as the doctor and the cardinal, at such extraordinary presence of mind in the midst of such horrible pain. Rodin, with his eyes fixed on the reverend father, seemed to wait with impatience for him to leave the room to execute his orders. Guessing the thought of Rodin, the doctor whispered Father d'Aigrigny, who went out.

'Come, reverend father,' said the doctor, 'we must begin again. This time, do not move.'

Rodin did not answer, but clasped his hands over his head, closed his eyes, and presented his chest. It was a strange, lugubrious, almost fantastic spectacle. The three priests, in their long black gowns, leaned over this body, which almost resembled a corpse, and blowing through their tubes into the chest of the patient, seemed as if pumping up his blood by some magic charm. A sickening odour of burnt flesh began to spread through the silent chamber, and each assistant heard a slight crackling beneath the smoking trivet ; it was the skin of Rodin giving way to the action of fire, and splitting open in four different parts of his chest. The sweat poured from his livid face, which it made to shine ; a few locks of his grey hair stood up stiff and moist from his temples. Sometimes the spasms were so violent, that the veins swelled on his stiffened arms, and were stretched like cords ready to break.

Enduring this frightful torture with as much intrepid resignation as the savage whose glory consists in despising pain, Rodin gathered his strength and courage from the hope—we had almost said the certainty—of life. Such was the make of this dauntless character, such the energy of this powerful mind, that, in the midst of indescribable torments, his one fixed idea never left him. During the rare intervals of suffering—for pain is equal even at this degree of intensity—Rodin still thought of the Rennepont inheritance, and calculated his chances, and combined his measures, feeling that he had not a minute to lose. Dr. Baleinier watched him with extreme attention, waiting for the effects of the reaction of pain upon the patient, who seemed already to breathe with less difficulty.

Suddenly Rodin placed his hand on his forehead, as if struck with some new idea, and, turning his head towards Dr. Baleinier, made a sign to him to suspend the operation,

'I must tell you, reverend father,' answered the doctor, 'that it is not half finished, and, if we leave off, the renewal will be more painful——'

Rodin made a sign that he did not care, and that he wanted to write.

'Gentlemen, stop a moment,' said Dr. Baleinier; 'keep down your moxas, but do not blow the fire.'

So the fire was to burn slowly, instead of fiercely, but still upon the skin of the patient. In spite of this pain, less intense, but still sharp and keen, Rodin, stretched upon his back, began to write, holding the paper above his head. On the first sheet he traced some alphabetic signs, part of a cypher known to himself alone. In the midst of the torture, a luminous idea had crossed his mind ; fearful of forgetting it amidst his sufferings, he now took note of it. On another paper he wrote the following, which was instantly delivered to Father d'Aigrigny : 'Send B. immediately to Faringhea, for the report of the last few days with regard to Djalma, and let B. bring it hither on the instant.' Father d'Aigrigny went out to execute this new order. The cardinal approached a little nearer to the scene of the operation, for, in spite of the bad odour of the room, he took delight in seeing the Jesuit half roasted, having long cherished against him the rancour of an Italian and a priest.

'Come, reverend father,' said the doctor to Rodin, 'continue to be admirably courageous, and your chest will free itself. You have still a bitter moment to go through—and then I have good hope.'

The patient resumed his former position. The moment Father d'Aigrigny returned, Rodin questioned him with a look, to which the reverend father replied by a nod. At a sign from the doctor, the four assistants began to blow through the tubes with all their might. This increase of torture was so horrible, that, in spite of his self control, Rodin gnashed his teeth, started convulsively, and so expanded his palpitating chest, that, after a violent spasm, there rose from his throat and lungs a scream of terrific pain—but it was free, loud, sonorous.

'The chest is free !' cried the doctor, in triumph. 'The lungs have play —the voice returns—he is saved !—Blow, gentlemen, blow ; and, reverend father, cry out as much as you please ; I shall be delighted to hear you, for it will give you relief. Courage ! I answer for the result. It is a wonderful cure. I will publish it by sound of trumpet.'

'Allow me, doctor,' whispered Father d'Aigrigny, as he approached Dr. Baleinier ; 'the cardinal can witness, that I claimed beforehand the publication of this affair—as a miraculous fact.'

'Let it be miraculous then,' answered Dr. Baleinier, disappointed—for he set some value on his own work.

On hearing he was saved, Rodin, though his sufferings were perhaps worse than ever, for the fire had now pierced the scarf-skin, assumed almost an infernal beauty. Through the painful contraction of his features shone the pride of savage triumph ; the monster felt that he was becoming once more strong and powerful, and he seemed conscious of the evils that his fatal resurrection was to cause. And so, still writhing beneath the flames, he pronounced these words, the first that struggled from his chest : 'I told you I should live !'

'You told us true,' cried the doctor, feeling his pulse ; 'the circulation is now full and regular, the lungs are free. The reaction is complete. You are saved.'

At this moment, the last shreds of cotton had burnt out. The trivets were withdrawn, and on the skeleton trunk of Rodin were seen four large round blisters. The skin still smoked, and the raw flesh was visible beneath. In one of his sudden movements, a lamp had been misplaced, and one of these burns was larger than the others, presenting as it were to the eye a double circle. Rodin looked down upon his wounds. After some seconds of silent contemplation, a strange smile curled his lips. Without changing his position, he glanced at Father d'Aigrigny with an expression impossible to describe, and said to him, as he slowly counted the wounds, touching them with his flat and dirty nail : 'Father d'Aigrigny, what an omen!— Look here ! one Rennepont—two Renneponts—three Renneponts—four Renneponts—where is then the fifth !—Ah ! here—-this wound will count for two. They are twins.'* And he emitted a little dry, bitter laugh. Father d'Aigrigny, the cardinal, and Dr. Baleinier, alone understood the sense of these mysterious and fatal words, which Rodin soon completed by a terrible allusion, as he exclaimed, with prophetic voice, and almost inspired air : 'Yes, I say it. The impious race will be reduced to ashes, like the fragments of this poor flesh. I say it, and it will be so. I said I would live—and I do live !'

CHAPTER XXXI.

VICE AND VIRTUE.

TWO days have elapsed since Rodin was miraculously restored to life. The reader will not have forgotten the house in the Rue Clovis, where the reverend father had an apartment, and where also was the lodging of Philemon, inhabited by Rose-Pompon. It is about three o'clock in the afternoon. A bright ray of light, penetrating through a round hole in the door of Mother Arsène's subterraneous shop, forms a striking contrast with the darkness of this cavern. The ray streams full upon a melancholy object. In the midst of fagots and faded vegetables, and close to a great heap of charcoal, stands a wretched bed ; beneath the sheet, which covers it, can be traced the stiff and angular proportions of a corpse. It is the body of Mother Arsène herself, who died two days before, of the cholera. The burials have been so numerous, that there has been no time to remove her remains. The Rue Clovis is almost deserted. A mournful silence reigns without, often broken by the sharp whistling of the north wind. Between the squalls, one hears a sort of pattering. It is the noise of the large rats, running to and fro across the heap of charcoal.

Suddenly, another sound is heard, and these unclean animals fly to hide themselves in their holes. Some one is trying to force open the door, which communicates between the shop and the passage. It offers but little resistance, and, in a few seconds, the worn-out lock gives way, and a woman enters. For a short time she stands motionless in the obscurity of the damp and icy cave. After a minute's hesitation, the woman advances, and the ray of light illumines the features of the Bacchanal Queen. Slowly, she approached the funeral couch. Since the death of Jacques, the alteration in the countenance of Cephyse had gone on increasing. Fearfully pale, with her fine black hair in disorder, her legs and feet naked, she was barely covered with an old patched petticoat and a very ragged handkerchief.

When she came near the bed, she cast a glance of almost savage assurance at the shroud. Suddenly she drew back, with a low cry of involuntary terror. The sheet moved with a rapid undulation, extending from the feet to the head of the corpse. But soon the sight of a rat, flying along

* Jacques Rennepont being dead, and Gabriel out of the field, in consequence of his donation, there remained only five persons of the family—Rose and Blanche, Djalma, Adrienne, and Hardy.

the side of the worm-eaten bedstead, explained the movement of the shroud. Recovering from her fright, Cephyse began to look for several things, and collected them in haste, as though she dreaded being surprised in the miserable shop. First, she seized a basket, and filled it with charcoal; then, looking from side to side, she discovered in a corner an earthen pot, which she took with a burst of ominous joy.

'It is not all, it is not all,' said Cephyse, as she continued to search with an unquiet air.

At last she perceived near the stove a little tin box, containing flint, steel, and matches. She placed these articles on the top of the basket, and took it in one hand, and the earthen pot in the other. As she passed near the corpse of the poor charcoal-dealer, Cephyse said, with a strange smile: 'I rob you, poor Mother Arsène, but my theft will not do me much good.'

Cephyse left the shop, reclosed the door as well as she could, went up the passage, and crossed the little courtyard which separated the front of the building from that part in which Rodin had lodged. With the exception of the windows of Philemon's apartment, where Rose-Pompon had so often sat perched like a bird, warbling Béranger, the other windows of the house were open. There had been deaths on the first and second floors, and, like many others, they were waiting for the cart piled up with coffins.

The Bacchanal Queen gained the stairs, which led to the chambers formerly occupied by Rodin. Arrived at the landing-place, she ascended another ruinous staircase, steep as a ladder, and with nothing but an old rope for a rail. She at length reached the half-rotten door of a garret, situated in the roof. The house was in such a state of dilapidation, that in many places the roof gave admission to the rain, and allowed it to penetrate into this cell, which was not above ten feet square, and lighted by an attic window. All the furniture consisted of an old straw mattress, laid upon the ground, with the straw peeping out from a rent in its ticking; a small earthenware pitcher, with the spout broken, and containing a little water, stood by the side of this couch. Dressed in rags, Mother Bunch was seated on the side of the mattress, with her elbows on her knees, and her face concealed in her thin, white hands. When Cephyse entered the room, the adopted sister of Agricola raised her head; her pale, mild face seemed thinner than ever, hollow with suffering, grief, misery; her eyes, red with weeping, were fixed on her sister with an expression of mournful tenderness.

'I have what we want, sister,' said Cephyse, in a low, deep voice; 'in this basket there is wherewith to finish our misery.'

Then, showing to Mother Bunch the articles she had just placed on the floor, she added: 'For the first time in my life, I have been a thief. It made me ashamed and frightened; I was never intended for that or worse. It is a pity,' added she, with a sardonic smile.

After a moment's silence, the hunchback said to her sister, in a heart-rending tone: 'Cephyse—my dear Cephyse—are you quite determined to die?'

'How should I hesitate?' answered Cephyse, in a firm voice. 'Come, sister, let us once more make our reckoning. If even I could forget my shame, and Jacques' contempt in his last moments, what would remain to me? Two courses only: first, to be honest, and work for my living. But you know that, in spite of the best will in the world, work will often fail, as it has failed for the last few days, and, even when I got it, I would have to live on four to five francs a week. Live? that is to say, die by inches. I know that already, and I prefer dying at once. The other course would be to live a life of infamy—and that I will not do. Frankly, sister, between frightful misery, infamy, or death, can the choice be doubtful? Answer me!'

Then, without giving Mother Bunch time to speak, Cephyse added, in an abrupt tone : "Besides, what is the good of discussing it ? I have made up my mind, and nothing shall prevent my purpose, since all that you, dear sister, could obtain from me, was a delay of a few days, to see if the cholera would not save us the trouble. To please you, I consented ; the cholera has come, killed every one else in the house, but left us. You see, it is better to do one's own business,' added she, again smiling bitterly. Then she resumed : ' Besides, dear sister, you also wish to finish with life.'

' It is true, Cephyse,' answered the sempstress, who seemed very much depressed ; ' but alone—one has only to answer for one's self—and to die with you,' added she, shuddering, ' appears like being an accomplice in your death.'

' Do you wish, then, to make an end of it, I in one place, you in another ? —that would be agreeable !' said Cephyse, displaying in that terrible moment the sort of bitter and despairing irony which is more frequent than may be imagined in the midst of mortal anguish.

' Oh, no, no !' said the other, in alarm, ' not alone—I will not die alone !'

' Do you not see, dear sister, we are right not to part ? And yet,' added Cephyse, in a voice of emotion, ' my heart almost breaks sometimes, to think that you will die like me.'

' How selfish !' said the hunchback, with a faint smile. ' What reasons have I to love life ? What void shall I leave behind me ?'

' But you are a martyr, sister,' resumed Cephyse. ' The priests talk of saints ! Is there one of them so good as you ? And yet you are about to die like me, who have always been idle, careless, sinful—while you were so hard-working, so devoted to all who suffered. What should I say ? You were an angel on the earth ; and yet you will die like me, who have fallen as low as a woman can fall,' added the unfortunate, casting down her eyes.

' It is strange,' answered Mother Bunch, thoughtfully. ' Starting from the same point, we have followed different roads, and yet we have reached the same goal—disgust of life. For you, my poor sister, but a few days ago, life was so fair, so full of pleasure and of youth ; and now it is equally heavy with us both. After all, I have followed to the end what was my duty,' added she, mildly. ' Agricola no longer needs me. He is married ; he loves, and is beloved ; his happiness is secured. Mdlle. de Cardoville wants for nothing. Fair, rich, prosperous—what could a poor creature like myself do for her ? Those who have been kind to me are happy. What prevents my going now to my rest ? I am so weary !'

' Poor sister !' said Cephyse, with touching emotion, which seemed to expand her contracted features ; ' when I think that, without informing me, and in spite of your resolution never to see that generous young lady, who protected you, you yet had the courage to drag yourself to her house, dying with fatigue and want, to try to interest her in my fate—yes, dying, for your strength failed on the Champs-Elysées.'

' And when I was able to reach the mansion, Mdlle. de Cardoville was unfortunately absent—very unfortunately !' repeated the hunchback, as she looked at Cephyse with anguish ; ' for the next day, seeing that our last resource had failed us, thinking more of me than of yourself, and determined at any price to procure us bread——'

She could not finish. She buried her face in her hands, and shuddered.

' Well, I did as so many other hapless women have done when work fails or wages do not suffice, and hunger becomes too pressing,' replied Cephyse in a broken voice ; ' only that, unlike so many others, instead of living on my shame, I shall die of it.'

' Alas ! this terrible shame, which kills you, my poor Cephyse, because you have a heart, would have been averted, had I seen Mdlle. de Cardoville, or had she but answered the letter which I asked leave to write to her at the porter's lodge. But her silence proves to me that she is justly hurt at my abrupt departure from her house. I can understand it ; she believes me guilty of the blackest ingratitude—for she must have been greatly offended not to have deigned to answer me—and therefore I had not the courage to write a second time. It would have been useless, I am sure ; for, good and just as she is, her refusals are inexorable when she believes them deserved. And besides, for what good ? It was too late ; you had resolved to die !'

'Oh, yes, quite resolved ; for my infamy was gnawing at my heart. Jacques had died in my arms despising me ; and I loved him—mark me, sister,' added Cephyse, with passionate enthusiasm, ' I loved him as we love only once in life !'

'Let our fate be accomplished, then !' said Mother Bunch, with a pensive air.

'But you have never told me, sister, the cause of your departure from Mdlle. de Cardoville's,' resumed Cephyse, after a moment's silence.

'It will be the only secret that I shall take with me, dear Cephyse,' said the other, casting down her eyes. And she thought, with bitter joy, that she would soon be delivered from the fear which had poisoned the last days of her sad life—the fear of meeting Agricola, informed of the fatal and ridiculous love she felt for him.

For, it must be said, this fatal and despairing love was one of the causes of the suicide of the unfortunate creature. Since the disappearance of her journal, she believed that the blacksmith knew the melancholy secret contained in its sad pages. She doubted not the generosity and good heart of Agricola ; but she had such doubts of herself, she was so ashamed of this passion, however pure and noble, that, even in the extremity to which Cephyse and herself were reduced—wanting work, wanting bread—no power on earth could have induced her to meet Agricola, in an attempt to ask him for assistance. Doubtless, she would have taken another view of the subject if her mind had not been obscured by that sort of dizziness to which the firmest characters are exposed when their misfortunes surpass all bounds. Misery, hunger, the influence, almost contagious in such a moment, of the suicidal ideas of Cephyse, and weariness of a life so long devoted to pain and mortification, gave the last blow to the sewing-girl's reason. After long struggling against the fatal design of her sister, the poor, dejected, broken-hearted creature finished by determining to share Cephyse's fate, and seek in death the end of so many evils.

'Of what are you thinking, sister ?' said Cephyse, astonished at the long silence. The other replied, trembling : 'I think of that which made me leave Mdlle. de Cardoville so abruptly, and appear so ungrateful in her eyes. May the fatality which drove me from her house have made no other victims ! may my devoted service, however obscure and powerless, never be missed by her, who extended her noble hand to the poor sempstress, and deigned to call me sister ! May she be happy—oh, ever happy !' said Mother Bunch, clasping her hands with the ardour of a sincere invocation.

'That is noble, sister—such a wish in such a moment !' said Cephyse.

'Oh,' said her sister, with energy, ' I loved, I admired that marvel of genius, and heart, and ideal beauty—I viewed her with pious respect—for never was the power of the Divinity revealed in a more adorable and purer creation. At least one of my last thoughts will have been of her.'

'Yes, you will have loved and respected your generous patroness to the last.'

'To the last !' said the poor girl, after a moment's silence. 'It is true—you are right—it will soon be the last !—in a few moments, all will be finished. See how calmly we can talk of that which frightens so many others !'

'Sister, we are calm because we are resolved.'

'Quite resolved, Cephyse ?' said the hunchback, casting once more a deep and penetrating glance upon her sister.

'Oh, yes, if you are only as determined as I am.'——'Be satisfied ; if I put off from day to day the final moment,' answered the sempstress, 'it was because I wished to give you time to reflect. As for me——' She did not finish, but she shook her head with an air of the utmost despondency.

'Well, sister, let us kiss each other,' said Cephyse ; 'and, courage !'

The hunchback rose, and threw herself into her sister's arms. They held one another fast in a long embrace. There followed a few seconds of deep and solemn silence, only interrupted by the sobs of the sisters, for now they had begun to weep.

'Oh, heaven ! to love each other so, and to part for ever !' said Cephyse. 'It is a cruel fate.'

'To part ?' cried Mother Bunch, and her pale, mild countenance, bathed in tears, was suddenly illumined with a ray of divine hope ; 'to part, sister ? oh, no ! What makes me so calm is the deep and certain expectation, which I feel here at my heart, of that better world where a better life awaits us. God, so great, so merciful, so prodigal of good, cannot destine His creatures to be for ever miserable. Selfish men may pervert His benevolent designs, and reduce their brethren to a state of suffering and despair. Let us pity the wicked and leave them ! Come up on high, sister ; men are nothing there, where God is all. We shall do well there. Let us depart, for it is late.'

So saying, she pointed to the ruddy beams of the setting sun, which began to shine upon the window.

Carried away by the religious enthusiasm of her sister, whose countenance, transfigured, as it were, by the hope of an approaching deliverance, gleamed brightly in the reflected sunset, Cephyse took her hands, and, looking at her with deep emotion, exclaimed, 'Oh, sister ! how beautiful you look now !'

'Then my beauty comes rather late in the day,' said Mother Bunch, with a sad smile.——'No, sister ; for you appear so happy, that the last scruples I had upon your account are quite gone.'

'Then let us make haste,' said the hunchback, as she pointed to the chafing-dish. ——'Be satisfied, sister—it will not be long,' said Cephyse. And she took the chafing-dish full of charcoal, which she had placed in a corner of the garret, and brought it out into the middle of the room.

'Do you know how to manage it ?' asked the sewing-girl, approaching.

'Oh ! it is very simple,' answered Cephyse ; 'we have only to close door and window, and light the charcoal.'

'Yes, sister ; but I think I have heard that every opening must be well stopped, so as to admit no current of air.'

'You are right, and the door shuts so badly.'

'And look at the holes in the roof.'——'What is to be done, sister ?'

'I will tell you,' said Mother Bunch. 'The straw of our mattress, well twisted, will answer every purpose.'

'Certainly,' replied Cephyse. 'We will keep a little to light our fire, and with the rest we will stop up all the crevices in the roof, and make filling for our doors and windows.'

Then, smiling with that bitter irony, so frequent, we repeat, in the most gloomy moments, Cephyse added, ' I say, sister, weather-boards at our doors and windows, to prevent the air from getting in—what a luxury ! we are as delicate as rich people.'

' At such a time, we may as well try to make ourselves a little comfortable,' said Mother Bunch, trying to jest like the Bacchanal Queen.

And with incredible coolness, the two began to twist the straw into lengths of braid, small enough to be stuffed into the cracks of the door, and also constructed large plugs, destined to stop up the crevices in the roof. While this mournful occupation lasted, there was no departure from the calm and sad resignation of the two unfortunate creatures.

CHAPTER XXXII.

SUICIDE.

CEPHYSE and her sister continued with calmness the preparations for their death.

Alas ! how many poor young girls, like these sisters, have been, and still will be, fatally driven to seek in suicide a refuge from despair, from infamy, or from a too miserable existence ! And upon society will rest the terrible responsibility of these sad deaths, so long as thousands of human creatures, unable to live upon the mockery of wages granted to their labour, have to choose between these three gulfs of shame and woe : a life of enervating toil and mortal privations, causes of premature death ; prostitution, which kills also, but slowly—by contempt, brutality, and uncleanness ; suicide— which kills at once.

In a few minutes, the two sisters had constructed, with the straw of their couch, the caulkings necessary to intercept the air, and to render suffocation more expeditious and certain.

The hunchback said to her sister, ' You are the taller, Cephyse, and must look to the ceiling ; I will take care of the window and door.'

' Be satisfied, sister ; I shall have finished before you,' answered Cephyse.

And the two began carefully to stop up every crevice through which a current of air could penetrate into the ruined garret. Thanks to her tall stature, Cephyse was able to reach the holes in the roof, and to close them up entirely. When they had finished this sad work, the sisters again approached, and looked at each other in silence.

The fatal moment drew near ; their faces, though still calm, seemed slightly agitated by that strange excitement which always accompanies a double suicide.

' Now,' said Mother Bunch, ' now for the fire !'

She knelt down before the little chafing-dish, filled with charcoal. But Cephyse took hold of her under the arm, and obliged her to rise again, saying to her, ' Let me light the fire—that is my business.'

' But, Cephyse——'

' You know, poor sister, that the smell of charcoal gives you the headache !'

At the simplicity of this speech, for the Bacchanal Queen had spoken seriously, the sisters could not forbear smiling sadly.

' Never mind,' resumed Cephyse ; ' why suffer more and sooner than is necessary ?'

Then, pointing to the mattress, which still contained a little straw, Cephyse added, ' Lie down there, good little sister ; when our fire is alight, I will come and sit down by you.'

'Do not be long, Cephyse.'——'In five minutes it will be done.'

The tall building, which faced the street, was separated by a narrow court from that which contained the retreat of the two sisters, and was so much higher, that, when the sun had once disappeared behind its lofty roof, the garret soon became dark. The light, passing through the dirty panes of the small window, fell faintly on the blue and white patch-work of the old mattress, on which Mother Bunch was now stretched, covered with rags. Leaning on her left arm, with her chin resting in the palm of her hand, she looked after her sister with an expression of heart-rending grief. Cephyse, kneeling over the chafing-dish, with her face close to the black charcoal, above which already played a little blueish flame, exerted herself to blow the newly-kindled fire, which was reflected on the pale countenance of the unhappy girl.

The silence was deep. No sound was heard but the panting breath of Cephyse, and, at intervals, the slight crackling of the charcoal, which began to burn, and already sent forth a faint, sickening vapour. Cephyse, seeing the fire completely lighted, and feeling already a little dizzy, rose from the ground, and said to her sister, as she approached her, 'It is done!'

'Sister,' answered Mother Bunch, kneeling on the mattress, whilst Cephyse remained standing, 'how shall we place ourselves? I should like to be near you to the last.'

'Stop!' said Cephyse, half executing the measures of which she spoke, 'I will sit on the mattress with my back against the wall. Now, little sister, you lie there. Lean your head upon my knees, and give me your hand. Are you comfortable so?'

'Yes—but I cannot see you.'——'That is better. It seems there is a moment—very short, it is true—in which one suffers a good deal. And,' added Cephyse, in a voice of emotion, 'it will be as well not to see each other suffer.'

'You are right, Cephyse.'——'Let me kiss that beautiful hair for the last time,' said Cephyse, as she pressed her lips to the silky locks which crowned the hunchback's pale and melancholy countenance, 'and then—we will remain very quiet.'

'Sister, your hand,' said the sewing-girl; 'for the last time, your hand—and then, as you say, we will move no more. We shall not have to wait long, I think, for I begin to feel dizzy. And you, sister?'

'Not yet,' replied Cephyse; 'I only perceive the smell of the charcoal.'

'Do you know where they will bury us?' said Mother Bunch, after a moment's silence.

'No. Why do you ask?'——'Because I should like it to be in Père-la-Chaise. I went there once with Agricola and his mother. What a fine view there is!—and then the trees, the flowers, the marble—do you know the dead are better lodged—than the living—and——'

'What is the matter, sister?' said Cephyse to her companion, who had stopped short, after speaking in a slow voice.

'I am giddy—my temples throb,' was the answer. 'How do you feel?'

'I only begin to be a little faint; it is strange—the effect is slower with me than you.'

'Oh! you see,' said Mother Bunch, trying to smile, 'I was always so forward. At school, do you remember, they said I was before the others. And now it happens again.'

'I hope soon to overtake you this time,' said Cephyse.

What astonished the sisters was quite natural. Though weakened by sorrow and misery, the Bacchanal Queen, with a constitution as robust as the other was frail and delicate, was necessarily longer than her sister in feeling the effects of the deleterious vapour. After a moment's silence, Cephyse resumed, as she laid her hand on the head she still held upon her knees, 'You say nothing, sister ! You suffer, is it not so?'

'No,' said Mother Bunch, in a weak voice ; 'my eyelids are heavy as lead —I am getting benumbed—I feel that I speak more slowly—but I have no acute pain. And you, sister?'

'Whilst you were speaking, I felt giddy—and now my temples throb violently.'——'As it was with me just now. One would think it was more painful and difficult to die !'

Then, after a moment's silence, the hunchback said suddenly to her sister, 'Do you think that Agricola will much regret me, and think of me for some time?'

'How can you ask?' said Cephyse, in a tone of reproach.——'You are right,' answered Mother Bunch, mildly ; 'there is a bad feeling in such a doubt—but if you knew——'

'What, sister?'——The other hesitated for an instant, and then said, dejectedly, 'Nothing.' Afterwards, she added, 'Fortunately, I die convinced that he will never miss me. He married a charming girl, who loves him, I am sure, and will make him perfectly happy.'

As she pronounced these last words, the speaker's voice grew fainter and fainter. Suddenly she started, and said to Cephyse, in a trembling, almost frightened tone, 'Sister !—hold me in your arms—I am afraid—everything looks dark—everything is turning round.' And the unfortunate girl, raising herself a little, hid her face in her sister's bosom, and threw her weak arms around her.

'Courage, sister !' said Cephyse, in a voice which was also growing faint, as she pressed her closer to her bosom ; 'it will soon be over.'

And Cephyse added, with a kind of envy, 'Oh! why does my sister's strength fail so much sooner than mine? I have still my perfect senses, and I suffer less than she does. Oh ! if I thought she would die first !—But, no —I will go and hold my face over the chafing-dish rather.'

At the movement Cephyse made to rise, a feeble pressure from her sister held her back. 'You suffer, my poor child !' said Cephyse, trembling.

'Oh, yes ! a good deal now—do not leave me !'——'And I scarcely at all,' said Cephyse, gazing wildly at the chafing-dish. 'Ah !' added she, with a kind of fatal joy ; 'now I begin to feel it—I choke—my head is ready to split.'

And indeed the destructive gas now filled the little chamber, from which it had, by degrees, driven all the air fit for respiration. The day was closing in, and the gloomy garret was only lighted by the reflection of the burning charcoal, which threw a red glare on the sisters, locked in each other's arms. Suddenly Mother Bunch made some slight convulsive movements, and pronounced these words in a failing voice : 'Agricola—Mademoiselle de Cardoville—Oh ! farewell !—Agricola—I——'

Then she murmured some unintelligible words ; the convulsive movements ceased, and her arms, which had been clasped round Cephyse, fell inert upon the mattress.

'Sister !' cried Cephyse, in alarm, as she raised Mother Bunch's head, to look at her face. 'Not already, sister !—And I ? and I?'

The sewing-girl's mild countenance was not paler than usual. Only her eyes, half-closed, seemed no longer to see anything, and a half-smile of mingled grief and goodness lingered an instant about her violet lips, from which stole the almost imperceptible breath—and then the mouth became motionless, and the face assumed a great serenity of expression.

'But you must not die before me !' cried Cephyse, in a heart-rending tone, as she covered with kisses the cold cheek. 'Wait for me, sister! wait for me!'

Mother Bunch did not answer. The head, which Cephyse let slip from her hands, fell back gently on the mattress.

'My God! It is not my fault, if we do not die together!' cried Cephyse in despair, as she knelt beside the couch, on which the other lay motionless.

'Dead!' she murmured in terror. 'Dead before me!—Perhaps it is, that I am the strongest. Ah! it begins—fortunately—like her, I see everything dark blue—I suffer—what happiness!—I can scarcely breathe. Sister?' she added, as she threw her arms round her loved one's neck; 'I am coming—I am here!'

At the same instant, the sound of footsteps and voices was heard from the staircase. Cephyse had still presence of mind enough to distinguish the sound. Stretched beside the body of her sister, she raised her head hastily.

The noise approached, and a voice was heard exclaiming, not far from the door: 'Good heavens! what a smell of fire!'

And, at the same instant, the door was violently shaken, and another voice exclaimed: 'Open! open!'

'They will come in—they will save me—and my sister is dead.—Oh, no! I will not have the baseness to survive her!'

Such was the last thought of Cephyse. Using what little strength she had left, she ran to the window and opened it—and, at the same instant that the half-broken door yielded to a vigorous effort from without, the unfortunate creature precipitated herself from that third story into the court below. Just then, Adrienne and Agricola appeared on the threshold of the chamber. In spite of the stifling odour of the charcoal, Mdlle. de Cardoville rushed into the garret, and, seeing the stove, she exclaimed; 'The unhappy girl has killed herself!'

'No, she has thrown herself from the window,' cried Agricola; for, at the moment of breaking open the door, he had seen a human form disappear in that direction, and he now ran to the window.

'Oh! this is frightful!' he exclaimed, with a cry of horror, as he put his hand before his eyes, and returned pale and terrified to Mdlle. de Cardoville.

But, misunderstanding the cause of his terror, Adrienne, who had just perceived Mother Bunch through the darkness, hastened to answer: 'No! she is here.'

And she pointed to the pale form stretched on the mattress, beside which Adrienne now threw herself on her knees. Grasping the hands of the poor sempstress, she found them as cold as ice. Laying her hand on her heart, she could not feel it beat. Yet, in a few seconds, as the fresh air rushed into the room from the door and window, Adrienne thought she remarked an almost imperceptible pulsation, and she exclaimed: 'Her heart beats! Run quickly for help! Luckily, I have my smelling bottle.'

'Yes, yes! help for her—and for the other too, if it is yet time!' cried the smith in despair, as he rushed down the stairs, leaving Mdlle. de Cardoville still kneeling by the side of the mattress.

CHAPTER XXXIII.

CONFESSIONS.

DURING the painful scene that we have just described, a lively emotion glowed in the countenance of Mdlle. de Cardoville, grown pale and thin with sorrow Her cheeks, once so full, were now slightly hollowed, whilst a faint line of transparent azure encircled those large black eyes, no longer so bright as formerly. But the charming lips, though contracted by painful anxiety, had retained their rich and velvet moisture. To attend more easily to Mother Bunch, Adrienne had thrown aside her bonnet, and the silky waves of her beautiful golden hair almost concealed her face as she bent over the mattress, rubbing the thin, ivory hands of the poor sempstress, completely called to life by the salubrious freshness of the air, and by the strong action of the salts which Adrienne carried in her smelling-bottle. Luckily, Mother Bunch had fainted, rather from emotion and weakness than from the effects of suffocation, the senses of the unfortunate girl having failed her before the deleterious gas had attained its highest degree of intensity.

Before continuing the recital of the scene between the sempstress and the patrician, a few retrospective words will be necessary. Since the strange adventure at the theatre of the Porte Saint-Martin, where Djalma, at peril of his life, rushed upon the black panther in sight of Mdlle. de Cardoville, the young lady had been deeply affected in various ways. For getting her jealousy, and the humiliation she had suffered in presence of Djalma—of Djalma exhibiting himself before every one with a woman so little worthy of him—Adrienne was for a moment dazzled by the chivalrous and heroic action of the prince, and said to herself : ‘In spite of odious appearances, Djalma loves me enough to brave death in order to pick up my nosegay.’

But with a soul so delicate as that of this young lady, a character so generous, and a mind so true, reflection was certain soon to demonstrate the vanity of such consolations, powerless to cure the cruel wounds of offended dignity and love.

‘How many times,’ said Adrienne to herself, and with reason, ‘has the prince encountered, in hunting, from pure caprice and with no gain, such danger as he braved in picking up my bouquet ! and then, who tells me he did not mean to offer it to the woman who accompanied him ?’

Singular (it may be) in the eyes of the world, but just and great in those of heaven, the ideas which Adrienne cherished with regard to love, joined to her natural pride, presented an invincible obstacle to the thought of her succeeding this woman (whoever she might be), thus publicly displayed by the prince as his mistress. And yet Adrienne hardly dared avow to herself, that she experienced a feeling of jealousy, only the more painful and humiliating, the less her rival appeared worthy to be compared to her.

At other times, on the contrary, in spite of a conscious sense of her own value, Mdlle. de Cardoville, remembering the charming countenance of Rose-Pompon, asked herself, if the bad taste and improper manners of this pretty creature resulted from precocious and depraved effrontery, or from a complete ignorance of the usages of society. In the latter case, such ignorance, arising from a simple and ingenuous nature, might in itself have a great charm ; and if to this attraction, combined with that of incontestable beauty, were added sincere love and a pure soul, the obscure birth, or neglected education of the girl might be of little consequence, and she might be capable of inspiring Djalma with a profound passion. If Adrienne hesitated to see a lost creature in Rose-Pompon, notwithstanding unfavourable appearances, it was because, remembering what so many travellers had related of Djalma’s greatness of soul, and recalling the conversation she had overheard between him and Rodin, she could not bring herself to believe that a man of such remarkable intelligence, with so tender a heart, so poetical, imaginative and enthusiastic a mind could be capable of loving a depraved and vulgar creature, and of openly exhibiting himself in public along with her. There was a mystery in the transaction, which Adrienne sought in vain to penetrate. These trying doubts, this cruel curiosity, only served to nourish Adrienne's fatal love ; and we may imagine her incurable despair, when she found that the indifference, or even disdain of Djalma, was unable to stifle a passion that now burned more fiercely than ever. Sometimes, having recourse to notions of fatality, she fancied that she was destined to feel this love, that Djalma must therefore deserve it, and that one day whatever was incomprehensible in the conduct of the prince would be explained to his advantage. At other times, on the contrary, she felt ashamed of excusing Djalma, and the consciousness of this weakness was for Adrienne a constant occasion for remorse and torture. The victim of all these agonies, she lived in perfect solitude.

The cholera soon broke out, startling as a clap of thunder. Too unhappy to fear the pestilence on her own account, Adrienne was only moved by the sorrows of others. She was amongst the first to contribute to those charitable donations, which were now flowing in from all sides in the admirable spirit of benevolence. Florine was suddenly attacked by the epidemic. In spite of the danger, her mistress insisted on seeing her, and endeavoured to revive her failing courage. Conquered by this new mark of kindness, Florine could no longer conceal the treachery in which she had borne a part. Death was about to deliver her from the odious tyranny of the people whose yoke weighed upon her, and she was at length in a position to reveal everything to Adrienne. The latter thus learned how she had been continually betrayed by Florine, and also the cause of the sewing-girl's abrupt departure. At these revelations, Adrienne felt her affection and tender pity for the poor sempstress greatly increase. By her command, the most active steps were taken to discover traces of the hunchback ; but Florine's confession had a still more important result. Justly alarmed at this new evidence of Rodin's machinations, Adrienne remembered the projects formed, when, believing herself beloved, the instinct of affection had revealed to her the perils to which Djalma and the other members of the Rennepont family were exposed. To assemble the race around her, and bid them rally against the common enemy, such was Adrienne's first thought, when she heard the confession of Florine. She regarded it as a duty to accomplish this project. In a struggle with such dangerous and powerful adversaries as Rodin, Father d'Aigrigny, the Princess de Saint-Dizier, and their allies, Adrienne saw not only the praiseworthy and perilous task of unmasking hypocrisy and cupidity, but also, if not a consolation, at least a generous diversion in the midst of terrible sorrows.

From this moment, a restless, feverish activity took the place of the mournful apathy in which the young lady had languished. She called round her all the members of her family capable of answering the appeal, and, as had been mentioned in the secret note delivered to Father d'Aigrigny, Cardoville House soon became the centre of the most active and unceasing operations, and also a place of meeting, in which the modes of attack and defence were fully discussed. Perfectly correct in all points, the secret note of which we have spoken stated, as a mere conjecture, that Mdlle. de Cardoville had granted an interview to Djalma. This fact was untrue, but the cause which led to the supposition will be explained hereafter. Far from such being the case, Mdlle. de Cardoville scarcely found, in attending to the great family interests now at stake, a momentary diversion from the fatal love, which was slowly undermining her health, and with which she so bitterly reproached herself.

The morning of the day on which Adrienne, at length discovering Mother Bunch's residence, came so miraculously to rescue her from death, Agricola Baudoin had been to Cardoville House to confer on the subject of Francis

Hardy, and had begged Adrienne to permit him to accompany her to the Rue Clovis, whither they repaired in haste.

Thus, once again, there was a noble spectacle, a touching symbol! Mdlle. de Cardoville and Mother Bunch, the two extremities of the social chain, were united on equal terms—for the sempstress and the fair patrician were equal in intelligence and heart—and equal also, because the one was the ideal of riches, grace, and beauty, and the other the ideal of resignation and unmerited misfortune—and does not a halo rest on misfortune borne with courage and dignity? Stretched on her mattress, the hunchback appeared so weak, that even if Agricola had not been detained on the ground-floor with Cephyse, now dying a dreadful death, Mdlle. de Cardoville would have waited some time, before inducing Mother Bunch to rise and accompany her to her carriage. Thanks to the presence of mind and pious fraud of Adrienne, the sewing-girl was persuaded that Cephyse had been carried to a neighbouring hospital, to receive the necessary succours, which promised to be crowned with success. The hunchback's faculties recovering slowly from their stupor, she at first received this fable without the least suspicion—for she did not even know that Agricola had accompanied Mdlle. de Cardoville.

'And it is to you, lady, that Cephyse and I owe our lives,' said she, turning her mild and melancholy face towards Adrienne, '*you*, kneeling in this garret, near this couch of misery, where I and my sister meant to die—for you assure me, lady, that Cephyse was succoured in time?'

'Be satisfied! I was told just now that she was recovering her senses.'

'And they told her I was living, did they not, lady? Otherwise, she would perhaps regret having survived me.'

'Be quite easy, my dear girl!' said Adrienne, pressing the poor hands in her own, and gazing on her with eyes full of tears; 'they have told her all that was proper. Do not trouble yourself about anything; only think of recovering—and I hope you will yet enjoy that happiness of which you have known so little, my poor child.'

'How kind you are, lady! After flying from your house—and when you must think me so ungrateful!'

'Presently, when you are not so weak, I have a great deal to tell you. Just now, it would fatigue you too much. But how do you feel?'

'Better, lady. This fresh air—and then the thought, that, since you are come—my poor sister will no more be reduced to despair; for I will tell you all, and I am sure you will have pity on Cephyse—will you not, lady?'

'Rely upon me, my child,' answered Adrienne, forced to dissemble her painful embarrassment; 'you know I am interested in all that interests you. But tell me,' added Mdlle. de Cardoville, in a voice of emotion, 'before taking this desperate resolution, did you not write to me?'

'Yes, lady.'

'Alas!' resumed Adrienne, sorrowfully; 'and when you received no answer—how cruel, how ungrateful you must have thought me!'

'Oh! never, lady, did I accuse you of such feelings; my poor sister will tell you so. You had my gratitude to the last.'

'I believe you—for I know your heart. But how then did you explain my silence?'——'I had justly offended you by my sudden departure, lady.'

'Offended!—Alas! I never received your letter.'

'And yet you know that I wrote to you, lady.'

'Yes, my poor girl; I know also, that you wrote to me at my porter's lodge. Unfortunately, he delivered your letter to one of my women, named Florine, telling her it came from you.'

'Florine ! the young woman that was so kind to me !'

'Florine deceived me shamefully : she was sold to my enemies, and acted as a spy on my actions.'

'*She !*—Good Heavens !' cried Mother Bunch. 'Is it possible ?'

'She herself,' answered Adrienne, bitterly; 'but, after all, we must pity as well as blame her. She was forced to obey by a terrible necessity, and her confession and repentance secured my pardon before her death.'

'Then she is dead—so young ! so fair !'——'In spite of her faults, I was greatly moved by her end. She confessed what she had done, with such heart-rending regrets. Amongst her avowals, she told me she had intercepted a letter, in which you asked for an interview that might save your sister's life.'

'It is true, lady ; such were the terms of my letter. What interest had they to keep it from you ?'

'They feared to see you return to me, my good guardian angel. You loved me so tenderly, and my enemies dreaded your faithful affection, so wonderfully aided by the admirable instinct of your heart. Ah ! I shall never forget how well-deserved was the horror with which you were inspired by a wretch whom I defended against your suspicions.'

'M. Rodin ?' said Mother Bunch, with a shudder.——'Yes,' replied Adrienne ; 'but we will not talk of these people now. Their odious remembrance would spoil the joy I feel in seeing you restored to life—for your voice is less feeble, your cheeks are beginning to regain a little colour. Thank God ! I am so happy to have found you once more ;—if you knew all that I hope, all that I expect from our reunion—for we will not part again —promise me that, in the name of our friendship.'

'I—your friend !' said Mother Bunch, timidly casting down her eyes.

'A few days before your departure from my house, did I not call you my friend, my sister ? What is there changed ? Nothing, nothing,' added Mdlle. de Cardoville, with deep emotion. 'One might say, on the contrary, that a fatal resemblance in our positions renders your friendship even dearer to me. And I shall have it, shall I not ? Oh, do not refuse it me—I am so much in want of a friend !'

'You, lady ? you in want of the friendship of a poor creature like me ?'

'Yes,' answered Adrienne, as she gazed on the other with an expression of intense grief ; 'nay, more, you are perhaps the only person, to whom I could venture to confide my bitter sorrows.' So saying, Mdlle. de Cardoville coloured deeply.

'And how do I deserve such marks of confidence ?' asked Mother Bunch, more and more surprised.

'You deserve it by the delicacy of your heart, by the steadiness of your character,' answered Adrienne, with some hesitation ; 'then—you are a woman—and I am certain you will understand what I suffer, and pity me.'

'Pity you, lady ?' said the other, whose astonishment continued to increase. 'You, a great lady, and so much envied—I, so humble and despised, pity you ?'

'Tell me, my poor friend,' resumed Adrienne, after some moments of silence, 'are not the worst griefs those which we dare not avow to any one, for fear of raillery and contempt ? How can we venture to ask interest or pity, for sufferings that we hardly dare avow to ourselves, because they make us blush ?'

The sewing-girl could hardly believe what she heard. Had her benefactress felt, like her, the effects of an unfortunate passion, she could not have held any other language. But the sempstress could not admit such a supposition ; so, attributing to some other cause the sorrows of Adrienne, she answered mournfully, whilst she thought of her own fatal love for Agricola, 'Oh ! yes, lady. A secret grief, of which we are ashamed, must be frightful —very frightful !'

'But then what happiness to meet, not only a heart noble enough to inspire complete confidence, but one which has itself been tried by a thousand sorrows, and is capable of affording you pity, support, and counsel ! —Tell me, my dear child,' added Mdlle. de Cardoville, as she looked attentively at Mother Bunch, 'if you were weighed down by one of those sorrows, at which one blushes, would you not be happy, very happy, to find a kindred soul, to whom you might entrust your griefs, and half relieve them by entire and merited confidence ?'

For the first time in her life, Mother Bunch regarded Mdlle. de Cardoville with a feeling of suspicion and sadness.

The last words of the young lady seemed to her full of meaning. 'Doubtless, she knows my secret,' said Mother Bunch to herself ; 'doubtless, my journal has fallen into her hands.—She knows my love for Agricola, or at least suspects it. What she has been saying to me is intended to provoke my confidence, and to assure herself if she has been rightly informed.'

These thoughts excited in the workgirl's mind no bitter or ungrateful feeling towards her benefactress ; but the heart of the unfortunate girl was so delicately susceptible on the subject of her fatal passion, that, in spite of her deep and tender affection for Mdlle. de Cardoville, she suffered cruelly at the thought of Adrienne's being mistress of her secret.

CHAPTER XXXIV.

MORE CONFESSIONS.

THE fancy, at first so painful, that Mdlle. de Cardoville was informed of her love for Agricola, was soon exchanged in the hunchback's heart, thanks to the generous instincts of that rare and excellent creature, for a touching regret, which showed all her attachment and veneration for Adrienne.

'Perhaps,' said Mother Bunch to herself, 'conquered by the influence of the adorable kindness of my protectress, I might have made to her a confession which I could make to none other, and revealed a secret which I thought to carry with me to my grave. It would, at least, have been a mark of gratitude to Mdlle. de Cardoville ; but, unfortunately, I am now deprived of the sad comfort of confiding my only secret to my benefactress. And then—however generous may be her pity for me, however intelligent her affection, she cannot—she, that is so fair and so much admired—she cannot understand how frightful is the position of a creature like myself, hiding in the depths of a wounded heart, a love at once hopeless and ridiculous. No, no—in spite of the delicacy of her attachment, my benefactress must unconsciously hurt my feelings, even whilst she pities me—for only sympathetic sorrows can console each other. Alas ! why did she not leave me to die ?'

These reflections presented themselves to the thinker's mind as rapidly as thought could travel. Adrienne observed her attentively ; she remarked that the sewing-girl's countenance, which had lately brightened up, was again clouded, and expressed a feeling of painful humiliation. Terrified at this relapse into gloomy dejection, the consequences of which might be serious, for Mother Bunch was still very weak, and, as it were, hovering on the brink of the grave, Mdlle. de Cardoville resumed hastily : ' My friend, do not you think with me, that the most cruel and humiliating grief admits of consolation, when it can be entrusted to a faithful and devoted heart ?'

'Yes, lady,' said the young sempstress, bitterly; 'but the heart which suffers in silence, should be the only judge of the moment for making so painful a confession. Until then, it would perhaps be more humane to respect its fatal secret, even if one had by chance discovered it.'

'You are right, my child,' said Adrienne, sorrowfully; 'if I choose this solemn moment to entrust you with a very painful secret, it is that, when you have heard me, I am sure you will set more value on your life, as knowing how much I need your tenderness, consolation, and pity.'

At these words, the other half raised herself on the mattress, and looked at Mdlle. de Cardoville in amazement. She could scarcely believe what she heard; far from designing to intrude upon her confidence, it was her protectress who was to make the painful confession, and who came to implore pity and consolation from her !

'What !' stammered she; 'you, lady.'——'I come to tell you that I suffer, and am ashamed of my sufferings. Yes,' added the young lady, with a touching expression, 'yes—of all confessions, I am about to make the most painful—I love—and I blush for my love.'

'Like myself !' cried Mother Bunch, involuntarily, clasping her hands together.

'I love,' resumed Adrienne, with a long-pent-up grief; 'I love, and am not beloved—and my love is miserable, is impossible—it consumes me—it kills me—and I dare not confide to any one the fatal secret !'

'Like me,' repeated the other, with a fixed look. 'She—a queen in beauty, rank, wealth, intelligence—suffers like me. Like me, poor unfortunate creature ! she loves, and is not loved again.'

'Well, yes ! like you, I love and am not loved again,' cried Mdlle. de Cardoville; 'was I wrong in saying, that to you alone I could confide my secret—because, having suffered the same pangs, you alone can pity them ?'

'Then, lady,' said Mother Bunch, casting down her eyes, and recovering from her first amazement, 'you knew——'

'I knew all, my poor child—but never should I have mentioned your secret, had I not had one to entrust you with, of a still more painful nature. Yours is cruel, but mine is humiliating. Oh, my sister !' added Mdlle. de Cardoville, in a tone impossible to describe, 'misfortune, you see, blends and confounds together what are called distinctions of rank and fortune—and often those whom the world envies are reduced by suffering far below the poorest and most humble, and have to seek from the latter pity and consolation.'

Then, drying her tears, which now flowed abundantly, Mdlle. de Cardoville resumed, in a voice of emotion : 'Come, sister ! courage, courage ! let us love and sustain each other. Let this sad and mysterious bond unite us for ever.'

'Oh lady ! forgive me. But now that you know the secret of my life,' said the workgirl, casting down her eyes, and unable to vanquish her confusion, 'it seems to me, that I can never look at you without blushing.'

'And why ? because you love Agricola ?' said Adrienne. 'Then I must die of shame before you, since, less courageous than you, I had not the strength to suffer and be resigned, and so conceal my love in the depths of my heart. He that I love, with a love henceforth deprived of hope, knew of that love and despised it—preferring to me a woman, the very choice of whom was a new and grievous insult, if I am not much deceived by appearances. I sometimes hope that I am deceived on this point. Now tell me—is it for you to blush ?'

'Alas, lady ! who could tell you all this ?'——'Which you only entrusted to your journal ? Well, then—it was the dying Florine who confessed her misdeeds. She had been base enough to steal your papers, forced to this odious act by the people who had dominion over her. But she had read your journal—and as every good feeling was not dead within her, your admirable resignation, your melancholy and pious love, had left such an impression on her mind, that she was able to repeat whole passages to me on her death-bed, and thus to explain the cause of your sudden disappearance—for she had no doubt that the fear of seeing your love for Agricola divulged had been the cause of your flight.'

'Alas! it is but too true, lady.'——'Oh, yes!' answered Adrienne, bitterly; 'those who employed the wretched girl to act as she did, well knew the effect of the blow. It was not their first attempt. They reduced you to despair, they would have killed you, because you were devoted to me, and because you had guessed their intentions. Oh! these black-gowns are implacable, and their power is great!' said Adrienne, shuddering.

' It is fearful, lady.'——' But do not be alarmed, dear child; you see, that the arms of the wicked have turned against themselves; for the moment I knew the cause of your flight, you became dearer to me than ever. From that time I made every exertion to find out where you were; after long efforts, it was only this morning that the person I had employed succeeded in discovering that you inhabited this house. Agricola was with me when I heard it, and instantly asked to accompany me.'

'Agricola!' said Mother Bunch, clasping her hands; 'he came——'

'Yes, my child—be calm. Whilst I attended to you, he was busy with your poor sister. You will soon see him.'

'Alas, lady!' resumed the hunchback, in alarm. ' He doubtless knows——'

' Your love? No, no; be satisfied. Only think of the happiness of again seeing your good and worthy brother.'

'Ah, lady! may he never know what caused me so much shame, that I was like to die of it. Thank God, he is not aware of it!'

'Then let us have no more sad thoughts, my child. Only remember, that this worthy brother came here in time to save us from everlasting regrets—and you from a great fault. Oh! I do not speak of the prejudices of the world, with regard to the right of every creature to return to heaven a life that has become too burdensome!—I only say that you ought not to have died, because those who love you, and whom you love, were still in need of your assistance.'

' I thought you happy; Agricola was married to the girl of his choice, who will, I am sure, make him happy. To whom could I be useful?'

' First, to myself, as you see—and then, who tells you that Agricola will never have need of you? Who tells you, that his happiness, or that of his family, will last for ever, and will not be tried by cruel shocks? And even if those you love had been destined to be always happy, could their happiness be complete without you? And would not your death, with which they would perhaps have reproached themselves, have left behind it endless regrets?'

' It is true, lady,' answered the other, ' I was wrong—the dizziness of despair had seized me—frightful misery weighed upon us—we had not been able to find work for some days—we lived on the charity of a poor woman, and her the cholera carried off. To-morrow or next day, we must have died of hunger.'

' Die of hunger!—and you knew where I lived!'

' I had written to you, lady, and, receiving no answer, I thought you offended at my abrupt departure.'

' Poor, dear child! you must have been, as you say, seized with dizziness in that terrible moment; so that I have not the courage to reproach you for doubting me a single instant. How can I blame you? Did I not myself think of terminating my life?'

'You, lady!' cried the hunchback.——'Yes, I thought of it—when they came to tell me, that Florine, dying, wished to speak to me. I heard what she had to say: her revelations changed my projects. This dark and mournful life, which had become insupportable to me, was suddenly lighted up. The sense of duty woke within me. You were no doubt a prey to horrible misery; it was my duty to seek and save you. Florine's confessions unveiled to me the new plots of the enemies of my scattered family, dispersed by sorrows and cruel losses; it was my duty to warn them of their danger, and to unite them against the common enemy. I had been the victim of odious manœuvres; it was my duty to punish their authors, for fear that, encouraged by impunity, these black-gowns should make other victims. Then the sense of duty gave me strength, and I was able to rouse myself from my lethargy. With the help of Abbé Gabriel, a sublime, oh! a sublime priest—the ideal of a true Christian—the worthy brother of Agricola—I courageously entered on the struggle. What shall I say to you, my child? The performance of these duties, the hope of finding you again, have been some relief to me in my trouble. If I was not consoled, I was at least occupied. Your tender friendship, the example of your resignation, will do the rest—I think so—I am sure so—and I shall forget this fatal love.'

At the moment Adrienne pronounced these words, rapid footsteps were heard upon the stairs, and a young, clear voice exclaimed: 'Oh! dear me, poor Mother Bunch! How lucky I have come just now! If only I could be of some use to her!'

Almost immediately, Rose-Pompon entered the garret with precipitation. Agricola soon followed the grisette, and, pointing to the open window, tried to make Adrienne understand by signs, that she was not to mention to the girl the deplorable end of the Bacchanal Queen. This pantomime was lost on Mdlle. de Cardoville. Adrienne's heart swelled with grief, indignation, pride, as she recognised the girl she had seen at the Porte-Saint-Martin in company with Djalma, and who alone was the cause of the dreadful sufferings she endured since that fatal evening. And, strange irony of fate! it was at the very moment when Adrienne had just made the humiliating and cruel confession of her despised love, that the woman, to whom she believed herself sacrificed, appeared before her.

If the surprise of Mdlle. de Cardoville was great, Rose-Pompon's was not less so. Not only did she recognise in Adrienne the fair young lady with the golden locks, who had sat opposite to her at the theatre, on the night of the adventure of the black panther, but she had serious reasons for desiring most ardently this unexpected interview. It is impossible to paint the look of malignant joy and triumph, that she affected to cast upon Adrienne. The first impulse of Mdlle. de Cardoville was to quit the room. But she could not bear to leave Mother Bunch at this moment, or to give, in the presence of Agricola, her reasons for such an abrupt departure, and moreover, an inexplicable and fatal curiosity held her back, in spite of her offended pride. She remained, therefore, and was about to examine closely, to hear and to judge, this rival, who had nearly occasioned her death, to whom, in her jealous agony, she had ascribed so many different aspects in order to explain Djalma's love for such a creature.

CHAPTER XXXV

THE RIVALS.

ROSE-POMPON, whose presence caused such deep emotion in Mdlle. de Cardoville, was dressed in the most showy and extravagant bad taste. Her very small, narrow, rose-coloured satin bonnet, placed so forward over her face as almost to touch the tip of her little nose, left uncovered behind half of her light, silky hair ; her plaid dress, of an excessively broad pattern, was open in front, and the almost transparent gauze, rather two honest in its revelations, hardly covered the charms of the form beneath.

The grisette having run all the way upstairs, held in her hands the ends of her large blue shawl, which, falling from her shoulders, had slid down to her wasp-like waist, and there been stopped by the swell of the figure. If we en‘er into these details, it is to explain how, at the sight of this pretty creature, dressed in so impertinent and almost indecent a fashion, Mdlle. de Cardoville, who thought she saw in her a successful rival, felt her indignation, grief, and shame redoubled.

But judge of the surprise and confusion of Adrienne, when Mdlle. Rose-Pompon said to her, with the utmost freedom and pertness, ' I am delighted to see you, madame. You and I must have a long talk together. Only I must begin by kissing poor Mother Bunch—with your permission, madame !'

To understand the tone and manner with which this word ' madame ' was pronounced, you must have been present at some stormy discussion between two Rose-Pompons, jealous of each other , then you would be able to judge how much provoking hostility may be compressed into the word ' madame,' under certain circumstances. Amazed at the impudence of Rose-Pompon, Mdlle. de Cardoville remained mute ; whilst Agricola, entirely occupied with the interest he took in the workgirl, who had never withdrawn her eyes from him since he entered the room, and with the remembrance of the painful scene he had just quitted, whispered to Adrienne, without remarking the grisette's effrontery, ' Alas, lady ! it is all over. Cephyse has just breathed her last sigh, without recovering her senses.'

' Unfortunate girl !' said Adrienne, with emotion ; and for the moment she forgot Rose-Pompon.

' We must keep this sad news from Mother Bunch, and only let her know it hereafter, with great caution,' resumed Agricola. ' Luckily, little Rose-Pompon knows nothing about it.'

And he pointed to the grisette, who was now stooping down by the side of the work girl. On hearing Agricola speak so familiarly of Rose-Pompon, Adrienne's amazement increased. It is impossible to describe what she felt ; yet, strangely enough, her sufferings grew less and less, and her anxiety diminished, as she listened to the chatter of the grisette.

' Oh, my good dear !' said the latter, with as much volubility as emotion, while her pretty blue eyes were filled with tears ; ' is it possible that you did so stupid a thing ? Do not poor people help one another ? Could you not apply to me ? You knew that others are welcome to whatever is mine, and I would have made a raffle of Philemon's bazaar,' added this singular girl, with a burst of feeling, at once sincere, touching, and grotesque ; ' I would have sold his three boots, pipes, boating-costume, bed, and even his great drinking-glass, and at all events you should not have been brought to such an ugly pass. Philemon would not have minded, for he is a good fellow ; and if he had minded, it would have been all the same. Thank heaven ! we are not married. I am only wishing to remind you that you should have thought of little Rose-Pompon.'

' I know you are obliging and kind, miss,' said Mother Bunch ; for she had heard from her sister that Rose-Pompon, like so many of her class, had a warm and generous heart.

'After all,' resumed the grisette, wiping with the back of her hand the tip of her little nose, down which a tear was trickling, 'you may tell me that you did not know where I had taken up my quarters. It's a queer story, I can tell you. When I say queer,' added Rose-Pompon, with a deep sigh, 'it is quite the contrary—but no matter. I need not trouble you with that. One thing is certain ; you are getting better—and you and Cephyse will not do such a thing again. She is said to be very weak. Can I not see her yet, M. Agricola?'

'No,' said the smith, with embarrassment, for Mother Bunch kept her eyes fixed upon him ; 'you must have patience.'

'But I may see her to-day, Agricola?' exclaimed the hunchback.

'We will talk about that. Only be calm, I entreat.'

'Agricola is right ; you must be reasonable, my good dear,' resumed Rose-Pompon ; 'we will wait patiently. I can wait too, for I have to talk presently to this lady ;' and Rose-Pompon glanced at Adrienne with the expression of an angry cat. 'Yes, yes ; I can wait ; for I long to tell Cephyse also that she may reckon upon me.' Here Rose-Pompon bridled up very prettily, and thus continued, 'Do not be uneasy ! It is the least one can do, when one is in a good position, to share the advantages with one's friends, who are not so well off. It would be a fine thing to keep one's happiness to one's self ! to stuff it with straw, and put it under a glass, and let no one touch it ! When I talk of happiness, it's only to make talk ; it is true in one sense ; but in another, you see, my good dear—— Bah ! I am only seventeen—but no matter—I might go on talking till to-morrow, and you would not be any the wiser. So let me kiss you once more, and don't be down-hearted—nor Cephyse either, do you hear ? for I shall be close at hand.'

And, stooping still lower, Rose-Pompon cordially embraced Mother Bunch. It is impossible to express what Mdlle. de Cardoville felt during this conversation, or rather during this monologue of the grisette on the subject of the attempted suicide. The eccentric jargon of Mdlle. Rose-Pompon, her liberal facility in disposing of Philemon's bazaar, to the owner of which (as she said) she was luckily not married—the goodness of her heart, which revealed itself in her offers of service—her contrasts, her impertinence, her drollery—all this was so new and inexplicable to Mdlle. de Cardoville, that she remained for some time mute and motionless with surprise. Such, then, was the creature to whom Djalma had sacrificed her !

If Adrienne's first impression at sight of Rose-Pompon had been horribly painful, reflection soon awakened doubts, which were to become shortly ineffable hopes. Remembering the interview she had overheard between Rodin and Djalma, when, concealed in the conservatory, she had wished to prove the Jesuit's fidelity, Adrienne asked herself if it was reasonable, if it was possible to believe, that the prince, whose ideas of love seemed to be so poetical, so elevated, so pure, could find any charm in the disjointed and silly chat of this young girl? Adrienne could not hesitate ; she pronounced the thing impossible, from the moment she had seen her rival near, and witnessed her style both of manners and conversation, which, without detracting from the prettiness of her features, gave them a trivial and not very attractive character. Adrienne's doubts with regard to the deep love of the prince for Rose-Pompon were hence soon changed to complete incredulity. Endowed with too much sense and penetration, not to perceive that this apparent connection, so inconceivable on the part of Djalma, must conceal some mystery, Mdlle. de Cardoville felt her hopes revive. As this consoling thought arose in her mind, her heart, until now so painfully oppressed, began once more to dilate ; she felt vague aspirations towards a better future ; and yet, cruelly warned by the past, she feared to yield too readily to a mere illusion, for she remembered the notorious fact that the prince had really appeared in public with this girl. But now that Mdlle. de Cardoville could fully appreciate what she was, she found the conduct of the prince only the more incomprehensible. And how can we judge soundly and surely of that which is enveloped in mystery ? And then a secret presentiment told her, that it would, perhaps, be beside the couch of the poor semptress, whom she had just saved from death, that, by a providential coincidence, she would learn the secret on which depended the happiness of her life.

The emotions which agitated the heart of Adrienne became so violent, that her fine face was flushed with a bright red, her bosom heaved, and her large, black eyes, lately dimmed by sadness, once more shone with a mild radiance. She waited with inexpressible impatience for what was to follow. In the interview, with which Rose-Pompon had threatened her, and which a few minutes before Adrienne would have declined with all the dignity of legitimate indignation, she now hoped to find the explanation of a mystery, which it was of such importance for her to clear up. After once more tenderly embracing Mother Bunch, Rose-Pompon got up from the ground, and, turning towards Adrienne, eyed her from head to foot, with the utmost coolness, and said to her, in a somewhat impertinent tone : " It is now our turn, madame '—the word ' madame ' still pronounced with the accent before described—' we have a little matter to settle together.'

' I am at your order,' answered Adrienne, with much mildness and simplicity.

At sight of the triumphant and decisive air of Rose-Pompon, and on hearing her challenge to Mdlle. de Cardoville, the worthy Agricola, after exchanging a few words with Mother Bunch, opened his eyes and ears very wide, and remained staring in amazement at the effrontery of the grisette ; then, advancing towards her, he whispered, as he plucked her by the sleeve : ' I say, are you mad ? Do you know to whom you speak ?'

' Well ! what then ? Is not one pretty woman worth another ? I say that for the lady. She will not eat me, I suppose,' replied Rose-Pompon, aloud, and with an air of defiance. ' I have to talk with madame, here. I am sure, she knows why and wherefore. If not, I will tell her ; it will not take me long.'

Adrienne, who feared some ridiculous exposure on the subject of Djalma, in the presence of Agricola, made a sign to the latter, and thus answered the grisette : ' I am ready to hear you, miss, but not in this place. You will understand why.'

' Very well, madame. I have my key. You can come to my apartments '—the last word pronounced with an air of ostentatious importance.

' Let us go then to your apartments, miss, since you will do me the honour to receive me there,' answered Mdlle. de Cardoville, in her mild, sweet voice, and with a slight inclination of the head, so full of exquisite politeness, that Rose-Pompon was daunted, notwithstanding all her effrontery.

' What, lady !' said Agricola to Adrienne ; ' you are good enough——'

' M. Agricola,' said Mdlle. de Cardoville, interrupting him, ' please to remain with our poor friend : I shall soon be back.'

Then, approaching Mother Bunch, who shared in Agricola's astonishment, she said to her : ' Excuse me for leaving you a few seconds. Only regain a little strength, and, when I return, I will take you home with me, dear sister.'

Then, turning towards Rose-Pompon, who was more and more surprised at hearing so fine a lady call the workgirl her sister, she added : 'I am ready whenever you please, mademoiselle.'

'Beg pardon, madame, if I go first to show you the way, but it's a regular break-neck sort of a place,' answered Rose-Pompon, pressing her elbows to her sides, and screwing up her lips, to prove that she was no stranger to polite manners and fine language. And the two rivals quitted the garret together, leaving Agricola alone with Mother Bunch.

Luckily, the disfigured remains of the Bacchanal Queen had been carried into Mother Arsène's subterraneous shop, so that the crowd of spectators, always attracted by any fatal event, had assembled in front of the house ; and Rose-Pompon, meeting no one in the little court she had to traverse with Adrienne, continued in ignorance of the tragical death of her old friend Cephyse. In a few moments the grisette and Mdlle. de Cardoville had reached Philemon's apartment. This singular abode remained in the same state of picturesque disorder in which Rose-Pompon had left it, when Ninny Moulin came to fetch her to act the heroine of a mysterious adventure.

Adrienne, completely ignorant of the eccentric modes of life of students and their companions, could not, in spite of the thoughts which occupied her mind, forbear examining, with a mixture of surprise and curiosity, this strange and grotesque chaos, composed of the most dissimilar objects—disguises for masked balls, skulls with pipes in their mouths, odd boots standing on book-shelves, monstrous bottles, women's clothes, ends of tobacco pipes, &c., &c. To the first astonishment of Adrienne succeeded an impression of painful repugnance. The young lady felt herself uneasy and out of place in this abode, not of poverty, but disorder ; whilst, on the contrary, the sewing-girl's miserable garret had caused her no such feeling.

Rose-Pompon, notwithstanding all her airs, was considerably troubled when she found herself alone with Mdlle. de Cardoville ; the rare beauty of the young patrician, her fashionable look, the elegance of her manners, the style, both dignified and affable, with which she had answered the impertinent address of the grisette, began to have their effect upon the latter, who, being moreover a good-natured girl, had been touched at hearing Mdlle. de Cardoville call the hunchback 'friend and sister.' Without knowing exactly who Adrienne was, Rose-Pompon was not ignorant that she belonged to the richest and highest class of society ; she felt already some remorse at having attacked her so cavalierly ; and her intentions, at first very nostile with regard to Mdlle. de Cardoville, were gradually much modified. Yet, being very obstinate, and not wishing to appear to submit to an influence that offended her pride, Rose-Pompon endeavoured to recover her assurance ; and, having bolted the door, she said to Adrienne : 'Pray do me the favour to sit down, madame '—still with the intention of showing that she was no stranger to refined manners and conversation.

Mdlle. de Cardoville was about mechanically to take a chair, when Rose-Pompon, worthy to practise those ancient virtues of hospitality, which regarded even an enemy as sacred in the person of a guest, cried out hastily : 'Don't take that chair, madame ; it wants a leg.'

Adrienne laid her hand on another chair.

'Nor that either ; the back is quite loose,' again exclaimed Rose-Pompon. And she spoke the truth ; for the chair-back, which was made in the form of a lyre, remained in the hands of Mdlle. de Cardoville, who said, as she replaced it discreetly in its former position : 'I think, miss, that we can very well talk standing.'

'As you please, madame,' replied Rose-Pompon, steadying herself the more bravely the more uneasy she felt. And the interview of the lady and the grisette began in this fashion.

CHAPTER XXXVI

THE INTERVIEW.

AFTER a minute's hesitation, Rose-Pompon said to Adrienne, whose heart was beating violently : 'I will tell you directly, madame, what I have on my mind. I should not have gone out of my way to seek you, but, as i happen to fall in with you, it is very natural I should take advantage of it.'

'But, miss,' said Adrienne, mildly, 'may I at least know the subject of the conversation we are to have together?'

'Yes, madame,' replied Rose-Pompon, affecting an air of still more decided confidence ; 'first of all, you must not suppose I am unhappy, or going to make a scene of jealousy, or cry like a forsaken damsel. Do not flatter yourself ! Thank heaven, I have no reason to complain of Prince Charming—that is the pet name I gave him—on the contrary, he has made me very happy. If I left him, it was against his will, and because I chose.'

So saying, Rose-Pompon, whose heart was swelling in spite of her fine airs, could not repress a sigh.

'Yes, madame,' she resumed, 'I left him because I chose—for he quite doted on me. If I had liked, he would have married me—yes, madame, married me—so much the worse, if that gives you pain. Though, when I say "so much the worse," it is true that I meant to pain you. To be sure I did—but then, just now when I saw you so kind to poor Mother Bunch, though I was certainly in the right, still I felt something. However, to cut matters short, it is clear that I detest you, and that you deserve it,' added Rose-Pompon, stamping her foot.

From all this it resulted, even for a person much less sagacious than Adrienne, and much less interested in discovering the truth, that Rose-Pompon, notwithstanding her triumphant airs in speaking of him whom she represented as so much attached to her, and even anxious to wed her, was in reality completely disappointed, and was now taking refuge in a deliberate falsehood. It was evident that she was not loved, and that nothing but violent jealousy had induced her to desire this interview with Mdlle. de Cardoville, in order to make what is vulgarly called a scene, considering Adrienne (the reason will be explained presently) as her successful rival. But Rose-Pompon, having recovered her good-nature, found it very difficult to continue the scene in question, particularly as, for many reasons, she felt overawed by Adrienne.

Though she had expected, if not the singular speech of the grisette, at least something of the same result—for she felt it was impossible that the prince could entertain a serious attachment for this girl—Mdlle. de Cardoville was at first delighted to hear the confirmation of her hopes from the lips of her rival ; but suddenly these hopes were succeeded by a cruel apprehension, which we will endeavour to explain. What Adrienne had just heard ought to have satisfied her completely. Sure that the heart of Djalma had never ceased to belong to her, she ought, according to the customs and opinions of the world, to have cared little if, in the effervescence of an ardent youth, he had chanced to yield to some ephemeral caprice for this creature, who was, after all, very pretty and desirable—the more especially as he had now repaired his error by separating from her.

Notwithstanding these good reasons, such an error of the senses would not have been pardoned by Adrienne. She did not understand that complete separation of the body and soul that would make the one exempt from the stains of the other. She did not think it a matter of indifference to toy with one woman whilst you were thinking of another. Her young, chaste, passionate love demanded an absolute fealty—a fealty as just in the eyes of heaven and nature as it may be ridiculous and foolish in the eyes of man. For the very reason that she cherished a refined religion of the senses, and revered them as an adorable and divine manifestation, Adrienne had all sorts of delicate scruples and nice repugnances, unknown to the austere spirituality of those ascetic prudes who despise vile matter too much to take notice of its errors, and allow it to grovel in filth, to show the contempt in which they hold it. Mdlle. de Cardoville was not one of those wonderfully modest creatures who would die of confusion rather than say plainly that they wished for a young and handsome husband, at once ardent and pure. It is true that they generally marry old, ugly, and corrupted men, and make up for it by taking two or three lovers six months after. But Adrienne felt instinctively how much of virginal and celestial freshness there is in the equal innocence of two loving and passionate beings—what guarantees for the future in the remembrance which a man preserves of his first love!

We say, then, that Adrienne was only half-satisfied, though convinced by the vexation of Rose-Pompon that Djalma had never entertained a serious attachment for the grisette.

'And why do you detest me, miss?' said Adrienne mildly, when Rose-Pompon had finished her speech.

'Oh! bless me, madame!' replied the latter, forgetting altogether her assumption of triumph, and yielding to the natural sincerity of her character; 'pretend that you don't know why I detest you!—Oh, yes! people go and pick bouquets from the jaws of a panther for people that they care nothing about, don't they? And if it was only that!' added Rose-Pompon, who was gradually getting animated, and whose pretty face, at first contracted into a sullen pout, now assumed an expression of real and yet half-comic sorrow.

'And if it was only the nosegay!' resumed she. 'Though it gave me a dreadful turn to see Prince Charming leap like a kid upon the stage, I might have said to myself: "Pooh! these Indians have their own way of showing politeness. Here, a lady drops her nosegay, and a gentleman picks it up and gives it to her; but in India it is quite another thing; the man picks up the nosegay, and does not return it to the woman—he only kills a panther before her eyes." Those are good manners in that country, I suppose; but what cannot be good manners anywhere is to treat a woman as I have been treated. And all thanks to you, madame!'

These complaints of Rose-Pompon, at once bitter and laughable, did not at all agree with what she had previously stated as to Djalma's passionate love for her; but Adrienne took care not to point out this contradiction, and said to her, mildly: 'You must be mistaken, miss, when you suppose that I had anything to do with your troubles. But, in any case, I regret sincerely that you should have been ill-treated by any one.'

'If you think I have been beaten, you are quite wrong,' exclaimed Rose-Pompon. 'Ah! well, I am sure! No, it is not that. But I am certain that, had it not been for you, Prince Charming would have got to love me a little. I am worthy the trouble, after all—and then there are different sorts of love—I am not so very particular—not even so much as that,' added Rose-Pompon, snapping her fingers.

'Ah!' she continued, 'when Ninny Moulin came to fetch me, and brought me jewels and laces to persuade me to go with him, he was quite right in saying there was no harm in his offers.'

'Ninny Moulin?' asked Mdlle. de Cardoville, becoming more and more interested; 'who is this Ninny Moulin, miss?'

'A religious writer,' answered Rose-Pompon, pouting; 'the right-hand man of a lot of old sacristans, whose money he takes on pretence of writing about morality and religion. A fine morality it is!'

At these words—'a religious writer'—'sacristans'—Adrienne instantly divined some new plot of Rodin or Father d'Aigrigny, of which she and Djalma were to have been the victims. She began vaguely to perceive the real state of the case, as she resumed: 'But, miss, under what pretence could this man take you away with him?'

'He came to fetch me, and said I need not fear for my virtue, and was only to make myself look pretty. So I said to myself: "Philemon's out of town, and it's very dull here all alone. This seems a droll affair; what can I risk by it?"—Alas! I didn't know what I risked,' added Rose-Pompon, with a sigh. 'Well! Ninny Moulin takes me away in a fine carriage. We stop in the Place du Palais-Royal. A sullen-looking man, with a yellow face, gets up in the room of Ninny Moulin, and takes me to the house of Prince Charming. When I saw him—la! he was so handsome, so very handsome, that I was quite dizzy-like; and he had such a kind, noble air, that I said to myself: "Well! there will be some credit if I remain a good girl now!"—I did not know what a true word I was speaking. I have been good—oh! worse than good.'

'What, miss! do you regret having been so virtuous?'

'Why, you see, I regret, at least, that I have not had the pleasure of refusing. But how can you refuse, when nothing is asked—when you are not even thought worth one little loving word?'

'But, miss, allow me to observe to you that the indifference of which you complain does not seem to have prevented your making a long stay in the house in question.'

'How should I know why the prince kept me there, or took me out riding with him, or to the play? Perhaps it is the fashion in his savage country to have a pretty girl by your side, and to pay no attention to her at all!'

'But why, then, did you remain, miss?'

'Why did I remain?' said Rose-Pompon, stamping her foot with vexation. 'I remained because, without knowing how it happened, I began to get very fond of Prince Charming; and what is queer enough, I, who am as gay as a lark, loved him because he was so sorrowful, which shows that it was a serious matter. At last, one day, I could hold out no longer. I said: "Never mind; I don't care for the consequences. Philemon, I am sure, is having his fun in the country." That set my mind at ease. So one morning, I dress myself in my best, all very pretty, look in my glass, and say: "Well, that will do—he can't stand that!" and, going to his room, I tell him all that passes through my head; I laugh, I cry—at last I tell him that I adore him. What do you think he answers, in his mild voice, and as cold as a piece of marble? Why, "Poor child—poor child—poor child!"' added Rose-Pompon, with indignation; 'neither more nor less than if I had come to complain to him of the toothache. But the worst of it is that I am sure, if he were not in love elsewhere, he would be all fire and gunpowder. Only now he is so sad, so dejected!'

Then, pausing a moment, Rose-Pompon added: 'No, I will not tell you that; you would be too pleased.' But, after another pause, she continued: 'Well, never mind; I will tell you, though;' and this singular girl looked at Mdlle. de Cardoville with a mixture of sympathy and deference. 'Why should I keep it from you? I began by riding the high horse, and saying that the prince wished to marry me; and I finish by confessing that he almost turned me out. Well, it's not my fault ; when I try to fib, I am sure to get confused. So, madame, this is the plain truth :—When I met you at poor Mother Bunch's, I was at first as angry as a little turkey-cock ; but when I heard you, that are such a fine great lady, speak so kindly to the poor girl, and treat her as your sister, do what I would, my anger began to go away. Since we have been here, I have done my utmost to get it up again ; but I find it impossible, and the more I see the difference between us, the more I perceive that Prince Charming was right in thinking so much of you. For you must know, madame, that he is over head and ears in love with you. I don't say so merely because he killed the panther for you at the Porte-Saint-Martin ; but if you knew all the tricks he played with your bouquet, and how he will sit up all night weeping in that room where he saw you for the first time—and then your portrait, that he has drawn upon glass, after the fashion of his country, and so many other things—the fact is, that I, who was fond of him, and saw all this, was at first in a great rage ; but afterwards it was so touching that it brought the tears into my eyes. Yes, madame, just as it does now, when I merely think of the poor prince. Oh, madame !' added Rose-Pompon, her eyes swimming in tears, and with such an expression of sincere interest, that Adrienne was much moved by it ; ' oh, madame, you look so mild and good, that you will not make this poor prince miserable. Pray love him a little bit ; what can it matter to you ?'

So saying, Rose-Pompon, with a perfectly simple, though too familiar, gesture, took hold of Adrienne's hand, as if to enforce her request. It had required great self-command in Mdlle. de Cardoville to repress the rush of joy that was mounting from her heart to her lips, to check the torrent of questions which she burned to address to Rose-Pompon, and to restrain the sweet tears of happiness that for some seconds had trembled in her eyes ; and, strangely enough, when Rose-Pompon took her hand, Adrienne, instead of withdrawing it, pressed the offered hand almost affectionately, and led her towards the window, as if to examine her sweet face more attentively.

On entering the room, the grisette had thrown her bonnet and shawl down upon the bed, so that Adrienne could admire the thick and silky masses of light hair that crowned the fresh face of the charming girl, with its firm, rosy cheeks, its mouth as red as a cherry, and its large blue laughing eyes ; and, thanks to the somewhat scanty dress of Rose-Pompon, Adrienne could fully appreciate the various graces of her nymph-like figure. Strange as it may appear, Adrienne was delighted at finding the girl still prettier than she had at first imagined. The stoical indifference of Djalma to so attractive a creature was the best proof of the sincerity of the passion by which he was actuated.

Having taken the hand of Adrienne, Rose-Pompon was herself confused and surprised at the kindness with which Mdlle. de Cardoville permitted this familiarity. Emboldened by this indulgence, and by the silence of Adrienne, who for some moments had been contemplating her with almost grateful benevolence, the grisette resumed : 'Oh, you will not refuse, madame ? You will take pity on this poor prince ?'

We cannot tell how Adrienne would have answered this indiscreet question of Rose-Pompon, for suddenly a loud, wild, shrill, piercing sound, evidently intended to imitate the crowing of a cock, was heard close to the door of the room.

Adrienne started in alarm ; but the countenance of Rose-Pompon, just now so sad, brightened up joyously at this signal, and, clapping her hands, she exclaimed, ' It is Philemon !'

' What—who ?' said Adrienne, hastily.

' My lover ; oh, the monster ! he must have come upstairs on tiptoe, to take me by surprise with his crowing. Just like him !'

A second cock-a-doodle-doo, still louder than the first, was heard close to the door. 'What a stupid, droll creature it is ! Always the same joke, and yet it always amuses me,' said Rose-Pompon.

And drying her tears with the back of her hand, she began to laugh like one bewitched at Philemon's jest, which, though well known to her, always seemed new and agreeable.

'Do not open the door,' whispered Adrienne, much embarrassed ; 'do not answer, I beg of you.'

'Though the door is bolted, the key is on the outside ; Philemon can see that there is some one at home.'

' No matter—do not let him in.'

' But, madame, he lives here ; the room belongs to him.'

In fact, Philemon, probably growing tired of the little effect produced by his two ornithological imitations, turned the key in the lock, and finding himself unable to open the door, said in a deep bass voice : 'What, dearest puss, have you shut yourself in ? Are you praying Saint-Flambard the return of Philly ?' (short for Philemon).

Adrienne, not wishing to increase, by prolonging it, the awkwardness of this ridiculous situation, went straight to the door and opened it, to the great surprise of Philemon, who recoiled two or three steps. Notwithstanding the annoyance of this incident, Mdlle. de Cardoville could not help smiling at sight of Rose-Pompon's lover, and of the articles he carried in his hand or under his arm.

Philemon was a tall fellow, with dark hair and a very fresh colour, and, being just arrived from a journey, he wore a white cap ; his thick, black beard flowed down on his sky-blue waistcoat ; and a short olive-coloured velvet shooting-coat, with extravagantly large plaid trousers, completed his costume. As for the accessories, which had provoked a smile from Adrienne, they consisted : first, of a portmanteau tucked under his arm, with the head and neck of a goose protruding from it ; secondly, of a cage held in his hand, with an enormous white rabbit all alive within it.

' Oh ! the darling white rabbit ! what pretty red eyes !' Such, it must be confessed, was the first exclamation of Rose-Pompon, though Philemon, to whom it was not addressed, had returned after a long absence ; but the student, far from being shocked at seeing himself thus·sacrificed to his long-eared companion, smiled complacently, rejoicing at the success of his attempt to please his mistress.

All this passed very rapidly. While Rose-Pompon, kneeling before the cage, was still occupied with her admiration of the rabbit, Philemon, struck with the lofty air of Mdlle. de Cardoville, raised his hand to his cap, and bowed respectfully as he made way for her to pass. Adrienne returned his salutation with politeness, full of grace and dignity, and, lightly descending the stairs, soon disappeared. Dazzled by her beauty, as well as impressed with her noble and lofty bearing, and curious to know how in the world Rose-Pompon had fallen in with such an acquaintance, Philemon said to her, in his amorous jargon : 'Dearest puss ! tell her Philly who is that fine lady ?'

'One of my school-fellows, you great satyr !' said Rose-Pompon, still playing with the rabbit.

Then, glancing at a box, which Philemon deposited close to the cage and the portmanteau, she added : ' I'll wager anything you have brought me some more preserves !'

' Philly has brought something better to his dear puss,' said the student, imprinting two vigorous kisses on the rosy cheeks of Rose-Pompon, who had at length consented to stand up ; ' Philly has brought her his heart.'

'Fudge!' said the grisette, delicately placing the thumb of her left hand on the tip of her nose, and opening the fingers, which she slightly moved to and fro. Philemon answered this provocation by putting his arm round her waist; and then the happy pair shut their door.

CHAPTER XXXVII.

SOOTHING WORDS.

DURING the interview of Adrienne with Rose-Pompon a touching scene took place between Agricola and Mother Bunch, who had been much surprised at Mdlle. de Cardoville's condescension with regard to the grisette. Immediately after the departure of Adrienne, Agricola had knelt down beside Mother Bunch, and said to her, with profound emotion : ' We are alone, and I can at length tell you what weighs upon my heart. This act is too cruel—to die of misery and despair, and not to send to me for assistance !'

' Listen to me, Agricola——'——' No, there is no excuse for this. What ! we called each other by the names of brother and sister, and for fifteen years gave every proof of sincere affection—and, when the day of misfortune comes, you quit life without caring for those you must leave behind—without considering that to kill yourself is to tell them they are indifferent to you !'

' Forgive me, Agricola ! it is true. I had never thought of that,' said the workgirl, casting down her eyes ; ' but poverty—want of work——'

' Misery ! want of work ! and was I not here ?' ——' And despair !'

' But why despair ? This generous young lady had received you in her house ; she knew your worth, and treated you as her friend—and just at the moment when you had every chance of happiness, you leave the house abruptly, and we remain in the most horrible anxiety on your account.'

' I feared—to be—to be a burden to my benefactress,' stammered she.

' You a burden to Mdlle. de Cardoville, that is so rich and good !'

' I feared to be indiscreet,' said the sewing-girl, more and more embarrassed.

Instead of answering his adopted sister, Agricola remained silent, and contemplated her for some moments with an undefinable expression ; then he exclaimed suddenly, as if replying to a question put by himself: ' She will forgive me for disobeying her.—I am sure of it.'

He next turned towards Mother Bunch, who was looking at him in astonishment, and said to her in a voice of emotion : ' I am too frank to keep up this deception. I am reproaching you—blaming you—and my thoughts are quite different.'

' How so, Agricola ?'——' My heart aches, when I think of the evil I have done you.'

' I do not understand you, my friend ; you have never done me any evil.'

' What ! never ? even in little things ? when, for instance, yielding to a detestable habit, I, who loved and respected you as my sister, insulted you a hundred times a day ?'

' Insulted me !'——' Yes—when I gave you an odious and ridiculous nickname, instead of calling you properly.'

At these words, Mother Bunch looked at the smith in the utmost alarm, trembling lest he had discovered her painful secret, notwithstanding the assurance she had received from Mdlle. de Cardoville. Yet she calmed herself a little when she reflected, that Agricola might of himself have thought of the humiliation inflicted on her by calling her Mother Bunch, and she answered him with a forced smile : ' Can you be grieved at so small a thing? It was a habit, Agricola, from childhood. When did your good and affectionate mother, who nevertheless loved me as her daughter, ever call me anything else?'

'And did my mother consult you about my marriage, speak to you of the rare beauty of my bride, beg you to come and see her, and study her character, in the hope that the instinct of your affection for me would warn you—if I made a bad choice? Did my mother have this cruelty?—No; it was I, who thus pierced your heart!'

The fears of the hearer were again aroused; there could be but little doubt that Agricola knew her secret. She felt herself sinking with confusion; yet, making a last effort not to believe the discovery, she murmured in a feeble voice: 'True, Agricola! It was not your mother, but yourself, who made me that request—and I was grateful to you for such a mark of confidence.'

'Grateful, my poor girl!' cried the smith, whilst his eyes filled with tears; 'no, it is not true. I pained you fearfully—I was merciless—heaven knows, without being aware of it!'

'But,' said the other, in a voice now almost unintelligible, 'what makes you think so!'

'Your love for me!' cried the smith, trembling with emotion, as he clasped Mother Bunch in a brotherly embrace.

'Oh, heaven!' murmured the unfortunate creature, as she covered her face with her hands, 'he knows all.'

'Yes, I know all,' resumed Agricola, with an expression of ineffable tenderness and respect: 'yes, I know all, and I will not have you blush for a sentiment, which honours me, and of which I feel so justly proud. Yes, I know all; and I say to myself with joy and pride, that the best, the most noble heart in the world is mine—will be mine always. Come, Magdalen; let us leave shame to evil passions. Raise your eyes, and look at me! You know, if my countenance was ever false—if it ever reflected a feigned emotion. Then look and tell me, if you cannot read in my features, how proud I am, Magdalen, how justly proud of your love!'

Overwhelmed with grief and confusion, Mother Bunch had not dared to look on Agricola; but his words expressed so deep a conviction, the tones of his voice revealed so tender an emotion, that the poor creature felt her shame gradually diminish, particularly when Agricola added, with rising animation: 'Be satisfied, my sweet, my noble Magdalen; I will be worthy of this love. Believe me, it shall yet cause you as much happiness as it has occasioned tears. Why should this love be a motive for estrangement, confusion, fear? For what is love, in the sense in which it is held by your generous heart? Is it not a continual exchange of devotion, tenderness, esteem, of mutual and blind confidence?—Why, Magdalen! we may have all this for one another—devotion, tenderness, confidence—even more than in times past; for, on a thousand occasions, your secret inspired you with fear and suspicion—while, for the future, on the contrary, you will see me take such delight in the place I fill in your good and valiant heart, that you will be happy in the happiness you bestow. What I have just said may seem very selfish and conceited; so much the worse! I do not know how to lie.'

The longer the smith spoke, the less troubled became Mother Bunch. What she had above all feared in the discovery of her secret was to see it received with raillery, contempt, or humiliating compassion; far from this, joy and happiness were distinctly visible on the manly and honest face of Agricola. The hunchback knew him incapable of deception; therefore she exclaimed, this time without shame or confusion, but rather with a sort of pride:

'Every sincere and pure passion is so far good and consoling as to end by deserving interest and sympathy, when it has triumphed over its first excess ! It is alike honourable to the heart which feels and that which inspires it !—Thanks to you, Agricola—thanks to the kind words, which have raised me in my own esteem—I feel that, instead of blushing, I ought to be proud of this love. My benefactress is right—you are right : why should I be ashamed of it ? Is it not a true and sacred love ? To be near you, to love you, to tell you so, to prove it by constant devotion, what did I ever desire more ? And yet shame and fear, joined with that dizziness of the brain which extreme misery produces, drove me to suicide !—But then some allowance must be made for the suspicions of a poor creature, who has been the subject of ridicule from her cradle. So my secret was to die with me, unless some unforeseen accident should reveal it to you ; and, in that case, you are right—sure of myself, sure of you, I ought to have feared nothing. But I may claim some indulgence ; mistrust, cruel mistrust of one's self, makes one doubt others also. Let us forget all that. Agricola, my generous brother, I will say to you, as you said to me just now, "Look at me ; you know my countenance cannot lie. Look at me ; see if I shun your gaze ; see if, ever in my life, I looked so happy"—and yet, even now, I was about to die !'

She spoke the truth. Agricola himself could not have hoped so prompt an effect from his words In spite of the deep traces which misery, grief, and sickness had imprinted on the girl's features, they now shone with radiant happiness and serenity, whilst her blue eyes, gentle and pure as her soul, were fixed, without embarrassment, on those of Agricola.

'Oh ! thanks, thanks !' cried the smith, in a rapture of delight : ' when I see you so calm, and so happy, Magdalen, I am indeed grateful.'

'Yes, I am calm, I am happy,' replied she ; 'and happy I shall be, for I can now tell you my most secret thoughts. Yes, happy ; for this day, which began so fatally, ends like a divine dream. Far from being afraid, I now look at you with hope and joy. I have again found my generous benefactress, and I am tranquil as to the fate of my poor sister. Oh ! shall we not soon see her ? I should like to take part in this happiness.'

She seemed so happy, that the smith did not dare to inform her of the death of Cephyse, and reserved himself to communicate the same at a more fitting opportunity. Therefore he answered : ' Cephyse, being the stronger, has been the more shaken ; it will not be prudent, I am told, to see her to-day.'

'I will wait then. I can repress my impatience, I have so much to say to you.'——' Dear, gentle Magdalen !'

'Oh, my friend !' cried the girl, interrupting Agricola, with tears of joy ; ' I cannot tell you what I feel, when I hear you call me Magdalen. It is so sweet, so soothing, that my heart expands with delight.'

'Poor girl ! how dreadfully she must have suffered !' cried the smith, with inexpressible emotion, ' when she displays so much happiness, so much gratitude, at being called by her own poor name !'

'But consider, my friend ; that word in your mouth contains a new life for me. If you only knew what hopes, what pleasures, I can now see gleaming in the future ! If you knew all the cherished longings of my tenderness !—Your wife, the charming Angela, with her angel face and angel-soul—oh ! in my turn, I can say to you, "Look at me, and see how sweet that name is to my lips and heart !" Yes, your charming, your good Angela will call me Magdalen—and your children, Agricola, your children ! —dear little creatures !—to them also I shall be Magdalen—their good Magdalen—and the love I shall bear them will make them mine, as well as their mother's—and I shall have my part in every maternal care—and

they will belong to us three ; will they not, Agricola ?—Oh ! let me, let me
weep ! These tears without bitterness do me so much good ; they are tears
that need not be concealed. Thank heaven ! thank you, my friend ! those
other tears are I trust dried for ever '

For some seconds, this affecting scene had been overlooked by an invisible witness. The smith and Mother Bunch had not perceived Mdlle.
de Cardoville standing on the threshold of the door. As Mother Bunch
had said, this day, which dawned with all under such fatal auspices, had
become for all a day of ineffable felicity. Adrienne, too, was full of joy,
for Djalma had been faithful to her, Djalma loved her with passion. The
odious appearances, of which she had been the dupe and victim, evidently
formed part of a new plot of Rodin, and it only remained for Mdlle. de
Cardoville to discover the end of these machinations.

Another joy was reserved for her. The happy are quick in detecting
happiness in others, and Adrienne guessed, by the hunchback's last words,
that there was no longer any secret between the smith and the sempstress.
She could not therefore help exclaiming, as she entered : ' Oh ! this will
be the brightest day of my life, for I shall not be happy alone !'

Agricola and Mother Bunch turned round hastily. ' Lady,' said the
smith, ' in spite of the promise I made you, I could not conceal from
Magdalen that I knew she loved me !'

' Now that I no longer blush for this love before Agricola, why should
I blush for it before you, lady, that told me to be proud of it, because it is
noble and pure ?' said Mother Bunch, to whom her happiness gave strength
enough to rise, and to lean upon Agricola's arm.

' It is well, my friend,' said Adrienne, as she threw her arms round her
to support her ; ' only one word, to excuse the indiscretion with which you
will perhaps reproach me. If I told your secret to M. Agricola——'

' Do you know why it was, Magdalen ?' cried the smith, interrupting
Adrienne. ' It was only another proof of the lady's delicate generosity. " I
long hesitated to confide to you this secret," said she to me this morning,
" but I have at length made up my mind to it. We shall probably find your
adopted sister ; you have been to her the best of brothers ; but many times,
without knowing it, you have wounded her feelings cruelly—and now that
you know her secret, I trust in your kind heart to keep it faithfully, and
so spare the poor child a thousand pangs—pangs the more bitter, because
they come from you, and are suffered in silence. Hence, when you speak
to her of your wife, your domestic happiness, take care not to gall that
noble and tender heart."—Yes, Magdalen, these were the reasons that led
the lady to commit what she calls an indiscretion.'

' I want words to thank you now and ever,' said Mother Bunch.

' See, my friend,' replied Adrienne, ' how often the designs of the wicked
turn against themselves. They feared your devotion to me, and therefore
employed that unhappy Florine to steal your journal——'

' So as to drive me from your house with shame, lady, when I supposed
my most secret thoughts an object of ridicule to all. There can be no
doubt such was their plan,' said Mother Bunch.

' None, my child. Well ! this horrible wickedness, which nearly caused
your death, now turns to the confusion of the criminals. Their plot is discovered—and, luckily, many other of their designs,' said Adrienne, as she
thought of Rose-Pompon.

Then she resumed, with heartfelt joy : ' At last, we are again united,
happier than ever, and in our very happiness we shall find new resources to
combat our enemies. I say *our* enemies—for all that love me are odious to
these wretches. But courage, the hour is come, and the good people will
have their turn.'

'Thank heaven, lady,' said the smith ; 'for my part, I shall not be wanting in zeal. What delight to strip them of their mask.'

'Let me remind you, M. Baudoin, that you have an appointment for to-morrow with M. Hardy.'——'I have not forgotten it, lady, any more than the generous offers I am to convey to him.'

'That is nothing. He belongs to my family. Tell him (what indeed I shall write to him this evening), that the funds necessary to reopen his factory are at his disposal ; I do not say so for his sake only, but for that of a hundred families reduced to want. Beg him to quit immediately the fatal abode to which they have taken him : for a thousand reasons he should be on his guard against all that surround him.'

'Be satisfied, lady. The letter he wrote to me in reply to the one I got secretly delivered to him, was short, affectionate, sad—but he grants me the interview I had asked for, and I am sure I shall be able to persuade him to leave that melancholy dwelling, and perhaps to depart with me, he has always had so much confidence in my attachment.'

'Well, M. Baudoin, courage !' said Adrienne, as she threw her cloak over the workgirl's shoulders, and wrapped her round with care. 'Let us be gone, for it is late. As soon as we get home, I will give you a letter for M. Hardy, and to-morrow you will come and tell me the result of your visit. No, not to-morrow,' she added, blushing slightly. 'Write to me to-morrow, and the day after, about twelve, come to me.'

✿ ✿ ✿ ✿ ✿ ✿

Some minutes later, the young sempstress, supported by Agricola and Adrienne, had descended the stairs of that gloomy house, and, being placed in the carriage by the side of Mdlle. de Cardoville, she earnestly entreated to be allowed to see Cephyse : it was in vain that Agricola assured her it was impossible, and that she should see her the next day. Thanks to the information derived from Rose-Pompon, Mdlle. de Cardoville was reason-ably suspicious of all those who surrounded Djalma, and she therefore took measures, that very evening, to have a letter delivered to the prince by what she considered a sure hand.

CHAPTER XXXVIII.

THE TWO CARRIAGES.

IT is the evening of the day on which Mdlle. de Cardoville prevented the sewing-girl's suicide. It strikes eleven ; the night is dark ; the wind blows with violence, and drives along great black clouds, which completely hide the pale lustre of the moon. A hackney-coach, drawn by two broken-winded horses, ascends slowly and with difficulty the slope of the Rue Blanche, which is pretty steep near the barrier, in the part where is situated the house occupied by Djalma.

The coach stops. The coachman, cursing the length of an interminable drive 'within the circuit,' leading at last to this difficult ascent, turns round on his box, leans over towards the front window of the vehicle, and says in a gruff tone to the person he is driving : 'Come ! are we almost there ? From the Rue de Vaugirard to the Barrière Blanche, is a pretty good stretch, I think, without reckoning that the night is so dark, that one can hardly see two steps before one—and the street-lamps not lighted because of the moon, which doesn't shine, after all !'

'Look out for a little door with a portico—drive on about twenty yards be-yond—and then stop close to the wall,' answered a squeaking voice, im-patiently, and with an Italian accent.

'Here is a beggarly Dutchman, that will make me as savage as a bear!' muttered the angry Jehu to himself. Then he added : 'Thousand thunders ! I tell you that I can't see. How the devil can I find out your little door?'

'Have you no sense? Follow the wall to the right, brush against it, and you will easily find the little door. It is next to No. 50. If you do not find it, you must be drunk,' answered the Italian, with increased bitterness.

The coachman only replied by swearing like a trooper, and whipping up his jaded horses. Then, keeping close to the wall, he strained his eyes in trying to read the numbers of the houses, by the aid of his carriage-lamps.

After some moments, the coach again stopped. 'I have passed No. 50, and here is a little door with a portico,' said the coachman. 'Is that the one.'——'Yes,' said the voice. 'Now go forward some twenty yards, and then stop.'

'Well ! I never——'——'Then get down from your box, and give twice three knocks at the little door we have just passed—you understand me ?—twice three knocks.'

'Is that all you give me to drink ?' cried the exasperated coachman.

'When you have taken me back to the Faubourg Saint-Germain, where I live, you shall have something handsome, if you do but manage matters well.'

'Ha ! now the Faubourg Saint-Germain ! Only that little bit of distance !' said the driver, with repressed rage. 'And I who have winded my horses, wanted to be on the boulevard by the time the play was out. Well, I'm blowed !' Then, putting a good face on his bad luck, and consoling himself with the thought of the promised drink-money, he resumed : 'I am to give twice three knocks at the little door ?'

'Yes ; three knocks first—then a pause—then three other knocks. Do you understand ?'

'What next ?'——'Tell the person who comes, that he is waited for, and bring him here to the coach.'

'The devil burn you !' said the coachman to himself, as he turned round on the box, and whipped up his horses, adding : 'this crusty old Dutchman has something to do with Freemasons, or, perhaps, smugglers, seeing we are so near the gates. He deserves my giving him in charge, for bringing me all the way from the Rue de Vaugirard.'

At twenty steps beyond the little door, the coach again stopped, and the coachman descended from the box to execute the orders he had received. Going to the little door, he knocked three times ; then paused, as he had been desired, and then knocked three times more. The clouds, which had hitherto been so thick as entirely to conceal the disk of the moon, just then withdrew sufficiently to afford a glimmering light, so that when the door opened at the signal, the coachman saw a middle-sized person issue from it, wrapped in a cloak, and wearing a coloured cap.

This man carefully locked the door, and then advanced two steps into the street. 'They are waiting for you,' said the coachman ; 'I am to take you along with me to the coach.'

Preceding the man with the cloak, who only answered him by a nod, he led him to the coach-door, which he was about to open, and to let down the step, when the voice exclaimed from the inside : 'It is not necessary. The gentleman may talk to me through the window. I will call you when it is time to start.'

'Which means that I shall be kept here long enough to send you to all the devils !' murmured the driver. 'However, I may as well walk about, just to stretch my legs.'

So saying, he began to walk up and down, by the side of the wall in which was the little door. Presently, he heard the distant sound of wheels, which soon came nearer and nearer, and a carriage, rapidly ascending the slope, stopped on the other side of the little garden-door.

'Come, I say! a private carriage!' said the coachman. 'Good horses those, to come up the Rue Blanche at a trot.'

The coachman was just making this observation, when, by favour of a momentary gleam of light, he saw a man step from the carriage, advance rapidly to the little door, open it, and go in, closing it after him.

'It gets thicker and thicker!' said the coachman. 'One comes out, and the other goes in.'

So saying, he walked up to the carriage. It was splendidly harnessed, and drawn by two handsome and vigorous horses. The driver sat motionless, in his great box-coat, with the handle of his whip resting on his right knee.

'Here's weather to drive about in, with such tidy dukes as yours, comrade!' said the humble hackney-coachman to this automaton, who remained mute and impassible, without even appearing to know that he was spoken to.

'He doesn't understand French—he's an Englishman. One could tell that by his horses,' said the coachman, putting this interpretation on the silence of his brother whip. Then, perceiving a tall footman at a little distance, dressed in a long grey livery coat, with blue collar and silver buttons, the coachman addressed himself to him, by way of compensation, but without much varying his phrase : 'Here's nice weather to stand about in, comrade!' On the part of the footman, he was met with the same imperturbable silence.

'They're both Englishmen,' resumed the coachman, philosophically ; and, though somewhat astonished at the incident of the little door, he recommenced his walk in the direction of his own vehicle.

While these facts were passing, the man in the cloak, and the man with the Italian accent continued their conversation, the one still in the coach, and the other leaning with his hand on the door. It had already lasted for some time, and was carried on in Italian. They were evidently talking of some absent person, as will appear from the following.

'So,' said the voice from the coach, 'that is agreed to ?'——'Yes, my lord,' answered the man in the cloak ; 'but only in case the eagle should become a serpent.'

'And, in the contrary event, you will receive the other half of the ivory crucifix I gave you.'——'I shall know what it means, my lord.'

'Continue to merit and preserve his confidence.'——'I will merit and preserve it, my lord, because I admire and respect this man, who is stronger than the strongest, by craft, and courage, and will. I have knelt before him with humility, as I would kneel before one of the three black idols that stand between Bowanee and her worshippers ; for his religion, like mine, teaches to change life into nothingness.'

'Humph!' said the voice, in a tone of some embarrassment ; 'these comparisons are useless and inaccurate. Only think of obeying him, without explaining your obedience.'

'Let him speak, and I perform his will ! I am in his hands like a corpse, as he himself expresses it. He has seen, he sees every day, my devotion to his interests with regard to Prince Djalma. He has only to say : "Kill him !"—and this son of a king——'

'For heaven's sake, do not have such ideas!' cried the voice, interrupting the man in the cloak. 'Thank heaven, you will never be asked for such proofs of your submission.'

'What I am ordered, I do. Bowanee sees me.'

'I do not doubt your zeal. I know that you are a loving and intelligent barrier, placed between the prince and many guilty interests ; and it is because I have heard of that zeal, of your skill in circumventing this young Indian, and, above all, of the motives of your blind devotion, that I have wished to inform you of everything. You are the fanatical worshipper of him you serve. That is well ; man should be the obedient slave of the god he chooses for himself.'——'Yes, my lord ; so long as the god remains a god.'

'We understand each other perfectly. As for your recompense, you know what I have promised.'——'My lord, I have my reward already.'

'How so ?'——'I know what I know.'

'Very well. Then as for secrecy——'——'You have securities, my lord.'

'Yes—and sufficient ones.'——'The interest of the cause I serve, my lord, would alone be enough to secure my zeal and discretion.'

'True ; you are a man of firm and ardent convictions.'——'I strive to be so, my lord.'

'And, after all, a very religious man in your way. It is very praiseworthy, in these irreligious times, to have any views at all on such matters—particularly when those views will just enable me to count upon your aid.'

'You may count upon it, my lord, for the same reason that the intrepid hunter prefers a jackal to ten foxes, a tiger to ten jackals, a lion to ten tigers, and the welmiss to ten lions.'

'What is the welmiss ?'——'It is what spirit is to matter, the blade to the scabbard, the perfume to the flower, the head to the body.'

'I understand. There never was a more just comparison. You are a man of sound judgment. Always recollect what you have just told me, and make yourself more and more worthy of the confidence of—your idol.'

'Will he soon be in a state to hear me, my lord ?'——'In two or three days, at most. Yesterday a providential crisis saved his life ; and he is endowed with so energetic a will, that his cure will be very rapid.'

'Shall you see him again to-morrow, my lord ?'——'Yes, before my departure, to bid him farewell.'

'Then tell him a strange circumstance, of which I have not been able to inform him, but which happened yesterday.'

'What was it ?'——'I had gone to the garden of the dead. I saw funerals everywhere, and lighted torches, in the midst of the black night, shining upon tombs. Bowanee smiled in her ebon sky. As I thought of that divinity of destruction, I beheld with joy the dead-cart emptied of its coffins. The immense pit yawned like the mouth of hell ; corpses were heaped upon corpses, and still it yawned the same. Suddenly, by the light of a torch, I saw an old man beside me. He wept. I had seen him before. He is a Jew—the keeper of the house in the Rue Saint-François—you know what I mean.' Here the man in the cloak started.

'Yes, I know ; but what is the matter ? why do you stop short ?'

'Because in that house there has been for a hundred and fifty years the portrait of a man whom I once met in the centre of India, on the banks of the Ganges.' And the man in the cloak again paused and shuddered.

'A singular resemblance, no doubt.'——'Yes, my lord, a singular resemblance—nothing more.'

'But the Jew—the old Jew ?'——'I am coming to that, my lord. Still weeping, he said to a gravedigger, "Well ! and the coffin ?"—"You were right," answered the man ; "I found it in the second row of the other grave. It had the figure of a cross on it, formed by seven black nails. But how could you know the place and the mark ? —"Alas ! it is no matter," replied the old Jew, with bitter melancholy. "You see that I was but too well informed on the subject. But where is the coffin ?"—" Behind the great tomb of black marble ; I have hidden it there. So make haste ; for, in the confusion, nothing will be noticed. You have paid me well, and I wish you to succeed in what you require." '

'And what did the old Jew do with the coffin marked with the seven black nails ?'

'Two men accompanied him, my lord, bearing a covered litter, with curtains drawn round it. He lighted a lantern, and, followed by these two men, went towards the place pointed out by the gravedigger. A stoppage, occasioned by the dead-carts, made me lose sight of the old Jew, whom I was following amongst the tombs. Afterwards I was unable to find him.'

'It is indeed a strange affair. What could this old Jew want with the coffin ?'——'It is said, my lord, that they use dead bodies in preparing their magic charms.'

'Those unbelievers are capable of anything—even of holding communication with the Enemy of mankind. However, we will look after this : the discovery may be of importance.'

At this instant a clock struck twelve in the distance.——'Midnight ! already ?'

'Yes, my lord.'——'I must be gone. Good-bye—but for the last time swear to me that, should matters so turn out, as soon as you receive the other half of the ivory crucifix I have just given you, you will keep your promise.'

'I have sworn it by Bowanee, my lord.'——'Do not forget that, to make all sure, the person who will deliver to you the other half of the crucifix is to say—come, what is he to say ?'

'He is to say, my lord : " There is many a slip 'twixt the cup and the lip."'

'Very well. Adieu ! secrecy and fidelity !'——'Secrecy and fidelity, my lord,' answered the man in the cloak.

Some seconds after, the hackney-coach started, carrying with it Cardinal Malipieri, one of the speakers in the above dialogue. The other, whom the reader has no doubt recognised as Faringhea, returned to the little garden-door of the house occupied by Djalma. At the moment he was putting the key into the lock, the door opened, to his great astonishment, and a man came forth. Faringhea rushed upon the unknown, seized him violently by the collar, and exclaimed : 'Who are you ? whence came you ?'

The stranger evidently found the tone of this question anything but satisfactory ; for, instead of answering, he struggled to disengage himself from Faringhea's hold, and cried out, in a loud voice : 'Help ! Peter !'

Instantly the carriage, which had been standing a few yards off, dashed up at full speed, and Peter, the tall footman, seizing the half-breed by the shoulders, flung him back several paces, and thus made a seasonable diversion in favour of the unknown.

'Now, sir,' said the latter to Faringhea, shaking himself, and still protected by the gigantic footman, 'I am in a state to answer your questions, though you certainly have a very rough way of receiving an old acquaintance. I am Dupont, ex-bailiff of the estate of Cardoville, and it was I who helped to fish you out of the water, when the ship was wrecked in which you had embarked.'

By the light of the carriage-lamps, indeed, the half-caste recognised the good, honest face of Dupont, formerly bailiff, and now house-steward, to Mdlle. de Cardoville. It must not be forgotten that Dupont had been the first to write to Mdlle. de Cardoville, to ask her to interest herself for Djalma, who was then detained at Cardoville Castle by the injuries he had received during the shipwreck.

'But, sir, what is your business here? Why do you introduce your-self clandestinely into this house?' said Faringhea, in an abrupt and suspicious tone.

'I will just observe to you that there is nothing clandestine in the matter. I came here in a carriage, with servants in the livery of my excellent mistress, Mdlle. de Cardoville, charged by her, without any disguise or mystery, to deliver a letter to Prince Djalma, her cousin,' replied Dupont, with dignity.

On these words, Faringhea trembled with mute rage, as he answered : 'And why, sir, come at this late hour, and introduce yourself by this little door ?'

'I came at this hour, my dear sir, because such was Mdlle. de Cardoville's command, and I entered by this little gate because there is every reason to believe that if I had gone round to the other I should not have been permitted to see the prince.'

'You are mistaken, sir,' replied the half-caste.

'It is possible : but as we knew that the prince usually passed a good portion of the night in the little saloon, which communicates with the greenhouse, and as Mdlle. de Cardoville had kept a duplicate key of this door, I was pretty certain, by taking this course, to be able to deliver into the prince's own hands the letter from Mdlle. de Cardoville, his cousin—which I have now had the honour of doing, my dear sir ; and I have been deeply touched by the kindness with which the prince deigned to receive me and to remember our last interview.'

'And who kept you so well informed, sir, of the prince's habits ?' said Faringhea, unable to control his vexation.

'If I have been well informed as to his habits, my dear sir, I have had no such correct knowledge of yours,' answered Dupont, with a mocking air ; 'for I assure you that I had no more notion of seeing you than you had of seeing me.'

So saying, M. Dupont bowed with something like mock politeness to the half-caste, and got into the carriage, which drove off rapidly, leaving Faringhea in a state of the utmost surprise and anger.

CHAPTER XXXIX.

THE APPOINTMENT.

THE morning after Dupont's mission to Prince Djalma, the latter was walking with hasty and impatient step up and down the little saloon, which communicated, as we already know, with the greenhouse from which Adrienne had entered when she first appeared to him. In remembrance of that day, he had chosen to dress himself as on the occasion in question ; he wore the same tunic of white cashmere, with a cherry-coloured turban, to match with his girdle ; his gaiters, of scarlet velvet, embroidered with silver, displayed the fine form of his leg, and terminated in small white morocco slippers, with red heels. Happiness has so instantaneous, and, as it were, material an influence upon young, lively, and ardent natures, that Djalma, dejected and despairing only the day before, was no longer like the same person. The pale, transparent gold of his complexion was no longer tarnished by a livid hue. His large eyes, of late obscured like black diamonds by a humid vapour, now shone with mild radiance in the centre of their pearly setting ; his lips, long pale, had recovered their natural colour, which was rich and soft as the fine purple flowers of his country.

Ever and anon, pausing in his hasty walk, he stopped suddenly, and drew from his bosom a little piece of paper, carefully folded, which he pressed to his lips with enthusiastic ardour. Then, unable to restrain the expression of his happiness, he uttered a full and sonorous cry of joy, and with a bound he was in front of the plate-glass which separated the saloon from the conservatory, in which he had first seen Mdlle. de Cardoville. By a singular power of remembrance, or marvellous hallucination of a mind possessed by a fixed idea, Djalma had often seen, or fancied he saw, the adored semblance of Adrienne appear to him through this sheet of crystal. The illusion had been so complete, that, with his eyes ardently fixed on the vision he invoked, he had been able, with the aid of a pencil dipped in carmine, to trace, with astonishing exactness, the profile of the ideal countenance which the delirium of his imagination had presented to his view.* It was before these delicate lines of bright carmine that Djalma now stood in deep contemplation, after perusing, and reperusing, and raising twenty times to his lips, the letter he had received the night before from the hands of Dupont. Djalma was not alone. Faringhea watched all the movements of the prince, with a subtle, attentive, and gloomy aspect. Standing respectfully in a corner of the saloon, the half-caste appeared to be occu-pied in unfolding and spreading out Djalma's sash, light, silky Indian web, the brown ground of which was almost entirely concealed by the exquisite gold and silver embroidery with which it was overlaid.

The countenance of the half-caste wore a dark and gloomy expression. He could not deceive himself. The letter from Mdlle. de Cardoville, de-livered by Dupont to Djalma, must have been the cause of the delight he now experienced, for, without doubt, he knew himself beloved. In that event, his obstinate silence towards Faringhea, ever since the latter had entered the saloon, greatly alarmed the half-caste, who could not tell what interpretation to put upon it. The night before, after parting with Dupont, he had hastened, in a state of anxiety easily understood, to look for the prince, in the hope of ascertaining the effect produced by Mdlle. de Cardo-ville's letter. But he found the parlour door closed, and when he knocked, he received no answer from within. Then, though the night was far ad-vanced, he had despatched a note to Rodin, in which he informed him of Dupont's visit and its probable intention. Djalma had indeed passed the night in a tumult of happiness and hope, and a fever of impatience quite impossible to describe. Repairing to his bedchamber only towards the morning, he had taken a few moments of repose, and had then dressed himself without assistance.

Many times, but in vain, the half-caste had discreetly knocked at the door of Djalma's apartment. It was only in the early part of the afternoon, that the prince had rung the bell to order his carriage to be ready by half-past two. Faringhea having presented himself, the prince had given him the order without looking at him, as he might have done to any other of his servants. Was this suspicion, aversion, or mere absence of mind on the part of Djalma? Such were the questions which the half-caste put to him-self with growing anguish ; for the designs of which he was the most active and immediate instrument, might all be ruined by the least suspicion in the prince.

'Oh ! the hours—the hours—how slow they are !' cried the young Indian, suddenly, in a low and trembling voice.

'The day before yesterday, my lord, you said the hours were very long,' observed Faringhea, as he drew near Djalma in order to attract his

* Some collectors of curiosities possess such sketches, the product of Indian art, distinguished by their primitive simplicity.

attention. Seeing that he did not succeed in this, he advanced a few steps nearer, and resumed : ' Your joy seems very great, my lord ; tell the cause of it to your poor and faithful servant, that he also may rejoice with you.'

If he heard the words, Djalma did not pay any attention to them. He made no answer, and his large black eyes gazed upon vacancy. He seemed to smile admiringly on some enchanting vision, and he folded his two hands upon his bosom, in the attitude which his countrymen assume at the hour of prayer. After some instants of contemplation, he said : ' What o'clock is it ?'—but he asked this question of himself, rather than of any third person.

' It will soon be two o'clock, my lord, said Faringhea.

Having heard this answer, Djalma seated himself, and hid his face in his hands, as if completely absorbed in some ineffable meditation. Urged on by his growing anxiety, and wishing at any cost to attract the attention of Djalma, Faringhea approached still nearer to him, and, almost certain of the effect of the words he was about to utter, said to him in a slow and emphatic voice : ' My lord, I am sure that you owe the happiness which now transports you to Mdlle. de Cardoville.'

Hardly had this name been pronounced, than Djalma started from his chair, looked the half-breed full in the face, and exclaimed, as if only just aware of his presence, ' Faringhea ! you here !—what is the matter?'

' Your faithful servant shares in your joy, my lord.'

' What joy ?'——' That which the letter of Mdlle. de Cardoville has occasioned, my lord.'

Djalma returned no answer, but his eye shone with so much serene happiness, that the half-caste recovered from his apprehensions. No cloud of doubt or suspicion obscured the radiant features of the prince. After a few moments of silence, Djalma fixed upon the half-caste a look half-veiled with a tear of joy, and said to him, with the expression of one whose heart overflows with love and happiness : ' Oh ! such delight is good—great— like heaven !—for it is heaven which——'

' You deserve this happiness, my lord, after so many sufferings.'

' What sufferings ?—Oh ! yes. I formerly suffered at Java ; but that was years ago.'

' My lord, this great good fortune does not astonish me. What have I always told you ? Do not despair ; feign a violent passion for some other woman, and then this proud young lady——'

At these words Djalma looked at the half-caste with so piercing a glance, that the latter stopped short ; but the prince said to him with affectionate goodness, ' Go on ! I listen.'

Then, leaning his chin upon his hand, and his elbow on his knee, he gazed so intently on Faringhea, and yet with such unutterable mildness, that even that iron soul was touched for a moment with a slight feeling of remorse.

' I was saying, my lord,' he resumed, ' that by following the counsels of your faithful slave, who persuaded you to feign a passionate love for another woman, you have brought the proud Mdlle. de Cardoville to come to you. Did I not tell you it would be so ?'

' Yes, you did tell me so,' answered Djalma, still maintaining the same position, and examining the half-caste with the same fixed and mild attention.

The surprise of Faringhea increased ; generally, the prince, without treating him with the least harshness, preserved the somewhat distant and imperious manners of their common country, and he had never before spoken to him with such extreme mildness. Knowing all the evil he had done the prince, and suspicious as the wicked must ever be, the half-caste thought for a moment, that his master's apparent kindness might conceal a snare. He continued, therefore, with less assurance, 'Believe me, my lord, this day, if you do but know how to profit by your advantages, will console you for all your troubles, which have indeed been great—for only yesterday, though you are generous enough to forget it, only yesterday you suffered cruelly—but you were not alone in your sufferings. This proud young lady suffered also !'

'Do you think so ?' said Djalma.——'Oh ! it is quite sure, my lord. What must she not have felt, when she saw you at the theatre with another woman !—If she loved you only a little, she must have been deeply wounded in her self-esteem ; if she loved you with passion, she must have been struck to the heart. At length, you see, wearied out with suffering, she has come to you.'

'So that, any way, she must have suffered—and that does not move your pity ?' said Djalma, in a constrained, but still very mild voice.

'Before thinking of others, my lord, I think of your distresses ; and they touch me too nearly to leave me any pity for other woes,' added Faringhea, hypocritically, so greatly had the influence of Rodin already modified the character of the Phansegar.

'It is strange !' said Djalma, speaking to himself, as he viewed the half-caste with a glance still kind, but piercing.

'What is strange, my lord ?'——'Nothing. But tell me, since your advice has hitherto prospered so well, what think you of the future ?'

'Of the future, my lord ?'——'Yes ; in an hour I shall be with Mdlle. de Cardoville.'

'That is a serious matter, my lord. The whole future will depend upon this interview.'——'That is what I was just thinking.'

'Believe me, my lord, women never love any so well, as the bold man who spares them the embarrassment of a refusal.'——'Explain more fully.'

'Well, my lord, they despise the timid and languishing lover, who asks humbly for what he might take by force.'

'But to day I shall meet Mdlle. de Cardoville for the first time.'

'You have met her a thousand times in your dreams, my lord ; and depend upon it, she has seen you also in her dreams, since she loves you. Every one of your amorous thoughts has found an echo in her heart. All your ardent adorations have been responded to by her. Love has not two languages, and, without meeting, you have said all that you had to say to each other. Now, it is for you to act as her master, and she will be yours entirely.'

'It is strange—very strange !' said Djalma, a second time, without removing his eyes from Faringhea's face.

Mistaking the sense which the prince attached to these words, the half-caste resumed : 'Believe me, my lord, however strange it may appear, this is the wisest course. Remember the past. Was it by playing the part of a timid lover that you have brought to your feet this proud young lady, my lord ? No, it was by pretending to despise her, in favour of another woman. Therefore, let us have no weakness. The lion does not woo like the poor turtle-dove. What cares the sultan of the desert for a few plaintiff howls from the lioness, who is more pleased than angry at his rude and wild caresses ? Soon submissive, fearful, and happy, she follows in the track of her master. Believe me, my lord—try everything—dare everything—and to-day you will become the adored sultan of this young lady, whose beauty all Paris admires.'

After some minutes' silence, Djalma, shaking his head with an expression of tender pity, said to the half-caste, in his mild, sonorous voice: 'Why betray me thus? Why advise me thus wickedly to use violence, terror, and surprise, towards an angel of purity, whom I respect as my mother? Is it not enough for you to have been so long devoted to my enemies, whose hatred has followed me from Java?'

Had Djalma sprung upon the half-caste with bloodshot eye, menacing brow, and lifted poniard, the latter would have been less surprised, and perhaps less frightened, than when he heard the prince speak of his treachery in this tone of mild reproach.

He drew back hastily, as if about to stand on his guard. But Djalma resumed, with the same gentleness, 'Fear nothing. Yesterday I should have killed you! But to-day happy love renders me too just, too merciful for that. I pity you, without any feeling of bitterness—for you must have been very unhappy, or you could not have become so wicked.'

'My lord!' said the half-caste, with growing amazement.

'Yes, you must have suffered much, and met with little mercy, poor creature, to have become so merciless in your hate, and proof against the sight of a happiness like mine. When I listened to you just now, and saw the sad perseverance of your hatred, I felt the deepest commiseration for you.'

'I do not know, my lord—but——' stammered the half-caste, and was unable to find words to proceed.——'Come, now—what harm have I ever done you?'

'None, my lord,' answered Faringhea.——'Then why do you hate me thus? why pursue me with so much animosity? Was it not enough to give me the perfidious counsel to feign a shameful love for the young girl that was brought hither, and who quitted the house disgusted at the miserable part she was to play?'

'Your feigned love for that young girl, my lord,' replied Faringhea, gradually recovering his presence of mind, 'conquered the coldness of——'

'Do not say that,' resumed the prince, interrupting him with the same mildness. 'If I enjoy this happiness, which makes me compassionate towards you, and raises me above myself, it is because Mdlle. de Cardoville now knows that I have never for a moment ceased to love her as she ought to be loved, with adoration and reverence. It was your intention to have parted us for ever, and you had nearly succeeded.'

'If you think this of me, my lord, you must look upon me as your most mortal enemy.'

'Fear nothing, I tell you. I have no right to blame you. In the madness of my grief, I listened to you and followed your advice. I was not only your dupe, but your accomplice. Only confess that, when you saw me at your mercy, dejected, crushed, despairing, it was cruel in you to advise the course that might have been most fatal to me.'

'The ardour of my zeal may have deceived me, my lord.'

'I am willing to believe it. And yet again to-day there were the same evil counsels. You had no more pity for my happiness than for my sorrow. The rapture of my heart inspires you with only one desire—that of changing this rapture into despair.'

'I, my lord!'——'Yes, you. It was your intention to ruin me—to dishonour me for ever in the eyes of Mdlle. de Cardoville. Now, tell me—why this furious hate? what have I done to you?'

'You misjudge me, my lord—and——'——'Listen to me. I do not wish you to be any longer wicked and treacherous. I wish to make you good. In our country, they charm serpents, and tame the wildest tigers. You are a man, with a mind to reason, a heart to love, and I will tame you too by gentleness. This day has bestowed on me divine happiness; you shall have good cause to bless this day. What can I do for you? what would you have—gold? You shall have it. Do you desire more than gold? Do you desire a friend, to console you for the sorrows that made you wicked, and to teach you to be good? Though a king's son, I will be that friend—in spite of the evil—ay, because of the evil you have done me. Yes; I will be your sincere friend, and it shall be my delight to say to myself: "The day on which I learned that my angel loved me, my happiness was great indeed—for, in the morning, I had an implacable enemy, and, ere night, his hatred was changed to friendship." Believe me, Faringhea, misery makes crime, but happiness produces virtue. Be happy!'

At this moment the clock struck two. The prince started. It was time to go on his visit to Adrienne. The handsome countenance of Djalma, doubly embellished by the mild, ineffable expression with which it had been animated whilst he was talking to the half-caste, now seemed illumined with almost divine radiance.

Approaching Faringhea, he extended his hand with the utmost grace and courtesy, saying to him, 'Your hand!'

The half-caste, whose brow was bathed with a cold sweat, whose countenance was pale and agitated, seemed to hesitate for an instant; then, over-awed, conquered, fascinated, he offered his trembling hand to the prince, who pressed it, and said to him, in their country's fashion, 'You have laid your hand honestly in a friend's; this hand shall never be closed against you. Faringhea, farewell! I now feel myself more worthy to kneel before my angel.'

And Djalma went out, on his way to the appointment with Adrienne. In spite of his ferocity, in spite of the pitiless hate he bore to the whole human race, the dark sectary of Bowanee was staggered by the noble and clement words of Djalma, and said to himself, with terror, 'I have taken his hand. He is now sacred for me.'

Then, after a moment's silence, a thought occurred to him, and he exclaimed, 'Yes—but he will not be sacred for him who, according to the answer of last night, waits for him at the door of the house.'

So saying, the half-caste hastened into the next room, which looked upon the street, and, raising a corner of the curtain, muttered anxiously to himself, 'The carriage moves off—the man approaches. Perdition! it is gone. and I see no more.'

CHAPTER XL.

ANXIETY.

BY a singular coincidence of ideas, Adrienne, like Djalma, had wished to be dressed exactly in the same costume as at their interview in the house in the Rue Blanche. For the site of this solemn meeting, so important to her future happiness, Adrienne had chosen, with habitual tact, the grand drawing-room of Cardoville House, in which hung many family portraits. The most apparent were those of her father and mother. The room was large and lofty, and furnished, like those which preceded it, with all the imposing splendour of the age of Louis XIV. The ceiling, painted by Lebrun, to represent the Triumph of Apollo, displayed his bold designing and vigorous colouring, in the centre of a wide cornice, magnificently carved and gilt, and supported at its angles by four large gilt figures, representing the Seasons. Huge panels, covered with crimson damask, and set in frames, served as the background to the family portraits which adorned this apartment. It is easier to conceive than describe the thousand conflicting emotions which agitated the bosom of Mdlle. de Cardoville as the moment approached for her interview with Djalma. Their meeting had been hitherto prevented by so many painful obstacles, and Adrienne was so well aware of the vigilant and active perfidy of her enemies, that even now she doubted of her happiness. Every instant, in spite of herself, her eyes wandered to the clock. A few minutes more, and the hour of the appointment would strike. It struck at last. Every reverberation was echoed from the depth of Adrienne's heart. She considered that Djalma's modest reserve had, doubtless, prevented his coming before the moment fixed by herself. Far from blaming this discretion, she fully appreciated it. But, from that moment, at the least noise in the adjoining apartments, she held her breath, and listened with the anxiety of expectation.

For the first few minutes which followed the hour at which she expected Djalma, Mdlle. de Cardoville felt no serious apprehension, and calmed her impatience by the notion (which appears childish enough to those who have never known the feverish agitation of waiting for a happy meeting), that perhaps the clocks in the Rue Blanche might vary a little from those in the Rue d'Anjou. But when this supposed variation, conceivable enough in itself, could no longer explain a delay of a quarter of an hour, of twenty minutes, of more, Adrienne felt her anxiety gradually increase. Two or three times the young girl rose, with palpitating heart, and went on tip-toe to listen at the door of the saloon. She heard nothing. The clock struck half-past three.

Unable to suppress her growing terror, and clinging to a last hope, Adrienne returned towards the fire-place, and rang the bell. After which she endeavoured to compose her features, so as to betray no outward sign of emotion. In a few seconds, a grey-haired footman, dressed in black, opened the door, and waited in respectful silence for the orders of his mistress. The latter said to him, in a calm voice, 'Andrew, request Hebe to give you the smelling-bottle that I left on the chimney-piece in my room, and bring it me here.' Andrew bowed ; but just as he was about to withdraw to execute Adrienne's order, which was only a pretext to enable her to ask a question without appearing to attach much importance to it in her servant's eyes, already informed of the expected visit of the prince, Mdlle. de Cardoville added, with an air of indifference, 'Pray, is that clock right ?'

Andrew drew out his watch, and replied, as he cast his eyes upon it, 'Yes, mademoiselle. I set my watch by the Tuileries. It is more than half-past three.'

'Very well—thank you !' said Adrienne, kindly.

Andrew again bowed ; but, before going out, he said to Adrienne, 'I forgot to tell you, lady, that Marshal Simon called about an hour ago ; but, as you were only to be at home to Prince Djalma, we told him that you received no company.'

'Very well,' said Adrienne. With another low bow, Andrew quitted the room, and all returned to silence.

For the precise reason that, up to the last minute of the hour previous to the time fixed for her interview with Djalma, the hopes of Adrienne had not been disturbed by the slightest shadow of doubt, the disappointment she now felt was the more dreadful. Casting a desponding look at one of the portraits placed above her, she murmured, with a plaintive and despairing accent, 'Oh, mother !'

Hardly had Mdlle. de Cardoville uttered the words than the windows were slightly shaken by a carriage rolling into the courtyard. The young lady started, and was unable to repress a low cry of joy. Her heart bounded at the thought of meeting Djalma, for this time she felt that he was really come. She was quite as certain of it as if she had seen him. She resumed her seat, and brushed away a tear suspended from her long eye-lashes. Her hand trembled like a leaf. The sound of several doors opening and shutting proved that the young lady was right in her conjecture. The gilded panels of the drawing-room door soon turned upon their hinges, and the prince appeared.

While a second footman ushered in Djalma, Andrew placed on a gilded table, within reach of his mistress, a little silver salver, on which stood the crystal smelling-bottle. Then he withdrew, and the door of the room was closed. The prince and Mdlle. de Cardoville were left alone together.

CHAPTER XLI.

ADRIENNE AND DJALMA.

THE prince had slowly approached Mdlle. de Cardoville. Notwithstanding the impetuosity of the Oriental's passions, his uncertain and timid step —timid, yet graceful—betrayed his profound emotion. He did not venture to lift his eyes to Adrienne's face ; he had suddenly become very pale, and his finely formed hands, folded over his bosom in the attitude of adoration, trembled violently. With head bent down, he remained standing at a little distance from Adrienne. This embarrassment, ridiculous in any other person, appeared touching in this prince of twenty years of age, endowed with an almost fabulous intrepidity, and of so heroic and generous a character, that no traveller could speak of the son of Kadja-sing without a tribute of admiration and respect. Sweet emotion ! chaste reserve ! doubly interesting if we consider that the burning passions of this youth were all the more inflammable, because they had hitherto been held in check.

No less embarrassed than her cousin, Adrienne de Cardoville remained seated. Like Djalma, she cast down her eyes ; but the burning blush on her cheeks, the quick heaving of her virgin bosom, revealed an emotion that she did not even attempt to hide. Notwithstanding the powers of her mind, by turns gay, graceful, and witty—notwithstanding the decision of her proud and independent character, and her complete acquaintance with the manners of the world—Adrienne shared Djalma's simple and enchanting awkwardness, and partook of that kind of temporary weakness, beneath which these two pure, ardent, and loving beings appeared sinking—as if unable to support the boiling agitation of the senses, combined with the intoxicating excitement of the heart. And yet their eyes had not met. Each seemed to fear the first electric shock of the other's glance—that invincible attraction of two impassioned beings—that sacred fire, which suddenly kindles the blood, and lifts two mortals from earth to heaven ; for it is to approach the Divinity, to give one's self up with religious fervour to the most noble and irresistible sentiment that he has implanted within us—the only sentiment that, in His adorable wisdom, the Dispenser of all good has vouchsafed to sanctify, by endowing it with a spark of His own creative energy.

Djalma was the first to raise his eyes. They were moist and sparkling. The excitement of passionate love, the burning ardour of his age, so long repressed, the intense admiration in which he held ideal beauty, were all expressed in his look, mingled with respectful timidity, and gave to the countenance of this youth an undefinable, irresistible character. Yes, irre•

sistible !—for, when Adrienne encountered his glance, she trembled in every limb, and felt herself attracted by a magnetic power. Already, her eyes were heavy with a kind of intoxicating langour, when, by a great effort of will and dignity, she succeeded in overcoming this delicious confusion, rose from her chair, and said to Djalma in a trembling voice : ' Prince, I am happy to receive you here.' Then, pointing to one of the portraits suspended above her, she added, as if introducing him to a living person : ' Prince—my mother !'

With an instinct of rare delicacy, Adrienne had thus summoned her mother to be present at her interview with Djalma. It seemed a security for herself and the prince, against the seductions of a first interview—which was likely to be all the more perilous, that they both knew themselves madly loved, that they both were free, and had only to answer to Providence for the treasures of happiness and enjoyment with which He had so magnificently endowed them. The prince understood Adrienne's thoughts ; so that, when the young lady pointed to the portrait, Djalma, by a spontaneous movement full of grace and simplicity, knelt down before the picture, and said to it in a gentle, but manly voice : ' I will love and revere you as my mother. And, in thought, my mother too shall be present, and stand like you, beside your child !'

No better answer could have been given to the feeling which induced Mdlle. de Cardoville to place herself, as it were, under the protection of her mother. From that moment, confident in Djalma, confident in herself, the young lady felt more at her ease, and the delicious sense of happiness replaced those exciting emotions, which had at first so violently agitated her.

Then, seating herself once more, she said to Djalma, as she pointed to the opposite chair : ' Pray take a seat, my dear cousin ; and allow me to call you so, for there is too much ceremony in the word prince ; and do you call me cousin also, for I find other names too grave. Having settled this point, we can talk together like old friends.'

'Yes, cousin,' answered Djalma, blushing.

'And, as frankness is proper between friends,' resumed Adrienne, ' I have first to make you a reproach,' she added, with a half-smile.

The prince had remained standing, with his arm resting on the chimney-piece, in an attitude full of grace and respect.

'Yes, cousin,' continued Adrienne, 'a reproach, that you will perhaps forgive me for making. I had expected you a little sooner.'——'Perhaps, cousin, you may blame me for having come so soon.'

'What do you mean ?'——'At the moment when I left home, a man, whom I did not know, approached my carriage, and said to me, with such an air of sincerity that I believed him : " You are able to save the life of a person who has been a second father to you. Marshal Simon is in great danger, and, to rescue him, you must follow me on the instant——"

'It was a snare,' cried Adrienne, hastily. ' Marshal Simon was here, scarcely an hour ago.'

'Indeed !' exclaimed Djalma, joyfully, and as if he had been relieved from a great weight. 'Then there will be nothing to sadden this happy day !'——'But, cousin,' resumed Adrienne, 'how came you not to suspect this emissary ?'

'Some words, which afterwards escaped from him, inspired me with doubts,' answered Djalma : ' but at first I followed him, fearing the marshal might be in danger—for I know that he also has enemies.'

'Now that I reflect on it, you were quite right, cousin, for some new plot against the marshal was probable enough ; and the least doubt was enough to induce you to go to him.'

' I did so—even though you were waiting for me.'

' It was a generous sacrifice ; and my esteem for you is increased by it, if it could be increased,' said Adrienne, with emotion. 'But what became of this man ?'

'At my desire, he got into the carriage with me. Anxious about the marshal, and in despair at seeing the time wasted, that I was to have passed with you, cousin, I pressed him with all sorts of questions. Several times, he replied to me with embarrassment, and then the idea struck me that the whole might be a snare. Remembering all that they had already attempted, to ruin me in your opinion, I immediately changed my course, The vexation of the man who accompanied me then became so visible, that I ought to have had no doubt upon the subject. Still, when I thought of Marshal Simon, I felt a kind of vague remorse, which you, cousin, have now happily set at rest.'

' Those people are implacable !' said Adrienne ; 'but our happiness will be stronger than their hate.'

After a moment's silence, she resumed, with her habitual frankness : ' My dear cousin, it is impossible for me to conceal what I have at heart. Let us talk for a few seconds of the past, which was made so painful to us, and then we will forget it for ever, like an evil dream.'

'I will answer you sincerely, at the risk of injuring myself,' said the prince.

' How could you make up your mind to exhibit yourself in public with——?'

'With that young girl ?' interrupted Djalma.

' Yes, cousin,' replied Mdlle. de Cardoville, and she waited for Djalma's answer with anxious curiosity.

'A stranger to the customs of this country,' said Djalma, without any embarrassment, for he spoke the truth, ' with a mind weakened with despair, and misled by the fatal counsels of a man devoted to my enemies, I believed, even as I was told, that, by displaying before you the semblance of another love, I should excite your jealousy, and thus——'

' Enough, cousin ; I understand it all,' said Adrienne hastily, interrupting Djalma in her turn, that she might spare him a painful confession. ' I too must have been blinded by despair, not to have seen through this wicked plot, especially after your rash and intrepid action. To risk death for the sake of my bouquet !' added Adrienne, shuddering at the mere remembrance. ' But one last question,' she resumed, 'though I am already sure of your answer. Did you receive a letter that I wrote to you, on the morning of the day in which I saw you at the theatre ?'

Djalma made no reply. A dark cloud passed over his fine countenance, and, for a second, his features assumed so menacing an expression, that Adrienne was terrified at the effect produced by her words. But this violent agitation soon passed away, and Djalma's brow became once more calm and serene.

' I have been more merciful than I thought,' said the prince to Adrienne, who looked at him with astonishment. ' I wished to come hither worthy of you, my cousin. I pardoned the man who, to serve my enemies, had given me all those fatal counsels. The same person, I am sure, must have intercepted your letter. Just now, at the memory of the evils he thus caused me, I, for a moment, regretted my clemency. But then, again, I thought of your letter of yesterday—and my anger is all gone.'

' Then the sad time of fear and suspicion is over—suspicion, that made me doubt of your sentiments, and you of mine. Oh, yes ! far removed from us be that fatal past !' cried Adrienne de Cardoville, with deep joy.

Then, as if she had relieved her heart from the last thought of sadness, she continued : ' The future is all our own—the radiant future, without cloud or obstacle, pure in the immensity of its horizon, and extending beyond the reach of sight !'

It is impossible to describe the tone of enthusiastic hope which accompanied these words. But suddenly Adrienne's features assumed an expression of touching melancholy, and she added, in a voice of profound emotion : ' And yet—at this hour—so many unfortunate creatures suffer pain !'

This simple touch of pity for the misfortunes of others, at the moment when the noble maiden herself attained to the highest point of happiness, had such an effect on Djalma, that involuntarily he fell on his knees before Adrienne, clasped his hands together, and turned towards her his fine countenance, with an almost daring expression. Then, hiding his face in his hands, he bowed his head without speaking a single word. There was a moment of deep silence. Adrienne was the first to break it, as she saw a tear steal through the slender fingers of the prince.

' My friend ! what is the matter ?' she exclaimed, as, with a movement rapid as thought, she stooped forward, and, taking hold of Djalma's hands, drew them from before his face. That face was bathed in tears.

' You weep !' cried Mdlle. de Cardoville, so much agitated that she kept the hands of Djalma in her own ; and, unable to dry his tears, the young Hindoo allowed them to flow like so many drops of crystal over the pale gold of his cheeks.

' There is not in this wide world a happiness like to mine !' said the prince, in his soft, melodious voice, and with a kind of exhaustion ; ' therefore do I feel great sadness, and so it should be. You give me heaven—and were I to give you the whole earth, it would be but a poor return. Alas ! what can man do for a divinity, but humbly bless and adore ? He can never hope to return the gifts bestowed : and this makes him suffer—not in his pride— but in his heart !'

Djalma did not exaggerate. He said what he really felt ; and the rather hyperbolical form, familiar to Oriental nations, could alone express his thought. The tone of his regret was so sincere, his humility so gentle and full of simplicity, that Adrienne, also moved to tears, answered him with an effusion of serious tenderness, ' My friend, we are both at the supreme point of happiness. Our future felicity appears to have no limits, and yet, though derived from different sources, sad reflections have come to both of us. It is, you see, that there are some sorts of happiness, which make you dizzy with their own immensity. For a moment, the heart, the mind, the soul, are incapable of containing so much bliss ; it overflows and drowns us. Thus the flowers sometimes hang their heads, oppressed by the too ardent rays of the sun, which is yet their love and life. Oh, my friend ! this sadness may be great, but it is also sweet !'

As she uttered these words, the voice of Adrienne grew fainter and fainter, and her head bowed lower, as if she were indeed sinking beneath the weight of her happiness. Djalma had remained kneeling before her, his hands in hers—so that as she thus bent forward, her ivory forehead and golden hair touched the amber-coloured brow and ebon curls of Djalma. And the sweet, silent tears of the two young lovers flowed together, and mingled as they fell on their clasped hands.

Whilst this scene was passing in Cardoville House, Agricola had gone to the Rue de Vaugirard, to deliver a letter from Adrienne to M. Hardy.

CHAPTER XLII.

'THE IMITATION.'

As we have already said, M. Hardy occupied a pavilion in the 'Retreat' annexed to the house in the Rue de Vaugirard, inhabited by a goodly number of the reverend fathers of the Company of Jesus. Nothing could be calmer and more silent than this dwelling. Every one spoke in whispers, and the servants themselves had something oily in their words, something sanctified in their very walk.

Like all that is subject to the chilling and destructive influences of these men, this mournfully quiet house was entirely wanting in life and animation. The boarders passed an existence of wearisome and icy monotony, only broken by the use of certain devotional exercises ; and thus, in accordance with the selfish calculation of the reverend fathers, the mind, deprived of all nourishment and all external support, soon began to droop and pine away in solitude. The heart seemed to beat more slowly, the soul was benumbed, the character weakened ; at last, all freewill, all power of discrimination, was extinguished, and the boarders, submitting to the same process of self-annihilation as the novices of the Company, became, like them, mere 'corpses' in the hands of the brotherhood.

The object of these manœuvres was clear and simple. They secured the means of obtaining all kinds of donations, the constant aim of the skilful policy and merciless cupidity of these priests. By the aid of enormous sums, of which they thus become the possessors or the trustees, they follow out and obtain the success of their projects, even though murder, incendiarism, revolt, and all the horrors of civil war, excited by and through them, should drench in blood the lands over which they seek to extend their dark dominion.

Such, then, was the asylum of peace and innocence in which François Hardy had taken refuge. He occupied the ground-floor of a summer-house, which opened upon a portion of the garden. His apartments had been judiciously chosen, for we know with what profound and diabolical craft the reverend fathers avail themselves of material influences, to make a deep impression upon the minds they are moulding to their purpose. Imagine a prospect bounded by a high wall, of a blackish grey, half-covered with ivy, the plant peculiar to ruins. A dark avenue of old yew-trees, so fit to shade the grave with their sepulchral verdure, extended from this wall to a little semicircle, in front of the apartment generally occupied by M. Hardy, Two or three mounds of earth, bordered with box, symmetrically cut, completed the charms of this garden, which in every respect resembled a cemetery.

It was about two o'clock in the afternoon. Though the April sun shone brightly, its rays, intercepted by the high wall of which we have spoken, could not penetrate into that portion of the garden, obscure, damp, and cold as a cavern, which communicated with M. Hardy's apartment. The room was furnished with a perfect sense of the comfortable. A soft carpet covered the floor ; thick curtains of dark green baize, the same colour as the walls, sheltered an excellent bed, and hung in folds about the glass-door, which opened on the garden. Some pieces of mahogany furniture, plain, but very clean and bright, stood round the room. Above the secretary, placed just in front of the bed, was a large ivory crucifix, upon a black velvet ground. The chimney-piece was adorned with a clock, in an ebony case, with ivory ornaments representing all sorts of gloomy emblems, such as hour-glasses, scythes, death's-heads, etc. Now imagine this scene in twilight, with its solitary and mournful silence, only broken at the hour of prayer by the lugubrious sound of the bells of the neighbouring chapel, and you will recognise the infernal skill, with which these dangerous priests know how to turn to account every external object, when they wish to influence the mind of those they are anxious to gain over.

And this was not all. After appealing to the senses, it was necessary to address themselves to the intellect—and this was the method adopted by the reverend fathers. A single book—but one—was left, as if by chance, within reach. This book was Thomas à Kempis' 'Imitation.' But as it might happen that M. Hardy would not have the courage or the desire to read this book, thoughts and reflections borrowed from its merciless pages, and written in very large characters, were suspended in black frames close to the bed, or at other parts within sight, so that, involuntarily, in the sad leisure of his inactive dejection, the dweller's eyes were almost necessarily attracted by them. To that fatal circle of despairing thoughts they confined the already weakened mind of this unfortunate man, so long a prey to the most acute sorrow. What he read mechanically, every instant of the day and night, whenever the blessed sleep fled from his eyes inflamed with tears, was not enough merely to plunge the soul of the victim into incurable despair, but also to reduce him to the corpse-like obedience required by the Society of Jesus. In that awful book may be found a thousand terrors to operate on weak minds, a thousand slavish maxims to chain and degrade the pusillanimous soul.

And now imagine M. Hardy carried wounded into this house ; while his heart, torn by bitter grief and the sense of horrible treachery, bled even faster than his external injuries. Attended with the utmost care, and thanks to the acknowledged skill of Dr. Baleinier, M. Hardy soon recovered from the hurts he had received when he threw himself into the embers of his burning factory. Yet, in order to favour the projects of the reverend fathers, a drug, harmless enough in its effects, but destined to act for a time upon the mind of the patient, and often employed for that purpose in similar important cases by the pious doctor, was administered to Hardy, and had kept him pretty long in a state of mental torpor. To a soul agonised by cruel deceptions, it appears an inestimable benefit to be plunged into that kind of torpor, which at least prevents one from dwelling upon the past. Hardy resigned himself entirely to this profound apathy, and at length came to regard it as the supreme good. Thus do unfortunate wretches, tortured by cruel diseases, accept with gratitude the opiate which kills them slowly, but which at least deadens the sense of pain.

In sketching the portrait of M. Hardy, we tried to give some idea of the exquisite delicacy of his tender soul, of his painful susceptibility with regard to anything base or wicked, and of his extreme goodness, uprightness, and generosity. We now allude to these admirable qualities, because we must observe, that with him, as with almost all who possess them, they were not, and could not be, united with an energetic and resolute character. Admirably persevering in good deeds, the influence of this excellent man was insinuating rather than commanding ; it was not by the bold energy and somewhat overbearing will, peculiar to other men of great and noble heart, that Hardy had realised the prodigy of his Common Dwelling-house ; it was by affectionate persuasion, for with him mildness took the place of force. At sight of any baseness or injustice, he did not rouse himself, furious and threatening ; but he suffered intense pain. He did not boldly attack the criminal, but he turned away from him in pity and sorrow. And then his loving heart, so full of feminine delicacy, had an irresistible longing for the blessed contact of dear affections ; they alone could keep it alive. Even as a poor, frail bird dies with the cold, when it can no longer lie close to its brethren, and receive and communicate the sweet warmth of the maternal nest. And now this sensitive organisation, this extremely susceptible nature, receives blow after blow from sorrows and deceptions, one of which would suffice to shake, if it did not conquer, the firmest and most resolute character. Hardy's best friend has infamously betrayed him. His adored mistress has abandoned him.

The house which he had founded for the benefit of his workmen, whom he loved as brethren, is reduced to a heap of ashes. What then happens? All the springs of his soul are at once broken. Too feeble to resist such frightful attacks, too fatally deceived to seek refuge in other affections, too much discouraged to think of laying the first stone of any new edifice—this poor heart, isolated from every salutary influence, finds oblivion of the world and of itself in a kind of gloomy torpor. And if some remaining instincts of life and affection, at long intervals, endeavoured to rouse themselves within him, and if, half-opening his mind's eye, which he had kept closed against the present, the past, and the future, Hardy looks around him—what does he see? Only these sentences, so full of terrible despair :

'Thou art nothing but dust and ashes. Grief and tears are thy portion. Believe not in any son of man. There are no such things as friendship or ties of kindred. All human affections are false. Die in the morning, and thou wilt be forgotten before night. Be humble—despise thyself—and let others despise thee. Think not, reason not, live not—but commit thy fate to the hands of a superior, who will think and reason for thee. Weep, suffer, think upon death. Yes, death! always death—that should be thy thought when thou thinkest—but it is better not to think at all. Let a feeling of ceaseless woe prepare thy way to heaven. It is only by sorrow that we are welcome to the terrible God whom we adore !'

Such were the consolations offered to this unfortunate man. Affrighted, he again closed his eyes, and fell back into his lethargy. As for leaving this gloomy retreat, he could not, or rather he did not desire to do so. He had lost the power of will ; and then, it must be confessed, he had finished by getting accustomed to this house, and liked it well—they paid him such discreet attentions, and yet left him so much alone with his grief—there reigned all around such a death-like silence, which harmonised closely with the silence of his heart ; and that was now the tomb of his last love, last friendship, last hope. All energy was dead within him ! Then began that slow, but inevitable transformation, so judiciously foreseen by Rodin, who directed the whole of this machination, even in its smallest details. At first alarmed by the dreadful maxims which surrounded him, M. Hardy had at length accustomed himself to read them over almost mechanically, just as the captive, in his mournful hours of leisure, counts the nails in the door of his prison, or the bars of the grated window. This was already a great point gained by the reverend fathers.

And soon his weakened mind was struck with the apparent correctness of these false and melancholy aphorisms.

Thus he read : ' Do not count upon the affection of any human creature' —and he had himself been shamefully betrayed.

' Man is born to sorrow and despair '—and he was himself despairing.

' There is no rest save in the cessation of thought '—and the slumber of his mind had brought some relief to his pain.

Peepholes, skilfully concealed by the hangings and in the wainscoting of these apartments, enabled the reverend fathers at all times to see and hear the boarders, and above all to observe their countenance and manner, when they believed themselves to be alone. Every exclamation of grief which escaped Hardy in his gloomy solitude, was repeated to Father d'Aigrigny by a mysterious listener. The reverend father, following scrupulously

Rodin's instructions, had at first visited his boarder very rarely. We have said, that when Father d'Aigrigny wished it, he could display an almost irre·sistible power of charming ; and accordingly he threw all his tact and skill into the interviews he had with Hardy, when he came from time to time to inquire after his health. Informed of everything by his spies, and aided by his natural sagacity, he soon saw all the use that might be made of the physical and moral prostration of the boarder. Certain beforehand that Hardy would not take the hint, he spoke to him frequently of the gloom of the house, advising him affectionately to leave it, if he felt oppressed by its monotony, or at all events to seek beyond its walls for some pleasure and amusement. To speak of pleasure and amusement to this unfortunate man, was in his present state to ensure a refusal, and so it of course happened. Father d'Aigrigny did not at first try to gain the recluse's confidence, nor did he speak to him of sorrow ; but every time he came, he appeared to take such a tender interest in him, and showed it by a few simple and well-timed words. By degrees, these interviews, at first so rare, became more frequent and longer. Endowed with a flow of honeyed, insinuating, and persuasive eloquence, Father d'Aigrigny naturally took for his theme those gloomy maxims, to which Hardy's attention was now so often directed.

Supple, prudent, skilful, knowing that the hermit had hitherto professed that generous natural religion which teaches the grateful adoration of God, the love of humanity, the worship of what is just and good, and which, dis·daining dogmas, professes the same veneration for Marcus Aurelius as for Confucius, for Plato as for Christ, for Moses as for Lycurgus—Father d'Aigrigny did not at first attempt to convert him, but began by incessantly reminding him of the abominable deceptions practised upon him ; and, instead of describing such treachery as an exception in life—instead of trying to calm, encourage, and revive this drooping soul—instead of ex-horting Hardy to seek oblivion and consolation in the discharge of his duties towards humanity, towards his brethren, whom he had previously loved and succoured—Father d'Aigrigny strove to inflame the bleeding wounds of the unfortunate man, painted the human race in the most atro-cious blackness, and, by declaring all men treacherous, ungrateful, wicked, succeeded in rendering his despair incurable. Having attained this object, the Jesuit took another step. Knowing Hardy's admirable goodness of heart, and profiting by the weakened state of his mind, he spoke to him of the consolation to be derived by a man overwhelmed with sorrow, from the belief that every one of his tears, instead of being unfruitful, was in fact agreeable to God, and might aid in the salvation of souls—the belief, as the reverend father adroitly added, that by faith alone can sorrow be made use-ful to humanity, and acceptable to Divinity.

Whatever impiety, whatever atrocious Machiavelism there was in these detestable maxims, which make of a loving-kind Deity a being delighted with the tears of his creatures, was thus skilfully concealed from Hardy's eyes, whose generous instincts were still alive. Soon did this loving and tender soul, whom unworthy priests were driving to a sort of moral suicide, find a mournful charm in the fiction, that his sorrows would at least be pro-fitable to other men. It was at first only a fiction ; but the enfeebled mind which takes pleasure in such a fable, finishes by receiving it as a reality, and by degrees will submit to the consequences. Such was Hardy's moral and physical state, when, by means of a servant who had been bought over, he received from Agricola Baudoin a letter requesting an interview. Alone, the workman could not have broken the band of the Jesuit's pleadings, but he was accompanied by Gabriel, whose eloquence and reasonings were of a most convincing nature to a spirit like Hardy's.

It is unnecessary to point out to the reader, with what dignified reserve Gabriel had confined himself to the most generous means of rescuing Hardy from the deadly influence of the reverend fathers. It was repugnant to the great soul of the young missionary, to stoop to a revelation of the odious plots of these priests. He would only have taken this extreme course, had his powerful and sympathetic words have failed to have any effect on Hardy's blindness. About a quarter of an hour had elapsed since Gabriel's departure, when the servant appointed to wait on this boarder of the reverend fathers entered and delivered to him a letter.

'From whom is this?' asked Hardy.——'From a boarder in the house, sir,' answered the servant, bowing.

This man had a crafty and hypocritical face ; he wore his hair combed over his forehead, spoke in a low voice, and always cast down his eyes. Waiting the answer, he joined his hands, and began to twiddle his thumbs. Hardy opened the letter, and read as follows :

'SIR,—I have only just heard, by mere chance, that you also inhabit this respectable house ; a long illness, and the retirement in which I live, will explain my ignorance of your being so near. Though we have only met once, sir, the circumstance which led to that meeting was of so serious a nature, that I cannot think you have forgotten it.'

Hardy stopped, and tasked his memory for an explanation, and not finding anything to put him on the right track, he continued to read :

'This circumstance excited in me a feeling of such deep and respectful sympathy for you, sir, that I cannot resist my anxious desire to wait upon you, particularly as I learn, that you intend leaving this house to-day—piece of information I have just derived from the excellent and worthy Abbé Gabriel, one of the men I most love, esteem, and reverence. May I venture to hope, sir, that just at the moment of quitting our common retreat to return to the world, you will deign to receive favourably the request, however intrusive, of a poor old man, whose life will henceforth be passed in solitude, and who cannot therefore have any prospect of meeting you, in that vortex of society which he has abandoned for ever. Waiting the honour of your answer, I beg you to accept, sir, the assurance of the sentiments of high esteem with which I remain, sir, with the deepest respect,

'Your very humble and most obedient servant,

'RODIN.'

After reading this letter and the signature of the writer, Hardy remained for some time in deep thought, without being able to recollect the name of Rodin, or to what serious circumstance he alluded.

After a silence of some duration, he said to the servant : 'M. Rodin gave you this letter?'——'Yes, sir.'

'And who is M. Rodin?'——'A good old gentleman, who is just recovering from a long illness, that almost carried him off. Lately, he has been getting better, but he is still so weak and melancholy, that it makes one sad to see him. It is a great pity, for there is not a better and more worthy gentleman in the house—unless it be you, sir,' added the servant, bowing with an air of flattering respect.

'M. Rodin?' said Hardy, thoughtfully. 'It is singular, that I should not remember the name, nor any circumstance connected with it.'

'If you will give me your answer, sir,' resumed the servant, 'I will take it to M. Rodin. He is now with Father d'Aigrigny, to whom he is bidding farewell.'——'Farewell?'

'Yes, sir, the post-horses have just come.'——'Post-horses for whom?' asked Hardy.

'For Father d'Aigrigny, sir.'——'He is going on a journey then!' said Hardy, with some surprise.

'Oh! he will not, I think, be long absent,' said the servant, with a confidential air, 'for the reverend father takes no one with him, and but very light luggage. No doubt, the reverend father will come to say farewell to you, sir, before he starts. But what answer shall I give M. Rodin?'

The letter, just received, was couched in such polite terms—it spoke of Gabriel with so much respect—that Hardy, urged moreover by a natural curiosity, and seeing no motive to refuse this interview before quitting the house, said to the servant : 'Please tell M. Rodin, that, if he will give himself the trouble to come to me, I shall be glad to see him.'

'I will let him know immediately, sir,' answered the servant, bowing as he left the room.

When alone, Hardy, while wondering who this M. Rodin could be, began to make some slight preparations for his departure. For nothing in the world would he have passed another night in this house ; and, in order to keep up his courage, he recalled every instant the mild, evangelical language of Gabriel, just as the superstitious recite certain litanies, with the view of escaping from temptation.

The servant soon returned, and said : 'M. Rodin is here, sir.

'Beg him to walk in.'

Rodin entered, clad in his long black dressing-gown, and with his old silk cap in his hand. The servant then withdrew. The day was just closing. Hardy rose to meet Rodin, whose features he did not at first distinguish. But, as the reverend father approached the window, Hardy looked narrowly at him for an instant, and then uttered an exclamation, wrung from him by surprise and painful remembrance. But, recovering himself from this first movement, Hardy said to the Jesuit, in an agitated voice : 'You here, sir? Oh, you are right! It was indeed a very serious circumstance that first brought us together.'

'Oh, my dear sir!' said Rodin, in a kindly and unctuous tone ; 'I was sure you would not have forgotten me.

CHAPTER XLIII.

PRAYER.

It will doubtless be remembered that Rodin had gone (although a stranger to Hardy) to visit him at his factory, and inform him of De Blessac's shameful treachery—a dreadful blow, which had only preceded by a few moments a second no less horrible misfortune ; for it was in the presence of Rodin that Hardy had learned the unexpected departure of the woman he adored. Painful to him must have been the sudden appearance of Rodin. Yet, thanks to the salutary influence of Gabriel's counsels, he recovered himself by degrees, and the contraction of his features being succeeded by a melancholy calm, he said to Rodin : 'I did not indeed expect to meet you, sir, in this house.'

'Alas, sir!' answered Rodin, with a sigh, 'I did not expect to come hither, probably to end my days beneath this roof, when I went, without being acquainted with you, but only as one honest man should serve another, to unveil to you a great infamy.'

'Indeed, sir, you then rendered me a true service ; perhaps, in that painful moment, I did not fully express my gratitude ; for, at the same moment in which you revealed to me the treachery of M. de Blessac——'

'You were overwhelmed by another piece of painful intelligence,' said

Rodin, interrupting M. Hardy; 'I shall never forget the sudden arrival of that poor woman, who, pale and affrighted, and without considering my presence, came to inform you that a person who was exceedingly dear to you had quitted Paris abruptly.'

'Yes, sir; and, without stopping to thank you, I set out immediately,' answered Hardy, with a mournful air.

'Do you know, sir,' said Rodin, after a moment's silence, 'that there are sometimes very strange coincidences?'

'To what do you allude, sir?'——'While I went to inform you that you were betrayed in so infamous a manner—I was myself——'

Rodin paused, as if unable to control his deep emotion, and his counte-nance wore the expression of such overpowering grief that Hardy said to him, with interest: 'What ails you, sir?'

'Forgive me,' replied Rodin, with a bitter smile. 'Thanks to the ghostly counsels of the angelic Abbé Gabriel, I have reached a sort of resignation. Still, there are certain memories which affect me with the most acute pain. I told you,' resumed Rodin, in a firmer voice, 'or was going to tell you, that the very day after that on which I informed you of the treachery practised against you, I was myself the victim of a frightful deception. An adopted son—a poor unfortunate child, whom I had brought up——' He paused again, drew his trembling hand over his eyes, and added: 'Pardon me, sir, for speaking of matters which must be indifferent to you. Excuse the in-trusive sorrow of a poor, broken-hearted old man!'

'I have suffered too much myself, sir, to be indifferent to any kind of sorrow,' replied Hardy. 'Besides, you are no stranger to me—for you did me a real service—and we both agree in our veneration for the same young priest.'

'The Abbé Gabriel!' cried Rodin, interrupting Hardy; 'ah, sir! he is my deliverer, my benefactor. If you knew all his care and devotion, during my long illness, caused by intense grief—if you knew the ineffable sweetness of his counsels——'

'I know them, sir,' cried Hardy; 'oh, yes! I know how salutary is the influence.'

'In his mouth, sir, the precepts of religion are full of mildness,' resumed Rodin, with excitement. 'Do they not heal and console? do they not make us love and hope, instead of fear and tremble?'

'Alas, sir! in this very house,' said Hardy, 'I have been able to make the comparison.'

'I was happy enough,' said Rodin, 'to have the angelic Abbé Gabriel for my confessor, or, rather, my confidant.'

'Yes,' replied Hardy, 'for he prefers confidence to confession.'

'How well you know him!' said Rodin, in a tone of the utmost sim-plicity. Then he resumed: 'He is not a man, but an angel. His words would convert the most hardened sinner. Without being exactly impious, I had myself lived in the profession of what is called Natural Religion; but the angelic Abbé Gabriel has, by degrees, fixed my wavering belief, given it body and soul, and, in fact, endowed me with faith.'

'Yes! he is a truly Christian priest—a priest of love and pardon!' cried Hardy.

'What you say is perfectly true,' replied Rodin; 'for I came here almost mad with grief, thinking only of the unhappy boy who had repaid my paternal goodness with the most monstrous ingratitude, and some-times I yielded to violent bursts of despair, and sometimes sank into a state of mournful dejection, cold as the grave itself. But, suddenly, the Abbé Gabriel appeared—and the darkness fled before the dawning of a new day.'

'You were right, sir ; there are strange coincidences,' said Hardy, yielding more and more to the feeling of confidence and sympathy, produced by the resemblance of his real position to Rodin's pretended one. 'And to speak frankly,' he added, ' I am very glad I have seen you before quitting this house. Were I capable of falling back into fits of cowardly weakness, your example alone would prevent me. Since I listen to you, I feel myself stronger in the noble path which the angelic Abbé Gabriel has opened before me, as you so well express it.'

'The poor old man will not then regret having listened to the first impulse of his heart, which urged him to come to you,' said Rodin, with a touching expression. ' You will sometimes remember me in that world to which you are returning ?'

'Be sure of it, sir ; but allow me to ask one question : You remain, you say, in this house ?'

'What would you have me do ? There reigns here a calm repose, and one is not disturbed in one's prayers,' said Rodin, in a very gentle tone. 'You see, I have suffered so much—the conduct of that unhappy youth was so horrible—he plunged into such shocking excesses—that the wrath of heaven must be kindled against him. Now I am very old, and it is only by passing the few days that are left me in fervent prayer that I can hope to disarm the just anger of the Lord. Oh ! prayer—prayer ! It was the Abbé Gabriel who revealed to me all its power and sweetness—and therewith the formidable duties it imposes.'

'Its duties are indeed great and sacred,' answered Hardy, with a pensive air.——' Do you remember the life of Rancey ?' said Rodin, abruptly, as he darted a peculiar glance at Hardy.

'The founder of La Trappe ?' said Hardy, surprised at Rodin's question. ' I remember hearing a very vague account, some time ago, of the motives of his conversion.'

'There is, mark you, no more striking an example of the power of prayer, and of the state of almost divine ecstasy, to which it may lead a religious soul. In a few words, I will relate to you this instructive and tragic history. Rancey—but I beg your pardon ; I fear I am trespassing on your time.'

' No, no,' answered Hardy, hastily ; 'you cannot think how interested I am in what you tell me. My interview with the Abbé Gabriel was abruptly broken off, and in listening to you I fancy that I hear the further development of his views. Go on, I conjure you.'

'With all my heart. I only wish that the instruction which, thanks to our angelic priest, I derived from the story of Rancey might be as profitable to you as it was to me.'

'This, then, also came from the Abbé Gabriel ?'——' He related to me this kind of parable in support of his exhortations,' replied Rodin. 'Oh, sir ! do I not owe to the consoling words of that young priest all that has strengthened and revived my poor old broken heart ?'

' Then I shall listen to you with a double interest.'

' Rancey was a man of the world,' resumed Rodin, as he looked attentively at Hardy ; 'a gentleman—young, ardent, handsome. He loved a young lady of high rank. I cannot tell what impediments stood in the way of their union. But this love, though successful, was kept secret, and every evening Rancey visited his mistress by means of a private staircase. It was, they say, one of those passionate loves which men feel but once in their lives. The mystery, even the sacrifice made by the unfortunate girl, who forgot every duty, seemed to give new charms to this guilty passion. In the silence and darkness of secrecy, these two lovers passed two years of voluptuous delirium, which amounted almost to ecstasy.'

At these words Hardy started. For the first time of late his brow was suffused with a deep blush ; his heart throbbed violently ; he remembered that he too had once known the ardent intoxication of a guilty and hidden love. Though the day was closing rapidly, Rodin cast a sidelong glance at Hardy, and perceived the impression he had made. 'Sometimes,' he continued, 'thinking of the dangers to which his mistress was exposed, if their connexion should be discovered, Rancey wished to sever these delicious ties ; but the girl, beside herself with passion, threw herself on the neck of her lover, and threatened him, in the language of intense excitement, to reveal and to brave all, if he thought of leaving her. Too weak and loving to resist the prayers of his mistress, Rancey again and again yielded, and they both gave themselves up to a torrent of delight, which carried them along, forgetful of earth and heaven !'

M. Hardy listened to Rodin with feverish and devouring avidity. The Jesuit, in painting, with these almost sensual colours, an ardent and secret love, revived in Hardy burning memories, which till now had been drowned in tears. To the beneficent calm produced by the mild language of Gabriel had succeeded a painful agitation, which, mingled with the reaction of the shocks received that day, began to throw his mind into a strange state of confusion.

Rodin, having so far succeeded in his object, continued as follows : 'A fatal day came at last. Rancey, obliged to go to the wars, quitted the girl ; but, after a short campaign, he returned, more in love than ever. He had written privately, to say he would arrive almost immediately after his letter. He came accordingly. It was night. He ascended, as usual, the private staircase which led to the chamber of his mistress ; he entered the room, his heart beating with love and hope. His mistress had died that morning !'

'Ah !' cried Hardy, covering his face with his hands, in terror.

'She was dead,' resumed Rodin. 'Two wax-candles were burning beside the funeral couch. Rancey could not, would not, believe that she was dead. He threw himself on his knees by the corpse. In his delirium, he seized that fair, beloved head, to cover it with kisses. The head parted from the body, and remained in his hands ! Yes,' resumed Rodin, as Hardy drew back, pale and mute with terror, 'yes, the girl had fallen a victim to so swift and extraordinary a disease, that she had not been able to receive the last sacraments. After her death, the doctors, in the hope of discovering the cause of this unknown malady, had begun to dissect that fair form——'

As Rodin reached this part of his narrative, night was almost come. A sort of hazy twilight alone reigned in this silent chamber, in the centre of which appeared the pale and ghastly form of Rodin, clad in his long black gown, whilst his eyes seemed to sparkle with diabolic fire. Overcome by the violent emotions occasioned by this story, in which thoughts of death and voluptuousness, love and horror, were so strangely mingled, Hardy remained fixed and motionless, waiting for the words of Rodin, with a combination of curiosity, anguish and alarm.

'And Rancey?' said he, at last, in an agitated voice, whilst he wiped the cold sweat from his brow.

'After two days of furious delirium,' resumed Rodin, 'he renounced the world, and shut himself up in impenetrable solitude. The first period of his retreat was frightful ; in his despair, he uttered loud yells of grief and rage, that were audible at some distance. Twice he attempted suicide, to escape from the terrible visions.'

'He had visions, then ?' said Hardy, with an increased agony of curiosity.

'Yes,' replied Rodin, in a solemn tone, 'he had fearful visions. He saw the girl who, for his sake, had died in mortal sin, plunged in the heat of the everlasting flames of hell ! On that fair face, disfigured by infernal tortures, was stamped the despairing laugh of the damned ! Her teeth gnashed with pain ; her arms writhed in anguish ! She wept tears of blood, and, with an agonised and avenging voice, she cried to her seducer : " Thou art the cause of my perdition—my curse, my curse be upon thee !"'

As he pronounced these last words, Rodin advanced three steps nearer to Hardy, accompanying each step with a menacing gesture. If we remember the state of weakness, trouble, and fear, in which M. Hardy was—if we remember that the Jesuit had just roused in the soul of this unfortunate man all the sensual and spiritual memories of a love, cooled, but not extinguished, in tears—if we remember, too, that Hardy reproached himself with the seduction of a beloved object, whom her departure from her duties might (according to the Catholic faith) doom to everlasting flames—we shall not wonder at the terrible effect of this phantasmagoria, conjured up in silence and solitude, in the evening dusk, by this fearful priest.

The effect on Hardy was indeed striking, and the more dangerous, that the Jesuit, with diabolical craft, seemed only to be carrying out, from another point of view, the ideas of Gabriel. Had not the young priest convinced Hardy that nothing is sweeter, than to ask of heaven forgiveness for those who have sinned, or whom we have led astray ? But forgiveness implies punishment ; and it was to the punishment alone that Rodin drew the attention of his victim, by painting it in these terrific hues. With hands clasped together, and eye fixed and dilated, Hardy trembled in all his limbs, and seemed still listening to Rodin, though the latter had ceased to speak. Mechanically, he repeated : ' My curse, my curse be upon thee !'

Then suddenly he exclaimed, in a kind of frenzy : 'The curse is on me also ! The woman, whom I taught to forget her sacred duties, and to commit mortal sin—one day—plunged in the everlasting flames—her arms writhing in agony—weeping tears of blood—will cry to me from the bottomless pit : " My curse, my curse be upon thee !"—One day,' he added, with redoubled terror, 'one day ?— who knows ? perhaps at this moment !—for if the sea voyage had been fatal to her—if a shipwreck—oh, God ! she too would have died in mortal sin—lost, lost, for ever !—Oh, have mercy on her, my God ! Crush me in Thy wrath—but have mercy on her—for I alone am guilty !'

And the unfortunate man, almost delirious, sank with clasped hands upon the ground.

' Sir,' cried Rodin, in an affectionate voice, as he hastened to lift him up, 'my dear sir—my dear friend—be calm ! Comfort yourself. I cannot bear to see you despond. Alas ! my intention was quite the contrary to that.'

' The curse ! the curse ! yes, she will curse me also--she, that I loved so much—in the everlasting flames !' murmured Hardy, shuddering, and apparently insensible to the other's words.

' But, my dear sir, listen to me, I entreat you,' resumed the latter ; 'let me finish my story, and then you will find it as consoling as it now seems terrible. For heaven's sake, remember the adorable words of our angelic Abbé Gabriel, with regard to the sweetness of prayer.'

At the name of Gabriel, Hardy recovered himself a little, and exclaimed, in a heart-rending tone : 'Ay ! his words were sweet and beneficent. Where are they now ? For mercy's sake, repeat to me those consoling words.'

' Our angelic Abbé Gabriel,' resumed Rodin, ' spoke to you of the sweetness of prayer——'——' Oh, yes ! prayer !'

'Well, my dear sir, listen to me, and you shall see how prayer saved Rancey, and made a saint of him. Yes, these frightful torments, that I have just described, these threatening visions, were all conquered by prayer, and changed into celestial delights.'

' I beg of you,' said Hardy, in a faint voice, ' speak to me of Gabriel, speak to me of heaven—but no more flames—no more hell—where sinful women weep tears of blood——'

' No, no,' replied Rodin ; and even as, in describing hell, his tone had been harsh and threatening, it now became warm and tender, as he uttered the following words : ' No ; we will have no more images of despair—for, as I have told you, after suffering infernal tortures, Rancey, thanks to the power of prayer, enjoyed the delights of paradise.'

' The delights of paradise ?' repeated Hardy, listening with anxious attention.

' One day, at the height of his grief, a priest, a good priest—another Abbé Gabriel—came to Rancey. Oh, happiness ! oh, providential change ! In a few days, he taught the sufferer the sacred mysteries of prayer—that pious intercession of the creature, addressed to the Creator, in favour of a soul exposed to the wrath of heaven. Then Rancey seemed transformed. His grief was at once appeased. He prayed ; and the more he prayed, the greater was his hope. He felt that God listened to his prayer. Instead of trying to forget his beloved, he now thought of her constantly, and prayed for her salvation. Happy in his obscure cell, alone with that adored remembrance, he passed days and nights in praying for her—plunged in an ineffable, burning, I had almost said amorous ecstacy.'

It is impossible to give an idea of the tone of almost sensual energy with which Rodin pronounced the word 'amorous.' Hardy started, changing from hot to cold. For the first time, his weakened mind caught a glimpse of the fatal pleasures of asceticism, and of that deplorable catalepsy, described in the lives of St. Theresa, St. Aubierge, and others.

Rodin perceived the other's thoughts, and continued : ' Oh ! Rancey was not now the man to content himself with a vague, passing prayer, uttered in the whirl of the world's business, which swallows it up, and prevents it from reaching the ear of heaven. No, no ; in the depths of solitude, he endeavoured to make his prayers even more efficacious, so ardently did he desire the eternal salvation of his mistress.'

' What did he do then—oh ! what did he do in his solitude ?' cried Hardy, who was now powerless in the hands of the Jesuit.——' First of all,' said Rodin, with a slight emphasis, ' he became a monk.'

' A monk !' repeated Hardy, with a pensive air.

' Yes,' resumed Rodin, ' he became a monk, because his prayers were thus more likely to be favourably accepted. And then, as in solitude our thoughts are apt to wander, he fasted, and mortified his flesh, and brought into subjection all that was carnal within him, so that, becoming all spirit, his prayers might issue like a pure flame from his bosom, and ascend like the perfume of incense to the throne of the Most High !'

' Oh ! what a delicious dream !' cried Hardy, more and more under the influence of the spell ; ' to pray for the woman we have adored, and to become spirit—perfume—light !'

' Yes ; spirit, perfume, light !' said Rodin, with emphasis. ' But it is no dream. How many monks, how many hermits, like Rancey, have, by prayers, and austerity, and macerations, attained a divine ecstacy ! and if you only knew the celestial pleasures of such ecstacies !—Thus, after he became a monk, the terrible dreams were succeeded by enchanting visions. Many times, after a day of fasting, and a night passed in prayers and macerations, Rancey sank down exhausted on the floor of his cell ! Then the spirit freed itself from the vile closs of matter. His senses were absorbed in pleasure ; the sound of heavenly harmony struck upon his ravished ear ; a bright, mild light, which was not of this world, dawned upon his half-closed eyes ; and, at the height of the melodious vibrations of the golden harps of the Seraphim, in the centre of a glory, compared to which the sun is pale, the monk beheld the image of that beloved woman——'

' Whom by his prayers he had at length rescued from the eternal flames ?' said Hardy, in a trembling voice.

' Yes, herself,' replied Rodin, with eloquent enthusiasm, for this monster was skilled in every style of speech. ' Thanks to the prayers of her lover, which the Lord had granted, this woman no longer shed tears of blood—no longer writhed her beautiful arms in the convulsions of infernal anguish. No, no ; still fair—oh ! a thousand times fairer than when she dwelt on earth—fair with the everlasting beauty of angels—she smiled on her lover with ineffable ardour, and, her eyes beaming with a mild radiance, she said to him in a tender and passionate voice : " Glory to the Lord ! glory to thee, O my beloved ! Thy prayers and austerities have saved me. I am numbered amongst the chosen. Thanks, my beloved, and glory !"—And therewith, radiant in her felicity, she stooped to kiss, with lips fragrant with immortality, the lips of the enraptured monk—and their souls mingled in that kiss, burning as love, chaste as divine grace, immense as eternity !'

' Oh !' cried Hardy, completely beside himself ; ' a whole life of prayer, fasting, torture, for such a moment—with her, whom I mourn—with her, whom I have perhaps led to perdition !'

' What do you say ? such a moment !' cried Rodin, whose yellow forehead was bathed in sweat, like that of a magnetiser, and who now took Hardy by the hand, and drew still closer, as if to breathe into him the burning delirium ; ' it was not once in his religious life—it was almost every day, that Rancey, plunged in divine ecstacy, enjoyed these delicious, ineffable, superhuman pleasures, which are to the pleasures of earth what eternity is to man's existence !'

Seeing, no doubt, that Hardy was now at the point to which he wished to bring him, and the night being almost entirely come, the reverend father coughed two or three times in a significant manner, and looked towards the door. At this moment, Hardy, in the height of his frenzy, exclaimed, with a supplicating voice : ' A cell—a tomb—and the Ecstatic Vision !'

The door of the room opened, and Father d'Aigrigny entered, with a cloak under his arm. A servant followed him, bearing a light.

 ❀ ❀ ❀ ❀ ❀   ❀

About ten minutes after this scene, a dozen robust men, with frank, open countenances, led by Agricola, entered the Rue de Vaugirard, and advanced joyously towards the house of the reverend fathers. It was a deputation from the former workmen of M. Hardy. They came to escort him, and to congratulate him on his return amongst them. Agricola walked at their head. Suddenly he saw a carriage with post-horses issuing from the gateway of the house. The postilion whipped up the horses, and they started at full gallop. Was it chance or instinct ?—the nearer the carriage approached the group of which he formed a part, the more did Agricola's heart sink within him.

The impression became so vivid that it was soon changed into a terrible apprehension ; and at the moment when the vehicle, which had its blinds down, was about to pass close by him, the smith, in obedience to a resistless impulse, exclaimed, as he rushed to the horses' heads : ' Help, friends ! stop them !'

' Postilion ! ten louis if you ride over him !' cried from the carriage the military voice of Father d'Aigrigny.

The cholera was still raging. The postilion had heard of the murder of the poisoners. Already frightened at the sudden attack of Agricola, he struck him a heavy blow on the head with the butt of his whip, which stretched him senseless on the ground. Then, spurring with all his might, he urged his three horses into a triple gallop, and the carriage rapidly disappeared, whilst Agricola's companions, who had neither understood his actions nor the sense of his words, crowded around the smith, and did their best to revive him.

CHAPTER XLIV.

REMEMBRANCES.

OTHER events took place a few days after the fatal evening in which M. Hardy, fascinated and misled by the deplorable, mystic jargon of Rodin, had implored Father d'Aigrigny on his knees to remove him far from Paris, into some deep solitude, where he might devote himself to a life of prayer and ascetic austerities. Marshal Simon, since his arrival in Paris, had occupied, with his two daughters, a house in the Rue des Trois-Frères. Before introducing the reader into this modest dwelling, we are obliged to recall to his memory some preceding facts. The day of the burning of Hardy's factory, Marshal Simon had come to consult with his father on a question of the highest importance, and to communicate to him his painful apprehensions on the subject of the growing sadness of his twin daughters, which he was unable to explain.

Marshal Simon held in religious reverence the memory of the Great Emperor. His gratitude to the hero was boundless, his devotion blind, his enthusiasm founded upon reason, his affection warm as the most sincere and passionate friendship. But this was not all.

One day the emperor, in a burst of joy and paternal tenderness, had led the marshal to the cradle of the sleeping King of Rome, and said to him, as he proudly pointed to the beautiful child : ' My old friend, swear to me that you will serve the son as you have served the father !'

Marshal Simon took and kept that vow. During the Restoration, the chief of a military conspiracy in favour of Napoleon II., he had attempted in vain to secure a regiment of cavalry, at that time commanded by the Marquis d'Aigrigny. Betrayed and denounced, the marshal, after a desperate duel with the future Jesuit, had succeeded in reaching Poland, and thus escaping a sentence of death. It is useless to repeat the series of events which led the marshal from Poland to India, and then brought him back to Paris after the Revolution of July—an epoch at which a number of his old comrades in arms had solicited and obtained from the government, without his knowledge, the confirmation of the rank and title which the emperor had bestowed upon him just before Waterloo.

On his return to Paris, after his long exile, in spite of all the happiness he felt in at length embracing his children, Marshal Simon was deeply affected on learning the death of their mother, whom he adored. Till the last moment, he had hoped to find her in Paris. The disappointment was dreadful, and he felt it cruelly, though he sought consolation in his children's affection.

But soon new causes of trouble and anxiety were interwoven with his life by the machinations of Rodin. Thanks to the secret intrigues of the reverend father at the Courts of Rome and Vienna, one of his emissaries, in a condition to inspire full confidence, and provided with undeniable evidence to support his words, went to Marshal Simon, and said to him : ' The son of the emperor is dying, the victim of the fears with which the name of Napoleon still inspires Europe.

'From this slow expiring, you, Marshal Simon, one of the emperor's most faithful friends, are able to rescue this unfortunate prince.

'The correspondence in my hand proves that it would be easy to open relations, of the surest and most secret nature, with one of the most influential persons about the King of Rome, and this person would be disposed to favour the prince's escape.

'It is possible, by a bold, unexpected stroke, to deliver Napoleon II. from the custody of Austria, which would leave him to perish by inches in an atmosphere that is fatal to him.

'The enterprise may be a rash one, but it has chances of success that you, Marshal Simon, more than any other, could change into certainties ; for your devotion to the emperor is well known, and we remember with what adventurous audacity you conspired, in 1815, in favour of Napoleon II.'

The state of languor and decline of the King of Rome was then in France a matter of public notoriety. People even went so far as to affirm that the son of the hero was carefully trained by priests, who kept him in complete ignorance of the glory of his paternal name ; and that, by the most execrable machinations, they strove day by day to extinguish every noble and generous instinct that displayed itself in the unfortunate youth. The coldest hearts were touched and softened at the story of so sad and fatal a destiny. When we remember the heroic character and chivalrous loyalty of Marshal Simon, and his passionate devotion to the emperor, we can understand how the father of Rose and Blanche was more interested than any one else in the fate of the young prince, and how, if occasion offered, he would feel himself obliged not to confine his efforts to mere regrets. With regard to the reality of the correspondence produced by Rodin's emissary, it had been submitted by the marshal to a searching test, by means of his intimacy with one of his old companions in arms, who had been for a long period on a mission to Vienna, in the time of the Empire. The result of this investigation, conducted with as much prudence as address, so that nothing should transpire, showed that the marshal might give his serious attention to the advances made him.

Hence, this proposition threw the father of Rose and Blanche into a cruel perplexity ; for, to attempt so bold and dangerous an enterprise, he must once more abandon his children ; whilst, on the contrary, if, alarmed at this separation, he renounced the endeavour to save the King of Rome, whose lingering death was perfectly true and well authenticated, the marshal would consider himself as false to the vow he had sworn to the emperor. To end these painful hesitations, full of confidence in the inflexible uprightness of his father's character, the marshal had gone to ask his advice ; unfortunately, the old republican workman, mortally wounded during the attack on M. Hardy's factory, but still pondering over the serious communication of his son, died with these words upon his lips : ' My son, you have a great duty to perform, under pain of not acting like a man of honour, and of disobeying my last will. You must, without hesitation——'

But, by a deplorable fatality, the last words, which would have completed the sense of the old workman's thought, were spoken in so feeble a voice as to be quite unintelligible. He died, leaving Marshal Simon in a worse state of anxiety, as one of the two courses open to him had now been formally condemned by his father, in whose judgment he had the most implicit and merited confidence. In a word, his mind was now tortured by the doubt whether his father had intended, in the name of honour and duty, to advise him not to abandon his children, to engage in so hazardous an enterprise, or whether, on the contrary, he had wished him to leave them for a time, to perform the vow made to the emperor, and endeavour at least to rescue Napoleon II. from a captivity that might soon be mortal.

This perplexity, rendered more cruel by certain circumstances, to be re-lated hereafter, the tragical death of his father, who had expired in his arms ; the incessant and painful remembrance of his wife, who had perished in a land of exile ; and finally, the grief he felt at perceiving the ever-growing sadness of Rose and Blanche, occasioned severe shocks to Marshal Simon. Let us add that, in spite of his natural intrepidity, so nobly proved by twenty years of war, the ravages of the cholera, the same terrible malady to which his wife had fallen a victim in Siberia, filled the marshal with involuntary dread. Yes, this man of iron nerves, who had coolly braved death in so many battles, felt the habitual firmness of his character give way at sight of the scenes of desolation and mourning which Paris offered at every step. Yet, when Mdlle. de Cardoville gathered round her the members of her family, to warn them against the plot of their enemies, the affectionate tenderness of Adrienne for Rose and Blanche appeared to exercise so happy an influence on their mysterious sorrow, that the marshal, forgetting for a moment his fatal regrets, thought only of enjoying this blessed change, which, alas ! was but of short duration. Having now recalled these facts to the mind of the reader, we shall continue our story.

CHAPTER XLV.

THE BLOCKHEAD.

WE have stated that Marshal Simon occupied a small house in the Rue des Trois-Frères. Two o'clock in the afternoon had just struck in the marshal's sleeping-chamber, a room furnished with military simplicity. In the recess, in which stood the bed, hung a trophy composed of the arms used by the marshal during his campaigns. On the secretary opposite was a small bronze bust of the emperor, the only ornament of the apartment. Out of doors the temperature was far from warm, and the marshal had become susceptible to cold during his long residence in India. A good fire there-fore blazed upon the hearth. A door, concealed by the hangings, and lead-ing to a back staircase, opened slowly, and a man entered the chamber. He carried a basket of wood, and advanced leisurely to the fireplace, before which he knelt down, and begun to arrange the logs symmetrically in a box that stood beside the hearth. After some minutes occupied in this manner, still kneeling, he gradually approached another door, at a little distance from the chimney, and appeared to listen with deep attention, as if he wished to hear what was passing in the next room.

This man, employed as an inferior servant in the house, had the most ridiculously stupid look that can be imagined. His functions consisted in carrying wood, running errands, etc. In other respects he was a kind of laughing-stock to the other servants. In a moment of good humour, Dago-bert, who filled the post of major-domo, had given this idiot the name of ' Loony' (lunatic), which he had retained ever since, and which he deserved in every respect, as well for his awkwardness and folly as for his unmeaning face, with its grotesquely flat nose, sloping chin, and wide, staring eyes. Add to this description a jacket of red stuff, and a triangular white apron, and we must acknowledge that the simpleton was quite worthy of his name.

Yet, at the moment when Loony listened so attentively at the door of the adjoining room, a ray of quick intelligence animated for an instant his dull and stupid countenance.

When he had thus listened for a short time, Loony returned to the fire-piace, still crawling on his knees ; then rising, he again took his basket half full of wood, and once more approaching the door at which he had listened, knocked discreetly. No one answered. He knocked a second time, and more loudly. Still there was the same silence.

Then he said, in a harsh, squeaking, laughable voice, ' Ladies, do you want any wood, if you please, for your fire ?'

Receiving no answer, Loony placed his basket on the ground, opened the door gently, and entered the next room, after casting a rapid glance around. He came out again in a few seconds, looking from side to side with an anxious air, like a man who had just accomplished some important and mysterious task.

Taking up his basket, he was about to leave Marshal Simon's room, when the door of the private staircase was opened slowly and with precaution, and Dagobert appeared.

The soldier, evidently surprised at the servant's presence, knitted his brows, and exclaimed abruptly, ' What are you doing here ?'

At this sudden interrogation, accompanied by a growl expressive of the ill-humour of Spoilsport, who followed close on his master's heels, Loony uttered a cry of real or pretended terror. To give, perhaps, an appearance of greater reality to his dread, the supposed simpleton let his basket fall on the ground, as if astonishment and fear had loosened his hold of it.

' What are you doing, numbskull ?' resumed Dagobert, whose countenance was impressed with deep sadness, and who seemed little disposed to laugh at the fellow's stupidity.

' Oh, M. Dagobert ! how you frighten me ! Dear me ! what a pity I had not an armful of plates, to prove it was not my fault if I broke them all.'

' I ask you what you are doing,' resumed the soldier.

' You see, M. Dagobert,' replied Loony, pointing to his basket, ' that I came with some wood to master's room, so that he might burn it, if it was cold—which it is.'

' Very well. Pick up your wood, and begone !'——' Oh, M. Dagobert ! my legs tremble under me. How you did scare me, to be sure !'

' Will you begone, brute ?' resumed the veteran ; and seizing Loony by the arm, he pushed him towards the door, while Spoilsport, with recumbent ears, and hair standing up like the quills of a porcupine, seemed inclined to accelerate his retreat.

' I am going, M Dagobert, I am going,' replied the simpleton, as he hastily gathered up his basket ; ' only please to tell the dog——'

' Go to the devil, you stupid chatterbox !' cried Dagobert, as he pushed Loony through the doorway.

Then the soldier bolted the door which led to the private staircase, and going to that which communicated with the apartments of the two sisters, he double-locked it. Having done this, he hastened to the alcove in which stood the bed, and taking down a pair of loaded pistols, he carefully removed the percussion caps, and, unable to repress a deep sigh, restored the weapons to the place in which he had found them. Then, as if on second thoughts, he took down an Indian dagger with a very sharp blade, and drawing it from its silver-gilt sheath, proceeded to break the point of this murderous instrument, by twisting it beneath one of the iron castors of the bed.

Dagobert then proceeded to unfasten the two doors, and, returning slowly to the marble chimney-piece, he leaned against it with a gloomy and pensive air. Crouching before the fire, Spoilsport followed with an attentive eye the least movement of his master. The good dog displayed a rare and intelligent sagacity. The soldier, having drawn out his handkerchief, let fall, without perceiving it, a paper containing a roll of tobacco. Spoilsport, who had all the qualities of a retriever of the Rutland race, took the paper between his teeth, and, rising upon his hind-legs, presented it respectfully to

Dagobert. But the latter received it mechanically, and appeared indifferent to the dexterity of his dog. The grenadier's countenance revealed as much sorrow as anxiety. After remaining for some minutes near the fire, with fixed and meditative look, he began to walk about the room in great agitation, one of his hands thrust into the bosom of his long blue frock-coat, which was buttoned up to the chin, and the other into one of his hind-pockets.

From time to time he stopped abruptly, and seemed to make reply to his own thoughts, or uttered an exclamation of doubt and uneasiness ; then, turning towards the trophy of arms, he shook his head mournfully, and murmured, ' No matter—this fear may be idle ; but he has acted so extra-ordinarily these two days, that it is at all events more prudent——'

He continued his walk, and said, after a new and prolonged silence, ' Yes, he must tell me. It makes me too uneasy. And then the poor children—it is enough to break one's heart.'

And Dagobert hastily drew his moustache between his thumb and fore-finger, a nervous movement, which with him was an evident symptom of extreme agitation. Some minutes after, the soldier resumed, still answering his inward thoughts, ' What can it be ? It is hardly possible to be the letters, they are too infamous ; he despises them. And yet—— But no, no—he is above that !'

And Dagobert again began to walk with hasty steps. Suddenly, Spoil-sport pricked up his ears, turned his head in the direction of the staircase-door, and growled hoarsely. A few seconds after, some one knocked at the door.

' Who is there ?' said Dagobert. There was no answer, but the person knocked again. Losing patience, the soldier went hastily to open it, and saw the servant's stupid face.

' Why don't you answer, when I ask who knocks !' said the soldier, angrily.

' M. Dagobert, you sent me away just now, and I was afraid of making you cross, if I said I had come again.'

' What do you want ? Speak then—come in, stupid !' cried the exaspe-rated Dagobert, as he pulled him into the room. ——' M. Dagobert, don't be angry—I'll tell you all about it—it is a young man.'

' Well ?'——' He wants to speak to you directly, M. Dagobert.'

' His name ?'——' His name, M. Dagobert ?' replied Loony, rolling about and laughing with an idiotic air.

' Yes, his name. Speak, idiot !'——' Oh, M. Dagobert ! it's all in joke that you ask me his name !'

' You are determined, fool that you are, to drive me out of my senses !' cried the soldier, seizing Loony by the collar. ' The name of this young man !'

' Don't be angry, M. Dagobert. I didn't tell you the name, because you know it.'——' Beast !' said Dagobert, shaking his fist at him.

' Yes, you do know it, M. Dagobert, for the young man is your own son. He is downstairs, and wants to speak to you directly—yes, directly.'

The stupidity was so well assumed, that Dagobert was the dupe of it. Moved to compassion rather than anger by such imbecility, he looked fixedly at the servant, shrugged his shoulders, and said, as he advanced towards the staircase, ' Follow me !'

Loony obeyed ; but, before closing the door, he drew a letter secretly from his pocket, and dropped it behind him without turning his head, saying all the while to Dagobert, for the purpose of occupying his attention, ' Your son is in the court, M. Dagobert. He would not come up—that's why he is still downstairs !'

. Thus talking, he closed the door, believing he had left the letter on the floor of Marshal Simon's room. But he had reckoned without Spoilsport. Whether he thought it more prudent to bring up the rear, or, from respectful deference for a biped, the worthy dog had been the last to leave the room, and, being a famous carrier, as soon as he saw the letter dropped by Loony, he took it delicately between his teeth, and followed close on the heels of the servant, without the latter perceiving this new proof of the intelligence and sagacity of Spoilsport.

———

CHAPTER XLVI.

THE ANONYMOUS LETTERS.

WE will explain presently what became of the letter, which Spoilsport held between his teeth, and why he left his master, when the latter ran to meet Agricola. Dagobert had not seen his son for some days. Embracing him cordially, he led him into one of the rooms on the ground-floor, which he usually occupied. 'And how is your wife?' said the soldier to his son.

'She is well, father, thank you.'

Perceiving a great change in Agricola's countenance, Dagobert resumed, 'You look sad. Has anything gone wrong since I saw you last?'——'All is over, father. We have lost him,' said the smith, in a tone of despair.

'Lost whom?'——'M. Hardy.'

'M. Hardy!—why, three days ago, you told me you were going to see him.'

'Yes, father, I have seen him—and my dear brother Gabriel saw him and spoke to him—how he speaks! with a voice that comes from the heart!—and he had so revived and encouraged him, that M. Hardy consented to return amongst us. Then I, wild with joy, ran to tell the good news to some of my mates, who were waiting to hear the result of my interview with M Hardy. I brought them all with me, to thank and bless him. We were within a hundred yards of the house belonging to the black-gowns——'

'Ah, the black-gowns!' said Dagobert, with a gloomy air. 'Then some mischief will happen. I know them.'

'You are not mistaken, father,' answered Agricola, with a sigh. 'I was running on with my comrades, when I saw a carriage coming towards us. Some presentiment told me that they were taking away M. Hardy.'

'By force!' said Dagobert, hastily.

'No,' answered Agricola, bitterly; 'no—the priests are too cunning for that. They know how to make you an accomplice in the evil they do you. Shall I not always remember how they managed with my good mother?'

'Yes, the worthy woman! there was a poor fly caught in the spider's web. But this carriage, of which you speak?'

'On seeing it start from the house of the black-gowns,' replied Agricola, 'my heart sank within me; and, by an impulse stronger than myself, I rushed to the horses' heads, calling on my comrades to help me. But the postilion knocked me down and stunned me with a blow from his whip. When I recovered my senses, the carriage was already far away.'

'You were not hurt?' cried Dagobert, anxiously, as he examined his son from top to toe.——'No, father; a mere scratch.'

'What did you next, my boy?'——'I hastened to our good angel, Mdlle. de Cardoville, and told her all. "You must follow M. Hardy on the instant," said she to me. "Take my carriage and post-horses. Dupont will accompany you; follow M. Hardy from stage to stage; should you succeed in overtaking him, your presence and your prayers may perhaps conquer the fatal influence that these priests have acquired over him."'

'It was the best advice she could give you. That excellent young lady is always right.'

'An hour after, we were upon our way, for we learned by the returned postilions, that M. Hardy had taken the Orleans road. We followed him as far as Etampes. There we heard, that he had taken a cross-road, to reach a solitary house in a valley, about four leagues from the highway. They told us that this house, called the Val-de-St. Hérem, belonged to certain priests, and that, as the night was so dark, and the road so bad, we had better sleep at the inn, and start early in the morning. We followed this advice, and set out at dawn. In a quarter of an hour, we quitted the high road for a mountainous and desert track. We saw nothing but brown rocks, and a few birch trees. As we advanced, the scene became wilder and wilder. We might have fancied ourselves a hundred leagues from Paris. At last we stopped in front of a large, old, black-looking house, with only a few small windows in it, and built at the foot of a high, rocky mountain. In my whole life, I have never seen anything so deserted and sad. We got out of the carriage, and I rang the bell. A man opened the door. "Did not the Abbé d'Aigrigny arrive here last night with a gentleman?" said I to this man, with a confidential air. "Inform the gentleman directly, that I come on business of importance, and that I must see him forthwith."—The man, believing me an accomplice, showed us in immediately ; a moment after, the Abbé d'Aigrigny opened the door, saw me, and drew back ; yet, in five minutes more, I was in presence of M. Hardy.'

'Well !' said Dagobert, with interest.

Agricola shook his head sorrowfully, and replied : 'I knew by the very countenance of M. Hardy, that all was over. Addressing me in a mild but firm voice, he said to me : "I understand, I can even excuse, the motives that bring you hither. But I am quite determined to live henceforth in solitude and prayer. I take this resolution freely and voluntarily, because I would fain provide for the salvation of my soul. Tell your fellows that my arrangements will be such as to leave them a good remembrance of me."— And as I was about to speak, M. Hardy interrupted me, saying : "It is useless, my friend. My determination is unalterable. Do not write to me, for your letters would remain unanswered. Prayer will henceforth be my only occupation. Excuse me for leaving you, but I am fatigued from my journey !" —He spoke the truth for he was as pale as a spectre, with a kind of wildness about the eyes, and so changed since the day before, as to be hardly the same man. His hand, when he offered it on parting from me, was dry and burning. The Abbé d'Aigrigny soon came in. "Father," said M. Hardy to him, "have the goodness to see M. Baudoin to the door."—So saying, he waved his hand to me in token of farewell, and retired to the next chamber. All was over ; he is lost to us for ever.'

'Yes,' said Dagobert, 'those black-gowns have enchanted him, like so many others.'

'In despair,' resumed Agricola, 'I returned hither with M. Dupont. This, then, is what the priests have made of M. Hardy—of that generous man, who supported nearly three hundred industrious workmen in order and happiness, increasing their knowledge, improving their hearts, and earning the benediction of that little people, of which he was the providence. Instead of all this, M. Hardy is now for ever reduced to a gloomy and unavailing life of contemplation.'

'Oh, the black-gowns !' said Dagobert, shuddering, and unable to conceal a vague sense of fear. 'The longer I live, the more I am afraid of them. You have seen what those people did to your poor mother ; you see what they have just done to M. Hardy ; you know their plots against my two poor orphans, and against that generous young lady. Oh, these people are very powerful ! I would rather face a battalion of Russian grenadiers, than a dozen of these cassocks. But don't let's talk of it ! I have causes enough beside for grief and fear.'

Then seeing the astonished look of Agricola, the soldier, unable to restrain his emotion, threw himself into the arms of his son, exclaiming, with a choking voice : ' I can hold out no longer. My heart is too full. I must speak ; and whom shall I trust, if not you ?'

' Father, you frighten me !' said Agricola. ' What is the matter?'

' Why, you see, had it not been for you and the two poor girls, I should have blown out my brains twenty times over—rather than see what I see—and dread what I do.'

' What do you dread, father ?'——' Since the last few days, I do not know what has come over the marshal—but he frightens me.'

' Yet, in his last interviews with Mdlle. de Cardoville——'

' Yes, he was a little better. By her kind words, this generous young lady poured balm into his wounds ; the presence of the young Indian cheered him ; he appeared to shake off his cares, and his poor little girls felt the benefit of the change. But for some days, I know not what demon has been loosed against this family. It is enough to turn one's head. First of all, I am sure that the anonymous letters have begun again.'

' What letters, father ?'——' The anonymous letters.'

' But what are they about ?'——' You know how the marshal hated that renegade, the Abbé d'Aigrigny. When he found that the traitor was here, and that he had persecuted the two orphans, even as he persecuted their mother to the death—but that now he had become a priest—I thought the marshal would have gone mad with indignation and fury. He wished to go in search of the renegade. With one word, I calmed him. " He is a priest," I said ; " you may do what you will, insult, or strike him—he will not fight. He began by serving against his country, he ends by becoming a bad priest. It is all in character. He is not worth spitting upon."—" But surely I may punish the wrong done to my children, and avenge the death of my wife," cried the marshal, much exasperated.—" They say, as you well know, that there are courts of law to avenge your wrongs," answered I ; " Mdlle. de Cardoville has lodged a charge against the renegade, for having attempted to confine your daughters in a convent. We must champ the bit, and wait." '

' Yes,' said Agricola, mournfully, ' and unfortunately there lacks proof to bring it home to the Abbé d'Aigrigny. The other day, when I was examined by Mdlle. de Cardoville's lawyer, with regard to our attempt on the convent, he told me that we should meet with obstacles at every step, for want of legal evidence, and that the priests had taken their precautions with so much skill, that the indictment would be quashed.'

' That is just what the marshal thinks, my boy, and this increases his irritation at such injustice.'

' He should despise the wretches.'

' But the anonymous letters !'——' Well, what of them, father ?'

' You shall know all. A brave and honourable man like the marshal, when his first movement of indignation was over, felt that to insult the renegade disguised in the garb of a priest, would be like insulting an old man or a woman. He determined therefore to despise him, and to forget him as soon as possible. But then, almost every day, there came by the post anonymous letters, in which all sorts of devices were employed, to revive and excite the anger of the marshal against the renegade, by reminding him of all the evil contrived by the Abbé d'Aigrigny against him and his family. The marshal was reproached with cowardice for not taking vengeance on this priest, the persecutor of his wife and children, the inso.ent mocker at his misfortunes.'

'And from whom do you suspect these letters to come, father?'——'I cannot tell—it is that which turns one's brain. They must come from the enemies of the marshal, and he has no enemies but the black-gowns.'

'But, father, since these letters are to excite his anger against the Abbé d'Aigrigny, they can hardly have been written by priests.'

'That is what I have said to myself.'——'But what, then, can be their object?'

'Their object? oh, it is too plain!' cried Dagobert. 'The marshal is hasty, ardent; he has a thousand reasons to desire vengeance on the rene·gade. But he cannot do himself justice, and the other sort of justice fails him. Then what does he do? He endeavours to forget, he forgets. But every day there comes to him an insolent letter, to provoke and exasperate his legitimate hatred, by mockeries and insults. Devil take me! my head is not the weakest—but, at such a game, I should go mad.'

'Father, such a plot would be horrible, and only worthy of hell!'

'And that is not all.'

'What, more?'——'The marshal has received other letters; those he has not shown me—but, after he had read the first, he remained like a man struck motionless, and murmured to himself: "They do not even respect that—oh! it is too much—too much!"—And, hiding his face in his hands, he wept.'

'The marshal wept!' cried the blacksmith, hardly able to believe what he heard.——'Yes,' answered Dagobert, 'he wept like a child.'

'And what could these letters contain, father?'——'I did not venture to ask him, he appeared so miserable and dejected.'

'But, thus harassed and tormented incessantly, the marshal must lead a wretched life.'

'And his poor little girls too! he sees them grow sadder and sadder, without being able to guess the cause. And the death of his father, killed almost in his arms! Perhaps, you will think all this enough; but, no! I am sure there is something still more painful behind. Lately, you would hardly know the marshal. He is irritable about nothing, and falls into such fits of passion, that——' After a moment's hesitation, the soldier resumed: 'I may tell this to you, my poor boy. I have just been upstairs, to take the caps from his pistols.'

'What, father!' cried Agricola; 'you fear——'——'In the state of exasperation in which I saw him yesterday, there is everything to fear.'

'What then happened?'——'Since some time, he has often long secret interviews with a gentleman, who looks like an old soldier, and a worthy man. I have remarked, that the gloom and agitation of the marshal are always redoubled after one of these visits. Two or three times, I have spoken to him about it; but I saw by his look, that I displeased him, and therefore I desisted.

'Well! yesterday, this gentleman came in the evening. He remained here till eleven o'clock, and his wife came to fetch him, and waited for him in a coach. After his departure, I went up to see if the marshal wanted anything. He was very pale, but calm; he thanked me, and I came down again. You know that my room is just under his. I could hear the marshal walking about, as if much agitated, and soon after he seemed to be knocking down the furniture. In alarm, I once more went upstairs. He asked me, with an irritated air, what I wanted, and ordered me to leave the room. Seeing him in that way, I remained; he grew more angry, still I remained; perceiving a chair and table thrown down, I pointed to them with so sad an air, that he understood me. You know that he has the best heart in the world, so, taking me by the hand, he said to me : " Forgive me for causing you this uneasiness, my good Dagobert ; but just now, I lost my senses, and gave way to a burst of absurd fury ; I think I should have thrown myself out of the window, had it been open. I only hope, that my poor dear girls have not heard me," added he, as he went on tip-toe to open the door which communicates with his daughters' bedroom. When he had listened anxiously for a moment, he returned to me, and said : " Luckily, they are asleep."—Then I asked him what was the cause of his agitation, and if, in spite of my precautions, he had received any more anonymous letters. " No," replied he, with a gloomy air ; " but leave me, my friend. I am now better. It has done me good to see you. Good-night, old comrade ! go downstairs to bed."—I took care not to contradict him ; but, pretending to go down, I came up again, and seated myself on the top stair, listening. No doubt, to calm himself entirely, the marshal went to embrace his children, for I heard him open and shut their door. Then he returned to his room, and walked about for a long time, but with a more quiet step. At last, I heard him throw himself on his bed, and I came down about break of day. After that, all remained tranquil.'

' But whatever can be the matter with him, father ?'

' I do not know. When I went up to him, I was astonished at the agitation of his countenance, and the brilliancy of his eyes. He would have looked much the same, had he been delirious, or in a burning fever—so that, when I heard him say, he could have thrown himself out of the window, had it been òpen, I thought it more prudent to remove the caps from his pistols.'

' I cannot understand it !' said Agricola. ' So firm, intrepid, and cool a man as the marshal, a prey to such violence !'

' I tell you that something very extraordinary is passing within him. For two days, he has not been to see his children, which is always a bad sign with him—to say nothing of the poor little angels themselves, who are miserable at the notion that they have displeased their father. They displease him ! If you only knew the life they lead, dear creatures ! a walk or ride with me and their companion, for I never let them go out alone, and, the rest of their time, at their studies, reading, or needlework—always together—and then to bed. Yet their duenna, who is, I think, a worthy woman, tells me, that sometimes at night, she has seen them shed tears in their sleep. Poor children ! they have hitherto known but little happiness,' added the soldier, with a sigh.

At this moment, hearing some one walk hastily across the courtyard, Dagobert raised his eyes, and saw Marshal Simon, with pale face and bewildered air, holding in his two hands a letter, which he seemed to read with devouring anxiety.

CHAPTER XLVII.

THE GOLDEN CITY.

WHILE Marshal Simon was crossing the little court with so agitated an air, reading the anonymous letter, which he had received by Spoilsport's unexpected medium. Rose and Blanche were alone together, in the sitting-room they usually occupied, which had been entered for a moment by Loony during their absence. The poor children seemed destined to a succession of sorrows. At the moment their mourning for their mother drew near its close, the tragical death of their grandfather had again dressed them in funereal weeds. They were seated together upon a couch, in front of their work-table. Grief often produces the effect of years. Hence, in a few months, Rose and Blanche had become quite young women. To the infantine grace of their charming faces, formerly so plump and rosy, but now pale and thin, had succeeded an expression of grave and touching sadness. Their large, mild eyes of limpid azure, which always had a dreamy character, were now never bathed in those joyous tears, with which a burst of frank and hearty laughter used of old to adorn their silky lashes, when the comic coolness of Dagobert, or some funny trick of Spoilsport, cheered them in the course of their long and weary pilgrimage.

In a word, those delightful faces, which the flowery pencil of Greuze could alone have painted in all their velvet freshness, were now worthy of inspiring the melancholy ideal of the immortal Ary Scheffer, who gave us Mignon aspiring to Paradise, and Margaret dreaming of Faust. Rose, leaning back on the couch, held her head somewhat bowed upon her bosom, over which was crossed a handkerchief of black crape. The light streaming from a window opposite, shone softly on her pure, white forehead, crowned by two thick bands of chestnut hair. Her look was fixed, and the open arch of her eyebrows, now somewhat contracted, announced a mind occupied with painful thoughts. Her thin, white little hands had fallen upon her knees, but still held the embroidery, on which she had been engaged. The profile of Blanche was visible, leaning a little towards her sister, with an expression of tender and anxious solicitude, whilst her needle remained in the canvas, as if she had just ceased to work.

'Sister,' said Blanche, in a low voice, after some moments of silence, during which the tears seemed to mount to her eyes, 'tell me what you are thinking of. You look so sad.'

'I think of the Golden City of our dreams,' replied Rose, almost in a whisper, after another short silence.

Blanche understood the bitterness of these words. Without speaking, she threw herself on her sister's neck, and wept. Poor girls! the Golden City of their dreams was Paris, with their father in it—Paris, the marvellous city of joys and festivals, through all of which the orphans had beheld the radiant and smiling countenance of their sire! But, alas! the Beautiful City had been changed into a place of tears, and death, and mourning. The same terrible pestilence which had struck down their mother in the heart of Siberia, seemed to have followed them like a dark and fatal cloud, which, always hovering above them, hid the mild blue of the sky, and the joyous light of the sun.

The Golden City of their dreams! It was the place, where perhaps one day their father would present to them two young lovers, good and fair as themselves. 'They love you,' he was to say; 'they are worthy of you. Let each of you have a brother, and me two sons.' Then what chaste, enchanting confusion for those two orphans, whose hearts, pure as crystal, had never reflected any image but that of Gabriel, the celestial messenger sent by their mother to protect them!

We can therefore understand the painful emotion of Blanche, when she heard her sister repeat, with bitter melancholy, those words which described their whole situation: 'I think of the Golden City of our dreams!'

'Who knows?' proceeded Blanche, drying her sister's tears; 'perhaps, happiness may yet be in store for us.'——'Alas! if we are not happy with our father by us—shall we ever be so!'

'Yes, when we rejoin our mother,' said Blanche, lifting her eyes to heaven.

'Then, sister, this dream may be a warning—it is so like that we had in Germany.'

'The difference being that then the Angel Gabriel came down from heaven to us, and that this time he takes us from earth, to our mother.'

'And this dream will perhaps come true, like the other, my sister. We dreamt that the Angel Gabriel would protect us, and he came to save us from the shipwreck.'

'And, this time, we dream that he will lead us to heaven. Why should not that happen also?'——'But to bring that about, sister, our Gabriel, who saved us from the shipwreck, must die also. No, no ; that must not happen. Let us pray that it may not happen.'

'No, it will not happen—for it is only Gabriel's good angel, who is so like him, that we saw in our dream.'

'Sister, dear, how singular is this dream !—Here, as in Germany, we have both dreamt the same—three times, the very same !'

'It is true. The Angel Gabriel bent over us, and looked at us with so mild and sad an air, saying: " Come, my children ! come, my sisters ! Your mother waits for you. Poor children, arrived from so far !" added he in his tender voice : " You have passed over the earth, gentle and innocent as two doves, to repose for ever in the maternal nest."'

'Yes, those were the words of the archangel,' said the other orphan, with a pensive air ; 'we have done no harm to any one, and we have loved those who loved us—why should we fear to die?'

'Therefore, dear sister, we rather smiled than wept, when he took us by the hand, and, spreading wide his beautiful white wings, carried us along with him to the blue depths of the sky.'

'To heaven, where our dear mother waited for us with open arms, her face all bathed in tears.'

'Oh, sweet sister ! one has not dreams like ours for nothing. And then,' added she, looking at Rose, with a sad smile that went to the heart, 'our death might perhaps end the sorrow, of which we have been the cause.'

'Alas ! it is not our fault. We love him so much. But we are so timid and sorrowful before him, that he may perhaps think we love him not.'

So saying, Rose took her handkerchief from her work-basket, to dry her tears ; a paper, folded in the form of a letter, fell out.

At this sight, the two shuddered, and pressed close to one another, and Rose said to Blanche, in a trembling voice : 'Another of these letters !— Oh, I am afraid ! It will doubtless be like the last.'

'We must pick it up quickly, that it may not be seen,' said Blanche, hastily stooping to seize the letter ; 'the people who take interest in us might otherwise be exposed to great danger.'

'But how could this letter come to us?'——'How did the others come to be placed right under our hand, and always in the absence of our duenna?'

'It is true. Why seek to explain the mystery? We should never be able to do so. Let us read the letter. It will perhaps be more favourable to us than the last.' And the two sisters read as follows :—

'Continue to love your father, dear children, for he is very miserable, and you are the involuntary cause of his distress. You will never know the terrible sacrifices that your presence imposes on him ; but, alas ! he is the victim of his paternal duties. His sufferings are more cruel than ever ; spare him at least those marks of tenderness, which occasion him so much more pain than pleasure. Each caress is a dagger-stroke, for he sees in you the innocent cause of his misfortunes. Dear children, you must not therefore despair. If you have enough command over yourselves, not to torture him by the display of too warm a tenderness, if you can mingle some reserve with your affection, you will greatly alleviate his sorrow. Keep these letters a secret from every one, even from good Dagobert, who loves you so much ; otherwise, both he and you, your father, and the unknown friend who is writing to you, will be exposed to the utmost peril, for your enemies are indeed formidable. Courage and hope ! May your father's tenderness be once more free from sorrow and regret !—That happy day is perhaps not so far distant. Burn this letter like all the others !'

The above note was written with so much cunning that, even supposing the orphans had communicated it to their father or Dagobert, it would at the worst have been considered a strange, intrusive proceeding, but almost excusable from the spirit in which it was conceived. Nothing could have been contrived with more perfidious art, if we consider the cruel perplexity in which Marshal Simon was struggling between the fear of again leaving his children and the shame of neglecting what he considered a sacred duty. All the tenderness, all the susceptibility of heart which distinguished the orphans, had been called into play by these diabolical counsels, and the sisters soon perceived that their presence was in fact both sweet and painful to their father ; for sometimes he felt himself incapable of leaving them, and sometimes the thought of a neglected duty spread a cloud of sadness over his brow. Hence the poor twins could not fail to value the fatal meaning of the anonymous letters they received. They were persuaded that, from some mysterious motive, which they were unable to penetrate, their presence was often importunate and even painful to their father. Hence the growing sadness of Rose and Blanche—hence the sort of fear and reserve which restrained the expression of their filial tenderness. A most painful situation for the marshal, who, deceived by inexplicable appearances, mistook, in his turn, their manner for indifference to him—and so, with breaking heart, and bitter grief upon his face, often abruptly quitted his children to conceal his tears !

And the desponding orphans said to each other : 'We are the cause of our father's grief. It is our presence which makes him so unhappy.'

The reader may now judge what ravages such a thought, when fixed and incessant, must have made on these young, loving, timid, and simple hearts, How could the orphans be on their guard against such anonymous communications, which spoke with reverence of all they loved, and seemed every day justified by the conduct of their father? Already victims of numerous plots, and hearing that they were surrounded by enemies, we can understand, how, faithful to the advice of their unknown friend, they forbore to confide to Dagobert these letters, in which he was so justly appreciated. The object of the proceeding was very plain. By continually harassing the marshal on all sides, and persuading him of the coldness of his children, the conspirators might naturally hope to conquer the hesitation which had hitherto prevented his again quitting his daughters to embark in a dangerous enterprise. To render the marshal's life so burdensome that he would desire to seek relief from his torments in any project of daring and generous chivalry, was one of the ends proposed by Rodin—and, as we have seen, it wanted neither logic nor possibility.

*   *   *   *   *   *

After having read the letter, the two remained for a moment silent and dejected. Then Rose, who held the paper in her hand, started up suddenly, approached the chimney-piece, and threw the letter into the fire, saying, with a timid air : 'We must burn it quickly, or perhaps some great danger will ensue.'

'What greater misfortune can happen to us,' said Blanche, despondingly, 'than to cause such sorrow to our father ? What can be the reason of it ?'

'Perhaps,' said Rose, whose tears were slowly trickling down her cheeks, he does not find us what he could have desired. He may love us well as the children of our poor mother, but we are not the daughters he had dreamed of. Do you understand me, sister?'

'Yes, yes—that is perhaps what occasions all his sorrow. We are so badly informed, so wild, so awkward, that he is no doubt ashamed of us; and, as he loves us in spite of all, it makes him suffer.'

'Alas! it is not our fault. Our dear mother brought us up in the deserts of Siberia as well as she could.'

'Oh! father himself does not reproach us with it; only it gives him pain.'

'Particularly if he has friends whose daughters are very beautiful, and possessed of all sorts of talents. Then he must bitterly regret that we are not the same.'

'Dost remember when he took us to see our cousin, Mdlle. Adrienne, who was so affectionate and kind to us, that he said to us, with admiration: " Did you notice her, my children? How beautiful she is, and what talent, what a noble heart, and therewith such grace and elegance !" '

'Oh, it is very true! Mdlle. de Cardoville is so beautiful, her voice is so sweet and gentle, that, when we saw and heard her, we fancied that all our troubles were at an end.'

'And it is because of such beauty, no doubt, that our father, comparing us with our cousin and so many other handsome young ladies, cannot be very proud of us. And he, who is so loved and honoured, would have liked to have been proud of his daughters.'

Suddenly Rose laid her hand on her sister's arm, and said to her, with anxiety: 'Listen! listen! they are talking very loud in father's bedroom.'

'Yes,' said Blanche, listening in her turn; 'and I can hear him walking. That is his step.'

'Good heaven! how he raises his voice; he seems to be in a great passion; he will perhaps come this way.'

And at the thought of their father's coming—that father who really adored them—the unhappy children looked in terror at each other. The sound of a loud and angry voice became more and more distinct; and Rose, trembling through all her frame, said to her sister: 'Do not let us remain here! Come into our room.'

'Why?'——'We should hear, without designing it, the words of our father—and he does not perhaps know that we are so near.'

'You are right. Come, come!' answered Blanche, as she rose hastily from her seat.——'Oh! I am afraid. I have never heard him speak in so angry a tone.'

'Oh! kind heaven!' said Blanche, growing pale, as she stopped involuntarily. 'It is to Dagobert that he is talking so loud.'——'What can be the matter—to make our father speak to him in that way?'

'Alas! some great misfortune must have happened.'——'Oh, sister! do not let us remain here! It pains me too much to hear Dagobert thus spoken to.'

The crash of some article, hurled with violence and broken to pieces in the next room, so frightened the orphans, that, pale and trembling with emotion, they rushed into their own apartment, and fastened the door. We must now explain the cause of Marshal Simon's violent anger.

CHAPTER XLVIII.

THE STUNG LION.

THIS was the scene, the sound of which had so terrified Rose and Blanche. At first alone in his chamber, in a state of exasperation difficult to describe,

Marshal Simon had begun to walk hastily up and down, his handsome, manly face inflamed with rage, his eyes sparkling with indignation, while on his broad forehead, crowned with short-cut hair that was now turning grey, large veins, of which you might count the pulsations, were swollen almost to bursting ; and sometimes his thick, black moustache was curled with a convulsive motion, not unlike that which is seen in the visage of a raging lion. And even as the wounded lion, in its fury, harassed and tortured by a thousand invisible darts, walks up and down its den with savage wrath, so Marshal Simon paced the floor of his room, as if bounding from side to side ; sometimes he stooped, as though bending beneath the weight of his anger ; sometimes, on the contrary, he paused abruptly, drew himself up to his full height, crossed his arms upon his vigorous chest, and with raised brow, threatening and terrible look, seemed to defy some invisible enemy, and murmur confused exclamations. Then he stood like a man of war and battle in all his intrepid fire.

And now he stamped angrily with his foot, approached the chimney-piece, and pulled the bell so violently that the bell-rope remained in his hand. A servant hastened to attend to this precipitate summons. ' Did you not tell Dagobert that I wished to speak to him ?' cried the marshal.

' I executed your grace's orders, but M. Dagobert was accompanying his son to the door, and——'——' Very well !' interrupted Marshal Simon, with an abrupt and imperious gesture.

The servant went out, and his master continued to walk up and down with impatient steps, crumpling, in his rage, a letter that he held in his left hand. This letter had been innocently delivered by Spoilsport, who, seeing him come in, had run joyously to meet him. At length the door opened, and Dagobert appeared. ' I have been waiting for you a long time, sirrah !' cried the marshal, in an irritated tone.

Dagobert, more pained than surprised at this burst of anger, which he rightly attributed to the constant state of excitement in which the marshal had now been for some time past, answered mildly : ' I beg your pardon, general, but I was letting out my son——'

' Read that, sir !' said the marshal abruptly, giving him the letter.

While Dagobert was reading it, the marshal resumed, with growing anger, as he kicked over a chair that stood in his way : ' Thus, even in my own house, there are wretches bribed to harass me with incredible perseverance. Well ! have you read it, sir ?'

' It is a fresh insult to add to the others,' said Dagobert, coolly, as he threw the letter into the fire.

' The letter is infamous—but it speaks the truth,' replied the marshal. Dagobert looked at him in amazement.

' And can you tell who brought me this infamous letter ?' continued the marshal. ' One would think the devil had a hand in it—for it was your dog !'

' Spoilsport ?' said Dagobert, in the utmost surprise.——' Yes,' answered the marshal, bitterly ; ' it is no doubt a joke of your invention.'

' I have no heart for joking, general,' answered Dagobert, more and more saddened by the irritable state of the marshal ; ' I cannot explain how it happened. Spoilsport is a good carrier, and no doubt found the letter in the house——'

' And who can have left it there ? Am I surrounded by traitors ? Do you keep no watch ? You, in whom I have every confidence ?'——' Listen to me, general——'

But the marshal proceeded, without waiting to hear him : ' What ! I have made war for five-and-twenty years, I have battled with armies, I have struggled victoriously through the evil times of exile and proscription, I have withstood blows from maces of iron—and now I am to be killed with pins ! Pursued into my own house, harassed with impunity, worn out, tortured every minute, to gratify some unknown, miserable hate !—When I say unknown, I am wrong—it is D'Aigrigny, the renegade, who is at the bottom of all this, I am sure. I have in the world but one enemy, and he is the man. I must finish with him, for I am weary of this—it is too much !'

'But general, remember he is a priest——'

'What do I care for that ? Have I not seen him handle the sword ? I will yet make a soldier's blood rise to the forehead of the traitor !'

'But, general——'——'I tell you, that I must be avenged on some one,' cried the marshal, with an accent of the most violent exasperation ; 'I tell you, that I must find a living representative of these cowardly plots, that I may at once make an end of him !—They press upon me from all sides ; they make my life a hell—you know it—and you do nothing to save me from these tortures, which are killing me as by a slow fire. Can I have no one, in whom to trust ?'

'General, I can't let you say that,' replied Dagobert, in a calm, but firm voice.——'And why not ?'

'General, I can't let you say that you have no one to trust to. You might end perhaps in believing it, and then it would be even worse for yourself, than for those who well know their devotion for you, and would go through fire and water to serve you. I am one of them—and you know it.'

These simple words, pronounced by Dagobert with a tone of deep conviction, recalled the marshal to himself ; for although his honourable and generous character might from time to time be embittered by irritation and grief, he soon recovered his natural equanimity. So, addressing Dagobert in a less abrupt tone, he said to him, though still much agitated : 'You are right. I could never doubt your fidelity. But anger deprives me of my senses. This infamous letter is enough to drive one mad. I am unjust, ungrateful—yes, ungrateful—and to you !'

'Do not think of me, general. With a kind word at the end, you might blow me up all the year round. But what has happened ?'

The general's countenance again darkened, as he answered rapidly : 'I am looked down upon, and despised !'

'You ?'——'Yes, I. After all,' resumed the marshal, bitterly. '.why should I conceal from you this new wound ? If I doubted you a moment, I owe you some compensation, and you shall know all. For some time past, I have perceived that, when I meet any of my old companions in arms, they try to avoid me——'

'What ! was it to this that the anonymous letter alluded ?'——'Yes ; and it spoke the truth,' replied the marshal, with a sigh of grief and indignation.

'But it is impossible, general—you are so loved and respected——'

'Those are mere words ; I speak of positive facts. When I appear, the conversation is often interrupted. Instead of treating me as an old comrade, they affect towards me a rigorously cold politeness. There are a thousand little shades, a thousand trifles, which wound the heart, but which it is impossible to notice——'

'What you are now saying, general, quite confounds me,' replied Dagobert. 'You assure me of it, and I am forced to believe you.'

'Oh, it is intolerable ! I was resolved to ease my heart of it ; so, this morning, I went to General d'Havrincourt, who was colonel with me in the Imperial Guard ; he is honour and honesty itself. I went to him with open heart. "I perceive," said I, "the coldness that is shown me. Some calumny must be circulating to my disadvantage. Tell me all about it. Knowing the attack, I shall be able to defend myself"——'

'Well, general?'——' D'Havrincourt remained impassible, ceremoniously polite. To all my questions he answered coldly : "I am not aware, my lord duke, that any calumny has been circulated with regard to you."—"Do not call me 'my lord duke,' my dear D'Havrincourt ; we are old fellow-soldiers and friends ; my honour is somewhat touchy, I confess, and I find that you and our comrades do not receive me so cordially as in times past. You do not deny it ; I see, I know, I feel it."—To all this D'Havrincourt answered, with the same coldness : "I have never seen any one wanting in respect towards you."—"I am not talking of respect," exclaimed I, as I clasped his hand affectionately, though I observed that he but feebly returned the pressure ; "I speak of cordiality, confidence, which I once enjoyed, while now, I am treated like a stranger. Why is it ? What has occasioned this change ?'—Still cold and reserved, he answered : "These distinctions are so nice, marshal, that it is impossible for me to give you any opinion on the subject."—My heart swelled with grief and anger. What was I to do ? To quarrel with D'Havrincourt would have been absurd. A sense of dignity forced me to break off the interview, but it has only confirmed my fears. Thus,' added the marshal, getting more and more animated, 'thus am I fallen from the esteem to which I am entitled, thus am I despised, without even knowing the cause ! Is it not odious ? If they would only utter a charge against me—I should at least be able to defend myself, and to find an answer. But no, no ! not even a word—only the cold politeness that is worse than any insult. Oh ! it is too much, too much ! for all this comes but in addition to other cares. What a life is mine, since the death of my father ! If I did but find rest and happiness at home—but no ! I come in, but to read shameful letters ; and still worse,' added the marshal, in a heart-rending tone, and after a moment's hesitation, 'to find my children grow more and more indifferent towards me. Yes,' continued he, perceiving the amazement of Dagobert, 'and yet they know how much I love them !'

'Your daughters indifferent ?' exclaimed Dagobert, in astonishment. 'You make them such a reproach ?'——'Oh ! I do not blame them. They have hardly had time to know me.'

'Not had time to know you ?' returned the soldier, in a tone of remonstrance, and warming up in his turn. 'Ah ! of what did their mother talk to them, except you ? and I too ! what could I teach your children except to know and love you ?'

'You take their part—that is natural—they love you better than they do me,' said the marshal, with growing bitterness. Dagobert felt himself so painfully affected, that he looked at the marshal without answering.

'Yes !' continued the other ; 'yes ! it may be base and ungrateful—but no matter !—Twenty times I have felt jealous of the affectionate confidence which my children display towards you, while with me they seem always to be in fear. If their melancholy faces ever grow animated for a moment, it is in talking to you, in seeing you ; while for me they have nothing but cold respect—and that kills me. Sure of the affection of my children, I would have braved and surmounted every difficulty——' Then, seeing that Dagobert rushed towards the door which led to the chamber of Rose and Blanche, the marshal asked : 'Where are you going ?'

'For your daughters, general.'——'What for ?'

'To bring them face to face with you—to tell them : "My children, your father thinks that you do not love him."—I will only say that—and then you will see.'

'Dagobert ! I forbid you to do it,' cried the marshal, hastily. ——'I don't care for that—you have no right to be unjust to the poor children,' said the soldier, as he again advanced towards the door.

'Dagobert, I command you to remain here,' cried the marshal.——'Listen to me, general. I am your soldier, your inferior, your servant, if you will, said the old grenadier, roughly ; 'but neither rank nor station shall keep me silent, when I have to defend your daughters. All must be explained— I know but one way—and that is to bring honest people face to face.'

If the marshal had not seized him by the arm, Dagobert would have entered the apartment of the young girls.

'Remain !' said the marshal, so imperiously, that the soldier, accustomed to obedience, hung his head, and stood still.

'What would you do ?' resumed the marshal. 'Tell my children, that I think they do not love me ? induce them to affect a tenderness they do not feel—when it is not their fault, but mine ?'

'Oh, general !' said Dagobert, in a tone of despair, 'I no longer feel anger, in hearing you speak thus of your children. It is such grief, that it breaks my heart !'

Touched by the expression of the soldier's countenance, the marshal continued, less abruptly : 'Come, I may be wrong ; and yet I ask you, without bitterness or jealousy, are not my children more confiding, more familiar, with you than with me ?'

'God bless me, general !' cried Dagobert ; 'if you come to that, they are more familiar with Spoilsport than with either of us. You are their father ; and, however kind a father may be, he must always command some respect. Familiar with me ! I should think so. A fine story ! What the devil should they respect in me, who, except that I am six feet high, and wear a moustache, might pass for the old woman that nursed them ?—and then I must say, that, even before the death of your worthy father, you were sad and full of thought ; the children have remarked that, and what you take for coldness on their part, is, I am sure, anxiety for you. Come, general ; you are not just. You complain, because they love you too much.'

'I complain, because I suffer,' said the marshal, in an agony of excitement. 'I alone know my sufferings.'

'They must indeed be grievous, general,' said Dagobert, carried further than he would otherwise have gone by his attachment for the orphans, 'since those who love you feel them so cruelly.'

'What, sir ! more reproaches ?'——'Yes, general, reproaches,' cried Dagobert. 'Your children have the right to complain of you, since you accuse them so unjustly.'

'Sir,' said the marshal, scarcely able to contain himself, 'this is enough— this is too much !'——'Oh, yes ! it is enough,' replied Dagobert, with rising emotion. 'Why defend unfortunate children, who can only love and submit ? Why defend them against your unhappy blindness ?'

The marshal started with anger and impatience, but then replied, with a forced calmness : 'I needs must remember all that I owe you—and I will not forget it, say what you will.'

'But, general,' cried Dagobert, 'why will you not let me fetch your children ?'

'Do you not see, that this scene is killing me ?' cried the exasperated marshal. 'Do you not understand, that I will not have my children witness what I suffer ? A father's grief has its dignity, sir ; and you ought to feel for and respect it.'

'Respect it ? no—not when it is founded on injustice !'——'Enough, sir— enough !'

'And not content with tormenting yourself,' cried Dagobert, unable any longer to control his feelings, 'do you know what you will do ? You will make your children die of sorrow. Was it for this, that I brought them to you from the depths of Siberia ?'

'More reproaches !'——'Yes ; for the worst ingratitude towards me, is to make your children unhappy.'

'Leave the room, sir !' cried the marshal, quite beside himself, and so terrible with rage and grief, that Dagobert, regretting that he had gone so far, resumed : 'I was wrong, general. I have perhaps been wanting in respect to you—forgive me—but——'

'I forgive you—only leave me !' said the marshal, hardly restraining himself.——'One word, general——'

'I entreat you to leave me—I ask it as a service—is that enough ?' said the marshal, with renewed efforts to control the violence of his emotions.

A deadly paleness succeeded to the high colour which during this painful scene had inflamed the cheeks of the marshal. Alarmed at this symptom, Dagobert redoubled his entreaties. 'I implore you, general,' said he, in an agitated voice, 'to permit me for one moment——'

'Since you will have it so, sir, I must be the one to leave,' said the marshal, making a step towards the door.

These words were said in such a manner, that Dagobert could no longer resist. He hung his head in despair, looked for a moment in silent supplication at the marshal, and then, as the latter seemed yielding to a new movement of rage, the soldier slowly quitted the room.

    ✧   ✧   ✧   ✧   ✧   ✧

A few minutes had scarcely elapsed since the departure of Dagobert, when the marshal, who, after a long and gloomy silence, had repeatedly drawn near the door of his daughters' apartment with a mixture of hesitation and anguish, suddenly made a violent effort, wiped the cold sweat from his brow, and entered the chamber in which Rose and Blanche had taken refuge.

CHAPTER XLIX.

THE TEST.

DAGOBERT was right in defending his children, as he paternally called Rose and Blanche, and yet the apprehensions of the marshal with regard to the coldness of his daughters, were unfortunately justified by appearances. As he had told his father, unable to explain the sad, and almost trembling embarrassment which his daughters felt in his presence, he sought in vain for the cause of what he termed their indifference. Now reproaching himself bitterly for not concealing from them his grief at the death of their mother, he feared he might have given them to understand that they would be unable to console him ; now supposing that he had not shown himself sufficiently tender, and that he had chilled them with his military sternness ; and now repeating with bitter regret, that, having always lived away from them, he must be always a stranger to them. In a word, the most unlikely suppositions presented themselves by turns to his mind, and whenever such seeds of doubt, suspicion, or fear, are blended with a warm affection, they will sooner or later develop themselves with fatal effect. Yet, notwithstanding this fancied coldness, from which he suffered so much, the affection of the marshal for his daughters was so true and deep, that the thought of again quitting them caused the hesitations which were the torment of his life, and provoked an incessant struggle between his paternal love and the duty he held most sacred.

The injurious calumnies, which had been so skilfully propagated, that men of honour, like his old brothers in arms, were found to attach some credit to them, had been spread with frightful pertinacity by the friends of the Princess de Saint-Dizier. We shall describe hereafter the meaning and object of these odious reports, which, joined with so many other fatal injuries, had filled up the measure of the marshal's indignation. Inflamed with anger, excited almost to madness by this incessant 'stabbing with pins' (as he had himself called it), and offended at some of Dagobert's words, he had spoken harshly to him. But, after the soldier's departure, when left to reflect in silence, the marshal remembered the warm and earnest expressions of the defender of his children, and a doubt crossed his mind, as to the reality of the coldness of which he accused them. Therefore, having taken a terrible resolution, in case a new trial should confirm his desponding doubts, he entered, as we before said, his daughters' chamber. The discussion with Dagobert had been so loud, that the sound of the voices had confusedly reached the ears of the two sisters, even after they had taken refuge in their bedroom. So that, on the arrival of their father, their pale faces betrayed their fear and anxiety. At sight of the marshal, whose countenance was also much agitated, the girls rose respectfully, but remained close together, trembling in each other's arms. And yet there was neither anger nor severity on their father's face—only a deep, almost supplicating grief, which seemed to say: 'My children, I suffer—I have come to you—console me, love me ! or I shall die !'

The marshal's countenance was at this moment so expressive, that, the first impulse of fear once surmounted, the sisters were about to throw themselves into his arms ; but remembering the recommendations of the anonymous letter, which told them how painful any effusion of their tenderness was to their father, they exchanged a rapid glance, and remained motionless. By a cruel fatality, the marshal at this moment burned to open his arms to his children. He looked at them with love, he even made a slight movement as if to call them to him ; but he would not attempt more, for fear of meeting with no response. Still the poor children, paralysed by perfidious counsels, remained mute, motionless, trembling !

'It is all over,' thought he, as he gazed upon them. 'No chord of sympathy stirs in their bosom. Whether I go—whether I remain—matters not to them. No, I am nothing to these children—since, at this awful moment, when they see me perhaps for the last time, no filial instinct tells them that their affection might save me still !'

During these terrible reflections, the marshal had not taken his eyes off his children, and his manly countenance assumed an expression at once so touching and mournful—his look revealed so painfully the tortures of his despairing soul—that Rose and Blanche, confused, alarmed, but yielding together to a spontaneous movement, threw themselves on their father's neck, and covered him with tears and caresses. Marshal Simon had not spoken a word ; his daughters had not uttered a sound ; and yet all three had at length understood one another. A sympathetic shock had electrified and mingled those three hearts. Vain fears, false doubts, lying counsel, all had yielded to the irresistible emotion, which had brought the daughters to their father's arms. A sudden revelation gave them faith, at the fatal moment when incurable suspicion was about to separate them for ever.

In a second, the marshal felt all this, but words failed him. Pale, bewildered, kissing the brows, the hair, the hands of his daughters, weeping, sighing, smiling all in turn, he was wild, delirious, drunk with happiness. At length, he exclaimed : 'I have found them—or rather, I had never lost them. They loved me, and did not dare to tell me so. I overawed them. And I thought it was my fault. Heavens ! what good that does ! what strength, what heart, what hope!—Ha ! ha !' cried he, laughing and weeping at the same time, whilst he covered his children with caresses ; 'they may despise me now, they may harass me now—I defy them all. My own blue eyes ! my sweet blue eyes ! look at me well, and inspire me with new life.'

'Oh, father ! you love us then as much as we love you ?' cried Rose, with enchanting simplicity.

'And we may often, very often, perhaps every day, throw ourselves on your neck, embrace you, and prove how glad we are to be with you ?'

'Show you, dear father, all the store of love we were heaping up in our hearts—so sad, alas ! that we could not spend it upon you ?'

'Tell you aloud all that we think in secret ?'

'Yes—you may do so—you may do so,' said Marshal Simon, faltering with joy ; 'what prevented you, my children ? But no ; do not answer ; enough of the past !—I know all, I understand all. You misinterpreted my gloom, and it made you sad ; I, in my turn, misinterpreted your sadness. But never mind ; I scarcely know what I am saying to you. I only think of looking at you—and it dazzles me—it confuses me—it is the dizziness of joy !'

'Oh, look at us, father ! look into our eyes, into our hearts,' cried Rose, with rapture.——'And you will read there, happiness for us, and love for you, sir !' added Blanche.

'Sir, sir ?' said the marshal, in a tone of affectionate reproach ; 'what does that mean ? Will you call me *father*, if you please ?'——' Dear father, your hand !' said Blanche, as she took it, and placed it on her heart.

'Dear father, your hand !' said Rose, as she took the other hand of the marshal. 'Do you believe now in our love and happiness ?' she continued.

It is impossible to describe the charming expression of filial pride in the divine faces of the girls, as their father, slightly pressing their virgin bosoms, seemed to count with delight the joyous pulsations of their hearts.

'Oh, yes ! happiness and affection can alone make the heart beat thus !' cried the marshal.

A hoarse sob, heard in the direction of the open door, made the three turn round, and there they saw the tall figure of Dagobert, with the black nose of Spoilsport reaching to his master's knee. The soldier, drying his eyes and moustache with his little blue cotton handkerchief, remained motionless as the god Terminus. When he could speak, he addressed himself to the marshal, and, shaking his head, muttered, in a hoarse voice, for the good man was swallowing his tears : 'Did I not tell you so ?'

'Silence !' said the marshal, with a sign of intelligence. 'You were a better father than myself, my old friend. Come and kiss them ! I shall not be jealous.'

The marshal stretched out his hand to the soldier, who pressed it cordially, whilst the two sisters threw themselves on his neck, and Spoilsport, according to custom wishing to have his share in the general joy, raised himself on his hind legs, and rested his fore-paws against his master's back. There was a moment of profound silence. The celestial felicity enjoyed during that moment, by the marshal, his daughters, and the soldier, was interrupted by the barking of Spoilsport, who suddenly quitted the attitude of a biped. The happy group separated, looked round, and saw Loony's stupid face. He looked even duller than usual, as he stood quite still in the doorway, staring with wide-stretched eyes, and holding a feather-broom under his arm, and in his hand the ever-present basket of wood.

Nothing makes one so gay as happiness ; and, though this grotesque figure appeared at a very unseasonable moment, it was received with frank laughter from the blooming lips of Rose and Blanche. Having made the marshal's daughters laugh, after their long sadness, Loony at once acquired a claim to the indulgence of the marshal, who said to him, good-humouredly: 'What do you want, my lad?'

'It's not me, my lord duke!' answered Loony, laying his hand on his breast, as if he were taking a vow, so that his feather-brush fell down from under his arm. The laughter of the girls redoubled.

'It is not you?' said the marshal.

'Here! Spoilsport!' Dagobert called, for the honest dog seemed to have a secret dislike for the pretended idiot, and approached him with an angry air.

'No, my lord duke, it is not me!' resumed Loony. 'It is the footman who told me to tell M. Dagobert, when I brought up the wood, to tell my lord duke, as I was coming up with the basket, that M. Robert wants to see him.'

The girls laughed still more at this new stupidity. But, at the name of Robert, Marshal Simon started.

M. Robert was the secret emissary of Rodin, with regard to the possible, but adventurous, enterprise of attempting the liberation of Napoleon II.

After a moment's silence, the marshal, whose face was still radiant with joy and happiness, said to Loony: 'Beg M. Robert to wait for me a moment in my study.'

'Yes, my lord duke,' answered Loony, bowing almost to the ground.

The simpleton withdrew, and the marshal said to his daughters, in a joyous tone, 'You see, that, in a moment like this, one does not leave one's children, even for M. Robert.'

'Oh! that's right, father!' cried Blanche, gaily; 'for I was already very angry with this M. Robert.'——'Have you pen and paper at hand?' asked the marshal.

'Yes, father; there on the table,' said Rose, hastily, as she pointed to a little desk near one of the windows, towards which the marshal now advanced rapidly.

From motives of delicacy, the girls remained where they were, close to the fire-place, and caressed each other tenderly, as if to congratulate themselves in private on the unexpected happiness of this day.

The marshal seated himself at the desk, and made a sign to Dagobert to draw near.

While he wrote rapidly a few words in a firm hand, he said to the soldier with a smile, in so low a tone that it was impossible for his daughters to hear: 'Do you know what I had almost resolved upon, before entering this room?'

'What, general?'——'To blow my brains out. It is to my children that I owe my life.' And the marshal continued writing.

Dagobert started at this communication, and then replied, also in a whisper: 'It would not have been with your pistols. I took off the caps.'

The marshal turned round hastily, and looked at him with an air of surprise. But the soldier only nodded his head affirmatively, and added: 'Thank heaven, we have now done with all those ideas!'

The marshal's only answer was to glance at his children, his eyes swimming with tenderness, and sparkling with delight; then, sealing the note he had written, he gave it to the soldier, and said to him, 'Give that to M. Robert. I will see him to-morrow.'

Dagobert took the letter, and went out. Returning towards his daughters, the marshal joyfully extended his arms to them, and said, 'Now, young ladies, two nice kisses for having sacrificed M. Robert to you. Have I not earned them?' And Rose and Blanche threw themselves on their father's neck.

About the time that these events were taking place at Paris, two travellers, wide apart from each other, exchanged mysterious thoughts through the breadth of space.

CHAPTER L.

THE RUINS OF THE ABBEY OF ST. JOHN THE BAPTIST.

The sun is fast sinking. In the depths of an immense piny wood, in the midst of profound solitude, rise the ruins of an abbey, once sacred to St. John the Baptist. Ivy, moss, and creeping plants, almost entirely conceal the stones, now black with age. Some broken arches, some walls pierced with ovals, still remain standing, visible on the dark background of the thick wood. Looking down upon this mass of ruins, from a broken pedestal, half-covered with ivy, a mutilated, but colossal statue of stone still keeps its place. This statue is strange and awful. It represents a headless human figure. Clad in the antique toga, it holds in its hand a dish, and on that dish is a head. This head is its own. It is the statue of St. John the Baptist and Martyr, put to death by wish of Herodias.

The silence around is solemn. From time to time, however, is heard the dull rustling of the enormous branches of the pine-trees, shaken by the wind. Copper-coloured clouds, reddened by the setting sun, pass slowly over the forest, and are reflected in the current of a brook, which, deriving its source from a neighbouring mass of rocks, flows through the ruins. The water flows, the clouds pass on, the ancient trees tremble, the breeze murmurs.

Suddenly, through the shadow thrown by the overhanging wood, which stretches far into endless depths, a human form appears. It is a woman. She advances slowly towards the ruins. She has reached them. She treads the once sacred ground. This woman is pale, her look sad, her long robe floats on the wind, her feet are covered with dust. She walks with difficulty and pain. A block of stone is placed near the stream, almost at the foot of the statue of St. John the Baptist. Upon this stone she sinks breathless and exhausted, worn out with fatigue. And yet, for many days, many years, many centuries, she has walked on unwearied.

For the first time, she feels an unconquerable sense of lassitude. For the first time, her feet begin to fail her. For the first time, she, who traversed, with firm and equal footsteps, the moving lava of torrid deserts, while whole caravans were buried in drifts of fiery sand—who passed, with steady and disdainful tread, over the eternal snows of Arctic regions, over icy solitudes, in which no other human being could live—who had been spared by the devouring flames of conflagrations, and by the impetuous waters of torrents— she, in brief, who for centuries had had nothing in common with humanity— for the first time suffers mortal pain.

Her feet bleed, her limbs ache with fatigue, she is devoured by burning thirst. She feels these infirmities, yet scarcely dares to believe them real. Her joy would be too immense ! But now, her throat becomes dry, contracted, all on fire. She sees the stream, and throws herself on her knees, to quench her thirst in that crystal current, transparent as a mirror. What happens then ? Hardly have her fevered lips touched the fresh, pure water, than, still kneeling, supported on her hands, she suddenly ceases to drink, and gazes eagerly on the limpid stream. Forgetting the thirst which devours her, she utters a loud cry—a cry of deep, earnest, religious joy, like a note of praise and infinite gratitude to heaven. In that deep mirror, she perceives that she has grown older.

In a few days, a few hours, a few minutes, perhaps in a single second, she has attained the maturity of age. She, who for more than eighteen centuries has been as a woman of twenty, carrying through successive generations the load of her imperishable youth—she has grown old, and may, perhaps, at length, hope to die. Every minute of her life may now bring her nearer to the last home ! Transported by that ineffable hope, she rises, and lifts her eyes to heaven, clasping her hands in an attitude of fervent prayer. Then her eyes rest on the tall statue of stone, representing St. John. The head, which the martyr carries in his hand, seems, from beneath its half-closed granite eye-lid, to cast upon the Wandering Jewess a glance of commiseration and pity. And it was she, Herodias, who, in the cruel intoxication of a pagan festival, demanded the murder of the saint ! And it is at the foot of the martyr's image, that, for the first time, the immortality, which weighed on her for so many centuries, seems likely to find a term !

'Oh, impenetrable mystery ! oh, divine hope !' she cries. 'The wrath of heaven is at length appeased. The hand of the Lord brings me to the feet of the blessed martyr, and I begin once more to feel myself a human creature. And yet it was to avenge his death, that the same heaven condemned me to eternal wanderings !

'Oh, Lord ! grant that I may not be the only one forgiven. May he—the artisan, who, like me, daughter of a king, wanders on for centuries—likewise hope to reach the end of that immense journey !

'Where is he, Lord ? where is he ? Hast thou deprived me of the power once bestowed, to see and hear him through the vastness of intervening space ? Oh ! in this mighty moment, restore me that divine gift—for the more I feel these human infirmities, which I hail and bless as the end of my eternity of ills, the more my sight loses the power to traverse immensity, and my ear to catch the sound of that wanderer's accents, from the other extremity of the globe !'

Night had fallen, dark and stormy. The wind rose in the midst of the great pine-trees. Behind their black summits, through masses of dark cloud, slowly sailed the silver disc of the moon. The invocation of the Wandering Jewess had perhaps been heard. Suddenly, her eyes closed— with hands clasped together, she remained kneeling in the heart of the ruins—motionless as a statue upon a tomb. And then she had a wondrous dream !

———

CHAPTER LI.

THE CALVARY.

THIS was the vision of Herodias : On the summit of a high, steep, rocky mountain, there stands a cross. The sun is sinking, even as when the Jewess herself, worn out with fatigue, entered the ruins of St. John's Abbey. The great figure on the cross—which looks down from this Calvary, on the mountain, and on the vast, dreary plain beyond—stands out white and pale against the dark, blue clouds, which stretch across the heavens, and assume a violet tint towards the horizon. There, where the setting sun has left a long track of lurid light, almost of the hue of blood—as far as the eye can reach, no vegetation appears on the surface of the gloomy desert, covered with sand and stones, like the ancient bed of some dried-up ocean. A silence as of death broods over this desolate tract. Sometimes, gigantic black vultures, with red unfeathered necks, luminous yellow eyes, stooping from their lofty flight in the midst of these solitudes, come to make their bloody feast on the prey they have carried off from less uncultivated regions.

How, then, did this Calvary, this place of prayer, come to be erected so far from the abodes of men ? This Calvary was prepared at a great cost by a repentant sinner. He had done much harm to his fellow-creatures, and, in the hope of obtaining pardon for his crimes, he had climbed this mountain on his knees, and become a hermit, and lived there till his death, at the foot of this cross, only sheltered by a roof of thatch, now long since swept away by the wind. The sun is still sinking. The sky becomes darker. The luminous lines on the horizon grow fainter and fainter, like heated bars of iron that gradually grow cool. Suddenly, on the eastern side of the Calvary, is heard the noise of some falling stones, which, loosened from the side of the mountain, roll down rebounding to its base. These stones have been loosened by the foot of a traveller, who, after traversing the plain below, has during the last hour been climbing the steep ascent. He is not yet visible—but one hears the echo of his tread—slow, steady, and firm. At length, he reaches the top of the mountain, and his tall figure stands out against the stormy sky.

The traveller is pale as the great figure on the cross. On his broad forehead a black line extends from one temple to the other. It is the cobbler of Jerusalem. The poor artisan, who, hardened by misery, injustice, and oppression, without pity for the suffering of the Divine Being who bore the cross, repulsed him from his dwelling, and bade him : ' GO ON ! GO ON ! GO ON !' And, from that day, the avenging Deity has in his turn said to the artisan of Jerusalem : ' GO ON ! GO ON ! GO ON !'

And he has gone on, without end or rest. Nor did the divine vengeance stop there. From time to time death has followed the steps of the wanderer, and innumerable graves have been even as mile-stones on his fatal path. And if ever he found periods of repose in the midst of his infinite grief, it was when the hand of the Lord led him into deep solitudes, like that where he now dragged his steps along. In passing over that dreary plain, or climbing to that rude Calvary, he at least heard no more the funeral knell, which always, always sounded behind him in every inhabited region.

All day long, even at this hour, plunged in the black abyss of his thoughts, following the fatal track—going whither he was guided by the invisible hand, with head bowed on his breast, and eyes fixed upon the ground, the wanderer had passed over the plain, and ascended the mountain, without once looking at the sky—without even perceiving the Calvary—without seeing the image upon the cross. He thought of the last descendants of his race. He felt, by the sinking of his heart, that great perils continued to threaten them. And in the bitterness of a despair wild and deep as the ocean, the cobbler of Jerusalem seated himself at the foot of the cross. At this moment a farewell ray of the setting sun, piercing the dark mass of clouds, threw a reflection upon the Calvary, vivid as a conflagration's glare. The Jew rested his forehead upon his hand. His long hair, shaken by the evening breeze, fell over his pale face—when, sweeping it back from his brow, he started with surprise—he, who had long ceased to wonder at anything. With eager glance he contemplated the long lock of hair that he held between his fingers. That hair, until now black as night, had become grey. He also, like unto Herodias, was growing older.

His progress towards old age, stopped for eighteen hundred years, had resumed its course. Like the Wandering Jewess, he might henceforth hope for the rest of the grave. Throwing himself on his knees, he stretched his hands towards heaven, to ask for the explanation of the mystery which filled him with hope. Then, for the first time, his eyes rested on the Crucified One, looking down upon the Calvary, even as the Wandering Jewess had fixed her gaze on the granite eye-lids of the Blessed Martyr.

The Saviour, his head bowed under the weight of his crown of thorns, seemed from the cross to view with pity and pardon the artisan, who for so many centuries had felt his curse—and who, kneeling, with his body thrown backward in an attitude of fear and supplication, now lifted towards the crucifix his imploring hands.

' Oh, Messiah !' cried the Jew, ' the avenging arm of heaven brings me back to the foot of this heavy cross, which thou didst bear, when, stopping at the door of my poor dwelling, thou wert repulsed with merciless harshness, and I said unto thee : " Go on ! go on !"—After my long life of wanderings, I am again before this cross, and my hair begins to whiten. Oh, Lord ! in thy divine mercy, hast thou at length pardoned me ? Have I reached the term of my endless march ? Will thy celestial clemency grant me at length the repose of the sepulchre, which, until now, alas ! has ever fled before me ?—Oh ! if thy mercy should descend upon me, let it fall likewise upon that woman, whose woes are equal to mine own ! Protect also the last descendants of my race ! What will be their fate ? Already, Lord, one of them—the only one that misfortune had perverted—has perished from the face of the earth. Is it for this that my hair grows grey ? Will my crime only be expiated when there no longer remains in this world one member of our accursed race ? Or does this proof of thy powerful goodness, Lord, which restores me to the condition of humanity, serve also as a sign of the pardon and happiness of my family ? Will they at length triumph over the perils which beset them ? Will they, accomplishing the good which their ancestor designed for his fellow-creatures, merit forgiveness both for themselves and me ? Or will they, inexorably condemned as the accursed scions of an accursed stock, expiate the original stain of my detested crime ?

' Oh, tell me—tell me, gracious Lord ! shall I be forgiven with them, or will they be punished with me ?'

    ☼   ☼   ☼   ☼   ☼   ☼

The twilight gave place to a dark and stormy night, yet the Jew continued to pray, kneeling at the foot of the cross.

CHAPTER LII.

THE COUNCIL.

THE following scene took place at Saint-Dizier House, two days after the reconciliation of Marshal Simon with his daughters. The princess is listening with the most profound attention to the words of Rodin. The reverend father, according to his habit, stands leaning against the mantelpiece, with his hands thrust into the pockets of his old brown great-coat. His thick, dirty shoes have left their mark on the ermine hearth-rug. A deep sense of satisfaction is impressed on the Jesuit's cadaverous countenance. Princess de Saint-Dizier, dressed with that sort of modest elegance which becomes a mother of the Church, keeps her eyes fixed on Rodin—for the latter has completely supplanted Father d'Aigrigny in the good graces of this pious lady. The coolness, audacity, lofty intelligence, and rough and imperious character of the ex-socius have overawed this proud woman, and inspired her with a sincere admiration. Even his filthy habits and often brutal repartees have their charm for her, and she now prefers them to the exquisite politeness and perfumed elegance of the accomplished Father d'Aigrigny.

' Yes, madame,' said Rodin, in a sanctified tone, for these people do not take off their masks even with their accomplices, ' yes, madame, we have excellent news from our house at St. Hérem. M. Hardy, the infidel, the freethinker, has at length entered the pale of the holy Roman Catholic and Apostolic Church.' Rodin pronounced these last words with a nasal twang, and the devout lady bowed her head respectfully.

'Grace has at length touched the heart of this impious man,' continued Rodin, 'and so effectually that, in his ascetic enthusiasm, he has already wished to take the vows which will bind him for ever to our divine Order.'

'So soon, father?' said the princess, in astonishment.

'Our statutes are opposed to this precipitation, unless in the case of a penitent *in articulo mortis*—on the very gasp of death—should such a person consider it necessary for his salvation to die in the habit of our Order, and leave us all his wealth for the greater glory of the Lord.'

'And is M. Hardy in so dangerous a condition, father?'

'He has a violent fever. After so many successive calamities, which have miraculously brought him into the path of salvation,' said Rodin, piously, 'his frail and delicate constitution is almost broken up, morally and physically. Austerities, macerations, and the divine joys of ecstasy, will probably hasten his passage to eternal life, and in a few days,' said the priest, shaking his head with a solemn air, 'perhaps ——'

'So soon as that, father?'——' It is almost certain. I have therefore made use of my dispensations, to receive the dear penitent, as *in articulo mortis*, a member of our divine Company, to which, in the usual course, he has made over all his possessions, present and to come—so that now he can devote himself entirely to the care of his soul, which will be one victim more rescued from the claws of Satan.'

'Oh, father!' cried the lady, in admiration ; 'it is a miraculous conversion. Father d'Aigrigny told me how you had to contend against the influence of Abbé Gabriel.'

'The Abbé Gabriel,' replied Rodin, 'has been punished for meddling with what did not concern him. I have procured his suspension, and he has been deprived of his curacy. I hear that he now goes about the cholera-hospitals to administer Christian consolation ; we cannot oppose that—but this universal comforter is of the true heretical stamp.'

'He is a dangerous character, no doubt,' answered the princess, 'for he has considerable influence over other men. It must have needed all your admirable and irresistible eloquence to combat the detestable counsels of this Abbé Gabriel, who had taken it into his head to persuade M. Hardy to return to the life of the world. Really, father, you are a second St. Chrysostom.'

'Tut, tut, madame !' said Rodin, abruptly, for he was very little sensible to flattery ; 'keep that for others.'

'I tell you that you're a second St. Chrysostom, father,' repeated the princess, with enthusiasm ; 'like him, you deserve the name of Golden Mouth.'

'Stuff, madame !' said Rodin, brutally, shrugging his shoulders ; 'my lips are too pale, my teeth too black, for a mouth of gold. You must be only joking.'

'But, father——'——' No, madame, you will not catch old birds with chaff,' replied Rodin, harshly. 'I hate compliments, and I never pay them.'

'Your modesty must pardon me, father,' said the princess, humbly ; 'I could not resist the desire to express to you my admiration, for, as you almost predicted, or at least foresaw, two members of the Rennepont family have, within the last few months, resigned all claim to the inheritance.'

Rodin looked at Madame de Saint-Dizier with a softened and approving air, as he heard her thus describe the position of the two defunct claimants.

For, in Rodin's view of the case, M. Hardy, in consequence of his donation and his suicidal asceticism, belonged no longer to this world.

The lady continued : ' One of these men, a wretched artisan, has been led to his ruin by the exaggeration of his vices. You have brought the other into the path of salvation, by carrying out his loving and tender qualities. Honour, then, to your foresight, father ! for you said that you would make use of the passions to attain your end.'

' Do not boast too soon,' said Rodin, impatiently. ' Have you forgotten your niece, and the Hindoo, and the daughters of Marshal Simon ? Have they also made a Christian end, or resigned their claim to share in this inheritance?'

' No, doubtless.'

' Hence, you see, madame, we should not lose time in congratulating ourselves on the past, but make ready for the future. The great day approaches. The first of June is not far off. Heaven grant we may not see the four surviving members of the family continue to live impenitent up to that period, and so take possession of this enormous property—the source of perdition in their hands—but productive of the glory of the Church in the hands of our Company !'——' True, father !'

' By the way, you were to see your lawyers on the subject of your niece?'

' I have seen them, father. However uncertain may be the chance of which I spoke, it is worth trying. I shall know to-day, I hope, if it is legally possible.'

' Perhaps then, in the new condition of life to which she would be reduced, we might find means to effect her conversion,' said Rodin, with a strange and hideous smile ; ' until now, since she has been so fatally brought in contact with the Oriental, the happiness of these two pagans appears bright and changeless as the diamond. Nothing bites into it, not even Faringhea's tooth. Let us hope that the Lord will wreak justice on their vain and guilty felicity !' This conversation was here interrupted by Father d'Aigrigny, who entered the room with an air of triumph, and exclaimed, ' Victory !'

' What do you say ?' asked the princess.

' He is gone—last night,' said Father d'Aigrigny.

' Who ?' said Rodin.——' Marshal Simon,' replied the abbé.

' At last !' said Rodin, unable to hide his joy.——' It was no doubt his interview with General d'Havrincourt which filled up the measure,' cried the princess, ' for I know he had a long conversation with the general, who, like so many others, believed the reports in circulation. All means are good against the impious !' added the princess, by way of moral.

' Have you any details ?' asked Rodin.——' I have just left Robert,' said Father d'Aigrigny. ' His age and description agree with the marshal's, and the latter travels with his papers. Only one thing has greatly surprised your emissary.'

' What is that ?' said Rodin.——' Until now, he had always to contend with the hesitations of the marshal, and had moreover noticed his gloomy and desponding air. Yesterday, on the contrary, he found him so bright with happiness, that he could not help asking him the cause of the alteration.'

' Well ?' said Rodin and the princess together, both extremely surprised.

' The marshal answered : " I am indeed the happiest man in the world ; for I am going joyfully to accomplish a sacred duty !"——'

The three actors in this scene looked at each other in silence.

' And what can have produced this sudden change in the mind of the marshal ?' said the princess, with a pensive air. ' We rather reckoned on sorrow and every kind of irritation to urge him to engage in this adventurous enterprise.'

'I cannot make it out,' said Rodin, reflecting; 'but no matter—he is gone. We must not lose a moment, to commence operations on his daughters. Has he taken that infernal soldier with him?'

'No,' said Father d'Aigrigny; 'unfortunately, he has not done so. Warned by the past, he will redouble his precautions; and a man, whom we might have used against him at a pinch, has just been taken with the contagion.'

'Who is that?' asked the princess.——'Morok. I could count upon him, anywhere and for anything. He is lost to us; for, should he recover from the cholera, I fear he will fall a victim to a horrible and incurable disease.'

'How so?'——'A few days ago, he was bitten by one of the mastiffs of his menagerie, and, the next day, the dog showed symptoms of hydrophobia.'

'Ah! it is dreadful,' cried the princess; 'and where is this unfortunate man?'

'He has been taken to one of the temporary hospitals established in Paris, for at present he has only been attacked with cholera. It is doubly unfortunate, I repeat, for he was a devoted, determined fellow, ready for anything. Now this soldier, who has the care of the orphans, will be very difficult to get at, and yet only through him can we hope to reach Marshal Simon's daughters.'

'That is clear,' said Rodin, thoughtfully.——'Particularly, since the anonymous letters have again awakened his suspicions,' added Father d'Aigrigny, 'and——'

'Talking of the anonymous letters,' said Rodin suddenly, interrupting Father d'Aigrigny, 'there is a fact that you ought to know; I will tell you why.'

'What is it?'——'Besides the letters that you know of, Marshal Simon has received a number of others unknown to you, in which, by every possible means, it is tried to exasperate his irritation against yourself—for they remind him of all the reasons he has to hate you, and mock at him, because your sacred character shelters you from his vengeance.'

Father d'Aigrigny looked at Rodin with amazement, coloured in spite of himself, and said to him: 'But for what purpose has your reverence acted in this manner?'

'First of all, to clear myself of suspicion with regard to the letters; then, to excite the rage of the marshal to madness, by incessantly reminding him of the just grounds he has to hate you, and of the impossibility of being avenged upon you. This, joined to the other emotions of sorrow and anger, which ferment in the savage bosom of this man of bloodshed, tended to urge him on to the rash enterprise, which is the consequence and the punishment of his idolatry for a miserable usurper.'

'That may be,' said Father d'Aigrigny, with an air of constraint; 'but I will observe to your reverence, that it was, perhaps, rather dangerous thus to excite Marshal Simon against me.'

'Why?' asked Rodin, as he fixed a piercing look upon Father d'Aigrigny.

'Because the marshal, excited beyond all bounds, and remembering only our mutual hate, might seek me out——'——'Well! and what then?'

'Well! he might forget that I am a priest——'——'Oh, you are afraid, are you?' said Rodin, disdainfully, interrupting Father d'Aigrigny.

At the words: 'You are afraid,' the reverend father almost started from his chair; but recovering his coolness, he answered: 'Your reverence is right; yes, I should be afraid under such circumstances; I should be afraid of forgetting that I am a priest, and of remembering too well that I have been a soldier.'

'Really?' said Rodin, with sovereign contempt. 'You are still no further than that stupid and savage point of honour? Your cassock has not yet extinguished the war-like fire? So that if this brawling swordsman, whose poor, weak head, empty and sonorous as a drum, is so easily turned with the stupid jargon of "Military honour, oaths, Napoleon II."—if this brawling bravo, I say, were to commit some violence against you, it would require a great effort, I suppose, for you to remain calm?'

'It is useless, I think,' said Father d'Aigrigny, quite unable to control his agitation, 'for your reverence to enter upon such questions.'

'As your superior,' answered Rodin, severely, 'I have the right to ask. If Marshal Simon had lifted his hand against you——'

'Sir,' cried the reverend father.——'There are no sirs here—we are only priests,' said Rodin, harshly.   Father d'Aigrigny held down his head, scarcely able to repress his rage.

'I ask you,' continued Rodin, obstinately, 'if Marshal Simon had struck you? Is that clear?'

'Enough! in mercy,' said Father d'Aigrigny, 'enough!'

'Or, if you like it better, had Marshal Simon left the marks of his fingers on your cheek?' resumed Rodin, with the utmost pertinacity.

Father d'Aigrigny, pale as death, ground his teeth in a kind of fury at the very idea of such an insult, while Rodin, who had no doubt his object in asking the question, raised his flabby eye-lids, and seemed to watch attentively the significant symptoms revealed in the agitated countenance of the ex-colonel.

At length, recovering partly his presence of mind, Father d'Aigrigny replied, in a forcedly calm tone : 'If I were to be exposed to such an insult, I would pray heaven to give me resignation and humility.'

'And no doubt heaven would hear your prayers,' said Rodin, coldly, satisfied with the trial to which he had just put him. 'Besides, you are now warned, and it is not very probable,' added he, with a grim smile, 'that Marshal Simon will ever return to test your humility. But if he were to return,' said Rodin, fixing on the reverend father a long and piercing look, 'you would know how to show this brutal swordsman, in spite of all his violence, what resignation and humility there is in a Christian soul!'

Two humble knocks at the door here interrupted the conversation for a moment. A footman entered, bearing a large sealed packet on a salver, which he presented to the princess. After this, he withdrew. Princess de Saint-Dizier, having by a look asked Rodin's permission to open the letter, began to read it—and a cruel satisfaction was soon visible on her face.

'There is hope,' cried she, addressing herself to Rodin : 'the demand is rigorously legal, and the consequences may be such as we desire. In a word, my niece may, any day, be exposed to complete destitution. She, who is so extravagant! what a change in her life!'

'We shall then no doubt have some hold on that untamable character,' said Rodin, with a meditative air ; 'for, till now, all has failed in that direction, and one would suppose some kinds of happiness are invulnerable,' added the Jesuit, gnawing his flat and dirty nails.

'But, to obtain the result we desire, we must exasperate my niece's pride. It is therefore absolutely necessary, that I should see and talk to her,' said the Princess de Saint-Dizier, reflecting.

'Mdlle. de Cardoville will refuse this interview,' said Father d'Aigrigny.

'Perhaps,' replied the princess. 'But she is so happy that her audacity must be at its height. Yes, yes—I know her—and I will write in such a manner, that she will come.'

'You think so?' asked Rodin, with a doubtful air.——'Do not fear it, father,' answered the lady, ' she will come. And her pride once brought into play, we may hope a good deal from it.'

'We must then act, lady,' resumed Rodin ; 'yes, act promptly. The moment approaches. Hate and suspicion are awake. There is not a moment to lose.'

'As for hate,' replied the princess, 'Mdlle. de Cardoville must have seen to what her law-suit would lead, about what she calls her illegal detention in a lunatic asylum, and that of the two young ladies in St. Mary's Convent. Thank heaven, we have friends everywhere ! I know from good authority, that the case will break down from want of evidence, in spite of the animosity of certain parliamentary magistrates, who shall be well remembered.'

' Under these circumstances,' replied Rodin, ' the departure of the marshal gives us every latitude. We must act immediately on his daughters.'

' But how ?' said the princess.——' We must see them,' resumed Rodin, 'talk with them, study them. Then we shall act in consequence.'

' But the soldier will not leave them a second,' said Father d'Aigrigny.

' Then,' replied Rodin, ' we must talk to them in presence of the soldier, and get him on our side.'

'That hope is idle,' cried Father d'Aigrigny. ' You do not know the military honour of his character. You do not know this man.'

' Don't I know him ?' said Rodin, shrugging his shoulders. ' Did not Mdlle. de Cardoville present me to him as her liberator, when I denounced you as the soul of the conspiracy ? Did I not restore to him his ridiculous imperial relic—his cross of honour—when we met at Dr. Baleinier's ? Did I not bring him back the girls from the convent, and place them in the arms of their father ?'

' Yes,' replied the princess ; ' but, since that time, my abominable niece has either guessed or discovered all. She told you so herself, father.'

' She told me, that she considered me her most mortal enemy,' said Rodin. ' Be it so. But did she tell the same to the marshal ? Has she even mentioned me to him ? and if she have done so, has the marshal communicated this circumstance to his soldier ? It may be so ; but it is by no means sure ; in any case, I must ascertain the fact ; if the soldier treats me as an enemy, we shall see what is next to be done—but I will first try to be received as a friend.'

' When ?' asked the princess.——' To-morrow morning,' replied Rodin.

' Good heaven, my dear father !' cried the Princess de Saint-Dizier, in alarm ; 'if this soldier were to treat you as an enemy—beware——'

' I always beware, madame. I have had to face worse enemies than he is,' said the Jesuit, showing his black teeth ; 'the cholera to begin with.'

'But he may refuse to see you, and in what way will you then get at Marshal Simon's daughters ?' said Father d'Aigrigny.

' I do not yet know,' answered Rodin. ' But as I intend to do it, I shall find the means.'

' Father,' said the princess, suddenly, on reflection, 'these girls have never seen me, and I might obtain admittance to them, without sending in my name.'

' That would be perfectly useless at present, madame, for I must first know what course to take with respect to them. I must see and converse with them, at any cost, and then, after I have fixed my plan, your assistance may be very useful. In any case, please to be ready to-morrow, madame, to accompany me.'——' To what place, father ?'

' To Marshal Simon's.'——' To the marshal's ?'

' Not exactly. You will get into your carriage, and I will take a hackney-coach. I will then try to obtain an interview with the girls, and, during that time, you will wait for me at a few yards from the house. If I succeed, and require your aid, I will come and fetch you ; I can give you my instructions, without any appearance of concert between us.'

' I am content, reverend father ; but, in truth, I tremble at the thought of your interview with that rough trooper.'

' The Lord will watch over his servant, madame !' replied Rodin. ' As for you, father,' added he, addressing the Abbé d'Aigrigny, ' despatch instantly to Vienna the note which is all prepared, to announce the departure and speedy arrival of the marshal. Every precaution has been taken. I shall write more fully this evening.'

☼   ☼   ☼   ☼   ☼   ☼

The next morning, about eight o'clock, the Princess de Saint-Dizier, in her carriage, and Rodin in his hackney-coach, took the direction of Marshal Simon's house.

CHAPTER LIII.

HAPPINESS

MARSHAL SIMON has been absent two days. It is eight o'clock in the morning. Dagobert, walking on tip-toe with the greatest caution, so as not to make the floor creak beneath his tread, crosses the room which leads to the bedchamber of Rose and Blanche, and applies his ear to the door of the apartment. With equal caution, Spoilsport follows exactly the movements of his master. The countenance of the soldier is uneasy, and full of thought. As he approaches the door, he says to himself : ' I hope the dear children heard nothing of what happened in the night ! It would alarm them, and it is much better that they should not know it at present. It might afflict them sadly, poor dears ! and they are so gay, so happy, since they feel sure of their father's love for them. They bore his departure so bravely ! I would not for the world that they should know of this unfortunate event.'

Then, as he listened, the soldier resumed : ' I hear nothing— and yet they are always awake so early. Can it be sorrow ?'

Dagobert's reflections were here interrupted by two frank, hearty bursts of laughter, from the interior of the bedroom.

' Come ! they are not so sad as I thought,' said the soldier, breathing more freely. ' Probably, they know nothing about it.'

Soon, the laughter was again heard with redoubled force, and the soldier, delighted at this gaiety, so rare on the part of 'his children,' was much affected by it : the tears started to his eyes at the thought that the orphans had at length recovered the serenity natural to their age ; then, passing from one emotion to the other, still listening at the door, with his body leaning forward, and his hands resting on his knees, Dagobert's lip quivered with an expression of mute joy, and, shaking his head a little, he accompanied with his silent laughter the increasing hilarity of the young girls. At last, as nothing is so contagious as gaiety, and as the worthy soldier was in an ecstasy of joy, he finished by laughing aloud with all his might, without knowing why, and only because Rose and Blanche were laughing. Spoilsport had never seen his master in such a transport of delight ; he looked at him for a while in deep and silent astonishment, and then began to bark in a questioning way.

At this well-known sound, the laughter within suddenly ceased, and a sweet voice, still trembling with joyous emotion, exclaimed : ' Is it you, Spoilsport, that have come to wake us ?' The dog understood what was said, wagged his tail, held down his ears, and, approaching close to the door, answered the appeal of his young mistress by a kind of friendly growl.

'Spoilsport,' said Rose, hardly able to restrain her laughter, 'you are very early this morning.'

'Tell us what o'clock it is, if you please, old fellow?' added Blanche.

'Young ladies, it is past eight,' said suddenly the gruff voice of Dagobert, accompanying this piece of humour with a loud laugh.

A cry of gay surprise was heard, and then Rose resumed : 'Good-morning, Dagobert.'

'Good-morning, my children. You are very lazy to-day, I must tell you.'

'It is not our fault. Our dear Augustine has not yet been to call us. We are waiting for her.'

'Oh ! there it is,' said Dagobert to himself, his features once more assuming an expression of anxiety. Then he returned aloud, in a tone of some embarrassment, for the worthy man was no hand at a falsehood : 'My children, your companion went out this morning—very early. She is gone to the country—on business—she will not return for some days—so you had better get up by yourselves for to-day.'

'Our good Madame Augustine !' exclaimed Blanche, with interest. 'I hope it is nothing bad, that has made her leave so suddenly—eh, Dagobert ?'

'No, no—-not at all—only business,' answered the soldier. 'To see one of her relations.'

'Oh, so much the better !' said Rose. 'Well, Dagobert, when we call, you can come in.'

'I will come back in a quarter of an hour,' said the soldier, as he withdrew ; and he thought to himself : 'I must lecture that fool Loony—for he is so stupid, and so fond of talking, that he will let it all out.'

The name of the pretended simpleton will serve as a natural transition, to inform the reader of the cause of the hilarity of the sisters. They were laughing at the numberless absurdities of the idiot. The girls rose and dressed themselves, each serving as lady's-maid to the other. Rose had combed and arranged Blanche's hair ; it was now Blanche's turn to do the same for her sister. Thus occupied, they formed a charming picture. Rose was seated before the dressing-table ; her sister, standing behind her, was smoothing her beautiful brown hair. Happy age ! so little removed from childhood, that present joy instantly obliterates the traces of past sorrow ! But the sisters felt more than joy ; it was happiness, deep and unalterable, for their father loved them, and their happiness was a delight, and not a pain to him. Assured of the affection of his children, he also, thanks to them, no longer feared any grief. To those three beings, thus certain of their mutual love, what was a momentary separation ? Having explained this, we shall understand the innocent gaiety of the sisters, notwithstanding their father's departure, and the happy, joyous expression, which now filled with animation their charming faces, on which the late fading rose had begun once more to bloom. Their faith in the future gave to their countenance something resolute and decisive, which added a degree of piquancy to the beauty of their enchanting features.

Blanche, in smoothing her sister's hair, let fall the comb, and, as she was stooping to pick it up, Rose anticipated her, saying : 'If it had been broken, we would have put it into the handle-basket.'

Then the two laughed merrily at this expression, which reminded them of an admirable piece of folly on the part of Loony.

The supposed simpleton had broken the handle of a cup, and when the governess of the young ladies had reprimanded him for his carelessness, he had answered : 'Never mind, madame ; I have put it into the handle-basket.'

'The handle-basket, what is that ?'——'Yes, madame ; it is where I keep all the handles I break off the things !'

'Dear me!' said Rose, drying her eyes; 'how silly it is to laugh at such foolishness.'——'It is so droll,' replied Blanche; 'how can we help it?'

'All I regret is, that father cannot hear us laugh.'——'He was so happy to see us gay!'

'We must write to him to-day, the story of the handle-basket.'——'And that of the feather-brush, to show that, according to promise, we kept up our spirits during his absence.'

'Write to him, sister? no, he is to write to us, and we are not to answer his letters.'——'True! well then, I have an idea. Let us address letters to him here; Dagobert can put them into the post, and, on his return, our father will read our correspondence.'

'That will be charming! What nonsense we will write to him, since he takes pleasure in it!'——'And we, too, like to amuse ourselves.'

'Oh, certainly! father's last words have given us so much courage.'

'As I listened to them, I felt quite reconciled to his going.'

'When he said to us: "My children, I will confide in you all I can. I go to fulfil a sacred duty, and I must be absent for some time; for though, when I was blind enough to doubt your affection, I could not make up my mind to leave you, my conscience was by no means tranquil. Grief takes such an effect on us, that I had not the strength to come to a decision, and my days were passed in painful hesitation. But now that I am certain of your tenderness, all this irresolution has ceased, and I understand how one duty is not to be sacrificed to another, and that I have to perform two duties at once, both equally sacred; and this I now do with joy, and delight, and courage!"'

'Go on, sister!' cried Blanche, rising to draw nearer to Rose. 'I think I hear our father, when I remember those words, which must console and support us during his absence.'

'And then our father continued: "Instead of grieving at my departure, you should rejoice in it, you should be proud and happy. I go to perform a good and generous act. Fancy to yourselves, that there is somewhere a poor orphan, oppressed and abandoned by all—and that the father of that orphan was once my benefactor, and that I had promised him to protect his son—and that the life of that son is now in peril—tell me, my children, would you regret that I should leave you to fly to the aid of such an orphan?"——'

'"No, no, brave father!" we answered; "we should not then be your daughters!"' continued Rose, with enthusiasm. '"Count upon us! We should be indeed unhappy if we thought that our sorrow could deprive thee of thy courage. Go! and every day we will say to ourselves proudly, 'It was to perform a great and noble duty that our father left us—we can wait calmly for his return.'"'

'How that idea of duty sustains one, sister!' resumed Rose, with growing enthusiasm. 'It gave our father the courage to leave us without regret, and to us the courage to bear his absence gaily!'

'And then, how calm we are now! Those mournful dreams, which seemed to portend such sad events, no longer afflict us.'——'I tell you, sister, this time we are really happy once for all.'

'And then, do you feel like me? I fancy, that I am stronger and more courageous, and that I could brave every danger.'——'I should think so! We are strong enough now. Our father in the midst, you on one side, I on the other——'

'Dagobert in the vanguard, and Spoilsport in the rear! Then the army will be complete, and let 'em come on by thousands!' added a gruff, but jovial voice, interrupting the girl, as Dagobert appeared at the half-open door of the room. It was worth looking at his face, radiant with joy; for the old fellow had somewhat indiscreetly been listening to the conversation.

'Oh! you were listening, Paul Pry!' said Rose, gaily, as she entered the adjoining room with her sister, and both affectionately embraced the soldier.

'To be sure, I was listening; and I only regretted not to have ears as large as Spoilsport's! Brave, good girls! that's how I like to see you—bold as brass, and saying to care and sorrow: "Right about face! march! go to the devil!"'

'He will want to make us swear, now,' said Rose to her sister, laughing with all her might.

'Well! now and then, it does no harm,' said the soldier; 'it relieves and calms one, when if one could not swear by five hundred thousand de——'

'That's enough!' said Rose, covering with her pretty hand the grey moustache, so as to stop Dagobert in his speech. 'If Madame Augustine heard you——'

'Our poor governess! so mild and timid,' resumed Blanche.——'How you would frighten her!'

'Yes,' said Dagobert, as he tried to conceal his rising embarrassment; 'but she does not hear us. She is gone into the country.'

'Good, worthy woman!' replied Blanche, with interest. 'She said something of you, which shows her excellent heart.'

'Certainly,' resumed Rose; 'for she said to us, in speaking of you, "Ah, young ladies! my affection must appear very little, compared with M. Dagobert's. But I feel, that I also have the right to devote myself for you."'

'No doubt, no doubt! she has a heart of gold,' answered Dagobert. Then he added to himself, 'It's as if they did it on purpose, to bring the conversation back to this poor woman.'——'Father made a good choice,' continued Rose. 'She is the widow of an old officer, who was with him in the wars.'

'When we were out of spirits,' said Blanche, 'you should have seen her uneasiness and grief, and how earnestly she set about consoling us.'——'I have seen the tears in her eyes when she looked at us,' resumed Rose. 'Oh! she loves us tenderly, and we return her affection. With regard to that, Dagobert, we have a plan as soon as our father comes back.'

'Be quiet, sister!' said Blanche, laughing. 'Dagobert will not keep our secret.' ——'He!'

'Will you keep it for us, Dagobert?'——'I tell you what,' said the soldier, more and more embarrassed; 'you had better not tell it me.'

'What! can you keep nothing from Madame Augustine?'——'Ah, Dagobert! Dagobert!' said Blanche, gaily holding up her finger at the soldier; 'I suspect you very much of paying court to our governess.'

'I pay court?' said the soldier—and the expression of his face was so rueful, as he pronounced these words, that the two sisters burst out laughing.

Their hilarity was at its height when the door opened, and Loony advanced into the room, announcing, with a loud voice, 'M. Rodin!' In fact, the Jesuit glided almost imperceptibly into the apartment, as if to take possession of the ground. Once there, he thought the game his own, and his reptile eyes sparkled with joy. It would be difficult to paint the surprise of the two sisters, and the anger of the soldier, at this unexpected visit.

Rushing upon Loony, Dagobert seized him by the collar, and exclaimed: 'Who gave you leave to introduce any one here, without my permission?'

'Pardon, M. Dagobert!' said Loony, throwing himself on his knees, and clasping his hands with an air of idiotic entreaty.

'Leave the room!—and you too!' added the soldier, with a menacing gesture, as he turned towards Rodin, who had already approached the girls, with a paternal smile on his countenance.

'I am at your orders, my dear sir,' said the priest, humbly ; and he made a low bow, but without stirring from the spot.

'Will you go ?' cried the soldier to Loony, who was still kneeling, and who, thanks to the advantages of this position, was able to utter a certain number of words, before Dagobert could remove him.

'M. Dagobert,' said Loony in a doleful voice, 'I beg pardon for bringing up the gentleman without leave ; but, alas ! my head is turned, because of the misfortune that happened to Madame Augustine !'

'What misfortune ?' cried Rose and Blanche together, as they advanced anxiously towards Loony.

'Will you go ?' thundered Dagobert, shaking the servant by the collar, to force him to rise.

'Speak—speak !' said Blanche, interposing between the soldier and his prey. 'What has happened to Madame Augustine ?'

'Oh,' shouted Loony, in spite of the cuffs of the soldier. 'Madame Augustine was attacked in the night with cholera, and taken——'

He was unable to finish. Dagobert struck him a tremendous blow with his fist, right on the jaw, and, putting forth his still formidable strength, the old horse-grenadier lifted him to his legs, and, with one violent kick bestowed on the lower part of his back, sent him rolling into the antechamber.

Then, turning to Rodin, with flushed cheek and sparkling eye, Dagobert pointed to the door with an expressive gesture, and said in an angry voice : 'Now, be off with you--and that quickly !'

'I must pay my respects another time, my dear sir,' said Rodin, as he retired towards the door, bowing to the young girls.

CHAPTER LIV.

DUTY.

RODIN, retreating slowly before the fire of Dagobert's angry looks, walked backwards to the door, casting oblique but piercing glances on the orphans, who were visibly affected by the servant's intentional indiscretion. (Dagobert had ordered him not to speak before the girls of the illness of their governess, and that was quite enough to induce the simpleton to take the first opportunity of doing so.)

Rose hastily approached the soldier, and said to him, 'Is it true—is it really true, that poor Madame Augustine has been attacked with the cholera ?'

'No—I do not know—I cannot tell,' replied the soldier, hesitating ; 'besides, what is it to you ?'

'Dagobert, you would conceal from us a calamity,' said Blanche. 'I remember now your embarrassment, when we spoke to you of our governess.'

'If she is ill, we ought not to abandon her. She had pity on our sorrows ; we ought to pity her sufferings.'

'Come, sister ; come to her room,' said Blanche, advancing towards the door, where Rodin had stopped short, and stood listening with growing attention to this unexpected scene, which seemed to give him ample food for thought.

'You will not leave this room,' said the soldier, sternly, addressing the two sisters.

'Dagobert,' replied Rose, firmly, 'it is a sacred duty, and it would be cowardice not to fulfil it.'

'I tell you that you shall not leave the room,' said the soldier, stamping his foot with impatience.

'Dagobert,' replied Blanche, with as resolute an air as her sister's, and with a kind of enthusiasm which brought the blood to her fair cheek, 'our father, when he left us, gave us an admirable example of devotion and duty. He would not forgive us were we to forget the lesson.'

'What !' cried Dagobert, in a rage, and advancing towards the sisters to prevent their quitting the apartment ; 'you think, that if your governess had the cholera, I would let you go to her under the pretext of duty ?—Your duty is to live, to live happy, for your father's sake—and for mine into the bargain—so not a word more of such folly !'

'We can run no danger by going to our governess in her room,' said Rose.

'And if there were danger,' added Blanche, 'we ought not to hesitate. So Dagobert, be good ! and let us pass.'

Rodin, who had listened to what precedes, with sustained attention, suddenly started, as if a thought had struck him ; his eye shone brightly, and an expression of fatal joy illumined his countenance.

'Dagobert, do not refuse !' said Blanche. 'You would do for us what you reproach us with wishing to do for another.'

Dagobert had, as it were, till now, stood in the path of the Jesuit and the twins, by keeping close to the door ; but, after a moment's reflection, he shrugged his shoulders, stepped on one side, and said, calmly : 'I was an old fool. Come, young ladies ; if you find Madame Augustine in the house, I will allow you to remain with her.' Surprised at these words, the girls stood motionless and irresolute.

'If our governess is not here, where is she, then?' said Rose.——'You think, perhaps, that I am going to tell you, in the excitement in which you are !'

'She is dead !' cried Rose, growing pale.——'No, no—be calm,' said the soldier, hastily ; 'I swear to you, by your father's honour, that she is not dead. At the first appearance of the disorder, she begged to be removed from the house, fearing the contagion for those in it.'

'Good and courageous woman !' said Rose, tenderly. 'And you will not allow us——'

'I will not allow you to go out, even if I have to lock you up in your room,' cried the soldier, again stamping with rage ; then, remembering that the blunderhead's indiscretion was the sole cause of this unfortunate incident, he added, with concentrated fury, 'Oh ! I will break my stick upon that rascal's back.'

So saying, he turned towards the door, where Rodin still stood, silent and attentive, dissembling with habitual impassibility the fatal hopes he had just conceived in his brain. The girls, no longer doubting the removal of their governess, and convinced that Dagobert would not tell them whither they had conveyed her, remained pensive and sad.

At sight of the priest, whom he had forgotten for the moment, the soldier's rage increased, and he said to him roughly : 'Are you still there ?'

'I would merely observe to you, my dear sir,' said Rodin, with that air of perfect good-nature which he knew so well how to assume, 'that you were standing before the door, which naturally prevented me from going out.'

'Well, now nothing prevents you—so file off !'——'Certainly, I will file off, if you wish it, my dear sir ; though I think I have some reason to be surprised at such a reception.'

'It is no reception at all—so begone !'

'I had come, my dear sir, to speak to you——'

'I have no time for talking.'——'Upon business of great importance.'

'I have no other business of importance than to remain with these children.'——'Very good, my dear sir,' said Rodin, pausing on the threshold. 'I will not disturb you any longer ; excuse my indiscretion. The bearer of excellent news from Marshal Simon, I came——'

'News from our father !' cried Rose, drawing nearer to Rodin.

'Oh, speak, speak, sir !' added Blanche.

'You have news of the marshal !' said Dagobert, glancing suspiciously at Rodin. 'Pray, what is this news ?'

But Rodin, without immediately answering the question, returned from the threshold into the room, and, contemplating Rose and Blanche by turns with admiration, he resumed : 'What happiness for me, to be able to bring some pleasure to these dear young ladies ! They are even as I left them, graceful, and fair, and charming—only less sad than on the day when I fetched them from the gloomy convent in which they were kept prisoners, to restore them to the arms of their glorious father !'

'That was their place, and this is not yours,' said Dagobert, harshly, still holding the door open behind Rodin.

'Confess, at least, that I was not so much out of place at Dr. Baleinier's,' said the Jesuit, with a cunning air. 'You know, for it was there that I restored to you the noble imperial cross you so much regretted—the day when that good Mdlle. de Cardoville only prevented you from strangling me by telling you that I was her liberator. Aye ! it was just as I have the honour of stating, young ladies,' added Rodin, with a smile ; 'this brave soldier was very near strangling me, for, be it said without offence, he has, in spite of his age, a grasp of iron. Ha, ha ! the Prussians and Cossacks must know that better than I !'

These few words reminded Dagobert and the twins of the services which Rodin had really rendered them ; and though the marshal had heard Mdlle. de Cardoville speak of Rodin as of a very dangerous man, he had forgotten, in the midst of so many anxieties, to communicate this circumstance to Dagobert. But this latter, warned by experience, felt, in spite of favourable appearances, a secret aversion for the Jesuit ; so he replied abruptly : 'The strength of my grasp has nothing to do with the matter.'

'If I allude to that little innocent playfulness on your part, my dear sir,' said Rodin, in the softest tone, approaching the two sisters with a wriggle which was peculiar to him ; 'if I allude to it, you see, it was suggested by the involuntary recollection of the little services I was happy enough to render you.' Dagobert looked fixedly at Rodin, who instantly veiled his glance beneath his flabby eyelids.

'First of all,' said the soldier, after a moment's silence, 'a true man never speaks of the services he has rendered, and you come back three times to the subject.'

'But, Dagobert,' whispered Rose, 'if he bring news of our father ?'

The soldier made a sign, as if to beg the girl to let him speak, and resumed, looking full at Rodin : 'You are cunning, but I'm no raw recruit.'

'I cunning ?' said Rodin, with a sanctified air.

'Yes, very. You think to puzzle me with your fine phrases ; but I'm not to be caught in that way. Just listen to me. Some of your band of blackgowns stole my cross ; you returned it to me. Some of the same band carried off these children ; you brought them back. It is also true that you denounced the renegade D'Aigrigny. But all this only proves two things : first, that you were vile enough to be the accomplice of these scoundrels ; and secondly, that, having been their accomplice, you were base enough to betray them. Now, those two facts are equally bad, and I suspect you most furiously. So march off at once ; your presence is not good for these children.'

'But, my dear sir——'——'I will have no buts,' answered Dagobert, in an angry voice. 'When a man of your look does good, it is only to hide some evil; and one must be on guard.'

'I understand your suspicions,' said Rodin coolly, hiding his growing disappointment, for he had hoped it would have been easy to coax the soldier; 'but, if you reflect, what interest have I in deceiving you? and in what should the deception consist?'

'You have some interest or other in persisting to remain here, when I tell you to go away.'——'I have already had the honour of informing you of the object of my visit, my dear sir.'

'To bring news of Marshal Simon?'——'That is exactly the case. I am happy enough to have news of the marshal. Yes, my dear young ladies,' added Rodin, as he again approached the two sisters, to recover, as it were, the ground he had lost, 'I have news of your glorious father!'

'Then come to my room directly, and you can tell it to me,' replied Dagobert.——'What! you would be cruel enough to deprive these dear ladies of the pleasure——'

'By heaven, sir!' cried Dagobert, in a voice of thunder, 'you will make me forget myself. I should be sorry to fling a man of your age down the stairs. Will you be gone?'

'Well, well,' said Rodin mildly, 'do not be angry with a poor old man. I am really not worth the trouble. I will go with you to your room, and tell you what I have to communicate. You will repent not having let me speak before these dear young ladies; but that will be your punishment, naughty man!'

So saying, Rodin again bowed very low, and, concealing his rage and vexation, left the room before Dagobert, who made a sign to the two sisters, and then followed, closing the door after him.

'What news of our father, Dagobert?' said Rose anxiously, when the soldier returned, after a quarter of an hour's absence.

'Well, that old conjuror knows that the marshal set out in good spirits, and he seems acquainted with M. Robert. How could he be informed of all this? I cannot tell,' added the soldier, with a thoughtful air; 'but it is only another reason to be on one's guard against him.'

'But what news of our father?' asked Rose.——'One of that old rascal's friends (I think him a rascal still) knows your father, he tells me, and met him five-and-twenty leagues from here. Knowing that this man was coming to Paris, the marshal charged him to let you know that he was in perfect health, and hoped soon to see you again.'

'Oh, what happiness!' cried Rose.

'You see, you were wrong to suspect the poor old man, Dagobert,' added Blanche. 'You treated him so harshly!'

'Possibly so; but I am not sorry for it.'——'And why?'

'I have my reasons; and one of the best is that, when I saw him come in, and go sidling and creeping round about us, I felt chilled to the marrow of my bones, without knowing why. Had I seen a serpent crawling towards you, I should not have been more frightened. I knew, of course, that he could not hurt you in my presence; but I tell you, my children, in spite of the services he has no doubt rendered us, it was all I could do to refrain from throwing him out of window. Now, this manner of proving my gratitude is not natural, and one must be on one's guard against people who inspire us with such ideas.'

'Good Dagobert, it is your affection for us that makes you so suspicious,' said Rose, in a coaxing tone; 'it proves how much you love us.'

CHAPTER LV.

THE IMPROVISED HOSPITAL.

AMONG a great number of temporary hospitals opened at the time of the cholera in every quarter of Paris, one had been established on the ground-floor of a large house in the Rue du Mont-Blanc. The vacant apartments had been generously placed by their proprietor at the disposal of the authorities ; and to this place were carried a number of persons, who, being suddenly attacked with the contagion, were considered in too dangerous a state to be removed to the principal hospitals.

Two days had elapsed since Rodin's visit to Marshal Simon's daughter. Shortly after he had been expelled, the Princess de Saint-Dizier had entered to see them, under a cloak of being a house-to-house visitor to collect funds for the cholera sufferers.

Choosing the moment when Dagobert, deceived by her ladylike demeanour, had withdrawn, she counselled the twins that it was their duty to go and see their governess, whom she stated to be in the hospital we now describe.

It was about ten o'clock in the morning. The persons who had watched during the night by the sick people, in the hospital established in the Rue du Mont-Blanc, were about to be relieved by other voluntary assistants.

'Well, gentlemen,' said one of those newly arrived, 'how are we getting on ? Has there been any decrease last night in the number of the sick ?'

'Unfortunately, no ; but the doctors think the contagion has reached its height.'——'Then there is some hope of seeing it decrease.'

'And have any of the gentlemen, whose places we come to take, been attacked by the disease ?'

'We came eleven strong last night ; we are only nine now.'

'That is bad. Were these two persons taken off rapidly ?'

'One of the victims, a young man of twenty-five years of age, a cavalry officer on furlough, was struck as it were by lightning. In less than a quarter of an hour he was dead. Though such facts are frequent, we were speechless with horror.'

'Poor young man !'——'He had a word of cordial encouragement and hope for every one. He had so far succeeded in raising the spirits of the patients, that some of them, who were less affected by the cholera than by the fear of it, were able to quit the hospital nearly well.'

'What a pity ! So good a young man ! Well, he died gloriously ; it requires as much courage as on the field of battle.'

'He had only one rival in zeal and courage, and that is a young priest, with an angelic countenance, whom they call the Abbé Gabriel. He is indefatigable ; he hardly takes an hour's rest, but runs from one to the other, and offers himself to everybody. He forgets nothing. The consolations which he offers come from the depths of his soul, and are not mere formalities in the way of his profession. No, no ; I saw him weep over a poor woman, whose eyes he had closed after a dreadful agony. Oh, if all priests were like him !'

'No doubt, a good priest is most worthy of respect. But who is the other victim of last night ?'——'Oh ! his death was frightful. Do not speak of it. I have still the horrible scene before my eyes.'

'A sudden attack of cholera ?'——'If it had only been the contagion, I should not so shudder at the remembrance.'

'What then did he die of ?'——'It is a string of horrors. Three days ago, they brought here a man, who was supposed to be only attacked with cholera. You have no doubt heard speak of this personage. He is the lion-tamer, that drew all Paris to the Porte-Saint-Martin.'

' I know the man you mean. Called Morok. He performed a kind of play with a tame panther.'

' Exactly so ; I was myself present at a similar scene, in which a stranger, an Indian, in consequence of a wager, it was said at the time, jumped upon the stage and killed the panther.'

' Well, this Morok, brought here as a cholera-patient, and indeed with all the symptoms of the contagion, soon showed signs of a still more frightful malady.'

' And this was——'——' Hydrophobia.'

' Did he become mad !'——' Yes ; he confessed, that he had been bitten a few days before by one of the mastiffs in his menagerie ; unfortunately, we only learnt this circumstance after the terrible attack, which cost the life of the poor fellow we deplore.'

' How did it happen, then ?'——' Morok was in a room with three other patients. Suddenly seized with a sort of furious delirium, he rose, uttering ferocious cries, and rushed raving mad into the passage. Our poor friend made an attempt to stop him. This kind of resistance increased the frenzy of Morok, who threw himself on the man that crossed his path, and, tearing him with his teeth, fell down in horrible convulsions.'

' Oh ! you are right. 'Twas indeed frightful. And, notwithstanding every assistance, this victim of Morok's——'

' Died during the night, in dreadful agony ; for the shock had been so violent, that brain-fever almost instantly declared itself.'

' And is Morok dead ?'——' I do not know. He was to be taken to another hospital, after being fast bound in the state of weakness which generally succeeds the fit. But, till he can be removed, he has been confined in a room upstairs.'

' But he cannot recover.'——' I should think he must be dead by this time. The doctors did not give him twenty-four hours to live.'

The persons engaged in this conversation were standing in an ante-chamber on the ground-floor, in which usually assembled those who came to offer their voluntary aid to the sick. One door of this room communicated with the rest of the hospital, and the other with the passage that opened upon the courtyard.

' Dear me !' said one of the two speakers, looking through the window. ' See what two charming girls have just got out of that elegant carriage. How much alike they are ! Such a resemblance is indeed extraordinary.'

' No doubt they are twins. Poor young girls ! dressed in mourning. They have perhaps lost father or mother.'

' One would imagine they are coming this way.

' Yes, they are coming up the steps.'

And indeed Rose and Blanche soon entered the antechamber, with a timid, anxious air, though a sort of feverish excitement was visible in their looks. One of the two men that were talking together, moved by the embarrassment of the girls, advanced towards them, and said, in a tone of attentive politeness : ' Is there anything I can do for you, ladies ?'

' Is not this, sir,' replied Rose, ' the infirmary of the Rue du Mont-Blanc?' ' Yes, miss.'

' A lady, called Madame Augustine du Tremblay, was brought here, we are told, about two days ago. Could we see her ?'

' I would observe to you, miss, that there is some danger in entering the sick-wards.'

' It is a dear friend that we wish to see,' answered Rose, in a mild and firm tone, which sufficiently expressed that she was determined to brave the danger.

'I cannot be sure, miss,' resumed the other, 'that the person you seek is here ; but, if you will take the trouble to walk into this room on the left, you will find there the good sister Martha ; she has the care of the women's wards, and will give you all the information you can desire.'

'Thank you, sir,' said Blanche, with a graceful bow ; and she and her sister entered together the apartment which had been pointed out to them.

'They are really charming,' said the man, looking after the two sisters, who soon disappeared from his view. 'It would be a great pity if——'

He was unable to finish. A frightful tumult, mingled with cries of alarm and horror, rose suddenly from the adjoining rooms. Almost instantly, two doors were thrown open, and a number of the sick, half-naked, pale, flesh-less, and their features convulsed with terror, rushed into the antechamber, exclaiming : 'Help ! help ! the madman !' It is impossible to paint the scene of despairing and furious confusion which followed this panic of so many affrighted wretches, flying to the only other door, to escape from the peril they dreaded, and there, struggling and trampling on each other to pass through the narrow entrance.

At the moment when the last of these unhappy creatures succeeded in reaching the door, dragging himself along upon his bleeding hands, for he had been thrown down and almost crushed in the confusion—Morok, the object of so much terror—Morok himself appeared. He was a horrible sight. With the exception of a rag bound about his middle, his wan form was entirely naked, and from his bare legs still hung the remnants of the cords he had just broken. His thick, yellow hair stood almost on end, his beard bristled, his savage eyes rolled full of blood in their orbits, and shone with a glassy brightness ; his lips were covered with foam ; from time to time, he uttered hoarse, guttural cries. The veins, visible on his iron limbs, were swollen almost to bursting. He bounded like a wild beast, and stretched out before him his bony and quivering hands. At the moment Morok reached the doorway, by which those he pursued made their escape, some persons, attracted by the noise, managed to close this door from without, whilst others secured that which communicated with the sick-wards.

Morok thus found himself a prisoner. He ran to the window to force it open, and throw himself into the courtyard. But, stopping suddenly, he drew back from the glittering panes, seized with that invincible horror which all the victims of hydrophobia feel at the sight of any shining object, par-ticularly glass. The unfortunate creatures whom he had pursued, saw him from the courtyard exhausting himself in furious efforts to open the doors that had just been closed upon him. Then, perceiving the inutility of his attempts, he uttered savage cries, and rushed furiously round the room, like a wild beast that seeks in vain to escape from its cage.

But, suddenly, those spectators of this scene, who had approached nearest to the window, uttered a loud exclamation of fear and anguish. Morok had perceived the little door which led to the closet occupied by Sister Martha, where Rose and Blanche had entered a few minutes before. Hoping to get out by this way, Morok drew the door violently towards him, and succeeded in half opening it, notwithstanding the resistance he experienced from the inside. For an instant, the affrighted crowd saw the stiffened arms of Sister Martha and the orphans, clinging to the door, and holding it back with all their might.

————

CHAPTER LVI

HYDROPHOBIA.

WHEN the sick people, assembled in the courtyard, saw the desperate efforts of Morok to force the door of the room which contained Sister Martha and the orphans, their fright redoubled. 'It is all over with Sister Martha!' cried they.

'The door will give way.'——'And the closet has no other entrance.'

'There are two young girls in mourning with her.'

'Come! we must not leave these poor women to encounter the madman. Follow me, friends!' cried generously one of the spectators, who was still blessed with health, and he rushed towards the steps to return to the antechamber.

'It's too late! it's only exposing yourself in vain,' cried many persons, holding him back by force.

At this moment, voices were heard, exclaiming: 'Here is the Abbé Gabriel.'——'He is coming downstairs. He has heard the noise.'

'He is asking what is the matter.'——'What will he do?'

Gabriel, occupied with a dying person in a neighbouring room, had, indeed just learned that Morok, having broken his bonds, had succeeded in escaping from the chamber in which he had been temporarily confined. Foreseeing the terrible dangers which might result from the escape of the lion-tamer, the missionary consulted only his courage, and hastened down, in the hope of preventing greater misfortunes. In obedience to his orders, an attendant followed him, bearing a brazier full of hot cinders, on which lay several irons, at a white heat, used by the doctors for cauterising, in desperate cases of cholera.

The angelic countenance of Gabriel was very pale; but calm intrepidity shone upon his noble brow. Hastily crossing the passage, and making his way through the crowd, he went straight to the antechamber door. As he approached it, one of the sick people said to him, in a lamentable voice: 'Ah, sir! it is all over. Those who can see through the window say that Sister Martha is lost.'

Gabriel made no answer, but grasped the key of the door. Before entering the room, however, he turned to the attendant, and said to him in a firm voice: 'Are the irons of a white heat?'——'Yes, sir.'

'Then wait here, and be ready. As for you, my friends,' he added, turning to some of the sick, who shuddered with terror, 'as soon as I enter shut the door after me. I will answer for the rest. And you, friend, only bring your irons when I call.'

And the young missionary turned the key in the lock. At this juncture, a cry of alarm, pity, and admiration rose from every lip, and the spectators drew back from the door, with an involuntary feeling of fear. Raising his eyes to heaven, as if to invoke its assistance at this terrible moment, Gabriel pushed open the door, and immediately closed it behind him. He was alone with Morok.

The lion-tamer, by a last furious effort, had almost succeeded in opening the door, to which Sister Martha and the orphans were clinging, in a fit of terror, uttering piercing cries. At the sound of Gabriel's footsteps, Morok turned round suddenly. Then, instead of continuing his attack on the closet, he sprang, with a roar and a bound, upon the newcomer.

During this time, Sister Martha and the orphans, not knowing the cause of the sudden retreat of their assailant, took advantage of the opportunity to close and bolt the door, and thus placed themselves in security from a new attack. Morok, with haggard eye, and teeth convulsively clenched, had rushed upon Gabriel, his hands extended to seize him by the throat. The missionary stood the shock valiantly. Guessing, at a glance, the intention of his adversary, he seized him by the wrists as he advanced, and, holding him back, bent him down violently with a vigorous hand. For a second, Morok and Gabriel remained mute, breathless, motionless, gazing on each other; then the missionary strove to conquer the efforts of the madman, who, with violent jerks, attempted to throw himself upon him, and to seize and tear him with his teeth.

Suddenly the lion-tamer's strength seemed to fail, his knees quivered, his livid head sank upon his shoulder, his eyes closed. The missionary, supposing that a momentary weakness had succeeded to the fit of rage, and that the wretch was about to fall, relaxed his hold in order to lend him assistance. But no sooner did he feel himself at liberty, thanks to his crafty device, than Morok flung himself furiously upon Gabriel. Surprised by this sudden attack, the latter stumbled, and at once felt himself clasped in the iron arms of the madman. Yet, with redoubled strength and energy, struggling breast to breast, foot to foot, the missionary in his turn succeeded in tripping up his adversary, and, throwing him with a vigorous effort, again seized his hands, and now held him down beneath his knee. Having thus completely mastered him, Gabriel turned his head to call for assistance, when Morok, by a desperate strain, succeeded in raising himself a little, and seized with his teeth the left arm of the missionary. At this sharp, deep, horrible bite, which penetrated to the very bone, Gabriel could not restrain a scream of anguish and horror. He strove in vain to disengage himself, for his arm was held fast, as in a vice, between the firm-set jaws of Morok.

This frightful scene had lasted less time than it has taken in the description, when suddenly the door leading to the passage was violently opened, and several courageous men, who had learned from the patients to what danger the young priest was exposed, came rushing to his assistance, in spite of his recommendation not to enter till he should call. The attendant was amongst the number, with the brazier and the hot irons. Gabriel, as soon as he perceived him, said to him, in an agitated voice, 'Quick, friend! your iron. Thank God I had thought of that.'

One of the men who had entered the room was luckily provided with a blanket; and the moment the missionary succeeded in wresting his arm from the clenched teeth of Morok, whom he still held down with his knee, this blanket was thrown over the madman's head, so that he could now be held and bound without danger, notwithstanding his desperate resistance. Then Gabriel rose, tore open the sleeve of his cassock, and laying bare his left arm, on which a deep bite was visible, bleeding, of a bluish colour, he beckoned the attendant to draw near, seized one of the hot irons, and, with a firm and sure hand, twice applied the burning metal to the wound, with a calm heroism which struck all the spectators with admiration. But soon so many various emotions, intrepidly sustained, were followed by a natural reaction. Large drops of sweat stood upon Gabriel's brow; his long light hair clung to his temples; he grew deadly pale, reeled, lost his senses, and was carried into the next room to receive immediate attention.

* * * * * *

An accidental circumstance, likely enough to occur, had converted one of the Princess de Saint-Dizier's falsehoods into a truth. To induce the orphans to go to the hospital, she had told them Gabriel was there, which at the time she was far from believing. On the contrary, she would have wished to prevent a meeting, which, from the attachment of the missionary to the girls, might interfere with her projects. A little while after the terrible scene we have just related, Rose and Blanche, accompanied by Sister Martha, entered a vast room, of a strange and fatal aspect, containing a number of women who had suddenly been seized with cholera.

These immense apartments, generously supplied for the purpose of a temporary hospital, had been furnished with excessive luxury. The room now

occupied by the sick women of whom we speak had been used for a ball-room.
The white panels glittered with sumptuous gilding, and magnificent pier-
glasses occupied the space between the windows, through which could be
seen the fresh verdure of a pleasant garden, smiling beneath the influence
of budding May. In the midst of all this gilded luxury, on a rich, inlaid floor
of costly woods, were seen arranged in regular order four rows of beds, of
every shape and kind, from the humble truckle-bed to the handsome couch
in carved mahogany.

This long room was divided into two compartments by a temporary partition, four or five feet in height. They had thus been able to manage the
four rows of beds. This partition finished at some little distance from either
end of the room, so as to leave an open space without beds, for the volunteer
attendants, when the sick did not require their aid. At one of these extremities of the room was a lofty and magnificent marble chimney-piece, ornamented with gilt bronze. On the fire beneath, various drinks were brewing
for the patients. To complete the singular picture, women of every class
took their turns in attending upon the sick, to whose sighs and groans they
always responded with consoling words of hope and pity. Such was the
place, strange and mournful, that Rose and Blanche entered together, hand
in hand, a short time after Gabriel had displayed such heroic courage in the
struggle against Morok. Sister Martha accompanied Marshal Simon's
daughters. After speaking a few words to them in a whisper, she pointed
out to them the two divisions in which the beds were arranged, and herself
went to the other end of the room to give some orders.

The orphans, still under the impression of the terrible danger from which
Gabriel had rescued them without their knowing it, were both excessively
pale ; yet their eyes were expressive of firm resolution. They had determined
not only to perform what they considered an imperative duty, but to prove
themselves worthy of their valiant father ; they were acting too for their
mother's sake, since they had been told that, dying in Siberia without receiving
the sacrament, her eternal felicity might depend on the proofs they gave of
Christian devotion. Need we add that the Princess de Saint-Dizier, following the advice of Rodin, had, in a second interview, skilfully brought about
without the knowledge of Dagobert, taken advantage of the excitable qualities of these poor, confiding, simple, and generous souls, by a fatal exaggeration of the most noble and courageous sentiments. The orphans having
asked Sister Martha if Madame Augustine du Tremblay had been brought to
this asylum within the last three days, that person had answered, that she
really did not know, but, if they would go through the women's wards, it would
be easy for them to ascertain. For the abominable hypocrite, who, in
conjunction with Rodin, had sent these two children to encounter a mortal
peril, had told an impudent falsehood when she affirmed that their governess had been removed to this hospital. During their exile, and their toilsome journey with Dagobert, the sisters had been exposed to many hard
trials. But never had they witnessed so sad a spectacle as that which now
offered itself to their view.

The long row of beds, on which so many poor creatures writhed in agony,
some uttering deep groans, some only a dull rattle in the throat, some raving
in the delirium of fever, or calling on those from whom they were about to
part for ever—these frightful sights and sounds, which are too much even for
brave men, would inevitably (such was the execrable design of Rodin and
his accomplices) make a fatal impression on these young girls, urged by the
most generous motives to undertake this perilous visit. And then—sad
memory ! which awoke, in all its deep and poignant bitterness, by the side
of the first beds they came to—it was of this very malady, the Cholera, that

their mother had died a painful death. Fancy the twins entering this vast room, of so fearful an aspect, and, already much shaken by the terror which Morok had inspired, pursuing their search in the midst of these unfortunate creatures, whose dying pangs reminded them every instant of the dying agony of their mother ! For a moment, at sight of the funereal hall, Rose and Blanche had felt their resolution fail them. A black presentiment made them regret their heroic imprudence ; and, moreover, since several minutes they had begun to feel an icy shudder, and painful shootings across the temples ; but, attributing these symptoms to the fright occasioned by Morok, their good and valiant natures soon stifled all these fears. They exchanged glances of affection, their courage revived, and both of them—Rose on one side of the partition, and Blanche on the other—proceeded with their painful task. Gabriel, carried to the doctors' private room, had soon recovered his senses. Thanks to his courage and presence of mind, his wound, cauterised in time, could have no dangerous consequences. As soon as it was dressed he insisted on returning to the women's ward, where he had been offering pious consolations to a dying person at the moment they had come to inform him of the frightful danger caused by the escape of Morok.

A few minutes before the missionary entered the room, Rose and Blanche arrived almost together at the term of their mournful search, one from the left, the other from the right-hand row of beds, separated by the partition which divided the hall into compartments. The sisters had not yet seen each other. Their steps tottered as they advanced, and they were forced, from time to time, to lean against the beds as they passed along. Their strength was rapidly failing them. Giddy with fear and pain, they appeared to act almost mechanically. Alas ! the orphans had been seized almost at the same moment with the terrible symptoms of cholera. In consequence of that species of physiological phenomenon, of which we have already spoken—a phenomenon by no means rare in twins, which had already been displayed on one or two occasions of their sickness—their organisations seemed liable to the same sensations, the same simultaneous accidents, like two flowers on one stem, which bloom and fade together. The sight of so much suffering, and so many deaths, had accelerated the development of this dreadful disease. Already, on their agitated and altered countenances, they bore the mortal tokens of the contagion, as they came forth, each on her own side, from the two subdivisions of the room in which they had vainly sought their governess. Until now separated by the partition, Rose and Blanche had not yet seen each other ; but, when at length their eyes met, there ensued a heart-rending scene.

CHAPTER LVII.

THE GUARDIAN ANGEL.

To the charming fresnness of the sisters' faces had succeeded a livid pallor. Their large blue eyes, now hollow and sunk in, appeared of enormous dimensions. Their lips, once so rosy, were now suffused with a violet hue, and a similar colour was gradually displacing the transparent carmine of their cheeks and fingers. It was as if all the roses in their charming countenances were fading and turning blue before the icy blast of death.

When the orphans met, tottering and hardly able to sustain themselves, a cry of mutual horror burst from their lips. Each of them exclaimed, at sight of the fearful change in her sister's features, ' Are you also ill, sister ?' And then, bursting into tears, they threw themselves into each other's arms, and looked anxiously at one another.

' Good heaven, Rose ! how pale you are !'——' Like you, sister.'

' And do you feel a cold shudder ?'——' Yes, and my sight fails me.'

' My bosom is all on fire.'——' Sister, we are perhaps going to die.'

' Let it only be together !'——' And our poor father ?'

' And Dagobert ?'——' Sister, our dream has come true !' cried Rose, almost deliriously, as she threw her arms round Blanche's neck. ' Look ! look ! the Angel Gabriel is here to fetch us.'

Indeed, at this moment, Gabriel entered the open space at the end of the room. ' Heavens ! what do I see ?' cried the young priest. ' The daughters of Marshal Simon !'

And, rushing forward, he received the sisters in his arms, for they were no longer able to stand. Already their drooping heads, their half-closed eyes, their painful and difficult breathing, announced the approach of death. Sister Martha was close at hand. She hastened to respond to the call of Gabriel. Aided by this pious woman, he was able to lift the orphans upon a bed reserved for the doctor in attendance. For fear that the sight of this mournful agony should make too deep an impression on the other patients, Sister Martha drew a large curtain, and the sisters were thus in some sort walled off from the rest of the room. Their hands had been so tightly clasped together, during a nervous paroxysm, that it was impossible to separate them. It was in this position that the first remedies were applied—remedies incapable of conquering the violence of the disease, but which at least mitigated for a few moments the excessive pains they suffered, and restored some faint glimmer of perception to their obscured and troubled senses. At this moment, Gabriel was leaning over the bed with a look of inexpressible grief. With breaking heart, and face bathed in tears, he thought of the strange destiny, which thus made him a witness of the death of these girls, his relations, whom but a few months before he had rescued from the horrors of the tempest. In spite of his firmness of soul, the missionary could not help shuddering as he reflected on the fate of the orphans, the death of Jacques Rennepont, and the fearful devices by which M. Hardy, retired to the cloistered solitude of St. Hérem, had become a member of the Society of Jesus almost in dying. The missionary said to himself, that already four members of the Rennepont family—his family—had been successively struck down by some dreadful fate ; and he asked himself with alarm, how it was that the detestable interests of the Society of Loyola should be served by a providential fatality? The astonishment of the young missionary would have given place to the deepest horror, could he have known the part that Rodin and his accomplices had taken, both in the death of Jacques Rennnepont, by exciting, through Morok, the evil propensities of the artisan, and in the approaching end of Rose and Blanche, by converting, through the Princess de Saint-Dizier, the generous inspirations of the orphans into suicidal heroism.

Roused for a moment from the painful stupor in which they had been plunged, Rose and Blanche half-opened their large eyes, already dull and faded. Then, more and more bewildered, they both gazed fixedly at the angelic countenance of Gabriel.

' Sister,' said Rose, in a faint voice, ' do you see the archangel—as in our dreams, in Germany ?'——' Yes—three days ago—he appeared to us.'

' He is come to fetch us.'——' Alas ! will our death save our poor mother from purgatory ?'

' Angel ! blessed angel ! pray God for our mother—and for us !' Until now, stupefied with amazement and sorrow, almost suffocated with sobs, Gabriel had not been able to utter a word. But, at these words of the orphans, he exclaimed : ' Dear children, why doubt of your mother's salvation? Oh! never did a purer soul ascend to its Creator. Your mother? I know from my adopted father, that her virtues and courage were the admiration of all who knew her. Oh! believe me; God has blessed her.'

'Do you hear, sister?' cried Rose, as a ray of celestial joy illumined for an instant the livid faces of the orphans. 'God has blessed our mother.'

'Yes, yes,' resumed Gabriel; 'banish these gloomy ideas. Take courage, poor children! You must not die. Think of your father.'

'Our father?' said Blanche, shuddering; and she continued, with a mixture of reason and wild excitement, which would have touched the soul of the most indifferent: 'Alas! he will not find us on his return. Forgive us, father! we did not think to do any harm. We wished, like you, to do something generous—to help our governess——'

'And we did not think to die so quickly, and so soon. Yesterday, we were gay and happy.'

'Oh, good angel! you will appear to our father, even as you have appeared to us. You will tell him, that, in dying—the last thought of his children—was of him.'

'We came here, without Dagobert's knowing it—do not let our father scold him.'——'Blessed angel!' resumed the other sister, in a still more feeble voice; 'appear to Dagobert also. Tell him, that we ask his forgiveness, for the grief our death will occasion him.'

'And let our old friend caress our poor Spoilsport for us—our faithful guardian,' added Blanche, trying to smile.

'And then,' resumed Rose, in a voice that was growing still fainter, 'promise to appear to two other persons, that have been so kind to us— good Mother Bunch—and the beautiful Lady Adrienne.'

'We forget none whom we have loved,' said Blanche, with a last effort. 'Now, God grant we may go to our mother, never to leave her more!'

'You promised it, good angel—you know you did—in the dream. You said to us: "Poor children—come from so far—you will have traversed the earth—to rest on the maternal bosom!"——'

'Oh! it is dreadful—dreadful! So young—and no hope?' murmured Gabriel, as he buried his face in his hands. 'Almighty Father! Thy views are impenetrable. Alas! yet why should these children die this cruel death?'

Rose heaved a deep sigh, and said in an expiring tone: 'Let us be buried together!—united in life, in death not divided——'

And the two turned their dying looks upon Gabriel, and stretched out towards him their supplicating hands.

'Oh, blessed martyrs to a generous devotion!' cried the missionary, raising to heaven his eyes streaming with tears. 'Angelic souls! treasures of innocence and truth! ascend, ascend to heaven—since God calls you to him, and the earth is not worthy to possess you!'

'Sister! father!' were the last words that the orphans pronounced with their dying voices.

And then the twins, by a last instinctive impulse, endeavoured to clasp each other, and their eyes half-opened to exchange yet another glance. They shuddered twice or thrice, their limbs stiffened, a deep sigh struggled from their violet-coloured lips. Rose and Blanche were both dead! Gabriel and Sister Martha, after closing the eyes of the orphans, knelt down to pray by the side of that funereal couch. Suddenly a great tumult was heard in the room. Rapid footsteps, mingled with imprecations, sounded close at hand, the curtain was drawn aside from this mournful scene, and Dagobert entered precipitately, pale, haggard, his dress in disorder. At sight of Gabriel and the Sister of Charity kneeling beside the corpses of his children, the soldier uttered a terrible roar, and tried to advance—but in vain—for, before Gabriel could reach him, Dagobert fell flat on the ground, and his grey head struck violently on the floor.

☼   ☼   ☼   ☼   ☼   ☼

It is night—a dark and stormy night. One o'clock in the morning has just sounded from the church of Montmartre. It is to the cemetery of Montmartre that is carried the coffin which, according to the last wishes of Rose and Blanche, contains them both. Through the thick shadow, which rests upon that field of death, may be seen moving a pale light. It is the gravedigger. He advances with caution ; a dark lantern is in his hand. A man wrapped in a cloak accompanies him. He holds down his head and weeps. It is Samuel. The old Jew—the keeper of the house in the Rue Saint-François. On the night of the funeral of Jacques Rennepont, the first who died of the seven heirs, and who was buried in another cemetery, Samuel had a similar mysterious interview with the gravedigger, to obtain a favour at the price of gold. A strange and awful favour ! After passing down several paths, bordered with cypress trees, by the side of many tombs, the Jew and the gravedigger arrived at a little glade, situated near the western wall of the cemetery. The night was so dark, that scarcely anything could be seen. After moving his lantern up and down, and all about, the gravedigger showed Samuel, at the foot of a tall yew-tree, with long black branches, a little mound of newly-raised earth, and said : ' It is here.'

' You are sure of it ?'——' Yes, yes—two bodies in one coffin ! it is not such a common thing.'

' Alas ! two in the same coffin !' said the Jew, with a deep sigh.——' Now that you know the place, what do you want more ?' asked the gravedigger.

Samuel did not answer. He fell on his knees, and piously kissed the little mound. Then rising, with his cheeks bathed in tears, he approached the gravedigger, and spoke to him for some moments in a whisper—though they were alone, and in the centre of that deserted place. Then began between those two men a mysterious dialogue, which the night enveloped in shade and silence. The gravedigger, alarmed at what Samuel asked him, at first refused his request.

But the Jew, employing persuasions, entreaties, tears, and at last the seduction of the jingling gold, succeeded in conquering the scruples of the gravedigger. Though the latter trembled at the thought of what he promised, he said to Samuel in an agitated tone : ' To-morrow night then, at two o'clock.'

' I shall be behind the wall,' answered Samuel, pointing out the place with the aid of the lantern. I will throw three stones into the cemetery, for a signal.'——'Yes, three stones—as a signal,' replied the gravedigger shuddering, and wiping the cold sweat from his forehead.

With considerable remains of vigour, notwithstanding his great age, Samuel availed himself of the broken surface of the low wall, and climbing over it, soon disappeared. The gravedigger returned home with hasty strides. From time to time, he looked fearfully behind him, as though he had been pursued by some fatal vision.

☼   ☼   ☼   ☼   ☼

On the evening after the funeral of Rose and Blanche, Rodin wrote two letters. The first, addressed to his mysterious correspondent at Rome, alluded to the deaths of Jacques Rennepont, and Rose and Blanche Simon, as well as to the cession of M. Hardy's property, and the donation of Gabriel—events which reduced the claimants of the inheritance to two— Mdlle. de Cardoville and Djalma. This first note, written by Rodin for Rome, contained only the following words : ' have from seven leaves two

Announce this result to the Cardinal-Prince. Let him go on. I advance—advance—advance!' The second note, in a feigned hand, was addressed to Marshal Simon, to be delivered by a sure messenger, and contained these few lines : ' If there is yet time, make haste to return. Your daughters are both dead. You shall learn who killed them.'

CHAPTER LVIII.

RUIN.

IT is the day after the death of Marshal Simon's daughters. Mdlle. de Cardoville is yet ignorant of the sad end of her young relatives. Her countenance is radiant with happiness, and never has she looked more beautiful ; her eye has never been more brilliant, her complexion more dazzlingly white, her lip of a richer coral. According to her somewhat eccentric custom of dressing herself in her own house in a picturesque style, Adrienne wears to-day, though it is about three o'clock in the afternoon, a pale green watered-silk dress, with a very full skirt, the sleeves and bodice slashed with rose-coloured ribbon, and adorned with white bugle-beads of exquisite workmanship ; while a slender net-work, also of white bugle-beads, concealing the thick plait of Adrienne's back-hair, forms an oriental head-dress of charming originality, and contrasts agreeably with the long curls which fall in front almost to the swell of the bosom. To the expression of indescribable happiness which marks the features of Mdlle. de Cardoville, is added a certain resolute, cutting, satirical air, which is not habitual to her. Her charming head, and graceful, swan-like neck, are raised in an attitude of defiance ; her small, rose-coloured nostrils seem to dilate with ill-repressed ardour, and she waits with haughty impatience for the moment of an aggressive and ironical interview. Not far from Adrienne is Mother Bunch. She has resumed in the house the place which she at first occupied. The young sempstress is in mourning for her sister, but her countenance is expressive of a mild calm sorrow. She looks at Mdlle. de Cardoville with surprise ; for never, till now, has she seen the features of the fair patrician impressed with such a character of ironical audacity. Mdlle. de Cardoville was exempt from the slightest coquetry, in the narrow and ordinary sense of the word. Yet she now cast an inquiring look at the glass before which she was standing, and, having restored the elastic smoothness to one of her long, golden curls, by rolling it for a moment round her ivory finger, she carefully effaced with her hands some almost imperceptible folds, which had formed themselves in the thick material of her elegant corsage. This, movement, and that of turning her back to the glass, to see if her dress sat perfectly on all points, revealed, in serpentine undulations, all the charms and graces of her light and elegant figure ; for, in spite of the rich fulness of her shoulders, white and firm as sculptured alabaster, Adrienne belonged to that class of privileged persons, who are able at need to make a girdle out of a garter.

Having performed, with indescribable grace, these charming evolutions of feminine coquetry, Adrienne turned towards Mother Bunch, whose surprise was still on the increase, and said to her, smiling : ' My dear Magdalen, do not laugh at my question—but what would you say to a picture, that should represent me as I am now ?'

' Why, lady——'——' There you are again, with your lady-ing,' said Adrienne, in a tone of gentle reproach.

' Well, then, Adrienne,' resumed Mother Bunch, ' I think it would be a charming picture, for you are dressed, as usual, with perfect taste.'

'But am I not better dressed than on other days, my dear poetess? I began by telling you that I do not ask the question for my own sake,' said Adrienne, gaily.

'Well, I suppose so,' replied Mother Bunch, with a faint smile. 'It is certainly impossible to imagine anything that would suit you better. The light green and the pale rose-colour, with the soft lustre of the white ornaments, harmonise so well with your golden hair, that I cannot conceive, I tell you, a more graceful picture.'

The speaker felt what she said, and she was happy to be able to express it, for we know the intense admiration of that poetic soul for all that was beautiful.

'Well !' went on Adrienne, gaily, 'I am glad, my dear, that you find me better dressed than usual.'

'Only,' said the hunchback, hesitating.——'Only?' repeated Adrienne, looking at her with an air of interrogation.

'Why, only,' continued the other, 'if I have never seen you look more pretty, I have also never observed in your features the resolute and ironical expression which they had just now. It was like an air of impatient defiance.'

'And so it was, my dear little Magdalen,' said Adrienne, throwing her arms round the girl's neck with joyous tenderness. 'I must kiss you, for having guessed it. You see, I expect a visit from my dear aunt.'

'The Princess de Saint-Dizier?' cried Mother Bunch, in alarm. 'That wicked lady, who did you so much evil?'——'The very same. She has asked for an interview, and I shall be delighted to receive her.'

'Delighted ?'——'Yes—a somewhat ironical and malicious delight, it is true,' answered Adrienne, still more gaily. 'You shall judge for yourself. She regrets her gallantries, her beauty, her youth—even her size afflicts the holy woman !—and she will see me young, fair, beloved—and above all thin—yes, thin,' added Mdlle. de Cardoville, laughing merrily. 'And you may imagine, my dear, how much envy and despair, the sight of a young, thin woman excites in a stout one of a certain age !'

'My friend,' said Mother Bunch, gravely, 'you speak in jest. And yet, I know not why, the coming of this princess alarms me.'

'Dear, gentle soul, be satisfied !' answered Adrienne, affectionately. 'I do not fear this woman—I no longer have any fear of her—and, to prove it to her confusion, I will treat her—a monster of hypocrisy and wickedness, who comes here, no doubt, on some abominable design—I will treat her as an inoffensive, ridiculous fat woman !' And Adrienne again laughed.

A servant here entered the room, and interrupted the mirth of Adrienne, by saying : 'The Princess de Saint-Dizier wishes to know if you can receive her ?'

'Certainly,' said Mdlle. de Cardoville ; and the servant retired. Mother Bunch was about to rise and quit the room ; but Adrienne held her back, and said to her, taking her hand, with an air of serious tenderness : 'Stay, my dear friend, I entreat you.'

'Do you wish it ?'——'Yes ; I wish—still in revenge, you know,' said Adrienne, with a smile, 'to prove to her highness of Saint-Dizier, that I have an affectionate friend—that I have, in fact, every happiness.'

'But, Adrienne,' replied the other, timidly, 'consider——'

'Silence ! here is the princess. Remain ! I ask it as a favour. The instinct of your heart will discover any snare she may have laid. Did not your affection warn me of the plots of Rodin ?'

Mother Bunch could not refuse such a request. She remained, but was about to draw back from the fire-place. Adrienne, however, took her by the hand, and made her resume her seat in the arm-chair, saying : 'My dear Magdalen, keep your place. You owe nothing to the lady. With me it is different ; she comes to my house.'

Hardly had Adrienne uttered these words, than the princess entered, with head erect, and haughty air (we have said, she could carry herself most loftily), and advanced with a firm step. The strongest minds have their side of puerile weakness ; a savage envy, excited by the elegance, wit, and beauty of Adrienne, bore a large part in the hatred of the princess for her niece ; and though it was idle to think of eclipsing Adrienne, and the Princess de Saint-Dizier did not seriously mean to attempt it, she could not forbear, in preparing for the interview she had demanded, taking more pains even than usual in the arrangement of her dress. Beneath her robe of shot silk, she was laced in and tightened to excess—a pressure which considerably increased the colour in her cheeks. The throng of jealous and hateful sentiments, which inspired her with regard to Adrienne, had so troubled the clearness of her ordinarily calm judgment, that, instead of the plain and quiet style, in which, as a woman of tact and taste, she was generally attired, she now committed the folly of wearing a dress of changing hues, and a crimson hat, adorned with a magnificent bird of paradise. Hate, envy, the pride of triumph—for she thought of the skilful perfidy with which she had sent to almost certain death the daughters of Marshal Simon—and the execrable hope of succeeding in new plots, were all expressed in the countenance of the Princess de Saint-Dizier, as she entered her niece's apartment.

Without advancing to meet her aunt, Adrienne rose politely from the sofa on which she was seated, made a half-curtsey, full of grace and dignity, and immediately resumed her former posture. Then, pointing to an arm-chair near the fire-place, at one corner of which sat Mother Bunch, and she herself at the other, she said : 'Pray sit down, your highness.' The princess turned very red, remained standing, and cast a disdainful glance of insolent surprise at the sempstress, who, in compliance with Adrienne's wish, only bowed slightly at the entrance of the Princess de Saint-Dizier, without offering to give up her place. In acting thus, the young sempstress followed the dictates of her conscience, which told her that the real superiority did not belong to this base, hypocritical, and wicked princess, but rather to such a person as herself, the admirable and devoted friend.

'Let me beg your highness to sit down,' resumed Adrienne, in a mild tone, as she pointed to the vacant chair. ——'The interview I have demanded, niece,' said the princess, 'must be a private one.'

'I have no secrets, madame, for my best friend ; you may speak in the presence of this young lady.'

'I have long known,' replied Madame de Saint-Dizier, with bitter irony, 'that in all things you care little for secrecy, and that you are easy in the choice of what you call your friends. But you will permit me to act differently from you. If you have no secrets, madame, I have—and I do not choose to confide them to the first comer.'

So saying, the pious lady glanced contemptuously at the sempstress. The latter, hurt at the insolent tone of the princess, answered mildly and simply:

I do not see what can be the great difference between the first and the last comer to Mdlle. de Cardoville's.'

'What ! can it speak !' cried the princess, insolently.

'It can at least answer, madame,' replied Mother Bunch, in her calm voice.

'I wish to see you alone, niece—is that clear?' said the princess, impatiently, to her niece.

'I beg your pardon, but I do not quite understand your highness,' said Adrienne, with an air of surprise. 'This young lady, who honours me with her friendship, is willing to be present at this interview, which you have asked for—I say she has consented to be present, for it needs, I confess, the kindest condescension in her to resign herself, from affection for me, to hear all the graceful, obliging, and charming things which you have no doubt come hither to communicate.'

'Madame——' began the princess, angrily.

'Permit me to interrupt your highness,' returned Adrienne, in a tone of perfect amenity, as if she were addressing the most flattering compliments to her visitor. 'To put you quite at your ease with the lady here, I will begin by informing you that she is quite aware of all the holy perfidies, pious wrongs, and devout infamies, of which you nearly made me the victim. She knows that you are a mother of the Church, such as one sees but few of in these days. May I hope, therefore, that your highness will dispense with this delicate and interesting reserve ?'

'Really,' said the princess, with a sort of incensed amazement, 'I scarcely know if I wake or sleep.'

'Dear me !' said Adrienne, in apparent alarm ; 'this doubt as to the state of your faculties is very shocking, madame. I see that the blood flies to your head, for your face sufficiently shows it ; you seem oppressed, confined, un-comfortable—perhaps (we women may say so between ourselves), perhaps you are laced a little too tightly, madame ?'

These words, pronounced by Adrienne with an air of warm interest and perfect simplicity, almost choked the princess with rage. She became crimson, seated herself abruptly, and exclaimed : 'Be it so, madame ! I prefer this reception to any other. It puts me at my ease, as you say.'

'Does it indeed, madame ?' said Adrienne, with a smile. 'You may now at least speak frankly all that you feel, which must for you have the charm of novelty ! Confess that you are obliged to me for enabling you, even for a moment, to lay aside that mask of piety, amiability, and goodness, which must be so troublesome to you.'

As she listened to the sarcasms of Adrienne (an innocent and excusable revenge, if we consider all the wrongs she had suffered), Mother Bunch felt her heart sink within her ; for she dreaded the malignity of the princess, who replied, with the utmost calmness : 'A thousand thanks, madame, for your excellent intentions and sentiments. I appreciate them as I ought, and I hope in a short time to prove it to you.'

'Well, madame,' said Adrienne, playfully, 'let us have it all at once. I am full of impatient curiosity.'

'And yet,' said the princess, feigning in her turn a bitter and ironical delight, 'you are far from having the least notion of what I am about to announce to you.'

'Indeed ! I fear that your highness's candour and modesty deceive you,' replied Adrienne, with the same mocking affability ; 'for there are very few things on your part that can surprise me, madame. You must be aware that from your highness I am prepared for anything.'

'Perhaps, madame,' said the princess, laying great stress on her words, 'if, for instance, I were to tell you that within twenty-four hours—suppose between this and to-morrow—you will be reduced to poverty——'

This was so unexpected, that Mdlle. de Cardoville started in spite of herself, and Mother Bunch shuddered.

'Ah, madame !' said the princess, with triumphant joy and cruel mildness, as she watched the growing surprise of her niece, 'confess that I have astonished you a little. You were right in giving to our interview the turn it has taken. I should have needed all sorts of circumlocution to say to you, "Niece, to-morrow you will be as poor as you are rich to-day." But now I can tell you the fact quite plainly and simply.'

Recovering from her first amazement, Adrienne replied, with a calm smile, which checked the joy of the princess: ' Well, I confess frankly, madame, that you have surprised me ; I expected from you one of those black pieces of malignity, one of those well-laid plots, in which you are known to excel, and I did not think you would make all this fuss about such a trifle.'

' To be ruined—completely ruined,' cried the princess, ' and that by to-morrow—you that have been so prodigal, will see your house, furniture, horses, jewels, even the ridiculous dresses of which you are so vain, all taken from you—do you call that a trifle ? You, that spend with indifference thousands of louis, will be reduced to a pension inferior to the wages you give your foot-boy—do you call that a trifle ?'

To her aunt's cruel disappointment, Adrienne, who appeared quite to have recovered her serenity, was about to answer accordingly, when the door suddenly opened, and, without being announced, Prince Djalma entered the room. A proud and tender expression of delight beamed from the radiant brow of Adrienne at sight of the prince, and it is impossible to describe the look of triumphant happiness and high disdain that she cast upon the Princess de Saint-Dizier. Djalma himself had never looked more hand-some, and never had more intense happiness been impressed on a human countenance. The Hindoo wore a long robe of white Cashmere, adorned with innumerable stripes of gold and purple ; his turban was of the same colour and material ; a magnificent figured shawl was twisted about his waist. On seeing the Indian, whom she had not hoped to meet at Mdlle. de Cardo-ville's, the Princess de Saint-Dizier could not at first conceal her extreme sur-prise. It was between these four, then, that the following scene took place.

———

CHAPTER LIX.

MEMORIES.

DJALMA, having never before met the Princess de Saint-Dizier at Adrienne's, at first appeared rather astonished at her presence. The princess, keeping silence for a moment, contemplated with implacable hatred and envy those two beings, both so fair and young, so loving and happy. Suddenly she started, as if she had just remembered something of great importance, and for some seconds she remained absorbed in thought.

Adrienne and Djalma availed themselves of this interval to gaze fondly on each other, with a sort of ardent idolatry, which filled their eyes with sweet tears. Then, at a movement of the Princess de Saint-Dizier, who seemed to rouse herself from her momentary trance, Mdlle. de Cardoville said to the young prince, with a smile : ' My dear cousin, I have to repair an omission (voluntary, I confess, and for good reasons), in never having before men-tioned to you one of my relations, whom I have now the honour to present to you. The Princess de Saint-Dizier !'

Djalma bowed ; but Mdlle. de Cardoville resumed, just as her aunt was about to make some reply : ' Her Highness of Saint-Dizier came very kindly to inform me of an event which is a most fortunate one for me, and of which I will speak to you hereafter, cousin—unless this amiable lady should wish to deprive me of the pleasure of making such a communication.'

The unexpected arrival of the prince, and the recollections which had suddenly occurred to the princess, had no doubt greatly modified her first plans : for, instead of continuing the conversation with regard to Adrienne's threatened loss of fortune, the princess answered, with a bland smile, that covered an odious meaning : ' I should be sorry, prince, to deprive my dear and amiable niece of the pleasure of announcing to you the happy news to which she alludes, and which, as a near relative, I lost no time in communicating to her. I have here some notes on this subject,' added the princess, delivering a paper to Adrienne, ' which I hope will prove, to her entire satisfaction, the reality of what I have announced to her.'

' A thousand thanks, my dear aunt,' said Adrienne, receiving the paper with perfect indifference ; ' these precautions and proofs are quite superfluous. You know that I always believe you on your word, when it concerns your good feeling towards myself.'

Notwithstanding his ignorance of the refined perfidy and cruel politeness of civilised life, Djalma, endowed with a tact and fineness of perception common to most natures of extreme susceptibility, felt some degree of mental discomfort as he listened to this exchange of false compliments. He could not guess their full meaning, but they sounded hollow to his ear ; and moreover, whether from instinct or presentiment, he had conceived a vague dislike for the Princess de Saint-Dizier. That pious lady, full of the great affair in hand, was a prey to the most violent agitation, which betrayed itself in the growing colour of her cheeks, her bitter smile, and the malicious brightness of her glance. As he gazed on this woman, Djalma was unable to conquer his rising antipathy, and he remained silent and attentive, whilst his handsome countenance lost something of its former serenity. Mother Bunch also felt the influence of a painful impression. She glanced in terror at the princess, and then imploringly at Adrienne, as though she entreated the latter to put an end to an interview of which the young sempstress foresaw the fatal consequences. But, unfortunately, the Princess de Saint-Dizier was too much interested in prolonging this conversation ; and Mdlle. de Cardoville, gathering new courage and confidence from the presence of the man she adored, took delight in vexing the princess with the exhibition of their happy loves.

After a short silence, the Princess de Saint-Dizier observed, in a soft and insinuating tone : ' Really, prince, you cannot think how pleased I was to learn by public report (for people talk of nothing else, and with good reason) of your chivalrous attachment to my dear niece ; for, without knowing it, you will extricate me from a difficult position.'

Djalma made no answer, but he looked at Mdlle. de Cardoville with a surprised and almost sorrowful air, as if to ask what her aunt meant to insinuate.

The latter, not perceiving this mute interrogation, resumed as follows : ' I will express myself more clearly, prince. You can understand that, being the nearest relative of this dear, obstinate girl, I am more or less responsible for her conduct in the eyes of the world ; and you, prince, seem just to have arrived on purpose, from the end of the earth, to take charge of a destiny which had caused me considerable apprehension. It is charming, it is excellent ; and I know not which most to admire, your courage or your good fortune.' The princess threw a glance of diabolical malice at Adrienne, and awaited her answer with an air of defiance.

' Listen to our good aunt, my dear cousin,' said the young lady, smiling calmly. ' Since our affectionate kinswoman sees you and me united and happy, her heart is swelling with such a flood of joy, that it must run over, and the effects will be delightful. Only have a little patience, and you will behold them in their full beauty. I do not know,' added Adrienne, in the most natural tone, ' why, in thinking of these outpourings of our dear aunt's affection, I should remember what you told me, cousin, of a certain viper in your country, which sometimes, in a powerless bite, breaks its fangs, and, absorbing its own venom, becomes the victim of the poison it distils. Come, my dear aunt, you that have so good and noble a heart, I am sure you must feel interested in the fate of those poor vipers.'

The princess darted an implacable look at her niece, and replied, in an agitated voice, 'I do not see the object of this selection of natural history. Do you, prince ?'

Djalma made no answer ; leaning with his arm on the mantelpiece, he threw dark and piercing glances upon the princess. His involuntary hatred of this woman filled his heart.

' Ah, my dear aunt !' resumed Adrienne, in a tone of self-reproach ; 'have I presumed too much on the goodness of your heart ? Have you not even sympathy for vipers ? For whom, then, have you any ? After all, I can very well understand it,' added Adrienne, as if to herself ; 'vipers are so thin. But, to lay aside these follies,' she continued, gaily, as she saw the ill-repressed rage of the pious woman, 'tell us at once, my dear aunt, all the tender things which the sight of our happiness inspires.'

' I hope to do so, my amiable niece. First, I must congratulate this dear prince, on having come so far to take charge, in all confidence, and with his eyes shut, of you, my poor child, whom we were obliged to confine as mad, in order to give a decent colour to your excesses. You remember the handsome lad, that we found in your apartment. You cannot be so faithless, as already to have forgotten his name ? He was a fine youth, and a poet—one Agricola Baudoin—and was discovered in a secret place, attached to your bed-chamber. All Paris was amused with the scandal—for you are not about to marry an unknown person, dear prince ; her name has been in every mouth.'

At these unexpected and dreadful words, Adrienne, Djalma, and Mother Bunch, though under the influence of different kinds of resentment, remained for a moment mute with surprise ; and the princess, judging it no longer necessary to repress her infernal joy and triumphant hatred, exclaimed, as she rose from her seat, with flushed cheek, and flashing eyes, ' Yes, I defy you to contradict me. Were we not forced to confine you, on the plea of madness ? And did we not find a workman (your lover) concealed in your bedroom ?'

On this horrible accusation, Djalma's golden complexion, transparent as amber, became suddenly the colour of lead ; his eyes, fixed and staring, showed the white round the pupil—his upper lip, red as blood, was curled in a kind of wild convulsion, which exposed to view the firmly-set teeth—and his whole countenance became so frightfully threatening and ferocious, that Mother Bunch shuddered with terror. Carried away by the ardour of his blood, the young Oriental felt a sort of dizzy, unreflecting, involuntary rage—a fiery commotion, like that which makes the blood leap to the brave man's eyes and brain, when he feels a blow upon his face. If, during that moment, rapid as the passage of the lightning through the cloud, action could have taken the place of thought, the princess and Adrienne, Mother Bunch and himself, would all have been annihilated by an explosion as sudden and fatal as that of the bursting of a mine. He would have killed the princess, because she accused Adrienne of infamous deception—he would have killed Adrienne, because she could even be suspected of such infamy —and Mother Bunch, for being a witness of the accusation—and himself, in order not to survive such horrid treachery. But, oh wonder ! his furious and bloodshot gaze met the calm look of Adrienne—a look so full of dignity and serene confidence—and the expression of ferocious rage passed away like a flash of lightning.

Much more : to the great surprise of the princess and the young work-girl, as the glances which Djalma cast upon Adrienne went (as it were) deeper into that pure soul, not only did the Indian grow calm, but, by a kind of transfiguration, his countenance seemed to borrow her serene expression, and reflect, as in a mirror, the noble serenity impressed on the young lady's features. Let us explain physically this moral revolution, as consoling to the terrified workgirl, as provoking to the princess. Hardly had the princess distilled the atrocious calumny from her venomous lips, than Djalma, then standing before the fireplace, had, in the first paroxysm of his fury, advanced a step towards her ; but, wishing as it were to moderate his rage, he held by the marble chimney-piece, which he grasped with iron strength. A convulsive trembling shook his whole body, and his features, altered and contracted, became almost frightful. Adrienne, on her part, when she heard the accusation, yielding to a first impulse of just indignation, even as Djalma had yielded to one of blind fury, rose abruptly, with offended pride flashing from her eyes ; but, almost immediately appeased by the consciousness of her own purity, her charming face resumed its expression of adorable serenity. It was then that her eyes met Djalma's. For a second, the young lady was even more afflicted than terrified at the threatening and formidable expression of the young Indian's countenance. ' Can stupid indignity exasperate him to this degree ?' said Adrienne to herself. ' Does he suspect *me*, then ?'

But to this reflection, as rapid as it was painful, succeeded the most lively joy, when the eyes of Adrienne rested for a short time on those of the Indian, and she saw his agitated countenance grow calm as if by magic, and become radiant and beautiful as before. Thus was the abominable plot of the Princess de Saint-Dizier utterly confounded by the sincere and confiding expression of Adrienne's face. That was not all. At the moment, when, as a spectator of this mute and expressive scene (which proved so well the wondrous sympathy of those two beings, who, without speaking a word, had understood and satisfied each other), the princess was choking with rage and vexation—Adrienne, with a charming smile and gesture, extended her fair hand to Djalma, who, kneeling, imprinted on it a kiss of fire, which sent a light blush to the forehead of the young lady.

Then the Hindoo, placing himself on the ermine carpet at the feet of Mdlle. de Cardoville, in an attitude full of grace and respect, rested his chin on the palm of one of his hands, and gazed on her silently, in a sort of mute adoration—while Adrienne, bending over him with a happy smile, ' looked at the babies in his eyes,' as the song says, with as much amorous complacency, as if the hateful princess had not been present. But soon, as if something were wanting to complete her happiness, Adrienne beckoned to Mother Bunch, and made her sit down by her side. Then, with her hand clasped in that of this excellent friend, Mdlle. de Cardoville smiled on Djalma, stretched adoringly at her feet, and cast on the dismayed princess a look of such calm and firm serenity, so nobly expressive of the invincible quiet of her happiness, and her lofty disdain of all calumnious attacks, that the Princess de Saint-Dizier, confused and stupefied, murmured some hardly intelligible words, in a voice trembling with passion, and, completely losing her presence of mind, rushed towards the door. But, at this moment, the hunchback, who feared some ambush, some perfidious plot in the background, resolved, after exchanging a glance with Adrienne, to accompany the princess to her carriage.

The angry disappointment of the Princess de Saint-Dizier, when she saw herself thus followed and watched, appeared so comical to Mdlle. de Cardoville, that she could not help laughing aloud ; and it was to the sound of contemptuous hilarity that the hypocritical princess, with rage and despair in her heart, quitted the house to which she had hoped to bring trouble and misery. Adrienne and Djalma were left alone. Before relating the scene which took place between them, a few retrospective words are indispensable. It will easily be imagined, that since Mdlle. de Cardoville and the Oriental had been brought into such close contact, after so many disappointments, their days had passed away like a dream of happiness. Adrienne had especially taken pains to bring to light, one by one, all the generous qualities of Djalma, of which she had read so much in her books of travels. The young lady had imposed on herself this tender and patient study of Djalma's character, not only to justify to her own mind the intensity of her love, but because this period of trial, to which she had assigned a term, enabled her to temper and divert the violence of Djalma's passion—a task the more meritorious, as she herself was of the same ardent temperament. For, in those two lovers, the finest qualities of sense and soul seemed exactly to balance each other, and heaven had bestowed on them the rarest beauty of form, and the most adorable excellence of heart, as if to legitimatise the irresistible attraction which drew and bound them together. What, then, was to be the term of this painful trial, which Adrienne had imposed on Djalma and on herself? This is what Mdlle. de Cardoville intended to tell the prince, in the interview she had with him, after the abrupt departure of the Princess de Saint-Dizier.

CHAPTER LX.

THE ORDEAL.

ADRIENNE DE CARDOVILLE and Djalma had remained alone. Such was the noble confidence which had succeeded in the Hindoo's mind to his first movement of unreflecting fury, caused by the infamous calumny, that, once alone with Adrienne, he did not even allude to that shameful accusation. On her side (touching and admirable sympathy of those two hearts!), the young lady was too proud, conscious of the purity of her love, to descend to any justification of herself. She would have considered it an insult both to herself and him. Therefore, the lovers began their interview, as if the princess had never made any such remark. The same contempt was extended to the papers, which the princess had brought with her, to prove the imminent ruin to which Adrienne was exposed. The young lady had laid them down, without reading them, on a stand within her reach. She made a graceful sign to Djalma to seat himself by her side, and accordingly he quitted, not without regret, the place he had occupied at her feet.

'My love,' said Adrienne, in a grave and tender voice, 'you have often impatiently asked me, when would come the term of the trial we have laid upon ourselves. That moment is at hand.'

Djalma started, and could not restrain a cry of surprise and joy ; but this almost trembling exclamation was so soft and sweet, that it seemed rather the expression of ineffable gratitude, than of exulting passion.

Adrienne continued : ' Separated—surrounded by treachery and fraud—mutually deceived as to each other's sentiments—we yet loved on, and in that followed an irresistible attraction, stronger than every opposing influence. But since then, in these days of happy retirement from the world, we have learned to value and esteem each other more. Left to ourselves in perfect freedom, we have had the courage to resist every temptation, that hereafter we might be happy without remorse. During these days, in which our hearts have been laid open to each other, we have read them thoroughly,

Yes, Djalma ! I believe in you, and you in me—I find in you all that you find in me—every possible human security for our future happiness. But this love must yet be consecrated ; and in the eyes of the world, in which we are called upon to live, marriage is the only consecration, and marriage enchains one's whole life.'

Djalma looked at the young lady with surprise.

'Yes, one's whole life ! and yet who can answer for the sentiments of a whole life ?' resumed Adrienne. ' A God, that could see into the future, could alone bind irrevocably certain hearts for their own happiness ; but, alas ! to human eyes the future is impenetrable. Therefore, to accept indissoluble ties, for any longer than one can answer for a present sentiment, is to commit an act of selfish and impious folly.'

Djalma made no reply, but, with an almost respectful gesture, he urged the speaker to continue.

'And then,' proceeded she, with a mixture of tenderness and pride, ' from respect for your dignity and mine, I would never promise to keep a law made by man against woman, with contemptuous and brutal egotism—a law, which denies to woman soul, mind, and heart—a law, which none can accept, without being either a slave or perjured—a law, which takes from the girl her name, reduces the wife to a state of degrading inferiority, denies to the mother all rights over her own children, and enslaves one human creature to the will of another, who is in all respects her equal in the sight of God !—You know, my love,' added the young lady, with passionate enthusiasm, ' how much I honour you, whose father was called the Father of the Generous. I do not then fear, noble and valiant heart, to see you use against me these tyrannical powers ; but, throughout my life, I never uttered a falsehood, and our love is too sacred and celestial to be purchased by a double perjury. No, never will I swear to observe a law, that my dignity and my reason refuse to sanction. If, to-morrow, the freedom of divorce were established, and the rights of women recognised, I should be willing to observe usages, which would then be in accordance with my conscience, and with what is just, possible, and humane.' Then, after a pause, Adrienne continued, with such deep and sweet emotion, that a tear of tenderness veiled her beauteous eyes : ' Oh ! if you knew, my love, what your love is to me : if you knew how dear and sacred I hold your happiness—you would excuse, you would understand, these generous superstitions of a loving and honest heart, which could only see a fatal omen in forms degraded by falsehood and perjury. What I wish, is, to attach you by love, to bind you in chains of happiness—and to leave you free, that I may owe your constancy only to your affection.'

Djalma had listened to the young girl with passionate attention. Proud and generous himself, he admired this proud and generous character. After a moment's meditative silence, he answered, in his sweet, sonorous voice, in an almost solemn tone : ' Like you, I hold in detestation, falsehood and perjury. Like you, I think that man degrades himself, by accepting the right of being a cowardly tyrant, even though resolved never to use the power. Like you, I could not bear the thought, that I owed all I most valued, not to your love alone, but to the eternal constraint of an indissoluble bond. Like you, I believe there is no dignity but in freedom. But you have said, that, for this great and holy love, you demand a religious consecration ; and if you reject vows, that you cannot make without folly and perjury, are there then others, which your reason and your heart approve ?— Who will pronounce the required blessing ? To whom must these vows be spoken ?'

'In a few days, my love, I believe I shall be able to tell you all. Every evening, after your departure, I have no other thought. I wish to find the means of uniting yourself and me—in the eyes of God, not of the law—without offending the habits and prejudices of a world, in which it may suit us hereafter to live. Yes, my friend ! when you know whose are the noble hands, that are to join ours together—who is to bless and glorify God in our union—a sacred union, that will leave us worthy and free—you will say, I am sure, that never purer hands could have been laid upon us. Forgive me, friend ! all this is in earnest—yes, earnest as our love, earnest as our happiness. If my words seem to you strange, my thoughts unreasonable, tell it me, love ! We will seek and find some better means, to reconcile that we owe to heaven, with what we owe to the world and to ourselves. It is said, that lovers are beside themselves,' added the young lady, with a smile, ' but I think that no creatures are more reasonable.'

' When I hear you speak thus of our happiness,' said Djalma, deeply moved, ' with so much calm and earnest tenderness, I think I see a mother occupied with the future prospects of her darling child—trying to surround him with all that can make him strong, valiant, and generous—trying to remove far from him all that is ignoble and unworthy. You ask me to tell you if your thoughts seem strange to me, Adrienne. You forget, that what makes my faith in our love, is my feeling exactly as you do. What offends you, offends me also ; what disgusts you, disgusts me. Just now, when you cited to me the laws of this country, which respect in a woman not even a mother's right—I thought with pride of our barbarous countries, where woman, though a slave, is made free when she becomes a mother. No, no ; such laws are not made either for you or me. Is it not to prove your sacred respect for our love, to wish to raise it above the shameful servitude that would degrade it ? You see, Adrienne, I have often heard say by the priests of my country, that there were beings inferior to the gods, but superior to every other creature. I did not believe those priests ; but now I do.' These last words were uttered, not in the tone of flattery, but with an accent of sincere conviction, and with that sort of passionate veneration and almost timid fervour, which mark the believer talking of his faith ; but what is impossible to describe, is the ineffable harmony of these almost religious words, with the mild, deep tone of the young Oriental's voice—as well as the ardent expression of amorous melancholy, which gave an irresistible charm to his enchanting features.

Adrienne had listened to Djalma with an indescribable mixture of joy, gratitude, and pride. Laying her hand on her bosom, as if to keep down its violent pulsations, she resumed, as she looked at the prince with delight : ' Behold him, ever the same !—just, good, great !—Oh, my heart ! my heart ! how proudly it beats. Blessed be God, who created me for this adored lover ! He must mean to astonish the world, by the prodigies of tenderness and charity, that such a love may produce. They do not yet know the sovereign might of free, happy, ardent love. Yes, Djalma ! on the day when our hands are joined together, what hymns of gratitude will ascend to heaven !—Ah ! they do not know the immense, the insatiable longing for joy and delight, which possesses two hearts like ours ; they do not know what rays of happiness stream from the celestial halo of such a flame !—Oh, yes ! I feel it. Many tears will be dried, many cold hearts warmed, at the divine fire of our love. And it will be by the benedictions of those we serve, that they will learn the intoxication of our rapture !'

To the dazzled eyes of Djalma, Adrienne appeared more and more an ideal being—partaking of the Divinity by her goodness, of the animal nature by passion—for, yielding to the intensity of excitement, Adrienne fixed upon Djalma looks that sparkled with love.

Then, almost beside himself, the Asiatic fell prostrate at the feet of the maiden, and exclaimed, in a supplicating voice : ' Mercy ! my courage fails me. Have pity on me ! do not talk thus. Oh, that day ! what years of my life would I not give to hasten it !'

' Silence ! no blasphemy. Do not your years belong to me ?'

' Adrienne ! you love me !'

The young lady did not answer ; but her half-veiled, burning glance, dealt the last blow to Djalma's reason. Seizing her hands in his own, he exclaimed, with a tremulous voice : 'That day, in which we shall mount to heaven, in which we shall be gods in happiness—why postpone it any longer ?'

' Because our love must be consecrated by the benediction of heaven.'

' Are we not free ?'

' Yes, yes, my love ; we are free. Let us be worthy of our liberty !'

'Adrienne ! mercy !'

' I ask you also to have mercy—to have mercy on the sacredness of our love. Do not profane it in its very flower. Believe my heart ! believe my presentiments ! to profane it would be to kill. Courage, my adored lover ! a few days longer—and then happiness—without regret, and without remorse !'

'And, until then, hell ! tortures without a name ! You do not, cannot know what I suffer when I leave your presence. Your image follows me, your breath burns me up ; I cannot sleep, but call on you every night with sighs and tears—just as I called on you, when I thought you did not love me—and yet I know you love me, I know you are mine. But to see you every day more beautiful, more adored—and every day to quit you more impassioned—oh ! you cannot tell——'

Djalma was unable to proceed. What he said of his devouring tortures, Adrienne had felt, perhaps even more intensely. Electrified by the passionate words of Djalma, so beautiful in his excitement, her courage failed, and she perceived that an irresistible languor was creeping over her. By a last chaste effort of the will, she rose abruptly, and hastening to the door, which communicated with Mother Bunch's chamber, she exclaimed : ' My sister ! help me !'

In another moment, Mdlle. de Cardoville, her face bathed in tears, clasped the young sempstress in her arms ; while Djalma knelt respectfully on the threshold he did not dare to pass.

CHAPTER LXI.

AMBITION.

A FEW days after the interview of Djalma and Adrienne, just described, Rodin was alone in his bed-chamber, in the house in the Rue de Vaugirard, walking up and down the room where he had so valiantly undergone the moxas of Dr. Baleinier. With his hands thrust into the hind-pockets of his great-coat, and his head bowed upon his breast, the Jesuit seemed to be reflecting profoundly, and his varying walk, now slow, now quick, betrayed the agitation of his mind.

' On the side of Rome,' said Rodin to himself, ' I am tranquil. All is going well. The abdication is as good as settled, and if I can pay them the price agreed, the Prince Cardinal can secure me a majority of nine voices in the conclave. Our General is with me ; the doubts of Cardinal Malipieri are at an end, or have found no echo. Yet I am not quite easy, with regard to the reported correspondence between Father d'Aigrigny and Malipieri. I

have not been able to intercept any of it. No matter ; that soldier's business is settled. A little patience and he will be wiped out.'

Here the pale lips were contracted by one of those frightful smiles, which
gave to Rodin's countenance so diabolical an expression.

After a pause, he resumed : ' The funeral of the freethinker, the philan-
thropist, the workman's friend, took place yesterday at St. Hérem. Francis
Hardy went off in a fit of ecstatic delirium. I had his donation, it is true ;
but this is more certain. Everything may be disputed in this world ; the
dead dispute nothing.'

Rodin remained in thought for some moments ; then he added, in a grave
tone : ' There remain this red-haired wench and her mulatto. This is the
twenty-seventh of May ; the first of June approaches, and these turtle-doves
still seem invulnerable. The princess thought she had hit upon a good
plan, and I should have thought so too. It was a good idea to mention the
discovery of Agricola Baudoin in the madcap's room, for it made the Indian
tiger roar with savage jealousy. Yes : but then the dove began to coo, and
hold out her pretty beak, and the foolish tiger sheathed his claws, and
rolled on the ground before her. It's a pity, for there was some sense in the
scheme.'

The walk of Rodin became more and more agitated. ' Nothing is more
extraordinary,' continued he, ' than the generative succession of ideas. In
comparing this red-haired jade to a dove (*colombe*), I could not help thinking of that infamous old woman, Sainte-Colombe, whom that big rascal
Jacques Dumoulin pays his court to, and whom the Abbé Corbinet will
finish, I hope, by turning to good account. I have often remarked, that,
as a poet may find an excellent rhyme by mere chance, so the germ of the
best ideas is sometimes found in a word, or in some absurd resemblance
like the present. That abominable hag, Sainte-Colombe, and the pretty
Adrienne de Cardoville, go as well together, as a ring would suit a cat, or a
necklace a fish. Well, there is nothing in it.'

Hardly had Rodin pronounced these words, than he started suddenly, and
his face shone with a fatal joy. Then it assumed an expression of meditative astonishment, as happens when chance reveals some unexpected discovery to the surprised and charmed inquirer after knowledge.

Soon, with raised head and sparkling eye, his hollow cheeks swelling with
joy and pride, Rodin folded his arms in triumph on his breast, and exclaimed : ' Oh ! how admirable and marvellous are these mysterious evolutions of the mind ; how incomprehensible is the chain of human thought,
which, starting from an absurd jingle of words, arrives at a splendid or
luminous idea ! Is it weakness ? or is it strength ? Strange—very strange !
I compare the red-haired girl to a dove—a colombe. That makes me think
of the hag, who traded in the bodies and souls of so many creatures. Vulgar
proverbs occur to me, about a ring and a cat, a fish and a necklace—and
suddenly, at the word NECKLACE, a new light dawns upon me. Yes : that
one word NECKLACE shall be to me a golden key, to open the portals of my
brain, so long foolishly closed.'

And, after again walking hastily up and down, Rodin continued : ' Yes, it is
worth attempting. The more I reflect upon it, the more feasible it appears. Only how to get at that wretch, Sainte-Colombe ? Well, there is
Jacques Dumoulin, and the other—where to find her ? That is the stumbling-
block. I must not shout before I am out of the wood.'

Rodin began again to walk, biting his nails with an air of deep thought.
For some moments, such was the tension of his mind, large drops of sweat
stood on his yellow brow. He walked up and down, stopped, stamped with
his foot, now raised his eyes as if in search of an inspiration, and now scratched

his head violently with his left hand, whilst he continued to gnaw the nails of the right. Finally, from time to time, he uttered exclamations of rage, despondency, or hope, as by turns they took possession of his mind. If the cause of this monster's agitation had not been horrible, it would have been a curious and interesting spectacle, to watch the labours of that powerful brain—to follow, as it were, on that shifting countenance, the progress and development of the project, on which he was now concentrating all the resources of his strong intellect. At length, the work appeared to be near completion, for Rodin resumed : Yes, yes ! it is bold, hazardous—but then it is prompt, and the consequences may be incalculable. Who can foresee the effects of the explosion of a mine ?'

Then, yielding to a movement of enthusiasm, which was hardly natural to him, the Jesuit exclaimed, with rapture : 'Oh, the passions ! the passions ! what a magical instrument do they form, if you do but touch the keys with a light, skilful, and vigorous hand ! How beautiful too is the power of thought ! Talk of the acorn that becomes an oak, the seed that grows up to the corn—the seed takes months, the acorn centuries, to unfold its splendours—but here is a little word in eight letters, necklace—and this word, falling into my brain but a few minutes ago, has grown and grown till it has become larger than any oak. Yes, that word is the germ of an idea, that, like the oak, lifts itself up towards heaven, for the greater glory of the Lord —such as they call Him, and such as I would assert Him to be, should I attain—and I shall attain—for these miserable Renneponts will pass away like a shadow. And what matters it, after all, to the moral order I am reserved to guide, whether these people live or die ? What do such lives weigh in the balance of the great destinies of the world ? while this inheritance which I shall boldly fling into the scale, will lift me to a sphere, from which one commands many kings, many nations—let them say and make what noise they will. The idiots—the stupid idiots ! or rather, the kind, blessed, adorable idiots ! They think they have crushed us, when they say to us men of the church : " You take the spiritual, but we will keep the temporal !"—Oh, their conscience or their modesty inspires them well, when it bids them not meddle with spiritual things ! They abandon the spiritual ! they despise it, they will have nothing to do with it—oh, the venerable asses ! they do not see, that, even as they go straight to the mill, it is by the spiritual that we go straight to the temporal. As if the mind did not govern the body ! They leave us the spiritual—that is, command of the conscience, soul, heart, and judgment—the spiritual—that is, the distribution of heaven's rewards, and punishments, and pardons—without check, without control, in the secrecy of the confessional—and that dolt, the temporal, has nothing but brute matter for his portion, and yet rubs his paunch for joy. Only, from time to time, he perceives, too late, that, if he has the body, we have the soul, and that the soul governs the body, and so the body ends by coming with us also—to the great surprise of Master Temporal, who stands staring with his hands on his paunch, and says : " Dear me ! is it possible ?"——'

Then, with a laugh of savage contempt, Rodin began to walk with great strides, and thus continued : 'Oh ! let me reach it—let me but reach the place of Sixtus V.—and the world shall see (one day, when it awakes) what it is to have the spiritual power in hands like mine—in the hands of a priest, who, for fifty years, has lived hardly, frugally, chastely, and who, were he pope, would continue to live hardly, frugally, chastely !'

Rodin became terrible, as he spoke thus. All the sanguinary sacrilegious, execrable ambition of the worst popes seemed written in fiery characters on the brow of this son of Ignatius. A morbid desire of rule seemed to stir up the Jesuit's impure blood ; he was bathed in a burning sweat, and a kind of nauseous vapour spread itself round about him. Suddenly, the noise of a travelling-carriage, which entered the courtyard of the house, attracted his attention. Regretting his momentary excitement, he drew from his pocket his dirty white and red cotton handkerchief, and dipping it in a glass of water, he applied it to his cheeks and temples, while he approached the window, to look through the half-open blinds at the traveller who had just arrived. The projection of a portico, over the door at which the carriage had stopped, intercepted Rodin's view.

'No matter,' said he, recovering his coolness : 'I shall know presently who is there. I must write at once to Jacques Dumoulin, to come hither immediately. He served me well, with regard to that little slut in the Rue Clovis, who made my hair stand on end with her infernal Béranger. This time, Dumoulin may serve me again. I have him in my clutches, and he will obey me.'

Rodin sat down to his desk, and wrote. A few seconds later, some one knocked at the door, which was double locked, quite contrary to the rules of the order. But, sure of his own influence and importance, Rodin, who had obtained from the General permission to be rid for a time of the inconvenient company of a socius, often took upon himself to break through a number of the rules. A servant entered, and delivered a letter to Rodin. Before opening it, the latter said to the man : 'What carriage is that which just arrived ?'

'It comes from Rome, father,' answered the servant, bowing.

'From Rome !' said Rodin, hastily ; and, in spite of himself, a vague uneasiness was expressed in his countenance. But, still holding the letter in his hands, he added : 'Who comes in the carriage ?'

'A reverend father of our blessed company.' Notwithstanding his ardent curiosity, for he knew that a reverend father, travelling post, is always charged with some important mission, Rodin asked no more questions on the subject, but, said, as he pointed to the paper in his hand : 'Whence comes this letter ?'

'From our house at St. Hérem, father.' Rodin looked more attentively at the writing, and recognised the hand of Father d'Aigrigny, who had been commissioned to attend M. Hardy in his last moments. The letter ran as follows :

'I send a despatch to inform your reverence of a fact which is perhaps more singular than important. After the funeral of M. Francis Hardy, the coffin, which contained his remains, had been provisionally deposited in a vault beneath our chapel, until it could be removed to the cemetery of the neighbouring town. This morning, when our people went down into the vault, to make the necessary preparations for the removal of the body—the coffin had disappeared.''

'That is strange, indeed,' said Rodin with a start. Then he continued to read :

'All search has hitherto been vain, to discover the authors of the sacrilegious deed. The chapel being, as you know, at a distance from the house, they were able to effect an entry without disturbing us. We have found traces of a four-wheeled carriage on the damp ground in the neighbourhood ; but, at some little distance from the chapel, these marks are lost in the sand, and it has been impossible to follow them any farther.''

'Who can have carried away this body ?' said Rodin, with a thoughtful air. 'Who could have any interest in doing so ?'

He continued to read :

'Luckily, the certificate of death is quite correct. I sent for a doctor from Etampes, to prove the disease, and no question can be raised on that point. The donation is therefore good and valid in every respect, but I think it best to inform your reverence of what has happened, that you may take measures accordingly, etc., etc.'

After a moment's reflection, Rodin said to himself: 'D'Aigrigny is right in his remark; it is more singular than important. Still, it makes one think. We must have an eye to this affair.'

Turning towards the servant, who had brought him the letter, Rodin gave him the note he had just written to Ninny Moulin, and said to him: 'Let this letter be taken instantly to its address, and let the bearer wait for an answer.'

'Yes, father.' At the moment the servant left the room, a reverend father entered, and said to Rodin, 'Father Caboccini of Rome has just arrived, with a mission from our General to your reverence.'

At these words, Rodin's blood ran cold, but he maintained his immovable calmness, and said simply, 'Where is Father Caboccini?'

'In the next room, father.'

'Beg him to walk in, and leave us,' said the other.

A second after, Father Caboccini of Rome entered the room, and was left alone with Rodin.

CHAPTER LXII.

TO A SOCIUS, A SOCIUS AND A HALF.

THE Reverend Father Caboccini, the Roman Jesuit who now came to visit Rodin, was a short man of about thirty years of age, plump, in good condition, and with an abdomen that swelled out his black cassock. The good little father was blind with one eye, but his remaining organ of vision sparkled with vivacity. His rosy countenance was gay, smiling, joyous, splendidly crowned with thick chestnut hair, which curled like a wax doll's. His address was cordial to familiarity, and his expansive and petulant manners harmonised well with his general appearance. In a second, Rodin had taken his measure of the Italian emissary; and as he knew the practice of his Company, and the ways of Rome, he felt by no means comfortable at sight of this jolly little father, with such affable manners. He would have less feared some tall, bony priest, with austere and sepulchral countenance, for he knew that the Company loves to deceive by the outward appearance of its agents; and, if Rodin guessed rightly, the cordial address of this personage would rather tend to show that he was charged with some fatal mission.

Suspicious, attentive, with eye and mind on the watch, like an old wolf expecting an attack, Rodin advanced, as usual, slowly and tortuously towards the little man, so as to have time to examine him thoroughly, and penetrate beneath his jovial outside. But the Roman left him no space for that purpose. In his impetuous affection, he threw himself right on the neck of Rodin, pressed him in his arms with an effusion of tenderness, and kissed him over and over again upon both cheeks, so loudly and plentifully that the echo resounded through the apartment. In his life Rodin had never been so treated. More and more uneasy at the treachery which must needs lurk under such warm embraces, and irritated by his own evil presentiments, the French Jesuit did all he could to extricate himself from the Roman's exaggerated tokens of tenderness. But the latter kept his hold; his arms, though short, were vigorous, and Rodin was kissed over and over again, till the little one-eyed man was quite out of breath. It is hardly necessary to state that these embraces were accompanied by the most friendly, affec-

tionate, and fraternal exclamations—all in tolerably good French, but with
a strong Italian accent, which we must beg the reader to supply for himself,
after we have given a single specimen. It will perhaps be remembered that,
fully aware of the danger he might possibly incur by his ambitious machinations, and knowing from history that the use of poison had often been
considered at Rome as a state necessity, Rodin, on being suddenly attacked
with the cholera, had exclaimed, with a furious glance at Cardinal Malipieri,
' I am poisoned !'

The same apprehensions occurred involuntarily to the Jesuit's mind as he
tried, by useless efforts, to escape from the embraces of the Italian emissary;
and he could not help muttering to himself, ' This one-eyed fellow is a great
deal too fond. I hope there is no poison under his Judas-kisses.' At last,
little Father Caboccini, being quite out of breath, was obliged to relinquish
his hold on Rodin's neck, who, readjusting his dirty collar, and his old
cravat and waistcoat, somewhat in disorder in consequence of this hurricane
of caresses, said in a gruff tone, ' Your humble servant, father, but you need
not kiss quite so hard.'

Without making any answer to this reproach, the little father riveted his
one eye upon Rodin with an expression of enthusiasm, and exclaimed,
whilst he accompanied his words with petulant gestures, ' At lazt I zee te
zuperb light of our zacred Company, and can zalute him from my heart—
vonse more, vonse more.'

As the little father had already recovered his breath, and was about to
rush once again into Rodin's arms the latter stepped back hastily, and held
out his arm to keep him off, saying, in allusion to the illogical metaphor employed by Father Caboccini, ' First of all, father, one does not embrace a
light—and then I am not a light—I am a humble and obscure labourer in
the Lord's vineyard.'

The Roman replied with enthusiasm (we shall henceforth translate his
gibberish), ' You are right, father, we cannot embrace a light, but we can
prostrate ourselves before it, and admire its dazzling brightness.'

So saying, Caboccini was about to suit the action to the word, and to
prostrate himself before Rodin, had not the latter prevented this mode of
adulation by seizing the Roman by the arm and exclaiming, ' This is mere
idolatry, father. Pass over my qualities, and tell me what is the object of
your journey.'

' The object, my dear father, fills me with joy and happiness. I have endeavoured to show you my affection by my caresses, for my heart is overflowing. I have hardly been able to restrain myself during my journey
hither, for my heart rushed to meet you. The object transports, delights,
enchants me——'

' But what enchants you ?' cried Rodin, exasperated by these Italian ex-
aggerations. ' What is the object ?'

' This rescript of our very reverend and excellent General will inform you,
my dear father.'

Caboccini drew from his pocket-book a folded paper, with three seals,
which he kissed respectfully, and delivered to Rodin, who himself kissed it
in his turn, and opened it with visible anxiety. While he read it, the countenance of the Jesuit remained impassible, but the pulsations of the arteries
on his temples announced his internal agitation. Yet he put the letter
coolly into his pocket, and looking at the Roman, said to him, ' Be it as our
excellent General has commanded !'

' Then, father,' cried Caboccini, with a new effusion of tenderness and
admiration, ' I shall be the shadow of your light, and, in fact, your second
self. I shall have the happiness of being always with you, day and night,

and of acting as your socius, since, after having allowed you to be without one for some time, according to your wish, and for the interest of our blessed Company, our excellent General now thinks fit to send me from Rome, to fill that post about your person—an unexpected, an immense favour, which fills me with gratitude to our General, and with love to you, my dear, my excellent father !'

' It is well played,' thought Rodin ; ' but I am not so soft, and 'tis only among the blind that your cyclops are kings !'

    ✿   ✿   ✿   ✿   ✿   ✿

The evening of the day in which this scene took place between the Jesuit and his new socius, Ninny Moulin, after receiving in presence of Caboccini the instructions of Rodin, went straight to Madame de la Sainte-Colombe's.

This woman had made her fortune at the time of the allies taking Paris, by keeping one of those ' pretty milliner's-shops,' whose ' pink bonnets ' have run into a proverb not extinct in these days when bonnets are not known. Ninny Moulin had no better well to draw inspiration from when, as now, he had to find out, as per Rodin's order, a girl of an age and appearance which, singularly enough, were closely resembling those of Mdlle. de Cardoville.

No doubt of Ninny Moulin's success in this mission, for the next morning Rodin, whose countenance wore a triumphant expression, put with his own hand a letter into the post.

This letter was addressed :

To M. Agricola Baudoin,
' No. 2, Rue Brise-Miche,
' Paris.'

CHAPTER LXII.

FARINGHEA'S AFFECTION.

It will, perhaps, be remembered that Djalma, when he heard for the first time that he was beloved by Adrienne, had, in the fulness of his joy, spoken thus to Faringhea, whose treachery he had just discovered, ' You leagued with my enemies, and I had done you no harm. You are wicked, because you are no doubt unhappy. I will strive to make you happy, so that you may be good. Would you have gold?—you shall have it. Would you have a friend ?—though you are a slave, a king's son offers you his friendship.'

Faringhea had refused the gold, and appeared to accept the friendship of the son of Kadja-sing. Endowed with remarkable intelligence, and extraordinary power of dissimulation, the half-breed had easily persuaded the prince of the sincerity of his repentance, and obtained credit for his gratitude and attachment from so confiding and generous a character. Besides, what motives could Djalma have to suspect the slave, now become his friend ? Certain of the love of Mdlle. de Cardoville, with whom he passed a portion of every day, her salutary influence would have guarded him against any dangerous counsels or calumnies of the half-caste, a faithful and secret instrument of Rodin, and attached by him to the Company. But Faringhea, whose tact was amazing, did not act so lightly ; he never spoke to the prince of Mdlle. de Cardoville, and waited unobtrusively for the confidential communications into which Djalma was sometimes hurried by his excessive joy. A few days after the interview last described between Adrienne and Djalma, and on the morrow of the day when Rodin, certain of the success of Ninny Moulin's mission to Sainte-Colombe, had himself put a letter in the post to the address of Agricola Baudoin, the half-caste, who for some time had appeared oppressed with a violent grief, seemed to get so much worse, that the prince, struck with the desponding air of the man, asked him kindly and repeatedly the cause of his sorrow. But Faringhea, while he gratefully thanked the prince for the interest he took in him, maintained the most absolute silence and reserve on the subject of his grief.

These preliminaries will enable the reader to understand the following scene, which took place about noon in the house in the Rue de Clichy occupied by the Hindoo. Contrary to his habit, Djalma had not passed that morning with Adrienne. He had been informed the evening before, by the young lady, that she must ask of him the sacrifice of this whole day, to take the necessary measures to make their marriage sacred and acceptable in the eyes of the world, and yet free from the restrictions which she and Djalma disapproved. As for the means to be employed by Mdlle. de Cardoville to attain this end, and the name of the pure and honourable person who was to consecrate their union, these were secrets which, not belonging exclusively to the young lady, could not yet be communicated to Djalma. To the Indian, so long accustomed to devote every instant to Adrienne, this day seemed interminable. By turns a prey to the most burning agitation, and to a kind of stupor, in which he plunged himself to escape from the thoughts that caused his tortures, Djalma lay stretched upon a divan, with his face buried in his hands, as if to shut out the view of a too enchanting vision. Suddenly, without knocking at the door, as usual, Faringhea entered the prince's apartment.

At the noise the half-caste made in entering, Djalma started, raised his head, and looked round him with surprise ; but, on seeing the pale agitated countenance of the slave, he rose hastily, and advancing towards him, exclaimed : 'What is the matter, Faringhea ?'

After a moment's silence, and as if struggling with a painful feeling of hesitation, Faringhea threw himself at the feet of Djalma, and murmured in a weak, despairing, almost supplicating voice : ' I am very miserable. Pity me, my good lord !'

The tone was so touching, the grief under which the half-breed suffered seemed to give to his features, generally fixed and hard as bronze, such a heart-rending expression, that Djalma was deeply affected, and, bending to raise him from the ground, said to him, in a kindly voice : ' Speak to me ! Confidence appeases the torments of the heart. Trust me, friend—for my angel herself said to me, that happy love cannot bear to see tears about him.'

' But unhappy love, miserable love, betrayed love—weeps tears of blood,' replied Faringhea, with painful dejection.——'Of what love dost thou speak? asked Djalma, in surprise.

' I speak of my love,' answered the half-caste, with a gloomy air.—— ' Of *your* love ?' said Djalma, more and more astonished ; not that the half-caste, still young, and with a countenance of sombre beauty, appeared to him incapable of inspiring or feeling the tender passion, but that, until now, he had never imagined him capable of conceiving so deep a sorrow.

' My lord,' resumed the half-caste, ' you told me, that misfortune had made me wicked, and that happiness would make me good. In those words, I saw a presentiment, and a noble love entered my heart, at the moment when hatred and treachery departed from it. I, the half-savage, found a woman, beautiful and young, to respond to my passion. At least I thought so. But I had betrayed you, my lord, and there is no happiness for a

traitor, even though he repent. In my turn, I have been shamefully betrayed.'

Then, seeing the surprise of the prince, the half-caste added, as if overwhelmed with confusion : ' Do not mock me, my lord ! The most frightful
tortures would not have wrung this confession from me ; but you, the son of
a king, deigned to call the poor slave your friend !'

' And your friend thanks you for the confidence,' answered Djalma. ' Far
from mocking, he will console you. Mock you ! do you think it possible ?'

' Betrayed love merits contempt and insult,' said Faringhea, bitterly.
' Even cowards may point at one with scorn—for, in this country, the sight
of the man deceived in what is dearest to his soul, the very life-blood of his
life, only makes people shrug their shoulders and laugh.'

' But are you certain of this treachery ?' said Djalma, mildly. Then he
added, with a visible hesitation, that proved the goodness of his heart :
' Listen to me, and forgive me for speaking of the past ! It will only be
another proof, that I cherish no evil memories, and that I fully believe in
your repentance and affection. Remember, that I also once thought, that
she, who is the angel of my life, did not love me—and yet it was false.
Who tells you, that you are not, like me, deceived by false appearances ?'

' Alas, my lord ! could I only believe so ! But I dare not hope it. My
brain wanders uncertain, I cannot come to any resolution, and therefore I
have recourse to you.'

' But what causes your suspicions ?'——' Her coldness, which sometimes
succeeds to apparent tenderness. The refusals she gives me in the name of
duty. Yes,' added the half-caste, after a moment's silence, ' she reasons
about her love—a proof, that she has never loved me, or that she loves me
no more.'

' On the contrary, she perhaps loves you all the more, that she takes into
consideration the interest and the dignity of her love.'

' That is what they all say,' replied the half-caste, with bitter irony, as he
fixed a penetrating look on Djalma ; ' thus speak all those who love weakly,
coldly ; but those who love valiantly, never show these insulting suspicions.
For them, a word from the man they adore is a command ; they do not
haggle and bargain, for the cruel pleasure of exciting the passion of their
lover to madness, and so ruling him more surely. No, what their lover asks
of them, were it to cost life and honour, they would grant it without hesitation—because, with them, the will of the man they love is above every other
consideration, divine and human. But those crafty women, whose pride it
is to tame and conquer man—who take delight in irritating his passion, and
sometimes appear on the point of yielding to it—are demons, who rejoice in
the tears and torments of the wretch, that loves them with the miserable
weakness of a child. While we expire with love at their feet, the perfidious
creatures are calculating the effects of their refusals, and seeing how far they
can go, without quite driving their victim to despair. Oh ! how cold and
cowardly are they, compared to the valiant, true-hearted women, who say
to the men of their choice : " Let me be thine to-day—and to-morrow, come
shame, despair, and death—it matters little ! Be happy ! my life is not worth
one tear of thine !"——'

Djalma's brow had darkened, as he listened. Having kept inviolable the
secret of the various incidents of his passion for Mdlle. de Cardoville, he
could not but see in these words a quite involuntary allusion to the delays
and refusals of Adrienne. And yet Djalma suffered a moment in his pride,
at the thought of considerations and duties, that a woman holds dearer than
her love. But this bitter and painful thought was soon effaced from the
oriental's mind, thanks to the beneficent influence of the remembrance of

Adrienne. His brow again cleared, and he answered the half-caste, who was watching him attentively with a sidelong glance : ' You are deluded by grief. If you have no other reason to doubt her you love, than these refusals and vague suspicions, be satisfied ! You are perhaps loved better than you can imagine.'

' Alas ! would it were so, my lord !' replied the half-caste, dejectedly, as if he had been deeply touched by the words of Djalma. ' Yet I say to myself : There is for this woman something stronger than her love—delicacy, dignity, honour, what you will—but she does not love me enough to sacrifice for me this something !'

' Friend, you are deceived,' answered Djalma, mildly, though the words affected him with a painful impression. ' The greater the love of a woman, the more it should be chaste and noble. It is love itself that awakens this delicacy and these scruples. He rules, instead of being ruled.'

' That is true,' replied the half-caste, with bitter irony. ' Love so rules me, that this woman bids me love in her own fashion, and I have only to submit.'

Pausing suddenly, Faringhea hid his face in his hands, and heaved a deep-drawn sigh. His features expressed a mixture of hate, rage, and despair, at once so terrible and so painful, that Djalma, more and more affected, exclaimed, as he seized the other's hand : ' Calm this fury, and listen to the voice of friendship ! It will disperse this evil influence. Speak to me !'

' No, no ! it is too dreadful !'——' Speak, I bid thee.'

' No ! leave the wretch to his despair !'——' Do you think me capable of that ?' said Djalma, with a mixture of mildness and dignity, which seemed to make an impression on the half-caste.

' Alas !' replied he, hesitating ; ' do you wish to hear more, my lord ?'

' I wish to hear all.'

' Well, then ! I have not told you all—for, at the moment of making this confession, shame and the fear of ridicule kept me back. You asked me what reason I had to believe myself betrayed. I spoke to you of vague suspicions, refusals, coldness. That is not all—this evening——'

' Go on !'——' This evening—she made an appointment—with a man that she prefers to me.'

' Who told you so ?'——' A stranger who pitied my blindness.'

' And suppose the man deceives you—or deceives himself ?'——' He has offered me proofs of what he advances.'

' What proofs ?'——' He will enable me this evening to witness the interview. " It may be," said he, " that this appointment may have no guilt in it, notwithstanding appearances to the contrary. Judge for yourself, have courage, and your cruel indecision will be at an end." '

' And what did you answer ?'——' Nothing, my lord. My head wandered as it does now, and I came to you for advice.'

Then making a gesture of despair, he proceeded with a savage laugh : ' Advice ? It is from the blade of my kandjiar that I should ask counsel ! It would answer : " Blood ! blood !" '

Faringhea grasped convulsively the long dagger attached to his girdle. There is a sort of contagion in certain forms of passion. At sight of Faringhea's countenance, agitated by jealous fury, Djalma shuddered—for he remembered the fit of insane rage, with which he had been possessed, when the Princess de Saint-Dizier had defied Adrienne to contradict her, as to the discovery of Agricola Baudoin in her bedchamber. But then, reassured by the lady's proud and noble bearing, Djalma had soon learned to despise the horrible calumny, which Adrienne had not even thought worthy of an answer. Still, two or three times, as the lightning will flash suddenly across the clearest sky, the remembrance of that shameful accusation had crossed the prince's mind, like a streak of fire, but had almost instantly vanished, in the serenity and happiness of his ineffable confidence in Adrienne's heart. These memories, however, whilst they saddened the mind of Djalma, only made him more compassionate with regard to Faringhea, than he might have been without this strange coincidence between the position of the half-caste and his own. Knowing, by his own experience, to what madness a blind fury may be carried, and wishing to tame the half-caste by affectionate kindness, Djalma said to him in a grave and mild tone : ' I offered you my friendship. I will now act towards you as a friend.'

But Faringhea, seemingly a prey to a dull and mute frenzy, stood with fixed and haggard eyes, as though he did not hear Djalma.

The latter laid his hand on his shoulder, and resumed : ' Faringhea, listen to me !'——' My lord,' said the half-caste, starting abruptly, as from a dream, ' forgive me—but——'

' In the anguish occasioned by these cruel suspicions, it is not of your kandjiar that you must take counsel—but of your friend.'——' My lord——'

' To this interview, which will prove the innocence or the treachery of your beloved, you will do well to go.'——' Oh, yes !' said the half-caste, in a hollow voice, and with a bitter smile ; ' I shall be there.'

' But you must not go alone.'——' What do you mean, my lord ?' cried the half-caste. ' Who will accompany me ?'

' I will.'——' You, my lord ?'

' Yes—perhaps; to save you from a crime—for I know how blind and un-just is the earliest outburst of rage.'——' But that transport gives us revenge !' cried the half-caste, with a cruel smile.

' Faringhea, this day is all my own. I shall not leave you,' said the prince, resolutely. ' Either you shall not go to this interview, or I will accompany you.'

The half-caste appeared conquered by this generous perseverance. He fell at the feet of Djalma, pressed the prince's hand respectfully to his fore-head and to his lips, and said : ' My lord, be generous to the end ! forgive me !'——' For what should I forgive you ?'

' Before I spoke to you, I had the audacity to think of asking for what you have just freely offered. Not knowing to what extent my fury might carry me, I had thought of asking you this favour, which you would not perhaps grant to an equal, but I did not dare to do it. I shrunk even from the avowal of the treachery I have cause to fear, and I came only to tell you of my misery—because to you alone in all the world I could tell it.'

It is impossible to describe the almost candid simplicity, with which the half-breed pronounced these words, and the soft tones, mingled with tears, which had succeeded his savage fury. Deeply affected, Djalma raised him from the ground, and said : ' You were entitled to ask of me a mark of friendship. I am happy in having forestalled you. Courage ! be of good cheer ! I will accompany you to this interview, and, if my hopes do not deceive me, you will find you have been deluded by false appearances.'

 ✿   ✿   ✿   ✿   ✿   ✿

When the night was come, the half-breed and Djalma, wrapped in their cloaks, got into a hackney-coach. Faringhea ordered the coachman to drive to the house inhabited by Sainte-Colombe.

CHAPTER LXIV.

AN EVENING AT SAINTE-COLOMBE'S.

LEAVING Djalma and Faringhea in the coach, on their way, a few words are indispensable before continuing this scene. Ninny Moulin, ignorant of the real object of the step he took at the instigation of Rodin, had, on the evening before, according to orders received from the latter, offered a considerable sum to Sainte-Colombe, to obtain from that creature (still singularly rapacious) the use of her apartments for a whole day. Sainte-Colombe, having accepted this proposition, too advantageous to be refused, had set out that morning with her servants, to whom she wished, she said, in return for their good services, to give a day's pleasure in the country. Master of the house, Rodin, in a black wig, blue spectacles, and a cloak, and with his mouth and chin buried in a worsted comforter—in a word, perfectly disguised—had gone that morning to take a look at the apartments, and to give his instructions to the half-caste. The latter, in two hours from the departure of the Jesuit, had, thanks to his address and intelligence, completed the most important preparations, and returned in haste to Djalma, to play with detestable hypocrisy the scene at which we have just been present.

During the ride from the Rue de Clichy to the Rue de Richelieu, Faringhea appeared plunged in a mournful reverie. Suddenly, he said to Djalma in a quick tone : ' My lord, if I am betrayed, I must have vengeance.'

' Contempt is a terrible revenge,' answered Djalma.

' No, no,' replied the half-caste, with an accent of repressed rage. ' It is not enough. The nearer the moment approaches, the more I feel I must have blood.'

' Listen to me——'——' My lord, have pity on me ! I was a coward to draw back from my revenge. Let me leave you, my lord ! I will go alone to this interview.'

So saying, Faringhea made a movement, as if he would spring from the carriage.

Djalma held him by the arm, and said : ' Remain ! I will not leave you. If you are betrayed, you shall not shed blood. Contempt will avenge and friendship will console you.'

' No, no, my lord ; I am resolved. When I have killed—then I will kill myself,' cried the half-caste, with savage excitement. ' This kandjiar for the false ones !' added he, laying his hand on his dagger. ' The poison in the hilt for me.'

' Faringhea——'——' If I resist you, my lord, forgive me ! My destiny must be accomplished.'

Time pressed, and Djalma, despairing to calm the other's ferocious rage, resolved to have recourse to a stratagem.

After some minutes' silence, he said to Faringhea : ' I will not leave you. I will do all I can to save you from a crime. If I do not succeed, the blood you shed be on your own head. This hand shall never again be locked in yours.'

These words appeared to make a deep impression on Faringhea. He breathed a long sigh, and, bowing his head upon his breast, remained silent and full of thought. Djalma prepared, by the faint light of the lamps reflected in the interior of the coach, to throw himself suddenly on the half-caste, and disarm him. But the latter, who saw at a glance the intention of the prince, drew his kandjiar abruptly from his girdle, and holding it still in its sheath, said to the prince in a half-solemn, half-savage tone : ' This dagger, in a strong hand, is terrible ; and in this phial is one of the most subtle poisons of our country.'

He touched a spring, and the knob at the top of the hilt rose like a lid, discovering the mouth of a small crystal phial concealed in this murderous weapon.

'Two or three drops of this poison upon the lips,' resumed the half-caste, 'and death comes slowly and peacefully, in a few hours, and without pain. Only, for the first symptom, the nails turn blue. But he who emptied this phial at a draught would fall dead, as if struck by lightning.'

'Yes,' replied Djalma ; 'I know that our country produces such mysterious poisons. But why lay such stress on the murderous properties of this weapon ?'

'To show you, my lord, that this kandjiar would ensure the success and impunity of my vengeance. With the blade I could destroy, and by the poison escape from human justice. Well, my lord ! this kandjiar—take it —I give it up to you—I renounce my vengeance—rather than render myself unworthy to clasp again your hand !'

He presented the dagger to the prince, who, as pleased as surprised at this unexpected determination, hastily secured the terrible weapon beneath his own girdle, whilst the half-breed continued, in a voice of emotion : ' Keep this kandjiar, my lord—and when you have seen and heard all that we go to hear and see—you shall either give me the dagger to strike a wretch— or the poison, to die without striking. You shall command ; I will obey.'

Djalma was about to reply, when the coach stopped at the house inhabited by Sainte-Colombe. The prince and the half-caste, well enveloped in their mantles, entered a dark porch, and the door was closed after them. Faringhea exchanged a few words with the porter, and the latter gave him a key. The two orientals soon arrived at Sainte-Colombe's apartments, which had two doors opening upon the landing-place, besides a private entrance from the courtyard. As he put the key into the lock, Faringhea said to Djalma, in an agitated voice : ' Pity my weakness, my lord—but, at this terrible moment, I tremble and hesitate. It were perhaps better to doubt—or to forget !'

Then, as the prince was about to answer, the half-caste exclaimed : 'No ! we must have no cowardice !' and, opening the door precipitately, he entered, followed by Djalma.

When the door was again closed, the prince and the half-caste found themselves in a dark and narrow passage. ' Your hand, my lord—let me guide you—walk lightly,' said Faringhea, in a low whisper.

He extended his hand to the prince, who took hold of it, and they both advanced silently through the darkness. After leading Djalma some distance, and opening and closing several doors, the half-caste stopped abruptly, and, abandoning the hand which he had hitherto held, said to the prince : ' My lord, the decisive moment approaches ; let us wait here for a few seconds.'

A profound silence followed these words of the half-caste. The darkness was so complete, that Djalma could distinguish nothing. In about a minute, he heard Faringhea moving away from him ; and then a door was suddenly opened, and as abruptly closed and locked. This circumstance made Djalma somewhat uneasy. By a mechanical movement, he laid his hand upon his dagger, and advanced cautiously towards the side, where he supposed the door to be.

Suddenly, the half-caste's voice struck upon his ear, though it was impossible to guess whence it came. ' My lord,' it said, ' you told me, you were my friend. I act as a friend. If I have employed stratagem to bring you hither, it is because the blindness of your fatal passion would otherwise have prevented your accompanying me. The Princess de Saint-Dizier named to you Agricola Baudoin, the lover of Adrienne de Cardoville. Listen—look—judge !'

The voice ceased. It appeared to have issued from one corner of the room. Djalma, still in darkness, perceived too late into what a snare he had fallen, and trembled with rage—almost with alarm.

' Faringhea !' he exclaimed ; ' where am I ? where are you ? Open the door on your life ! I would leave this place instantly.'

Extending his arms, the prince advanced hastily several steps, but he only touched a tapestried wall ; he followed it, hoping to find the door, and he at length found it ; but it was locked, and resisted all his efforts. He continued his researches, and came to a fire-place with no fire in it, and to a second door, equally fast. In a few moments, he had thus made the circle of the room, and found himself again at the fire-place. The anxiety of the prince increased more and more. He called Faringhea, in a voice trembling with passion. There was no answer. Profound silence reigned without, and complete darkness within. Ere long, a perfumed vapour, of indescribable sweetness, but very subtle and penetrating, spread itself insensibly through the little room in which Djalma was. It might be, that the orifice of a tube, passing through one of the doors of the room, introduced this balmy current. At the height of angry and terrible thoughts, Djalma paid no attention to this odour—but soon the arteries of his temples began to beat violently, a burning heat seemed to circulate rapidly through his veins, he felt a sensation of pleasure, his resentment died gradually away, and a mild, ineffable torpor crept over him, without his being fully conscious of the mental transformation that was taking place. Yet, by a last effort of the wavering will, Djalma advanced once more to try and open one of the doors ; he found it indeed, but at this place the vapour was so strong, that its action redoubled, and, unable to move a step further, Djalma was obliged to support himself by leaning against the wall.*

Then a strange thing happened. A faint light spread itself gradually through an adjoining apartment, and Djalma now perceived, for the first time, the existence of a little round window, in the wall of the room in which he was. On the side of the prince, this opening was protected by a slight but strong railing, which hardly intercepted the view. On the other side a thick piece of plate-glass was fixed at the distance of two or three inches from the railing in question. The room, which Djalma saw through this window, and through which the faint light was now gradually spreading, was richly furnished. Between two windows, hung with crimson silk curtains, stood a kind of wardrobe, with a looking-glass front ; opposite the fireplace, in which glowed the burning coals, was a long, wide divan, furnished with cushions.

In another second a woman entered this apartment. Her face and figure were invisible, being wrapped in a long, hooded mantle, of peculiar form, and a dark colour. The sight of this mantle made Djalma start. To the pleasure he at first felt succeeded a feverish anxiety, like the growing fumes of intoxication. There was that strange buzzing in his ears which we experience when we plunge into deep waters. It was in a kind of delirium that Djalma looked on at what was passing in the next room. The woman who had just appeared entered with caution, almost with fear. Drawing aside one of the window curtains, she glanced through the closed blinds into the

* See the strange effect of haskeish. To the effect of this is attributed the kind of hallucination which seized on those unhappy persons, whom the Prince of the Assassins (the Old Man of the Mountain) used as the instruments of his vengeance.

street. Then she returned slowly to the fire-place, where she stood for a moment pensive, still carefully enveloped in her mantle. Completely yielding to the influence of the vapour, which deprived him of his presence of mind—forgetting Faringhea, and all the circumstances that had accompanied his arrival at this house—Djalma concentrated all the powers of his attention on the spectacle before him, at which he seemed to be present as in a dream.

Suddenly Djalma saw the woman leave the fire-place and advance towards the looking-glass. Turning her face towards it, she allowed the mantle to glide down to her feet. Djalma was thunderstruck. He saw the face of Adrienne de Cardoville. Yes, Adrienne, as he had seen her the night before, attired as during her interview with the Princess de Saint-Dizier—the light green dress, the rose-coloured ribbons, the white bead ornaments. A network of white beads concealed her back-hair, and harmonised admirably with the shining gold of her ringlets. Finally, as far as the Hindoo could judge through the railing and the thick glass, and in the faint light, it was the figure of Adrienne, with her marble shoulders and swan-like neck, so proud and so graceful. In a word, he could not, he did not doubt that it was Adrienne de Cardoville. Djalma was bathed in a burning dew, his dizzy excitement increased, and, with bloodshot eye and heaving bosom, he remained motionless, gazing almost without the power of thought. The young lady, with her back still turned towards Djalma, arranged her hair with graceful art, took off the network which formed her head-dress, placed it on the chimney-piece, and began to unfasten her gown; then, withdrawing from the looking-glass, she disappeared for an instant from Djalma's view.

'She is expecting Agricola Baudoin, her lover,' said a voice, which seemed to proceed from the wall of the dark room in which Djalma was.

Notwithstanding his bewilderment, these terrible words, 'She is expecting Agricola Baudoin, her lover,' passed like a stream of fire through the brain and heart of the prince. A cloud of blood came over his eyes, he uttered a hollow groan, which the thickness of the glass prevented from being heard in the next room, and broke his nails in attempting to tear down the iron railing before the window.

Having reached this paroxysm of delirious rage, Djalma saw the uncertain light grow still fainter, as if it had been discreetly obscured, and, through the vapoury shadow that hung before him, he perceived the young lady returning, clad in a long white dressing-gown, and with her golden curls floating over her naked arms and shoulders. She advanced cautiously in the direction of a door which was hid from Djalma's view. At this moment, one of the doors of the apartment in which the prince was concealed was gently opened by an invisible hand. Djalma noticed it by the click of the lock, and by the current of fresh air which steamed upon his face, for he could see nothing. This door, left open for Djalma, like that in the next room, to which the young lady had drawn near, led to a sort of antechamber communicating with the stairs, which some one now rapidly ascended, and, stopping short, knocked twice at the outer door.

'Here comes Agricola Baudoin. Look and listen!' said the same voice that the prince had already heard.

Mad, intoxicated, but with the fixed idea and reckless determination of a madman or a drunkard, Djalma drew the dagger which Faringhea had left in his possession, and stood in motionless expectation. Hardly were the two knocks heard before the young lady quitted the apartment, from which streamed a faint ray of light, ran to the door of the staircase, so that some faint glimmer reached the place where Djalma stood watching, his dagger in his hand. He saw the young lady pass across the antechamber, and approach the door of the staircase, where she said in a whisper : 'Who is there ?'

'It is I—Agricola Baudoin,' answered, from without, a manly voice.

What followed was rapid as lightning, and must be conceived rather than described. Hardly had the young lady drawn the bolt of the door, hardly had Agricola Baudoin stepped across the threshold, than Djalma, with the bound of a tiger, stabbed as it were at once, so rapid were the strokes, both the young lady, who fell dead on the floor, and Agricola, who sank, dangerously wounded, by the side of the unfortunate victim. This scene of murder, rapid as thought, took place in the midst of a half obscurity. Suddenly the faint light from the chamber was completely extinguished, and a second after, Djalma felt his arm seized in the darkness by an iron grasp, and the voice of Faringhea whispered : 'You are avenged. Come ; we can secure our retreat.' Inert, stupefied at what he had done, Djalma offered no resistance, and let himself be dragged by the half-caste into the inner apartment, from which there was another way out.

*   *   *   *   *   *

When Rodin had exclaimed, in his admiration of the generative power of thought, that the word NECKLACE had been the germ of the infernal project he then contemplated, it was, that chance had brought to his mind the remembrance of the too famous affair of the diamond necklace, in which a woman, thanks to her vague resemblance to Queen Marie Antoinette, being dressed like that princess, and favoured by the uncertainty of a twilight, had played so skilfully the part of her unfortunate sovereign, as to make the Cardinal Prince de Rohan, though familiar with the court, the complete dupe of the illusion. Having once determined on his execrable design, Rodin had sent Jacques Dumoulin to Sainte-Colombe, without telling him the real object of his mission, to ask this experienced woman to procure a fine young girl, tall, and with red hair. Once found, a costume exactly resembling that worn by Adrienne, and of which the Princess de Saint-Dizier gave the description to Rodin (though herself ignorant of this new plot), was to complete the deception. The rest is known, or may be guessed. The unfortunate girl, who acted as Adrienne's double, believed she was only aiding in a jest. As for Agricola, he had received a letter, in which he was invited to a meeting that might be of the greatest importance to Mdlle. de Cardoville.

———

CHAPTER LXV.

THE NUPTIAL BED.

THE mild light of a circular lamp of oriental alabaster, suspended from the ceiling by three silver chains, spreads a faint lustre through the bedchamber of Adrienne de Cardoville. The large ivory bedstead, inlaid with mother-of-pearl, is not at present occupied, and almost disappears beneath snowy curtains of lace and muslin, transparent and vapoury as clouds. On the white marble mantelpiece, from beneath which the fire throws ruddy beams on the ermine carpet, is the usual basket filled with a bush of red camellias, in the midst of their shining green leaves. A pleasant aromatic odour, rising from a warm and perfumed bath in the next room, penetrates every corner of the bedchamber. All without is calm and silent. It is hardly eleven o'clock. The ivory door, opposite to that which leads to the bath-room, opens slowly. Djalma appears. Two hours have elapsed since he committed a double murder, and believed that he had killed Adrienne in a fit of jealous fury.

The servants of Mdlle. de Cardoville, accustomed to Djalma's daily visits, no longer announced his arrival, and admitted him without difficulty, having received no orders to the contrary from their mistress. He had never before entered the bedchamber, but, knowing that the apartment the lady occupied was on the first floor of the house, he had easily found it. As he entered that virgin sanctuary, his countenance was pretty calm, so well did he control his feelings ; only a slight paleness tarnished the brilliant amber of his complexion. He wore that day a robe of purple cashmere, striped with silver—a colour which did not show the stains of blood upon it. Djalma closed the door after him, and tore off his white turban, for it seemed to him as if a band of hot iron encircled his brow. His dark hair streamed around his handsome face. He crossed his arms upon his bosom, and looked slowly about him. When his eyes rested on Adrienne's bed, he started suddenly, and his cheek grew purple. Then he drew his hand across his brow, hung down his head, and remained standing for some moments in a dream, motionless as a statue.

After a mournful silence of a few seconds' duration, Djalma fell upon his knees, and raised his eyes to heaven. The Asiatic's countenance was bathed in tears, and no longer expressed any violent passion. On his features was no longer the stamp of hate, or despair, or the ferocious joy of vengeance gratified. It was rather the expression of a grief at once simple and immense. For several minutes he was almost choked with sobs, and the tears ran freely down his cheeks.

'Dead ! dead !' he murmured, in a half-stifled voice. 'She, who this morning slept so peacefully in this chamber ! And I have killed her. Now that she is dead, what is her treachery to me ? I should not have killed her for that. She had betrayed me ; she loved the man whom I slew—she loved him ! Alas ! I could not hope to gain the preference,' added he, with a touching mixture of resignation and remorse ; 'I, poor, untaught youth— how could I merit her love ? It was my fault that she did not love me ; but, always generous, she concealed from me her indifference, that she might not make me too unhappy—and for that I killed her. What was her crime ? Did she not meet me freely ? Did she not open to me her dwelling ? Did she not allow me to pass whole days with her ? No doubt she tried to love me, and could not. I loved her with all the faculties of my soul, but my love was not such as she required. For that, I should not have killed her. But a fatal delusion seized me, and, after it was done, I woke as from a dream. Alas ! it was not a dream : I have killed her. And yet—until this evening—what happiness I owed to her—what hope—what joy ! She made my heart better, nobler, more generous. All came from her,' added the Indian, with a new burst of grief. 'That remained with me—no one could take from me that treasure of the past—that ought to have consoled me. But why think of it ? I struck them both—her and the man—without a struggle. It was a cowardly murder—the ferocity of the tiger that tears its innocent prey !'

Djalma buried his face in his hands. Then, drying his tears, he resumed, 'I know, clearly, that I mean to die also. But my death will not restore her to life !'

He rose from the ground, and drew from his girdle Faringhea's bloody dagger ; then, taking the little phial from the hilt, he threw the blood-stained blade upon the ermine carpet, the immaculate whiteness of which was thus slightly stained with red.

'Yes,' resumed Djalma, holding the phial with a convulsive grasp, 'I know well that I am about to die. It is right. Blood for blood ; my life for hers. How happens it that my steel did not turn aside ? How could I kill her ?—but it is

done—and my heart is full of remorse, and sorrow, and inexpressible tenderness—and I have come here—to die !

' Here, in this chamber,' he continued, ' the heaven of my burning visions !'
And then he added, with a heart-rending accent, as he again buried his face in
his hands, ' Dead ! dead !'

' Well ! I too shall soon be dead,' he resumed, in a firmer voice. ' But, no !
I will die slowly, gradually. A few drops of the poison will suffice ; and, when
I am quite certain of dying, my remorse will perhaps be less terrible. Yesterday, she pressed my hand when we parted. Who could have foretold me
this ?' The Indian raised the phial resolutely to his lips. He drank a few
drops of the liquor it contained, and replaced it on a little ivory table
close to Adrienne's bed.

' This liquor is sharp and hot,' said he. ' Now I am certain to die.
Oh ! that I may still have time to feast on the sight and perfume of
this chamber—to lay my dying head on the couch where she has reposed.

Djalma fell on his knees beside the bed, and leaned against it his
burning brow. At this moment, the ivory door, which communicated with
the bath-room, rolled gently on its hinges, and Adrienne entered. The young
lady had just sent away her woman, who had assisted to undress her. She
wore a long muslin wrapper of lustrous whiteness. Her golden hair, neatly
arranged in little plaits, formed two bands, which gave to her sweet face an
extremely juvenile air.. Her snowy complexion was slightly tinged with rose-
colour, from the warmth of the perfumed bath, which she used for a few
seconds every evening. When she opened the ivory door, and placed
her little naked foot, in its white satin slipper, upon the ermine carpet,
Adrienne was dazzlingly beautiful. Happiness sparkled in her eyes, and
adorned her brow. All the difficulties relative to her union with Djalma
had now been removed. In two days she would be his. The sight of
the nuptial chamber oppressed her with a vague and ineffable languor.
The ivory door had been opened so gently, the lady's first steps were so
soft upon the fur-carpet, that Djalma, still leaning against the bed, had
heard nothing. But suddenly a cry of surprise and alarm struck upon
his ear. He turned round abruptly. Adrienne stood before him.

With an impulse of modesty, Adrienne closed her night-dress over her
bosom, and hastily drew back, still more afflicted than angry at what she
considered a guilty attempt on the part of Djalma. Cruelly hurt and
offended, she was about to reproach him with his conduct, when she perceived the dagger, which he had thrown down upon the ermine carpet.
At sight of this weapon, and the expression of fear and stupor which
petrified the features of Djalma, who remained kneeling, motionless, with
his body thrown back, his hands stretched out, his eyes fixed and wildly
staring—Adrienne, no longer dreading an amorous surprise, was seized
with an indescribable terror, and, instead of flying from the prince, advanced several steps towards him, and said, in an agitated voice, whilst she
pointed to the kandjiar, ' My friend, why are you here? what ails you? why
this dagger ?'

Djalma made no answer. At first, the presence of Adrienne seemed
to him a vision, which he attributed to the excitement of his brain, already
(it might be) under the influence of the poison. But when the soft voice
sounded in his ears—when his heart bounded with the species of electric
shock, which he always felt when he met the gaze of that woman so ardently beloved—when he had contemplated for an instant that adorable face, so fresh
and fair, in spite of its expression of deep uneasiness—Djalma understood that
he was not the sport of a dream, but that Mdlle. de Cardoville was really before
his eyes.

Then, as he began fully to grasp the thought that Adrienne was not dead, though he could not at all explain the prodigy of her resurrection, the Hindoo's countenance was transfigured, the pale gold of his complexion became warm and red, his eyes (tarnished by tears of remorse) shone with new radiance, and his features, so lately contracted with terror and despair, expressed all the phases of the most ecstatic joy. Advancing, still on his knees, towards Adrienne, he lifted up to her his trembling hands, and, too deeply affected to pronounce a word, he gazed on her with so much amazement, love, adoration, gratitude, that the young lady, fascinated by those inexplicable looks, remained mute also, motionless also, and felt, by the precipitate beating of her heart, and by the shudder which ran through her frame, that there was here some dreadful mystery to be unfolded.

At last, Djalma, clasping his hands together, exclaimed with an accent impossible to describe, ' Thou art not dead !'

' Dead !' repeated the young lady, in amazement.

' It was not thou, really not thou, whom I killed ? God is kind and just !'

And as he pronounced these words with intense joy, the unfortunate youth forgot the victim whom he had sacrificed in error.

More and more alarmed, and again glancing at the dagger, on which she now perceived marks of blood—a terrible evidence, in confirmation of the words of Djalma—Mdlle. de Cardoville exclaimed, ' You have killed some one, Djalma ! Oh ! what does he say ? It is dreadful !'

' You are alive—I see you—you are here,' said Djalma, in a voice trembling with rapture. ' You are here—beautiful ! pure ! for it was not you ! Oh, no ! had it been you, the steel would have turned back upon myself.'

' You have killed some one ?' cried the young lady, beside herself with this unforeseen revelation, and clasping her hands in horror. ' Why ? whom did you kill ?'

' I do not know. A woman that was like you—a man that I thought your lover—it was an illusion, a frightful dream—you are alive—you are here !'

And the oriental wept for joy.

' A dream ? but no, it is not a dream. There is blood upon that dagger !' cried the young lady, as she pointed wildly to the kandjiar. ' I tell you there is blood upon it !'——' Yes. I threw it down just now, when I took the poison from it, thinking that I had killed you.'

' The poison !' exclaimed Adrienne, and her teeth chattered convulsively. ' What poison ?'——' I thought I had killed you, and I came here to die.'

' To die ? Oh ! wherefore ? who is to die ?' cried the young lady, almost in delirium.——' I,' replied Djalma, with inexpressible tenderness, ' I thought I had killed you—and I took poison.'

' You !' exclaimed Adrienne, becoming pale as death. ' You !'

' Yes.'

' Oh ! it is not true !' said the young lady, shaking her head.——' Look !' said the Asiatic. Mechanically, he turned towards the bed—towards the little ivory table, on which sparkled the crystal phial.

With a sudden movement, swifter than thought, swifter, it may be, than the will, Adrienne rushed to the table, seized the phial, and applied it eagerly to her lips.

Djalma had hitherto remained on his knees ; but he now uttered a terrible cry, made one spring to the drinker's side, and dragged away the phial, which seemed almost glued to her mouth.

' No matter ! I have swallowed as much as you,' said Adrienne, with an air of gloomy triumph.

For an instant. there followed an awful silence. Adrienne and Djalma gazed upon each other, mute, motionless, horror-struck. The young lady was the first to break this mournful silence, and said in a tone which she tried to make calm and steady, 'Well ! what is there extraordinary in this ? You have killed, and death must expiate your crime. It is just. I will not survive you. That also is natural enough. Why look at me thus ? This poison has a sharp taste—does it act quickly ! Tell me, my Djalma !'

The prince did not answer. Shuddering through all his frame, he looked down upon his hands. Faringhea had told the truth ; a slight violet tint appeared already beneath the nails. Death was approaching, slowly, almost insensibly, but not the less certain. Overwhelmed with despair at the thought that Adrienne, too, was about to die, Djalma felt his courage fail him. He uttered a long groan, and hid his face in his hands. His knees shook under him, and he fell down upon the bed, near which he was standing.

'Already ?' cried the young lady in horror, as she threw herself on her knees at Djalma's feet. 'Death already ? Do you hide your face from me ?'

In her fright, she pulled his hands from before his face. That face was bathed in tears.

'No, not yet,' murmured he, through his sobs. 'The poison is slow.'

'Really !' cried Adrienne, with ineffable joy. Then, kissing the hands of Djalma, she added tenderly, 'If the poison is slow, why do you weep ?'

'For you ! for you !' said the Indian, in a heart-rending tone.

'Think not of me,' replied Adrienne, resolutely. 'You have killed, and we must expiate the crime. I know not what has taken place ; but I swear by our love that you did not do evil for evil's sake. There is some horrible mystery in all this.'

'On a pretence which I felt bound to believe,' replied Djalma, speaking quickly, and panting for breath, 'Faringhea led me to a certain house. Once there, he told me that you had betrayed me. I did not believe him, but I know not what strange dizziness seized upon me—and then, through a half-obscurity, I saw you——'

'Me !'——'No—not you—but a woman resembling you, dressed like you, so that I believed the illusion—and then there came a man—and you flew to meet him—and I—mad with rage—stabbed her, stabbed him, saw them fall—and so came here to die. And now I find you only to cause your death. Oh, misery ! misery ! that you should die through me !'

And Djalma, this man of formidable energy, began again to weep with the weakness of a child. At sight of this deep, touching, passionate despair, Adrienne, with that admirable courage which women alone possess in love, thought only of consoling Djalma. By an effort of superhuman passion, as the prince revealed to her this infernal plot, the lady's countenance became so splendid with an expression of love and happiness, that the East Indian looked at her in amazement, fearing for an instant that he must have lost his reason.

'No more tears, my adored !' cried the young lady, exultingly. 'No more tears—but only smiles of joy and love ! Our cruel enemies shall not triumph !'——'What do you say ?'

'They wished to make us miserable. We pity them. Our felicity shall be the envy of the world !'——'Adrienne—bethink you——'

'Oh ! I have all my senses about me. Listen to me, my adored ! I now understand it all. Falling into a snare, which these wretches spread for you, you have committed murder. Now, in this country, murder leads to infamy, or the scaffold—and to-morrow—to-night, perhaps—you would be thrown into prison. But our enemies have said : "A man like Prince Djalma does not wait for infamy—he kills himself. A woman like Adrienne de Cardoville does not survive the disgrace or death of her lover—she prefers to die. Therefore a frightful death awaits them both ;" said the black-robed men ; "and that immense inheritance, which we covet——" '

'And for you—so young, so beautiful, so innocent—death is frightful, and these monsters triumph !' cried Djalma. 'They have spoken the truth !'

'They have lied !' answered Adrienne. 'Our death shall be celestial. This poison is slow—and I adore you, my Djalma !'

She spoke those words in a low voice, trembling with passionate love, and, leaning upon Djalma's knees, approached so near, that he felt her warm breath upon his cheek. As he felt that breath, and saw the humid flame that darted from the large, swimming eyes of Adrienne, whose half-opened lips were becoming of a still deeper and brighter hue, the Indian started—his young blood boiled in his veins—he forgot everything—his despair, and the approach of death, which as yet (as with Adrienne) only showed itself in a kind of feverish ardour. His face, like the young girl's, became once more splendidly beautiful.

'Oh, my lover ! my husband ! how beautiful you are !' said Adrienne, with idolatry. 'Those eyes—that brow—those lips—how I love them !— How many times has the remembrance of your grace and beauty, coupled with your love, unsettled my reason, and shaken my resolves—even to this moment, when I am wholly yours !—Yes, heaven wills that we should be united. Only this morning, I gave to the apostolic man, that was to bless our union, in thy name and mine, a royal gift—a gift, that will bring joy and peace to the heart of many an unfortunate creature. Then what have we to regret, my beloved ? Our immortal souls will pass away in a kiss, and ascend, full of love, to that God who is all love !'

'Adrienne !'——'Djalma !'

* * * * * *

The light, transparent curtains fell like a cloud over that nuptial and funereal couch. Yes, funereal ; for, two hours after, Adrienne and Djalma breathed their last sigh in a voluptuous agony.

———

CHAPTER LXVI.

A DUEL TO THE DEATH.

ADRIENNE and Djalma died on the 30th of May. The following scene took place on the 31st, the eve of the day appointed for the last convocation of the heirs of Marius de Rennepont. The reader will no doubt remember the room occupied by M. Hardy, in the 'house of retreat' in the Rue de Vaugirard—a gloomy and retired apartment, opening on a dreary little garden, planted with yew-trees, and surrounded by high walls. To reach this chamber, it was necessary to cross two vast rooms, the doors of which, once shut, intercepted all noise and communication from without. Bearing this in mind, we may go on with our narrative. For the last three or four days, Father d'Aigrigny occupied this apartment. He had not chosen it, but had been induced to accept it, under most plausible pretexts, given him at the instigation of Rodin. It was about noon. Seated in an arm-chair, by the window opening on the little garden, Father d'Aigrigny held in his hand a newspaper, in which he read as follows, under the head of 'Paris':

'Eleven P.M.—A most horrible and tragical event has just excited the greatest consternation in the quarter of the Rue de Richelieu. A double murder has been committed, on the persons of a young man and woman. The girl was killed on the spot, by the stroke of a dagger ; hopes are entertained of saving the life of the young man. The crime is attributed to jealousy. The officers of justice are investigating the matter. We shall give full particulars to-morrow.'

When he had read these lines, Father d'Aigrigny threw down the paper, and remained in deep thought.

'It is incredible,' said he, with bitter envy, in allusion to Rodin. 'He has attained his end. Hardly one of his anticipations has been defeated. This family is annihilated, by the mere play of the passions, good and evil, that he has known how to set in motion. He said it would be so. Oh ! I must confess,' added Father d'Aigrigny, with a jealous and hateful smile, 'that Rodin is a man of rare dissimulation, patience, energy, obstinacy, and intelligence. Who would have told me a few months ago, when he wrote under my orders, a discreet and humble socius, that he had already conceived the most audacious ambition, and dared to lift his eyes to the Holy See itself? that, thanks to intrigues and corruption, pursued with wondrous ability, these views were not so unreasonable ? Nay, that this infernal ambition would soon be realised, were it not that the secret proceedings of this dangerous man have long been as secretly watched ?—Ah !' sneered Father d'Aigrigny, with a smile of irony and triumph, ' you wish to be a second Sixtus V., do you ? And, not content with this audacious pretension, you mean, if successful, to absorb our Company in the Papacy, even as the Sultan has absorbed the Janissaries. Ah ! you would make *us* your stepping-stone to power ! And you have thought to humiliate and crush me with your insolent disdain ! But patience, patience : the day of retribution approaches. I alone am the depository of our General's will. Father Caboccini himself does not know that. The fate of Rodin is in my hands. Oh ! it will not be what he expects. In this Rennepont affair, (which, I must needs confess, he has managed admirably), he thinks to outwit us all, and to work only for himself. But to-morrow——'

Father d'Aigrigny was suddenly disturbed in these agreeable reflections. He heard the door of the next room open, and, as he turned round to see who was coming, the door of the apartment in which he was turned upon its hinges. Father d'Aigrigny started with surprise, and became almost purple. Marshal Simon stood before him. And, behind the marshal, in the shadow of the door, Father d'Aigrigny perceived the cadaverous face of Rodin. The latter cast on him one glance of diabolical delight, and instantly disappeared. The door was again closed, and Father d'Aigrigny and Marshal Simon were left alone together. The father of Rose and Blanche was hardly recognisable. His grey hair had become completely white. His pale, thin face had not been shaved for some days. His hollow eyes were bloodshot and restless, and had in them something wild and haggard. He was wrapped in a large cloak, and his black cravat was tied loosely about his neck. In withdrawing from the apartment, Rodin had (as if by inadvertence) double-locked the door on the outside. When he was alone with the Jesuit, the marshal threw back his cloak from his shoulders, and Father d'Aigrigny could see two naked swords, stuck through a silk handkerchief which served him as a belt.

Father d'Aigrigny understood it all. He remembered how, a few days before, Rodin had obstinately pressed him to say what he would do if the marshal were to strike him in the face. There could be now no doubt that he, who thought to have held the fate of Rodin in his hands, had been brought by the latter into a fearful peril ; for he knew that, the two outer rooms being closed, there was no possibility of making himself heard, and that the high walls of the garden only bordered upon some vacant lots. The first thought which occurred to him, one by no means destitute of probability, was that Rodin, either by his agents at Rome, or by his own incredible penetration, had learned that his fate depended on Father d'Aigrigny, and hoped therefore to get rid of him, by delivering him over to the inexorable vengeance of the father of Rose and Blanche. Without speaking a word, the marshal unbound the handkerchief from his waist, laid the two swords upon the table, and, folding his arms upon his breast, advanced slowly towards Father d'Aigrigny. Thus these two men, who through life had pursued each other with implacable hatred, at length met face to face—they, who had fought in hostile armies, and measured swords in single combat, and one of whom now came to seek vengeance for the death of his children. As the marshal approached, Father d'Aigrigny rose from his seat. He wore that day a black cassock, which rendered still more visible the pale hue, which had now succeeded to the sudden flush on his cheek. For a few seconds, the two men stood face to face without speaking. The marshal was terrific in his paternal despair. His calmness, inexorable as fate, was more impressive than the most furious burst of anger.

'My children are dead,' said he at last, in a slow and hollow tone. 'I come to kill you.'

'Sir,' cried Father d'Aigrigny, 'listen to me. Do not believe——'

'I must kill you,' resumed the marshal, interrupting the Jesuit; 'your hate followed my wife into exile, where she perished. You and your accomplices sent my children to certain death. For twenty years you have been my evil genius. I must have your life, and I will have it.'

'My life belongs, first, to God,' answered Father d'Aigrigny, piously, 'and then to who likes to take it.'

'We will fight to the death in this room,' said the marshal; 'and, as I have to avenge my wife and children, I am tranquil as to the result.'

'Sir,' answered Father d'Aigrigny, coldly, 'you forget that my profession forbids me to fight. Once I accepted your challenge—but my position is changed since then.'

'Ah !' said the marshal, with a bitter smile; 'you refuse to fight because you are a priest ?'——' Yes, sir—because I am a priest.'

'So that, because he is a priest, a wretch like you may commit any crime, any baseness, under shelter of his black gown ?'

'I do not understand a word of your accusations. In any case, the law is open,' said Father d'Aigrigny, biting his pale lips, for he felt deeply the insult offered by the marshal ; 'if you have anything to complain of, appeal to that law, before which all are equal.'

Marshal Simon shrugged his shoulders in angry disdain. 'Your crimes escape the law—and, could it even reach you, that would not satisfy my vengeance, after all the evil you have done me, after all you have taken from me,' said the marshal ; and, at the memory of his children, his voice slightly trembled ; but he soon proceeded, with terrible calmness : 'You must feel that I now only live for vengeance. And I must have such revenge as is worth the seeking—I must have your coward's heart palpitating on the point of my sword. Our last duel was play ; this will be earnest—oh ! you shall see.'

The marshal walked up to the table, where he had laid the two swords. Father d'Aigrigny needed all his resolution to restrain himself. The implacable hate which he had always felt for Marshal Simon, added to these insults, filled him with savage ardour. Yet he answered, in a tone that was still calm : 'For the last time, sir, I repeat to you, that my profession forbids me to fight.'

'Then you refuse ?' said the marshal, turning abruptly towards him.

'I refuse.'

'Positively ?'——' Positively. Nothing on earth should force me to it.'

'Nothing?'——'No, sir; nothing.'

'We shall see,' said the marshal, as his hand fell with its full force on the cheek of Father d'Aigrigny.

The Jesuit uttered a cry of fury; all his blood rushed to his face, so roughly handled; the courage of the man (for he was brave), his ancient military ardour, carried him away; his eyes sparkled, and, with teeth firmly set, and clenched fists, he advanced towards the marshal, exclaiming : 'The swords! the swords!'

But suddenly, remembering the appearance of Rodin, and the interest which the latter had in bringing about this rencounter, he determined to avoid the diabolical snare laid by his former socius, and so gathered sufficient resolution to restrain his terrible resentment.

To his passing fury succeeded a calm, full of contrition ; and, wishing to play his part out to the end, he knelt down, and, bowing his head and beating his bosom, repeated: 'Forgive me, Lord, for yielding to a movement of rage! and, above all, forgive him who has injured me!'

In spite of his apparent resignation, the Jesuit's voice was greatly agitated. He seemed to feel a hot iron upon his cheek, for never before in his life, whether as a soldier or a priest, had he suffered such an insult. He had thrown himself upon his knees, partly from religious mummery, and partly to avoid the gaze of the marshal, fearing that, were he to meet his eye, he should not be able to answer for himself, but give way to his impetuous feelings. On seeing the Jesuit kneel down, and on hearing his hypocritical invocation, the marshal, whose sword was in his hand, shook with indignation.

'Stand up, scoundrel!' he said, 'stand up, wretch!' And he spurned the Jesuit with his boot.

At this new insult, Father d'Aigrigny leaped up, as if he had been moved by steel springs. It was too much; he could bear no more. Blinded with rage, he rushed to the table, caught up the other sword, and exclaimed, grinding his teeth together : 'Ah! you will have blood. Well, then! it shall be yours—if possible!'

And the Jesuit, still in all the vigour of manhood, his face purple, his large grey eyes sparkling with hate, fell upon his guard with the ease and skill of a finished swordsman.

'At last!' cried the marshal, as their blades were about to cross.

But once more reflection came to damp the fire of the Jesuit. He remembered how this hazardous duel would gratify the wishes of Rodin, whose fate was in his hands, and whom he hated perhaps even more than the marshal. Therefore, in spite of the fury which possessed him, in spite of his secret hope to conquer in this combat, so strong and healthy did he feel himself, and so fatal had been the effects of grief on the constitution of Marshal Simon, he succeeded in mastering his rage, and, to the amazement of the marshal, dropped the point of his sword, exclaiming : 'I am a minister of the Lord, and must not shed blood. Forgive me, heaven! and, oh! forgive my brother also.'

Then, placing the blade beneath his heel, he drew the hilt suddenly towards him, and broke the weapon into two pieces. The duel was no longer possible. Father d'Aigrigny had put it out of his own power to yield to a new burst of violence, of which he saw the imminent danger. Marshal Simon remained for an instant mute and motionless with surprise and indignation, for he also saw that the duel was now impossible. But, suddenly, imitating the Jesuit, the marshal placed his blade also under his heel, broke it in half, and picking up the pointed end, about eighteen inches in length, tore off his black silk cravat, rolled it round the broken part so as to form a handle, and said to Father d'Aigrigny: 'Then we will fight with daggers.'

Struck with this mixture of coolness and ferocity, the Jesuit exclaimed :
' Is this then a demon of hell ?'

' No ; it is a father, whose children have been murdered,' said the marshal,
in a hollow voice, whilst he fitted the blade to his hand, and a tear stood in
the eye, that instantly after became fierce and ardent.

The Jesuit saw that tear. There was in this mixture of vindictive rage
and paternal grief something so awful, and yet so sacred, that for the first
time in his life Father d'Aigrigny felt fear—cowardly, ignoble fear—fear for
his own safety. While a combat with swords was in question, in which
skill, agility, and experience are such powerful auxiliaries to courage, his
only difficulty had been to repress the ardour of his hate—but when he
thought of the combat proposed, body to body, face to face, heart to heart,
he trembled, grew pale, and exclaimed : ' A butchery with knives ?—never !'

His countenance and the accent betrayed his alarm, so that the marshal
himself was struck with it, and fearing to lose his revenge, he cried : ' After
all, he is a coward ! The wretch had only the courage or the vanity of a
fencer. This pitiful renegade—this traitor to his country—whom I have
cuffed, kicked—yes, kicked, most noble marquis !—shame of your ancient
house—disgrace to the rank of gentleman, old or new—ah ! it is not hypocrisy, it is not calculation, as I at first thought—it is fear ! You need the
noise of war, and the eyes of spectators to give you courage——'

' Sir—have a care !' said Father d'Aigrigny, stammering through his
clenched teeth, for rage and hate now made him forget his fears.——' Must
I then spit on you, to make the little blood you have left rise to your face ?'
cried the exasperated marshal.

' Oh ! this is too much ! too much !' said the Jesuit, seizing the pointed
piece of the blade that lay at his feet.——' It is not enough,' said the marshal,
panting for breath. ' There, Judas !' and he spat in his face.

' If you will not fight now,' added the marshal, ' I will beat you like a dog,
base child-murderer !'

On receiving the uttermost insult which can be offered to an already insulted man, Father d'Aigrigny lost all his presence of mind, forgot his
interests, his resolutions, his fears, forgot even Rodin—felt only the frenzied
ardour of revenge—and, recovering his courage, rejoiced in the prospect of a
close struggle, in which his superior strength promised success over the enfeebled frame of the marshal—for, in this kind of brutal and savage combat,
physical strength offers an immense advantage. In an instant, Father d'Aigrigny had rolled his handkerchief round the broken blade, and rushed upon
Marshal Simon, who received the shock with intrepidity. For the short time
that this unequal struggle lasted—unequal, for the marshal had since some
days been a prey to a devouring fever, which had undermined his strength—
the two combatants, mute in their fury, uttered not a word or a cry. Had any
one been present at this horrible scene, it would have been impossible for
him to tell how they dealt their blows. He would have seen two heads—
frightful, livid, convulsed—rising, falling, now here, now there—arms, now
stiff as bars of iron, and now twisting like serpents—and, in the midst of the
undulations of the blue coat of the marshal and the black cassock of the
Jesuit, from time to time the sudden gleam of the steel. He would have
heard only a dull stamping, and now and then a deep breath. In about two
minutes at most, the two adversaries fell, and rolled one over the other.
One of them—it was Father d'Aigrigny—contrived to disengage himself with
a violent effort, and to rise upon his knees. His arms fell powerless by his
side, and then the dying voice of the marshal murmured : ' My children !
Dagobert !'——'I have killed him,' said Father d'Aigrigny, in a weak voice ;
' but I feel—that I am wounded—to death.'

Leaning with one hand on the ground, the Jesuit pressed the other to his bosom. His black cassock was pierced through and through, but the blades, which had served for the combat, being triangular and very sharp, the blood, instead of issuing from the wounds, was flowing inwards.

'Ch ! I die—I choke,' said Father d'Aigrigny, whose features were already changing with the approach of death.

At this moment, the key turned twice in the door, Rodin appeared on the threshold, and, thrusting in his head, he said in a humble and discreet voice : 'May I come in?'

At this dreadful irony, Father d'Aigrigny strove to rise, and rush upon Rodin ; but he fell back exhausted ; the blood was choking him.

'Monster of hell !' he muttered, casting on Rodin a terrible glance of rage and agony. 'Thou art the cause of my death.'

'I always told you, my dear father, that your old military habits would be fatal to you,' answered Rodin with a frightful smile. 'Only a few days ago, I gave you warning, and advised you to take a blow patiently from this old swordsman—who seems to have done with that work for ever, which is well —for the scripture says: "All they that take the sword shall perish with the sword." And then this Marshal Simon might have had some claim on his daughter's inheritance. And, between ourselves, my dear father, what was I to do ? It was necessary to sacrifice you for the common interest ; the rather, that I well knew what you had in pickle for me to-morrow. But I am not so easily caught napping.'

'Before I die,' said Father d'Aigrigny, in a failing voice, 'I will unmask you.'——'Oh, no, you will not,' said Rodin, shaking his head with a knowing air ; 'I alone, if you please, will receive your last confession.'

'Oh ! this is horrible,' moaned Father d'Aigrigny, whose eyes were closing. 'May God have mercy on me, if it is not too late !—Alas ! at this awful moment, I feel that I have been a great sinner——'

'And, above all, a great fool,' said Rodin, shrugging his shoulders, and watching with cold disdain the dying moments of his accomplice.

Father d'Aigrigny had now but a few minutes more to live. Rodin perceived it, and said : 'It is time to call for help.' And the Jesuit ran, with an air of alarm and consternation, into the courtyard of the house.

Others came at his cries ; but, as he had promised, Rodin had only quitted Father d'Aigrigny as the latter had breathed his last sigh.

✿   ✿   ✿   ✿   ✿   ✿

That evening, alone in his chamber, by the glimmer of a little lamp, Rodin sat plunged in a sort of ecstatic contemplation, before the print representing Sixtus V. The great house clock struck twelve. At the last stroke, Rodin drew himself up in all the savage majesty of his infernal triumph, and exclaimed : 'This is the first of June. There are no more Renneponts !— Methinks, I hear the hour from the clock of St. Peter's at Rome striking !'

CHAPTER LXVII.

A MESSAGE.

WHILE Rodin sat plunged in ambitious reverie, contemplating the portrait of Sixtus V., good little Father Caboccini, whose warm embraces had so much irritated the first-mentioned personage, went secretly to Faringhea, to deliver to him a fragment of an ivory crucifix, and said to him, with his usual air of jovial good-nature : 'His Excellency Cardinal Malipieri, on my departure from Rome, charged me to give you this only on the 31st of May.'

The half-caste, who was seldom affected by anything, started abruptly, almost with an expression of pain. His face darkened, and, bending upon the little father a piercing look, he said to him : 'You were to add something.'

'True,' replied Father Caboccini ; 'the words I was to add are these : " There is many a slip 'twixt the cup and the lip."

'It is well,' said the other. Heaving a deep sigh, he joined the fragment of the ivory crucifix to a piece already in his possession ; it fitted exactly.

Father Caboccini looked at him with curiosity, for the cardinal had only told him to deliver the ivory fragment to Faringhea, and to repeat the above words. Being somewhat mystified with all this, the reverend father said to the half-caste : 'What are you going to do with that crucifix ?'

'Nothing,' said Faringhea, still absorbed in painful thought.

'Nothing ?' resumed the reverend father, in astonishment. 'What, then, was the use of bringing it so far ?'

Without satisfying his curiosity, Faringhea replied : 'At what hour to-morrow does Father Rodin go to the Rue Saint-François ?'——'Very early.'

'Before leaving home, he will go to say prayers in the chapel ?'

'Yes, according to the habit of our reverend fathers.'

'You sleep near him ?'

'Being his socius, I occupy the room next to his.'

'It is possible,' said Faringhea, after a moment's silence, 'that the reverend father, full of the great interests which occupy his mind, might forget to go to the chapel. In that case, pray remind him of this pious duty.'

'I shall not fail.'

'Pray do not fail,' repeated Faringhea, anxiously.——'Be satisfied,' said the good little father ; 'I see that you take great interest in his salvation.'

'Great interest.'——'It is very praiseworthy in you. Continue as you have begun, and you may one day belong completely to our Company,' said Father Caboccini, affectionately.

'I am as yet but a poor auxiliary member,' said Faringhea, humbly ; 'but no one is more devoted to the Society, body and soul. Bowanee is nothing to it.'——'Bowanee ! who is that, my good friend ?'

'Bowanee makes corpses which rot in the ground. The Society makes corpses which walk about.'——'Ah, yes ! Perindè ac cadaver—they were the last words of our great saint, Ignatius de Loyola. But who is this Bowanee ?'

'Bowanee is to the Society what a child is to a man,' replied the Asiatic, with growing excitement. 'Glory to the Company—glory ! Were my father its enemy, I would kill my father. The man whose genius inspires me most with admiration, respect, and terror—were he its enemy, I would kill, in spite of all,' said the half-caste, with an effort. Then, after a moment's silence, he looked full in Caboccini's face, and added : 'I say this, that you may report my words to Cardinal Malipieri, and beg him to mention them to——'

Faringhea stopped short. 'To whom should the cardinal mention your words ?' asked Caboccini.

'He knows,' replied the half-caste, abruptly. 'Good-night !'——'Good-night, my friend ! I can only approve of your excellent sentiments with regard to our Company. Alas ! it is in want of energetic defenders, for there are said to be traitors in its bosom.'

'For those,' said Faringhea, 'we must have no pity.'

'Certainly,' said the good little father ; 'we understand one another.

'Perhaps,' said the half-caste. 'Do not, at all events, forget to remind Father Rodin to go to chapel to-morrow morning.'

'I will take care of that,' said Father Caboccini.

The two men parted. On his return to the house, Caboccini learned that a courier, only arrived that night from Rome, had brought despatches to Rodin.

CHAPTER LXVIII.

THE FIRST OF JUNE.

THE chapel belonging to the house of the reverend fathers, in the Rue de Vaugirard, was gay and elegant. Large panes of stained glass admitted a mysterious light ; the altar shone with gold and silver ; and at the entrance of this little church, in an obscure corner beneath the organ-loft, was a font for holy water in sculptured marble. It was close to this font, in a dark nook where he could hardly be seen, that Faringhea knelt down, early on the 1st of June, as soon indeed as the chapel doors were opened. The half-caste was exceedingly sad. From time to time he started and sighed, as if agitated by a violent internal struggle. This wild, untameable being, possessed with the monomania of evil and destruction, felt, as may be imagined, a profound admiration for Rodin, who exercised over him a kind of magnetic fascination. The half-caste, almost a wild beast in human form, saw something supernatural in the infernal genius of Rodin. And the latter, too sagacious not to have discovered the savage devotion of this wretch, had made, as we have seen, good use of him, in bringing about the tragical termination of the loves of Adrienne and Djalma. But what excited to an incredible degree the admiration of Faringhea, was what he knew of the Society of Jesus. This immense, occult power, which undermined the world by its subterraneous ramifications, and reached its ends by diabolical means, had inspired the half-caste with a wild enthusiasm. And if anything in the world surpassed his fanatical admiration for Rodin, it was his blind devotion to the Company of Ignatius de Loyola, which, as he said, could make corpses that walk about. Hid in the shadow of the organ-loft, Faringhea was reflecting deeply on these things, when footsteps were heard, and Rodin entered the chapel, accompanied by his socius, the little one-eyed father.

Whether from absence of mind, or that the shadow of the organ-loft completely concealed the half-caste, Rodin dipped his fingers into the font without perceiving Faringhea, who stood motionless as a statue, though a cold sweat streamed from his brow. The prayer of Rodin was, as may be supposed, short ; he was in haste to get to the Rue Saint-François. After kneeling down with Father Caboccini for a few seconds, he rose, bowed respectfully to the altar, and returned towards the door, followed by his socius. At the moment Rodin approached the font, he perceived the tall figure of the half-caste standing out from the midst of the dark shadow ; advancing a little, Faringhea bowed respectfully to Rodin, who said to him, in a low voice : ' Come to me at two o'clock.'

So saying, Rodin stretched forth his hand to dip it into the holy water ; but Faringhea spared him the trouble, by offering him the sprinkling-brush, which generally stood in the font.

Pressing between his dirty fingers the damp hairs of the brush, which the half-caste held by the handle, Rodin wetted his thumb and forefinger, and, according to custom, traced the sign of the cross upon his forehead. Then, opening the door of the chapel, he went out, after again repeating to Faringhea : ' Come to me at two o'clock.'

Thinking he would also make use of the sprinkling-brush, which Faringhea, still motionless, held with a trembling hand, Father Caboccini stretched out his fingers to reach it, when the half-breed, as if determined to confine his favours to Rodin, hastily withdrew the instrument. Deceived in his expectation, Father Caboccini lost no time in following Rodin, whom he was not to leave that day for a single moment, and, getting into a hackney-coach with him, set out for the Rue Saint-Francois. It is impossible to describe the look which the half-breed fixed upon Rodin as the latter quitted the chapel. Left alone in the sacred edifice, Faringhea sank upon the stones, half kneeling, half crouching, with his face buried in his hands. As the coach drew near the quarter of the Marais, in which was situated the house of Marius de Rennepont, a feverish agitation, and the devouring impatience of triumph, were visible on the countenance of Rodin. Two or three times he opened his pocket-book, and read and arranged the different certificates of death of the various members of the Rennepont family; and from time to time he thrust his head anxiously from the coach-window, as if he had wished to hasten the slow progress of the vehicle.

The good little father, his socius, did not take his eye off Rodin, and his look had a strange and crafty expression. At last the coach entered the Rue Saint-François, and stopped before the iron-studded door of the old house, which had been closed for a century and a half. Rodin sprang from the coach with the agility of a young man, and knocked violently at the door, whilst Father Caboccini, less light of foot, descended more prudently to the ground. No answer was returned to the loud knocking of Rodin. Trembling with anxiety, he knocked again. This time, as he listened attentively, he heard slow steps approaching. They stopped at some distance from the door, which was not yet opened.

'It is keeping one upon red-hot coals,' said Rodin, for he felt as if there was a burning fire in his chest. He again shook the door violently, and began to gnaw his nails according to his custom.

Suddenly the door opened, and Samuel, the Jew guardian, appeared beneath the porch. The countenance of the old man expressed bitter grief. Upon his venerable cheeks were the traces of recent tears, which he strove to dry with his trembling hands, as he opened the door to Rodin.

'Who are you, gentlemen?' said Samuel.——'I am the bearer of a power of attorney from the Abbé Gabriel, the only living representative of the Rennepont family,' answered Rodin, hastily. 'This gentleman is my secretary,' added he, pointing to Father Caboccini, who bowed.

After looking attentively at Rodin, Samuel resumed: 'I recognise you, sir. Please to follow me.' And the old guardian advanced towards the house in the garden, making a sign to the two reverend fathers to follow.

'That confounded old man kept me so long at the door,' said Rodin to his socius, 'that I think I have caught a cold in consequence. My lips and throat are dried up, like parchment baked at the fire.'

'Will you not take something, my dear, good father? Suppose you were to ask this man for a glass of water,' cried the little one-eyed priest, with tender solicitude.

'No, no,' answered Rodin; 'it is nothing. I am devoured by impatience. That is all.'

Pale and desolate, Bathsheba, the wife of Samuel, was standing at the door of the apartment she occupied with her husband, in the building next the street. As the Jew passed before her, he said, in Hebrew: 'The curtains of the Hall of Mourning?'——'Are closed.'——'And the iron casket?'

'Is prepared,' answered Bathsheba, also in Hebrew.

After pronouncing these words, completely unintelligible to Rodin and Caboccini, Samuel and Bathsheba exchanged a bitter smile, notwithstanding the despair impressed on their countenances.

Ascending the steps, followed by the two reverend fathers, Samuel entered the vestibule of the house, in which a lamp was burning. Endowed with an excellent local memory, Rodin was about to take the direction of the Red Saloon, in which had been held the first convocation of the heirs, when Samuel stopped him, and said : ' It is not that way.'

Then, taking the lamp, he advanced towards a dark staircase, for the windows of the house had not been unbricked.

' But,' said Rodin, ' the last time, we met in a saloon on the ground floor.'

' To-day, we must go higher,' answered Samuel, as he began slowly to ascend the stairs.

' Where to? higher !' said Rodin, following him.——' To the Hall of Mourning,' replied the Jew, and he continued to ascend.

' What is the Hall of Mourning ?' resumed Rodin, in some surprise.

' A place of tears and death,' answered the Israelite ; and he kept on ascending through the darkness, for the little lamp threw but a faint light around.

' But,' said Rodin, more and more astonished, and stopping short on the stairs, ' why go to this place ?'——' The money is there,' answered Samuel, and he went on.

' Oh ? if the money is there, that alters the case,' replied Rodin ; and he made haste to regain the few steps he had lost by stopping.

Samuel continued to ascend, and, at a turn of the staircase, the two Jesuits could see by the pale light of the little lamp, the profile of the old Israelite, in the space left between the iron balustrade and the wall, as he climbed on with difficulty above them. Rodin was struck with the expression of Samuel's countenance. His black eyes, generally so calm, sparkled with ardour. His features, usually impressed with a mixture of sorrow, intelligence, and goodness, seemed to grow harsh and stern, and his thin lips wore a strange smile.

' It is not so very high,' whispered Rodin to Caboccini, ' and yet my legs ache, and I am quite out of breath. There is a strange throbbing too in my temples.'

In fact, Rodin breathed hard, and with difficulty. To this confidential communication, good little Father Caboccini, in general so full of tender care for his colleague, made no answer. He seemed to be in deep thought.

' Will we soon be there ?' said Rodin, impatiently, to Samuel.

' We are there,' replied the Israelite.

' And a good thing too,' said Rodin.——' Very good,' said the Jew.

Stopping in the midst of a corridor, he pointed with the hand in which he held the lamp to a large door from which streamed a faint light. In spite of his growing surprise, Rodin entered resolutely, followed by Father Caboccini and Samuel. The apartment in which these three personages now found themselves was very large. The daylight only entered from a belvedere in the roof, the four sides of which had been covered with leaden plates, each of which was pierced with seven holes, forming a cross, thus :

✿
✿ ✿ ✿
✿
✿
✿

Now, the light being only admitted through these holes, the obscurity would have been complete, had it not been for a lamp, which burned on a large massive slab of black marble, fixed against one of the walls. One would have taken it for a funeral chamber, for it was all hung with black curtains, fringed with white. There was no furniture, save the slab of black marble we have already mentioned. On this slab, was an iron casket, of the manufacture of the seventeenth century, admirably adorned with open work, like lace made of metal.

Addressing Rodin, who was wiping his forehead with his dirty handkerchief, and looking round him with surprise, but not fear, Samuel said to
him : 'The will of the testator, however strange it may appear, is sacred
with me, and must be accomplished in all things.'

'Certainly,' said Rodin ; 'but what are we to do here ?'——'You will know
presently, sir. You are the representative of the only remaining heir of the
Rennepont family, the Abbé Gabriel de Rennepont ?'

'Yes, sir, and here are my papers,' replied Rodin.——'To save time,' resumed Samuel, 'I will, previous to the arrival of the magistrate, go through
the inventory of the securities contained in this casket, which I withdrew
yesterday from the custody of the Bank of France.'

'The securities are there ?' cried Rodin, advancing eagerly towards the
casket.

'Yes, sir,' replied Samuel, 'as by the list. Your secretary will call them
over, and I will produce each in turn. They can then be replaced in the
casket, which I will deliver up to you in presence of the magistrate.'

'All this seems perfectly correct,' said Rodin.

Samuel delivered the list to Father Caboccini, and, approaching the casket, touched a spring, which was not seen by Rodin. The heavy lid flew
open, and, while Father Caboccini read the names of the different securities,
Samuel showed them to Rodin, who returned them to the old Jew, after a
careful examination. This verification did not last long, for this immense
fortune was all comprised, as we already know, in eight government
securities, five hundred thousand francs in bank-notes, thirty-five thousand
francs in gold, and two hundred and fifty francs in silver—making in all an
amount of two hundred and twelve millions, one hundred and seventy-five
thousand francs. When Rodin had counted the last of the five hundred
bank-notes, of a thousand francs each, he said, as he returned them to
Samuel : 'It is quite right. Two hundred and twelve millions, one hundred
and seventy-five thousand francs !'

He was no doubt almost choked with joy, for he breathed with difficulty,
his eyes closed, and he was obliged to lean upon Father Caboccini's arm, as
he said to him in an altered voice : 'It is singular. I thought myself proof
against all such emotions ; but what I feel is extraordinary.'

The natural paleness of the Jesuit increased so much, and he seemed so
much agitated with convulsive movements, that Father Caboccini exclaimed :
'My dear father, collect yourself ; do not let success overcome you thus.'

Whilst the little one-eyed man was attending to Rodin, Samuel carefully
replaced the securities in the iron casket. Thanks to his unconquerable
energy, and to the joy he felt at seeing himself so near the term of his labours,
Rodin mastered this attack of weakness, and drawing himself up, calm and
proud, he said to Caboccini : 'It is nothing. I did not survive the cholera,
to die of joy on the first of June.'

And, though still frightfully pale, the countenance of the Jesuit shone with
audacious confidence. But now, when Rodin appeared to be quite recovered,
Father Caboccini seemed suddenly transformed. Though short, fat, and
one-eyed, his features assumed on the instant so firm, harsh, and commanding
an expression, that Rodin recoiled a step as he looked at him. Then Father
Caboccini, drawing a paper from his pocket, kissed it respectfully, glanced
sternly at Rodin, and read as follows, in a severe and menacing tone :

'"On receipt of the present rescript, the Reverend Father Rodin will
deliver up all his powers to the Reverend Father Caboccini, who is alone
commissioned, with the Reverend Father d'Aigrigny, to receive the inheritance of the Rennepont family, if, in His eternal justice, the Lord should restore this property, of which our Company has been wronged.

' " Moreover, on receipt of the present rescript, the Reverend Father Rodin, in charge of a person to be named by the Reverend Father Caboccini, shall be conveyed to our house in the town of Laval, to be kept in strict seclusion in his cell until further orders." '

Then Father Caboccini handed the rescript to Rodin, that the latter might read the signature of the General of the Company. Samuel, greatly interested by this scene, drew a few steps nearer, leaving the casket half-open. Suddenly, Rodin burst into a loud laugh—a laugh of joy, contempt and triumph, impossible to describe. Father Caboccini looked at him with angry astonishment ; when Rodin, growing still more imperious and haughty, and with an air of more sovereign disdain than ever, pushed aside the paper with the back of his dirty hand, and said : ' What is the date of that scribble ?'

' The eleventh of May,' answered Father Caboccini in amazement.

' Here is a brief, that I received last night from Rome, under date of the eighteenth. It informs me that I am appointed GENERAL OF THE ORDER. Read !'

Father Caboccini took the paper, read it, and remained thunderstruck. Then, returning it humbly to Rodin, he respectfully bent his knee before him. Thus seemed the ambitious views of Rodin accomplished. In spite of the hatred and suspicion of that party, of which Cardinal Malipieri was the representative and the chief, Rodin, by address and craft, audacity and per-. suasion, and in consequence of the high esteem in which his partisans at Rome held his rare capacity, had succeeded in deposing his General, and in procuring his own elevation to that eminent post. Now, according to his calculation, aided by the millions he was about to possess, it would be but one step from that post to the pontifical throne. A mute witness of this scene, Samuel smiled also with an air of triumph, as he closed the casket by means of the spring known only to himself. That metallic sound recalled Rodin from the heights of his mad ambition to the realities of life, and he said to Samuel in a sharp voice : ' You have heard ? These millions must be delivered to me alone.'

He extended his hands eagerly and impatiently towards the casket, as if he would have taken possession of it, before the arrival of the magistrate. Then Samuel in his turn seemed transfigured, and, folding his arms upon his breast, and drawing up his aged form to its full height, he assumed a threatening and imposing air. His eyes flashed with indignation, and he said in a solemn tone : ' This fortune—at first the humble remains of the inheritance of the most noble of men, whom the plots of the sons of Loyola drove to suicide—this fortune, which has since become royal in amount, thanks to the sacred probity of three generations of faithful servants—this fortune shall never be the reward of falsehood, hypocrisy and murder. No ! the eternal justice of heaven will not allow it.'

' Of murder ? what do you mean, sir ?' asked Rodin, boldly.

Samuel made no answer. He stamped his foot, and extended his arm slowly towards the extremity of the apartment. Then Rodin and Father Caboccini beheld an awful spectacle. The draperies on the wall were drawn aside, as if by an invisible hand. Round a funeral vault, faintly illumined by the blueish light of a silver lamp, six dead bodies were ranged upon black biers, dressed in long black robes. They were : Jacques Rennepont— François Hardy—Rose and Blanche Simon—Adrienne and Djalma. They appeared to be asleep. Their eyelids were closed, their hands crossed over their breasts. Father Caboccini, trembling in every limb, made the sign of the cross, and retreating to the opposite wall, buried his face in his hands. Rodin, on the contrary, with agitated countenance, staring eyes, and hair standing on end, yielding to an invincible attraction, advanced towards

those inanimate forms.   One would have said that these last of the Renneponts had only just expired.   They seemed to be in the first hour of the
eternal sleep.*

'Behold those whom thou hast slain !' cried Samuel, in a voice broken
with sobs.   'Yea ! your detestable plots caused their death—and, as they
fell one by one, it was my pious care to obtain possession of their poor
remains, that they may all repose in the same sepulchre.   Oh ! cursed—
cursed—cursed—be thou who hast killed them !   But their spoils shall escape
thy murderous hands.'

Rodin, still drawn forward in spite of himself, had approached the funeral
couch of Djalma.   Surmounting his first alarm, the Jesuit, to assure himself
that he was not the sport of a frightful dream, ventured to touch the hands
of the Asiatic—and found that they were damp and pliant, though cold as
ice.

The Jesuit drew back in horror.   For some seconds, he trembled convulsively.   But, his first amazement over, reflection returned, and, with reflection
came that invincible energy, that infernal obstinacy of character, that gave
him so much power.   Steadying himself on his legs, drawing his hand across
his brow, raising his head, moistening his lips two or three times before he
spoke—for his throat and mouth grew ever drier and hotter, without his
being able to explain the cause—he succeeded in giving to his features an
imperious and ironical expression, and, turning towards Samuel, who wept in
silence, he said to him, in a hoarse, guttural voice : 'I need not show you the
certificates of their death.   There they are in person.'   And he pointed with
his bony hand to the six dead bodies.

At these words of his General, Father Caboccini again made the sign of
the cross, as if he had seen a fiend.

'Oh, my God !' cried Samuel ; 'thou hast quite abandoned this man.
With what a calm look he contemplates his victims !'

'Come, sir !' said Rodin, with a horrid smile ; 'this is a natural waxwork
exhibition, that is all.   My calmness proves my innocence—and we had best
come at once to business.   I have an appointment at two o'clock.   So let
us carry down this casket.'

He advanced towards the marble slab.   Seized with indignation and horror, Samuel threw himself before him, and, pressing with all his might on a
knob in the lid of the casket—a knob which yielded to the pressure—he exclaimed : 'Since your infernal soul is incapable of remorse, it may perhaps
be shaken by disappointed avarice.'

'What does he say ?' cried Rodin. 'What is he doing ?'——'Look !' said
Samuel, in his turn assuming an air of savage triumph.   'I told you, that
the spoils of your victims should escape your murderous hands.'

Hardly had he uttered these words, before through the open-work of the
iron casket rose a light cloud of smoke, and an odour as of burnt paper spread
itself through the room.   Rodin understood it instantly.   'Fire !' he exclaimed, as he rushed forward to seize the casket.   It had been made fast
to the heavy marble slab.

'Yes, fire,' said Samuel.   'In a few minutes, of that immense treasure
there will remain nothing but ashes.   And better so, than that it should belong to you or yours.   This treasure is not mine, and it only remains for me
to destroy it—since Gabriel de Rennepont will be faithful to the oath he has
taken.'

'Help ! water ! water !' cried Rodin, as he covered the casket with his
body, trying in vain to extinguish the flames, which, fanned by the current

* Should this appear incredible, we would remind the reader of the marvellous
discoveries in the art of embalming—particularly Dr. Gannal's.

of air, now issued from the thousand apertures in the lid ; but soon the intensity of the fire diminished, a few threads of blueish smoke alone mounted upwards—and then, all was extinct.

The work was done ! Breathless and faint, Rodin leaned against the marble slab. For the first time in his life, he wept ; large tears of rage rolled down his cadaverous cheeks. But suddenly, dreadful pains, at first dull, but gradually augmenting in intensity, seized on him with so much fury, though he employed all his energy to struggle against them, that he fell on his knees, and, pressing his two hands to his chest, murmured with an attempt to smile : ' It is nothing. Do not be alarmed. A few spasms —that is all. The treasure is destroyed—but I remain General of the Order. Oh ! I suffer. What a furnace !' he added, writhing in agony. ' Since I entered this cursed house, I know not what ails me. If—I had not lived on roots—water—bread—which I go myself to buy—I should think—I was poisoned—for I triumph—and Cardinal Malipieri has long arms. Yes—I still triumph—for I will not die—this time no more than the other—I will not die !'

Then, as he stretched out his arms convulsively, he continued : ' It is fire that devours my entrails. No doubt, they have tried to poison me. But when ? but how ?'

After another pause, Rodin again cried out, in a stifled voice : 'Help ! help me, you that stand looking on—like spectres !—Help me, I say !'

Horror struck at this dreadful agony, Samuel and Father Caboccini were unable to stir.

' Help !' repeated Rodin, in a tone of strangulation. ' This poison is horrible.—But how——' Then, with a terrific cry of rage, as if a sudden idea had struck him, he exclaimed : ' Ha ! Faringhea—this morning—the holy water —he knows such subtle poisons. Yes—it is he—he had an interview with Malipieri. The demon !—Oh ! it was well played. The Borgias are still the same. Oh ! it is all over. I die. They will regret me, the fools !—Oh ! hell ! hell ! The Church knows not its loss—but I burn—help !'

They came to his assistance. Quick steps were heard upon the stairs, and Dr. Baleinier, followed by the Princess de Saint-Dizier, appeared at the entrance of the Hall of Mourning. The princess had learned vaguely that morning the death of Father d'Aigrigny, and had come to question Rodin upon the subject. When this woman, entering the room, suddenly saw the frightful spectacle that offered itself to her view—when she saw Rodin writhing in horrible agony, and, further on, by the light of the sepulchral lamp, those six corpses—and, amongst them, her own niece, and the two orphans whom she had sent to meet their death—she stood petrified with horror, and her reason was unable to withstand the shock. She looked slowly round her, and then raised her arms on high, and burst into a wild fit of laughter. She had gone mad ! Whilst Dr. Baleinier supported the head of Rodin, who expired in his arms, Faringhea appeared at the door ; remaining in the shade, he cast a ferocious glance at the corpse of the Jesuit. ' He would have made himself the chief of the Company of Jesus, to destroy it,' said he ; ' with me, the Company of Jesus stands in the place of Bowanee. I have obeyed the cardinal !'

EPILOGUE

CHAPTER I.

FOUR YEARS AFTER.

FOUR years had elapsed, since the events we have just related, when Gabriel de Rennepont wrote the following letter to Abbé Joseph Charpentier, curate of the Parish of Saint-Aubin, a hamlet of Sologne :

'Springwater Farm,
'June 2nd, 1836.

' Intending to wr..e to you yesterday, my dear Joseph, I seated myself at the little old black table, that you will remember well. My window looks, you know, upon the farm-yard, and I can see all that takes place there. These are grave preliminaries, my friend, but I am coming to the point. I had just taken my seat at the table, when, looking from the window, this is what I saw. You, my dear Joseph, who can draw so well, should have been there to have sketched the charming scene. The sun was sinking, the sky serene, the air warm and balmy with the breath of the hawthorn, which, flowering by the side of a little rivulet, forms the edge which borders the yard. Under the large pear-tree, close to the wall of the barn, sat upon the stone bench my adopted father, Dagobert, that brave and honest soldier whom you love so much. He appeared thoughtful, his white head was bowed on his bosom ; with absent mind, he patted old Spoilsport, whose intelligent face was resting on his master's knees. By his side was his wife, my dear adopted mother, occupied with her sewing ; and near them, on a stool, sat Angela, the wife of Agricola, nursing her last born child, while the gentle Magdalen, with the eldest boy in her lap, was occupied in teaching him the letters of the alphabet. Agricola had just returned from the fields, and was beginning to unyoke his cattle, when, struck, like me, no doubt, with this picture, he stood gazing on it for a moment, with his hand still leaning on the yoke, beneath which bent submissive the broad foreheads of his two large black oxen. I cannot express to you, my friend, the enchanting repose of this picture, lighted by the last rays of the sun, here and there broken by the thick foliage. What various and touching types ! The venerable face of the soldier—the good, loving countenance of my adopted mother—the fresh beauty of Angela, smiling on her little child—the soft melancholy of the hunchback, now and then pressing her lips to the fair, laughing cheek of Agricola's eldest son— and then Agricola himself, in his manly beauty, which seems to reflect so well the valour and honesty of his heart ! Oh, my friend ! in contemplating this assemblage of good, devoted, noble, and loving beings, so dear to each other, living retired in a little farm of our poor Sologne, my heart rose towards heaven with a feeling of ineffable gratitude. This peace of the family circle—this clear evening, with the perfume of the woods and wild flowers wafted on the breeze—this deep silence, only broken by the murmur of the neighbouring rill—all affected me with one of these passing fits of vague and sweet emotion, which one feels but cannot express. You well know it, my friend, who, in your solitary walks, in the midst of your immense plains of flowering heath, surrounded by forests of fir trees, often feel your eyes grow moist, without being able to explain the cause of that sweet melancholy, which I, too, have often felt, during those glorious nights passed in the profound solitudes of America.

' But, alas ! a painful incident disturbed the serenity of the picture. Suddenly I heard Dagobert's wife say to him : " My dear—you are weeping !"

' At these words, Agricola, Angela, and Magdalen gathered round the soldier. Anxiety was visible upon every face. Then, as he raised his head abruptly, one could see two large tears trickle down his cheek to his white moustache. " It is nothing, my children," said he, in a voice of emotion ; " it is nothing. Only, to-day is the first of June—and this day four years——" He could not complete the sentence ; and, as he raised his hands to his eyes, to brush away the tears, we saw that he held between his fingers a little bronze chain, with a medal suspended to it. That is his dearest relic. Four years ago, almost dying with despair at the loss of the two angels, of whom I have so often spoken to you, my friend, he took from the neck of Marshal Simon, brought home dead from a fatal duel, this chain and medal which his children had so long worn. I went down instantly, as you may suppose, to endeavour to soothe the painful remembrances of this excellent man ; gradually, he grew calmer, and the evening was passed in a pious and quiet sadness.

' You cannot imagine, my friend, when I returned to my chamber, what cruel thoughts came to my mind, as I recalled those past events, from which I generally turn away with fear and horror. Then I saw once more the victims of those terrible and mysterious plots, the awful depths of which have never been penetrated, thanks to the deaths of Father d'A. and Father R., and the incurable madness of Madame de St.-D., the three authors or accomplices of the dreadful deeds. The calamities occasioned by them are irreparable ; for those who were thus sacrificed to a criminal ambition, would have been the pride of humanity by the good they would have done. Ah, my friend ! if you had known those noble hearts ; if you had known the projects of splendid charity, formed by that young lady, whose heart was so generous, whose mind so elevated, whose soul so great ! On the eve of her death, as a kind of prelude to her magnificent designs, after a conversation, the subject of which I must keep secret, even from you, she put into my hands a considerable sum, saying, with her usual grace and goodness : " I have been threatened with ruin, and it might perhaps come. What I now confide to you will at least be safe—safe for those who suffer. Give much—give freely—make as many happy hearts as you can. My happiness shall have a royal inauguration !" I do not know whether I ever told you, my friend, that, after those fatal events, seeing Dagobert and his wife reduced to misery, poor " Mother Bunch " hardly able to earn a wretched subsistence, Agricola soon to become a father, and myself deprived of my curacy, and suspended by my bishop, for having given religious consolations to a Protestant, and offered up prayers at the tomb of an unfortunate suicide—I considered myself justified in employing a small portion of the sum intrusted to me by Mdlle. de Cardoville in the purchase of this farm in Dagobert's name.

' Yes, my friend, such is the origin of my fortune. The farmer to whom these few acres formerly belonged, gave us the rudiments of our agricultural education, and common sense, and the study of a few good practical books, completed it. From an excellent workman, Agricola has become an equally excellent husbandman ; I have tried to imitate him, and have put my hand also to the plough : there is no derogation in it, for the labour which provides food for man is thrice hallowed, and it is truly to serve and glorify God, to cultivate and enrich the earth He has created. Dagobert, when his first grief was a little appeased, seemed to gather new vigour from this healthy life of the fields ; and, during his exile in Siberia, he had already learned to till the ground. Finally, my dear adopted mother and sister, and Agricola's good wife, have divided between them the household cares ; and God has blessed this little colony of people, who, alas ! have been sorely tried by misfortune, and who now only ask of toil and solitude, a quiet, laborious, innocent life, and oblivion of great sorrows. Sometimes, in our winter evenings, you have been able to appreciate the delicate and charming mind of the gentle " Mother Bunch," the rare poetical imagination of Agricola, the tenderness of his mother, the good sense of his father, the exquisite natural grace of Angela. Tell me, my friend, was it possible to unite more elements of domestic happiness? What long evenings have we passed round the fire of crackling wood, reading, or commenting on a few immortal works, which always warm the heart, and enlarge the soul! What sweet talk have we had, prolonged far into the night! And then Agricola's pastorals, and the timid literary confidences of Magdalen! And the fresh, clear voice of Angela, joined to the deep manly tones of Agricola, in songs of simple melody! And the old stories of Dagobert, so energetic and picturesque in their warlike spirit! And the adorable gaiety of the children, in their sports with good old Spoilsport, who rather lends himself to their play than takes part in it—for the faithful, intelligent creature seems always to be looking for somebody, as Dagobert says—and he is right. Yes, the dog also regrets those two angels, of whom he was the devoted guardian!

' Do not think, my friend, that our happiness makes us forgetful. No, no ; not a day passes without our repeating, with pious and tender respect, those names so dear to our heart. And these painful memories, hovering for ever about us, give to our calm and happy existence that shade of mild seriousness which struck you so much. No doubt, my friend, this kind of life, bounded by the family circle, and not extending beyond, for the happiness or improvement of our brethren, may be set down as selfish ; but, alas ! we have not the means—and though the poor man always finds a place at our frugal table, and shelter beneath our roof, we must renounce all great projects of fraternal action. The little revenue of our farm just suffices to supply our wants. Alas ! when I think over it, notwithstanding a momentary regret, I cannot blame my resolution to keep faithfully my sacred oath, and to renounce that great inheritance, which, alas ! had become immense by the death of my kindred. Yes, I believe I performed a duty, when I begged the guardian of that treasure to reduce it to ashes, rather than let it fall into the hands of people, who would have made an execrable use of it, or to perjure myself by disputing a donation which I had granted freely, voluntarily, sincerely. And yet, when I picture to myself the realisation of the magnificent views of my ancestor—an admirable Utopia, only possible with immense resources—and which Mdlle. de Cardoville hoped to carry into execution, with the aid of M. François Hardy, of Prince Djalma, of Marshal Simon and his daughters, and of myself—when I think of the dazzling focus of living forces, which such an association would have been, and of the immense influence it might have had on the happiness of the whole human race—my indignation and horror, as an honest man and a Christian, are excited against that abominable Company, whose black plots nipped in their bud all those great hopes, which promised so much for futurity. What remains now of all these splendid projects? Seven tombs. For my grave also is dug in that mausoleum, which Samuel has erected on the site of the house in the Rue Neuve-Saint-François, and of which he remains the keeper—faithful to the end!

    ✧   ✧   ✧   ✧   ✧   ✧

'I had written thus far, my friend, when I received your letter. So, after having forbidden you to see me, your bishop now orders that you shall cease to correspond with me. Your touching, painful regrets have deeply moved me, my friend. Often have we talked together of ecclesiastical discipline, and of the absolute power of the bishops over us, the poor working clergy, left to their mercy without aid or remedy. It is painful, but it is the law of the church, my friend, and you have sworn to observe it. Submit as I have submitted. Every engagement is binding upon the man of honour! My poor, dear Joseph! would that you had the compensations which remained to me, after the rupture of ties that I so much value. But I know too well what you must feel—I cannot go on—— I find it impossible to continue this letter, I might be bitter against those whose orders we are bound to respect. Since it must be so, this letter shall be my last. Farewell, my friend! farewell for ever. My heart is almost broken.

'GABRIEL DE RENNEPONT.'

CHAPTER II.

THE REDEMPTION.

DAY was about to dawn. A rosy light, almost imperceptible, began to glimmer in the east; but the stars still shone, sparkling with radiance, upon the azure of the zenith. The birds awoke beneath the fresh foliage of the great woods; and, with isolated warblings, sang the prelude of their morning-concert. A light mist rose from the high grass, bathed in nocturnal dew, while the calm and limpid waters of a vast lake reflected the whitening dawn in their deep, blue mirror. Everything promised one of those warm and joyous days, that belong to the opening of summer.

Half-way up the slope of a hill, facing the east, a tuft of old, moss-grown willows, whose rugged bark disappeared beneath the climbing branches of wild honeysuckle and harebells, formed a natural harbour; and on their gnarled and enormous roots, covered with thick moss, were seated a man and a woman, whose white hair, deep wrinkles, and bending figures, announced extreme old age. And yet this woman had only lately been young and beautiful, with long black hair overshadowing her pale forehead. And yet this man had, a short time ago, been still in the vigour of his age. From the spot where this man and woman were reposing, could be seen the valley, the lake, the woods, and, soaring above the woods, the blue summit of a high mountain, from behind which the sun was about to rise. This picture, half-veiled by the pale transparency of the morning twilight, was pleasing, melancholy, and solemn.

'Oh, my sister!' said the old man to the woman, who was reposing with him beneath the rustic arbour formed by the tuft of willow-trees; 'oh, my sister! how many times during the centuries in which the hand of the Lord carried us onward, and, separated from each other, we traversed the world from pole to pole—how many times we have witnessed this awaking of nature with a sentiment of incurable grief!—Alas! it was but another day of wandering—another useless day added to our life, since it brought death no nearer!'

'But now what happiness, oh, my brother! since the Lord has had mercy on us, and, with us, as with all other creatures, every returning day is a step nearer to the grave. Glory to Him! yes, glory!'

'Glory to Him, my sister! for since yesterday, when we again met, I feel that indescribable langour which announces the approach of death.'

'Like you, my brother, I feel my strength, already shaken, passing away in a sweet exhaustion. Doubtless, the term of our life approaches. The wrath of the Lord is satisfied.'

'Alas, my sister! doubtless also, the last of my doomed race, will, at the same time, complete our redemption by his death; for the will of heaven is manifest, that I can only be pardoned, when the last of my family shall have disappeared from the face of the earth. To him, holiest amongst the holiest—was reserved the favour of accomplishing this end—he who has done so much for the salvation of his brethren !'

'Oh, yes, my brother ! he who has suffered so much, and without complaining, drunk to the dregs the bitter cup of woe—he, the minister of the Lord, who has been his Master's image upon earth—he was fitted for the last instrument of this redemption !'

'Yes, for I feel, my sister, that, at this hour, the last of my race, touching victim of slow persecution, is on the point of resigning his angelic soul to God. Thus, even to the end, have I been fatal to my doomed family. Lord, if Thy mercy is great, Thy anger is great likewise !'

'Courage and hope, my brother ! Think how after the expiation cometh pardon, and pardon is followed by a blessing. The Lord punished, in you and your posterity, the artisan rendered wicked by misfortune and injustice. He said to you : "Go on ! without truce or rest—and your labour shall be vain—and every evening, throwing yourself on the hard ground, you shall be no nearer to the end of your eternal course !"—And so, for centuries, men without pity have said to the artisan : "Work ! work ! work ! without truce or rest—and your labour shall be fruitful for all others, but fruitless for yourself—and every evening, throwing yourself on the hard ground, you shall be no nearer to happiness and repose ; and your wages shall only suffice to keep you alive in pain, privation, and poverty !"'

'Alas ! alas ! will it be always thus ?'——'No, no, my brother ! and instead of weeping over your lost race, rejoice for them—since their death was needed for your redemption, and in redeeming you, heaven will redeem the artisan, cursed and feared by those who have laid on him the iron yoke. Yes, my brother ! the time draweth nigh—heaven's mercy will not stop with us alone. Yes, I tell you ; in us will be rescued both the WOMAN and the SLAVE of these modern ages. The trial has been hard, brother ; it has lasted throughout eighteen centuries ; but it will last no longer. Look, my brother ! see that rosy light, there in the east, gradually spreading over the firmament ! Thus will rise the sun of the new emancipation—peaceful, holy, great, salutary, fruitful, filling the word with light and vivifying heat, like the day-star that will soon appear in heaven !'

'Yes, yes, my sister ! I feel it. Your words are prophetic. We shall close our heavy eyes just as we see the aurora of the day of deliverance—a fair, a splendid day, like that which is about to dawn. Henceforth I will only shed tears of pride and glory for those of my race, who have died the martyrs of humanity, sacrificed by humanity's eternal enemies—for the true ancestors of the sacrilegious wretches, who blaspheme the name of Jesus by giving it to their Company, were the false Scribes and Pharisees, whom the Saviour cursed !—Yes ! glory to the descendants of my family, who have been the last martyrs offered up by the accomplices of all slavery and all despotism, the pitiless enemies of those who wish to think, and not to suffer in silence—of those that would fain enjoy, as children of heaven, the gifts which the Creator has bestowed upon all the human family. Yes, the day approaches—the end of the reign of our modern Pharisees—the false priests, who lend their sacrilegious aid to the merciless selfishness of the strong against the weak, by daring to maintain in the face of the exhaustless treasures of the creation, that God has made man for tears, and sorrow, and suffering—the false priests, who are the agents of all oppression, and would bow to the earth, in brutish and hopeless humiliation, the brow of every creature. No, no ! let man lift his head proudly ! God made him to be noble and intelligent, free and happy.'

'Oh, my brother ! your words also are prophetic. Yes, yes ! the dawn of that bright day approaches, even as the dawn of the natural day which. by the mercy of God, will be our last on earth.'——'The last, my sister ; for a strange weakness creeps over me, all matter seems dissolving in me, and my soul aspires to mount to heaven.'

'Mine eyes are growing dim, brother ; I can scarcely see that light in the east, which lately appeared so red.'——'Sister ! it is through a confused vapour that I now see the valley—the lake—the woods. My strength fails me.'

'Blessed be God, brother ! the moment of eternal rest is at hand.

'Yes, it comes, my sister ! the sweetness of the everlasting sleep takes possession of my senses.'

'Oh, happiness ! I am dying.'——'These eyes are closing, sister !'

'We are then forgiven !'——'Forgiven !'

'Oh, my brother ! may this Divine redemption extend to all those who suffer upon the earth !'——'Die in peace, my sister ! The great day has dawned—the sun is rising—behold !'

'Blessed be God !'——'Blessed be God !'

    *   *   *   *   *   *

And at the moment when those two voices ceased for ever, the sun rose, radiant and dazzling, and deluged the valley with its beams.

To M. C—— P——.

To you, my friend, I dedicated this book. To inscribe it with your name, was to assume an engagement that, in the absence of talent, it should be at least conscientious, sincere, and of a salutary influence, however limited. My object is attained. Some select hearts, like yours, my friend, have put into practice the legitimate association of labour, capital, and intelligence, and have already granted to their workmen a proportionate share in the profits of their industry. Others have laid the foundations of Common Dwelling-houses, and one of the chief capitalists of Hamburg has favoured me with his views respecting an establishment of this kind, on the most gigantic scale.

As for the dispersion of the members of the Company of Jesus, I have taken less part in it than other enemies of the detestable doctrines of Loyola, whose influence and authority were far greater than mine.

Adieu, my friend. I could have wished this work more worthy of you ; but you are indulgent, and will at least give me credit for the intentions which dictated it.

Believe me,

Yours truly,

EUGENE SUE.

Paris, 25th August, 1845.

THE END.

BILLING AND SONS, PRINTERS, GUILDFORD

Other fantasy titles from Dedalus include:

The Arabian Nightmare – Robert Irwin £5.95 (hardback)
The Revenants – Geoffrey Farrington £3.95
The Illumination of Alice J. Cunningham – Lyn Webster £5.95
Mr Narrator – Pat Gray £4.95
The Golem – Gustav Meyrink £4.95
La-Bas – J. K. Huysmans £4.95
The Cathedral – J. K. Huysmans £6.95
Les Diaboliques – Barbey D'Aurevilly £4.95
Baron Munchausen – Erich Raspe £4.95
The Red Laugh – Leonid Andreyev £4.95
The Little Angel – Leonid Andreyev £4.95

Forthcoming titles include:

The Acts of the Apostates – Geoffrey Farrington £6.95
The Memoirs of the Year 2500 – Louis-Sebastian Mercier £6.95
Seraphita – Balzac £4.95
Micromegas – Voltaire £4.95